SECRETS

AND

LIES

THE LePAGE LEGACY

AN EXPLOSIVE EXPOSÉ OF NORTH AMERICA's SECRET FREEMASONRY PAST

BY: FIRTH BOWSER AYOTTE

CONTENTS

PART 2

INTRODUCTION

DURING THE LAST CENTURY, THE LEPAGE FAMILY NAME FLOURISHED WITH MUCH VIGOR AND VALOR AS HUMANLY POSSIBLE WHILE A LARGE PERCENTAGE OF THEM STOOD OUT FROM THE CROWD. IN THE 1940'S AND 1950'S FOR EXAMPLE, ERNEST LEPAGE OF RIMOUSKI, QUEBEC WENT ON TO BECOME ONE OF CANADA'S MOST LEADING EXPERTS IN THE FIELD OF BOTANY. BORN NOT VERY FAR FROM THE OLD ANCESTRAL HOMESTEAD IN RIMOUSKI ON JUNE 1ST, 1905 HE WAS ORIGINALLY ORDAINED A PRIEST AND SERVED AS AN ASSISTANT PARISH PRIEST IN HIS HOME TOWN UNTIL 1933. BETWEEN THE YEARS 1936-61, HE TAUGHT AT THE ECOLE MOYENNE D'AGRICULTURE ALSO LOCATED IN THIS LITTLE FRANCOPHONE COMMUNITY OF RIMOUSKI. IN 1943, ERNEST LEPAGE AND ANOTHER ENTHUSIASTIC COLLEAGUE OF PLANT LIFE, ARTHEME DUTILLY, BEGAN THEIR RESEARCH STUDIES ON ARCTIC AND SUBARCTIC FLORA, CONCENTRATING MOST OF THEIR ENDEAVORS ON THE JAMES BAY REGION OF NORTHERN QUEBEC. THROUGHOUT THEIR TRIPS BETWEEN THE YEARS 1945-64, THEY DOCUMENTED THEIR FINDINGS IN SO MUCH DETAIL THAT BOTH OF THEM BECAME INSTANT PUBLISHED AUTHORS. IT WAS REPORTEDLY DURING THESE EXTENSIVE TRIPS TO QUEBEC'S NORTHLAND THAT THE PAIR'S PERSONAL INTERESTS IN THE COLLECTION OF DRIED PLANTS AS SPECIMENS ENABLED THEM TO CONDUCT FURTHER RESEARCH AT HOME AMONGST THE FLORA AND FOINA ALONG THE BANKS OF THE ST. LAWRENCE RIVER.

ALTHOUGH ERNEST LEPAGE SUFFERED FROM AN ASSORTMENT OF HEALTH PROBLEMS, HE STILL PUSHED ONWARDS WITH HIS RESEARCH STUDIES AND CONTINUED WITH HIS WRITINGS UNTIL BEING OVER TAKEN BY A THROMBOSIS (BLOOD CLOT) IN 1976 WHICH LEFT HIM PARTIALLY PARALYZED. UNABLE TO CONDUCT FURTHER STUDIES ON THE SUBJECT HE LOVED SO DEEPLY, ERNEST LEPAGE WAS SAID TO HAVE DONATED HIS EXTENSIVE HERBARIUM AND BOTANICAL COLLECTION TO THE RESEARCH LIBRARY AT LAVAL UNIVERSITY. DESPITE THE FACT THAT HE DIED ON JANUARY 4TH, 1981 IN RIMOUSKI AT THE AGE OF 75, HIS LEGACY

LIVED ON AS IT IS WELL DOCUMENTED THAT HE MADE A VALUABLE CONTRIBUTION TO BOTANICAL KNOWLEDGE HERE IN CANADA.

OTHER TWENTIETH CENTURY CONTRIBUTIONS TO CANADIAN SOCIETY AS A WHOLE BY THE LEPAGE FAMILY NAME INCLUDED CRYSTALLOGRAPHER YVON LEPAGE BORN IN MORLAIX, FRANCE ON OCTOBER 7TH, 1943. DURING THE LATE 1960'S AND MOST OF THE 1970'S, THIS MEMBER OF THE FAMILY TREE FURTHERED HIS RESEARCH STUDIES AT ECOLE POLYTECHNIQUE IN MONTREAL AND BECAME PART OF ITS LECTURE CIRCUIT, 1967-73. AFTER WHICH, HE WENT ONTO POSTDOCTORAL SERVICES AT MCGILL UNIVERSITY 1974-77 AND BECAME A PUBLISHED AUTHOR/CO-AUTHOR ON A HOST OF SCIENTIFIC PUBLICATIONS RANGING ON AN ASSORTMENT OF TOPICS; GEOMETRICAL CRYSTALLOG, X-RAY DIFFRACTION PHYSICS, DIFFRACTOMETRY, STRUCTURE AND CRYSTAL CHEMISTRY, AND INORGANIC COMPOUNDS JUST TO NAME A FEW.

ON THE LESS EXTENSIVE SCALE OF THE LEPAGE SPECTRUM, OTHER FAMILY MEMBERS INSTANTLY COME TO MIND. INDIVIDUALS SUCH AS FRENCH CANADA'S ACTOR/DIRECTOR/PLAYWRIGHT ROBERT LEPAGE. BORN IN QUEBEC CITY IN 1957, THIS MEMBER OF THE LEPAGE FAMILY LITERALLY ROCKED THE ENGLISH CANADIAN ESTABLISHMENT AS A VAST MAJORITY OF HIS CREATIONS WERE PURPOSELY DESIGNED TO MAKE THE AUDIENCES THINK OUTSIDE THE BOX OF THE NORMAL THOUGHT PROCESSES. IN OTHER WORDS, THINKING FOR YOURSELF AND NOT ALLOWING SOMEONE ELSE TO DO THE THINKING FOR YOU!!!

AFTER RECEIVING EXTENSIVE THEATRE TRAINING IN BOTH QUEBEC AND PARIS, FRANCE — HE PROVED HIMSELF TO BE THAT OF A VISIONARY OF SORTS. IN FACT, SOME OF HIS EARLIEST RECORDED PERFORMANCES IN THE 1980'S WERE SAID TO HAVE ENABLED AUDIENCES TO SEE THINGS FROM DIFFERENT PERSPECTIVES AS EVERY ONCE IN AWHILE, TWO DIFFERENT VERSIONS OF THE SAME PLAY /OR SCENE WOULD BE ACTED OUT. THROUGHOUT HIS PROFESSIONAL CAREER, ROBERT LEPAGE KEPT HONING HIS SKILLS BY EXPERIMENTING WITH A VARIATION OF HUMANISTIC ATTRIBUTES AS PART OF HIS CRAFT.

IN 1991 FOR INSTANCE, HIS NEW SOLO PRODUCTION CALLED "NEEDLES AND OPIUM "OPENED IN CANADA'S CAPITAL CITY OF OTTAWA. WRITTEN, PERFORMED AND DESIGNED BY ROBERT LEPAGE HIMSELF, THE CREATION EXPLORED SURREALISM, EXISTENTIALISM, JAZZ AND OTHER CULTURAL DEVELOPMENTS OF THE TWENTIETH CENTURY THAT A NARRATIVE INSPIRED BY THE CONNECTIONS HE REPORTEDLY SAW BETWEEN TWO OF THE WORLD'S MOST GIFTED ARTISTS; THE FRENCH WRITER AND FILM-MAKER JEAN COCTEAU AND THE AMERICAN JAZZ TRUMPETER MILES DAVIS. WHILE RESEARCHING THE LIVES OF THESE TWO ICONS, IT WAS SOON DISCOVERED THAT THE TWO MEN IN QUESTION ACTUALLY HAD SOMETHING IN COMMON; DRUGS. COCTEAU WAS SAID TO HAVE BEEN ADDICTED TO OPIUM WHILE DAVIS WAS HOOKED ON

HEROIN. HENCE, THE NAME OF THE PERFORMANCE. AS THE SHOW OPENED, ROBERT LEPAGE PLAYED THE MAIN CHARACTERS; DAVIS WAS REPRESENTED BY THE PLANGENT SOUND OF HIS TRUMPET AND PROJECTED PHOTOGRAPHS OF HIM. THROUGHOUT MOST OF THE PERFORMANCE, ROBERT LEPAGE WORKED IN MIDAIR AS HE WHISKED ABOUT IN A HARNESS THAT SUSPENDED HIM ABOVE THE STAGE FLOOR BECAUSE AT THE TIME, COCTEAU APPARENTLY SPENT A LARGE PORTION OF HIS LIFE ABOARD A TRANSATLANTIC FLIGHT GOING BETWEEN HIS HOME COUNTRY AND NEW YORK. WITH THE APPLICATION OF CONDUCTING THE PERFORMANCE IN MIDAIR, IT REPORTEDLY SYMBOLIZED THE FACT THAT COCTEAU WAS ACTUALLY CAUGHT BETWEEN TWO WORLDS. THE HARNESS ITSELF ALSO FACILITATED THE SPECTACULAR EFFECT OF FREE FALL AS IMAGES OF SKYSCRAPERS WERE PROJECTED ON A SCREEN AT THE REAR OF THE STAGE, THUS GENERATING THAT SPECIFIC ILLUSION.

AS PART OF A MINIATURE WORLD TOUR, THIS EXACT SAME PERFORMANCE OPENED IN NEW YORK CITY AND LONDON, ENGLAND IN 1992; RECEIVING GREAT REVIEWS IN THE UNITED STATES. BUT WHEN ROBERT LEPAGE PERFORMED THE PIECE AT THE ROYAL NATIONAL THREATRE IN LONDON DURING THE MONTH OF MAY, THERE WAS NO CHEERING BY THE CRITICS AS THEY HAD ALMOST IMMEDIATELY LABELED HIM AS BEING FAR TOO EXTREME FOR THEIR LIKING. THIS WAS BY NO MEANS THE FIRST TIME THAT THE BRITISH AUDIENCE AT THE ROYAL NATIONAL THREATRE STUBBED THEIR NOSES AT THE FRANCOPHONE PERFORMER.

DURING HIS JULY 1992 PRODUCTION OF SHAKESPEARE'S "A MID-SUMMER NIGHT'S DREAM", HE ADDED A LITTLE TWIST /OR TWO MUCH TO THE DISMAY OF THE ONLOOKERS. IN KEEPING WITH HIS TRADITIONAL ANTICS OF DOING JUST ABOUT ANYTHING IN ORDER TO GET THE AUDIENCE TO THINK FOR THEMSELVES, THE ACTORS WERE INSTRUCTED TO FOCUS ALL OF THEIR ATTENTION ONTO THE DESIRED AFFECT OF THE PERFORMANCE WHICH WAS TOTALLY CENTERED AROUND AN UNCONVENTIONAL SETTING; A CIRCULAR POOL OF MUD. AUDIENCE MEMBERS IN THE FIRST THREE ROWS OF THE THEATRE WERE REPORTEDLY HANDED RAINCOATS TO HELP PROTECT THEMSELVES FROM THE WET SPRAY THAT LITERALLY SPLATTERED THE ENTIRE STAGE AREA DURING THE INITIAL PERFORMANCE. ACCORDING TO SOME OF ENGLAND'S CRITICS, THE SPRAY VIRTUALLY SYMBOLIZED THE LEPAGE FAMILY'S USUAL MUD SLINGING TACTICS AT AUTHORITY FIGURES.

NEEDLESS TO SAY, ROBERT LEPAGE'S HIGHLY CONTROVERSIAL PRODUCTION RECEIVED MUCH CRITICISM AS THE BRITISH CONDEMNED HIS ACTIONS FOR NOT ONLY BEING IN BAD TASTE BUT ALSO BEING TOTALLY UNJUSTIFIABLE AS WELL. THEY FURTHER ACCUSED HIM OF MALIGNING THEIR LITERARY HERITAGE BY BELITTLING SHAKESPEARE'S GOOD NAME.

During the scheduled referendum election of 1995 on Quebec's possible separation from the rest of Canada, all levels of government (federal, provincial and municipal) were said to have showered him with riches in order to help launch his various productions. Further to this, just as Robert LePage's one-man production titled "The Far Side of the Moon" was preparing to tour English Canada in the year 2002, the separatist government of the Province of Quebec donated $25,000.00 to the cause just so that some of its performances could be conducted in French. It should also be stated that this member of the LePage family tree has been the recipient of numerous prestigious awards, including the Order of Canada in 1994.

It goes without saying that some members of the LePage family tree never tend to wonder too far away from the conventional way of thinking on a daily basis. In using Montreal's actress and director Monique LePage of the 1950's and 1960's as an example, it is learned that throughout the vast majority of her professional career, she not only got involved with theatre productions but also played in several CBC television productions as well. Further to this, she was the recipient of many awards and honors. Which in turn, enabled yet another member of the family tree (Roland LePage) to further hone their skills in a 1970's play which was performed at Ontario's Tarragon Theatre; Le Temps d'une vie. As was the case of Pierrette LePage who was a renowned pianist when she married Bruce Mather, the composer/pianist/educator of McGill University.

Surprisingly, the LePage name can also be found in a very unlikely location within Canadian literary history. Of all places, the Twentieth Century teachings and philosophies of logic and reason. In French Canada, the LePage's of Quebec exercised their uncanny ability to creatively write a few books on logic and the history of its creation, (Francois LePage), as it pertained to the Province of Quebec during the 1960's and 1970's. And by the time the 21ST Century exposed itself, yet another member of the LePage family dynasty found themselves filming the pages of our country's no so glamorous past in the CBC production of **Canada: A People's History**. In the second half of Episode 15 and the full copulation of Episode 16 of this great film undertaking, Marquis LePage was responsible for both the writing and directing of these two CBC episodes.

Growing up as a child in northern New Brunswick, I was forever being reminded of my French Roman Catholic heritage. Despite this, most of my childhood friends were English Protestants

AS I FELT MORE AT EASY WITH THEM – HELL, I EVEN WENT A PROTESTANT SCHOOL. DURING THE VERY LAST YEARS OF LIVING IN NEW BRUNSWICK AS A YOUNG TWELVE-YEAR-OLD, I WAS FORCED TO ATTEND A FRENCH ROMAN CATHOLIC SCHOOL THAT WAS RUN BY NUNS. OBVIOUSLY, I WAS NOT AT ALL IMPRESSED BECAUSE EVEN BACK THEN I FOUND THE FRENCH TO BE FAR TOO PRETENTIOUS. IT WASN'T UNTIL MY PARENTS DECIDED TO MOVE TO GIBSONS, BRITISH COLUMBIA DURING MONTREAL'S INTERNATIONAL EXPEDITION YEAR OF EXPO 67 THAT I WAS ACTUALLY ABLE TO DISASSOCIATE MYSELF FROM FRENCH CANADA. BUT ONCE AMONGST THOSE IN ENGLISH CANADA ON THE SUNSHINE COAST, I STILL COULDN'T ESCAPE MY FRENCH ORIENTED ROOTS AS EVEN IN THIS TINY COMMUNITY OF GIBSONS, THE LEPAGE FAMILY NAME HAD A VERY WELL ESTABLISHED PAST.

AS THE STORY GOES, SOMETIME DURING THE TURN OF THE TWENTIETH CENTURY GEORGE GIBSON SENIOR WAS SAID TO HAVE SOLD A PIECE OF LAND TO THE LEPAGE'S GLUE COMPANY SO THAT THEY COULD CONSTRUCT A LARGE FACTORY FOR THE PROCESSING OF GLUE FROM DOGFISH LIVERS. THE BUILDING ITSELF STOOD ON PILINGS AT THE HIGH TIDE WATER MARKER ON THE SHORELINE. ANTICIPATING MUCH SUCCESS IN THEIR ENDEAVORS, A SMALL BUILDING WAS ALSO ERECTED AS A DWELLING AND NOT LONG AFTERWARDS, A TWO STOREY RESIDENTIAL BUILDING WAS CONSTRUCTED AS THE COMPANY WAS NOW FLOURISHING IN THE NEWLY ESTABLISHED SETTLEMENT OF GIBSON'S LANDING. BUT LIKE ANYTHING ELSE IN LIFE, THE GLUE FACTORY'S EXISTENCE WAS SHORT LIVED AS IT WAS FORCED OUT OF BUSINESS DUE TO LEGAL ARGUMENTS OF THE GLUE COMPANY'S FORMER PARTNERS IN THE UNITED STATES.

ALTHOUGH THE FACTORY WAS BUILT IN 1900 /OR 1901, IT WASN'T ACTUALLY DEMOLISHED UNTIL THREE-QUARTERS OF A CENTURY LATER AS BY THIS TIME PERIOD THE BUILDING HAD BECOME A HAVEN FOR THE HIPPIES AND BEATNIKS OF THE 1960'S ERA TO EXERCISE THEIR USAGE OF LSD, MARIJUANA AND OTHER ILLUSIVE DRUGS. ACCORDING TO CERTAIN GIBSONS RESIDENTS, THE OLD FACTORY WAS NOTHING BUT A COMPLETE EYE SORE AND A DISGRACE TO THE COMMUNITY AS BY THIS TIME PERIOD THE VILLAGE OF GIBSONS HAD BEEN PLAYING AN IMPORTANT ROLE ON THE WORLD STAGE THANKS TO THE CBC WEEKLY TELEVISION SERIES KNOWN AS "THE BEACHCOMBERS". VIEWERS WORLDWIDE SLOWLY BEGAN FLOCKING INTO THE COMMUNITY WANTING TO MET NICK ADONIDAS (BRUNO GERUSSI), RELIC (ROBERT CLOTHIER), JESSE (PAT JOHN) AND THE ENTIRE MOLLY'S REACH GANG.

BUT TO THE VAST MAJORITY OF THOSE LIVING IN THE COMMUNITY, THE FILMING OF THE SERIES DURING THE SPRING AND SUMMER MONTHS WAS NOTHING MORE THAN A CONSTANT INTERRUPTION OF DAILY LIFE WHILE FLAG CREWS COULD BE FOUND DAY IN AND DAY OUT STOPPING ALL OF THE TRAFFIC IN THE LOWER SECTION OF THE VILLAGE WHERE MOLLY'S REACH WAS LOCATED,

DOWN ON THE GOVERNMENT WHARF AREA. NEVER BEING A GREAT FAN OF THE SERIES ITSELF, IT WASN'T UNTIL SOME YEARS LATER THAT I BEGAN TO APPRECIATE AS TO HOW THEIR NEVER-ENDING PRESENCE OVER THE NINETEEN YEARS OF BEING AIRED GLOBALLY, (OCTOBER 1972 TO APRIL 1991), HELPED MOLD MY PERSONALITY INTO WHAT IT IS TODAY; A PESSIMIST THROUGH AND THROUGH. EVEN WHEN THE NEW AND IMPROVED BEACHCOMBERS MADE A COME-BACK AS A CBC TV MOVIE ON PRIME TIME TELEVISION MONDAY, NOVEMBER 25TH, 2002 – I COULDN'T BE BOTHERED WASTING MY TIME WATCHING IT AS THERE WERE FAR MORE IMPORTANT DETAILS OF HISTORY THAT COULD HAVE BEEN USED AS A WAY AND MEANS OF ENTERTAINING A SOMEWHAT BORED AND ILLUSIONAL WORLD AUDIENCE.

AS A TEENAGER IN THE VILLAGE OF GIBSONS, (OCTOBER 27TH, 1967 AND ONWARDS), I WAS CONSTANTLY REMINDED BY OTHERS AS TO HOW PROUD OF A NAME THAT SOME OF MY ANCESTORS HAD AND THAT I MUST HAVE BEEN EXTREMELY HONORED IN CARRYING ON THAT FAMILY TRADITION. THE TWO MOST PROMINENT NAMES THAT THESE GIBSONS RESIDENTS ALWAYS MENTIONED WERE OF COURSE ALBERT EDWARD LEPAGE OF THE A.E. LEPAGE REAL ESTATE FAME AND HIS KIN, WILLIAM NELSON LEPAGE, THE FOUNDER OF THE INFAMOUS STICKY GLUE SUBSTANCE THAT WAS FIRST FORMULATED IN THE 1870'S FROM THE SKINS OF DOGFISH. NOT WANTING TO PARTAKE IN THE GLORIFYING OF THE FAMILY NAME, I CONSTANTLY CURSED THE LEPAGE NAME AND DENOUNCED HAVING ANYTHING TO DO WITH THE LEPAGE'S OF PRINCE EDWARD ISLAND, THE BIRTH PLACE OF BOTH THE REAL ESTATE TYCOON AND THE GLUE GURU.

ALTHOUGH I DIDN'T WANT TO ACKNOWLEDGE THEIR ACTUAL EXISTENCE, THEIR HUMBLE BEGINNING WERE SOMEWHAT KNOWN TO ME. FOR INSTANCE, ALBERT E. LEPAGE FIRST STARTED SELLING HOUSES IN TORONTO JUST BEFORE THE OUTBREAK OF THE FIRST WORLD WAR, (1913), AND WAS REPORTEDLY RESPONSIBLE FOR UP LIFTING THE ONCE TARNISHED REPUTATION OF HIS COLLEAGUES BY SUPPOSEDLY IMPLEMENTING HONESTY AND INTEGRITY INTO THE PROFESSION. AT THE TIME, BEING A REALTOR WAS CLASSIFIED AS BEING A BOTTOM FEEDER ON THE FOOD CHAIN; THE LOWEST POSSIBLE FORM OF HUMAN EXISTENCE. AT THE CLOSE OF THE WAR, HE WAS SAID TO HAVE BEEN THE DRIVING FORCE TO END THE BAD PRACTICES USED IN REAL ESTATE AND BECAME INSTRUMENTAL IN THE ESTABLISHING OF THE TORONTO REAL ESTATE BOARD THAT OF WHICH HE BECAME ITS PRESIDENT IN 1928. ONE YEAR LATER, (1929), THIS MEMBER OF THE LEPAGE FAMILY NAME WAS BUILDING SMALL FIVE BEDROOM HOUSES (BUNGALOWS) AND SELLING THEM AS FAST AS THEY COULD BE CONSTRUCTED.

BY THE 1940'S, A.E. LEPAGE WAS SUBDIVIDING PRESTIGIOUS PROPERTIES AND SELLING PROPERTY LOTS AS WHOLE SUBDIVISIONS SOON BEGAN TO EMERGE

OUT OF THE ASHES AT THE END OF THE SECOND WORLD WAR AS THE ENTIRE COUNTRY WAS NOW REAPING THE BENEFITS OF ECONOMIC SPLENDOR. AFTER CELEBRATING 40 YEARS IN THE REAL ESTATE BUSINESS AND AFTER ACCUMULATING A TREMENDOUS FORTUNE, A.E. LePAGE SOLD HIS COMPANY IN 1953 WHICH AT THE TIME OFFERED ITS SERVICES TO CLIENTELE WITHIN A TWENTY-MILE RADIUS OF METRO TORONTO. ONCE THE COMPANY WAS SOLD, IT WENT ON TO BECOME ONE OF THE LARGEST REAL ESTATE OPERATIONS IN THE COUNTRY AS IT NOT ONLY CONTINUED TO BE ACTIVELY INVOLVED IN BOTH RESIDENTIAL HOUSE SALES AS WELL AS ASSEMBLING SUBDIVISIONS IN AND AROUND THE TORONTO AREA BUT IT ALSO EXTENDED ITS PHILOSOPHY ON A NATIONAL LEVEL FROM THE EAST COAST RIGHT ACROSS TO THE PACIFIC SHORES OF VANCOUVER ISLAND, INCORPORATING COMMERCIAL SALES AS IT WENT ALONG. THE COMPANY, A.E. LePAGE LTD. REPORTEDLY DID THE BULK OF THE APPRAISAL WORK FOR THE CONSTRUCTION OF THE ST. LAWRENCE SEAWAY, (THE ACTUAL CONSTRUCTION TAKING PLACE THROUGHOUT MOST OF THE 1950's). NEARLY TEN YEARS AFTER THE OFFICIAL OPENING OF THE ST. LAWRENCE SEAWAY IN 1959, A.E. LePAGE DIED ON JUNE 4TH, 1968.

IN 1984, A.E. LePAGE LTD. MERGED WITH ROYAL TRUST TO BECOME KNOWN AS ROYAL LePAGE REAL ESTATE SERVICES LTD., **ROYAL LePAGE**. WITH THEIR COMBINED ASSESSES, (ALSO WITH THE FORMATION OF ROYAL LePAGE COMMERCIAL INC.), ROYAL LePAGE BECAME KNOWN AS ONE OF THE COUNTRY'S LEADING CONGLOMERATES EMPLOYING MORE THAN NINE-THOUSAND PEOPLE WITH A REPORTED 500 OFFICES THROUGHOUT CANADA – LATER ESTABLISHING REAL ESTATE OFFICES HERE ON THE SUNSHINE COAST AS WELL.

LIKE THE REAL ESTATE TYCOON, HIS RELATIVE THE GLUE GURU HAD A VERY INTERESTING BEGINNING AS WELL. WHILE STILL IN HIS VERY EARLY TWENTIES, WILLIAM NELSON LePAGE BEGAN EXPERIMENTING WITH THE POSSIBILITY OF IMPROVING THE USAGE OF GLUE. AT THE TIME, MOST OF THE COMMERCIAL GLUES USED CONSISTED LARGELY OF A MIXTURE OF GELATIN AND ANIMAL BONES AND HIDES THAT REQUIRED HEATING BEFORE USING THEM. THIS ESSENTIALLY WAS A PAIN IN THE ASS FOR MOST OF ITS USERS AND HAVING ACCESS TO AN OVER ABUNDANCE OF CODFISH SKINS, THE SON OF A P.E.I. FARMER SOON BEGAN FORMULATING VARIOUS CONCOCTIONS TO IMPROVE THE GLUE. AS A YOUNG MAN, WILLIAM N. LePAGE REALIZED THAT HIS LIFE WAS GOING NOWHERE FAST AS LONG AS HE REMAINED IN CANADA. SO, HE REPORTEDLY MIGRATED TO THE STATE OF MASSACHUSETTS WHERE HE WAS SAID TO HAVE WORKED IN VARIOUS VOCATIONS (TINSMITH, MERCHANT AND CHEMIST). IT WAS DURING THIS TIME PERIOD IN ROCKPORT, MASSACHUSETTS THAT HE SOON DISCOVERED THAT THE FISH SKINS DISCARDED BY THE AREA'S FISHING INDUSTRY COULD ACTUALLY BE PROCESSED BY USING VINEGAR AND OTHER COMPONENTS TO MAKE AN ADHESIVE

THAT NOT ONLY HAD A LONG SHELF LIFE BUT ALSO WAS MUCH EASIER TO USE THAN THE OTHER GLUES USED AT THE TIME.

IT ALMOST IMMEDIATELY BECAME APPARENT TO WILLIAM NELSON LEPAGE THAT HE WAS ONTO SOMETHING THAT WAS LITERALLY GOING TO BE MAKING HIM A VERY WEALTHY MAN AND BEGAN THE TASK OF SEEKING A PARTNER /OR TWO WHO WOULD BE IN A POSITION TO BANK ROLL THE VENTURE THAT HE HAD IN MIND. BEFORE LONG, THE RUSSIAN CEMENT COMPANY WAS FORMED AND IN 1880, A NEWER VERSION OF THE GLUE WAS INTRODUCED FOR HOME USAGE. THE HOME VERSION KNOWN AS LEPAGE'S LIQUID GLUE WAS AN OVER NIGHT SUCCESS AS ITS ADHESIVE QUALITIES COULD BE USED FOR JUST ABOUT ANYTHING THAT NEEDED MENDING. BY 1882, TWO NEW AMERICAN PARTNERS CAME ON BOARD AS MORE MONEY HAD TO BE GENERATED FOR EXPANSION PURPOSES. IN EIGHT SHORT YEARS, (1880-87), THE LEPAGE'S GLUE COMPANY SOLD AN ESTIMATED 50 MILLION BOTTLES WORLDWIDE AND THE MONEY KEPT ROLLING IN AS TONS UPON TONS OF FISH PARTS WERE USED TO MAKE THIS RATHER STICKY SUBSTANCE. DURING THE 1890'S, WILLIAM NELSON LEPAGE REPORTEDLY SOLD HIS SHARE OF THE COMPANY BUT MAINTAINED THE RIGHTS TO THE NAME OF THE GLUE WHEREAS OVER THE COURSE OF TIME SIMPLY BECAME ONE SINGLE HOUSEHOLD WORD WHICH WAS TO BE RECOGNIZED ON A GLOBAL SCALE – LEPAGE.

IN 1897, THE GLUE GURU MOVED TO BRITISH COLUMBIA (VANCOUVER) WHERE HE HAD HOPED TO RE-ESTABLISH HIMSELF BY MATCHING HIS EARLIER SUCCESSES. DUE TO THE FACT THAT GIBSON'S LANDING WAS A THRIVING LOGGING AND FISHING COMMUNITY, IT WAS CHOSEN AS A LOCATION TO INSTITUTE A CANADIAN ENTITY ON THE PACIFIC COAST. HENCE, A PARCEL OF LAND WAS PURCHASED FROM THE GIBSON FAMILY AND CONSTRUCTION OF A LARGE GLUE FACTORY WAS NOW UNDERWAY. BUT THINGS WERE NOT MEANT TO BE AS HIS FORMER PARTNERS IN THE UNITED STATES SOUGHT LEGAL OWNERSHIP OF THE LEPAGE FAMILY NAME. THE RATHER LENGTHY AND COSTLY LEGAL BATTLE WHICH HAD ENSUED, PROVED ITSELF TO BE THE DOWNFALL OF WILLIAM NELSON LEPAGE AS HE REPORTEDLY LOST THE ARGUMENT MERELY BECAUSE OF THE FACT THAT ACCORDING TO THE JUDICIAL SYSTEM SOUTH OF THE 49TH PARALLEL OF LATITUDE, HE WASN'T AN AMERICAN CITIZEN WHICH LITERALLY MEANT THAT HIS FORMER PARTNERS COULD DO AS THEY DAMN WELL PLEASED WITH THE FRENCH ORIENTED NAME. UNABLE TO FULLY UTILIZE THE FAMILY NAME ON HIS GIBSON'S LANDING GLUE PRODUCT, WILLIAM NELSON LEPAGE WAS FORCED TO CEASE OPERATIONS FORTHWITH.

ALTHOUGH THIS MEMBER OF THE LEPAGE FAMILY TREE WAS ONE OF THE ORIGINAL FOUNDING MEMBERS OF THE ROYAL VANCOUVER YACHT CLUB IN COAL HARBOUR, HE STILL DIED A POPPER ON SEPTEMBER 16TH, 1919 AS THE INVENTOR OF THE HOUSEHOLD GLUE LITERALLY LOST THE VAST MAJORITY OF

HIS FORTUNE TO HIS AMERICAN COUNTERPARTS. DURING THE 1940's, (1941), THE AMERICANIZED WING OF LEPAGE'S INC. SET UP A CANADIAN BASE OF OPERATION IN MONTREAL AND EVENTUALLY MOVED TO TORONTO TEN YEARS LATER. BY 1960, LEPAGE'S LTD. WAS FORMED IN CANADA AS A SEPARATE ENTITY FROM LEPAGE'S U.S.A. AND LEPAGE'S U.K. HENKEL CORPORATION OF GERMANY.

TO THIS VERY DAY, NO MEMBER OF THE LEPAGE FAMILY HAS LEGAL JURISDICTIONAL RIGHTS TO THEIR OWN SURNAME WITHOUT PROPER AUTHORIZATION. IT IS LARGELY DUE TO THIS REASON AS TO WHY I, BENOIT LEPAGE HAVE PURPOSELY WRITTEN THE CONTENTS OF THIS BOOK IN THE THIRD PERSON, UNDER A PSEUDONYM, WITH A COMBINATION OF INTEGRATED FAMILY NAMES AS BEING THE AUTHOR BECAUSE THE TWO CORPORATE ENTITIES (ROYAL LEPAGE AND LEPAGE'S INC.) CONTROL ALL ASPECTS OF THE FAMILY NAME ON A LEGAL BASIS AND IN ORDER FOR ME TO GET MY POINT ACROSS — IT SEEMED TO BE THE MOST LOGICAL APPROACH TO THE TASK THAT OF WHICH I HAD DEDICATED 13 YEARS OF MY LIFE RESEARCHING AND COMPLYING INTO MANUSCRIPT FORM (LATE FALL 1989 TO DECEMBER 31ST, 2002).

Chapter 1 - DIEU ET MON DROIT

Although the history of the LePage family name living on the North American Continent is supposedly that of nobility, pride and honor, it's far from the actual truth. The first family member to set sail from France was an unscrupulous individual who oddly enough had the nobility title of LePage dit Chaudron despite the fact that he was merely a cook in the services of the Dutchesse de Nevers. Ironic as it may seem to most of today's present members of the LePage family name of both Canada and the United States, this renegade of the family tree had no influence on anyone whatsoever, as he was nothing more than a common criminal, an assassin who rendered his services to the highest bidder.

Using the pretext of being one of France's self-righteous members of a most honorable fraternity, LePage dit Chaudron mingled amongst the elite seeking his next exploitable prey. It's not exactly certain as to who were his victims and/or who paid for his valuable services, the only thing that is for certain is the fact that in 1542, he was taken from his prison cell in France and forced to set sail across the high seas to Canada as a member of the Roberval expedition — Roberval, being of course none other than Jean-Francois de La Rocque de Roberval. The French explorer who was interestingly enough commissioned by the King of France (Francois the First) to establish a Roman Catholic colony in the name of the Almighty Himself. The King was even willing to sacrifice the lives of its criminals taken from the prisons and forced to join Roberval's expedition.

According to French historians, the prisoners had the most deplorable reputations that France had ever seen. Two of whom were said to be paid assassins, LePage and his fellow hitman Louis de Villaine. It's obvious to say that Canada was going to be the French version of the British penal colony like in Australia. The saving

GRACE FOR CANADA WAS THAT THIS ILL-CONCEIVED EXPEDITION ONLY LASTED A FEW MONTHS. INTERESTINGLY, JACQUES CARTIER WAS TO ACT AS ROBERVAL'S GUIDE BUT FOR SOME REASON /OR ANOTHER, THE EXPERIENCED SAILOR GOT IMPATIENT AND SET SAIL WITHOUT THE ROBERVAL PARTY IN MAY OF 1541.

ONE YEAR LATER, CARTIER AND THE ROBERVAL EXPEDITION MET AT ST. JOHN'S, NEWFOUNDLAND. DESPITE THE KING'S REQUEST FOR JACQUES CARTIER TO SERVE AS GUIDE, ROBERVAL WAS GIVEN THE ONE FINGER SALUTE AND CARTIER RETURNED BACK TO FRANCE. APPARENTLY, AT THIS TIME PERIOD OF HISTORY ROBERVAL WAS ASSOCIATED WITH AN INDIVIDUAL (BIDOUX DE LARTIQUE) WHO WAS SAID TO BE SAILING THE SEVEN SEAS AS A PIRATE. AND DUE TO HIS FRIENDSHIP WITH THE KNOWN BUCCANEER, ROBERVAL WAS HAVING A LOT OF DIFFICULTY TRYING TO ORGANIZE HIS EXPEDITION. FORCED TO SELL SOME PROPERTIES AND BORROW MONEY FROM HIS RELATIVES, RUMORS SPREAD LIKE WILDFIRE THROUGHOUT THE STREETS OF FRANCE THAT ROBERVAL HIMSELF WAS INVOLVED WITH THE SEIZURE OF ENGLISH SHIPS ON THE OPEN SEAS. UPON HEARING SOME OF THE RUMORS AND TALL TALES THAT WERE CIRCULATING ABOUT, THE ENGLISH AMBASSADOR QUICKLY COMPLAINED TO THE FRENCH KING, WHO IN TURN LAUGHED IT OFF AS MERE GOSSIP. AS IT SO HAPPENED, WHILE ROBERVAL WAS BUSY MAKING HIS PREPARATIONS FOR THE VOYAGE – THE SPANIARDS WERE SOMEWHAT DISPLEASED ABOUT WHAT WAS BEGINNING TO UNFOLD AND ONE OF CHARLES THE FIFTH'S SPIES HAD INFORMED HIM THAT ROBERVAL'S DESTINATION WAS CANADA, (CHARLES V BEING THE RULER OF SPAIN WHO FAILED TO UNITE PROTESTANTS AND ROMAN CATHOLICS AS ONE SEPARATE ENTITY).

BE THAT AS IT MAY, THE ROBERVAL EXPEDITION SET SAIL IN THE SPRING OF 1542 WITH 200 ILL PREPARED FRENCH COLONISTS (LESS THAN HALF OF WHICH WERE CONVICTS TAKEN FROM THEIR PRISON CELLS). THE CROSSING REPORTEDLY LASTED FROM APRIL 16TH TO JUNE 8TH, ON WHICH DATE THE UNHAPPY MEETING TOOK PLACE AT ST. JOHN'S. ALONG WITH SUPPLYING ROBERVAL WITH VOLUNTEER PRISONERS TO HELP POPULATE HIS FRENCH ROMAN CATHOLIC COLONY, THE KING OF FRANCE ALSO FITTED HIM WITH THREE SHIPS. AFTER PARTING COMPANY IN NEWFOUNDLAND, THE EXPEDITION NAVIGATED ITS WAY UP THE ST. LAWRENCE AND DROPPING ANCHOR AT CHARLESBOURG-ROYAL ON THE CAP ROUGE WHERE CARTIER HAD ALREADY BUILT A FORT.

IRONICALLY, ROBERVAL BUILT A FORTIFIED HOUSE ON HIS PENAL COLONY TO EITHER KEEP HIS VOLUNTEER PRISONERS IN /OR PERHAPS TO KEEP ANY DISSIDENT VOLUNTEERS OUT. BEING THE SORT OF PERSON THAT HE ACTUALLY WAS, ROBERVAL HAD VISIONS OF FINDING PRECIOUS STONES AND GOLD, AND RETURNING BACK TO FRANCE A WEALTHY MAN – HE SOON BEGAN EXPLORING THE COUNTRY SIDE LOOKING FOR HIS VAST FORTUNES ALONG THE BANKS OF THE ST. LAWRENCE RIVER. AND SINCE HE ALREADY KNEW THAT HIS CREW

WERE HARDEN CRIMINALS, IT'S SAFE TO SAY THAT THE FORTIFIED HOUSE WAS MORE THAN LIKELY DESIGNED TO PROTECT THE VAST FORTUNES THAT HE WAS HOPING TO COLLECT WHILE RESIDING IN CANADA.

AS WINTER WAS SETTING IN, ROBERVAL HAD A REBELLION ON HIS HANDS, FAMINE AND SICKNESS CAUSED THE REMAINING SURVIVORS TO NOT ONLY QUESTION HIS AUTHORITY, BUT HIS SANITY AS WELL. ACCUSED OF TREATING THEM IN A MUST CRUEL AND UNJUST FASHION, "MICHAEL GAILLON WAS HANGED FOR HIS THEFT "THE RECORD BOOK STATED, WHILE OTHERS WERE "PUT IN IRONS "/OR WHIPPED FOR THEIR OFFENSES. FURTHER STATED IN THE DOCUMENT;"... FORCING THEM TO WORK; OTHERWISE THEY WERE DEPRIVED OF FOOD AND DRINK. IF ANYONE FAILED IN HIS DUTY, ROBERVAL HAD HIM PUNISHED. ONE DAY HE HAD SIX OF THEM HANGED AND SOME HE ORDERED TO BE BANISHED TO AN ISLAND, IN LEG-IRONS, BECAUSE THEY HAD BEEN CAUGHT IN PETTY THEFTS INVOLVING NOT MORE THAN FIVE SOUS. OTHERS, BOTH MEN AND WOMEN WERE FLOGGED FOR THE SAME OFFENSE."

IN YET ANOTHER TWIST OF IRONY, MOST HISTORIANS EXCUSE ROBERVAL'S ACTIONS BY STATING THAT HIS FRENCH COLONY WAS COMPOSED PRINCIPALLY OF HABITUAL CRIMINALS AND THAT HE HAD NO OTHER CHOICE BUT TO DISPLAY SUCH TERRIBLE SEVERITY. BUT THAT IN ITSELF DID NOT EXONERATE HIM FOR WHAT HE DID TO HIS OWN FLESH AND BLOOD DURING THE EXPEDITION. AS THE STORY GOES, MARGUERITE DE LA ROCQUE AND HER YOUNG MALE LOVER'S ACTIONS DURING THE VOYAGE WAS SAID TO HAVE ENRAGED SIEUR ROBERVAL SO MUCH THAT HE LITERALLY BOOTED THEM OFF THE SHIP AND BANISHED THEM TO AN ISLAND (ILE DES DEMONS) IN THE ST. LAWRENCE RIVER NEAR THE MOUTH OF THE RIVIERE SAINT-PAUL. THE SERVANT-GIRL DAMIENNE ALSO ACCOMPANIED THEM ON THEIR LITTLE ISLAND PARADISE. WHILE LIVING IN EXILE ON THE ISLAND, MARGUERITE GAVE BIRTH TO A CHILD, WHO DIED. NOT LONG AFTERWARDS, THE YOUNG LOVER DIED AS DID THE SERVANT-GIRL. THE SOLE SURVIVOR, SIEUR ROBERVAL'S BANISHED KIN, MARGUERITE, WAS LATER PICKED UP BY A PASSING FISHER'S BOAT AND BROUGHT HER BACK TO FRANCE WITH THEM.

NEEDLESS TO SAY, BEFORE THE INCIDENT MARGUERITE DE LA ROCQUE WAS VERY CLOSE TO SIEUR ROBERVAL BUT AFTERWARDS, THAT RELATIONSHIP WAS VIRTUALLY NON-EXISTENT. COINCIDENTLY, MARGUERITE WAS CO-OWNER OF THE SAME PROPERTIES OF WHICH ROBERVAL ALSO OWNED. WITHIN THREE YEARS OF HIS RETURN BACK TO FRANCE, SIEUR ROBERVAL'S HOLDINGS WERE MORTGAGED AND HIS CHATEAU THREATENED WITH SEIZURE. LIKE HIS BUCCANEER BUDDY BIDOUX DE LARTIQUE, JEAN-FRANCOIS DE LA ROCQUE DE ROBERVAL DIDN'T REALLY GIVE A DAMN AS TO WHOSE TOES HE STEPPED ON IN ORDER TO GET RICH QUICK.

Knowing full well that Roberval was defiantly involved in piracy activities in the English Channel when he was originally granted the commission by the King of France, Jacques Cartier swallowed his pride and got involved with a rescue mission to help save Roberval and his remaining survivors; returning them back to France — a rescue mission that had Cartier and Roberval at odds with one another once again. Apparently, both parties in question had two different tales to tell about the events that unfolded. In 1544, both Cartier and Roberval stood before a tribunal established to examine the accounts of what actually happened. Jacques Cartier was the victor and sometime later, Roberval fell prey to an assassin — there is no evidence to lay blame on who was responsible for his death. All that is known is that while Roberval was coming out of a Calvinist meeting one night in 1560, he and his fellow Protestants were attacked and Roberval lay dead at a street corner in Paris. Jean-Francois de La Rocque de Roberval thus became one of the first victims of the Wars of Religion.

Coincidently, there is also no evidence on hand to say for certain if LePage dit Chaudron /or even Louis de Villaine perished in Canada /or if they returned back to France with the remaining survivors of Roberval's ill-conceived expedition of 1542 — even family records are somewhat sketchy on this little detail!!!

One also might be excused for asking yet another obvious question pertaining as to why such a devoted Protestant, who was also an active pirate at sea was put in charge of a bunch of Roman Catholics trying to set-up housekeeping in Canada in the first place. Well, like anything else in life its not what you know but rather who you know. As it so happens, Sieur Roberval actually came from a very respectable family in the south of France. His father was none other than Bernard de La Rocque dit Couillaud, the governor at Carcassonne — dear old dad was also the seigneur of Chatelrein and of Isabeau de Poitiers. Roberval's father spent a good portion of his time as a gentleman of the King's household (an ambassador as well as an officer). It was there whereupon Roberval first met Prince Francois before becoming King of France and was ordained the young Prince's protector.

Unfortunately, as a Protestant convert, Roberval had to flee the country for fear of losing his life in 1535. The only thing that saved his sorry ass was the friendship that he had with the King. Not long afterwards, Roberval returned back to France and once again continued living under the King's roof. Upon his return he

ALMOST IMMEDIATELY DENOUNCED THE PROTESTANT FAITH BY BECOMING A CATHOLIC AND CONVINCED THE FRENCH MONARCHY THAT HIS INTENTIONS WERE HONORABLE. IN DOING SO, ROBERVAL CONCEIVED THE IDEA OF GAINING MATERIAL WEALTH IN THE UNEXPLORED FRONTIER OF NORTH AMERICA AND STARTED FINE TUNING HIS DOG AND PONY SHOW FOR THE FRENCH KING. AFTER HEARING THE SELF-RIGHTEOUS DRIBBLE FROM ROBERVAL AND FEELING SORRY FOR HIM, THE KING OF FRANCE APPOINTED HIS FORMER PROTECTOR THE LIEUTENANT-GENERAL OF CANADA IN CHARGE OF SPREADING THE ROMAN CATHOLIC FAITH. KNOWING THAT ROBERVAL WAS BY NO MEANS A PROPER SAILOR, HE HAD TO BE ASSIGNED A CREW THAT WERE KNOWLEDGEABLE OF WHAT TROUBLES MAYBE AHEAD. BUT THE KING WAS UNABLE TO FIND WELL EXPERIENCED SAILORS WHO WERE WILLING TO SAIL UNDER ROBERVAL'S COMMAND. HAVING NO OTHER ALTERNATIVE, THE KING, THEN, DECIDED TO OPEN UP HIS PRISON CELLS ASKING FOR VOLUNTEERS. IN ESSENCE, THOSE SELECTED WERE GIVEN A CHOICE; THE GUILLOTINE /OR THE SEA VOYAGE.

SINCE ITS FIRST CONCEPTION, CANADA WAS DESTINED TO BECOME A SYSTEM OF SEGREGATION AS THE SEIGNIORIAL REGIME OF FRANCE PITTED MAN AGAINST HIS RELIGIOUS CONVICTIONS. TWENTY-EIGHT MONTHS PRIOR TO SIEUR ROBERVAL'S SETTING SAIL, THE KING PUT TO PAPER THE TERMS OF HIS COMMISSION ON JANUARY 15TH, 1540. AS IT TURNS OUT, THE FRENCH MONARCHY WANTED ROBERVAL TO ESTABLISH A COLONY BASED ON THE MODEL OF THEIR **SEIGNIORAL TENURE**. HE WAS NOT ONLY TO POPULATE THIS COLONY WITH THE OFFSPRING OF HIS SO-CALLED EXPERIENCED CREW, BUT HE WAS ALSO TO ESTABLISH THE SEIGNIORIAL SYSTEM FOR THE PURPOSE OF AGRICULTURAL NEEDS OF ITS PEOPLE FOR FUTURE GENERATIONS.

BY THE TERMS OF HIS COMMISSION, ROBERVAL WAS GIVEN THE AUTHORITY TO TAKE POSSESSION OF CANADA AND CLAIM IT AS PART OF FRANCE'S NEWFOUND TERRITORY. HE WAS TO IMMEDIATELY INTRODUCE THE CATHOLIC FAITH AND ITS CHRISTIAN TEACHINGS, AS WELL AS TO INSTITUTE LAWS AND OFFICERS OF THE JUSTICE SYSTEM IN ORDER THAT THE NEW RESIDENTS OF QUEBEC CONDUCT THEMSELVES IN GOOD BEHAVIOR AND AT THE SAME TIME, FEAR THE ALMIGHTY GOD. THE KING THUSLY BESTOWED AMPLE POWERS ONTO SIEUR ROBERVAL AS QUEBEC'S NEW LORD AND MASTER BEFORE SENDING HIM OFF ONTO HIS JOURNEY ACROSS THE HIGH SEAS. ESSENTIALLY, ROBERVAL AND THOSE INCORPORATED AS PART OF HIS ADMINISTRATIVE ENTOURAGE WERE GIVEN THE DIVINE RIGHT TO DO WHATEVER THEY WANTED AND NO ONE HAD THE POWER TO EVEN QUESTION THAT AUTHORITY. JEAN-FRANCOIS DE LA ROCQUE DE ROBERVAL AND HIS ENTIRE ADVISORY GROUP HAD A MONOPOLY OF THE COUNTRY AND ITS TRADE AS LONG AS THEY DEEMED IT SO. ALL OTHERS WERE PROHIBITED FROM INTERFERING DIRECTLY AND/OR INDIRECTLY WITH THE EVERYDAY AFFAIRS OF THE NEW COLONY. EVEN VISITING THE COLONY WAS

PROHIBITED WITHOUT PROPER AUTHORIZATION. NOT EVEN THE EXPERIENCED SAILOR JACQUES CARTIER COULD SET FOOT ONTO CANADIAN SOIL WITHOUT FIRST RECEIVING ROBERVAL'S PERMISSION.

SIEUR ROBERVAL WAS TO BECOME CANADA'S VERY FIRST FRENCH DICTATOR HIDING BEHIND THE CLOAK OF THE FRENCH KING'S RELIGIOUS BELIEFS AND ALL THAT IT STOOD FOR. ON FEBRUARY 16TH, 1540 ROBERVAL TOOK THE FRATERNAL OATH OF OFFICE AS FRANCE'S ROMAN CATHOLIC REPRESENTATIVE FOR THE TERRITORY IN THE NEW WORLD KNOWN NOWADAYS BY ALL AS THE PROVINCE OF QUEBEC.

ONLY FIFTY-SIX YEARS AFTER THE SOMEWHAT FAILURE OF THE ROBERVAL EXPEDITION, THE FRENCH MONARCHY WAS AT IT AGAIN. AS BEFORE, HARDEN CRIMINAL WERE TAKEN FROM THEIR PRISON CELLS IN FRANCE AND FORCED TO SET SAIL ACROSS THE SEAS. THE VOYAGE OF 1542 COMPRISING OF 40 CRIMINALS AND THE 1598 VOYAGE CONSISTING OF A BAND OF 60 CONVICTS.

ON JANUARY 12TH, 1598 ROBERVAL'S COMMISSION WAS TRANSFERRED OVER TO THE MARQUIS DE LA ROCHE, A CATHOLIC NOBLEMAN OF BRITTANY WHO PETITIONED THE KING OF FRANCE TO PERMIT HIM TO COLONIZE CANADA. LIKE ROBERVAL, ALL THE MARQUIS WANTED FROM THE FRENCH KING WAS THE RIGHT TO HAVE A MONOPOLY ON THE COUNTRY'S TRADE. THE MARQUIS WAS THUSLY GIVEN THE SAME POWERS AS HIS PREDECESSOR — TO BESTOW ONTO OTHERS LAND GRANTS AND TITLES OF DISTINCTION SUCH AS BARONS, VICE-COUNTS AND ANY OTHER TITLE OF NOBILITY THAT HE SO DESIRED IN ORDER TO ACCOMPLISH THE FRENCH DREAM OF A CIVILIZED NATION FOR ITS PEOPLE.

IRONICALLY, SOME YEARS PREVIOUS TO THIS THE MARQUIS DE LA ROCHE HAD RECEIVED THE BLESSING OF THE FRENCH MONARCHY AND HAD BEEN COMMISSIONED TO ESTABLISH A COLONY IN NEWFOUNDLAND BUT DUE TO THE CIRCUMSTANCES BEYOND HIS CONTROL, HE WAS FORCED TO ABANDON HIS PLANS AS MISFORTUNE TOOK OVER EVEN BEFORE HIS SHIPS WERE ABLE TO LEAVE THE FRENCH DOCKS, AT LEAST THAT'S WHAT HISTORIANS WISH US TO BELIEVE IS TRUE. THE FACT OF THE MATTER IS, THE MARQUIS HAD MUCH INFLUENCE ON THE FRENCH MONARCHY AND IN 1598 THEY GAVE HIM YET ANOTHER CHANCE AFTER SCREWING THEM OVER ON THE NEWFOUNDLAND PROPOSAL — BUT THIS TIME HE HAD TO PROVE HIS WORTHINESS. AS BEFORE, THE ONLY OBSTACLE IN THE MARQUIS' WAY WAS THE FACT THAT HE COULDN'T FIND PEOPLE STUPID ENOUGH TO JOIN HIM ON THE VOYAGE. NO MATTER WHO HE TALKED WITH, THE ANSWER WAS ALWAYS THE SAME AS HE COULDN'T CONVINCE ANY OF THE RESPECTABLE FRENCHMEN OF FRANCE TO ACCOMPANY HIM TO THE NEW TERRITORY OF CANADA. THE FRENCH NOBILITY WAS NOT THE LEAST BIT INTERESTED IN RISKING THEIR LIVES JUST FOR THE MERE SAKE OF CIVILIZING THE PAGAN HEATHENS OF CANADA'S WILDERNESS. ONCE THE VOLUNTEER PRISONERS WERE ON BOARD AND SUITABLE SECONDARY NOBLES

WERE FOUND (NOBILITY IN NAME ONLY), THE MARQUIS' EXPEDITION OF 1598 SET SAIL FOR THE NEW WORLD.

IT'S REPORTED THAT THE MARQUIS DE LA ROCHE MADE TWO SEPARATE VOYAGE TO THE NEW WORLD IN 1598. THE FIRST CONSISTING OF THREE-HUNDRED MEN AND WOMEN, MAINLY OF THE CRIMINAL TYPE NATURE AS NO MEMBER OF NOBILITY IN FRANCE WANTED TO EVEN ATTEMPT TO SETTLE THE UNEXPLORED BARREN LANDS OF CANADA. APPARENTLY, AFTER THE LARGER OF LA ROCHE'S VESSELS WAS WRECKED FOR SOME REASON /OR ANOTHER, HIS EXPEDITION RETURNED BACK TO FRANCE. ACCORDING TO SOME HISTORIANS, THE MARQUIS DE LA ROCHE'S FIRST ATTEMPTED VOYAGE FAILED LARGELY TO HIS HAVING AN INEXPERIENCED CREW. BE THAT AS IT MAY, LATER IN THAT SAME YEAR YET ANOTHER ATTEMPT WAS MADE. THIS TIME, A MUCH LARGER BAND OF CONVICTS WAS ORGANIZED. THE MARQUIS AND HIS NEWLY ACQUIRED CREW OF CONVICTS THUSLY SET-UP HOUSEKEEPING OFF THE NOVA SCOTIA COASTLINE AND LANDED HIS PARTY ON SABLE ISLAND WHILE HE SCOUTED AROUND FOR A SUITABLE PLACE TO ESTABLISH A SETTLEMENT ON NOVA SCOTIA'S MAINLAND. BUT LIKE ANYTHING ELSE IN LIFE, IT WASN'T MEANT TO BE AS A SUDDEN STORM FORCED HIM TO SET SAIL BACK TO FRANCE. INTERESTINGLY, ACCORDING TO SOME WELL RESPECTED HISTORIANS – THE MARQUIS PERISHED ON SABLE ISLAND ALONG WITH HIS VOLUNTEER PRISONERS. WHILE OTHER HISTORIANS CLEARLY STATE THAT THE MARQUIS BARELY SURVIVED THE GALE FORCE WINDS OF THE ATLANTIC. BUT THE FACT OF THE MATTER IS, WHILE THE MARQUIS WAS OUT SCOUTING AROUND TO ESTABLISH A SETTLEMENT ALONG THE SHORES OF NOVA SCOTIA, HE ABANDONED HIS FORCED VOLUNTEER CREW AS SOON AS THE SEVERE STORM APPEARED OVER THE HORIZON AND HEADED BACK TO FRANCE. AFTERALL, THE VAST MAJORITY OF THEM LEFT BEHIND WERE ONLY HARDENED CRIMINALS AND WHO REALLY CARED IF THEY LIVED /OR DIED ANYWAYS.

FIVE YEARS AFTER THE SO-CALLED MAROONING AND/OR SUBSEQUENT DEATH OF THE MARQUIS DE LA ROCHE ON SABLE ISLAND, LESS THAN A DOZEN SURVIVORS WERE FOUND ON THE ALMOST BARREN ISLAND PARADISE. PERHAPS THE HISTORIANS HAD GOOD REASON FOR LYING ABOUT WHAT REALLY HAPPENED BUT THAT STILL DIDN'T GIVE THEM THE RIGHT TO CREATE THE ILLUSION THAT THE MARQUIS DE LA ROCHE DIED A HERO WHEN IN FACT HE WAS NOTHING BUT A COWARD WITH HIS OWN HIDDEN AGENDA TO FULFILL. THE REMAINING SURVIVORS THUSLY MADE ALLEGATIONS THAT THE MARQUIS FEARED FOR HIS OWN SAFETY AND FLED THE STORM LEAVING THEM, THE CONVICTS TO FEND FOR THEMSELVES. LIKE ROBERVAL, THE MARQUIS OBVIOUSLY ASSUMED THAT THERE WOULD BE NO ONE LEFT ALIVE TO EXPLAIN THE TRUE DETAILS OF HIS COWARDLY DEEDS AS THE VAST MAJORITY OF HISTORIANS AIDED AND ABETTED WITH THE ILLUSION IN ORDER TO JUSTIFY THE SELF-SERVING FRENCH ROMAN CATHOLIC DIVINE MISSION FROM GOD. BY THIS TIME PERIOD OF COURSE,

France laid claim to Newfoundland, Labrador and the Maritimes, including Nova Scotia.

In 1599, another attempt was made to settle the New World by the French Roman Catholics. But unlike all of the other previous attempts, this one was somewhat successful. It was a time period of Canadian history that saw the fur trade in its infancy. A fraternal transaction was thusly agreed upon which gave a monopoly to Pontgrave of St. Malo, on the coast of Brittany, and Pierre Chauvin of Honfleur, under the strict condition that they bring fifty colonists each year to the newfound territory of France. The exact same privileges of establishing feudal lordships that were applied to Roberval and the Marquis de La Roche also applied here as well. According to historians, Pontgrave, who was already familiar with the St. Lawrence River, wanted to establish a trading post some distance up river, but his partner Chauvin preferred Tadoussac, near the gulf. Nevertheless, sixteen men were designated to be left at the established trading post of Chauvin's choosing in the fall of 1600 to collect furs from the Indians. But when Pontgrave's partner returned to Canada the following summer to check up on his men, he found the trading post at Tadoussac totally deserted.

It appears that the survivors of the trading post befriended the Indians and took refuge with them in the wilderness of Quebec. Therefore marking the actual beginning of Quebec's mixed Franco-Indian bloodlines as it is well documented that the survivors of the trading post did in fact mingle with the native peoples of the Rimouski and Riviere-du-Loup regions of the Province. Despite this little known fact of history, the majority of the French Roman Catholic genealogical research data for the Province of Quebec dismisses all of this as being a true reflection of Quebec's past simply because of the fact that the Catholic Church has never sanctioned fornication with the Indians. In cross-referencing the names related to the LePage's of Quebec for example, the Cyr and Poirier families – only the Cyr family members seemed to openly admit to being that of North American Indian bloodlines.

By 1608, France found it necessary to implement a system of government when Samuel de Champlain marked the site of the first building that was to be constructed in Quebec City on July 3RD. Needless to say, it was the exact same system of government that Roberval, the Marquis de La Roche and the Tadoussac trading post settlement concepts were suppose to have had established. Like a male canine, the French marked their territory in order to spread good

CHEER AND EDUCATE THOSE WHO WORSHIPED PAGAN GODS. COINCIDENTLY, IT IS STATED BY MOST HISTORIANS THAT THE SEIGNIORIAL REGIME IN CANADA DIDN'T BEGIN UNTIL THE EARLY PARTS OF THE 1600'S. THEY BASE THIS THEORY ON THE LACK OF A PAPER TRAIL DURING THE SO-CALLED PREVIOUS FAILED ATTEMPTS BY THE FRENCH MONARCHY AND CHAMPLAIN'S FINAL ESTABLISHING OF THE SETTLEMENT AT THE FUTURE SITE OF QUEBEC CITY. LOUIS HEBERT, A FRENCH DOCTOR OF MEDICINE FROM PARIS IS ACCREDITED AS HAVING THE FIRST GRANTED SEIGNIORY IN NEW FRANCE IN 1623. THIS DESPITE THE FACT THAT HEBERT BROUGHT HIS ENTIRE FAMILY (WIFE AND THREE CHILDREN) TO CANADA SIX YEARS PREVIOUSLY AND WAS GRANTED PERMISSION BY SAMUEL DE CHAMPLAIN TO BUILD HIMSELF A HOUSE NOT VERY FAR FROM A FORT THAT HAD BEEN CONSTRUCTED AT THE SITE WERE CHAMPLAIN HIMSELF HAD ORIGINALLY MARKED IN 1608. REPORTEDLY, HEBERT'S HOUSE WAS SAID TO BE A ONE STORY STONE STRUCTURE THAT MEASURED TWENTY FEET WIDE AND FORTY FEET IN LENGTH AND AROUND THIS STONE DWELLING, THE FRENCH DOCTOR APPARENTLY HAD ESTABLISHED THE IDEAL LITTLE MODEL FARM. CHAMPLAIN WAS SAID TO BE SO IMPRESSED WITH THE DOCTOR'S EFFORTS IN MAKING CANADA THE NEW HOME FOR HIS ENTIRE FAMILY THAT HE WAS SAID TO HAVE ACCORDED HEBERT SEIGNIORIAL RIGHTS ON FEBRUARY 4TH, 1623 AND THE DOCUMENT ITSELF WAS THUSLY NOTED IN THE RECORD BOOKS SIGNED BY FRENCH NOBILITY THE DUC DE MONTMORENCI, THE VICEROY OF NEW FRANCE. IT WASN'T UNTIL THREE YEARS LATER THAT THE BUREAUCRATIC WHEELS OF THE FRENCH MONARCHY IN FRANCE CONFIRMED THE LAND TRANSACTION AS BEING SUCH. BETWEEN THE YEARS 1633 AND 1663, THERE WERE AN ESTIMATED SIXTY SEIGNIORIAL ESTATES GRANTED, THAT OF WHICH LESS THAN HALF WERE ISSUED TO SOME RATHER SHADY CHARACTERS.

BEFORE MOVING ON, ONE OTHER DISCREPANCY CONCERNING CANADA'S PAST MUST BE RAISED. CONTRARY AS TO WHAT SOME HISTORIANS WISH US TO BELIEVE, THE FACT OF THE MATTER IS THAT ACCORDING TO FRANCE'S VISION OF CANADA, IT WAS GOING TO BE CONSISTING LARGELY OF MURDERERS, RAPISTS AND THIEVES. THE FACT THAT A RENEGADE LEPAGE SET FOOT ONTO CANADIAN SOIL SOME 120 YEARS BEFORE THEY ACTUALLY SETTLED ALONG THE BANKS OF THE ST. LAWRENCE RIVER IN 1664 CANNOT BE DISPUTED BY ANYONE NO MATTER WHO MAKES THE CLAIM!!!

FURTHERMORE, LESS THAN TWENTY YEARS AFTER THE FIRST LEPAGE'S OF FRANCE SETTLED ON THE BANKS OF THE ST. LAWRENCE YET ANOTHER RENEGADE OF THE NOBLE FAMILY TREE URGED THE KING OF ENGLAND (CHARLES THE FIRST) TO ACT SWIFTLY IN THE APPROPRIATION OF CANADA AND PARTS OF THE UNITED STATES AS BRITAIN'S NEW TERRITORY. IN AS SUCH, A SCHEME WAS PUT FORWARD BY LOUIS LEPAGE DE L'OMESNIL (IN FRENCH NO LESS) OFFERING A MAP AND A DETAILED DESCRIPTION OF THE ST. LAWRENCE, THE GREAT LAKES,

THE MISSISSIPPI AND FLORIDA. EMPHASIS WAS PUT ON APPROPRIATING THESE LANDS IN THE NAME OF HUMANITY. IT'S OBVIOUS TO SAY THAT LOUIS LEPAGE DE L'OMESNIL DISAPPROVED OF WHAT WAS UNFOLDING BEHIND THE SCENES IN THE ROMAN CATHOLIC CHURCH'S NEW WORLD ORDER AND WAS TOTALLY PREPARED TO ABANDON HIS FRENCH NOBLE ANCESTRY IN FAVOR OF ENGLISH RULE.

WITH THAT BEING STATED, LET US NOW PUT FORWARD OTHER PIECES OF THE PUZZLE THAT EVEN THE LEPAGE'S THEMSELVES HAVE KEPT HIDDEN FOR SO MANY CENTURIES. ACCORDING TO THE ANCIENT CRAFT HISTORY OF THIS DISTINGUISHED FAMILY NAME, THE LEPAGE'S IN FRANCE WERE SUPPOSEDLY OF NOBLE BLOODLINE WHERE THEY HELD LARGE TRACTS OF LAND AND OWNED MANY BUSINESS VENTURES. FOR HUNDREDS UPON HUNDREDS OF YEARS, THEY WERE TREATED WITH RESPECT AND CONTINUED TO EXPAND THEIR ROYAL DOMAIN THROUGHOUT FRANCE AND EVENTUALLY CANADA. THE FIRST LEPAGE TO SUPPOSEDLY SETTLE IN THIS COUNTRY ORIGINALLY CAME FROM ILE DE FRANCE WHERE THEY HELD ESTATES AND MANORS. OF THIS FAMILY TREE, THEY BRANCHED OUT TO LIMOUSIN BUT THE MAIN COMPONENT OF THE FAMILY MOVED TO NORMANDY IN THE FIFTEENTH CENTURY. THE FAMILY ALSO BRANCHED OUT TO NIVERNILS AND OF THIS MIGRATION, GERMAIN AND LOUIS LEPAGE (SONS OF ETIENNE LEPAGE AND NICOLE BERTHELOT) SAILED TO THE NEWLY ACCLAIMED TERRITORY OF NEW FRANCE SETTLING ALONG THE BANKS OF THE ST. LAWRENCE RIVER IN 1664. ANOTHER MEMBER OF THIS DISTINGUISHED FAMILY NAME, BARTHELEMY LEPAGE SOON FOLLOWED AND MARRIED AT THE SETTLEMENT OF QUEBEC IN 1696. FROM THERE, THE HISTORY OF THE LEPAGE FAMILY TREE SEEMS TO GET A LITTLE VAGUE AS DIFFERENT VERSIONS OF THE FAMILY TREE ARE TOLD DEPENDING TOTALLY AS TO WHO'S TELLING THE STORY. FOR THAT REASON, ALL THE FACTS MUST BE BASED ON THE DOCUMENTATION THAT'S BEEN MADE AVAILABLE AND NOTHING ELSE.

LIKE THE 1544 TRIBUNAL OF ROBERVAL'S EXPEDITION, A CAREFUL ANALYSIS OF THE DOCUMENTATION MUST BE TAKEN IN ORDER TO SEPARATE THE FACTS FROM FAIRY TALES CONJURED UP BY CERTAIN MEMBERS OF THIS NOBLE AND SELF-RIGHTEOUS FAMILY IN A FEEBLE ATTEMPT TO KEEP THE BULK OF THE INFORMATION A WELL HIDDEN FAMILY SECRET. WHERE DOES ONE BEGIN IN TRYING TO EXPLAIN THIS PHENOMENON OF CANADIAN HISTORY THAT HAS UNFOLDED FOR SO MANY YEARS THAT HAS CAUSED EVEN THE LEPAGE FAMILY THEMSELVES TO EDIT AND REVISE THE TRUE FACTS AS A WAY AND MEANS OF DENYING WHAT HAS ACTUALLY HAPPENED THROUGHOUT THE CENTURIES. THE MOST HUMANE WAY MAYBE BY SIMPLY STATING THAT THE FACTS ESSENTIALLY SPEAK FOR THEMSELVES AND ARE SET IN STONE WITHIN THE NATIONAL ARCHIVES OF CANADA IN OTTAWA, AS WELL AS THE NATIONAL ARCHIVES OF QUEBEC IN QUEBEC CITY.

Right from the very beginning of time, excluding the paid assassin LePage dit Chaudron of course, the LePage's of Quebec controlled the destiny of its people, (whites as well as natives). As soon as they stepped off the ships from France and planted their feet firmly into the Francophone soil, they became instant lords and masters ruling the masses. Whatever they said was the law as they saw it, if anyone disputed their divine right by God, then, there was literally hell to pay. As the LePage's settled along the banks of the St. Lawrence, they promoted the teachings and philosophies of the Catholic faith and continued acquiring more and more land in the Rimouski, Quebec City and Montreal regions in order to spread the French monarchy's religious beliefs onto others.

Like in France, the new territory in French Canada was to be blessed with two separate classifications of people; those who have and those who have not. In as such, the LePage's began building their empires by taking full advantage of those who were having financial difficulties, as well as pulling whatever fraternal strings that they could as a way and means of obtaining various properties. On July 18TH, 1694 Rene LePage de Sainte-Claire acquired the title of more land located in Rimouski (Rene LePage was the son of Germain LePage). This seigneury ran along the St. Lawrence River bank for about six miles and went to the depth of yet another six miles. It should also be noted that the Ile Saint-Barnabe and all of the adjoining Islands, (small ones included) were incorporated as part of this land transaction. No money was said to have changed hands as the LePage's exchanged a tract of land that they had been previously granted at Saint-Francois on Ile d'Orleans.

Throughout his life time as seigneur of Rimouski, Rene LePage de Sainte-Claire continued to wheel and deal. Where ever someone was having money problems, he always managed to be the recipient of the land. Such was the case in 1705 when Charlotte-Francoise Junchereau de Saint-Denis had no choice but to sell her properties on the Metis River to the seigneur of Rimouski. Apparently, she too was a wheeler dealer of sorts carrying out transactions in her own name as well as using straw men to help close the deals. Unfortunately for her, she was forced to sell off her holdings that were inherited from her first husband due to a debt that she owed to a certain member of Quebec's upper society who just happened to be an associate of the LePage family dynasty. To top it all off, Charlotte-Francoise was also involved with lengthy legal battles in both Canada and in France which lasted from 1704 to

1713. After exhausting all legal avenues at her disposal, the King of France demanded that she discontinue her fruitless efforts and had her deported back to New France. To most of Quebec's male elite population, she was seen as a very dangerous competitor as she never knew when to call it quits. To that end, what ever debts she owed were slowly being called in for payment in full as her rivals decided to whip her out financially. That of which, the seigneur of Rimouski took full advantage of.

Although Rene LePage de Sainte-Claire was a ruthless businessman, he was by no means the only member of this prominent noble family to operate their financial empire in this manner. His son, Louis LePage de Sainte-Claire born on August 22ND, 1690, was cut from the exact same fraternal Roman Catholic cloth. Barely twenty-years-old, this member of the LePage family tree entered the Seminary of Quebec and on April 6TH, 1715 was ordained a priest in the Cathedral of Quebec. And since the LePage's of the New World were destined by divine intervention to rule their own little part of Quebec, as soon as Louis LePage de Sainte-Claire was ordained a priest, he was also appointed priest of the parish of Saint-Francois-de-Sales on Ile Jesus which literally opened the fraternity doors for LePage's to acquire more massive land grants in the name of the Almighty God Himself. It seems that the LePage's of Quebec were determined to create any type of facade in order to guarantee their divine seat at the right hand of God, even if that meant doing it from within the confines of the Roman Catholic Church itself.

Interestingly, after the death of Rene LePage yet another one of heirs took over the reigns of power at Rimouski and seemed to show a little bit more compassion to some of its inhabitants. Shortly before 1728, Pierre LePage dit St. Barnabe (the new seigneur of Rimouski) was said to have sold a piece of land supposedly at a cheap price, to a direct descendant of Jacques Cartier who was not only illiterate but also suffered from epileptic seizures. The descendant of this famous explorer, Toussaint Cartier would eventually be known as the hermit of Saint-Barnabe as he was said to have purchased the property on the Ile Saint-Barnabe with the full intention of wanting to be left alone. To some of Rimouski's population, the hermit had his fill of the madness surrounding the everyday activities of Quebec's powers that be and he simply wanted to live his life away from it all living in seclusion. Cartier lived on the Island for nearly forty years before coming to his death on January 30TH, 1767.

Ironically, historians to this very day dispute that the hermit was in fact related to Jacques Cartier. The reasoning that they give is that he was far too busy exploring as there apparently is no record of Jacques Cartier even fathering a child in accordance to Roman Catholic Church archives – as a direct result of this, history books state time and time again that the explorer never had any children. Considering the fact that these exact same historians clearly stated that the seigniorial regime in Canada didn't actually begin until sometime after both the Roberval and the Marquis de La Roche expeditions as well as after the establishing of the Tadoussac, including the so-called maroon death of the Marquis on Sable Island along with his volunteer prisoners, anything that they say supposedly of historical value must be taken with a very large grain of salt. They are either nuts /or merely fools not willing to accept a little known aspect of human nature known as illegitimate children. Maybe it has something to with their Roman Catholic upbringing /or perhaps even it's their outright ignorance to the truth??? In total honesty, it sounds more like a combination of the two. Afterall, Canada's Franco-Indian past had already proven the fact that a stiff rock hard erect penis has absolutely no guilt attached to it whatsoever and the historians therefore exploited this little known fact for all that it was worth. That is to say unless the Roman Catholic Church was willing to sanction the existence of illegitimate children as being part and parcel of human sexual relations!!!

Coincidently, only those families close to the King of France had the privilege of being bestowed with certain booties – all they had to do was ask for them and they would receive. Such was the case when sometime in the early 1700's, (on /or thereabouts 1725) when a member of the LePage's family tree who had migrated to Louisiana , Antoine-Simon LePage du Pratz, asked for and received a favor from the French monarchy that caused such an up roar throughout the entire French North American Continent that others demanded justice be served. For his services rendered as being one of the King's most favored fraternity members, Antoine-Simon LePage was rewarded with an increase in his salary as one of the French monarchy's doctors. At the time, most of the doctors and surgeons living in the colonies ruled by France were receiving a base salary of 600 livres while LePage, a mere botanist was receiving more than three times that amount (2,000 livres). Needless to say, fully experienced members of the medical profession were totally

OUTRAGED AT THE FAVORITISM THAT WAS BEING BESTOWED ONTO LEPAGE THAT THEY QUICKLY DEMANDED EQUAL PAY FOR THEIR SERVICES AS WELL.

AS IT TURNS OUT, THIS MEMBER OF THE LEPAGE FAMILY TREE (1689-1775) HAD BEEN COMMISSIONED BY THE KING OF FRANCE TO COMPILE VARIOUS PIECES OF DOCUMENTATION IN LOUISIANA IN PREPARATION FOR A SOON TO BE RELEASED BOOK DEPICTING THE FRENCH VERSION OF HOW FRANCE CIVILIZED THE BAYOU (1718-1758) AND BROUGHT PROSPERITY TO ITS PEOPLE. HIS WRITINGS; HISTOIRE DE LA LOUISIANA WAS PUBLISHED IN 1758 AND BY THE TIME THE FRENCH SURRENDERED LOUISIANA TO SPAIN IN 1763, THE LEPAGE'S OF LOUISIANA BEARING THE TITLE OF NOTABLE DISTINCTION (DU PRATZ) SIMPLY BECAME KNOWN AS DUPRATZ AS IT WAS SAID TO HAVE SOUNDED MORE CAJAN. AND WHEN THE UNITED STATES CONGRESS PASSED INTO LAW THE LOUISIANA PURCHASE OF 1803, THE MAJORITY OF THE REMAINING MEMBERS OF THE LEPAGE CLAN DROPPED THE "LE "OF THEIR SURNAME AND MERELY BECAME KNOWN AS PAGE AND/OR PAIGE. IT WAS AS THOUGH THE LEPAGE'S SOUTH OF THE 49TH PARALLEL OF LATITUDE ALSO HAD SOMETHING TO HIDE AND WERE WILLING TO SACRIFICE ALL TRACES OF THEIR FRENCH ROMAN CATHOLIC TIES TO THE MONARCHY IN FRANCE. WHICH WHILE RESEARCHING THE FAMILY TREE RAISED THE VERY QUESTION AS TO WHY THEY WERE SO ASHAMED OF THEIR HERITAGE IN FRENCH LOUISIANA???

MEANWHILE, BACK IN CANADA THE LEPAGE'S CONTINUED BUILDING UP THEIR LITTLE TIN-GOD EMPIRES BY EXPLOITING THE PEOPLE AND RAPING THE LAND OF ITS WEALTH. THE MOST NOTORIOUS OF THIS FACTION WAS NONE OTHER THAN LOUIS LEPAGE DE SAINTE-CLAIRE, WHO TOOK FULL ADVANTAGE OF HIS POSITION WITH THE CATHOLIC CHURCH IN ORDER TO PROSPER BOTH FINANCIALLY AS WELL AS POLITICALLY. ONLY FIVE YEARS AFTER BEING ORDAINED A PRIEST ON ILE JESUS, LOUIS LEPAGE DE SAINTE-CLAIRE ACQUIRED THE SEIGNEURY OF TERREBONNE (SEPTEMBER 12TH, 1720) AND WAS INSTANTLY UNDER FIRE AS CHARGES OF DERELICTION OF HIS DUTIES AS CANON OF SAINT-FRANCOIS-DE-SALES SOON EMERGED. APPARENTLY, THE CRITICISM CAME NOT ONLY FROM HIS PARISHIONERS BUT FROM THE CATHOLIC CHURCH OFFICIALS AS WELL. BEFORE LONG, ABBE LEPAGE (AS HE WAS SIMPLY REFERRED TO BY ALL) STOOD BEFORE THE FRENCH COURTS EXPLAINING HIS REPEATED ABSENCES FROM CHURCH SERVICES AND ALL OTHER MEETINGS HELD BY THE CATHEDRAL OF QUEBEC. BEING THE SILVER TONGUED FRENCH ROMAN CATHOLIC THAT HE WAS, ABBE LEPAGE REPORTEDLY DEFENDED HIMSELF BY STATING IN ESSENCE THAT HE HAD LAND TO ATTEND TOO AND THAT HE HAD NO TIME FOR THE UNPLEASANTNESS RHETORIC OF HIS RELIGIOUS CONGREGATION. HE, OF COURSE USED A MORE DIPLOMATIC TERM WHEN STATING HIS CASE TO THE SEIGNIORIAL COURT (THE ROYAL COURT AT THE TIME) PLEADING WITH THEM THAT HIS ESTATE REQUIRED HIS NEVER-ENDING PRESENCE.

The charges reportedly came to light on October 19TH, 1728 when the secretary-treasurer of the Cathedral of Quebec, Canon Charles Plante complained of LePage's negligence of his duties to the parishioners. Be that as it may, Abbe LePage was never convicted of the charges and was allowed to continue to do as he damn well pleased until a year later when the Catholic Church officials asked him to comply with the wishes of his parish congregation to be in good attendance of his religious duties. After being given the ultimatum of choosing between his religious convictions and prospects of making it rich, Abbe LePage resigned from his religious portfolio as parish priest and continued exploiting the people of Quebec and its natural resources. Even though the charges were properly documented and investigated by the Catholic Church, some historians interestingly enough insist that Canon Louis LePage de Sainte-Claire was a caring and compassionate individual who always managed to find the time for his parishioners. Oddly enough, within months of first acquiring the land at Terrebonne, Abbe LePage appealed to the Roman Catholic Church for help during various absences of his duties. An assistant was dispatched in the spring of 1721 but later canceled by the fall, September 18TH. Ironically, he was uplifted to the prestigious portfolio of Canon and was given extra responsibilities to fulfill. These additional duties obviously did not suit him as he continued building his empire by raping the land and exploiting anyone who dare tried stopping him.

There is ample evidence on hand to prove beyond a shadow of a doubt that the LePage's of Quebec had much influence on the French monarchy and the Roman Catholic Church, Abbe LePage in particular. Less than a year after obtaining the seigneury supposedly for the sum of 10,000 livres, the Abbe de Sainte-Claire was deemed Canon on June 9TH, 1721 and was given permission by the Catholic Church to reside on his property at Terrebonne for the sole purpose of developing it. The seigneury then consisted of an area about six miles square just northeast of Montreal. Prior to his acquisition of Terrebonne, Abbe LePage received a land grant in January of 1719 from the Seminary of Quebec on Ile Jesus. After acquiring the taste of being an important land owner, he soon gained possession of other properties in February and March of the following year. By 1723, Abbe LePage was so far out of control as he became more and more money hungry, seeking more and more land that would enable him to have more and more power over the inhabitants of his domains. Before long, he began subleasing land to the inhabitants of his

SEIGNIORIES WITH THE USUAL MONETARY CONDITIONS STIPULATED, WHEREBY CANON LEPAGE WAS TO REIGN SUPREME OVER HIS EMPIRE. AND WHILE ALL THIS WAS GOING ON, THE ROMAN CATHOLIC CHURCH OFFICIALS KEPT TURNING A BLIND EYE AS IT WAS OBVIOUSLY INTERFERING WITH HIS RELIGIOUS DUTIES. BY 1736, HIS SOVEREIGNTY POWERS REACHED AN ESTIMATED 81 CENTENARIES AND CONTINUED TO GROW FOR THE NEXT FEW YEARS. ACCORDING TO MOST OF THE PROVINCE OF QUEBEC'S FRENCH-SPEAKING HISTORIANS, ABBE LEPAGE WAS A VISIONARY OF SORTS AS HE WAS SAID TO HAVE BROUGHT NEW HOPE TO ITS FRANCOPHONE POPULATION. BUT THE TRUTH OF THE MATTER IS, ABBE LEPAGE WAS NOTHING MORE THAN AN OPPORTUNIST WHO AS IT JUST SO HAPPENED, HAD LOTS OF FRIENDS IN VERY HIGH PLACES BOTH RELIGIOUSLY AS WELL AS POLITICALLY!!!

THROUGHOUT HIS ENTIRE LIFETIME, LOUIS LEPAGE DE SAINTE-CLAIRE WAS CONSTANTLY STEPPING OVER THE LINE MAKING THE FRENCH POWERS THAT BE ADOPT A WAIT-AND-SEE APPROACH WHEN TRYING TO DISCIPLINE HIM. IT IS BELIEVED IN SOME FAMILY CIRCLES THAT THE LEPAGE'S OF QUEBEC FELT THAT THEY WERE LITERALLY ABOVE THE LAW AND COULD DO ABSOLUTELY NO WRONG. CASE IN POINT; AS THE SHIPS WERE THE MEANS OF BOTH TRADE AND TRAVEL, THE SHIPYARDS SOON BECAME THE HUB OF WAGE-LABOR AND BEFORE LONG, QUEBEC WAS PRODUCING WARSHIPS FOR THE FRENCH NAVY. IN 1731, ABBE LEPAGE SECURED A CONTRACT WITH THE KING OF FRANCE TO SUPPLY OAK AND PINE PLANKING TO THE SHIPYARDS FOR THE CONSTRUCTION OF VESSELS IN BOTH CANADA AND FRANCE. BUT IN ORDER TO FULFILL HIS CONTRACTUAL OBLIGATIONS HE HAD TO FIRST GET HIS BOUNDARIES AT TERREBONNE EXTENDED TO ENCOMPASS TIMBER RESERVES THAT WERE NOT ON HIS PROPERTY. THE SEIGNEUR OF TERREBONNE PROMPTLY OBTAINED A GRANT FROM THE FRENCH MONARCHY TO A PIECE OF LAND APPROXIMATELY SIX MILES DEEP ADJOINING HIS SEIGNEURY. STILL FALLING SOMEWHAT SHORT OF THE AMOUNT OF TIMBER THAT WAS NEEDED, HE THEN FORMED A PARTNERSHIP WITH CLEMENT DE SABREVOUS DE BLEURY, AN INDIVIDUAL WHO HAD ACQUIRED A RATHER SHADY REPUTATION AMONGST QUEBEC'S ELITE. THE PAIR, THEN EXTRACTED 2,000 FEET OF OAK TIMBER FROM PROPERTIES NOT OWNED BY THEM. ONCE THE TIMBER WAS ILLEGALLY OBTAINED, A FEW OF THE TOWNSFOLK BECAME SOMEWHAT CHOCKED AT WHAT HAD TRANSPIRED AND JUST AS THEY HAD MANAGED TO STIR UP A PUBLIC OUTCRY ABOUT THE ORDEAL, AN ORDINANCE WAS THUSLY ISSUED GIVING THESE NAVAL CONTRACTORS THE POWER TO HARVEST ANY OAK TIMBERS FROM THE PROPERTIES TO WHICH HAD BEEN PREVIOUSLY PILLAGED BY ABBE LEPAGE AND HIS ASSOCIATE.

THIS WAS BY NO MEANS THE ONLY TIME PERIOD THAT OF WHICH THE FRENCH MONARCHY TURNED A BLIND EYE ON THE EVERYDAY ACTIVITIES THAT SEEMED TO FOLLOW THE LEPAGE FAMILY NO MATTER WHERE THEY WENT AND/

OR WHO THEY WERE DEALING WITH ON A BUSINESS LEVEL. UNDER THE TERMS OF BOTH THE KING OF FRANCE AND THE CATHOLIC CHURCH, IT WAS STRICTLY PROHIBITED BY LAW FOR ANY INDIVIDUAL IN THE COLONY TO ESTABLISH A COMMUNITY WHEREBY THE KING HIMSELF WAS NOT THE SUPREME BEING. EVEN THOUGH THEY FORBID IT, ABBE LEPAGE CREATED A SMALL VILLAGE ON THE RIVIERE DES MILLE-ILES WHERE HE REIGNED SUPREME AND NOT THE FRENCH MONARCHY. ON HIS DOMAIN, HE BUILT A STONE CHURCH, A PRESBYTERY WHICH SERVED AS THE SEIGNIORIAL DWELLING, FOUR FLOUR MILLS AND A SAWMILL. GILLES HOCQUART, THE COLONY'S FINANCIAL COMMISSIONER WAS SO IMPRESSED WITH WHAT ABBE LEPAGE HAD DONE ON HIS TERREBONNE LAND HOLDINGS THAT HE DEEMED IT NOTEWORTHY AND ALLOWED IT TO FLOURISH OVER THE YEARS. IT SHOULD ALSO BE STATED THAT ACCORDING TO SOME CANADIAN HISTORIANS, THE LEPAGE NAME IS LINKED TO MUCH OF THE EFFORTS TOWARDS ESTABLISHING AN ASSORTMENT OF INDUSTRIES THAT HELPED CARVE THE MOSAIC OF OUR NATION BY INTRODUCING DIGNITY AND HONESTY INTO THE UNEXPLORED FRONTIER OF THE QUEBEC BUSINESS COMMUNITY. THAT OF WHICH IS VERY HARD TO IMAGINE CONSIDERING THE FACT THAT THE COUNTLESS PIECES OF DOCUMENTATION INDICATES JUST THE OPPOSITE HAS OCCURRED OVER AND OVER AGAIN. BE THAT AS IT MAY, THE LEPAGE DYNASTY PROCEEDED TO GROW AS THEY CONTINUED RECEIVING FINANCIAL BACKING FROM BOTH THE FRENCH MONARCHY AND THE ROMAN CATHOLIC CHURCH.

ON OCTOBER 30TH, 1730 ABBE LEPAGE DISPATCHED A RATHER LENGTHY REPORT TO THE KING'S FINANCIAL REPRESENTATIVE COMPLAINING OF THE TRAVESTIES ASSOCIATED WITH DOING BUSINESS SHORT OF FUNDS AS WELL AS LACKING THE PROPER WORKFORCE OF SKILLED TRADESMEN. **"SCARCITY OF MONEY IS THE REASON WHY THERE ARE SUCH DIFFICULTIES IN THE WAY OF SUCCEEDING IN DIFFERENT ENTERPRISES IN CANADA TODAY. "OF WHICH HE EMPHASIZED "IN THE SUCCEEDING IN THE DIFFERENT UNDERTAKING ... SIMPLY COME FROM THE SCARCITY OF MONEY AND MEN. "**HIS REPORT PROPOSED THAT IF THE KING WERE TO BUILD A GREATER NUMBER OF SHIPS IN QUEBEC, IT **"WOULD CAUSE AN INFLUX OF MONEY INTO THE COLONY "AND "WOULD PROMOTE COMPETITION"**.

IN A DESPERATE ATTEMPT TO DISTANCE ANY PAPER TRAIL THAT SUCH A PROPOSAL WAS IN FACT THE BRAIN CHILD OF ABBE LEPAGE AS A WAY AND MEANS OF EXTRACTING MORE MONEY OUT OF THE FRENCH MONARCHY, SOME HISTORIANS STATE THAT THE PROPOSAL DULY SUBMITTED WAS NOT EVEN CONSIDERED, LET ALONE TAKEN SERIOUSLY. BUT YET IT IS DOCUMENTED THAT THE SHIPYARDS IN QUEBEC PRODUCED A NUMBER OF WARSHIPS, INCLUDING ONE CARRYING THIRTY-SIX CANNONS. IT'S ALSO A WELL KNOWN AND PROVEN FACT OF CANADIAN HISTORY THAT IN 1739, A WAR VESSEL OF 500 TONS KNOWN AS THE **"CANADA "**WAS BEING BUILT AND IN THAT SAME YEAR SHIPYARD

WORKERS BUILT AN ADDITIONAL TEN MERCHANT SHIPS. THE FORESTS OF THE ST. LAWRENCE RIVER VALLEY SUPPLIED THE OAK AND PINE TIMBERS NEEDED, WHILE THE IRON-MINES AND FORGES OF SAINT-MAURICE NEAR TROIS RIVIERE PROVIDED THE NAILS AND IRON WORKS. DURING THIS TIME PERIOD OF HISTORY, THE LEPAGE'S HAD ACCUMULATED VAST FORTUNES AND HAD MOST OF QUEBEC'S ELITE IN THEIR BACK POCKETS. NEEDLESS TO SAY, ONE DOES NOT CLIMB THE FRATERNAL LADDER OF SUCCESS WITHOUT STEPPING ON A FEW TOES. AND AS IT TURNS OUT, THE LEPAGE'S STEPPED ON A FEW TOO MANY ON THEIR WAY UP TO THE TOP. EVEN THOUGH HIS REPORT WAS IN FACT TAKEN SERIOUSLY BUT WASN'T IMPLEMENTED UNTIL A FEW YEARS LATER, THE FRENCH MONARCHY'S PLANS OF PROSPERITY FOR QUEBEC DID NOT INCLUDE THE LIKES OF THE LEPAGE'S AS THEY HAD ALREADY PROVEN THEMSELVES UNTRUSTWORTHY AND TOTALLY INCAPABLE OF TREATING OTHERS ON A EQUAL PLAYING FIELD. WHILE ON THE KING'S FRATERNITY BLASKLIST, ABBE LEPAGE WAS ON THE VERGE OF BANKRUPTCY IN 1736 AS HIS LUMBER BUSINESS PRODUCED A MEAGER EXISTENCE AND HIS OTHER ENTERPRISES WEREN'T DOING MUCH BETTER. WAS THIS TO BE PAY-BACK TIME FOR THE LEPAGE'S OF QUEBEC FOR ALL OF THOSE OCCASIONS WHERE IN WHICH THEY STEPPED OUT OF LINE THUS FORCING EITHER THE KING OF FRANCE /OR THE CATHOLIC CHURCH TO BAIL THEM OUT OF TROUBLE TIME AND TIME AGAIN.

FEELING SORRY FOR HIS FRIEND AND ALL OF THOSE SUFFERING FROM THE DIRE CONSEQUENCES OF THE KING'S NON-COMPASSIONATE ATTITUDE TOWARDS THE FRENCH COLONY, (SO HISTORIANS WISH US TO BELIEVE), HOCQUART SUPPOSEDLY PLEADED WITH THE MONARCHY AS HE WAS SAID TO HAVE BELIEVED THAT UNLESS SOME SORT OF FINANCIAL INJECTION WAS PUT INTO THE RATHER SLUGGISH ECONOMY OF CANADA, ALL WOULD BE LOST. "I KNOW, MY LORD, THAT THE EXPENDITURES OF THE KING MAKES IN SUPPORT OF THIS COLONY ARE GREAT, AND THAT THEY ARE EVEN A BURDEN ON THE MARINE, "HE EXPLAINED, "BUT ... THE COLONY IS TO BECOME STILL MORE USEFUL TO FRANCE THROUGH THE CULTIVATION OF TOBACCO, THE CONSTRUCTION OF SHIPS, THE MINING OF IRON ANS COPPER: BUT THE EFFORT THAT WILL BE MADE HERE CAN PRODUCE AN EFFORT ONLY SLOWLY, IF HIS MAJESTY DOES NOT CONSENT TO HELP US. "IN THE SAME YEAR THAT ABBE LEPAGE SERIOUSLY CONSIDERED GOING INTO BANKRUPTCY, THE COLONY'S FINANCIAL COMMISSIONER DECIDED TO SAIL TO FRANCE IN ORDER TO APPEAL PERSONALLY TO THE KING. BETWEEN THE YEARS 1736 AND 1741, THE FRENCH MONARCHY INVESTED HEAVILY IN THE GROWTH OF VARIOUS INDUSTRIES OF QUEBEC ASSOCIATED WITH THE SHIPBUILDING. MORE THAN 500,000 LIVRES IN CROWN FUNDS WERE THUSLY FUNNELED THROUGH CERTAIN COMPANIES IN ORDER TO PROMOTE RAPID GROWTH IN THE SHIPBUILDING INDUSTRY. OF WHICH IT WAS LATER DISCOVERED THAT A GOOD PORTION OF THESE FUNDS HAD FALLEN INTO THE WRONG HANDS AND ALMOST

INSTANTLY BECAME KNOWN AS ONE OF QUEBEC'S FIRST POLITICAL SCANDALS OF THAT CENTURY.

IN 1736, ABBE LEPAGE'S GOOD FRIEND GILLES HOCQUART CONVINCED THE FRENCH MONARCHY TO INVEST 110,000 LIVRES IN THE SAINT-MAURICE IRONWORKS AND IN ADDITION TO THAT, THEY SOMEHOW MANAGED TO RECEIVE MORE MONIES THAN WHAT THEY WERE ORIGINALLY ENTITLED TO RECEIVE. IN TOTAL, 192,627 LIVRES MADE ITS WAY INTO THE COMPANY'S BANK ACCOUNT, MONIES THAT THE CROWN DEMANDED BE PAID BACK WITH INTEREST. APPARENTLY, EVERYTHING STARTED UNRAVELING FOR THE SAINT-MAURICE IRONWORKS COMPANY WHEN IT WAS ACCIDENTLY DISCOVERED THAT ONE OF ITS OWN FINANCIAL OFFICERS HAD MISAPPROPRIATED FUNDS DESTINED FOR THE DOMAINE D'OCCIDENT. WHEN IT WAS LEARNED THAT AN ESTIMATED 64,302 LIVRES APPEARED OUT OF NOWHERE ON THE COMPANY BOOKS AS UNEXPLAINED MONIES FROM THE FRENCH MONARCHY, EVERYONE INVOLVED BEGAN BACKPEDALING, ONE BLAMING THE OTHER. BEFORE LONG, (1740), THE KING OF FRANCE DEMANDED REPAYMENT AND ONE YEAR LATER, THE SAINT-MAURICE IRONWORKS WENT INTO BANKRUPTCY BECOMING THE PROPERTY OF THE FRENCH MONARCH.

IN ORDER TO FULLY UNDERSTAND AS TO WHAT EXACTLY WENT WRONG, IT MUST BE MADE CRYSTAL CLEAR THAT GILLES HOCQUART OPERATED IN THE CAPACITY OF BOTH THE FRENCH MONARCHY'S FINANCIAL ADVISOR AS WELL AS A PRIVATE INVESTOR. HE NOT ONLY ASSISTED ABBE LOUIS LEPAGE DE SAINTE-CLAIRE IN ESTABLISHING A SAWMILL ON HIS SEIGNEURY OF TERREBONNE BUT HE ALSO ACTED AS A STRAW MAN FOR MOST OF QUEBEC'S BUSINESS VENTURES. IN 1740, HE INVESTED 3,000 LIVRES OF HIS OWN MONEY INTO THE SAINT-MAURICE IRONWORKS. HE ALSO ASSISTED THE COMPANY'S PARTNERS IN ACQUIRING ADDITIONAL LAND GRANTS IN THE VICINITY OF THE IRONWORKS AND HELPED FACILITATE THE TRANSPORTATION OF IRON DESTINED FOR PARTS OF CANADA AND FRANCE.

FURTHERMORE, BY THE TIME THE FRENCH MONARCHY BEGAN INVESTING LARGE AMOUNTS OF MONEY INTO THE SHIPBUILDING INDUSTRY THE KING'S FINANCIAL ADVISOR FAVORED CERTAIN CLIENTS OVER OTHERS. BY USING WHATEVER INFLUENCE THAT HE HAD, THE COLONY'S FINANCIAL COMMISSIONER BLOCKED EVERY EFFORT THAT ABBE LEPAGE WAS MAKING IN ORDER TO STAY OUT OF BANKRUPTCY. DUE TO BEING CONSTANTLY PLAGUED WITH MONEY PROBLEMS, THE DEDICATED ROMAN CATHOLIC CANON ATTEMPTED TO RIDE ON THE COAT TAILS OF THE FINANCIAL COMMISSIONER BY ESTABLISHING AN IRONWORKS ON HIS SEIGNEURY. ON JULY 12TH, 1738 HE FORMED A PARTNERSHIP WITH THE D'AILLEBOUST BROTHERS OF MONTREAL. THE LEPAGE NAME WAS ONCE AGAIN GOING TO RISE TO THE TOP, SO FAMILY MEMBERS THOUGHT AT THE TIME. BUT THEIR DREAMS OF PROSPERITY WERE SOON SHATTERED AS GILLES HOCQUART

INFORMED THE FRENCH MONARCHY THAT ABBE LEPAGE'S PROPOSED IRONWORKS AT TERREBONNE CONSTITUTED NOTHING BUT TROUBLE FOR THE SAINT-MAURICE COMPANY AS THERE LITERALLY WASN'T ENOUGH MONEY TO GO AROUND AND IN THE END WOULD DO MORE HARD THAN GOOD.

AS PREVIOUSLY STATED, THE LEPAGE'S OF QUEBEC FELT THAT THEY WERE ABOVE THE LAW AND COULD DO NO WRONG. IN A VERY INTERESTING TWIST OF IRONY, THE TABLES FINALLY TURNED ON THEM AS ABBE LEPAGE NEGLECTED TO OBTAIN THE KING'S PERMISSION TO EXTRACT THE ORE ON HIS TERREBONNE SEIGNEURY. INSTEAD OF APPROACHING THE FRENCH MONARCHY FOR THE AUTHORIZATION TO DO SO, THE DEVOTED ROMAN CATHOLIC RECEIVED PERMISSION FROM THE CHURCH ITSELF. DESPITE THE FACT THAT THE KING OF FRANCE KNEW OF THE EXISTENCE OF THIS LITTLE KNOWN DETAIL, HE STILL ISSUED A ROYAL ORDER FOR ABBE LEPAGE TO CEASE AND DECEITS ALL OF HIS ACTIVITIES. FORCED TO ABANDON HIS IRONWORKS PROJECT, THE PARTNERS IN MONTREAL OBTAINED AN ANNULMENT RELINQUISHING THEIR INVOLVEMENT ON SEPTEMBER 29TH, 1739 AND DEMANDED REPAYMENT OF ALL THE MONIES ADVANCED TO HIM. NOT HAVING THE FUNDS AVAILABLE, LEPAGE WAS OBLIGATED UNDER THE TERMS OF HIS CONTRACT OF PARTNERSHIP TO SURRENDER HIS SAWMILL FOR A PERIOD OF EIGHT YEARS. WHILE IN THE PROCESS OF LOSING HIS EMPIRE, ABBE LOUIS LEPAGE DE SAINTE-CLAIRE MADE ONE FINAL ATTEMPT TO RISE TO POWER AS HE PLEADED WITH THE AUTHORITIES TO ALLOW HIM TO TAKE-OVER THE SAINT-MAURICE IRONWORKS, WHICH AT THIS TIME PERIOD WAS IN THE EXACT SAME FINANCIAL BIND AS LEPAGE HIMSELF. UNABLE TO CONVINCE THE KING OF FRANCE THAT HIS FAMILY NAME WAS IN GOOD STANDING WITH CREDITORS IN BOTH CANADA AS WELL AS IN THE MOTHERLAND, LEPAGE'S PROPOSAL WAS FLATLY REFUSED. NOW ON THE ROAD TO FINANCIAL RUIN, HE WAS THEN FORCED TO SELL OFF ALL OF HIS HOLDINGS.

ON JANUARY 15TH, 1745 ABBE LEPAGE SOLD HIS TERREBONNE SEIGNEURY TO SIEUR LOUIS DE LA CORNE FOR 60,000 LIVRES, TO WHICH AN ANNUAL 1,000 LIVRES WAS ADDED AND WAS TO CONTINUE UNTIL HIS DEATH. AT THE TIME, HIS SEIGNEURY WAS WORTH AN ESTIMATED 150,000 LIVRES. IN THE FINAL ANALYSIS, "THE STATEMENT OF HIS DEBTS ATTACHED TO THE BILL OF SALE SHOWED THE SUM OF 55,268 LIVRES. "AFTER BEING ABLE TO REGAIN POSSESSION OF HIS SAWMILL, (THE EIGHT YEAR TERM EXPIRING), LEPAGE MADE ONE MORE ATTEMPT TO RISE TO THE TOP OF QUEBEC'S ELITE SOCIETY. HE ESTABLISHED A SAWMILL ON THE RIVIERE DES MILLE-ILES WHICH ONCE AGAIN PROVED ITSELF TO BE A TOTAL DISASTER AS BUSINESS DECLINED RAPIDLY. IN A SELF-IMPOSED EXILE MANNER DURING 1750, HE RETREATED TO THE PRESBYTERY OF SAINT-LOUIS-DE-TERREBONNE WHERE HE DIED ON DECEMBER 3RD, 1762 AT THE AGE OF 72.

With the tables finally turning on them in 1739, the LePage's of Quebec were at a loss. Like a game of political dominoes, the various land holdings help by them over the years soon started to crumble and fall one-by-one. In a feeble attempt to save face, both Abbe Louis LePage and Rene LePage de Sainte-Claire were raised to the status of sainthood in the Province of Quebec as certain members of the Roman Catholic faith began rewriting their dirty family deeds hoping to hide the truth for all eternity. To this very day, statues and monuments can be found along the banks of the St. Lawrence depicting the generous efforts of the good family name of the LePage's in La Belle Province de Quebec. Afterall, it was their God given right to rule over the peasantry population of their domain!!!

Chapter 2 - MOI BEAU PAYS DE QUEBEC

Throughout the ages there has been many individuals of stature raised to sainthood whereas glorious monuments were constructed (Churches and such) in their honor. In most, if not in all cases, a religion is nothing more than a way and means of controlling a person's own thoughts, ambitions and/or ideas. For instance, historically the Holy Bible is said to contain the most accurate ancient history of mankind and is also said to be the only of its kind in existence today. The Bible is further said to be a well kept record of God's superior wisdom and is also said to contain truthful answers to important questions having to do with man's existence on the planet earth. Accordingly, some religions firmly believe that the Almighty God (the Supreme Being and/or the Creator of the Universe) was also the Bible's author. Within the religious doctrine of these zealots, they preach that the Almighty God merely used human beings as writers of his teachings and philosophies, allowing them by his powerful and superior force to set to pen and paper what he was inspiring them to write. In examining the Bible's actual worthiness, it is therefore not only concluded that the Bible is a very unusual piece of work ever compiled but it is also very different in yet another way and that being of course that its origins are among the oldest writings composed by man dating back some 3,500 years. The Bible is thusly considered by most scientists, historians, archaeologists, geographers and language experts to be many centuries older than any other record book ever written. The Bible was supposedly written about a thousand years before Buddha and Confucius and some two-thousand years before Muhammad. It is also said that there were an estimated 13,000 hand written sections of

THE BIBLE AND/OR PARTS OF IT IN EXISTENCE IN HEBREW AND GREEK; SOME OF WHICH DATING AS FAR BACK TO THE TIME OF ITS ORIGINAL WRITINGS.

CONTRARY AS TO WHAT SOME HISTORIANS MAY SAY IS TRUE WHEN THE OLD TESTAMENT WAS ORIGINALLY CONCEIVED, IT WAS ACTUALLY WRITTEN ON BOTH THE SKINS OF LAMBS AS WELL AS PAPYRUS /OR PAPER AS IT WERE, MANUFACTURED FROM THE PITHS OF PLANTS. AT THE TIME, NOT MANY PEOPLE COULD READ AND EVEN FEWER COULD ACTUALLY WRITE. TO MAKE MATTERS EVEN WORST, THE WRITINGS WERE SAID TO BE IN THE FORM OF MORE THAN 500 DIFFERENT LANGUAGES WHEN HEBREW SCHOLARS FIRST BEGAN TRANSLATING THEM IN 260 B.C. AND THUSLY CONTINUED WITH THEIR TRANSLATION EFFORTS UNTIL APPROXIMATELY 130 B.C. IT'S ACCURACY AT BEST IS BY NO MEANS PRECISE AS MANY REVISIONS HAVE BEEN INITIALLY MADE THROUGHOUT THE MANY CENTURIES AS EDUCATED SCHOLARS BEGAN PUTTING THEIR OWN SPIN ON WHAT THE BIBLE WAS ACTUALLY SAYING.

THE FIRST TRANSLATION FROM THE HEBREW LANGUAGE INTO ANOTHER LANGUAGE (AT LEAST ONE THAT WAS RECORDED) WAS IN CHALDEE, WHICH INTERESTINGLY ENOUGH WAS SAID TO BE THE LAW AT THE TIME AND WAS ULTIMATELY READ TO THE KING OF PERSIA. THE ORIGINAL OF THIS NEW TRANSLATION WAS COINCIDENTLY SAID TO BE LOST, WHILE THE OLDEST OF THESE TRANSLATIONS HAD BEEN PRESERVED WHICH WAS MADE AT ALEXANDRIA IN EGYPT (260 B.C.) AND IS CALLED THE SEPTUAGINT, FROM A SUPPOSITION THAT IT WAS MADE BY SEVENTY TRANSLATORS. ADDITIONAL TRANSLATIONS OF THE HOLY SCRIPTURES WAS MADE BY ONKELOS, ALSO IN CHALDEE, A.D. 150. THIS SAME AUTHOR OF THE SCRIPTURES, WHOSE NAME IN GREEK WAS AQUILA, ALSO TRANSLATED THE OLD TESTAMENT INTO GREEK, A.D. 160. IRONICALLY, THIS WORK WAS ORIGINALLY INTENDED TO CORRECT THE ERRORS OF THE SEPTUAGINT, WHICH AS IT JUST SO HAPPENED WAS TRANSLATED BY SEVERAL PERSONS, SOME OF WHOM WERE SAID NOT TO BE EQUAL TO THE TASK AS THEY HAD THEIR OWN PERSONAL AGENDA TO FULFILL. BESIDES THIS LITTLE KNOWN FACT OF HUMAN HISTORY, THE STATE OF PUBLIC OPINION AT THE TIME PERMITTED THE TRANSLATORS TO PUT THEIR OWN SPIN ON WHATEVER RELIGIOUS TEXT THEY SAW FIT INSTEAD OF FOLLOWING THE NORMAL THOUGHT PERTAINING TO THE ACTUAL LITERAL TEXT. ADDING MORE CONFUSION TO BIBLICAL TEXT, THE SEPTUAGINT WENT THROUGH FURTHER REVISIONS (THEODOTION) AND ABOUT THAT SAME TIME PERIOD, (THE SECOND CENTURY), SYMMACHUS MADE A VERSION OF THE HOLY SCRIPTURES IN GREEK FOR THE USE OF THE EBIONITES, WHICH ODDLY ENOUGH WAS SAID TO BE THE MOST CORRECT AND PUREST OF ALL THE RELIGIOUS WRITINGS IN ITS DICTION.

IN THE TIME OF THE APOSTLES THERE WERE MANY COPIES OF THE GOSPELS FOR THE USE OF THE CHURCH IN THE DIFFERENT CITIES, IN THE LANGUAGES OF THE LOCALITIES; GREEK, LATIN, HEBREW, SYRIAC, COPTIC, ETHIOPIC and Arabic. As fate would have it, the majority of the authors of these religious translations are still unknown to this very day. The Ethiopic version was written in the sacred Jeez, the dialect of Axum, in the Fourth Century. The Coptic and Memphitic versions were made soon after, and the Coptic is still used in Egypt today. The Syriac, also called Peshito, was made from the Hebrew and Greek about A.D. 200, and had become almost obsolete as early as the Fourth Century. These religious writings contained the whole Bible, with the Apocrypha. Paul of Tela made a version of the Septuagint at Alexandria, A.D. 617, which was said to be extremely literal, every Greek word being rendered by one in Syriac. The Thebaic version, which was written in the common dialect used in Egypt was made in the Third Century but before long ceased to be used especially among persons of intellect who preferred the more elegant Coptic. The Gothic version was made about A.D. 383, by Ulphilas. For a time, there was a copy of the original edition of this Biblical writing in Upsal, Sweden. The great works of Origen were said to have consumed twenty-eight years of his life, and consist of homilies and commentaries supposedly written with every bit of scholarship and untiring research that could possibly be mustered expending its arm into all the lands of the Holy Scriptures. It is also said that he first arranged four versions on the same page for comparison purposes of the text that had been translated. After comparing them with one another in order to choose the most accurate, a new and improved version was then selected, one being better than the other. These four different versions of the same page that were first written and then compared for correctness were as follows; 1) Septuagint; 2) Aquila; 3) Symmachus; 4) Theodotion. After comparing these to one another, he added two others to the mix, making what was later to be known as the Hexapla (six parts). Some portions of the Gospels were in eight different versions. The whole literary works comprised of nearly fifty volumes folio, coincidently that of which only a very few are said to be in existence nowadays.

Since the dawning of time, man has attempted to revise actual Biblical text time and time again; the Veneto Greek version is yet an example of such translations dated A.D. 875. Tertullian (born A.D. 160, died 245) once described a Latin version of the Gospels as having influenced a great degree of the popular speech of the day, elevating it to a much higher standard of excellence. To many of the scholars, if the languages of the human race were to improve themselves, so was Biblical text destined to change. Accordingly,

THE OLD TESTAMENT WAS SAID TO BE TRANSLATED INTO LATIN IN ORDER TO PRESERVE ITS AUTHENTICITY BEFORE THE CRUCIFIXION BUT THERE SEEMS TO BE NO ACTUAL RECORD OF SUCH A TRANSLATION. GRANTED, INDIRECT EVIDENCE MAY BE SEEN IN THE SIMILARITY OF STYLE OF THE OLD AND NEW TESTAMENTS AS THEY ARE FOUND IN THE VERSION WHICH WAS USED BEFORE JEROME'S WAS MADE. EVER SINCE MAN FIRST USED FIRE TO COOK HIS FOOD AND KEEP WARM, THE HOLY SCRIPTURES HAVE GONE THROUGH COUNTLESS REVISIONS AND/OR TRANSLATIONS AS A WAY AND MEANS OF CONTROLLING THE MASSES. THE EXTENSIVE INFLUENCE OF THE SCRIPTURES ON THE HUMAN RACE IN THE EARLY AGES CAN BE EASILY DEDUCED FROM THE OFTEN REPEATED USAGE OF QUOTATIONS THAT HAVE PLAGUED THE WHOLE BIBLE FROM THE FRONT PAGE ALL THE WAY TO ITS LAST WORDS NO MATTER WHAT LANGUAGE NOR WHO TRANSLATED IT . THE SO-CALLED GREAT SCHOLARS WHO WANTED TO PROVE THEIR SUPERIORITY OVER OTHERS SUCCEEDED IN MAKING WHAT IS SAID TO BE THE MOST VALUABLE VERSION OF THE SCRIPTURES WAS IN THE LATIN TONGUE AND WAS COMPOSED BY JEROME, WHOSE NAME AS WRITTEN IN LATIN WAS EUSEBIUS HIERONYMUS SOPHRONIUS (BORN A.D. 329 AT STRIDON, DIED 420 AT BETHLEHEM). IT IS SAID THAT HE WAS A STUDENT AND A TRAVELER FROM HIS YOUTH, AND A PATIENT GATHERER OF KNOWLEDGE SERVICEABLE IN HIS GREAT UNDERTAKING IN ALL PARTS OF THE CHRISTIAN WORLD. JEROME'S VERSION OF THE HOLY SCRIPTURES WAS READ BY ALL FOR MORE THAN EIGHT CENTURIES AS RELIGIOUS INSTITUTIONS SLOWLY BEGAN GAINING A STRANGLEHOLD ONTO THE PEOPLE.

SINCE ITS FIRST CONCEPTION OVER 2,000 YEARS AGO, THE BIBLE HAS BEEN RE-EDITED AND/OR REVISED MORE TIMES THAN WHAT MOST PEOPLE CAN EVER IMAGINE. UNSATISFIED WITH ITS BIBLICAL TEXT, WHEN THE HOLY SCRIPTURES WENT THROUGH A COMPLETE DURING THE LATTER HALF OF THE FOURTH CENTURY THE POWERS THAT BE HAD VISIONS OF GRANDEUR IN THEIR EYES (THE ROMAN REPUBLIC HAD LONG SINCE BECAME KNOWN AS THE ROMAN EMPIRE, OF WHICH GREECE, PALESTINE AND EGYPT WERE PROVINCES), AND PROPHESIED THAT THE BIBLE BE RE-TRANSLATED FROM MANUSCRIPTS OF HEBREW, GREEK AND OLD LATIN TO SOMETHING THAT OF WHICH EVERYONE COULD ACTUALLY UNDERSTAND. DURING THIS SAME TIME PERIOD, ROME HAD BECOME COMPLETELY CHRISTIANIZED WITH THE CHURCH BEING THE CENTER OF ITS CHRISTIANIZATION AND THEREFORE A NEED SOON DEVELOPED TO HAVE BOTH OF THE TESTAMENTS (OLD AND NEW) TRANSLATED INTO A COMMON LANGUAGE OF ITS PEOPLE, NEW LATIN /OR VULGATE LATIN. AFTER SPENDING MANY YEARS COLLECTING THE MANUSCRIPTS, EUSEBIUS HIERONYMUS SOPHRONIUS MET WITH HIS SMALL CIRCLE OF LEARNED FRIENDS (JEWISH RABBIS AND CHRISTIAN SCHOLARS), AND BEGAN THE TASK OF RE-TRANSLATING THE OLD AND NEW TESTAMENTS INTO A COMMON LANGUAGE OF WHICH ANY

LITERATE LATIN-SPEAKING PERSON COULD UNDERSTAND. COINCIDENTLY, THE AUTHOR OF THE NEW BIBLICAL TEXT, EUSEBIUS HIERONYMUS SOPHRONIUS WAS GRACIOUSLY REWARDED FOR HIS TRANSLATION WORKS AS HE WAS ELEVATED TO THE STATURE OF A BISHOP AND WAS EXTREMELY RECOGNIZED AS BEING THE MOST KNOWLEDGEABLE MAN OF RELIGIOUS HISTORY THAT THE CHURCH HAD EVER SEEN, HE WAS THUSLY ANOINTED AS BEING THE BIG KHAUNA OF A SMALL MONASTERY IN BETHLEHEM.

FURTHER TRANSLATIONS OF THE HOLY SCRIPTURES BEGAN TO TAKE PLACE IN AND/OR ABOUT THE YEAR A.D. 860, IN A POETICAL NARRATIVE OF THE LIFE OF JESUS. THIS WORK OF TRANSLATING THE BIBLE IN GERMANY WAS UNDERTAKEN BY OTFRIED WEISSENBURG. PSALMS, CANTICLES AND GENESIS WERE ALSO DONE IN METER SOON AFTER. A POETICAL VERSION OF THE HISTORICAL LITERARY WORKS APPEARED IN THE THIRTEENTH CENTURY. MARTIN LUTHER'S VERSION OF BIBLICAL TEXT WAS MADE BY THE ASSISTANCE OF MELANCTHON AND OTHERS (AUROGALLUS, BUGENHAGEN, JONAS AND CREVZIGER) WHO WANTED TO PUT THEIR OWN INTERPRETATIONS AS BEING THE TRUE WORD AND GLORY OF **GOD**. AS LEADER OF THE REFORMERS, LUTHER PUBLICALLY CRITICIZED THE ROMAN CATHOLIC CHURCH BY QUESTIONING THE AUTHORITY OF THE PAPACY WHICH IN TURN LED TO HIS BEING EXCOMMUNICATED IN 1521. NOT LONG AFTER HIS ATTACKS OF HERESY AGAINST THE CATHOLIC CHURCH AND HIS UNWILLINGNESS TO RECANT WHAT HE WAS SAYING, MARTIN LUTHER AND HIS FELLOW REFORMERS BEGAN THE TASK OF THEIR GERMAN TRANSLATION OF THE BIBLE (1521-2). WITH THIS ONE SIMPLE ACT OF DEFIANCE, STANDING UP TO THE ENDLESS ABUSES OF RELIGIOUS DOCTRINE THAT HAD PLAGUED THE CATHOLIC CHURCH FOR MANY CENTURIES, A RELIGIOUS MOVEMENT WAS BORN WHICH ENDED IN THE FORMATION OF THE PROTESTANT CHURCHES. WITH THE PUBLICATION OF LUTHER'S VERSION OF PROTESTANT BIBLICAL TEXT, IT HELPED PAVE THE WAY FOR OTHER PUBLICATIONS TO SOON FOLLOW. THERE ARE ALSO VERSIONS IN LOW GERMAN (1533), DANISH (1550), SWEDISH (1526), ICELANDIC (1540), BY THORLAK SKULESON (1644), DUTCH (1648) AND POMERANIAN (1588). SLOWLY BUT SURELY, THE ROMAN CATHOLIC CHURCH WAS LOSING ITS FOOTHOLD ON ITS CITIZENRY AS HUNDREDS OF THOUSANDS BEGAN CONVERTING TO PROTESTANTISM. IN 1579, THE REFORMED CHURCH PUBLISHED A SLIGHTLY REVISED VERSION OF LUTHER'S ORIGINAL WORKS AND ANOTHER FOR THE SWISS IN 1665. ONLY TWENTY-EIGHT YEARS PREVIOUS TO THE SWISS PUBLICATION, THE REFORMERS PUBLISHED YET ANOTHER, THE SYNOD OF DORT IN 1637.

INTERESTINGLY, SINCE GERMANY WAS THE BIRTH PLACE OF THE LUTHERAN DOCTRINE WHICH BROUGHT INTO QUESTION THE SUPREMACY OF THE PAPACY, IT ONLY MADE SENSE THAT THEY WOULD ALSO TRANSLATE THE VULGATE VERSION OF THE SCRIPTURES INTO THEIR MOTHER TONGUE. THIS DEED WAS

EXECUTED AT LEIPSIC IN 1527. TWO-HUNDRED AND SIXTEEN YEARS LATER (1743), CHRISTOPHER SAUR PRINTED A BIBLE IN GERMAN AT GEORGETOWN, PENNSYLVANIA WHICH WAS THE FIRST BIBLE PRINTED IN AMERICA NEXT TO JOHN ELIOT'S BIBLE WHICH WAS TRANSLATED INTO AN ALGONQUIAN LANGUAGE IN AN ATTEMPT TO CIVILIZE THE PAGAN INDIAN WORSHIPERS DURING THE MID-1600'S. ELIOT BEGAN WORKING ON HIS TRANSLATED VERSION OF THE HOLY SCRIPTURES IN 1661 AND ONLY TWO YEARS LATER (1663) HAD HIS VERSION OF THE BIBLE PRINTED IN THE INDIAN LANGUAGE. IT WAS ELIOT'S BELIEF THAT COME HELL /OR HIGH WATER, THE ALGONQUIAN INDIANS OF NORTH AMERICA WERE GOING TO BE ACCEPTING THE WHITEMAN'S WAY OF LIFE BY BECOMING TRUE CHRISTIANS AND NOT THE PAGAN IDOL WORSHIPERS THAT THEY HAD BECOME WITH THE PASSAGE OF TIME.

IT HAS BEEN PROVEN THUS FAR THAT THE BIBLE HAS BEEN RE-EDITED AND REVISED MANY, MANY TIMES AS IT WENT THROUGH ITS VARIOUS STAGES OF TRANSLATIONS. THE FIRST RECORDED TRANSLATION OF THE HOLY SCRIPTURES INTO THE ENGLISH LANGUAGE WAS THE WORK OF CAEDMON, WHO RENDERED THE WHOLE BIBLE, FROM GENESIS TO REVELATION, INTO ALLITERATIVE VERSE, A.D. 680. NOT LONG AFTERWARDS, ALDHELM (BISHOP OF SHERBORNE) RENDERED THE PSALMS INTO VERSE. BEDE TRANSLATED JOHN'S GOSPEL (A.D. 735), AND ALFRED THE GREAT (DIED A.D. 901) WROTE AND THEN PUBLISHED THE FOUR CHAPTERS OF LAWS FROM THE BOOK OF EXODUS SIMPLY BECAUSE OF THE FACT THAT HE ENVISIONED GRANDEUR IF THE YOUTH POPULATION OF HIS KINGDOM WERE ABLE TO READ THE ENGLISH SCRIPTURES. IT IS ALSO SAID THAT ALFRED THE GREAT HAD A BOOK OF EXTRACTS FROM THE PSALMS AND OTHER BOOKS MADE FOR USAGE IN HIS FAMILY. REPORTEDLY, THE OLDEST VERSION OF THE ANGLO-SAXON GOSPELS IS CALLED THE DURHAM BOOK, OF WHICH HAD BEEN CARBON DATED AND IS SAID TO BE FROM A.D. 688.

LIKE THE ANGLO-SAXONS, THE NORMANS ALSO PUT THEIR OWN SPIN ON BIBLICAL TEXT. HISTORICALLY, THE NORMANS WERE NO FRIENDS OF THE ENGLISH AND REFUSED TO EDUCATE THEIR PEOPLE IN THE ANGLO-SAXON DIALECT. AS FAR AS THAT GOES, THEY ONLY TRANSLATED A FEW SECTIONS OF THE BIBLE BUT DID EDUCATE THE PEOPLE IN RELIGIOUS MATTERS BY THE USE OF MIRACLE-PLAYS AND PICTURES. THE REAL CONTROVERSY OCCURRED DURING THE THIRTEENTH CENTURY WHEN THE HOLY SCRIPTURES WERE TRANSLATED INTO NORMAN-FRENCH. NEEDLESS TO SAY, THE ENGLISH WERE NOT AT ALL AMUSED AS THE RELIGIOUS RIVALRY SOON ESCALATED OUT OF CONTROL IN THE FORM OF AN INQUISITION FOR SUPERIORITY OVER THE MASSES.

THROUGHOUT THE ENTIRE MIDDLE AGES, THE BIBLE BECAME THE GAUNTLET BY WHICH MAN'S INHUMANITY TO MAN WAS TO BE HEIGHTENED AS IT BECAME KNOWN AS THE OFFICIAL BOOK BY WHICH THE HUMAN RACE WAS TO RECEIVE ITS ONLY SALVATION. AS MAN'S INHUMANITY TO HIS FELLOW

BEINGS INCREASED AT A DRAMATIC PACE ALL IN THE NAME OF RELIGION, THE HOLY SCRIPTURES ONCE AGAIN WENT THROUGH MORE RE-EDITING AND/OR REVISING AS BEING THE BIBLE OF THE CATHOLIC CHURCH IN WESTERN EUROPE AND GREAT BRITAIN. WITH EVER INCREASING TENSIONS, A NUMBER OF ROMAN CATHOLIC ENGLISH-SPEAKING SCHOLARS LEFT THE CHURCH AND SOON BEGAN SPREADING THEIR WINGS INTO THE FORMATION OF THEIR OWN RELIGIONS; PROTESTANTISM. AS THEY FLED TO ESCAPE PERSECUTION, IT BECAME APPARENT TO THE CATHOLIC CHURCH THAT A NEW BIBLE HAD TO BE WRITTEN INTO ENGLISH. DURING THE REIGN OF QUEEN ELIZABETH I, AN ENGLISH VERSION OF THE HOLY SCRIPTURES WAS THUS WRITTEN SOLELY TO COUNTERACT THE FUNDAMENTAL TEACHINGS OF THE PROTESTANT FAITH. IN 1582, THE ROMAN CATHOLIC CHURCH HAD BIBLICAL TEXT TRANSLATED INTO ENGLISH AND PUBLISHED THEIR VERSION OF THE NEW TESTAMENT AT RHEIMS AND TWENTY-EIGHT YEARS LATER (1610) ISSUED A REVISED VERSION OF THE OLD TESTAMENT WHICH WAS SIMPLY CALLED THE DOUAY VERSION. THE DOUAY VERSION OF THE HOLY SCRIPTURES INTERESTINGLY ENOUGH WAS TRANSLATED FROM THE LATIN VULGATE AND NOT FROM THE ORIGINAL GREEK. ACCORDINGLY, THE AUTHORS OF THE OLD TESTAMENT (CARDINAL WILLIAM ALLEN, GREGORY MARTIN AND RICHARD BRISTON) PUBLISHED THEIR VERSION OF BIBLICAL TEXT AT DOUAY, HENCE THE NAME. FOR MORE THAN 300 YEARS, THE DOUAY VERSION WAS THE FAVORED TEXT USED BY THE ROMAN CATHOLIC CHURCH AS BEING THE AUTHORIZED STANDARD VERSION IN ENGLISH.

WITH THE CATHOLIC CHURCH ATTEMPTING TO MAINTAIN A SOMEWHAT DELUSIONAL STRANGLEHOLD ON ITS CITIZENRY, THE KING OF ENGLAND (JAMES THE FIRST) IN 1606 INSTRUCTED A PURITAN, DR. JOHN REYNOLDS TO SELECT FIFTY-FOUR SCHOLARS TO IMPROVE BIBLICAL TEXT SO THAT PROTESTANTISM WOULD REIGN SUPREME. FORTY-EIGHT OF THE LEARNED MEN WERE ASSIGNED TO RE-WRITING THE NEW TRANSLATION. AMONG THESE SCHOLARS WERE MEN WHO HELD IMPORTANT PORTFOLIOS WITHIN THE CHURCH ITSELF; ANDREWS, BARLOW, MONTAGUE, OVERAL AND SARAVIA. LIKE ALL THE OTHERS, THE PURITANS ALSO HELD PRESTIGIOUS POSITIONS WITHIN THE PROTESTANT MOVEMENT AS WELL, AMONG THEM WERE REYNOLDS, CHADERTON AND LIVLIE. UNFORTUNATELY, THERE WERE NO ACTUAL RECORDS KEPT PERTAINING TO THE VARIOUS MEETINGS OF THE TRANSLATORS. APPARENTLY, THE ONLY RECORDED DOCUMENTS SEEMS TO BE THE PROCEDURE THEY USED IN ORDER TO ACHIEVE THE FINAL TASK OF PUBLICATION. WHEN EACH OF THE INDIVIDUALS GATHERED TOGETHER TO DISCUSS AND EXAMINE WHAT THEY HAD TRANSLATED, ONE MEMBER OF THE GROUP WOULD READ HIS VERSION OF BIBLICAL TEXT WHILE THE OTHERS HELD IN THEIR HANDS SOME VERSION OF THE SCRIPTURES IN EITHER ONE OF THE LEARNED LANGUAGES AND IF THEY FELT THAT AN ERROR / OR FALSE STATEMENT WAS MADE, THEN AND ONLY THEN WERE THEY TO SPEAK

UP. IF NOTHING WAS SAID, THE READER CONTINUED READING WITHOUT BEING INTERRUPTED. THIS PROCEDURE WENT ON DAY IN AND DAY OUT FOR THREE SOLID YEARS. IT IS SAID THAT THE INTRODUCTION AND ARGUMENT OF EACH BOOK WAS WRITTEN BY THOMAS BILSON, BISHOP OF WINCHESTER AND DR. MILES SMITH. COINCIDENTLY, DR. SMITH WENT ON TO BECOME KNOWN AS BISHOP OF GLOUCESTER. THESE NEW AND IMPROVED TRANSLATIONS OF THE HOLY SCRIPTURES WERE COMPLETED AND PUBLISHED IN 1611 AT LONDON BY ROBERT BARKER; PRINTER TO THE KING OF ENGLAND.

ALTHOUGH THE EARLIEST EXISTING FRAGMENTS OF SOME PORTIONS OF THE BIBLE ACTUALLY BEING TRANSLATED INTO ENGLISH ARE REPORTED TO HAVE TAKEN PLACE DURING THE EIGHTH CENTURY AND POSSIBLY AS EARLY AS EVEN THE SEVENTH (AS IN SOME INSTANCES PERTAINING TO PARAPHRASES WRITTEN BY CAEDMON), THE FIRST FULL TEXT AND TRANSLATION IS SAID NOT TO HAVE OCCURRED UNTIL JOHN WYCLIFFE, AN ENGLISH THEOLOGIAN WHO WAS EDUCATED AT BALLIOL COLLEGE, UNIVERSITY OF OXFORD, BEGAN A MOVEMENT THAT LITERALLY WAS IN DIRECT OPPOSITION AS TO WHAT THE HOLY SCRIPTURES ACTUALLY CONTAINED IN ACCORDANCE TO THE CATHOLIC FAITH. WYCLIFFE'S ENGLISH VERSION OF THE BIBLE WERE TRANSLATED INTO MANUSCRIPT FORM IN 1382 AND WASN'T PUBLISHED INTO A FULL TEXT UNTIL ELEVEN YEARS AFTER HIS DEATH, (1395). AFTER JOHN WYCLIFFE'S DEATH IN 1584, HIS TEACHINGS BEFORE LONG BEGAN TO SPREAD LIKE WILDFIRE ENGULFING EVERYTHING THAT STOOD IN ITS PATH. ALTHOUGH HIS BIBLE WAS MOSTLY CIRCULATED AMONGST HIS FOLLOWERS, CALLED LOLLARDS AND/OR LOLLARDISM, HIS PHILOSOPHIES SOON LEAD TO OTHER FORMS OF PROTESTANTISM WHICH ULTIMATELY MEANT RELIGIOUS REFORMATION. WHICH IN TURN CAUSED MUCH TURMOIL FOR THE CATHOLIC CHURCH AND IN MAY OF 1415, A REVIEW OF WYCLIFFE'S HERESIES LEAD TO A DECREE BEING ISSUED FOR HIS BODY TO BE DISINTERRED AND BURNED, CONDEMNING HIS ETERNAL SOUL TO THE DEPTHS OF HELL. THIS DECREE WAS ISSUED BY THE ROMAN CATHOLIC COUNCIL OF CONSTANCE AND EVENTUALLY CARRIED OUT IN 1428. THE CONDEMNATION CAME ABOUT LARGELY DUE TO THE FACT THAT WYCLIFFE'S PROTESTANT TEACHINGS REPRESENTED THE COMPLETE BREAK-UP OF THE CATHOLIC CHURCH AS HE HAD ALSO BEEN URGING HIS FOLLOWERS NOT TO WORSHIP THE FALSE GODS OF THE CATHOLIC FAITH AS HE BELIEVED THAT MANKIND COULD GOVERN THEMSELVES WITHOUT THE AID OF POPES AND PRELATES. THE SPECIFIC PURPOSE OF THE COUNCIL WAS TO PUT AN END TO THE QUESTION AS TO WHICH RELIGION WAS SUPERIOR OVER THE OTHER. IN THE EYES OF THE CATHOLICS, ANY OTHER FORM OF RELIGION WAS INFERIOR AND THOSE WHO OPPOSED THE ROMAN CATHOLIC FAITH WERE QUITE OFTEN KILLED FOR THEIR SUBVERSIVE BELIEFS.

One-hundred years later another Biblical scholar, William Tyndale began translating portions of the Holy Scriptures that were based on the Hebrew and Greek manuscripts instead of on the Vulgate Latin that had been previously translated by the Roman Catholics during the latter half of the Fourth Century. Tyndale's version of the Bible, together with the earlier translations of Wycliffe are said to have formed the basic foundation of the Authorized King James version of 1611 which had originally taken place in 1535 when Myles Coverdale, yet another noted Biblical scholar, issued the first completed printed English version of the Bible based on the religious translation findings of Tyndale and other previous translations. Be that as it may, Tyndale's version of Biblical text was bitterly opposed by the Roman Catholic Church which in the end resulted in Tyndale's being imprisoned for several years and eventually condemned to death for his heresies. In 1536, William Tyndale was put to death at Villefort, near Brussels where his body burned to ashes. Tyndale's Biblical theory was that every part of the Scriptures had one sense only, and he kept that always in his view as he translated from the original Hebrew and Greek writings knowing full well that promenaded omissions had taken place in all of the other previous translations. Even one of Tyndale's most faithful assistant's, John Fry, couldn't escape being burned at the stake for taking part in the heresy. Fry was terminated at Smithford, England in 1552 while another assistant, the Monk William Roye was put to death for the same offense in Portugal one year later. It is also interesting to note that Myles Coverdale, a priest, barely escaped being torched himself. While in prison for the exact same offense as all the others, he edited an edition of the Bible in 1535, which was dedicated to the King of England. Accordingly, Coverdale declared that he hadn't changed so much as one word for the benefit of one religion over the other but instead made it more concise in its actual wording as he believed that the previous authors made errors while interpreting its true meaning. This was the first edition of the entire Bible that was printed in English, and was also the very first authorized version. It was reportedly published in six volumes, folio, with marginal notes and cross-references, and illustrated with many wood-cuts.

It is duly recorded in the history books that Coverdale preached extensively against certain ecclesiastical practices of the Catholic faith, notably confession and image worship. The chief attribute to Coverdale's version of the Bible was said to be his felicitous

PHRASEOLOGY, MUCH OF WHICH WAS INCORPORATED WITHIN THE CONTEXT OF HIS RE-EDITED HOLY SCRIPTURES. AND IN 1538 HAD BEEN COMMISSIONED BY THOMAS CROMWELL, A.K.A. LORD CROMWELL, SECRETARY TO HENRY THE EIGHTH AND VICAR-GENERAL IN CHURCH AFFAIRS WHO'S DUTY IT WAS TO OVERSEE THE FIRST EVER OFFICIAL PUBLISHED BIBLE FOR THE ANGLICAN CHURCH. THIS PUBLISHED EDITION, THEN KNOWN AS THE GREAT BIBLE WAS COMPLETED IN 1539. STILL NOT SATISFIED WITH ITS BIBLICAL TEXT, COVERDALE WAS ORDERED BY CROMWELL AND THE BRITISH MONARCHY TO REVISE THE GREAT BIBLE EVEN FURTHER IN 1540. AFTER REFUSING TO COMPLY WITH THE WISHES OF THE MONARCHY, HISTORY BOOKS THEN STATE THAT COVERDALE LATER ON IN THAT SAME YEAR FLED ENGLAND FEARING FOR HIS OWN SAFETY AS CROMWELL'S ENEMIES HAD INSTANTLY LABELED THE PAIR AS TRAITORS OF THE STATE. AS FATE WOULD HAVE IT, CROMWELL WAS BEHEADED IN 1540 BY THE BRITISH MONARCHY ITSELF AS HE HAD BEEN THE ROYAL ADVISOR TO THE KING AND WAS THUSLY GIVEN MANY RELIGIOUS RESPONSIBILITIES, INCLUDING CHANGING BIBLICAL TEXT AS TO WHAT THE KING HIMSELF PERCEIVED AS BEING THE TRUE WORD OF GOD.

ACCORDING TO HISTORIANS, CROMWELL'S EXECUTION HAD APPARENTLY TAKEN PLACE PARTLY BECAUSE OF HIS ROLE IN ARRANGING THE KING'S UNSUCCESSFUL MARRIAGE WITH ANN BOLEYN, THE DAUGHTER OF SIR THOMAS BOLEYN, WHO WAS LATER ANOINTED THE EARL OF WILTSHIRE AND ORMOND. CROMWELL APPARENTLY NEGOTIATED THE TERMS OF THE MARRIAGE AND IN JANUARY OF 1533, THE BRITISH MONARCHY WAS SECRETLY UNITED WITH HIS NEW BRIDE. ALMOST INSTANTLY, HENRY VIII GREW TIRED OF HIS WIFE AND WAS OUT ON THE PROWL TRYING TO FIND A NEW ONE. HENRY THE EIGHTH NOT ONLY HAD A ROAMING EYE FOR MEMBERS OF THE OPPOSITE SEX BUT HE WAS ALSO DELUSIONAL, SUFFERING FROM VISIONS OF GRANDEUR AS WELL. ON MAY 2ND, 1536 HIS PARANOID SCHIZOPHRENIC ACTIVITIES SOON TOOK FULL CONTROL OF HIM WHEN HE HAD HIS WIFE ANNE OF CLEVES, IMPRISONED IN THE TOWER OF LONDON ON TRUMPED UP CHARGES OF ADULTERY WITH HER BROTHER AND ONLY DAYS LATER CONVICTED OF HIGH TREASON AS THE KING FELT THAT THERE EXISTED A CONSPIRACY TO TOPPLE HIM. THEN, ON MAY 19TH OF THAT SAME YEAR, HENRY HAD HIS WIFE BEHEADED. IT WAS LITERALLY THE KING'S WAY OF DIVORCING HER AS HIS FIFTH WIFE. AND SINCE NO ONE DARED QUESTION THE SANITY OF THE BRITISH MONARCHY, CATHERINE HOWARD WAS ALSO BEHEADED SIX YEARS LATER TO MAKE WAY FOR YET ANOTHER MARRIAGE THAT TOOK PLACE IN 1543. DUE TO THE FACT THAT HE HAD A SEXUAL APPETITE THAT WAS NOT SANCTIONED BY THE ROMAN CATHOLIC CHURCH, THE CATHOLICS NOT BELIEVING IN DIVORCE, HENRY VIII CREATED THE CHURCH OF ENGLAND AND SEVERED ALL TIES WITH ROME, (NO PUN INTENDED). ACCORDING TO THE MAJORITY OF HISTORIANS, HENRY THE

Eighth was a man of scholarship who was said to have encouraged the arts. But if the truth be told in its proper light, he was just like all the others that walked before him, a manipulator of Biblical text who always wanted things done his way. Historically, anyone who disagreed with Henry was simply thrown into a prison cell, then, when the time was right, they had their heads chopped off.

As Henry the Eighth's religious advisor, Cromwell was being pressured to have Biblical text in the Great Bible revised in accordance as to what the British monarchy wanted it to say. Originally, the monarchy decreed that England have their own Bible by August 1ST, 1536 but those working on it didn't follow through on what the British royals were dictating to them. Tyndale's version was edited by John Rogers who is said to have assumed the name Thomas Matthewe as a disguise because of the enemies of Tyndale, whose intimate friend he was. This edition followed Tyndale's version as far as the end of Chronicles, and that of Rogers for the rest. Accordingly, there were many wood-cuts that embellished both the Old and New Testaments, the book of Revelation having one to each of its chapters. Cromwell was given a copy in 1538 and asked if the King would be able to decree its contents as being England's official Biblical text. The British monarchy granted it to be so and issued a royal proclamation informing its people that they were to use this version of the Bible in their churches as it was England's mother tongue; English. Since England was still under the Roman Catholic domain, Church officials strongly opposed the printing of the Bible in English and used whatever means they could muster in an attempt to quash these acts of heresy. One tactic used by the Catholic Church was to prevent its free distribution and usage by the people. But the people all over England gathered in crowds in the streets /or where ever they could to hear the book being read to them.

Being the sort of person that he was, Henry the Eighth even took it one step further by asking permission from Francois the First to print an English Bible in France. Permission was thusly granted, the works were forwarded under the care of Coverdale. But religion being what it is, their endeavors were defeated by the Inquisition and the whole edition of 2,500 copies were ordered to be burned. After being forced to go back to the drawing board, the works were once again ready to be printed in 1539. By this time period, Henry's superiority in the boudoir was on the verge of impotence. In a desperate attempt to reign supreme once more, Cromwell was

TOLD TO CHANGE BIBLICAL TEXT SO THAT LITTLE HENRY WOULD BE ABLE TO SEXUALLY EXPLOIT OTHER WOMEN. KNOWING HOW UNSTABLE THE BRITISH MONARCHY ACTUALLY WAS, CROMWELL FEARED FOR HIS OWN LIFE AND ORDERED COVERDALE TO MAKE THE NECESSARY CHANGES. NOT LONG AFTER THE DEATHS OF MYLES COVERDALE AND LORD CROMWELL IN 1540, THE ROMAN CATHOLIC CHURCH STRENGTHENED THEIR OPPOSITION TO ENGLAND'S WANTS AND DESIRES OF HAVING THEIR OWN BIBLE. BY AN ACT OF PARLIAMENT A LAW WAS PASSED ABOLISHING TYNDALE'S VERSION OF BIBLICAL TEXT CITING THAT IT NOT ONLY CONTAINED COUNTLESS ERRORS BUT ENCOURAGED HUMAN BEINGS TO ACT IN MANY EVIL WAYS, HERESIES AND MISCHIEFS BEING THE DESTRUCTIVE FORCE UPON THE HARMONY AND PEACEFUL NATURE OF THE CATHOLIC FAITH. UNDER THIS PIECE OF LEGISLATION THE OWNER OF THE PUBLISHING HOUSE (WHITECHURCH AND GRAFTON) WAS THEREFORE IMPRISONED, FINED A VERY LARGE AMOUNT OF MONEY AND LATER RELEASED ONLY AFTER A HEAVY BOND WAS AGREED UPON. GRAFTON WAS NOT ONLY PROHIBITED FROM PRINTING ENGLISH BIBLES BUT HIS PUBLISHING HOUSE WAS ALSO ORDERED NOT TO SELL THEM. WITH THEIR LONG REACHING TENTACLES OF RELIGION, THE ROMAN CATHOLIC CHURCH WAS ABLE TO MAKE IT ILLEGAL FOR PERSONS TO HAVE IN THEIR POSSESSION /OR EVEN READ WYCLIFFE'S, TYNDALE'S AND COVERDALE'S VERSIONS OF THE HOLY SCRIPTURES – IT WASN'T UNTIL EDWARD THE SIXTH'S REIGN MANY GENERATIONS LATER THAT THESE SAID RESTRICTIONS WERE EVENTUALLY REMOVED.

FURTHER TO ALL OF THIS BICKERING TAKING PLACE FROM WITHIN THE RELIGIOUS INSTITUTIONS THEMSELVES, IT WAS ALSO ORDERED THAT PARSONS AND OTHERS IN THE CHURCH SERVICE READ SCRIPTURES IN BOTH LATIN AND ENGLISH, WITH THE PARAPHRASE OF ERASMUS IN ENGLISH AND THAT THE MASS ITSELF ALSO BE SAID IN ENGLISH AS WELL. THE LITURGY AS IT WERE, WAS FINALIZED AND PASSED AS AN ACT OF PARLIAMENT IN 1549.

BY THE TIME QUEEN MARY CAME ONTO THE SCENE IN 1553, THE CATHOLIC FAITH WAS ONCE AGAIN RESTORED IN ENGLAND AS BEING THE SUPERIOR RELIGION. AS A SYMBOLIC GESTURE OF GOOD FAITH, JOHN ROGERS WAS BURNED AT THE STAKE AND MANY PROTESTANT SCHOLARS AND EDUCATED THEOLOGIANS WERE THUSLY DRIVEN INTO EXILE. UPON THEIR ARRIVAL IN GENEVA, MANY OF THE EXILED BECAME INSPIRED AS TO WHAT HAD HAPPENED TO THEM AND BEGAN THE TASK OF WRITING THEIR OWN VERSION OF BIBLICAL TEXT. AN EDITION OF THE WHOLE BIBLE (OMITTING THE APOCRYPHA) WAS PRINTED IN GENEVA IN 1560, IN ENGLISH. FOR SIXTY YEARS, THE GENEVA BIBLE WAS THE FAVORED BIBLICAL TEXT OF THE PROTESTANTS, ONLY TO BE REPLACED BY YET ANOTHER AUTHORIZED VERSION PAYING TRIBUTE TO KING JAMES THE FIRST'S MENTOR HENRY VIII.

It goes without saying that throughout the ages there has been billions upon billions of individuals who fell prey to the war of religion; Tyndale, Fry, Roye, Rogers and Cromwell are only a few of them that history wishes to immortalize. In using Thomas Cromwell and those who served under him, Henry the Eighth was virtually altering the course of religious text as at that time period of history divorcing one's wife was totally unheard of for both the Roman Catholics as well as the Protestants. In both of these religions, divorce was prohibited by the word of the **Lord thy GOD**. To that end, Coverdale's English version of the Holy Scriptures and subsequent publication of the authorized King James version opened up the flood gates for divorce to take place. Coincidently, just before Cromwell's head was detached from his body, he is said to have denounced Protestantism and instantly converted back to the Roman Catholic faith in order to receive its right to passage, (the final sacrament).

It is also interesting to note that the great undertaking of having an official publication of the Bible in tribute to Henry VIII was first brought up during conversation at a conference that was taking place at Hampton Court in 1604 and received the immediate support of the King; James the First. Forty-eight highly educated Protestant scholars then began the task of analyzing the oldest original manuscript versions and studying translations in Greek, Latin, Syrian, Hebrew and Chaldean. By 1611, the task had been completed and the Bible was published. Ironically, even the Protestants kept making revisions of their own Biblical text from time to time. In fact, the situation got so far out of control that drastic swift action had to be taken in order to either slow down /or prevent any further changes from occurring as every religion's sect had been putting their own interpretation /or spin on what they perceived as being the true word of **GOD**.

Prior to the United States gaining their independence from England during the American Revolutionary War, the entire North American Continent was controlled by only two well known worldwide religions; Roman Catholic and/or Protestant. France controlled parts of the Continent where devoted French Roman Catholics lived while the English-speaking portions were Protestants. Those parts of the country where in which the mother tongue was English, had their Bibles supplied by England. At the time of American Independence in 1776, only two separate editions of the Bible had been published in the United States; John Eliot's

VERSION PRINTED IN THE ALGONQUIAN LANGUAGE IN 1663 AND CHRISTOPHER SAUR'S VERSION IN THE GERMAN LANGUAGE PRINTED IN 1743. ONLY SIX YEARS AFTER GAINING THEIR INDEPENDENCE FROM THE BRITISH MONARCHY, THE UNITED STATES OF AMERICA HAD ITS OWN BIBLE PUBLISHED IN ENGLISH BY ROBERT AITKEN AT PHILADELPHIA IN 1782. LESS THAN TEN YEARS LATER, OTHER PUBLISHING HOUSES SET BIBLICAL TEXT TO PRINT IN THE ENGLISH LANGUAGE; ISAIAH THOMAS AT WORCESTER, MASSACHUSETTS IN 1791 AND ISAAC COLLINS AT TRENTON, NEW JERSEY IN THE SAME YEAR. BY THE MID-1800'S, THE HOLY SCRIPTURES HAD BEEN REVISED AND RE-WRITTEN SO MANY TIMES IN THE UNITED STATES THAT IT WAS HARD TO DISTINGUISH FACT FROM FICTION WITHIN THE BIBLE ITSELF AS ONE SECTION WOULD BE OMITTED AND ANOTHER PUT IN ITS PLACE TO SUIT THE WHIMS OF THOSE WHO HAD A HIDDEN RELIGIOUS AGENDA TO FULFILL.

IN 1870, DRASTIC RELIGIOUS ACTION WAS EXECUTED AS A GROUP OF BRITISH AND AMERICAN SCHOLARS WERE SELECTED BY THE CONVOCATION OF CANTERBURY TO RE-EDIT AND REVISE BIBLICAL TEXT SUPPOSEDLY FOR ONE LAST TIME. THIS REVISED NEW TESTAMENT WAS PUBLISHED IN 1881 WHILE THEIR REVISED OLD TESTAMENT WASN'T RELEASED UNTIL FOUR YEARS LATER, (1885). THESE REVISIONS WERE SAID TO BE A NECESSITY IN ORDER TO KEEP AN ENGLISH TRANSLATION IN MAIN STREAM OF LIVING, CONTEMPORARY SPEECH AS IT WERE. ACCORDINGLY, THE KING JAMES VERSION WHICH HAD BEEN WRITTEN IN WORDS NORMALLY USED DURING THE SEVENTEENTH CENTURY AND NOT WELL UNDERSTOOD BY THOSE OF THE NINETEENTH CENTURY WAS SAID TO BE AS TO WHERE THE MAIN PROBLEM LIED. SO, WITH THAT UNDERSTANDING THE INNER CIRCLE OF THE BRITISH AND AMERICAN EDUCATED ELITE ALLIED FORCES PUT THEIR COLLECTIVE THOUGHTS TO PEN AND PAPER AND RE-WROTE BIBLICAL TEXT.

LIKE ANYTHING ELSE IN LIFE, THE TRUE CONTENT OF THINGS JUST SEEMS TO GET LOST IN THE TRANSLATION AS THE EDUCATED ONES TRIED TO PROVE THEIR SUPERIORITY OVER ALL INDIVIDUALS WHO WERE PERCEIVED AS BEING INFERIOR TO THE INTELLIGENTSIA. BY THE TWENTIETH CENTURY, FURTHER REVISIONS WERE MADE TO BIBLICAL TEXT; MOULTON'S THE READER'S BIBLE, SMITH AND GOODSPEED'S AMERICAN TRANSLATION, AND MOFFAT'S NEW TRANSLATION ARE PRIME EXAMPLES OF SUPERIOR INTERPRETATIONS VERSUS A LAYMAN'S OWN PERSONAL INTERPRETATIONS. TO EVEN ADD MORE CONFUSION TO BIBLICAL TEXT, THE JERUSALEM BIBLE WHICH WAS FIRST PUBLISHED IN FRENCH IN 1956 WHICH ACTED AS THE OFFICIAL TEXT FOR USE IN ROMAN CATHOLIC LITURGY WAS REVISED TEN YEARS LATER AS IT WAS TRANSLATED INTO ENGLISH AND FURTHER REVISIONS WERE EXPECTED TO OCCUR JUST AS THE 21ST CENTURY WAS BEGINNING TO UNFOLD.

By all account, the Bible is the most widely distributed and translated book in all of mankind's history. According to the 1988 edition of the Gluiness Book of World Records, an estimated 2.5 billion copies were printed between the years 1815 and 1975, and has been translated into more than 1,800 different languages and/or dialects. Further to this, the Bible is also said to be accessible to at least 98 percent of the world's population. To this very day, no other history book has ever made the best-sellers list with such zeal and prolific success on a worldwide scale as the Holy Scriptures.

When the King of France (Francois I) attempted to establish a French Roman Catholic colony in Quebec during the 1540's by cleaning out his prison cells, Protestantism had spread throughout the world like wildfire thus causing much unrest for the Catholic Church. In an attempt to prove its superiority over the Protestants, the Roman Catholic Church in conjunction with the King of France (as both Church and state were one in the same), conceived a master plan to establish a colony based on the model of their *Seignioral Tenure* whereas Canada was destined to become the envy of all. But the half-baked French Roman Catholic idea had far too many loopholes in it to be executed properly that numerous attempts had taken place. One in fact could say that the French weren't as smart as they had originally anticipated since English Protestants in the end gained control of Canada thus throwing the French themselves into total chaos for many generations thereafter. Contrary as to what some members of the LePage family tree of Quebec may wish to be true, they too were thrown into chaos as the Protestant take-over of Canada in 1763 set the wheels in motion for their religious, political and/or financial ruin. To some, their only salvation was to remain devoted to the Catholic Church while others collaborated with the Protestants playing both ends against the middle. Perhaps the demise of the Roman Catholic plan was destined to fail right from the very beginning as less than fifty years after Samuel de Champlain's marking of the site where the construction of a building was to take place in Quebec City during the summer of 1608, French Roman Catholics in Montreal began fighting amongst themselves for control of the Catholic Church in 1657; one group wanting more to say than the other.

It apparently all began when the Roman Catholic Church in France seriously started contemplating the idea of establishing a Seminary on the Island of Montreal for the purpose of theological studies for those who wanted to enter the priesthood. The Church

THUSLY SENT FOUR PRIESTS OF THE SULPICIAN ORDER, (A SOCIETY THAT HAD A SOLE PURPOSE OF TRAINING THOSE WHO WANTED TO BE PRIESTS) TO MONTREAL; DE QUEYLUS, SOUART, D'ALLET AND GALINIER. THE SULPICIANS WERE SAID TO BE SECULAR PRIESTS, THE CREAM OF THE ROMAN CATHOLIC CROP AS IT WERE, WHO WERE NOT ONLY FINE TUNED GENTLEMEN BUT INDIVIDUALS OF HIGH CALIBER WHO COULD NOT BE BOUGH-OFF AS THEY WERE ALSO SAID NOT TO BE WORSHIPERS OF MATERIAL OBJECTS. THE LOWER CLASS OF ROMAN CATHOLICS ON THE OTHER HAND WERE FULL AWARE OF THE FACT THAT THE SULPICIANS HAD AMPLE FUNDS AS THEY WERE PAID DIRECTLY FROM THE CHURCH IN FRANCE, WHILE THOSE ON THE LOWER SCALE BARELY HAD ENOUGH MONEY TO PAY AS TO WHAT THE CHURCH AND STATE EXPECTED THE PARISHIONERS TO DISH OUT ON A DAILY BASIS. THE CATHOLIC CHURCH WAS SAID TO BE HATED BY MOST, IF NOT ALL OF QUEBEC'S LOWER CLASSES NOT ONLY BECAUSE OF THE FACT THAT THE PRIESTS REGULATED THE AFFAIRS OF THEIR DAILY LIVES BUT ALSO DUE TO THE FACT THAT THEY (THE CHURCH AND THEIR COUNTERPARTS) WERE LANDED PROPRIETORS, LORDS OF MANORS, TITHE OWNERS, AND ADMINISTRATORS IN THE NEW WORLD (QUEBEC AND LOUISIANA). WHILE THE MIDDLE AND UPPER CLASSES REAPED THE WEALTH OF THE SEIGNIORAL SYSTEM, THE POOR SUFFERED FROM THE COLD AND HUNGER AS THE CANONS, (THE CHURCH CLERGY) ATE WELL AND THOUGHT NOTHING OF FATTENING THEMSELVES LIKE PIGS THAT WERE SOON GOING TO BE SLAUGHTER FOR AN EASTER FEAST. THIS RESENTMENT ESCALATED EVEN FURTHER AS CHURCH OFFICIALS IN FRANCE SET THE WHEELS IN MOTION FOR THE ESTABLISHING OF A PERMANENT HEAD OF THE CHURCH IN CANADA. BEFORE LONG, THE SULPICIAN ORDER AND THE JESUITS, (ANOTHER ROMAN CATHOLIC SOCIETY THAT WAS OUT TO EDUCATE THE IGNORANCE OF OTHERS IN ACCORDANCE TO CATHOLIC DOCTRINE), WERE AT EACH OTHERS THROATS AS ONE GROUP WANTED MORE TO SAY AS TO HOW CHRISTIANITY WAS TO FLOURISH IN THE NEW WORLD. WITH THE SCHISM BREWING IN THE BACKGROUND, THE CATHOLIC CHURCH HAD TO ACT QUICKLY AND IN THE SUMMER OF 1657 THE FOUR MEMBERS OF THE SULPICIAN ORDER ARRIVED IN NEW FRANCE.

UPON THEIR ARRIVAL, THEY FOUND THEMSELVES EMBROILED IN A BITTER DISPUTE THAT WAS CAUSING SO MUCH DISSECTION BETWEEN ALL ROMAN CATHOLICS FROM MONTREAL TO QUEBEC CITY AND BACK AGAIN. IT WAS LARGELY DUE TO THIS ANIMOSITY THAT CONVINCED CHURCH OFFICIALS THAT A HOME GROWN HEAD-OF-STATE HAD TO BE IMPLEMENTED. BUT LITTLE DID ANYONE REALIZE THAT THE SCHISM WOULD ESCALATE SO FAR OUT OF CONTROL AS IT DID WHEN TALK BEGAN TO CIRCULATE THAT THE ISLAND OF MONTREAL WAS BEING TRANSFERRED INTO THE CARE OF THE SULPICIANS, PERHAPS THIS IS WHY IT TOOK FOUR YEARS TO DO SO. ACTING QUICKLY, ONE OF THE ORIGINAL FOUR, ABBE DE QUEYLUS WAS APPOINTED SUPERIOR OF THE SULPICIAN MISSIONS

IN CANADA. NOT AT ALL IMPRESSED WHAT WAS GOING ON, THE JESUITS SOON BECAME ENRAGED AT THE APPOINTMENT AS QUEYLUS HIMSELF WAS A MAN OF CONSIDERABLE PERSONAL WEALTH WHICH IN ITSELF WAS HYPOCRITICAL IN NATURE. CHURCH OFFICIALS IN FRANCE WERE PAVING THE WAY FOR ABBE DE QUEYLUS TO BECOME CANADA'S FIRST BISHOP AS IT WAS BELIEVED THAT HE WAS A MAN OF HIGH CHARACTER AND UNDOUBTABLY PERCEIVED AS BEING CAPABLE OF HANDLING THE JOB. BUT ALL THIS FELL TO THE WAY SIDE AS NOT LONG AFTER HIS ARRIVAL, QUEYLUS APPARENTLY GAVE TWO SERMONS THAT WERE SAID TO HAVE INFLAMED THE POWERS THAT BE IN QUEBEC AS WELL AS IN FRANCE ITSELF. WITH HIS POSSIBLE APPOINTMENT OF BEING THE BIG KHAUNA FOR ALL OF CANADA, QUEYLUS LOST ALL TRACK OF REALITY AS HE ASSUMED HIMSELF TO BE SAFELY SEATED IN THE SADDLE AND BEGAN LASHING OUT AT THE JESUITS CALLING THEM THE MOST PAGAN FORM OF CHRISTIANITY ON THE FACE OF THE EARTH. THE JESUITS IN TURN ACCUSED QUEYLUS OF WARRING THEM MORE SAVAGELY THAN THE IROQUOIS INDIANS. WITH HIS APPOINTMENT NOW HANGING IN THE BALANCE, ABBE DE QUEYLUS CONTINUED TO BASH THE JESUITS AT ANY OPPORTUNE MOMENT THAT HE HAD, BOTH IN HIS SERMONS AS WELL AS ON THE STREETS. THE SITUATION WAS SO FAR OUT OF CONTROL THAT THE ROMAN CATHOLIC CHURCH OFFICIALS HAD NO CHOICE BUT TO LOOK FOR YET ANOTHER FINE TUNED GENTLEMAN AMONGST THEIR SO-CALLED CREAM OF THE ROMAN CATHOLIC CROP. QUEYLUS' REPLACEMENT, FRANCOIS XAVIER DE LAVAL DE MONTMORENCY (A.K.A. ABBE DE MONTIGNY) ARRIVED INTO CANADA IN JUNE OF 1659 AND ANOINTED AS QUEBEC'S BISHOP NOT LONG AFTERWARDS.

COINCIDENTLY, BISHOP LAVAL WAS EDUCATED AT THE JESUIT COLLEGES IN FRANCE, LA FLECHE AND PARIS AND ORDAINED ON MAY 1ST, 1647. AFTER REALIZING THAT THE CATHOLIC CHURCH APPOINTED SOMEONE TO THE POST THAT HE WAS ORIGINALLY DESTINED TO HOLD BY DIVINE INTERVENTION, QUEYLUS EXPRESSED HIS DISPLEASURE TO THE NEW BISHOP. AFTER QUARRELING WITH BISHOP LAVAL AND THE JESUITS OF QUEBEC, ABBE DE QUEYLUS LEFT CANADA FOR FRANCE MADDER THAN A HATTER — BY WAY OF A SHIP SAILING TO THE MOTHERLAND. LAVAL, IN TURN REQUESTED QUEYLUS' IMMEDIATE RETURN TO FACE THE MUSIC. SINCE CHURCH AND STATE WERE ONE IN THE SAME, THE KING OF FRANCE WHO SANCTIONED LAVAL'S APPOINTMENT AS BISHOP REFUSED TO ALLOW QUEYLUS TO LEAVE FRANCE ONCE HE ARRIVED. FEELING THOROUGHLY ANNOYED AT THE FACT THAT HE WAS DUMPED FOR A WEALTHIER AND MORE SUBDUED CLASS OF PERSONALITY, QUEYLUS DISOBEYED THE KING BY HEADING IMMEDIATELY TO ROME IN ORDER TO OBTAIN SUPPORT FOR HIS JUST CAUSE OF OVERTHROWING LAVAL AS BISHOP. AFTER GAINING THE SUPPORT NEEDED, QUEYLUS THEN WHEN BACK TO THE NEW WORLD TO PROVE THAT HIS CAUSE WAS TOTALLY JUSTIFIED. AS IT TURNS OUT, THE KING APPARENTLY

SUBMITTED A DISPATCH REQUESTING QUEYLUS' IMMEDIATE RETURN TO THE MOTHERLAND WITHIN ONLY A FEW WEEKS OF HIS BEING OUT ON THE LAM AFTER FIRST BATTLING IT OUT WITH BISHOP LAVAL.

THE ANIMOSITY BETWEEN LAVAL AND QUEYLUS WAS SO EVIDENT THAT BISHOP LAVAL EVEN PERSUADED THE GOVERNOR OF QUEBEC TO SENT A SQUAD OF FRENCH SOLDIERS TO ARREST HIM AFTER THE TWO PARTIES IN QUESTION HAD THEIR LITTLE SQUABBLE THAT CAUSED QUEYLUS TO STORM OUT OF LAVAL'S OFFICE ALL IN A HUFF. THE FRENCH SOLDIERS WERE ORDERED TO BRING THE DISTRAUGHT ABBE BACK TO THE BISHOP'S OFFICE IN QUEBEC CITY TO FACE THE WRATH THAT WAS GOING TO BE BESTOWED ONTO HIM. BUT IT WAS WAY TOO LATE, HE HAD ALREADY BOARDED A SHIP HEADING FOR FRANCE. THIS IRONICALLY IS A PART OF HISTORY THAT MOST HISTORIANS DISAGREE ON AS SOME SAY THAT QUEYLUS INITIALLY RETURNED BACK TO LAVAL'S OFFICE TO FACE THE MUSIC ON HIS ON FREE WILL AND ACCORD WHEREBY THEY PURPOSELY LEAVE OUT THE MOST CRUCIAL PIECE OF THIS RELIGIOUS PUZZLE. BE THAT AS IT MAY, BISHOP LAVAL WAS NOT AT ALL IMPRESSED WITH QUEYLUS' ANTICS OF QUESTIONING HIS AUTHORITY IN NEW FRANCE AND COULD NOT PERMIT SUCH MISBEHAVING TO CONTINUE AS THE PARISHIONERS THEMSELVES ALSO BEGAN QUESTIONING THE SUPREMACY OF THE CHURCH. IN THE END, IT WOULD LATER BE A *LETTRE DE CACHET* DISPATCHED FROM THE KING THAT INITIALLY ENABLED QUEYLUS TO TAKE THE EASY WAY OUT AS BY THIS TIME PERIOD, EVEN HE WAS BECOMING WELL AWARE OF THE FACT THAT THINGS WERE JUST A LITTLE BIT OUT OF CONTROL. THE PROTESTING ABBE, THEN, BEGRUDGINGLY BOARDED THE NEXT AVAILABLE SHIP HEADING BACK TO FRANCE.

IT IS ALSO INTERESTING TO NOTE THAT AMONGST THOSE WHO SUPPORTED QUEYLUS' CAUSE TO OVERTHROW THE JESUIT BISHOP LAVAL IN CANADA , OTHER THAN THE SULPICIAN ORDER ITSELF OF COURSE, WAS THE GALLICAN PARTY OF THE CATHOLIC CHURCH WHO WERE A GROUP OF RELIGIOUS ZEALOTS TRYING TO GAIN CONTROL OF THE CHURCH IN FRANCE. SINCE FRANCOIS XAVIER DE LAVAL DE MONTMORECY WAS A MAN OF GREAT WEALTH AND NOBILITY IN FRANCE, HIS ABILITY TO REACH FAR ACROSS THE ATLANTIC OCEAN ESSENTIALLY ENABLED HIM TO UTILIZE WHATEVER INFLUENCES THAT HE HAD WITH VARIOUS MEMBERS OF THE UPPER ECHELONS OF FRENCH SOCIETY TO HAVE HIS RIVAL FACE THE MUSIC IN CANADA. WHILE THE KING WAS VISITING THE SOUTHERN FRONTIER OF FRANCE, WHERE HE WOULD MET AND LATER MARRY THE INFANTA OF SPAIN, THE KING WAS PERSUADED TO WRITE A LETTER TO QUEYLUS REQUESTING HIS IMMEDIATE RETURN TO THE MOTHERLAND. DISREGARDING THE KING'S WISHES TO STAY PUT ONCE RETURNING TO FRANCE, QUEYLUS SET OUT FOR ROME AS HE HAD COME TO THE FULL REALIZATION THAT HE WAS NOW IN DEEP SHIT WITH THE FRENCH MONARCHY AND HAD HIGH HOPES OF WINNING THE POPE'S SUPPORT CONCERNING THE GROWING

CONTROVERSY. ANTICIPATING SUCH TROUBLE, QUEYLUS HAD BEEN TOLD BY HIS SUPPORTERS IN ROME THAT THE INNER PAPAL CIRCLE WERE SECRET SUPPORTERS OF JANSENISM, YET ANOTHER FACTION TRYING TO GAIN CONTROL OF THE CHURCH. THE CATHOLIC CHURCH WAS OBVIOUSLY FALLING APART AT THE SEAMS AS THEY WERE CONSTANTLY AT ODDS WITH THEIR OWN BRETHREN FROM WITHIN THE PAPACY ITSELF. UPON HIS ARRIVAL TO SEE THE VATICAN SUPPORTERS, QUEYLUS RECEIVED A SOMEWHAT LUKEWARM RECEPTION.

NOT TAKING *"NO "*FOR AN ANSWER, ABBE DE QUEYLUS STATED HIS CASE AND GRADUALLY WON SOME SUPPORT FOR HIS CLAIMS, CITING THAT THE SULPICIAN ORDER WAS INDEPENDENT FROM THE ROMAN CATHOLIC CHURCH AND THAT THE CHURCH ITSELF HAD NO JURISDICTIONAL POWERS OVER THEM. AFTER SOME DELIBERATION, HE WAS GIVEN BULLS FROM THE ***CONGREGATION OF THE DATERIE***, AN OFFICE OF THE CURIA, CONFIRMING THE INDEPENDENCE OF THE SULPICIAN MEMBERSHIP IN MONTREAL. HAVING THE DOCUMENTATION THAT HE NEEDED TO TOPPLE BISHOP LAVAL, THE DISOBEDIENT SULPICIAN HOPPED ONTO A SHIP SAILING TO CANADA. WITH THE DOCUMENTED BULLS UNDER HIS ARM, QUEYLUS ARRIVED AT QUEBEC ON AUGUST 3RD, 1661 AND MADE HIS WAY TO LAVAL'S OFFICE. NOW, IT WAS BISHOP LAVAL'S TURN TO BE MADDER THAN A HATTER AS QUEYLUS WAS GOING DIRECTLY FOR THE BISHOP'S JUGULAR VEIN. IN A TOTAL STATE OF PANIC, BISHOP LAVAL CHARGED THAT THE BULLS WERE OBTAINED BY ABBE DE QUEYLUS BY FRAUDULENT AND MISREPRESENTATION MEANS. AN ORDER WAS THUSLY ISSUED PROHIBITING THE DISSIDENT FROM LEAVING QUEBEC UNTIL THE FRENCH MONARCHY HAD BEEN INFORMED OF HIS ILLEGAL ENTRY BACK INTO NEW FRANCE. APPARENTLY, VICOMTE D'ARGENSON (THE GOVERNOR OF QUEBEC) WAS SUPPOSEDLY GOING TO ARREST QUEYLUS BUT DIDN'T HAVE THE HEART TO DO SO AS HE WAS SAID TO HAVE MIXED FEELINGS ABOUT THE ENTIRE SCENARIO AND THEREFORE WAS CONSTANTLY DRAGGING HIS FEET IN THE NUMEROUS ATTEMPTS OF TRYING TO DETAIN QUEYLUS. AS SOON AS LAVAL HAD BEEN MADE AWARE OF WHAT ABBE DE QUEYLUS HAD IN HIS POSSESSION AND WHAT HE WAS GOING TO BE DOING WITH THEM, BISHOP LAVAL WAS OVER COME WITH ANXIETY. HE ONLY WAITED FOR A DAY TO PASS BEFORE SENDING A HARSHLY WORDED PEREMPTORY TO THE GOVERNOR TO HAVE QUEYLUS DETAINED. BY THE TIME D'ARGENSON FINALLY MADE UP HIS MIND AS TO HOW TO DEAL WITH THE SITUATION AT HAND, ABBE DE QUEYLUS HAD ALREADY OBTAINED PASSAGE OUT OF QUEBEC CITY BY WAY OF A CANOE. UNDER THE CLOAK OF DARKNESS, HE MADE HIS WAY UP THE RIVER TO MONTREAL AND WAITED AROUND TO FIGURE OUT HIS NEXT LINE OF ATTACK ON BISHOP LAVAL. APPARENTLY, THIS IS WHERE THE HISTORIANS GET THEIR FACTS ALL MIXED UP AS LAVAL HAD HEARD RUMORS THAT QUEYLUS HAD FLED TO MONTREAL AND NOW, THE GOVERNOR WAS FINALLY SENDING A SQUAD OF SOLDIERS TO BRING HIM BACK. SINCE LAVAL FEARED THAT HE WAS

GOING TO BE TOPPLED BY ABBE DE QUEYLUS RIGHT FROM THE OUTSET OF HIS APPOINTMENT AS BEING THE NEW BISHOP, LAVAL ALMOST IMMEDIATELY BEGAN SENDING WRATHFUL MESSAGES TO FRANCE INSISTING THAT OVER THE COURSE OF TIME HE MIGHT NEED ASSISTANCE IN TONING DOWN THE RHETORIC ACTIONS OF HIS OPPONENT. ONCE IT WAS LEARNED THAT THE DISOBEDIENT SULPICIAN WAS HEADING FOR ROME TO GAIN SUPPORT FOR HIS CAUSE, BOTH CHURCH OFFICIALS IN FRANCE AND THE FRENCH MONARCHY KNEW EXACTLY AS TO WHAT QUEYLUS WAS UP TOO. THE KING THUSLY COMMANDED THE GOVERNOR OF QUEBEC TO SUPPORT BISHOP LAVAL EVERY STEP OF THE WAY; NO MATTER WHAT THE REQUEST!!!

CONTEMPLATING AS TO WHAT HIS NEXT MANEUVER WAS GOING TO BE WHILE IN MONTREAL, QUEYLUS WAS CAPTURED BY THE GOVERNOR'S SOLDIERS AND BROUGHT BACK TO QUEBEC CITY. HE WAS THEN BEGRUDGINGLY SENT BACK TO FRANCE ON THE FIRST AVAILABLE SHIP LEAVING PORT. ALL DOCUMENTATION THAT HE HAD IN HIS POSSESSION WAS IMMEDIATELY CONFISCATED WHEN HE WAS ARRESTED AND THE BULLS FROM THE *CONGREGATION OF DATERIE* WERE WITHDRAWN THUS GIVING NO VOLUBILITY WHATSOEVER TO HIS CLAIMS. BY HOOK /OR BY CROOK, BISHOP LAVAL WAS GOING TO REMAIN SEATED AT THE RIGHT HAND OF **GOD** AS THE OVERSEER OF THE ROMAN CATHOLIC CHURCH IN CANADA. TOTALLY DISILLUSIONED BY THE WHOLE ORDEAL, QUEYLUS ONLY REMAINED IN FRANCE FOR A SHORT PERIOD OF TIME IN A SOMEWHAT UNHAPPY SEMI-OBSCURITY STATE STEWING OVER LAVAL'S WIN. BUT BISHOP LAVAL'S WIN WAS TO BE SHORT LIVED AS HE TOO SOON BEGAN TO SHOW SIGNS OF HIS ARROGANCE AND RESIGNED HIS POSTING IN 1688, ILL HEALTH WAS GIVEN BY THE HISTORIANS AS BEING THE MAIN CONTRIBUTING FACTOR OF HIS RESIGNATION. BUT IF THAT WAS INDEED THE CASE, THEN, WHY IS IT THAT QUEYLUS RETURNED BACK TO CANADA THAT VERY SAME YEAR AND RESUMED HIS POSITION AS SUPERIOR OF THE SULPICIANS AND BECAME LAVAL'S VICAR-GENERAL IN MONTREAL. COINCIDENTLY, HISTORIANS STATE CATEGORICALLY THAT PEACE HAD BEEN ESTABLISHED BETWEEN THE TWO PRELATES BUT IN ALL LIKELIHOOD A COMPROMISE WAS MORE THAN LIKELY REACHED AS ABBE DE QUEYLUS WAS NOT THE SORT OF PERSON TO LET THINGS SQUEAK BY AS EASILY AS TO WHAT SOME MAY WISH US TO BELIEVE IS TRUE.

DURING THE FIRST YEARS OF THE 21ST CENTURY, BIBLICAL TEXT WAS SLATED TO GO THROUGH YET ANOTHER TRANSFORMATION AS THE EDUCATED ONES WANTED TO MAKE MORE CHANGES THAT ONCE AGAIN WERE TO CHALLENGE THE SUPERIORITY OF THE ROMAN CATHOLIC CHURCH ITSELF; THE DEAD SEA SCROLLLS. THE SCROLLS WERE ORIGINALLY FOUND BY A BEDOUIN SHEPHERD BOY IN CAVES AT QUMRAN, A SMALL VILLAGE IN THE MIDDLE EAST, ON THE NORTHWESTERN SHORE OF THE DEAD SEA, (JORDAN), IN 1947. NOT LONG AFTER THEY WERE FOUND, THE SCROLLS VIRTUALLY BECAME A GROWING

CONTROVERSY THAT PITTED JEWS AND ROMAN CATHOLICS AGAINST ONE ANOTHER EVEN FURTHER AS THE SCROLLS CONTENTS WERE SAID TO CONTAIN WRITINGS THAT DIFFERED WITH THE ACCEPTED CHRISTIAN TEACHINGS AND PHILOSOPHIES – WHICH ULTIMATELY COULD HAVE TOTALLY ROCKED THE RELIGIOUS FOUNDATION OF THE CATHOLIC CHURCH /OR EVEN POSSIBLY DESTROYED IT ALTOGETHER. TO THAT END, THE ROMAN CATHOLIC CHURCH THEN BEGAN A PROPAGANDA PROGRAM IN A FEEBLE ATTEMPT TO PREVENT THE CONTENTS FROM EVER BEING REVEALED UNTIL FURTHER ANALYSIS HAD BEEN CONDUCTED ON ITS AUTHENTICITY AND A TOTAL ACCEPTABLE TRANSLATION COULD BE FINALIZED AS A WAY AND MEANS OF NOT ANNIHILATE THE CHURCH ITSELF. WITH COUNTLESS DECADES OF SHEER SECRECY ON THE ROMAN CATHOLIC CHURCH'S PART CAME MANY CONSPIRACY THEORIES AS TO WHY THEY (THE CATHOLICS) WERE HOLDING OUT. THROUGHOUT THE MANY, MANY YEARS AFTER THE SCROLLS WERE FOUND IN THE CAVES, MUCH SCANDAL CLAD RHETORIC HAD BEEN PUBLISHED THAT CHURCH OFFICIALS HAD NO CHOICE BUT TO AGREE TO HAVE THE HOLY SCRIPTURES REVISED ONE LAST TIME. IN SEPTEMBER OF 2001, THE PAPACY ENDED THE MANY DECADES OF SECRECY AND OBSTRUCTION OF THE SCROLLS CONTENTS BY GIVING THE RELIGIOUS NOD TO HAVE THE CHANGES REVEALED IN THE BIBLE BASED ON THE DEAD SEA SCROLLS' LATEST REVELATIONS. THE CHANGES WERE EXPECTED TO TAKE FIVE (5) YEARS TO COMPLETE AND ACCORDING TO SOME OF THE POPE'S KEEPERS OF ROMAN CATHOLIC DOCTRINE, THE SCROLLS WERE TO LAY TO REST THE CONTROVERSY AS THE ENTIRE PICTURE OF THE ORIGINS OF CHRISTIANITY WAS SAID TO BE INCORPORATED IN THE NEW AND IMPROVED VERSION OF THE HOLY SCRIPTURES. WITH THE ROMAN CATHOLIC CHURCH'S APPROVAL, EDUCATED SCHOLARS OF THEOLOGY THEN BEGAN MAKING VARIOUS REVISIONS TO BIBLICAL TEXT ONCE AGAIN AND NATURALLY, ALL CHANGES WERE SUBJECT TO FINAL APPROVAL BY THE KEEPERS OF ROMAN CATHOLIC CHURCH DOCTRINE.

BEFORE ACCEPTING THE NEW 21ST CENTURY CHANGES TO BIBLICAL TEXT AS BEING A TRUE FACT OF MAN'S EXISTENCE ON THE PLANET EARTH, A PERSON SHOULD ALSO CONSIDER THIS. ACCORDING TO THE ROMAN CATHOLIC CHURCH ARCHIVES, THE PROTESTANT HERO WILLIAM OF ORANGE RECEIVED SUBSTANTIAL SUMS OF MONEY FROM THE ROMAN CATHOLIC POPE INNOCENT XI IN THE LATTER PARTS OF THE 1600'S. THE PONTIFF, APPARENTLY WANTED TO SEE A END TO THE RULE OF ENGLAND'S JAMES II AND PREFERRED THAT A MORE SUBDUED RULER BE PUT IN HIS PLACE, WILLIAM OF ORANGE, JAMES' SON-IN-LAW. AS FAR AS THE ROMAN CATHOLIC POPE WAS CONCERNED, JAMES II WAS WAY TOO CHUMMY WITH KING LOUIS XIV OF FRANCE, WHOSE RELATIONS WITH THE CATHOLIC CHURCH WAS ON SHAKY GROUND FOR THE TIME BEING AS KING LOUIS' HATRED FOR PROTESTANTS WAS SAID TO BE RUBBING THE PONTIFF THE WRONG WAY. JAMES THE SECOND, ON THE OTHER

HAND WAS ATTEMPTING TO SET UP HIS OWN ROMAN CATHOLIC DYNASTY IN ENGLAND WHERE HE WOULD REIGN SUPREME INSTEAD OF POPE INNOCENT XI. OBVIOUSLY, BOTH THE KINGS OF FRANCE AND ENGLAND HAD SOMETHING IN COMMON AS THE TWO MONARCHY LEADERS BEGAN DISREGARDING WHAT THE POPE HAD TO SAY ABOUT ANYTHING WHILE ATTEMPTING TO BE THE BIG KHAUNA OF THEIR OWN DESIGNATED DOMAINS. TO THAT END, (THE ENDS JUSTIFYING THE MEANS OF COURSE), POPE INNOCENT XI THEN BEGAN FUNNELING LARGE AMOUNTS OF MONEY TOWARDS THE PROTESTANT CAUSE OF OVERTHROWING THE ROMAN CATHOLIC RULE OF KING JAMES II OF ENGLAND. IT IS SAID THAT THE PROTESTANT LEADER RECEIVED HIS FUNDING THROUGH INTERMEDIARIES CLOSE TO THE WEALTHY FAMILY OF BENEDETTO ODESCALCHI, INNOCENT'S CHRISTIAN NAME BEFORE HE WAS ORDAINED POPE. THE MONETARY TRANSFERS, EQUIVALENT TO AN ESTIMATED 7.5 MILLION DOLLARS IN TODAY'S CURRENCY, WERE CONTAINED IN NUMEROUS VOLUMES OF MANUSCRIPTS KEPT FOR CENTURIES IN THE CELLAR OF A PALACE BELONGING TO THE ODESCALCHI FAMILY AND WEREN'T MADE AVAILABLE TO HISTORIANS UNTIL THE ROMAN CATHOLIC CHURCH DECIDED TO MAKE THE VARIOUS CHANGES TO THE HOLY SCRIPTURES.

NEEDLESS TO SAY, THERE HAS BEEN MANY SECRETS AND LIES PASSED DOWN THROUGH THE AGES IN THE NAME OF RELIGION THAT SOMETIMES IT COMES BACK TO BITE THEM IN THE ASS. EVEN THE CATHOLIC CHURCH IS NOT IMMUNE TO THIS LITTLE KNOWN FACT OF HISTORY. WHOSE TO SAY THAT SOME SORT OF COMPROMISE HAD NOT BEEN REACHED CONCERNING THE TRUE CONTENTS OF THE DEAD SEA SCROLLS THAT WOULD ALLOW THE ROMAN CATHOLIC CHURCH TO SAVE FACE AS EVEN THE VATICAN ITSELF HAS A TEND OF PLAYING BOTH ENDS AGAINST THE MIDDLE FROM TIME TO TIME THUS ALLOWING THEM TO MAINTAIN THEIR FACADE OF REIGNING SUPREME OVER ALL OTHER FORMS OF RELIGION — RELIGIOUSLY SPEAKING THUS FAR, ONE RELIGION IN ESSENCE IS JUST AS BAD AS THE OTHER!!!

Chapter 3 - Je Me Souviens

Like the gate keepers of Roman Catholic Church doctrine, the history of Canada has a very intriguing past (religiously as well as politically). Unfortunately for Canadians, most of this history has been drastically watered down by both French and English-speaking historians throughout the many centuries. For instance, during the time period of France's establishing of the seignorial system on the North American Continent in the 1600's and well into the next century, many of the wealthier families of New France had either Indian and/or Black house slaves. Among some of the earliest recorded owners of slaves in Canada was none other than the Sieur de Monts, a.k.a. Pierre du Guast, a Protestant convert gentleman and pillar of nobility from France. De Monts was appointed the French King's Lieutenant-General for the colonies along the Atlantic coast from the 40TH to the 46TH parallels, his authority is said to have extended as far south as to where today's modern day Philadelphia is situated. During the summer of 1604, de Monts's first colony on the Island of St. Croix (where the river of the same name enters into the Bay of Fundy) was established. Amongst its inhabitants were both Huguenots and Roman Catholics (priest and pastor) as de Monts himself was a devoted Huguenot. Buildings were constructed and seeds planted in the sandy soil during that summer. By the summer of the following year, the little colony moved itself clear across the Bay of Fundy to the luscious meadows of Port Royal in the Annapolis Valley in what is now known as Nova Scotia. Apparently the colony had endured much hardship during the first year, starvation due to the lack of winter supplies and the dreaded break-out of scurvy that literally whipped out two-fifths of the colony's population. De Monts is said to have taken it as a sign from the Almighty God that St. Croix was not a suitable location for a permanent settlement.

By 1608, de Monts was granted a monopoly of the North American fur trade industry and thusly began his trading privileges for that season along the banks of the St. Lawrence River. Calculating a hefty rate of return on his investments, de Monts erected several buildings and warehouses along the St. Lawrence were the Indians were to be the main instruments of his obtaining a large profit margin. Interestingly, one member of de Monts expedition to Port Royal in 1606 was a Black slave who went by the name of Mathieu d'Acosta. As fate would have it, the actual ownership of this slave was subject of a lawsuit at one time /or another in Rouen, France. D'Acosta was said to be an invaluable asset to the Sieur de Monts as he acted as an interpreter for the French with the Mi'kmaq Indians along the eastern Atlantic coastline.

Other recorded slave transactions in Canada took place while the French were attempting to establish their God given right to reign supreme on the North American Continent. Duly recorded at Champlain's new settlement of Quebec City in 1629 is the sale of a young Blackman (Louis) from Madagascar to one Le Bailly from an English commander who later on that year would force the surrender of a trading post that literally gave him full control of French Canada. By the time the trading post was up and running at full capacity in 1628, there were only seventy-six settlers living around its fortified walls cultivating small portions of land and carpenters, brought out from France had just started constructing a water-mill. During that summer, a fleet of English ships appeared in the St. Lawrence demanding the surrender of the post. Their commander, David Kirke dropped anchor and waited for the French to respond to his request. The stalemate lasted all winter long as the French weren't about ready to give in to the English demands. Holding out as long as they could, the French had no choice but to surrender the trading post once winter ended. They had managed to survive the cold winter months on a diet of eels, ground peas and the little remaining stocks of grain that they had harvested before Kirke showed up onto the scene. Little did they (the French) realize at the time of their surrender, religious hostilities in Europe had already ended, the French and the English were on speaking terms for the time being. In exchange for an arrangement to pay the dowry of Charles the First's French Queen, (Henrietta Maria), France once again gained control of Canada. Charles I of course being the father of Pope Innocent XI's favorite English King, James the Second.

It goes without saying that even the French had a problem controlling their slaves. It in fact became such an issue that in the spring of 1676 the powers that be prohibited the slaves from leaving their master's service under the penalty of pillory for the first offense, and for the second attempt of abandoning their master, the offender was to be severely beaten with rods and then branded with the French monogram fleur-de-lys. This cruel and inhumane form of punishment was bestowed onto many a slave (both Indians and Blacks alike throughout French North America), who attempted to run away from the clutches of their masters. Obviously, the French weren't as compassionate a people as to what some historians have led us to believe over the many, many centuries.

By the time France's so-called arch-enemy William of Orange forced James II to vacate his throne in 1689 (with the secret financial backing of the Roman Catholic Church), the question of obtaining the King of France's permission to own slaves in Canada was just in the process of receiving a royal decree. The main argument for allowing French Canada and other regions south of the 49th parallel to have slaves was the old adage of manufacturing and working the fields. The French even began a sobbing campaign for good measure saying that slave ownership was allowed in the West Indies so why not North America as well. In the end, the possession of Black slaves for New France was fully authorized. But to most of the French living in North America, owning Black slaves was a luxury that not many of them could actually afford since there was an over abundance of Indian slaves out there to be had free for the taking. Just to clarify this bit of Canadian history, the ownership of an Indian slave was called a *Pani* which originated from the name Pawnee as many of the first Indian slaves of the previous years were brought into the fur trade from the Ohio Valley regions as guides as well as a cheap work force for the French traders.

In 1705, the French monarchy in France appointed the son of a financially secure family to act as Quebec's new guardian of law — Jacques Raudot was the son of Jean Raudot, seignior of Bazarne and Coudray, and Marguerite Talon, a distant relative of Jean Talon. While acting as the Intendant of New France, history books tell us that he not only encouraged its inhabitants to become more educated but was also said to have been an advocate for industry and trade as well as administrating the colony with conspicuous success. But if Jacques Raudot was such a great humanitarian as to what some historians wish us to believe, then, why is it that in 1709

HE INITIATED AN ORDINANCE CITING "THAT ALL PAINS AND NEGROES WHO HAVE BEEN PURCHASED, OR SHALL BE HEREAFTER, SHALL BELONG IN FULL PROPERTY AS SLAVES TO THOSE WHO HAVE PURCHASED THEM. "PROOF OF ACTUAL OWNERSHIP OF SLAVES DIDN'T COME INTO BEING UNTIL A DECADE LATER WHEN RAUDOT'S SUCCESSOR MICHEL BEGON DE LA PICARDIERE APPEARED ON THE SCENE.

JUST LIKE HIS PREDECESSOR, BEGON WAS AN ADVOCATE OF BOTH INDUSTRY AND TRADE AND SOON BEGAN USING HIS NEWLY ACQUIRED POSITION TO MAKE LARGE AMOUNTS OF MONEY OFF THE SWEAT OF OTHERS. OPERATING AS THE INTENDANT OF NEW FRANCE FROM THE CONFINES OF HIS VAST LAND HOLDINGS, BEGON SET THE WHEELS IN MOTION TO PUT AN END TO INDIAN SLAVERY BY FIRST ARGUING THAT THE ONLY REASON FOR PROSPERITY OF THE WEST INDIES WAS LARGELY DUE TO THE FACT OF HAVING A BLACK SLAVE LABOR FORCE. HIS NEXT LINE OF DEFENSE WAS THE UTILIZING OF FRANCE'S NEED FOR MORE MONEY FROM THE SALE OF BLACK SLAVES INSISTING THAT IF THE COLONIES OF NORTH AMERICA HAD BLACK SLAVES, THEN THE COLONIES' INHABITANTS WOULD HAVE NO NEED FOR THE HIRING OF DAY-LABORERS. IT WAS THEN DECREED THAT ALL OWNERS OF INDIAN SLAVES HAD TO PROVE ACTUAL OWNERSHIP. TO SOME, THIS DEED OF HUMANITY WAS A GOOD THING BUT TO OTHERS, A HIDDEN AGENDA EXISTED.

ONE OF THE OTHER ISSUES THAT BEGON HAD TO DEAL WITH WAS THE RAMPANT CORRUPTION AND OUTRIGHT MISUSE OF POWER THAT HAD EXISTED ON MOST, IF NOT ALL OF THE SEIGNIORIES. AT THE TIME, A LARGE MAJORITY OF THE SEIGNIORS DIDN'T LIKE THE IDEA OF JUMPING THROUGH THE KING'S COUNTLESS HOOPS ANY TIME THEY WANTED TO DO SOMETHING, SO OTHER MEANS WERE CONCEIVED THUS ALLOWING THEM TO BYPASS ALL OF THE BUREAUCRATIC RED TAPE OF THE FRENCH MONARCHY. FROM THERE, THINGS JUST SEEMED TO ESCALATE OUT OF CONTROL. THE SITUATION IN FACT GOT SO BAD THAT IN 1717, THE INTENDANT BEGON COMPLAINED TO THE KING ABOUT THE ABUSES AND VARIOUS ATTEMPTS WERE MADE TO PUT AN END TO THEM WITH NO SUCCESS WHATSOEVER. FEELING TOTALLY FRUSTRATED AT THE SEIGNIORS UNWILLINGNESS TO CONFORM TO THE LAWS OF THE LAND, THE SO-CALLED COMPASSIONATE BEGON DECIDED TO HIT THE SEIGNIORS RIGHT WHERE IT COUNTED THE MOST, IN THE POCKET BOOK. THIS IN ESSENCE IS WHAT SET HIM OFF ONTO THE PATH OF TRYING TO END INDIAN SLAVERY, COMPASSION AND/OR HUMANITARIAN REASONS HAD ABSOLUTELY NOTHING TO DO WITH IT. ACCORDINGLY, HISTORIANS WRITE THAT MICHEL BEGON LATER ON IN LIFE MENDED HIS WAYS OF USING UNSCRUPULOUS TACTICS FOR HIS OWN GAIN BY BECOMING A STRONG ADVOCATE FOR AGRICULTURE, FISHING, COMMERCE AS WELL AS THE FUR TRADE. COINCIDENTLY, BOTH JACQUES RAUDOT AND MICHEL BEGON WERE ISSUED LAND GRANTS FROM THE KING AND OPERATED THEIR DESIGNATED SEIGNIORIES WITH THE AID OF SLAVES WHILE RESIDING

IN NEW FRANCE. SO MUCH FOR THE THEORY OF BEING AN ADVOCATE OF AGRICULTURE, FISHING, COMMERCE AND THE FUR TRADE!!!

SINCE THE DAWNING OF TIME IT HAS BEEN PART OF HUMAN NATURE TO TELL HALF-TRUTHS AS WELL AS OUTRIGHT LIES, SUPPOSEDLY FOR THE GOOD OF ALL. AND SINCE THIS WAS PART OF FRENCH CANADA'S PAST NOT TOO MANY HISTORIANS WERE WILLING TO PUBLICIZE THE FACT THAT THE FRENCH IN CANADA WILLINGLY TOOK PART IN INDIAN SLAVES AS BELONGING TO THEM, THEIR PROPERTY. MOST HISTORIANS DOWN PLAYED THE ISSUE BY ONLY SKIMMING THE SURFACE, THEN OPENLY CRITICIZING THE BRITISH FOR THEIR BLATANT DISREGARD FOR HUMAN LIFE BY USING BLACK SLAVES STRICTLY AS A COMMODITY. BUT IN REALITY, BOTH THE FRENCH AND THE ENGLISH VIEWED THE SLAVES AS AN INFERIOR RACE OF PEOPLE TO BE EXPLOITED TO THE FULLEST EXTENT OF HUMAN EXISTENCE. FOR INSTANCE, WHEN THE BRITISH TOOK-OVER FULL JURISDICTIONAL POWERS OF CANADA IN 1760 THEY SIGNED THEIR NAMES TO THE ***ARTICLES OF CAPITULATION*** AT MONTREAL ON SEPTEMBER 8TH. HIDDEN AWAY IN ARTICLE NUMBER 47 OF THIS SURRENDER DOCUMENT IS A VERY INTERESTING PIECE OF CANADIAN HISTORY: **"NEGROES AND PANIS OF BOTH SEXES SHALL RETAIN THEIR STATUS AS SLAVES IN THE POSSESSION OF THE FRENCH AND CANADIANS TO WHOM THEY BELONG; THESE SHALL BE FREE TO KEEP THEM IN THEIR SERVICE IN THE COLONY OR TO SELL THEM."**

CONTRARY AS TO WHAT SOME HISTORIANS WISH US TO BELIEVE, MANY INDIAN SLAVES FELL PREY TO THE WHITEMAN. IN FACT, NOT A HELL OF A LOT OF INFORMATION IS OUT THERE PERTAINING TO INDIAN SLAVERY PRIOR TO THE ENGLISH TAKE-OVER. IT WAS AS THOUGH THE FRENCH HAD NOTHING TO DO WITH INDIAN SLAVERY AS IT WAS ALL THE ENGLISH'S FAULT AND NOT THEIR'S THAT SLAVERY ITSELF HAD FLOURISHED IN NORTH AMERICA.

BE THAT AS IT MAY, A LARGE NUMBER OF INDIAN SLAVES UNDER THE AUSPICES OF HOUSE-SLAVES AND/OR DOMESTIC SERVANTS SERVED THEIR MASTERS WELL DURING THE DAYS OF THE FRENCH SEIGNORIAL REGIME AND WELL PAST THE EARLY DAYS OF THE ENGLISH TAKE-OVER. JUST TO GIVE AN EXAMPLE AS TO HOW WIDESPREAD THE USAGE OF INDIAN SLAVERY ACTUALLY WAS, DURING THE YEAR 1761 ONE-TENTH OF ALL BURIALS REGISTERED IN MONTREAL WERE INDIAN SLAVES. OBVIOUSLY, THE ONLY WAY AN INDIAN SLAVE WAS TO BE FREED FROM HIS/OR HER BONDAGE WAS TO BE BURIED AS THEIR CAPTURES WERE NOT ABOUT READY TO SET THEM FREE. ONCE THE BRITISH GAINED CONTROL OF CANADA, SLAVERY OF BLACKS WAS THE MORE PREFERRED CHOICE AS THE ENGLISH WERE NOW IN CHARGE OF THINGS. ALTHOUGH THE FRENCH IN CANADA STILL PREFERRED INDIAN SLAVES OVER BLACKS, THEY TOO HAD NO CHOICE BUT TO KNUCKLE DOWN TO THE WHIMS OF THE POWERS THAT BE AS ALL AVENUES OF OBTAINING AN INDIAN SLAVE WERE SLOWLY EVAPORATING. GRANTED, A FEW OF THE FRENCH WERE STILL ABLE TO OBTAIN AN INDIAN SLAVE FOR THE RIGHT

AMOUNT OF MONEY IF THEY KNEW A HIGH RANKING ENGLISH ECCENTRIC AS A LARGE MAJORITY OF THE BRITISH ELITE NORTH OF THE 49TH PARALLEL HAD EITHER INDIAN /OR BLACK SLAVES, SOMETIMES THEY HAD BOTH. THE OWNERSHIP OF SLAVES (INDIAN AND/OR NEGRO) IN CANADA DIDN'T BECOME AN ILLEGAL ACTIVITY UNTIL THE VERY LATE 1700'S WHEN A MOVEMENT FOR POLITICAL REFORM BEGAN TO REAR ITS UGLY HEAD ONCE MORE. THE FRENCH IN LOWER CANADA AND THE ENGLISH IN UPPER CANADA WERE BOTH TRYING TO RULE THE ROOST IN AN ATTEMPT TO PROVE THEIR SUPERIORITY OVER THE OTHER. NATURALLY, THE FRENCH DIDN'T LIKE TO BE TOLD WHAT TO DO BY THE ENGLISH AND VICE VERSA. AT THE TIME, FRENCH CANADA'S POPULATION WAS 160,000 STRONG WITH A VOLATILE MIX OF FRANCO-INDIAN BLOODLINES WHILE ENGLISH CANADA HAD A POPULATION OF LESS THAN 30,000 PURITANS, NO INDIAN BLOOD SUPPOSEDLY FLOWED THROUGH THEIR VEINS (THEY WERE THE PUREST OF THE PURE).

IN 1793, JEAN ANTOINE PLANTE, A FRENCH ROMAN CATHOLIC REPRESENTATIVE IN THE LEGISLATIVE ASSEMBLY OF LOWER CANADA INTRODUCED THE "BILL FOR THE ABOLITION OF SLAVERY IN LOWER CANADA" BUT THE BILL ITSELF WAS BLOCKED BY SLAVE OWNERS WHO OPPOSED THE LEGISLATION — IN A SERIES OF COURT DECISIONS THAT SOON FOLLOWED, (BETWEEN THE YEARS 1797-1803), THEY UNDERMINED THE LEGALITY OF THE RIGHT TO THE POSSESSION OF SLAVES. NEEDLESS TO SAY, THESE COURT DECISIONS WERE MET WITH RESISTANCE AS HOWLS OF PROTEST COULD BE HEARD THROUGHOUT FRENCH CANADA. IN FACT, A PETITION OF SORTS WAS CIRCULATED BY A NUMBER OF MONTREAL'S CITIZENRY STATING THAT THEY **"HAVE PURCHASED AT GREAT COST A CONSIDERABLE NUMBER OF PANI AND NEGRO SLAVES ... THAT WHICH ... HAVE BECOME REFRACTORY THROUGH A SPIRIT OF DISOBEDIENCE WITH WHICH THEY ARE IMBUED, UNDER THE PRETEXT THAT NO SLAVERY EXISTS IN THIS COUNTRY. "**THE ENGLISH-SPEAKING POPULATION LIVING IN MONTREAL WERE EXTREMELY UPSET WITH THE FRENCH AS ACCORDING TO THEM (FRENCH ROMAN CATHOLIC CANADA), THE ENGLISH WERE EXPLOITING THE COUNTRY'S NATURAL RESOURCES BY EMPLOYING A CHEAP WORK FORCE UNDER THE DISGUISE OF THE SLAVE TRADE. HOW PATHETIC CAN A SITUATION BE, THERE FRENCH CANADIANS STOOD POINTING FINGERS AT THE BRITISH FOR IMPALING OTHER HUMAN BEINGS WHILE IN BONDAGE. PERHAPS THIS IS WHERE SOME HISTORIANS GOT THE IDEA THAT FRENCH ANCESTRAL HAD NO FRATERNAL CONNECTIONS TO CANADA'S SLAVERY PAST. THE LAST KNOWN PUBLIC SALE OF A SLAVE WAS SAID TO HAVE TAKEN PLACE IN MONTREAL IN 1797, THAT OF WHICH THE COURTS EVENTUALLY ANNULLED.

MEANWHILE IN UPPER CANADA MEASURES WERE BEING TAKEN IN 1793 TO PREVENT FURTHER EXPLOITATION OF THE SLAVES AS WELL AS TO LIMITING THEIR SERVICES TO WITHIN THE TERRITORY AND NO FURTHER. LIKE FRENCH

Canada, slave owners opposed the pending legislation every stop of the way. The Lieutenant-Governor of Upper Canada, John Graves Simcoe reportedly stated that "the greatest resistance ... to the Slave Bill, many plausible arguments being brought forward in respect to the dearness of labor and the difficulty of obtaining servants."

The introductory portion of the Slave Bill read as follows:

"Whereas it is unjust that a people
who enjoy freedom by law should
encourage the introduction of slaves,
and whereas it is highly expedient
to abolish slavery in the Province
so far as the same may gradually
be done without violating private
property, be it enacted ... in order to
prevent the continuation of slavery
within this Province children born of
slaves should be supported until they
reached the age of twenty-five years,
when each should be entitled to
discharge from further service, while
any issue born of such children shall
be entitled to all rights and privileges
of free-born subjects."

At the same time period that Upper Canada was in the midst of limiting the ownership of slaves, its territorial boundaries were being over-run by American immigrants (1790 to 1812) who swore allegiance to no one as they had their own ideas as to how Canada was to be established, politically as well as religiously. Residents of Upper Canada thus felt totally threatened by the American invaders and a campaign soon grew to import more of their own kind from England emerged. Before long, English Canada's puritan population was increased with each passing year. By 1824 the population of Upper Canada had increased to 150,000 and by 1830, it reached 213,000. Ten years later, the population grew to 430,000. Interestingly, the population of French Canada also increased to an estimated 700,000 people.

Contrary as to what English Canada may have thought of French Canada at the time, when it came to the exploitation of slaves these two races of people were on the exact same page. The puritans of Upper Canada continued to obtain the services of slaves well into the 1800's. The process of phasing out slavery in Canada was in fact so

SLOW THAT ENGLISH CANADA BECAME THE LAUGHING STOCK OF THE ENTIRE COUNTRY. WHILE MOST HISTORIANS BEGAN TAKING PART IN HIDING THE TRUE FACTS CONCERNING THE FRATERNAL INSTITUTION OF SLAVERY IN CANADA, (IT IN EFFECT HAD PLAGUED BOTH THE ENGLISH AND FRENCH-SPEAKING PEOPLES FOR AT LEAST TWO HUNDRED YEARS), THIS VALUABLE PART OF CANADA: A PEOPLE'S HISTORY WAS RARELY EVER TALKED ABOUT AGAIN.

ANOTHER INTERESTING PIECE OF OUR COUNTRY'S FOLKLORE IS THE FACT THAT MASSIVE LAND GRANTS STILL CONTINUED TO BE ISSUED EVEN AFTER THE ENGLISH TAKE-OVER OF CANADA. THESE LAND GRANTS WERE GIVEN TO ENGLISHMEN WHO WERE SAID TO BE DESERVING OF LAND AS THEY WERE LOYAL TO THE BRITISH MONARCHY. FOR EXAMPLE, ON THE BAIE DE CHALEURS THE FIRST SEIGNIORY WAS ACTUALLY LOCATED IN THE NORTHERN REGIONS OF NEW BRUNSWICK ON THE BANKS OF THE RESTIGOUCHE RIVER – NOT VERY FAR FROM WHERE SOME MEMBERS OF THE LEPAGE'S OF QUEBEC WOULD EVENTUALLY REPLANT THEMSELVES AFTER SIR JOHN A. MACDONALD'S DREAM OF CONFEDERATION WAS EXECUTED IN 1867. THE LAND WAS ORIGINALLY GRANTED TO FRENCH CANADIANS BUT WAS LATER SAID TO BE TAKEN AWAY BY THE ENGLISH. "BY AN ACT OF FEALTY AND HOMAGE MADE ON THE 3RD OF JUNE 1736 BY JEAN CLAUDE LOUET, ACTING FOR HIS WIFE, ANNE MORIN, WHO WAS THE WIDOW OF RENE D'ENEAU, AND ALSO ON BEHALF OF CAPTAIN RENE D'ENEAU, HER SON, JOINT-OWNERS OF THE FIEF D'ENEAU, HE PRODUCED AN ORDINANCE SIGNED BY THE INTENDANT HOCQUART DATED THE 28TH OF MARCH 1691, AND DECLARED THAT HIS TITLES TO THE LAND HAD BEEN TAKEN AWAY BY THE ENGLISH. "LOUET, THEN PETITIONED THE FRENCH POWERS THAT BE AND REGAINED POSSESSION OF HIS FAMILY'S SEIGNIORY ON THE RESTIGOUCHE ONLY AFTER THE HEIRS OF THE LATE RENE D'ENEAU AND LOUIS DE BUADE (A.K.A. COUNT DE FRONTENAC THE GOVERNOR OF NEW FRANCE) AGREED THAT THE REINSTATEMENT OF THE LANDS WERE TO TAKE PLACE. APPARENTLY THERE WAS AN AGREEMENT IN PLACE WITH THE TWO FAMILIES (RENE D'ENEAU AND COUNT FRONTENAC) THAT STIPULATED AS TO WHERE THE BOUNDARIES OF THIS SEIGNIORY WAS TO BEGIN AS WELL AS TO END. THE D'ENEAU FAMILY SEIGNIORY WHICH WAS KNOWN AS CLORIDON WAS RESTRICTED TO EXIST BETWEEN THE RIVERS PORCEPIC AND THE RESTIGOUCHE ITSELF, ITS BOUNDARIES WERE PROHIBITED FROM EXTENDING BEYOND THAT POINT. INTERESTINGLY, THE GOVERNOR OF NEW FRANCE WHO WAS FIRST APPOINTED TO HIS PRESTIGIOUS PORTFOLIO IN 1672 ALSO TOOK FULL ADVANTAGE OF THE FREE LAND AS HE TOO ESTABLISHED A SEIGNIORY IN NEW BRUNSWICK WHERE HE THEN BECAME THE BIG KHAUNA OF THE MIRAMICHI. PERHAPS THIS IS WHY THE D'ENEAU FAMILY LOST POSSESSION OF THE LAND IN 1691 AS THE ACTING GOVERNOR OF NEW FRANCE WHO WAS SAID TO BE A DIRECT DESCENDENT OF NOBILITY IN FRANCE HAD SOMETHING ELSE IN MIND

FOR NEW BRUNSWICK AS FOR SOME REASON /OR ANOTHER THERE IS NO REAL PAPER TRAIL TO SPEAK OF AS TO WHY RENE D'ENEAU'S LAND WAS TAKEN AWAY BY THE ENGLISH IN THE FIRST PLACE. AFTERALL, THE FRENCH DID HAVE A TENDENCY OF BLAMING THE ENGLISH FOR JUST ABOUT EVERYTHING THAT WAS GOING ON AT THE TIME.

ON THE QUEBEC SIDE OF THE BAIE DE CHALEURS THE FIRST FRENCH SEIGNIORY WAS A LAND GRANT ISSUED ON APRIL 23RD, 1697 AT BONAVENTURE. THIS GRANT WAS SUBMITTED TO ONE SIEUR DE LA CROIX BY FRONTENAC HIMSELF AND WAS SITUATED AT THE MOUTH OF BONAVENTURE RIVER WHICH FACED THE BAIE DE CHALEURS. OTHER SEIGNIORIES ALONG THE BAIE DE CHALEURS ON THE QUEBEC SIDE INCLUDED PORT DANIEL AND GRAND PABOS. THE SEIGNIORY AT PORT DANIEL WAS ALSO GRANTED TO ONE RENE D'ENEAU (1696) WHILE THE SEIGNIORY AT GRAND PABOS WAS GRANTED TO RENE HUBERT A MONTH EARLIER ON NOVEMBER 4TH, 1696 AND IN MAY OF THE FOLLOWING YEAR (MAY 31ST, 1697) THE SEIGNIORY OF JACQUES COCHU WAS ISSUED.

WITHIN ONLY MONTHS OF THE BRITISH TAKE-OVER OF CANADA, THE ENGLISH BEGAN THEIR MASSIVE LAND GRANT CAMPAIGN TO ENGLISHMEN LOYAL TO THE MONARCHY. IN 1762, THE SEIGNIORY OF "MALBAIE "(MURRAY BAY) WAS GIVEN TO CAPTAIN JOHN NAIRN AND THE SEIGNIORY OF "MOUNT MURRAY "WAS GIVEN TO A CAPTAIN FRASER, BOTH OF WHOM WERE OFFICERS WITH THE BRITISH FORCES. BOTH OF THESE TRANSACTIONS WERE DONE SO WITH THE AUTHORIZATION FROM GENERAL JAMES MURRAY, THE NEW GOVERNOR OF THE COLONIES. FURTHER LAND GRANTS WERE ISSUED TO OTHER OFFICERS AFTER A ROYAL PROCLAMATION WAS ISSUED ON OCTOBER 7TH, 1763 WHICH ALLOWED LAND GRANTS TO BE DESIGNATED TO OFFICERS AS A REWARD FOR THEIR MILITARY /OR NAVAL SERVICES AS FRANCE GAVE UP MORE AND MORE OF CANADA. THIS WAS SOON TO BE FOLLOWED BY YET ANOTHER PROCLAMATION (DECEMBER 7TH, 1763) WHICH ALLOWED EVEN MORE LANDS TO BE GRANTED TO OFFICERS FOR THEIR SERVICES RENDERED. IT WAS A FREE-FOR-ALL AS LANDS AS FAR SOUTH AS FLORIDA WERE NOW COMING UNDER BRITISH CONTROL AND THE ENGLISH WERE DESTINED TO REIGN SUPREME AS THEY BEGAN ESTABLISHING A MILITARY PRESENCE WITH THEIR LAND GRANTS TO OFFICERS LOYAL TO THE FRATERNAL CAUSE. MASSIVE CONFUSION SOON FOLLOWED AS ALL OF THE SEIGNIORIES GIVEN TO THE BRITISH OFFICERS HAD ENGLISH LAWS AND CUSTOMS ATTACHED TO THEM WHILE THE REMAINING FRENCH SEIGNIORIES WERE HAVING A HARD TIME ADAPTING TO THE NEW WAYS. THE SITUATION WAS SO POORLY PLANNED THAT ON SEPTEMBER 17TH, 1764 THE ENGLISH HAD NO CHOICE BUT TO ESTABLISH A SYSTEM OF COURTS TO KEEP THE PEACE AS CIVIL UNREST WAS STARTING TO BREW. GENERAL JAMES MURRAY INSTITUTED TWO COURT SYSTEMS - A SUPERIOR COURT, WHERE

CASES WERE TO BE DECIDED ACCORDING TO THE LAWS OF ENGLAND AND THE REGULATIONS OF THE PROVINCE, AND AN INFERIOR COURT, FOR THE TRIAL OF LESS IMPORTANT CASES TO TAKE PLACE WHERE JURIES MIGHT BE SUMMONED ON WHICH FRENCH CANADIANS WERE QUALIFIED TO SERVE AND FRENCH ADVOCATED WERE PERMITTED TO PRACTICE LAW.

BUT LIKE ANYTHING ELSE IN CANADA, THE GENERAL CONFUSION AND DISCONTENT ESCALATED EVEN FURTHER AS JUDGES AND OFFICIALS APPOINTED TO THE NEW COURTS WERE OF BRITISH DESCENT. INDIVIDUALS WHO KNEW VERY LITTLE OF THE FRENCH CULTURE AND IN MOST CASES, DIDN'T REALLY GIVE A DAMN /OR EVEN CARE ONE WAY /OR THE OTHER AS TO HOW FRENCH CANADA FELT ABOUT ANYTHING WERE NOW IN CHARGE OF DISBURSING JUSTICE. THIS ENRAGED FRENCH CANADIANS EVEN MORE, ESPECIALLY CONSIDERING THE FACT THAT IT WAS WELL KNOWN AT THE TIME THAT GENERAL MURRAY HAD NO TOLERANCE WHATSOEVER FOR THE FRENCH. HE APPARENTLY VIEWED MOST OF THEM AS BEING AN EXTREMELY IGNORANT RACE OF PEOPLE WHO LACKED THE ABILITY TO READ /OR WRITE. BUT YET ANY TIME A ROYAL PROCLAMATION CAME INTO BEING THAT AFFECTED THE GENERAL POPULATION, NOTICES WERE POSTED ON THE CHURCH DOORS. ONE IN FACT COULD SAY THAT MURRAY'S OWN IGNORANCE WAS AIDING AND ABETTING THE CONFUSION!!!

THIS WAS BY NO MEANS AN ISOLATED CASE WHERE THE ENGLISH GOVERNOR'S STUPIDITY REIGNED SUPREME. FOR EXAMPLE, WHEN MURRAY ESTABLISHED HIS NEW SYSTEM OF COURTS BY WAY OF THE PROCLAMATION DATED SEPTEMBER 17TH, 1764 HE INADVERTENTLY USED TERMINOLOGY THAT EVEN THE BRITISH PEOPLE THEMSELVES HAD A HARD TIME IN DETERMINING ITS TRUE MEANING. BRITISH NOBILITY THUS BEGAN FIGHTING AMONGST THEMSELVES IN ATTEMPTING TO RE-DEFINE THE MEANING FOR MANY YEARS THEREAFTER. WITH MORE AND MORE CIVIL UNREST BREWING, THE IMMEDIATE PASSAGE OF A BILL TO RE-ESTABLISH THE OLD FRENCH CIVIL CODE CAME INTO BEING, TERMED THE QUEBEC ACT, IT WAS FIRST INTRODUCED INTO THE HOUSE OF LORDS ON MAY 2ND, 1774 AND RECEIVED THE ROYAL ASSENT ON JUNE 22ND OF THAT SAME YEAR.

FEELING THAT THEY HAD SOMEWHAT SUBDUED THE FRENCH IN CANADA, THE BRITISH CONTINUED WITH THEIR CAMPAIGN OF GRANTING MASSIVE LAND GRANTS TO ENGLISHMEN THAT THEY FELT WERE DESERVING OF IT. SOME OF THE ONCE OWNED PROPERTIES OF THE FRENCH WERE THEN RE-ISSUED TO ENGLISHMEN LOYAL TO THE BRITISH MONARCHY. ON JULY 4TH, 1788 THE RIGHT HONORABLE LORD DORCHESTER (A.K.A. GENERAL GUY CARLTON) ISSUED A MASSIVE LAND GRANT TO JOHN SCHOOLBRED AT BONAVENTURE BAY. THIS LAND GRANT CONSISTED OF SEVERAL TRACTS AND PARCELS OF LAND FACING THE BAIE DE CHALEURS, IT ALSO INCLUDED SEVERAL SMALL PARCELS THAT WERE SCATTERED ALL ALONG THE GASPE PENINSULA. FURTHER TO

THIS, ON AUGUST 19TH, 1797 A MASSIVE LAND GRANT WAS ISSUED TO YET ANOTHER ENGLISHMAN LOYAL TO THE FRATERNAL CAUSE. FOR HIS PATRIOTISM TO ENGLAND, NICHOLAS AUSTIN WAS GRANTED 62,621 ACRES OF LAND IN THE TOWNSHIP OF POTTON. BETWEEN THE YEARS 1775 AND 1792 COUNTLESS OTHER LAND GRANTS WERE ALSO GIVEN, THESE GRANTS WERE SUBMITTED TO ENGLISHMEN IN WESTERN CANADA (ONTARIO), THE MARITIME PROVINCES AND THE EASTERN TOWNSHIPS OF QUEBEC.

AS THE GROWING TREND OF ENGLISHMEN RECEIVING FREEHOLD LANDS CONTINUALLY INCREASED AMONG THOSE LIVING IN FRENCH CANADA, MORE AND MORE DISCONTENT BEGAN TO FESTER. FRENCH CANADIANS WERE NOT AT ALL IMPRESSED WITH THE WAY IN WHICH THE BRITISH WERE CONDUCTING BUSINESS AS NOT ONE SINGLE INSTANCE COULD BE FOUND WHEREAS A LAND GRANT WAS ISSUED FROM THE CROWN TO A FRENCHMAN BETWEEN THE YEARS 1775 TO 1792. THE OUTRIGHT HATRED SOON ESCALATED EVEN FURTHER AS FRENCH CANADA (CHARLES DE LANAUDIERE) PETITIONED THE GOVERNOR OF CANADA IN 1778 POSING THE QUESTION OF OWNERSHIP TO HIS LANDS. THE PETITION WAS REFERRED TO A COMMITTEE IN WHICH THEY SAT ON IT FOR YEARS, THEN, IN 1790 A FURTHER INVESTIGATION WAS CONDUCTED WHICH RESULTED IN SOME RATHER STARTLING FACTS CONCERNING THE VARIOUS DIFFERENCES BETWEEN THE TENURE-IN-FREE AND COMMON SOCAGE AMONGST THE TWO CLASSES OF PEOPLE. IN EARLY SEPTEMBER, 1790, THE COMMITTEE INVESTIGATING LANAUDIERE'S COMPLAINT BEGAN MAKING INQUIRIES REGARDING THE NUMBER OF SEIGNIORIES GRANTED WHILE UNDER BRITISH CONTROL AS WELL AS THE LEGAL CONDITIONS STIPULATED BY THE CROWN CONCERNING EACH ONE OF THE LAND GRANTS ISSUED. THE END RESULT OF THE SUBSEQUENT PETITION WAS THE SLOW PACED PROCESS OF FREEHOLD LANDS FOR THE FRENCH AS WELL. IN 1791, THE CONSTITUTIONAL ACT WAS PASSED ALLOWING FOR THE ESTABLISHMENT OF UPPER AND LOWER CANADA. IN ENGLISH CANADA (UPPER CANADA) THE CIVIL AND CRIMINAL LAWS OF ENGLAND CAME INTO BEING, WHICH INCLUDED THE OWNERSHIP OF FREEHOLD LANDS. FRENCH CANADA ON THE OTHER HAND HAD TO WAIT NEARLY TWENTY YEARS BEFORE THEY TOO WOULD BE GRANTED FREEHOLD TITLE TO THEIR LANDS.

COINCIDENTLY, AS THE FATE OF CANADA WAS BEING DECIDED BY THE CONTENTS OF THE TREATY OF PARIS (CONCLUDED ON FEBRUARY 10TH, 1763) WHEREAS THE KING OF FRANCE GAVE UP ALL CLAIM TO ACADIA WHICH ALSO INCLUDED THE ISLAND OF CAPE BRETON AND ALL OTHER LANDS IN AND AROUND THE GULF AND RIVER OF THE ST. LAWRENCE, MANY FRENCH CANADIANS TOOK ADVANTAGE OF THE OPPORTUNITY EXTENDED TO THEM BY SELLING THEIR LANDS TO THE ENGLISH AND HEADING BACK TO FRANCE. THIS WAS TAKING PLACE JUST AS AN INFLUX OF ENGLISH SETTLERS BEGAN TO

FLOCK INTO THE COUNTRY SIDES EAGER TO PURCHASE THE LANDS THAT THE FRENCH ONCE VIEWED AS BEING A PROFITABLE INVESTMENT, BUT LATER SOLD AT A GREAT LOSS JUST TO BE ABLE TO ACQUIRE SHIP PASSAGE SO THAT THEY COULD HIGH TAIL IT THE HELL OUT OF THE COUNTRY RATHER THAN SWEAR ALLEGIANCE TO THE BRITISH MONARCHY.

WITH THE BLATANT THEFT OF INDIAN LANDS, (FIRST BY THE FRENCH, THEN, BY THE ENGLISH), ALL OF CANADA'S ABORIGINAL PEOPLES BECAME A DISENFRANCHISED RACE. IT IS WITHOUT A DOUBT THAT BOTH THE FRENCH AND THE ENGLISH REGARDED THE INDIANS AS NON-PERSONS, THIS WAS APPARENTLY THE CASE AT THE CLOSE OF THE SEVEN YEARS' WAR IN 1763 WHEN THE BRITISH BY WAY OF A ROYAL PROCLAMATION PREVENTED THE OHIO VALLEY COUNTRY SIDE FROM BEING SETTLED BY EUROPEANS SO THAT THEY COULD FURTHER EXPLOIT THE FUR TRADE. TO THAT END, THE TREATY OF FORT STANWYX IN 1768 STIPULATED THAT THE LANDS NORTHWEST OF THE OHIO RIVER WERE TO REMAIN IN THE POSSESSION OF THE ABORIGINAL PEOPLES. OBVIOUSLY, AS LONG AS THE BRITISH REQUIRED THE SERVICES OF THE INDIANS, ESPECIALLY DURING THE WARS AGAINST THE FRENCH AND THE AMERICANS, ALL WAS WELL IN PARADISE AS THEY (THE ENGLISH) PRETENDED TO DEAL WITH THE ABORIGINALS IN GOOD FAITH. WHILE OUT ON THE FRONTIER WITH THE INDIANS NEGOTIATING THE VARIOUS ALLIANCES WITH THEM, BRITISH RULERS IN ENGLAND WERE BUSY PASSING SPECIFIC PIECES OF LEGISLATION ALLOWING THEM TO TREAT THE ABORIGINALS AS A SUBJECT RACE OF PEOPLE. SIR WILLIAM JOHNSTON, AN AGENT ACTING FOR THE BRITISH DURING THE NEGOTIATION STAGES WITH THE SIX NATION INDIANS REPORTEDLY STATED IN HIS OFFICIAL CORRESPONDENCE THAT IF THE INDIANS THEMSELVES HAD LEARNED OF WHAT WAS ACTUALLY UNFOLDING IN ENGLAND, DIRE CONSEQUENCES WOULD HAVE HAD OCCURRED. AS FAR AS THE INDIANS WERE CONCERNED, THEY REGARDED THEMSELVES AS BEING TRUE ALLIES AND FRIENDS TO THE BRITISH.

WITH SLIGHT-OF-HAND, THE INDIANS WERE LED TO BELIEVE THAT THEY WERE GOING TO BE TREATED AS EQUALS AND THEIR ALLIES (THE ENGLISH) WERE SUPPOSEDLY TREATING THEM AS SUCH AS THE LANDS OF WHICH THEY TRADITIONALLY HUNTED IN WERE GUARANTEED TO REMAIN IN THEIR POSSESSION. NOT ONCE DID IT EVER CROSS THE MINDS OF THE INDIANS THAT THE BRITISH WERE LYING TO THEM AS IT AFTERALL WAS INCORPORATED AS PART AND PARCEL OF A TREATY AGREEMENT. BUT TO THE ENGLISH, TREATY RIGHTS TO LAND WAS THE VEHICLE IN WHICH WAS TO BE USED TO OBTAIN THE SERVICES OF THE INDIANS AS IT LONG AGO HAD BEEN ADOPTED AS MERELY A POLICY OF DECEPTION, THE MEANS TO AN END. ONCE THE WAR WITH THE AMERICANS HAD ENDED, BRITISH RULERS SECRETLY BEGAN NEGOTIATING WITH THE AMERICANS AND BEHIND THE INDIAN POPULATION'S BACKS SURRENDERED

TO THE UNITED STATES ALL THE LANDS PLEDGED TO REMAIN IN ABORIGINAL TITLE INCORPORATED WITHIN THE TREATY OF FORT STANWYX.

UPON REALIZING THAT THEY HAD BEEN BETRAYED BY THE ENGLISH AND DESPITE NUMEROUS ATTEMPTS BY THE BRITISH TO DOWN PLAY WHAT HAD ACTUALLY OCCURRED, INDIAN LEADERS PROTESTED BITTERLY TO THE ACT OF BETRAYAL. THE BRITISH ON THE OTHER HAND QUICKLY BEGAN DEFENDING THEIR ACTIONS BY INSISTING THAT THE ENGLISH MONARCHY WOULD NEVER ALLOW SUCH A DIRTY DEED TO HAVE OCCURRED IN THE FIRST PLACE AS THE MONARCHY WAS SAID TO BE A SACRED INSTITUTION AND THAT ITS WORD WAS AS GOOD AS GOLD, (FOOL'S GOLD NO DOUBT). NEEDLESS TO SAY, THE MOHAWK CHIEF, THAYENDANEGEA - A.K.A. JOSEPH BRANT WAS NOT AMUSED. TO APPEASE THE PROTESTING INDIAN LEADER, THE BRITISH ACCORDED BRANT AND HIS PEOPLE OF THE SIX NATIONS CONFEDERACY THE LAND LYING SIX MILES ON EACH SIDE OF THE GRAND RIVER WHICH EMPTIED INTO LAKE ERIE, NEAR THE PRESENT CITY OF BRANTFORD. NOT LONG AFTER THE LANDS WERE GRANTED TO THEM, WHITE SETTLERS WERE ISSUED LAND GRANTS WITHIN THE JURISDICTIONAL BOUNDARIES OF BRANT'S DESIGNATED RESERVATION. OF ALL THE LAND ACCORDED TO BRANT AND THE SIX NATIONS CONFEDERACY BY THE BRITISH AS PAYMENT FOR THE BETRAYAL CONCERNING THE FORT STANWYX TREATY, THEY WERE ONLY ABLE TO RETAIN A FIFTEENTH OF THE ORIGINAL LANDS GIVEN TO THEM. AS MANY TIMES BEFORE, THE WHITEMAN LIED TO THEM. JOSEPH BRANT ON THE OTHER HAND SHOULD HAVE KNOWN BETTER ANYWAYS SINCE HE HIMSELF WAS SAID TO HAVE HAD WHITEMAN'S BLOOD FLOWING THROUGH HIS VEINS. BRANT WAS SIR WILLIAM JOHNSON'S BROTHER-IN-LAW, HIS SISTER MOLLY MARRIED JOHNSON IN A TRADITIONAL MOHAWK MARRIAGE CEREMONY.

IN YET ANOTHER QUIRK OF FATE WAS THE FACT THAT THIS ENTIRE ORDEAL ENABLED BRANT'S HALF-BREED INDIAN SON (JOHN BRANT) TO GET INVOLVED WITH FEDERAL POLITICS AS HE WAS ELECTED IN 1832 TO THE UPPER CANADA ASSEMBLY ONLY TO HAVE HIS ELECTION INTO PUBLIC OFFICE DECLARED NULL AND VOID BY THE BRITISH MONARCHY ON THE GROUNDS THAT THE SETTLERS WHO ELECTED HIM HELD LEASES OBTAINED FROM THE ELDER BRANT AS THE COURTS HAD ALREADY DECIDED THAT THE TITLE IN FEE SIMPLE (OUTRIGHT OWNERSHIP) DID NOT BELONG TO THE INDIANS IN THE FIRST PLACE. SO MUCH FOR THE BRITISH MONARCHY BEING AN HONORABLE INSTITUTION!!!

AS PART OF OUR COUNTRY'S HERITAGE; **CANADA: A PEOPLE'S HISTORY**, WE TEND TO FIRST TAKE THE LAND FROM THE INDIANS, THEN GIVE THEM A SMALL PORTION OF IT BACK AS COMPENSATION, THEN, ONCE AGAIN TAKE SOME OF IT BACK FROM THEM AS WE, THE WHITMAN SOME WHERE ALONG THE LINE ASSUME THAT THE INDIAN HAS BEEN OVERLY COMPENSATED. THAT IS EXACTLY AS TO HOW OUR NATION GOT TO WHERE IT IS TODAY AS IT WAS ORIGINALLY

OPENED UP TO BE SETTLED BY EUROPEANS AS MASSIVE EXPROPRIATION LAND GRANTS WERE GIVEN TO THE WHITE FOLK WHILE THE INDIAN WAS BANISHED TO THE RESERVATIONS. OUR NATION'S VERY OWN HISTORY, HAS PROVEN TIME AND TIME AGAIN THAT BOTH THE FRENCH AND THE ENGLISH FIRMLY BELIEVED THAT THEY WERE RELIEVING THE INDIANS FROM THE BURDEN OF TITLE TO THE LANDS WHEN IN FACT THE INDIANS LOST POSSESSION OF THEIR LANDS BY FRAUD, MISREPRESENTATION AND LEGALIZED THEFT.

EVEN THE ROMAN CATHOLIC CHURCH TOOK PART IN THIS CONCEPT OF DECEIT AND DECEPTION AS IT ACQUIRED IN PERPETUITY THE OWNERSHIP OF MILLIONS OF ACRES OF LAND WHERE CANADA'S ABORIGINAL PEOPLES ONCE HUNTED, TRAPPED AND FISHED. UNDER THE FRENCH SEIGNIORIAL SYSTEM, THE ROMAN CATHOLIC CHURCH HAD ABSOLUTE POWERS OVER ITS PARISHIONERS. BUT EVERY ONCE IN A WHILE A MORE KINDRED SPIRIT KICKS IN AS WAS THE CASE WHEN THE CHURCH FIRST ATTEMPTED TO IMPOSE ITS TITHE ONTO ITS PARISHIONERS IN 1663, A LARGE MAJORITY OF THEM SAW IT AS BEING FAR TOO EXPENSIVE FOR THEIR LIKING AND FLATLY REFUSED TO PAY. YEARS LATER, PARISHIONERS WOULD EVENTUALLY START DIGGING INTO THEIR POCKETS AND HANDING MONEY OVER TO THE CHURCH. THIS OCCURRED ONLY DUE TO THE FACT THAT THE ROMAN CATHOLIC CHURCH AGREED TO DECREASE ITS TITHE FROM A ONE-TENTH OF ALL MONIES EARNED IN 1663 TO ONE-THIRTEENTH, THEN DOWN TO ONE-TWENTY-SIXTH BY 1679. ALL OTHER ATTEMPTS BY THE CHURCH TO INCREASE THE TITHE WERE DEFEATED FOR MANY YEARS THEREAFTER. OBVIOUSLY, THE INHABITANTS OF NEW FRANCE WERE BEING TAXED TO DEATH BETWEEN WHAT THE ROMAN CATHOLIC CHURCH WANTED THEM TO PAY AND WHAT THEY WERE EXPECTED TO DISH OUT TO THE SEIGNIORIES, THE ADDITIONAL MONIES THAT THE CHURCH WAS TRYING TO EXTORT OUT OF THEM JUST HAPPENED TO BE THE CATALYSIS FOR THEIR FRUSTRATIONS. THIS IN ESSENCE MEANT THAT THE PRIESTS IN THOSE COMMUNITIES HAD NO CHOICE BUT TO TIGHTEN UP THEIR BELTS AS IT WAS OUT OF THE TITHE ITSELF THAT THE PRIESTS WERE PAID.

THE ROMAN CATHOLIC CHURCH EVEN WENT SO FAR AS TO ENCOURAGE ITS PARISHIONERS TO PAY TRIBUTE TO THE SEIGNIOR THAT THEY WERE WORKING UNDER. THIS TRIBUTE WAS TO TAKE PLACE ON THE FIRST OF MAY EACH YEAR WHEN THE INHABITANTS OF THE SEIGNIORIES WERE TO SHOW THEIR APPRECIATION BY THROWING A SHIN-DIG OF SORTS FOR THE BIG KHAUNA OF THE ESTATE. THE FESTIVITIES ALWAYS STARTED THE EXACT SAME WAY EACH AND EVERY YEAR WHERE THE TENANTS OF THE SEIGNIORY WERE EXPECTED TO APPEAR IN FRONT OF THE MANOR TO ERECT A MAY-POLE, SUPPOSEDLY UNBEKNOWNST TO THE SEIGNIOR AND HIS FAMILY. ONCE THE MAY-POLE WAS UP, WHICH THEY ALWAYS BROUGHT WITH THEM, TWO OF THE ELDEST MEN WOULD THEN BE SENT TO GET THE SEIGNIOR'S PERMISSION TO PAY TRIBUTE TO

HIM. UPON THEIR RETURN, THEY WOULD MAKE IT KNOWN OF THEIR SUCCESS AND A FEW KIND WORDS WERE THEN STATED CONCERNING THE SEIGNIOR BY WAY OF A PRAYER. CARRYING A MUSKET, A DELEGATION THEN ESCORTED THE TWO ELDEST MEN OF THE SEIGNIORY (ONE CARRYING A SMALL GOBLET WHILE THE OTHER BROUGHT A BOTTLE OF BRANDY) WHICH SIGNIFIED THE SEIGNIOR'S APPROVAL OF THE FESTIVE OCCASION. AS THE SEIGNIOR AND HIS FAMILY REACHED THE DOORWAY OF THE MANOR AND PROCEEDED TO STEP OUTSIDE, SHOUTS OF **"LONG LIVE THE KING!"** FOLLOWED BY **"LONG LIVE THE SEIGNIOR! "**CAME FROM THE GROUP OF EAGER PARTY GOERS THAT WERE GATHERED AROUND THE MAY-POLE. AFTER A FEW MORE POMPOUS RITUALS, THE SEIGNIOR THEN INVITED HIS VISITORS INTO THE MANOR WHERE THEY WERE SUPPLIED WITH MUCH FOOD AND DRINK, (WINE FOR THE WOMEN AND BRANDY FOR THE MEN). WHILE THE DANCING AND MUSIC WAS STILL GOING ON, AN ENDLESS STREAM OF THE SEIGNIOR'S GUESTS KEPT JUMPING UP FROM WHERE THEY WERE SEATED, SEIZING THEIR GUNS, AND RUSHING OUT THE DOOR TO FIRE AT THE MAY-POLE, THEN RETURNING TO THEIR PLACES FROM WHICH THEY WERE SEATED. FOLLOWING THIS LITTLE RITUAL, GAMES AND OLD FRENCH SONGS COMPLETED THE DAYS ENTERTAINMENT SCHEDULE.

ONE MIGHT BE EXCUSED FOR ASKING THE QUESTION AS TO WHY SUCH A FORM OF HOMAGE WAS ORDAINED BY THE CATHOLIC CHURCH AS THE ACT ITSELF SEEMED SO PAGAN LIKE IN ITS DESIGN. BUT THE REALITY OF IT ALL WAS THE FACT THAT MOST OF THE PRIVILEGES ENJOYED BY THE FRENCH SEIGNIOR WERE DEEPLY ROOTED WITH HIS RELIGIOUS DUTIES. TO MOST OF THE INHABITANTS RESIDING IN AND AROUND THE SEIGNIORS' MANOR, PAYING SUCH A TRIBUTE TO A TYRANT WAS HYPOCRITICAL IN NATURE. TO THAT END, THEY PETITIONED THE INTENDANT OF NEW FRANCE TO RELIEVE THEM FROM IT. IN 1709, A SPECIAL EDICT WAS ISSUED RESTRICTING AS TO WHICH SEIGNIORS WERE TO RECEIVE THE RIGHTS OF BEING HONORED.

RELIGIOUSLY SPEAKING, WHEN IT CAME TO HYPOCRISY ALL FORMS OF RELIGION WERE EXACTLY THE SAME AS THEY (THE RELIGIOUS INSTITUTIONS) VIEWED THE NORTH AMERICAN NATIVE POPULATION AS BEING NOTHING BUT PAGANS WHO NEEDED SOME REFINING. THIS IN ITSELF WAS TO BE THEIR JUSTIFICATION FOR EXECUTING A LARGE-SCALE MISSIONARY EFFORT TO CIVILIZE THE SAVAGE BEASTS. NOT SURPRISING IS THE FACT THAT THE GREATEST ABUSERS OF ALL WAS THE CATHOLIC CHURCH AND ITS CLOSE TIES TO THE FRENCH MONARCHY. WHILE THE CHURCH WAS REGARDED AS BEING GLADLY ACCEPTED BY THE MAJORITY OF THE PEOPLE OF NEW FRANCE, IT DID ANNOY THE HELL OUT OF A GROUP OF CERTAIN FRENCH CANADIANS WHICH BECAME KNOWN HISTORICALLY AS THE *COUREURS DE BOIS* - THE UNLICENCED FUR BOOTLEGGERS WHO LATER ON CREATED SO MUCH TROUBLE FOR THE POWERS THAT BE IN CANADA. THESE RENEGADE FRENCH CANADIANS, ACCORDINGLY

MARRIED INDIAN WOMEN AND FATHERED A RACE OF SWARTHY HALF-BREEDS. EACH YEAR, THE *COUREURS DE BOIS* DESCENDED FROM THE WILDERNESS SURROUNDING QUEBEC CITY, TROIS RIVIERES AND MONTREAL EAGER TO SPEND THEIR MONEY ON WINE, WOMEN, SONG AND VICE (THEY HAD THEM ALL BY JESUS CHRIST). AFTER CREATING HAVOC IN THESE COMMUNITIES, THEY WOULD DISAPPEAR ONCE AGAIN INTO THE WILDERNESS – REPEATING THIS EXACT SAME RITUAL YEAR AFTER YEAR. THE CATHOLIC CHURCH VIEWED THIS ACT OF DEGRADATION AS BEING BOTH IMMORAL AND UNCONTROLLABLE AS THE VAST MAJORITY OF THE *COUREURS DE BOIS* WERE YOUNG WORKMEN WHO DESERTED THE DICTATORIAL TYRANNICAL PRACTICES OF THE SEIGNIORIES OF NEW FRANCE FOR A MORE ADVENTUROUS LIFESTYLE WHICH THE CHURCH HAD NO JURISDICTIONAL POWERS OVER. ALTHOUGH THE CATHOLIC CHURCH WAS PORTRAYING ITSELF AS BEING THE MORE SUPERIOR WAY TO LIVE, MOST OF THE INHABITANTS LIVING IN AND AROUND THE SURROUNDING AREAS OF THE SEIGNIOR'S MANOR WERE BARELY ABLE TO SUPPORT THEIR OWN FAMILIES, TOO POOR TO EVEN BE ABLE TO PAY WHATEVER AMOUNT THE CHURCH TITHE MIGHT HAVE BEEN. AS THE ROMAN CATHOLIC CHURCH GOT TO BE MORE AND MORE FASCIST WITH EACH PASSING YEAR, COUNTLESS YOUNG MEN WORKING THE LAND BELONGING TO SOMEONE ELSE GAVE THE CHURCH THE ONE FINGER SALUTE AND MOVED ON.

IN THE EARLY DAYS OF THE *COUREURS DE BOIS*, IT WAS DEEMED TO BE THAT OF AN HONORABLE VOCATION AS MANY OF THE SEIGNIORS WHO WERE ISSUED LAND GRANTS GLADLY GAVE UP THE STRUGGLE WITH THE LAND FOR A MORE SUBDUED WAY OF LIVING SEEKING THE WEALTH AND FREEDOM THAT THE FUR TRADE OFFERED THEM. AS THE FUR TRADE BEGAN SHIFTING INTO HIGH GEAR WESTWARD INTO THE TERRITORY OCCUPIED BY THE INDIANS, THE CATHOLIC CHURCH BECAME LESS AND LESS INTERESTED IN ACKNOWLEDGING THE IMPORTANT ROLE THAT THE *COUREURS DE BOIS* WERE PLAYING IN CANADA: A PEOPLE'S HISTORY. TWO OF CANADA'S MORE HONORABLE MEMBERS OF THIS PROFESSION, SIEUR DE MEDARD CHOUART GROSEILLIERS AND HIS BROTHER-IN-LAW PIERRE ESPRIT RADISSON RISKED LIFE AND LIMB FOR THE PEACE AND TRANQUILITY OF THE WILDERNESS INSTEAD OF THE BOURGEOISIE TACTICS OF CHURCH AND STATE.

IN 1642 /OR THEREABOUTS, GROSEILLIERS CAME TO NORTH AMERICA WHERE HE WAS LATER ISSUED A LAND GRANT IN CANADA KNOWN AS THE GOOSEBERRY PATCH, THE SEIGNIOR'S NAME WAS EVENTUALLY ADOPTED AS THE OFFICIAL TITLE OF THE ESTATE. WITHIN ONLY A FEW SHORT YEARS OF BEING ISSUED THE LAND GRANT, HE ENTERED THE FUR TRADE AND HIS LIFE EXPERIENCES AS AN OFFICIAL *COUREURS DE BOIS* TOOK OFF FROM THERE AND WAS LATER JOINED BY HIS BROTHER-IN-LAW. LIKE GROSEILLIERS, PIERRE ESPRIT RADISSON MIGRATED TO CANADA IN 1651 AND WAS ISSUED A LAND GRANT

ON THE BANKS OF THE ST. LAWRENCE RIVER (TROIS RIVIERES) WHERE THE TWO SEIGNIORS BEGAN SECRETLY VENTURING OUT INTO THE WILDERNESS IN ORDER TO MAKE SOME EXTRA CASH. BEFORE LONG, THE PAIR OF ADVENTURERS WERE OUT EXPLORING THE COUNTRY SIDE CHARTING NEW TERRITORY THAT WOULD EVENTUALLY PROVE TO BE A VERY VALUABLE ASSET FOR THE FUR TRADE INDUSTRY. AS FATE WOULD HAVE IT, GROSEILLIERS AND RADISSON WERE ENVIED BY THEIR FRIENDS IN THE SETTLEMENTS AND NOT LONG AFTER THAT, A STEADY STREAM OF YOUNG MEN BEGAN LEAVING THE DICTATORIAL PRACTICES OF THE SEIGNIORIES BEHIND. ACCORDINGLY, THIS WAS DEEMED TO BE THE BEGINNING OF THE END OF THE MOST HONORABLE VOCATION THAT CANADA HAD TO OFFER AS EVERYONE AND THEIR DOG NOW WANTED TO GET IN ON THE ACT. AS FAR AS THE CHURCH WAS CONCERNED, THE NEW STOCK OF *COUREURS DE BOIS* WERE IRRESPONSIBLE LAZY INDIVIDUALS WHO WERE AFRAID OF A GOOD HARD DAY'S WORK ALWAYS QUESTIONING THE SUPERIORITY OF FRENCH AUTHORITY OVER THEM. WITH THEIR JOVIAL AND CARE-FREE OUTLOOK ON LIFE, THE NEW STOCK OF ADVENTURERS SOON GAINED THE CONFIDENCE AND FRIENDSHIP OF THE INDIANS AS THEY DISCARDED THE AUTHORITY OF THE SETTLED COMMUNITIES AND THE CHURCH ITSELF. AT THE CLOSE OF THE 1600'S, THERE WERE IN EXCESS OF A COUPLE OF HUNDRED MEMBERS OF THE *COUREURS DE BOIS* OUT THERE TAKING FULL ADVANTAGE OF THE LUCRATIVE FUR TRADE INDUSTRY. BY ALL ACCOUNT, THESE FUR TRADE BOOTLEGGERS FATHERED MANY CHILDREN (FRANCO-INDIANS) THROUGHOUT QUEBEC AND THE MARITIME PROVINCES THUS ENABLING THE COUNTRY TO FLOURISH WELL INTO THE 21ST CENTURY. QUEBEC'S HALF-BREED INDIAN PAST IN FACT CAN BE EASILY IDENTIFIED BY THE ESTABLISHMENT OF SUCH COMMUNITIES AS GRAND-METIS, METIS-SUR-MUER, ST.-OCTAVE-DE-METIS AND OF COURSE ST. JOSEPH-DE-LEPAGE. ALL OF THESE COMMUNITIES HAVE ONE THING IN COMMON, AN ABORIGINAL HISTORY THAT HAS BEEN WELL HIDDEN OVER THE COURSE OF TIME.

THE ROMAN CATHOLIC CHURCH IN CANADA HAS ALWAYS REMAINED A POWERFUL FORCE TO BE RECKONED WITH AS IT TO THIS VERY DAY HAS NOT LOST THE CONFIDENCE OF THE MASSES OF PEOPLE UNDER ITS NEVER- ENDING SPELL. THROUGHOUT ITS EXISTENCE IN THIS COUNTRY, THE CATHOLIC CHURCH HAS BEEN EDUCATING THE VAST MAJORITY OF FRENCH CANADIANS (FRANCO-INDIANS AS WELL) IN A HALF-ASSED FASHION AS A WAY AND MEANS OF WATERING DOWN THE TRUTH. UTILIZING THE IGNORANCE OF ITS PARISHIONERS TO SATISFY ITS OWN AGENDA, THE CHURCH BEGAN ACQUIRING LARGE AMOUNTS OF LAND THAT WERE TO BE HELD IN PERPETUITY AND TAX FREE SINCE THEY, THE CATHOLIC CHURCH WAS A TOTALLY RECOGNIZED RELIGION. WHILE UNDER THIS CLOAK OF DECEIT AND DECEPTION, THE ROMAN CATHOLIC CHURCH'S BLATANT DISREGARD FOR THE INDIANS ESCALATED AS MORE AND MORE OF THE ABORIGINAL PEOPLES LANDS WERE TRANSFERRED INTO THE OWNERSHIP OF THE

Church. Case in point; while the Jesuits were out trying to civilize the savage Indians many of their writings proved beyond the shadow of a doubt that they blamed the *COUREURS DE BOIS* for the demise of the aboriginal way of life claiming that all of the dishonesty and licentious conduct of the adventurers were holding the religious convictions of the native peoples back. Then, on the flip side of the hypercritical religious coin there's the list of land grants issued to the Jesuits by the King of France while trying to establish a French Roman Catholic presence in New France.

The following lands were held by the Jesuit Order in the various communities of New France;

Charlesbourg	119,720 arpents
Lorette	23,944 arpents
Sillery	8,979 arpents
Isle-aux-Ruaux	360 arpents
Cap-de-la-Magdelaine	282,240 arpents
Batiscan	282,240 arpents
La-Prairie-de-la-Magdelaine	56,448 arpents
St. Gabriel	104,850 arpents
Isle St.Christophe	80 arpents
Pachiriny	585 arpents
La Vacherie	73 arpents
St. Nicholas	1,180 arpents
Tadoussac	6 arpents
Totalling	**880,705 ARPENTS**

Other land holdings held by the Church and its various Fraternal Orders were as follows;

The Bishop and Seminary of Quebec	693,324 arpents
Sulpitians	250,191 arpents
Ursulines of Quebec	164,616 arpents
Les Soeurs Grises	42,336 arpents
General Hospital at Quebec	28,497 arpents
Ursulines of Trois Rivieres	30,909 arpents
Hotel-Dieu at Quebec	14,112 arpents
Recollets	945 arpents
General Hospital at Montreal	404 arpents
Totalling	**1,225,334 ARPENTS**

After adding it all up, the Roman Catholic Church in Canada had a grand total of 2,106,309 arpents of land in the colony of New France and it wanted much more as it only controlled about a quarter of all the granted lands issued by the various Kings of

France. Of all the lands granted to the Roman Catholic Church under the French seigniorial system, over two-million acres once converted from arpents, the aboriginal peoples were destined to become slaves of religious bondage on the same lands that they once roamed free on. Afterall, it was the French who were chosen by God to reign supreme in the New World.

But when the British officially took-over control of Canada, the French Roman Catholic Church was thrown into total chaos as their superiority was no being ruled by Protestants. This naturally forced the Catholic Church to oppose the incoming doctrine of the English seigniors who as it so happened paid no tithes whatsoever to their Protestant Church leaders. The Catholic Church deemed this practice to be absolutely intolerable as it threatened the very existence of its reigning powers over the people and threatened further Church revenues. While the French seigniors subleased portions of their land to other French Roman Catholics who in turn paid a tithe to the Church, English seigniors were busy subleasing to other English Protestants. The additional monies that the Protestants were able to keep for themselves, allowed them to purchase the necessary items to work the land in preparation for harvest. Obviously, English settlers were being encouraged to grow new products (including hemp), while the French inhabitants grew more jealous of their English neighbors who soon lavished on a great economic lifestyle.

As religious tensions mounted between the French and the English settlers, the Roman Catholic Church soon began losing its stranglehold onto the people. The Jesuits' large land holdings in Canada were eventually transferred into the care of the British Government with the stipulation that all revenues derived from the said properties would be used strictly for educational purposes. With its back up against the wall, the Catholic Church was at a loss as to what tactic was going to be able to salvage the ownership of the remaining 1,225,334 arpents of land that they legally held title too. Their salvation came in the form of the Quebec Act of 1774 which recognized the status of the Roman Catholic Church of Canada. The Jesuit Order was later restored by Pope Pius VII and in 1842 a small number of them returned to Canada. The question of acquiring their once held properties soon arose and before long, (1888), a compensation package gave the Jesuits possession of some of the lands as well as $ 400,000.00 for the loss of the majority of their estates.

Between the years 1793 and 1811, over three-million acres of land were issued in the form of land grants to a couple of hundred favored applicants. It was supposedly the only way that the English Protestants were going to surpass the French population of Lower Canada. The English seigniors, then in turn sold some of the land to the European settlers that were immigrating to Canada for a nice profit. To many of the country's population, French and English, this constituted abuse of power at its highest level and before long words of corruption were being whispered from the lips of all Canadian citizens. As public opinion spread like wildfire throughout the country side, the powers that be began looking into the abuses in the land department whose own bureaucratic officials violated the laws set forth in the provisions of the Constitutional Act of 1791 whereby one-seventh of the ungranted lands of the Colony were to be reserved for the support of a Protestant clergy. By the time the land department's officials granted the lands to a couple hundred of the selected few, there was no longer anymore suitable land available for the placement of immigrants, disbanded soldiers /or even the Protestant clergy.

Realizing that their own seigniorial system was highly flawed, the British authorities passed a piece of legislation in 1822 (commonly known as the Canada Trade Act) which in essence was the first step towards abolishing the **Seignioral Tenure** system in our country. The Act itself was later revised and then once again passed into law in 1825 known as the **"Canada Trade and Tenures Act"**. There were future revisions to refine the legislation even more. This refinement was finalized when the two separate ruling classes merged into one entity in 1840 under the auspices of the **Canada Act**, more commonly known as the Act of Union because by the provisions set out in the Act itself, the two Provinces (Upper and Lower Canada) were to be united with equal representation in a joint legislature. Although this union was supposedly designed to automatically abolish the feudal regime in Canada once and for all, it still exist to this very day in certain regions of our country – a person merely has to open one's eyes to witness it!!!

Coincidently, one of Quebec's well known hero's, Louis Joseph Papineau was by no means in favor of the proposed union of Upper and Lower Canada. Although he supposedly professed admiration for the British institutions, he did not like the idea of French Canada being controlled by the English – he ironically preferred the United States of America over British rule. A lawyer by vocation,

HE WAS FIRST ELECTED TO THE FRENCH ASSEMBLY IN 1808 WHEN HE WAS BUT TWENTY-TWO- YEARS-OLD. HE ALSO SERVED AS A MAJOR IN THE CANADIAN MILITIA DURING THE WAR OF 1812 AND WAS PRESENT WHEN BROCK AND TECUMSEH CAPTURED DETROIT. PAPINEAU WAS ELECTED SPEAKER OF THE LEGISLATIVE ASSEMBLY IN 1815. BUT THINGS REALLY STARTED TO UNRAVEL FOR HIM WHILE HE WAS THE ELECTED REPRESENTATIVE FOR MONTREAL WEST IN THE LOWER CANADA LEGISLATURE, 1814-37. LOUIS JOSEPH APPARENTLY INSTIGATED AN ARMED ATTACK AGAINST THE BRITISH GOVERNMENT OF CANADA IN NOVEMBER OF 1837. HE WAS THUS FORMERLY CHARGED WITH HIGH TREASON AND A PRICE TAG OF $ 4,000.00 WAS THUS PLACED ON HIS HEAD, DEAD /OR ALIVE. IN ORDER TO ESCAPE THE CLUTCHES OF HIS FOES, PAPINEAU ELUDED THEM BY FLEEING TO THE UNITED STATES ON NOVEMBER 23RD, 1837 JUST AS THINGS WERE STARTING TO ESCALATE OUT OF CONTROL BETWEEN THE FRENCH AND THE ENGLISH WHICH IGNITED AN ALL OUT CIVIL WAR. PAPINEAU WAS EVEN DENOUNCED BY THE ROMAN CATHOLIC CHURCH, THE MONSEIGNEUR JEAN JACQUES LARTIGUE WHO JUST HAPPENED TO BE ONE OF PAPINEAU'S OWN RELATIVES, (A COUSIN) – WITH A BOUNTY ON HIS HEAD AND THE CATHOLIC CHURCH TRYING TO PERSUADE HIM TO SURRENDER, HE FIRST FLED TO THE U.S., THEN, ONTO PARIS, FRANCE.

PAPINEAU REPORTEDLY LIVED IN PARIS FROM 1839 TO 1845 WHERE HE WAS SAID TO HAVE FREQUENTED MANY SOCIAL GATHERINGS, LITERARY CLUBS AND POLITICAL FRATERNITY MEETINGS. SOMETIME IN 1845, HE WAS ALLOWED TO RETURN BACK TO CANADA UNDER TERMS OF AMNESTY AS HE HAD PROCLAIMED HIMSELF TO BE A TOTALLY CHANGED MAN. HE RE-ENTERED THE POLITICAL ARENA AS AN ELECTED PUBLIC OFFICIAL, ST. MAURICE 1848-51, AND DEUX MONTAGNES 1852-54. AFTER FAILING TO BE RE-ELECTED IN 1854, HE RETIRED HIMSELF TO HIS MANOR AT MONTEBELLO, QUEBEC WHERE HE REMAINED UNTIL HIS DEATH ON SEPTEMBER 23RD, 1871.

IN ORDER TO FULLY UNDERSTAND AS TO WHICH DIRECTION LOUIS JOSEPH PAPINEAU WAS ACTUALLY COMING FROM, A COUPLE OF WELL KNOWN FACTORS MOST BE PRESENTED. FIRST OF ALL, IN THE PROVINCE OF QUEBEC THE PAPINEAU NAME IS SYNONYMOUS FOR A COUPLE OF RATHER INTERESTING REASONS. IN 1801 HIS FATHER, JOSEPH PAPINEAU PURCHASED THE SEIGNIORY OF LA PETITE NATION ON THE OTTAWA RIVER AT MONTEBELLO FROM THE QUEBEC SEMINARY AND BEGAN RAISING HIS TWO SONS; LOUIS JOSEPH AND DENIS BENJAMIN – THE SEIGNIORY WAS ORIGINALLY GRANTED TO MONSEIGNEUR DE LAVAL IN 1674. WHILE THE ELDEST SON WAS OUT RAISING OLD HELL WITH ENGLISH CANADA, DENIS PAPINEAU WAS BUSY PLAYING BOTH ENDS AGAINST THE MIDDLE AS A WAY AND MEANS OF GETTING ENGLISH CANADA TO RECOGNIZE THE FRENCH LANGUAGE AS BEING OFFICIALLY USED IN THE UNITED CANADA LEGISLATIVE ASSEMBLY. ALTHOUGH HE DID NOT SHARE THE SAME RADICAL FRANCOPHONE

IDEAS AS HIS RENEGADE BROTHER, DENIS WAS SAID TO HAVE BEEN ABLE TO ELEVATE FRENCH IDEAS INTO THE GOVERNMENTAL POWER STRUCTURE AS HE REPRESENTED THE OTTAWA COUNTY IN THE LEGISLATIVE ASSEMBLY OF THE UNITED CANADA BETWEEN THE YEARS 1842-47. FURTHER TO HIS BEING AN ELECTED PUBLIC OFFICIAL THAT BASICALLY ALLOWED HIM TO EASE THE BILL OF FRENCH USAGE IN THE PARLIAMENTARY PROCEDURES, DENIS PAPINEAU ALSO SERVED AS COMMISSIONER OF CROWN LANDS IN 1844-47 AS THE FRENCH HAD ALWAYS COMPLAINED OF NOT BEING FAIRLY TREATED WHEN IT CAME TO LAND GRANT DISBURSEMENTS AND/OR GOVERNMENTAL POSTINGS WHILE UNDER BRITISH RULE.

IT WAS REPORTEDLY SAID TO BE IN LOUIS JOSEPH PAPINEAU'S OWN PERSONAL OPINION THAT THE BRITISH WAY OF DOING THINGS CONCERNING ALL ASPECTS OF FRENCH LIVE WAS BEING CONDUCTED IMPROPERLY – THE FRENCH ELITE WANTING TO PRESERVE THEIR OLD WAY OF GOVERNING, INCLUDING THEIR SEIGNIORY POWERS OVER THE PEASANTRY OF THEIR ESTATES AND VAST LAND HOLDINGS. THEY ALSO FELT THAT THEIR RELIGION, LANGUAGE AND CUSTOMS WERE IN DANGER OF BEING EVENTUALLY ELIMINATED BY THE ENGLISH AND THE **CANADA TRADE ACT** WAS GOING TO BE THE FIRST NAIL DRIVEN INTO FRENCH CANADA'S COFFIN. ONCE THE BRITISH AUTHORITIES PASSED IT INTO LAW IN 1822, LOUIS JOSEPH LED A REVOLT AGAINST THE PROPOSED UNION OF THE TWO CANADA'S AND AS FRUSTRATIONS GREW TO ITS FINAL PEAK IN 1834, HE INTRODUCED HIS FAMOUS RESOLUTIONS INSISTING THAT THE ENGLISH WAY OF DEALING WITH FRENCH CANADA HAD TO CHANGE /OR ELSE WIDE SPREAD DISSECTION WAS GOING TO BE OCCURRING THROUGHOUT THE LAND. WITH HIS NINETY-TWO RESOLUTIONS, PAPINEAU ATTEMPTED TO CHANGE THE OPINIONS OF THE BRITISH GOVERNMENT THAT CONTROLLED ALL OF THE POLITICAL AND ECONOMICAL AFFAIRS OF BOTH UPPER AND LOWER CANADA.

OF THESE NINETY-TWO RESOLUTIONS, NUMBERS FIFTY-SIX TO SIXTY-TWO DEALT STRICTLY WITH LAND TENURE. THEY OPENLY CRITICIZED THE LEGISLATION PASSED BY THE ENGLISH IMPERIAL PARLIAMENT IN THEIR BID TO CHANGE THE FORM OF HOLDING LANDS IN A UNITED CANADA. THESE RESOLUTIONS WERE SAID TO HAVE BEEN THE EXACT SAME GRIEVANCES THAT OF WHICH FRENCH CANADIANS HAD FELT EVER SINCE THE BRITISH DEFEATED THEM ON THE PLAINS OF ABRAHAM. APPARENTLY, THE SEVENTY-FIFTH RESOLUTION DEALT WITH THE ASPECTS OF FAVORITISM THAT HAD MANAGED TO CREEP INTO THE COUNTRY'S ENGLISH ADMINISTRATION AS CORRUPTION WAS SO WIDE SPREAD AT THE TIME. IN 1823, AN AUDIT WAS CONDUCTED ON THE FINANCIAL AFFAIRS OF THE ADMINISTRATION AND IT WAS SOON DISCOVERED THAT A RATHER LARGE SUM OF MONEY HAD BEEN EMBEZZLED, NEARLY 100,000 POUNDS /OR APPROXIMATELY A QUARTER OF A MILLION DOLLARS CANADIAN. BOTH FRENCH CANADA AND THE BRITISH GOVERNMENT IN ENGLAND

BLAMED OUR COUNTRY'S GOVERNOR (A.K.A. SIR GEORGE RAMSAY, 9TH EARL OF DALHOUSIE) AND HIS REPRESENTATIVES FOR THE LOSS OF THE MONIES AS THERE WERE NO REAL CONTROLS OVER WHO COULD SPEND WHAT, WHERE. AS THE FINGERS WERE BEING POINTED AT ENGLISH CANADA'S ADMINISTRATION, LOUIS JOSEPH PAPINEAU REPORTEDLY BOLTED FROM HIS SEAT IN THE ASSEMBLY TO EXECUTE A VIOLENT ATTACK ON HIS EMINENCE LORD DALHOUSIE WHO AT THE TIME WAS MAKING ALL SORTS OF EXCUSES AS TO WHY THE MONEY COULD NOT BE TRACED THROUGH CONVENTIONAL CHANNELS. PERHAPS THIS WAS WHY PAPINEAU POINTED OUT IN HIS SEVENTY-FIFTH RESOLUTION THE FACT THAT WHILE THE FRENCH POPULATION IN LOWER CANADA WAS 525,000 AND THOSE OF BRITISH ORIGIN WERE ONLY 75,000 STRONG, THE ENGLISH HELD ONE-HUNDRED AND FIFTY-SEVEN POSTINGS IN THE PUBLIC OFFICES OF THE COUNTRY AND THE MAJORITY RACE OF PEOPLE ONLY HELD FORTY-SEVEN. PAPINEAU'S RHETORIC WAS OBVIOUSLY CONTAGIOUS AS THE VAST MAJORITY OF QUEBEC'S FRANCOPHONE PEOPLE FELT AS THOUGH THEY WERE A DISENFRANCHISED RACE LIVING IN THEIR OWN HOMELAND AND THEY DEMANDED IMMEDIATE CHANGES /OR AT LEAST BE PERMITTED TO STEP INTO A TIME MACHINE WHICH WOULD HAVE ALLOWED ITS FRENCH POPULATION THE LUXURY OF REACQUAINTING THEMSELVES WITH THEIR OLD CUSTOMS OF BEING THE BIG KHAUNA IN HOPES OF HAVING FRATERNAL POWERS RE-IMPLEMENTED.

UPON HEARING THE NEWS THAT LOUIS JOSEPH PAPINEAU AND HIS FELLOW RENEGADE POLITICIANS HAD SUBMITTED THEIR LONG LIST OF GRIEVANCES DIRECTLY TO THE BRITISH GOVERNMENT IN LONDON, ENGLAND FOR ITS APPROVAL, AN ENGLISH FRATERNITY MEMBER BROTHER JOHN MOLSON — ONE OF THE MOST POWERFUL BUSINESSMEN IN MONTREAL — ISSUED A STERN WARNING TO PAPINEAU AND HIS FRENCH BRETHRENSHIP TELLING THEM THAT THEY SHOULDN'T BE SO DAMN UNGRATEFUL BECAUSE IN THE END, THEIR OUTRIGHT ARROGANCE JUST MIGHT LEAD TO THEIR OWN DOWNFALL IN DUE TIME!!!

Chapter 4 - Le Pays de Droit Francais

In a desperate attempt to prove their superiority over all breathing things, mainly the British and the French peasantry population working the lands on the French seigniories, Canada's Roman Catholic elite were ordained to the status of nobility. All other living beings, especially the Indians and the Negroes didn't really matter as they were said to be far too inferior of a race of people to be even calculated into the equation as far as the French Roman Catholics were concerned. The first real well known title-bearing noblesse in Canada was Jean Talon, the Intendant of New France who officially came to colonize the country in 1665. Having visions of grandeur, three small communities were established – Bourg Royal, Bourg-La-Reine and Bourg Talon became successful enterprises and then flourishing villages. In 1667, Jean Talon began contemplating the establishment of three more communities which involved three separate seignories that he owned. By 1671, he requested permission from the King of France so that he would be able to unite the said properties into one entity which would enable him to maintain the title and dignities of a baron, which he wanted to name Des Islets. The Intendant of New France was not only granted permission to unite his three properties into one but he was also dubbed the Baron des Islets.

Although Intendant Talon was deemed to be the Baron des Islets, it appears that the title of distinction was only to humor him as he was constantly blowing his own horn while writing to the King's representative asking for permission to unite his properties. As it turns out, Talon suggested in his letter to the King that he, (the King) might be pleased to grant some sort of title honoring the gallant efforts being conducted in the New World concerning its

COLONIZATION. THE KING OF FRANCE, THEN, GAVE TALON AUTHORIZATION TO AMALGAMATE HIS PROPERTIES AND ESTABLISH THREE ROYAL VILLAGES WHICH WERE TO BE FOUNDED INTO ONE FIEF WHICH IN TURN WAS TO BECOME DES ISLETS. THIS IN ITSELF GAVE THE INTENDANT OF NEW FRANCE AUTHORIZATION TO CALL HIMSELF THE BARON DES ISLETS WHILE ROAMING THE COUNTRY SIDE WITH HIS NOSE UP IN THE AIR SNUBBING THOSE WHO HAD NO TIME FOR THAT SORT OF FOOLISH NONSENSE.

TALON'S OWN SEIGNIORY ON THE ST. CHARLES RIVER INTERESTINGLY ENOUGH BECAME TO BE KNOWN AS THE FIRST CANADIAN EXPERIMENTAL FARM, WITH MODEL BARNS AND OTHER FARM BUILDINGS. HISTORICALLY, IS IT SAID THAT THE INTENDANT TALON NOT ONLY IMPROVED THE BREED OF LIVE STOCK BY IMPORTING BETTER HORSES, CATTLE AND SHEEP, BUT HE ALSO IMPORTED THE METHODS OF CULTIVATION. UNBEKNOWNST TO TALON HIMSELF, HE WAS ALSO RESPONSIBLE FOR SOMETHING ELSE THAT WAS THE BIRTH CHILD OF HIS OWN PERSONAL ZEALOUSNESS THAT WAS RUNNING AMOK THAT FORCED MANY YOUNG MEN WORKING ON THE SEIGNIORIES TO SEEK THE COMFORT AND COMPANIONSHIP OF THE INDIANS. WHILE RULING NEW FRANCE WITH AN IRON CLAD FIST AND HAVING NO TOLERANCE WHATSOEVER FOR THE LOWER CLASSES OF PEOPLE, TALON SCRUTINIZED ALL ASPECTS OF THEIR LIVES. ACCORDINGLY, HE INCORPORATED A SYSTEM OF GOVERNING BODIES "PATERNALISTIC "THAT VIRTUALLY TOLD ALL INHABITANTS WHEN THEY COULD EAT, DRINK AND BE MERRY. HELL, THE DICTATOR TALON EVEN TOLD THE INHABITANTS OF NEW FRANCE WHO THEY COULD HAVE SEXUAL RELATIONS WITH AND WHO THEY COULD NOT!!!

IN HIS ATTEMPT TO CREATE A SUPER WHITE RACE OF PEOPLE FOR QUEBEC ITSELF, NO INDIAN AND/OR NEGRO BLOODLINES WERE PERMITTED, SHIP LOADS OF YOUNG WOMEN AND GIRLS WERE SENT FROM FRANCE AS BOUNTY IMMIGRANTS OF THE CROWN – HISTORICALLY KNOWN AS THE **"KING'S GIRLS"**. EACH ONE OF THESE FEMALES WERE PROMISED A SUM OF MONEY, DOMESTIC ANIMALS AND A LAND GRANT SO THAT THEY MIGHT SET UP HOUSEKEEPING AND ESTABLISH A HOME ONCE THEY WERE MARRIED. ALL UNMARRIED MEN LIVING IN NEW FRANCE WERE GIVEN FIFTEEN DAYS TO SNAG ONE OF THE FEMALES ABOARD THE SHIPS UPON ITS ARRIVAL AND MARRY THEM. IF THE UNMARRIED MAN FAILED TO FULFILL TALON'S PLAN OF POPULATING QUEBEC WITH ITS ARYAN BLOODLINE, A HEAVY FINE WAS IMPOSED UPON THEM. ALL AVENUES OF ESTABLISHING A SUPER WHITE RACE IN THE NEW WORLD WAS PROMPTLY EXECUTED. FATHERS OF MARRIAGEABLE SONS AND DAUGHTERS WERE HEAVILY PENALIZED IF THEIR CHILDREN WERE NOT MARRIED AND OUT OF THE HOUSE BY SPECIFIC AGES - THE BOYS HAD TO BE MARRIED AND HAVE HOMESTEADS OF THEIR OWN AT THE AGE OF TWENTY AND THE GIRLS AT THE AGE OF EIGHTEEN. WITH HIS KLANSMEN TYPE RACIST POLICIES OF POPULATING FRENCH NORTH

Americia, the numbers of settlers practically doubled itself within only two short years.

Less than two years after his being dubbed the Baron, Talon went back to France and soon began boasting to his royal master the good deeds and/or accomplishments performed by him while living in the New World. The French King, agreeing with him, elevated Talon in 1675 to a higher stature as his barony in New France was now dubbed a courtship which was to be called the courtship of Orsainville. Baron des Islets then became known as the Count d'Orsainville. Upon his death in 1694, all of the vast fortunes that he had accumulated over the many years of his life (both land and money) went to his heirs. The properties in Canada were eventually sold off and/or donated to charities to maintain Jean Talon's presence in Quebec as the Count d'Orsainville. In fact, one of the last remaining properties held by Talon's heirs was handed over to the City of Quebec in 1896 which in turn became known as Victoria Park.

In 1668, the French Roman Catholic monarchy set the wheels in motion to grant yet still another baronial title onto its master class; Charles Le Moyne, who was made Baron de Longueuil. Like his fraternity brother Talon, Charles Le Moyne also had illusions of grandeur as he fortified his seignorial manor-house assuming the presence of a medieval castle which he ironically called Chateau Le Moyne de Longueuil. Only a few years prior to his being elevated to the pedestal of Baron, Charles Le Moyne arrived into Canada like everyone else wanting to get rich quick to show the folks back home in motherland just how good things were in the New World. Le Moye was the son of an innkeeper in France with no ties whatsoever to nobility. Once he arrived in Canada, he took up residence in Montreal were on a few occasions he rendered his services out to a couple of that community's elite population against the Indians of the wilderness. Some years later, he was issued a land grant on the south shore of the St. Lawrence almost opposite the Island of Montreal where he build a solid stone masonry structure flanked by four strong towers which enabled him to ward off any unwanted guests.

Although the Baron de Longueuil only got to enjoy his prestigious title for a short time period, (he was born in 1626 and reportedly died in 1685), his eldest son Charles assumed the title and lands bequeathed to him. On his father's estate, Charles Jr. erected supposedly one of the best equipped mills in the neighborhood of

Montreal and further to this, he build roads throughout the estate willed to him on his father's death bed. Wanting full recognition for his gallant efforts, the King of France was asked to consider a request for the baronial status as junior's seigniory was now the ideal estate to be envied by others. In 1700, Charles Jr. was permitted to consolidate all of his extensive land holdings into the Barony of Longueuil. One-hundred and eighty years later (1880), Her Majesty Queen Victoria recognized the existence of Charles Cilmore Grant as being the seventh Baron of Longueuil. To this very day, the prestigious title of nobility lives on in the Le Moyne family tree of Quebec.

Perhaps the most interesting of all noblesse oblige in New France was that of Francois Berthelot, who in 1676 became known as the Count de Saint-Laurent. This courtship comprised the Island of Orleans, just below Quebec City. Originally, the Island was granted to the Jesuits but in 1675, the Bishop Laval exchanged it with Francois Berthelot for his seigniory of Isle Jesus, at Montreal. Berthelot, then took possession of his new domain and in the following year was raised to the stature of Comte de Saint-Laurent. Apparently, it had been incorporated within the agreement of exchange that this elevation of power and title were to take place. And once the King learned of this, he was not at all impressed with what Laval had done as only he (the King) had the power to do so. Which in effect put an end to any other courtship titles being executed in New France. In total, the French Roman Catholic's only issued two courtships in Canada; Jean Talon Count d'Orsainville and the one issued to Francois Berthelot.

After the fiasco finally died down, the French monarchy was confined to handing out its prestigious titles of barons to less and less people. Previously to this, everyone who had been granted land wanted to be elevated to a higher plain of nobility. New France was said to have had so many men of distinction walking around that nothing was getting done in the fields as everyone was far too busy trying to impress the hell out of one another with their various titles and/or placements in French society. The situation in fact was so far out of control that in 1687, the Intendant Gilles Hocquart of Champigny pleaded with the King of France not to grant any more titles of nobility as the passing of distinguished titles was making beggars out of everyone.

With everyone and their dog being elevated to nobility in some form/or another; Michel de Saint-Martin was known as the Marquis

DE MISCOU WHILE ROBERT GIFFARUD WAS REFERRED TO AS THE MARQUIS DE BEAUPORT (SO NAMED AFTER THEIR SEIGNIORIES), EVERYTHING STARTED TO UNRAVEL AS THE SO-CALLED BLUE BLOODS OF QUEBEC SPENT LESS AND LESS TIME LOOKING AFTER THEIR ESTATES. OF ALL THE PRESTIGIOUS TITLES GRANTED TO PEOPLE LIVING IN NEW FRANCE, ONLY A SMALL HANDFUL ACTUALLY CAME FROM BLUE BLOOD STOCK. THEY WERE THE FAMILIES OF JACQUES LENEUF DE LA POTERIE, CHARLES LE GARDEUR DE TILLY, JEAN-BAPTISTE LE GARDEUR DE REPENTIGNY AND CHARLES D'ALLEBOUST DE MUSSEAUX. ALL OF THESE MEN WERE KNOWN NOBLEMEN BEFORE THEY HEADED TO THE NEW WORLD FROM FRANCE AND CONTRARY AS TO WHAT SOME HISTORIANS MAY TRY TELLING US, THEIR TITLES OF NOBILITY HAD ABSOLUTELY NOTHING TO DO WITH THE ESTABLISHING OF CANADA PER SE AS FRANCE'S FRENCH NOBILITY ACTUALLY HAD SOMETHING ELSE IN MIND FOR ITS PEOPLE. TO SAY THE LEAST, THIS BIT OF CANADIAN HISTORY HAS BEEN DRASTICALLY ALTERED OVER THE CENTURIES AS THE VAST MAJORITY OF HISTORIANS GLORIFY OUR COUNTRY'S NOBILITY AS THOUGH THEY BORE THE TITLES AS FINE OUTSTANDING PILLARS OF BOTH CHURCH AND STATE. BUT THE FACTS SPEAK FOR THEMSELVES AND CANNOT BE DISPUTED BY ANYONE, CANADA'S SO-CALLED FRENCH NOBILITY WAS NOTHING BUT A JOKE FROM START TO FINISH AS IT WAS ONLY THE MEANS TO AN END. THOSE WHO WERE ELEVATED TO THE STATURE OF NOBILITY WERE MERELY ARTIFICIAL IMPLANTS OF DISTINCTION. BEFORE LONG, THESE MEN OF SO-CALLED BLUE BLOOD OF NEW FRANCE CEASED TO WORK ON THEIR SEIGNIORIES AS THEY TRIED TO LIVE THE LIVES OF COUNTRY GENTLEMEN WHICH IN THE END WAS DRIVING THE COUNTRY CLOSER AND CLOSER TO THE BRINK OF ECONOMIC RUIN. IN MANY CASES, THEIR PROPERTIES BECAME SO DESTITUTE THAT THEY HAD NO CHOICE BUT TO APPEAL TO THE KING OF FRANCE FOR ASSISTANCE.

THE MORE WELL OFF SEIGNIORAL NOBLESSE ON THE OTHER HAND MANAGED TO AVOID THE RIGGERS OF HIGH DEBTS BY PLAYING BOTH ENDS AGAINST THE MIDDLE AT ALL TIMES. ACCORDING TO HISTORIANS, MANY OF NEW FRANCE'S FRENCH ELITE WERE QUITE WELL OFF FINANCIALLY — SUCH AS THE FAMILIES OF LE MOYNE, LE BER, LEPAGE, ROBINEAU, VILLERAY, LOTBINIERE, SOREL AND/OR SAUREL, AND A HOST OF OTHERS. WHICH IN TURN ENABLED THEM TO SUPPOSEDLY SERVE THEIR TITLES OF DISTINCTION WELL. FOR INSTANCE, JACQUES LE BER WAS THE RICHEST MAN IN MONTREAL WHO HAD ACQUIRED THE SEIGNIORY OF SAINT PAUL'S ISLAND. UPON TAKING POSSESSION OF HIS NEWLY ACQUIRED ESTATE HE INSTANTLY DUBBED HIMSELF SIEUR DE SENNEVILLE.

LE BER WAS A MERCHANT OF MONTREAL WHO HAD AMASSED A VAST FORTUNE THROUGH SOMEWHAT CRAFTY MEANS AND WAS SAID TO HAVE PAID A RATHER HEFTY FEE TO ASSUME THE TITLE OF LORD OF THE MANOR OF SENNEVILLE. THEN OF COURSE THERE'S NOEL LANGLOIS, WHO WAS COMMISSIONED BY THE

KING TO LOOK FOR TIMBER FOR THE ROYAL NAVY. LIKE JACQUES LE BER AND ALL THE OTHERS, LANGLOIS WANTED TO BE RECOGNIZED AS A GENTLEMAN. WHILE CLIMBING HIS WAY UP TO THE TOP OF THE FRATERNITY LADDER, HE BEGAN HONING HIS SOCIAL SKILLS. ON MAY 25TH, 1677 LANGLOIS ACQUIRED THE SEIGNIORY OF SAINT-JEAN-PORT-JOLI WHERE HE ALMOST IMMEDIATELY WENT FROM BEING A VERY SKILLED CARPENTER TO THAT OF AN ABSOLUTE LAY ABOUT. COINCIDENTLY, HE BECAME KNOWN IN FRENCH CANADA AS THE LAZY ENGLISH GENTLEMAN AS THE LAND LATER PASSED INTO THE HANDS OF THE DE GASPE FAMILY WHO WERE SAID TO BE NEVER AT ALL IMPRESSED WITH NOEL LANGLOIS IN THE FIRST PLACE.

IT IS NOT THE INTENTION OF THESE PAGES TO GLORIFY THE FRENCH NOBLESSE IN ANY WAY, SHAPE /OR FORM AS IT IS ALL PURE TRIPE TO BEGIN WITH. THE MAIN PURPOSE OF THIS CHAPTER IS TO HELP SET THE RECORD STRAIGHT BY LETTING IT BE KNOWN THAT UNDER THE SEIGNIORIAL SYSTEM OF THE FRENCH MONARCHY, THE RECIPIENT OF A NOBILITY TITLE WAS GRANTED BY LAW THAT HIS /OR HER CHILDREN WOULD GAIN POSSESSION OF ALL THAT IS BEQUEATHED TO THEM UPON THE DEMISE OF THE SO-CALLED BLUE BLOODS OF CANADA. CASE IN POINT; THE SEIGNIORY OF SOREL (/OR SAUREL) PROVED BEYOND A DOUBT THAT IT VIRTUALLY PAID TO BE ISSUED SUCH A TITLE OF DISTINCTION — THIS SEIGNIORY, WHICH IS NOW THE PRESENT SITE OF THE CITY OF SOREL IN THE PROVINCE OF QUEBEC WAS ORIGINALLY ISSUED IN 1672 TO PIERRE DE SAUREL, A CAPTAIN IN THE CARIGNAN REGIMENT. WHEN HE DIED TEN YEARS LATER, HIS ESTATE WAS LEFT IN LIMBO AND THUS THE SUBJECT OF A RATHER LENGTHY LITIGATION AS NO DIRECT HEIRS WERE SAID TO BE FOUND. MANY YEARS LATER, IT WAS EVENTUALLY AWARDED TO CLAUDE DE RAMEZAY, THE GOVERNOR OF TROIS RIVIERES AND MONTREAL. NOW, THIS IS WHERE THINGS GET REALLY INTERESTING CONSIDERING THE FACT THAT BOTH ABBE LEPAGE AND THE DE RAMEZAY FAMILY HAD THEIR OWN SAWMILLS IN OPERATION AND WERE SUPPLYING TIMBERS TO QUEBEC'S SHIPBUILDING INDUSTRY, THAT IS UNTIL THE KING BLACKLISTED THE LEPAGE'S. LIKE ABBE LEPAGE'S MILL, THE DE RAMEZAY OPERATION WAS CUTTING BOTH PLANKS AND BEAMS. DE RAMEZAY'S MILL WAS ESTIMATED TO BE PUTTING OUT 8,000 FEET OF PLANKING A YEAR AND AT LEAST 4,000 BEAMS ON AN ANNUALLY BASIS. BUT UNLIKE LEPAGE, CLAUDE DE RAMEZAY AND HIS FAMILY WAS INCLUDED IN THE FRENCH MONARCHY'S PLAN OF PROSPERITY FOR QUEBEC AS HE WAS COMMISSIONED BY THE KING OF FRANCE TO SUPPLY MORE AND MORE TIMBERS TO THE SHIPBUILDING INDUSTRY. BY 1739, THERE WERE AN ESTIMATED SEVENTY SAWMILLS IN OPERATION SUPPLYING THE TIMBERS THAT WERE NEEDED. THE DE RAMEZAY FAMILY WENT ON TO BECOME ONE OF QUEBEC'S LARGEST LUMBER MAGNATES AS THEY BEGAN PRODUCTION ON A GRAND SCALE HAVING WORKMEN

MAKING MASTS AT HIS MILLS ON BAIE ST. PAUL, AT SOREL AS WELL AS OTHER PLACES OUTSIDE OF MONTREAL.

APPARENTLY, SIEUR DE RAMEZAY HAD SO MUCH MONEY THAT HE HAD CONSTRUCTED A MEDIEVAL TYPE CASTLE ON HIS SEIGNIORY. THE CASTLE ITSELF WAS DUBBED THE CHATEAU DE RAMEZAY AS THE SIEUR DE RAMEZAY ALSO WANTED FULL RECOGNITION FOR HIS GALLANT EFFORTS AS BEING ONE OF MONTREAL'S MOST POWERFUL ELITE GENTLEMEN. LIKE ALL THE OTHERS BEFORE HIM, DE RAMEZAY FIRMLY BELIEVED THAT YOU WEREN'T SOMEONE UNLESS YOU WERE OF NOBILITY. IRONICALLY, NOT TOO MANY YEARS PRIOR TO HIS BECOMING ONE OF THE WEALTHIEST MEN IN MONTREAL, ONE OF HIS OWN RELATIVES LODGED A COMPLAINT WITH THE KING OF FRANCE'S INTENDANT WHINING ABOUT HOW CERTAIN INHABITANTS OF THEIR SEIGNIORY AT SOREL WERE REFUSING TO SEND HARVESTED GRAIN TO THE SEIGNIOR'S SOREL FLOUR MILL. AT THE TIME, THE SEIGNIORS HAD THE MILLING RIGHTS OF ALL THE GRAIN THAT WAS TO BE PRODUCED ON THEIR ESTATES. THIS ALSO INCLUDED THE GRAIN OF THE SUBLEASED LANDS ON THE ESTATE AS WELL. WITH THE EXTENSION OF THESE MILLING RIGHTS, THE CENTENARIES WERE BOUND BY THEIR CONTRACTUAL OBLIGATIONS TO GRIND ALL GRAIN IN THE SEIGNIOR'S MILL — PAYING THE SEIGNIOR A SHARE OF THE PROCEEDS, USUALLY ONE-FOURTEENTH OF ALL THE FLOUR PRODUCED. THE END RESULT OF THE COMPLAINT WAS THE ISSUING OF AN ORDER PROHIBITING THE INHABITANTS OF DE RAMEZAY'S SOREL SEIGNIORY FROM HAVING THEIR WHEAT GROUND ELSEWHERE AND FURTHER IMPOSING A FINE OF TEN LIVRES ONTO THOSE WHO DID. SOMETIMES THE MASTERS OF THE ESTATES WERE SO PETTY THAT THEY EVEN COMPLAINED ABOUT THE INHABITANTS UNLAWFUL FISHING ON THEIR SEIGNIORIES. SUCH WAS THE CASE ON FEBRUARY 18TH, 1750, WHEN AN EDICT WAS ISSUED REGARDING YET ANOTHER COMPLAINT BY THE DE RAMEZAY FAMILY CONCERNING THE INHABITANTS OF SOREL'S ILLEGAL FISHING OF WATERS THAT THE DE RAMEZAY'S FELT WAS NO ONE'S RIGHT BUT THEIR OWN TO FISH IN. NEEDLESS TO SAY, THE EDICT SIDED WITH THE DE RAMEZAY'S AND FINED THOSE OF HIS INHABITANTS TEN LIVRES FOR DOING SO. FURTHER TO THIS, ANY FUTURE UNAUTHORIZED FISHERS WERE ALSO TO BE FINED TEN LIVRES AS WELL AS HAVING ALL OF THEIR FISHING GEAR CONFISCATED IN THE PROCESS OF GETTING CAUGHT. ALL RULES AND REGULATIONS ALWAYS FAVORED THE MASTERS OF THE ESTATE AND NOT THOSE WHO INITIALLY WORKED HARD TOILING THE LAND.

IT IS ALSO INTERESTING TO NOTE THAT THE SEIGNIORY THAT WAS ORIGINALLY GRANTED TO MONSIEUR PIERRE DE SAUREL ON OCTOBER 21ST, 1672 ACTUALLY DID IN FACT HAVE A HUMBLE BEGINNING. SHORTLY AFTER HIS ARRIVAL INTO CANADA, HE WAS SENT TO CONSTRUCT A FORT AT THE MOUTH OF THE RICHELIEU RIVER. PICKING THE LOCATION AS TO WHERE THE

FORT WAS TO BE BUILT, DE SAUREL LATER CHOSE THE EXACT SAME LOCATION TO ERECT HIS SEIGNIORY AFTER THE COMPLETION OF HIS SERVICE AND THE SUBSEQUENT DISBANDMENT OF HIS REGIMENT. NEARLY SIXTY YEARS AFTER HIS DEATH, THE SEIGNIORY WAS ALLOWED TO EXPAND ITS BOUNDARIES UNDER THE STEWARDSHIP OF MESDEMOISELLES ANGELIQUE-LOUISE AND ELIZABETH DE RAMEZAY (JUNE 18TH, 1739). THIS EXPANSION CONTAINED ALL OF THE REMAINING LANDS BEHIND THE SOREL SEIGNIORY AND FURTHER LANDS GRANTED WERE TO INCLUDE SOME OF THE SMALL ISLANDS IN LAKE SAINT PETER WHICH HAD NOT BEEN ISSUED TO PIERRE DE SAUREL. IN ACTUAL FACT, IT INCLUDED ALL THE ISLANDS OF THE CHANNEL OF ISLE PLATTE.

ACCORDING TO THE HISTORY BOOKS, JEAN-BAPTISTE NICOLAS ROCH DE RAMEZAY (THE SON OF CLAUDE DE RAMEZAY) SUCCEEDED LOUIS-JOSEPH MONTCALM, DUBBED THE MARQUIS DE MONTCALM AS BEING THE GRAND-POOH-BAH IN PREVENTING THE BRITISH FROM INVADING CANADA. THE MARQUIS, NOT WANTING TO BE RULED BY THE ENGLISH WHILE THE SIEUR DE RAMEZAY DIDN'T REALLY CARE ONE WAY /OR THE OTHER AS TO WHO WAS IN CHARGE SINCE HE WAS SAID TO HAVE BEEN PLAYING BOTH ENDS AGAINST THE MIDDLE MOST OF HIS LIFE ANYWAYS. AFTER THE MARQUIS DE MONTCALM WAS MORTALLY WOUNDED ON THE PLAINS OF ABRAHAM ON SEPTEMBER13TH, 1759 AND SUBSEQUENTLY DYING BY NIGHT FALL, SIEUR DE RAMEZAY WAS NOW IN CHARGE OF THE FRENCH TROOPS. AS THE NEW GOVERNING BODY, DE RAMEZAY REPORTEDLY DIDN'T HAVE THE HEART FOR FURTHER RESISTANCE AS HE SOON BEGAN CONTEMPLATING HIS OPTIONS. WHILE MONTCALM'S SECOND-IN-COMMAND (FRANCOIS GASTON DE LEVIS, A.K.A. CHEVALIER DE LEVIS) WAS ALMOST AT THE GATES OF THE CITY WITH HIS RE-ENFORCEMENTS, THE SIEUR DE RAMEZAY SURRENDERED THE CITY OF QUEBEC AND THE ENTIRE SURROUNDING COUNTRY SIDE TO THE BRITISH. ON SEPTEMBER 18TH, HE SIGNED HIS NAME TO THE ***ARTICLES OF CAPITULATION*** WHICH GAVE THE ENGLISH SOLE POSSESSION OF CANADA. TWO DAYS AFTER SIGNING HIS NAME TO THE CAPITULATION OF QUEBEC, SIEUR DE RAMEZAY REPORTEDLY LEFT FOR FRANCE LEAVING FRENCH CANADA TO FEND FOR ITSELF.

COINCIDENTLY, CLAUDE DE RAMEZAY ORIGINALLY CAME TO CANADA IN 1685 WHERE HE RAISED HIS CHILDREN, HE IS SAID TO WHAT HAD AS MANY AS SIXTEEN OF THEM. FIVE YEARS AFTER HIS ARRIVAL, (1690), HE WAS APPOINTED GOVERNOR OF TROIS RIVIERES AND COMMANDER OF THE FRENCH TROOPS IN 1699, AND ELEVATED TO THAT OF NOBILITY IN 1705, (AWARDED THE CROSS OF ST. LOUIS). AFTER SERVING A SHORT STINT AS GOVERNOR OF MONTREAL, (1704-24), HE BECAME THE ADMINISTRATOR OF NEW FRANCE, (1714-16). WHILE LIVING AT HIS CASTLE, THE CHATEAU DE RAMEZAY, CLAUDE DE RAMEZAY BEGAN SETTING THE STAGE FOR MANY OF HIS SONS TO BE THE MAIN PLAYERS IN. UPON HIS DEATH ON AUGUST 1ST, 1724 THE MILITARY REIGNS

OF POWER WERE THUSLY HANDED DOWN TO JEAN-BAPTISTE WHO, AT THE TIME WAS ONLY SIXTEEN- YEARS-OLD. BY THIS TIME PERIOD OF COURSE, JEAN-BAPTISTE WAS ALREADY SERVING IN THE MONTREAL GARRISON. TWO YEARS AFTER HIS FATHER'S DEATH, HE WAS PROMOTED TO LIEUTENANT AND IN 1734, HE BECAME A CAPTAIN. JUST LIKE HIS FATHER BEFORE HIM, JEAN-BAPTISTE NICOLAS ROCH DE RAMEZAY WAS ELEVATED TO NOBILITY IN 1748 AS HE TOO WAS ALSO AWARDED WITH THE CROSS OF ST. LOUIS. AND BY THE FOLLOWING YEAR, (1749), BECAME QUEBEC CITY'S NEW MAYOR. IN 1758, HE WAS PROMOTED TO LIEUTENANT IN THE KING'S ARMY. AFTER SIGNING HIS NAME TO THE SURRENDER DOCUMENT, THIS SO-CALLED BLUE BLOOD OF CANADA FLED TO LA ROCHELLE, FRANCE NEVER MORE TO RETURN. HE REPORTEDLY DIED AT BLAYE, NEAR BORDEAUX, FRANCE ON MAY 7TH, 1777.

IN THE FINAL ANALYSIS, THE SOREL SEIGNIORY THAT WAS ONCE GRANTED TO PIERRE DE SAUREL, AND FINALLY AWARDED TO THE SIEUR CLAUDE DE RAMEZAY MANY YEARS LATER, WAS EVENTUALLY PURCHASED IN 1781 BY SIR FREDRICK HALDIMAND FOR AN UNSPECIFIED USE OF THE BRITISH GOVERNMENT. THIS IS THE EXACT SAME BRITISH SOLDIER WHO IRONICALLY ENOUGH TOOK POSSESSION OF MONTREAL FROM THE FRENCH IN 1760. HALDIMAND, THEN WENT ON TO BECOME THE ACTING GOVERNOR OF THE TROIS RIVIERES DISTRICT AND EVENTUALLY ITS GOVERNOR (1762-65). FREDRICK HALDIMAND WAS KNIGHTED SIR FREDRICK IN 1785 SUPPOSEDLY FOR HIS EFFORTS OF DEFUSING THE SERIOUS FRICTIONS THAT HAD EXISTED BETWEEN THE FRENCH AND BRITISH INHABITANTS OF CANADA WHILE HE SERVED AS LORD DORCHESTER'S GOVERNOR-IN-CHIEF OF CANADA (1778-84).

NOT ALL OF CANADA'S FRENCH-SPEAKING POPULATION WELCOMED THE IDEA OF PICKING UP THEIR WEAPONS IN ORDER TO WARD OFF A BRITISH TAKE-OVER, IF TRUTH BE TOLD FOR WHAT ACTUALLY EXISTED — THEY ACTED JUST LIKE DE RAMEZAY AND GREETED THEM WITH ARMS OPENED WIDE. AT THE FORMER SEIGNIORY OF ABBE LEPAGE LOCATED AT TERREBONNE FOR EXAMPLE, THE TENANTS APPARENTLY INFORMED THE SEIGNIOR (SIEUR LOUIS DE LA CORNE) THAT UPON THE ENGLISH TAKE-OVER OF CANADA, THEY PERCEIVED THEMSELVES AS BEING WARDS OF ENGLAND AND NOT THAT OF FRANCE. THIS WAS APPARENTLY STATED WHEN THE SEIGNIOR OF TERREBONNE ATTEMPTED TO FORCE HIS TENANTS TO SEE THINGS HIS WAY — THEY SWARMED AROUND HIM LIKE LOCUS WHICH COMPELLED HIM TO FLEE FOR HIS LIFE BACK TO MONTREAL. THINGS THEN ESCALATED EVEN FURTHER UPON HIS DEPARTURE AS HE THREATENED TO RETURN WITH SOLDIERS AND FORCE THEM TO COMPLY WITH HIS WISHES. THEY, THEN ARMED THEMSELVES VOWING TO FIGHT FORCE WITH BRUTE FORCE AS THE SEIGNIOR'S TENANTS REFUSED OUTRIGHT TO TAKE PART IN THE FIGHT AGAINST THE BRITISH /OR ANYONE ELSE WHO WAS TRYING TO TAKE-OVER THE COUNTRY. AS FAR AS THE FRENCH TENANTS WERE

CONCERNED, ALTHOUGH THEY PERCEIVED THEMSELVES AS BEING SUBJECTS OF ENGLAND, THE RACIAL TENSIONS THAT WERE BREWING BETWEEN THE BRITISH, THE FRENCH AND THE AMERICANS WAS NONE OF THEIR DAMNED BUSINESS – IT WAS STRICTLY BETWEEN THE POWERS THAT BE AND NO ONE ELSE. AT THE TIME, FRANCE HAD FORMED AN ALLIANCE WITH THE AMERICAN REVOLUTIONARIES AND THE FRENCH SEIGNIORS AUTOMATICALLY ASSUMED THAT THEIR TENANTS WOULD JOIN IN THE CAUSE TO PREVENT AN ENGLISH /OR EVEN AN AMERICAN TAKE-OVER AS THE UNITED STATES WAS TRYING TO TAKE FULL ADVANTAGE OF FRENCH CANADA'S DIRE SITUATION.

THROUGHOUT QUEBEC'S FRENCH SEIGNIORAL SYSTEM THIS EXACT SAME RHETORIC AND/OR LOGICAL REASONING WAS BEING REPEATED OVER AND OVER AGAIN, FOLLOWED BY OF COURSE THE TAKING UP OF ARMS DEFYING THE WISHES OF THE VARIOUS SEIGNIORS WHO WANTED THEIR TENANTS TO WAGE WAR AGAINST THE AMERICAN ARMIES THAT HAD INVADED THE TERRITORY NORTH OF THE 49TH PARALLEL. IF THE SO-CALLED BLUE BLOODS OF CANADA WANTED TO TAKE UP ARMS AGAINST THE UNITED STATES, THEN, THEY WERE GOING TO HAVE TO DO IT ALL ON THEIR OWN AS THE LOWER CLASS OF THE POPULATION ESSENTIALLY HAD ENOUGH OF THE BLUE BLOODS CONSTANT WHINING AND SNIVELING EVERY TIME THINGS DIDN'T GO AS TO WHAT THE FRENCH MASTERS HAD ORIGINALLY PLANNED AND/OR ANTICIPATED. APPARENTLY, THIS WAS SUPPOSEDLY DEFUSED BY SIR FREDRICK HALDIMAND AS HE BEGAN INTRODUCING HARSH METHODS TO STEAM THE SEEDS OF VIOLENCE THAT WAS ERUPTING ON THE VAST MAJORITY OF THE FRANCOPHONE SEIGNIORIES WHILE HE WAS LORD DORCHESTER'S GOVERNOR-IN-CHIEF OF CANADA.

IN SPEAKING OF THE UNITED STATES AND THEIR FORMED ALLIANCE WITH FRANCE, THE HISTORY OF THIS INTERCOURSE AND SUBSEQUENT MARRIAGE OF THE TWO SOUTH OF THE 49TH PARALLEL WAS NO BETTER THAN WHAT WAS UNFOLDING IN THE NORTH. FOR INSTANCE, ON MAY 28TH, 1664 THE POWERS THAT BE IN FRANCE FORMED A NEW COMMERCIAL ORGANIZATION THAT WAS SUPPOSEDLY GOING TO BRING GREAT RICHES TO BOTH CHURCH AND STATE. THE COMMERCIAL VENTURE, KNOWN AS THE COMPANY OF THE WEST INDIES WAS TO ASSIST FRANCE IN ACQUIRING ITS SHARE OF THE GROWING COMMODITIES TRADE THAT WAS DEVELOPING IN EUROPE AND ABROAD. NEEDLESS TO SAY, THE HISTORY OF THIS COMPANY IS RIDDLED WITH GREED AND CORRUPTION, BUT THAT'S YET ANOTHER STORY. OF ALL THE CORRUPTION THAT HAD PLAGUED THIS COMPANY, WE'RE ONLY INTERESTED IN THE ONES ASSOCIATED WITH THE COMPANY OF THE WEST INDIES' GRANTED JURISDICTIONAL TRADING RIGHTS OF CANADA, WHICH AS IT SO HAPPENED REACHED AS FAR AS THE FROZEN FRONTIER OF THE ARCTIC TO THE SOUTHERN MOST TIP OF FLORIDA. THESE JURISDICTIONAL RIGHTS ALSO INCLUDED LOUISIANA, WHERE IN WHICH TWO MEMBERS OF THE LEPAGE FAMILY TREE PLANTED THEIR SEEDS FOR MANY

GENERATIONS TO GROW UNDER; ANTOINE-SIMON LEPAGE DU PRATZ AND JEAN-BAPTISTE LEPAGE DU PRATZ (TWO FRATERNITY BLOOD BROTHERS).

THROUGHOUT THE LAND THAT OF WHICH THE COMPANY HAD JURISDICTIONAL TRADING RIGHTS, IT ALSO ACTED AS THE ENFORCERS OF LAW. WHEN SOMEONE DISAGREED, THEY WERE DEALT WITH EXPEDIENTLY BY WAY OF A FRATERNAL *STAR CHAMBER*. UNDER THE KING OF FRANCE'S AUTHORITY, THE COMPANY OF THE WEST INDIES POSSESSED THE RIGHT TO ESTABLISH TRIBUNALS AS WELL AS TO EXECUTE THE TRIBUNAL'S FINDINGS AND/OR JUDGEMENTS — THIS RANGING FROM FINES BEING LEVIED ON THE SEIGNIORIES TO THE BRUTAL BEATING OF SLAVES. THE ENFORCERS OF THE KING'S LAW WERE A RUTHLESS BUNCH OF BASTARDS HAVING NO TOLERANCE WHATSOEVER FOR THOSE CLASSES OF PEOPLE WHO CONTINUALLY QUESTIONED THE SUPREMACY OF FRENCH ROMAN CATHOLIC AUTHORITY OVER THEM — THE MORE DEFIANT A PERSON WAS, THE HARSHER THE PENALTY. THESE ENFORCERS OF THE FRENCH MONARCHY'S FRATERNITY LAW, KNOWN HISTORICALLY AS MEMBERS OF THE SOVEREIGN COUNCIL WERE SUPPOSEDLY MEN OF GREAT DISTINCTION, A HIGHER CALIBER OF SOCIETY AS IT WERE. BUT IN REALITY, THESE SO-CALLED BLUE BLOODS MERELY WANTED TO PROVE TO OTHERS THAT THEY WERE SIMPLY HOLIER THAN THOU.

INTERESTINGLY ENOUGH, DURING THE FALL OF 1666 THE COMPANY RELINQUISHED ITS RIGHT OF MAKING LAND GRANTS AS APPARENTLY THE WANNABE'S STARTED ABUSING THEIR POWERS BY ISSUING GRANTS TO THEIR CLOSEST FRIENDS. IT WAS BAD ENOUGH THAT THESE SUPPOSED MEN OF HIGH CALIBER WERE BEING BESTOWED WITH PRIVILEGES OF COVERING TRADE (MINES, FORESTS, FISHING AND SLAVERY) AND BEING APPOINTED JUDGE, JURY AND EXECUTIONER OF ITS PEOPLE, BUT TO ALSO ALINE THEMSELVES WITH THEIR OWN KIND WAS JUST A LITTLE TOO MUCH FOR MOST TO BARE. THE REVAMPING OF THE LAND GRANT SYSTEM, WHICH COINCIDENTLY ALSO MEANT REVISING THE JUDICIAL SYSTEM AS WELL LEAD TO THE CREATION OF THE SEIGNIORIAL JUSTICE SYSTEM. INSTEAD OF THE MEMBERS OF THE SOVEREIGN COUNCIL ISSUING LAND GRANTS AND PASSING JUDGEMENT ONTO OTHERS, THEY WERE TO ACT STRICTLY AS THE ENFORCERS. THE INTENDANT, APPOINTED BY THE KING NOW WAS IN CHARGE OF ISSUING ALL LAND GRANTS AND THE SEIGNIOR WAS TO ACT AS THE JURY. THE INTENDANT, PASSED JUDGEMENT ON WHAT THE JURY (THE SEIGNIOR OF THE ESTATE) WANTED WHILE THE SOVEREIGN COUNCIL ENFORCED THE JUDGEMENT HANDED DOWN. THE SITUATION HADN'T IMPROVED AT ALL, IT MERELY WENT FROM BAD TO WORST AS IT WAS STILL A *STAR CHAMBER* OF SORTS. ALTHOUGH THESE CHANGES WERE MADE, THE COMPANY OF THE WEST INDIES STILL HAD THE FINAL SAY ABOUT ISSUES REGARDING WHO WAS DEEMED TO BE FIT AND PROPER FOR LAND DEVELOPMENT AND TRADE. IT WAS THE SAME OLD STORY, THE RICH GOT RICHER WHILE THE POOR GOT POORER.

With the political landscape of the Company of the West Indies shifting into high gear, it soon began exploiting the vast regions of its domain raping the land of its wealth. Before long, dissension amongst the so-called blue bloods began to emerge as one group of people wanted more power than the other. Even though it was a very viable business venture, the constant bickering of those ruling the roost lead to its dismal failure in December of 1674 when the King of France revoked its trading privileges. According to some historians, the Company lost well in excess of three and a half million livres during its ten years of existence and handed out only a few land grants between the years 1664 and 1666. Accordingly, it is stated that these two factors (monies owed to them and not enough land grants issued) contributed to its own demise. But in reality, other factors were at play; such as the rampant corruption of those in charge of the Company itself. Be that as it may, new life was breathed into the Company as its privileges were later re-instated and differences were set aside. With the rebirth came newfound hope for the future as more and more of the country's wealth was exploited by the ruling classes. In Louisiana for example, the Company under the stewardship of Jean-Baptiste LePage du Pratz was able to flourish as the sale of Black slaves became his speciality. Now known primarily as the Company of the Indies, it attempted to rule French Louisiana with so much vigor and valor that yet another member of the LePage family tree had to be called in to help water down the true facts as they unfolded on a daily basis. One of the French monarchy's most valued Roman Catholic patron saints, Antoine-Simon LePage du Pratz was commissioned to write the history of Louisiana in accordance as to what the King of France wanted it to say.

Contrary as to what the history books may say about the LePage's of Louisiana, (kind to both Indians and Negroes alike), they in fact were not only notorious for exploiting those who were deemed to be an inferior race of people but also fathered many of their children. And since fathering illegitimate children wasn't sanctioned by the Roman Catholic Church, the actual existence of their offspring was totally denied by all. Case in point; it's a well known and proven fact of history that two members of the upper echelon in Louisiana were having sexual relations with the Natchez Indian women and fathered many of their children; Jean-Baptiste LePage du Pratz and Marc-Antoine La Loire des Ursins.

The native community was in fact said to be so interwoven with Franco-Indian blood that the two races soon began to mistrust one another. The situation escalated even further when the Company of the Indies implemented one of the most racist policies of its time and Jean-Baptiste LePage sided with his masters, turning his back on those who he supposedly viewed as being equal to him. Obviously, this member of the LePage family tree had no trouble weighing his options which in effect allowed him to side with his master (the Company of the Indies) as it apparently is one of the LePage family traits to collaborate with those who are in power. This disowning of those who were supposedly his equal came about mainly because of the fact that a large number of slaves (both Indians and Blacks) were constantly running away from the Company of the Indies. The Indians, running back to their own villages with a couple of the Black slaves along side them. The villagers, concealing the refugees from the enforcers of law, shrugged their shoulders and shook their heads saying that they hadn't seen any of the escapees. Being totally chocked at what was happening, (profits not being recouped due to slaves running away all the time), Company brass asked all the native tribes in the Natchez region to arrest all fugitives, Indian /or Black, promising to reward those who did so with guns, blankets and Limburg cloth. Further to this, the Company of the Indies promised to pardon the Indians who had fled, if they had returned with Black slaves in tow. The Blacks on the other hand weren't to be so lucky as the Company's enforcers had be instructed to maintain the law by way of beating them with rods and then branding them with hot irons depicting the fleur-de-lys emblem onto their foreheads. Before long, hatred divided both the Indians and the Blacks, which for many generations prior to this having transpired had been at ease with each other.

The Company of the Indies implemented this policy of racial segregation because it firmly believed that the Black's hatred for the Indians who had betrayed them and handed them over to the French authorities would drive a huge wedge between the two races of people. This way, Black slavery would be able to flourish amongst the French colonies of New France from the Arctic to the most southerly point of Florida. Then, the not so unexpected occurred on June 1ST, 1730 when a group of Blacks massacred the Indian population of Natchez; killing men, women and children. With the Natchez Indian Nation's blood on his hands, Jean-Baptiste LePage du Pratz was put in charge of keeping track of all chronological

EVENTS FOR THE COLONY IN NEW ORLEANS WHILE HIS FRATERNITY BROTHER PUT THEM IN MANUSCRIPT FORM PERTAINING AS TO HOW THE KING OF FRANCE SAW THE EVENTS OF THE DAY UNFOLD.

WHEN IT CAME DOWN TO THE NITTY GRITTY OF BUSINESS DEALING FOR THE COMPANY OF THE INDIES, JEAN-BAPTISTE LEPAGE HAD A SILVER TONGUE, A GIFT FOR THE GAB. DURING THIS TIME PERIOD IN LOUISIANA, RACIAL TENSIONS WERE ALSO AT AN ALL TIME HIGH WITH OTHER DIFFERENT GROUPS OF PEOPLE AS THE FRENCH WERE ALWAYS OUT THERE TRYING TO PROVE THEIR SUPERIORITY OVER OTHERS. GERMAN SETTLERS FOR EXAMPLE FIRST MOVED FURTHER UP RIVER (THE MISSISSIPPI RIVER) TO AVOID PERSECUTION BY THE MAJORITY OF THE FRENCH, WHO OCCUPIED MOST OF THE SOUTHERN TERRITORY OF LOUISIANA. AMPLE EVIDENCE IS DOCUMENTED IN PASSENGER AND IMMIGRATION LISTS INDEX ABOARD SHIPS HEADING TO NORTH AMERICA FROM EUROPE AS THE NAME SPATHELFER APPARENTLY HAS MANY WAYS OF BEING WRITTEN AS THEY ORIGINALLY CAME FROM DIFFERENT REGIONS OF GERMANY; SPATHELFER/SPATHILFER – IT'S EVEN SOMETIMES WRITTEN SIMPLY AS SPATHELF. WHICH EVER WAY THE NAME WAS SPELT, MOST, IF NOT ALL OF THE GERMAN SETTLERS FACED A HOST OF OBSTACLES BY THE TIME THEY REACHED THE SHORES OF LOUISIANA. ACCORDING TO THE FRENCH, THE GERMAN SETTLERS THREATENED THE VERY EXISTENCE OF THEIR LOUISIANIAN CULTURE AS IT HAD BEEN ASSUMED THAT MOST OF THE GERMAN IMMIGRANTS WERE EITHER PROTESTANTS /OR JEWISH.

NOTWITHSTANDING, IN THE BEGINNING (1722 /OR THEREABOUTS) THE GERMAN SETTLERS OF LOUISIANA ALWAYS DID THEIR OWN WORK ON THE SMALL FARMS THAT WERE ALLOTTED TO THEM BY THE COMPANY OF THE INDIES, GROWING FOOD CROPS, RAISING POULTRY AND CATTLE. BUT AFTER A FEW YEARS, THEY ADOPTED THE FRENCH WAY OF LIFE BECAUSE INTERMARRIAGE SOON BROUGHT THE TWO DIFFERENT RACES OF PEOPLE TOGETHER. AS IT TURNS OUT, THE MAJORITY OF THE GERMAN SETTLERS WERE ROMAN CATHOLIC AND POSED NO INITIAL THREAT WHATSOEVER TO FRENCH LOUISIANA. GRANTED, A FEW OF THEM WERE IN FACT PROTESTANTS BUT PRESSURE WAS SOON ADDED FROM FAMILY MEMBERS AND THE CATHOLIC CHURCH TO CONVERT LEAVING THEIR EVIL LUTHERAN WAYS IN THE LURCH. NOT LONG AFTER THE FIRST INTERMARRIAGE OF THE FRENCH AND GERMAN PEOPLES, LEPAGE DU PRATZ MANAGED TO PERSUADE THE GERMAN SETTLERS TO ACQUIRE THE SERVICES OF BLACK SLAVES.

IRONICALLY, WHILE JEAN-BAPTISTE LEPAGE DU PRATZ WAS THE MANAGER OF THE COMPANY OF THE INDIES IN THE LOUISIANA TERRITORY, HE WAS ALWAYS LOOKING FOR AN ANGLE TO BOOST HIS OWN REPUTATION AND THE GERMAN SETTLERS WERE MERELY THE MEANS TO AN END. IN OCTOBER OF 1726, APPLICATIONS WERE MADE FOR BLACK SLAVES AND LEPAGE WAS MORE

THAN WILLING TO OBLIGE THEM. AFTERALL, BY THIS TIME PERIOD THE COMPANY WAS LOSING MONEY HAND OVER FIST DUE TO MISMANAGEMENT AND BAD DECISION-MAKING ON HIS PART AND SOMETHING HAD TO BE DONE IN ORDER FOR HIM TO SAVE FACE. BY YEAR'S END, THE COMPANY OF THE INDIES DID SAME SOLE-SEARCHING AS ALLEGATIONS OF MANAGERIAL NEGLECT BY JEAN-BAPTISTE LEPAGE DU PRATZ SOON ESCALATED OUT OF CONTROL. FEELING THAT HE HAD DONE ABSOLUTELY NOTHING WRONG, HE PETITIONED THE COMPANY ON JANUARY 2ND, 1727 PROTESTING HIS REMOVAL AS MANAGER. THIS IN ITSELF EXPLAINS AS TO WHY HE DISOWNED HIS THE FRANCO-INDIAN CHILDREN THAT HE HAD FATHERED WHILE BEDDING DOWN WITH THE NATCHEZ INDIAN WOMEN AS HE WAS ONLY INTERESTED IN SAVING HIS OWN SORRY ASS. THE FACT THAT HE WAS TURNING HIS BACK ON HIS OWN FLESH AND BLOOD WAS INSIGNIFICANT AS FAR AS HE WAS CONCERNED. DISOWNING ONE'S OWN CHILDREN IS YET ANOTHER LEPAGE FAMILY TRAIT AND HAS BEEN SO SINCE THE BEGINNING OF TIME.

IN REALITY, THE LEPAGE'S OF LOUISIANA WERE NOTHING BUT WANNABE REJECTS OF QUEBEC. FOR INSTANCE, JUST PRIOR TO JEAN-BAPTISTE LEPAGE DU PRATZ'S ASSUMING THE MANAGEMENT OF THE COMPANY OF THE INDIES, THE BLACK POPULATION OF FRENCH LOUISIANA WAS SUFFERING FROM SCURVY AND THEIR HEALTH WAS WORSENING WITH EACH PASSING DAY. DUE TO THIS FAILING HEALTH ISSUE, THE PRICE THAT THE COMPANY WAS GETTING FOR THE BLACK SLAVES (USUALLY MORE THAN 1,000 LIVRES) WAS GETTING LESS AND LESS EVEN THOUGH THEY (THE COMPANY) HAD PAID A MUCH HIGHER PRICE FOR THEM. IT WAS REPORTEDLY STATED THAT IF SUCH SALES WERE TO CONTINUE MUCH LONGER, IT WAS GOING TO BE FORCING THE COMPANY OF THE INDIES INTO SHEER BANKRUPTCY. ALMOST IMMEDIATELY AFTER HE ASSUMED THE MANAGEMENT POST OF THE COMPANY, LEPAGE BEGAN BOOSTING OF HAVING FOUND A CURE FOR THE ILLNESS AND THE SALE AUCTIONS WERE ALLOWED TO RESUME DESPITE THE FACT THAT A LARGE MAJORITY OF THEIR SYMPTOMS HAD GOTTEN WORSE CAUSING MANY OF THEM TO DIE NOT LONG AFTER BEING SOLD. ACCORDING TO SOME HISTORIANS, LEPAGE HAD A GENUINE INTEREST IN THEIR ILLNESS AND BEGAN TREATING THE BLACKS WITH CARE AND COMPASSION. THIS IS THE SAME LEPAGE WHO IN 1726 IS SAID TO HAVE INVENTED A COTTON GIN THAT WORKED WONDERS BUT LATER ADMITTED PRIVATELY TO HIS CLOSEST FRIENDS AND FAMILY MEMBERS THAT IN REALITY IT FAILED MISERABLY.

PRIOR TO LEPAGE'S TAKING OVER OF THE COMPANY OF THE INDIES IN FRENCH LOUISIANA, A VERY SMALL PERCENTAGE OF THE COMPANY'S HABITANTS HAD BLACK SLAVES ON THEIR SEIGNIORIES — THE SLAVES THAT THEY DID HAVE WERE MOSTLY INDIAN SLAVES. UNDER THE STEWARDSHIP OF JEAN-BAPTISTE LEPAGE DU PRATZ, EACH AND EVERY SEIGNIOR WAS TO BE ASSIGNED A SLAVE HOUSEHOLD COMPRISING OF BLACK SERVANTS. AS FAR AS THAT GOES, BLACK

SLAVES WERE EVEN FORCED TO SERVE REFRESHMENTS TO THE CREWS OF SHIPS ARRIVING FROM FRANCE AND ORDERED TO ANSWER TO ANY OF THEIR BECKON CALLS; SEXUALLY AND/OR OTHERWISE.

ALL-TOO-OFTEN, THE LEPAGE'S OF LOUISIANA WERE MORE INTERESTED IN FULFILLING THEIR OWN VISIONS OF GRANDEUR AND NOTHING ELSE MATTERED. FOR EXAMPLE, UNDER THE FRENCH REGIME IN BOTH CANADA AND LOUISIANA, INDIAN AND BLACK SLAVES ALIKE HAD NO LEGAL STATUS TO OWN PROPERTY WHATSOEVER. THEY WERE SUBJECTED TO CONTINUOUS SURVEILLANCE, TOLD WHEN TO EAT, DRINK AND BE MERRY. EVEN WHEN THEY WOULD GO INTO TOWN TO SELL THE PROCEEDS THAT THEIR MASTERS HAD PRODUCED ON THE SEIGNIORIES, THE SLAVES WERE WATCHED LIKE HAWKS. POORLY FED AND UNDERNOURISHED, BLACK SLAVES OFTEN PROTESTED THE WAY IN WHICH THE FRENCH MASTERS WERE TREATING THEM. FIRST BY SYSTEMATICALLY REFUSING TO WORK, THEN WHEN THAT FAILED, SOME WOULD EVEN RESORT TO TRYING TO POISON THEIR MASTERS. BUT IN MOST OF THE CASES, IF THE LORD OF THE MANOR WASN'T WILLING TO LISTEN TO THEIR GRIEVANCES BLACK SLAVES QUITE OFTEN SOUGHT COMPENSATION BY STEALING SOMETHING FROM THE MASTER, THEN RUNNING AWAY FROM THEM. JEAN-BAPTISTE LEPAGE DU PRATZ WAS SAID TO HAVE REGARDED THIS ACT AS AN ELEMENTARY REFLEX OF A CREATURE WHO HAD NOTHING OF HIS OWN AND THEREFORE HAD NO QUALMS WHATSOEVER OF IMPOSING A BEATING WITH RODS ON THE RUNAWAY SLAVES AS WELL AS THEIR BEING BRANDED ON THE FOREHEAD WITH A HOT IRON. SO MUCH FOR THIS MEMBER OF THE LEPAGE FAMILY DYNASTY BEING SUCH A CARING AND CONCERN HUMANITARIAN DESPITE WHAT HISTORIANS WISH US TO BELIEVE IS TRUE.

THEN OF COURSE, THERE'S THE ANTICS OF THE OTHER LEPAGE LIVING DOWN ON THE BAYOU WRITING ONLY WHAT THE FRENCH MONARCHY WANTED HIM TO PUT IN MANUSCRIPT FORM. WHILE STUDYING THE CUSTOMS, LANGUAGE AND CEREMONIES OF THE NATIVE PEOPLES, ANTOINE-SIMON LEPAGE DU PRATZ WAS OFFERED AN INDIAN WOMAN TO BED DOWN WITH. ACCORDING TO THESE SAME HISTORIANS, THIS MEMBER OF THE LEPAGE FAMILY TREE IS SAID TO HAVE DECLINED THE OFFER MADE TO HIM BECAUSE HE WAS SUPPOSEDLY DEEPLY DEVOTED TO THE ROMAN CATHOLIC CHURCH DOCTRINE – THE HISTORIANS DESCRIBE IT BY STATING THAT THE NATIVE WOMAN WAS AN INDIAN PRINCESS AND THAT LEPAGE WANTED TO BE EVER SO LOYAL TO HIS SUPERIORS AS HE HAD A GENUINE INTEREST IN PRESERVING THE HISTORY OF LOUISIANA. IN ALL LIKELIHOOD ANTOINE-SIMON LEPAGE DID TAKE THE INDIAN CHIEF UP ON HIS OFFER AS IT WOULD HAVE BEEN A DIRECT INSULT TO THE TRIBE'S ABORIGINAL CUSTOM NOT TO DO SO. BESIDES THAT, WHEN IT COMES DOWN TO HAVING SEXUAL INTERCOURSE WITH AN INDIAN WOMAN, THE LEPAGE'S NEVER GAVE IT A SECOND THOUGHT AS THIS TOO IS PART OF THEIR BUILT-IN FAMILY

CHARACTERISTIC — TEPEE CREEPING WAS A NORMAL RITUAL FOR THE LePAGE'S OF BOTH LOUISIANA AND QUEBEC. AND ONCE A CHILD WAS BORN FROM THE SEXUAL COUPLING, THE BIOLOGICAL FATHER MERELY DENIED HAVING ANY SEXUAL RELATIONS WITH THAT WOMAN AS SUCH ACTIONS (ILLEGITIMATE CHILDREN BORN OUT OF WEDLOCK) WAS NOT SANCTIONED BY THE CHURCH. IT WAS AFTERALL THE ROMAN CATHOLIC THING TO DO; DENY, DENY, DENY!!!

IF ANTOINE-SIMON LePAGE DU PRATZ WAS SO INTERESTED IN PRESERVING THE TRUE HISTORY OF LOUISIANA AS TO WHAT SOME HISTORIANS SUGGEST, THEN, WHY IS IT THAT HIS OWN PERSONAL BIGOTED VIEW POINTS INSISTED THAT THE BLACK POPULATION BE TREATED IN A TOTALLY DIFFERENT MANNER FROM THE REST OF THE PEOPLE SIMPLY BECAUSE OF THE FACT THAT THEY SAW THINGS NOT QUITE THE SAME WAY AS THE WHITEMAN. HE REPORTEDLY STATED: **"THE NEGROES MUST BE GOVERNED DIFFERENTLY FROM THE EUROPEANS, NOT BECAUSE THEY ARE BLACK, NOR BECAUSE THEY ARE SLAVES; BUT BECAUSE THEY THINK DIFFERENTLY FROM WHITE MEN.** "IRONICALLY, LePAGE'S OPINION WAS TAKEN INTO CONSIDERATION WHEN THE KING OF FRANCE, LOUIS XV, ENACTED THE BLACK CODE OF CONDUCT ONTO THE NEGRO POPULATION OF FRENCH LOUISIANA IN MARCH OF 1724, BETTER KNOWN TO HISTORICALLY AS **CODE NOIR.**

THE PRIMARY PURPOSE OF THE BLACK CODE WAS ORIGINALLY TO CONTROL THE EVER INCREASING NUMBER OF SLAVES IN THE COLONY. HARSH RESTRICTIONS WERE IMPOSED ONTO THE BLACK SLAVES IN ORDER TO PREVENT INSURRECTIONS AND SUPPOSEDLY TO CURTAIL THE TORTURE OF SLAVES ONCE THEY WERE RE-CAPTURED AFTER RUNNING AWAY FROM THE SHACKLES OF THEIR FRENCH MASTERS. THE CODE NOIR ALSO ATTEMPTED TO CONVERT BLACK SLAVES TO THE ROMAN CATHOLIC FAITH AS IT WAS SEEN AS THE SUPERIOR RELIGION AND THE PRACTICING OF OTHER RELIGIONS IN THE NEW WORLD WAS NOT TO BE TOLERATED. THE ROYAL ROMAN CATHOLIC DECREE EVEN PROHIBITED WHITES FROM HAVING SEXUAL RELATIONS WITH THE BLACK POPULATION AS THEY (THE BLACKS) WERE REGARDED AS INFERIOR RACE OF PEOPLE BY ANY FRENCH STANDARD — BLACKS WERE THEREFORE ENCOURAGED TO MARRY THEIR OWN KIND. BUT THE FRENCH BEING WHO THEY ARE, DID SET ASIDE PROVISIONS IN THEIR LITTLE BLACK BOOK OF RACISM EXONERATING THOSE OF LOUISIANA'S MALE ELITE WHO HAD A TENDENCY OF HAVING SEXUAL INTERCOURSE WITH THEIR BLACK FEMALE SLAVES. IN THE EVENT THAT A CHILD WAS TO BE BORN OF A FREE FATHER AND A SLAVE MOTHER, THEN THAT CHILD WAS TO BE CONSIDERED A SLAVE. BUT IF THE FATHER WAS A SLAVE AND THE MOTHER NOT A SLAVE, THEN THE CHILD WAS TO BE CONSIDERED A FREE BORN PERSON — IT ALWAYS DEPENDED TOTALLY AS TO WHAT THE MOTHER'S STATUS WAS AT THE TIME OF THE CHILD'S BIRTH.

Coincidently, Antoine-Simon LePage du Pratz urged the baptism of all slaves (Indians as well as Blacks) in accordance to his Roman Catholic faith. In doing so, he was guaranteed his rightful seat at the right hand of both the King of France as well as the Almighty God Himself. As previously stated, this member of the LePage family tree was one of the King's favorite in Louisiana. While attempting to make his fortune down on the Bayou, he was given a tract of land not long after his arrival in 1714, but the dampness and the constant flooding soon forced him to give up his estate and relocate his abode from on the Bayou St. John to one near Fort Rosalie among the Natchez Indian people. Later, he was granted a duchy in the Arkansas region after pleasing the French monarchy with some of his special fraternity thoughts of enlightenment. As he proved his worthiness to the King of France, Antoine-Simon LePage began exploring the interior of Louisiana taking notes as he went on his journey.

In 1726, he was appointed the overseer of a plantation near New Orleans belonging to the Company of the Indies. But as time went on, all the responsibilities got to be far too much for him to handle as he had more pressing things on his mind such as writing a manuscript depicting how prosperous Louisiana was under French rule. By 1734, LePage's business venture proved itself to be nothing but a disaster as he too operated on a helter-skelter philosophy that was far too costly and his post at the plantation was abolished altogether. The plantation was now so far in debt that it was eventually handed over to the King. With his tail neatly tucked between his legs, Antoine-Simon LePage du Pratz returned back to France (La Rochelle) ending his twenty year reign of terror in French Louisiana, (1714-34).

While back in France, Antoine-Simon LePage was busy mingling with the French elite once again. If he wasn't living it up with the rich and famous, he was writing down what the King wanted him to have in his manuscripts. In 1758, his version of the true history of French Louisiana was first published in Paris and a few years later (1763), it was translated into English in London. Once his books were published, a three volume project, he simply vanished off the LePage family history books never to be heard from again until his death in 1775.

To the uninformed everything mentioned thus far maybe of no importance whatsoever but once an individual calculates various equations into the mix, everything comes into clear focus. For instance, when the United States Government began contemplating

THE PURCHASE OF LOUISIANA FROM FRANCE FOR $ 15,000,000.00 (U.S.) IN 1803, MANY AMERICANS PROTESTED BITTERLY AGAINST THE PRESIDENT'S PAYING EVEN THREE-MILLION DOLLARS FOR IT. AS FAR AS THE MAJORITY OF THE AMERICAN POPULATION WAS CONCERNED, THE LOUISIANA TERRITORY WAS A WORTHLESS PIECE OF SWAMP LAND AND WILDERNESS INCAPABLE OF SUSTAINING ANY FORM OF HUMAN EXISTENCE AND THEY THEREFORE URGED THEIR PRESIDENT (THOMAS JEFFERSON) TO RECONSIDER WHAT HE WAS ABOUT READY TO DO. THEY VIEWED THE MOVE BY THE FRENCH AS A TACTIC TO FORCE THE UNITED STATES INTO BANKRUPTCY AS EVEN THEY (THE AMERICANS) DIDN'T HAVE ACCESS TO THAT AMOUNT OF CASH!!!

ALTHOUGH THE AMERICANS BROKE AWAY FROM GREAT BRITAIN ONLY A FEW YEARS PREVIOUSLY, AN ENGLISH BANKING INSTITUTION (THE HOUSE OF BARING IN LONDON) WAS WILLING TO FRONT THE MONIES NEEDED FOR THE LAND TRANSACTION FOR A SMALL NOMINAL FEE OF COURSE. AND SINCE THE UNITED STATES OF AMERICA STILL HAD A GOOD LINE OF CREDIT, THE HOUSE OF BARING THUSLY MADE ARRANGEMENTS WITH FRANCE AND ENGLAND FOR THE AMERICANS TO BE ABLE TO MAKE BOTH A LUMP SUM PAYMENT AS WELL AS MONTHLY PAYMENTS AS AGREED UPON BY THE PARTIES INVOLVED. IRONICALLY, AS FRANCE AND ENGLAND WERE ALWAYS AT ODDS WITH ONE ANOTHER, THE BRITISH GOVERNMENT GAVE THEIR APPROVAL OF THE SALE UNDER THE CONDITION THAT IN THE EVENT OF WAR BREAKING OUT BETWEEN THE TWO COUNTRIES (FRANCE AND GREAT BRITAIN), ENGLAND HAD THE OPTION TO DEPLOY TROOPS TO THE NEWFOUND TERRITORY FOR ITS IMMEDIATE CAPTURE. IT IS SAID THAT ONCE THE KING OF ENGLAND (GEORGE III) LEARNED OF THE TERMS OF SALE, HE WAS OVER COME WITH JOY AS PROSPECTS OF INVADING AMERICAN SOIL LOOKED VERY PROMISING AS FRANCE'S RULING POWER WAS NOTHING BUT A LITTLE TIN-GOD WHO WANTED TO RULE THE WORLD.

AS FRANCE WAS BEING STRIPPED OF ITS AMERICAN CONTINENTAL POSSESSION, TENSIONS BEGAN TO MOUNT BETWEEN THE THREE PARTIES ALMOST IMMEDIATELY. WEIGHING HER OPTIONS, ENGLAND SERIOUSLY BEGAN CONTEMPLATING SENDING IN TROOPS TO CAPTURE NEW ORLEANS AS A SOMEWHAT COCKY FRATERNITY LEADER KNOWN HISTORICALLY AS NAPOLEON BONAPARTE (KNIGHTS OF MALTA) BEGAN PICKING A FIGHT WITH THE BRITISH MONARCHY. DESPITE THE FACT THAT IT WAS NAPOLEON WHO SOLD LOUISIANA TO THE AMERICANS AND WAS WELL AWARE OF THE TERMS OF SALE, HE PERSISTENTLY ANNOYED THE HELL OUT OF THE ENGLISH. AS IT TURNS OUT, BONAPARTE WAS USING ALL OF THE MONIES RECEIVED TO FINANCE HIS WAR ON GREAT BRITAIN AND THE REST OF THE WORLD. IT EVEN GOT TO THE POINT WHERE HE WAS SAID TO HAVE MANAGED TO CONVINCE THE AMERICANS TO ATTACK BRITISH SOIL IN 1812 AS THEY (THE UNITED STATES) FEARED AN ENGLISH INVASION TO CONSUMMATE THE VIOLATION OF THE TERMS OF SALE.

Unfortunately, this is one little detail of American history that not too many historians wanted to openly admit to having had existed in the first place.

It should also be stated that the terms of the sale for the Louisiana territory was the brain child of England's Lord Hawkesbury, (a.k.a. Charles Jenkinson, Baron of Hawkesbury and Earl of Liverpool). Under the terms of sale, $ 11,250,000.00 was to be paid outright to France's Knights of Malta protector and the remaining balance of $ 3,750,000.00 was to be paid directly to the citizens of the United States of America, monies owed by France. With the acquisition of the Louisiana territory, it became quite apparent to both England and France that the Americans would eventually seek to expand their boundaries beyond the 828,000 square miles of land incorporated within the purchase itself. As far as the United States of America was concerned, the Louisiana Purchase left Canada wide open, free for the taking as England had proven once and for all that everything was up for grabs as its honor and integrity took a back seat if the price was right. According to the Americans, both France and Great Britain had exposed the United States and its people to the many evils of the world by way of forcing its views onto others. Wanting absolutely nothing to do with either one of them, the United States of America forged onwards and upwards with their dreams of doing things their way and on their own terms!!!

Before long, the territory of Louisiana was divided up into two separate regions; the Territory of Orleans and the District of Louisiana. The Territory of Orleans went on to become known as the State of Louisiana while the District of Louisiana lead the way for the establishing of fourteen further States in the American Union. Their dreams of *"Manifest Destiny "*were finally showing signs of becoming a reality.

In yet another twist of irony, at the same time that Napoleon had managed to convince the Americans to attack British soil in 1812, Louisiana was admitted into the Union as the 18^(TH) State on April 30^(TH) of that same year. Almost immediately after that, battle lines were drawn as war erupted on the Canadian border when American troops tried to acquire Canada as their newly acquired trophy. The little French Emperor must have been laughing his fool head off as England had been at war with France from 1796 to 1814-15, with a brief truce intervening in 1802 just long enough for him to throw the Americans a bone peaking their interest in wanting to acquire the Louisiana territory. As far as Napoleon was concerned,

It was obviously an easy maneuver to achieve as there still existed a lot of animosity between England and the United States regarding unresolved fraternity issues that had transpired over the American Revolutionary War for Independence from the British monarchy. Utilizing the hatred that the Americans had for their British counterpart, Bonaparte played both ends against the middle as a way and means of getting exactly what he wanted out of the two parties in question.

This tactic was extremely evident when U.S. President Jefferson sent two of his right hand mento France to seal the fraternal deal with the French Emperor; Robert R. Livingston and James Monroe. Upon their arrival, all hell broke loose as the little tin-god of France increased his initial price from 10 million (U.S.) to 15 million. Wanting so desperately to obtain the land, the American envoy agreed to the set price given. Once Jefferson learned that a secret agreement had been finalized without his prior approval, he reportedly became enraged. Apparently, the envoy had no authorization to go as high as they did because Jefferson and the U.S. Congress had only given approval of 10 million dollars and no more. Further to this little set back, it now meant that additional financial resources would now have to be extracted from the British money makers in London (the House of Baring) which in essence was putting the United States Government behind the fraternal eight ball. A position that of which Jefferson didn't like to be in at all as it literally meant that someone else in a foreign country was now calling the shots and/or pulling the fraternity puppetry strings.

According to some historians, Napoleon Bonaparte was said to be in a hurry to sell off the property as he needed the money to deploy his troops against the British monarchy and that if he sold the Louisiana territory to the United States, it would financially strap them for many years to come thus preventing them from joining forces with the English. Sounds like a good bed time fairy tale and nothing more because in reality, the little tin-god of France knew exactly as to what he was doing. As it turned out, by the time the American envoy reached Paris – Bonaparte had already instructed his French Minister of Foreign Affairs (Charles Maurice de Talleyrand-Perigord) to sell them all of Louisiana /or nothing at all. Originally, the Americans only wanted to acquire one of the following from the French Emperor;

1) THE PURCHASE OF EASTERN AND WESTERN FLORIDA AND NEW ORLEANS;
2) THE PURCHASE OF NEW ORLEANS ALONE;
3) THE PURCHASE OF LAND ON THE EASTERN BANK OF THE MISSISSIPPI RIVER TO BUILD AN AMERICAN PORT; /OR
4) THE ACQUISITION OF PERPETUAL RIGHTS OF NAVIGATION AND DEPOSIT.

APPARENTLY, THE AMERICANS HAD BEEN NEGOTIATING FOR SOME TIME WITH FRANCE IN A BID TO REACH SOME SORT OF DEAL WITH NAPOLEON IN THE PAST BUT THE LITTLE FRENCH FRATERNITY LEADER WASN'T QUITE READY TO PLAY HIS TRUMP CARD UNTIL THE TIMING WAS RIGHT. ITS OBVIOUS TO SAY THAT THE FRENCH EMPEROR HAD THE AMERICANS ALL FIGURED OUT RIGHT FROM THE VERY BEGINNING. THE END RESULT OF BONAPARTE'S TACTIC WAS REACHED ON APRIL 30TH, 1803 AS A TREATY AND TWO CONVENTIONS WERE DULY ENTERED INTO AN AGREEMENT BETWEEN THE AMERICAN AND THE FRENCH GOVERNMENTS BY WHICH FRANCE AGREED TO SELL ALL OF THE LOUISIANA TERRITORY TO THE UNITED STATES FOR THE SUM OF SIXTY-MILLION FRANCS TO BE PAID DIRECTLY TO FRANCE AND TWENTY-MILLION FRANCS TO BE PAID TO THE CITIZENS OF THE UNITED STATES THAT WERE DUE FROM FRANCE; FOR SUPPLIES, EMBARGOES, AND PRIZES MADE AT SEA. ALSO INCORPORATED WITHIN THE AGREEMENT WERE FURTHER CONSIDERATIONS OF CERTAIN STIPULATIONS IN FAVOR OF THE FRENCH INHABITANTS OF THE CEDED TERRITORY AND CERTAIN COMMERCIAL PRIVILEGES SECURED TO FRANCE.

ONCE THE UNITED STATES OBTAINED POSSESSION OF THE LOUISIANA TERRITORY, VERY LITTLE CHANGES WERE MADE TO THE **CODE NOIR**. CONTRARY AS TO WHAT OUR AMERICAN COUSINS SOUTH OF THE 49TH PARALLEL MAY WISH TO BE TRUE, BLACK SLAVERY UNDER THE FRENCH REGIME WAS NOTHING IN COMPARISON AS TO WHAT HAPPENED TO THE BLACK POPULATION AFTER THE LOUISIANA PURCHASE. IN FACT, VARIOUS REVISIONS WERE MADE ONLY A FEW YEARS AFTER THE INITIAL PURCHASE WHEREAS MANY OF THE ORIGINAL PROVISIONS SET OUT BY THE FRENCH WERE RETAINED. UNDER THE AMERICAN BANNER OF EQUALITY AND JUSTICE FOR ALL, BLACK SLAVERY STILL FLOURISHED – BLACK SLAVERY IN THE LOUISIANA TERRITORY THUSLY BECAME KNOWN AS AN AMERICAN DILEMMA AS THOSE BORN INTO BONDAGE ATTEMPTED TO REMOVE THE SHACKLES OF THEIR MASTERS. THE HARDER THEY FOUGHT TO BE TREATED FAIRLY UNDER THE LAW OF SIMPLE HUMAN KINDNESS, THE MORE RESISTANT THE LAWS OF THE LAND BECAME. TREATED LIKE CATTLE, THE VAST MAJORITY OF THE WHITE POPULATION LIVING IN THE LOUISIANA TERRITORY (FRENCH AND AMERICANS ALIKE) SAW ALL BLACKS AS NON-PERSONS WHO HAD NO HUMAN

RIGHTS WHATSOEVER. ACCORDING TO THEM, THE AMERICANS, IT WAS THEIR GOD GIVEN RIGHT TO OWN BLACK SLAVES.

MEANWHILE IN CANADA, THINGS WERE NO BETTER AS THE BRITISH MONARCHY DISPENSED WITH MORE AND MORE INDIAN LAND TO ENGLISH SUBJECTS LOYAL TO THE CROWN AS PART OF ITS LEGALIZED VERSION OF GENOCIDE. IN UPPER CANADA FOR EXAMPLE – 3,200,000 ACRES WERE GRANTED TO MEMBERS OF THE UNITED EMPIRE LOYALISTS AS THEY WERE REFUGEES FROM THE UNITED STATES WHO HAD INITIALLY SETTLED IN CANADA PRIOR TO 1787. FURTHER LAND GRANTS WERE ISSUED TO THEIR CHILDREN WHO ACTED AS MILITIAMEN FOR THE CROWN, (730,000 ACRES), WHILE 450,000 ACRES WERE ISSUED TO DISCHARGED SOLDIERS AND SAILORS; 255,000 ACRES TO MAGISTRATES AND BARRISTERS; 136,000 ACRES TO EXECUTIVE COUNCILLORS AND THEIR FAMILIES; 50,000 ACRES TO FIVE LEGISLATIVE COUNCILLORS AND THEIR FAMILIES; 36,000 ACRES TO CLERGYMEN AS PRIVATE PROPERTY; 264,000 ACRES TO PERSONS CONTRACTED OUT TO SURVEY THE LANDS; 92,526 ACRES TO OFFICERS OF THE ARMY AND NAVY; 500,000 ACRES FOR THE ENDOWMENT OF SCHOOLS; 48,520 ACRES TO COLONEL THOMAS TALBOT FOR HIS MANY YEARS OF DEDICATED SERVICE AS A SOLDIER FOR THE CROWN; 12,000 ACRES TO THE HEIRS OF GENERAL BROCK AND 12,000 ACRES TO DOCTOR JACOB MOUNTAIN, A FORMER ANGLICAN BISHOP OF QUEBEC WHO WAS FIRST ANOINTED THE BIG CHEESE OF THE NEW ANGLICAN DIOCESES OF LA BELLE PROVINCE IN 1793.

FURTHER TO THIS, THE ENGLISH GOVERNING BODY ALSO CONTINUED DISHING OUT LAND GRANTS IN FRENCH CANADA TO THOSE LOYAL TO THE BRITISH MONARCHY; 450,000 ACRES TO MILITIAMEN; 72,000 ACRES TO EXECUTIVE COUNCILLORS; 48,000 ACRES TO SIR ROBERT SHORE MILNES FOR HIS SERVICES RENDERED WHILE STILL ACTING AS LIEUTENANT-GOVERNOR OF LOWER CANADA 1797-1808; 100,000 ACRES TO ELMER CUSHING IN 1798 AS A REWARD FOR GIVING INFORMATION PERTAINING TO HIGH TREASONOUS BEHAVIOR OF THOSE LIVING IN FRENCH CANADA; 200,000 ACRES TO OFFICERS AND SOLDIERS OF THE CROWN AND AN ESTIMATED 1,457,209 ACRES FOR THE PURPOSE OF ESTABLISHING EASTERN TOWNSHIPS.

IN 1823, A BUSINESS-MINDED POET AND NOVELIST FROM AYRSHIRE, SCOTLAND (JOHN GALT) FOUNDED THE CANADA COMPANY AND WITH SHARES HELD BY SOME OF ENGLAND'S MOST POWERFUL ELITE BUSINESSMEN, RECEIVED UNTOLD THOUSANDS OF ACRES OF GRANTED CROWN LANDS FOR THE DEVELOPMENT OF TOWN SITES THROUGHOUT ONTARIO. AND THEN YEARS LATER, THE OUTRIGHT THEFT OF INDIAN LANDS CONTINUED UNDER THE STEWARDSHIP OF GALT'S SON, ALEXANDER TILLOCH GALT, AS THE BRITISH AMERICA LAND COMPANY RECEIVED A LAND GRANT OF 800,000 ACRES IN LOWER CANADA TO DEVELOP AT WILL AS EASTERN TOWNSHIPS IN LA BELLE PROVINCE.

CHAPTER 5 - LA FAMILLE LePAGE APRES LA CONFEDERATION CANADIENNE

Not only the natives were restless as the new Nation of Canada was in the midst of being formulated by Sir John A. MacDonald and the founding forefathers contemplated as to what the contents of the British North America Act of 1867 was going to be protecting under British law. At the time, Quebec's French-speaking Roman Catholics were totally appalled at the very thought of being incorporated by an Act of Parliament that would literally be forcing them into complying with the British monarchy. It is for this reason as to why certain members of the Province's Francophone elite band together and diplomatically attempted to scuttle MacDonald's dream of a Confederation. The French, not wanting to be controlled by an inept Protestant who was said to be an active member in the Ancient Craft of Freemasonry.

With tension mounting between the two classifications of people, a series of events began to unfold in both Canada and south of the 49TH parallel. In the United States, various forces were at play to take specific regions of Canada under its wing and make them part of the American Republic. Hostility, therefore began to emerge from all flanks and something had to be done mightily quickly, if not sooner. Secret meetings and fraternal rituals were conducted by Quebec's French power elite, thusly conceiving a master plan and then having it executed. The first order of business was to put an end to any prospects of an American take-over, then, to deal outright with the Protestant formation of a united Confederation for Canada.

By the time the British North America Act received **ROYAL ASSENT** from England in March of 1867, Canada had already been invaded by the United States more times than one can possibly imagine. According to most historians, during this time period of our history (commencing from the defeat by the English at the Plains of Abraham to the time of the Royal Assent over one hundred years later) the United States of America only attempted to invade Canada twice, using the excuse that the little insurrections didn't really count as they were far too minute to even be considered to be anything serious; an invasion is an invasion no matter what the size! The first noted invasion is said to have occurred while the American Declaration of Independence was still nine months in the future when yet another said member of the Ancient Craft who was also the Commander-in-Chief of the American revolutionary army (Fraternity Brother George Washington), chose Benedict Arnold to lead one column of battle hardened troops to invade Canada, and General Richard Montgomery another. On November 13TH, 1775 Montgomery marched into Montreal and gave the residents four hours to surrender on his terms, he called for a provincial convention "to elect delegates to the Continental Congress and declared Canada the fourteenth American colony. "On December of that same year, General Montgomery and Arnold joined forces and stormed Quebec City under the cover of a raging blizzard. Montgomery was killed, Arnold was wounded and the American forces were driven back to the United States. By all account, the America Freemasonry leaders south of the 49TH parallel saw Canada as a mere trophy to be captured just so that they would be able to proudly display her over a fireplace mantel.

When fraternity leader John Adams became the second President of the United States in 1797, he reportedly made some very interesting statements regarding Canada's future. "The unanimous voice of the Continent is that Canada must be ours, "he declared from Philadelphia, "Canada must be taken." At this time, a large percentage of those occupying seats within the U.S. political arena were fellow members of the Ancient Craft of Freemasonry as they had dreams of fulfilling their God given right to control all of the North American Continent. The Freemasonry controlled United States of the America's then sent a couple of their top notched fraternity Master Mason Brethren up to Montreal to organize elections in what they called the "Liberated territory. "One of these Master Masons being of course Benjamin Franklin, who ironically signed

HIS NAME TO THE AMERICAN DECLARATION OF INDEPENDENCE ONLY A FEW YEARS PREVIOUSLY. ONCE IN MONTREAL, FRANKLIN ALMOST IMMEDIATELY SET UP HIS PRINTING PRESS AND BEGAN TURNING OUT PAMPHLETS AND MANIFESTOES. HE ASSURED THE PEOPLE OF QUEBEC THAT **"THE GOVERNMENT OF EVERYTHING RELATIVE TO THEIR RELIGION AND CLERGY WOULD BE LEFT IN THE HANDS OF THE GOOD PEOPLE OF THE PROVINCE.** "BUT IT WAS FAR TOO LATE FOR BENJAMIN FRANKLIN AND THE REST OF THE MASONIC ORDER, THE AMERICAN TROOPS WERE FLEEING IN RETREAT FROM QUEBEC AS OPPOSING FORCES WERE AGAINST THEIR DREAMS OF ACQUIRING CANADA AS A SET OF ANTLERS OVER THEIR FIREPLACE MANTEL.

THEN, THIRTY-SIX YEARS LATER, ON JUNE 23RD, 1812 THE UNITED STATES IS SAID TO HAVE INVADED CANADA FOR A SECOND TIME WHEN THEY DECLARED WAR ON BRITAIN, HOPING TO TAKE CANADA AWAY FROM THE ENGLISH WHILE THEY WERE TIED DOWN WITH THEIR WAR AGAINST NAPOLEON. ONE MUST NOT FORGET AS TO WHAT WAS PREVIOUSLY STATED CONCERNING THE LOUISIANA PURCHASE OF 1803 AS ALL OF THIS IS INTERCONNECTED CONTRARY AS TO WHAT HISTORIANS WANT US TO BELIEVE IS TRUE. WHILE U.S. PRESIDENT THOMAS JEFFERSON WAS BUSY NEGOTIATING WITH BONAPARTE AND HE, (NAPOLEON) WHISPERED IN THE AMERICAN PRESIDENT'S EAR TO INVADE BRITISH SOIL, JEFFERSON WAS REPORTEDLY TO HAVE STATED SOME YEARS LATER: **"THE ACQUISITION OF CANADA THIS YEAR WILL BE A MERE MATTER OF MARCHING.** "AND IN THAT SAME YEAR (1812), HENRY CLAY, THE SPEAKER OF THE U.S. HOUSE OF REPRESENTATIVES, INTERESTINGLY DECLARED: **"THE MILITIA OF KENTUCKY ARE ALONE COMPETENT TO PLACE MONTREAL AND UPPER CANADA AT OUR FEET. I AM NOT FOR STOPPING AT QUEBEC OR ANYWHERE ELSE, BUT I WOULD TAKE THE WHOLE CONTINENT FROM THEM AND ASK NO FAVORS. I WISH TO SEE NO PEACE 'TILL WE DO. GOD HAS GIVEN US THE POWER AND THE MEANS AND WE ARE TO BLAME IF WE DO NOT USE THEM."** THE U.S. ARMY UNDER GENERAL HULL CROSSED THE DETROIT RIVER AND ATTACKED CANADA WITH 2,500 TROOPS AND THE WAR WHICH WOULD DECIDE THE DESTINY OF HALF THE CONTINENT WAS THUSLY ON.

THE AMERICANS HAD HIGH HOPES OF GAINING CONTROL OF CANADA IN THE WAR OF 1812, BUT THEIR DREAMS WERE SHATTERED BY A VERY UNLIKELY UNION NORTH OF THE 49TH PARALLEL. TWO OF THE GREATEST MILITARY COMMANDERS IN THE HISTORY OF NORTH AMERICA DEFENDED CANADA'S HONOR. THE FIRST WAS BRITISH GENERAL ISAAC BROCK AND THE SECOND WAS NONE OTHER THAN A MERE SHAWNEE CHIEF NAMED TECUMSEH. AT THE BEGINNING OF THE WAR, BROCK FOUND WIDESPREAD DISBELIEF THAT CANADA WOULD EVER BE ABLE TO RESIST THE AMERICAN MENACE. WRITING FROM YORK, (TORONTO), HE WROTE: "MY SITUATION IS MOST CRITICAL, NOT FROM ANYTHING THE ENEMY CAN DO, BUT FROM THE DISPOSITION OF THE PEOPLE ...

A full belief posses - them that this province must inevitably succumb - this proposition is fatal to every exertion - legislators, magistrates, militia officers, all have imbibed the idea. "At a war council meeting, almost all of the British commanders felt it would be foolish to attack the Americans. But Tecumseh reportedly stated that it in fact could be done under certain favorable circumstances. Brock, then listened as to what Tecumseh had in mind for the American Army as he knew full well that everything depended on swift and bold actions, and with the Indian leader's decision that the best defense against the United States was a good offense, they at least had a good fighting chance of actually pulling it off. With this being acceptable to Brock, he rallied his troops. "Gentlemen," he said, "we shall cross the river. We gain nothing by delay. We are committed to a war in which the enemy must always be our superior in numbers and ammunition. "His 300 Canadian militiamen all disguised in red coats symbolizing British forces joined Tecumseh's 600 warriors and together they set out to change history by attacking the Americans on their own soil at Detroit thus embarrassing the hell out of them for many generations thereafter.

Before they reached the fort at Detroit, Brock sent out a man bearing a fictitious dispatch to an area where he was sure to be captured. The dispatch stated that 5,000 Indians were on their way to join the attach on United States soil at Fort Detroit. When the Americans captured the man and searched him, they found the falsified message. Tecumseh reportedly had his men cross a clearing in single file in full view of the Detroit troops and then circled back through the dense woods and crossed again. This ritual was said to be repeated over and over again as it went on all day long. As far as the Americans occupying the fort at the time were concerned, thousands upon thousands of Indians were preparing to attack and in their haste, sent an officer out with a white flag of surrender, August 16TH, 1812. Using a combination of limited attack and a brilliant strategy conceived by an inferior mind of an Indian, the 900 human beings compelled the complete surrender of General Hull and his 2,500 American troops. They captured Fort Detroit which commanded the whole of west-central North American Continent. Needless to say, the initial attack upon the United States on their own soil which eventually lead to the capture of this same soil, affected the entire war as it was a major blow to American morale as they to this very day don't like the idea of openly admitting to the fact that a mere Indian beat them at their own game of warfare.

General Brock and Tecumseh rode side-by-side into the fort at Detroit as the American flag was lowered. It apparently was a moving ceremony for all involved, and Brock was, of course immortalized in legend in Canadian history despite the fact that it was the Shawnee Indian leader who originally saved Canada from an American Masonic take-over. For his gallant and brilliant services at Detroit, General Isaac Brock was knighted **"SIR** "Isaac and was proclaimed as being the main hero who had deterred the American dream of **"Manifest Destiny"**. Brock was killed in the morning of October 13TH, 1812 while rallying the retreating British forces for an assault and victory on the American invader's position at the historic Battle of Queenston Heights, where his memorial column stands to this very day. Almost a year later, in the Battle of Moravian Town the British forces broke under a U.S. Cavalry charge of 3,500 men. The British General Proctor turned and fled for his life. The 300 Indian warriors, however, stood and fought till they were overwhelmed and that's where Tecumseh met his death.

Originally, Proctor had agreed to allow the Shawnee Chief to fire the first shot. Holding their position in the swamp lands, (the British to the right of them), Tecumseh found himself totally deserted by his English allies and fully surrounded by the enemy. As the enemy's riflemen dismounted from their horses, gun fire could be heard and the warriors lay dead as their lifeless bodies fell to the wet spongy ground beneath their feet. Prior to Proctor's abandoning the Indian warriors, both he and Tecumseh had shaken hands symbolizing their alliance as to which one of them was going to discharge the signal that the Americans were in the right position to be fired upon. But the Indian Chief never did have that opportunity as Proctor and his cowardly troops fled the scene. Tecumseh, to whom Canadians owe plenty, along with Sir Isaac Brock, the very existence of our own country, lies in an unmarked grave.

The only positive thing that came out of death of Tecumseh and his Indian warriors was the fact that it ended General Proctor's military career once and for all as his dishonorable actions gave the Americans complete possession of the Lakes Erie and Huron as well as the undisturbed wilderness lands of the western frontier. Thus striking a tremendous blow for the British military command. Unfortunately for Canada, it gave the United States newfound hope in achieving their dreams of being able to have our country as its newly acquired trophy. Coincidently, not too many Canadian

HISTORIANS ARE WILLING TO ADMIT AS TO WHAT HAD OCCURRED IN THE SWAMP LANDS SURROUNDING THE BATTLE OF MORAVIAN TOWN. IN MOST CASES THEY SIMPLY FORGET TO MENTION THE FACT THAT THE BRITISH GENERAL DESERTED HIS POST AND LEFT THE INDIANS OUT THERE TO BE SLAUGHTERED WHILE THEY, THE INDIANS FOUGHT TO DEFEND CANADA UNDER THE UNION JACK.

IN JULY OF 1813, THE AMERICANS PILLAGED AND BURNED YORK, THEN THE CAPITAL OF UPPER CANADA. BUT THE COURSE OF THE WAR HAD ALREADY BEEN SET - THE CANADIAN AND BRITISH FORCES FOR VICTORY WERE ALREADY PUT IN MOTION, THE CANADIANS, WHEN THEY GOT TO WASHINGTON, D.C. A YEAR LATER, BURNED THE WHITE HOUSE IN REVENGE FOR THE BURNING OF YORK. AT THE TIME, WASHINGTON WAS STILL A STRUGGLING SMALL COMMUNITY WITH AN ESTIMATED POPULATION OF ABOUT 8,000 PEOPLE, MOST OF WHICH WERE WHITE INHABITANTS WHO HAD BLACK SLAVES. AS THE STORY GOES, ONCE THE CANADIAN AND BRITISH FORCES ARRIVED INTO THE AMERICAN CAPITAL ON AUGUST 24TH, 1814 FIRES WERE BEING LIT SUPPOSEDLY AT CERTAIN STRATEGY POINTS. WHILE PRIVATE HOMES WERE BURNING, PLACES OF BUSINESS WERE FIRST LOOTED THEN SET ON FIRE. NOTHING WAS SAID TO BE SACRED AND/OR SPARED AS HORSES AND OTHER ANIMALS OWNED BY AMERICANS WERE KILLED IN THE MAYHEM OF DISORDERLY CONDUCT. AS THE TERROR AND CONFUSION ESCALATED TO EPIDEMIC PROPORTIONS, CITIZENS OF WASHINGTON (WHITES AS WELL AS BLACKS) REPORTEDLY HELPED THEMSELVES TO WHATEVER THE LOOTING CANADIAN AND BRITISH SOLDIERS LEFT BEHIND. STILL HAVING THE GLAZE OF REVENGE IN THEIR EYES, ONTO THE GOVERNMENT BUILDINGS THEY WENT WITH TORCHES IN HAND. GOVERNMENT OFFICES WERE FIRST RANSACKED, WITH PAPERS SCATTERED THROUGHOUT, CHAIRS AND OTHER FURNISHINGS THROWN OUTSIDE THROUGH CLOSED WINDOWS AND INTO THE STREETS BELOW — THE OFFICES WERE THEN SET ON FIRE. LIKE A STRIKE OF LIGHTING SETTING THE WHOLE COMMUNITY ON FIRE, THE AMERICAN CAPITAL WAS ABLAZE. ONCE ALL THE CHAOS AND CONFUSION HAD FINALLY CALMED DOWN AND ALL THE SMOKE HAD CLEARED AWAY, AN ASSESSMENT OF THE SITUATION WAS CONDUCTED. THE ENTIRE TOWN LOOKED AS THOUGH IT HAD BEEN STRUCK BY A TREMENDOUS TORNADO AS JUST ABOUT EVERYTHING LAY IN RUIN. THE ONLY PUBLIC BUILDING THAT REMAINED COMPLETELY UNTOUCHED WAS THE GENERAL POST OFFICE AND THE PATENT OFFICE WHICH WERE BOTH UNDER THE SAME ROOF. ALTHOUGH THEY WERE ACTUALLY RUNNING AMOK, HISTORIANS TO THIS VERY DAY STILL INSIST THAT THE MAYHEM WAS CONDUCTED IN AN ORDERLY FASHION AS BY THIS TIME PERIOD OF HISTORY, CANADIANS TOOK PRIDE IN HAVING HAD BUILT A SOLID REPUTATION OF RESISTING A U.S. FREEMASONRY TAKE-OVER.

BUT IF THE ATTACK ON WASHINGTON, D.C. WAS AS WELL ORCHESTRATED AS TO WHAT HISTORIANS WISH US TO BELIEVE IS TRUE, THEN, WHY IS IT THAT IN THE MIDST OF ALL THE CHAOS AND CONFUSION NEARLY ONE-HUNDRED

British soldiers were killed during an accidental explosion. The massive explosion occurred down near the docks when one of the British soldiers set a building on fire that acted as an ammunition warehouse for the American Army. With a tremendous loud explosion, many houses in the vicinity had their walls and roofs scorned with bullets and mortar fire as the ammunition; consisting mostly of quantities of shot, shell, hand-grenades and gun powder went off like a cluster bomb spreading its bullets like a machine gun. Even some of the American historians watered down the events that occurred during the burning of Washington as they too stated that upon the burning of their Capital, the Canadian and British forces returned to Canada without serious loss. The War of 1812, is therefore marked down in our history books as being the defeat of the second American invasion of Canada despite the fact that from a political point of view, the Americans saw the War of 1812 as being their "Second War for Independence "for political independence from the British.

To the uninformed, this discrepancy in our history books is seen as no real big deal but once the Freemasonry connections are exposed for all to see, then, it causes a person to shake their heads in total disbelief. For instance, by the time Sir John A. MacDonald was attempting to formulate a United Confederation, fraternal relations between the American Freemasons (moderns) and the English Freemasons (ancients) had already reached an all time low – the British Freemasons of course controlling Canada. And to make matters even worse, Quebec's French Freemasons (the Knights of Malta) wanted absolutely nothing to do with either one of them. This, therefore set off an internal battle from within the Masonic Order itself. According to their own literature, territorial disagreements were totally normal in the world of Freemasonry and were usually caused due to dissension amongst their own ranks. When this occurred, it was classified as schism which meant that its members of a specific Grand Lodge, (established Grand Lodge in either England, France /or the United States) were competing for the recognition of a disputed territory.

Here on the North American Continent, the first great schism of Freemasonry occurred in England when Master Masons fought amongst themselves which apparently was to be the stepping stone that inspired the American Revolutionary War for Independence from the British monarchy. With the *ANCIENTS* "and the *MODERNS* "at odds with one another, Canada was soon viewed

AS A TROPHY FOR THE VICTOR. THIS IN ITSELF PUT CANADA'S SOVEREIGN JURISDICTION UP ON THE AUCTION BLOCK AS MEMBERS OF THE MASONIC ORDER TRIED TO OUT FLANK ONE ANOTHER. AS DISSENSION GREW, CERTAIN LEADING BUSINESS FAMILIES IN QUEBEC ORGANIZED THEMSELVES AND SIGNED THE MONTREAL ANNEXATION MANIFESTO CALLING FOR THE UNION WITH THE UNITED STATES. ONE THOUSAND OF CANADA'S WEALTHIEST FAMILIES LIVING IN AND AROUND MONTREAL SIGNED THE ANNEXATION MANIFESTO. AMONG THE SIGNATORIES INCLUDED THE REDPATH FAMILY OF THE SUGAR FAME AND THE MOLSON BREWING FAMILY, NAMES STILL FAMILIAR TO CANADIAN SOCIETY OF THE 21ST CENTURY. THESE ANNEXATIONISTS SCORNED THE ONES THEY CALLED THE "RADICAL DEMOCRATS "WHO WANTED AN INDEPENDENT CANADA NOT CONTROLLED BY AN AMERICAN POWER SOUTH OF THE 49TH PARALLEL. NEEDLESS TO SAY, THE U.S. FREEMASONRY GOVERNING BODY WAS NATURALLY INVOLVED WITH THE MOVEMENT AS THEY DID NOT WANT THEIR BRITISH FRATERNITY COUNTERPART TO MAINTAIN THE CONTROL THAT THEY HAD ON THE COUNTRY. EVIDENCE SOON EMERGED THAT ON ONE PECULIAR OCCASION, AN AMERICAN SECRET SERVICE AGENT PAID OUT IN EXCESS A TOTAL OF $ 30,000.00 (U.S.) TO HELP PERSUADE CANADIAN POLITICIANS IN VOTING IN FAVOR FOR ANNEXATION. ($ 5,000 WAS PAID TO A NEWSPAPER EDITOR, $5,000 TO AN ATTORNEY-GENERAL, $ 5,000 TO AN INSPECTOR-GENERAL, AND $ 15,000 TO A MEMBER OF THE NEW BRUNSWICK ASSEMBLY TO PUSH THE ANNEXATION MOVEMENT IN CANADA). THE AMERICANS FREEMASONS THOUGHT THAT CANADA WAS THEIR'S FOR THE TAKING AND EVEN WENT SO FAR AS TO INTRODUCE LEGISLATION THAT WOULD ENABLE A SPEEDY TAKE-OVER. ON JULY 22ND, 1866 A BILL WAS TABLED IN THE U.S. CONGRESS CALLING FOR "ADMISSION OF THE STATES OF NOVA SCOTIA, NEW BRUNSWICK, CANADA EAST AND CANADA WEST, AND FOR THE ORGANIZATION OF THE TERRITORIES OF SELKIRK, SASKATCHEWAN AND COLUMBIA, AS STATES AND TERRITORIES OF THE UNITED STATES OF AMERICA. "BUT AT THE TIME THIS WAS ALL UNFOLDING SOUTH OF THE BORDER, THE INDIAN AND METIS PEOPLES OF CANADA'S WESTERN PLAINS WERE BEGINNING TO EXPRESS THEIR DISMAY AND MISTRUST WITH ALL FORMS OF WHITE GOVERNMENT. AND UNBEKNOWNST TO EVERYONE INVOLVED, AS BEFORE, A PERSON WITH INDIAN BLOODLINES WAS TO PLAY A VERY IMPORTANT ROLE IN AVOIDING AN AMERICAN INVASION.

THINKING THAT IT WAS THEIR GOD GIVEN RIGHT TO RULE SUPREME IN CANADA, THE UNITED STATES GOVERNMENT ENLISTED THE SERVICES OF ONE OF THEIR OPERATIVE AGENTS, JAMES WICKES TAYLOR, (A.K.A. SASKATCHEWAN TAYLOR) BECAUSE OF HIS REPORTED KNOWLEDGEABLE SKILLS PERTAINING TO THE ENDS JUSTIFYING THE MEANS IN THE FREEMASONRY WORLD. HE WAS SENT TO FORT GARRY AND ORDERED TO MAKE THE RED RIVER REGION AMERICAN TERRITORY AT ANY COST TO HUMAN LIFE IF NEED BE. FROM HIS COMMAND

POST AT FORT GARRY IN 1868, TAYLOR WROTE: "THE AMERICANIZATION OF THE FERTILE BELT IS INEVITABLE. INDEED IT IS FOR THE INTEREST OF THE SETTLERS HERE THAT ANNEXATION SHOULD TAKE PLACE AT ONCE. "AS FAR AS HE WAS CONCERNED, THE ONLY WAY TO POLITICAL UNION WAS THROUGH COMMERCIAL UNION. HE THEN WROTE IN A DETAILED PLAN THE VARIOUS STEPS THAT NEEDED TO TAKE PLACE FOR CONTINENTAL UNION WHICH WAS SAID TO HAVE BEEN PRESENTED TO THE U.S. GOVERNMENT FOR ITS APPROVAL. WHEN LOUIS RIEL SEIZED POWER IN MANITOBA, THE AMERICAN ANNEXATION MOVEMENT THOUGHT THAT AN OPPORTUNITY WAS AT HAND AND THEY RUSHED TO TAKE IT. THE AMERICAN GENERAL OSCAR MALMOS ARRIVED IN WINNIPEG AS THE NEW AMERICAN CONSUL. THE HEADQUARTERS OF WHAT WAS KNOWN AS THE AMERICAN PARTY WAS SET UP IN A HOTEL IN WINNIPEG, AND "AMID THE JUBILATION OF AMERICANS DRINKING TOASTS TO THE ANNEXATION OF CANADA, THE AMERICAN FLAG WAS RAISED OVER THE HOTEL. "ON FEBRUARY 8TH, 1870 THE ST. PAUL PRESS WROTE: "THE RED RIVER REVOLUTION IS A TRUMP CARD IN THE HANDS OF AMERICAN DIPLOMACY IF RIGHTLY PLAYED."

INTERESTINGLY, THE FORMER GOVERNOR OF MINNESOTA, WILLIAM MARSHALL, WAS REPORTED TO HAVE PLEDGED FINANCIAL BACKING TO THE CAUSE IF LOUIS RIEL DECLARED ANNEXATION TO THE UNITED STATES. IN ADDITION TO FINANCIALLY FURNISHING THE MEANS AS WELL AS THE GUNS FOR THE JUST CAUSE, A TOTAL OF $4,000,000.00 (U.S.) WAS ALSO PLEDGED TO ANNEX WESTERN CANADA INTO THE AMERICAN MASONIC FOLD. FURTHER TO THIS, AN AMERICAN BUSINESSMAN BY THE NAME OF ROBINSON ARRIVED IN MANITOBA AND BEGAN PUBLISHING A PAPER WHICH HE IRONICALLY CALLED "THE NEW NATION. "THE FRONT PAGE HEADLINES OF THE PAPER ODDLY ENOUGH READ: "CONSOLIDATION: ONE FLAG, ONE EMPIRE "AND "NATURAL LINES MUST PREVAIL."AT THAT MOMENT THE FUTURE OF ALL NORTH AMERICA WEST OF THE GREAT LAKES CLEAR UP TO THE ARCTIC CIRCLE HUNG IN THE BALANCE. FROM OTTAWA SIR JOHN A. MACDONALD WROTE: "IT IS QUITE EVIDENT TO ME THAT THE U.S. GOVERNMENT IS RESOLVED TO DO ALL IT CAN, SHORT OF WAR, TO GET POSSESSION OF THE WESTERN TERRITORY, AND WE MUST MAKE IMMEDIATE AND VIGOROUS STEPS TO COUNTERACT THEM. "BUT SIR JOHN A. WAS WAY TOO LATE, THE CANADIAN GOVERNMENT HAD FEWER THAN ONE-HUNDRED MEN IN MANITOBA. THEN, ON APRIL 20TH, 1870 FRATERNITY BROTHER ZACHARIAH CHANDLER, THE SENIOR SENATOR FROM MICHIGAN, ROSE IN THE U.S. SENATE STATING THE FOLLOWING: "THOUGH CANADA WAS A MERE SPECK ON THE MAP, IT WAS AN INTOLERABLE NUISANCE. AND IF IT EVER REACHED THE PACIFIC, IT WOULD BECOME A STANDING MENACE, THAT WE OUGHT NOT TO TOLERATE. BUT FENIANS AND FRONTIERSMEN WERE MARCHING NORTH AND BEHIND THEM WAS THE STRONGEST MILITARY POWER ON EARTH. MR. PRESIDENT, THIS CONTINENT IS OURS."

While all of this fraternal schism was going on, Louis Riel was only twenty-five-years-old, but he stood his ground. He ordered the American flag lowered over Fort Garry and shut down the American newspaper. And when the advanced military party crossed the border south of Winnipeg, they were met by Riel's General, Ambrose LePine, with 200 well-armed Metis horsemen, who arrested, disarmed, and escorted the Americans back across the border. For his role in saving two-thirds of the entire land mass of present-day Canada, Louis Riel later met his Masonic reward on a scaffold in a miserable Regina jail. His body was shipped in the same manner as U.S. President Lincoln's assassin, in a box car on a midnight freight train out of Regina to Winnipeg where he was buried and where he rests today.

Not too many Canadians nowadays fully realize as to how much hatred and animosity actually existed in those days because of what Sir John A. was trying to achieve by his proposed concept of Confederation and the schism that it created between Freemasons themselves. The schism, in fact was the direct result of two political assassinations; one here in Canada (D'Arcy McGee) and the other in the United States (Abraham Lincoln). For example, in April of 1865, John Wilkes Booth made his way into Ford's Theater where the American President had been watching a play, ironically called "Our American Cousin." At approximately 10:20 P.M. raising his high-caliber derringer, Booth placed the muzzle close to U.S. President Lincoln's head, pulled the trigger and quickly exited the building. With the execution-style assassination, the victim's head fell forward and then sideways as he slumped in his chair, Lincoln died on April 15TH. Many days later, when Booth was eventually captured, then shot and killed, U.S. secret service agents interestingly found a draft Canadian bank note in the amount of three-hundred dollars. It was later discovered that Booth had been in Montreal not long before the assassination of the American President. In some circles, it is believed that John Wilkes Booth was an active member of a secret fraternity that had a mandate of protecting their ideals to the extreme and exterminating those who stood in its path, otherwise known historically as the Carbonari hit squad of the Ancient Craft of Freemasonry.

In a viscous attempt to hide the true details of history, the vast majority of North America's historians wish us to believe that the only reason as to why the U.S. President was assassinated consisted largely due to his intentions of eliminating slavery in the United

States. That in itself only played a very small role in Lincoln's assassination as there were many other factors involved that over the many years since his death, historians have managed to delete the existence of Freemasonry schismatic activity as being behind the initial American conspiracy plot to eliminate their own President. To begin with, if the American Civil War was initially about freeing the slaves as to what historians have been telling us for nearly 150 years now, then, why is it that following January 1st, 1863, not long after Lincoln signed his name to the **EMANCIPATION PROCLAMATION** document designed to free slaves — an all out mutiny erupted within his Union Army??? Men from within Lincoln's own military forces who had originally enlisted to help save the Union from a Confederate take-over were reportedly having their doubts about remaining in combat and **"swore that they would not stand up and fight just to free niggers and make them their social equal."** Apparently, thousands upon thousands of soldiers then deserted and even fewer refused to enlist as recruiting fell off everywhere. The American people to whom Lincoln was once seen as a living icon soon started to evaporate as many of them became disgusted with him for changing the original cause of their just war which consisted primarily of Freemasonry corruption from within the American Federal Government itself and then without warning, the dynamics of the Civil War was changed into something that it wasn't.

While Lincoln was President of the United States, four slave States had remained with the North, (Delaware, Maryland, Missouri and Kentucky). They were classified as the border States separating the North and the South. Lincoln apparently feared that if he had originally come down with a firm hand on slavery, the conflict would have driven them to join the Confederacy thus strengthening the South. But as the months passed and public opinion was being dictated by the newspapers, the American President reportedly turned to his comrades asking: **"If slavery isn't wrong, nothing is wrong, and I have never felt more certain in my life that I was doing right. "**The American President, then signed his name to the document that instantly gave freedom to three and a half million slaves of the North. Throughout the land, the American President was being denounced by just about everyone. To most of the U.S. population all of Lincoln's policies had failed miserably and they wanted the insane butchery of the soldiers stopped at any cost. And at any cost, they, the people, apparently did not mean by the

FREEING OF THE SLAVES AS TO WHAT HISTORIANS HAVE BEEN SAYING SINCE THE AMERICAN CIVIL WAR BECAME NOTHING MORE THAN FOLKLORE AND/ OR LEGEND.

ORIGINALLY, THE CIVIL WAR WAS ABOUT GOVERNMENTAL CORRUPTION FROM WITHIN LINCOLN'S OWN FEDERAL GOVERNMENT, IT WAS A WAR BETWEEN OPPOSING FREEMASONRY VIEWS; SCHISM. AS THE U.S. PRESIDENT'S POPULARITY WITH THE PEOPLE WAS REACHING AN ALL TIME LOW, OPPOSING FORCES FROM WITHIN HIS OWN REPUBLICAN PARTY SOUGHT TO HAVE HIM REMOVED FROM THE WHITE HOUSE AS THEIR COMMANDER-IN-CHIEF. ONLY MONTHS AFTER SIGNING HIS NAME TO THE DOCUMENT TO FREE THE SLAVES, A SENATE REVOLT ENSUED AND THEY HAULED HIM IN ON THE CARPET DEMANDING THAT EITHER HIS POLICIES HAD TO CHANGE /OR HE AND HIS ENTIRE CABINET HAD TO VACATE THE PRESIDENTIAL PALACE. THIS, BEING A HUMILIATING BLOW TO THE PRESIDENT OF THE UNITED STATES WAS SAID TO HAVE BEEN TOTALLY DUMBFOUNDED WHILE HE STOOD THERE BEING RAKED OVER THE COALS BY HIS OWN FRATERNITY BRETHREN, LINCOLN SWORE TO MEND HIS EVIL WAYS AND VOWED NOT TO ROAM OFF THE BEATEN PATH ANY FURTHER. ABE'S COLLEAGUES WERE SAID TO HAVE REGRETTED THE FACT THAT THEY HAD NOMINATED HIM FOR THE PRESIDENCY AS THEY NOW WANTED HIS HEAD ON A SILVER PLATTER, HE HAD BETRAYED THEM.

JUST TO GIVE AN EXAMPLE AS TO HOW FAR APART THE UNITED STATES PRESIDENT AND HIS FELLOW FRATERNITY BRETHREN ACTUALLY WERE, IN FEBRUARY OF 1865, WHILE THE CONFEDERACY WAS ALREADY CRUMBLING INTO PIECES, AND GENERAL ROBERT E. LEE'S SURRENDER WAS STILL ONLY A FEW MONTHS AWAY, LINCOLN PROPOSED THAT THE U.S. FEDERAL GOVERNMENT PAY THE SOUTHERN STATES $400,000,000.00 FOR THEIR BLACK SLAVES. UNBEKNOWNST TO THE AMERICAN PRESIDENT, EVERY MEMBER OF HIS CABINET DID NOT LIKE THE IDEA OF DISHING OUT SUCH A LARGE SUM OF MONEY JUST TO HELP FREE THE SLAVES. ONCE LINCOLN REALIZED THIS, HE REPORTEDLY DROPPED THE WHOLE ISSUE AND NEVER BROUGHT IT UP EVER AGAIN. BY THIS TIME PERIOD OF COURSE, MORE SOLDIERS HAD BEEN FOUND TO REPLACE THOSE WHO HAD DESERTED. THE RECRUITMENT OF ADDITIONAL TROOPS WAS ACHIEVED BY FIRST OFFERING MORE MONEY TO THOSE WHO HAD ORIGINALLY REFUSED TO TAKE UP ARMS JUST TO HELP **"FREE NIGGERS "**AND IF THAT FAILED, PROMISES OF NO COURT MARTIAL FOR DESERTION SOON CLINCHED THE DEAL. FURTHER TO ALL OF THIS HAVING TRANSPIRED, MONTHS PREVIOUSLY (SUMMER OF 1864) AS THE FRATERNITY WHEELS WERE PUT IN MOTION WITH THE FEDERAL ELECTIONS ALREADY IN THE WORKS, THE AMERICAN PRESIDENT WAS SAID TO BE THAT OF A COMPLETELY CHANGED MAN; IN MIND, IN BODY AS WELL AS IN HIS POLITICAL POLICIES.

Contrary as to what American historians may wish us to believe is true, one only has to read Lincoln's first inaugural address (March 4TH, 1861) where he is quoted in saying the following: *"I have no purpose, directly or indirectly, to interfere with the institution of slavery in the United States where it now exists. I believe I have no lawful right to do so, and I have no inclination to do so* "And not long after taking office, a delegation of Chicago's moral majority ministers reportedly showed up at the White House urging Lincoln to free the slaves as it was said to be God's will. The U.S. President then informed the group that if the Almighty God wanted the slaves freed, then, the supreme deity had better come directly to the White House in person instead of dispatching the message through a third party by way of Chicago. It goes without saying that the religious zealots were not at all impressed with their new President-elect.

Then of course there's the well documented paper trail that occurred between U.S. President Abraham Lincoln and Horace Greeley, an American journalist who was adding political pressure to try and convince him into making the Civil War something that it wasn't. Greeley reportedly used his printing press influences to not only attempt to sway public opinion but Lincoln's policies as well. It was in Greeley's opinion that slavery was wrong and he publically stated it so, time and time again in his newspaper columns. While the American Civil War was reaching its thirteenth month, Greeley began his vicious attack on Lincoln's inability to do the most humane act of kindness by freeing the slaves as the war dragged on. The attacks on the U.S. President was a continual bombardment of Lincoln's policies being indecisive and inept for the times. The most notable of Horace Greeley's attacks interestingly enough came in an article that was so affectionately entitled **"THE PRAYER OF TWENTY MILLIONS** "referring to the estimated twenty-million Black slaves that were said to be keeping the American economy afloat while the American States fought it out on the battle fields, (August 20TH, 1862). Only a few days had passed when the U.S. President decided to answer Greeley's New York Tribune newspaper article in the form of an unconditional rebuttal which in essence became one of the most well publicized classics of wartime literature - clear, terse, and vigorous, which over the last few centuries just seemed to disappear off the face of the earth as historians twisted and bent the facts to suit their own hidden agenda. At the close of Lincoln's reply to Greeley's comments, these most memorable words can be found:

"My paramount object in this struggle to save the Union, and is not either to save or destroy slavery. If I could save the Union without freeing any slave, I would do it; and if I could save it by freeing all the slaves, I would do it; and if I could save it by freeing some and leaving others alone, I would also do that. What I do about slavery and the colored race, I do because I believe it helps to save the Union; and what I forbear, because I do not believe it would help to save the Union. I shall do less whenever I shall believe what I am doing hurts the cause, and I shall do more whenever I shall believe doing more will help the cause. I shall try to correct errors when shown to be errors, and I shall adopt new views so fast as they shall appear to be true views.

I have here stated my purpose according to my view of official duty; and I intend no modification of my oft-expressed personal wish that all men everywhere could be free."

Apparently, Abraham Lincoln had a firm belief that if he was able to save the Union, he would also be able to prevent slavery from spreading even further thus allowing it to die a natural death in the process. But on the other hand, if the Union was to be totally annulated, it didn't really matter in the end as in all likelihood it would have perished centuries later anyways. Great logic there Mr. President!!!

But after caving into the much added political pressure bestowed onto him by Greeley and the printing press, Lincoln began having second thoughts as to why things should continue exactly as they were as an election year was fast approaching. Hoping to save his political career, the American President signed his name to the Emancipation Proclamation and hoped for the best. Within only months of his signing the document that now officially converted the Civil War from being one of corruption within the Federal Government to one of freeing the slaves, a group of Virginia Freemasons who just happened to be slave barons, financially funded a secret fraternity whose main objective was to assassinate the U.S. President. And in December of 1864, an advertisement reportedly was placed in a Selma, Alabama newspaper asking the general public to help fund the cause to terminate Lincoln's Presidency by way of an assassination for his deeds of betrayal. As his popularity plummeted, the U.S. President soon became worrisome as all prospects of his being re-elected looked bleak. After the American public went to

THE POLLS TO CAST THEIR VOTES, THE BALLOTS WERE COUNTED. LINCOLN WAS RETURNED TO THE OFFICE AS PRESIDENT BY THE SKIN OF HIS TEETH (200,000 VOTES). DESPITE THIS, SOME AMERICAN CITIZENS VIEWED IT AS BEING NOTING BUT A WELL RIGGED ELECTION CAMPAIGN. WITH NEWFOUND HOPE FOR THE FUTURE, AMERICAN HISTORIANS DEEMED THE CIVIL WAR A VICTORY ON APRIL 9TH, 1865 AND PROCLAIMED IT AS BEING A WAR TO FREE ALL SLAVES. LESS THAN A WEEK LATER, THE NEWLY RE-ELECTED AMERICAN PRESIDENT FELL PREY TO AN ASSASSIN'S BULLET. COINCIDENTLY, THROUGHOUT LINCOLN'S FIRST TERM AS PRESIDENT OF THE UNITED STATES, MANY FREEMASONRY BRETHREN HELD HIGH PROFILE POSTINGS IN HIS FEDERAL GOVERNMENT; WILLIAM H. SEWARD WAS HIS SECRETARY OF STATE WHILE ANDREW JACKSON TOOK OVER THE REIGNS OF POWER AFTER LINCOLN'S DEATH. FRATERNITY BROTHER JACKSON NEVER APPOINTED A VICE-PRESIDENT — IN FACT, THE VICE-PRESIDENTIAL OFFICE REMAINED EMPTY THROUGHOUT JACKSON'S FRATERNAL TERM IN OFFICE AND BROTHER SEWARD MAINTAINED HIS PORTFOLIO AS SECRETARY OF STATE.

FURTHERMORE, ONLY A FEW HOURS BEFORE THE AMERICAN PRESIDENT WAS ASSASSINATED AT FORD'S THEATER, LINCOLN APPARENTLY ATTENDED A CABINET MEETING IN WHICH HE HAD STATED THE FOLLOWING TO HIS COLLEAGUES: "ENOUGH LIVES HAVE BEEN SACRIFICED. WE MUST EXTINGUISH OUR RESENTMENTS IF WE EXPECT HARMONY AND UNION. "ABE'S PARADOX WAS WHOLEHEARTEDLY APPLAUDED BY HIS SECRETARY OF STATE, WILLIAM H. SEWARD. AT THE SAME TIME THAT LINCOLN LAY DYING ON THE THEATER FLOOR, SECRETARY SEWARD WAS STABBED WHILE IN BED, AND WAS REPORTEDLY NOT EXPECTED TO LIVE. RUMORS SOON SPREAD LIKE A GROWING CANCER, PEOPLE WERE SURE THAT THE CONFEDERATES HAD CREPT INTO THE CAPITAL AND BEGAN TO WIPE OUT THE GOVERNMENT OFFICIALS WITH ONE SWIFT BLOW. MYSTERIOUS MESSENGERS WERE REPORTED TO BE DASHING THROUGH THE RESIDENTIAL DISTRICTS SENDING MORSE CODES, "STRIKING THE PAVEMENT TWO SHORT STACCATO RAPS, THRICE REPEATED, "AS IT WAS SAID TO BE THE DANGER CRY OF A SECRET FRATERNITY; THE UNION LEAGUE. UPON HEARING THE RAPPING SOUNDS, MEMBERS OF THE ANCIENT CRAFT AROSE FROM THEIR BEDS, "GRASPING THEIR RIFLES AND RUSHED WILDLY INTO THE STREETS. "ANGRY LYNCH MOBS SOON CONGREGATED HOLDING TORCHES DEMANDING IMMEDIATE ACTION: "BURN THE THEATER!"... "HANG THE TRAITOR!"... "KILL THE REBELS!" IT WAS A NIGHT OF ABSOLUTE AND COMPLETE MADNESS!!!

WHILE THE MOBS GATHERED IN THE STREETS, VICE-PRESIDENT ANDREW JACKSON WAS REPORTEDLY SAID TO HAVE BEEN "SPRAWLED ON HIS BED STONE-DRUNK "AND "HIS HAIR MATTED WITH MUD. "AT THE TIME MOST OF THE REPUBLICANS IN LINCOLN'S CABINET CONSIDERED JACKSON TO BE AN EXTREME LEFT RADICAL, A SOUTHERN SYMPATHIZER AS WELL AS AN ACTIVE MEMBER OF THE UNION LEAGUE. WITH NO ONE ABLE TO TAKE CONTROL OF

THE MADNESS THAT FOLLOWED LINCOLN'S EXECUTION-STYLE SHOOTING, THE REIGNS OF POWER WERE INSTANTLY GRASPED BY ABE'S SECRETARY OF WAR, EDWARD M. STANTON. ALL THE FORCES WERE CALLED IN; THE U.S. SECRET SERVICE, SPIES ASSOCIATED WITH THE BUREAU OF MILITARY JUSTICE, MILITARY SOLDIERS, WASHINGTON D.C.'S POLICE FORCE, AND CIVILIAN MILITIA MEMBERS. STANTON'S DRAGNET PATROLLED THE AREAS OF THE CITY, HE ORDERED EVERYONE CONNECTED WITH THE FORD'S THEATER UNDER ARREST PENDING AN IMMEDIATE INVESTIGATION. THE ENTIRE CITY HAD PICKETS WRAPPED AROUND IT, THE AMERICAN CAPITAL WAS UNDER A STATE OF SIEGE. THE SEARCH FOR LINCOLN'S PAID ASSASSIN WAS NOW ON, ABE LINCOLN DIED AT A LITTLE AFTER TWENTY PAST SEVEN THE NEXT MORNING, SATURDAY, APRIL 15TH, (7:22 A.M.).

THE DRAGNET WAS LOOKING FOR ONE SUSPECT, A FAILED ACTOR BY THE NAME OF JOHN WILKES BOOTH. "THE INSTANT THAT BOOTH FIRED AT LINCOLN, MAJOR RATHBONE "WHOM WAS SITTING IN THE PRESIDENTIAL BOX WITH ABE, "LEAPED UP AND GRABBED THE ASSASSIN. "BOOTH SLASHED AT HIM WITH A BOWIE-KNIFE, "CUTTING DEEP GASHES IN THE MAJOR'S ARM." THE MAJOR COULDN'T HOLD ONTO THE ASSAILANT, BOOTH SPRANG OVER THE RAILING OF THE BOX AND LEAPED TO THE STAGE FLOOR, TWELVE FEET BELOW. AS HE JUMPED, BOOTH CAUGHT HIS SPUR IN THE FOLDS OF THE AMERICAN UNION FLAG THAT DRAPED OVER THE PRESIDENT'S BOX, HE "FELL AWKWARDLY, AND BROKE THE SMALL BONE IN HIS LEG. "HOBBLING ACROSS THE STAGE IN EXCRUCIATING PAIN, SHOUTING "SIC SEMPER TYRANNIS "THE MOTTO OF THE STATE OF VIRGINIA MEANING; **THUS EVER TO TYRANTS**, BOOTH STABBED A MUSICIAN WHO ACCIDENTLY STEPPED INTO HIS PATH AND KNOCKED AN ACTRESS TO THE FLOOR AS HE DASHED OUT THE BACK STAGE DOOR AND MOUNTED A WAITING HORSE.

LATER THAT NIGHT, BOOTH MET A FELLOW COMRADE (DAVY HEROLD) AT THEIR DESIGNATED RENDEZVOUS POINT, AND THE TWO RACED ONWARD TO VIRGINIA ON HORSEBACK. BY MIDNIGHT, THEY DECIDED TO HAVE A PIT STOP AT A FRIENDLY WATERING HOLE IN SURRATTVILLE. AFTER DRINKING "A DOLLAR'S WORTH OF WHISKY; THEN, BOASTING THAT THEY HAD SHOT LINCOLN," THEY MOUNTED THEIR HORSES AND "SPURRED ON INTO THE DARKNESS. "JUST BEFORE DAYBREAK (SATURDAY MORNING) THE TWO DESPERADOS "REINED UP IN FRONT OF THE HOUSE OF A COUNTRY PHYSICIAN "THAT WENT BY THE NAME OF MUDD, DOCTOR SAMUEL MUDD. THE GOOD DOCTOR LIVED TWENTY MILES SOUTHEAST OF THE CAPITAL CITY, THERE WERE NO TELEGRAPH LINES NOR ANY RAILWAY SYSTEM IN THIS REMOTE DISTRICT, NO ONE KNEW OF LINCOLN'S ASSASSINATION. DOCTOR MUDD ATTENDED TO BOOTH'S BROKEN LEG, AS WOULD ANY PHYSICIAN. BOOTH AND HEROLD SLEPT ALL THAT DAY AT DOCTOR MUDD'S HOUSE, BUT AS DARKNESS DREW NEAR, THEY URGED TO

ROAM. BOOTH SHAVED OFF HIS MUSTACHE AND DISGUISED HIMSELF WITH "A SET OF FALSE WHISKERS, "PAID THE DOCTOR $ 25.00 FOR HIS SERVICES, THEN, HE AND HIS FELLOW ASSASSIN MOUNTED THEIR HORSES AND ROAD OFF. THAT WAS THE FIRST AND LAST TIME THE GOOD DOCTOR HAD EVER SEEN JOHN WILKES BOOTH.

NINE DAYS LATER, AT 3:30 A.M. APRIL 25TH, YANKEE TROOPERS ARRIVED IN FRONT OF A FARMHOUSE IN VIRGINIA LOOKING FOR THE TWO CONSPIRATORS. THE TROOPS QUICKLY SURROUNDED THE HOUSE, GUNS WERE POINTED AT EVERY WINDOW AND DOOR. A LIEUTENANT BAKER BANGED THE BUTT OF HIS PISTOL ON THE PORCH, THE OWNER OF THE FARM, RICHARD GARRETT AROSE FROM HIS BED, CANDLE IN HAND AND UNBOLTED THE DOOR. BAKER DEMANDED THAT GARRETT "HAND OVER BOOTH, "AS HE REPORTEDLY GRABBED THE FARMER BY THE THROAT AND POINTED A PISTOL AT HIS HEAD. BAKER AND HIS TROOPS HAD BEEN IN HOT PURSUIT OF BOOTH AND HEROLD AFTER PICKING UP CLUES A COUPLE OF DAYS BEFOREHAND OF THEIR WHEREABOUTS. AS BAKER COCKED HIS PISTOL, THE OLD MAN TREMBLED IN FEAR, GARRETT "SWORE THAT THE STRANGERS WERE NOT IN THE HOUSE, "HE TOLD BAKER THAT THEY WERE IN THE WOODS. KNOWING THAT IT WAS A LIE, "THE TROOPERS JERKED HIM OUT OF THE DOORWAY, DANGLED A ROPE IN HIS FACE, AND THREATENED TO STRING HIM UP AT ONCE TO A LOCUST TREE IN THE YARD. "THAT'S WHEN ONE OF GARRETT'S SONS AWOKE FROM HIS SLEEP AND TOLD THE TROOPERS THAT THE TWO MEN WERE IN THE TOBACCO BARN. THE YANKS THEN RUSHED TOWARDS THE BARN AND SURROUNDED IT. "FOR FIFTEEN OR TWENTY MINUTES THE NORTHERN OFFICERS ARGUED WITH BOOTH "DEMANDING HIS SURRENDER. BOOTH APPARENTLY SHOUTED BACK THAT HE WAS A CRIPPLE AND ASKED THEM TO "GIVE A LAME MAN A SHOW "OFFERING TO EMERGE FROM THE BARN FIGHTING WITH GUNS BLAZING. DAVEY HEROLD ON THE OTHER HAND WANTED TO SURRENDER, BOOTH THEN BECAME TOTALLY DISGUSTED WITH HIS CO-CONSPIRATOR, "YOU DAMN COWARD, "HE SHOUTED, "GET OUT OF HERE. I DON'T WANT YOU TO STAY. "HEROLD DASHED OUT OF THE BARN WITH HIS HANDS IN FRONT OF HIM PLEADING FOR MERCY. AS HE CONTINUED WITH HIS CRY FOR MERCY, HEROLD SWORE THAT HE HAD NOTHING TO DO WITH LINCOLN'S ASSASSINATION, IN FACT, HE STATED THAT HE "LIKED MR. LINCOLN'S JOKES. "DAVY HEROLD WAS THEN TIED TO A TREE, COLONEL CONGER "THREATENED TO GAG HIM UNLESS HE CEASED HIS SILLY WHIMPERING."

WITH BOOTH REFUSING TO SURRENDER, THE STAGE WAS NOW SET FOR HIS CAPTURE. WHEN ASKED ONCE AGAIN TO COME OUT PEACEFULLY, HE IMMEDIATELY SHOUTED BACK THAT "SURRENDER "WAS NOT A WORD RECOGNIZED IN HIS VOCABULARY. HE FURTHER INFORMED THEM THAT THEY HAD BETTER PREPARE A STRETCHER FOR HIM AS A MARK OF "ONE MORE STAIN ON THE GLORIOUS OLD BANNER. "CONGER ORDERED ONE OF GARRETT'S BOYS

TO PILE DRY BRUSH AGAINST THE BARN IN AN ATTEMPT TO SMOKE HIM OUT. BOOTH REALIZED WHAT WAS GOING ON, AND HE THEN WHISPERED THROUGH THE CRACKS OF THE BARN TELLING THE BOY THAT HE WOULD SHOOT HIM DEAD RIGHT THERE ON THE SPOT IF HE CONTINUED DOING SO — THE BOY DID STOP, BUT IT WAS FAR TOO LATE, COLONEL CONGER "PULLED A WISP OF HAY THROUGH A CRACK AND LIGHT IT WITH A MATCH. "THE GARRETT BARN WAS ORIGINALLY BUILT FOR TOBACCO, "WITH SPACINGS FOUR INCHES WIDE LEFT TO LET IN THE AIR. "IT WAS THROUGH THESE CRACKS THAT THE UNION SOLDIERS "SAW BOOTH PICK UP A TABLE TO FIGHT THE MOUNTING FIRE."

THE TROOPERS HAD STRICT ORDERS TO TAKE BOOTH ALIVE, THE FEDERAL GOVERNMENT DIDN'T WANT HIM DEAD: "IT WANTED TO HAVE A BIG TRIAL AND THEN HANG HIM. "LIKE LOUIS RIEL, BOOTH WAS CONDEMNED TO DIE LONG BEFORE HIS TRIAL. IF IT WASN'T FOR THE FACT THAT "A HALF-CRACKED SERGEANT - ' BOSTON ' CORBETT, A RELIGIOUS FANATIC "JOHN WILKES BOOTH WOULD HAVE BEEN ABLE TO STAND TRIAL. EACH AND EVERY TROOPER "HAD BEEN WARNED REPEATEDLY NOT TO SHOOT WITHOUT ORDERS. "WITH THE BARN IN FLAMES, CORBETT WAS SAID TO HAVE SEEN "BOOTH THROW AWAY HIS CRUTCH, DROP HIS CARBINE, RAISE HIS REVOLVER, AND SPRING FOR THE DOOR." THE RELIGIOUS ZEALOT WAS POSITIVE THAT BOOTH WAS GOING TO SHOOT HIS WAY OUT AND "MAKE A LAST, DESPERATE DASH FOR LIBERTY, FIRING AS HE RAN. "CORBETT INSISTED THAT HE HAD A VISION FROM GOD ALMIGHTY INSTRUCTING HIM TO SHOOT BOOTH IN AN ATTEMPT TO PREVENT FURTHER DESTRUCTION. ACTING AS JUDGE, JURY AND EXECUTIONER, "CORBETT STEPPED FORWARD, RESTED HIS PISTOL ACROSS HIS ARM, TOOK AIM THROUGH THE CRACK, PRAYED FOR BOOTH'S SOUL, AND PULLED THE TRIGGER."

BOOTH WAS FATALLY WOUNDED AS HE LAY FACE DOWN IN THE HAY — ROARING FLAMES MOVED RAPIDLY ACROSS THE BARN, BAKER WAS EAGER TO HAUL THE DYING MAN OUT OF THE PATH OF THE FLAMES. HE RUSHED INTO THE BURNING BUILDING AND LEAPED UPON THE WOUNDED ASSASSIN, WRENCHING THE REVOLVER FROM HIS CLINCHED FIST. BOOTH WAS QUICKLY CARRIED TO THE FARMHOUSE PORCH. A SOLDIER WAS ORDER TO MOUNT HIS HORSE AND FETCH A DOCTOR THAT LIVED THREE MILES DOWN THE ROAD AT PORT ROYAL. AS BOOTH LAY THERE ON THE PORCH FLOOR, UNABLE TO SPEAK, (HIS THROAT SEEMED TO BE PARALYZED AND HE COULDN'T SWALLOW). HIS LIPS WERE MOISTENED BY MRS. GARRETT'S SISTER "MISS HALLOWAY "WHO WAS BOARDING AT THE FARMHOUSE. MISS HALLOWAY WAS SAID TO HAVE CONSIDERED BOOTH TO BE A ROMANTIC ACTOR AS WELL AS A GREAT LOVER. SHE SAID, "HE MUST BE CARED FOR TENDERLY, "AND HAD A MATTRESS HAULED ONTO THE PORCH FOR HIM TO LIE UPON AND EVEN BROUGHT OUT ONE OF HER OWN PILLOWS, "PUT IT UNDER HIS HEAD, "TOOK HER HANDKERCHIEF DIPPED IT IN WATER AND BEGAN MOISTENING HIS LIPS. IT SEEMED TO BE A SCRIPT

WRITTEN BY A GROUP OF HOLLYWOOD MOVIE PRODUCERS AS IT HAD ALL OF THE ELEMENTS OF A GREAT BOX OFFICE HIT. SHE REPORTEDLY PAMPERED BOOTH FOR TWO AND A HALF HOURS AS HE STRUGGLED WITH DEATH. BOOTH EVEN URGED COLONEL CONGER TO PRESS FIRMLY DOWN ON HIS THROAT AS HE CRIED OUT IN AGONY: "KILL ME! KILL ME! "AS THE YOUNG ACTOR PLEADED WITH THE COLONEL HE HAD ONE LAST REQUEST, BOOTH WANTED TO SEND A MESSAGE TO HIS MOTHER: "TELL HER ... I DID ... WHAT I THOUGHT ... WAS BEST ... AND THAT I DIED ... FOR MY COUNTRY."

AS THE FINAL CURTAIN CALL DREW NEAR, BOOTH ASKED TO HAVE HIS HANDS RAISED SO THAT HE COULD SEE THEM. THEY WERE TOTALLY PARALYZED, HE MUTTERED, "USELESS! USELESS! "THOSE WERE SAID TO BE HIS LAST WORDS, HE DIED JUST AS THE SUN SHONE BRIGHT OVER THE LOCUST TREES IN GARRETT'S YARD. BOOTH'S "JAW DREW SPASMODICALLY AND OBLIQUELY DOWNWARD, HIS EYEBALLS ROLLED TOWARD HIS FEET AND BEGAN TO SWELL ... AND WITH A SORT OF GURGLE, AND SUDDEN CHECK, HE STRETCHED HIS FEET AND THREW BACK HIS HEAD. "IT WAS EXACTLY 7:00 A.M. (APRIL 26TH), "HE DIED WITHIN TWENTY-TWO MINUTES OF THE TIME OF DAY LINCOLN HAD DIED. "CORBETT'S "BULLET HAD STRUCK BOOTH IN THE BACK OF THE HEAD, JUST AN INCH BELOW THE SPOT WHERE HE HIMSELF "HAD SHOT ABE LINCOLN. THE ATTENDING DOCTOR, "CUT OFF A CURL OF BOOTH'S HAIR, AND GAVE IT TO MISS HALLOWAY. "SHE ALSO KEPT THE BLOOD STAINED PILLOW-SLIP ON WHICH BOOTH LAID HIS HEAD.

BOOTH HAD HARDLY STOPPED BREATHING BEFORE DETECTIVES WERE KNEELING TO SEARCH HIS BODY FOR FURTHER INCRIMINATING EVIDENCE. ON HIS PERSON, THEY REPORTEDLY FOUND A PIPE, A BOWIE-KNIFE, A DAIRY, TWO REVOLVERS, A COMPASS GREASED WITH CANDLE WAX, A DIAMOND PIN, A NAIL FILE, PHOTOGRAPHS OF FIVE GORGEOUS WOMEN WHO WERE SAID TO HAD WORSHIPED THE GROUND THAT HE WALKED ON: "FOUR WERE ACTRESSES: EFFIE GERMON, ALICE GREY, HELEN WESTERN AND ' PRETTY FAY BROWN'." ODDLY ENOUGH, THE FIFTH WOMAN APPARENTLY WAS THE DAUGHTER OF ONE OF WASHINGTON D.C.'S MOST WELL RESPECTED FAMILIES, WHOSE NAME THE U.S. SECRET SERVICE REFUSED TO DISCLOSE SUPPOSEDLY "OUT OF RESPECT FOR HER DESCENDANTS. "BUT THE MOST IMPORTANT ITEM THE DETECTIVES DISCOVERED IN ONE OF BOOTH'S POCKETS, CONSISTED OF A BANK NOTE DRAFT FROM A CANADIAN BANK IN THE AMOUNT OF ABOUT THREE-HUNDRED DOLLARS. THIS IN ITSELF RAISED MANY QUESTIONS FOR THE U.S. SECRET SERVICE, QUESTIONS SUCH AS WHAT THE HELL BOOTH WAS DOING WITH A CANADIAN BANK NOTE??? DID THIS MEAN THAT THERE WAS A CANADIAN CONNECTION IN THE CONSPIRACY TO ASSASSINATE THE AMERICAN PRESIDENT??? WAS THE CORRUPT TORY ADMINISTRATION OF SIR JOHN A. MACDONALD INVOLVED IN THE AMERICAN DILEMMA??? NEEDLESS TO SAY, THE ANSWERS TO THESE AND

MANY OTHER QUESTIONS ARE LOST FOREVER IN THE UNTOLD PAGES OF HISTORY. TO SOME WHO ARE HISTORY BUFFS, THE MERE FACT THAT LIEUTENANT BAKER HAD A COUSIN OF WHOM WAS CLOSELY CONNECTED WITH THE U.S. SECRET SERVICE AS WELL AS TO THE SECRETARY OF WAR, SENDS SHIVERS DOWN THEIR SPINS. ESPECIALLY, AS TO WHAT UNFOLDED AFTER BOOTH'S INITIAL DEATH!!!

AS THE NEWS TRAVELED OF BOOTH'S DEATH AND HIS BODY WAS BEING TRANSPORTED FIRST BY MIDNIGHT EXPRESS, THEN, BY GUNBOAT TO THE CAPITAL, THE CHIEF OF THE U.S. SECRET SERVICE, COLONEL BAKER RUSHED TO THE SECRETARY OF WAR WITH THE INFORMATION THAT HE HAD LEARNED. BAKER FURTHER INFORMED STANTON THAT A WOMAN HAD A LOCK OF BOOTH'S HAIR. WAR SECRETARIAT EDWARD M. STANTON WAS SOMEWHAT SHOCKED AT HEARING THE NEWS OF BOOTH'S HAIR BECOMING A COLLECTOR'S ITEM AND FEARED THAT HE WOULD BE MADE AN INSTANT MARTYR: "EVERYONE OF BOOTH'S HAIRS, "HE CRIED "WILL BE CHERISHED AS A RELIC BY THE REBELS. "STANTON FIRMLY BELIEVED THAT "THE ASSASSINATION OF LINCOLN WAS A SINISTER PLOT CONCEIVED "AND EXECUTED BY THE CONFEDERACY, HE WAS SAID TO HAVE FEARED THAT THEY WOULD ATTEMPT TO CAPTURE BOOTH'S BODY AND USE IT AS A CRUSADE TO FUEL THE FIRE OF THE SLAVERY ISSUE. HE, THEN, ORDERED BOOTH'S BODY TO BE DISPOSED OF, IT WAS TO BE A SECRET RITUALISTIC BURIAL, NO MOURNERS, NO FLOWERS, AND MOST IMPORTANTLY, NO TEARS. STANTON ISSUED HIS ORDERS TO HIS MOST TRUST WORTHY MEN, AND THAT SAME EVENING, COLONEL BAKER AND HIS COUSIN LIEUTENANT LA FAYETTE C. BAKER EXECUTED STANTON'S ORDERS. THEY TRANSPORTED BOOTH'S BODY INCASED IN A PINE GUNBOX LOADED ABOARD A SKIFF AND DRIFTED DOWN THE POTOMAC RIVER.

AS THE TWO AMERICAN GOVERNMENTAL PUPPETS DRIFTED DOWNSTREAM, A CURIOUS CROWD GATHERED ON THE SHORE AND WATCHED THEM DRIFT FOR ABOUT TWO MILES. BY THE TIME TOTAL DARKNESS HAD FALLEN, THE SPOT WHERE BOOTH'S BODY WAS TO REST HAD BEEN FINALLY REACHED. HIS BODY WAS TO BE INCASED WITHIN THE SOLID MASONRY WALLS OF THE OLD PENITENTIARY THAT THE FEDERAL GOVERNMENT WAS USING FOR THEIR ARSENAL. JOHN WILKES BOOTH WAS BURIED IN A SHALLOW HOLE IN THE SOUTHWEST CORNER OF A LARGE ROOM IN WHICH THE GOVERNMENT STORED ITS AMMUNITION. BY THE NEXT MORNING "EXCITED MEN WITH GRAPPLING HOOKS WERE DRAGGING THE POTOMAC "LOOKING FOR BOOTH'S BODY. LITTLE DID THEY REALIZE THAT HE WAS BURIED ON DRY LAND AT GEESEBOROUGH POINT JUST AHEAD OF THEM BEHIND THE SWAMP IN THE OLD BURIAL-GROUNDS WHERE THE ARMY CAST ITS CONDEMNED HORSES AND DEAD MULES.

BOOTH'S FELLOW CONSPIRATORS, MINUS THE GROUP OF VIRGINIA FREEMASONS OF COURSE, WERE TRIED AND CONVICTED OF TREASON AGAINST THE GOVERNMENT OF THE UNITED STATES OF AMERICA, THEY WERE

PUNISHED BY DEATH /OR LIFE IMPRISONMENT FOR THEIR DIRTY DEEDS AGAINST THE POWERS THAT BE. DOCTOR SAMUEL MUDD WAS AMONG THOSE INCARCERATED FOR HIS SO-CALLED INVOLVEMENT WITH THE ASSASSINATION OF THE AMERICAN PRESIDENT, HE WAS SENTENCED TO LIFE BEHIND BARS WITH NO CHANCES OF PAROL. MUDD'S ONLY CRIME IN LINCOLN'S ASSASSINATION WAS MENDING BOOTH'S BROKEN LEFT LEG. MUDD'S WIFE BEGGED THE NEW AMERICAN PRESIDENT, ANDREW JACKSON TO FREE HER HUSBAND CITING THAT HE HAD NO PART OF BOOTH'S ASSASSINATION PLOT. AFTER A NUMBER OF YEARS, DOCTOR SAMUEL MUDD WAS RELEASED AND PARDONED BY THE PRESIDENT. APPARENTLY, MRS. MUDD HAD CIRCULATED A PETITION DEMANDING HIS IMMEDIATE RELEASE. THIS WAS A TIME PERIOD IN U.S. HISTORY WHEN MOST, IF NOT ALL THE AMERICAN FREEMASONS HAD LOTS OF POLITICAL CLOUT WITHIN THE JUDICIAL SYSTEM AND WERE PRETTY WELL ALLOWED TO DO AS THEY DAMN WELL PLEASED IF WENT UNCHALLENGED. FOR EXAMPLE, NOT VERY LONG AFTER LINCOLN'S ASSASSINATION BOOTH'S FAMILY AND FRIENDS WANTED HIS BODY EXHUMED FROM THE SITE AS TO WHERE THEY (THE GOVERNMENT OF THE UNITED STATES) HAD BURIED HIM BUT THE NEW AMERICAN PRESIDENT REFUSED TO DO SO. AFTER MUCH PRESSURE WAS ADDED THROUGHOUT HIS TERM, PRESIDENT ANDREW JACKSON ISSUED AN ORDER ON FEBRUARY 15TH, 1869 TO HAVE BOOTH'S BODY DUG UP SO THAT IT COULD BE TAKEN TO BALTIMORE AND REBURIED IN THE BOOTH FAMILY PLOT IN GREENMOUNT CEMETERY.

JUST TO GIVE ONE MORE EXAMPLE AS TO HOW MUCH POLITICAL CLOUT THE AMERICA FREEMASONS ACTUALLY HAD AT THAT TIME PERIOD OF U.S. HISTORY AND CONTINUED TO DO SO FOR MANY YEARS THEREAFTER — IN THE EARLY PARTS OF 1886, A FRENCHMAN NAMED ANTOINE-AMEDEE-MARIE-VINCENT MANCE DE VALLAMBROSA, (A.K.A. THE MARQUIS DE MORES) MADE HIS WAY FROM FRANCE TO THE DAKOTA BADLANDS AT THE AGE OF TWENTY-FIVE. UPON HIS ARRIVAL INTO THE UNITED STATES OF AMERICA VIA NEW YORK CITY, THE MARQUIS SCOUTED AROUND FOR A BRIDE WHO HAD ACCESS TO VAST FORTUNES AS HE HIMSELF WAS SAID TO HAVE SOMEWHAT LIMITED FINANCIAL RESOURCES. HE, THEN, MARRIED MEDORA VON HOFFMAN, THE DAUGHTER OF A RICH NEW YORK CITY BANKER AND IN THREE SHORT YEARS BUILT ONE OF THE MOST ELABORATE SHEEP AND CATTLE RANCHES THAT THE WESTERN UNITED STATES HAD EVER SEEN AT THAT TIME PERIOD. THE MARQUIS EVEN BUILT A TOWN, MEDORA IN HONOR OF HIS WIFE ON THE LITTLE MISSOURI RIVER, WHICH HAD INCORPORATED WITHIN ITS JURISDICTIONAL BOUNDARIES A TWENTY-SIX ROOM CHATEAU WITH A GIGANTIC FRENCH-ENGLISH-GERMAN LIBRARY AND TWENTY SERVANTS TO CATER TO THE WHIMS OF HIS LORDSHIP. FURTHER TO THIS, HE ERECTED AN EXPENSIVE SLAUGHTERHOUSE COSTING APPROXIMATELY $ 250,000.00 TO BUILD; A REFRIGERATOR-CAR COMPANY, WITH ICE PLANTS AT

TWELVE POINTS ALONG THE NORTHERN PACIFIC RAILROAD; A STRING OF STORES IN NEW YORK CITY TO SELL BEEF DIRECTLY FROM THE SLAUGHTERHOUSE; AND A 225 MILE STAGE COACH LINE CONNECTING THE NEWLY CONSTRUCTED TOWN OF MEDORA AND THE METROPOLIS OF DEADWOOD.

THE MARQUIS' FAST PACE LIFESTYLE BROUGHT HIM INTO CONTACT WITH MANY OF AMERICA'S RICH AND MOST POWERFUL FAMILIES LIVING AT THE TIME. BUT IT SEEMS THAT ONE OF THE MOST BAZAAR RELATIONSHIPS THAT THE MARQUIS HAD WAS THE ONE THAT HE HAD WITH HIS NEIGHBOR, THEODORE ROOSEVELT (THE SOON TO BE PRESIDENT OF THE UNITED STATES OF AMERICA). AS THE STORY GOES, THE MARQUIS WAS ALWAYS ARGUING WITH ROOSEVELT ABOUT SOMETHING /OR ANOTHER OVER RANGE PROBLEMS CONCERNING EITHER THE SHEEP /OR THE CATTLE. MORE THE SHEEP THAN ANYTHING ELSE AS THEY HAD A TENDENCY TO EAT THE GRASS RIGHT DOWN TO THE ROOTS AND THIS APPARENTLY ANNOYED THE HELL OUT OF THE PRESIDENT TO BE. ALTHOUGH THEY CONSTANTLY ARGUED BITTERLY, THE MARQUIS STILL MAINTAINED HIS FRIENDSHIP WITH ROOSEVELT AND QUITE OFTEN INVITED HIM OVER TO DINE AT THE CHATEAU. ITS SAFE TO SAY THAT THE MARQUIS KNEW SOMETHING ABOUT ROOSEVELT THAT MOST HISTORIANS WEREN'T WILLING TO TALK ABOUT. TO THE COMMON FOLK LIVING ON THE WESTERN PLAINS OF THE DAKOTA'S, THE CLUE WAS PROUDLY DISPLAYED BY TEDDY ROOSEVELT IN HIS MALTESE CROSS RANCH BUILDINGS THAT WERE CONSTRUCTED ON LANDS THAT DID NOT LEGALLY BELONG TO HIM. AT THE TIME, HOMESTEAD LAND GRANTS COMPRISING OF ONE-HUNDRED AND SIXTY ACRES WERE BEING ISSUED TO PERSONS WHO WANTED TO LAY A CLAIM AND SETTLE THE WEST. ROOSEVELT, BEING WHO HE WAS NOT ONLY NEGLECTED TO MAKE AN APPLICATION FOR THE LANDS CONCERNING HIS MALTESE CROSS RANCH BUT HE EVEN ACQUIRED MORE ILLEGAL LAND AND BUILD THE ELKHORN RANCH UP FROM SCRATCH. BOTH OF ROOSEVELT'S SEIGNIORIES WERE OBTAINED THROUGH ILLEGAL MEANS AND FALSE PRETENSES. THE SOON TO BE PRESIDENT OF THE UNITED STATES DIDN'T REALLY GIVE A DAMN AS IT WAS ONLY LANDS THAT WERE ONCE OCCUPIED BY THE INDIANS ANYWAYS AND AS FAR AS HE WAS CONCERNED, THEY (THE INDIANS) DIDN'T BELONG IN HIS FRATERNAL PLANS OF "MANIFEST DESTINY".

AS THE ROOSEVELT DYNASTY FLOURISHED, THE MARQUIS DE MORES WAS FORCED TO ACCEPT FAILURE AS EACH AND EVERY ONE OF HIS ENTERPRISES FELL PREY TO THE UNSCRUPULOUS TACTICS TEDDY AND HIS FRATERNITY CRONIES. IN 1889, THE MARQUIS LEFT THE UNITED STATES LEAVING ALL OF HIS BUSINESS VENTURES IN THE CARE OF OTHERS AS HE HEADED BACK TO FRANCE. ACCORDING TO HISTORIANS, ONCE IN FRANCE THE MARQUIS SUPPOSEDLY GOT INVOLVED WITH THE UGLY ANTI-SEMITIC POLITICS OF THE DREYFUS ERA AND MET HIS DEATH AT THE HANDS OF SOME ARAB ASSASSINS IN NORTH AFRICA. THE DREYFUS ERA BEING OF COURSE THAT TIME PERIOD OF FRENCH HISTORY

WHEN ONE OF FRANCE'S MOST WELL RESPECTED JEWISH MILITARY OFFICERS, ALFRED DREYFUS IN 1893 BEGAN COLLECTING DOCUMENTATION THAT HE WASN'T SUPPOSE TO HAVE IN HIS POSSESSION. APPARENTLY, ONCE HE FULLY REALIZED WHAT HE HAD IN HIS HOT LITTLE HANDS HE REPORTEDLY WROTE A SCATHING EXPOSÉ OF THE EXISTENCE OF A FREEMASONRY CONSPIRACY OF SORTS (A DOCKET OF SCHEDULED FRATERNITY MANEUVERS) THAT CONTAINED MILITARY DOCUMENTS THAT HE WAS SUPPOSE TO BE DELIVERING TO THE GERMAN EMBASSY IN PARIS. INSTEAD OF DOING WHAT HE WAS ORIGINALLY ORDERED TO DO, DREYFUS SET TO PEN AND PAPER WHAT HE HAD ACCIDENTLY DISCOVERED. ONE YEAR LATER, HE WAS CONVICTED OF TREASON AND ALMOST IMMEDIATELY ANTI-SEMITISM RHETORIC WAS ON THE LIPS OF JUST ABOUT EVERYONE IN EUROPE.

ALTHOUGH MOST, IF NOT ALL OF WHAT TAKES PLACE INSIDE A MEETING OF THE MASONIC FRATERNITY IS SECRET, SOME OF THEIR WORKS, CALLED "ESOTERIC "MAY NOT EVEN BE WRITTEN — AND THAT OF WHICH CAN BE WRITTEN DOWN FOR ALL TO SEE IS SIMPLY CALLED "EXOTERIC "WORKS. IT APPEARS AS THOUGH THESE SECRET WORKS HAVE BEEN THE CASE FOR MOST OF WHAT HAS UNFOLDED THROUGHOUT THE FREEMASONRY HISTORY OF NORTH AMERICA. EVEN THOUGH THE MASONIC MEETINGS WERE CLASSIFIED AS CONFIDENTIAL, IT STILL HASN'T STOPPED THE PUBLICATION OF WELL OVER TWENTY-FIVE-THOUSAND VOLUMES ON THE SUBJECT OF THEIR TEACHINGS FOR THE LAST 200 /OR 300 YEARS.

WITH ALL OF THIS BEING STATED AND WITH THE FRATERNITY STAGE FINALLY SET, ITS NOW TIME TO SHED A LITTLE LIGHT ON WHY QUEBEC'S FRANCOPHONE POPULATION IN THE LAST FORTY /OR FIFTY YEARS HAS BEEN PUSHING FOR FULL RECOGNITION AS BEING A **"DISTINCT SOCIETY"**. LIKE ANYTHING ELSE IN CANADA, THIS TOO IS CONNECTED TO THE PAST — IT RESPECTIVELY GOES HAND-IN-HAND WITH THE ESTABLISHMENT OF THE OLD SEIGNIORIAL REGIME OF DAYS-GONE-BY AS THE INTERCOURSE AND MARRIAGE OF QUEBEC'S FRENCH FREEMASONRY IS THAT OF A VERY INTERESTING HISTORY, ESPECIALLY SINCE ITS ALL CONNECTED TO THE ROMAN CATHOLIC CHURCH. BUT IN ORDER TO FULLY UNDERSTAND THIS TWISTED FRENCH WEB OF DECEIT AND CORRUPTION, A BRIEF LOOK INTO THE QUEBEC ACT OF 1774 MUST BE INTRODUCED. TO BEGIN WITH, THE QUEBEC ACT WAS A BRITISH ACT OF PARLIAMENT WHICH GUARANTEED FRENCH CANADIANS THE FREE EXERCISE OF THEIR RELIGION, THE ENJOYMENT OF THEIR CIVIL RIGHTS AND THE PROTECTION OF THEIR OWN CIVIL LAWS AND CUSTOMS. THE FRENCH WERE SUPPOSEDLY UNACCUSTOMED TO THE AFFAIRS OF ENGLISH GOVERNMENT AND WERE THEREFORE GIVEN THE KIND OF GOVERNMENT THAT THEY COULD UNDERSTAND. FRENCH RATHER THAN ENGLISH LEGAL TRADITIONS WERE THUSLY INSTITUTED AND ROMAN CATHOLICISM BECAME QUEBEC'S LEGALLY RECOGNIZED RELIGION. THE

BOUNDARIES OF THE COLONY WERE AUTOMATICALLY EXTENDED WESTWARD AND SOUTHWARD; SOUTH INTO THE OHIO VALLEY AND WEST TO THE MISSISSIPPI.

NEEDLESS TO SAY, MASONIC BROTHER GEORGE WASHINGTON AND HIS AMERICAN FRATERNITY BRETHREN WERE NOT AT ALL IMPRESSED BY THIS AS THEY THEMSELVES WERE PLANNING TO SEVER ALL TIES WITH THE BRITISH GRAND LODGE IN LONDON AND SEEK A DIVORCE FROM THE MONARCHY ALTOGETHER BUT NOW, YET ANOTHER BLOODY OBSTACLE WAS PUT IN THEIR WAY. TO MOST PEOPLE AT THE TIME, THE QUEBEC ACT WAS INTERPRETED AS BEING A THREAT TO THE ENGLISH-SPEAKING COLONIES IN CANADA WHICH VIRTUALLY MEANT AN END TO ALL PROSPECTS OF SELF-GOVERNMENT, A LIMITATION OF THE COLONISTS' LEGAL RIGHT AS ANGLICANS AND THE ENCOURAGEMENT OF ROMAN CATHOLICISM. THERE WAS ALSO CONSTANT STRIFE BETWEEN THE CONQUERING ENGLISH AND THE CONQUERED FRANCOPHONES, THE OBJECT OF WHICH WAS SUPPOSEDLY DESIGNED TO AMALGAMATE THE TWO RACES, AND TO PUT AN END TO IT ONCE AND FOR ALL. IN 1791, THE BRITISH PARLIAMENT THUSLY DIVIDED CANADA INTO TWO SEPARATE PROVINCES; LOWER CANADA / OR QUEBEC, FOR THE FRENCH AND UPPER CANADA FOR THE ENGLISH, MANY OF WHOM HAD FLED TO FROM THE UNITED STATES AT THE CLOSE OF THE AMERICAN REVOLUTIONARY WAR. AT LEAST, THAT'S WHAT THE HISTORY BOOKS HAVE BEEN SAYING FOR SOME 200 YEARS NOW.

MASONICALLY SPEAKING, QUEBEC'S HISTORY IS MUCH MORE INTERESTING THAN WHAT HISTORIANS HAVE BEEN TELLING US. IN THIS PROVINCE, THERE ARE MANY FRATERNITY HEROES, FRENCH AS WELL AS ENGLISH. ONE OF ENGLAND'S VERY OWN LEGENDARY FIGURES FOR EXAMPLE, SIR JOHN JOHNSON (1742-1830), THE SON OF SIR WILLIAM JOHNSON (1714-74) AND CATHERINE WISENBERG. HE WAS SAID TO HAVE BEEN BORN ON THE BANKS OF THE MOHAWK RIVER, ABOUT TWENTY-FIVE MILES WEST OF SCHENECTADY, NEW YORK AND WAS KNIGHTED SIR JOHN MANY YEARS LATER AFTER TAKING OVER HIS FATHER'S ESTATES AND BARONETCY IN THE MOHAWK VALLEY IN 1774 UPON HIS FATHER'S DEATH. ACCORDINGLY, HE TOOK PART IN THE FRENCH AND INDIAN WARS AS WELL AS IN THE BORDER WARFARE DURING THE AMERICAN REVOLUTIONARY WAR FOR INDEPENDENCE. HE ALSO WAS RESPONSIBLE FOR ORGANIZING A LOYALIST REGIMENT KNOWN HISTORICALLY AS THE QUEEN'S ROYAL GREENS, WHICH HE WAS SAID TO HAVE LED AT THE BATTLE OF ORISKANY, AND IN THE MANY RAIDS (1778-80) ON CHERRY VALLEY AND IN THE MOHAWK VALLEY. SIR JOHN JOHNSON WAS MADE BRIGADIER-GENERAL OF THE PROVINCIAL TROOPS IN 1782 AND THUS MOVED FROM THE UNITED STATES TO CANADA WHERE HE INTERESTINGLY OBTAINED THE PORTFOLIO OF SUPERINTENDENT-GENERAL OF INDIAN AFFAIRS FOR BRITISH NORTH AMERICA FROM 1791 UNTIL HIS DEATH ON JANUARY 4TH, 1830. BESIDES GIVING HIM THE PRESTIGIOUS POSTING OF INDIAN CONTROL AGENT, THE ROYAL BRITISH MONARCHY GAVE SIR JOHN

EXTENSIVE LAND GRANTS, TO REPLACE THE MOHAWK VALLEY SEIGNIORIES WHICH HAD BEEN CONFISCATED BY THE OPPOSING FORCES. IRONICALLY, SIR JOHN JOHNSON HAD PLAYED A MAJOR ROLE IN THE VARIOUS INDIAN MASSACRES OF WHICH FORMED SOME OF THE MOST BLOODIES INCIDENTS IN OUR HISTORY THAT ANY WAR COULD HAVE POSSIBLY GENERATED. THIS, DESPITE THE FACT THAT HIS VERY OWN FATHER MARRIED AN INDIAN WOMAN IN A TRADITIONAL MOHAWK CEREMONY (MOLLY BRANT). PERHAPS HE WAS TAKING HIS ANGER OUT ON THE INDIANS AS IT WAS BELIEVED AT THE TIME THAT SIR WILLIAM HAD BASICALLY DISGRACED THE GOOD FAMILY NAME BY MARRYING A MERE INDIAN.

BE THAT AS IT MAY, SIR JOHN JOHNSON WAS INITIATED INTO FREEMASONRY AT THE ROYAL LODGE LOCATED ON ST. JAMES STREET IN LONDON, ENGLAND, HOLDING THE WARRANT NO. 31 OF THE GRAND LODGE OF ENGLAND (THE MODERNS) ABOUT THE YEAR 1767. JOHNSON LATER AFFILIATED WITH ST. PATRICK'S LODGE NO. 4 AT JOHNSTOWN, NEW YORK, WHICH COINCIDENTLY WAS FOUNDED BY HIS FATHER. BY 1771, SIR JOHN HAD BEEN SELECTED PROVINCIAL GRAND MASTER OF NEW YORK, THUSLY MAKING HIM THE FIFTH GRAND MASTER OF THE COLONY OF THE STATE OF NEW YORK. UNFORTUNATELY, THERE ARE NO RECORDS TO BE HAD OF THE OFFICIAL ACTS OF SIR JOHN IN THIS CAPACITY, EXCEPT THE CHARTERING OF A LODGE AT SCHENECTADY IN 1774, AND TWO MILITARY LODGES, ONE IN 1775, AND THE OTHER IN 1776. IT IS BELIEVED THAT ONE OF SIR JOHN JOHNSON'S ESTABLISHED MILITARY LODGES IS IN FACT THE ACTUAL FORMATION OF THE UNITED STATES MILITARY ACADEMY KNOWN TO ALL AS **"WEST POINT"**. FURTHERMORE, ON MAY 5TH, 1788 A WARRANT WAS ISSUED BY THE EARL OF EFFINGHAM, ACTING ON BEHALF OF THE GRAND MASTER OF ENGLAND (MODERNS), APPOINTING SIR JOHN AS THE PROVINCIAL GRAND MASTER OF CANADA. ODDLY ENOUGH, IT IS REPORTED THAT HE HELD THIS TITLE UNTIL HIS DEATH IN 1830. COINCIDENTLY, ACCORDING TO THE MASONIC ORDER'S OWN LITERATURE, THE FIRST AMERICAN INDIAN TO JOIN THE ANCIENT CRAFT OF FREEMASONRY WAS NONE OTHER THAN JOSEPH BRANT, THE MOHAWK CHIEF. HE WAS REPORTEDLY INITIATED IN LODGE NO. 417 MEETING AT THE FALCON PUBLIC HOUSE, PRINCESS STREET, LEICESTER FIELDS IN LONDON, ENGLAND. HIS MASONIC CERTIFICATE IS DULY DATED APRIL 26TH, 1776. FURTHER TO THIS INTERESTING REVELATION, IT IS ALSO NOTED THAT IN CANADA ON /OR ABOUTS 1797, MASONIC LODGE NO. 11 WAS FOUNDED IN THE MOHAWK VILLAGE NOW KNOWN AS BRANTFORD, WITH JOSEPH BRANT AS ITS MASTER. OF ITS MEMBERSHIP WERE THE MOHAWK INDIANS OF BRANT'S SIX NATIONS CONFEDERACY.

GETTING BACK TO SIR JOHN JOHNSON'S SUPPOSED PLACEMENT OF BEING THE PROVINCIAL GRAND MASTER OF ALL CANADA UNTIL HIS DEATH FOR A SECOND /OR TWO, WHEN HIS ROYAL HIGHNESS PRINCE EDWARD, (LATER DUBBED THE DUKE OF KENT) ARRIVED INTO THE NEWLY FORMED

TERRITORIES OF UPPER AND LOWER CANADA IN MARCH OF 1792, ALL HELL BROKE LOOSE WHEN THE OFFICIAL TITLE WAS DULY TRANSFERRED OVER TO THE PRINCE AS HE WAS INSTALLED AS PROVINCIAL GRAND MASTER BY THE "ANCIENTS "GRAND LODGE OF ENGLAND. THE REASON GIVEN WAS SAID TO BE LARGELY DUE TO THE FACT THAT WHILE MOST OF THE "MODERNS" LODGES WERE SUPPOSEDLY DECLINING IN ITS MEMBERSHIP, SOME WERE TRANSFERRING THEIR ALLEGIANCE TO THE ANCIENTS GRAND LODGE. BUT IF THE TRUTH BE TOLD IN ITS PROPER LIGHT, THIS SCHISM OCCURRED MOSTLY DUE TO THE FACT THAT THE AMERICAN FREEMASONS "THE MODERNS "WERE SEVERING ALL TIES WITH ENGLAND ALTOGETHER AND THE BRITISH GRAND LODGE WAS NOT AT ALL AMUSED. FOR INSTANCE, ST. PAUL'S LODGE IN MONTREAL WAS WARRANTED BY THE PROVINCIAL GRAND LODGE OF QUEBEC IN 1770, AND REMAINED LOYAL TO THE "MODERNS" UNTIL 1797, WHEN IT, TOO, WAS FORCED TO SCUM TO THE PRESSURE AND TOOK AN "ANCIENTS "WARRANT. FROM THIS DATE (1797), SIR JOHN JOHNSON'S POSTING OF PROVINCIAL GRAND MASTER OF ALL CANADA WAS THAT OF AN EMPTY OFFICE AS DISSENSION GREW BETWEEN THE TWO GOVERNING FREEMASONRY BODIES. AS THE TENSION MOUNTED, A MEDIATOR WAS APPOINTED TO HELP DEFUSE THE VOLATILE FRATERNITY SITUATION – SIR GEORGE PREVOST WAS THUS GRANTED THE PORTFOLIO AS THE GOVERNOR-GENERAL OF QUEBEC. IN THE SAME YEAR OF HIS TAKING OFFICE, (1812), THE INSTITUTION OF PREVOST LODGE NO. 8 IN DUNHAM, QUEBEC TOOK PLACE. THERE WERE NOW THREE FREEMASONRY FORCES FIGHTING FOR POLITICAL CONTROL OF LOWER CANADA; THE BRITISH ANCIENTS LODGERY, THE AMERICAN MODERNS LODGERY AND THE INSTITUTION OF PREVOST'S FRANCOPHONISM.

AS THIS TUG-OF-WAR SOON ESCALATED TO EPIDEMIC PROPORTIONS, SIR GEORGE PREVOST WAS CALLED BACK TO ENGLAND ON APRIL 3RD, 1815 TO FACE COURT MARTIAL CHARGES FOR HIS INVOLVEMENT IN THE INTRODUCING OF MASONIC FRANCOPHONISM TO QUEBEC'S POPULATION. HE APPARENTLY DIED A WEEK BEFORE HE WAS TO FACE TRIAL, (JANUARY 5TH, 1816). A PAINTING OF SIR GEORGE PREVOST PROUDLY HANGS IN THE NATIONAL ASSEMBLY OF THE GOVERNMENT OF THE PROVINCE OF QUEBEC IN QUEBEC CITY TO THIS VERY DAY.

IT WASN'T UNTIL 1813 THAT THE DIFFERENCES OF OPINION BY THE AMERICAN AND BRITISH FREEMASONS WERE FINALLY SETTLED BY THE AMALGAMATION OF THE TWO GRAND LODGES IN ENGLAND AND THUS FORMED THE UNITED GRAND LODGE OF ENGLAND. IT IS ALSO IMPORTANT TO STATE THAT SIR JOHN JOHNSON WAS AN ANGLICAN AND THAT HIS NAME WAS LISTED AS A PEW-HOLDER OF CHRIST'S CHURCH IN MONTREAL, AS EARLY AS 1789. ON JANUARY 8TH, 1830 SIR JOHN WAS BURIED WITH FULL HONORS, MILITARY AS WELL AS MASONIC. COINCIDENTLY, ON THE SAME DAY OF HIS FUNERAL,

A special meeting of the Provincial Grand Lodge of Montreal was held "for the purpose of assisting at the interment of the late R.W. Bro. Sir John Johnson "interestingly with the Provincial Grand Master "R.W. Bro. John Molson, presiding."

After completing their secret rituals, a procession was formed with a gun-carriage in tow, and proceeded to Christ's Church, and thence to the banks of the St. Lawrence River, "where the body was embarked for the purpose of being conveyed to the family vault" at the top of Mount Johnson. In attendance were John Molson, Provincial Grand Master; Turton Penn, Deputy Provincial Grand Master; William Badgley, Senior Grand Warden; J. Guthrie Scott, Junior Grand Warden; Horatio Gates, Grand Treasurer; Henry MacKenzie, Grand Registrar; Fredrick Griffen, Grand Director of Ceremonies, and many of the Fraternity Brethren from St. Paul's and St. George's Lodgery of Montreal. It is also important to note that some in attendance were active military personnel during the American Revolutionary War. Horatio Gates for example was a professional British Officer in General Edward "Braddock's Alumni" fraternity forces. As were; George Washington, Daniel Boone, Thomas Gage, Christopher Gist, Daniel Morgan and Sir William Johnson, along with many other well respected Masonic military commandos of the American Revolution.

Furthermore, Horatio Gates and John Molson were the founding forces behind the establishing of the banking system of Lower Canada. During the War of 1812-14 for instance, the Molson family and others became actively engaged in profitable banking operations by buying bills of exchange at heavy discount in Montreal and disposing of them at a profit in Quebec. After having acquired a taste for an abundance of money, nine Montreal merchants band together and signed articles of forming an association that was to then become the first permanent bank in Canadian history. On June 23RD, 1817 the Bank of Montreal received its Charter and by 1859, the Masonic controlled banking system established branches in New York State, and in 1870, opened its first overseas office in London, England. In 1855, yet another Charter secured the Molson family Bank and in October of 1924, the Bank of Montreal made arrangements to take-over the Molson's Bank investments — the merger took place on January 25TH, 1925.

Both the Molson's Bank and the Bank of Montreal became the backbone of many fraternity business ventures. While Freemasonry Brother Gates ventured in the import of groceries and liquors,

Brother Molson began experimenting with barley and malt liquors. In 1786, fraternity Brother Molson began production of Molson's ale and in 1817, established one of Canada's first luxury hotels, the Mansion House, in the former residence of Sir John Johnson. It was Montreal's elite social center until it was destroyed by fire in 1821, and it was succeeded by yet another Molson hostelry seven years later, (1828), the New Mansion House, which ironically was also destroyed by fire in 1833. Although the Molson family of Quebec were regarded as pillars of the community and highly respected Anglo-Saxons, all was not well when it came to dealing with the French. To the majority of Quebec's French-speaking population, John Molson represented the upper class of Englanders living in Montreal, that of which he sat in the Lower Canada Legislature from 1816-20 and was appointed to the Provincial Legislative Council in 1832. In accordance to what Masonic literature has to say on this topic, apparently from 1813 to 1855, the United Grand Lodge of England with the assistance of the Americans, manipulated Quebec and its people to rid the Province of its Francophone ties. In the eyes of English-speaking Freemasons, Quebec was to be that of "Protestant Christianity ... one flag ... one language. "From 1855 to 1869, the Grand Lodge of Canada (Upper Canada; Ontario) was the controlling Masonic power in Quebec, but with the birth of a united Confederation as proposed by MacDonald came the agitation for a separation of the Grand Lodge. Several meetings were held in an attempt to ward off schism from within the fraternity itself and finally, on the 20TH of October, 1869 the Grand Lodge of Quebec was formed by twenty-eight of the recognized Warranted Lodges then operating within French Canada.

Like Masonic brethren's Johnson, Gates and Molson, Quebec's Francophone hero Sir George Prevost also had an impressive dossier. Not long after Prevost entered into the British Army, he was promoted to Captain (1784). By 1790, he became a Major in the Queen's Royal American Army. During the Napoleonic Wars, Prevost spent some years in the West Indies, first on active service in St. Vincent (1794-96), then, with the rank of Brigadier-General, as military Governor of St. Lucia, 1798-1801. By 1802, he was appointed Governor of the Dominican Republic and in 1805, was knighted as a Baron. Three years thereafter, he was appointed to the portfolio of Lieutenant-Governor of Nova Scotia, with the military rank of Lieutenant-General. Prevost administrated the affairs of the Province until 1811, when he was transferred to Quebec as its

ACTING GOVERNMENTAL ADMINISTRATOR. ALTHOUGH PROVOST WAS SWORN INTO OFFICE IN OCTOBER OF 1811, HE REPORTEDLY DIDN'T ACTUALLY TAKE OFFICE UNTIL SOME NINE MONTHS LATER, (JULY OF 1812). THUS GIVING HIM AMPLE TIME TO LAY THE FOOTING FOUNDATION OF HIS OWN PERSONAL FREEMASONRY INSTITUTION. ACCORDING TO WHAT HISTORY BOOKS TELL US, AS COMMANDER-IN-CHIEF OF THE BRITISH FORCES IN CANADA DURING THE AMERICAN-CANADIAN WAR OF 1812, PREVOST WAS SUPPOSEDLY RESPONSIBLE FOR TWO OF THE MOST HUMILIATING EPISODES OF THE WAR ITSELF; THE WITHDRAWAL AFTER THE SUCCESSFUL ATTACK ON SACKETT'S HARBOR AND THE DISASTROUS DEFEAT AT PLATTSBURG.

BUT IN REALITY, HE WAS BEING PENALIZED FOR SOMETHING EVEN MORE SINISTER THAN THAT. FOR EXAMPLE, PRIOR TO THE SUMMER OF 1814, ENGLAND HAD BEEN UNABLE TO SEND TROOPS INTO CANADA DUE TO ITS PREOCCUPATION WITH THE WARS AGAINST NAPOLEON. BUT ONCE THE FALLEN FRENCH KNIGHTS OF MALTA EMPEROR HAD BEEN BANISHED TO ELBA IN APRIL OF THAT YEAR, SIXTEEN-THOUSAND WELL SEASONED SOLDIERS HAD BEEN SENT TO CANADA. MANY OF WHOM WERE VETERANS OF WELLINGTON'S PENINSULAR ARMIES, (WELLINGTON BEING OF COURSE A BRITISH MEMBER OF FREEMASONRY HIMSELF). IN AN ATTEMPT TO EXECUTE AN OFFENSIVE ATTACK, AN ESTIMATED FOURTEEN-THOUSAND MEN, UNDER PREVOST, WERE SENT TO PLATTSBURG. PREVOST, REPORTEDLY INSISTED THAT THE TROOPS SECURE COMMAND OF LAKE CHAMPLAIN BEFORE ATTACKING OTHER STRATEGY POINTS. ORDERS WERE THEN GIVEN TO ATTACK THE AMERICAN NAVAL FORCES WHICH PROVED TO BE FATAL AS THE BRITISH TROOPS WERE DEFEATED. AT NINE O'CLOCK IN THE MORNING OF SEPTEMBER 11TH, 1814 THE PEACEFUL SURROUNDINGS OF THE LAKE WERE DISTURBED AS SOUNDS OF GUN FIRE APPEARED OFF THE HARBOR OF PLATTSBURG. AFTER ONLY A FEW SHORT HOURS, HALF PAST ELEVEN, SHOUTS OF VICTORY COULD BE HEARD ALL ALONG THE AMERICAN LINES AS THE BRITISH FORCES SLOWLY BEGAN TO SURRENDER. WHEN ALL THE GUNS WERE FINALLY SILENT AND THE WOUNDED BE BEING ATTENDED TOO, BODY COUNTS WERE TALLIED. UPON THE LAKE, AMERICAN LOSS WAS ONE-HUNDRED AND TEN WHILE THE BRITISH LOSS WAS ONE-HUNDRED AND NINETY-FOUR. BUT ON LAND, THINGS WERE MUCH WORSE FOR THE ENGLISH. WHILE THE AMERICAN LOSS WAS ONLY ONE-HUNDRED AND NINETEEN, THE BRITISH HAD LOST AN ESTIMATED TWO-THOUSAND-FIVE-HUNDRED SOLDIERS. AS HEAD OF THE FOURTEEN-THOUSAND MEN THAT HAD INITIALLY ENTERED THE TERRITORY OF THE UNITED STATES IN PREPARATION FOR BATTLE, PREVOST WAS USED AS A SCAPEGOAT AS SOMEONE HAD TO PAY THE PRICE FOR THE STAGGERING HISTORIC LOSSES.

THE EVENTS SURROUNDING THE SACKETT'S HARBOR ORDEAL SEEM TO PROVE THIS AS BEING IN DEED THE CASE. FOR EXAMPLE, ONLY WEEKS PREVIOUS TO THE PLATTSBURG MASSACRE OF THE BRITISH TROOPS, PREVOST

WAS IN CHARGE OF NEARLY THIRTEEN-THOUSAND SOLDIERS WHEN HE SENT ELEVEN-THOUSAND OF THEM TO ADVANCE ON AMERICAN TROOPS THAT WERE WELL POSITIONED NEAR SACKETT'S HARBOR. WHILE THOSE BRITISH TROOPS ADVANCED FORWARD, PREVOST AND SIXTEEN-HUNDRED MEN OF DUKE WELLINGTON'S WELL SEASONED ARMY BROUGHT UP THE REAR FLANK. THE AMERICANS WHO WERE IN WAITING HAD AN EXCESS OF ONLY FIVE-THOUSAND-FIVE-HUNDRED TROOPS IN PLACE BUT HAD MANAGED TO OBTAIN A GREAT STRATEGY LOCATION TO HELP WIN THE BATTLE. BY THE TIME PREVOST AND HIS MEN RETURNED ONTO THE SCENE, A HEAVY ARTILLERY FIRE WAS ALREADY IN PROGRESS. FOR NEARLY THREE DAYS, PREVOST AND HIS MEN WERE PINNED DOWN UNABLE TO MAKE A MOVE WITHOUT BEING SLAUGHTERED. WAITING FOR THE RIGHT MOMENT TO JOIN IN ON THE ATTACK, PREVOST AND HIS MEN REPORTEDLY WAITED AND WAITED. THEN, WHEN THE MOMENT AROSE, INSTEAD OF ORDERING HIS COLUMNS AT ONCE TO JOIN IN THE ACTION, PREVOST WAITED UNTIL THE WRONG TIME PERIOD BEFORE ISSUING THE COMMAND. AND WHEN IT APPEARED THAT HIS TROOPS WERE GOING TO BE BUTCHERED, HE IMMEDIATELY ORDERED THEM TO RETREAT. ALMOST INSTANTLY, DISSENSION AMONGST HIS MEN EMERGED AS SOME OF THEM REPORTEDLY BROKE THEIR SWORDS IN HALF VOWING NEVER TO SERVE UNDER HIS COMMAND EVER AGAIN. APPARENTLY, A GOOD PORTION OF HIS TROOPS PREFERRED TO DIE IN BATTLE THEN TO REMAIN ALIVE IN DISGRACE AND DISAPPOINTMENT AS THEY RETURNED FROM BATTLE UNSCATHED. THOSE WHO PREFERRED DYING IN BATTLE SOON BEGAN MAKING ALLEGATIONS OF PREVOST'S INITIAL ACTIONS AS BEING COWARDLY IN NATURE.

INTERESTINGLY, MOST HISTORIANS TODAY STILL CAN'T EVEN AGREE ON WHAT LATER UNFOLDED AS CHARGES OF SERIOUS INCOMPETENCE WERE MADE AGAINST SIR GEORGE PREVOST BY ONE COMMODORE JAMES YEO, (A.K.A. SIR JAMES YEO), WHO WAS ASSOCIATED WITH PREVOST IN MANY OTHER WAYS THAN BEING WITH HIM DURING THE ATTACK ON SACKETT'S HARBOR. ACCORDING TO THE VAST MAJORITY OF HISTORIANS, WITHIN ONLY DAYS OF THE ORDEAL AT SACKETT'S HARBOR UNFOLDING, PREVOST WAS SAID TO HAVE ACQUIRED A REPUTATION OF INDECISION'S AND WEAKNESS WHILE IN BATTLE.

IN ORDER TO FULLY UNDERSTAND PREVOST'S COURT MARTIAL CHARGES, A FURTHER ANALYSIS INTO QUEBEC'S FREEMASONRY PAST MUST NOW BE INTRODUCED. WHEN ROBERVAL, THE MARQUIS DE LA ROCHE , JACQUES CARTIER AND SAMUEL DE CHAMPLAIN FIRST SET FOOT ONTO CANADIAN SOIL, THEY BROUGHT WITH THEM THE FUNDAMENTAL PRINCIPLES AND TEACHINGS OF THE ORDERS OF ST. JOHN OF JERUSALEM, RHODES AND MALTA. UNIVERSALLY KNOWN AS THE MASONIC ORDER OF MALTA, WHICH HAD BEEN ESTABLISHED ON A SMALL ISLAND IN THE MEDITERRANEAN SEA AT THE CLOSE OF THE ELEVENTH CENTURY. ALTHOUGH OCCUPYING ONLY 170 SQUARE MILES, THIS LITTLE ISLAND PARADISE POSSESSED MUCH POWER FOR SEVERAL CENTURIES.

Prior to 1530, it was occupied mostly by the Knights Templar, which were said to have ceased to exist once the Crusades had finished with them. From 1530 to 1798, the Island was occupied by the Knights of Hospitalers, then also called the Knights of Malta. Just like the Knights Templar, these Knights of Malta became one of the most powerful forces in European Affairs. In France, its influence was felt in the highest places and it played an important role in the foundation of establishing a French Roman Catholic presence in Canada.

Although Quebec was first explored by Cartier in 1534, and various attempts were made to set up housekeeping after that, the territory itself wasn't really Masonically claimed until Champlain received a commission from Charles de Bourbon, Comte de Soissons, a Prince of Royal French bloodlines and the Protector of the Knights of Malta, who later acquired for Samuel de Champlain his portfolio as Viceroy of the new colony. Supposedly after numerous failures in attempting to colonize the new frontier, French nobility formed the Company of One Hundred Associations in 1627. Most of the Associations' members had close fraternity connections with the Order of Malta – Armand-Jean du Plessis de Richelieu, the main organizer of the Company for example had an uncle who was the Ambassador of the Order to the King of France, the Commandeer de La Porte, and with whom he kept close contact. Richelieu's mother, Suzanne de La Porte, was the sister of the Order's Grand Master. At the head of the One Hundred Associations, Richelieu placed his nephew Isaac de Razilly, an ordained member of the Knights of Malta who in turn soon recruited two other relatives and various confreres of the fraternal Order, Charles Huault de Montmagny, a high officer in the Priory of France, and Henri Languilliers de Poincy. Other members included; Noel Brulart de Sillery, a man of great wealth, and of course, the royal messengers of the King of France, the LePage's. Once in the New World, the LePage's became Masonic writers who were kept extremely busy by complying the various pieces of data pertaining to New France's Freemasonry past. In fact, the Masonic literature itself stated this as being the case as they, the LePage's "occupied themselves in the accumulation of cashiers or rituals of Masonic degrees." The LePage family's Ancient Craft of French Freemasonry contributions are contained in the various pages of Volumes 1 and 2 of the Encyclopedia of Freemasonry published by the Masonic History Company of the United States of the America's in 1924.

By 1636, Montmagny became the Viceroy of Quebec, Razilly the Governor of Acadia, and Poincy ruler of the West Indies. Richelieu and his three cousins were said to have had spent their youth in the armies of Malta and pledged allegiance to their King, the Grand Master and Protector of Malta. Poincy apparently was the first to prove his loyalty. Upon the termination of his term as Governor, he arranged the purchase (from the King of France) of the Island of St. Christopher (now St. Kitts) by the Order of Malta, and the flag of Malta flew over the land in the new Maltese Island. Razilly on the other hand had his reservations because Acadia had been set aside strictly as a reserve for the fur trade. Notwithstanding this, he attempted to establish a colony under the Order of Malta on the Atlantic Coast near where Halifax now stands. After the reported collapse of Richelieu's Company in 1641, Montmagny made financial arrangements for the purchase of the bankrupt venture by the Order of Malta from the King of France. Montmagny had full intentions of establishing the Order in Quebec, but according to what history books tell us, the plan fell through for the lack of money. If this is supposedly the case, then, why is it that not long after the 1641 bankruptcy of Richelieu's Company, the Knights of Malta announced that they were going to be colonizing Canada. Furthermore, contrary as to what historians state as being a true fact of our country's past, when Louis Riel and his Metis followers seized power and took control of Fort Garry, they hoisted up the flag of Malta!!!

It is very clear that Charles Huault de Montmangny played a very important role in the formation of Quebec and its distinction from the British Royal monarchy. When he built the first Chateau St. Louis, Montmangny placed the cross of Malta in its facade. The Cross of Malta is best known as the "Maltese Cross. "A cross of eight points, which was worn by the Knights of the Order. It is heroically described as "a cross pattee, but the extremity of each pattee notched at a deep angle. "When the Chateau was destroyed in 1784, the Maltese Cross was found amongst the rubble, and it now can reportedly be seen incorporated into the main entrance at the Chateau Frontenac Hotel in Quebec City.

Like Montmangny, Noel Brulart de Sillery also played an important role in laying the French Freemasonry foundations in Quebec. As the extremely rich person that he was, and having served the French King as his Ambassador to Spain in 1614 and to Rome in 1622, de Sillery used his Masonic influence where ever he could.

While in Rome for example, he courted the papacy for Richelieu, the New World that the Knights of Malta wanted to create was to have the blessing of the Pope in order for the proper flourishing of Roman Catholicism. De Sillery was a loyal member of the Knights of Malta and in 1637, he reportedly sent Montmangny a very large sum of money that was needed to help establish a settlement not far from Quebec City which was said to have had twelve large families as well as a number of Algonkian Indian slaves living within its boundaries. It was to be Quebec's first established Roman Catholic Missionary set up by the Masonic Order's Knights of Malta. Further to this, de Sillery also reportedly sent Montmangny twenty workmen from France to build the village that was to become the Quebec suburb of Sillery.

Contrary as to what some historians may say is true, the Knights of Malta had a hell of a lot of political and religious clout at that time period of history. For example, according to the Roman Catholic Church records; Samuel de Champlain married the twelve-year-old daughter of Nicholas Boulle, an extremely wealthy Huguenot who catered to the French monarchy's every whim. The marriage ceremony reportedly took place in the Church of St. Germain l'Auxerrois in Paris (1610) where twelve-year-old Helene Boulle and forty-three-year Samuel de Champlain reportedly exchanged their vows. The intercourse and marriage of this couple was fully sanctioned by not only the King of France but by the Roman Catholic Church as well. The main stipulation of the marriage was that once Champlain's twelve-year-old bride had been broken-in, she was to convert to the Roman Catholic faith before being able to join her husband in Canada. Champlain's good friend Pierre du Guast (Sieur de Monts) acted as the official witness to the marital union. Further to this, because of her very young age it was also stipulated in the marital agreement that Champlain's twelve-year-old bride was to remain with her parents for at least two years before being able to set sail for Canada as she required more time to mature. Madame de Champlain was said to be twenty-two-years-old when she was finally permitted to migrate to Canada and set up housekeeping with four of her own personal female servants in tow. Due to the fact that her father had lots of money, reportedly giving a dowry of six-thousand livres, she was as spoiled as they came.

Once in Canada, she was instantly exposed to the many hardships of living on the frontier and was said to have whined constantly about it. Very little is actually known about Champlain's married

LIFE AND THE VERY UNHAPPY WOMAN OF WHOM HE CALLED HIS WIFE AS CHAMPLAIN PURPOSELY NEGLECTED TO WRITE ANYTHING DOWN IN HIS DAILY JOURNALS CONCERNING HIS ROCKY MARRIAGE. ALL THAT IS KNOWN, AT THE END OF HER FOUR YEARS OF LIVING IN THE HOSTILE LANDS OF CANADA, SHE HAD HER FILL AND PACKED UP ALL OF WHAT SHE OWNED AND HEADED BACK TO FRANCE IN 1624 NEVER MORE TO RETURN. ITS SAFE TO SAY THAT SAMUEL DE CHAMPLAIN WAS MISERABLE AS OLD HELL BECAUSE NOWHERE IN HIS JOURNALS COULD IT BE FOUND IF HIS YOUNG WIFE HAD GIVEN BIRTH TO ANY OF HIS CHILDREN. BE THAT AS IT MAY, NOT LONG AFTER HIS WIFE RETURNED BACK TO FRANCE SHE WAS SAID TO HAVE ENTERED A CONVENT AND EVENTUALLY BECAME AN URSULINE NUN, TAKING THE NAME HELENE D'AUGUSTIN. SHE REPORTEDLY FOUNDED A CONVENT AT MEAUX AND DIED IN 1654. IT IS ALSO SAID BY SOME HISTORIANS THAT RIGHT FROM THE VERY BEGINNING OF HER WANTING TO BECOME A NUN, SAMUEL DE CHAMPLAIN REFUSED TO GIVE HIS BLESSING ON HER NEWFOUND ENDEAVORS BUT SHE DID IT DESPITE HIS FORBIDDING HER TO DO SO. CHAMPLAIN REPORTEDLY TOOK HIS BITTER RESENTMENT FOR HER RIGHT TO HIS GRAVE ON DECEMBER 25TH, 1635.

AS A TRIBUTE TO SAMUEL DE CHAMPLAIN'S FREEMASONRY ACHIEVEMENTS MANY OF QUEBEC'S RULERS WORE THE CROSS OF THE ORDER OF MALTA. INTERESTINGLY ENOUGH, AFTER HIS DEATH FRANCOPHONE LEADERS BEGAN STRUTTING THEIR STUFF EVEN FURTHER. CHAMPLAIN'S TEMPORARY GOVERNORSHIP REPLACEMENT WAS VICEROY BRAS-DE-FAR DE CHATEAUFORT, WHICH WAS FRENCH LITERALLY MEANING, "IRON ARM OF THE STRONG CASTLE." CHAMPLAIN WAS ORIGINALLY APPOINTED GOVERNOR IN 1632 BY LOUIS XIII AND RETURNED TO QUEBEC TO FILL HIS POST – THIS QUEBEC ICON WAS ALSO RESPONSIBLE FOR THE WRITING OF MANY OF HIS MASONIC ADVENTURES DESCRIBING THEM IN MINUTE DETAIL. LIKE CHAMPLAIN AND CHARLES DE BOURBON, OTHER FRENCH FREEMASONS MOLDED THE **NEW WORLD** INTO SOMETHING THAT OF WHICH WAS GOING TO BE TAKING HUNDREDS OF YEARS TO FINALIZE ON A GRAND SCALE. ARMAND-JEAN DU PLESSIS DE RICHELIEU FOR INSTANCE BEING OF MASONIC NOBLE BLUE BLOOD WAS APPOINTED TO THE PORTFOLIO OF FRANCE'S SECRETARY OF STATE IN 1616, CARDINAL (1622) AND CHIEF MINISTER (1624) TO THE KING OF FRANCE. RICHELIEU'S FOREIGN POLICY WAS AIMED AT WORLD DOMINATION. IN THE EARLY 1630'S HE JOINED THE ALLIED FORCES OF THE NETHERLANDS, THE GERMAN STATES AND SWEDEN IN AN ATTEMPT TO FULFILL THE DREAM OF MAKING IT A REALITY AND WAGED WAR ON SPAIN, WHICH COINCIDENTLY CAUSED A HUGE FINANCIAL CRISIS FOR FRANCE. IN 1635, RICHELIEU FOUNDED THE FRENCH MILITARY ACADEMY. AND IN THE EARLY 1700'S, THE FRENCH KNIGHTS OF MALTA ESTABLISHED QUEBEC'S VERY OWN FIRST SERVICE/SOCIAL-CLUB, THE MAISON DE RICHELIEU WHICH ODDLY ENOUGH WAS LATER AMALGAMATED WITH HOTEL-DIEU DE

Quebec. The main purpose of the Maison de Richelieu at the time was to help promote French involvement of professional men and business people while looking after the mental, moral and physical well being of children, especially the under privileged. The motto: "Peace and Brotherhood "thusly became the rantings of French Canada throughout the Eighteenth and Nineteenth Centuries. But everything just seemed to fall apart once Sir John A. MacDonald formed the Royal North West Mounted Police in 1873 to help keep the Indian up-risings under full control, the police motto was designed as; *MAINTAIN LE DROIT*, (Uphold the Right). The majestic head of the Buffalo dominated the mounties first official crest. Ironically, the buffalo was a symbol of power and authority to many, while others saw it as nothing more than a bloody nuisance and decided that it had to be exterminated in order to make a large profit. While the Hudson's Bay Company traded supplies, guns and ammunition for the buffalo skins, the Canadian Pacific Railway was busy paying Canada's aboriginal peoples a nominal fee to collect buffalo bones, (usually for way less than what the CPR would later re-sell them for). Once the bones were collected, the railway company sold them to the United States for fertilizer at a reported $ 7.00 a ton.

When the Island of Malta was officially annexed by England in 1814 during the Napoleonic Wars, it thus transformed Quebec and Canada into the British Royal motto of their divine right to rule. Canada's Royal North West Mounted Police was therefore designed to maintain that rule under God's Nation. The Hotel-Dieu de Quebec was thusly instituted as a guarantee of the protection of Quebec's sovereign right as a **"DISTINCT SOCIETY "**in accordance to the philosophy of the Knights of Malta and the British Government's enactment of the Quebec Act of 1774, which recognized the Francophone population as such. The Hotel-Dieu de Quebec was originally conceived long before the English take-over of Canada, dating as far back as 1637 when the Duchesse d'Aiguillon secured financial funding for one of the first hospitals to be established in New France. Construction began a year later and by August of 1639, the first hospital (Hotel-Dieu de Quebec) opened its doors on the North American Continent. At the close of the Nineteenth Century, the Hotel-Dieu de Quebec had branched out virtually throughout most regions of French Canada, including some regions of English Canada as well, such as New Brunswick, Ontario and even south of the 49TH parallel into the United States of the America's (Winooski,

Vermont). With the collaboration of the Maison de Richelieu and the Hotel-Dieu de Quebec, the French Freemasons of Quebec were able to execute their fundamental practices of brotherly love onto an unsuspecting population. This despite the fact that according to most historians, French Freemasonry in La Belle Province never contributed a hell of a lot when it came to Canadian Masonic activities. Coincidently, once the British took full control of the Island of Malta, the French Freemasonry Knights of Malta were expelled altogether from the little Island but by 1998, they were allowed to return and re-establish themselves one again as a powerful force to be reckoned with.

Throughout the history of Quebec's Freemasonry past, the LePage's were right there every step of the way writing down the cahiers and the various Masonic degrees. From the very moment they migrated from France, the LePage's mingled amongst the elite in both Quebec and Louisiana. By 1663, the French-speaking population of Quebec was only five-hundred. But during the next decade, France began issuing massive land grants as an incentive to help populate their newfound territory — about two-thousand migrants accepted the challenge. And in 1675, it was estimated that there was seven-thousand French-speaking people in the New World. Nearly one-hundred years later (1755), approximately ten-thousand French Acadians (Nova Scotia, New Brunswick and Prince Edward Island) who were said to never be impressed with the British monarchy as they flatly refused to swear an oath of allegiance to the King of England were promptly deported by English Canada. After finding refuge in Louisiana, the French race soon flourished down on the Bayou.

By the early 1800's, most of the LePage's began migrating to various regions of the North American Continent. In 1819, Alexander Claude Angelique LePage settled in Philadelphia and ten years later Fredrick LePage, an influential shipping agent hung his shingle in St. John's, Newfoundland. Some years later, Wilfred Alexander LePage, a real estate broker and land developer moved to Sarasota, Florida. Other high rollers of the fraternity included Alphonse LePage, an Insurance Company Executive from Montreal and Robert Morris Page, Physicist with the United States Naval Research Lab located in Washington, D.C. With their family tree branching out to all aspects of living, the LePage name is synonymous as they became prominent in social, cultural, religious and political affairs that helped carve the history of both Church and State. Many of

WHOM WENT ON TO CREATE THEIR OWN LITTLE NICHE IN THE FREEMASONRY WORLD AS THEY WILLINGLY TOOK PART IN AIDING AND ABETTING IN THE JUST CAUSE OF THE **NEW WORLD ORDER.** FOR INSTANCE, AS TIME DRAGGED ON QUEBEC'S FRENCH POPULATION BEGAN TO REALIZE THAT THEY WERE GETTING THE SHORT END OF THE FREEMASONRY STICK. UPON THE CLOSE OF THE SECOND WORLD WAR, A REVISED LINE OF ATTACK WAS THUSLY INITIATED AND ON SEPTEMBER 19TH, 1945 A SOMEWHAT WATERED DOWN VERSION OF THE HOTEL-DIEU DE QUEBEC WAS ESTABLISHED IN OTTAWA BY FRATERNITY BROTHER ARTHUR DESJARDINS AND SIXTEEN RICHELIEU ASSOCIATION SOCIAL CLUBS. AND FIVE YEARS LATER, (1950), THE EUROPEAN GRAND MASTER OF THE KNIGHTS OF MALTA, PRINCE CHIGI WAS SENT ON A MISSION TO THE PROVINCE OF QUEBEC TO ONCE AGAIN HAVE THE FRENCH FREEMASONRY KNIGHTS OF MALTA DICTATING POLITICAL AND RELIGIOUS POLICIES. WHILE IN MONTREAL, FIVE FRATERNITY KNIGHTS WERE CHOSEN AND QUEBEC'S SUPREME COURT CHIEF JUSTICE THIBAUDEAU RINFRET WAS SELECTED AS ITS OVERSEER. INTERESTINGLY, IN 1944 THE PRESTIGIOUS RINFRET RECEIVED THE PORTFOLIO AS THE CHIEF JUSTICE OF CANADA AND UPON HIS RETIREMENT TEN YEARS LATER, HE WAS ASSIGNED BY THE GOVERNMENT OF MAURICE DUPLESSIS TO DRAFT A REVISION OF THE PROVINCE'S CIVIL CODE. AT THE TIME, THE FRENCH PROVINCIAL GOVERNMENT OF DUPLESSIS WAS THE MOST CORRUPT GOVERNMENTAL REGIME IN EXISTENCE WITHIN ALL OF CANADA. HIS GOVERNMENT COULD BE EASILY BOUGHT OFF FOR THE RIGHT AMOUNT OF MONEY!!!

BY 1957, THE FRENCH MASONIC KNIGHTS OF MALTA HAD INSTITUTED THEMSELVES INTO A CHARITABLE ORGANIZATION PROMOTING INTEREST IN THE FIELD OF FIRST-AID TRAINING. IT ALSO INFILTERED THE CATHOLIC SCHOOL SYSTEM AND OTHER ROMAN CATHOLIC INSTITUTIONS. BESIDES SUPPLYING FIRST-AID TREATMENT TO CHURCH PERSONNEL AND ALL OF THEIR FUNCTIONS, IT ALSO DID CHARITY WORK WITHIN THE COMMUNITIES. ITS MEMBERSHIP ROSTER HAD FORTY OF QUEBEC'S MOST POWERFUL POLITICAL PEOPLE AS ITS FRENCH KNIGHTS, AS WELL AS HIGH PROFILE RELIGIOUS PERSONNEL INCLUDING THE CARDINAL ARCHBISHOP OF MONTREAL. BUT THE MOST INTERESTING TRUE FACT OF CANADIAN HISTORY HAS NOT YET BEEN MENTIONED — AND THAT BEING OF COURSE THE FACT THAT SINCE IT HAD TO RECEIVE CONSCRIPTION BACK INTO THE FRATERNITY FOLD, IT WAS INCORPORATED BY THE PARLIAMENT OF CANADA AS THE ORDER OF THE HOSPITAL OF ST. JOHN OF JERUSALEM /OR IN SHORT, THE ST. JOHN AMBULANCE ASSOCIATION. IT SHOULD ALSO BE STATED THAT IN FULL RECOGNITION OF THEIR GALLANT EFFORTS TOWARDS CHARITY WORK THROUGHOUT THE VARIOUS REGIONS OF THE WORLD, POPE JOHN XXIII ORDAINED THE FREEMASONRY INSTITUTION OF THE KNIGHTS OF MALTA AS BEING A NOTABLE FORM OF RELIGIOUS ENTITY AS WELL AS BEING

A noble order of chivalry. Unlike the days-gone-by, the modern day Knights didn't have to hide their membership from the Roman Catholic Church. By the time Pope John XXIII instituted the reformation of Vatican II, (1962-65), diplomatic relations with the Vatican had been somewhat subdued as both the Knights of Malta and the religious leaders in the papacy were collaborating with one another on an assortment of issues. As a fully recognized religious entity, the Knights of Malta maintained hospitals, first-aid centers and facilities to care for war casualties and refugees. They wore a black cloak on which an eight-pointed Maltese Cross was clearly visible. By the later 1960's, the membership roster of the Knights of Malta in La Belle Province de Quebec was reportedly an estimated 8,000 strong.

In an interesting twist of ironic fate, during the corrupt administration years of Maurice Duplessis, Soviet Union diplomats based here in Canada during the Second World War considered the Province of Quebec to be a hotbed of anti-Soviet sentiment. Newspapers within the Province were apparently writing an assortment of articles criticizing the Stalinist regime of the Soviet People's Republic saying that the diplomats based in Canada were sending scathing reports back to Moscow concerning Quebec's leading journalists and political figures. Although Duplessis was labeled by the Francophone population of Quebec as being a fascist supporter and was further described by his own political party (the Union Nationale Party) as being the **FUHRER** of the Province, the vast majority of French Canada were in favor of Duplessis largely due to the fact that both fascism and anti-Semitism was fully supported by the Roman Catholic Church during the 1930's, 40's and 50's. To that end, a secular faction of the Catholic Church was established to help fight Communism well into the 21ST Century; **OPUS DEI**.

Perhaps it was due to the Roman Catholic Church's establishing of this secret fraternity that enabled the LePage name to be found in the archives of the British Secret Intelligence Service (MI5) and its Security Service (MI6), including both of their American counterparts the CIA and the FBI as being possible Soviet agents during the Cold War. While the U.S. Senator Joseph McCarthy was just beginning to get his witch hunt of Communism infiltration of the American Federal Government underway during the 1950's, the KGB (Soviet military intelligence) had already initiated its recruiting campaign in both Great Britain and the United States. In England for example, the KGB targeted British politicians into the

FOLD. AMONG THOSE TARGETED WAS TOM DRIBERG, AN ACTIVE JOURNALIST TURNED POLITICIAN WHO WAS ALSO A MEMBER OF THE LABOR PARTY AS WELL AS AN ELECTED MP (MEMBER OF PARLIAMENT). HE WAS THE LABOR PARTY'S NATIONAL EXECUTIVE FROM 1949 TO 1974 AND ITS CHAIRMAN IN 1957-58. DRIBERG WAS REPORTEDLY RECRUITED AS AGENT **LePAGE** BECAUSE OF HIS PROMISCUOUS HOMOSEXUAL ACTIVITIES THAT APPARENTLY WAS AN OPEN BOOK IN GREAT BRITAIN AS WELL AS IN A FEW OTHER COUNTRIES; SUCH AS THE UNITED STATES AND THE SOVIET UNION. THE MAIN REASON FOR HIS EASY RECRUITMENT WAS THE FACT THAT WHILE STILL IN HIS TEENAGE YEARS DRIBERG JOINED THE COMMUNIST PARTY AND ONE YEAR PREVIOUS TO BEING INITIATED AS A SOVIET SPY, A GROUP OF WESTERN HEMISPHERE POLITICIANS WERE VISITING MOSCOW (TOM DRIBERG OF COURSE BEING ONE OF THEM). USING MALE /OR FEMALE OPERATIVES TO SEDUCE THE WESTERN POLITICIANS, THEN TAKING PHOTOGRAPHS OF THEIR SEXUAL INTERLUDES, THE KGB BLACKMAILED THEM INTO SUBMISSION.

THE RECRUITMENT OF AGENT **LePAGE** ON THE OTHER HAND WAS MUCH EASIER THAN WHAT WAS ORIGINALLY ANTICIPATED BECAUSE HE KNOWINGLY COMPROMISED HIS SITUATION BY PAYING A VISIT TO "A LARGE UNDERGROUND URINAL JUST BEHIND THE METROPOLE HOTEL, OPEN ALL NIGHT, FREQUENTED BY HUNDREDS OF QUESTING SLAV HOMOSEXUALS - STANDING THERE IN RIGID EXHIBITIONIST ROWS, MOTIONLESS SAVE FOR THE HASTY GROPE AND THE ANXIOUS OR BECKONING GLANCE OVER THE SHOULDER - AND TENDED ONLY BY AN OLD WOMAN CLEANER WHO NEVER SEEMED TO NOTICE WHAT WAS GOING ON. "ALTHOUGH THE ELDERLY WOMAN FAILED TO NOTICE THE INDISCRETIONS OF THE BRITISH POLITICIAN IN THE PUBLIC WASHROOM FACILITIES, THE KGB WERE NOT ABOUT READY TO LET IT PASS THEM BY. WELL AWARE OF WHO HE WAS AS WELL AS HIS SEXUAL PREFERENCES, THEY CONFRONTED DRIBERG WITH HIS VARIOUS SEXUAL ENCOUNTERS. TO MAKE MATTERS EVEN WORSE FOR THE EASY RECRUITMENT OF SOVIET AGENT **LePAGE** WAS THE FACT THAT EITHER ON THAT SAME EVENING /OR ON OTHER SUBSEQUENT EVENINGS IN MOSCOW, HE APPARENTLY HAD YET ANOTHER SEXUAL RELATIONSHIP WITH HOMOSEXUAL MEN. KNOWING THIS, THE KGB USED IT FOR THEIR ADVANTAGE AND SOON AFTERWARDS, AGENT **LePAGE** WAS USING HIS PROPAGANDA SKILLS BY WRITING A SHORT BIOGRAPHY CONTAINING A DISINGENUOUS STUDY OF FELLOW SOVIET SPY GUY BURGESS CLEARING THE AIR PERTAINING TO BURGESS NOT BEING AN AGENT FOR THE KGB — GUY BURGESS OF COURSE BEING ONE OF THE KGB'S MOST CELEBRATED AGENTS. IN FACT, HE WAS ONE OUT OF A GROUP OF FIVE YOUNG CAMBRIDGE UNIVERSITY GRADUATES WHO BY THE SECOND WORLD WAR BECAME KNOWN AS THE MAGNIFICENT FIVE: ANTONY BLUNT, GUY BURGESS, JOHN CAIRNCROSS, DONALD MACLEAN AND KIM PHILBY.

With the publication of agent **LePAGE's** masterpiece "Guy Burgess: A Portrait with Background "in 1956, other propaganda works were soon to follow — set to pen and paper such as "Ruling Passions "for example which was an autobiography of the life and times of Tom Driberg published in the mid-1970's. From 1956 to 1968, Driberg acted as agent **LePAGE** for the KGB influencing the British Parliament whenever he could. The Soviet spy remained under MI5/MI6 and CIA operative surveillance well past 1968 when he reportedly first began severing all ties with the KGB by restricting his meeting with Soviet diplomats and intelligence officers under diplomatic cover, then, breaking off contact altogether. His decision to quit the KGB soon followed with the decision to retire from the political arena. This decision was apparently an easy one to make as Soviet agent **LePAGE** had suffered a mild heart attack and was having an ever increasing sexual appetite for the young boys of the Island of Cyprus while on tour as chairman of the British Parliamentary Labor Party in January of 1968. The British politician had turned into a sexual predator of young children and as before, the KGB was going to take full advantage of it. By the mid-1970's, the Soviet agent/pedophile not only disappeared off the surveillance radar of the various spy agencies (British, Russian and/or American) but he also withdrew from society soon after retiring from politics altogether, turning into a virtual recluse. The only reason as to why the Soviet spy was able to continually molest young children was largely due to the fact that he too had lots of friends in extremely high places and his colleagues simply turned a blind eye to all of it.

Contrary to popular belief, religion has always played a very important role in the never-ending politics of Freemasonry on a global scale. In Quebec for example, Freemasonry and Roman Catholicism go hand-in-hand. For many generations after its formation, the Grand Lodge of Quebec had become a leader in improving the Catholic/Masonic relationship all thanks to General George Prevost and his establishing of the Francophonism to the Ancient Craft. It oddly enough became so successful that on April 28TH, 1989 a special concert was held in the Notre Dame Basilica (one of North America's largest Catholic Churches, located in old Montreal) which has a seating capacity of 3,500. The McGill Chamber Orchestra furnished the musical accompaniment of Mozart's Masonic Music Concert while Fraternity Brother Xavier Varnus, a highly respected Master Mason and world class organ virtuoso, performed the organ solos. The concert was a dedication

OF MOZART'S MUSIC, IN QUOTING THE GRAND LODGE OF QUEBEC AND ITS ADVERTISING BULLETIN: **"THIS WILL BE THE FIRST TIME IN NORTH AMERICA THAT SUCH A PROGRAM HAS EVER BEEN PRESENTED FOR THE PUBLIC."**

DURING 1989, THERE WERE MANY FREEMASONRY AND ROMAN CATHOLIC UNITED ACTIVITIES BEING ENJOYED BY ALL IN OTHER REGIONS OF THE COUNTRY. IN EARLY AUGUST FOR EXAMPLE, IN FRATERNITY BROTHER JOHN DIEFENBAKER'S HOMETOWN OF PRINCE ALBERT, SASKATCHEWAN "THE KNIGHTS OF COLUMBUS JOINED WITH THE MASONIC ORDER AND LAID A CORNERSTONE OF THE NEW ST. JOSEPH'S CATHOLIC CHURCH. "THERE WERE REPORTEDLY OVER FOUR-HUNDRED PARISHIONERS ATTENDING IN ADDITION TO THE MEMBERS OF THE CRAFT AND THE KNIGHTS OF COLUMBUS JOINING IN ON THE FESTIVITIES. EVEN A ROMAN CATHOLIC CHURCH IN MARKATO, MINNESOTA HOPPED INTO BED WITH THE MASONIC BROTHERHOOD OF MAN AS ITS IMPERIAL SHRINERS PREPARED FOR THE COLLABORATION DURING A SPECIAL DINNER MEETING IN THE EARLY PARTS OF 1989. THE INTERCOURSE AND MARRIAGE THAT TOOK PLACE WITH THE SHRINERS ASSOCIATION AND OTHER FRATERNITY BRETHREN, A ROMAN CATHOLIC PRIEST, WHO WAS ALSO AN ACTIVE MEMBER IN THE MARKATO MASONIC LODGE NO. 12 AS WELL AS THE KNIGHTS OF COLUMBUS, APPEALED "TO HIS FELLOW FRATERNALISTS ON BOTH SIDES TO JOIN TOGETHER TO FIGHT PREJUDICE. "IRONICALLY, DURING HIS PRESENTATION ON UNITY THE ROMAN CATHOLIC PARISH PRIEST CALLED HIMSELF A "RARE SPECIMEN "AND HAD HIGH HOPES OF RECONCILIATION.

ONE-HUNDRED YEARS PRIOR TO ALL OF THIS UNFOLDING, IF A ROMAN CATHOLIC WALKED INTO A ROOM AN A PROTESTANT WAS PRESENT — EITHER THE CATHOLIC WALKED RIGHT OUT AGAIN /OR IF THE CATHOLIC REMAINED, THE PROTESTANT WOULD LEAVE; NEITHER HAD A TOLERANCE FOR ONE ANOTHER. THIS FORNICATION BY WAY OF INBREEDING — ROMAN CATHOLIC AND MASONIC RELATIONSHIPS — MANY YEARS LATER WAS THE MAIN CHARACTERISTIC OF A GOOD PORTION OF QUEBEC'S FRENCH FAMILIES AS THEY BEGAN MAKING VARIOUS ATTEMPTS TO QUASH SIR JOHN A. MACDONALD'S DREAMS OF A CONFEDERATION WITHIN THE DOMAIN OF FRENCH CANADA. WITH GROWING DISSENSION AND SCHISM RUNNING AT A HIGH FEVERISH PACE, PIERRE FORTIN, A POLITICIAN FOR THE DISTRICT OF RIMOUSKI AND THE GASPE PENINSULA REGIONS OF THE PROVINCE WAS ELECTED INTO PARLIAMENT. IN HIS DEBUT SPEECH TO OTTAWA, (FEBRUARY 23RD, 1878), HE REPORTEDLY STATED THAT HIS FRENCH RIDING IN RIMOUSKI-GASPE HAD THEIR OWN GOVERNMENT AND APPARENTLY, VERY POLITELY TOLD THE GOVERNMENT OF CANADA WHAT THEY COULD DO WITH THEIR RACIAL SEGREGATION POLICIES FOR FRENCH QUEBEC.

IT'S INTERESTING TO NOTE THAT ACCORDING TO THE RECORDS OF THE LEPAGE FAMILY TREE, THE FORTIN AND THE LEPAGE FAMILIES WERE RELATED TO ONE ANOTHER THROUGH VARIOUS COLLABORATIONS. ACCORDING TO THE

RECORDS OF THE LEPAGE'S LINEAGE FOR EXAMPLE, IT IS DULY RECORDED AS EARLY AS THE LATE 1600'S THAT BOTH OF THESE FRANCOPHONE FAMILIES ASSOCIATED WITH ONE ANOTHER. IN FACT, RENE LEPAGE, THE FIRST SEIGNEUR OF RIMOUSKI MARRIED MARIE MADELEINE GANGNON (1686), SHE WAS THE DAUGHTER OF PIERRE GANGNON AND BARBE FORTIN. THEN NEARLY A FULL CENTURY LATER, AUGUST 22ND, 1785 CAPTAIN JOSEPH LEPAGE OF RIMOUSKI MARRIED ONE THRESES FORTIN OF CAP-ST.-IGNACE. THE INTERCOURSE AND MARRIAGE OF THESE TWO FRENCH QUEBEC FAMILIES THROUGHOUT THE CENTURIES HAVE PRODUCED MANY OFFSPRING OF DISTINCTION, BOTH POLITICALLY AS WELL AS RELIGIOUSLY. FURTHERMORE, ACCORDING TO DOCUMENTS CONTAINED IN THE LEPAGE FAMILY'S OWN ARCHIVES, THEY WERE NOT AT ALL IMPRESSED WITH THE POLITICAL AFFAIRS OF THE PROTESTANT ADMINISTRATION OF SIR JOHN A. MACDONALD AND THOSE WHO FOLLOWED HIM. PERHAPS THIS IS THE REASON AS TO WHY THE FEDERAL GOVERNMENT'S NATIONAL ARCHIVES BRANCH IN OTTAWA HAS COMPILED AN ABUNDANCE OF ASSORTED FILES ON THE LEPAGE'S OF CANADA SINCE CONFEDERATION. OR, MAYBE ITS SIMPLY A WAY OF KEEPING THE RECORD STRAIGHT IF SOMEONE MERELY WANTED TO KNOW THE TRUTH SINCE THE LEPAGE'S THEMSELVES HAVE A TENANCY OF OMITTING AND/OR CHANGING THE FACTS AS THEY HAD OCCURRED JUST TO SUIT THEIR OWN WHIMS AS A WAY AND MEANS OF FULFILLING THEIR MANY HIDDEN SECRET AGENDAS AS PROPHESIED BY THE ALMIGHTY GOD HIMSELF.

BE THAT AS IT MAY, NOT ONE MEMBER OF THE LEPAGE FAMILY ITSELF CAN EVER DISPUTE THE FACTS AS THEY STAND TODAY. IT SEEMED THAT ONCE THE PRISON GATES WERE SPRUNG OPEN IN FRANCE AND THE ASSASSIN LEPAGE DIT CHAUDRON WAS FORCED TO SET SAIL WITH THE ROBERVAL EXPEDITION OF 1542, IT LITERALLY SET THE WHEELS IN MOTION FOR ALL OTHER LEPAGE'S TO FOLLOW THROUGHOUT THE MANY CENTURIES OF CANADA'S ACTUAL EXISTENCE. THEIR NOT SO GLAMOROUS FREEMASONRY PAST IS A TWISTED WEB OF SECRETS AND LIES THAT HAVE BEEN PASSED DOWN FROM GENERATION TO GENERATION THAT JUST MANAGED TO FIT INTO THE SCHEME OF THINGS, REQUIRING MUCH UNRAVELING IN ORDER TO PUT DOWN TO PEN AND PAPER. AS ONE MEMBER OF THE LEPAGE'S SOON DISCOVERED WHILE RESEARCHING HIS OWN FAMILY LINEAGE TRYING TO TRACE HIS ABORIGINAL BLOODLINES. KNOWING FULL WELL THAT HIS GREAT GRANDMOTHER (ON THE LEPAGE'S SIDE) WAS AN INDIAN WOMAN FROM THE PROVINCE OF QUEBEC, HE KEPT RUNNING INTO A BRICK WALL EACH AND EVERY TIME HE ASKED FAMILY MEMBERS ABOUT HER. BEING A FANATIC WHEN IT CAME TO OBTAINING A PAPER TRAIL, NO STONE WAS LEFT UNTURNED AS HIS QUEST FOR ONE SIMPLY QUESTION SOON EVOLVED INTO A MASSIVE UNDERTAKING THAT HE KNEW IN THE END WOULD CAUSE HIM TO BE OSTRACIZED BY HIS OWN FAMILY MEMBERS. BUT HE DIDN'T CARE AS IT BECAME MORE APPARENT TO HIM AS TO WHY HE PERSONALLY HAD ALWAYS FELT MORE

COMPASSIONATE TOWARDS CANADA'S FIRST NATION PEOPLES THAN THAT OF THE WHITEMAN. SOMETIMES A FAMILY TREE CAN GET SOMEWHAT DISTORTED IF ALL THE FACTS ARE NOT COLLECTED FOR PROPER ANALYSIS. AT FIRST GLANCE HIS FAMILY LINEAGE SEEMED SIMPLE AND STRAIGHT FORWARD ENOUGH AS THE GENERATIONS GREW;

ETIENNE LEPAGE/NICOLE BERTHELOT

LA FAMILLE LEPAGE AU CANADA .... GERMAIN LEPAGE		(1634)
LA FAMILLE LEPAGE AU CANADA .... RENE LEPAGE		(1656)
LA FAMILLE LEPAGE AU CANADA .... PIERRE LEPAGE SR.		(1687)
LA FAMILLE LEPAGE AU CANADA .... PIERRE LEPAGE JR.		(1724)
LA FAMILLE LEPAGE AU CANADA .... CHARLES LEPAGE		(1753)
LA FAMILLE LEPAGE AU CANADA .... HONORAT LEPAGE		(1795)
LA FAMILLE LEPAGE AU CANADA .... OCTAVE LEPAGE		(1828)
LA FAMILLE LEPAGE AU CANADA .... AMABLE LEPAGE		(1853)
LA FAMILLE LEPAGE AU CANADA .... DONAT LEPAGE		(1888)
LA FAMILLE LEPAGE AU CANADA .... HECTOR LEPAGE		(1928)
LA FAMILLE LEPAGE AU CANADA .... BENOIT LEPAGE		(1954)

BUT LIKE ANYTHING ELSE THAT THE LEPAGE'S HAD A HAND IN, THINGS ARE NOT QUITE AS SIMPLE AND STRAIGHT FORWARD AS THEY MAY SEEM TO BE. FOR INSTANCE, THE PAPER TRAIL NORMALLY ASSOCIATED WITH THE MANY GENERATIONS OF LEPAGE'S IN CANADA IT IS SOON DISCOVERED THAT CHARLES LEPAGE MARRIED A WOMAN NAMED MARIE-ANNE DION ON JULY 8TH, 1781 AND ONE PIERRE LEPAGE III (THE SON OF PIERRE LEPAGE JR. 1724) MARRIED GENEVIEVE DION (THE SISTER OF MARIE-ANNE DION) ON AUGUST 30TH, 1779. BOTH WOMEN WERE THE DAUGHTERS OF JEAN-BAPTISTE DION AND GENEVIEVE MORISSET. AND TO FURTHER COMPLICATE THE GENE POOL YEARS LATER, OTHER GENERATIONS OF LEPAGE'S ALSO MARRIED INTO A SAME FAMILY SCENARIO THUS MAKING THE MIX VERY VOLATILE IN NATURE. NOT ONLY THOSE CIRCUMSTANCES WERE THE CAUSE OF A CLANDESTINE LINEAGE, HONORAT LEPAGE AND HIS FIRST COUSIN, EVODE LEPAGE (THE SON OF PIERRE LEPAGE III AND GENEVIEVE DION BAPTISED OCTOBER 8TH, 1787) FOR EXAMPLE BOTH MARRIED INTO THE LEVASSEUR FAMILY. HONRAT MARRIED FRANCOISE LEVASSEUR ON FEBRUARY 15TH, 1819 AND EVODE LEPAGE MARRIED ANGELEQUE LEVASSEUR ONLY A FEW YEARS PREVIOUSLY, JUNE 22ND, 1812. BOTH FRANCOISE AND ANGELEQUE WERE THE DAUGHTERS OF JEAN LEVASSEUR AND JUDITH DRAPEAU. WITH THE GENE POOL DEPLETING WITH EACH PASSING GENERATION, THE LEPAGE'S OF CANADA SEEMED TO BE HEADING FOR SOME VERY TURBULENT WATERS IN THE NOT TOO DISTANT FUTURE. PERHAPS THIS WAS WHY THEY CHANGED PARTNERS AS OFTEN AS THEY DID AND BEGAN THEIR

TEPEE CREEPING ADVENTURES AS A WAY AND MEANS OF REFURBISHING THE GENE POOL AS WITH SO MUCH INNER COUPLING OCCURRING AMONGST THEIR OWN KIND, NOTHING BUT DIRE CONSEQUENCES LAY AHEAD FOR THE FUTURE GENERATIONS.

BY THE TIME THE EARLY 1800'S GENERATION OF LEPAGE'S WERE BEING BORN, CANADA WAS IN THE MIDST OF A GREAT UPHEAVAL AS FRENCH AND ENGLISH CANADA SOON BEGAN TO DESPISE ONE ANOTHER EVEN MORE. MOST OF THE FRENCH ROMAN CATHOLICS WANTED NOTHING TO DO WITH THE BRITISH MONARCHY AS THEY (THE FRENCH) FELT THAT THE ENGLISH COULD NOT BE TRUSTED. SOME IN FACT BECAME TOTALLY DISGUSTED WITH THE BRITISH THAT THEY MIGRATED TO THE UNITED STATES IN ORDER TO BREAK AWAY FROM THE CLUTCHES OF ENGLAND. SUCH WAS THE CASE WHEN OCTAVE LEPAGE VENTURED IN MASSACHUSETTS TO RAISE HIS FAMILY IN THE EARLY 1880'S. AT THE TIME, THE DOMINION OF CANADA WAS BARELY FOURTEEN-YEARS-OLD; 1881. BUT BY NOVEMBER 10TH, 1887 OCTAVE WAS NEGOTIATING A LAND TRANSACTION IN BALMORAL, NEW BRUNSWICK – A SMALL NORTHERN NEW BRUNSWICK COMMUNITY THAT WAS GOING TO EVENTUALLY ENABLE HIS OFFSPRING TO RE-ESTABLISH THEMSELVES AS SO-CALLED DEVOTED FRENCH ROMAN CATHOLIC CANADIAN CITIZENS ONCE AGAIN; **DEED NUMBER: 3499** REGISTERED 09/03/1888 AND BY DECEMBER 28TH,1890 A SECOND LAND TRANSACTION WAS REGISTERED; **DEED NUMBER: 5881**. WHILE RESIDING AT FALL RIVER, MASSACHUSETTS THE LEPAGE'S ALSO BEGAN ESTABLISHING THEMSELVES AS NEWFOUND AMERICANS. ALTHOUGH AMABLE LEPAGE (THE SON OF OCTAVE LEPAGE) WAS BORN AND MARRIED IN FRENCH CANADA, HE TOO VENTURED WITH HIS FATHER INTO MASSACHUSETTS IN 1881 TO WORK IN THE TEXTILE INDUSTRY AS FRENCH CANADIANS FELT THAT THEY WERE GETTING THE SHORT END OF SIR JOHN A. MACDONALD'S CONFEDERATION STICK. IN FACT, A COUPLE OF AMABLE LEPAGE'S CHILDREN WERE BORN AT THE NEW DIGS IN MASSACHUSETTS; JOSEPH-AIME LEPAGE JULY 24TH, 1882 AND JOSEPH (BLANC) LEPAGE NOVEMBER 8TH, 1883. BY THE TIME JOSEPH-DONAT LEPAGE WAS BORN (JANUARY 5TH, 1888), THE LEPAGE'S OF MASSACHUSETTS HAD JUST MOVED FROM FALL RIVER TO BALMORAL TO LIVE AMONGST THE ACADIANS OF NORTHERN NEW BRUNSWICK.

IN TOTAL AMABLE LEPAGE HAD TEN (10) CHILDREN, THREE OF WHOM REPORTEDLY DIED NOT LONG AFTER BIRTH; FLORA 1881/DENISE 1889/ANGELA 1901. THE SURVIVING CHILDREN WENT ON TO RAISE FAMILIES OF THEIR OWN IN NORTHERN NEW BRUNSWICK, WITH THE EXCEPTION OF CHARLES LEONIDE LEPAGE AND JOSEPH (BLANC) LEPAGE WHO MOVED TO JACKSONBOROS, ONTARIO IN 1924. CHARLES REPORTEDLY HAD TWELVE (12) CHILDREN IN ALL, THREE OF WHOM DIED; JOSEPH-ROMUALD-ADELARD BORN FEBRUARY 4TH, 1902 ONLY TO DIE DAYS LATER, FEBRUARY 15TH, 1902; LAURA BORN

September 5th, 1915, died fifteen years later in June of 1930; Joseph-Benoit born September 11th, 1922 and dying on September 25th of that same year. Joseph (Blanc) LePage on the other hand only had one (1) child that died at a very young age; Joseph-Auguste born April 2nd, 1915, died February 11th, 1916. In total, Blanc had seven (7) living children. Other members of the LePage's of northern New Brunswick also had large families of their own. The sixth living child of Amable LePage (Octave LePage born on August 9th, 1890 in Balmoral) for example had thirteen (13) children, two (2) of whom died at a young age; Honore born February 19th, 1914, died only days later on February 23rd; Rene born January 17th, 1925, died October 2nd, 1926.

Joseph-Donat LePage and his wife Marie-Genevieve Poirier, Emma for short, had the (10) children, two (2) of whom died early on in life; Ida-Catherine-Eloisa born April 11th, 1916, died February 7th, 1920 and of course Joseph-Romain-Benoit born November 12th, 1914, died in Sicily during the Second World War in 1942. The remaining children;

Leo	born	July 3rd, 1912
Laura	born	April 11th, 1916
Germaine	born	October 7th, 1920
Rolande	born	October 16th, 1922
Anita	born	September 13th, 1924
Louis	born	February, 28th, 1926
Mathias	born	May 28th, 1928
Hector	born	May 28th, 1928

also went on to have children of their own. The youngest of Donat's sons, Hector Joseph LePage had seven (7) children, one (1) of whom died, Lorna Catherine LePage, not long after being born in 1956, she was only three months old.

Ironically, the history of the LePage family tree really got watered down after Donat LePage married Emma Poirier on September 25th, 1911 as they (the LePage's of northern New Brunswick) now had more family secrets to hide. One naturally being their migration from French Canada to the United States and another being the fact that Emma Poirier was the child of a Mi'kmaq Indian woman from Maria, Quebec, (Marie Eliza Cyr). According to an 1891 census taken by the Canadian Federal Government, one James T. Poirier is registered as being a farmer living at Charlo Station (a small farming

COMMUNITY NOT VERY FAR FROM BALMORAL) WHILE MARIE CYR IS LISTED AS BEING AN INN KEEPER IN THE TINY INDIAN VILLAGE OF MARIA, QUEBEC ON THE GASPE PENINSULA. CHARLO STATION WAS JUST ACROSS THE BAY, (BAIE DE CHALEURS) FROM THE INDIAN VILLAGE, A GOOD HALF DAYS ROWING IN A NEWFOUNDLAND DORY BOAT. THE BAIE DE CHALEURS SEPARATES NORTHERN NEW BRUNSWICK FROM THE PROVINCE OF QUEBEC.

NOT MUCH IS ACTUALLY KNOWN ABOUT JAMES T. POIRIER THE FARMER EXCEPT THE FACT THAT ONCE HIS FIRST WIFE DIED FOR SOME REASON /OR ANOTHER, HE GOT INVOLVED WITH MARIE CYR AND ONCE HE GREW TIRED OF HER, HE GOT INVOLVED WITH YET ANOTHER WOMAN; MELANIE MERCIER. AS THE STORY GOES, JAMES POIRIER SUPPOSEDLY MARRIED MARIE CYR BUT THAT IN ITSELF IS HIGHLY UNLIKELY BASICALLY BECAUSE OF THE FACT THAT EVEN AT THAT TIME PERIOD OF OUR COUNTRY'S HISTORY THE CATHOLIC CHURCH STILL DIDN'T SANCTION FORTIFICATION WITH THE INDIANS AND NO OFFICIAL MARRIAGE CERTIFICATE COULD BE FOUND ANYWHERE IN THE FAMILY RECORDS. BESIDES THAT, THE LEPAGE'S OF NORTHERN NEW BRUNSWICK WERE NOT ABOUT READY TO ACCEPT A MERE INDIAN INTO THE FAMILY FOLD. PERHAPS THIS IS WHY EMMA POIRIER DENOUNCED HER NATIVE HERITAGE AS SHE SO DESPERATELY WANTED TO BE ACCEPTED BY ALL THE LEPAGE'S, THUS MAKING HER TOTALLY ASHAMED OF HER INDIAN BLOODLINE FOR SAKE OF WANTING TO FIT IN. ACCORDINGLY, MARIE ELIZA CYR WAS NEVER ACCEPTED AS BEING PART OF THE LEPAGE FAMILY AS THOSE WHO TOLERATED HER PRESENCE SIMPLY REFERRED TO HER AS MADAME CYR, NOTHING LESS THAN A TOKEN FAMILY INDIAN. ONLY ON THOSE SPECIAL OCCASIONS WAS SHE CALLED MADAME POIRIER /OR EVEN GRAND-MERE AS FAR AS THAT GOES.

LIKE THE LEPAGE'S OF QUEBEC AND FORMERLY OF MASSACHUSETTS, BOTH THE POIRIER AND CYR FAMILY NAMES GO WAY BACK INTO CANADIAN HISTORY TRACING THEIR ROOTS TO THE 1600'S. THROUGHOUT THE HISTORY OF THESE QUEBEC FAMILY NAMES, MANY LEPAGE'S MARRIED INTO THEIR FAMILIES. IN FACT, ONE OF JAMES T. POIRIER'S OTHER DAUGHTERS, ELIZABETH (BESSIE) POIRIER FROM HIS THIRD SEXUAL COUPLING, MARRIED ONE AMABLE LEPAGE, THE SON OF JOSEPH-AIME LEPAGE ON AUGUST 10TH, 1937. NEEDLESS TO SAY, MARRYING THEIR OWN KIND HAD BEEN THE TREND OVER THE MANY CENTURIES AS NOTHING ELSE WAS TO BE TOLERATED. WITH THAT BEING LOGICALLY INGRAINED IN THEIR HUMAN PSYCHE, MANY A LEPAGE MARRIED THEIR OWN 1ST AND 2ND COUSINS — SOME IN FACT MARRIED DIRECTLY FROM THE SAME FAMILY TREE. AS INBREEDING SOON BECAME A NORMAL PRACTICE FOR SOME OF THE LEPAGE'S, IT WAS NOT ONLY HIDDEN FROM PLAIN PUBLIC VIEW BUT WAS ALSO KEPT IN THE DARK FROM THE CATHOLIC CHURCH AS HAVING SEXUAL RELATIONS SO CLOSE TO THE FAMILY TREE WAS HIGHLY DISCOURAGED BY THE CHURCH AND ITS FALSE IDOL GOD; THE POPE. EVEN AT THAT TIME PERIOD,

THE ROMAN CATHOLIC CHURCH ATTITUDE WAS THAT IF THE CHURCH DIDN'T KNOW ANYTHING ABOUT IT, THEN, IT DIDN'T REALLY MATTER IN THE LONG RUN – A DON'T ASK, DON'T TELL POLICY OF ENLIGHTENMENT.

BUT BY THE TIME THE CHANGING OF THE GUARD CAME INTO BEING (A BABY BOOMER), THE UNANSWERED QUESTIONS OF YEARS PAST HAD TO BE EXPLAINED IN FULL DETAIL AS THIS MEMBER OF THE FAMILY TREE BEGAN SEARCHING FOR THE TRUTH AS HE HAD FINALLY REACHED THE CROSSROADS OF HIS LIFE AND WASN'T AT ALL SATISFIED WITH THE DIRECTION IT HAD TAKEN. MARRIED, THEN, DIVORCED AND UNABLE TO SEE HIS HALF-BREED INDIAN DAUGHTER, HE FELT BOTH GUILTY AND REJECTED ALL AT THE SAME TIME. GUILTY FOR ABANDONING HIS DAUGHTER WHILE SHE WAS STILL ONLY FIVE YEARS OLD AND REJECTED BECAUSE NO ONE REALLY UNDERSTOOD HIM AND HOW HE WAS FEELING ABOUT IT AT THE TIME. KNOWING FULL WELL THAT HE CAME FROM A HIGHLY DYSFUNCTIONAL FRENCH ROMAN CATHOLIC FAMILY, HE SOON BEGAN HAVING FLASHBACKS OF HIS PAST AND THE ANSWERS TO MANY OF HIS QUESTIONS WERE EITHER IGNORED /OR SHRUGGED OFF AS BEING THE RANTING OF AN IDIOT HELL BENT ON DESTROYING WHAT REMAINED OF HIS IMMEDIATE FAMILY. TO SOME, HE MERELY WANTED TO BE THE CENTER OF ATTENTION CITING THAT HE WAS HAVING ILLUSIONS OF GRANDEUR.

IT IS ALSO INTERESTING TO NOTE THAT CONTRARY AS TO WHAT SOME MEMBERS OF THE LEPAGE FAMILY ACROSS CANADA MAY WISH TO BE TRUE, NO ONE CAN DENY THE FACT THAT THEY AND THEIR ROMAN CATHOLIC CHURCH CONNECTIONS HAD A HAND IN DICTATING WHAT THE GOVERNING BODY OF THE NEWLY FORMED PROVINCE OF MANITOBA WAS GOING TO BE DURING THE METIS UP-RISING OF 1869 UNDER THE LEADERSHIP OF LOUIS RIEL.

FOR INSTANCE, ON JULY 1ST, 1847 FRANCOISE LEPAGE (ONE OF THE DAUGHTERS OF A 7TH GENERATION OF LEPAGE'S IN CANADA, LOUIS LEPAGE OF RIMOUSKI), MARRIED ONE JOSEPH-CHARLES TACHE, A WELL RESPECTED PHYSICIAN TURNED POLITICIAN. TO SOME FAMILY MEMBERS, IT WAS MERELY A MARRIAGE OF POLITICAL CONVENIENCE. AT THE AGE OF TWENTY-SEVEN, TACHE WAS ELECTED BY ACCLAMATION TO THE LEGISLATURE ASSEMBLY OF THE PROVINCE OF CANADA FOR THE DISTRICT OF RIMOUSKI ON JANUARY 24TH, 1848. NEEDLESS TO SAY, TACHE RETURNED TO THE ASSEMBLY IN 1851, ALSO BY ACCLAMATION AND HE NARROWLY ESCAPED DEFEAT IN 1854. DURING THE LATER PARTS OF 1856, TACHE WAS FORCED TO VACATE HIS SEAT IN THE LEGISLATIVE ASSEMBLY AS ALLEGATIONS OF CORRUPTION AND DERELICTION OF HIS POLITICAL DUTIES SPREAD THROUGHOUT LA BELLE PROVINCE DE QUEBEC. EVEN THOUGH HE WAS MADE A FRATERNAL KNIGHT OF THE LEGION OF HONOR BY THE KING OF FRANCE (NAPOLEON III) IN 1855, IT STILL MADE NO DIFFERENCE AS TACHE WAS ACCUSED OF BEING MORE INTERESTED IN DEALING WITH THE FRATERNITY CONCERNS AND INTERESTS OF BOTH THE

French monarchy and the Roman Catholic Church than those of his own constituency.

As rumors of his political demise began to circulate, Tache resigned his seat in December of 1856 to avoid public humiliation and the penalty of impeachment by his duly elected peers. Shortly after his resignation out of the political arena, he was ironically anointed head of a newly formed newspaper, Le Courrier du Canada, which was to be first issued on February 2ND, 1857. It goes without saying that the daily newspaper had a mandate to mold the views and opinions of the people of Quebec as Tache set to print his ideas for the roles of both Church and state. Without a doubt, Joseph-Charles Tache used the printing press as a way and means of defeating Sir John A. MacDonald's dream of the Confederation of the British North American colonies of Canada. He reportedly stirred up the emotions of his readership by denouncing the injustices of the British system and the threat it represented in the foreseeable future to the survival of the Francophone Nation of Quebec. In his series of articles which appeared in Le Courrier du Canada from July 7TH to October 27TH, 1857 Tache fully documented his scheme for constitutional recommendations for the preservation of the French Roman Catholic identity under the proposed British Confederation of the Dominion of Canada. Coincidently, Tache's newspaper articles were also published in book form the following year and Sir John A. MacDonald would eventually incorporate a good portion of its contents into the British North America Act of 1867.

It should also be stated that Tache remained head of the daily newspaper until October 31ST, 1859 whereupon for some reason /or another, his employment was thusly terminated. Within only a few days of this termination order, he became an inspector of prisons and asylums for the Province of Canada and in 1864, Tache was appointed Deputy Minister of Agriculture and Statistics. He spent twenty-four years as being a senior civil servant in Ottawa and was reportedly responsible for writing many books on an assortment of topics pertaining to the preservation of French Canada under English rule while at the same time maintaining his prestigious governmental posting. Oddly enough, in 1854 Tache had one of his most infamous books published; **"A PLAN FOR THE COMMUTATION OF THE SEIGNIORIAL TENURE "**which contained some rather interesting statistics and other related documentation pertaining to lands (Indian lands) held by the LePage's of Quebec and other

PROMINENT FRANCOPHONE FAMILIES, INCLUDING MASSIVE LAND HOLDINGS HELD BY THE ROMAN CATHOLIC CHURCH. ALTHOUGH TACHE WASN'T REALLY A GREAT SUPPORTED OF SIR JOHN A. MACDONALD'S DREAM OF A UNITED FRONT FOR CONFEDERATION AND WAS SAID TO HAVE OPENLY CRITICIZED THE BRITISH PROPOSAL WHENEVER HE HAD A CHANCE TO DO SO, THE MAIN REASON AS TO WHY HE WAS GIVEN SUCH AN IMPORTANT PORTFOLIO WITHIN MACDONALD'S ADMINISTRATION WAS LARGELY DUE TO THE FACT THAT JOSEPH-CHARLES TACHE WAS THE NEPHEW OF ONE OF THE CANADIAN PRIME MINISTER'S BEST LONGTIME FRIENDS, SIR ETIENNE PASCHAL TACHE. LIKE ANYTHING ELSE IN THE FREEMASONRY WORLD, IT'S NOT WHAT YOU KNOWN BUT RATHER WHO YOU KNOW. IT WASN'T AS THOUGH QUEBEC'S MASONIC ANCIENT CRAFT MEMBERS DIDN'T KNOW WHAT THEY WERE DOING AS THEY HAD MANAGED TO MANIPULATE THEIR WAY INTO THE HEARTS AND MINDS OF THE FRANCOPHONE POPULATION OF FRENCH CANADA. AFTERALL, PLAYING BOTH ENDS AGAINST THE MIDDLE FOR MERE SURVIVAL WAS THE FRENCH ROMAN CATHOLIC THING TO DO. ACCORDING TO THE RECORDS OF THE LEPAGE FAMILY TREE, PIERRE LEPAGE THE THIRD (LA FAMILLE LEPAGE AU CANADA, BORN AT RIMOUSKI IN 1750), EXCHANGED MARRIAGE VOWS WITH GENEVIEVE DION IN 1779 AT THE FAMILY PLANTATION. SHE APPARENTLY WAS A RELATIVE OF SOME SORT TO THE TACHE FAMILY, MOST LIKELY ON JOSEPH-CHARLES TACHE MOTHER'S SIDE OF THE FAMILY AS ONE CHARLES DION APPEARS TO BE LISTED AS HIS GRAND-FATHER.

ONE MUST ALWAYS KEEP IN MIND THAT SOMETIMES WHILE TRACING THE FAMILY TREE THERE'S THE POSSIBILITY THAT PANDORA'S BOX MIGHT BE OPENED EVER SO SLIGHTLY IN ORDER TO FIND THE TRUTH ASSOCIATED WITH ONE'S OWN LINEAGE. AS SOON AS THE LEPAGE NAME WAS CROSS-REFERENCED FOR ANY POSSIBLE POLITICAL AND/OR RELIGIOUS ACTIVITY WEST OF OTTAWA, THE METIS OF MANITOBA AUTOMATICALLY EMERGED OUT OF THE DARKNESS. WHILE ON HIS QUEST TO TRACE HIS NATIVE BLOODLINE ON THE WESTERN PLAINS OF THE CANADIAN FRONTIER, "THE METIS IN THE CANADIAN WEST", NOTHING PREPARED HIM FOR WHAT CRAWLED FROM UNDERNEATH THE LID OF PANDORA'S BOX. AS IT SO HAPPENED, JOSEPH-CHARLES TACHE WAS THE ELDER BROTHER OF ALEXANDRE-ANTONIN TACHE, WHO IRONICALLY WAS RESPONSIBLE FOR ESTABLISHING THE ROMAN CATHOLIC FAITH IN MANITOBA JUST AS LOUIS RIEL AND HIS BAND OF METIS FOLLOWERS WERE TELLING THE CANADIAN FEDERAL GOVERNMENT WHERE TO SHOVE THEIR LAND EXPANSION POLICY FOR THE DOMINION OF CANADA IN 1869. THE MONSEIGNEUR TACHE FIRST ENTERED INTO THE REALM OF THE CATHOLIC CLERGY IN SEPTEMBER OF 1833 AND BECAME ANOINTED AS THE COMMANDER-IN-CHIEF OF THE METIS PEOPLE OF ST. BONIFACE IN 1845. THIRTEEN YEARS LATER, (1858), MONSEIGNEUR TACHE SELECTED LOUIS RIEL AND TWO OTHER YOUNG HALF-

BREED MEN, LOUIS SCHMID AND DANIEL MCDOUGALL, TO COMPLETE THEIR STUDIES ON THE CATHOLIC FAITH. ALL THREE WERE THEN SENT TO THE BEST FRANCOPHONE COLLEGES IN QUEBEC'S ST. LAWRENCE RIVER VALLEY AT MONTREAL, ST. HYACINTHE AND TROIS RIVIERES. THIS WAS THE SAME TIME PERIOD IN CANADIAN HISTORY WHEREAS THE HUDSON'S BAY COMPANY RULED SUPREME IN THE WEST AND MONSEIGNEUR TACHE WAS ALWAYS ACTING AS MEDIATOR FOR THE TWO PARTIES; THE HUDSON'S BAY COMPANY AND THE METIS. ACCORDING TO HUDSON'S BAY COMPANY ARCHIVES, THE TWO PARTIES IN QUESTION TOLERATED ONE ANOTHER PURELY FOR ECONOMICAL REASONS AND TACHE WAS PLAYING BOTH ENDS AGAINST THE MIDDLE AS HATRED AND ANIMOSITY BEGAN TO FLOURISH EACH AND EVERY TIME THE METIS TRADED FURS FOR RIFLES.

CONTRARY AS TO WHAT HISTORIANS TELL US, IT WAS A HUDSON'S BAY COMPANY POLICY THAT IF AN INDIAN AND/OR A HALF-BREED WANTED TO PURCHASE A RIFLE BY WAY OF TRADING OFF ANIMAL PELTS, THEN, THE PELTS HAD TO BE STACKED ON THE FLOOR AND MUST BE EQUIVALENT TO THE HEIGHT OF THE RIFLE WHEN IT'S STANDING UPRIGHT. THE LONGER THE RIFLE, THE HIGHER THE STACK OF PELTS!!! NOT SURPRISING, RIEL AND TACHE DIDN'T SEE EYE TO EYE MOST OF THE TIME AS THE ROMAN CATHOLIC CHURCH LEADER ALWAYS ADVISED THE METIS TO YIELD TO THE WISHES OF THE HUDSON'S BAY COMPANY. THIS ILL-ADVISED RHETORIC ESCALATED EVEN FURTHER AS THE MONSEIGNEUR AND HIS RELIGIOUS INSTITUTION PLEADED WITH LOUIS RIEL INSISTING THAT IT WAS GOD'S WILL TO ALLOW THE CONTINUATION OF SIR JOHN A.'S DREAM OF LAND EXPANSION DURING THE 1869 INSURRECTION. IN THE END, RIEL FELT BETRAYED BY THE CATHOLIC CHURCH AND HELD MONSEIGNEUR TACHE FULLY RESPONSIBLE FOR THAT ACT OF BETRAYAL. ACCORDING TO CANADIAN HISTORIANS, THE DEMIGOD MONSEIGNEUR TACHE WANTED BOTH THE CHURCH AND THE PROVINCE OF MANITOBA TO BE BUILT ON THE QUEBEC MODEL SUPPOSEDLY WHEREBY THE CATHOLICS AND THE PROTESTANTS WERE TO CO-EXIST IN PEACEFUL HARMONY. BUT THE FACT OF THE MATTER IS, THE QUEBEC MODEL WAS NOTHING MORE THAN A DUPLICATE COPY OF FRANCE'S **"SEIGNIORAL TENURE "**WHEREAS THE ROMAN CATHOLIC CHURCH AND THE SEIGNIORS RULED SUPREME OVER THE MASSES.

IN REALITY, MONSEIGNEUR TACHE'S SO-CALLED QUEBEC MODEL HAD ABSOLUTELY NOTHING TO DO WITH THE PEACEFUL CO-EXISTENCE OF THE VARIOUS RELIGIOUS DENOMINATIONS. THAT IN ITSELF WAS MERELY A FICTITIOUS STORY THAT WAS CONJURED UP BY THE POWERS THAT BE IN A DESPERATE ATTEMPT TO WATER DOWN WHAT WAS REALLY HAPPENING BEHIND THE RELIGIOUS SCENES AS THE ROMAN CATHOLICS, THE PROTESTANTS AND BOTH OF THEIR FREEMASONRY AFFILIATED ENTITIES ULTIMATELY DUELED IT OUT FOR FULL CONTROL OF CANADA. WHY ELSE WOULD THE CATHOLIC CHURCH END

UP WITH A GRAND TOTAL OF 2,106,309 ARPENTS OF LAND IN THE COLONY OF NEW FRANCE AND THEN FIGHT TO MAINTAIN THOSE HOLDINGS ONCE THE BRITISH PROTESTANTS GAINED CONTROL OF THE REIGNS OF POWER AFTER THEY (THE FRENCH) WERE DEFEATED AT THE PLAINS OF ABRAHAM, THEN, BREATHED A COLLECTIVE SIGH OF RELIEF ONCE THE QUEBEC ACT OF 1774 WAS IMPLEMENTED – CANADA'S FATE (PIVOTAL BATTLE IN THE FRENCH-BRITISH STRUGGLE FOR NORTH AMERICA) WAS SUPPOSEDLY DECIDED ON THE PLAINS OF ABRAHAM. THERE'S A HELL OF A LOT MORE TO CANADA'S RELIGIOUS PAST THAN WHAT HISTORIANS HAVE BEEN FALSELY TELLING US THROUGHOUT THE MANY CENTURIES. ESPECIALLY CONSIDERING THE FACT THAT THE ROMAN CATHOLIC CHURCH WAS TOTALLY WILLING TO SACRIFICE THE HALF-BREED INDIAN POPULATION OF MANITOBA JUST SO THAT THEY WOULD BE ABLE TO INCREASE THEIR MASSIVE LAND HOLDINGS BY EXTENDING ITSELF ONTO CANADA'S WESTERN PRAIRIES.

AND AGAIN, CONTRARY AS TO WHAT SOME HISTORIANS HAVE BEEN TELLING US, IT WAS IN MONSEIGNEUR TACHE'S OWN PERSONAL OPINION THAT THE EVOLUTION OF THE CATHOLIC CHURCH IN THE NEWLY FORMED PROVINCE OF MANITOBA DICTATED ONE MAIN PRIORITY; STRENGTHENING THE FRENCH-SPEAKING CATHOLIC ELEMENT. HE APPARENTLY MADE HIS OPINION KNOWN IN JULY OF 1872 AS HE URGED THE ROMAN CATHOLIC BISHOPS OF QUEBEC TO ENCOURAGE MORE FRANCOPHONE SETTLERS TO MOVE OUT WEST TO THE WESTERN PLAINS OF MANITOBA. ONLY FOUR MONTHS PRIOR TO THIS, A LETTER WAS WRITTEN BY LOUIS LEPAGE (THE LORD AND MASTER OF THE OLD RIMOUSKI SEIGNIORIAL) TO MONSEIGNEUR TACHE DATED MARCH 14TH, 1872 WHEREBY THE SELF-RIGHTEOUS FRENCH ROMAN CATHOLIC RIMOUSKI PLANTATION OWNER OPENLY CRITICIZED THE ANTICS OF THE METIS PEOPLE STATING THAT THEY WERE EASILY INFLUENCED BY THE TASTE OF ALCOHOL AND THAT THEIR DEEDS OF WILDNESS WERE TOTALLY INEXCUSABLE. THIS MEMBER OF THE LEPAGE FAMILY TREE REPORTEDLY CONDEMNED THE ACTIONS OF THE METIS PEOPLE TO THE BITTER END BY FURTHER STATING THAT THEIR ACTS OF LAWLESSNESS HAD TO BE FULLY CONTAINED BEFORE THE CATHOLIC CHURCH LOST THE REMAINING STRANGLEHOLD THAT IT HAD OVER THE MASSES. CURIOUS AS OLD HELL AS TO WHY ONE OF HIS OWN ANCESTORS WOULD USE WHATEVER RELIGIOUS AND/OR POLITICAL INFLUENCES THAT THEY COULD MUSTER IN AN ATTEMPT OF KEEPING THE HALF-BREED INDIAN POPULATION OF WESTERN CANADA AT BAY, THE LEPAGE BABY BOOMER BORN IN 1954 DUG A LITTLE DEEPER INTO FAMILY ARCHIVES AND SOON DISCOVERED MORE HIDDEN SECRETS. FROM THERE, EVERYTHING JUST SEEMED TO FALL INTO PLACE AS MORE AND MORE FAMILY LIES STARTED TO UNRAVEL THEMSELVES AS THE LEPAGE'S OF CANADA CONTINUED HIDING UNDER THE CLOAK OF **CATHOLICISM**.

Not everyone was fooled by the French Roman Catholic tactic of deceit and deception as a way and means of hiding the truth. For example, while the LePage's of northern New Brunswick created the illusion that they were far more superior than the English Protestants, the eldest son of Donat LePage; Jacques-Amable-Leon LePage was forced to flee New Brunswick in 1936 /or 1937 as the Provincial Police's rum running branch of the RCMP were hot on his trail for illegal activities of bootlegging and other immoral acts. As fate would have, the renegade LePage migrated immediately to the Province of British Columbia were he spent his remaining years living in the rich luxurious parts of West Vancouver. His two other brothers moved to British Columbia some years later; Louis in 1955 and Hector in 1967 (both of whom chose Gibson's Landing to raise their immediate families) — it seemed that the further west of Manitoba they migrated, the less interested the baby boomer generation of LePage's living in Canada became in their French Roman Catholic ties. Within any family pedigree chart, a generation usually consist on an average time frame in which children are ready to replace parents — reckoned at 1/3 of a century /or at 30 years as a time-measure — procreation, propagation of the species, begetting / or being begotten.

It wasn't until researching the family tree that Hector LePage and Wilma Thompson's eldest son began to fully understand as to how dysfunctional his French Roman Catholic family had been for many, many generations. For instance, Hector and Wilma's marriage was basically doomed right from the very beginning as both the LePage's and the Thompson's had a run-in with one another at their wedding reception in 1952 as it was being held at the home of Blanche and Everett Thompson (Wilma's parents). Everett Thompson reportedly grabbed Donat LePage, (Hector's father) by the scruff of the neck and the seat of the pants and commenced to throw him out the door. This ordeal unfolded largely due to the fact that Donat LePage and John Goulette (one of Wilma's relatives) were speaking French in a house that was owned by an English-speaking family. Further to this, ninety-eight percent of those attending the reception were also English-speaking persons. When it came down to such infractions of English rights being violated by the French, Everett Thompson (an Irish Roman Catholic) didn't play favoritism. He apparently even threatened to throw one of his own relatives (John Goulette) out the door as well if he continued speaking French in an English household. This little incident obviously set the stage for many

MORE RUN-INS THAT THE LEPAGE'S AND THE THOMPSON'S WERE TO HAVE OVER THE YEARS. ALTHOUGH THE LEPAGE'S OF NORTHERN NEW BRUNSWICK WERE BUSY CREATING THE ILLUSION OF SUPERIORITY OVER ENGLISH CANADA, THE THOMPSON'S KNEW OTHERWISE AS IT WAS ONE OF JOHN GOULETTE'S BROTHERS WHO REPORTEDLY WORKED FOR THE PROVINCIAL POLICE'S RUM RUNNING BRANCH OF THE RCMP THAT WERE TRYING TO APPREHEND LEO LEPAGE FOR HIS ILLEGAL ACTIVITIES. THROUGHOUT HER ENTIRE MARRIAGE, WILMA LEPAGE WAS CONSTANTLY RIDICULED AND BELITTLED BY THE LEPAGE'S OF NORTHERN NEW BRUNSWICK AS THEY FELT THAT SHE WAS NOT GOOD ENOUGH TO BECOME A MEMBER OF THIS FRANCOPHONE FAMILY. BEING OF ANGLO-SAXON ANCESTRY WAS SOMETHING ELSE THAT THE LEPAGE'S OF NORTHERN NEW BRUNSWICK WOULD NOT TOLERATE.

WILMA AND HECTOR LEPAGE'S ELDEST SON, JOSEPH EDWARD BENJAMIN (BABY BOOMER BENOIT JOSEPH LEPAGE) WAS BORN DURING A HURRICANE IN SEPTEMBER OF 1954; HURRICANE EDNA. WHILE IN LABOR, WILMA NOTIFIED HER MOTHER (BLANCHE THOMPSON) LETTING HER KNOW THAT THE UNBORN FUTURE HELL RAISER OF THE LEPAGE FAMILY DYNASTY WAS ABOUT TO COME INTO THE WORLD DURING THE MIDST OF THE STORM. REQUIRING ASSISTANCE TO BRING SATAN'S UNBEGOTTEN SON INTO THE WORLD, MRS. THOMPSON NEVER HESITATED AS SHE QUICKLY BEGAN TELEPHONING AROUND TO GET IN CONTACT WITH AN AMBULANCE, A TAXI CAB /OR EVEN THE FIRE DEPARTMENT. BUT HER EFFORTS WERE FUTILE AS THE GALE FORCE WINDS WERE SMASHING WINDOWS AND RIPPING ROOFS OFF THE TOPS OF HOUSES THUS SENDING EVERYONE INTO A STATE OF SHEER PANIC. EVERY MEANS OF EMERGENCY TRANSPORT WERE KEPT EXTREMELY BUSY DUE TO THE RAGING FORCE WINDS OF THE HURRICANE THAT VIRTUALLY SENT COLD HEARTED SHIVERS DOWN EVERYONE'S SPINE. HAVING NO OTHER ALTERNATIVE, THE MEANS OF EMERGENCY TRANSPORT TO THE NORTHERN NEW BRUNSWICK HOSPITAL IN DALHOUSIE WAS LEFT IN THE CARE OF THE TELEPHONE OPERATOR. AS THE RAGING WINDS HOWLED AND HOUSES CRACKLED UNDER THE TREMENDOUS PRESSURE, THE SOUND OF AN EMERGENCY VEHICLE'S SIREN COULD BE HEARD IN THE FAINT DISTANCE. THE DALHOUSIE RCMP THEN APPEARED ON THE SCENE WHERE THEY TRANSPORTED THE EXPECTING MOTHER AND HER UNBORN CHILD TO THE HOSPITAL. ONCE THE STORM WAS OVER, NEWSPAPER REPORTERS TRIED TO FIND OUT WHO THE TWO POLICE OFFICERS WERE THAT BROUGHT THE PREGNANT WOMAN TO THE HOSPITAL BUT DUE TO LEGAL REASONS REFRAINED FROM DEVOLVING THEIR NAMES. DAYS LATER, THE LOCAL NEWSPAPER, THE DALHOUSIE NEWS HAD STORIES OF THE HURRICANE AND OF THE WOMAN'S ORDEAL WITH THE POLICE AS THEY JOURNEYED THROUGH THE STORM.

Chapter 6 - TO BE AN INDIAN, IN A WHITEMAN'S WORLD

To be a Canadian born North American Indian /or even a Metis in this country, is to be an individual with all of man's humanistic needs and abilities attached to it. But in order to do so, it also means to be different at the same time. *"It is to speak different languages, draw different pictures, tell different tales and to rely on a set of values developed in a different world. Canada is rich for its Indian component, although there have been times when diversity seemed of little value to many Canadians. But to a Canadian Indian today is to be someone different in another way. It is to be someone apart-apart in law, apart in the provision of government services, and too often, apart in social contacts. To be a Canadian Indian is to lack power - the power to act as the owner of your lands, the power to spend your own money, and too often the power to change your own conditions. Not always, but too often, to be an Indian is to be without, training or technical skills, and above all, without those feelings of dignity and self-confidence that a man must have if he is to walk with his head held high. All of these conditions of the Indians are the product of history and have nothing to do with their abilities and capacities. Indian relations with other Canadians began with special treatment by government and society, and special treatment has been the rule since Europeans first settled in Canada. Special treatment has made the Indians a community disadvantaged and apart."*

With the whiteman's setting sail to the New World, it became quite apparent that to be an Indian on the North American Continent was to be a race of people captured and enslaved in accordance to rules and regulations of economic, social and political bondage: *"To be an Indian must be to be free-free to develop Indian culture in*

EVER SINCE THE WHITE EUROPEANS FIRST SETTLED IN THIS COUNTRY, THE WAY IN WHICH THEY HAVE TREATED OUR NATION'S NATIVE PEOPLES IS SOMEWHAT QUESTIONABLE ESPECIALLY CONSIDERING THE FACT THAT OVER THE MANY CENTURIES, THE MAJORITY OF THE TRUTH HAS BEEN DRASTICALLY WATERED DOWN BY THE POWERS THAT BE IN ORDER TO SAVE FACE. BUT IN YET ANOTHER TWIST OF IRONY, SUCH UNFAIR TREATMENT BY THE WHITES CAN BE EASILY TRACED IN THE PUBLIC ARCHIVES OF CANADA. FOR EXAMPLE, ON MAY 2ND, 1670 A ROYAL CHARTER FROM ENGLAND GRANTED SOLE TRADING RIGHTS IN THE HUDSON BAY DRAINAGE BASIN, (RUPERT'S LAND) TO THE HUDSON'S BAY COMPANY OF ENGLAND AT THE REQUEST OF QUEBEC'S TWO MOST HONORABLE MEMBERS OF THE **COUREURS DE BOIS** (GROSEILLIERS AND HIS BROTHER-IN-LAW RADISSON). THE HUDSON'S BAY COMPANY HAD MANY MEMBERS AND ASSOCIATES, AMONG ITS SHAREHOLDERS WAS THE ROYAL FAMILY IN GREAT BRITAIN. IRONICALLY, THE BRITISH MONARCHY ALSO OWNED SHARES IN THE ROYAL AFRICAN COMPANY, WHICH WAS DESIGNED FOR THE SLAVE TRADE BUSINESS, WHILE THE HUDSON'S BAY COMPANY WAS ESTABLISHED TO EXPLOIT THE WEALTH IN THE FURS THAT WERE AVAILABLE IN CANADA. ONCE THE ROYAL CHARTER WAS ISSUED, IT GAVE THE BAY COMPANY VIRTUALLY A MONOPOLY THROUGHOUT THE ENTIRE WESTERN INTERIOR OF CANADA. THE BUSINESS VENTURE THUS BECAME KNOWN AS ONE OF THE MOST POWERFUL FORCES UNDER BRITISH RULE. WITHIN THE **CHARTER**, IT GAVE SPECIAL TREATMENT TO THE INDIANS. WHEREAS, AN INDIAN WAS UNDER THE DIRECT RULE OF THE HUDSON'S BAY COMPANY FOR ANY WRONGDOINGS, AND COULD NOT BE CHARGED WITH MURDER OF ANOTHER INDIAN AND/OR A WHITEMAN UNDER THE JURISDICTION OF THE BAY; IF AN INDIAN COMMITTED AN INDECENT ACT SUCH AS A MURDER, THEN HE /OR SHE WAS UNDER THE CARE OF THE INDIAN TRIBAL COUNCIL.

BY THE MID-1800'S, A SMALL BATTLE FROM WITHIN THE HUDSON'S BAY COMPANY MEMBERSHIP ENSUED AS A FEW OF THE SHAREHOLDERS WANTED CONTROL OF THE COMPANY'S LAND ASSETS AS A WAY AND MEANS OF EXPANDING THE COUNTRY'S JURISDICTIONAL BORDERS. AFTER MUCH DELIBERATION IN 1870, THE HUDSON'S BAY COMPANY SURRENDERED ITS CHARTER TO SIR JOHN A. MACDONALD, RECEIVING IN RETURN $ 1.7 MILLION, A GIGANTIC TWENTY-FIVE MILLION ACRES OF FERTILE LAND WHICH IT DEEMED TO BE VERY IMPORTANT FOR ITS SURVIVAL FOR THE FUTURE, BLOCKS OF LAND SURROUNDING ITS POSTS AND SURFACE RIGHTS TO MANY MINERAL RICH AREAS. THE HUDSON'S BAY COMPANY THUS BECAME A PRIVATE CORPORATION, BUILDING ITS EMPIRE AS IT EXPLOITED THE LAND AND ITS PEOPLE ALONG THE WAY. BEFORE LONG, THE HONORABLE HUDSON'S BAY GREW INTO A MULTI-NATIONAL CORPORATION,

WITH TIES IN RAILWAY, MINING, OIL AND GAS EXPLORATION, REAL ESTATE DEVELOPMENT, ETC., ETC. ALTHOUGH IT BECAME KNOWN AS A CANADIAN ENTITY, IT STILL MAINTAINED ITS FREEMASONRY CONNECTIONS IN MERRY OLE ENGLAND.

OBVIOUSLY, THE COURSE OF HISTORY WAS LITERALLY CHANGED BY THE SALE OF RUPERT'S LAND AS THE DREAM THAT FREEMASONRY BROTHER SIR JOHN A. HAD WAS NOW A REALITY. BEFORE 1850, INDIAN LEGISLATION HAD BEEN INCOMPLETE, ENACTED AND UNENFORCEABLE, BUT AFTERWARDS TWO OBJECTIVES SUPPOSEDLY EMERGED; 1) PROTECTION OF INDIANS FROM DESTRUCTIVE ELEMENTS OF "WHITE SOCIETY", AND 2) PROTECTION OF INDIAN LANDS UNTIL INDIAN PEOPLE WERE ABLE TO OCCUPY AND PROTECT THEM IN THE SAME WAY AS OTHER CITIZENS. BUT IN FACT, MOST OF THE CHANGES IN INDIAN LEGISLATION DURING THE POST-CONFEDERATION PERIOD WERE TO BENEFIT "WHITE SOCIETY", RATHER THAN THOSE OF THE INDIAN AND METIS RACES OF PEOPLE. AN EXAMPLE OF THIS BLATANT DISREGARD FOR THE NATIVE PEOPLES RIGHTS WAS EXERCISED IN DECEMBER OF 1761 AS A ROYAL PROCLAMATION BY HIS MAJESTY THE KING OF ENGLAND (GEORGE III) STATED THAT THE INDIANS FILED MANY COMPLAINTS OF WHITE SETTLERS TAKING POSSESSION OF THEIR LANDS THAT OF WHICH WERE **TREATY LANDS** RESERVED TO THE INDIANS BY HIS MAJESTY THE KING. INTERESTINGLY ENOUGH, THE KING'S ROYAL PROCLAMATION HAD THE FOLLOWING AS ITS CLOSING STATEMENT: **"AND IF ANY PERSON OR PERSONS HAVE POSSESSED THEMSELVES OF ANY PART OF THE SAME TO THE PREJUDICE OF THE SAID INDIANS IN THEIR CLAIMS BEFORE SPECIFIED OR WITHOUT LAWFUL AUTHORITY, THEY ARE HEREBY REQUIRED FORTHWITH TO REMOVE, AS THEY WILL OTHERWISE BE PROSECUTED WITH THE UTMOST RIGOUR OF LAW."**

IN YET ANOTHER **ROYAL PROCLAMATION** DATED OCTOBER 7TH, 1763 IT SETS DOWN SPECIFIC SETTLEMENT GUIDELINES TO FORM THREE NEW COLONIES. THESE NEW COLONIES WOULD LATER BE KNOWN AS ENGLISH CONTROLLED UPPER AND LOWER CANADA, (ONTARIO AND QUEBEC) AND THE EASTERN SEABOARD OF THE UNITED STATES. FURTHERMORE, THESE NEW COLONIES WERE TO EXTEND THEMSELVES INTO PROVINCES AND STATES CONTROLLED BY OFFICERS AND SOLDIERS OF THE AMERICA'S. LAND STOLEN FROM THE INDIANS WERE THEREFORE GRANTED TO WHITE SETTLERS LOYAL TO THE BRITISH MONARCHY:

"TO EVERY PERSON HAVING THE RANK OF A FIELD OFFICER - **5,000** ACRES
TO EVERY CAPTAIN - **3,000** ACRES
TO EVERY SUBALTERN OR STAFF OFFICER - **2,000** ACRES
TO EVERY NON-COMMISSION OFFICER - **200** ACRES
TO EVERY PRIVATE MAN - **50** ACRES."

WAS THIS TO BE AN ACT ON THE BRITISH MONARCHY'S PART TO PREVENT AN INDIAN UPRISING FOR THE STEALING OF THEIR TRADITIONAL LANDS THAT THEY LITERALLY HELD FOR THOUSANDS UPON THOUSANDS OF YEARS PRIOR TO THE WHITEMAN SETTING FOOT ON NORTH AMERICAN SOIL??? BE THAT AS IT MAY, THE OCTOBER 7TH PROCLAMATION WENT ON TO SAY THE FOLLOWING WORDS:

"AND WE DO FURTHER EXPRESSLY ENJOIN AND REQUIRE ALL OFFICERS WHATEVER, AS WELL MILITARY AS THOSE EMPLOYED IN THE MANAGEMENT AND DIRECTION OF INDIAN AFFAIRS, WITHIN THE TERRITORIES RESERVED AS AFORESAID CHARGED WITH TREASON, MISPRISIONS OF TREASON, MURDER, OR OTHER FELONIES OR MISDEMEANORS, SHALL FLY FROM JUSTICE AND TAKE REFUGE IN THE SAID TERRITORY, AND TO SEND THEM UNDER A PROPER GUARD TO THE COLONY WHERE THE CRIME WAS COMMITTED OF WHICH THEY STAND ACCUSED, IN ORDER TO TAKE TRIAL FOR THE SAME."

BY 1821, VARIOUS REGULATIONS WERE INTRODUCED REGULATING THE FUR TRADE AND ESTABLISHING A CRIMINAL AND CIVIL JURISDICTION WITHIN CERTAIN PARTS OF THE AMERICA'S. THESE WERE THE YEARS OF CONSTANT FEUDING BETWEEN THE HUDSON'S BAY COMPANY AND THE NORTH WEST TRADING COMPANY OF MONTREAL. DUE TO THE GREED OF THE SETTLERS AND TRAVELERS, BOTH UPPER AND LOWER CANADA AS WELL AS ITS UNEXPLORED INTERIOR WAS PLAGUED WITH VIOLENCE EXTENDING TO LOSS OF LIVES, AND DESTRUCTION OF PROPERTY. IT WAS A WAR BETWEEN MONEY AND POWER — VIRTUALLY A WAR BETWEEN THE INDIAN WAY OF LIFE AND THE WHITEMAN'S WAY. ON JUNE 10TH, 1857 AN ACT TO ENCOURAGE THE GRADUAL CIVILIZATION OF INDIAN TRIBES WAS INTRODUCED. THIS ACT WAS SUPPOSEDLY DESIGNED TO PROTECT THE INDIANS, AT LEAST THAT'S WHAT HISTORIANS WANT US TO BELIEVE AS BEING A TRUE FACT OF CANADIAN HISTORY!!!

CASE IN POINT; ON JANUARY 3RD, 1849 A CHARTER OF GRANT WAS GIVEN TO THE HUDSON'S BAY COMPANY TO EXPLOIT THE RESOURCES OF BRITISH COLUMBIA'S VANCOUVER ISLAND. THE GRANT WAS NATURALLY ISSUED BY GREAT BRITAIN AND IT SOON BECAME THE GROUNDWORK OF A NEW POLITICAL ENTITY IN THE ENGLISH REALM WEST OF THE ROCKY MOUNTAINS. IN THAT SAME YEAR, ALL OF VANCOUVER ISLAND WAS PROCLAIMED TO BE BRITISH TERRITORY AND BEFORE LONG, THEY LAID CLAIM TO THE QUEEN CHARLOTTE ISLANDS AS WELL. IN 1850, THE WHITE COLONIAL INHABITANTS WERE GIVEN EQUAL REPRESENTATION BY THE POWERS THAT BE WITH THE SEAT OF GOVERNMENT AT NEW WESTMINSTER. DURING THIS TIME PERIOD OF COLONIAL DEVELOPMENT ON VANCOUVER ISLAND, THE MAINLAND TERRITORY WAS DEEMED TO BE INDIAN LANDS SUBJECT TO THE SOLE AUTHORITY OF THE HUDSON'S BAY COMPANY.

On August 20TH, 1858 by Imperial Edict all the lands that were still deemed to be Indian lands were named **"British Columbia "**with boundaries very much as to what we see today. In one foul swoop, the whiteman laid claim to all lands within the jurisdictional boundaries of British Columbia and the Indians had no say about it whatsoever – no referendum was held by the powers that be to help decide the fate of the territorial Indian population.

With the outright theft of Indian lands, the white inhabitants of Vancouver Island demanded that the seat of power be shifted from New Westminister to the most southerly tip of the Island. Although their numbers were few, mostly officers of the British military and employees of the Hudson's Bay Company, they managed to whin enough to convince the British Parliament in London, England to migrate its governing body from New Westminister to Victoria on the Pacific. In the following year, (1859), representatives of the British Columbia colony of Vancouver Island unlawfully entered onto Indian lands, (James Bay Reserve), and re-claimed part of it as their own deeming it to be the future site of the newly acquired territorial Capital Government Buildings. Although the inner harbor lands were designated as being part of the Indian Reserve lands in accordance to an 1850 treaty of which the Hudson's Bay Company willing signed with the Lekwungen, the original First Nation inhabitants of Victoria, it didn't seem to matter as the whiteman went ahead despite this and re-claimed part of the land for their own use. This blatant disrespect for the treaties signed by both the whiteman and the Indians continued as more and more of the James Bay Reserve lands became part and parcel of the Government of British Columbia's Parliament Buildings. As the growing controversy unfolded, white inhabitants essentially threatened to sever all political ties with the colony on the mainland unless it agreed to move the seat of power to Victoria. That of which, an agreement was finally reached in 1868. And some years later, (1893), the new and improved British Columbia Parliament Buildings project was underway, taking five full years to complete where it now stands in all of its splendor for the entire world to glorify in absolute awe. In total, the new Government Buildings in Victoria expropriated 10.6 acres of land from the Indians just so that its seat of power would have a pristine view of the inner harbor as it dictated how British Columbia's aboriginal peoples were going to remain in the shackles of their bondage.

At the time of British Columbia's first being civilized by the whiteman, the Hudson's Bay Company was solely responsible for establishing English settlements on Vancouver Island as part of its trading licence agreement with the British monarchy. Because of this being stipulated, the Hudson's Bay Company began making various land transactions (via treaty agreements) with the aboriginal peoples of Vancouver Island for colonial settlement and industrial development. Between the years 1850 and 1854 the acting representative for the Hudson's Bay Company, Freemasonry Brother James Douglas made a series of fourteen of these treaty land transactions with the Indians of Vancouver Island. One of the first treaties ever signed by British fraternity Brother Douglas was the treaty in which set out the land where the Province's Legislature now stands as part of the James Bay Indian Reserve. It is estimated that Masonic Brother James Douglas and his silver tongued tactics managed to expropriate 358 square miles of land around Victoria, Sannich, Sooke, Nanaimo and Port Hardy, all of these naturally are parts of Vancouver Island. Coincidently, in 1856 Douglas conducted a somewhat rather detailed census of Vancouver Island's native population where in which it had been calculated that the entire indigenous population was 33,873 persons; men, women and children. Although some historians attempt to tell us that Douglas seized the reins of power on his own free will and accord by appointing himself governor of the colony, supposedly in the best-interest of white society, he was in fact instructed by the British Government to do whatever was necessary for the future colonization of its newfound trophy of Vancouver Island. These treaty practices were eventually discontinued after 1854 as the white settlers on Vancouver Island began their whining tactic with the British colonial office in New Westminister and all monetary funds were immediately tightened. According to the historians, these funds were hard to come-by largely due to Vancouver Island's slow rate of population growth and development. Naturally, that was only part of what was going on behind the Freemasonry scenes as Brother Douglas and his other Masonic cronies began manipulating their way into having the seat of power moved to Victoria on the Pacific. Doctor John Sebastian Helmcken for example was only one of seven members elevated into the first assembly of B.C.'s Legislature in 1856. The good doctor ironically married Cecilia Douglas in 1853, (one of James Douglas' daughters), and was later anointed Speaker at the Assembly's first sitting. In their capacity of being the newly

FORMED MASONIC GOVERNING BODY ON VANCOUVER ISLAND, DOUGLAS AND HIS FRATERNITY BRETHREN LATER RE-CLAIMED LAND THAT WAS ONCE GIVEN TO THE LEKWUNGEN INDIANS AND ALMOST IMMEDIATELY RE-NAMED IT "GOVERNMENT RESERVE "LANDS FOR LEGAL REASONS AND THE REST AS THEY SAY IS HISTORY!!!

AFTER FIRST RE-CLAIMING THE LAND, THEN, RE-NAMING IT (1859), CONSTRUCTION OF THE WANTED SEAT OF POWER BEGAN IN THE FOLLOWING YEAR. THOSE BUILDINGS, KNOWN HISTORICALLY AS THE BIRD CAGES ODDLY ENOUGH MARKED A FULL YEAR OF HIGH RACIAL TENSION BETWEEN THE WHITE SETTLERS AND THE NATIVE PEOPLES. REPORTEDLY, THOUSANDS OF MEMBERS OF THE ABORIGINAL TRIBES LIVING THROUGHOUT THE COASTAL REGIONS OF VANCOUVER ISLAND AND THE QUEEN CHARLOTTE ISLANDS TRAVELED TO VICTORIA TO TRADE THEIR WARES WITH THE WHITEMAN. ACCORDING TO HISTORIANS, WHITE SETTLERS SUPPOSEDLY WANTED THE INDIANS ESCORTED OUT OF VICTORIA AS THEY FEARED THAT AN OUT BREAK OF SMALLPOX WOULD VIRTUALLY WHIP OUT THE COMMUNITY'S ANGLO-SAXON POPULATION. THEN OF COURSE, THERE'S THE OTHER SIDE OF THE STORY WHERE THE INDIANS WERE BEGINNING TO FULLY REALIZE THAT THE WHITEMAN WAS STEALING THE LAND RIGHT FROM UNDERNEATH THEIR FEET (AUGUST 20TH, 1858 IMPERIAL EDICT BY THE BRITISH GOVERNMENT) AND THEY WERE NOT AT ALL IMPRESSED WITH THIS MANIPULATION TACTIC OF DECEIT AND DECEPTION WANTING SOME SORT OF RESTITUTION. TENSIONS WERE SAID TO BE SO HIGH THAT AT ONE POINT, THE ROYAL NAVY'S GUNBOATS REPORTEDLY SEALED OFF THE INNER HARBOR AND LANDED ONE-HUNDRED BRITISH TROOPS AS A WAY AND MEANS OF KEEPING THE PEACE. FURTHER TO THIS, THE SITUATION GOT EVEN MUCH WORST FOR ALL PARTIES INVOLVED AS TWO HAIDA CHIEFS WERE ACCUSED OF BRUTALLY MURDERING ANOTHER ABORIGINAL (A TONGASS CHIEF) AND AS THE ROYAL BRITISH MARINES HUNTED THEM DOWN, TENSIONS SOON REACHED THE BOILING POINT WHEN THE TWO HAIDA CHIEFS WERE SHOT AND KILLED WHILE RESISTING ARREST. WHITE SETTLERS FROM ALL OVER THE SANNICH PENINSULA QUICKLY TOOK SHELTER IN THE COMMUNITY'S FORT (FORT VICTORIA) AS ALL HELL BROKE LOOSE BETWEEN THE BRITISH TROOPS AND THE ABORIGINAL PEOPLES. FOR HIS DEED OF LEGALLY EXPROPRIATING INDIAN LAND AND ESTABLISHING A STRONG FREEMASONRY PRESENCE IN VICTORIA ON THE PACIFIC WHILE FIRST ACTING AS THE REPRESENTATIVE OF THE HUDSON'S BAY COMPANY IN 1849 AND THEN AS THE BRITISH GOVERNMENT'S GOVERNOR OF VANCOUVER ISLAND (1851 TO 1864), MASONIC ORDER'S BROTHER JAMES DOUGLAS WAS KNIGHTED SIR JAMES DOUGLAS IN 1863 BY QUEEN VICTORIA AND HE QUICKLY ROSE THROUGH THE FRATERNITY RANKS IN THE HISTORY BOOKS AS A MAN A GREAT VISION. ACCORDING TO THE HISTORIANS, FRATERNITY BROTHER DOUGLAS DIDN'T RECEIVE HIS OFFICIAL TITLE OF B.C.'S

GOVERNORSHIP UNTIL NOVEMBER 19TH, 1858, THREE FULL MONTHS AFTER THE PASSING INTO BRITISH LAW THE LEGALIZED THEFT OF INDIAN LANDS. BUT IN RETROSPECT TO HIS SUPPOSEDLY BEING A VISIONARY, IT SEEMS THAT THE ONLY REAL GREAT CONTRIBUTION THAT SIR JAMES DOUGLAS ACTUALLY MADE TO SOCIETY AS A WHOLE WAS WHEN HE DECLARED VICTORIA A FREE PORT JUST PRIOR TO HIS RETIRING AS GOVERNOR SO THAT IMPORTERS BRINGING FOREIGN CARGOS INTO THE PORT WOULD NO LONGER HAVE TO PAY A CUSTOMS DUTY TAX TO THE POWERS THAT BE IN NEW WESTMINSTER. THIS MANEUVER ESSENTIALLY GAVE THE VANCOUVER ISLAND COLONY THE LEVERAGE IT NEEDED TO HAVE THE SEAT OF POWER SHIFTED, AND THAT'S EXACTLY AS TO WHAT HAPPENED IN 1868 WHEN YET ANOTHER MASTER MASON, BROTHER DOCTOR JOHN SEBASTIAN HELMCKEN WON THE DEBATE WITH HIS FRATERNITY BRETHREN ON THE MAINLAND.

ALTHOUGH MEMBERS OF THE ANCIENT MASONIC CRAFT ON VANCOUVER ISLAND WERE UNITED IN THEIR EFFORTS OF HAVING THE SEAT OF POWER SHIFTED FROM NEW WESTMINISTER TO VICTORIA ON THE PACIFIC, WHEN IT CAME DOWN TO THE ISSUE OF WHETHER /OR NOT BRITISH COLUMBIA SHOULD BE JOINING THE FREEMASONRY CAUSE OF A UNITED FRONT TOWARDS CONFEDERATION MANY MEMBERS WERE DEAD SET AGAINST IT. ACCORDING TO THE HISTORIANS, THE GREATEST OPPONENT TO SIR JOHN A. MACDONALD'S DREAM OF CONFEDERATION WAS NONE OTHER THAN HELMCKEN HIMSELF AND HE REPORTEDLY ACTED AS SPOKESMAN FOR THE ANTI-CONFEDERATION FORCES IN BRITISH COLUMBIA. CONTRARY AS TO WHAT THE HISTORY BOOKS MAY SAY AS BEING A TRUE FACT OF THE PAST, THE GOOD DOCTOR AND HIS FREEMASONRY BUDDIES ACTUALLY BEGAN THEIR PREPARATIONS AGAINST JOINING CANADA IN 1866 AND BY APRIL OF 1869 A PETITION BEGAN TO CIRCULATE IN NEW WESTMINISTER FOR BRITISH COLUMBIA TO JOIN THE UNITED STATES INSTEAD. THE PETITION WAS DRAWN UP AND ADDRESSED TO THE PRESIDENT OF THE UNITED STATES (ULYSSES S. GRANT). IT WAS SAID TO BE SIGNED BY MANY OF NEW WESTMINISTER'S BUSINESS COMMUNITY WHO IRONICALLY CLAIMED TO BE LOYAL BRITISH SUBJECTS NOT AT ALL IMPRESSED WITH THE STATE OF AFFAIRS IN THE BRITISH COLUMBIA TERRITORY. BY FALL OF THAT SAME YEAR, A SECOND PETITION WAS CIRCULATED IN VICTORIA ALSO ADDRESSED TO THE AMERICAN PRESIDENT, CALLING ONTO HIM TO ASSIST IN FACILITATING THE ANNEXATION OF BRITISH COLUMBIA AND FURTHER ASKING HIM TO NEGOTIATE WITH THE BRITISH GOVERNMENT FOR THE TRANSFER OF THE COLONY OF VICTORIA ON THE PACIFIC INTO THE AMERICAN MASONIC FAMILY. THIS PETITION WAS SIGNED BY FORTY-THREE PERSONS, MAINLY MEMBERS OF THE MASONIC ORDER WHO WERE EITHER BUSINESSMEN AND/OR PROMINENT CITIZENS OF THE COLONY. COINCIDENTLY, THIS SECOND PETITION WAS HANDED OVER TO VINCENT COLLYER, A SPECIAL INDIAN COMMISSIONER

FOR THE ALASKA ABORIGINAL TRIBES WHO JUST HAPPENED TO BE HEADED DOWN TO SAN FRANCISCO, CALIFORNIA THEN ONWARDS TO WASHINGTON, D.C. – COLLYER APPARENTLY PROMISED HIS VANCOUVER ISLAND FRATERNITY BRETHREN THAT HE WOULD PRESENT THE PETITION IN PERSON TO THE U.S. PRESIDENT WITH A STATEMENT OF WHAT THE BRETHRENSHIP WANTED FROM THE AMERICANS IN RETURN. ON DECEMBER 29TH, 1869 THE PETITION WAS FORMALLY PRESENTED TO THE PRESIDENT AND BY SEPTEMBER 1ST OF THE FOLLOWING YEAR, (1870), A SUPPLEMENTARY LIST OF SIXTY-ONE ADDITIONAL SIGNATURES WAS FORWARDED TO U.S. PRESIDENT GRANT.

OF THE ONE-HUNDRED AND FOUR SIGNATURES SUBMITTED TO THE ANNEXATION PETITION, MANY OF WHOM WERE ESSENTIALLY THE MOVERS AND SHAKERS OF CAPITALISM, FREEMASONRY BROTHER HENRY FREDERICK HEISTERMAN WAS THE PRIMARY INSTIGATOR FOR ANNEXATION BY THE UNITED STATES WHILE FRATERNITY BROTHER HELMCKEN VOCALIZED THE GROUPS DISCONTENT WITH PROSPECTS /OR THE LACK THEREOF IN JOINING CONFEDERATION. ONLY A FEW YEARS PREVIOUS TO BOTH OF THESE ANCIENT CRAFT MEMBERS OF THE MASONIC ORDER REALLY STIRRING UP THE FRATERNAL POT AGAINST FELLOW FREEMASONS WANTING TO FORM A CANADIAN CONFEDERATION, RUMORS BEGAN TO EMERGE THAT GREAT BRITAIN AND THE UNITED STATES OF THE AMERICA'S WERE NEGOTIATING SOME SORT OF DEAL BEHIND CLOSED DOORS FOR THE IMMEDIATE CESSION OF BRITISH COLUMBIA INTO THE AMERICAN MASONIC FAMILY UNDER THE AUSPICES OF "**MANIFEST DESTINY**". BUT ONCE THE NEWS OF THE ACQUISITION OF ALASKA BY THE UNITED STATES BECAME PUBLIC KNOWLEDGE, IT ULTIMATELY BROUGHT THE LAMENT OF BRITISH COLUMBIA'S ANNEXATION BY THE AMERICANS TO A HEAD. IN JULY OF 1867, A PETITION TO QUEEN VICTORIA WAS CIRCULATED ON VANCOUVER ISLAND ASKING HER ROYAL MAJESTY TO EITHER SHIT /OR GET THE HELL OFF THE POT BECAUSE IF THE PEOPLE OF BRITISH COLUMBIA DIDN'T RECEIVE SOME KIND OF A RESPONSE FROM THE MONARCHY ITSELF, THE ENTIRE TERRITORY WAS DESTINED TO BECOME PART OF THE AMERICAN LANDSCAPE:

> "EITHER, THAT YOUR MAJESTY'S GOVERNMENT MAY BE PLEASED TO RELIEVE US IMMEDIATELY OF THE EXPENSE OF OUR EXCESSIVE STAFF OF OFFICIALS, ASSIST IN THE ESTABLISHMENT OF A BRITISH STEAM-LINE WITH PANAMA, SO THAT IMMIGRATION FROM ENGLAND MAY REACH US, AND ALSO ASSUME THE DEBTS OF THE COLONY
>
> OR, THAT YOUR MAJESTY WILL GRACIOUSLY PERMIT THE COLONY TO BECOME A PORTION OF THE **UNITED STATES**."

NEEDLESS TO SAY, THE COLONIAL OFFICE IN LONDON, ENGLAND WAS NOT AT ALL AMUSED WHEN IT INITIALLY RECEIVED THE PETITION. NOR WERE

THEY IMPRESSED WITH THE CONTENTS OF A PRIVATE LETTER TO THE DUKE OF BUCKINGHAM REPORTEDLY WRITTEN BY THE GOVERNOR OF VANCOUVER ISLAND AND ALL OF BRITISH COLUMBIA (FREDERICK SEYMOUR) WHICH DESCRIBED THE SAD STATE OF AFFAIRS AS WELL AS THE PEOPLES MOOD:

> *"THERE IS A SYSTEMATIC AGITATION GOING ON IN THIS TOWN IN FAVOR OF ANNEXATION TO THE UNITED STATES. IT IS BELIEVED THAT MONEY FOR ITS MAINTENANCE IS PROVIDED FROM SAN FRANCISCO. AS YET, HOWEVER, NOTHING HAS REACHED ME OFFICIALLY ON THE SUBJECT, AND SHOULD ANY PETITION ON THE SUBJECT, I WILL KNOW HOW TO ANSWER IT BEFORE I TRANSMIT THE PETITION TO YOUR GRACE. ON THE MAINLAND THE QUESTION OF ANNEXATION IS NOT MOOTED ..."*

THE REACTION OF THE COLONIAL OFFICE TO THE WHOLE UGLY MESS (DATED SEPTEMBER 16TH, 1867) WAS TO SAY THE LEAST SOMEWHAT SOMBER TO THE GRIEVANCES OF THOSE COMPLAINANTS:

> "AS TO THE FUTURE IT IS NO DOUBT THAT HIGH TAXATION, DISTRESS AND WANT OF ASSISTANCE FROM HOME, WILL PROBABLY CAUSE THE AMERICAN POPULATION OF THESE COLONIES TO KEEP FOR ANNEXATION, A PORPOSE WH WH SOON BECOME IRRESISTIBLE EXCEPT AT A COST *FAR GREATER THAN A WORTH OF THE FEE SIMPLE OF THE COLONY. ON THE OTHER HAND IF THE COLONIES EVER FIND THAT THE ANNEXATION THREAT IS SATISFACTORY IN EXTRACTING MONEY FROM US, THEY WILL PLUNDER US INDEFINITELY BY IT ... I SUPPOSE THE QUESTION TO BE* (IN THE LONG RUN) IS B.C. TO FORM PART OF THE U.S., OR OF CANADA; AND IF WE DESIRE TO PROMOTE THE LATTER ALTERNATIVE WHAT FORM OF EXPENDITURE OR NON-EXPENDITURE *IS LIKELY TO FACILITATE OR PAVE THE WAY."*

ACCORDINGLY, ONCE THE COLONIAL OFFICE LET IT BE KNOWN THAT IT WASN'T GOING TO BE BULLIED INTO MAKING ANY DEALS IN ORDER TO PREVENT BRITISH COLUMBIA FROM JOINING THE UNITED STATES AS THE BRITISH MONARCHY ITSELF FAVORED AMALGAMATION WITH CANADA ANYWAYS, THE ANNEXATION MOVEMENT PICKED UP SPEED AS FRATERNITY BROTHERS HELMCKEN AND HEISTERMAN SEIZED THE REIGNS OF POWER FOR THEIR JUST CAUSE ONCE GOVERNOR SEYMOUR DIED ON JUNE 10TH, 1869. IRONICALLY ACCORDING TO THE HISTORIANS, THE ANTI-CONFEDERATIONISTS LOST A KEY SUPPORTER WHEN SEYMOUR DIED AND MOST OF THE WIND WAS SUPPOSEDLY TAKEN OUT OF THEIR SAILS AS A NEW GOVERNOR WAS APPOINTED TO REPLACE THE NOW DEARLY DEPARTED ONE. THE NEW GOVERNOR OF BRITISH COLUMBIA, ANTHONY MUSGRAVE WAS REPORTEDLY TO HAVE BEEN NOT ONLY A STRONG ADVOCATE OF CONFEDERATION BUT ALSO A GOOD FRIEND

OF MACDONALD'S AS WELL. HIS MANDATE WAS TO MAKE BRITISH COLUMBIA PART OF MACDONALD'S FREEMASONRY FAMILY AS QUICKLY AS HUMANLY POSSIBLE; NO IF'S, AND'S /OR BUT'S ABOUT IT. BUT THE ONE THING THAT THE HISTORIANS FAILED TO MENTION WAS THE FACT THAT LIKE CANADA'S FIRST PRIME MINISTER, MUSGRAVE HIMSELF WAS SAID TO BE AN ACTIVE MEMBER OF THE ANCIENT CRAFT AND ALINED HIMSELF WITH FELLOW FREEMASONS WHO WERE IN FAVOR OF MAKING MASONIC BROTHER MACDONALD'S DREAM OF A UNITED CONFEDERATION A FULL BLOWN REALITY. AND CONTRARY AS TO WHAT THESE SAME HISTORIANS HAVE BEEN WRITING IN THE HISTORY BOOKS TELLING US AS TO HOW AND WHY THE ANIMOSITY CONCERNING THIS ISSUE ALL BEGAN IS PURELY BULLSHIT ON THEIR PART. THE FACT REMAINS NOW AND FOREVER THAT THE QUESTION OF WHETHER /OR NOT BRITISH COLUMBIA SHOULD HAVE HAD JOINED CANADA /OR THE UNITED STATES ALL UNFOLDED LARGELY DUE TO THE FACT THAT LIKE THE AMERICAN FREEMASONS, SOME OF BRITISH COLUMBIA'S MASTER MASONS WANTED TO GOVERN THEIR OWN AFFAIRS BY ESTABLISHING AN INDEPENDENT GRAND LODGE HERE IN BRITISH COLUMBIA BUT THE POWERS THAT BE IN ENGLAND WERE RESISTING THE MOVE EVERY STEP OF THE WAY INSISTING THAT IT WAS IN THE BEST-INTEREST OF EVERYONE THAT THEY BE THE ONLY GOVERNING POWER DICTATING THE LIVES OF OTHERS. THIS DESIRE TO ESTABLISH AN INDEPENDENT GRAND LODGE OF BRITISH COLUMBIA IS EASILY VERIFIED BY REVIEWING THE LIST OF THE ONE-HUNDRED AND FOUR SIGNATURES ON THE ANNEXATION PETITIONS THAT WERE PRESENTED TO THE AMERICAN PRESIDENT AND CROSS-REFERENCING THEM WITH KNOWN MEMBERS OF FREEMASONRY OF DAYS-GONE-BY. WHILE CROSS-REFERENCING THESE FAMILY NAMES, SOME OF THEM TO THIS VERY DAY ARE HIGHLY RESPECTED IN THE PROVINCE OF BRITISH COLUMBIA AND STILL VERY ACTIVE IN FREEMASONRY DURING THE 21ST CENTURY.

FRATERNITY BROTHER HENRY F. HEISTERMAN FOR EXAMPLE SERVED AS THE GRAND LODGE OF BRITISH COLUMBIA'S GRAND SECRETARY FROM 1871 TO 1873 AND ACTED AS ITS GRAND TREASURER FROM 1885 UNTIL HIS DEATH IN VICTORIA ON AUGUST 29TH, 1896. WHILE THE ANNEXATION PETITION WAS BEING CIRCULATED THROUGHOUT VANCOUVER ISLAND IN 1869, HE WAS ACTING IN THE CAPACITY OF THE GRAND SECRETARY OF THE PROVINCIAL GRAND LODGE OF BRITISH COLUMBIA WHICH AT THE TIME WAS UNDER THE JURISDICTIONAL POWERS OF THE GRAND LODGE OF SCOTLAND. ANOTHER VERY INTERESTING NAME ON THE ANNEXATION PETITION THAT SENDS ALARM BELLS RINGING, ISAAC OPPENHEIMER WHO AT THE TIME WAS A MEMBER OF THE MASONIC ORDER'S AMERICAN FRATERNITY LODGERY; UNION LODGE NO. 58, SACRAMENTO, CALIFORNIA. ONCE BRITISH COLUMBIA BECAME PART OF FREEMASONRY BROTHER MACDONALD'S DREAM OF A UNITED CONFEDERATION, OPPENHEIMER JOINED CARIBOO LODGE NO. 469 AND WHEN THE GOLDFIELDS

OF BARKERVILLE REFUSED TO SHARE ANY MORE OF ITS WEALTH, HE MIGRATED FROM THE PROVINCE'S INTERIOR BACK DOWN TO THE LOWER MAINLAND IN 1879 AND ALMOST IMMEDIATELY JOINED VANCOUVER AND QUADRA LODGE NO. 2. WHERE IN WHICH ISAAC AND HIS BROTHER DAVID SOON BECAME HIGHLY RESPECTED POLITICAL FIGURES IN ALL OF VANCOUVER AS BOTH SERVED ON THE CITY COUNCIL DURING THE 1880'S WHILE FRATERNITY BROTHER DAVID WAS EVENTUALLY ELEVATED TO THE MAYOR'S CHAIR IN DECEMBER OF 1887 AND SERVED THAT PORTFOLIO UNTIL JANUARY OF 1892. OTHER MASTER MASONS WHO SIGNED THEIR NAMES TO THE ANNEXATION PETITION WERE; JOSEPH DESPARD PEMBERTON, WOLFF HOFFMAN, LEWIS LEWIS, PETER OUSTERHOUT, ELI HARRISON SR., JOSEPH LOEWEN, EMIL SUTO, R.H. ADAMS, K.J.F. BECKER, H.M. COHEN, D.F. FEE, G.C. KEAYS, C.B. SWEENY, M.W. WAITT AND MANY OTHERS OF THE FRATERNITY CRAFT.

ACCORDING TO THE MASONIC ORDER'S OWN LITERATURE, IN JANUARY OF 1869 THREE OF THE INDIVIDUALS WHO INITIALLY SIGNED THEIR NAMES TO THE ANNEXATION PETITION; R.H. ADAMS, HENRY F. HEISTERMAN AND M.W. WAITT WERE ALSO TRYING TO ESTABLISH AN INDEPENDENT GRAND LODGE FOR BRITISH COLUMBIA. APPARENTLY, THE MEMBERS OF FREEMASONRY WHO ATTENDED THE SCOTTISH LODGES WERE IN FAVOR OF THE PROPOSAL BUT THOSE ATTENDING THE ENGLISH LODGES WERE OPPOSED. WITH THE DISSECTION GROWING BETWEEN THESE TWO MASONIC FACTIONS, HEISTERMAN AND HIS FELLOW BRETHREN QUICKLY TURNED TO THE UNITED STATES TO HELP RESOLVE THE ISSUE THAT WAS SETTING BRITISH COLUMBIA'S FREEMASONS AGAINST ONE ANOTHER. BY SPRING OF 1870, FREEMASONRY TENSIONS REACHED AN ALL TIME HIGH AS BY THIS TIME PERIOD THE MAJORITY OF BRITISH COLUMBIA'S NON-MASONIC POPULATION STRONGLY SUPPORTED ANNEXATION BY THE UNITED STATES AS THEY REPORTEDLY PREFERRED IT OVER WHAT MACDONALD AND THE BRITISH MONARCHY HAD IN STORE FOR THE PROVINCE. FEARING INADEQUATE REPRESENTATION BY OTTAWA, THE ANNEXATION MOVEMENT GAINED MOMENTUM AS MORE AND MORE OF BRITISH COLUMBIA'S WHITE POPULATION VOICED THEIR INTEREST IN JOINING THE UNITED STATES OF AMERICA INSTEAD OF CANADA.

THESE WERE VERY TRYING TIMES FOR THE MEMBERS OF THE MASONIC ORDER AS IT PITTED BRETHREN AGAINST BRETHREN. ACCORDING TO THE HISTORIANS, THE PETITION AND SUBSEQUENT LETTERS FROM THE VICTORIA MERCHANTS ASKING PERMISSION TO JOIN THE UNITED STATES ANGERED SEVERAL COLONIAL OFFICERS, AMONG THEM THE ATTORNEY-GENERAL HENRY CREASE AND THE COMMISSIONER OF LANDS AND WORKS JOSEPH TRUTCH. THESE TWO INDIVIDUALS ACCORDING TO SOME HISTORIANS ORIGINALLY OPPOSED CONFEDERATION BUT LATER CHANGED THEIR MINDS ONCE THE ANNEXATION PETITION WAS DULY SUBMITTED TO THE AMERICAN PRESIDENT AND THEY

WERE SAID TO HAVE EVENTUALLY JOINED THE NEWLY APPOINTED GOVERNOR (MUSGRAVE) IN HIS EFFORTS TO DEFUSE THE ANNEXATION MOVEMENT. BY THE WAY, FRATERNITY BROTHER JOSEPH WILLIAM TRUTCH WAS BRITISH COLUMBIA'S FIRST LIEUTENANT-GOVERNOR ASSUMING THE PORTFOLIO ON JULY 5TH, 1871. ALTHOUGH HE BECAME A MASTER MASON PRIOR TO HIS ARRIVAL IN BRITISH COLUMBIA IN 1859, HE WASN'T KNIGHTED SIR JOSEPH WILLIAM TRUTCH UNTIL THIRTY YEARS LATER, (1889). HIS FREEMASONRY COMRADE, HENRY PERING PELLEW CREASE ALSO BECAME A MEMBER OF THE MASONIC ORDER PRIOR TO HIS ARRIVAL AS WELL IN 1859 AND WAS ANOINTED ATTORNEY-GENERAL IN 1864 WHERE HE REMAINED FOR SIX YEARS UNTIL BEING APPOINTED TO THE SUPREME COURT OF BRITISH COLUMBIA IN 1870. UPON HIS RETIREMENT FROM THE BENCH IN 1896, BROTHER CREASE WAS KNIGHTED SIR HENRY.

DESPITE THE FACT THAT BRITISH COLUMBIA'S FREEMASONS WERE AT WAR WITH THEMSELVES, MOST, IF NOT ALL THE HISTORIANS DOWN PLAYED THE ORDEAL BY NOT MENTIONING ONE WORD OF THE SCHISM THAT EXISTED BETWEEN THE TWO PARTIES IN QUESTION. THE HISTORY BOOKS MERELY SKIMMED THE SURFACE OF THE VERY TURBULENT WATERS ATTRIBUTING THE DISCONTENT AS BEING SOMETHING THAT IT WASN'T AND THEN SAYING BY JANUARY OF 1871, THE NEGOTIATED TERMS OF BRITISH COLUMBIA'S JOINING CONFEDERATION HAD BEEN AGREED UPON AND IN APRIL OF THAT SAME YEAR, THE AGREEMENT WAS SENT TO LONDON FOR ITS APPROVAL. THE BRITISH, THEN, REPORTEDLY AUTHORIZED ITS TERMS AND ON JULY 20TH, 1871 BRITISH COLUMBIA OFFICIALLY ENTERED INTO CANADA'S CONFEDERATION. BUT WHAT THESE SAME HISTORIANS NEGLECTED TO MENTION WAS THE FACT THAT ACCORDING TO THE JANUARY 1871 NEGOTIATED TERMS OF AGREEMENT, BRITISH COLUMBIA WAS ALSO PERMITTED TO HAVE ITS OWN INDEPENDENT GRAND LODGE AS THE TWO BRANCHES OF THE ANCIENT MASONIC CRAFT (SCOTTISH AND ENGLISH RITE LODGERY) DECIDED TO SET ASIDE THEIR FRATERNAL DIFFERENCES OF OPINION AND ALLOW THE GRAND LODGE OF BRITISH COLUMBIA TO BE ESTABLISHED. ON OCTOBER 21ST, 1871 A CONVENTION WAS HELD IN VICTORIA ON THE PACIFIC WHICH IN THE END RESULTED IN THE ORGANIZATION OF THE PRESENT GRAND LODGE OF BRITISH COLUMBIA. WITH THE DIFFERENCES OF OPINIONS SHELVED FOR THE TIME BEING, BRITISH COLUMBIA'S FREEMASONRY MEMBERSHIP SOON LOOKED TO THE FUTURE AS THEY WELCOMED THE TWENTIETH CENTURY WITH ARMS OPENED WIDE. THAT IS TO SAY UNTIL THE HALF-BREED POPULATION UNDER LOUIS RIEL BEGAN SPOILING ALL OF IT FOR THEM.

LIKE THE LEKWUNGEN INDIANS OF THE JAMES BAY RESERVE, THE METIS PEOPLES OF CANADA'S WESTERN PRAIRIES IN 1869 FEARED THE LOSS OF THEIR LIVELIHOOD AND LAND RIGHTS AS A RESULT OF AN INFLUX OF "WHITE "SETTLERS WHO WERE MIGRATING INTO THE RED RIVER COLONY. IN

A measure to prevent further unrest, the Government of Canada under the leadership of Sir John A. MacDonald deployed a further military presence by implementing the Militia Act (originally passed into law on May 22ND, 1868) to the regions of western Canada as the Metis posed a very serious threat in a small part of the North West Territory which the Canadian Federal Government had acquired from the Hudson's Bay Company. The Metis settlers, fearing the loss of their property rights and totally chocked at the high-handed treatment that they had received from Canadian surveyors, established a Provincial Government at Fort Garry under the leadership of Louis Riel. With the two opposing views of how Canada was to be formed as a nation, both British troops as well as the Canadian Militia were deployed to settle the political unrest of the Indian up-rising. Amongst those members of the militia sent to Fort Garry by the Canadian Government was none other than the Commander of the 42ND "Brockville "Battalion Captain Thomas Scott.

Once the Canadian Federal Government regained control of the western prairie Red River Settlement, it implemented additional steps that were supposedly designed to prevent further unrest by the Metis peoples of the West. Clause thirty-one of the Manitoba Act of May 12TH, 1870 authorized that one-million-four-hundred-thousand acres of ungranted lands be made available for Manitoba's half-breed population; the Metis. But as per usual, the Canadian Federal Government reneged on the transaction virtually turning their backs on the Metis of Manitoba as they became a disenfranchised race of people in their own homeland. And by 1885, a second Metis insurrection unfolded in Saskatchewan at the Battle of Batoche which took place for four days; May 9-12. (This too was under the leadership of Louis Riel). After the insurrection was finally contained by MacDonald's semi-military force, the Royal North West Mounted Police, Riel later surrendered to the powers that be putting his fate in the hands of the Almighty God as to what the English Freemasonry Government of Canada had in store for him. Knowing full well that his former spiritual advisor, the Archbishop Tache and his Roman Catholic Francophone population of Quebec considered themselves to be the superior race of people living in Canada, Louis Riel wrote a rather lengthy letter to the Archbishop from his prison cell in Regina while waiting his trial, (July 24TH, 1885). In his letter, Riel appointed Archbishop Tache the supreme pontiff of Canada's newfound Roman Catholic Church

AS THE CHURCH ITSELF RIGHT FROM THE VERY BEGINNING OF THE FIRST INSURRECTION HAD TURNED ITS BACK ON THE HALF-BREED POPULATION AND PUBLICALLY DENOUNCED RIEL'S VIEWS AS BEING THE RANTINGS OF AN INSANE INDIVIDUAL. IN 1876-77 WHILE TRYING TO FIGURE OUT EXACTLY AS TO WHAT THE CATHOLIC CHURCH REALLY MEANT TO HIM, LOUIS RIEL REPORTEDLY SPENT TWENTY MONTHS IN THE MENTAL ASYLUMS OF CANADA AND BOTH THE ROMAN CATHOLIC CHURCH AND THE CANADIAN FEDERAL GOVERNMENT USED THIS LITTLE FACTOR FOR THEIR FULL ADVANTAGE. THAT OF WHICH GOVERNMENTAL OFFICIALS WERE MADE WELL AWARE OF WHERE WITHIN THE MENTAL HEALTH SYSTEM RIEL ACTUALLY WAS AS ARCHBISHOP TACHE'S ELDEST BROTHER JOSEPH-CHARLES TACHE WAS THE INSPECTOR OF ALL THE ASYLUMS FOR THE GOVERNMENT OF CANADA AT THE TIME.

BY THE TIME LOUIS RIEL'S TRIAL BEGAN, THE FREEMASONRY POWERS THAT BE DECIDED TO USE HIS TIME SERVED IN THE ASYLUMS AS BEING SIGNS OF AN INSANE PERSON HELL BENT ON OVER-THROWING THE GOVERNMENT OF CANADA. THE QUESTION OF HIS SANITY THUS BECAME THE STEPPING STONE OF RIEL'S DOWNFALL AS OTTAWA WANTED HIM TO PAY THE FULL PRICE OF HIS WRONGDOINGS WITH HIS OWN LIFE. AFTERALL, HE WAS MERELY A HALF-BREED INDIAN WHO NEVER CONTRIBUTED ONE DAMN THING TO "WHITE SOCIETY "AS A WHOLE. POSING AS A THREAT TO NATIONAL SECURITY BECAUSE OF WHAT HE KNEW OF THE SO-CALLED BENEVOLENT EFFORTS OF THE MASONIC ORDER, LOUIS RIEL WAS CONVICTED OF TREASONOUS ACTIONS AGAINST THE FREEMASONRY GOVERNMENT OF CANADA.

UPON HEARING THE NEWS OF HIS CONVICTION, FRENCH ROMAN CATHOLICS DEMANDED THAT THE CANADIAN FEDERAL GOVERNMENT RELEASE HIM IMMEDIATELY. HAVING NO SYMPATHY WHATSOEVER FOR FRENCH CANADA AND THEIR KIND, PRIME MINISTER SIR JOHN A. MACDONALD REPORTEDLY STATED: "HE SHALL HANG THOUGH EVERY DOG IN QUEBEC BARK IN HIS FAVOR. "AND WHEN NEWS FINALLY TRAVELED THAT RIEL WAS EXECUTED, FRENCH CANADA'S REACTION WAS SOMEWHAT MIXED TO SAY THE LEAST; WHILE MOST MOURNED, OTHERS CHEERED. DESPITE THE FACT THAT LOUIS RIEL WAS TRYING TO FREE BOTH THE INDIAN AND FRANCO-INDIAN POPULATION FROM THE SHACKLES OF THEIR CAPTURES, MANY OF QUEBEC'S ELECTED POLITICIANS SIDED WITH MACDONALD SAYING THAT THE EXECUTION WAS TOTALLY JUSTIFIABLE. HOWLS OF REVENGING RIEL'S DEATH SOON FILLED THE STREETS OF FRENCH CANADA AS ANTI-MASONIC RHETORIC BECAME THE BATTLE CRY OF MANY GRIEVING FRENCHMEN. AS AN ESTIMATED FIFTY-THOUSAND OF FRENCH CANADA'S FREE CITIZENS GATHERED AT A MASSIVE MEETING ON THE CHAMP DE MARS IN QUEBEC CITY ON NOVEMBER 22ND, 1885 CRIES OF VENGEANCE COULD BE HEARD. IT WAS AT THIS EXACT SAME RALLY THAT ONE OF QUEBEC'S ELECTED OFFICIALS, WILFRID LAURIER, DECLARED THAT IF HE HAD BEEN LIVING ON THE

BANKS OF THE SASKATCHEWAN RIVER AMONG THE FRENCH METIS HE TOO WOULD HAVE SHOULDERED HIS MUSKET ALONG WITH HIS FELLOW BRETHREN AGAINST RIEL AND HIS BAND OF RENEGADES. THIS STATEMENT WOULD LATER COME BACK AND BITE LAURIER IN THE ASS AS HE FAILED TO MAINTAIN HIS SEAT OF POWER DURING THE 1887 FEDERAL ELECTION.

IRONICALLY IN 1897, WILFRID LAURIER WAS DUBBED SIR WILFRID AS HE MADE THE FRATERNITY CUT AND WAS GRANTED THE PRESTIGIOUS PORTFOLIO OF GRAND OFFICER DE LA LEGION D'HONNEUR, (THE LEGION OF HONOR IS AN OFFSHOOT FRATERNAL ORDER OF THE KNIGHTS OF MALTA INSTITUTED BY NAPOLEON IN 1802). ONLY 30 YEARS PREVIOUS TO LAURIER BEING KNIGHTED, HE HAD BEEN PUSHING FOR QUEBEC'S SEPARATION FROM SIR JOHN A.'S ATTEMPTS OF FORMING A UNITED CONFEDERATION. FROM DECEMBER 1866 UNTIL SOMETIME IN MARCH OF THE FOLLOWING YEAR, FRATERNITY BROTHER WILFRID LAURIER WAS THE EDITOR-IN-CHIEF OF A NEWSPAPER (LE DEFRICHEUR) IN ARTHABASKAVILLE, QUEBEC, DURING WHICH TIME PERIOD MACDONALD AND HIS FELLOW CRAFTSMEN WERE PUTTING THE FINISHING TOUCHES ON THE BRITISH NORTH AMERICA ACT IN LONDON, ENGLAND. IN LAURIER'S EDITORIALS, HE WARNED THE GOVERNMENT OF CANADA THAT IF THEY CONTINUED WITH THEIR PLANS OF UNIFICATION, VIOLENCE AND BLOODSHED WOULD BE ON THEIR HANDS AS THE PEOPLE OF QUEBEC WERE NOT ABOUT READY TO SIT IDLY BY WHILE CONFEDERATION WAS BEING RAMMED DOWN THE THROATS OF FRENCH CANADA. HE THEREFORE URGED QUEBEC TO SEVER TIES WITH ENGLAND AND PURSUE ITS OWN INDEPENDENCE.

WHILE FRENCH CANADA REPORTEDLY MOURNED THE DEATH OF LOUIS RIEL, ENGLISH CANADA CHEERED WHOLE HEARTEDLY AND CELEBRATED IN THE STREETS CALLING FOR FURTHER ACTION TO BE TAKEN AGAINST ALL FORMS OF FRENCH AGGRESSION. NEWSPAPER EDITORIALS SOON GOT ONTO THE BANDWAGON INSISTING THAT THE CANADIAN FEDERAL GOVERNMENT CONTINUE WITH ITS HEAVY HANDED APPROACH TO THE CONSTANT DISRUPTIONS OF FRENCH CANADA AND ITS HALF-BREED INDIAN POPULATION OF CHRONIC WHINERS. THE NEWSPAPERS, EVEN WENT SO FAR AS TO PUBLICALLY STATE THAT THE FRENCH WERE NOTHING BUT A BURDEN ON THE TREASURY OF CANADA AS ONTARIO TAXPAYERS WERE SAID TO BE PAYING THREE-FIFTHS OF THE COUNTRY'S TAXES AND THAT NINE-TENTHS OF ALL THE MONIES COLLECTED WERE GOING TO THE SOLDIERS AND THE POLICE OFFICERS TO FIGHT THE METIS REBELS ON THE WESTERN PRAIRIES. JUST MONTHS PRIOR TO RIEL'S EXECUTION, THE FOLLOWING PARTIAL EDITORIAL WAS PUBLISHED IN THE APRIL 20TH, 1885 ISSUE OF THE TORONTO EVENING NEWS WHICH BASICALLY EXPRESSED THE SENTIMENTS OF THE VAST MAJORITY OF ENGLISH-SPEAKING CANADIANS AT THE TIME:

"WE ARE SICK OF THE FRENCH CANADIANS WITH THEIR PATRIOTIC BLABBER AND THEIR CONSPIRACIES AGAINST THE TREASURY AND THE PEACE OF WHAT WITHOUT THEM MIGHT BE A UNITED CANADA ... WITH QUEBEC HOLDING THE BALANCE OF POWER CANADA ISN'T SAFE A MOMENT. THE CONSTITUTION, OR THE BRITISH NORTH AMERICA ACT, WHICH IS OUR ALLEGED CONSTITUTION, MUST BE ALTERED SO AS TO DEPRIVE THESE VENAL POLITICIANS OF THEIR POWERS OR ELSE CONFEDERATION WILL HAVE TO GO. AS FAR AS WE ARE CONCERNED, AND WE ARE CONCERNED, AND WE ARE AS MUCH CONCERNED FOR THE GOOD OF CANADA AS ANY ONE ELSE, QUEBEC COULD GO OUT OF THE CONFEDERATION TO-MARROW AND WE WOULD NOT SHED A TEAR EXCEPT JOY. IF ONTARIO WERE A TRIFLE MORE LOYAL TO HERSELF SHE WOULD NOT STAND QUEBEC'S MONKEY BUSINESS ANOTHER MINUTE."

ACCORDING TO THE HISTORIANS, DURING RIEL'S TRIAL HE SUFFERED FROM HALLUCINATIONS OF POLITICAL AND RELIGIOUS RANTINGS BUT AFTER HIS TRIAL HAD BEEN COMPLETED AND HE WAS SENTENCED TO THE GALLOWS, LOUIS RIEL SUPPOSEDLY RENOUNCED ALL OF HIS HERESIES AGAINST THE CATHOLIC CHURCH AS HE WAS OFTEN SAID TO HAVE BEEN BABBLING INCOHERENTLY MOST OF THE TIME ANYWAYS, AND DIED A FAITHFUL ROMAN CATHOLIC IN ORDER TO RECEIVE THE FINAL SACRAMENT PRIOR TO BEING EXECUTED ON NOVEMBER 16TH, 1885.

ACCORDINGLY, IT IS BELIEVED IN SOME GOVERNMENTAL CIRCLES THAT DUE TO BOTH OF THE INSURRECTIONS, RIEL SET THE WHEELS IN MOTION FOR POSITIVE CHANGES TOWARDS INDIAN LEGISLATION. BUT IF THAT IS INDEED THE CASE, THEN, WHY IS IT THAT THESE SO-CALLED POSITIVE CHANGES WERE NOT IMPLEMENTED UNTIL FEBRUARY 11TH, 1986 WHEN THE GOVERNMENT OF CANADA FIRST TABLED BILL C-93 INTO THE HOUSE OF COMMONS – SELF-GOVERNMENT LEGISLATION FOR THE SECHELT, BRITISH COLUMBIA INDIAN BAND. SOME ONE-HUNDRED YEARS PRIOR TO THE SECHELT INDIAN BAND'S BEING AUTHORIZED BY THE FEDERAL GOVERNMENT TO CONTROL THEIR OWN DESTINY, THE GOVERNMENT OF CANADA BEGAN PURSUING A TRANSITIONAL INDIAN POLICY BY SEEKING TO PROTECT INDIAN INTERESTS YET GRADUALLY MAKING THE NATIVE PEOPLE AWARE OF THE IMPORTANCE OF BECOMING MORE INDEPENDENT AS A PEOPLE. AS FAR AS THAT GOES, THERE NEVER WAS ONE PIECE OF LEGISLATION THAT TREATED THE INDIANS OF CANADA FAIRLY, LET ALONE AS HUMAN BEINGS!!!

RIGHT FROM THE VERY BEGINNING OF TIME, THE NATIVE PEOPLES HAVE BEEN UNJUSTLY TREATED BY THE POWERS THAT BE. FOR EXAMPLE, LOUIS RIEL AND HIS BAND OF HALF-BREED REBELLIOUS FOLLOWERS WERE NOT THE ONLY ONES RAISING HELL AGAINST CONFEDERATION AND THE STEALING OF THE

BASIC RIGHTS OF PEOPLE. BY 1864-65, THE PLAN TO UNITE BRITISH NORTH AMERICA INTO A FEDERATION HAD AROUSED THE OPPOSITION OF THE MARITIME COLONIES FOR SEVERAL REASONS. THEY REALIZED THAT THEY WOULD BE A MINORITY IN THE PROPOSED UNION AND THAT THEIR INTERESTS MIGHT BE SUBVERTED BY THE MAJORITY IN ONTARIO AND QUEBEC. ECONOMICALLY, THE COLONIES BY THE SEA ALSO STOOD TO LOOSE BY CONFEDERATION. THEY WERE; OF NECESSITY, WEDDED TO FREE TRADE FOR THEY DEPENDED UPON LUMBERING, MINING, SHIPBUILDING AND FISHING FOR A LIVELIHOOD EXPORTING THEIR PRODUCT AND IMPORTING MUCH OF WHAT THEY CONSUMED. CANADA, ON THE OTHER HAND, WAS PROTECTIONIST, AND IT SEEMED LIKELY THAT ITS TARIFF WALL WOULD BE STRETCHED AROUND THE NEW CONFEDERATION. NOVA SCOTIA PARTICULARLY DISLIKED THE FINANCIAL TERMS OF THE UNION, FEARING THAT ITS GOVERNMENT WOULD LOOSE HALF OF ITS INCOME AND WOULD LACK MONEY TO SUPPORT SUCH ESSENTIAL FUNCTIONS AS EDUCATION AND PUBLIC WORKS. FOR THESE REASONS AND MANY OTHERS, MOST NOVA SCOTIANS PREFERRED TO REMAIN AS THEY WERE, A SEPARATE COLONY, RATHER THAN TO JOIN THE PROPOSED UNION BY FRATERNITY BROTHER SIR JOHN A. MACDONALD.

JOSEPH HOWE, THUSLY BECAME KNOWN AS THE FIRST REBEL AGAINST CONFEDERATION AS HE WAS ANOINTED LEADER OF THE LEAGUE OF THE MARITIME PROVINCES TO CARRY ON THE FIGHT AGAINST A UNITED BRITISH NORTH AMERICA; FROM THE OFFICES OF PARLIAMENT IN OTTAWA, TO THE OFFICES IN LONDON, ENGLAND. HOWE'S FIRST LINE OF ATTACK WAS TO ATTEMPT TO PREVENT THE PASSAGE OF THE BRITISH NORTH AMERICA ACT BY THE IMPERIAL PARLIAMENT /OR AT LEAST TO HAVE THE ACT AMENDED SO THAT IT WOULD NOT INCLUDE NOVA SCOTIA. AS PER USUAL, THE MARITIME PROVINCES AND THEIR RHETORIC OF PROTEST HAD LITTLE /OR NO IMPACT WHATSOEVER ON LONDON NOR ON OTTAWA. THUS, NOVA SCOTIA BECAME PART OF THE DOMINION OF CANADA DESPITE THE FACT THAT IT DIDN'T WANT ANY PART OF A UNITED CANADA. HOWE AND HIS FOLLOWERS CONTINUED TO CRITICIZE AND CONDEMN THE TORY ADMINISTRATION OF MACDONALD. BUT DUE TO THE FACT THAT JOSEPH HOWE WAS A TRUE BLUE CANADIAN POLITICIAN, HE FRIGHTENED EASILY. ONCE THE OUTBURST OF BEING DISLOYAL TO THE FRATERNITY AND THE BRITISH MONARCHY BECAME THE RHETORIC OF THE DAY, HOWE DENOUNCED HIS REBELLION AND IN NOVEMBER OF 1868 SUDDENLY ANNOUNCED THAT HE COULD NO LONGER REMAIN IN THE ANTI-CONFEDERATION MOVEMENT AND LATER ACCEPTED A POLITICAL POSTING IN SIR JOHN A.'S TORY CABINET. IT IS ALSO INTERESTING TO NOTE THAT MACDONALD AND HIS ADMINISTRATION HAD SPENT A SMALL FORTUNE IN ITS ATTEMPTS TO WIN HOWE'S LOYALTY TO THE CONFEDERATED DOMINION OF CANADA CONCEPT.

Be that as it may, as animosity increased against Sir John A. MacDonald's dreams of a Confederation, the people of Nova Scotia contemplated the issue of annexation with the United States as they went to the polls voting on the issue. Nova Scotia was literally divided down the middle as a good portion of its townsfolk wanted nothing to do with the Federal Government's plans of a united front. Ironically, at the exact same time that the Metis of Manitoba were beginning the 1869 up-rising against the stealing of their lands and livelihood, the Nova Scotia based League of the Maritime Provinces changed its name to the Annexation League, (June 12th, 1869). It reportedly even went so far as to issue a manifesto declaring that its members wanted to be left out of any proposed plans of a Confederation within the Dominion of Canada:

> "Our hope of commercial prosperity, material development, and permanent peace lies in closer relations with the United States. Therefore, be it resolved that every legitimate means should be used by members of this convention to sever our connections with Canada and to bring about a union on fair equitable terms with **the American Republic.**"

Just like the annexation movement of British Columbia, the Nova Scotia insurrection had the financial backing of the money makers, movers and shakers of our nation. Owners of financial institutions and just about all of the business owners in the Maritime Provinces were said to be supporters of the cause. Interestingly, due to this being a factor in both cases they were never classified as being official insurrections nor were they classified as being actual acts of treason against the Government of Canada. To that end, Canadian historians duly labeled the Nova Scotia insurrection as the **"Nova Scotia Affair"** as that is exactly as to what Sir John A. Macdonald himself referred to it as being. In accordance to what historians wish us to believe is true, they ironically classify Joseph Howe as being one of Canada's greatest political figures, while at the same time publically stating that Louis Riel was an insane individual who acted immorally against the Government of Canada. By 1872, the issue of annexation in Nova Scotia lost all of the wind in its sails and the remaining members of the movement gave the insurrection a proper burial as they consented to Ottawa's demands of a united Confederation. On July 6th, 1885 a formal charge of treason was laid against Riel, then jailed at Regina. This was the beginning of that trial which was to have much drastic consequences, not only

FOR RIEL HIMSELF, BUT FOR CANADA AS A WHOLE. AFTER BEING FOUND GUILTY BY THE POWERS THAT BE, THE METIS LEADER WAS EXECUTED FOR HIS TREASONIST BEHAVIOR AGAINST THE GOVERNING FREEMASONRY BODY OF SIR JOHN A. MACDONALD.

BETWEEN THE YEARS 1892 AND 1894, THE INDIAN ACT IMPOSED STRICT CONTROLS ON THE NATIVE PEOPLES AND INCREASED THE POWERS OF LOCAL INDIAN AGENTS. CLAUSE FOUR OF THE INDIAN ACT IN 1894 FOR INSTANCE EMPOWERED THE STOPPAGE OF FUNDS TO AN INDIAN SEPARATED FROM HIS WIFE AND FAMILY, EITHER BY HIS OWN CONDUCT /OR BY IMPRISONMENT, AND TO APPLY THE SAID FUNDS TO SUPPORT THE WIFE AND FAMILY. WHILE CLAUSE SEVEN PERMITTED A POLICE CONSTABLE TO ARREST AS WELL AS DETAIN WITHOUT WARRANT "ANY PERSON OR INDIANS FOUND GAMBLING, OR DRUNK, OR WITH INTOXICANTS IN HIS POSSESSION "ON A RESERVE. CLAUSE EIGHT THEREFORE EMPOWERED INDIAN AGENTS TO EX OFFICIO JUSTICES OF THE PEACE FOR INDIAN ACT OFFENSES AND CERTAIN SECTIONS OF THE 1892 CRIMINAL CODE OF CANADA.

AT THIS POINT, IT SHOULD BE STATED THAT WHEN THE ROYAL NORTH WEST MOUNTED POLICE WAS FIRST INTRODUCED IN 1873, THEY WERE DESIGNED STRICTLY TO BE INDIAN CONTROL AGENTS. FOR EXAMPLE, AS A SMALL BAND OF INDIANS AND THEIR METIS BLOOD BROTHERS ON THE WESTERN PRAIRIES MOUNTED OPPOSITION TO SIR JOHN A. MACDONALD'S DREAM OF LAND EXPANSION, SOME SORT OF MILITARY FORCE SEPARATE TO THAT OF THE BRITISH MILITARY TROOPS HAD TO BE CREATED AS NATIVE RESISTANCE WAS GROWING STRONGER WITH EACH PASSING DAY. AND IN ORDER FOR THE TORY ADMINISTRATION TO ACHIEVE ITS GOAL OF A UNITED FRONT, SIR JOHN A. TURNED TO THE IRISH MOUNTED CONSTABULARY FOR GUIDANCE. LIKE IRELAND'S IRISH MOUNTED CONSTABULARY, THE ROYAL NORTH WEST MOUNTED POLICE HAD A MANDATE OF KEEPING THE COUNTRY BRITISH AT ANY COST, EVEN IF IT HAD TO TRACK DOWN DISSIDENTS LIKE A MAD DOG. THEIR HIDDEN AGENDA THEREFORE WAS TO BE THAT OF INDIAN CONTROL AGENTS, THIS REALITY WAS EXPOSED IN A LETTER THAT THE CANADA'S FIRST PRIME MINISTER WROTE TO A FRIEND OF HIS BY THE NAME OF ROSE; THIS LETTER IS ALSO CONTAINED IN THE SESSIONAL PAPERS AND THE CANADIAN ARCHIVES. SIR JOHN A. WROTE: **"THE INDIANS AND THE METIS OF THE NORTHWEST WILL BE HELD DOWN WITH A FIRM HAND TILL THE WEST IS OVER-RUN AND CONTROLLED BY WHITE SETTLERS. "**COINCIDENTLY, PRIOR TO THE FORMATION OF THE ROYAL NORTH WEST MOUNTED POLICE FORCE BEING IMPLEMENTED THE BRITISH TROOPS WERE THE ENFORCERS OF THE LAW UNTIL 1877, WHEN MACDONALD DECIDED TO MAKE THE MOUNTED POLICE FORCE WHOLLY RESPONSIBLE FOR LAW AND ORDER. ACCORDINGLY, MOST OF OUR COUNTRY'S HISTORIANS HAVE

FORGOTTEN TO MENTION THAT LITTLE DETAIL OF OUR NATIONS HISTORICAL PAST WHILE WRITING CANADA: A PEOPLE'S HISTORY.

THE ORIGINAL JUDICIAL POWERS THAT WERE GIVEN TO THE CANADIAN SEMI-MILITARY POLICE FORCE ALSO MEANT THAT THEY NOT ONLY HAD THE LEGAL RIGHT TO ARREST A SUSPECT, BUT PROSECUTE AND JUDGE THEM AS WELL. THIS WAS BY NO MEANS AND ORDINARY POLICE FORCE — IT WAS TOTALLY CONTROLLED BY OTTAWA AND HAD ALL JURISDICTIONAL POWERS IN WESTERN CANADA AS WELL AS IN THE ARCTIC. NO LOCAL AUTHORITY IN ANY PROVINCE AND/OR TERRITORY COULD TELL THEM WHAT TO DO /OR WHO THEY COULD NOT ARREST /OR HUNT DOWN. IN ESSENCE, IT WAS TO BE SIR JOHN A.'S ELITE ENFORCERS OF THE LAW TO HELP KEEP THE SAVAGE INDIANS OF CANADA AT BAY. COINCIDENTLY, JUST LIKE FRENCH LOUISIANA'S COMPANY OF THE WEST INDIES, MACDONALD'S TORY CABINET WAS THAT OF A FRATERNAL *STAR CHAMBER* OF SORTS AS IT FORCED ITS VIEWS ONTO OTHERS BY IMPOSING "AN AUTOCRATIC AND TYRANNICAL POWER UPON THE FREE PEOPLE OF ONTARIO. MACDONALD HIMSELF WAS A NEW KING JAMES II - SIGNIFICANTLY, JAMES WAS THE MONARCH DEPOSED IN THE GLORIOUS REVOLUTION OF 1688, WHEN THE TRIUMPH OF PARLIAMENT OVER AUTOCRATIC MONARCHY WAS CONFIRMED IN ENGLAND."

HISTORICALLY, CANADA'S FIRST PRIME MINISTER DESIGNED HIS STAR CHAMBER SIMILAR TO THAT OF THE BRITISH MODEL ***"COURT OF STAR CHAMBER*** "THAT EXISTED DURING THE FIRST SEVENTEEN YEARS OF JAMES THE FIRST'S REIGN WHICH EVENTUALLY HAD TO BE MODIFIED BY THE BRITISH PARLIAMENT LARGELY DUE TO THE FACT THAT JAMES I'S STAR CHAMBER REPORTEDLY STEPPED OVER THE LEGAL JUDICIAL RIGHTS AND PRIVILEGES OF HIS MONARCHY. AT THE TIME, JAMES THE FIRST WAS ALSO WELL KNOWN FOR HIS SELLING TITLES OF DISTINCTION TO MEMBERS OF ENGLAND'S UPPER SOCIETY AS A GUARANTEE OF FULFILLING THE EXECUTED DESIRE OF HIS SECRET CHAMBER'S HIDDEN AGENDA. THE PRACTICE OF SELLING TITLES OF DISTINCTION IN FACT BECAME VERY PROFITABLE IN THE END FOR THE BRITISH MONARCHY AS AT THE TIME, BARONIES WERE SOLD FOR 10,000 POUNDS, VICECOUNTS FOR 15,000 POUNDS AND EARLDOMS FOR 20,000 POUNDS. LIKE THE FRENCH MONARCHY, THE BRITISH ROYALS ALSO HAD THEIR OWN POLITICAL/RELIGIOUS AGENDA TO MAKE A REALITY AS IT WAS SAID TO BE GOD'S WILL TO DO SO AND BOTH PARTIES IN QUESTION PERCEIVED THEMSELVES AS BEING UNTOUCHABLE AND UNSTOPPABLE. TO THAT END, MACDONALD'S VERSION OF THE *STAR CHAMBER* OF COURSE USED WHATEVER MEANS WERE NECESSARY TO EXTERMINATE THOSE WHO STOOD IN HIS WAY OF EXECUTING HIS DREAMS OF A UNITED CANADIAN FRONT. AND AS PER USUAL, THIS NATION'S VERY OWN HISTORIANS ALSO FORGOT TO MENTION THIS LITTLE DETAIL AS BEING A FACT OF OUR COUNTRY'S HERITAGE WHILE SETTING TO PEN AND PAPER CANADA'S HISTORICAL PAST.

It is very interesting to note that according to the North West Mounted Police's own archives, the records clearly indicated that the majority of the arrests made were on the Indian and Metis peoples of our nation. And further to this, the RNWMP's first Commissioner (1873-76) was reportedly Lieutenant-Colonel George Arthur French, who apparently had been an officer of the Irish Mounted Constabulary. Only months prior to his posting, Lieutenant-Colonel French established a Canadian Militia gunnery school at Kingston, Ontario, (1871), and was later knighted for his services rendered. With the establishing of the police force it soon began to execute the motto of upholding the British monarchy's divine right to reign supreme with the utmost vigor as humanly possible by recruiting individuals who only had a dislike for the Indians, Metis, immigrants and French Canadians. Individuals who had no prejudices whatsoever against those races of people were therefore discouraged from applying for the job as being a Mounted Police Officer.

Unbeknownst to the general population of Canada, since its first conception the Royal North West Mounted Police have had two well known missions; one public and the other no so public. Behind the borage of bold faced lies by historians as they portrayed the RNWMP as mere keepers of law and order on Canadian soil while riding high in the saddle wearing their red regalia and always getting their man. After Sir John A. MacDonald made his semi-military police force solely responsible for imposing law and order in 1877, history has proven beyond a shadow of a doubt that the North West Mounted Police (including its successor the Royal Canadian Mounted Police) used surveillance and more than they would like to admit too, forceful control of all minorities who as it so happens simply didn't fit into the British mold of things to come. In reality, the RNWMP focused its concerns on four main groups of people living in Canada;

1) All immigrants entering the country from Europe.

2) Americans who were setting up housekeeping in Canada.

3) Indian and Metis peoples as they collectively stood up for their rights.

4) Organized labor as they demanded fair treatment in the workplace.

Oddly enough, a book /or two have been published in recent years confirming the fact that the North West Mounted Police viewed the native peoples of our nation as an inferior race of people: "Many members of the police regarded Indians as being inferior beings to be tolerated only as long as they stayed out of the way. "In yet another twist of never-ending irony, it was the Royal North West Mounted Police's own ignorance of the law that lead to a revamping of its public image and the changing of its name during a labor strike in 1919. Between the years 1877 and 1914, the RNWMP were used an estimated thirty-three times against striking workers, which resulted in numerous arrests, incarcerations and physical injuries. They even reportedly established spies and informants gradually making their way up the ranks of the union movement. This practice was widely used by the RNWMP as cart blanche while the Canadian Federal Government turned a blind eye on their everyday activities. During the trials of the leaders of the Winnipeg General Strike of 1919, the courts soon learned that the RNWMP themselves conspired against the union movement. Although everyone on the picket lines were either born in England /or here in Canada, the North West Mounted Police reportedly labeled them as being radicals with a subversive agenda. They, (the RNWMP) made references in their files stating that the strikers posed a threat to Canadian society.

Needless to say, when all of this was disclosed in a court of law, hostility amongst the North West Mounted Police and the labor movement increased even higher than before. In fact, it reached such a critical boiling point that the Government of Canada had to intervene and make legislative changes that virtually became the turning point for the RNWMP. In October of 1919, the Prime Minister of Canada (Borden-Meighen government) introduced legislation into the House of Commons changing the Royal North West Mounted Police into the Royal Canadian Mounted Police. By this time period, instead of the semi-military force only having jurisdictional powers in western Canada and in the unexplored regions of the Arctic, it now had jurisdiction nationwide with the exact same mandate of keeping the country British. Not too many historians are willing to admit that the chain of events which unfolded during the Winnipeg General Strike of 1919 was largely due to the fact that both the Government of Canada and the RNWMP firmly believed that the union movement was a plot to overthrow the government and replace it with a socialistic regime controlled by the Soviet Socialist Republic of Russia, (USSR). Logic and reason

OF THE FACT THAT BASIC HUMAN RIGHTS WERE BEING VIOLATED BY BOTH THE RNWMP AND THE CANADIAN FEDERAL GOVERNMENT WAS OF NO INTEREST / OR CONCERN AS THE POWERS THAT BE INSISTED THAT A BOLSHEVIK TAKE-OVER OF CANADA WAS AT HAND AND LIKE THE NATIVE PEOPLES OF CANADA, IT HAD TO BE QUASHED WITH A FIRM IRON FIST.

DURING THE YEARS 1905 AND 1911, THE CANADIAN FEDERAL GOVERNMENT HAD DOUBTS WHETHER INDIANS WOULD EVER BECOME SUFFICIENTLY ADVANCED TO COMPETE WITH "WHITE SOCIETY". THEREFORE GENERATING AMENDMENTS (1910) IN THE INDIAN ACT ITSELF, (9-10 EDWARD VII, CHAPTER 28) REGARDING PROTECTION OF INDIAN LANDS, SUPERVISION OF INDIAN CONTRACTUAL OBLIGATION AND PROTECTION OF GOODS AND/ OR FUNDS ACQUIRED THROUGH TREATY. PARLIAMENT PASSED **SPECIAL LEGISLATION** FOR SOME SURRENDERS AND FOR EXPROPRIATION OF RESERVES NEAR TOWNS /OR CITIES. FOR EXAMPLE, IT PASSED THE ST. PETER'S RESERVE ACT IN 1916 TO CONFIRM THE LANDS SURRENDER OF ST. PETER'S RESERVE OF 1907. IN ADDITION, AN ACT RESPECTING THE SONGHEES INDIAN RESERVE IN 1911 FINALIZED THE EXPROPRIATION OF THE SONGHEES RESERVE IN VICTORIA, BRITISH COLUMBIA.

ANOTHER IMPORTANT AMENDMENT IN 1911 CONCERNED EXPROPRIATION OF INDIAN RESERVE LANDS NEAR /OR WITHIN TOWNS /OR CITIES OF LESS THAN TEN-THOUSAND PEOPLE, (SECTION 49A) THUS CONSTITUTED A RADICAL DEPARTURE FROM PREVIOUS LEGISLATION CONCERNING INDIAN RIGHTS AND INDIAN LANDS. BOTH THE CANADIAN FEDERAL GOVERNMENT AND OPPOSITION MEMBERS IN THE HOUSE OF COMMONS REALIZED THIS IN THE POLICY — MEMBERS OF THE HOUSE OF COMMONS CLAIMED THAT IT OVER-RODE THE INDIAN TREATY RIGHTS. BUT PARLIAMENT STEADFASTLY CONTINUED TO VIOLATE THE TREATY DESPITE THE OPPOSITION. THE INDIAN ACT AMENDMENTS OF 1914, (4-5 GEORGE V, CHAPTER 35) DEALT WITH EXPROPRIATION AS WELL, BUT MORE IMPORTANTLY WITH THE WITHDRAWAL OF HALF-BREEDS FROM THE TREATY. THE FIRST CLAUSE OF THE LEGISLATION ENABLED THE GOVERNOR-IN-COUNCIL TO DECLARE PROPERLY EQUIPPED INSTITUTION AS AN INDUSTRIAL /OR BOARDING SCHOOL FOR INDIANS. THE SECOND CLAUSE EMPOWERED THE GOVERNOR-IN-COUNCIL TO "EXPROPRIATE" FOR SCHOOL PURPOSES. CLAUSE EIGHT OF THE 1914 LEGISLATION FORCED INDIANS TO PARTICIPATE IN WHITEMAN DANCES, RODEOS, AND OTHER EXHIBITIONS SUBJECT TO THE INDIAN AGENTS CONSENT IN THE WESTERN PROVINCES AND TERRITORIES. THE CANADIAN GOVERNMENT FELT THAT ALL OF THE OTHER EVENTS THAT THE NATIVES NORMALLY PARTICIPATED IN, SUCH AS THE POTLATCH, OFFERED "EVIL "TEMPTATIONS TO THE INDIANS AND WERE SAID TO HAVE ULTIMATELY DISRUPTED WORK THAT WERE SCHEDULED TO TAKE PLACE ON THE RESERVATIONS. THIS DESPITE THE FACT THAT ACCORDING TO

THE NATIVE PEOPLES OWN CUSTOMS AND TRADITIONS, THE POTLATCH PLAYED A VERY IMPORTANT ROLE MAINTAINING THEIR PRIDE AS A PEOPLE. ACCORDINGLY, THE POTLATCH SERVED FOUR PRIMARY FUNCTIONS FOR ITS PEOPLE AS A WAY AND MEANS OF RESTORING ITS PRIDE AND GLORY;

1) IT PROVIDED A MEANS WHEREBY AN INDIVIDUAL COULD ACHIEVE FAME AND BY WHICH HIS FAME COULD BE COMPARED ACCURATELY WITH THE ACHIEVEMENTS OF OTHERS. THE PRINCIPLE WAS SIMPLISTIC IN NATURE -THE MORE GIVE AWAY, THE GREATER THE PRESTIGE OF THE DONOR.

2) THE PUBLIC BESTOWAL OF GIFTS WAS NECESSARY TO VALIDATE EVERY TYPE OF ACTIVITY. A MARRIAGE, THE CONSTRUCTION OF A BUILDING /OR DECORATION OF A HOUSE, THE TRANSMISSION OF A NAME, THE PERFORMANCE OF A CEREMONIAL DANCE /OR A RITUAL OF MOURNING WAS TOTALLY MEANINGLESS UNLESS VALIDATED BY A PRESENT TO EVERY SPECTATOR, WHO THUS BECAME A LEGAL WITNESS OF THE TRANSACTION. THE GREATER THE VALUE OF THE GOODS DISTRIBUTED, THE GREATER THE STRENGTH /OR WORTH OF WHATEVER WAS BEING VALIDATED.

3) SINCE IT WAS NOT CUSTOMARY FOR AN INDIVIDUAL TO DECLINE A GIFT GIVEN, ONE COULD SHAME HIS RIVAL BY OUTDOING HIM IN LAVISHED GENEROSITY. QUITE OFTEN, PAST DISAGREEMENTS COULD BE SETTLED BY WAY OF THE POTLATCH AS ONE INDIVIDUAL TRIES TO OUT DO THE OTHER.

4) THE POTLATCH, IN ESSENCE PROVIDED A TYPE OF INVESTMENT THAT WAS RATHER UNIQUE TO THE NATIVE COMMUNITY AS THE INDIVIDUAL RECEIVING A GIFT WAS AUTOMATICALLY EXPECTED TO RETURN IT WITH MUCH GREATER VALUE OF A GIFT, UNLESS HE WAS WILLING TO BE PUBLICALLY HUMILIATED BY HIS RIVAL.

ALTHOUGH THE PRINCIPLE OF THE POTLATCH WAS KNOWN MAINLY THROUGHOUT THE PACIFIC COASTAL INDIAN POPULATION OF BRITISH COLUMBIA, THE CANADIAN FEDERAL GOVERNMENT PROCLAIMED ITS PRINCIPLES AS BEING AN EVIL PAGAN RITUAL AND BANNED ITS PRACTICE. ODDLY ENOUGH, SOME HISTORIANS STATE THAT BY ALL ACCOUNT THE CANADIAN GOVERNMENT DEEMED THE PRACTICE OF THE POTLATCH A TOTAL WASTE OF MATERIALS AND GOODS AS IT'S DISRUPTIVE EFFECTS COULD BE FELT THROUGHOUT THE NATIVE COMMUNITIES.

AFTER THE FIRST WORLD WAR, VARIOUS OTTAWA POLITICIANS AGREED THAT THE INDIAN ACT ON EDUCATION HAD TO BE CHANGED. THE HONORABLE ARTHUR MEIGHEN AND DEPUTY SUPERINTENDENT-GENERAL

Duncan Campbell Scott both felt that more Indians would become citizens under Canadian law if they were offered guidance through schooling. Scott then explained this concept of legalized genocide of our country's First Nation Peoples to a Special Committee of the House of Commons that was examining the Indian Act amendments of 1920:

"I want to get rid of the Indian problem. I do not think as a matter of fact, that this country ought to continuously protect a class of people who are able to stand alone. This is my whole point. I do not want to pass into the citizens' class people who are paupers. This is not the intention of the Bill. But after one hundred years, after being in close contact with civilization it is enervating to the individual or a band to continue in the state of tutelage, when he or she or they are able to take their position as British citizens or Canadian citizens, to support themselves and stand alone. That has been the whole purpose of Indian education and advancement since the earliest times. One of the very earliest enactment's was to provide for the enfranchisement of the Indian. So it is written in our law that the Indian was eventually to become enfranchised.

Our object is to continue until there is not a single Indian in Canada that has not been absorbed into the body politic and there is no Indian question, and no Indian Department, that is the whole object of this Bill."

The Indian Act amendments of 1924, (14-15 George V, Chapter 47) placed the Canadian Inuit Peoples of the Arctic under the control of Indian Affairs. Up to this time the Federal Government had only provided small amounts of assistance for relief when the Eskimos were short of food and supplies. Other than that, no services similar to those given to Indians were extended to them. The Canadian Federal Government then questioned if there should be a section in the Indian Act declaring that the Inuit were Indians for administration purposes. The original proposal of legalized genocide included **"ESKIMO "**in the same definition of **"INDIAN"** and the Honorable Arthur Meighen, was said to have objected strongly as he knew full well that both of these races of people were different from one another in an assortment of ways, mostly

CULTURALLY IF NOTHING ELSE. IN THE HOUSE OF COMMONS DEBATE OF JUNE 30TH, 1924, MEIGHEN STATED:

"I SHOULD NOT LIKE TO SEE THE SAME POLICY PRECISELY APPLIED TO THE ESKIMO AS WE HAVE APPLIED TO THE INDIAN. I OBJECT TO NURSING. I REALLY THINK THE NURSING OF OUR INDIANS HAS HURT THEM. THE BEST POLICY WE CAN ADOPT TOWARDS THE ESKIMO IS TO LEAVE THEM ALONE ... AFTER SEVENTY-FIVE YEARS OF TUTELAGE AND NURSING ... (THE INDIANS) ARE STILL HELPLESS ON OUR HANDS."

REPORTEDLY, OTHER MEMBERS THEREFORE AGREED, AND THE LEGISLATION PASSED AS TO READ THE WORDS IN EFFECT AS, "INDIAN AFFAIRS SHALL HAVE CHARGE OF ESKIMO AFFAIRS, "WITH NO MENTION WHATSOEVER OF PROPERTY /OR THE APPLICATION OF THE INDIAN ACT LEGISLATION ONTO THE INUIT OF CANADA'S FAR NORTHERN REGIONS. IT IS INTERESTING TO FURTHER NOTE THAT ARTHUR MEIGHEN WAS FIRST ANOINTED PRIME MINISTER OF CANADA IN 1920 AFTER MASONIC BROTHER ROBERT BORDEN RESIGNED HIS POST IN TOTAL DISGRACE, BUT MEIGHEN'S REIGN WAS SHORT LIVED AS IT ONLY LASTED FOR ABOUT A YEAR. HE THEN OBTAINED THE SAME PORTFOLIO ONCE AGAIN IN 1926 (FOR ONLY A FEW DAYS) AS THE GOVERNMENT OF CANADA WAS IN THE MIDST OF SCHISM FROM WITHIN ITS OWN FRATERNITY ORGANIZATION. DISGUSTED AND SOMEWHAT DISILLUSIONED ABOUT THE WHOLE POLITICAL ARENA, MEIGHEN RETIRED FROM POLITICS SHORTLY THEREAFTER BUT WAS LATER APPOINTED TO THE CANADIAN SENATE, (1932).

WHEN THE GOVERNMENT OF CANADA AGAIN PASSED LEGISLATION IN 1927, (REVISED STATUTES OF CANADA, CHAPTER 48) OUR COUNTRY WAS ENJOYING A PERIOD OF ECONOMIC BOOM BOTH AT HOME AND ABROAD. THE INDIAN ACT'S SECTION OF ESKIMO AFFAIRS WAS TO BE AMENDED IN SUCH A WAY THAT EVEN MEIGHEN HIMSELF WAS NOT AT ALL IMPRESSED WITH. BY 1930, THE INUIT PEOPLES OF CANADA'S UNEXPLORED FROZEN NORTHERN FRONTIER BECAME PART OF THE GOVERNMENT'S PLAN OF LEGALIZED GENOCIDE. WHEREAS, THE SUPERINTENDENT-GENERAL CHARLES A. STEWARD ADVISED MEMBERS OF THE HOUSE OF COMMONS ON MARCH 31ST, THAT THERE WERE NO INDIAN AFFAIRS OFFICIALS IN THE REGIONS INHABITED BY THE INUIT. HE FURTHER MAINTAINED THAT THE NORTH-WEST TERRITORIES COUNCIL AND THE DEPARTMENT OF THE INTERIOR SHOULD CONTROL ALL ESKIMO MATTERS.

IN THE 1920'S, MASSIVE DEVELOPMENT OF NATURAL RESOURCES, ESPECIALLY IN LUMBERING AND MINING, CAUSED THE THREE PRAIRIE PROVINCES TO DEMAND CONTROL OF THEIR OWN RESOURCES. THE FOUNDING PROVINCES AT CONFEDERATION HAD RETAINED CONTROL OF THEIR LANDS, FORESTS, AND MINERALS, BUT THE FEDERAL GOVERNMENT STILL HAD FULL CONTROL OVER THE RESOURCES IN THE NORTH-WEST TERRITORIES AND/OR RUPERT'S

LAND OUT OF WHICH LATER ROSE THE NEW PROVINCES OF MANITOBA, SASKATCHEWAN AND ALBERTA. IT WASN'T UNTIL MAY 30TH, 1930 THAT PARLIAMENT AGREED TO THE TRANSFER OF NATURAL RESOURCES TO THESE PROVINCES. NATURALLY, THE CANADIAN GOVERNMENT MADE PROVISIONS FOR FULFILLMENT OF INDIAN RESERVE LAND ENTITLEMENT UNDER TREATY AND TO ENABLE INDIANS TO HUNT, FISH AND TRAP FOR FOOD AT ALL TIMES OF THE YEAR. INTERESTINGLY, INTERPRETATION OF THESE RIGHTS WERE SUBJECT TOO MANY COURT DECISIONS IN LATER YEARS.

AS THE 1930'S PROGRESSED INTO A DECADE OF DESPAIR FOR ALL RACES OF PEOPLE, (INDIAN, ESKIMO, WHITE AND/OR BLACK) THE INDIAN AFFAIRS BRANCH ALMOST INSTANTLY BECAME FULLY AWARE OF THE PECULIAR-ECONOMICAL AND LEGAL POSITION OF THE INDIAN POPULATION IN CANADIAN SOCIETY. IT ACKNOWLEDGED THAT THE MAJORITY OF THE INDIANS SUFFERED EXTREME ECONOMIC HARDSHIP DURING THE DEPRESSION BECAUSE MOST EMPLOYERS TENDED TO VIEW THEM AS PUBLIC CHARGES WHO DID NOT NEED STEADY JOBS AND THEREFORE REFUSED TO EMPLOY THEIR SERVICES. THE GOVERNMENT OF CANADA REPORTEDLY SEARCHED FOR SOME MEANS TO ENCOURAGE WHITE INDIVIDUAL ENTERPRISES TO HIRE NATIVES AS THEY (THE CANADIAN FEDERAL GOVERNMENT) WANTED TO REMOVE THE STATE OF DEPENDENCY OF WHICH SO MANY WHITE CITIZENS VIEWED AS BEING UN-NECESSARY. HAVING NO OTHER ALTERNATIVE AT THEIR DISPOSAL, THE GOVERNMENT OF CANADA AMENDED THE INDIAN ACT ONCE MORE IN 1938 WHICH INSTITUTED A "REVOLVING LOAN FUND "FOR INDIAN PEOPLE (2 GEORGE VI, CHAPTER 31). MEMBERS OF THE HOUSE OF COMMONS AND THE SENATE WERE SAID TO HAVE VIEWED THIS AMENDMENT WITH MIXED FEELINGS, BUT MOST MEMBERS AGREED WITH THE AMENDMENT IN PRINCIPLE AS ITS MAIN FUNCTION WAS IDENTICAL TO THAT OF THE COMPANY OF THE INDIES, TO DRIVE AN EVEN HUGER WEDGE BETWEEN THE TWO RACES OF PEOPLE (NATIVES AND NON-NATIVES), THUS FORCING THE INDIAN TO CONVERT TO THE WHITEMAN'S WAY OF LIVING BY SHAMING THE SAVAGE BEAST OUT OF HIM.

ON APRIL 2ND, 1951 A SPECIAL COMMITTEE WAS APPOINTED TO CONSIDER A NEW PIECE OF LEGISLATION THAT LITERALLY WAS TO PUT WHITE CANADIANS INTO A COMPLETE TAIL SPIN, INCLUDING THE THIRTY-TWO-YEAR-OLD NEWLY NAMED ROYAL CANADIAN MOUNTED POLICE. AS BILL 79 WAS BEING REVIEWED, THE COMMITTEE MADE A FEW MINOR CHANGES BUT MAINTAINED THE SPECIFIC WORDINGS THAT IN EVERY INSTANCE THE INDIANS WOULD BE GRANTED GREATER OPPORTUNITY FOR SELF-GOVERNMENT. THE BILL PASSED WITH THE APPROVAL OF THE SENATE ON JUNE 5TH, 1951 AND RECEIVED THE SEAL OF **ROYAL ASSENT** SOME FIFTEEN DAYS LATER. THE NEW INDIAN ACT DID NOT DIFFER IN MANY RESPECTS FROM PREVIOUS LEGISLATION. FOR EXAMPLE; THE 1951 ACT REMOVED PROVISIONS RESPECTING EXPROPRIATION

AND REMOVAL OF RESERVES NEXT TO TOWNS OR CITIES AND LEASING OF RESERVE LANDS TO NON-INDIANS. BUT IT RETAINED A CONDITIONAL PERMIT SYSTEM FOR SALE /OR BARTER OF ANIMALS AND FARM PRODUCE BY INDIANS ON RESERVES IN WESTERN CANADA. THE NEW INDIAN ACT LEGISLATION HAD A LOT OF PITFALLS, REQUIRING SOME CLARIFICATION AND REVISION. DURING THE NEXT DECADE, PARLIAMENT PASSED CERTAIN AMENDMENTS TO MAKE GOOD STATUTE. AMENDMENTS IN 1953 FOR INSTANCE DEALT WITH LOANS TO INDIANS FOR THE PURCHASE OF FARM EQUIPMENT AND OTHER FARMING ASPECTS. THE AMENDMENTS ALSO CONCERNED THE SALE AND SURRENDERED LANDS, AS WELL AS THE RIGHT TO SEIZE MINERALS /OR OTHER RESOURCES UNLAWFULLY TAKEN FROM RESERVES.

ON JULY 24TH, 1956 THE CANADIAN FEDERAL GOVERNMENT INTENDED TO TIDY UP A FEW POINTS THAT WERE UNDER FIRE IN THE 1951 ACT. THEY DEALT WITH THE INDIAN STATUS, APPLICATION OF THE ACT, MEMBERSHIP OF ILLEGITIMATE CHILDREN, BAND TRANSFERS AND ADMISSIONS, LOCATION TICKETS, LAND SURRENDER, EXPENDITURE AND RECOVERY OF INDIAN FUNDS, SCHOOLING AND INTOXICANTS. THE INDIAN ACT OF 1951 CONTINUED TO DRAW CRITICISM FROM ALL WALKS OF LIFE THROUGHOUT THE ENTIRE 1950'S AND WELL INTO THE EARLY 1960'S. THE CANADIAN FEDERAL GOVERNMENT IN FACT FELT SO CONFIDENT THAT THE COUNTRY'S ABORIGINAL POPULATION WERE GOING TO REMAIN SHACKLED TO THE INDIAN ACT FOR THEIR ENTIRE LIVES BECAUSE IN THE LATE 1940'S AND EARLY 1950'S, IT BEGAN USING NATIVE CHILDREN IN THE RESIDENTIAL SCHOOLS AS PART OF AN EXPERIMENT TO FIND OUT EXACTLY WHAT WOULD HAPPEN IF ABORIGINAL CHILDREN WERE DENIED THE BASIC DENTAL TREATMENT AND CARE THAT THEY NEEDED. WITH THAT BEING THE MINISTRY OF HEALTH AND WELFARE CANADA'S MAIN DRIVING FORCE, GOVERNMENTAL SCIENTISTS BEGAN TINKERING WITH THE NATIVE CHILDREN'S DIETS MAKING SURE THAT THE FOODS THEY WERE EATING WERE EITHER LACED WITH SUGAR PROMOTING RAPID TOOTH DECAY /OR ADDED VITAMINS TO FIND THE TRUE EFFECTS OF THEM IN A SOMEWHAT UNDESIRABLE DIET. THE CANADIAN FEDERAL GOVERNMENT HEALTH OFFICIALS FIRST SUPPLIED FLOUR LOADED WITH ADDED VITAMINS IN 1949-50, THEN, THEY WITHDREW THE VITAMIN SUPPLEMENTS SO THE RESULTS COULD BE STUDIED FOR ITS FULL IMPACT AS THE NATIVE CHILDREN CONTINUED EATING AN ASSORTMENT OF SUGAR LACED FOODS. THE PRIMARY OBJECTIVE OF THE RESEARCH STUDIES ON THE INDIAN RESIDENTIAL SCHOOL CHILDREN WAS "TO EVOLVE METHODS FOR IMPROVING HEALTH, NOT ONLY OF THE SCHOOL CHILDREN, BUT OF THE WHOLE POPULATION. "ONCE AGAIN, OUR COUNTRY'S ABORIGINAL PEOPLES WERE BEING USED AS GUINEA PIGS IN THE BEST-INTEREST OF "WHITE SOCIETY". THE GOVERNMENT OF CANADA REPORTEDLY PLAYED **GOD** FOR FIVE YEARS AS THE EXPERIMENTS WERE CONDUCTED IN FOUR

RESIDENTIAL SCHOOLS IN BRITISH COLUMBIA AND ONTARIO. AS THE DATA WAS BEING COLLECTED, GOVERNMENTAL SCIENTISTS BEGAN TO FULLY UNDERSTAND THE EFFECTS OF VITAMIN C AND FLUORIDE ON THE HUMAN BODY. AND SINCE THE ABORIGINAL CHILDREN WERE OFFICIALLY WARDS OF BOTH THE CANADIAN FEDERAL GOVERNMENT AND THE RELIGIOUS INSTITUTIONS OPERATING THE RESIDENTIAL SCHOOLS, NONE OF THE NATIVE PARENTS WERE INFORMED OF THE RESEARCH STUDIES THAT THE FEDERAL DEPARTMENT OF INDIAN AFFAIRS HAD AUTHORIZED TO BE CONDUCTED ON THEIR CHILDREN.

WITH THE HIGHLY CONTROVERSIAL EXPERIMENT RESEARCH STUDIES BEHIND THEM, THE DEPARTMENT OF INDIAN AFFAIRS BEGAN CONDUCTING A SERIES OF OPINION COLLECTION FROM ABORIGINAL POPULATION DURING THE MID-1960'S AS A WAY AND MEANS OF INTRODUCING FURTHER LEGISLATIVE CHANGES TO THE INDIAN ACT. THIS PROCESS WAS CONDUCTED IN A SERIES OF COUNTRY-WIDE CONSULTATION MEETINGS. THEN, IN JUNE OF 1969 THE INFAMOUS **WHITE PAPER ON INDIAN POLICY** WAS TABLED IN THE HOUSE OF COMMONS. IT WAS ODDLY ENOUGH INTRODUCED BY THE HONORABLE JEAN CHRETIEN – AT THE TIME CHRETIEN WAS THE LIBERAL MINISTER OF INDIAN AFFAIRS AND NORTHERN DEVELOPMENT. INTERESTINGLY, THE **WHITE PAPER** AS IT WAS SO RESPECTFULLY DUBBED COVERED THE FOLLOWING ISSUES CONCERNING CANADA'S FIRST NATION PEOPLES:

1) THE LEGAL STRUCTURE - LEGISLATION AND CONSTITUTIONAL BASES OF DISCRIMINATION MUST BE REMOVED.

2) THE INDIAN CULTURE - THERE MUST BE POSITIVE RECOGNITION BY EVERYONE OF THE UNIQUE CONTRIBUTION OF THE INDIAN CULTURE TO CANADIAN SOCIETY.

3) PROGRAMS AND SERVICES - SERVICES MUST COME THROUGH THE SAME CHANNELS AND FROM THE SAME GOVERNMENT AGENCIES FOR ALL CANADIANS.

4) ENRICHED SERVICES - THOSE WHO ARE FURTHEST BEHIND MUST BE HELPED THE MOST.

5) CLAIMS AND TREATIES - LAWFUL OBLIGATIONS MUST BE RECOGNIZED.

6) INDIAN LANDS - CONTROL OF INDIAN LANDS SHOULD BE TRANSFERRED TO THE INDIAN PEOPLE."

IT GOES WITHOUT SAYING THAT THE INDIAN PEOPLE REJECTED THESE PROPOSALS AND IN 1970, FACED WITH NEAR UNANIMOUS OPPOSITION, THE FEDERAL GOVERNMENT SHELVED THE **WHITE PAPER POLICY**. THE INDIAN PEOPLE REPORTEDLY MADE THEIR OBJECTIONS CLEAR IN PUBLICATIONS SUCH AS THE **"RED PAPER "**(INDIAN ASSOCIATION OF ALBERTA), "WAHBUNG" (MANITOBA INDIAN BROTHERHOOD) AND HAROLD CARDINAL'S, **CITIZEN'S**

PLUS AND **THE UNJUST SOCIETY**. THE BASIC REASON AS TO WHY THE INDIAN PEOPLE REJECTED THE **"WHITE PAPER "**WAS SIMPLY BECAUSE THEY WANTED THE INDIAN ACT TO REMAIN, BUT WITH SIGNIFICANT CHANGES. IN HAROLD CARDINAL'S BOOK ENTITLED **"THE UNJUST SOCIETY"**, HE STATED THE FOLLOWING ON PAGE 161:

"IRONICALLY, THE WHITE PAPER CONCLUDES BY TALKING ABOUT THE IMPLEMENTATION PROCESS, CALLING UPON INDIAN ORGANIZATIONS AT BOTH PROVINCIAL AND FEDERAL LEVELS TO ASSIST. IT STATES; ' THE GOVERNMENT PROPOSES TO ASK THAT THE ASSOCIATIONS ACT AS THE PRINCIPLE AGENCIES THROUGH CONSULTATION AND NEGOTIATIONS WOULD BE CONDUCTED, BUT EACH BAND WOULD BE CONSULTED ABOUT GAINING OWNERSHIP TO ITS LAND HOLDINGS. ' IT IS DIFFICULT TO ENVISION ANY RESPONSIBLE INDIAN ORGANIZATION WILLING TO PARTICIPATE IN A PROPOSAL THAT PROMISES TO TAKE THE RIGHTS OF ALL INDIANS AWAY AND ATTEMPT TO DEFINE AND LEGISLATE INDIANS OUT OF EXISTENCE. IT IS A STRANGE GOVERNMENT AND A STRANGE MENTALITY THAT WOULD HAVE THE GALL TO ASK THE INDIAN TO HELP IMPLEMENT ITS PLAN TO PERPETRATE CULTURAL GENOCIDE ON THE INDIANS OF CANADA. IT IS LIKE ASKING THE DOOMED MAN ON THE GALLOWS IF HE WOULD MIND PULLING THE LEVER THAT TRIPS THE TRAP."

THE 1970'S WERE THE YEARS OF HIGH DOSES OF TENSION BETWEEN THE OTTAWA POLITICIANS, THE FIRST NATION PEOPLES AND THE WHITE POPULATION OF CANADA AS A WHOLE. EVERYONE WAS ANGRY ABOUT SOMETHING /OR ANOTHER. THIS ANGER THAT PEOPLE FELT WAS VERY EVIDENT IN THE FAR REACHES OF THE CANADIAN NORTH, TOWARDS THE DEVELOPMENT OF THE ARCTIC AND THE LACK OF NATIVE RIGHTS IN THEIR OWN HOMELAND. BECAUSE OF THIS BUILT-UP ANGER AROSE SUCH ORGANIZATIONS AS; THE INDIAN BROTHERHOOD OF THE NORTHWEST TERRITORIES, THE DENE NATION DECLARATION OF RIGHTS, THE INUIT TAPIRISAT OF CANADA, AND THE COMMITTEE FOR ORIGINAL PEOPLES ENTITLEMENT. ALL NATIVE PEOPLES NORTH OF THE 60TH PARALLEL STOOD IN DEFIANCE OF WHAT THE CANADIAN FEDERAL GOVERNMENT HAD IN STORE FOR THEM BY WAY OF A LEGALIZED GENOCIDE.

IN 1974, THE CANADIAN LIBERAL GOVERNMENT OF PIERRE ELLIOT TRUDEAU APPOINTED A ONE MAN **ROYAL COMMISSION**, UNDER MR. JUSTICE THOMAS BERGER. THE BERGER INQUIRY WAS TO EXAMINE THE RIGHT-OF-WAY TO CONSTRUCT A PROPOSED GAS PIPELINE DOWN THE MACKENZIE VALLEY IN THE NORTHWEST TERRITORIES. BUT THE ONE MAN COMMISSION EXPOSED A MUCH GREATER PIECE OF INFORMATION, THAT BERGER HIMSELF

OBSERVED. IN AN INTERVIEW IN FEBRUARY OF 1975 WITH MARTIN O'MALLEY OF THE TORONTO BASED GLOBE AND MAIL, JUDGE BERGER STATED THAT "IT IS NOT JUST ABOUT A GAS PIPELINE; IT RELATES TO THE WHOLE FUTURE OF THE **NORTH**." THE REASON FOR HIS STATEMENT WAS DUE TO THE FACT THAT THE INQUIRY PROVIDED THE PLATFORM FROM WHICH RACIAL ANGER GREW. IT PROMOTED RACISM, NATIVE PEOPLES AGAINST OTHER NATIVES AND WHITES, WHITE PEOPLE AGAINST NATIVE NORTHERNERS. IT LATER REPORTEDLY EXTENDED TO A HATE-THE-WHITE-MAN CAMPAIGN AS ALL WHITE PEOPLE LIVING IN THE ARCTIC WERE TOLD TO GO BACK DOWN SOUTH WHERE THEY BELONGED. DURING THE WHOLE DURATION OF THE INQUIRY, THE NATIVE PEOPLE OF THE NORTHERN COMMUNITIES WERE CONCERNED WITH WHAT THE PIPELINE WOULD DO TO THE LAND, THE PEOPLE, THE ANIMALS, AND MOST IMPORTANTLY WHO WOULD BENEFIT BY SUCH A PIPELINE **"NORTHERNERS"** WHO LIVED THERE /OR THE **"SOUTHERNERS "**WHO HAD A WELL KNOWN REPUTATION OF RAPING THE LAND OF ITS WEALTH AND STRIPPING IT BARE BEFORE GIVING IT BACK TO THE INDIAN. ONE-BY-ONE, THE NORTHERN NATIVE COMMUNITIES TOLD BERGER OF THEIR WAYS OF LIVING BEFORE THE WHITEMAN FORCED HIS OWN INTERRUPTED LIFESTYLE ONTO THE ABORIGINAL PEOPLES OF THE FAR NORTH;

ALEXIS POTFIGHTER	DETAH, SEPTEMBER 15TH, 1974
LOUIS MOOSENOSE	LAC LA MARTRE, SEPTEMBER 24TH, 1974
AMEN TAILBONE	RAE LAKES, SEPTEMBER 30TH, 1974
WILLIE MACDONALD	FORT MCPHERSON, JANUARY 13TH, 1975
PHILIP BLAKE	FORT MCPHERSON, JULY 9TH, 1975
FRANK T'SELEIE	FORT GOOD HOPE, AUGUST 5TH, 1975
RENE LAMOTHE	FORT SIMPSON, SEPTEMBER 9TH, 1975

THE MORE DEFIANT THE NATIVES OF THE NORTHWEST TERRITORIES BECAME, THE MORE PRESSURE WAS BEING ADDED ONTO THE ONE MAN ROYAL COMMISSION TO SUBMIT HIS RECOMMENDATIONS TO THE REIGNING LIBERAL TRUDEAU REGIME. BUT NO MATTER WHICH NORTHERN COMMUNITY BERGER HAD HIS HEARINGS IN, THE MESSAGE WAS CLEARLY ALWAYS THE SAME; **NO PIPELINE WAS TO BE CONSTRUCTED AS LONG AS THE CANADIAN FEDERAL GOVERNMENT REFUSED TO SETTLE THE NATIVE LAND CLAIMS ISSUE NORTH OF THE 60TH PARALLEL.** THE SUMMER OF 1975 PROVED ITSELF AS BEING ONE OF THE MOST INTERESTING TIMES FOR NOT ONLY THE NATIVE PEOPLES OF THE NORTHWEST TERRITORIES BUT OF ALL CANADA AS WELL. IT MARKED THE OFFICIAL BIRTH

OF THE INDIAN BROTHERHOOD OF THE NWT MANIFESTO, AND THE DENE NATION MANIFESTO. HISTORICALLY, THESE DOCUMENTS WERE SAID TO BE BASED ON THE COMMUNIST REVOLUTIONARY IDEOLOGY OF MAO TSE TUNG AND THE REVOLUTIONARY EXPERIENCES OF SUCH COUNTRIES AS TANZANIA, CUBA AND ODDLY ENOUGH, NORTHERN IRELAND. THE INDIAN MOVEMENT WAS THEREFORE FIGHTING FIRE WITH FIRE AS ALL OTHER AVENUES WEREN'T PRODUCING MUCH PROGRESS, EXTREME TIMES REQUIRING EXTREME MEASURES, SOMETHING OF WHICH THE NORTHERN NATIVES LEARNED OFF THE WHITEMAN AFTER BEING AN OPPRESSED PEOPLES EVER SINCE THE DAWNING OF TIME. PERHAPS IT WAS FOR THIS REASON THAT THE SUMMER OF 1975 ALSO WAS THE BIRTH OF AN RCMP REPORT THAT WAS PUBLISHED IN OTTAWA, THAT WENT INTO SOME DETAIL STATING THAT THE GREATEST THREAT TO CANADIAN SECURITY CAME FROM THE COUNTRY'S INDIAN PEOPLE, FROM THE SO-CALLED **"RED POWER MOVEMENT"**.

THE REPORT, ENTITLED **"RED POWER - CANADA"** ESSENTIALLY GOT ITS HUMBLE BEGINNINGS DURING JANUARY OF 1973 AS THE RCMP SECURITY SERVICE (CANADA'S FORMER SURVEILLANCE DIVISION OF THE RCMP) BEGAN CORRESPONDENCE WITH ITS COMMANDING OFFICERS OF THE INTELLIGENCE SECTIONS ALL ACROSS CANADA IN AN ATTEMPT TO COMPLY A **"RED POWER"** PHOTOGRAPH ALBUM OF OUR COUNTRY'S SUBVERSIVE AND/OR RADICAL NATIVE POPULATION, A BOOK OF WHO'S WHO NATION WIDE. IN A LETTER FROM THE COMMISSIONER OF THE RCMP DATED APRIL 5TH, 1973, **"RE: <u>RED POWER-CANADA</u>"** THE COMMISSIONER'S OFFICE REITERATED THE IMPORTANCE OF ESTABLISHING SUCH AN ELABORATE PHOTO ALBUM OF NATIVE EXTREMISTS AS THE AMERICAN INDIAN MOVEMENT WAS SLOWLY GAINING MOMENTUM HERE IN CANADA AND DEEMED THE SITUATION TO BE VERY CRITICAL AS MEMBERS OF A.I.M. HAD BEEN UNDER SURVEILLANCE AS THEY CRISSCROSSED THE COUNTRY PROMOTING SUPPORT FOR THEIR CAUSE SOUTH OF THE 49TH PARALLEL.

"THE APPEARANCE OF THE AMERICAN INDIAN MOVEMENT (AIM) AND ITS UNIFYING FACTOR IN THE INDIAN COMMUNITY HAS RESULTED IN CROSS COUNTRY TRAVEL BY INDIVIDUALS IN WHICH WE MAINTAIN AN INTEREST. TO ASSIST IN THE IDENTIFICATION OF THESE PERSONS A **"RED POWER "** *PHOTOGRAPH ALBUM IS BEING SET UP. ATTACHED IS A BLANK COPY OF THE LIST OF INDIVIDUAL THEY FEEL SHOULD BE INCLUDED IN THIS ALBUM IT IS REALIZED THAT AS OUR INVESTIGATIONS IN THIS ASPECT OF THE INDIAN COMMUNITY IS IN THE EARLY STAGES, IT WILL BE DIFFICULT TO SELECT INDIVIDUALS TO BE INCLUDED. PLEASE BEAR IN MIND THAT ONCE ESTABLISHED, IT WILL, AS FURTHER INFORMATION BECOMES AVAILABLE, BE A SIMPLE MATTER TO DELETE THOSE INDIVIDUALS IN WHOM WE NO LONGER MAINTAIN AN INTEREST. THIS ALBUM IS TO CONTAIN INDIVIDUALS WHOM*

YOU FEEL MAY BE INVOLVED IN ACTS OF VIOLENCE OR WHOSE MOVEMENTS WE SHOULD BE MONITORING. PERSONS WHO TRAVELLED TO WOUNDED KNEE, S.D. OR BELONG TO AIM WOULD BE LIKELY CANDIDATES FOR INCLUSION."

THE RCMP COMMISH'S OFFICE THEN INSTRUCTED ALL OF THE POLICE DIVISIONS ACROSS CANADA, FROM THE EASTERN SHORES OF ST. JOHN'S, NEWFOUNDLAND TO VICTORIA ON THE PACIFIC TO IMMEDIATELY PROVIDE THE NAMES AND PHOTOGRAPHS OF THOSE INDIVIDUALS OF WHOM THEY PERCEIVED AS BEING SUBVERSIVE/MILITANT CRIMINAL MINDED PERSONS WHO MAY END UP POSING AS A THREAT TO CANADIAN NATIONAL SECURITY.

"BECAUSE WE LIKE TO HAVE THIS ALBUM IN USE AS QUICKLY AS POSSIBLE, PLEASE PROVIDE INFORMATION WHICH YOU POSSESS AT THE PRESENT TIME ON THOSE TO BE PLACED IN THE ALBUM, FURTHER DATA CAN BE SUPPLIED AT A LATER DATE. DIVISIONS WILL SUBMIT THE INFORMATION ON FORM C-237 ON THE INDIVIDUAL'S FILE. IT WILL BE THE RESPONSIBILITY OF THIS 'H.Q.' TO COMPLETE THE FORM AND PROVIDE ALL DIVISIONS WITH A COPY."

BUT AS FAR AS BENOIT J. LEPAGE WAS CONCERNED, THE MOST IMPORTANT INFORMATION CONTAINED IN THE APRIL 5TH, 1973 LETTER FROM THE RCMP COMMISSIONER'S OFFICE TO THE COMMANDING OFFICERS OF THE INTELLIGENCE SECTIONS ALL ACROSS CANADA WERE THE CLOSING WORDS JUST BEFORE THE COMMISH SIGNED OFF: ***"A COPY OF THIS REPORT IS BEING PROVIDED TO THE D.C.I. WHO MAY WISH TO PROVIDE COPIES TO HIS FIELD PERSONNEL. IT IS REQUESTED THAT THE CONTENTS OF THE ATTACHED NOT BE DISSEMINATED OUTSIDE THE FORCE."*** WITH THIS ONE BRIEF STATEMENT, THE GIBSONS SHIT DISTURBER KNEW FULL WELL THAT ALL THE INFORMATION PERTAINING TO THE **"RED POWER - CANADA"** REPORT ITSELF WOULD NEVER SEE THE LIGHT OF DAY EVER AGAIN IN ITS ENTIRETY NO MATTER AS TO HOW HARD HE TRIED TO OBTAIN A COPY OF IT AS THE REPORT WAS OBVIOUSLY MEANT FOR INTERNAL USAGE ONLY AND NOT FOR CIVILIAN EYES TO SCRUTINIZE.

THE 1975 **"RED POWER - CANADA"** REPORT WAS THE CREATION OF THE INFAMOUS RCMP SECURITY SERVICE WHICH WAS EVENTUALLY TAKEN OVER BY THE CANADIAN SECURITY INTELLIGENCE SERVICE (A.K.A. CSIS), CANADA'S VERY OWN SPY AGENCY. IRONICALLY, ONCE CSIS TOOK OVER THE ACTIVITIES FORMERLY CONDUCTED BY THE RCMP A LARGE QUANTITY OF RECORDS WERE ALSO HANDED OVER TO CSIS PERTAINING TO THE POLITICAL AFFILIATION OF CANADA'S NATIVE AND NON-NATIVE POPULATIONS. THE **"RED POWER - CANADA"** REPORT INTERESTINGLY ENOUGH WAS DEEMED TO BE THAT OF HISTORICAL VALUE AND WAS THEREFORE TRANSFERRED TO THE NATIONAL ARCHIVES OF CANADA. WHICH IN ITSELF RAISED SUSPICIONS THAT PERHAPS THE POWERS THAT BE WERE ATTEMPTING TO HIDE THE REPORT IN

A VIRTUAL MOUNTAIN OF ARCHIVAL DOCUMENTATION. ONE WOULD ASSUME THAT SUCH A CONTROVERSIAL REPORT WOULD NORMALLY BE SENT TO THE FEDERAL GOVERNMENT'S NATIONAL LIBRARY ALLOWING THE WHITE CITIZENRY AN OPPORTUNITY TO THUMB THROUGH ITS CONTENTS AS THE REPORT ITSELF WOULD HAVE STIRRED UP THE EMOTIONS OF THE ENTIRE COUNTRY'S WHITE POPULATION INTO A FEEDING FRENZY OF HATRED AGAINST ALL NATIVE PEOPLES OF CANADA. THEN, AS NOW, THE RCMP MANDATE TOWARDS THE FIRST NATION PEOPLES IS THAT OF INDIAN CONTROL AGENTS AND NOTHING ELSE. BUT SINCE THE REPORT WAS SENT TO NATIONAL ARCHIVES AND NOT THE LIBRARY, IT CAN THEREFORE BE CONCLUDED THAT THE **"RED POWER - CANADA"** REPORT WAS STRICTLY DESIGNED FOR INTERNAL USAGE ONLY; A WAY AND MEANS OF KEEPING THE INDIANS OF CANADA AT BAY. AFTERALL, WHAT A BETTER WAY OF DENYING THE REPORT'S ACTUAL EXISTENCE THEN BY PLACING IT IN THE CARE OF THE COUNTRY'S ARCHIVES, A BUREAUCRATIC MAZE OF HISTORICAL PROPORTION THAT REQUIRES REFERENCE NUMBERS /OR CATALOGUE NUMBERS TO RETRIEVE THE DOCUMENTATION FROM ITS ARCHIVAL CLUTCHES — NO REFERENCE NUMBER LITERALLY MEANT THAT NO DOCUMENT WAS GOING TO BE FOUND.

WHILE RESEARCHING HIS ANCESTRAL LINEAGE AND TRYING TO TRACE HIS NATIVE BLOODLINES THROUGH THE CANADIAN FEDERAL GOVERNMENT'S NATIONAL ARCHIVES IN OTTAWA, THE BRITISH COLUMBIA RESIDENT (BENOIT LEPAGE) HAD HIGH HOPES IN BEING ABLE TO RECEIVE A PHOTO-COPY OF THIS VERY CONTROVERSIAL PIECE OF DOCUMENTATION FOR FURTHER RESEARCH PURPOSES. FIRST BY WRITING TO THE RCMP ACCESS COMMISSIONER IN OTTAWA, THEN, THE NATIONAL ARCHIVES OF CANADA TO WHICH HE HAD BEEN REFERRED TOO, AND FINALLY CSIS. AS IT SO HAPPENS, CSIS SENT HIM BACK TO NATIONAL ARCHIVES. WHILE ATTEMPTING TO OBTAIN A COPY OF THE REPORT **"RED POWER - CANADA"** FROM THE POWERS THAT BE, ADDITIONAL RCMP REPORTS WERE ACCIDENTLY DISCOVERED. IN THE NATIONAL ARCHIVES FOR EXAMPLE, AN RCMP SURVEILLANCE REPORT OF ALL PROTESTS AND DEMONSTRATIONS HELD BY THE NORTH AMERICAN INDIAN MOVEMENT BETWEEN THE YEARS 1973 TO 1977 WAS ALL THAT THE ARCHIVAL RESEARCHERS COULD FIND WITHOUT HAVING A COMPLETE REFERENCE /OR CATALOGUE NUMBER TO USE AS A STARTING POINT IN ORDER TO LOCATE THE REQUESTED REPORT BEING SOUGHT — A PARTIAL CATALOGUE NUMBER WASN'T GOOD ENOUGH AS THE REPORT'S CONTENTS WERE LITERALLY SEVERED FROM ONE ANOTHER. AND BY THE TIME CSIS HAD FINALLY RESPONDED TO HIS REQUEST FOR A PHOTO-COPY OF THE REPORT, **"RED POWER - CANADA"** LEPAGE WAS THUSLY INFORMED THAT THE 1975 REPORT COULD NOT BE FOUND AND THAT IT WAS HIGHLY PROBABLE THAT HE SIMPLY HAD THE NAME OF THE SAID REPORT WRONG AS THE ONLY THING THAT CSIS RESEARCHERS

COULD FIND WAS A REPORT TITLED **"PRIORITIES IN POLICING - TERRORISM AND V.I.P. SECURITY"**. ODDLY ENOUGH, IT WAS LARGELY DUE TO BOTH OF THESE PIECES OF DOCUMENTED REPORTS ON CANADA'S SO-CALLED **"RED POWER MOVEMENT** "THAT THE RCMP DEEMED THE GREATEST TO CANADIAN SECURITY COMING FROM THE COUNTRY'S VERY OWN INDIAN POPULATION. WITH THE SURVEILLANCE OF ALL THEIR ANTI-WHITE GOVERNMENTAL ACTIVITIES UNDER AN RCMP SECURITY SERVICE MICROSCOPE, THE SURVEILLANCE WAS THEREFORE USED AS A STEPPING STONE FOR THE PUBLICATION OF THE **"RED POWER - CANADA"** REPORT THAT OF WHICH THE **"RED POWER** "PHOTOGRAPH ALBUM HAD STATED ONLY TWO YEARS PREVIOUSLY.

BE THAT AS IT MAY, IN 1975 YET ANOTHER RCMP REPORT SURFACED IN OTTAWA THAT OF WHICH CANADA'S INDIAN PEOPLE WERE CLASSIFIED AS NOTHING MORE THAN A GROUP OF TERRORIST AND LIKE CANADA'S VERY FIRST PRIME MINISTER, THE RCMP WANTED TO USE A FIRM HAND IN ORDER TO KEEP THE PEACE WHEN DEALING WITH THEM. THIS REPORT **"PRIORITIES IN POLICING - TERRORISM AND V.I.P. SECURITY** "EVEN WENT SO FAR AS TO COMPARE THE INDIAN MOVEMENT FOR EQUALITY AND JUSTICE TO THAT OF THE FRONT DE LIBERATION QUÉBÉCOIS (A.K.A. FLQ), *"WHEREAS THE F.L.Q. CHOSE BOMBINGS AND FINALLY IN 1970, KIDNAPING AND MURDER AS THEIR TOOLS. "*

THE REPORT WENT AS FOLLOWS ON THE STATED COMPARISON:

> *"DURING THE LATE 1960's, AS A RESULT OF VARIOUS CULTURAL, SOCIAL AND ECONOMIC CONDITIONS (VIETNAM WAR, MOVEMENT FOR QUEBEC INDEPENDENCE, UNEMPLOYMENT, RACISM AND LACK OF RESPONSE BY THE ' ESTABLISHMENT ' TO THESE PROBLEMS) NUMEROUS EXTREMISM GROUPS FORMED IN CANADA AND THE U.S.A. MANY FOLLOWED THE TRADITIONAL MARXIST-LENINIST LINE WHICH REGARDS TERRORISM AS A LEGITIMATE REVOLUTIONARY WEAPON. THESE CLOSE-KNIT ORGANIZATIONS ADVOCATED CONFRONTATION AND (ARMED CONFLICT) WITH THE ' ESTABLISHMENT ' WITH THE LONG RANGE VIEW TO OVERTHROWING THE ' CAPITALIST 'SYSTEM, REPLACING IT WITH THEIR VERSION OF UTOPIA.*
>
> *WHILE THESE GROUPS WERE RELATIVELY VERBAL IN CANADA, TERRORISTS IN THE U.S.A. ENGAGED IN SPORADIC ACTS OF VIOLENCE. BOMBING OF SYMBOLIC TARGETS, BANK ROBBERIES AND VIOLENT CONFRONTATION WITH POLICE WERE COMMON PLACE. THE WEATHER UNDERGROUND (THE WEATHERMAN) AND BLACK PANTHER ORGANIZATIONS EMERGED AS THE PRINCIPAL AMERICAN GROUPS WHILE IN CANADA, THE COMMUNIST PARTY OF CANADA - MARXIST/LENINIST (MAOISTS) AND THE FRONT DE LIBERATION*

Québécois (FLQ) became prominent in revolutionary circles. The Maoists practice violent confrontation whereas the F.L.Q. chose bombings and finally in 1970, kidnaping and murder as their tools.

By 1970, Canadian extremism groups appeared to suffer pains and a lack of direction and by-in-large, moved to obscurity with only the Maoists and F.L.Q. remaining as a threat. The October 1970 action of the F.L.Q. in the kidnaping of the British Trade Commissioner and the Quebec Labour Minister and the subsequent murder of the latter, was their last violent act of note. Tremendous government pressure was successful in countering the F.L.Q. attempt to overthrow capitalism and force the separation of Quebec from Canada. The Maoist movement has since faded and is no longer considered a threat.

During the period in question many American extremists, fleeing from U.S. authorities, found sanctuary in Canada. They came with the help of local militants, using false documents and faded into our society. The important point is the possible influence these fugitives may have had on would be extremists in Canada.

The Red Power movement in North America is an excellent example of such influence. Dating from the early 1970's the American Indian Movement (A.I.M.) has shown an open defiance of laws in the United States. Some of their confrontations, i.e. the occupation of the Indian Affairs Building in Washington and Wounded Knee, was openly supported and physically participated in by Canadian Indians. The movement slowly spread across a number of confrontations, some violent, with Canadian Indians who have often been morally and physically supported by their American brothers.

The Canadian Red Power Movement has emerged as the principal threat to national stability. Their strive is not to overthrow our Government but to equitable treatment by society, satisfaction on native land claims, and social and economic rights. Currently their efforts towards these goals is escalating and if their demands are not quickly satisfied, it is conceivable that Indian militants may well seek to achieve their objectives through violence.

During the past few months information has been received of some Indian militants stock-piling arms and making open threats of violence. There have been numerous occupations of government buildings and blockade of traffic on highways and railroad lines. Recently the Canadian Indian Movement conducted various confrontations, illustrating an adeptness at planning and organization that was missing in past militant activities: Leadership is now evidence. There is a good possibility that if Government is not responsive to their demands, drastic escalation from their protest and demonstration philosophy to a more violent stance could ensue. The current direction to militancy by a minority of Canadian Indians has had an impact on the movement of our senior government officials. A few years ago, certainly before the F.L.Q. kidnaping in Quebec during 1970, Cabinet Members traveled across our nation freely. Currently, proposed trips must be studied and security requirements judged in light of available intelligence indicating the possibility of violence being directed against them.

The F.L.Q. and other Canadian right and left wing extremist groups are relatively quiet, and not considered a threat in the foreseeable future. A word of caution, however. We have seen in other Nations that extremist organizations can quickly grow into an active terrorist role given the proper cause and situation. It has been said that in advance industrial societies such as ours, political terrorists are unlikely to win support except in conditions of extreme social and economic crisis. Including inflation, unemployment and wide spread labour unrest could be the condition that would eventually breed terrorism in this country."

When reading this report with an open mind, it seems that the greatest fear that the RCMP actually had was the awakening of the "sleepers", individuals who were fast asleep and would more than likely be woken up by the rhetoric being used by various native groups and without hesitation and/or provocation would eventually join forces with the militant Indians and their cause of seeking justice and equality under the whiteman's law. Although the term "sleepers" was only used in the documentation associated with **"PRIORITIES IN POLICING - TERRORISM AND V.I.P. SECURITY"** it was easily applied to the **"RED POWER - CANADA"** report as well as to the RCMP surveillance activities of **"PROTESTS AND DEMONSTRATIONS BY NORTH AMERICAN INDIANS 1973 TO 1977"**.

In the surveillance report of all protests and demonstrations held by the North American Indian Movement on Parliament Hill between those years, various native groups from across Canada and the United States were instantly labeled as being extremists and militant in nature. The entire report was purged beyond belief with such words as; **"PRIORITY/SECRET"** and/or "CONFIDENTIAL" stamped all over it. In some cases, a warning was also stamped stating that "This is a classified cyber message. All replies or reference to it **MUST** bear the security classification stamped hereon, unless down graded by the proper authority. **YOUR TELEPHONE IS NOT SECURE.** The content or any portion of this message irrespective of classification is **NOT** to be discussed over the telephone."

In reviewing this surveillance report, it becomes abundantly clear that the powers that be feared the Red Power Movement and everything that it stood for; equality and justice under the law. This in itself is not a mere exaggeration nor is it an illusion because within the documentation associated with the RCMP's surveillance on the native population of Canada, the so-called radicals and/or subversives challenged the whiteman's authority over them as a people. In essence, Canada's First Nation Peoples were treated like second class citizens of our country and the whiteman continued to do as they damn well pleased as the natives were afterall perceived as not being equal under the law. As various native groups stood up in defiance to that ill-conceived concept on inequality, Canada's RCMP maintained their God given right to govern as Indian control agents for the Federal Government and thusly classified the defiant natives as **"NATIVE EXTREMISM - CANADA"** for surveillance purposes.

Just to give an example as to how out of touch the powers that be actually were with Canada's First Nation Peoples during this time period of our country's history, the RCMP classified the actions of fifty to sixty native Indians as a subversive operation by a group of **"NATIVE EXTREMISM** "from the St. Regis Reserve, (Cornwall, Ontario), who gathered in the auditorium of the National Museum of Man in Ottawa (August 30TH, 1977 at 10:00 A.M.) to collect the human remains of an archeological excavation held during the week of the 8TH to the 12TH of August 1977 in the Williamsburg, Ontario area. The group of so-called **"NATIVE EXTREMISM** "congregated with the sole purpose of reclaiming the remains of sixteen native bodies from the National Museum that of which were legally excavated in accordance to the whiteman laws of the land. Further

TO THIS, THE EXCAVATION TOOK PLACE ON SACRED NATIVE BURIAL GROUNDS THAT THE MUSEUM ITSELF REFUSED TO RECOGNIZE AS SUCH. A MUSEUM OFFICIAL WAS REPORTEDLY QUOTED IN STATING PUBLICALLY THAT THE REMAINS WERE FROM A VILLAGE SITE NEAR WILLIAMSBURG AND THAT ALL THE VILLAGERS DIED SOMETIME BETWEEN THE ARRIVAL OF JACQUES CARTIER IN 1534 AND SAMUEL DE CHAMPLAIN IN 1603. AT THE TIME OF THIS GRAVE ROBBERY BY THE NATIONAL MUSEUM OF MAN, IT WAS UNCERTAIN AS TO WHETHER THE VILLAGERS DIED OF A WHITEMAN'S DISEASE, SUCH AS SMALLPOX, /OR IF THEY DIED IN BATTLE WITH OTHER TRIBES.

A DEBATE THUSLY ENSUED BETWEEN THE NATIVE GROUP AND MUSEUM OFFICIALS AS TO WHO HAD LEGAL RIGHT TO THE SKELETAL REMAINS AND BONE FRAGMENTS. DUE TO THE FACT THAT APPROXIMATELY A DOZEN MEDIA OUTLET REPORTERS WERE EAVESDROPPING ON THE DISCUSSIONS CONSISTING PRINCIPALLY OF LEGAL AND TECHNICAL CONDITIONS FOR THE RELEASE OF THE HUMAN REMAINS TO THE RIGHTFUL CUSTODY OF SO-CALLED "NATIVE EXTREMISM", THE NATIONAL MUSEUM HAD NO CHOICE BUT TO LISTEN TO THE RADICAL DEMANDS OF THE NATIVE GROUP AND EVENTUALLY AGREED TO RETURN THE HUMAN REMAINS TO THE ST. REGIS INDIAN BAND. FIVE HOURS AFTER THE SUBVERSIVE NATIVE GROUP ARRIVED IN OTTAWA, A SYMBOLIC RED PICK-UP TRUCK WAS BACKED UP BEHIND ONE OF THE MUSEUM'S BLUE VAN'S CONTAINING THE REMAINS, AND A LARGE GREY BOX WAS THUSLY TRANSFERRED TO THE INDIANS' VEHICLE. INSIDE THE WOODEN BOX WERE SMALLER CARDBOARD BOXES CONTAINING THE CONTENTS OF INDIVIDUAL GRAVES.

IT GOES WITHOUT SAYING THAT THE FIFTY TO SIXTY NATIVE INDIANS FROM THE ST. REGIS RESERVE THAT THE RCMP CLASSIFIED AS CONSISTING OF **"NATIVE EXTREMISM "**WERE SOMEWHAT ANNOYED BY THE WHITEMAN'S WAY OF DOING THINGS, ESPECIALLY WHEN IT CAME TO STEALING FROM THEIR SACRED BURIAL GROUNDS ALL IN THE NAME OF SCIENCE. THE NATIVES OBVIOUSLY FELT THAT THE NATIONAL MUSEUM OF MAN HAD BEEN GUILTY OF NOTHING LESS THAN GRAVE ROBBING. COINCIDENTLY, AT THE TIME, FIVE OF EIGHT MUSEUM OF MAN DISPLAY HALLS WERE MADE UP OF CANADIAN NATIVE ARTIFACTS STOLEN FROM THEIR RIGHTFUL OWNERS. ALTHOUGH THE NATIVE GROUP FROM THE ST. REGIS RESERVE HAD LEGITIMATE REASONS FOR BEING THERE (AUDITORIUM OF THE NATIONAL MUSEUM OF MAN), AND WERE WELL WITHIN THEIR LEGAL RIGHTS TO DEMAND THE IMMEDIATE RETURN OF THE SKELETAL REMAINS AND BONE FRAGMENTS, THE RCMP SURVEILLANCE DOCUMENTATION HAD THIS TO SAY ON THE CLOSING OF EVENTS:

"THIS EVENT WAS A LEGAL DEMONSTRATION HEADED BY THE ELECTED CHIEF OF THE ST. REGIS RESERVE AND ALSO INCLUDED FACTIONS OF THE LONGHOUSE. THERE WERE SOME SUSPECTED AIM SYMPATHIZERS IN THE

INTERESTINGLY, EVEN AT THIS TIME PERIOD OF CANADIAN HISTORY IT WAS NOT UNUSUAL FOR A MUSEUM TO RETURN ARTIFACTS TO TRIBES WHICH HAD CLAIMED OWNERSHIP. THIS WAS ALSO TRUE WHEN IT CAME TO ARCHEOLOGICAL DIGS AS THE NATIONAL MUSEUM WAS MERELY PUSHING THE ENVELOPE AS THERE EXISTED AT THE TIME A BIT OF A FLAW IN THE LAW THAT OF WHICH ALLOWED THE WHITEMAN TO RAPE AND PILLAGE TRADITIONAL NATIVE BURIAL GROUNDS AS THEY (THE WHITEMAN) SAW FIT ALL IN THE NAME OF SCIENCE. AFTERALL, THE INDIANS WERE AN INFERIOR RACE OF PEOPLE AS DICTATED BY THE POWERS THAT BE AND HAS BEEN WRITTEN AS SUCH EVER SINCE EUROPEANS FIRST SET FOOT ON NORTH AMERICAN SOIL. BE THAT AS IT MAY, DURING THE INITIAL DEBATE OF RIGHTFUL OWNERSHIP OF THE HUMAN REMAINS, ARCHEOLOGISTS AT THE NATIONAL MUSEUM OF MAN WANTED TO STUDY THE BONES FOR SCIENTIFIC RESEARCH BUT THE ST. REGIS BAND DEMANDED THAT THE REMAINS BE RETURNED TO THEM IMMEDIATELY FOR REBURIAL ON THE RESERVE.

TO FURTHER ILLUSTRATE AS TO HOW OUT OF TOUCH THE POWERS THAT BE ACTUALLY WERE WITH CANADA'S FIRST NATION PEOPLES DURING THIS TIME PERIOD OF OUR COUNTRY'S HISTORY, THIS IS WHAT THE RCMP SURVEILLANCE DOCUMENTATION HAD TO SAY ON THE EXACT SAME DAY THAT THE GROUP OF **"NATIVE EXTREMISM "**CONGREGATED IN THE AUDITORIUM OF THE NATIONAL MUSEUM OF MAN:

ALSO CONTAINED IN THE RCMP SURVEILLANCE FILES PERTAINING TO THE ACTIVITIES OF **"NATIVE EXTREMISM - CANADA "**IS INFORMATION ASSOCIATED WITH YET ANOTHER VIOLATION OF SACRED NATIVE BURIAL GROUNDS BY THE WHITEMAN ALL IN THE NAME OF SCIENCE. THIS TIME, IT INVOLVED THE ROYAL ONTARIO MUSEUM AND THEIR ARCHEOLOGICAL DIG ON THE 375 YEAR OLD INDIAN BURIAL GROUNDS AT GRIMSBY, ONTARIO. THE ILLEGAL DIG TOOK PLACE DURING EXCAVATION PREPARATIONS OF A DEVELOPMENT PROJECT THAT THE OWNER OF THE PROPERTY HAD BEEN TRYING TO DEVELOP FOR SEVEN AND A HALF YEARS PRIOR TO THIS DIG OCCURRING. APPARENTLY, THE NEUTRAL INDIAN BURIAL GROUNDS WERE SMACK IN THE MIDDLE OF THE LAND SLATED FOR DEVELOPMENT AS A SUBDIVISION. THE BURIAL GROUND SITE WAS DISCOVERED PURELY BY ACCIDENT BY AN AMATEUR ARROW HEAD HUNTER DURING THE THANKSGIVING WEEKEND OF OCTOBER 1976 AND UPON HEARING OF THE FIND, THE ROYAL ONTARIO MUSEUM OF TORONTO SENT A CREW TO EXAMINE AS TO WHAT HAD BEEN UNEARTHED BY THE EXCAVATION PREP WORKERS.

FOR APPROXIMATELY TWO AND A HALF WEEKS, VARIOUS NATIVE GROUPS PREVENTED THE ROYAL ONTARIO MUSEUM FROM DOING ANYTHING FURTHER AT THE BURIAL GROUNDS. THE NATIVES, HAVING A WAIT-AND-SEE APPROACH TO THE SITUATION WERE SEEKING LEGAL COUNSEL AND THE POSSIBILITY OF DECLARING THE BURIAL GROUND SITE HISTORICAL UNDER CANADIAN LAW, HELD A SIT-IN AT THE ROYAL ONTARIO MUSEUM IN ATTEMPTS TO STALL THE DIG AS LONG AS THEY POSSIBLY COULD. AS TENSIONS MOUNTED, AN AGREEMENT WAS FINALLY REACHED THAT WOULD ALLOW THE MUSEUM TEAM TO BASICALLY SKIM THE BURIAL GROUND SURFACE IN ORDER TO DETERMINE THE EXACT AGE OF THE BURIAL GROUNDS FOR HISTORICAL PURPOSES ONLY. NO BONES WERE TO BE DISTURBED FROM THEIR RESTING PLACE, NOR WERE THEY TO BE REMOVED FROM THE SITE. ONCE THIS TASK HAD BEEN COMPLETED, MUSEUM OFFICIALS WERE HOPEFUL THAT THE INDIANS WOULD EVENTUALLY AGREE TO HAVE SOME OF THE HUMAN REMAINS REMOVED FROM THE BURIAL SITE SO THAT THEY COULD BE PROPERLY CLASSIFIED AS TO THEIR POINT OF ORIGIN. BUT IT WAS NOT MEANT TO BE!!!

THE HEAD ARCHEOLOGIST IN CHARGE OF THE MUSEUM'S ARCHEOLOGICAL TEAM WAS THUSLY ORDERED BY THE ROYAL ONTARIO MUSEUM'S BOARD OF DIRECTORS TO BEGIN EXCAVATING HUMAN REMAINS /OR LEAVE THE SITE ALTOGETHER. NEEDLESS TO SAY, THE MUSEUM WAS LOSING LOTS OF MONEY AT A FAST CLIP WITH ALL OF ITS ARCHEOLOGICAL CREW MEMBERS SITTING AROUND DOING NOTHING WHILE LEGAL BEAGLES FOR BOTH SIDES, NATIVES AS WELL AS THE MUSEUM, TRIED TO ARRIVE AT SOME SORT OF MUTUAL AGREEMENT FOR THE REMOVAL OF THE BONES FOR SCIENTIFIC STUDY. IN THE MEANTIME, THE OWNER/DEVELOPER OF THE PROPOSED SUBDIVISION WAS THREATENING

TO BULLDOZE THE ENTIRE SITE THUSLY PUTTING AN END TO THE WHOLE UGLY AFFAIR. TENSIONS MOUNTED EVEN FURTHER WHEN A REPRESENTATIVE OF THE UNION OF ONTARIO INDIANS BEGAN RATHER LENGTHY DISCUSSIONS WITH THE HEAD ARCHEOLOGIST IN CHARGE OF THE MUSEUM'S CREW WHEREAS THE HEAD OVERSEER ENDED UP TELLING THE INDIAN REPRESENTATION THAT HE HAD NO AUTHORITY WHATSOEVER OVER HIM TO HALT WORK AT THE SITE. THE REPRESENTATIVE, BEING AN INDIAN ACT SPECIALIST PLACED THE OVERSEER UNDER CITIZEN'S ARREST AND SUBSEQUENTLY CHARGED HIM WITH TWO COUNTS UNDER THE CEMETERIES ACT AND ONE COUNT UNDER THE CRIMINAL CODE OF CANADA. COINCIDENTLY, THE HEAD ARCHEOLOGIST IN CHARGE OF THE MUSEUM'S CREW WAS ALSO THE CURATOR OF THE MUSEUM. PERHAPS THIS IS WHY HE CHOSE TO OBEY THE BOARD OF DIRECTORS WHICH IN ESSENCE CAUSED THE CONTROVERSY AT THE GRIMSBY DIG SITE TO BLOW UP IN THE MUSEUM'S FACE. LISTENING TO HIS BOSSES, BONES WERE NOT ONLY EXTRACTED FROM THE PLACE OF REST BUT WERE ALSO NOT TAKEN DIRECTLY TO THE MUSEUM FOR FUTURE RESEARCH STUDY AND ANALYSIS. THE HUMAN REMAINS WERE SIMPLY PUT IN CLOTH BAGS, TOSSED IN A VEHICLE AND STORED IN A MOTEL ROOM PENDING FURTHER ARRANGEMENTS FOR THEIR TRANSPORT TO THE MUSEUM. THIS IN ESSENCE IS WHAT ENRAGED THE NATIVE POPULATION THE MOST, TOTAL DISRESPECT FOR THE TREATMENT AND CARE OF THEIR ANCESTRAL REMAINS.

IN COURT, THE CURATOR OF THE ROYAL ONTARIO MUSEUM PLEAD GUILTY TO TWO CHARGES FOR THE REMOVAL OF INDIAN REMAINS AND WAS FINED $ 50.00 ON EACH SUMMARY CONVICTION. THE CHARGE UNDER THE CRIMINAL CODE OF CANADA WAS STAYED BY THE CROWN. THE UNREPENTANT ARCHEOLOGIST FELT THAT HE WAS A VICTIM OF JURISDICTIONAL PROBLEMS AS A MERE INDIAN REPRESENTATIVE HAD PLACED HIM UNDER CITIZEN'S ARREST WHILE IN CHARGE OF THE ILLEGAL DIG AT THE OLD BURIAL SITE. ON THIS TOPIC, CITIZEN'S ARREST BY AN INDIAN REPRESENTATIVE, THE RCMP SURVEILLANCE DOCUMENT USED A VERY INTERESTING TERMINOLOGY TO DESCRIBE IT AS BEING **"RACIAL INTELLIGENCE"**. OBVIOUSLY, THE RCMP WERE OFF IN THEIR OWN LITTLE WORLDS FILLED WITH THEIR USUAL HOLIER THAN THOU RHETORIC.

IT SHOULD ALSO BE STATED THAT FURTHER CONTAINED IN THE SURVEILLANCE FILES PERTAINING TO THE ACTIVITIES OF **"NATIVE EXTREMISM - CANADA "**IS INFORMATION CONCERNING THE RCMP'S STRONG BELIEF AS TO WHERE THE COUNTRY'S RED POWER MOVEMENT WAS GETTING ITS IDEAS FROM AS WELL AS CONCERNS OF WHERE THE MOVEMENT ITSELF WAS RECEIVING ITS FINANCIAL RESOURCES FROM. THE INDIAN BROTHERHOOD OF THE NORTHWEST TERRITORIES FOR EXAMPLE OVER A FIVE YEAR PERIOD RECEIVED SOME $ 7 MILLION FROM THE CANADIAN FEDERAL GOVERNMENT AND IN ADDITION TO THAT, $ 240,000.00 FROM THE INTERNATIONAL ORGANIZATION

OXFAN AND $ 35,000.00 FROM THE ANGLICAN CHURCH OF CANADA. IN OCTOBER OF 1974, THE RCMP DULY NOTED THAT:

> *"THERE CAN BE NO DOUBT THAT CHURCH GROUPS SUCH AS THE UNITARIANS, QUAKERS AND THE COUNCIL OF CHURCHES WILL BACK THE NATIVE ACTION AS THEY HAVE BACKED SIMILAR ACTIONS IN THE PAST. IF A HARD STAND WAS TAKEN BY THE GOVERNMENT THESE PEOPLE WOULD LIKELY BECOME QUITE VOCAL IN THEIR SUPPORT BY THE SOCIAL ACTIVITIES IN THEIR MIDST"*

THIS SAME OCTOBER 2ND, 1974 SURVEILLANCE DATA FURTHER STATED THAT ONLY SOME LOCALLY OWNED AND OPERATED MEDIA OUTLETS WERE GIVING THE NATIVE'S RED POWER MOVEMENT SUPPORT IN THEIR CAUSE BY REPORTING EVENTS AND THAT A LARGE MAJORITY OF THE CANADIAN PRESS THEMSELVES WERE NOT LENDING A HAND IN THAT SUPPORT. FOR EXAMPLE: *"OUR WINDSOR SECURITY SERVICE ADVISE THAT THE PRESS IN THEIR AREA FEELS THAT THE INDIANS WERE USED BY THE COMMUNIST PARTY OF CANADA."*

TO MAKE MATTERS EVEN WORSE, SOME SIX AND A HALF MONTHS PRIOR TO THIS OCTOBER SURVEILLANCE DOCUMENT BEING COMPILED, YET ANOTHER PIECE OF RCMP SECURITY SERVICE DOCUMENTATION WAS UNDER TAKEN: *"DURING THE MONTHS OF FEBRUARY AND MARCH 1974 THE SECURITY SERVICE RECEIVED INFORMATION RELATING TO THE ACTIVITIES OF MEMBERS OF THE AMERICAN INDIAN MOVEMENT (A.I.M.) AND INDIVIDUALS WITHIN THE INDIAN EXTREMIST COMMUNITY. IN EDMONTON, ALBERTA A POWWOW WAS HELD ON THE 27 FEBRUARY 1974 IN RECOGNITION OF THE FIRST ANNIVERSARY OF WOUNDED KNEE."*

INTERESTINGLY ENOUGH, THIS COMMUNIQUE WAS WRITTEN TO THE HONORABLE WARREN ALLMAND, THEN-SOLICITOR GENERAL OF CANADA, GIVING HIM AN UPDATE ON THE SUBVERSIVE ACTIVITIES OF CANADA'S NATIVE POPULATION. THE CORRESPONDENCE GAVE THE SOLICITOR GENERAL A ROUGH BREAKDOWN OF WHAT THE FIRST NATION PEOPLES HAD IN STORE FOR THEM (WHITE SOCIETY) BY WAY OF PROTESTS AND DEMONSTRATIONS FOR THOSE TWO MONTHS OF 1974, A SCHEDULED MASSIVE INDIAN DEMONSTRATION ALONG THE CANADA-U.S. BORDER TO PROTEST THE FEDERAL GOVERNMENT'S REFUSAL TO HONOR THE JAY TREATY WHICH WAS INITIALLY DESIGNED TO SETTLE CERTAIN NATIVE LAND CLAIMS ISSUES OF THE LATE 1700's. THE RCMP's COMMUNIQUE TO THE GOVERNMENT OF CANADA REPRESENTATIVE EXPRESSED CONCERNS THAT BOTH FACTIONS OF THE **RED POWER MOVEMENT "**IN CANADA AS WELL AS THE UNITED STATES WOULD END UP EXECUTING THEIR PLANS AT THE EXACT SAME TIME PERIOD WHICH *"WILL SIMULTANEOUSLY CLOSE ALL BORDER POINTS."*

Given the fact that the surveillance files covered a full five year period of time (1973 to the end of 1977) and displayed many upon many protests and demonstration by Canada's First Nation Peoples nation wide, it is virtually impossible to include all of them in this Chapter. For that reason and that reason alone, the most impressive ones will be set to print in order to give further examples as to how out of touch the powers that be actually were when it came down to dealing with the concerns of our country's native population. That is to say of course providing that all of the facts can be determined amongst the purged files in order for the truth to be told.

During the course of those years that the RCMP Security Service kept track of all the protests and demonstrations held by Canada's aboriginal peoples, Metis included, the surveillance files document an assortment of native concerns. In July of 1974 demonstrations being organized by a group of aboriginal women from Caughnawaga, Quebec protesting the fact that Indian women lost their status as Indians once they married a non-native and on February 15TH, 1977 yet another group of aboriginals occupied a Federal Government building in Toronto, Ontario protesting the way in which native concerns were not being addressed by the elected officials, (aboriginal as well as white). This occupation of a Federal Government building was in preparation for a scheduled conference amongst the Presidents of four native organizations and governmental dignitaries in August of that year.

Hell, even British Columbia's native population made the cut into the RCMP surveillance files in 1975 as a large number of aboriginals became more and more discontent with the political situation of the Provincial Government's lack of concern involving native rights and pending land claim issues – it should be noted that in the Province of B.C., the natives remained restless for many, many years. Once the New Democratic Party took office in 1972 under the stewardship of Dave Barrett, aboriginals were hopeful that the socialists would address their concerns and settle the land claims issue forthwith. A person in fact could say that the die was cast for our country's First Nation Peoples in 1973 when the Supreme Court of Canada ruled in favor of B.C.'s native peoples' rights when it stated categorically that aboriginal title to lands still existed in Canadian law regardless of which political party was holding the reigns of power in Victoria on the Pacific; Calder versus Attorney-General of British Columbia – Calder being of course Frank Calder,

THE HEREDITARY CHIEF OF THE NISGA'A NATION. BY THE TIME THE CASE WAS BEING HEARD BEFORE THE COURTS, CALDER WAS AN ELECTED MLA IN THE PROVINCIAL NDP GOVERNMENT. AT THE TIME OF THE NEW DEMOCRATISTS TAKING CONTROL OF THE REIGNS OF POWER, THE PROVINCIAL COFFERS WERE IN A HUGE SURPLUS AND THE PROVINCIAL ECONOMY WAS IN FULL BLOOM – DURING THE THREE YEARS OF INEPT SOCIALIST RULE (1972 TO THE END OF 1975), THE EXPENDITURES OF THE PROVINCIAL GOVERNMENT DOUBLED AND REVENUES FAILED TO COME ANYWHERE NEAR THE SOCIALIST'S SPENDING HABITS OF THE NEW DEMOCRATS. THE NDP REGIME OF DAVE BARRETT PUT THE ENTIRE PROVINCE INTO CHAOS AS THE ECONOMY SLOWED DOWN DRAMATICALLY AND A HODGEPODGE OF SOCIALIST RULES AND REGULATIONS WERE INTRODUCED INTO THE LEGISLATURE AS A WAY AND MEANS OF KEEPING THE MASSES, BOTH NATIVE AND NON-NATIVE, UNDER FULL CONTROL BY THE POWERS THAT BE.

IN ACCORDANCE TO THE RCMP SURVEILLANCE DOCUMENTATION DATED MAY 2ND, 1975:

"CONFRONTATION POLITICS PRACTICED BY A GROWING NUMBER OF B.C. NATIVES CONTINUES TO DOMINATE AND REGULATE THE NATIVE COMMUNITY IN BRITISH COLUMBIA. RECURRING DEMONSTRATIONS, OCCUPATIONS, AND SELECTED TRAIN BLOCKADES ENDURE AS THE FORMS UTILIZED BY NATIVE MILITANTS TO MANIFEST THEIR DISSATISFACTION AT GOVERNMENT RESPONSE TO THEIR CLAIMS AND GRIEVANCES. NUMEROUS PLANNING SESSIONS AND CHIEF COUNCILS HAVE FOR THE MOST PART ENDORSED THE POLICY OF CONFRONTATION POLITICS AS A UTILITARIAN PROCEDURE FOR ENUMERATING DEMANDS."

ON MAY 1ST, 1975 A PEACEFUL DEMONSTRATION WAS HELD AT THE LEGISLATIVE GROUNDS IN VICTORIA, B.C. THAT OF WHICH APPROXIMATELY TWO-HUNDRED NATIVES ATTENDED IN AN ORDERLY FASHION. NO WEAPONS / OR BATONS WERE NOTED TO BE IN THE POSSESSION OF THE PROTESTORS. THE SURVEILLANCE DATA FURTHER STATED THAT PLACARDS WERE CARRIED BY THE DEMONSTRATORS AND SPEECHES WERE GIVEN. AT THE CONCLUSION OF THE DEMONSTRATION THE RCMP QUOTED THE MASTER OF CEREMONIES' CLOSING MESSAGE TO HIS FELLOW PROTESTORS: ***"THANK YOU ALL FOR COMING SO FAR PROVES WE ARE UNITED; GO BACK TO YOUR RESERVES AND TELL YOUR PEOPLE SIMPLY WE HAVE IN THE PAST BEEN DISSATISFIED WITH GOVERNMENT ACTION AND WE HAVE A LONG HARD FIGHT FOR HERITAGE."***

ACCORDING TO THE SURVEILLANCE FILES, THERE WERE OTHER MAY 1ST DEMONSTRATIONS OCCURRING IN BRITISH COLUMBIA DURING THE YEAR 1975. A PEACEFUL OCCUPATION OF THE FEDERAL DEPARTMENT OF INDIAN AND NORTHERN DEVELOPMENT PREMISES TOOK PLACE SIMULTANEOUSLY

AT WILLIAMS LAKE, VERNON AND KAMLOOPS. FURTHER TO THESE BEING EXECUTED, THE STEWART-TREMBLEUR INDIAN BAND CHOSE TO BLOCKADE THE BRITISH COLUMBIA RAILWAY LINE AT TACHE, B.C. THE BLOCKADE WENT UP AS A WAY AND MEANS OF GETTING THE ATTENTION OF BOTH THE FEDERAL AND PROVINCIAL GOVERNMENTS AS THE INDIAN BAND HAD ISSUES THAT THEY WANTED RESOLVED CONCERNING LAND CLAIMS. IN QUOTING THE SURVEILLANCE FILES:

"THE NATIVES CLAIM THEY WILL MAINTAIN THE BLOCKADE UNTIL A SETTLEMENT IS REACHED FOR INDIAN CLAIMS OF SEVEN MILLION DOLLARS AND A 3 TO 1 LAND EXCHANGE FOR 378 ACRES TAKEN BY THE RAILROAD. MEMBERS OF FT. ST. JAMES DETACHMENT DO NOT FEAR VIOLENCE IS PROBABLE AND OPINE THAT *LOCAL NATIVES DO NOT HAVE THE INTELLIGENCE TO FORMULATE OR CARRY OUT ANY ELABORATE PLANS ON THEIR OWN. THE PRESENT CONCERN IS THAT SHOULD PROTESTS AND DEMONSTRATIONS SPREAD IN THE FT. ST. JAMES AREA AND ROADS TO FT. ST. JAMES BE BLOCKED BY NATIVE RADICALS THE POSSIBILITY OF WHITE BACKLASH IS VERY REAL. LOCAL MEDIAREPORTS INDICATE THAT B.C. RAILWAY HAVE NO INTENTION OF RUNNING THE INDIAN BLOCKADE.*"

NEEDLESS TO SAY, THIS OPINIONATED RACIST RHETORIC *"LOCAL NATIVES DO NOT HAVE THE INTELLIGENCE TO FORMULATE OR CARRY OUT ANY ELABORATE PLANS ON THEIR OWN* "IS AN ALL TO COMMON BELIEF WITHIN THE RCMP AND HAS BEEN SO SINCE ITS FIRST CONCEPTION BY SIR JOHN A. MACDONALD WELL OVER A CENTURY AGO. IN ADDING FUEL TO THIS VERY VOLATILE FIRE, THE SURVEILLANCE FILES SUGGESTED THAT THE MAY 1ST, 1975 PROTEST DEMONSTRATION HELD ON THE LEGISLATIVE GROUNDS IN VICTORIA HAD EVERY INTENTION OF ACTUALLY WANTING TO OCCUPY THE LEGISLATIVE BUILDINGS AND THAT ACCORDING TO THEIR PRELIMINARY INFORMATION, THE SQUAMISH INDIAN BAND WAS OPERATING THROUGH THE SQUAMISH INDIAN BAND ACTION COMMITTEE AND THE AMERICAN INDIAN MOVEMENT, AND THAT THEY WERE THE MAIN ORGANIZERS OF THE EVENT IN EFFECT HAVING A HIDDEN AGENDA THAT INVOLVED TAKING OVER THE LEGISLATIVE BUILDINGS: "RECENT EVENTS IN BRITISH COLUMBIA WOULD TEND TO SUPPORT THE THEORY THAT THE DEMONSTRATORS WILL BE A DETERMINED AND ORGANIZED GROUP WHO WILL NOT BACK DOWN. IF IN FACT THIS ANALYSIS HAS CREDIBILITY AND ENTRY TO THE LEGISLATIVE BUILDINGS IS PROHIBITED, IT IS SUGGESTED THE ELEMENTS FOR A DISTASTEFUL CONFRONTATION WOULD PREVAIL ... IT IS REQUESTED THAT THE INFORMATION *CONTAINED ABOVE NOT BE DISSEMINATED OUTSIDE YOUR DEPARTMENT WITHOUT PRIOR CONSULTATION WITH THE ORIGINATOR.*"

ONLY MONTHS PRIOR TO THE PUBLICATION OF THE RCMP SECURITY SERVICE SURVEILLANCE REPORT TITLED "RED POWER - CANADA" YET

ANOTHER COMMUNIQUE WAS DISPATCHED TO THE POWERS THAT BEIN OTTAWA. THIS TIME, IT INVOLVED THE MANY SUBVERSIVE ACTIVITIES OF BRITISH COLUMBIA'S NATIVE POPULATION. DATED APRIL 4TH, 1975 THE SOMEWHAT RATHER LENGTHY PURGED RCMP COMMUNIQUE LISTED VARIOUS ITEMS OF GREAT INTEREST TO THEM AND WENT AS FOLLOWS:

"TACTICAL MANEUVERS UNDERTAKEN BY NATIVE ACTIVISTS HAVE ALTERED APPRECIABLY DURING THE PAST YEARS. THE PASSIVE SYSTEMATIC APPROACH TO RESOLVING GRIEVANCES THROUGH SANCTIONED BODIES AND FORMAL CHANNELS OF COMMUNICATION IS SEEN BY A SECTOR OF THE NATIVE COMMUNITY AS RESTRICTIVE, TIME CONSUMING, AND ULTIMATELY INEFFECTUAL. CONVERSELY, A GROWING LEGACY OF MILITANT DIRECT CONFRONTATION WITH ESTABLISHED AUTHORITY HAS REAPED CONCESSIONS, OPENED HERETOFORE CLOSED DOORS AND, MOST IMPORTANTLY, AFFORDED THE OPPORTUNITY FOR NATIVE MILITANTS TO ARTICULATE NATIVE GRIEVANCES AND DEMANDS. THE ACCRUED BENEFITS ARE VERY VISIBLE TO THE YOUNG NATIVE ACTIVIST. HIS LOT IS AT THE BOTTOM OF THE SOCIETAL LADDER, THEREFORE, ANY CONCESSIONS HOWEVER INSIGNIFICANT IS PROGRESSIVE.

2. THESE CONCESSIONS HAVE RESULTED FROM MILITANT CONFRONTATION SUCH AS ANACINABE PARK, CACHE CREEK, AND THE NATIVE PEOPLES CARAVAN WHICH CULMINATED IN THE ' RIOT ' ON PARLIAMENT HILL. SINGULARLY, THE CONCESSIONS GRANTED APPEAR MINIMAL, BUT CHRONICLED THEY FORM THE BASIS FOR A LEGACY OF ACTION, PROJECTED BY IMPETUOUS AD HOC NATIVE LEADERS AS THE ONLY METHOD THAT WILL BE EFFECTUAL IN OBTAINING RESULTS. THIS SMALL GROUP OF ' FIREBRANDS ' HAVE BEEN SUCCESSFUL IN ILLUMINATING THE CONFRONTATIVE TACTIC AS BEING SYNONYMOUS TO QUICK RESULTS.

3. FOLLOWING THIS TACTIC, SOME OF THE LEGITIMATE OR STRUCTURED NATIVE ORGANIZATIONS ARE CONSIDERING ABANDONING THE NEGOTIATIVE FOR THE CONFRONTATIVE PHILOSOPHY. THE REASON (S) FOR THIS TACTICAL CHANGE BY LEGITIMATE ORGANIZATIONS CAN ONLY BE SPECULATED AT THIS TIME. IT IS APPARENT THAT THE RADICALS HAVE GAINED A DEGREE OF STATUS AMONG THEIR OWN PEOPLE AND POSSIBLY THE LEGITIMATE HIERARCHY FORESEE AN EROSION OF THEIR AUTHORITY AND POWER IF THEY CONTINUE TO EXERCISE THE TRADITIONAL AND ACCEPTED MEANS TO SOLUTION. SECONDLY, FORMAL CHANNELS INVOLVE BUREAUCRATIC TIME FRAMES WHICH RUN CONTRARY TO THE PHILOSOPHY OF IMMEDIATE REDRESS OF GRIEVANCES, DEMANDED BY NATIVE LEADERS. ANOTHER EQUATION COULD INCLUDE THE INFUSION OF RADICAL MINDED PERSONS INTO THE CONTROLLING FIBRE OF THESE ORGANIZATIONS. REGARDLESS OF THE REASONS, RECENT EVIDENCE HAS

INDICATED A GROWING MILITANT ATTITUDE IN THE SPEECH AND WRITINGS OF SOME OF THESE LEGITIMATE ORGANIZATIONS.

4. THE PARTICULAR PATTERN OF NATIVE ACTIVITIES IN BRITISH COLUMBIA DURING THE PAST SIX MOTHS HAS FOLLOWED A SIMILAR ROUTE TO THAT OUTLINED ABOVE. PRESENT ACTIVITIES BY THE LEGITIMATE ORGANIZATIONS INDICATE A GROWING MILITANCY WITH CONFRONTATION AS THE EPOCHAL NORM. A DETERMINED EFFORT HAS BEEN UNDERTAKEN TO SOLIDIFY AND PRESENT A UNIFIED FRONT FOR THE PURPOSE OF ARTICULATING DEMANDS. A WORKING ACCORD HAS BEEN CEMENTED WHEREBY THE UNION OF BRITISH COLUMBIA INDIAN CHIEFS (UBCIC) AND THE BRITISH COLUMBIA ASSOCIATION OF NON-STATUS INDIANS (BCANSI) HAVE AGREED TO PURSUE GOALS FROM A UNIFIED FRONT.

5. AT PRESENT TIME, THE PRIMARY ISSUE CONCERNS 'CUT-OFF LANDS' AND, SECONDLY, ABORIGINAL LAND CLAIMS. NUMEROUS MEETINGS BETWEEN UBCIC AND BCANSI WERE CONVENED DURING MARCH 1975, AT WHICH TIME A GENERAL CONSENSUS WAS ARRIVED AT WHEREBY FAILING GOVERNMENT ACTION ON THE 'CUT-OFF LANDS' ISSUE, A PROTRACTED VIOLENT CAMPAIGN WOULD BE LAUNCHED STARTING IN APRIL 1975. HAS ESPOUSED STRONG MILITANT ACTION AGAINST THE B.C. GOVERNMENT FOR THE GOVERNMENT'S INEXCUSABLE INDIFFERENCE TO THE NATIVE PEOPLES TWO BASIC ISSUES; LAND CUT-OFF RESTITUTION AND ABORIGINAL RIGHTS.

A GROWING AWARENESS AMONG NATIVE INDIANS IN B.C. MAY RESULT IN ACTION AND VIOLENCE THAT WILL SURPRISE INDIAN LEADERS THEMSELVES. THESE STATEMENTS ECHO THE SENTIMENTS AND EXEMPLIFY A GROWING DETERMINATION BY B.C. NATIVES TO ACQUIRE WHAT THEY BELIEVE IS RIGHTFULLY THEIRS. THE ATTITUDE AND INTENT OF NATIVE LEADERS IN B.C. APPEARS TO HAVE REACHED THE CRITICAL STAGE OF EXERCISING THEIR INFLUENCE AND POWER TO COUNSEL AND LEAD THE GRASS ROOTS PEOPLES TOWARD VIOLENT CONFRONTATION IN ORDER TO EXTRACT IMMEDIATE RESPONSE AND RECTIFICATION OF THEIR DEMANDS. FAILURE TO CONCLUDE SATISFACTORY SOLUTIONS TO NATIVE GRIEVANCES IN A REASONABLE TIME FRAME WILL LIKELY RESULT IN AN INTENSIFICATION OF CONFRONTATION POLITICS BEING PRACTICED BY NATIVE ELEMENTS. RECURRING INCIDENTS OF THIS NATURE WILL INEVITABLY LEAD TO AN EVENT THAT RESULTS IN SACRIFICE OF HUMAN LIFE; A CONSEQUENCE THAT WILL ONLY IGNITE AND FUEL FURTHER CONFRONTATION.

6. THE SITUATION IN THE REMAINDER OF CANADA APPEARS RELATIVELY STABLE AT THIS TIME."

Beyond this point, the remaining contents of the dispatched communique to the powers that be in Ottawa are totally purged. It is further labeled **"SECRET"** as to where it originated from within British Columbia's RCMP Security Service Division. It goes without saying that the RCMP felt totally threatened by Canada's First Nation Peoples and ultimately feared the final outcome of the pending land claims issue nation wide. To give further examples to stipulate as to how threatened the RCMP actually were towards our country's native population, during the late 1960's a small group of Canada's First Nation activists were directly involved with protests and demonstrations protesting American involvement in the Vietnam War. With aboriginals putting their own grievances on the back burner, the RCMP had no choice but to take notice. In fact, it reportedly raised so much interest with the RCMP that they were able to maintain further surveillance on all associated subversives (both native and non-native alike). Contained within the surveillance files (March 7TH, 1969), it is duly noted that one of the protestors in question had her name mentioned on an open letter addressed to the Prime Minister "dated **21 Nov. 68, RE: FACULTY COMMITTEE FOR PEACE IN VIETNAM."** And that this same person in 1972 was, according to the RCMP Security Service surveillance documentation, a reporter "believed to be with the Montreal Star newspaper."

Perhaps it was largely due to this collaboration of natives and non-natives during the protest demonstrations of the Vietnam War that caused the RCMP Security Service to classify all native demonstrations organized by Quebec's First Nation Peoples as **"RED POWER - QUEBEC."** In accordance to the surveillance files, this terminology of Quebec's Red Power Movement first appeared in the purged documentation on December 4TH, 1973 involving a protest demonstration in Ottawa concerning the James Bay Project in northern Quebec and the flooding of traditional aboriginal lands that enabled white society of the southern portions of the Province to acquire an over abundance of hydro electric power. Nowhere else in the purged surveillance files can the words **"RED POWER - QUEBEC"** be found other than on that one specific occasion where a brief summary of native concerns are given over the James Bay Project itself. The surveillance document pertaining to Quebec's Red Power Movement was interestingly formulated after the RCMP Security Service completed their surveillance vigil on a few of our country's First Nation Peoples who in the past protested the American

INVOLVEMENT OF THE VIETNAM WAR. THESE SAME SURVEILLANCE VIGILS ALSO INCLUDED KEEPING TABS ON THE WHITE SUBVERSIVES WHO INTERESTINGLY ENOUGH HAD FORMED A STRONG BOND WITH THE ABORIGINALS DURING THE VIETNAM WAR PROTEST YEARS.

IN REVIEWING THE CONTENTS OF THE 1973-77 SURVEILLANCE FILES, THE **"RED POWER "**PHOTOGRAPH ALBUM, AS WELL AS THE 1975 REPORT ON TERRORISM AS IT PERTAINED TO V.I.P. SECURITY FOR CANADIAN POLITICIANS, IT BECOMES OBVIOUSLY CLEAR THAT THESE THREE PIECES OF VERY IMPORTANT DOCUMENTATION TOGETHER ALLOWED THE RCMP TO COME TO THE IMMEDIATE CONCLUSION THAT OUR COUNTRY'S INDIAN POPULATION WAS NOW BECOMING THE GREATEST THREAT TO CANADIAN SECURITY AS THEY, THE NATIVES STOOD UP IN DEFIANCE TO THE POWERS THAT BE. IN THE NATIVE PEOPLES ATTEMPT TO REMOVE THE SHACKLES OF THEIR CAPTURES, THE RCMP GAVE BIRTH TO THE HIGHLY CONTROVERSIAL SURVEILLANCE REPORT **"RED POWER - CANADA"** WHICH ESSENTIALLY WAS DESIGNED TO HOLD THE ABORIGINAL PEOPLES OF CANADA AT BAY IN ORDER TO AVOID SETTLING THE LAND CLAIMS ISSUE WHEREBY DENYING ITS FINAL RESOLUTION THEREOF WOULD AFTERALL BE IN THE BEST-INTEREST OF WHITE SOCIETY IN GENERAL.

IN SPEAKING OF THE BEST-INTEREST OF **"WHITE SOCIETY "**AND ALL OF ITS MANY HYPOCRISIES RIGHT ACROSS THE COUNTRY, THE CANADIAN FEDERAL GOVERNMENT'S INDIAN AFFAIRS AND NORTHERN DEVELOPMENT DEPARTMENT DURING THE MID-1970'S EMBARKED ON A NEW PROGRAM DESIGNED TO SUPPOSEDLY GIVE STATUS INDIANS A GREATER VOICE IN DECISION-MAKING AND MORE EQUALITY IN THE GOVERNMENT-INDIAN RELATIONSHIP. BUT IN REALITY, THE GOVERNMENT OF CANADA WAS ATTEMPTING TO DEFUSE THE VOLATILE SITUATION THAT THE RCMP'S SECURITY SERVICE BRANCH WAS REPORTING TO BE AT ITS CRITICAL STAGE OF DEVELOPMENT. THE NEW INDIAN POLICY WAS UNVEILED BY THE DEPARTMENT OF INDIAN AFFAIRS IN SEPTEMBER OF 1976 AND ACCORDINGLY, IT WAS SAID TO BE AN EFFECTIVE MEASURE THAT WAS DESIGNED TO WORK WITH THE NATIVE LEADERS AND THEIR ORGANIZATIONS INSTEAD OF WORKING AGAINST THEM AND BY GRADUALLY TRANSFERRING PROGRAM MANAGEMENT TO BAND COUNCILS. THE JOINT PARTICIPATION APPROACH, WAS APPROVED BY THE FEDERAL LIBERAL CABINET AND WAS THE POLICY FOR ALL DEPARTMENTS AND AGENCIES DEALING WITH STATUS INDIANS. THIS WAS TO BE FOLLOWED BY A ONE YEAR REVIEW COMMITTEE TO BE CARRIED OUT BY THE MINISTER OF INDIAN AFFAIRS AND HIS DEPARTMENT AT THE REQUEST OF THE CABINET. BASICALLY, A PREVIOUS INTERNAL GOVERNMENTAL REPORT CALLED FOR INCREASED CONSULTATION BETWEEN STATUS INDIANS AND THEIR REPRESENTATIVE ASSOCIATIONS AND THE DEPARTMENT. THIS, WAS TO HAPPEN AT THE FEDERAL LEVEL THROUGH THE JOINT CABINET-NATIONAL INDIAN BROTHERHOOD COMMITTEE, WITH CONSENSUS FILTERING UP TO IT FROM

THE BAND COUNCIL AND THE REGIONAL LEVELS. FURTHERMORE, PROGRAMS AND RESOURCES OF THE DEPARTMENT WERE TO BE HANDED OVER TO NATIVE BANDS AS THEY BECAME CAPABLE OF HANDLING THEIR OWN AFFAIRS AND THEIR POWERS OF INDEPENDENCE WAS TO BE GREATLY INCREASED BY REVISIONS TO THE INDIAN ACT. SUCH REVISIONS WERE SAID TO HAVE TOP PRIORITY OF THE JOINT COMMITTEE, ITS SUB-COMMITTEE AS WELL AS WITHIN THE VARIOUS WORKING GROUPS.

ALTHOUGH THE INTERNAL GOVERNMENTAL REPORT DID NOT SET OUT SPECIFIC PROGRAMS IT DID HOWEVER EMPHASIZE THAT PROGRAMS WERE TO HAVE SENSITIVE AND FLEXIBLE PRINCIPLES THAT OF WHICH WERE TO BE APPLIED IN A VARIETY OF SITUATIONS AND COMMUNITIES. IN ACCORDANCE TO THE REPORT SUCH AN APPROACH HAD A NUMBER OF IMPORTANT ADVANTAGES WHEREAS IT WOULD ESSENTIALLY BE GIVING THE INDIAN LEADERS A SENSE OF FALSE SECURITY BY GIVING THEM AND THEIR GROUPS FREEDOM OF CHOICE, SUPPOSEDLY INCREASING RESPONSIBILITIES AND ACCOUNTABILITY ON BOTH SIDES. IN DOING SO, IT WAS SAID TO GIVE REAL CREDIBILITY TO THE PROMISE OF PARTICIPATION THUS BUILDING THE SELF-CONFIDENCE AND SELF-RELIANCE OF INDIAN LEADERS AT ALL LEVELS. BUT MOST IMPORTANTLY THE REPORT STRESSED THE FACT THAT ONCE CONSENSUS WAS ACHIEVED AT ALL LEVELS, THAN AND ONLY THAN COULD COMPLETE AUTONOMY BE SUCCESSFUL.

AND JUST WHEN EVERYONE THOUGHT THAT THEY HAD IT ALL FIGURED IT, MORE CONFUSION WAS ADDED TO THE ISSUE IN AUGUST OF 1977 WHEN THEN-PRIME MINISTER PIERRE ELLIOT TRUDEAU WENT OVER THE NORTHERN DEVELOPMENT MINISTER'S HEAD BY ISSUING HIS OWN POLICY PAPER ON THE NORTH. THE POLICY PAPER ON THE POLITICAL DEVELOPMENT IN THE NORTH THAT THE THEN-NORTHERN DEVELOPMENT MINISTER WARREN ALLMAND ORIGINALLY CONCEIVED, WAS SCHEDULED TO BE RELEASED ON JULY 4TH OF THAT YEAR BUT THE PAPER THAT THE MINISTER BROUGHT TO CABINET FOR APPROVAL WAS REPORTEDLY REJECTED BY THE HOUSE OF COMMONS MEMBERS. TRUDEAU, THEN TOOK THE MATTER INTO HIS OWN HANDS AND REWROTE THE PAPER WITH HELP OF SENIOR DEPARTMENTAL OFFICIALS. PRIME MINISTER TRUDEAU'S VERSION OF THE POLICY PAPER WAS TWENTY PAGES LONG AND COVERED ISSUES ON NATIVE SELF-GOVERNMENT, NON RENEWABLE RESOURCES, CONSTITUTIONAL DEVELOPMENT, PROTECTION OF NATIVE RIGHTS, A RESIDENCY CLAUSE FOR VOTING, NATIVE STATES, TERRITORIAL DIVISION AND/OR PROVINCIAL STATUS. INTERESTINGLY ENOUGH, ACCORDING TO TRUDEAU'S POLICY PAPER ON THE POLITICAL DEVELOPMENT OF THE NORTHWEST TERRITORIES IT WAS A CONCEPT OF DIVIDING THE NWT INTO REGIONS THAT WOULD BE CONTROLLED BY A SINGLE RACE OF PEOPLE. THE CANADIAN VERSION OF POLICY RACIAL SEGREGATION THAT OF WHICH WAS PRACTICED IN THE REPUBLIC OF SOUTH AFRICA – OUR VERY OWN VERSION OF AN APARTHEID

SYSTEM WITH A BIT OF A TWIST, REVERSE DISCRIMINATION FOR ALL WHITE CANADIANS LIVING NORTH OF THE 60TH PARALLEL.

TRUDEAU'S POLICY PAPER FOR THE NORTHWEST TERRITORIES WAS BASED ON THE TERRITORIAL GOVERNMENT'S SUBMISSION OF A LIST OF PRIORITIES FOR THE NORTH. HIS POLICY OF POLITICAL DEVELOPMENT FOR THE NWT CURTAILED ISSUES OF RACIAL SEGREGATION THAT OF WHICH WERE NORMALLY PRACTICED IN SOUTH AFRICA THAT WERE GREATLY CRITICIZED BY MEMBERS OF THE UNITED NATIONS. AT THE TIME OF TRUDEAU'S INFAMOUS POLICY PAPER FOR THE ARCTIC, BOTH THE YUKON AND NORTHWEST TERRITORIES HAD MANY CONSTITUTIONAL RELATED DISAGREEMENTS WITH THE GOVERNMENT OF CANADA THAT REQUIRED A LOT OF IRONING OUT. THE PAPER NOTED IN ITS INTRODUCTION: "CONSTITUTIONAL PROBLEMS HAVE ASSUMED INCREASING IMPORTANCE IN THE NORTHWEST TERRITORIES AND YUKON AS THE TERRITORIAL GOVERNMENTS EVOLVED AND THE VARIOUS NATIVE GROUPS FORMULATED THEIR LAND CLAIMS."

ACCORDING TO THE POLICY PAPER, "MOST OF THE PRESSURES AND TENSIONS PREVALENT IN THE NWT DERIVE FROM THREE MAIN FACTORS;

1) THE GENERAL DEMAND FOR A GREATER DEGREE OF SELF-GOVERNMENT WHETHER AT TERRITORIAL OR COMMUNITY LEVEL;
2) THE DETERMINATION OF NATIVE PEOPLES, INDIAN, INUIT AND METIS, TO GET RECOGNITION AND POWER LARGELY THROUGH THE SETTLEMENT OF THEIR LAND CLAIMS;
3) THE URGENT NEED FOR DIRECTION AND PACING IN THE DEVELOPMENT OF ECONOMY IN ALL PARTS OF THE NORTHWEST TERRITORIES, LONG DOMINATED BY THE VAGARIES AND FLUCTUATIONS OF NON-RENEWABLE RESOURCE OPERATIONS."

TRUDEAU'S POLICY PAPER EMPHASIZED THAT: "THESE THREE FACTORS HAVE BEEN VERY MUCH IN PLAY DURING THE RATHER LENGTHY BERGER COMMISSION HEARINGS AND ARE PRODUCING DISRUPTIVE FORCES WHICH INTERACT AND RELATE TO HOW THE NORTHWEST TERRITORIES WILL EVOLVE POLITICALLY OVER THE NEXT DECADE."

ON THE ISSUE OF NATIVE SELF-GOVERNMENT THE POLICY STATED THAT "THE FEDERAL GOVERNMENT HAS CONCLUDED THE TIME HAS COME TO TAKE ENABLING NORTHERNERS TO GOVERN THEMSELVES IN WAYS OF THEIR OWN CHOOSING. "THIS WAS TO BE ACHIEVED THROUGH A "FULL, FRANK AND SYSTEMATIC CONSULTATION "WITH RECOGNIZED LEADERS OF THE TERRITORIAL GOVERNMENT, NATIVE COMMUNITIES AND NATIVE GROUPS THROUGH A FEDERAL GOVERNMENT APPOINTED SPECIAL REPRESENTATIVE COMMISSION. THE POLICY PAPER STATED: "LEGISLATIVE AUTHORITY AND GOVERNMENTAL

JURISDICTION ARE NOT ALLOCATED IN CANADA ON GROUNDS THAT DIFFERENTIATE BETWEEN THE PEOPLE ON THE BASIS OF RACE. "HOWEVER, THE PAPER INDICATED THAT THE FEDERAL GOVERNMENT WAS LOOKING AT SPLITTING THE NORTHWEST TERRITORIES INTO THREE REGIONS. IT SUGGESTED THAT THE MAINLAND MIGHT BE DIVIDED INTO EASTERN AND WESTERN TERRITORIES, EACH WITH ITS OWN GOVERNMENT. THE OTHER SUGGESTION WAS THAT THE RESOURCE RICH, BUT LARGELY UNPOPULATED ARCTIC ISLANDS MIGHT COMPROMISE A THIRD TERRITORY FULLY UNDER FEDERAL GOVERNMENT CONTROL. THE BASIS IN WHICH TRUDEAU ACKNOWLEDGED THE DIVISION OF THE NWT WAS MOSTLY DUE TO ITS SIZE AND WIDESPREAD REGIONAL DIFFERENCES; LANGUAGE, CULTURE, LIFESTYLE, ECONOMIC NEEDS AND RESOURCE REVENUES.

THE PAPER WENT ON STATING: "JURISDICTION IS PLACED IN THE HANDS OF GOVERNMENT THAT ARE RESPONSIBLE, DIRECTLY OR INDIRECTLY, TO THE PEOPLE, AGAIN, WITHOUT REGARD TO RACE. THESE ARE THE PRINCIPLES THAT THE GOVERNMENT CONSIDERS IT ESSENTIAL TO MAINTAIN FOR ANY POLITICAL REGIME OR GOVERNMENTAL STRUCTURE IN THE NORTHWEST TERRITORIES. "THE POLICY PAPER THEN EXPLAINED THE POSSIBILITY OF PROVINCIAL STATUS BEING THROUGH THE DEMOCRATIC PROCESS BUT ACKNOWLEDGED THE FACT THAT PRESSURE WAS BEING ADDED ON THE ISSUE IN BOTH TERRITORIES, "IT DOES NOT HAVE WHOLE-HEARTED SUPPORT IN EITHER TERRITORY, CERTAINLY NOT FROM NATIVE GROUPS, WHO SEE IT AS A THREAT TO THEIR SPECIAL IDENTITY AND POLITICAL POSITION." FURTHERMORE, THE CANADIAN FEDERAL GOVERNMENT WAS TOTALLY PREPARED TO ENTER INTO NEGOTIATIONS ABOUT RESTRUCTURING OF THE POLITICAL INSTITUTIONS AND POWERS IN THE NORTH, INCLUDING THE TRANSFER OF FEDERAL RESPONSIBILITIES AND PROGRAMS TO THE TERRITORIAL GOVERNMENT LEVEL.

TRUDEAU'S POLICY PAPER FOR THE NORTHLAND FURTHER STATED: "NATIONAL INTEREST DICTATES THAT THE FEDERAL GOVERNMENT MAINTAIN ITS OWNERSHIP AND CONTROL OF THE POTENTIALLY SIGNIFICANT NON-RENEWABLE RESOURCES, "NOT THAT THE TERRITORIAL GOVERNMENT ASKED FOR THE TRANSFER OF ALL SURFACE AND SUB-SURFACE LAND RESOURCES. BUT THE PAPER ITSELF DID ACCEPT IN PRINCIPLE A CONCEPT OF REVENUE SHARING INDICATING THAT IT "SHOULD OCCUR "AS A RESULT OF LAND CLAIM SETTLEMENTS ON THE BASIS OF A GOVERNMENT-TO-GOVERNMENT AGREEMENT. TRUDEAU'S PAPER THEN SUGGESTED THAT THE GOVERNMENT OF CANADA MAINTAIN TOTAL OWNERSHIP OF THE ARCTIC ISLANDS, BUT DID CONSIDER THAT THE OWNERSHIP AND CONTROL OF THE RENEWABLE RESOURCES AND OTHER LANDS BE TRANSFERRED INTO THE TERRITORIAL GOVERNMENTS HANDS AND OTHER CLAIM SETTLEMENTS BE TRANSFERRED TO NORTHERN NATIVE GROUPS. "THE NEED TO KNOWN ABOUT CANADA'S FRONTIER RESERVES IS AN IMPORTANT ELEMENT

IN THE GOVERNMENT'S ENERGY AND RESOURCES POLICIES, "IS HOW THE PRIME MINISTER'S POLICY PAPER DESCRIBED IT.

PRIME MINISTER TRUDEAU'S POLICY PAPER ALSO INDICATED THAT WHILE THE FEDERAL GOVERNMENT WAS NOT WILLING TO CONSIDER A TEN /OR FIFTEEN YEAR RESIDENCY CLAUSES THAT NATIVE ORGANIZATIONS WERE CALLING FOR IN THE ESTABLISHING OF VOTING RIGHTS, IT WAS WILLING TO CONSIDER RESIDENCY REQUIREMENTS WITH A VIEW TO INTRODUCING A MEASURE OF STABILITY IN THE POLITICAL AND ECONOMICAL SITUATION IN THE TERRITORIAL AND LOCAL LEVELS. THIS WAS LARGELY DUE TO THE INFLUX OF THE WHITE POPULATION INTO THE NORTHLAND WHO WERE REPORTEDLY BEING GIVEN ALL OF THE GOOD PAYING JOBS WHILE MOST OF THE NATIVE PEOPLES LIVING THERE WERE BEING FORCED TO ACCEPT JOBS THAT PAID MINIMUM WAGES. IN USING THE POLICY PAPER'S TERMS, "GREATER STABILITY REQUIRED IN FRONTIER AREAS. "THE TRUDEAU LIBERAL GOVERNMENTAL REGIME WAS ALSO WILLING TO LOOK AT SYSTEMS OF ESTABLISHING ELECTORAL BOUNDARIES WHICH WOULD "REFLECT THE COMMUNITY OF INTEREST IN VARIOUS REGIONS. "THE FEDERAL GOVERNMENT POLICY PAPER SUGGESTED THE ESTABLISHING OF A WARD SYSTEM IN COMMUNITIES WITH ONE-THOUSAND /OR MORE RESIDENTS TO ENSURE NATIVE REPRESENTATION IN CIVIL ELECTIONS. IT WAS ALSO SUGGESTED THAT AN ADVISORY BOARD BE SET UP AT THE TERRITORIAL LEVEL WHICH WAS TO CONSULT WITH ALL INTERESTED PARTIES BEFORE MAKING DECISIONS REGARDING THE RIGHTS AND INTERESTS OF NATIVE PEOPLES. WHILE RECOGNIZING THE INDIAN AND ESKIMO IDENTITY AND STATUS, THE PAPER FURTHER NOTED THAT THE CONCEPTS ON RESIDENCY REQUIREMENTS THAT WERE PROPOSED BY THE TWO NATIVE BROTHERHOODS WENT FAR BEYOND THE POLICY THAT THE FEDERAL GOVERNMENT WAS PREPARED TO FOLLOW. IRONICALLY, THE POLICY PAPER FURTHER STATED THAT IT WOULD GO SOME DISTANCE TOWARDS MEETING THE WISHES OF SOME OF THE INDIAN AND ESKIMO POPULATION.

TRUDEAU'S POLICY PAPER SUGGESTED THAT "REPRESENTATIVE GOVERNMENT COULD BE HEAVILY DECENTRALIZED BY THE TRANSFER OF MORE AUTHORITY TO THE INDIVIDUAL COMMUNITIES "AND FURTHER GRANTING THEM THE OPTION OF ESTABLISHING REGIONAL INSTITUTIONS WHICH WERE TO BE AN AMALGAMATION OF COMMUNITY EFFECT IN SUCH AREAS AS EDUCATION, LAND USE CONTROL, GAME MANAGEMENT AND RENEWABLE RESOURCE DEVELOPMENT. THE POLICY PAPER EVEN STATED THAT IT WAS WILLING TO REALIGN SOME POWERS AND FUNCTIONS BETWEEN THE TERRITORIAL, FEDERAL AND COMMUNITY LEVELS, BUT REFUSED OUTRIGHT TO RELINQUISH ITS POWERS RELATING TO THE MINERAL RICH RESOURCES, ESPECIALLY IN THE MINING INDUSTRY. TRUDEAU'S VERSION OF THE POLITICAL DEVELOPMENT IN THE ARCTIC ALSO REFUSED TO GIVE BOTH THE YUKON AND NORTHWEST TERRITORIES PROVINCIAL STATUS, BUT DID SUGGEST THAT OTHER POSSIBILITIES WERE WORTH EXPLORING. AS

AN ALTERNATIVE TO PROVINCEHOOD FOR THE NORTHWEST TERRITORIES, A GREATER DEGREE OF SELF-DETERMINATION WAS OFFERED.

- "IN RECOGNITION OF THE LEGITIMATE ASPIRATIONS AND DESIRES OF ALL RESIDENTS OF THE NORTHWEST TERRITORIES TO TAKE CHARGE OF THEIR OWN AFFAIRS, THE FEDERAL GOVERNMENT IS PREPARED, IN ADDITION TO OTHER MATTERS ALREADY MENTIONED IN THIS STATEMENT, TO ENGAGE IN CONSULTATION ABOUT THE FOLLOWING STEPS RELATIVE TO A PHASED EXTENSION OF RESPONSIBLE GOVERNMENT:
- THE RESTRUCTURING OF POLITICAL INSTITUTIONS AND POWERS, INCLUDING BUT NOT LIMITED TO THE COMPOSITION AND JURISDICTION OF THE TERRITORIAL COUNCIL, THE COMPOSITION AND ROLE OF EXECUTIVE COMMITTEE CONTINUING RESPONSIBILITIES AND ROLE OF THE COMMISSIONER, AND RESERVED POWERS OF THE MINISTER AND GOVERNOR-IN-COUNCIL;
- THE TRANSFER AND DELEGATION OF FEDERAL RESPONSIBILITIES AND PROGRAMS TO THE TERRITORIAL GOVERNMENT;
- THE DEVOLUTION OF RESPONSIBILITIES, POWERS AND FUNCTIONS FROM TERRITORIAL GOVERNMENT TO COMMUNITY WITH THE SUGGESTION OPTION FOR THE CREATION OF REGIONAL INSTITUTIONS."

THE IMMEDIATE REACTION OF THE TERRITORIAL GOVERNMENT COUNCIL MEMBERS TO THE PRIME MINISTER'S INTERVENTION AND POLICY WAS THAT OF UTTER DELIGHT. THE THEN-TERRITORIAL HOUSE SPEAKER DAVID SEARLE REPORTEDLY STATED THAT THE PRIME MINISTER SHOULD HAVE BEEN CONGRATULATED FOR NOT ONLY HAVING THE GONADS TO INTRODUCE SUCH A POLICY PAPER FOR THE ARCTIC BUT ALSO FOR APPOINTING A CLOSE FRIEND AND ALLY (BUD DRURY) AS SPECIAL REPRESENTATIVE COMMISSIONER FOR CONSTITUTIONAL DEVELOPMENT. IT WAS IN THE SPEAKER OF THE HOUSE'S OPINION THAT SUCH A MANEUVER WAS LONG OVERDUE FOR THE NORTHWEST TERRITORIES. TO MOST OF THE NWT'S WHITE POPULATION LIVING IN THE WESTERN REGIONS (HAY RIVER, YELLOWKNIFE, NORMAN WELLS AND INUVIK), IT WAS A CRYSTAL CLEAR SIGN THAT THE CANADIAN FEDERAL GOVERNMENT REJECTED THE INDIAN BROTHERHOOD'S INTERPRETATION OF A NORTHERN DESIGN CONCEPT OTHERWISE KNOWN AS THE DENE NATION CONCEPT AND SOMEHOW MANAGED TO BALANCE IT OUT EVENLY TAKING INTO ACCOUNT ALL ASPECTS OF NORTHERN LIVING. AT LEAST, THAT'S WHAT EVERYONE THOUGHT AT THE TIME!!!

IN RESPONSE TO TRUDEAU'S POLICY PAPER, THE THEN-PRESIDENT OF THE ESKIMO BROTHERHOOD, (INUIT TAPIRISAT OF CANADA) STATED: "IT IS OBVIOUS THAT THE FEDERAL GOVERNMENT DOES NOT UNDERSTAND WHAT HAS BEEN HAPPENING IN THE NORTH OVER THE LAST FEW YEARS." THE ESKIMO

Brotherhood leader, Michael Amarook criticized the document which he described as intending to "tinker with the existing (colonial) government system in the North, "but at the same time, "leaving it basically unchanged. "The Inuit Tapirisat of Canada (ITC) was struggling for decolonization and self-determination by establishing a separate territorial state in the eastern Arctic which was to become known as the **"Nunavut Territory"**. Amarook believed that the main cause behind the Prime Minister of Canada's pulling the rug from under Warren Allmand's feet was largely due to the fact that there was a backlash from within the Liberal Cabinet itself once the Minister of Indian Affairs and Northern Development had learned that Trudeau was in the process of appointing Bud Drury to head the Constitutional Development Commission. Bud Drury as it so happened, was a former member of the Northwest Territorial Council as well as a former Senior Cabinet Member of Prime Minister Trudeau's administration when he was put in charge of the Constitutional Development Commission.

Oddly enough, the ITC was encouraged by Trudeau's concept of dividing the Northwest Territories into regions on the grounds of common interests such as distinction of language, culture and lifestyles. "Assuming that actual boundaries are negotiable, there is no reason why the proposed Nunavut Territory could not be created under those guidelines. "This was largely due to the fact that only one year previous to the Prime Minister's policy paper being unveiled, the representative of the Inuit Tapirisat of Canada suggested that the Northwest Territories be divided into two territories which would eventually become provinces. ITC's then-president James Arvaluk, in the spring of 1976 reportedly made a presentation to the Federal Cabinet in a very low key manner saying that his people living in the eastern Arctic wanted to be full partners in "this country." Unlike the Indian Brotherhood, the Eskimo population were not asking for handouts per se, they simply wanted to share the land with all Canadians. "Rather, we are offering to share our land with the rest of the Canadian population in return for a recognition of rights and a say in the way the land is to be used. "Mr. Arvaluk submitted a seventy page proposal to Prime Minister Trudeau and his Cabinet members. It was the result of a three year research study conducted by the Inuit Tapirisat of Canada. The proposal called for the immediate establishing of a Nunavut Territory in the eastern Arctic, it was backed up with seventy-five pounds of documented research. "We are simply asking you to help us take the first step in

THE DIRECTION OF REGIONAL SELF-GOVERNMENT THAT WILL BE RESPONSIVE TO THE NEEDS OF THE INUIT WHO, AT PRESENT, MAKE UP THE MAJORITY OF THE POPULATION."

THE ITC PROPOSAL DID EMPHASIZE THAT THE INUIT OF THE NORTHWEST TERRITORIES DID HAVE "EXTENSIVE CLAIMS UPON THE BASIS OF RIGHTS TO LANDS AND WATERS IN THE NORTHWEST TERRITORIES, THE YUKON TERRITORY AND THE OFFSHORE SEABED AND SUBSOIL IN CANADA." THE TRUDEAU REGIME UNDER NO CIRCUMSTANCES COULD DISPUTE THE ESKIMO CLAIM, AFTERALL, IT WAS A WELL KNOWN AND PROVEN FACT OF HISTORY THAT THE INUIT LIVED IN THE ARCTIC LONG BEFORE THE INDIANS AND MOST DEFINITELY THOUSANDS UPON THOUSANDS OF YEARS BEFORE THE WHITEMAN. UNDER THE ITC PROPOSAL, THE YUKON WAS TO REMAIN A SEPARATE ENTITY /OR PROVINCE, WHILE THE NWT WAS TO BE DIVIDED INTO AN AREA SOUTH OF THE TREELINE BELONGING TO THE DENE AND THE NORTHERN AREA TO BE KNOWN AS **"NUNAVUT"** WHICH IS INUKTITUT MEANING, **"OUR LAND"**.

IN THEIR QUEST FOR "ENTRANCE TO CONFEDERATION "THEY CALLED FOR "STRONG CONTROL "OVER HUNTING, TRAPPING AND FISHING; SURFACE TITLE TO APPROXIMATELY 250,000 SQUARE MILES; ALL ROYALTIES FROM THE DEVELOPMENT OF INUIT LANDS, AND THREE PERCENT ROYALTIES FROM SURFACE (DEEPER THAN 1,500 FEET) AND OFFSHORE FOR THE BALANCE OF THE NUNAVUT TERRITORY. THEY WANTED TO BE "VERY INVOLVED "IN ALL GOVERNMENTAL ACTIVITIES AFFECTING ITS ESKIMO POPULATION, ESPECIALLY IN THE AREAS OF LAND USE PLANNING AND MANAGEMENT. THE ITC PROPOSAL CALLED FOR THE ESTABLISHING OF AN IMPROVED SOCIAL AND ECONOMIC BASE FOR ITS PEOPLE, THE ESTABLISHING OF AN INUIT DEVELOPMENT CORPORATION WAS SUGGESTED. PRIME MINISTER TRUDEAU REPORTEDLY EXTENDED HIS CONCERNS ABOUT "THE ATTITUDE AND APPROACH "IN WHICH THE ESKIMO PEOPLE OF THE ARCTIC USED TO HELP PUSH THEIR POINT TO HOME BASE; THE GOVERNMENT OF CANADA FUNDED THE INUIT TAPIRISAT OF CANADA TO RESEARCH THEIR CLAIM. AND WHEN THE PROPOSAL WAS PUT FORWARD, TRUDEAU WAS SAID TO HAVE MIXED NO WORDS OF SYMPATHY WHEN HE GAVE FAIR WARNING THAT IN ALL LIKELIHOOD HE AND HIS CABINET "MIGHT NOT BE ABLE TO MOVE "AS QUICKLY AS THE ITC WOULD HAVE HAD WANTED THEM TOO.

ONCE THE ITC MADE THEIR PROPOSAL TO THE FEDERAL LIBERALS, THEY (THE ITC) WERE LED TO BELIEVE THAT THE FUTURE POLICY STATEMENTS OF THE CANADIAN GOVERNMENT WERE TO BE THAT OF POLITICAL REFORM FOR THE NORTHWEST TERRITORIES. THUS DESIGNING A CLEAR DECLARATION THAT THE GOVERNMENT OF CANADA SUPPORTED POLITICAL SELF-DETERMINATION FOR ALL NATIVE PEOPLES, (DENE, ESKIMO AND METIS). BUT INSTEAD, THE PRIME MINISTER'S STATEMENT WAS SPRUNG ONTO THE NATIVE PEOPLES OF THE

NWT without warning and it seemed to say that the Government of Canada was determined that the population North of the 60TH parallel would not have self-determination.

In the eyes of the Northwest Territories' Indian Brotherhood, the Federal Government's new policy paper attempted to ignore many years of aboriginal history and reserved the progress of northern peoples in the struggle for their rights. The Brotherhood further argued that the government had opted to entrench colonization in the North rather than supporting the decolonization of the northern people. Furthermore, they saw the policy paper as a concept to preserve the stranglehold of the Federal Government over northern resources and to make the task of self-determination by the northern population impossible. As far as the Indian Brotherhood was concerned, the Federal Government's **THREE-NATION** proposal was an attempt to maintain control of colonial powers in the Northwest Territories. In the words of the Brotherhood, "the cabinet document deliberately distorts and misrepresents the proposal of the Dene as 'ethnic' and 'racial'. "The Indian Brotherhood also pointed out that the Federal Government document suggested that there was no relationship between political rights and the survival of cultural rights. To this suggestion the Brotherhood stated that it was totally "absurd".

The Indian Brotherhood then issued a press release condemning Prime Minister P.E. Trudeau's rewritten policy paper by praising Judge Thomas Berger's Report and criticizing the Federal Government for "blatantly "ignoring the Berger recommendations by endorsing "the view of the North as a frontier to be exploited, rather than a homeland. "It further regarded the policy paper as being an attempt to "unilaterally abolish the right of the Dene and other Northern peoples to negotiate their place in Confederation ... Once again, solutions have been imposed on the native peoples against their wishes and interests. In the place of self-determination political jurisdictions, the cabinet has proposed a proliferation of meaningless boards, committees and advisory councils, all controlled by the Federal Government."

The Indian Brotherhood's then-president, George Erasmus openly admitted that the policy paper itself showed that the native people themselves had a lot of work to do before being able to adopt a "new plan of action. "The NWT Indian Brotherhood's press release interestingly concluded by saying: "the Dene recognize that this

PAPER REPRESENTS JUST ONE MORE CHAPTER IN THEIR STRUGGLE FOR SELF-DETERMINATION."

Trudeau's version of the political development in the Arctic refused to even consider the recommendations made by others, hypocrisy and outright fascist tactics was the theme of the Canadian Prime Minister. It seemed that Trudeau's attitude was that "ethnic "governments were not un-Canadian as long as they were powerless and impoverished. To further execute his policy paper for the north country, Prime Minister Pierre Elliot Trudeau was thus to play the role that of Sir John A. MacDonald. Like our nation's first Prime Minister, it was to be a concept of deceit and deception. Trudeau announced the appointment of the Honorable Charles (Bud) Drury as his special representative to consult and to examine ways of improving existing structures, institutions and systems of government in the Northwest Territories. The main formula being of course **"CONSTITUTIONAL DEVELOPMENT"**. The Trudeau deception of a constitutional development task force in the North was designed in such a way to bypass the Minister of Northern Development and was to report directly to the Prime Minister himself. This task force was similar to the one held in the mid-1960's which started the **NWT** and the **YUKON** on the road towards responsible government. That of which, the Legislative Assembly of the Northwest Territories advocated in the early parts of the mid-1970's; **"THE CARROTHERS REPORT"**.

By 1977, most /or all of the recommendations made by the Carrothers Commission Report were either rejected /or simply not implemented. The following were its key recommendations;

- Recommended that the Commissioner be chairman of the Legislative Assembly and preside over it;
- Recommended that the Commissioner be paid a stipend as a first charge of the NWT Consolidated Revenue Fund so that his salary would appear as part of the Territorial budget;
- Recommended that the Commissioner have the power to dissolve Council;
- Recommended that the Commissioner have the power to vote at Council sessions;
- Recommended that the Deputy Commissioner be appointed by the Commissioner;

- Recommended that "at an appropriate time", the Deputy Commissioner be chosen from among the elected members of the Legislature;
- Recommended that the name of the Council be changed to the Legislative Assembly of the Northwest Territories;
- Recommended that the Legislative Assembly be composed of 18 persons, 14 elected and 4 appointed;
- Recommended that there be created a Northwest Territories Development Board and that there be established a Northwest Territories Development Corporation;
- Recommended that there be a Department of Lands and Resources, with jurisdiction over game, forestry, agriculture and surface rights to land in and adjacent to settlements;
- Recommended that political, economic and social development of the Northwest Territories be subject to public review not more than 10 years after tabling of the report of the Advisory Commission on the Development of Government in the Northwest Territories, 1966, and that the provision for review be incorporated in the Northwest Territories Act.

By the end of that summer, (1977), the Constitutional Development Committee of the Liberal Government of Canada reviewed the Territorial Government's list of priorities for the North and the Trudeau appointment of fraternity Brother Drury soon followed. This announcement was made Wednesday morning August 3RD, by Trudeau himself, simultaneously as he announced his own version as to how the Arctic was going to be fitting into his masterplan of the Canadian Constitution Act of 1982. Under much pressure, then-Northern Development Minister Warren Allmand acceded to the Territorial Government Council's demand towards responsible government, but rejected the idea that Council appoint the person to head up the Commission, claiming that it was his Ministry's responsibility to do so and no on else's. As the political tug-of-war continued, the Canadian Prime Minister once again took matters into his own hands and announced as to whom would be in charge of the Constitutional Development Commission as P.E. Trudeau was determined to be written down in the history books as being Canada's Constitutional white knight in bright shining armor. Trudeau's announcement literally left the Northern Development Minister out in the cold as Mr. Drury was ordered to report directly to the Office of the Prime Minister and no one

ELSE — THE CANADIAN PRIME MINISTER WAS NOW HAVING A PISSING CONTEST WITH HIS NORTHERN AFFAIRS MINISTER. MANY NORTHERN RESIDENTS SAW TRUDEAU'S DICTATORIAL POLICY AS BEING TOTALLY HYPOCRITICAL, SAYING "THAT REPORTING DIRECTLY TO THE PRIME MINISTER GIVES APPROPRIATE PRIORITY TO A CONSTITUTIONAL ISSUE OF NATIONAL IMPORTANCE AND PUTS THINGS INTO PROPER PERSPECTIVE. "IN THE EYES OF MANY LIVING IN THE ARCTIC, THE FEDERAL GOVERNMENT'S DOCUMENT ON THE POLITICAL DEVELOPMENT IN THE NORTHWEST TERRITORIES WAS ACTUALLY A RESPONSE TO THE DENE NATION DEFEATING THE PROPOSED MACKENZIE VALLEY PIPELINE.

THE FOLLOWING WERE THE TERMS OF REFERENCE FOR THE DRURY COMMISSION THAT OF WHICH OUR VERY OWN CANADIAN PRIME MINISTER PIERRE ELLIOT TRUDEAU HELPED SET-UP:

"IN NO WAY RESTRICTING THE GENERALITY OF THE FOREGOING, THE SPECIAL REPRESENTATIVE IS AUTHORIZED TO INCLUDE ON HIS AGENDA FOR CONSULTATION THE FOLLOWING SPECIFIC THINGS;

1) POSSIBLE DIVISION OF THE NORTHWEST TERRITORIES ON THE BASIS OF FUNCTIONAL FACTORS, INCLUDING ECONOMIC, SOCIO-CULTURE AND OTHER RELEVANT FACTORS, BUT EXCLUDING POLITICAL DIVISIONS AND EXPAND POLITICAL STRUCTURES BASED SOLELY ON DISTINCTIONS OF RACE;

2) PHASED RESTRUCTURING OF POLITICAL INSTITUTIONS IN THE NORTHWEST TERRITORIES TO ACHIEVE A GREATER DEGREE OF RESPONSIBLE GOVERNMENT, INCLUDING BUT NOT LIMITED TO CONSIDERATION OF THE COMPOSITION AND JURISDICTION OF THE TERRITORIAL COUNCIL, THE COMPOSITION AND ROLE OF THE EXECUTIVE COMMITTEE, THE CONTINUING RESPONSIBILITIES AND ROLE OF THE COMMISSIONER, AND RESERVED POWERS OF THE MINISTER AND GOVERNOR-IN-COUNCIL;

3) TRANSFER AND DELEGATION OF FEDERAL RESPONSIBILITIES AND PROGRAMS TO THE TERRITORIAL GOVERNMENTS;

4) DEVOLUTION OF RESPONSIBILITIES, POWERS AND FUNCTIONS FROM THE TERRITORIAL GOVERNMENT TO COMMUNITIES, WITH COMMUNITY OPTION OF CREATING REGIONAL INSTITUTIONS FOR SPECIFIC PURPOSES;

5) STATUTORY AND OTHER SAFEGUARDS FOR PROTECTING NATIVE INTERESTS, INCLUDING LANGUAGE, CULTURAL AND TRADITIONAL PURSUITS;

6) ARRANGEMENTS FOR PROMOTING NATIVE PARTICIPATION IN GOVERNMENT AT VARIOUS LEVELS, INCLUDING RESIDENCE REQUIREMENTS, CONSTITUENCY BOUNDARIES, A MUNICIPAL WARD

SYSTEM, REPRESENTATION ON SUBSIDIARY BODIES AND IN THE PUBLIC
SERVICE;

7) THE POLITICAL ROLE IN ANY OF NATIVE INSTITUTIONS FOR ECONOMIC
DERIVING FROM CLAIMS SETTLEMENTS;

8) CONTINUING FEDERAL OWNERSHIP AND MANAGEMENT OF NON-
RENEWABLE RESOURCES, WITH SHARING OF RESOURCE REVENUES;

9) DECENTRALIZATION OF SURFACE LAND USE AND MANAGEMENT
PROCEDURES WITH INSTITUTIONALIZED ARRANGEMENTS FOR JOINTLY-
PLANNED ECONOMIC DEVELOPMENT;

10) APPROPRIATE FINANCIAL ARRANGEMENTS TO SUPPORT THE
FOREGOING."

COINCIDENTLY, WHEN TRUDEAU BECAME CANADA'S SELECTED GOVERNMENTAL LEADER IN THE LATE 1960'S, HE APPOINTED HIS FRATERNAL FRIEND BUD DRURY TO THE TREASURY BOARD AS ITS CHANCELLOR. BY 1974, DRURY BECAME MINISTER OF PUBLIC WORKS CANADA, WHICH HE MAINTAINED UNTIL HIS SOMEWHAT CLOUDY DEPARTURE SOME TIME LATER. IN 1976, THE LIBERAL LOYALIST BUD DRURY REPORTEDLY USED HIS GOVERNMENTAL CONNECTIONS IN AN ATTEMPT TO INFLUENCE A SUPREME COURT JUDGE. WHEN IT WAS LEARNED THAT BUDDY BOY HAD TELEPHONED A JUDGE WHO WAS HEARING A CONTEMPT-OF-COURT CHARGE AGAINST FELLOW CABINET MINISTER ANDRE OUELLET, HE SUBMITTED HIS RESIGNATION BUT IT WAS SAID TO BE REFUSED BY PRIME MINISTER TRUDEAU AND THE INNER CIRCLE. DUE TO MUCH PRESSURE ADDED BY THE OPPOSITION FORCES, DRURY QUIT THE CABINET LATER THAT YEAR. BY 1978, HE RESIGNED FROM THE HOUSE OF COMMONS AND WAS APPOINTED CHAIRMAN OF YET ANOTHER USELESS LIBERAL GOVERNMENT INQUIRY, THE NATIONAL CAPITAL COMMISSION.

MEANWHILE BACK IN THE NORTHWEST TERRITORIES DURING THE MID-MONTH OF NOVEMBER 1977, THE INVISIBLE DRURY COMMISSION MADE ITS PRESENCE FELT IN THE NORTHLAND. IT OPENED A PERMANENT OFFICE IN YELLOWKNIFE AND SCHEDULED BOTH PUBLIC AND PRIVATE MEETINGS TO SEE WHAT ADDITIONAL DAMAGE IT COULD ACCOMPLISH NORTH OF THE 60TH PARALLEL. THE TRUDEAU-DRURY COMMISSION MANDATE WAS TO PUT A POLITICAL END TO THE NORTHERN NATIVE LAND CLAIMS ISSUE, ALL CLAIMS WERE IRONICALLY TO BE FILTERED MAINLY THROUGH THE DRURY INQUIRY AND NOT WITH THE LAND CLAIMS NEGOTIATORS FOR THE DEPARTMENT OF INDIAN AND NORTHERN AFFAIRS. A ROOKIE LIBERAL FLUNKY WAS DESIGNATED AS BUD DRURY'S MAIN GOVERNMENTAL GOFER, THE FLUNKY WAS NONE OTHER THAN THE POLITICAL HOPEFUL GEORGE BRADEN. AS THE FEDERAL GOVERNMENT'S CONSTITUTIONAL DEVELOPMENT COMMITTEE STRETCHED INTO ITS SECOND YEAR, THE POLITICAL DOORS WERE PROPPED WIDE OPEN FOR BRADEN AS HE

SOON BECAME KNOWN AS THE SELECTED LIBERAL GOLDEN BOY OF TRUDEAU'S REGIME (A.K.A. A LIBERAL PUPPET IN THE FRATERNAL SCHEME OF NEW THINGS TO COME). IN LATE 1979, GEORGE BRADEN BECAME A DULY ELECTED MEMBER OF THE NORTHWEST TERRITORIAL GOVERNING BODY FOR YELLOWKNIFE NORTH. MLA GEORGE BRADEN'S YELLOWKNIFE NORTH RIDING CONSISTED MAINLY OF A NORTHERN NATIVE POPULATION; RAINBOW VALLEY, DETAH AND THE OLD SECTION OF THE OTTAWA CONTROLLED CITY OF YELLOWKNIFE. HE QUICKLY CLIMBED TO THE TOP OF THE POLITICAL LADDER AS GOVERNMENT LEADER AND LATER RESPONSIBLE FOR THE JUSTICE DEPARTMENT FOR ALL THE NORTHWEST TERRITORIES, INCLUDING THE EASTERN AND WESTERN REGIONS OF THE ARCTIC. BY ALL ACCOUNT, BRADEN WAS THE PERFECT FEDERAL GOVERNMENT PUPPET FOR THE LIBERAL GOVERNMENT OF CANADA.

DRURY SUBMITTED HIS REPORT IN MARCH OF 1980 RECOMMENDING THAT LOCAL NORTHWEST TERRITORIAL GOVERNMENTS HAVE A GREATER ROLE, "WITH A SMALLER ROLE FOR OTTAWA "AND WAS REVIEWED BY THE CANADIAN FEDERAL GOVERNMENT AS A STEP IN THE RIGHT DIRECTION. BUT FOR MANY OF THE RESIDENTS LIVING NORTH OF THE 60TH PARALLEL, THE REPORT WAS NOTHING BUT A CRUEL JOKE BEING PLAYED ON ALL CANADIANS. BOTH TRUDEAU AND DRURY WERE HEAVILY CRITICIZED BY NATIVE GROUPS AND WHITES ALIKE!!! AT THE TIME BUD'S REPORT WAS ISSUED, HE WAS SERVING AS CHAIRMAN OF THE CAPITAL COMMISSION IN OTTAWA, A JOB THAT REQUIRED JUGGLING THE INTERESTS OF THE FEDERAL GOVERNMENT, THE CITY OF OTTAWA AND CITIZEN GROUPS. AFTER SUFFERING TWO MASSIVE STROKES IN A SPAN OF THREE MONTHS DURING CANADA'S CONSTITUTIONAL YEAR, DRURY REACHED SEMI-RETIREMENT STATUS BUT STILL REMAINED ON THE FRATERNAL GOVERNMENTAL PAYROLL. ON THE WEEKEND OF JANUARY 11TH, 1991 BUD DRURY DIED AT THE AGE OF 78, HE WAS THUS BURIED WITH FULL BRETHRENSHIP HONORS. IT SHOULD ALSO BE NOTED THAT BUD'S GOVERNMENTAL CAREER FIRST SHOT OUT LIKE A GIGANTIC SECRET CANNON AFTER THE DIEFENBAKER ADMINISTRATION. HE BECAME THE LIBERAL PARTY'S BRIGHT SHINING ETERNAL LIGHT OF TRUTH ON L.B. PEARSON'S GOVERNMENTAL TEAM DURING THE DYING DAYS OF DIEFENBAKERISM. ACCORDING TO THE MEDIA, BUD DRURY WAS ONE OF CANADA'S MOST HIGHLY RESPECTED MEN IN THE GOVERNMENT. IRONICALLY, IN 1965 THE PROMINENT MR. DRURY WAS ONE OF THE MAIN NEGOTIATING OFFICERS PUSHING FOR A FREE-TRADE PACKAGE WITH THE AMERICANS IN THE AUTOMOTIVE INDUSTRY.

IN THE SPRING OF 1982, TWO VERY IMPORTANT HISTORICAL EVENTS UNFOLDED BEFORE EVERYONE'S EYES;

1) THE VOTING OF THE FEDERAL GOVERNMENT'S PROPOSAL TO DIVIDE THE NORTHWEST TERRITORIES INTO SEPARATE ENTITIES,

2) THE BRINGING HOME OF THE CANADIAN CONSTITUTION ACT.

PRIME MINISTER P.E. TRUDEAU WAS THUSLY HAILED AS OUR COUNTRY'S CONQUERING HERO ON APRIL 17TH, 1982 AS THE MEDIA PROCLAIMED THE DAY AS BEING "A DAY OF POETRY AND PAGEANTRY" AS HE AND QUEEN ELIZABETH II SIGNED THE ROYAL PROCLAMATION TO CANADA'S NEW CONSTITUTION. HER MAJESTY SIGNED FIRST, FOLLOWED BY PIERRE TRUDEAU AND THE MINISTER OF JUSTICE JEAN CHRETIEN, AND FINALLY THE REGISTRAR-GENERAL ANDRE OUELLET WITH SECRETARY OF STATE GERALD REGAN THEN SIGNING HIS NAME AS WITNESS TO THE HISTORICAL EVENT. IRONICALLY, NOT ALL CANADIANS LIKED THE NEW VERSION OF THE BRITISH NORTH AMERICA ACT. AS FAR AS QUEBECKERS AND THE NATIVE POPULATION OF CANADA WERE CONCERNED, THEY WERE GETTING SEVERELY SCREWED OVER BY THE NEW CANADIAN CONSTITUTION. INCORPORATED IN THE NEW ACT FOR EXAMPLE, WERE ISSUES RELATING TO NATIVE RIGHTS THROUGH FEDERAL-PROVINCIAL CONFERENCES. THE COUNTRY'S NATIVE PEOPLES FELT THAT THE GOVERNMENT OF CANADA HAD BETRAYED THEM BY INCORPORATING THE CLAUSE THAT ENTRENCHED THE EXISTING ABORIGINAL AND TREATY RIGHTS. TO THE NATIVES, IT SOUNDED SUSPICIOUSLY LIKE A FURTHER EROSION OF THEIR CLAIMS TO LAND AND VALUABLE RESOURCES.

INSTEAD OF PARTICIPATING IN THE FESTIVE CELEBRATION ON PARLIAMENT HILL, NATIVES REPORTEDLY STAGED PROTESTS ALL ACROSS THE COUNTRY.

THE CANADIAN MEDIA INSTANTLY PROCLAIMED THE NEW CONSTITUTION AS THE "REBIRTH OF A NATION "MOVING CANADA SUPPOSEDLY ONE STEP FURTHER AWAY FROM ITS COLONIAL HERITAGE. HUNDREDS OF THOUSANDS OF TOTALLY UNAWARE CITIZENS RALLIED AROUND THE OLD FLAG POLE SIGNING "O CANADA! "MILITARY BANDS PLAYED "GOD SAVE THE QUEEN "AS A TWENTY-ONE GUN SALUTE WAS GIVEN TO COMMEMORATE THE OCCASION. PRIME MINISTER TRUDEAU DESCRIBED THE NEW CONSTITUTION AS "AS ACT OF DEFIANCE AGAINST THE HISTORY OF MANKIND. "IN THE MEANTIME JUST ACROSS THE OTTAWA RIVER, FOUR-HUNDRED ANGRY QUEBEC FLAG-WAVING PROTESTERS CHANTED THEIR DISCONTENT WITH SEPARATIST SLOGANS AND QUEBEC NATIONALIST SONGS. DURING ONE OCCASION, THE CANADIAN FLAG WAS LITERALLY USED AS A DOORMAT FOR PEOPLE TO WIPE THEIR FEET. THE PROVINCE OF QUEBEC REFUSED TO ENDORSE THE HAILED DOCUMENT THAT SUPPOSEDLY GUARANTEED EQUALITY TO ALL CANADIANS UNDER ITS CHARTER.

AS THE QUEEN OF ENGLAND PRESIDED AT THE OTTAWA PROPAGANDA CEREMONIES, THE CANADIAN MEDIA SEEMED TO BE ON THE DEFENSIVE, (THAT IS, DEFENDING THE NEW CONSTITUTION). THE WESTERN CANADA CONCEPT, "A POLITICAL PARTY WHICH PROPOSED WESTERN INDEPENDENCE "WAS UNDER

FIRE. MEDIA MEMBERS AUTOMATICALLY CLASSIFIED THE WESTERN CANADA CONCEPT GROUP AS "A PRAIRIE PARADOX "ATTEMPTING TO SEPARATE THE COUNTRY. PARTY LEADERS WERE REPORTEDLY ASKED: "WHAT ABOUT THE PARADOX OF SWEARING ALLEGIANCE TO THE CROWN WHILE OPPOSING THE CONSTITUTION WHICH QUEEN ELIZABETH CAME ALL THE WAY TO OTTAWA TO APPROVE? "TO THIS QUESTION THE ANSWER WAS SIMPLY:"SHE'S A FIGUREHEAD, LET'S FACE IT, I DOUBT IT IF HER MAJESTY HAS EVER READ THE CONSTITUTION OR KNOWS WHAT THE QUARREL IS ABOUT THE CONSTITUTION. "THE MEDIA'S NEXT TASK WAS TO COMMENT ON THE WESTERN INDEPENDENTISTS NOT ONLY BELIEVING THAT THE QUEEN WAS MERELY A FIGUREHEAD BUT FURTHER IMPLIED THAT THE GROUP HAD ONE OF THEIR OWN CULT LIKE FIGUREHEAD AND PREFERRED TO IDOL WORSHIP THAT INSTEAD. IN SHORT, TRUDEAU'S CONSTITUTION ACT OF 1982 WAS GLORIFIED AS NEWSPAPERS RIGHT ACROSS THE COUNTRY PUBLISHED ITS TEXT FOR ALL CANADIANS TO READ AND BE PROUD OF AND FURTHER PROCLAIMED PRIME MINISTER P.E. TRUDEAU THE CONQUERING HERO.

AS CANADIANS WERE BEING DAZZLED BY PRIME MINISTER TRUDEAU'S POLITICAL DOG AND PONY SHOW, NEWSPAPERS IN LONDON, ENGLAND CLAIMED THAT QUEEN ELIZABETH ACTUALLY PREFERRED TO ATTEND A HORSE SHOW RATHER THAN ATTEND THE OTTAWA CELEBRATIONS. ACCORDING TO THE DAILY MIRROR, QUEEN ELIZABETH WROTE A LETTER TWO WEEKS BEFOREHAND TO THE DUKE OF BEAUFORT SAYING THAT SHE PREFERRED BEING AT THE ANNUAL THREE-DAY BADMINTON HORSE TRIALS. THE NEWSPAPER INTERVIEWED COL. FRANK WELDON, THE DIRECTOR OF THE TRIALS, IN WHICH HE STATED: "SHE SAID SHE HAD TRIED TO GET THE DATES OF HER VISIT TO CANADA CHANGED, BUT TO NO AVAIL. "THE NEWSPAPER SAID WELDON'S REMARKS "ARE BOUND TO UPSET THE CANADIANS. "IT WAS IN COL. WELDON'S OWN PERSONAL OPINION THAT "THE QUEEN HAS A DREARY AND UNPLEASANT JOB TO DO AT PRESENT."

ONLY DAYS BEFORE THE SIGNING OF THE ROYAL PROCLAMATION, (APRIL 14TH), NORTHERN RESIDENTS WENT TO DESIGNATED POLLING STATIONS TO CAST THEIR VOTE ON TERRITORIAL DIVISION. BOTH THE VOTING PROCEDURE AND THE SIGNING OF THE PROCLAMATION WENT HAND-IN-HAND AS ONE WAS TO FEED OFF THE OTHER, THUS ENABLING TRUDEAU TO HAVE HIS FIFTEEN MINUTES IN THE LIMELIGHT ON A GRAND SCALE. YELLOWKNIFE, HAY RIVER AND INUVIK, COMMUNITIES WITH A **"WHITE MAJORITY"** VOTED WITH A STRONG UNITED VOICE SAYING **"NO"** TO TRUDEAU'S DIVISION CONCEPT. IRONICALLY, EVEN SOME NATIVE COMMUNITIES IN THE MACKENZIE VALLEY ALSO VOTED **"NO"** DESPITE THE RHETORIC BY INDIAN LEADERS URGING THEM TO SAY "YES". WHEN ALL THE BALLOTS WERE FINALLY COUNTED, THE PRESIDENT OF THE INDIAN BROTHERHOOD ATTRIBUTED THOSE BALLOTS THAT HAD BEEN MARKED WITH A "NO "VOTE AS BEING DUE TO THE FACT THAT MOST OF

THE ABORIGINALS WERE OUT ON THE LAND AT THE TIME OF THE PLEBISCITE AND THEY DIDN'T FULLY UNDERSTAND ITS MEANING. WITH THE VOTE JUST FALLING SHORT OF ITS REQUIRED PERCENTAGE – ONLY FIFTY-SIX PERCENT OF THE VOTES TALLIED IN THE WESTERN ARCTIC WERE IN FAVOR OF DIVIDING THE NORTHWEST TERRITORIES INTO SEPARATE REGIONS. THE INUIT OF THE EASTERN ARCTIC ON THE OTHER HAND VOTED WITH A SOLID RESOUNDING **"YES"** FOR DIVISION AS NINETY PERCENT OF ITS ELIGIBLE VOTERS TURNED OUT AT THE POLLS.

NOT EVERYONE LIVING NORTH OF THE 60TH PARALLEL WAS OVERJOYED WITH ENTHUSIASM. YELLOWKNIFE CENTER MLA BOB MACQUARRIE FOR EXAMPLE WHO REPORTEDLY SCRUTINIZED THE RESULTS AS THEY WERE PINNED ON THE WALLS IN A CONGESTED CONFERENCE ROOM AT ONE OF YELLOWKNIFE'S HOTELS FOR ALL TO SEE, LOOKED AT THE RESULTS IN TOTAL DISBELIEF SHAKING HIS HEAD TO-AND-FRO SAYING: "THIS MEANS THE END OF THE NORTHWEST TERRITORIES AS WE KNOW IT. "EVEN GOVERNMENT LEADER GEORGE BRADEN HAD A HARD TIME ACCEPTING THE RESULTS: "THIS RESULT MATCHES THE WORSE-CASE SCENARIO ... HOW DO WE INTERPRET THIS? "EAST VOTES "YES", WEST BASICALLY VOTES "NO". HOURS LATER, THE SITUATION GOT MUCH WORSE AS RESIDENTS IN INUVIK CONJUGATED AND HIRED A LAWYER TO TAKE THE PLEBISCITE ORDER TO COURT. THE MOVE TO CHALLENGE THE FEDERAL GOVERNMENT'S TERRITORIAL DIVISION CONCEPT CAME FROM INUVIK'S LONGTIME RESIDENT DOUG BILLINGSLEY. AT THE TIME, BILLINGSLEY WAS A HARDWARE STORE OWNER AND A MEMBER OF THE INUVIK TOWN COUNCIL. IN HIS EARLIER YEARS, DOUG WAS A MEMBER OF THE UNITED CHURCH OF CANADA PASTORAL MINISTRY. LIKE MANY WHITE RESIDENTS OF THE NWT, DOUG BILLINGSLEY WAS OUTRAGED ABOUT THE FEDERAL GOVERNMENT'S RULING THAT REQUIRED ELIGIBLE VOTERS TO HAVE LIVED IN THE NORTHWEST TERRITORIES FOR A THREE YEAR TERM BEFORE BEING ABLE TO VOTE IN THE TERRITORIAL DIVISION PLEBISCITE. THE LONG BUT NOT FORGOTTEN RETIRED PASTOR BILLINGSLEY STATED: "IT'S AN ATTEMPT TO DISENFRANCHISE ESSENTIALLY SOUTHERN CANADIANS. AND IT'S AT VARIANCE WITH THE MOBILITY RIGHTS GUARANTEED IN THE NEW CONSTITUTION. WE BETTER CLARIFY RIGHT NOW WHETHER THIS PART OF CANADA IS GOING TO BE CONSIDERED DIFFERENT FROM THE REST OF THE COUNTRY. "NORTHERN TEMPERS FLARED EVEN HIGHER AS SIGNS OF A RIGGED VOTE SOON EMERGED IN THE WESTERN ARCTIC BUT WAS IMMEDIATELY DOWN PLAYED BY THE NORTHERN MEDIA OUTLETS AS THEIR LIFELINE CAME FROM THE MONIES SPENT BY THE FEDERAL AND TERRITORIAL GOVERNMENTS ON PAID ADVERTISING.

JUST AS QUEEN ELIZABETH AND HER FRATERNAL COUNTERPARTS WERE SIGNING THE HISTORICAL DOCUMENT IMPLEMENTED BY THE TRUDEAU REGIME, LEGISLATIVE ASSEMBLY MEMBER BOB MACQUARRIE PARADED THE

STREETS OF YELLOWKNIFE WEARING A BLACK ARMBAND MOURNING THE DEATH OF THE BRITISH NORTH AMERICA ACT AND THE END OF WHITE RULE IN THE NORTHWEST TERRITORIES. MACQUARRIE REPORTEDLY SAW THE WRITING ON THE WALL, THIS LONE MOURNER WOULD LATER CONCEDE TO THE NORTHERN POLITICAL SCENE AND JOIN FORCES WITH HIS WESTERN CONSTITUTIONAL COMMITTEE COLLEAGUES BY HELPING IN THE ESTABLISHING OF A WESTERN ARCTIC TERRITORY FOR THE INDIAN BROTHERHOOD OF THE NORTHWEST TERRITORIES.

WHAT THE AVERAGE CANADIAN CITIZEN DOESN'T FULLY REALIZE IS THAT THE CONTENTS OF THE CONSTITUTION ACT OF 1982 GAVE THE OFFICE OF THE PRIME MINISTER MUCH POWER, ALTHOUGH THE LIMITS OF HIS POWERS HAVE NEVER BEEN PRECISELY DEFINED, TRUDEAU'S OWN LIBERAL REIGN OF TERROR HAD DONE MUCH TO ENHANCE BOTH THE PRESTIGE AND THE POWER. IN MARCH OF 1985, THE MINISTER OF INDIAN AND NORTHERN AFFAIRS, DAVID CROMBIE, THEN-MINISTER OF THE DAY, ANNOUNCED THAT THE PEOPLE OF THE NORTHWEST TERRITORIES WOULD BE GOING BACK TO THE POLLS IN 1987 TO VOTE ONCE MORE ON TERRITORIAL DIVISION. IT WAS PURELY A TACTIC OF DIVIDE AND CONQUER AS THE NATIVE PEOPLES ALL ACROSS CANADA WERE TOLD BY THE CANADIAN FEDERAL GOVERNMENT THAT THEIR CONCERNS OF SELF-GOVERNMENT AND SELF-DETERMINATION WOULD EVENTUALLY BE ACHIEVED BUT FIRST, THE NWT RESIDENTS HAD TO VOTE IN FAVOR OF TERRITORIAL DIVISION. THE OTTAWA POWERS THAT BE WERE FORCING THE NATIVE POPULATION INTO A CORNER BY BLACKMAILING THEM AS WELL, MANY NORTHERN RESIDENTS AT FIRST DIDN'T KNOWN WHAT TO THINK. BUT OTTAWA'S BLOOD STAINED HANDS SOON CAME DOWN WITH A FIRM FIST AS RESIDENTS IN COPPERMINE AND CAMBRIDGE BAY PROTESTED THE CANADIAN FEDERAL GOVERNMENT'S CONCEPT OF NATIVE GENOCIDE. OTTAWA SUPPRESSED THE ESKIMO UP-RISING BY HOLDING SEMINARS, DEBATES AND CONFERENCES EXPLAINING ITS GENUINE INTEREST FOR THE NORTHERN POPULATION.

ON THURSDAY, MARCH 12TH, 1987 THE GOVERNMENT OF THE NORTHWEST TERRITORIES ANNOUNCED THAT THE RESIDENTS OF THE NORTHLAND WOULD BE GOING BACK TO THE POLLS ON MAY 20TH OF THAT YEAR TO DECIDE ONCE AND FOR ALL THE ISSUE OF THE BOUNDARY LINE THAT WAS TO SEPARATE THE ARCTIC AS DICTATED BY P.E. TRUDEAU. JUST DAYS BEFORE THE PROPOSED VOTE, NATIVE LEADERS IN THE ARCTIC BAND TOGETHER WITH A FIRM AND LOUD VOICE INFORMING OTTAWA THAT THERE WOULD BE NO VOTE ON TERRITORIAL DIVISION UNTIL THE NATIVE LAND CLAIMS ISSUE WAS FIRST SETTLED. THOSE VERY WORDS SHOOK THE POLITICAL FRAMEWORK OF THE OTTAWA ESTABLISHMENT LIKE A GIGANTIC EARTHQUAKE AS THE CANADIAN FEDERAL GOVERNMENT SCRAMBLED FOR COVER BECAUSE ALL OF THEIR BACK ROOM WHEELING AND DEALING WAS NOW UNRAVELING AS NATIVES ONCE AGAIN

STOOD UP IN DEFIANCE AS TO WHAT HAD BEEN WRITTEN AS BEING LEGALLY BINDING BY THE POWERS THAT BE!!!

AT THIS POINT IT SHOULD ALSO BE NOTED THAT IN THE SPRING OF 1983, EVERYTHING STARTED TO UNRAVEL FOR GEORGE BRADEN AS WELL WHEN A YELLOWKNIFE RESIDENT (TREVOR BURROUGHS) CONFRONTED THE THEN- MINISTER OF JUSTICE FOR THE NORTHWEST TERRITORIES REGARDING GOVERNMENTAL ABUSES WITHIN THE AIR INDUSTRY NORTH OF THE 60TH PARALLEL. APPARENTLY AT THE TIME, BURROUGHS HAD AMPLE DOCUMENTATION VERIFYING THE FACT THAT FEDERAL AND/OR TERRITORIAL OFFICIALS AND/OR EMPLOYEE WERE INVOLVED WITH BRIBES, KICKBACKS, PAY-OFFS AND INFLUENCE PEDDLING. THE YELLOWKNIFE RESIDENT, THEN GAVE THE DOCUMENTATION TO THE SAID MINISTER OF JUSTICE WHO REPORTEDLY SAT ON IT FOR MONTHS ON END DOING ABSOLUTELY NOTHING. BUT DUE TO THE FACT THAT AN ELECTION WAS JUST AROUND THE CORNER, BURROUGHS TEAMED UP WITH YELLOWKNIFE'S TED MEHLER WHO HAD ACQUIRED A WELL KNOWN REPUTATION IN THE WESTERN ARCTIC FOR MAKING ALL POLITICAL FIGURES TOW THE LINE WHEN IT CAME TO STAYING ON THE PATH OF RIGHTEOUSNESS. MEHLER, GOT ALL THE NECESSARY INFORMATION FROM TREVOR AND THEN BEGAN TAKING THE APPROPRIATE LEGAL ACTION AGAINST THE MINISTER OF JUSTICE, BRADEN WAS THUS FACED WITH BREACH OF TRUST CHARGES.

BUT ON SEPTEMBER 7TH, 1983 BRADEN ANNOUNCED THAT HE WAS RESIGNING HIS POSITION AND RETIRING FROM TERRITORIAL POLITICS. THE GEORGE BRADEN SCANDAL BECAME SUCH A HOT POLITICAL ISSUE THAT IT WAS TOTALLY SUPPRESSED FROM THE MEDIA AND BY SPRING OF THE FOLLOWING YEAR, THE FEDERAL MINISTER OF JUSTICE AND ATTORNEY-GENERAL OF CANADA INTERVENED ALL CHARGES, **(STAY OF PROCEEDINGS)**, CITING LACK OF EVIDENCE. THE NORTHWEST TERRITORIAL GOVERNMENT COULDN'T AFFORD ANOTHER WIN BY TED MEHLER. THE GOVERNMENTAL HYPOCRISY GREW EVEN STRONGER AS BRADEN WAS SHIPPED OUT OF YELLOWKNIFE SOUTH TO VANCOUVER, BRITISH COLUMBIA TO JOIN FORCES WITH STUART HODGSON, THE EX-COMMISSIONER OF THE NORTHWEST TERRITORIES. HODGSON WAS GRANTED THE PRESTIGIOUS PORTFOLIO AS CHAIRMAN OF THE BRITISH COLUMBIA TRANSIT SYSTEM, AT AN ANNUAL INCOME OF WELL OVER $100,000.00, EXCLUDING EXPENSES. HIS SIDEKICK, ROD MORRISON WAS GRANTED THE POSITION OF CORPORATION MANAGER. BOTH HODGSON AND MORRISON STEPPED DOWN AS HEAD GOVERNMENTAL PUPPET MASTERS OF THE NORTHWEST TERRITORIES IN THE EARLY PARTS OF THE 1980'S AS B.C.'S REIGNING SOCRED GOVERNMENT WELCOMED THEM WITH OPEN ARMS. ONCE THE DISGRACED FORMER JUSTICE MINISTER GEORGE BRADEN ARRIVED IN VANCOUVER, HE WAS PUT IN CHARGE OF THE NORTHWEST TERRITORIAL PAVILION FOR EXPO 86. HIS OFFICIAL TITLE WAS; **"COMMISSIONER OF**

THE NWT PAVILION". And when things finally cooled down in Yellowknife and Braden impressed the hell out of various friends and colleagues in the political arena, he then returned back to the northland and was duly appointed Deputy Minister of Economic Development and Tourism. And what about Trevor Burroughs, you might be asking??? Well like anything else in the Northwest Territories, for his wanting of justice within the aviation industry in the Arctic, he found himself appearing before the Territorial courts in Yellowknife. Sometime during Trevor's ordeal of seeking justice, he was faced with losing his small aviation company. In the Arctic there exist an unwritten code of conduct, if you chose to rock the political boat you must be totally prepared to suffer the full consequences. Hence, instead of the Territorial Government's Department of Justice taking legal action against George Braden and the corrupt governmental officials and employees, the Department of Justice took swift legal action against Trevor for blowing the whistle.

By the time George Braden was whisked away out of town, many northern residents soon forgot all about the Braden scandal as the Yellowknife RCMP began investigating the illegal sale of two Eskimo infants. The twins were born on May 3RD, 1984 at the Yellowknife hospital to a single mother, they were delivered to their new parents in Westaskawin, Alberta eight days later. Rumors spread like wildfire in the northern Capital City that the biological father of the children was a twenty-eight-year-old white youth activist who had cycled across the country from May 30TH to August 11TH,1983 promoting a political voice for northern teenagers was somehow connected to the scandal. But in two separate accounts, sources that wished to remain anonymous told an entirely different story than that of the Yellowknife rumor mill. Apparently, the mother was seriously thinking about keeping the children but due to much pressure added by members of her religious congregation, "Pentecostal Church" a pre-arranged private adoption was organized with the assistance of her church leaders.

The Pentecostal Pastor and his wife informed the mother that she was unfit to take care of the children and that they would be much better off in a good Christian home. Confused about what to do, the mother reportedly left the twins in the care of a nurse who worked at the hospital as the mother was said to have needed time to decide the fate of her new born babies. Ironically, the nurse was also a member of the Pentecostal Church. The confused mother

APPARENTLY THOUGHT THAT SHE WOULD BE ABLE TO MAINTAIN CONTACT WITH HER CHILDREN, EVEN AFTER THEY WERE ADOPTED. AFTER THINKING IT OVER FOR A COUPLE OF DAYS, THE MOTHER DECIDED THAT SHE WANTED TO KEEP HER TWINS. BUT THERE WAS MUCH RESISTANCE BY HER CONGREGATION MEMBERS.

ALLEGATIONS EXISTED THAT A SUBSTANTIAL AMOUNT OF MONEY CHANGED HANDS IN THE PRIVATE ADOPTION PROCEEDINGS. NO ONE KNEW EXACTLY WHAT AMOUNT, NOR WHO ACTUALLY RECEIVED IT, THE MOTHER /OR THE CHURCH LEADERS. AT THE TIME, PRIVATE ADOPTIONS WERE VERY ATTRACTIVE IN THE NORTHLAND DUE TO THE FACT THAT THE LEGAL SYSTEM WAS SO DAMN SLACK AND/OR CORRUPT. THERE WAS NO PROTECTIVE GUIDELINES FOR EITHER THE CHILD NOR THE MOTHER IN A CASH TRANSACTION. THE ILLEGAL SALE OF THE ANIKINA TWINS THUSLY RAISED MANY QUESTIONS ABOUT THE TERRITORIAL GOVERNMENT'S ACTUAL INVOLVEMENT. THE GOVERNMENT OF THE NORTHWEST TERRITORIES' THEN-SUPERINTENDENT OF CHILD WELFARE, DIANE DOYLE INTERESTINGLY ENOUGH REVEALED THAT SOCIAL SERVICES PEOPLE HAD BECOME FULLY AWARE OF THE MOTHER'S PLIGHT BUT CHOSE TO DO NOTHING ABOUT IT. ACCORDINGLY, MUCH PRESSURE WAS BEING ORCHESTRATED BY THE PENTECOSTAL CHURCH MEMBERS AS SOCIAL SERVICES FOR THE NWT HAD A STRICT POLICY OF PLACING NATIVE CHILDREN IN NATIVE HOMES NORTH OF THE 60TH PARALLEL. NON-NATIVE FAMILIES WERE NOT PERMITTED TO ADOPT A NATIVE CHILD, NOR WERE NON-RESIDENTS OF THE ARCTIC ALLOWED TO ADOPT EITHER A NATIVE /OR NON-NATIVE CHILD. AND AT THAT SAME TIME PERIOD OF HISTORY, THE NORTHWEST TERRITORIES HAD A THREE-YEAR LONG WAITING LIST. CHILD WELFARE SERVICES, (A.K.A. SOCIAL SERVICES) STATED THAT THERE WERE FEW CAUCASIAN /OR NATIVE INFANTS AVAILABLE FOR ADOPTION. THE SOCIAL SERVICES PEOPLE WERE SAID TO BE NOT ACCEPTING APPLICATIONS FOR CAUCASIAN INFANTS. THE REAL MONEY MAKER APPARENTLY WAS IN THE HANDLING OF NATIVE INDIAN AND ESKIMO INFANT COMMODITIES. YEARS LATER, (1991), YELLOWKNIFE'S REGIONAL SUPERINTENDENT DIANE DOYLE FACED CRIMINAL CHARGES OF FORGERY AND FRAUD INVOLVING THE MISAPPROPRIATION OF $ 271,000.00 IN CHILD-WELFARE CHEQUES. AS IT TURNED OUT, OVER A PERIOD OF TWO YEARS DOYLE PREPARED A SERIES OF PHONY SOCIAL-ASSISTANCE AND CHILD-WELFARE CHEQUES WHILE HOLDING DOWN HER $ 84,000.00 A-YEAR PORTFOLIO.

IN THE NORTHWEST TERRITORIES, THERE ARE ONLY THREE WAYS TO ADOPT A CHILD. CUSTOM ADOPTION ARE IN A HISTORICAL AGREEMENT USED BY MANY NORTHERN CULTURAL PEOPLES, DENE AS WELL AS INUIT. CHILDREN ARE OFTEN GIVEN TO (ADOPTED BY) OTHER FAMILY MEMBERS. ONE OPTION IS THAT THE PARENTS OF A NATIVE MALE CHILD MAY GIVE HIM TO A FAMILY IF THEY ALREADY HAVE SONS AND THE OTHER FAMILY DOES NOT. TRADITIONALLY, A MALE IS

NEEDED IN EVERY HOUSEHOLD TO HELP SUPPORT THE FAMILY. OR, THE CHILD MAY BE GIVEN TO AN OLDER COUPLE TO TAKE CARE OF THEM IN LATER YEARS. THIS ARRANGEMENT IS LEGALLY RECOGNIZED BY THE GOVERNING BODIES, THE MAIN FUNCTION OF THE SOCIAL SERVICES DEPARTMENT IS TO ENSURE THAT ALL THE PAPER WORK IS PROPERLY CARRIED OUT. CHILDREN WHO HAVE BEEN REMOVED FROM THEIR HOMES, AND ARE PERMANENT WARDS OF THE TERRITORIAL GOVERNMENT ARE ADOPTED THROUGH THE SOCIAL SERVICES SYSTEM. THE PROCESS IS LONG AND CONTAINS A MOUNTAIN OF BUREAUCRATIC RED TAPE. ON THE OTHER HAND IN A PRIVATE ADOPTION, A MOTHER MAKES ARRANGEMENTS AND SIGNS AN AGREEMENT GIVING THE CUSTODY OF HER CHILD, (USUALLY UNBORN) TO A SPECIFIC COUPLE. THIS ARRANGEMENT IS ALSO A LEGAL BINDING CONTRACT ONCE THE AGREEMENT IS SIGNED. IN ACCORDANCE TO THE TERRITORIAL LAW AT THE TIME, NOTIFICATION OF RELEASING CHILDREN FOR ADOPTION WAS A REQUIREMENT, EVEN IN A PRIVATE ARRANGEMENTS. THE AGREEMENT OF ADOPTIONS WAS ORIGINALLY DRAFTED INTO THE TERRITORIAL CHILD WELFARE ORDINANCE MORE THAN A CENTURY AGO. BUT OVER THE MANY YEARS, VARIOUS INFRACTIONS TOOK PLACE AND ADDITIONAL LEGISLATION HAD TO BE INTRODUCED. SECTION 99, SUBSECTION (1) OF THE ORDINANCE FOR EXAMPLE STATES: "ANY PERSON OTHER THAN THE SUPERINTENDENT WHO GIVES OR RECEIVES OR AGREES TO GIVE OR RECEIVE ANY PAYMENT OR REWARD EITHER DIRECTLY OR INDIRECTLY, TO PROCURE OR ASSIST IN PROCURING A CHILD FOR THE PURPOSE OF ADOPTION, IS GUILTY OF AN OFFENCE AND LIABLE UPON SUMMARY CONVICTION TO A FINE OF NOT MORE THAN $ 200.00, OR IN DEFAULT OF PAYMENT A MAXIMUM OF SIX MONTHS IMPRISONMENT. "WHILE SUBSECTION (2) STATED: "NO PROSECUTION SHALL BE COMMENCED UNDER THIS SECTION EXCEPT WITH THE CONSENT OF THE COMMISSIONER." AS THE 1984 RCMP INVESTIGATION DREW TO A CLOSING CHAPTER, SO DID ALL PROSPECTS OF CHARGES BEING LAID AGAINST THE PENTECOSTAL CHURCH LEADERS WHO HAD SPENT FORTY YEARS OF THEIR NATURAL LIVES PREACHING TO THE NATIVE POPULATION OF THE NORTHLAND.

IN THE ARCTIC, THE VARIOUS CHURCHES PLAYED A VERY IMPORTANT ROLE IN THE DEVELOPMENT OF ITS FAR REACHING NORTHLAND. WHEN IT CAME TO SCHOOLING AND RELIGIOUS INSTITUTIONS, (USUALLY ROMAN CATHOLIC /OR PROTESTANT MISSIONARIES WITH RESIDENTIAL SCHOOLING AVAILABLE), THE NATIVE PEOPLES WERE FORCED TO SPEAK AND WRITE ENGLISH /OR FRENCH. THEY WERE STRICTLY FORBIDDEN TO SPEAK THEIR OWN NATIVE LANGUAGES AND THEY WERE ALSO NOT ALLOWED TO WORSHIP IN THEIR OWN NORMAL/ TRADITIONAL WAYS. THE NATIVE PEOPLES OF CANADA WERE THUSLY FORCED TO ADOPT THE WHITEMAN'S WAY OF LIFE. IT'S ESTIMATED THAT WHEN CHRISTOPHER COLUMBUS ARRIVED ON THE SHORES OF NORTH AMERICA IN 1492, THERE WERE 70 MILLION INDIANS LIVING IN THE AMERICA'S. SOME 150 YEARS LATER,

THE INDIAN POPULATION HAD DROPPED TO 12 MILLION. IN 1800, IT WAS ESTIMATED THAT THE INDIAN POPULATION OF THE CONTINENTAL UNITED STATES WAS ONE MILLION. AND AFTER THE AMERICANS HAD COMPLETED THEIR BLOODY MARCH ACROSS THE CONTINENT, THEY REPORTEDLY TOOK A COMPLETE CENSUS IN 1890, WHERE IT WAS SOON DISCOVERED THAT THE INDIAN POPULATION IN THE ENTIRE UNITED STATES OF THE AMERICA'S HAD BEEN REDUCED TO 250,000. CANADA ON THE OTHER HAND HAD A MORE DIPLOMATIC AND HUMANE WAY OF GETTING RID OF ITS INDIAN PROBLEM, LEGALIZED NATIVE GENOCIDE!!!

Chapter 7 - RED POWER – CANADA

We, as human beings are often afraid to face the many realities of the world and in doing so, an escape goat is quite often found. Sometimes the reality of it all has far too many ramifications attached to it and we, therefore search for ways of rejecting it. The fact of the matter is now and forever, our country's aboriginal peoples were here first; long before the whiteman set foot onto North American soil. And the whiteman in return, waged a war of genocide onto the First Nation Peoples by continually hiding behind the auspices of National Security and stacks upon stacks of purged files and/or reports originally created by the RCMP Security Service as they acted as Indian control agents for the Canadian Federal Government.

It wasn't until the whiteman first set foot onto the fertile soil of the North American Continent that all the chaos and confusion actually began as to who was the more superior race of people as well as who had legal title of the lands now occupied by the new invaders. With the whiteman claiming squatters rights, the aboriginal peoples of Canada were thusly placed into bondage and forced to obey the new masters who now had jurisdictional powers over them so deemed by Indian Act legislation and the whiteman's **GOD** given right to reign supreme. Ever since the Roberval expedition's first attempt to establish a French Roman Catholic colony in 1542 with volunteer prisoners from France's correctional facilities, the whiteman has virtually treated our country's native peoples with the utmost disrespect and inequality to that of the Black population south of the 49TH parallel, such as in Louisiana during the 1700's under the stewardship of the LePage family dynasty; Company of the Indies. In accordance to both Canadian and American history, it has been proven time and time again that the white Anglo-Saxon population saw themselves as being the more superior race of people and that the Blacks, along with the aboriginals – were perceived as being

216

THE INFERIOR ONES. ADAPTING THIS SOMEWHAT RACIST PHILOSOPHY TO THE FORMATION OF THE ROYAL NORTH WEST MOUNTED POLICE IN 1873, CANADA'S FIRST PRIME MINISTER, SIR JOHN A. MACDONALD SET TO PEN AND PAPER HIS PLAN FOR WHITE DOMINATION. HE WROTE: "THE INDIANS AND METIS OF THE NORTHWEST WILL BE HELD DOWN WITH A FIRM HAND TILL THE WEST IS OVER-RUN AND CONTROLLED BY WHITE SETTLERS, "IN A LETTER TO A FRIEND OF HIS BY THE NAME OF ROSE. AS STATED PREVIOUSLY, THIS LETTER IS ALSO CONTAINED IN OUT COUNTRY'S NATIONAL ARCHIVES.

CONTRARY AS TO WHAT HISTORIANS MAY SAY AS BEING A TRUE FACT OF THIS COUNTRY'S HISTORICAL HERITAGE, WHILE STUDYING ALL OF THE TWISTING AND TURNING OF CANADA'S FREEMASONRY PAST ADDITIONAL ENLIGHTENMENT IS INSTANTLY BESTOWED UPON ANYONE WHO RESEARCHES IT. FOR EXAMPLE, ONE OF THE OLDEST LIVING ORGANISMS OF ENGLISH FREEMASONRY INFILTRATION IS THE ROYAL-LOYAL ORDER OF ORANGISM. BUT IN ORDER TO GET THE FULL PICTURE OF THE "LAISSEZ-FAIRE", SOME BACKGROUND INFORMATION MUST BE GIVEN FIRST. WILLIAM THE FIRST, (1533-84) BETTER KNOWN HISTORICALLY AS WILLIAM THE SILENT, PRINCE OF ORANGE AND COUNT OF NASSAU, WAS THE FOUNDING FOREFATHER OF A VERY POWERFUL/RELIGIOUS FRATERNITY FORCE WHICH DEVOTED ITSELF TO THE ASSERTION OF THE LIBERTIES OF THE NETHERLANDS AND THE AGITATION OF SPANISH TROOPS AS WELL – THE REVOLT OF THE NETHERLANDS AND THE BIRTH OF HOLLAND. IN 1579, WILLIAM OF ORANGE BROUGHT ABOUT THE FORMATION OF THE UNION OF UTRECHT, WHICH COMPRISED OF THE PROVINCES OF HOLLAND, ZEELAND, UTRECHT, FRIESLAND, AND OVERYSSEL – THUS MARKING THE BIRTH OF THE DUTCH REPUBLIC. THE ORANGE FAMILY – SUPPORTED BY THE POORER CLASSES – PROMISED TO DEVELOP MONARCHICAL INSTITUTIONS IF GIVEN THE CHANCE. IN 1584 AS WILLIAM OF ORANGE BEGAN PUSHING FOR CONSTITUTIONAL DEVELOPMENT AND/OR REFORM IN THE DUTCH REPUBLIC, HIS LIFE WAS THEREFORE TERMINATED (MURDERED) BY THE OPPOSING FORCES; THE ROMAN CATHOLICS.

ONE-HUNDRED AND FIVE YEARS LATER, WILLIAM THE THIRD OF GREAT BRITAIN WAS KING OF ENGLAND, SCOTLAND AND IRELAND, (FROM 1689 TO 1702). HE WAS THE POSTHUMOUS SON OF WILLIAM II OF ORANGE (1626-50) AND MARY (1631-60) THE ELDEST DAUGHTER OF CHARLES THE FIRST OF ENGLAND – CHARLES I BEING OF COURSE THE GRANDSON OF MARY QUEEN OF SCOTS. BY THIS TIME FRAME OF HISTORY, WILLIAM THE FIRST'S PROTESTANT POLITICAL FORCES WERE STRONG AND FLOURISHING WITH EACH PASSING DECADE – ESPECIALLY IN THE LATTER PARTS OF THE 1600'S WHEN ROMAN CATHOLIC POPE INNOCENT XI STARTED SENDING WILLIAM III OF ORANGE LARGE AMOUNTS OF MONEY TO HELP SPONSOR THE PROTESTANT CAUSE OF OVERTHROWING THE ROMAN CATHOLIC RULE OF KING JAMES II OF ENGLAND.

Accordingly, William III's official British title of distinction was "William of Orange, King and protector of English Freemasonry." It is also interesting to note that in 1677, William III married his cousin, Princess Mary – incest by Royal Decree at its highest fraternity form!!!

By 1690, Orange Lodgery had been formed by Freemasonry Protestants in Ireland. Freemasonry in Northern Ireland, Armagh County, where Masonic Orangism was first established, is a very touchy topic to most of today's present day historians. No one really wanted to admit to the fact that all of the political and religious turmoil of Northern Ireland was actually a turf war between Protestant Freemasons and Roman Catholic Freemasons. It is for this reason that early records of Irish Freemasonry has been deleted from most, if not all fraternity literature.

Ironically, during the year 1911 in Ireland some rather interesting new information came to light; "a contemporary newspaper has been discovered, which gives an account of the installation of the Earl of Rosse as Grand Master of Ireland in June, 1725; and this account is so worded as to leave little room for doubt that the Grand Lodge of Ireland has already been in existence long enough to develop a complete organization of Grand Officers with at least six subordinate Lodges under its jurisdiction. "

As fate would have it, the name of the Masonic Orange force was based upon the Protestant support of William the Third, who reportedly gained possession of the British throne in 1689 after his Illuminati members succeeded in ousting the French friendly Roman Catholic Stuart King; James the Second. The Masonic Order of Orangism grew rapidly, establishing Lodgery throughout the British Commonwealth, including Canada and the United States. By 1795, the Orange Lodge of Belfast was active in creating chaos for the Irish Catholics and with the sunset of the 1700's, the secret fraternity of the Orange Order tallied a membership list of slightly over two-hundred thousand worldwide. By the mid-1800's, its membership roster had increased tenfold – the United States had three million registered members, Great Britain 400,000; Canada 200,000 and Ireland having over 50,000 fraternity members with a ferocious appetite of growing stronger as it was ultimately forced to continue its political/religious activities underground. Members of Orangism Freemasonry in Ireland took blood oaths of keeping the republic free from all forms of the Catholic faith. According to the Roman Catholic Church itself, the main function of Orangism was to force their views of anti-Catholic rhetoric onto others while keeping all Protestant opinions in the forefront and having an ultimate goal to "de-Christianize "the population of Ireland and the rest of the world. The Orangemen, were thus charged with being anti-Catholic bigots and were reportedly forced by British Parliament to suspend all their fraternal activities in Ireland from 1813 to 1828. While operating as an underground network, more and more of Ireland's Protestant population became interested in its fraternal anti-Catholic activities. By the mid-1840's, the Orange Lodgery membership became influential among farmers, skilled workers, and professional men and before long, had established Lodges for both men and women. In North America, a Grand Lodge of Orangism was instituted at Brockville, Upper Canada in the year 1830 – its fundamental principles were to defend Protestant Christianity and to unite the British Empire under one God, one flag and one language.

Orange Masonic Lodgery here in Canada has a very interesting history to say the least. For instance, during Louis Riel's first rebellion (1869-70), the Metis incarcerated various members of Freemasonry's Orangemen. These individuals ironically enough were very prominent and outstanding citizens of the Canadian establishment – two of these individuals were of course Doctor John Christian Schultz and Captain Thomas Scott of Sir John A. MacDonald's 42ND Brockville Battalion of the Canadian Militia. Doctor Schultz was reportedly a fine towering journalist and medical surgeon, who later went on to become a representative in the Freemasonry controlled Tory House of Commons in 1871, then, onto the Senate in 1882, and finally, he was appointed Lieutenant-Governor of Manitoba in July of 1888. Fraternity Brother Schultz held his Masonic portfolio until September of 1895 whereby he received the prestigious portfolio of King's Counsel by way of knighthood. Oddly enough, just like many of British Columbia's members of the Masonic Order at the time of Riel's insurrection, Schultz's manifestation was Manitoba's annexation with the United States but the Metis uprising sort of put the kibosh on that little maneuver. Once the good doctor escaped from Riel's jailhouse, he began recruiting sympathizers and warmongers willing to participate in controlling Canada's savage Indian population.

Like Schultz, Thomas Scott was an arrogant bigot and loyal Protestant British subject – the Captain of Sir John A. MacDonald's 42ND Brockville Battalion was imprisoned in December of 1869 but

LATER ESCAPED ALONG WITH DOCTOR SCHULTZ. SCOTT WAS RE-CAPTURED AND LATER EXECUTED AFTER HE REPORTEDLY STATED THAT IF GIVEN THE CHANCE, HE WOULD KILL RIEL WITH HIS BARE HANDS ONCE THE OPPORTUNITY SHOWED ITSELF — LIKE DOCTOR SCHULTZ AND SIR JOHN A. MACDONALD, THOMAS SCOTT WAS ALSO AN ACTIVE MEMBER OF FREEMASONRY. SCOTT APPARENTLY ATTEMPTED TO ASSASSINATE THE HALF-BREED REBELLION LEADER WHEN THE OPPORTUNITY REARED ITS UGLY HEAD, AND FOR THIS REASON, LOUIS RIEL DECIDED TO MAKE THOMAS SCOTT'S DEATH "A DELIBERATE ACT OF POLICY." RIEL FOUND HIM GUILTY OF DISORDERLY CONDUCT BY BEING INVOLVED IN OFFENSIVE ACTIONS AGAINST THE PEOPLE AND THE PROVINCIAL GOVERNMENT OF MANITOBA AND THUSLY ORDERED THE DEATH PENALTY — LOUIS RIEL WASN'T OVERLY CONCERNED THAT HE WAS ABOUT TO EXECUTE A MEMBER OF THE ANCIENT CRAFT OF FREEMASONRY. ON MARCH 4TH, 1870 FRATERNAL BROTHER THOMAS SCOTT WAS PULLED FROM HIS JAIL CELL AND DRAGGED BEFORE A FIRING SQUAD — BY THIS DEED, RIEL WAS SENDING A CLEAR MESSAGE TO THE BRETHERNSHIP IN OTTAWA. AS SCOTT FACED HIS HALF-BREED EXECUTIONERS, HIS CRY FOR MERCY: "THIS IS COLD-BLOODED MURDER!" ROCKED THE CANADIAN FREEMASONRY FOUNDATIONS OF SIR JOHN A. AND HIS FRATERNITY CRONIES.

THE AFTERMATH THAT SOON FOLLOWED WAS LARGELY DUE TO PRESSURE ADDED ONTO THE FREEMASONRY ADMINISTRATION OF SIR JOHN A. MACDONALD BY DOCTOR SCHULTZ AND HIS FELLOW ORANGEMEN. ONLY A FEW YEARS PREVIOUS TO HIS INCARCERATION, FRATERNITY BROTHER SCHULTZ WAS THE WORSHIPFUL MASTER AT THE FORT GARRY MASONIC LODGERY. MASONIC CONTROLLED NEWSPAPERS IN ENGLISH CANADA SOON DEMANDED RIEL'S BLOOD AS MEETINGS WERE QUICKLY ESTABLISHED TO AVENGE THE COLD-BLOODED MURDER OF FREEMASONRY BROTHER THOMAS SCOTT. NEWSPAPER HEADLINES SUCH AS "RED RIVER OUTRAGE "DID NOTHING BUT HELP STIR UP EMOTIONS AND ALMOST GUARANTEED A FULL HOUSE AT THE DESIGNATED MEETING HALLS OF ONTARIO. FURTHER NEWSPAPERS PUBLICIZED ENGLISH CANADA'S OUTRAGE ASKING THE PUBLIC TO ATTEND THE VARIOUS MEETINGS THROUGHOUT ONTARIO AND SEEK VENGEANCE FOR SCOTT'S EXECUTION BY RIEL. "TO AFFORD LOYAL PEOPLE AN OPPORTUNITY TO EXPRESSING THEIR DEEP INDIGNATION AT THE VILE CRIMES COMMITTED IN RUPERT'S LAND, BY IMPRISONING AND MURDERING BRITISH AND CANADIAN SUBJECTS. THE HONOR OF ENGLAND WAS NEVER OUTRAGED WITH IMPUNITY, AND NEVER WILL BE. LET CANADA NOT BE DEGRADED, THE HONOR OF THE COUNTRY MUST BE MAINTAINED, THE BLOOD OF THE MARTYRED SCOTT MUST NOT CRY IN VAIN FOR VENGEANCE. LET CANADA SPEAK OUT NOW, AND LET THE ASSASSIN RIEL FEEL THAT A CANADIAN MUST BE LIKE AN ANCIENT ROMAN, FREE FROM INJURY WHEREVER HE GOES. THE MEN THAT WENT TO MAGADALLA CAN GO TO THE

Red River. Come all Loyal Men to the meeting, this is the common cause of all Canadians ... **A ROPE FOR THE MURDERER RIEL! ... GOD SAVE THE QUEEN!"**

Sir John A. MacDonald and his Freemasonry Protestant thugs thus passed judgement on the Roman Catholic half-breed Indian leader – fraternity Brother Schultz and other members of the Masonic faith such as Brother Donald A. Smith reportedly screamed for justice in Freemasonry Brother Thomas Scott's assassination calling for no treaty and no negotiations to be conducted with the half-breed Metis "murderers "and "traitors "of Riel's "rebels." This is the same Donald Smith that according to historians was a fine outstanding pillar of the Protestant community as he was both a politician as well as a financier who helped Canadian Prime Minister MacDonald build his railway across our country at great expense to taxpayers. In fact, Smith assisted fraternity brethren George Stephen and William Van Horne in setting up the financial structure of the Canadian Pacific Railway syndicate scam, (a.k.a. Pacific Scandal of the CPR). In 1886, Donald A. Smith was knighted for his services in the illocution of the transcontinental railway – 1ST Baron of Strathcona and Mount Royal was his official Masonic title of distinction. Lord Strathcona was reportedly the largest shareholder in Freemasonry Brother John Molson's Bank of Montreal and because of this, was named its vice-president in 1882 and president five years later, (1887). By 1896, he was elevated to the prestigious portfolio of being the Canadian High Commissioner to London and in the following year, he became historically as the baron of all baron's, Baron Strathcona and Mount Royal. It should also be stated that Smith was the one who drove the last spike at Craigellachie (November 7TH, 1885) signifying the completion of the CPR's rail-line. As fate would have, the spike was later stolen and eventually made its way to Yellowknife in the Northwest Territories through diplomatic channels.

To further enhance fraternity documentation, between the years 1880-87 the CPR's corporate lawyer was none other than John Joseph Cadwell Abbott. For services rendered in setting the CPR up under the governmental wing of the Dominion of Canada, Abbott not only received knighthood from England, but he was also chosen to become Canada's third Prime Minister once Sir John A. finally kicked the old fraternity bucket on June 6TH, 1891. Interestingly, Sir Abbott was initiated into Freemasonry in 1847, some forty-four years before reaching the Canadian Prime Ministership. It is also

INTERESTING TO NOTE THAT CANADA'S SECOND PRIME MINISTER, ALEXANDER MACKENZIE WAS ALSO BELIEVED TO HAVE BEEN AN ACTIVE MEMBER OF THE ANCIENT CRAFT BUT LATER BROKE AWAY AND REPORTEDLY REFUSED KNIGHTHOOD NOT ONCE /OR TWICE, BUT THREE TIMES IN TOTAL BECAUSE OF HIS SINCERE OPINION THAT HIS FELLOW BRETHREN WERE DOING MORE HARM THAN GOOD. PERHAPS THIS IS WHY MACKENZIE'S NAME WAS TAKEN OFF THE MASONIC MEMBERSHIP ROSTER AS HE WAS DEEMED TO HAVE BEEN A THREAT TO THE FRATERNITY AND ITS FIRM BELIEF THAT IT WAS GOD'S WILL THAT ENGLISH FREEMASONRY SHOULD REIGN SUPREME IN CANADA.

AND TO FURTHER CAPITALIZE ON THE MASONIC ORDER'S ENDEAVORS PERTAINING TO FRATERNAL BROTHER SIR JOHN CHRISTIAN SCHULTZ AND HIS GOOD NAME, ONE OF THE THREE CLOSELY LINKED LAKES WEST OF BAKER LAKE IN THE THELON RIVER BASIN OF THE NORTHWEST TERRITORIES IS CALLED SCHULTZ LAKE. IT IRONICALLY WAS NAMED SO BY JOSEPH BURR TYRRELL, A HIGHLY RESPECTED CANADIAN CITIZEN AND DEVOTED EXPLORER OF CANADA'S NORTHLAND. IT SHOULD ALSO BE STATED THAT J.B. TYRRELL WAS AN ACTIVE MASTER MASON AS WELL. TYRRELL WAS A LONGTIME MEMBER OF THE MASONIC CRAFT, HE WAS INITIATED INTO THE BUILDER'S LODGE NO. 177 IN OTTAWA ON MAY, 10TH, 1889. BY 1910, HE DEMITTED TO BECOME A "CHARTER MEMBER" OF UNIVERSITY LODGE NO. 496 IN TORONTO, AND CONTINUED TO BE AN ACTIVE MEMBER UNTIL HIS DEATH ON AUGUST 26TH, 1957. BROTHER TYRRELL WASN'T YOUR AVERAGE RUN-OF-THE-MILL FREEMASONRY EXPLORER BY ANY MEANS — DURING THE SUMMER OF 1938, HE ORGANIZED THE FIRST MEETING OF A MASONIC LODGE IN CANADA'S FAR NORTH. THE HISTORICAL MEETING WAS HELD "NORTH OF THE ARCTIC CIRCLE AT COPPERMINE, N.W.T. ON AUGUST 30TH, 1938" AND SINCE YELLOWKNIFE WAS DESIGNATED BY OTTAWA TO BECOME A FREEMASONRY STRONGHOLD COMMUNITY AND CAPITAL CITY, THE COPPERMINE MASTER MASONS REPLANTED THEIR FRATERNAL ROOTS IN YELLOWKNIFE AND THE MASONIC ORDER'S YELLOWKNIFE LODGE NO. 162 WAS THEREFORE BORN.

FRATERNAL BROTHER TYRRELL'S FREEMASONRY CONTRIBUTIONS TO CANADIAN SOCIETY REPORTEDLY DIDN'T STOP THERE. DUE TO THE FACT THAT HE WAS A MINING ENGINEER AS WELL AS A GEOLOGIST, TYRRELL HAD THE OPPORTUNITY TO DO MUCH EXPLORING. WHILE OUT ON THE BARREN LANDS OF CANADA, HE FOUND THE SKULL AND BONES OF A NEW TYPE OF DINOSAUR; THE ALBERTO SAURUS SARCOPHAGUS WHICH WAS DISCOVERED NEAR DRUMHELLER, ALBERTA. IT SHOULD ALSO BE NOTED THAT DRUMHELLER HAS TWO MASONIC LODGES; DRUMHELLER LODGE NO. 146 AND SYMBOL LODGE NO. 93. IN ACCORDANCE TO FREEMASONRY, TYRRELL MADE MANY OTHER CONTRIBUTIONS TO THE CANADIAN MASONIC ENTITY. IN 1893 FOR EXAMPLE, HE AND HIS BROTHER JAMES, ALONG WITH THREE METIS AND THREE INDIANS

TRAVELED BY CANOE AND SNOWSHOE FROM ATHABASKA TO CHESTERFIELD INLET AND DOWN THE COAST OF HUDSON'S BAY AT CHURCHILL. TYRRELL AND HIS ENTOURAGE BARELY SURVIVED THE THREE-THOUSAND MILE TRIP BUT REPORTEDLY WIDENED THE SCIENTIFIC KNOWLEDGE OF GLACIATION AND PLANT LIFE FORMATIONS. ON MARCH 22ND, 1989 THE MASONIC CONTROLLED GOVERNMENT OF CANADA ISSUED A POSTAGE STAMP COMMEMORATING THE EXPLORATION OF CANADA'S RICHES BY HONORING FRATERNITY BROTHER JOSEPH BARR TYRRELL (1858-1957).

BY THE SUMMER OF 1990, THE MASONIC SERVICE ASSOCIATION OF THE UNITED STATES SUPPLIED THE FOLLOWING MEMBERSHIP STATISTICS FOR THE ENGLISH CANADIAN GRAND LODGES;

ALBERTA	11,824
BRITISH COLUMBIA	19,435
MANITOBA	8,500
NEW BRUNSWICK	6,623
NOVA SCOTIA	8,832
ONTARIO	89,053
PRINCE EDWARD ISLAND	1,181
QUEBEC	8,595
SASKATCHEWAN	8,406

THE SUM TOTAL OF THE ENGLISH-SPEAKING FREEMASONRY LIST OF MEMBERS WAS THUS AN ESTIMATED 162,449 THROUGHOUT CANADA. THIS LIST OBVIOUSLY DID NOT INCLUDED OTHER OFFSHOOTS OF FREEMASONRY SUCH AS THOSE OF FRENCH CANADA AS THESE TWO FACTIONS OF THE MASONIC ORDER WERE STILL NOT ON SPEAKING TERMS WITH ONE ANOTHER. ODDLY ENOUGH, NEWFOUNDLAND WASN'T ADDED TO THE AMERICAN MASONIC SERVICE ASSOCIATION'S MEMBERSHIP STATISTICS LIST BECAUSE ACCORDING TO FREEMASONRY'S OWN DOCUMENTATION ON THE POLITICAL AFFAIRS OF THE PROVINCE OF NEWFOUNDLAND, THE MASTER MASONS LIVING ON "THE ROCK "WEREN'T GOVERNED BY THE MASONIC CONTROLLED FACTIONS OF OTTAWA NOR THOSE OF WASHINGTON, D.C. BUT RATHER THE PRIME MINISTER OF ENGLAND AND HER BRITANNIC MAJESTY QUEEN ELIZABETH THE SECOND – THERE WAS REPORTEDLY NO PROVINCIAL GRAND LODGE OF NEWFOUNDLAND.

FURTHERMORE, ACCORDING TO THE AMERICAN ASSOCIATION DATA, THE MEMBERSHIP IN THE U.S. FREEMASONRY LODGERY WAS DRASTICALLY DROPPING. FOR EXAMPLE, IN 1959 THERE WERE 4,103,161 MEMBERS REGISTERED IN THE AMERICAN MASONIC ORDER. THIRTY YEARS LATER, (1989), THE ROSTER REACHED AN ALL TIME LOW OF 2.7 MILLION MEMBERS – AND ONCE AGAIN,

THIS CALCULATED AMERICAN MEMBERSHIP ROSTER DID NOT INCLUDE THE MANY FRATERNITY OFFSHOOTS OF THE MASONIC ORDER SUCH AS THOSE OF BLACK FREEMASONRY FOR EXAMPLE. THE MASONIC SERVICE ASSOCIATION OF THE UNITED STATES BASICALLY STIPULATED THAT IF THE MEMBERSHIP PERFORMANCE TRENDS OF THE LAST THIRTY YEARS WAS ANY INDICATION OF WHERE AMERICAN FREEMASONRY WAS GOING TO BE IN THE FUTURE, ITS OUTLOOK FOR THE YEAR 2000 AND BEYOND WAS BLEAK TO SAY THE LEAST. COINCIDENTLY, BY THE BEGINNING OF THE 1990's, THE MASONIC SUPREME COUNCIL OF THE UNITED STATES OF THE AMERICA'S RESPONDED SWIFTLY BY DEVELOPING A "CALL TO ACTION "PROGRAM. ONE OF THE MAJOR ELEMENTS WAS TO INITIATE A SERIES OF FOCUS GROUP MEETINGS WITH THOSE WHO HAD THE ULTIMATE AUTHORITY AND ACCOUNTABILITY FOR FREEMASONRY WITHIN "OUR JURISDICTION "OF THE WORLD. BY MID-SUMMER 1990, FREEMASONRY WAS UNDER FIRE BY CHRISTIANITY, "OF ANTI-MASONRY HAS CREATED A SMALL STORM WITHIN RELIGIOUS AND FRATERNAL CIRCLES."

NOW YOU MIGHT BE ASKING YOURSELVES AS TO WHAT ANY OF THIS FREEMASONRY INFORMATION HAS TO DO WITH OUR COUNTRY'S NATIVE **RED POWER MOVEMENT** OF THE TWENTIETH CENTURY. WELL TO PUT IT BLUNTLY, THE ANSWER IS RATHER SIMPLE REALLY CONSIDERING THE FACT THAT SIR JOHN A. MACDONALD'S ROYAL NORTH WEST MOUNTED POLICE FORCE WAS MODELED AFTER THE IRISH MOUNTED CONSTABULARY WHO'S MANDATE IT WAS TO KEEP IRELAND UNDER BRITISH PROTESTANT CONTROL. AND SINCE IT WAS ENGLAND'S **GOD** GIVEN RIGHT TO REIGN SUPREME, THE MASONIC CONTROLLED GOVERNMENT OF CANADA ENACTED PIECES OF INDIAN ACT LEGISLATION THAT OF WHICH THE NORTH WEST MOUNTED POLICE (INCLUDING THEIR SUCCESSOR THE RCMP) WERE TO BE UTILIZED AS INDIAN CONTROL AGENTS FOR THE DOMINION OF CANADA, THE POWERS THAT BE CONSTANTLY REFUSING TO TREAT ABORIGINALS AS THEIR SOCIAL EQUAL. AN INDIVIDUAL ALWAYS HAS TO REMEMBER ONE VERY IMPORTANT FACT OF OUR COUNTRY'S INTERESTING HISTORICAL PAST WHEN IT COMES TO THE MASONIC ORDER AND THEIR FRATERNITY, "FREEMASONRY IS NOT A SINGLE-MINDED ORGANIZATION. IT IS A MULTITUDE OF STRUCTURES, GROUPS, AND UNITS THAT ARE TIED TOGETHER BY A COMMON HISTORICAL TRADITION." AFTER HUNDREDS OF YEARS AS AN OPPRESSED PEOPLES IN THE LAND OF WHICH THEY WERE THE ORIGINAL INHABITANTS, THE NATIVE PEOPLES OF CANADA SLOWLY BEGAN STANDING UP IN DEFIANCE OF THEIR CAPTURES. THE CAPTURES ON THE OTHER HAND, HAVING A PHILOSOPHY OF THE ENDS JUSTIFYING THE MEANS THUSLY FELT THREATENED AS VARIOUS NATIVE ORGANIZATIONS WERE INSTANTLY LABELED AS BEING RADICALS, SUBVERSIVES, EXTREMISTS, TERRORISTS, ETC., ETC., ETC.

It should further be noted that many native organizations right across Canada during the 1970's had white advisors that were also under constant surveillance by the RCMP Security Service. This included Melville Watkins, advisor to the Indian Brotherhood of the Northwest Territories and formerly a prominent member of the federal New Democratic Party's "waffle group", a socialist political party membership who kept changing both their policies and minds depending totally upon which way the wind was blowing at the time. Watkins acted as a consultant for the Indian Brotherhood in Yellowknife for two years during the mid-1970's. It was under the authorship of a team of white advisors led by Melville Watkins that the Dene Nation Manifesto of the Northwest Territories for independence was born during the summer of 1975. Apparently, the Manifesto was originally drafted as a discussion paper as a way and means of letting the powers that be in Ottawa know that the Indian population North of 60 were not going to sit idly by allowing the whiteman to continue raping the land of its wealth and pollute the pristine Arctic while chasing that allusive almighty dollar. The Dene, North of the 60TH parallel were essentially putting the Federal Government on notice, letting them know that they (the natives) wanted to govern themselves rather than be controlled by Federal bureaucrats and the racist polices of the Government of Canada under the Indian Act.

Accordingly, the Manifesto was suppose to effectively execute "a peaceful war "that the NWT Indian Brotherhood was initially waging against the Government of Canada and white society in general. "As aboriginal people within a white society," the draft portion stated, "we have been made Canadians by decree and not by our free choice. "The Manifesto then went on to say the following: "The people of the African country, Tanzania, were, like the Dene people, also invaded by a white colonial government. Today they are independent and they say this about development: ' Any action which does not increase the people's say in running their own lives is not development and holds them down, even if the action brings them a little better health and a little more bread '."

Well aware of how their views were regarded by white society up in the Arctic, the offices of the Indian Brotherhood in Yellowknife had posters of Che Guevara splattered all over its walls and field workers representing aboriginal peoples of Canada's northern regions were sent out with copies of Mao Tse-Tung's little red book promoting the Chairman's revolutionary rhetoric. It goes without

SAYING THAT THE RCMP SECURITY SERVICE WAS NOT AT ALL IMPRESSED WITH THE SAD STATE OF AFFAIRS OF **"NATIVE EXTREMISM "**THAT WAS BEING EXERCISED BY THE INDIAN BROTHERHOOD OF THE NORTHWEST TERRITORIES. NOR WERE THEY IMPRESSED WITH THE TACTICS BEING USED BY SUCH YOUNG NATIVE LEADERS AS GEORGE ERASMUS, RICHARD NERYSOO, JAMES WAHSHEE AND GEORGE BARNABY. ALL OF THESE INDIVIDUALS AT ONE TIME /OR ANOTHER WERE EITHER PRESIDENT AND/OR VICE-PRESIDENT OF THE BROTHERHOOD DURING THE 1970'S. ESPECIALLY DISHEARTENING TO THE RCMP WAS THE FACT THAT ONLY WEEKS BEFORE THE INDIAN BROTHERHOOD'S PEACEFUL WAR BEING WAGED AGAINST THE GOVERNMENT OF CANADA, THEY (THE POWERS THAT BE) WERE TAKEN SOMEWHAT OFF GUARD AS A DECREE STATING THE ULTIMATE DEMISE OF THE MAOIST MOVEMENT IN CANADA HAD OCCURRED AND THAT IT WAS IN THE RCMP SECURITY SERVICE'S OWN PROFESSIONAL OPINION THAT THE COMMUNIST REVOLUTIONARY IDEOLOGY OF THE SAID MOVEMENT WAS "NO LONGER CONSIDERED A THREAT."

ON JULY 19^(TH), 1975 THE DENE DECLARATION (STATEMENT OF RIGHTS) WAS PASSED AT THE 2^(ND) JOINT GENERAL ASSEMBLY OF THE INDIAN BROTHERHOOD OF THE NORTHWEST TERRITORIES AND THE METIS ASSOCIATION OF THE NWT AT FORT SIMPSON IN THE NORTHWEST TERRITORIES. THIS IN ESSENCE THREW THE RCMP SECURITY SERVICE IN OTTAWA INTO A COMPLETE TAILSPIN AS ABORIGINALS NORTH OF 60 WERE RE-DEFINING DEMOCRATIC PROCEDURE AND THE PROCESS TO BE USED IN ORDER TO SETTLE THE LAND CLAIMS ISSUE IN THE UNEXPLORED FRONTIER OF THE CANADIAN ARCTIC.

CONTRARY AS TO WHAT MOST WHITE PEOPLE MAY THINK TO BE TRUE, THE DENE OF THE NORTHWEST TERRITORIES HAVE EXISTED FOR THOUSANDS UPON THOUSANDS OF YEARS AND IT WASN'T UNTIL OCTOBER OF 1969 THAT THEY OFFICIALLY FORMED THE INDIAN BROTHERHOOD – IN ACCORDANCE TO THE WHITEMAN'S RULES AND REGULATIONS THAT IS – IN AN ATTEMPT TO SET THE WHEELS IN MOTION TO GOVERN THEMSELVES AS A PEOPLE. ONLY SEVEN YEARS AFTER ITS FIRST CONCEPTION, THE INDIAN BROTHERHOOD SUBMITTED AN AGREEMENT-IN-PRINCIPLE BETWEEN THE DENE NATION AND THE GOVERNMENT OF CANADA WHICH READ IN PART: "THE DENE HAVE THE RIGHT TO RECOGNITION, SELF-DETERMINATION, AND ON-GOING GROWTH AND DEVELOPMENT AS A PEOPLE AND AS A NATION."

THE AGREEMENT-IN-PRINCIPLE WENT ON TO RE-DEFINE THE TERMS IN WHICH, "THE DENE, AS ABORIGINAL PEOPLE, HAVE THE RIGHT TO RETAIN OWNERSHIP OF SO MUCH OF THEIR TRADITIONAL LANDS, AND UNDER SUCH TERMS, AS TO ENSURE THEIR INDEPENDENCE AND SELF-RELIANCE, TRADITIONALLY, ECONOMICALLY AND SOCIALLY, AND THE MAINTENANCE OF WHATEVER OTHER RIGHTS THEY HAVE, WHETHER SPECIFIED IN THIS AGREEMENT OR NOT. "FURTHER STIPULATED IN THIS WRITTEN AGREEMENT WERE THE

TERMS FOR WHICH THE GOVERNMENT OF CANADA WAS TO COMPENSATE THE DENE PEOPLE FOR PAST USAGE OF DENE LANDS BY NON-DENE LIVING NORTH OF THE 60TH PARALLEL AND THAT THE SAID GOVERNMENT OF CANADA "WILL FINANCE THE ESTABLISHMENT OF NEW DENE COMMUNITIES IN CASES WHERE EXISTING COMMUNITIES ARE INHABITED BY SIGNIFICANT NUMBERS OF NON-DENE AND A SIGNIFICANT PROPORTION OF THE DENE COMMUNITY WISHES TO RE-ESTABLISH THEMSELVES ELSEWHERE."

NEEDLESS TO SAY, THE INDIAN BROTHERHOOD OF THE NORTHWEST TERRITORIES HAD THE CANADIAN FEDERAL GOVERNMENT BY THE SHORT HAIRS AND WERE NOT PREPARED TO LET GO AS THEY SLOWLY BEGAN SQUEEZING OTTAWA'S GONADS INTO SUBMISSION.

INTERESTINGLY ENOUGH, WHILE BRITISH COLUMBIA RESIDENT BENOIT J. LEPAGE WAS WAITING TO OBTAIN A PHOTO-COPY OF THE RCMP'S HIGHLY CONTROVERSIAL 1975 SURVEILLANCE REPORT **"RED POWER - CANADA"** FROM THE NATIONAL ARCHIVES IN OTTAWA, THE CHEAM INDIAN BAND OF THAT PROVINCE'S UPPER FRASER VALLEY REGION BEGAN HOSTILE NEGOTIATIONS WITH THE GOVERNMENT OF B.C. AS A DISPUTE OVER LAND USE IN THE ROSEDALE-AGASSIZ AREA ERUPTED AROUND AN INTERSECTION OF A MAJOR HIGHWAY THAT OF WHICH NATIVES WERE THREATENING TO BLOCKADE IF GOVERNMENT AUTHORITIES REFUSED TO ARRIVE AT A REASONABLE AGREEMENT FOR COMPENSATION OF LANDS STOLEN BY THE POWERS THAT BE, MANY, MANY YEARS PREVIOUSLY. THE LAND DISPUTE ISSUE IN QUESTION APPARENTLY WENT BACK SOME 40-PLUS YEARS, (1953), AS VARIOUS PROVINCIAL GOVERNMENTS OF DAYS-GONE-BY KEPT STALLING IN ATTEMPTS NOT TO RESOLVE THE LAND CLAIMS ISSUE. WEARING ARMY CAMOUFLAGED BATTLE FATIGUES, MORE THAN A DOZEN WARRIORS FIRST SHUT OFF ROAD ACCESS TO ALL FORMS OF VEHICLE TRAFFIC USING A SECONDARY ROAD THAT PASSED THROUGH THEIR LANDS WHICH CONNECTED THE COMMUNITIES OF AGASSIZ AND CHILLIWACK TO ONE ANOTHER, A SCENIC ROUTE USED BY AT LEAST 40 TO 50 VEHICLES A DAY.

THEN, DURING THE EASTER WEEKEND OF APRIL 2000, TENSIONS MOUNTED ON THE BLOCKADE AS A LEAKED PROVINCIAL GOVERNMENT MEMO MADE ITS WAY INTO THE HANDS OF THE CHEAM BAND CHIEF. THE MEMO, COMING FROM A VERY RELIABLE SOURCE FROM WITHIN THE ABORIGINAL AFFAIRS MINISTRY OF THE NDP GOVERNMENT SUGGESTED THAT THE THEN-PREMIER OF THE PROVINCE, UJJAL DOSANJH WAS TOTALLY PREPARED TO USE THE BLOCKAGE AS A CONFRONTATIONAL TOOL FOR IMPROVING THE GOVERNMENT'S SAGGING APPROVAL RATINGS AS A WAY AND MEANS OF BEING RE-ELECTED IN THE UPCOMING GENERAL ELECTION STATED TO TAKE PLACE SOMETIME DURING THE SPRING OF 2001. THE PREMIER'S OFFICE WAS OBVIOUSLY PREPARED TO MAKE AN EXAMPLE OF THE CHEAM FIRST NATION PEOPLES AS DOSANJH HIMSELF TOOK MUCH PRIDE IN TAKING A TOUGH APPROACH WITH PROTESTERS AS ATTORNEY-

GENERAL OF BRITISH COLUMBIA DURING THE MONTH-LONG STAND-OFF AT GUSTAFSEN LAKE NEAR 100 MILE HOUSE ONLY FIVE YEARS PREVIOUSLY.

NATURALLY, THE POWERS THAT BE IN VICTORIA DENIED KNOWING ANYTHING OF THE MEMO'S ACTUAL EXISTENCE AS WELL AS ITS POINT OF ORIGIN. TO THOSE MANNING THE BLOCKADE, THE LEAKING OF THE GOVERNMENTAL MEMO WAS MERELY A TACTIC OF MANIPULATION BEING USED BY THE SOCIALIST GOVERNMENT THAT OF WHICH WAS DESIGNED TO HAVE A TWOFOLD EFFECT. ONE BEING OF COURSE, THE USING OF THE NATIVE BLOCKADE AS PAWNS IN DOSANJH'S PLAN OF RAISING THE NDP'S POPULARITY WITH THE VOTERS AND THE SECOND, BEING AN ATTEMPT TO SCARE OFF THE DISSENTIENT INDIANS FOR STANDING THEIR GROUND IN DEFIANCE TO WHITE GOVERNMENTAL POLICY OF NOT WANTING TO SETTLE THE LAND CLAIMS ISSUE WITHIN THE PROVINCE OF BRITISH COLUMBIA. LIKE THE MANY WARS OF BLOODSHED LAUNCHED AGAINST THE NATIVE PEOPLES OF NORTH AMERICA BY WHITE SOCIETY OF YEARS PAST, ABORIGINALS THROUGHOUT BRITISH COLUMBIA BANNED TOGETHER LENDING THEIR MORAL AND FINANCIAL SUPPORT BEHIND THE CHEAM INDIAN BAND'S BLOCKADE AGAINST THEIR OPPRESSORS AS THE PARTICIPANTS PREPARED THEMSELVES FOR A LONG DRAWN OUT STAND-OFF THAT QUITE POSSIBLY WOULD LEAD TO MORE BLOODSHED ON THE FRONTLINES OF THE BLOCKADE ITSELF. THE PREMIER'S OFFICE ON THE OTHER HAND, REITERATED TIME AND TIME AGAIN THAT NO FURTHER NEGOTIATIONS WERE TO TAKE PLACE AS LONG AS THE BLOCKADE REMAINED INTACT.

ACCORDINGLY, THE NDP PROVINCIAL GOVERNMENT VIEWED THE MILITANT ACTIONS OF THE CHEAM FIRST NATION PEOPLES AS AN ACT OF TERRORISM AGAINST ALL PEOPLES OF BRITISH COLUMBIA AND STEADFAST REFUSED TO NEGOTIATE UNTIL THE NATIVES SURRENDERED TO DEMANDS OF THE POWERS THAT BE. AFTERALL, HISTORY WAS BELIEVED TO HAVE PROVEN OVER AND OVER THAT ABORIGINAL PEOPLES OF CANADA WERE FAR MORE INFERIOR THAN ANY OTHER RACE OF PEOPLE LIVING ON THE NORTH AMERICAN CONTINENT – WITH THE EXCEPTION OF THE BLACKS OF COURSE. DUE TO THE FACT THAT BOTH CSIS AND THE RCMP DIDN'T LIKE THE IDEA OF MEDIA OUTLETS LENDING SUPPORT TO THE ABORIGINAL CAUSE OF WANTING THE NATIVE LAND CLAIMS ISSUE RESOLVED EXPEDITIOUSLY, AS ANY FURTHER NEWS COVERAGE CONCERNING THE BLOCKADE ITSELF WOULD HAVE CAUSED THE "SLEEPERS" TO WAKE UP AND SHAKE THEIR HEADS IN TOTAL DISBELIEF, A BASIS FUNDAMENTAL NEWS BLACKOUT WAS IMPLEMENTED UNTIL THE INDIAN MILITANTS MANNING THE BLOCKADE AGREED TO DISBURSE.

WHILE ALL OF THIS WAS UNFOLDING DURING THE MONTH OF APRIL IN THE YEAR 2000, THE TOPIC OF THE DAY IN GIBSONS LIKE ANY OTHER COMMUNITY IN THE PROVINCE OF BRITISH COLUMBIA WAS CONCERNING THE ACTIONS OF THOSE ON THE BLOCKADE ITSELF – TO THE VAST MAJORITY OF THAT COMMUNITY'S

WHITE POPULATION, THE NATIVE RADICALS RESPONSIBLE FOR ERECTING AND MAINTAINING THE BLOCKADE SHOULD HAVE BEEN EITHER THROWN IN JAIL / OR SHOT ON THE SPOT. Knowing that he had passionate feelings about Canada's aboriginal people and their plight, anytime Benoit LePage walked into one of that community's coffee shops and the blockade was being discussed freely by the establishment's clientele, Gibsons residents would look directly at him voicing their opinion of the blockade. Bitting down on his tongue, he'd simply smile, not saying a word about anything as he quietly sipped on his coffee because when it came down to expressing his own personal opinion on any topic — perceived as a know-it-all by most of its residents — no one in Gibsons really wanted to hear anything that he had to say; especially when it came to the oppression of aboriginals by white society.

Seven weeks after the Cheam First Nation Peoples first blocked road access to local traffic on the secondary road that passed through their lands, LePage received word from the National Archives of Canada stating that the report he had requested could not be found anywhere in the Federal Government archives. This in itself was by no means a surprise to him, even though he had furnished archival researchers with the proper reference numbers to help locate the requested report. It was apparent to the author of the Access to Information Request Form that the powers that be were hiding behind a thin veil of secrecy as the surveillance report contained very specific pieces of documentation that revealed as to how paranoid and threatened the RCMP actually were when it came to Canada's First Nation Peoples and what lay ahead for the whiteman if all of the country's land claim issues were to be settled.

Curious as old hell as to how he was going to be able to actually obtain a photo-copy of this somewhat non-existent report, LePage purchased a 750 ml bottle of Lamb's Navy Rum (26 oz) and began searching the recesses of his mind for a possible solution to the dilemma. While in a slightly intoxicated state, he remembered while living up in the Arctic during the early 1980's reading a couple of old northern newspapers from the mid-1970's, (News of the North and the Yellowknifer), where delegates from the Indian Brotherhood had attended some sort of United Nations conference in Geneva during the summer of 1975 /or thereabouts. A few days later, he was faced with another piece of startling information as the powers that be in Ottawa then began insisting that the report requested **"RED POWER - CANADA""** did not exist. In their haste to defuse

THE PUSHY/ARROGANT ANTICS OF THE PERSON REQUESTING A PHOTO-COPY OF THE SAID STATED NON-EXISTENT REPORT, AN INVESTIGATING OFFICER FOR THE FEDERAL GOVERNMENT'S OFFICE OF THE INFORMATION COMMISSIONER INADVERTENTLY RESPONDED TO BENOIT'S MARCH 10TH, 2000 COMPLAINT OF CSIS NOT FULFILLING HIS QUEST FOR DATA BY MAILING HIM PHOTO-COPIES OF THREE NEWSPAPER ARTICLES DATING BACK TO AUGUST 7TH, 1975, (GLOBE AND MAIL, OTTAWA JOURNAL AS WELL AS AN UNNAMED MONTREAL NEWSPAPER), WHICH UNBEKNOWNST TO THEM WOULD SET THE GIBSONS SHIT DISTURBER OFF ONTO YET ANOTHER VERY INTERESTING PATH OF DISCOVERY.

ACCORDING TO ONE OF THE PHOTO-COPIED NEWSPAPER ARTICLES THAT THE OFFICE OF THE INFORMATION COMMISSIONER OF CANADA HAD SENT HIM, THE REPORT **"PRIORITIES IN POLICING - TERRORISM AND V.I.P. SECURITY** "WAS SUPPOSEDLY A CONFIDENTIAL REPORT THAT WAS PREPARED BY THE RCMP SECURITY SERVICE FOR THE OFFICE OF THE SOLICITOR-GENERAL OF CANADA WHICH WAS LATER TO BE SUBMITTED TO THE UNITED NATIONS FOR IN-DEPTH DISCUSSIONS AT THEIR INTERNATIONAL CRIME PREVENTION CONFERENCE IN GENEVA DURING THE MONTH OF SEPTEMBER 1975, (THE FIFTH CONGRESS ON CRIME PREVENTION). OTHER THAN THE HIGH RATES OF CRIME ON A GLOBAL SCALE, THE UNITED NATIONS CONFERENCE DELEGATES WERE ALSO SCHEDULED TO DISCUSS WAYS OF DEALING WITH SUCH ISSUES ASSOCIATED WITH DOMESTIC TERRORISM FROM WITHIN A COUNTRY'S OWN MILITANT POPULATION (NATIVE AS WELL AS NON-NATIVE). THE SAID STATED CONFIDENTIAL DOCUMENT WAS SUPPOSEDLY TO MAKE ITS DEBUT DURING A SCHEDULED UNITED NATIONS SUMMER 1975 CRIME CONFERENCE IN TORONTO, ONTARIO BUT PORTIONS OF ITS CONTENTS WERE MYSTERIOUSLY LEAKED TO THE NEWS MEDIA BEFOREHAND WHICH COINCIDENTLY CAUSED THE RCMP NOT ONLY MUCH EMBARRASSMENT BUT ALSO FORCED THEM INTO DAMAGE CONTROL MODE ALL AT THE SAME TIME.

AN OTTAWA RCMP SPOKESMAN, INSPECTOR JOHN POIRIER PUBLICALLY DENOUNCED THE CONTENTS OF THE REPORT ON AUGUST 6TH, 1975 STATING THAT THE RED POWER MOVEMENT POSED TO INITIAL THREAT TO CANADIAN SECURITY AND FURTHER DEEMED THE REPORT'S TERMINOLOGY AS BEING INACCURATE. POIRIER INTERESTINGLY ENOUGH ALSO DENOUNCED THE MONTREAL NEWPAPER'S ALLEGATIONS OF THE REPORT BEING A CONFIDENTIAL DOCUMENT CALLING IT "TOTALLY FALSE."

IN HIS ATTEMPT TO DOWN PLAY THE SERIOUSNESS OF THE REPORT'S CONTENTS AND ITS CONFIDENTIALITY, RCMP INSPECTOR POIRIER FURTHER STATED THAT THE REPORT ITSELF WAS INTENDED TO DEMONSTRATE TO THE UNITED NATIONS THAT THE CANADIAN INDIAN DRIVE FOR MORE EQUITABLE TREATMENT WAS POLITICALLY MOTIVATED AND THEREFORE A POLITICAL ISSUE THAT SHOULD BE ADDRESSED BY THE POLITICIANS AND NOT THE RCMP AND

THEIR DESIGNATED MANDATE. THE RCMP WERE OBVIOUSLY ATTEMPTING TO WHITEWASH NOT ONLY THE CONTENTS OF THE REPORT BUT ALSO OF THE FACT AS TO THEIR ROLE AS INDIAN CONTROL AGENTS FOR THE CANADIAN FEDERAL GOVERNMENT AS THE UNITED NATIONS MORE THAN LIKELY WOULD HAVE HAD LOTS TO SAY ABOUT IT — ESPECIALLY NOW SINCE THE REPORT'S CONTENTS WERE MADE PUBLIC. TO FURTHER ENHANCE THE FALSENESS OF THE REPORT'S CONTENTS, POIRIER ALSO STATED PUBLICALLY THAT THE REPORT ITSELF WAS BASED ON SPECULATION AND THAT THEY (THE RCMP) HAD NO REAL HARD EVIDENCE TO BACK-UP AS TO WHAT THE REPORT WAS ESSENTIALLY SAYING.

EVEN THE CANADIAN FEDERAL GOVERNMENT GOT IN ON THE ACT BY DENOUNCING THE RCMP'S ACTIONS FOR JUMPING THE GUN AS IT WERE — A REPRESENTATIVE FOR THE SOLICITOR-GENERAL OF CANADA IN 1975 STATED THAT CONTRARY AS TO WHAT THE RCMP DOCUMENT MAY HAVE STATED / OR IMPLIED ABOUT INDIAN MILITANTS STOCKPILING WEAPONS, SOMETHING THAT OF WHICH THE SOLICITOR-GENERAL'S OFFICE HAD BEEN PREVIOUSLY INFORMED ABOUT BY THE RCMP; "THERE IS NO KNOWN CACHE OF WEAPONS. NO SUCH CACHE HAS EVER BEEN FOUND, OR EVIDENCE OF ONE. THAT IS SPECULATION."

THE SITUATION THEN WENT FROM BAD TO WORSE FOR THE RCMP AS NATIONAL COVERAGE OF THE SOMEWHAT CONTROVERSIAL REPORT GAINED MORE AND MORE NOTORIETY AS MEDIA OUTLETS THROUGHOUT NORTH AMERICA PICKED UP ON THE STORY BROADCASTING IT WORLDWIDE. TO MOST CANADIAN ABORIGINALS WHO REMEMBERED HEARING THE NEWS OVER A QUARTER CENTURY AGO, IT BECAME KNOWN TO THEM AS THE GREATEST RCMP BLUNDER OF THE TWENTIETH CENTURY — AN RCMP PUBLIC RELATIONS NIGHTMARE THAT HAD ESSENTIALLY BACKFIRED NOT ONLY BECAUSE OF THE RCMP'S INCOMPETENCE BUT ALSO DUE TO THEIR OWN PERSONAL BIGOTRY TOWARDS CANADA'S FIRST NATION PEOPLES AND THE NATIVE VISION QUEST FOR JUSTICE AND FAIR TREATMENT UNDER CANADIAN LAW.

IN PREPARATION FOR THE UNITED NATIONS' IN-DEPTH DISCUSSION ON DOMESTIC TERRORISM AT THE GENEVA CONFERENCE, THE RCMP IRONICALLY COMPILED SEVEN SPECIFIC REPORTS ON POSSIBLE THREATS TO CANADIAN SECURITY. REPORTS THAT OF WHICH THEY, (THE RCMP), DEEMED TO BE MERELY WORKING PAPERS IN PROGRESS THAT WERE TO BE SUPPOSEDLY RELEASED TO THE MEDIA FOR PUBLIC SCRUTINY AS SURVEILLANCE OF THESE GROUPS HAD BEEN AN ONGOING THING. THE INDIAN MILITANT ISSUE ENCLOSED IN THE REPORT "PRIORITIES IN POLICING - TERRORISM AND V.I.P. SECURITY" INTERESTINGLY ENOUGH ONLY TOOK UP THREE-QUARTERS OF A PAGE IN THAT ONE SPECIFIC REPORT OF WHICH RCMP INSPECTOR POIRIER WAS REFERRING TOO. OBVIOUSLY, THE **"RED POWER - CANADA"** REPORT WAS ONE OF THOSE SO-CALLED WORKING PAPERS IN PROGRESS AS IT WENT INTO MUCH

GREATER DETAIL BACKING UP THE CONTENTS OF THE SPECULATIVE REPORT SINCE IT INITIALLY WAS TO BE PART AND PARCEL OF AN ORAL PRESENTATION BY CANADIAN AUTHORITIES TO THE UNITED NATIONS. IN FACT POIRIER HIMSELF OPENLY ADMITTED TO THE MEDIA (MONTREAL'S UNNAMED NEWSPAPER) THAT THE **"PRIORITIES IN POLICING - TERRORISM AND V.I.P. SECURITY** "REPORT "COULD NOT STAND ALONE "AS IT CONTAINED SOME "BROAD SWEEPING STATEMENTS."

IN CROSS REFERENCING VARIOUS NAMES OF THE ABORIGINAL COMMUNITY AS BEING POSSIBLE DELEGATES TO THE UNITED NATIONS' IN-DEPTH DISCUSSIONS OF DOMESTIC TERRORISM, IT BECOMES ABUNDANTLY CLEAR THAT CANADA'S NATIVE POPULATION DID IN FACT HAVE LEGAL REPRESENTATION AT THE 1975 GENEVA CONFERENCE. PERHAPS THIS IS WHY A GOOD PORTION OF THE NATIVE PEOPLES LIVING NORTH OF THE 60TH PARALLEL WERE WELL AWARE OF THE ACTUAL EXISTENCE OF THE **"RED POWER - CANADA"** REPORT CONTRARY AS TO WHAT CSIS WANTED THE GIBSONS, B.C. RESIDENT TO BELIEVE WAS TRUE. FOR MANY, MANY YEARS, (1930'S THROUGH TO THE 1990'S), NORTHERN NATIVES (INDIAN AS WELL AS ESKIMO AND METIS) COMPARED THE NORTHWEST TERRITORIES TO THAT OF THE BLACK PEOPLES SITUATION IN SOUTH AFRICA WHERE WHITE GOVERNMENT AND WHITE SOCIETY IN GENERAL CONTROLLED EVERYTHING, INCLUDING ALL OF THE GOOD PAYING JOBS AS WELL AS ALL PROSPECTS OF SELF-DETERMINATION AND HOME-RULE. TO THOSE ABORIGINALS WHO KNEW THE EXISTENCE OF THE **"RED POWER - CANADA"** REPORT, IT SIMPLY CONFIRMED THE FACT THAT OF WHITE GOVERNMENTAL DISCRIMINATION AGAINST ALL NATIVE PEOPLES OF CANADA. SOMETHING THAT OF WHICH THE UNITED NATIONS WOULD MOST LIKELY NOT HAVE TOLERATED IF THEY WERE TO BECOME MADE AWARE OF CANADA'S APARTHEID SYSTEM THAT WAS BEING REINFORCED WITH RCMP SURVEILLANCE ON ALL SO-CALLED SUBVERSIVE/ RADICAL **"NATIVE EXTREMISM** "AND THEIR WHITE SYMPATHIZERS BY CANADIAN FEDERAL GOVERNMENT FRATERNAL SANCTIONS.

NOT ONLY CANADIAN ABORIGINALS WERE UNDER CONSTANT SURVEILLANCE BY THE RCMP, AMERICAN NATIVES WERE AS WELL AS SOON AS THEY CROSSED THE CANADA-U.S. BORDER. RUSSELL MEANS AND DENNIS BANKS, THE FORMER LEADERS OF THE AMERICAN INDIAN MOVEMENT WHO HELPED EXECUTE THE ARMED TAKE-OVER OF A TINY INDIAN VILLAGE KNOWN AS WOUNDED KNEE, ON THE OGLALA SIOUX PINE RIDGE RESERVATION IN SOUTH DAKOTA, (THE SITE OF THE MASSACRE OF 300 INDIANS BY U.S. CAVALRY FORCES IN DECEMBER OF 1890), WERE PRIME CANDIDATES FOR SURVEILLANCE AS FAR AS THE RCMP SECURITY SERVICE WAS CONCERNED. THE SIEGE AT WOUNDED KNEE TOOK PLACE IN AN ATTEMPT TO OVERTHROW A CORRUPT TRIBAL CHIEF, THE SIEGE LASTED TEN WEEKS AND BEGAN TO UNFOLD ITSELF ON FEBRUARY 27TH, 1973 AS WELL OVER 200 ARMED A.I.M. SUPPORTERS CAPTURED THE SETTLEMENT

TAKING ELEVEN HOSTAGES WHO LIVED IN AND AROUND THE AREA. ALTHOUGH THE HOSTAGES WERE RELEASED ONLY DAYS LATER (MARCH 1ST), THE INSURRECTION OF WOUNDED KNEE LASTED UNTIL MAY 8TH WHEN ALL OF THE REMAINING RENEGADE INDIANS (ABOUT 120 OF THEM) SURRENDERED TO U.S. FEDERAL AGENTS. DURING THE SEVENTY-DAY STAND-OFF, ONE ABORIGINAL WAS SHOT AND TWO FBI AGENTS WERE DEAD.

THE AMERICAN INDIAN MOVEMENT LEADERS PROMPTLY STATED THAT THE 1973 SIEGE OF WOUNDED KNEE WAS THEIR WAY OF DRAWING ATTENTION TO THE CONTINUED MISTREATMENT OF ALL ABORIGINALS BY THE U.S. FEDERAL GOVERNMENT; POOR LIVING CONDITIONS ON THE RESERVATION DUE TO THE LACK OF EDUCATION, EMPLOYMENT AND HOUSING, BROKEN TREATIES AND THE LOSS OF LANDS STOLEN FROM THEM BY THE WHITEMAN. RUSSELL MEANS WAS INDITED ON MAY 2ND, 1973 FOR ALLEGEDLY TRANSPORTING ARMS ACROSS STATE LINES FOR THE SOLE PURPOSE OF INCITING A RIOT. LATER, U.S. FEDERAL AGENTS WOULD LAY ADDITIONAL CHARGES. BOTH RUSSELL MEANS AND DENNIS BANKS WERE SUBSEQUENTLY INDITED AND BROUGHT TO TRIAL IN SAINT PAUL, MINNESOTA ON CHARGES OF ASSAULT, LARCENY AND CONSPIRACY. THE TRIAL, LASTING EIGHT LONG MONTHS FAILED TO CONVICT THE TWO MEN AND THEY WERE FREED IN SEPTEMBER OF 1974 AFTER A UNITED STATES DISTRICT JUDGE, (JUDGE FRED NICHOL), DISMISSED ALL CHARGES LAID AGAINST THEM ARISING FROM THE OCCUPATION OF WOUNDED KNEE. APPARENTLY, THE INSURRECTION HAD PROVEN ITSELF TO BE THAT OF A JUST CAUSE AND FEDERAL AUTHORITIES COULDN'T PROVE OTHERWISE. LEONARD PELTIER ON THE OTHER HAND WASN'T SO LUCKY AS HE HAD BEEN CHARGED AND CONVICTED OF MURDERING TWO FBI AGENTS (RAY WILLIAMS AND JACK COLER), AND WAS SENTENCED TO LIFE IN PRISON. PELTIER WAS ALSO A PROMINENT NATIVE LEADER WITH A.I.M., AFTER BEING CHARGED IN THE DEATHS OF THE TWO AGENTS HE FLED TO CANADA AND WAS LATER EXTRADITED BACK TO THE U.S.

A CANADIAN INDIAN WOMAN, ANNA MAE PICTOU-AQUASH REPORTEDLY ALSO PLAYED AN IMPORTANT ROLE IN THE AMERICAN INDIAN MOVEMENT AS SHE QUICKLY ROSE UP THROUGH THE RANKS IN THE 1970'S AND WAS UNDER CONSTANT SURVEILLANCE BY THE RCMP'S SECURITY SERVICE ANYTIME SHE RE-ENTERED CANADA. ANNA MAE WAS AN INDIAN WARRIOR OF SORTS AS SHE PARTICIPATED AT THE WOUNDED KNEE INSURRECTION BUT WAS SHOT DEAD ON A RISE OF LAND WHERE THE PRAIRIE MEETS THE INHOSPITABLE BADLANDS OF SOUTH DAKOTA IN DECEMBER OF 1975 WHEN A .32-CALIBER BULLET RIPPED THROUGH HER SKULL. THE THIRTY-YEAR-OLD MI'KMAQ ACTIVIST WAS SHOT EXECUTION-STYLE, IN THE BACK OF THE HEAD. HER EXECUTIONER (S), THEN LEFT HER BODY AT THE BOTTOM OF THE STEEP RIDGE WHERE IT REMAINED FOR MANY, MANY DAYS AND WAS TOTALLY UNRECOGNIZABLE WHEN FOUND. IRONICALLY, THE NOVA SCOTIA BORN NATIVE WOMAN USED THE PLIGHT OF

THE AMERICAN INDIAN AS A CATALYST TO EXPOSE THE MANY HORRORS OF BEING AN INDIAN IN A WHITEMAN'S WORLD BUT LITTLE DID SHE REALIZE THE DANGEROUS PATH THAT SHE WAS ON WOULD END HER LIFE AT SUCH A VERY YOUNG AGE. TO THOSE INDIVIDUALS WHO KNEW HER THE MOST, RUSSELL MEANS AND OTHERS, THEY FIRMLY BELIEVED THAT ANNA MAE PICTOU-AQUASH MAY HAVE BEEN MISTAKENLY IDENTIFIED AS BEING AN INFORMANT FOR THE FBI REGARDING THE SHOOTING DEATHS OF TWO FBI AGENTS DURING A SHOOTOUT BETWEEN AUTHORITIES AND A.I.M. MEMBERS THAT HAD OCCURRED PRIOR TO HER DEMISE AND WAS EVENTUALLY EXECUTED BY HER OWN PEERS.

NEEDLESS TO SAY, CANADIAN AUTHORITIES NORTH OF THE 49TH PARALLEL DIDN'T WANT ANOTHER ANNA MAE PICTOU-AQUASH TYPE EXECUTION-STYLE DEATH TO OCCUR AS THEY FEARED THE WORST FOR OUR COUNTRY AND COMPLIED DOCUMENTATION AFTER DOCUMENTATION THAT WAS TO BE THE MAIN COMPONENT OF THE **"RED POWER - CANADA"** SURVEILLANCE REPORT OVER ITS PROJECTED COURSE OF TIME. THE HIGHLY CONTROVERSIAL SO-CALLED NON-EXISTENT 1975 REPORT ITSELF HAD A DESIGNATION OF BEING PIECEMEAL AUTOMATICALLY ATTACHED IT – MAKING ITS WAY TO THE NATIONAL ARCHIVES OF CANADA NEVER TO SEE THE LIGHT OF DAY IN COMPLETE TACT. ALTHOUGH LEPAGE HAD THE PROPER REFERENCE AND/OR CATALOGUE NUMBERS TO HELP OBTAIN A PHOTO-COPY OF THE SAID REPORT, IT PROVED TO BE TOTALLY FUTILE AS CSIS KEPT INSISTING THAT HE HAD THE WRONG NAME OF THE REPORT ORIGINALLY REQUESTED WHILE ARCHIVAL RESEARCHERS LOOKED HIGH AND LOW IN THE MOUNTAINS OF ARCHIVAL DOCUMENTATION BUT STILL COULDN'T FIND ANY TRACE OF IT IN THEIR DESIGNATED LOCATIONS ASSOCIATED WITH THE SAID REFERENCE AND/OR CATALOGUE NUMBERS. DUE TO THE FACT THAT THE POWERS THAT BE WERE CONTINUALLY HIDING BEHIND A THIN VEIL OF SECRECY, A MORE RADICAL APPROACH TO THE SITUATION HAD TO BE EXECUTED DURING THE SUMMER MONTHS OF THE YEAR 2000 IN ORDER TO OBTAIN A COPY OF THE SAID STATED NON-EXISTENT REPORT FOR HIS RESEARCH STUDIES.

NOT TAKING "NO "FOR AN ANSWER AS TO WHY THE REPORT COULDN'T BE FOUND, HE ENLISTED THE SERVICES OF B.C.'S UNITED NATIVE NATIONS AND OTHER ABORIGINAL ORGANIZATIONS SUCH AS THE ASSEMBLY OF FIRST NATIONS LOCATED IN THE COUNTRY'S NATIONAL CAPITAL CITY OF OTTAWA. HELL, HE EVEN WENT SO FAR AS TO DEMAND A FULL REVIEW AS TO WHY CANADA'S OWN SPY AGENCY CSIS REFUSED TO FULFILL HIS REQUEST FOR A PHOTO-COPY OF THE EXTREMELY CONTROVERSIAL NON-EXISTENT REPORT, (FEDERAL COURT OF CANADA VIA THE SOLICITOR-GENERAL OF CANADA AS WELL AS OTTAWA'S SECURITY INTELLIGENCE REVIEW COMMITTEE). HIS ONLY RECOURSE TO GET THE INFORMATION THAT HE WAS SEEKING WAS THROUGH THE FEDERAL COURT FOR A REVIEW OF THE MATTER INVESTIGATED BY THE CANADIAN

Security Intelligence Service as he had been advised to do so by the Information Commissioner's Office. A procedure that of which had no guarantee of him actually receiving the documentation being requested even after dishing out large amounts of money for lawyer fees, etc., etc. It was obvious to the Gibsons shit disturber that CSIS and those withholding the highly volatile document were using the judicial system for their own advantage by stonewalling him every step of the way.

Well aware that his pushy/arrogant self-righteous tactics wouldn't accomplish anything, he forged onwards despite this little known factor as he had already come to the conclusion that it was an unobtainable commodity through proper governmental channels and therefore, had no other alternative but to adopt a totally unconventional means of achieving his goal. A letter to the United Nations in New York City was promptly submitted in August of the year 2000 — as were his letters requesting assistance from the aboriginal community to commemorate the occasion of the report's initial birth 25 years previously. Determined to obtain some sort of paper trail of the report's original contents, he even submitted a letter to the governmental wing of the Indian Brotherhood of the Northwest Territories in Yellowknife asking for their help in tracking the report down, (the Dene Nation).

It wasn't until some weeks later that LePage got the shock of his life while thumbing through an old set of 1970's Funk & Wagnalls Encyclopedia looking for something totally unrelated. There it was in plain view for all the world to see on page 397 in the 1976 Yearbook (Events of 1975) describing some of the United Nations' political involvements for that year as they celebrated their 30TH anniversary by becoming the center of media attention worldwide arising from the political/terrorist activities of the Palestine Liberation Organization (P.L.O.) in the Middle East:

> "...the fifth Congress on Crime Prevention, which was to be held in Toronto, **Canada, had to be transferred to Geneva when the Canadian government proposed postponement rather than accept the presence of P.L.O. envoys."**

It was only then that everything came into complete focus as to why the secrecy and the denial of the **"RED POWER - CANADA"** report's actual existence by CSIS and the Solicitor-General's Office. Not only Canada's very own spy agency had lots to hide but so did the Canadian Federal Government. It was largely due to these factors

THAT LePAGE PREPARED HIMSELF FOR THE BAD NEWS THAT HE KNEW WOULD BE FORTHCOMING. EXCEPTING THE FACT THAT THE SAID STATED REPORT WAS GOING TO BE CLASSIFIED AS **TOP SECRET** AND/OR **CONFIDENTIAL** FOR **NATIONAL SECURITY** REASONS, THUS MAKING IT ABSOLUTELY IMPOSSIBLE FOR HIM /OR ANYONE ELSE TO OBTAIN A PHOTO-COPY IN ITS ENTIRETY, BENOIT HOPED THAT HE WAS WRONG. WITH PROSPECTS OF HIS TELEPHONE BEING TAPPED AND MAIL SCANNED, THE GIBSONS, B.C. RESIDENT CONTINUED TO FORGE ONWARDS DESPITE ALL OF THESE POSSIBLE RAMIFICATIONS AND ACCEPTING THE FULL CONSEQUENCES OF HIS OWN ACTIONS, WHATEVER THEY MIGHT BE!!!

AFTER ARRIVING AT THE CONCLUSION THAT THE REPORT **"RED POWER - CANADA"** WAS INDEED GOING TO BE AN UNOBTAINABLE COMMODITY, HE HAD HIGH HOPES THAT THE POSSIBILITY EXISTED THAT PERHAPS THE UNITED NATIONS HAD SOMETHING TO OFFER ON WHAT WAS BEING SOUGHT IN HIS OWN BIRTH COUNTRY. NOT LONG AFTER REQUESTING ASSISTANCE FROM THE UNITED NATIONS IN NEW YORK CITY, AN OVER ABUNDANCE OF INFORMATION WAS SOON AT HIS DISPOSAL FROM THE U.N. CENTER FOR INTERNATIONAL CRIME PREVENTION IN VIENNA, AUSTRIA, EXCLUDING OF COURSE THE **"RED POWER - CANADA"** REPORT. HE NOT ONLY RECEIVED THE ENTIRE CONTENT PACKAGE PERTAINING TO THE 1975 CONFERENCE ITSELF, BUT HE ALSO RECEIVED THE NAMES OF THE PARTICIPANTS AS WELL AS THE LIST OF ITEMS DISCUSSED BY THE DELEGATES AND THEIR RESPECTIVE GOVERNING BODIES.

ACCORDING TO THE DOCUMENTATION INCORPORATED WITHIN THE UNITED NATIONS DATA, ALL FACETS OF CRIME WERE DISCUSSED AT THE CONFERENCE — INCLUDING WHITE COLLAR CRIME AND CORRUPTION, PRICE-FIXING, ILLEGAL MONOPOLY AND ANY OTHER VIOLATIONS OF REGULATORY LAWS THAT WERE INTERPRETED AS BEING PART AND PARCEL OF "ORGANIZED CRIME". EVEN ASPECTS OF CRIMINAL ACTIVITY ASSOCIATED WITH MOTORIZED TRAFFIC (HUMAN SMUGGLING /OR OTHER CONTRABAND) AS WELL AS DRUG AND ALCOHOL RELATED CRIMES — ALL TAKING UP A LARGE PORTION OF THE AGENDA. THE CONFERENCE DELEGATES EVEN WENT SO FAR AS TO RE-DEFINE THE LAW ENFORCEMENT **CODE OF ETHICS** AS WELL AS THE EVER INCREASING ROLE OF THE POLICE IN TERMS OF CRIME PREVENTION AND SOCIAL ACTIVITIES. FURTHER DISCUSSIONS INVOLVED THE ARREST AND DETENTION OF CRIMINALS PERTAINING TO THEIR HUMAN RIGHTS AS SET OUT BY THE UNITED NATIONS. IN FACT, THE TREATMENT OF OFFENDERS AND/OR ALLEGED OFFENDERS WAS DISCUSSED AT LENGTH, ALSO PERTAINING TO THE UNITED NATIONS DEFINITION. IT GOES WITHOUT SAYING THAT THE DISCUSSIONS ON TERRORISM WERE FAR THE MOST INTERESTING OF ALL TOPICS TALKED ABOUT AS DELEGATES UNANIMOUSLY AGREED THAT A MORE CLEAR/CONCISE DEFINITION OF THE WORD HAD TO BE IMPLEMENTED.

In accordance to the documentation obtained from the United Nations Center for International Crime Prevention, the 1975 conference delegates suggested that "terrorism "or "terrorist "as it was then described had three distinctive classifications: "first, acts committed by an individual in an international situation, for instance the unlawful interference with an aircraft in flight, whether intended for personal gain or because of phychopathology; secondly, acts similar to the first but committed by groups; thirdly, acts which appeared similar to the first two but which were committed to further not the private ends of the actors but some cause to which they felt committed. "Other than wanting a clear-cut definition of the word, the participants of the 1975 conference were also in agreement to rid the world of all forms of terrorist activities "but there was also agreement that politically inspired violence, committed for the sake of gaining national independence or ethnic recognition or security, could not be expected to recede until the underlying causes had been satisfactorily dealt with."

In addition to that, the conference delegates also were in "agreement that measures should be studied with a view to strengthening the forces of criminal justice against the first two types of terrorism by (a) extending universal jurisdictions to all such crimes (as already existed in the case of air piracy) — for example, the taking of innocent persons as hostages and attacks against public buildings with explosives — especially if those crimes endangered the lives of innocent persons; (b) strengthening extradition laws and observing them more completely; and (c) strengthening the technical co-operation of agencies such as the International Criminal Police Organization (**INTERPOL**) by increasing both the number of nations participating and the mutual exchange of information."

The attending participants felt so confident in what they had accomplished during the 1975 Geneva conference (September 1-12) concerning domestic and international terrorism that it was proposed that the United Nations also arrange for a commentary on all relevant conventions, (international and/or otherwise), which in essence was to ensure that all in attendance were fully aware of the new scientific and legal definition as interpreted by the delegates.

In total, Canada had 14 governmental delegates, which included Warren Allmand, at the time he was Solicitor-General of Canada and G.W. Pritchett, the then-Assistant Commissioner

OF THE ROYAL CANADIAN MOUNTED POLICE, (THE SOLICITOR-GENERAL WAS REPORTEDLY HEAD OF THE CANADIAN DELEGATION). THERE WERE ALSO WELL OVER 40 INDIVIDUAL PARTICIPANTS REPRESENTING CANADA AS A WHOLE AT THE CONFERENCE – THEY INCLUDED OTHER GOVERNMENTAL BODIES AS WELL AS WORLDWIDE RECOGNIZED NON-PROFIT ORGANIZATIONS SUCH AS *THE SALVATION ARMY, THE JOHN HOWARD SOCIETY AND THE SEVEN STEP SOCIETY.* ALL THREE OF THESE NON-PROFIT ORGANIZATIONS HAD A VERY STRONG DEDICATED NATIVE FOLLOWING IN BOTH THE NORTHWEST TERRITORIES AND THE YUKON AT THE TIME OF THE GENEVA CONFERENCE, ESPECIALLY IN YELLOWKNIFE. ALL OF THOSE INDIVIDUALS WHO PARTICIPATED AT THE 1975 GENEVA CONFERENCE WERE PERSONS ASSOCIATED WITH ABORIGINAL RIGHTS TO SELF-DETERMINATION; GARY YOUNGMAN FOR EXAMPLE AT THE TIME WAS AN ABORIGINAL RIGHTS LAW STUDENT AND EXECUTIVE ASSISTANT FOR BRITISH COLUMBIA'S NATIVE COURTWORKERS COUNSELING ASSOCIATION (VANCOUVER). AFTER ATTENDING THE CONFERENCE, THE YOUNG INEXPERIENCED LAW STUDENT WENT ON TO BECOME ONE OF BRITISH COLUMBIA'S MOST LEADING EXPERTS IN THE FIELD OF ABORIGINAL RIGHTS AS HE DEALT STRICTLY WITH ASPECTS OF TREATY NEGOTIATIONS AND SUCH FOR THE PROVINCE'S NATIVE PEOPLES.

IN YET ANOTHER TWIST OF IRONY, ITS ALSO INTERESTING TO NOTE THAT FEDERALLY, CANADA'S ABORIGINAL PEOPLES WERE REPRESENTED BY ISSER SMITH – THEN WITH THE SOCIAL SERVICES DIVISION OF INDIAN AND ESKIMO AFFAIRS PROGRAM FOR THE CANADIAN GOVERNMENT IN OTTAWA. OBVIOUSLY, THE FEDERAL GOVERNMENT WANTED TO MAKE IT PUBLIC AT THE UNITED NATIONS CONFERENCE THAT THEY WERE NOT WILLING TO ADHERE TO ANY FORM OF DEGRADATION EXPRESSED BY **"NATIVE EXTREMIST "**THAT THE ABORIGINAL COMMUNITY AND THEIR INDIAN BROTHERHOODS MAY HAVE HAD HOPED TO EXECUTE AT THE CONFERENCE ITSELF – LIKE THE WELL PUBLICIZED LEAKED REPORT **"PRIORITIES IN POLICING - TERRORISM AND V.I.P. SECURITY "**ONE CAN ONLY SPECULATE AS TO WHAT THE CANADIAN FEDERAL GOVERNMENT WAS ACTUALLY UP TOO.

BUT ONCE FURTHER INVESTIGATION INTO THE LIST OF INDIVIDUAL PARTICIPANTS IS ANALYZED WITH AN OPEN MIND, IT ISN'T LONG BEFORE A PERSON BEGINS TO FULLY REALIZE THAT SOMETHING ELSE WAS AT PLAY HERE. FOR EXAMPLE, ALSO IN ATTENDANCE AT THE 1975 GENEVA CONFERENCE WERE A FEW BRITISH COLUMBIA'S WELL RECOGNIZED DISTINGUISHED NAMES; JOHN HOGARTH, THEN-CHAIRMAN OF THE POLICE COMMISSION FOR THE PROVINCIAL GOVERNMENT, AND ROBERT STEWART, THEN-EXECUTIVE OFFICER ALSO WITH THE POLICE COMMISSION OF BRITISH COLUMBIA – AND OF COURSE, B.C.'S ALEX MACDONALD, THEN-ATTORNEY-GENERAL OF THE PROVINCE. ALSO IN ATTENDANCE WAS FRANCIS JOSEPH PREVOST, THEN-

Director of Courts Planning and Facilities for Alex MacDonald's NDP Department of the Attorney-General's Office – British Columbia's NDP government remained in power until December 22ND, 1975, after which the Social Credit Party regained control of the Province under the leadership of Bill Bennett.

The list of individual participants was virtually a list of who's who that literally brought a huge smile to the Gibsons shit disturber's face as he now had a more clear understanding as to why the powers that be in Ottawa (CSIS and others) were constantly hiding behind a shroud of secrecy and denying the very existence of the **"RED POWER - CANADA"** surveillance report. At this point it should be noted that according to the United Nations documentation, both of British Columbia's Police Commission representatives, John Hogarth and Robert Stewart initially acted as Canada's consultants during the United Nations 1975 Geneva conference.

While reading through the data submitted by the United Nations, the entire history of how the Fifth Congress on Crime Prevention had been organized two years previously with an execution date already set for September of 1975 as well as why Toronto, Ontario had been selected as the designated location for the conference became crystal clear. "For a period of two years to the Congress, organizational meetings were held periodically at Ottawa, Toronto and the United Nations Secretariat. "As far as the U.N. itself was concerned, Toronto seemed to be the most logical place as the Congress time frame was set for every five years and Canada was more than willing to play host to the crime conference as it wanted further worldwide recognition for being portrayed as a peace making nation standing up for a concept known as democracy and at the same time not willing to tolerate any forms of domestic terrorism thusly exercised by the FLQ only a few years previously. Perhaps the Canadian Federal Government saw a window of opportunity and decided to utilize it by wanting to play host to the international crime conference as playing this very important role, (fighting against terrorism and other forms of human right violations), would be justified in calling its own country's aboriginal peoples a group of terrorist threatening the stability of the nation. Afterall, it was now Canada's turn at the international Crime Prevention podium as the first four Congresses were held in other countries; Geneva 1955, London 1960, Stockholm 1965 and Kyoto 1970.

It is also interesting to note that with Canada's requesting for a one year postponement of the Fifth Congress and thusly putting the U.N. time frame out of sequence (the International Crime Prevention conferences are held every five years without fail), the Canadian Federal Government actually proved itself to be totally selfish and undeserving of what the United Nations and all of its members were attempting to accomplish on a global scale — world peace. To that end, Canada was left out of the fraternal loop for many, many years as other countries got to play host;

The Sixth Congress	Caracas, Venezuela (August 25TH - September 5TH, 1980)
The Seventh Congress	Milan, Italy (August 26TH - September 6TH, 1985)
The Eighth Congress	Havana, Cuba (August 27TH - September 7TH, 1990)
The Ninth Congress	Cairo, Egypt (April 29TH - May 8TH, 1995)
The Tenth Congress	Vienna, Austria (April 10TH - 17TH, 2000)

Just to let it be known as to how corrupt and genocidal Canada really was concerning its own aboriginal peoples, at the 1980 International Crime Prevention Conference held in Venezuela during the summer months; the Socialist country's leader under Fidel Castro proposed that conference delegates vote on a resolution forcing all of the attending nations to prevent political and/or other abuses of power within their own country's boundaries. The proposed draft tabled by the Cubans entitled "Prevention of the abuse of power", that of which in the end was passed during a roll-call vote of 45 to 20, with 16 abstentions.

The voting was as follows;
IN FAVOR:
Algeria, Brazil, Bulgaria, Burma, Central African Republic, China, Cuba, Czechoslovakia, Democratic Yemen, Ecuador, Egypt, El Salvador, Ethiopia, Gabon, German Democratic Republic, Ghana, Hungary, India, Iraq, Lesotho, Libyan Arab Jamahiriya, Morocco, Mozambique, Nepal, Nigeria, Panama, Papua New Guinea, Paraguay, Peru, Philippines, Poland, Rwanda, Sri Lanka, Sudan, Surinmae,

Tongo, Trinidad and Tobago, Tunisia, Union of Socialist Republics, United Republic of Tanzania, Venezuela, Yemen, Yugoslavia, Zambia.

AGAINST:

Argentina, Belgium, Chile, Denmark, Finland, France, Germany, Federal Republic of Ireland, Israel, Italy, Japan, Netherlands, Norway, Portugal, San Marino, Spain, Sweden, Switzerland, United Kingdom of Great Britain and Northern Ireland, United States.

ABSTAINING:

Australia, Austria, Bathados, Canada, Costa Rica, Greece, Guatemala, Holy See, Indonesia, Jamaica, Malta, Saint Vincent and the Grenadines, Singapore, Thailand, Turkey, Uruguay.

The mere fact that Canada abstained from voting while both Italy and the United States voted against the adoption of the draft resolution is totally hypocritical to say the least. Ironically, only a year previous to the Cuban delegation tabling the said stated proposal of preventing abuse of political power, disgruntled American citizens were up in arms concerning a scandal of political corruption allegedly involving six U.S. Congressmen – while Italian federal politicians on the other hand were deeply involved not only with outright corruption and blackmail but cold-blooded murder as well. Contrary to public belief, both of these countries scandals (Italy and the United States) were somewhat related to one another by way of a couple of rather interesting aspects, that of which Canada was well aware of at the time and didn't want to rock the fraternity boat at the 1980 Crime Prevention Conference.

While the conference was being held in Caracas, Venezuela everyone in the United States was being hit with so much political bullshit that it became very difficult to tell fact from fiction. It was Ronald Reagan's 1980 Presidential election campaign, a failed Hollywood actor who was now wanting to be President of the most powerful nation in the world. At one point during Reagan's campaigning for the Oval Office, the Moral Majority felt totally threatened as they saw the wannabe President as Satan wanting to gain control of the American people in a desperate attempt to corrupt the very fiber of American society – Ronald Reagan was also an active member of the Ancient Craft of Freemasonry as well as a willing participant in the fraternal just cause of a one world government. By June of 1979, the evangelical movement had organized themselves into a very powerful force in a bid to

PREVENT THE AMERICAN FREEMASONS OF HAVING THEIR PUPPET ANOINTED AS PRESIDENT. IN JUST SIXTEEN SHORT MONTHS, THEY HAD SIGNED UP 72,000 MINISTERS AND FOUR MILLION MEMBERS IN WAITING, ESTABLISHING CHAPTERS IN ALL 50 OF THE U.S. STATES – IT WAS DURING THIS TIME PERIOD THAT THE MORAL MAJORITY RAISED MORE THAN $5 MILLION FOR THE SOLE PURPOSE OF POLITICALLY PROSELYTIZING THE FREEMASONS OF THE UNITED STATES OF THE AMERICA'S. EVANGELICAL-FUNDAMENTALIST PREACHERS SUCH AS BILLY GRAHAM, ORAL ROBERTS AND JERRY FALWELL SOON BEGAN CONDEMNING BOTH THE REPUBLICAN AND DEMOCRAT POLITICAL PARTIES FOR THEIR ILL-CONCEIVED CONCEPTS OF DEMOCRACY AND VOWED TO REPLACE IT WITH A SO-CALLED "BORN-AGAIN "CHRISTIAN GOVERNMENT.

THE 1980 U.S. PRESIDENTIAL ELECTION WAS NO DOUBT A RELIGIOUS BATTLE FIELD FOR BOTH THE AMERICAN FREEMASONS AND THEIR DO NO WRONG COUNTERPART, THE HIGHLY MORAL ONES. BUT THE MORAL MAJORITY WAS NO MATCH FOR MASONIC BROTHER RONALD REAGAN AS HE HAD THE ULTIMATE UPPER HAND, FRIENDS IN EXTREMELY HIGH PLACES. INTERESTING AS IT MAYBE, FALWELL AND OTHER CONSERVATIVE EVANGELICALS ADOPTED A PRESIDENTIAL PLATFORM SIMILAR TO THAT OF THE REPUBLICANS WHICH IN FACT THE MORAL MAJORITY HAD A HAND IN SHAPING. DURING THE SUMMER OF 1980, A GALLUP POLL ESTIMATED THAT FIFTY-TWO PERCENT OF THE NATION'S POPULATION FAVORED JIMMY CARTER OVER BROTHER REAGAN. COINCIDENTLY, DURING THE EARLY 1970'S THE FREEMASONRY ENTITY KNOWN AS THE BILDERBERG (A.K.A. THE ILLUMINOIDS) HAND PICKED THE ONE TERM GOVERNOR OF GEORGIA, JIMMY CARTER TO BECOME PRESIDENT OF THE UNITED STATES. AT THE TIME, BROTHER CARTER HAD BEEN AN ACTIVE MEMBER OF FRATERNITY BROTHER DAVID ROCKEFELLER'S TRILATERAL COMMISSION WHOSE MANDATE IT WAS TO SEEK GLOBAL DOMINATION. ONLY MONTHS BEFORE THE NOVEMBER 1980 PRESIDENTIAL DEADLINE, ALL OF THE OLD BLACK AND WHITE MOVIES THAT RONALD REAGAN EVER MADE HIT THE TELEVISION AIRWAVES AS BROTHER REAGAN WAS NOW THE MORE FAVORED WANNABE PRESIDENT FOR THE 1980'S DECADE. IT LITERALLY WAS A CASE OF BRAINWASHING THE PEOPLE IN THE BEST-INTEREST OF THE NATION. BUT ALL WAS NOT WELL IN THE U.S. PARADISE AS MANY ANTI-REAGAN FACTIONS TOOK TO THE STREETS VERBALIZING THEIR DISCONTENT BY STATING PUBLICALLY THAT IF THEY WANTED AN ACTOR AS PRESIDENT, THEN, THEY PREFERRED MORE TO HAVE VOTED FOR RICARDO MONTALBAN.

JUST AS THINGS SEEMED TO BE TAKING A MORE SUBDUED DIRECTION, ALL HELL BROKE LOOSE ONLY WEEKS BEFORE THE NOVEMBER 4TH, 1980 PRESIDENTIAL VOTING DAY AS EVIDENCE EMERGED ON FBI VIDEO TAPE EXPOSING PENNSYLVANIA CONGRESSMAN MICHAEL (OZZIE) MYERS OF ACCEPTING A $50,000.00 BRIBE. DURING THE SUMMER, THE FEDERAL JUSTICE

Department was investigating a series of high profile prosecutions involving six Congressmen who were allegedly on the take. At the time of his eventual conviction, Myers insisted that he had done nothing wrong, criminally and/or otherwise. Congressman Myers was fighting to save his political career as the House of Representatives viewed the tapes and thusly passed judgement upon him stating that it was the most deplorable act that they had ever encountered since throwing out two Confederate members as traitors in 1861. In a four-hour debate, the Ethics Committee Chairman Charles Bennett of Florida urged that Ozzie Myers be expelled due to the fact that the integrity of the entire House of Representatives was now at stake — while other members of the Ethics Committee pleaded for leniency insisting that he (Myers) was merely a misguided politician unable to distinguish the difference between right and wrong. As he stood before the Committee, not once did Myers ever deny taking the money — he openly admitted to accepting it, insisting that he never had any intention of doing anything in return. According to him, he was simply play-acting as it was in his own personal opinion that he had been set up right from the very beginning. Myers had the firm belief that his colleague's did not give him a fair hearing and accused them of lynching him. In yet another twist of irony, Myers later reportedly compared his conviction to a man sitting on death row taking his last breath of air as his brethren reached down hitting the button as though he had been strapped into an electric chair. But in the end, the vote to expel Myers was 376 to 30.

Only a matter of days later, another Republican representative was being crucified!!!

Maryland's eastern shore representative Robert Bauman, pleaded not guilty in a Washington court to a sexual solicitation charge for trying to pick-up a sixteen-year-old boy near Capital Hill. Like Myers, Bauman attempted to salvage his political career. Bauman's line of defense was the usage of alcohol and that because of it, he could not recollect the true circumstances of the situation. According to him, the incident occurred at a time period of his life when he was suffering from acute alcoholism. Bauman promised the court that he would enter a six-month treatment program, after which, all charges were dropped. With reference to his political career, Bauman merely stated that he would allow the citizens of his district to pass judgement on him and no one else. As it so happens, Robert Bauman was Ronald Reagan's main campaign leader in

Maryland during election maneuvers to overthrow the Presidential palace of Jimmy Carter.

While the United States was going to hell in a hand basket during the 1980 Presidential election, trouble was brewing in Italy as the upper echelons of the Italian government was in the midst of being toppled for being involved in various aspects of organized crime. It was said to be a gradual build up (1980-81) that literally brought down the coalition government of Arnaldo Forlani during the early parts of 1981. Right from the outset, media outlets worldwide called it the scandal of all scandals. Then-Italian Prime Minister Forlani was a member of a four-party coalition government ironically known as the Christian Democrats. He and many members of his political party loyalists were also members of the Italian Freemasonry's Roman Catholic P-2 Lodge. Then as now, the P-2 Lodge is one of the most powerful Italian propaganda machines of the Ancient Craft still in existence to this very day. Not long after the Italian government was toppled, it was soon made public that it occurred only because of the fact that the British Secret Intelligence Service (MI5) and its Security Service (MI6) were the driving forces behind the coup d'etat.

According to the Masonic Order's own literature, the United Grand Lodge of England didn't recognize the Italian P-2 Lodge until 1973. To say the least, this is somewhat puzzling especially considering the fact that under Masonic guidelines on a global scale politics and religion are one in the same — simply put, it is the politics of religion. Originally, the P-2 Lodge was constituted a "Propaganda "Lodge under the Grand Orient of Italy — an elite Lodge, which counted among its members some of the most powerful political figures of Europe and the free-world.

The P-2 Lodge itself was first designed in 1966 to be instituted as a Lodge for respectable Freemasons, thus making them accountable to the Masonic Order. But in later years, the Propaganda Lodge was re-named Raggruppamento Gelli Propaganda Due; P-2. The new image of the Lodge was a tribute to Lucio Gelli, a very wealthy Italian textile manufacturer who had been Raised to Sublime Master Mason in a very short time period of just two years. Gelli was the first Italian citizen to have ever acquired the power and prestige of the Masonic Order in such an extremely short period of time. He reportedly fought for the fascists in the Spanish Civil War and was said to be a passionate supporter of Benito Mussolini during World War II. Fraternity Brother Gelli had an outstanding reputation of

USING EXTORTION AND BLACKMAIL TACTICS IN PUBLIC AFFAIRS TO GET WANT HE WANTED. IN USING THE POLITICAL CHARMS THAT HE ULTIMATELY POSSESSED, GELLI INCREASED THE P-2 MEMBERSHIP TENFOLD AND DURING HIS REIGN OF TERROR IN THE FRATERNITY, HE WAS SAID TO HAVE EMBEZZLED MONEY FROM THE MASONIC DUES THAT OF WHICH THE MEMBERSHIP PAID DIRECTLY TO THE ORDER ITSELF.

BY 1976, FREEMASONRY BROTHER LUCIO GELLI WAS UNDER INVESTIGATION BY THE ITALIAN AUTHORITIES FOR HIS POSSIBLE CRIMINAL ACTIVITIES AND AS THE ROME PUBLIC PROSECUTOR BEGAN SNOOPING INTO THE MASONIC ORDER'S FINANCIAL BANKING PROCEDURES A FEW YEARS LATER, WHICH EVENTUALLY FOUND ITS WAY INTO THE VATICAN CITY BANKING SYSTEM AS WELL, THE GUILTY PARTIES OF P-2 THUSLY SCRAMBLED FOR COVER BY LEAVING THE COUNTRY. ONE OF ITS LOYALIST, MICHELE SINDONA WAS EVENTUALLY ARRESTED IN NEW YORK CITY ON CHARGES OF FRAUD. GELLI IRONICALLY FLEW TO THE UNITED STATES TO TESTIFY THAT FRATERNITY BROTHER SINDONA WAS SIMPLY AN INNOCENT VICTIM OF A COMMUNIST PLOT AND TO FURTHER CONFUSE THE ISSUE AT HAND, GELLI ALSO ATTENDED MASONIC BROTHER RONALD REAGAN'S PRESIDENTIAL INAUGURATION IN JANUARY OF 1981. IT SHOULD ALSO BE STATED THAT BOTH SINDONA AND GELLI HAD KNOWN MAFIA CONNECTIONS AND THAT SINDONA REPORTEDLY INTRODUCED GELLI IN WASHINGTON, D.C. TO THE U.S. REPUBLICAN PARTY'S NATIONAL COMMITTEE IN 1980. FACING FEDERAL COURT PROSECUTION IN 1980, SINDONA APPEALED TO THE FREEMASONRY BROTHERHOOD FOR HELP – AT THE TIME, LUCIO GELLI WAS P-2'S GRAND MASTER.

IN THE MEANTIME, THE ITALIAN AUTHORITIES WERE STILL INVESTIGATING THE FRATERNITY AND THEIR HIGHLY ILLEGAL ACTIVITIES. THE PROBE ALSO INVESTIGATED THE EVENTS AND CIRCUMSTANCES LEADING TO THE MURDER OF SINDONA'S LIQUIDATOR OF HIS FINANCIAL EMPIRE-DYNASTY. WITHIN HOURS OF GELLI'S APPEAL TO THE U.S. FEDERAL COURTS FOR LENIENCY, "A FAKED KIDNAPING WAS STAGED IN NEW YORK AND SINDONA DISAPPEARED. "IN MARCH OF 1981 WHEN EVIDENCE EVENTUALLY EMERGED LINKING GELLI TO FRATERNITY BROTHER SINDONA'S VANISHING ACT, MASONIC BROTHER GELLI AND HIS WIFE ALSO DISAPPEARED OFF THE FACE OF THE EARTH.

A WARRANT WAS THUS ISSUED FOR GELLI'S ARREST ON CHARGES OF POLITICAL, MILITARY AND INDUSTRIAL ESPIONAGE. ONE ADDITIONAL CHARGE WAS ISSUED, ENDANGERING THE SECURITY OF THE STATE OF ITALY. BY THIS TIME PERIOD OF COURSE, ALL OF GELLI'S DOCUMENTS HAD BEEN REVIEWED BY THE ITALIAN AUTHORITIES AND THEY WERE NOW GETTING THE FULL LOGISTICS OF WHAT THE MASONIC P-2 GROUP WAS ACTUALLY UP TOO.

AMONG THE DOCUMENTATION CONFISCATED BY THE AUTHORITIES WAS A LIST CONTAINING THE NAMES OF ONE- THOUSAND OF ITALY'S MOST POWERFUL

AND INFLUENTIAL PEOPLE, ALL ACTIVE MEMBERS OF THE MASONIC P-2 LODGE. As Italian authorities reportedly sifted through the ten heavy piles of Gelli's fraternity papers, it became very clear that the Masonic P-2 Lodge literally controlled the puppetry strings of the Christian Democrat government of Prime Minister Forlani. Howls of rage soon demanded the Italian Government's resignation, the Christian Democrats attempted to save face but to no avail. By June of 1981, Italy had its first non-Christian Democratic government since the Second World War — a coalition government made up of five separate parties, (Communists, Socialists, Republicans, Radicals and Neo-Fascists, most of whom were suspected in still being active members of the Masonic P-2 Lodge). Accordingly, the Masonic P-2 and all of its corrupt Freemasons had infiltrated most of Italy's governmental structures. Officials in Washington and London (CIA, FBI, MI5 and MI6) were mainly concerned with national security and thus placed a grave distance between themselves and the scandal by suppressing whatever information they possibly could.

Italy's P-2 Affair also linked Lucio Gelli with the attempted assassination of Pope John Paul II in May of 1981. All of a sudden, Gelli was classified as being a KGB agent by the powers that be in a feeble attempt to water down the Freemasonry influence of the Masonic P-2 group as secret intelligence service experts decreed that the plot was inspired by the Communist political forces. According to what British Intelligence sources leaked to the media, "Gelli was recruited by the KGB soon after he set about the task of building up Raggruppamento Gelli Propaganda Due. "From the information that was purposely leaked out, the Italian Masonic P-2 Lodge supposedly became "a KGB-sponsored program aimed at destabilizing Italy, "and weakening its NATO capability. As far as London and Washington were concerned, the Communist and their KGB agents were involved in the largest conspiracy in the world; global domination. Ironically, most of the Communist followers marched to the exact same Freemasonry drum beat of the United States and Great Britain.

By Masonic definition, the Grand Orient of Italy was as follows: "Most of the Grand Lodges established by the Latin races, such as those of France, Spain, Italy, and South American States, are called Grand Orients. The word is thus, in sense, synonymous with Grand Lodges; but these Grand Orients have often a more extensive obedience than Grand Lodges, frequently exercising jurisdiction over the highest degrees, from which English and American Grand

Lodges refrain ... Grand Orient is also used in English, and especially American Masonry to indicate the seat of the Grand Lodge of the highest Masonic powers. "As any free footing capitalist can clearly see with their own eyes, someone was lying about who did what in this Freemasonry P-2 scandal of all scandals!!!

This was by no means the first time that organized crime had infiltrated the Italian government. For example in July of 1990, news media outlets worldwide were not only shocked and horrified to hear that the American departmental branch wing of the CIA was involved in Italian terrorism as well as the assassination of Swedish Prime Minister Olaf Palme. As it turns out, the U.S. Central Intelligence Agency financially backed the neo-fascist political activities of the Masonic P-2 Lodge towards committing terrorist acts in Italy during the mid-to-late 1980's – allegations that of which the CIA naturally flatly denied having any part in. The allegations themselves were made by an ex-CIA agent (Dick Brenneke) on Italian television airwave. Brenneke's charges were supported by yet another agent who also claimed that the CIA financially supported the Masonic P-2 fraternity for its part in the killing of the Swedish Prime Minister.

Only days later, two-hundred people linked to the Mafia in southern Italy were promptly elected to regional and city councils. In an Italian parliamentary anti-Mafia commission report, the role of organized crime had been drastically watered down and in some cases, it was flatly denied of having ever existed. The commission probed Mafia infiltration into southern local governments following the gangland killing of eight candidates who were up for election in Calabria and Campania. The report itself stated that fifty-three of the candidates in the Campania region, surrounding Naples, had family ties /or other links to the Mafia clans. More than one-hundred of the newly elected governing bodies of Italy that were anointed with governmental positions had convictions for crimes connected with public administrations, including bribery and other forms of corruption.

With all of this decay of the political and moral fiber of both Italy and the United States, is it any wonder as to why Canada **ABSTAINED** itself from voting at the United Nations conference in favor of the Cuban delegation's resolution of preventing abuse of power from within a country's own jurisdictional boundaries. Coincidently, even the history of how the United Nations came

INTO BEING HAS SOMEWHAT OF A CORRUPT PAST CONTRARY AS TO WHAT SOME MAY SAY IS TRUE!!!

CASE IN POINT; IN 1919 FOR EXAMPLE, THE BRITISH GOVERNMENT SIGNED THE BALFOUR DECLARATION STATING THAT IT WAS IN THE ENGLISH GOVERNMENT'S OPINION THAT A NATIONAL HOME BE ESTABLISHED FOR THE JEWISH POPULATION OF THE WORLD IN THE HOLY LAND (PALESTINE) WITHOUT PREJUDICE TO THE CIVIL AND RELIGIOUS RIGHTS OF THE NON-JEWISH PEOPLE ALREADY LIVING THERE. ON DECEMBER 11TH OF THAT SAME YEAR, BRITISH TROOPS WERE SENT INTO THE HOLY LAND TO KEEP THE PEACE AS IT WERE. BUT LESS THAN A MONTH LATER, THE SUPREME ALLIED COMMAND FORCES BEGAN TAKING THE APPROPRIATE ACTIONS IN MAINTAINING CONTROL OF THEIR NEWFOUND RELIGIOUS WEALTH OF THE MIDDLE EAST — THEN, THE FREEMASONS OF THE WORLD BAND TOGETHER AND FORMULATED THE FRATERNITY LEAGUE OF NATIONS. ODDLY ENOUGH, THE IDEA OF FORMING THE LEAGUE WAS FIRST SUGGESTED BY U.S. PRESIDENT WOODROW WILSON ON JANUARY 8TH, 1918 AND IN THE NEW 1988 LEXICON WEBSTER'S ENCYCLOPEDIC DICTIONARY ON THE ENGLISH LANGUAGE, THE FOLLOWING IS IRONICALLY STATED: **"ALTHOUGH PRESIDENT WILSON WAS ONE OF THE CHIEF ARCHITECTS OF THE ORGANIZATION, THE U.S.A. REFUSED TO JOIN.** "WHAT WASN'T DARE MENTIONED IN WEBSTER'S NEW REVISED VERSION OF HISTORY WAS THE MAIN REASON AS TO WHY U.S. ELECTED OFFICIALS REFUSED TO RATIFY THE MASONIC FRATERNAL MERGER OF NATIONS. THIS WAS REPORTEDLY A TIME PERIOD IN THE UNITED STATES OF THE AMERICA'S HISTORY WHEN THE AMERICAN FREEMASONS DIDN'T CONTROL THE MAJORITY OF THE VOTES IN EITHER CONGRESS /OR THE SENATE, AND NO ONE, NOT EVEN THE LEXICOGRAPHERS WANTED TO ADMIT TO THIS DISMAL FAILURE. HISTORIANS THEREFORE WISH US TO BELIEVE THAT THE REASON AS TO WHY THE UNITED STATES REFUSED TO JOIN THE LEAGUE OF NATIONS WAS LARGELY DUE TO THE FACT THAT THERE WAS A DISCREPANCY IN THE GUIDELINES PROTECTING THE INTEGRITY OF ITS MEMBERS — ALL MEMBERS OF THE MASONIC ORDER'S FRATERNAL MERGE HAD TO AGREE WITH ARTICLE X OF ITS RESOLUTIONS, PLEDGING THEMSELVES **"TO RESPECT AND PRESERVE AS AGAINST EXTERNAL AGGRESSION THE TERRITORIAL INTEGRITY AND EXISTING POLITICAL INDEPENDENCE OF ALL MEMBERS OF THE LEAGUE.** "IRAQ REPORTEDLY JOINED THE MASONIC FOLD IN 1932, AND TWO YEARS LATER, SO DID THE SOVIET UNION (THE USSR). THROUGHOUT ITS SHORT EXISTENCE, THE UNITED STATES STEADFASTLY REFUSED TO JOIN THE LEAGUE BUT SEVEN YEARS LATER, (1939), THE SOVIETS WERE KICKED OUT OF THE MASONIC FAMILY AND WITH THE USSR OUT OF THE FREEMASONRY FOLD, U.S. PRESIDENT ROOSEVELT SOON BEGAN INSTITUTING THE AMERICAN VERSION OF A **NEW WORLD ORDER** THAT WAS TO BE MAINLY CONTROLLED BY AMERICAN FREEMASONS. ON APRIL 18TH, 1946 A GROUP OF MASONIC DELEGATES MET AT THE 21ST SESSION OF

THE LEAGUE OF NATIONS' ASSEMBLY IN GENEVA AND TRANSFERRED ALL OF ITS RECORDS, ASSETS AND PROPERTIES TO THE NEWLY FORMED UNITED NATIONS IN NEW YORK CITY. AT THE TIME OF THE TRANSFER OF ITS SEAT POWER ONTO AMERICAN SOIL, THE NET WORTH VALUE OF THE LEAGUE'S HOLDINGS WERE ESTIMATED IN BEING 11.7 MILLION DOLLARS.

TWELVE MONTHS AFTER THE POMPOUS, ARROGANT/SELF-RIGHTEOUS GIBSONS SHIT DISTURBER ENLISTED THE SERVICES OF THE VARIOUS NATIVE ORGANIZATION TO HELP TRACK DOWN THE SO-CALLED NON-EXISTENT REPORT, THE HEAD OF THE ASSEMBLY OF FIRST NATIONS, QUEBEC'S MATTHEW COON COME, STOOD BEFORE THE UNITED NATIONS WORLD CONFERENCE AGAINST RACISM IN DURBAN, SOUTH AFRICA (AUGUST 31ST TO SEPTEMBER 7TH, 2001) LETTING IT BE KNOWN THAT THE GREATEST VIOLATORS OF ABORIGINAL PEOPLES HUMAN RIGHTS IN THE ENTIRE WORLD WAS THE CANADIAN FEDERAL GOVERNMENT AND ITS VARIOUS GOVERNMENTAL DEPARTMENTS. LEADING A SIX-MEMBER ASSEMBLY OF FIRST NATIONS DELEGATION AT THE CONFERENCE, COON COME AND HIS NATIVE FOLLOWERS BEGAN CRITICIZING THE SOCIAL CONDITIONS OF CANADA'S ABORIGINAL PEOPLE LIVING IN AND OFF THE RESERVES AND OTTAWA'S UNWILLINGNESS TO SETTLE THE LAND CLAIMS ISSUE. THE GOVERNMENT OF CANADA IN THE PAST HAD PAINTED A ROSY PICTURE AT OTHER PREVIOUS CONFERENCES TIME AND TIME AGAIN, AND NATIVE GROUPS RIGHT ACROSS THE COUNTRY BY THIS TIME PERIOD HAD ENOUGH OF OTTAWA'S CONSTANT LYING TO THE UNITED NATIONS BY SAYING THAT EVERYTHING WAS NOT HUNKY DORY WITH CANADA'S INDIGENOUS PEOPLES LIVING IN A WHITEMAN'S WORLD.

THE NATIVE LEADER AND HIS DELEGATION KNEW FULL WELL THAT CONTRARY AS TO WHAT THE CANADIAN FEDERAL GOVERNMENT HAD BEEN SAYING ABOUT THE INTERCOURSE AND SUPPOSED MARRIAGE OF THE INDIGENOUS PEOPLES INTO THE FRATERNAL **FAMILY OF MAN**, THINGS IN REALITY WERE BY NO MEANS AS TO WHAT OTTAWA HAD PERCEIVED THEM TO BE. THE FEDERAL JUSTICE DEPARTMENT WAS BEING SWAMPED WITH COURT CASES IN BRITISH COLUMBIA, THE NORTHWEST TERRITORIES AND THE YUKON CONCERNING PENDING COURT PROCEEDINGS INVOLVING TREATY RIGHTS, LAND CLAIMS, SEX ABUSE CLAIMS ARISING FROM RESIDENTIAL SCHOOLS, HUNTING AND FISHING RIGHTS AND A LONG LIST OF OTHER GRIEVANCES (AN ESTIMATED 20,000 TO 60,000 PEOPLE HAD BEEN EXPECTED TO FILE LEGAL COURT PAPERS RESULTING FROM RESIDENTIAL SCHOOL ABUSES ALONE). THERE WERE SAID TO BE SO MANY CASES BEFORE THE COURTS NATION WIDE THAT BELIEVE IT /OR NOT, THERE WASN'T ENOUGH LAWYERS AROUND TO HANDLE THE CASE LOADS. BECAUSE OF THIS, OTTAWA HAD TO HIRE MORE PEOPLE WITH THE EXPERTISE OF HANDLING ABORIGINAL LEGAL CASES. KNOWING ALL OF THIS, QUEBEC'S NATIVE LEADER WANTED THE UNITED NATIONS TO KNOWN THAT DESPITE OTTAWA'S ATTEMPTS

OF PAINTING A NICE ROSY PICTURE AND THAT THEY (THE CANADIAN FEDERAL GOVERNMENT) HAD EVERYTHING UNDER FULL CONTROL AS CANADA'S INDIGENOUS PEOPLES OF THE 21ST CENTURY HELD NO THREAT TO NATIONAL SECURITY – CONTRARY AS TO WHAT THE **"RED POWER - CANADA"** REPORT OF PREVIOUS YEARS MAY HAVE STATED.

TO THAT END, ABORIGINAL LEADER MATTHEW COON COME SOON BEGAN REFRESHING EVERYONE MEMORY ON CANADA: A PEOPLES HISTORY AS ALL ASPECTS OF HUMAN RIGHTS BEING VIOLATED BY THE WHITEMAN EVER SINCE THE ROBERVAL EXPEDITION OF 1542 WERE BROUGHT UP AT THE ANTI-RACISM CONFERENCE. ISSUES SUCH AS CANADA'S INDIAN SLAVERY PAST UNDER BOTH THE FRENCH AND THE ENGLISH, A TOPIC THAT OF WHICH MOST CANADIANS TO THIS VERY DAY DISCREDIT AS BEING PURE NONSENSE. AFTER HUNDREDS OF YEARS AS BEING AN OPPRESSED RACE OF PEOPLE, CANADA'S ABORIGINAL PEOPLES WERE REMOVING THE SHACKLES OF THEIR BONDAGE BY USING THE WHITEMAN'S OWN LAWS AGAINST THEM THUS POSING THE ULTIMATE THREAT TO CANADIAN NATIONAL SECURITY.

RIGHT FROM THE VERY BEGINNING OF THE SCHEDULED EIGHT DAY CONFERENCE IN SOUTH AFRICA, IT WAS EXPECTED TO CONSIST OF A MUCH HEATED DEBATE AS PARAGRAPH 27 OF THE UNITED NATIONS DRAFT DECLARATION ON RACISM STATED THAT WHEN THE DELEGATES USED THE TERM INDIGENOUS PEOPLES, IT WAS NOT TO BE "CONSTRUED AS HAVING ANY IMPLICATIONS AS TO RIGHTS UNDER INTERNATIONAL LAW. "AS MANY TIMES BEFORE, JUST WHEN EVERYONE HAD FIGURED OUT EXACTLY AS TO HOW THE GAME WAS TO BE PLAYED OUT, THE U.N. WENT AND MOVED THE GOAL POST. IT WAS AS THOUGH THE UNITED NATIONS HAD ANTICIPATED THAT THE CONFERENCE WAS GOING TO BE USED AS A SOAP BOX TO EXPRESS THE RACIST POLICIES OF THE VARIOUS DELEGATIONS PROSPECTIVE HOMELANDS AND THEIR COUNTRY'S GOVERNING BODIES, AND THE U.N. DIDN'T REALLY WANT TO HEAR ANY OF IT – SO MEETINGS WERE HELD BEHIND CLOSED DOORS AND THE GOAL POST WAS THUSLY MOVED. COON COME IMMEDIATELY BEGAN CRITICIZING THE MANOEUVRE SAYING THAT THE UNITED NATIONS ORGANIZATION WAS LITERALLY TELLING ALL INDIGENOUS PEOPLES OF THE WORLD THAT THEIR BASIC FUNDAMENTAL HUMAN RIGHTS WERE NOT ONLY UP FOR NEGOTIATIONS BUT WERE ALSO AT THE FULL DISCRETION OF U.N. INTERPRETATION. QUEBEC'S NATIVE LEADER EVEN WENT SO FAR AS TO ACCUSE THE U.N. OF HAVING ITS OWN HIDDEN AGENDA AS THE UNITED NATIONS ITSELF HAD DECREED THAT INDIGENOUS PEOPLES HUMAN RIGHTS WERE BY NO MEANS UNIVERSAL DESPITE WHAT U.N. OFFICIALS HAD BEEN SAYING RIGHT FROM THE VERY BEGINNING OF ITS FIRST CONCEPTION NEARLY A CENTURY AGO!!!

WITH THE SHIFTING TO THE PREVAILING WINDS IN THE 21ST CENTURY, HOWLS OF RAGE SOON FILLED THE GIGANTIC CONFERENCE ROOM AS

DELEGATES (BETWEEN 15,000 TO 20,000 OF THEM) FROM MORE THAN 150 COUNTRIES EXPRESSED DISCONTENT WITH THEIR PROSPECTIVE COUNTRY'S RACIST GOVERNING POLICIES. AS NEARLY A THOUSAND JOURNALISTS FROM AROUND THE WORLD LOOKED ON, TENSIONS MOUNTED WITH EVERY PASSING MINUTE. LIKE A TERRORIST BOMB ATTACK THAT WAS ABOUT TO BE DROPPED ONTO AN UNSUSPECTING CROWD OF PEOPLE, WORDS OF SHEER ANGER WERE BEING EXPRESSED BY JUST ABOUT EVERYONE. THE CONFERENCE ITSELF WAS SO FAR OUT OF CONTROL THAT MANY COUNTRIES SIMPLY WALKED OUT ALTOGETHER — IN FACT ONE OF THE WORLD'S MOST RACIST COUNTRIES, THE UNITED STATES OF AMERICA, BUGGED OUT ONLY AFTER A FEW DAYS AND IN ORDER TO SAVE FACE, CANADIAN DELEGATES (GOVERNMENTAL AS WELL AS PRIVATE) WERE BEING URGED TO DO THE SAME. MEDIA OUTLETS IN CANADA ALMOST IMMEDIATELY BEGAN PORTRAYING MATTHEW COON COME AS BEING A HYPOCRITE FOR WHAT HE WAS SAYING ABOUT HIS COUNTRY'S PAST IMPLYING THAT HE HAD HIS FACTS OF CANADIAN HISTORY ALL TWISTED AND DISTORTED JUST AS A WAY AND MEANS OF FULFILLING HIS OWN AGENDA; IMPLICATIONS OF CANADA'S ABORIGINAL PEOPLES' UNWILLINGNESS TO LET BYGONES-BE-BYGONES SOON EMERGED. EVEN OUR VERY OWN COUNTRY'S CANADIAN PRIME MINISTER GOT IN ON THE ACT BY SUGGESTING THAT THE QUEBEC NATIVE LEADER HAD A SLIGHTLY DIFFERENT VIEW OF THINGS AS HE (JEAN CHRETIEN) HAD ATTEMPTED TO ABOLISH INDIAN RESERVATIONS WHILE ACTING AS THE INDIAN AFFAIRS MINISTER IN THE LATE 1960'S. OUR THEN-CANADIAN PRIME MINISTER WAS OBVIOUSLY REFERRING TO HIS **WHITE PAPER ON INDIAN POLICY** THAT WAS ASKING THE NATIVE POPULATION TO ASSIST THE FEDERAL GOVERNMENT IN PUTTING A NOOSE AROUND THEIR OWN NECKS AND THEN PULLING THE LEVER THAT TRIPPED THE TRAP DOOR OF THE GALLOWS.

AS COON COME EXPLAINED MORE AND MORE OF CANADA'S UNSAVORY PAST, MEDIA OUTLETS IN HIS OWN HOMELAND BEGAN ACCUSING HIM OF USING INFLAMMATORY LANGUAGE THAT IN THE END WAS GOING TO BE DOING MORE HARM THAN GOOD. IN A FEEBLE ATTEMPT TO WHITEWASH WHAT THE NATIVE LEADER WAS SAYING TO THE ENTIRE WORLD IN FRONT OF ALL THOSE JOURNALISTS, CANADIAN MEDIA OUTLETS ALMOST IMMEDIATELY WENT INTO DAMAGE CONTROL MODE BY COMPARING THE TREATMENT OF MINORITY GROUPS SOUTH OF THE 49TH PARALLEL. ACCORDINGLY, IT WAS THUSLY STATED THAT THE UNITED STATES BY FAR HAD ONE OF THE WORST HISTORICAL TRACK RECORDS IN THE WORLD FOR THE WAY IN WHICH THEY TREATED MINORITY GROUPS; ABORIGINALS, NEGROES, AND ALL OTHER MINORITY GROUPS. THE CANADIAN MEDIA EVEN WENT SO FAR AS TO IMPLY THAT THE AMERICANS WERE IN MORE OF A DENIAL OF THEIR HISTORICAL PAST THAN WHAT CANADIANS WERE; FRIDAY, SEPTEMBER 7TH, 2001 ISSUE OF THE VANCOUVER SUN, PAGE A17: **"A NATION IN DENIAL".**

Like a good game of Canadian hockey being played out on an international ice rink where the winner was to claim the **Stanley Cup** for all eternity but the goal tender kept moving the net around in order to prevent a score to be had, the conference soon went into overtime as tensions mounted even higher. The overtime period didn't end until sometime later, over twenty-four hours behind schedule. Which in itself proved to be a long stressful ordeal for the players, some two-hundred non-governmental Canadian organizations attended the hockey play-off. And what of the Stanley Cup you maybe asking – the United Nations decided to hold it for safe keeping as no winner was declared at the world conference on racism.

Less than a week after Matthew Coon Come literally informed the United Nations of all the travesties that Canada's First Native Peoples had been enduring under the watchful eye of the governmental sanctions of an apartheid system, all prospects of Benoit LePage's hopes of ever obtaining a photo-copy of the **"RED POWER - CANADA"** report was soon dashed once and for all. The Canadian Federal Government's wing of protecting all aspects of National Security began to tighten as the powers that be in both Canada and the United States (under the auspices of terrorist attacks launched on September 11TH, 2001) implemented anti-terrorist security procedures as domestic and/or international terrorism was now said to be on the increase. Here in Canada, it became quite apparent that the powers that be feared the worst as native leaders right across the country had effectively put the Canadian Federal Government on notice that they were no longer prepared to sit idly by while white society continued waging its war of genocide on the country's original inhabitants. With native land claims and self-determination being the main driving force behind Coon Come's speeches at the United Nations conference, the Government of Canada was now backed into a corner and something had to be done mighty quickly in order to off-set its everlasting consequences.

In the following weeks after 9/11, police forces nation wide were given new powers to help stem the tide of terrorism, it went into effect almost immediately – **PEACE** and **SECURITY** of all Canadians being of course the driving force behind it as the United States feared further attacks on its home front by well known international terrorist groups. While the Canadian citizenry remained in the **"sleepers "**state of consciousness, Matthew Coon Come's words were soon forgotten as the general population of the western free-world remained glued to their television sets as

The events of September 11TH, 2001 were constantly being played out on all of the airwaves like a bad film that the movie industry in Hollywood was broadcasting because it was the only one that they had ever produced. Bombarded by the television airwaves as the terrorists attacks of 9/11 played out over and over again for weeks and months on end, people became mesmerized by all of it and before long, its brainwashing effect had a psychological impact on the human psyche. With the wool virtually being pulled over their eyes as an extra measure, making sure that the "SLEEPERS" wouldn't dare wake-up, Canada as well as the United States brought into law anti-terrorist legislation that was going to make the witch hunt hearings of Senator Joseph McCarthy of the 1950's a cake walk in comparison. The Federal Government of Canada then began dishing out billions and billions of tax dollars for CSIS to spy on the Canadian population by way of surveillance, phone taps and/or whatever means that the spy agency deemed to be appropriate for the just cause. Leaving no stone unturned, anyone and everyone was now considered to be an enemy of the state; natives as well as non-natives.

Less than six months prior to the 9/11 terrorist attacks on American soil, the Canadian Federal Government in their great wisdom decided to set the fraternal bureaucratic wheels in motion to overhaul the Indian Act. This blatant inept Federal plan to make 21ST Century changes to the Act naturally annoyed the majority of the country's aboriginal peoples because Ottawa being who and what they are, also implemented a plan to divide and conquer the native population as some First Nations Peoples were in favor of the changes while others simply wanted the Act itself abolished completely. The Federal Government supposedly wanted to fine-tune the Indian Act in order to update band voting systems as well as to balance the interests of residents both on and off reserves. Further to this, Federal bureaucrats also wanted to make changes so that local Indian band administrations would be held more accountable to governmental bean counters. In other words, Ottawa wanted Canada's aboriginal peoples to remain in bondage, shackled to the Indian Act and at the full mercy of the Department of Indian Affairs and all of those who were employed by it. Reportedly, more than two-hundred meetings were held from May to July 2001 when the talks were put on hold for a short time period.

For those aboriginals who wanted the Indian Act abolished, it meant that the Canadian Federal Government had absolutely

NO INTENTION OF ALLOWING NATIVES THE RIGHT TO SELF-DETERMINATION VIA SELF-GOVERNMENT NOR THE RIGHT TO SOCIAL AND ECONOMIC JUSTICE VIA ABORIGINAL AND TREATY RIGHTS. MOST IMPORTANTLY, TO THOSE ABORIGINALS IT MEANT THAT THE GOVERNMENT OF CANADA HAD ABSOLUTELY NO INTENTION OF EVER SETTLING THE NATIVE LAND CLAIMS ISSUE ON A NATIONAL SCALE. PERHAPS IT WAS FOR THESE REASONS THAT THE NATIVE LEADERS THREATENED TO BRING THE COUNTRY TO A COMPLETE STANDSTILL BY ERECTING ROAD BLOCKADES RIGHT ACROSS CANADA IF OTTAWA BUREAUCRATS DIDN'T CEASE AND DESIST WITH THEIR SCHEME OF IMPOVERISHING THE NATIVE POPULATION INTO POLITICAL AND ECONOMICAL BONDAGE. THIS THREAT WAS FIRST INITIATED ON JULY 18TH, 2001 BY CHIEF LAWRENCE PAUL OF THE MILLBROOK FIRST NATION PEOPLES NEAR TRURO, NOVA SCOTIA WHILE ONE-THOUSAND DELEGATES AND THREE-HUNDRED CHIEFS OF THE ASSEMBLY OF FIRST NATIONS MET AT A CONVENTION IN HALIFAX. AT THE GATHERING, THEY VOTED UNANIMOUSLY TO URGE THE FEDERAL GOVERNMENT TO STOP CONSULTATIONS WITH ABORIGINALS ON THE PENDING CHANGES TO THE INDIAN ACT: "WE'LL BLOCK THE HIGHWAY FROM PRINCE EDWARD ISLAND TO VANCOUVER ... YOU HAVEN'T GOT ENOUGH POLICE TO STOP OVER 600 FIRST NATIONS ... WE CAN BRING CANADA TO A STANDSTILL, "CONCLUDING WITH "BUT WE DO NOT WANT TO GO THAT ROUTE."

BOTH THE NATIVE LEADERS AND THE DELEGATES THUSLY PASSED A RESOLUTION EMPHASIZING THAT OTTAWA MUST FOCUS MORE ON SELF-GOVERNMENT, ABORIGINAL AND TREATY RIGHTS, AND PRESSING SOCIAL AND ECONOMIC NEEDS OF ALL ABORIGINAL PEOPLES. THEIR THREAT OF A NATIONAL BLOCKADE WAS FURTHER BACKED BY GIVING THE CANADIAN FEDERAL GOVERNMENT THE STANDARD THIRTY DAYS TO ABANDON THE TALKS ON CHANGES TO THE INDIAN ACT, OTHERWISE, THE TAIL END OF THE RESOLUTION WAS GOING TO BE EXECUTED FORTHWITH: "THE FIRST NATIONS OF CANADA SHALL BE FORCED TO ENGAGE IN AN AGGRESSIVE STRATEGIC PLAN OF ACTION AT THE LOCAL, NATIONAL AND INTERNATIONAL LEVELS. "THAT'S ESSENTIALLY WHY MATTHEW COON COME WAS MAKING HIS PRESENTATION AT THE UNITED NATIONS WORLD CONFERENCE AGAINST RACISM IN DURBAN, SOUTH AFRICA A COUPLE OF MONTHS LATER AS IT WAS PART AND PARCEL OF THE RESOLUTION ADOPTED AT THE HALIFAX CONVENTION.

MEANWHILE AT THE OTHER END OF THE COUNTRY, BRITISH COLUMBIA'S NATIVE LEADERS HAD ALREADY DEVISED A DIRECT ACTION PLAN THAT ULTIMATELY WAS DESIGNED TO BRING THE WHITE POWER STRUCTURE TO ITS ECONOMIC KNEES; BLOCKING ROADS AND/OR FERRIES. AS PER USUAL, THE PROVINCE OF BRITISH COLUMBIA WAS WAY AHEAD OF THE REST OF THE CANADIAN PROVINCES AS ONLY A FEW MONTHS PRIOR TO THE ASSEMBLY OF FIRST NATIONS CONVENTION IN HALIFAX ABORIGINAL LEADERS WERE FORCED

TO CONCEIVE AN ACTION PLAN THAT WOULD ENABLE B.C. NATIVES TO FLEX THEIR POLITICAL MUSCLES AS THE NEWLY ELECTED LIBERAL GOVERNMENT OF BRITISH COLUMBIA (ELECTED MAY OF 2001) WITH A VOW TO HOLD A PUBLIC PLEBISCITE ON NATIVE LAND CLAIMS. THE NEWLY ELECTED LIBERAL B.C. GOVERNMENT PUBLICALLY STATED THAT A LOT OF BRITISH COLUMBIANS FELT LEFT OUR OF THE TREATY PROCESS AND THEY, THE LIBERAL GOVERNMENT WANTED TO HOLD A REFERENDUM ON THE SUBJECT ALLOWING ALL BRITISH COLUMBIANS A FINAL SAY ON THE ISSUE OF WHETHER /OR NOT THE ABORIGINAL POPULATION SHOULD BE COMPENSATED FOR LANDS SUPPOSEDLY LEGALLY SURRENDERED TO THE WHITEMAN ON AUGUST 20TH, 1858 BY AN IMPERIAL BRITISH GOVERNMENT EDICT. SIX MONTHS AFTER THIS PREJUDICIAL STATEMENT-OF-CLAIM BY ENGLAND, (FEBRUARY 14TH, 1859), THE NEWLY ANOINTED GOVERNOR, JAMES DOUGLAS PROCLAIMED THAT ALL THE LANDS WITHIN BRITISH COLUMBIA ITSELF — AND ALL MINERALS BELOW THE SURFACE — BELONGED TO THE BRITISH IMPERIAL CROWN. DESCRIBING THE INDIAN LAND AS "UNOCCUPIED", THE PROCLAMATION STATED IN PART: "ALL THE LANDS IN BRITISH COLUMBIA, AND ALL THE MINES AND MINERALS THEREIN, BELONG TO THE CROWN IN FEE. "PERCEIVING THEMSELVES AS THE LORD OF THE MANOR IN THEIR NEWFOUND TROPHY CASE — LAND NOT RESERVED FOR TOWNSITES AND/OR INDIAN RESERVATIONS IN THE UNOCCUPIED TERRITORY OF THE INDIANS WAS THEN MADE AVAILABLE TO PROSPECTIVE BUYERS AT A PRICE TAG OF TEN SHILLINGS PER ACRE.

BY THE 21ST CENTURY, THE MAJORITY OF WHITE BRITISH COLUMBIANS WANTED THE NATIVE LAND CLAIMS ISSUE RESOLVED AS LONG AS IT DIDN'T INVOLVE THE POSSIBILITY OF THEY THEMSELVES LOSING ANY PORTION OF THE LANDS PURCHASED BY THEM AND/OR INHERITED FROM THEIR WHITE EUROPEAN ANCESTORS. NOTWITHSTANDING, TO BE AN INDIAN IN A WHITEMAN'S WORLD LITERALLY MEANT BEING HELD HOSTAGE IN BONDAGE AND AT THE MERCY OF INDIAN ACT LEGISLATION ITSELF. TO THAT END, MOST BRITISH COLUMBIANS DISAGREED WITH THE NATIVES AND FELT THAT ABORIGINALS WERE HOLDING B.C. HOSTAGE BY ACTING LIKE A BUNCH OF TERRORISTS. ACCORDINGLY, THE BULK OF THE WHITE POPULATION WANTED THE NATIVES TREATED LIKE A GROUP OF TERRORISTS AS LONG AS THE INDIANS CONTINUED TO ACT AS SUCH BY DEMANDING COMPENSATION FOR THE STOLEN LANDS THAT THEIR ABORIGINAL ANCESTORS ONCE OCCUPIED PRIOR TO AUGUST 20TH, 1858. SOME BRITISH COLUMBIANS EVEN STIPULATED THAT THE NATIVES SHOULD CHOOSE THEIR WORDS OF WAR VERY CAREFULLY AS THEY (WHITE TERRORIST FACTIONS) WERE TOTALLY PREPARED TO FIGHT AGAINST ALL PROSPECTS OF SETTLING THE LAND CLAIMS ISSUE. OTHER WHITE FACTIONS, WANTED BOTH THE FEDERAL AND PROVINCIAL GOVERNMENTS TO CONSIDER THE IMMEDIATE CUT-OFF OF ANY

TRANSFER MONEY AND/OR SERVICES, INCLUDING POSTAL SERVICES, TO INDIAN BANDS CLAIMING NOT TO BE CANADIAN.

WITH THE BOX OF FRUIT LOOPS VIRTUALLY SCATTERED ALL OVER HELL'S CREATION, THE WHITE LUNATIC FRINGE INCREASED THEIR RACIST RHETORIC BY FORCING THE NEWLY ELECTED PROVINCIAL GOVERNMENT TO MAKE GOOD ON ITS PROMISE TO HOLD A REFERENDUM ON LAND CLAIMS. BEFORE LONG, THE CANADIAN FEDERAL GOVERNMENT LET IT BE KNOWN THAT THEY WERE NOT AT ALL IMPRESSED WITH B.C.'S INTENTIONS OF HOLDING A REFERENDUM ON THE NATIVE LAND CLAIMS ISSUE. IN FACT, OTTAWA'S THEN-FEDERAL MINISTER OF INDIAN AFFAIRS, (ROBERT NAULT), INSISTED THAT HE DIDN'T LIKE IT ONE BIT BUT WAS RESIGNED TO WAIT-AND-SEE AS TO WHAT THE PROVINCIAL GOVERNMENT ITSELF HAD IN STORE FOR THE NATIVES ONCE THE PLEBISCITE WENT TO THE PEOPLE FOR A VOTE. AS FAR AS OTTAWA WAS CONCERNED, THE B.C. LIBERAL'S PROPOSED REFERENDUM WAS GOING TO STALL THE TREATY TALKS EVEN FURTHER THUS ALLOWING A FREE-FOR-ALL WINDOW OF OPPORTUNITY TO OCCUR WHICH IN ESSENCE WAS GOING TO CREATE THE ILLUSION THAT THE TALKS HAD FALLEN APART AND NOTHING GOOD WAS EVER GOING TO COME OUT OF IT ANYWAYS. AT THE TIME, THE PROVINCE OF BRITISH COLUMBIA HAD A TOTAL OF FORTY-FOUR DIFFERENT TREATIES ON THE TABLE THAT WERE VERY CLOSE TO BEING FINALIZED (AGREEMENTS-IN-PRINCIPLE) AND WITH A REFERENDUM IN THE AIR, CHANCES OF A FINAL RESOLUTION WAS NEXT TO NON-EXISTENT. THE B.C. LIBERAL'S AT ONE TIME EVEN PLEADED WITH OTTAWA TO JOIN FORCES WITH THEM TO PUT AN END TO ALL PROSPECTS OF NATIVE SELF-GOVERNMENT BY TAKING THE NISGA'A TREATY TO THE SUPREME COURT OF CANADA CITING CONSTITUTIONAL GROUNDS.

WITH ALL OF THE POLITICAL CHAOS AND CONFUSION HAPPENING RIGHT ACROSS THE COUNTRY CONCERNING THE WHITEMAN'S UNWILLINGNESS TO ALLOW ABORIGINALS TO CONTROL THEIR OWN DESTINY, A WOMEN'S COALITION GROUP (THE FAMOUS 5 FOUNDATION) BEGAN COLLECTING SIGNATURES ON A PETITION URGING THE CANADIAN FEDERAL GOVERNMENT TO CHANGE THE LYRICS OF **"O CANADA"**. ACCORDING TO THE COALITION GROUP SOME OF THE LYRICS WERE SEXIST IN NATURE AND HAD TO BE CHANGED AS QUICKLY AS POSSIBLE, IF NOT SOONER. THE OFFENDING VERSION OF CANADA'S NATIONAL ANTHEM BEING OF COURSE;

O CANADA!
OUR HOME AND NATIVE LAND!
TRUE PATRIOT LOVE IN ALL THY SONS COMMAND.
WITH GLOWING HEARTS WE SEE THEE RISE,
THE TRUE NORTH STRONG AND FREE!
FROM FAR AND WIDE,

The coalition group wanted the Government of Canada to remove the phrase "in all thy sons command. "Wanting it to be replaced with lyrics such as "True patriot love in all of us command" /or "in all our command "/or even "in all our lives command. "It goes without saying that the 21ST Century political correctness was actually losing all touch with reality itself because not long after the women's coalition group began urging Ottawa to change the so-called sexist lyrics of our country's anthem, other factions of the lunatic fringe (white Anglo-Saxons) were chocking on the words "Our home and **NATIVE LAND!** "As far as they were concerned, Canada was not native land and never would be if they had anything to say about it.

With racial tensions flying fast and furious, the Federal Government must have finally realized as to where the assorted fruit loops were actually coming from because not long after the scattering of the box all over hell's creation, Ottawa decided to put consultation on changes to the Indian Act on hold until both parties (government and native leaders) decided how to proceed with the talks. This decision naturally came after the passing of a resolution by the Assembly of First Nations at their Halifax convention only two weeks previously. Ottawa bureaucrats also must have realized that the native peoples would have made good on the threat of a nation wide blockade. Afterall, aboriginals learned long ago as to how the whiteman speaks with a fork-tongue and could only relate to issues with some sort of brute force instantly attacked to it. Something that of which B.C. natives fully realized in 1859 when representatives of the whiteman's government first entered onto their lands (James Bay Reserve) and began construction of the Government Buildings for the Colony of Vancouver Island; the whiteman giveth and the whiteman taketh away!!!

After taking their lessons from the whiteman, (the whiteman hiding behind the shield of its own laws), two small B.C. Indian bands filed a lawsuit on Friday, August 24TH, 2001 with the Supreme Court of British Columbia claiming ownership of the land on which the Province's Legislature was sitting. The Esquimalt and Songhees bands submitted a writ asking the B.C. Supreme Court for unspecified damages and a declaration that the Province was trespassing on

Indian land and that both the Federal and Provincial Governments breached their duty to protect the bands' interests. Just like in the Northwest Territories, the Vancouver Island aboriginals had the whiteman's government by the gonads and were now squeezing them into submission. If the B.C. Liberals were going to hold a referendum on aboriginal rights to the native land claims issue, it was going to cost the Province and its people dearly, especially now that an extremely racist political party was in power at the Legislature in Victoria on the Pacific.

In speaking of extreme prejudices, on Thursday, November 21ST, 1996 a five-year investigation into the horrors of church-run, state-regulated Indian residential schools was released to the general public. The Royal Commission on Aboriginal Peoples of Canada revealed that the Federal Government's Ministry of Indian Affairs Canada wanted to "kill the Indian in the child "and in order to do so, the Department of Indian Affairs Canada drove a wedge between the children and "the old unimprovable people "by forcing them to sever all ties with their families and aboriginal culture. The mere use of this tactic raised the question as to who were the actual savages in Canadian society, the church-run schools that were allowed to constantly abuse the native children to "civilize" and "elevate" them /or the Government of Canada for the implementing of its tactics of genocide on the Indian population. The Royal Commission was established in the very early 1990's by the Federal Government of the day under the watchful eye of the then-Canadian Prime Minster Brian Mulroney after the stand-off at Oka, Quebec. The Commission's mandate was to examine all aspects of Indian life as a way and means of finding out exactly as to what causes Canada's aboriginal peoples to take up arms against white society in general.

During the five-year long investigation, the Commission had access to many secret government files which essentially exposed the existence of a conspiracy of sorts between the Government of Canada and the various religious institutions as they (the Canadian Federal Government) wanted to rid itself of the Indian problem. The religious institutions on the other hand, simply wanted to Christianize the savage beast out of the pagan worshipers while building up their religious land holdings in the name of a supreme deity. And since both of the parties in question had their own specific agendas to fulfill, it only made sense that a collaboration of efforts be put forward as Church and state are actually one in the same. Even while the Royal Commission was conducting its investigation

PROCEDURES VARIOUS RELIGIOUS INSTITUTIONS BEGAN TO WORRY A LITTLE BIT AS THEY (THE COMMISSION) WEREN'T LEAVING ANY STONE UNTURNED AS IT LITERALLY PUT ALL RELIGIONS UNDER A MICROSCOPE, PROTESTANT AS WELL AS ROMAN CATHOLIC. ONE OF THE COMMISSION'S INVESTIGATORS, FORMER PRESIDENT OF THE INDIAN BROTHERHOOD OF THE NORTHWEST TERRITORIES GEORGE ERASMUS WAS ALREADY WISE TO MOST OF THE HEART-WRENCHING TRAVESTIES OF CULTURAL GENOCIDE IMPLEMENTED BY THE POWERS THAT BE.

WHEN THE COMMISSION FINALLY RELEASED ITS FINDINGS IN THE FORM OF A FOUR-THOUSAND PAGE REPORT, IT BECAME CRYSTAL CLEAR THAT A LARGE MAJORITY OF TODAY'S PRESENT ADULT NATIVE POPULATION FELL PREY TOO MUCH PHYSICAL, SEXUAL AND EMOTIONAL ABUSE WHILE THEY WERE YOUNG STUDENTS ATTENDING THE RESIDENTIAL SCHOOLS. THE COMMISSION INTERESTINGLY ENOUGH ALSO UNCOVERED THE FACT THAT BOTH THE GOVERNMENT OF CANADA AND THE VARIOUS RELIGIOUS INSTITUTIONS HAD RACIST POLICIES IN PLACE WHEN DEALING WITH ABORIGINAL CHILDREN DATING AS FAR BACK TO THE DAYS OF SIR JOHN A. MACDONALD. IN 1879 MACDONALD'S GOVERNMENT DECIDED TO SET UP CHURCH-RUN BOARDING SCHOOLS IN ORDER TO REMOVE THE SAVAGE BEAST THAT WAS IN THEM AND THEN BEGAN ASSIMILATING THEM INTO WHITE CULTURE. RIGHT FROM THE VERY TIME ANGLICAN, CATHOLIC, METHODIST AND PRESBYTERIAN MISSIONARIES BEGAN ESTABLISHING RESIDENTIAL SCHOOLS DURING THE TRYING TIMES OF SIR JOHN A.'S FORMING A UNITED CONFEDERATION, THE FREEMASONRY GOVERNMENT OF CANADA'S MAIN INTENTION WAS NOT TO EDUCATE THE INDIAN CHILD BUT RATHER TO GET RID OF THE SAVAGE TENANCIES THAT THEY HAD BEEN BORN WITH. THIS WAS ACHIEVED BY FIRST SEPARATING THE CHILDREN FROM THEIR FAMILIES, THEN, FORBIDDING THEM TO USE THE ABORIGINAL LANGUAGES THAT THEY HAD BEEN TAUGHT AND LASTLY, BY PUNISHING THEM IN THE MOST INHUMANE FORMS OF DISCIPLINE THAT WAS OFTEN MORE SAVAGE THAN THOSE OF WHOM WERE BEING HELD IN BONDAGE. WHILE THE GOVERNMENT OF CANADA AND THE VARIOUS RELIGIOUS INSTITUTIONS WERE TRYING TO KILL THE INDIAN IN OUR COUNTRY'S ABORIGINAL POPULATION, IT WAS BUSINESS AS USUAL AS THE BRUTALITY WAS ALLOWED TO CONTINUE THROUGHOUT CANADA'S HISTORY AS A NATION UNDER **GOD**.

ACCORDING TO THE 1996 REPORT SUBMITTED BY THE ROYAL COMMISSION ON ABORIGINAL PEOPLES, MANY OF THE BRUTAL BEATINGS AND EMOTIONAL TRAUMA LED TO A NUMBER OF INDIAN CHILDREN'S DEATHS THAT WERE TOTALLY INEXCUSABLE AND THAT SOMEONE HAD TO BE HELD ACCOUNTABLE IN THE END. SOME OF THEIR FINDINGS WERE AS FOLLOWS; DURING THE YEAR 1907 FOR EXAMPLE, A LIMITED SURVEY OF A FRACTION OF THE RESIDENTIAL SCHOOLS FOUND THAT ONE-QUARTER OF THE 1,500 STUDENTS NEVER LEFT THE SCHOOLS ALIVE. A RESIDENTIAL SCHOOL IN BRITISH COLUMBIA, ON

KUPER ISLAND (NORTH OF SALTSPRING ISLAND) REPORTEDLY HAD A FORTY PERCENT DEATH RATE OVER ITS SHORT 25 YEAR HISTORY. AND IN THAT SAME YEAR, A NATIVE STUDENT (CHARLIE CLINES) LOST HIS TOES TO FROSTBITE AFTER FLEEING HIS SCHOOL AT NORWAY HOUSE IN MANITOBA, TO ESCAPE EIGHT YEARS OF BEATINGS FOR WETTING THE BED. ALSO IN THAT YEAR, (1907), AT A PRESBYTERIAN RESIDENTIAL SCHOOL RUNAWAY BOYS WERE TIED BEHIND A BUGGY AND FORCED TO RUN THE TWELVE KILOMETERS BACK TO THE SCHOOL. AND IN 1925 AT THE ANGLICAN MACKAY SCHOOL IN MANITOBA, AN ABORIGINAL BOY FLED BAREFOOT AND ALMOST COMPLETELY NAKED AFTER BEING SEVERELY BEATEN UNTIL HE WAS BLACK AND BLUE. A NON-NATIVE MAN WHO HAD SEEN THE CHILD THREATENED TO CONTACT THE AUTHORITIES IF THE TREATMENT OF ABORIGINAL CHILDREN AT THE RESIDENTIAL SCHOOL DIDN'T IMPROVE – HIS EXACT WORDS ODDLY ENOUGH WERE THAT HE WOULD CONTACT "THE SPCA LIKE HE WOULD IF A DOG WAS ABUSED."

FURTHER TO THIS, THE COMMISSION'S REPORT FOUND THAT "THE DEEPEST SECRET OF ALL - THE PERVASIVE SEXUAL ABUSE OF THE CHILDREN" WAS RARELY EVER MENTIONED IN THE DEPARTMENT OF INDIAN AFFAIRS FILES AS THEY (THE GOVERNMENT OF CANADA) MERELY TURNED A BLIND EYE WHILE THE LEADERS OF THE RELIGIOUS INSTITUTIONS BECAME GOVERNMENTAL PROTECTED SEXUAL PREDATORS OF YOUNG INDIAN CHILDREN. HIDING BEHIND THEIR SELF-RIGHTEOUSNESS AND A SHROUD OF RELIGIOUS SECRECY, THE GOVERNMENT SANCTIONED PEDOPHILE MEMBERSHIP CONTINUED RUNNING THE RESIDENTIAL SCHOOLS, SEXUALLY EXPLOITING THE INDIAN CHILDREN FOR MANY, MANY GENERATIONS. OBVIOUSLY, THE WHITE RELIGIOUS ONES AND THEIR VARIOUS CHURCHES HAD LOTS TO LOSE IF THE SAVAGE INDIANS WERE EVER TO BECOME A CIVILIZED RACE OF PEOPLE LAUNCHING LEGAL ACTION AGAINST THE GUILTY PARTIES INVOLVED!!!

ALTHOUGH THE MAJORITY OF THE RESIDENTIAL SCHOOLS ACROSS CANADA WEREN'T PHASED OUT UNTIL THE LATE 1960's /OR EARLY 1970's, RESIDENTIAL SCHOOLS IN OUR COUNTRY'S UNEXPLORED NORTHERN FRONTIER NORTH OF THE 60TH PARALLEL DIDN'T SEE ITS DOORS CHAINED SHUT UNTIL NEARLY THE EMERGING OF THE 21ST CENTURY. THIS TRANSPIRED LARGELY DUE TO THE FACT THAT PANDORA'S BOX WAS PRIED WIDE OPEN BY THE RELEASE OF THE ROYAL COMMISSION'S REPORT AND THEREFORE SET THE STAGE FOR A LONG LIST OF LAWSUITS AGAINST THOSE RELIGIOUS INSTITUTIONS RESPONSIBLE FOR RUNNING THE BOARDING SCHOOLS. ONCE THE REPORT SAW THE LIGHT OF DAY IN 1996, ONE OF THE LAST RESIDENTIAL SCHOOLS IN CIVILIZED CANADA; ON THE GORDON RESERVE JUST NORTH OF REGINA IN THE PROVINCE OF SASKATCHEWAN WAS CLOSED FOR GOOD AND SUBSEQUENTLY TORN DOWN – THE RESIDENTIAL SCHOOLS IN THE COUNTRY'S FAR REACHES OF THE NORTHLAND SOON FOLLOWED.

Four years after the Royal Commission on Aboriginal Peoples released its finding to the general public, the number of individual lawsuits reached 6,324 and climbed even higher once the various religious institutions began to publically voice their concerns at the large number of physical abuse cases that were now before the courts right across the country essentially saying that in the end, the legal process was going to be forcing their churches into bankruptcy!!!

To this very day, the damage of the sexual and physical abuse that our country's aboriginal population had endured at the hands of the various religious institutions can be felt throughout the land as more and more of the travesties were fully disclosed at the court proceedings of sexual abuse cases as they became public knowledge. From St. John's, Newfoundland to Victoria on the Pacific and even up in the far reaches of the Arctic (Inuvik, Yellowknife, Whitehorse and Frobisher Bay), the Canadian judicial system of became swamped with countless lawsuits pertaining to sexual abuses while under the care of the religious institutions operating the residential schools within our country. For its part in allowing the abuses to go unreported for all of those years, the Canadian Federal Government's Ministry of Indian Affairs apologized to the native population in 1998 and established a $350 million healing fund hoping that the money would pacify the once savage Indians of our nation.

As the court proceedings disclosed the many horrors of life for an Indian child at the residential schools, many of British Columbia's aboriginal peoples pondered what other legal actions could be taken in order to have absolute and total justice served onto the whiteman's way of exploiting the First Nation Peoples. One-by-one, Indian bands within the Provincial jurisdictional boundaries filed lawsuits against the Government of British Columbia for outright theft of their lands. On Thursday, March 7TH, 2002 the Haida First Nation Peoples launched a legal claim to the Queen Charlotte Islands stating that they not only owned the land but were also legally entitled to its offshore oil and gas reserves. Then on the following day, the Tsawwassen First Nation Peoples filed for an injunction seeking to shut down two of B.C.'s most widely used docks that sat right in front of their reserve lands; the Provincial Government's ferry terminal and a super port operated by the Vancouver Port Authority. Almost immediately, the white citizenry of British Columbia began to fully realize the implications of the

PENDING COURT ACTIONS AND WHAT IT VIRTUALLY MEANT IF THE JUDICIAL SYSTEM AGREED WITH BOTH THE HAIDA AND TSAWWASSEN FIRST NATION PEOPLES AS A WHOLE. THE FACT THAT THE POWERS THAT BE DIDN'T LAY CLAIM TO THE QUEEN CHARLOTTE ISLANDS UNTIL 1849 AND THE REST OF THE ENTIRE PROVINCE NINE YEARS LATER (1858 IMPERIAL EDICT) WAS OF NO SIGNIFICANCE WHATSOEVER TO THE WHITE POPULATION OF BRITISH COLUMBIA AS THEY DEEMED THE LAWSUITS AS BEING ABSOLUTE AND UTTER NONSENSE. TO THE UNINFORMED WHITEMAN, THE ACTIONS TAKEN BY THE PROVINCE'S INDIAN POPULATION WAS SEEN AS A WAY AND MEANS OF GETTING SOMETHING FOR NOTHING. AFTERALL, HISTORY HAD ALREADY PROVEN THAT THE INDIANS WERE AN INFERIOR RACE OF PEOPLE INCAPABLE OF HAVING THE INTELLIGENCE TO FORMULATE /OR CARRY OUT ANY ELABORATE PLANS ON THEIR OWN.

WITH THE QUESTION OF ACTUAL OWNERSHIP OF INDIAN LANDS IN THE MIDST OF BEING ANSWERED BY THE WHITEMAN'S OWN JUDICIAL SYSTEM, THE LIBERAL GOVERNMENT OF BRITISH COLUMBIA MADE GOOD ON ITS PROMISE OF HOLDING A REFERENDUM ON ABORIGINAL RIGHTS TO THE NATIVE LAND CLAIMS ISSUE IN THE SPRING OF 2002 BY MAILING OUT REFERENDUM QUESTIONNAIRE PACKAGES. AND JUST LIKE ALL OF THE OTHER SO-CALLED DEMOCRATIC PLEBISCITES HELD IN THIS COUNTRY, THE QUESTIONS PUT FORWARD WERE WORDS OF A DOUBLE EDGED SWORD HAVING ONE SPECIFIC MEANING FOR THE PROVINCE'S CITIZENRY WHILE HAVING JUST THE OPPOSITE FOR THE POWERS THAT BE IN VICTORIA ON THE PACIFIC. IN FACT, ONE OF THE QUESTIONS ASKED ACTUALLY CONTAINED A DOUBLE NEGATIVE QUESTION THAT EVEN STUMPED SOME OF BRITISH COLUMBIA'S NATIVE SUPPORTERS. FOR INSTANCE IN QUESTION NUMBER 1, IF A PRIVATE LAND OWNER FELT THAT HIS /OR HER PROPERTY SHOULD NOT BE EXPROPRIATED FOR THE PURPOSE OF SETTLING THE LAND CLAIMS ISSUE, THEY WERE TO ANSWER **"YES "**TO THE QUESTION. BUT IF THE QUESTION WAS MISINTERPRETED /OR MISUNDERSTOOD IN ANY WAY, SHAPE /OR FORM, TO THE PRIVATE LAND OWNER IT WAS APPARENT THAT THE ANSWER WAS A FIRM **"NO"** INSISTING THAT HIS /OR HER PROPERTY WAS NOT TO BE EXPROPRIATED AS PART AND PARCEL OF THE TREATY SETTLEMENTS. THIS ESSENTIALLY WAS NO ACCIDENT OF FATE AS THE FRATERNAL GOVERNMENT OF BRITISH COLUMBIA INITIALLY SET OUT TO CONFUSE THE PEOPLE OF THE PROVINCE ANYWAYS AS A WAY AND MEANS OF FULFILLING THEIR OWN HIDDEN AGENDA BECAUSE ALL OF THE QUESTIONS ON THE REFERENDUM QUESTIONNAIRE WERE AS CONFUSING AS THE FIRST.

UPON FURTHER ANALYSIS OF THE QUESTIONNAIRE ITSELF, ALARM BELLS WERE INSTANTLY SOUNDED AS SOON AS THE ELECTORAL POPULATION CRACKED OPEN THEIR REFERENDUM PACKAGES. NUMBERS 1 AND 3 ENSURED THAT NEITHER PRIVATE NOR CROWN LANDS WERE TO BE PART OF THE TREATY PROCESS, WHILE QUESTIONS 2 AND 4 MADE ALL EXISTING AND/OR PROPOSED

INDUSTRY/TOURISM A SACRED COW THAT WAS NOT TO BE DISTURBED BY THE LAND CLAIMS ISSUE. FURTHERMORE, QUESTIONS 5 AND 6 MADE DAMN SURE THAT THE FORM OF WHICH THE NATIVE PEOPLES WERE GOING TO BE TAKING IN THEIR ATTEMPTS OF INSTITUTING SELF-GOVERNMENT WOULD IN THE END BE NO BETTER THAN THAT OF A MUNICIPALITY, WHICH QUESTION 7 ENABLED THE GOVERNMENT OF B.C. TO ASSIST IN THE SETTING UP OF YET ANOTHER LEVEL OF GOVERNMENT THAT MORE THAN LIKELY WOULD NOT BE ABLE TO SURPASS THE PROVINCIAL GOVERNMENT'S OWN JURISDICTIONAL POWERS – WITH THE FRATERNAL GOVERNMENT OF BRITISH COLUMBIA OBVIOUSLY HAVING THE FINAL SAY IN ALL POLITICAL MATTERS BOTH BIG AND SMALL. AND LASTLY, QUESTION NUMBER 8, MAKING DAMN SURE THAT ALL SETTLEMENT PACKAGES CONCERNING THE LAND CLAIMS ISSUE DID NOT TAKE THE FORM OF A CASH SETTLEMENT WHICH IN TURN WOULD HAVE LITERALLY FORCED THE PROVINCE OF BRITISH COLUMBIA INTO SHEER BANKRUPTCY.

UTILIZING THE CHARTER OF RIGHTS AND FREEDOMS UNDER THE CANADIAN CONSTITUTION ACT OF 1982, WHICH IN ESSENCE GAVE THE POWERS THAT BE IN VICTORIA ON THE PACIFIC FULL CONSTITUTIONAL GROUNDS OF EXERCISING DEMOCRATIC PROCESS, THE GOVERNMENT OF BRITISH COLUMBIA SET THE FRATERNITY WHEELS IN MOTION FOR THESE HEINOUS ACTS OF DISCRIMINATION TO TAKE PLACE AGAINST THE PROVINCE'S ABORIGINAL PEOPLES. UNREASONABLE AND ARBITRARY DISCRIMINATORY ACTIONS OF OTHER INDIVIDUALS AND/OR GROUPS OF PEOPLE, BE THEY GOVERNMENTAL, JUDICIAL AND/OR OTHERWISE, WERE ONCE AGAIN TELLING OUR COUNTRY'S FIRST INHABITANTS WHEN TO EAT, DRINK AND/OR BE MERRY. ALTHOUGH BRITISH COLUMBIA PROFESSED ITSELF AS BEING A VERY DIPLOMATIC OPEN SOCIETY DIVERSE IN MANY CULTURES OF THE WORLD, FOR THE PROVINCE'S NATIVE PEOPLES, NOTHING HAD REALLY CHANGED AS THEY WERE STILL SHACKLED TO THEIR MASTERS BED POST AND TOLD TO CATER TO THE WHIMS OF SERVITUDE.

AS FAR AS THE VAST MAJORITY OF BRITISH COLUMBIA'S POPULATION WAS CONCERNED, THE QUESTIONS PUT FORWARD ON THE TREATY REFERENDUM PROPOSAL WAS INITIALLY A QUESTIONNAIRE WHICH CONSTITUTED RACISM AND THEREFORE WAS NOT EVEN WORTHY OF RECEIVING A RESPONSE. TO THAT END, ON APRIL 2ND, 2002 THE PROVINCIAL GOVERNMENT MAILED OUT 2,127,829 REFERENDUM PACKAGES TO THE PROVINCE'S ELIGIBLE VOTERS AND BY THE MIDDLE OF THE FOLLOWING MONTH, (MAY 15TH BEING OF COURSE THE MAIL-IN DEADLINE FOR THE REFERENDUM ITSELF), ONLY 763,480 BALLOTS WERE RETURNED TO THE POWERS THAT BE IN VICTORIA. ALTHOUGH THIS FIGURE REPRESENTED LESS THAN ONE-THIRD OF ALL THE REFERENDUM BALLOTS THAT THE BRITISH COLUMBIA GOVERNMENT HAD SENT OUT TO THE ELECTORAL POPULATION, THE GOVERNING POWERS STILL INSISTED THAT THE PEOPLE OF B.C. WERE SAID TO HAVE SPOKEN WITH A RESOUNDING **"NO "**VOTE

CONCERNING THE ACTUAL SETTLING OF THE PROVINCE'S NATIVE LAND CLAIMS ISSUE. THE LIBERAL GOVERNMENT'S CLAIM INSISTING THAT ANYWHERE BETWEEN 84 TO 94 PERCENT OF THE POPULATION OF BRITISH COLUMBIA SUPPORTED THE PROVINCIAL GOVERNMENT'S STANCE ON THE ISSUE OF HOW ABORIGINAL PEOPLES WERE GOING TO BE TREATED WHILE UNDER AN OLD BOYS NETWORK OF STEWARDSHIP. HOWLS OF OUTRAGE WERE SOON HEARD FROM JUST ABOUT EVERY PART OF BRITISH COLUMBIA AS ITS PEOPLE (NATIVE AND NON-NATIVE) CONDEMNED THE PROVINCIAL LIBERALS' INTERPRETATION OF THE REFERENDUM RESULTS AS THEY WERE MADE PUBLIC. TO THOSE WHO FLATLY REFUSED TO PARTICIPATE IN THE "ONE-SIDED AND AMATEURISH" TACTIC OF TRYING TO CON THE GENERAL POPULATION INTO VOTING THE GOVERNMENT'S WAY, THE PROVINCIAL LIBERAL FRATERNITY DOG AND PONY SHOW WAS PRETTY WELL A TOTAL WASTE OF BOTH TIME AND MONEY AS FAR AS GENERAL PUBLIC WAS CONCERNED – COSTING THE TAXPAYERS OF THE PROVINCE OF B.C. AN ESTIMATED 10 MILLION DOLLARS.

TO MOST BRITISH COLUMBIANS, THE WEASEL TYPE WORDING OF THE QUESTIONNAIRE WAS ESPECIALLY HARD TO SWALLOW CONSIDERING THE FACT THAT AS THEY KNEW THE LAW IN ACCORDANCE TO FORMER PRIME MINISTER TRUDEAU'S CANADIAN CONSTITUTION ACT OF 1982, THE GOVERNMENT OF BRITISH COLUMBIA HAD NO REAL JURISDICTIONAL POWERS OVER ITS ABORIGINAL POPULATION AND THEREFORE WASTED ALL THOSE MILLIONS OF TAX DOLLARS ON SOMETHING THAT WAS TOTALLY UNENFORCEABLE. COINCIDENTLY, MOST, IF NOT ALL OF THE QUESTIONS RAISED BY THE REFERENDUM QUESTIONNAIRE (PRIVATE PROPERTY RIGHTS TO PENDING AND/ OR NON-PENDING TAX EXEMPTIONS) WERE SAID TO HAVE BEEN WAY BEYOND THE POLITICAL POWERS OF THE RULING PROVINCIAL LIBERAL PARTY AND WERE FURTHER SAID TO HAVE BEEN A MATTER FOR THE FEDERAL LIBERAL PARTY TO IRON OUT AND NOT THAT OF THE PROVINCIAL LIBERALS. BEFORE LONG, THE REFERENDUM WAS BEING LABELED AS A DUMB MOVE ON THE GOVERNMENT OF BRITISH COLUMBIA'S PART AND HENCE A NEW TERMINOLOGY CAME INTO BEING AS **"REFERENDUMB "**SOON BECAME TO RHETORIC OF THE DAY BY THOSE WHO OPPOSED ITS LONG TERM IMPLICATIONS.

WITH ONLY 35.83 PERCENT OF THE PROVINCE'S ELIGIBLE VOTERS DICTATING AS TO HOW THEY FELT ON THE NATIVE LAND CLAIMS ISSUE, THE GOVERNMENT OF BRITISH COLUMBIA PROCLAIMED THE REFERENDUM A SUCCESS STATING THAT AN OVERWHELMING MAJORITY OF THE MINORITY THAT ACTUALLY PARTICIPATED REPORTEDLY VOTED **"YES"** TO ALL OF THE EIGHT QUESTIONS ON THE BALLOT WHICH IN TURN VOICED A RESOUNDING NEGATIVE RESPONSE CONCERNING THE ACTUAL SETTLING OF THE PROVINCE'S NATIVE LAND CLAIMS ISSUE. ACCORDING TO THE POWERS THAT BE IN VICTORIA ON THE PACIFIC, THE VOTERS THEREFORE GAVE THE GOVERNMENT OF THE DAY A

MANDATE FOR A HARD LINE APPROACH ON ALL FUTURE NEGOTIATIONS WITH B.C.'s First Nation Peoples.

How ironic, when the whiteman wanted the land that the Indians had, the land was simply taken away from them, then and only then were the necessary changes made to the whiteman laws making the actual theft of the Indian lands legally binding in a court of law. But when the Indians ultimately stood up in defiance to the whiteman's own laws demanding that the stolen lands be returned, the whiteman all of a sudden gathers his brethren around him telling them that in accordance to the democratic process under the Canadian Charter they had lots to loose if this inferior race of people were allowed to take possession of the lands once occupied by their ancestors for thousands upon thousands of years prior to the 1858 Imperial Edict actually being implemented. The whiteman, therefore made the minor adjustments necessary that would allow the more superior race of people to reign supreme while forcing the inferior ones to beg like a dog for a bone.

Contrary as to what the fraternal Government of B.C. was saying regarding the end results of the referendum, the vast majority of British Columbians didn't even bother filling in their ballots because they apparently realized that it was a totally stacked deck in favor of the powers that be in Victoria the instant that the questionnaire was scrutinized by them. Some residents of the Province, (slightly more than 7 percent of the respondents), spoiled their ballots before returning their democratic vote to the government, while others simply turfed the referendum packages in their round filing cabinet where it actually belonged; in the garbage can!!!

Reportedly, more than 40,000 British Columbians sent their ballots to aboriginal leaders province-wide in protest to the government's attempts of derailing the native land claim treaty negotiations. The mail-in referendum itself was such a hot button topic for most of the general population that countless protests and demonstrations were soon being executed throughout various regions of the Province where both natives and non-natives alike burned their ballots in total disbelief as to what the powers that be in Victoria on the Pacific were attempting to pull off all in the name of democracy. Sechelt Indian Band leaders for instance urged residents of the Sunshine Coast to destroy their ballots rather than vote against the native land claims issue — as did a large majority of other Indian Bands throughout the Province of British Columbia. Boycotting the referendum vote at the time seemed like

THE ONLY LOGICAL AND HUMANE THING TO DO AS THE ENTIRE FUTURE OF THE PROVINCE'S FIRST NATION PEOPLES WAS NOW AT THE PERIL OF ITS VERY EXISTENCE AS THE GOVERNMENT OF THE DAY WAS TRYING TO GET ALL BRITISH COLUMBIANS INVOLVED WITH SOAKING THEIR HANDS IN ABORIGINAL BLOOD FOR THE SAKE OF DEMOCRACY. CONSIDERED BY ALL ACCOUNTS OF BEING NOTHING BUT A SHAM TREATY REFERENDUM, ALL IT REALLY ACCOMPLISHED WAS TO FUEL THE FIRE THAT ENABLED THE GENERAL POPULATION OF B.C.'s OUTRAGE TO ESCALATE EVEN FURTHER WHEN THE ANGLICAN CHURCH PUBLICALLY DENOUNCED THE WAY IN WHICH THE FRATERNAL GOVERNMENT OF BRITISH COLUMBIA WAS SODOMIZING THE INDIAN PEOPLE.

IN THE USUAL HIGH AND MIGHTY RHETORIC OF ALL RELIGIOUS INSTITUTIONS, A SERMON WAS GIVEN DURING SUNDAY SERVICES ON APRIL 7TH, 2002 – WHILE STANDING IN FRONT OF PARISHIONERS AT CHRIST CHURCH CATHEDRAL IN VANCOUVER – ANGLICAN CHURCH LEADERS LET IT BE KNOWN WHERE THE PROTESTANTS STOOD ON THE TOPIC OF THE MAIL-IN REFERENDUM. AT THE BEGINNING OF THE CHURCH SERVICE, A PASTORAL LETTER ON THE SELF-RIGHTEOUS SUBJECT WAS READ OUT ALOUD FROM ALL FOUR BISHOPS OF B.C. AND THE YUKON TERRITORY URGING ITS CONGREGATION MEMBERS TO VOTE **"NO "**TO ALL OF THE REFERENDUM QUESTIONS, INSISTING THAT THE MERE THOUGHT OF A GOVERNMENT IMPOSING SUCH RESTRICTIONS ONTO A PEOPLE WAS TOTALLY IRRESPONSIBLE IN NATURE. THE PASTORAL LETTER OF CONDEMNATION WAS REPORTEDLY READ AT EACH AND EVERY ANGLICAN CHURCH IN THE PROVINCE ASKING SOME 300,000 ANGLICANS TO LET THE GOVERNMENT OF BRITISH COLUMBIA KNOWN EXACTLY AS TO WHERE THE PROTESTANT FAITH STOOD ON THE ISSUE OF GOVERNMENTAL DECREE OF SODOMIZATION ON THE TREATY PROCESS. THE PROTESTANT CHURCH THEN BEGAN FORMING A CHURCH TASK FORCE WHICH WAS DESIGNED STRICTLY FOR SHOW AS IT WAS SAID TO HAVE HAD A RELIGIOUS MANDATE IN REVIEWING THE LEGITIMACY OF THE REFERENDUM ITSELF. WITHIN ONLY A MATTER OF HOURS, A COALITION OF SORTS WAS FORMULATED AS BY THIS TIME PERIOD MOST BRITISH COLUMBIANS HAD AN AXE TO GRIND WITH THE GOVERNMENT OF THE PROVINCE – IT WAS VIRTUALLY A COALITION OF DISGRUNTLED TAXPAYERS FROM THE LABOR MOVEMENT, WOMEN'S RIGHTS GROUPS, HUMAN RIGHTS GROUPS AND EVEN ENVIRONMENTALISTS, WHO WANTED TO EXPRESS THEIR CONCERNS IN THE WAY WHICH THE GOVERNMENT OF BRITISH COLUMBIA WAS CONDUCTING ITS OUTLANDISH GENOCIDAL WAR ON THE PROVINCE'S FIRST NATION PEOPLES.

WITH THE SCATTERING OF THE SELF-RIGHTEOUS BOX OF FRUIT LOOPS ALL OVER HELL'S CREATION ONCE AGAIN, MOST BRITISH COLUMBIANS SOON BEGAN QUESTIONING THE ANGLICAN CHURCH'S REACTION TO THE TREATY REFERENDUM CITING THAT A DOUBLE STANDARD HAD ACTUALLY MANAGED TO

REAR ITS UGLY HEAD AS THE CHURCH WAS ONCE AGAIN TRYING TO DICTATE POLICY AS IT DID DURING DAYS-GONE-BY FROM ITS PULPITS. TO THE VAST MAJORITY OF THE PROVINCE'S POPULATION, THE MOST HYPOCRITICAL OF ALL WAS THE FACT THAT WHILE ALL OF SEXUAL ABUSES AND OTHER IMMORAL ACTS OF DEGRADATION WERE BEING PERFORMED BY THE RELIGIOUS SEXUAL PERVERTS OF THE ROMAN CATHOLIC AND PROTESTANT FAITHS, THE ANGLICAN CHURCH MAINTAINED ITS CODE OF SILENCE HOPING THAT THE SEXUAL PREFERENCES OF ITS PASTORS FOR YOUNG NATIVE CHILDREN (BOTH MALE AND FEMALE) WOULD GO UNNOTICED. AS FAR AS MOST BRITISH COLUMBIANS WERE CONCERNED, THE ANGLICAN CHURCH HAD NO DAMN BUSINESS INTERFERING WITH B.C.'S POLITICS AS THEIR BISHOPS ATTEMPTED TO TAKE THE HIGH MORAL GROUND WHILE THEIR RELIGIOUS INSTITUTION WAS ON THE VERGE OF BANKRUPTCY BECAUSE OF THE TREMENDOUS AMOUNT OF PEDOPHILES FOUND WITHIN ITS OWN ORGANIZATION. THE ANGLICAN CHURCH WAS IN THE MIDST OF BEING SUED BY THE VERY SAME PEOPLE THAT THEY HAD CLAIMED TO RESPECT IN THEIR PASTORAL LETTER CONDEMNING THE GOVERNMENT OF THE DAY FOR SODOMIZING THE PROVINCE'S INDIAN POPULATION ON THE TREATY PROCESS. THE FACT REMAINED PURE AND SIMPLE, MOST, IF NOT ALL OF THE ANGLICAN CHURCH PEDOPHILES' VICTIMS WERE ABORIGINAL CHILDREN WHO FELL PREY TO THE RELIGIOUS ONES AND THEIR TWISTED/DEMENTED SEXUAL APPETITES FOR YOUNG INDIAN CHILDREN.

IN SPEAKING OF WHITEMAN HYPOCRISY, FIVE OF THE PROVINCE'S ABORIGINAL LEADERS AND A GROUP OF NATIVE ELDERS ATTEMPTED TO PREVENT THE REFERENDUM RESULTS FROM BEING COUNTED – KNOWING FULL WELL THAT ONCE THE FINAL BALLOTS WERE TALLIED AND DULY REGISTERED IN THE RECORD BOOKS BY ELECTIONS B.C., ALL WOULD BE LOST. IN THEIR ATTEMPT TO HAVE THE B.C. SUPREME COURT PASS JUDGEMENT MAKING THE REFERENDUM NULL AND VOID AS AN OUTRIGHT VIOLATION OF THEIR ABORIGINAL RIGHTS UNDER THE CANADIAN CHARTER, ALL OF THEIR TRADITIONAL CHANTING FOR SOCIAL EQUALITY FELL ON DEAF EARS AS EVEN THE COURTS SIDED WITH THE FRATERNAL GOVERNMENT OF BRITISH COLUMBIA AND ALLOWED THE COUNT TO TAKE PLACE. ACCORDING TO THE SUPREME COURT OF BRITISH COLUMBIA, THE ABORIGINALS DID NOT ESTABLISH SUFFICIENT EVIDENCE THAT WOULD HAVE VERIFIED THEIR CLAIM "THAT IRREPARABLE HARM WILL RESULT FROM THE REFERENDUM VOTE BEING COUNTED." IN ESSENCE, THE SUPREME COURT OF BRITISH COLUMBIA ENDORSED THE LEGALIZATION OF THE GENOCIDAL WAR THAT THE FRATERNAL GOVERNMENT OF B.C. HAD WAGED AGAINST THE PROVINCE'S FIRST NATION PEOPLES. THIS LITERALLY MARKED THE BEGINNING OF THE END FOR ALL BRITISH COLUMBIA'S NATIVE POPULATION AS ELECTIONS B.C. THUSLY SUBMITTED ITS REPORT TO THE PROVINCIAL GOVERNMENT WHICH IN TURN PROCLAIMED THAT THE REFERENDUM WAS VICTORIOUS IN ITS FLAWLESS FRATERNITY DESIGN. DESPITE THE FACT OF THE LOW TURNOUT

REGARDING THE REFERENDUM'S PROPOSAL QUESTIONNAIRE, THE END RESULTS OF THE REFERENDUM ITSELF WERE LEGALLY BINDING ON THE GOVERNMENT'S PART UNDER LEGISLATION PERTAINING TO THE REFERENDUM ACT OF THE PROVINCE. WHICH ESSENTIALLY MEANT THAT THE WHITEMAN'S GOVERNMENT COULD NOW INCORPORATED ITS OWN INTERPRETATIONS INTO ALL OF THE TREATY NEGOTIATIONS AS THE PROVINCE'S INDIAN PEOPLE WERE ABOUT TO BE SODOMIZED EVEN FURTHER BY THE MORE SUPERIOR RACE OF PEOPLE.

SINCE ALL OF THIS HAS LITERALLY UNFOLDED BEFORE EVERYONE'S VERY EYES IN JUST A SHORT TIME SPAN (THE LATTER PARTS OF THE TWENTIETH CENTURY AS WELL AS THE EARLY YEARS OF THE 21ST CENTURY), IT THEREFORE POSES A RATHER INTERESTING AND FUNDAMENTAL QUESTION PERTAINING TO THE SO-CALLED NON-EXISTENT REPORT **"RED POWER - CANADA"** WHICH REPORTEDLY STATED CATEGORICALLY THAT THE GREATEST THREAT TO CANADIAN SECURITY CAME FROM WITHIN THE COUNTRY'S VERY OWN INDIAN POPULATION AS THEY ATTEMPTED TO SETTLE THE NATIVE LAND CLAIMS ISSUE ON A NATIONAL SCALE. IT THUSLY MAKES A PERSON SIT BACK AND CONTEMPLATE AS TO WHAT LIFE HAS IN STORE FOR THE ENTIRE HUMAN RACE AS THE REMAINING YEARS OF THE 21ST CENTURY SLOWLY BEGINS TO SHED ITS REPTILIAN SKIN!!!

PART 2

KNOWLEDGE IS POWER

Chapter 8 - Through a Masonic Looking Glass

Democracy is a great concept, but it seems that over the last 40 or 50 years it has been replaced by a pure dictatorship. Take the Liberal administration of Lester B. Pearson and the great Canadian flag controversy of the early 1960's for example. In 1963, Canada's then-Prime Minister informed the public that he wanted the nation to have its own flag — Pearson wanted to have a political statement informing Canadians that we, as a society were not British nor were we Americans. The Dominion of Canada had been using Britain's Union Jack /or the British Red Ensign, (which was actually the flag for the British merchant marines). There was no doubt about it, the vast majority of the Canadian population in English Canada was that of British descendant. But Pearson's new flag proposal split Canadians even further apart. For months on end, the bitter argument enraged British loyalists and thus created more animosity between the Anglo-Canadians, the Francophone population and the Canadian establishment itself. Prime Minister Pearson supposedly wanted to decolonize the Dominion of Canada, thus moving its economic ties even closer to those south of the 49TH parallel. If Canada and its people were to survive economically, then Canadians had no choice but to become just like the Americans; loud, obnoxious and self-serving.

While Pearson helped lay the foundation for the American's "Manifest Destiny", Conservative opposition leader John Diefenbaker was totally outraged at the maneuver. Dief the Chief demanded that the Union Jack remain, thus symbolizing the British founding race of people. Not long after Pearson announced his great American dream to the disgruntled Canadian population, he pushed his dictatorial dream onto the Royal Canadian Legion fraternity at its

1963 ANNUAL CONVENTION. PRIME MINISTER PEARSON RECEIVED NOTHING BUT BOOS AND HISSES FROM THE LEGIONARIES, CANADIANS MARCHED TO WAR UNDER THE RED ENSIGN AND/OR THE UNION JACK. THE ROYAL CANADIAN LEGION THUS REFUSED TO ENDORSE THE MAPLE LEAF, LEGIONARIES WANTED NOTHING TO DO WITH PEARSON'S DISLOYAL REGARD FOR THE BRITISH MONARCHY. IN THE EYES OF MANY WAR VETERANS, THERE COULD BE NO FLAG WITHOUT THE UNION JACK. IN FACT, THEY FELT THAT CANADA LOST ITS BRITISH HERITAGE ONCE THE MAPLE LEAF WAS UNVEILED AS THE COUNTRY'S GLORY BANNER. AS PEARSON PUSHED HARDER FOR HIS FLAG, HE WAS CALLED BOTH A TRAITOR AND A COMMUNIST. DIEFENBAKER PROTESTED PEARSON'S NEW FLAG PROPOSAL TO THE BITTER END, BUT TO NO AVAIL. MANY BRITISH SUBJECTS LITERALLY WANTED THE CANADIAN PRIME MINISTER'S HEAD ON A SILVER PLATTER. PROTESTS WERE EXECUTED ON PARLIAMENT HILL AS THE CONTROVERSY ALMOST IMMEDIATELY HEATED UP. ON JUNE 15TH, 1964 THE GREAT FLAG DEBATE FOUND ITS WAY INTO THE HOUSE OF COMMONS. EVERYONE INSTANTLY GOT ONTO THE BANDWAGON AS DOZENS UPON DOZENS OF SUGGESTIONS AND/OR IDEAS WERE SUBMITTED, MOST OF WHICH INCLUDED VARIOUS ETHNIC SYMBOLS, (BEAVERS, CROWNS, CROSSES, SCOTTISH THISTLE AND EVEN AN IRISH SHAMROCK). BACK THEN, CANADIANS DEFINITELY DIDN'T FULLY UNDERSTAND THE POLITICAL BACKGROUND OF THEIR OWN COUNTRY — ALL WAS FORGOTTEN!!!

IN A PARLIAMENTARY DEBATE MANNER, 308 SPEECHES WERE MADE, THAT LITERALLY DRAGGED ON FOR WEEKS. AS THE DEBATE CAME TO A CLOSE, THE FLAG CONTROVERSY WAS REFERRED TO AN ALL-PARTY COMMITTEE — CANADIANS WERE GOING TO BE GETTING THIS NEW FLAG WHETHER THEY WANTED IT /OR NOT, (SO MUCH FOR DEMOCRACY). BY MID-FEBRUARY 1965, THE DOMINION OF CANADA HOISTED ITS NEW RED-AND-WHITE MAPLE LEAF FOR ALL THE WORLD TO SEE. PRIME MINISTER PEARSON LOOKED ONWARD AS THE "GOLDARN RAG" OF DECOLONIZATION LAID IMPOTENT IN A LIGHT BREEZE ABOVE THE PEACE TOWER ON PARLIAMENT HILL. THE DESIGN OF THE FLAG ITSELF WAS STOLEN FROM OTHER SOURCES, THERE WAS NOTHING ORIGINAL ABOUT THIS SO-CALLED NATIONAL GLORY BANNER SO DEEMED TO BE THE CANADIAN FLAG. APPARENTLY, THE SINGLE RED MAPLE LEAF WORN BY VANCOUVER, B.C. RUNNER PERCY WILLIAMS IN THE 1920 WORLD GAMES WAS MERELY APPLIED TO A WHITE FIELD WITH RED BORDERS. PEARSON IN FACT LIKED THE DESIGN SO MUCH THAT HE INVOKED CLOSURE IN THE HOUSE OF COMMONS TO CUT OFF FURTHER DEBATE CONCERNING THE NEW FLAG AND CANADIANS WERE GOING TO ACCEPT IT AS BEING THEIR NEW FLAG EVEN IF IT MEANT THE IMMEDIATE DEMISE OF CANADA AS A NATION UNDER GOD THE FATHER.

WITH THE FLAG CONTROVERSY BEHIND HIM, PEARSON PREPARED CANADIANS FOR THE NEXT PHASE OF THE AMERICAN VERSION OF "**MANIFEST**

Destiny". A young charismatic maverick politician from the Province of Quebec was purposely selected as leader of the Liberal Party of Canada. Ironically, when this tin-god-like person was first anointed as our country's Prime Minister in 1968, many Canadians saw him as the nation's own personal savior, Canada's very own version of John F. Kennedy as it were. Within any political organization and/or party that wishes to deceive the people by having for its objective the establishment of an elected dictatorship, first there must be an instrument capable of fulfilling its purpose. It must, then, be firmly anchored to its object so that it is impossible for it to drift, the first thing needed, is a clear statement of what the object actually is. It must be clear because the party seeking votes can only gain its object through men and women who throughly understand what the object is. Those individuals who hold the idea that it is the "leader "or representative who is the source of power are, of course, quite logical in adopting an "object" that will appeal to the greatest numbers. In such a case all that is wanted is shoulders to climb upon. The "leader "being the strength of the organization, it is quite sufficient that they understand the object of the organization, the others do not matter.

But within a true democratic political organization, the case is very different. The first principle of such is that it is the average workers as a class who must fight the battle to remove the shackles of their bondage; it is they who must be strong, since their servants and delegates can be strong only with their strength. The logic of this is that the fitness of the political party for its purpose depends upon the quality and strength, not of the "leader "but rather of its own membership. The essential, then, of the political party is a clear and definitely stated **OBJECT**. Since society is automatically divided into two distinct classifications, one of which is enslaved to the other, one of which exploits, preys upon the other; all political parties in Canada have a stated hidden objective. (The interest of one class is to maintain its position of dominance, while the interest of the other class is to escape from the clutches of servitude).

Those who want to hold public office, who are determined to get their feet firmly planted on the floor of the House of Commons and/or a Provincial Legislature are not particularly fussy as to how they do it and thus claim that the emancipation of the average working class need not stand up in defiance to the powers that be. The reason for this is easily seen, the only way in which they would be able to set foot into the political arena is by denying the actual

EXISTENCE OF A NEED FOR A REVOLT BY THE WORKING CLASS. REVOLUTION AND CLASS STRUGGLE OF COURSE ARE NECESSARILY CONNECTED AS THEY GO HAND-IN-HAND WHEN ATTEMPTING TO REMOVE THE SHACKLES OF ONE'S OWN BONDAGE. THE GRADUALIST THEREFORE, IN ORDER THAT HE /OR SHE MAY GET HIS /OR HER FEET PLANTED ON THE FLOOR OF A LEGISLATURE /OR THE HOUSE OF COMMONS WITH THE HELP OF NON-REVOLUTIONARY VOTES, IS FORCED TO DENY THE REVOLUTION BECAUSE THAT IMPLIES RECOGNIZING THE EXISTENCE OF A CLASS STRUGGLE. THOSE, HOWEVER, WHO REALIZE THE FACTS OF THE POLITICAL SITUATION, KNOW THAT THE WORKERS WOULD NOT BE DRIVEN TO SEEK EMANCIPATION BUT FOR THE CLASS ANTAGONISM; HENCE THEY ARE DRIVEN TO ACCEPT THE CLASS STRUGGLE AS THE VERY BASIS OF THEIR OWN ACTION.

THERE IS THE SHEET ANCHOR OF THE REVOLUTIONARY PARTY, IT IS THIS WHICH BEYOND ALL ELSE SECURES TO THE CONSCIOUSLY ORGANIZED WORKING CLASS THE EFFICIENCY OF THEIR ORGANIZATION FOR ITS REVOLUTIONARY PURPOSE. WHILE ADHERENCE TO THIS VITAL PRINCIPLE REMAINS ONE OF THE CONDITIONS OF MEMBERSHIP, IT CAN NEVER BECOME THE PLAYTHING OF THE LEADERS AND/OR DICTATORS. A MEMBERSHIP HOLDING TO THAT CLAUSE HAS A GAUGE WHEREWITH TO MEASURE ANY PERSON'S ACTION, AND AN INSTRUMENT TO FIRE HIM /OR HER OUT WITH, IF HE /OR SHE BE FOUND WANTING. THE FIRST SIGN OF COMPROMISE, THE FIRST INDICATION OF ALLIANCE WITH THE ENEMY, THE FIRST PARTICLE OF EVIDENCE THAT A MEMBER HAS BECOME THE TOOL OF ANY SECTION OF THE MASTER CLASS, AND HE /OR SHE IS DEALT WITH BY A MEMBERSHIP IMBUED WITH THE PRINCIPLE OF CLASS STRUGGLE.

BASED UPON SUCH PRINCIPLES AS THESE, THE POLITICAL PARTY OF THE WORKING CLASS CANNOT DRIFT AWAY FROM THE **OBJECT**, AND MUST REMAIN A SOUND ORGANIZATION, AN INSTRUMENT CAPABLE OF ACHIEVING ITS PURPOSE. JUST AS IT CAN ONLY BE COMPOSED OF REVOLUTIONARY MEN AND WOMEN CONSCIOUS OF THEIR CLASS POSITION AND THE REMEDY FOR IT, THE MEN AND WOMEN WHO ALONE ARE CAPABLE OF ACHIEVING THE SOCIAL REVOLUTION, SO IT IS CAPABLE OF CREATING SUCH A CLASS CONSCIOUS WORKING CLASS, BY ITS CLEAR CUT, CLASS STRUGGLE, REVOLUTIONARY POLICY. THIS POLICY LEAVES NO DOUBT AS TO THE ENEMY, IT LEAVES NO DOUBT AS TO THE CHARACTER OF THE STRUGGLE THAT DICTATES IT. AND ABOVE ALL ELSE, IT LEAVES NO DOUBT AS TO THE STRENGTH OF THE REVOLUTIONARY MOVEMENT.

FOR WHEN EVERY VOTE IS ASKED FOR ITS OPPOSITION TO LIBERAL AND TORY, IN OPPOSITION TO THE SOCIAL-DEMOCRATIC PARTY AND THE INDEPENDENTS, IN OPPOSITION TO REFORMISTS CONFUSION AND VOTE CATCHING SLOGANS, ASKED FOR EVERY VOTE WILL BE FOUND A SOUND VOTE. A VOTE WHICH OWES THE MASTER CLASS NOTHING, AND FROM WHICH THEY CAN TAKE NOTHING AWAY, A VOTE BACKED BY THE REVOLUTIONARY FORCE OF

THE VOTER, AND THEREFORE A VOTE TO STRIKE FEAR INTO THE HEARTS OF ALL EXPLOITERS. THE POLITICAL MACHINERY THAT EXPLOITS THE PEOPLE MUST BE CAPTURED BY THE PEOPLE, THE WORKERS, BY ORGANIZING THEMSELVES INTO A NEW POLITICAL PARTY, HAVE FOR ITS **OBJECT** THE OVERTHROW OF THE PRESENT SOCIAL SYSTEM AND THE ESTABLISHMENT OF A SYSTEM OF SOCIETY BASED ON COMMON OWNERSHIP OF THE MEANS OF LIVING. THESE STATEMENTS AND MANY LIKE THEM HAVE BEEN PREACHED IN THE PAST, BUT LONG FORGOTTEN BY THE SOCIAL-DEMOCRATS OF THE NEW MILLENNIUM AS POLITICAL BACK ROOM WHEELING AND DEALING IS THE FLAVORED CHOICE OF THE 21ST CENTURY.

WITHIN THE CONCEPT OF A TRUE DEMOCRACY PROCESS, THE VOTE IS TO BE THE PREFERRED WEAPON OF CHOICE. ON THAT NOTE, ONE MUST INQUIRE THEREFORE; WHAT IS THE REAL NATURE OF THE VOTE???

AT ONE TIME MEN SUPPORTED THEIR INTERESTS BY SHEER BRUTE FORCE OF ARMS, GRADUALLY, IT WAS RECOGNIZED THAT, OVER ALL THINGS BEING EQUAL, POWER RESTS WITH NUMBERS. FROM THIS TO THE IDEA THAT THOSE WHO POSSESS MILITANT POWER CAN EXPRESS IT JUST AS EFFECTIVELY AND MUCH MORE CONVENIENTLY BY A VOTE THAN BY A BLOW, IS BUT ONE SINGLE STEP. THUS THE VOTE HAS BEEN IN EXISTENCE AT THE VERY DAWN OF AUTHENTIC HISTORY. IN REALITY, (UNDER A TRUE DEMOCRATIC PROCESS), A VOTE IS SEEN AS NOTHING MORE THAN A CROSS ON A SCRAP PIECE OF PAPER, IN THIS RESPECT IT IS VERY SIMILAR TO THAT OF A BANK NOTE. A BANK NOTE OF ITSELF IS PRACTICALLY VALUELESS. IT DERIVES ITS "BANK NOTE VALUE "ENTIRELY FROM THE PUBLIC CONFIDENCE IN THE SECURITY AT THE BACK OF IT. WHERE ANY DOUBT EXISTS AS TO THIS, THE FACT IS INDICATED IN THE DEPRECIATION OF THE "VALUE "OF THE PAPER MONEY. OR, IN CANADA'S CASE, THE LOONIE / TWOONIE!!!

IT IS EXACTLY THE SAME WITH THE VOTE. NO SEGMENT OF SOCIETY OBTAINS VOTING POWER UNTIL IT PROVES BY STRUGGLE THAT ITS DEMANDS CANNOT BE IGNORED. IT THEN BECOMES TO THE ADVANTAGE OF THE DOMINANT CLASS TO PERMIT THESE DEMANDS TO BE EXPRESSED THROUGH THE BALLOT BOX RATHER THAN THROUGH THE DISRUPTIVE AND WASTEFUL CHANNEL OF OPEN STRUGGLE.

THE VALUE OF THE VOTE IS THEREFORE MEASURED BY THE PERSON BEHIND THE VOTE.

WITH THAT BEING SO, THEN, IT IS CLEAR THAT IT IS NOT THE ELECTED REPRESENTATIVE WHO IS THE ALL IMPORTANT FACTOR HERE, BUT RATHER THE QUALITY OF THE VOTE WHICH PUTS HIM /OR HER INTO PLACE. WHAT, THEN, MUST BE QUALITY OF THE VOTE??? SURELY THE QUALITY OF THE VOTE WILL ENABLE IT TO AFFECT ITS PURPOSE. THE REVOLUTIONARY PURPOSE OF COURSE BEING REVOLUTION, THE VOTE CAST FOR THE REVOLUTIONARY

REPRESENTATIVE MUST BE REVOLUTIONARY VOTES. THEY MUST BE VOTES OF THOSE WHO UNDERSTAND THE NEED FOR REVOLUTION, DESIRE IT, AND ARE DETERMINED TO ACHIEVE IT. BUT WHAT ARE THE RESPECTIVE POSITIONS OF MEN AND WOMEN RETURNED TO PARLIAMENT /OR OTHER ELECTED PUBLIC BODIES BY VOTES OF THIS QUALITY AND THOSE ELECTED BY VOTES OF THE POLITICALLY UNINFORMED WHO DO NOT CLEARLY UNDERSTAND WHAT IT IS THEY WANT???

THE FORMER IS THE SERVANT OF HIS /OR HER CONSTITUENTS. UNDERSTANDING THE POSITION, THEY ARE ABLE TO DIRECT THEIR COURSE OF ACTION, HENCE THEY ARE ESSENTIALLY THE MASTER. IF HE /OR SHE PLAYS THEM FALSE, IF HE /OR SHE DEPARTS FROM THE REVOLUTIONARY PATH, THEY KNOW IT AT ONCE, AND SEIZE THE FIRST OPPORTUNITY OF DEALING WITH HIM /OR HER. ON THE OTHER HAND, SUCH A REPRESENTATIVE KNOWS THAT IN ALL SOUND REVOLUTIONARY ACTION HE /OR SHE HAS FULL SUPPORT OF THOSE WHOSE DELEGATE HE /OR SHE IS, AND HENCE BECOMES THE STRONG AND EFFICIENT SERVANT OF A STRONG MASTER. WHILE THE REPRESENTATIVE OF THE POLITICALLY UNINFORMED IS IN AN ENTIRELY DIFFERENT POSITION. AS HE /OR SHE GETS THEIR VOTES ON ALL MANNER OF VAGUE PRETEXTS AND PROMISES, THE ONLY SAFE COURSE FOR THEM TO TAKE IS A VAGUE WOBBLE / OR FLIP FLOP FROM TIME TO TIME. A DEFINITE COURSE IN ANY DIRECTION WOULD RESULT IN THE ALIENATION OF SUPPORT. THEY THEREFORE DARE NOT TO ATTEMPT TO TAKE A REVOLUTIONARY ACTION, WHATEVER THEIR VIEWS MAYBE, FOR ALL FORMS OF HUMAN CONSCIOUSNESS ARE IN THEIR FOLLOWING EXCEPT REVOLUTIONISTS, THE REVOLUTIONIST DOES NOT FOLLOW. SUCH A REPRESENTATIVE IS IN A POSITION TO SELL HIS /OR HER ELECTORS DOWN THE RIVER FOR A MERE PITTANCE DEPENDING UPON CONFUSION FOR HIS /OR HER PLACE IN GOVERNMENT, THEIR BEST CHANCE OF MAINTAINING THE POLITICAL POSTING IS TO PRESERVE THE SAID STATED CONFUSION AT ANY COST. THIS SUITS THE CAPITALIST AND ITS SYSTEM OF GOVERNING VERY WELL, FOR THEIR CHIEF CONCERN IS THAT THE WORKERS SHALL NOT KNOW WHO THEIR ENEMIES ACTUALLY ARE. THEREFORE, THE POLITICAL PARTIES OF THE CAPITALIST CLASS WELCOME SUCH REPRESENTATIVES OF **LABOR**, THEY KNOW THERE IS NO REVOLUTIONARY FORCE BEHIND THEM.

THE FIRST ESSENTIAL, THEN, OF HAVING A VOTE OF REVOLUTIONARY QUALITY IS TO HAVE A WORKING CLASS THAT THROUGHLY UNDERSTANDS ITS POSITION IN SOCIETY, THAT THROUGHLY REALIZES THE HOPELESSNESS OF ANY ENDEAVOR TO IMPROVE MATERIALLY THAT POSITION UNDER THE PRESENT SOCIAL SCHEME, AND THAT THEREFORE IS THROUGHLY RESOLVED TO ABOLISH THE SYSTEM AND REPLACE IT WITH ONE BASED ON **SOCIALIST** IDEOLOGY. ONE THAT REFUSES TO DROP ITS RED-NECK SOCIALIST PHILOSOPHY BY WANTING TO BECOME KNOWN AS SOCIAL-DEMOCRATS.

THESE socialistic attributes of a class struggle between those who have versus those who have not has been in existence ever since the dawning of time, at least since the building of the great pyramids in Egypt thousands of years ago. The pharaohs, with their somewhat pagan rituals of worshiping gods such as Horus and Osiris, (Horus the sun-god, while Osiris being the god of the underworld and judge of the dead) – see **EGYPTIAN BOOK OF THE DEAD**, forced slaves to build pyramids in dedication to them and their gods in preparation for life into the hereafter as it was believed by the pharaohs that it was their preordained destiny to rule the world. Then, as now, the fraternal Order of Freemasonry has been in existence since that time period in some form /or another; Knights of Saint John, Knights of Malta, Knights Templar. Since the building of these great pyramids, the Masonic Order has flourished as one of the most powerful political forces in the entire world, today having a membership roster involving many governmental leaders who understand what the **OBJECT** of the organization actually is and are more than willing to publically acknowledge their predetermined mandate of global domination.

Granted, it wasn't always the case with the passage of time; from the building of the pyramids by such great men as Kings Solomon and Ramses to modern day empire builders, the religious institution of Freemasonry was modified ever so slightly and driven underground as the various forces of the day (Christianity) opposed the religious teaching of the Craft. To most religions, Protestant as well as Roman Catholic, the Masonic Order represented the anti-Christ and viewed their teachings of Freemasonry as witchcraft and/or black magic. As man progressed through the many centuries, so did the Masonic Order and the ways in which other religious institutions regarded Masonry and its practices. A collaboration of sorts was thusly implemented as both Protestants and Catholics alike began jumping onto the fraternal bandwagon of global domination via "The Brotherhood of Man – under the Fatherhood of God."

Seven years prior to the outbreak of the Second World War (1932), a book was published in Ireland titled, "The Framework of a Christian State "written by the well known and highly respected Rev. E. Cahill, S.J. in tribute to **HIS HOLINESS POPE PIUS XI**. The book itself was a scathing expose of Freemasonry on a global scale as the Catholic Church condemned the actions of the Masonic Order – not only in Ireland but throughout the world – for their Satanist behavior while glorifying the deeds of Christianity by way of the Roman Catholic Church. Although the contents of the book kept repeating itself (all 670-plus pages) as to the evils of Protestant Freemasonry, the Roman Catholics proved themselves to be no better than those who they condemned to the bowels of hell's inferno on the concluding pages of the book while defending the occupation of Ireland by Irish Catholics. Interestingly enough, pages 673 and 674 of the Roman Catholic Church propaganda hardcovered book "The Framework of a Christian State "read as follows:

"From all the above it is clear that the seriousness and pressing nature of the social question in Ireland can hardly be exaggerated. The question is one which affects the highest interests of the whole English-speaking world and even of the Catholic Church itself. Although the English-speaking countries now contain between 25,000,000 and 30,000,000 Catholics, Ireland is the only country among them (if we except the French-speaking provinces of Canada) that contains a practically homogeneous Catholic population with an historical past. That Catholic population, now in peril, is one of the main sources of supply of priests and religious of both sexes for the whole English-speaking world. It is in a sense, and to a certain extent, the very center and source of the Catholic life of a scattered Catholic population of more than 25,000,000 souls. Its failure, or serious weakening, would be a disaster to them and to the Catholic Church.

To rescue the Irish Catholic nation from the perils by which it is now menaced a now social system organized in accordance with Catholic principles and tradition must be gradually built up; and it is this objective rather than at applying palliatives here and there, that the social reformer in Ireland should consistently direct his efforts. For it is certain that nothing else and nothing less can ultimately save the nation, and at the same time preserve intact the wondrous faith and substantial goodness of the people. The faith and religious fervor of the Irish people (probably unsurpassed in any country of the world) forms the great counterbalancing element in the present depressing situation. For their Catholic faith is still as strong as ever, and the traditional habit of fidelity to religious duties has not so far been affected.

THE PEOPLE HAVE NOW SUBSTANTIALLY REGAINED THE OWNERSHIP OF THE LAND OF IRELAND. UNDER THE NEW POLITICAL CONDITIONS THE CATHOLIC IRISH, OVER THE GREATER PORTION OF THE COUNTRY, HAVE SECURED, BESIDES, SUBSTANTIAL CONTROL OF THE CIVIL ADMINISTRATION. HENCE, WHAT WAS IMPOSSIBLE DURING THE LAST FOUR CENTURIES HAS NOW BECOME FEASIBLE — NAMELY, TO INAUGURATE A SOCIAL RECONSTRUCTION UPON AN IRISH CATHOLIC BASIS. A NATIONAL MOVEMENT FOR SUCH A RECONSTRUCTION COULD IN A COMPARATIVELY SHORT TIME CHANGE THE WHOLE NATIONAL OUTLOOK AND USHER IN A NEW ERA OF PROSPERITY AND SOCIAL PEACE."

AND IN BOTH IRELAND AND NORTH AMERICA SOME 57 YEARS LATER, THE WAR BETWEEN PROTESTANT FREEMASONRY AND THE ROMAN CATHOLIC CHURCH WAS STILL RAGING ON — SAME OLD, SAME OLD — NOTHING HAD ACTUALLY CHANGED IN THAT TIME PERIOD. FOR EXAMPLE, ACCORDING TO MASONIC LITERATURE ON THIS SUBJECT OF CONTINUAL RELIGIOUS BICKERING BETWEEN THE TWO FACTIONS INVOLVED **"A FRATERNITY UNDER FIRE"**, WHICH WAS FIRST PUBLISHED IN THE SHORT TALK BULLETIN (NOVEMBER 1989) BY THE MASONIC SERVICE ASSOCIATION OF THE UNITED STATES, THEN AGAIN IN THE AMERICAN ISSUE OF THE NORTHERN LIGHT (VOLUME 21 NO. 1 FEBRUARY 1990) IRONICALLY TITLED; **A WINDOW FOR FREEMASONRY**. WITH THE ANIMOSITY BETWEEN THE MASONIC ORDER AND THEIR RELIGIOUS OPPONENTS, THE OPPOSING FORCES SEEMED TO HAVE FORGOTTEN THAT THE TWO ENTITIES IN QUESTION WERE TOTALLY COMPATIBLE WITH EACH OTHER AS "FREEMASONRY IS NOT, IN AND OF ITSELF, A CHRISTIAN ORGANIZATION. RATHER, IT IS ONE THAT NUMBERS AMONG ITS MEMBERS MANY WHO ARE CHRISTIAN. ONE OF OUR GREAT STRENGTHS IS THE ABILITY TO ACCEPT THOSE OF DIFFERING FAITHS INTO OUR FELLOWSHIP. "BUT WITH THE PASSAGE OF TIME, "FREEMASONRY HAS COME UNDER ATTACK FROM SOME SEGMENTS OF CHRISTIANITY, PARTICULARLY THOSE CONSIDERED TO BE ' FUNDAMENTALISTS.' IT IS TO THOSE MEMBERS OF THE MASONIC FRATERNITY WHO ARE CHRISTIAN THAT THIS SHORT TALK IS PRIMARILY ADDRESSED. MANY MASONS HAVE HAD TO AGONIZE OVER CHOOSING BETWEEN THEIR CHRISTIAN FAITH AND THEIR MASONIC MEMBERSHIP, BELIEVING THE TWO TO BE IN CONFLICT. IT IS HOPED THAT THIS SHORT TALK WILL BE A SOURCE OF COMFORT AND UNDERSTANDING TO THOSE WHO ARE IN SUCH TURMOIL AS WELL AS INFORMATIVE AND A GUIDE TO THOSE WHO HAVE QUESTIONS ABOUT THE ROLE OF THE MASON WITH RESPECT TO HIS RELIGIOUS BELIEFS. THIS SHORT TALK IS DIRECTLY ADDRESSING THE CHRISTIAN, BUT THE TRUTH IT CONTAINS APPLIES TO ALL WHO BELIEVE AND SERVE ONE **GOD!**"

The Literature then went on to say: "The recent revival, by fundamental Christianity, of anti-Masonry has created a small storm within both religious and fraternal circles. Over the past two years, I have listened to, watched on TV or read every program, article and item concerning the modern day anti-Masonic movement that has been called to my attention. It has been good for me. I have reexamined my own membership in all of my 'other than the Church' commitments. I have reached a considered decision that Freemasonry is not now or never has been detrimental to my Christian faith and doctrine. In fact my fraternal relationship have strengthened and assisted me in my ministry as well as in my personal faith and life ... It is disturbing that the opponents of Freemasonry are, in effect attacking that which is supportive of Christian faith. The 'Christians' anti-masonic leaders are not only inaccurate in their attack on Freemasonry but they are, in my opinion, making a far more serious attack on the basic Christian faith under whose banner they claim to operate. How do I respond to these attacks? What do I say? I do not respond directly to the attacker. The attacker is shrewd. He attacks the weak spot of his enemy. In our case that weakest spot is not, as the attacker would have you believe and thus defend, in our rituals, customs and traditions. It is in the members themselves who have had only a ritualistic education about Freemasonry. Where Freemasonry has instructed its candidates in its history, purpose and intent and where a local lodge is going about its business with pride and dignity, there is very little that anti-Masonic groups can do to destroy the craft."

Coincidently, the literature **A FRATERNITY UNDER FIRE** was originally composed by the Rev. Forrest D. Haggard, 33RD degree of the Masonic Order, who had been the pastor of the Overland Park (Kansas) Christian Church since 1953 and was interestingly the Grand Master of Masons in Kansas in 1974-75. He was also the published author of a book titled "The Clergy and the Craft", published in 1970. Not unlike his counterpart, the Rev. Cahill was also the author of a couple of other interesting literary works; "Freemasonry and the Anti-Christian Movement "as well as "Ireland's Peril", both of which were anti-Masonic creations sanctioned by the Roman Catholic Church.

It is without a doubt that for more than 2,000 years, the Freemasonry concept of establishing a **New World Order** has had literally thousands upon thousands of disagreements and/or skirmishes that cost many a people their lives throughout the ages.

APPARENTLY, DISSENSION AMONGST ITS OWN MEMBERSHIP WAS A COMMON OCCURRENCE. FOR INSTANCE, SOME NINE WEEKS BEFORE THE AMERICAN PRESIDENT ABRAHAM LINCOLN WAS ASSASSINATED, THOMAS D'ARCY MCGEE, THE ORATOR OF THE CONFEDERATION MOVEMENT HERE IN CANADA, HAD URGED AN EXPANSION OF A CANADIAN MADE UNION WHILE EMPHASIZING THE EXISTENCE OF AN AMERICAN THREAT IF THE CANADIAN UNION HAD NOT BEEN ACHIEVED, SOMETHING THAT OF WHICH MCGEE HAD BEEN PREACHING ABOUT FOR A COUPLE OF YEARS PRIOR TO HIS UNTIMELY DEMISE. IN A SPEECH FEBRUARY 9TH, 1865 HE STATED: "THE POLICY OF OUR NEIGHBORS TO THE SOUTH OF US HAS ALWAYS BEEN AGGRESSIVE. THERE HAS ALWAYS BEEN A DESIRE AMONGST THEM FOR ACQUISITION OF NEW TERRITORY ... THEY COVETED FLORIDA, AND SEIZED IT; THEY COVETED LOUISIANA, AND PURCHASED IT; THEY COVETED TEXAS, AND STOLE IT; AND THEY PICKED A QUARREL WITH MEXICO, WHICH ENDED THEIR GETTING CALIFORNIA. THEY SOMETIMES PRETEND TO DESPISE THESE COLONIES AS PRIZES BENEATH THEIR AMBITION; BUT HAD NOT THE STRONG ARM OF ENGLAND OVER US, WE SHOULD NOT HAVE HAD A SEPARATE EXISTENCE. THE ACQUISITION OF CANADA WAS THE FIRST AMBITION OF AMERICAN CONFEDERACY, AND NEVER CEASED TO BE SO, WHEN HER TROOPS WERE A HANDFUL AND HER NAVY SCARCE A SQUADRON. IT IS LIKELY TO BE STOPPED NOW, WHEN SHE COUNTS HER GUNS AFLOAT BY THE THOUSANDS AND HER TROOPS BY HUNDREDS OF THOUSANDS?"

IRONICALLY, THOMAS D'ARCY MCGEE LIVED FOR A NUMBER OF YEARS IN THE UNITED STATES (NEW YORK AND BOSTON) BEFORE MOVING TO CANADA. HE INITIALLY MIGRATED NORTH OF THE 49TH PARALLEL IN 1857 AT THE INVITATION OF SOME VERY HIGH PROFILE LEADING IRISH-CATHOLICS LIVING IN MONTREAL AS THEY FIRMLY BELIEVED THAT MCGEE WOULD HAVE BEEN AN IDEAL PLAYER FOR THEIR FRATERNAL CAUSE. AFTERALL, HE WAS ONCE DEEPLY INVOLVED IN AN IRISH UP-RISING IN THE HOMELAND AND HAD TO FLEE THE COUNTRY FEARING FOR HIS LIFE BY DISGUISING HIMSELF AS A PRIEST, HE ESCAPED TO NEW YORK, (1848). TEN YEARS LATER, HE ENTERED CANADIAN POLITICS AS AN INDEPENDENT, FIRST IN THE LEGISLATIVE ASSEMBLY OF CANADA, AND AFTER 1867, IN THE CANADIAN HOUSE OF COMMONS. DURING HIS STAY IN CANADA, MCGEE PISSED OFF A LOT OF HIS FRATERNITY BRETHREN BY BECOMING HIGHLY CRITICAL OF THEIR POLITICAL/TERRORIST ACTIVITIES AGAINST SIR JOHN A. MACDONALD'S DREAM OF A CONFEDERATION UNDER BRITISH RULE. APPARENTLY, HE FIRST DENOUNCED THE IRISH BROTHERHOOD IN 1866 AND SLOWLY BUT SURELY BEGAN WASHING HIS HANDS OF THEM ALTOGETHER. IN IRELAND, THE FENIAN BROTHERHOOD WAS BETTER KNOWN AS THE IRISH REPUBLICAN BROTHERHOOD, A SECRET FRATERNITY WHOSE MANDATE WAS TO PUT AN END TO BRITISH RULE IN THEIR MOTHERLAND. AS THE TURBULENCE IN IRELAND BETWEEN IRISH-CATHOLICS AND THE

English monarchy grew even stronger during the 1848 rebellion for an independent homeland, it also saw the strengthening of yet another secret fraternity, the Masonic Orange Order, which was re-instituted in 1795 to further defend Protestant succession to the throne in Britain.

As the hostilities escalated, all forms of racism and/or hatred soon began to emerge as Irish-Catholics and Protestants battled it out for fraternal control of Ireland. For those who had the good fortune to escape the animosity in the motherland by migrating to both Canada and the United States, the movement only grew stronger as the new immigrants began supplying their Irish Brethren in the homeland with money and arms from North American counterparts. The Canada/U.S. connection was so strong that the Fenian Brotherhood established headquarters in New York City and not long after that, off-shoot organisms soon began to sprout up north of the 49TH parallel. In 1865, the American Fenians set their fraternity sights on trying to gain political control of Canada as an estimated 35,000 Fenian troops prepared themselves for an armed invasion by strategically stationing themselves at various locations along the Canadian border. Hearing of this unsanctioned Freemasonry invasion northward, the U.S. Masonically controlled Federal Government intercepted large quantities of ammunition sent to the border and confiscated all munitions, and arrested many of the Fenian officers and their troops. The American Fenians, in fact attempted two other invasions – in 1870 and once again in 1871. Both of which were also foiled by the U.S. Freemasonry forces of the Federal Government.

For his vision of wanting to see a Protestant Freemason's dream of a Canadian union under British rule, just after having made a speech in Parliament on April 7TH, 1868, early in the morning, Thomas D'Arcy McGee was shot at the door of his boarding house on Sparks Street in downtown Ottawa. A young Fenian, Patrick James Whelan was later convicted of the assassination and then duly executed for his crime.

It goes without saying that Thomas D'Arcy McGee knew the risk that he was taking by speaking out against the Irish-Catholic Brotherhood in favor of a more subdued Protestant one under British rule. In fact, he feared more as to what kind of a future lay ahead for Canada under the American Masonic administration than that of an Irish /and or even an English one. In a desperate attempt to prevent Canada from forming a united fraternal front by way

OF A CONFEDERATION, THE AMERICAN'S PURCHASED ALASKA IN MARCH OF 1867. WHILE THE ENGLISH MONARCHY WAS BUSY SIGNING THE DOCUMENTS THAT WERE TO BECOME KNOWN AS THE BRITISH NORTH AMERICA ACT OF MARCH 29TH, 1867 THE AMERICAN SECRETARY OF STATE , WILLIAM SEWARD, AND A RUSSIAN MINISTER WERE UP UNTIL THE WEE HOURS OF THE MORNING COMPLETING THEIR AGREEMENT FOR THE PURCHASE OF ALASKA. THIS DOCUMENT WAS REPORTEDLY SIGNED AT ABOUT 3 O'CLOCK IN THE MORNING ON MARCH 30TH, 1867. IT WENT TO THE MASONICALLY CONTROLLED SENATE A FEW HOURS LATER, AS THEY, THE AMERICANS HAD EVERY INTENTION OF MAKING THEIR **GOD** GIVEN RIGHT TO REIGN SUPREME A REALITY BY ATTEMPTING TO OCCUPY THE ENTIRE NORTH AMERICAN CONTINENT, "**MANIFEST DESTINY**."

NOT LONG AFTER THE TERMS OF THE ALASKAN PURCHASE WERE BROUGHT TO THE AMERICAN SENATE FOR ITS APPROVAL, THE PURCHASE AGREEMENT WAS RATIFIED BY A VOTE OF 37-2. NEWSPAPERS SOUTH OF THE 49TH PARALLEL THEN PROCLAIMED THE NEW TERRITORY OF ALASKA AS BEING AMERICAN SOIL AND OPENLY ADMITTED OF HOPING TO GAIN ALL OF THE TERRITORY BETWEEN ALASKA AND THE UNITED STATES. ONE NEWSPAPER, "THE MORNING POST" EVEN TOOK IT A STEP FURTHER BY STATING THAT THE REASON FOR THE PURCHASING OF ALASKA WAS NOT FOR THE INTRINSIC VALUE OF ALASKA ITSELF, BUT RATHER FOR THE SOLE PURPOSE OF ACQUIRING THE TERRITORY SOUTH OF IT.

AS CANADA'S FIRST BIRTHDAY PRESENT, AT THE PASSING OF THE BRITISH NORTH AMERICA ACT, THE U.S. CONGRESS PASSED A RESOLUTION OF EXTREME CONCERN CONDEMNING THE FORMATION OF CANADA AS A SEPARATE NATION ON THEIR NORTHERN BOUNDARY. AS IRONIC AS IT MAY SEEM, ONLY TWENTY-THREE HOURS BEFORE THE AMERICAN PURCHASE OF ALASKA, THE PRESIDENTIAL ELECTION SLOGAN OF THE UNITED STATES WAS "FIFTY-FOUR FORTY OR FIGHT. "IT WAS A DECLARATION STATING THAT THE AMERICANS WERE CLAIMING ALL OF THE WEST COAST OF NORTH AMERICA CLEAR UP TO ALASKA. IRONICALLY, IN DEFEATING THIS CAMPAIGN SLOGAN, JOHN L. O'SULLIVAN, THE FAMOUS AMERICAN NEWSPAPER EDITOR, COINED A PHRASE THAT WOULD RUN THROUGH AMERICAN POLITICS AND LITERALLY SOW FEAR INTO THE HEARTS AND SOULS OF ALL CANADIANS. O'SULLIVAN SO PROUDLY PROCLAIMED FOR ALL THE WORLD TO SEE: "AWAY, AWAY WITH ALL THESE COBWEB TISSUES OF RIGHTS OF DISCOVERY, EXPLORATION, SETTLEMENT, AND CONTIGUITY. THE AMERICAN TITLE IS BY RIGHT OF OUR MANIFEST DESTINY TO OVERSPREAD AND POSSESS THE WHOLE OF THE CONTINENT WHICH PROVIDENCE HAS GIVEN US. TEXAS, I REPEAT, IS SECURE, AND SO NOW WHO'S THE NEXT CUSTOMER? SHALL IT BE CALIFORNIA, OR SHALL IT BE CANADA?"

THE AMERICAN DREAM OF "**MANIFEST DESTINY** "BY DIVINE INTERVENTION TOOK YET ANOTHER DRASTIC TURN FOR THE WORST WHILE THE SOON TO BE

Metis leader Louis Riel was still knee high to a grasshopper. Being true believers in their **GOD** given right to reign supreme, the U.S. Federal Government began its renewed war on Mexico from whom it seized one third of Mexico's entire territory including the ports of San Diego, Los Angeles and San Francisco and all of the Mexican provinces of California and New Mexico. At the time, there was a movement afoot in the United States interestingly called **All-of-Mexico Movement** which was ultimately pushing the American administration of the President Polk to take all of the Mexican territory. As far as the neighbors north of the 49TH parallel were concerned, as long as the Americans were picking on someone else, Canada was in the clear. But trouble was once again brewing in paradise north as certain leading Freemasonry business families in Montreal began organizing themselves in an attempt to force annexation with the United States. In 1849, a group of Masonically connected political conservatives signed the Montreal Annexation Manifesto calling for union with the Americans as one-thousand of the wealthiest families in Montreal signed the Annexation Manifesto (some very highly profiled family names still known to Canadians to this very day). And naturally, the U.S. Masonic governing body south of the 49TH parallel were directly involved with this movement as they so desperately wanted Canada as its newfound trophy.

Sometimes repeating one's self on certain aspects of our country's historical past can't be helped as it is often used as a way and means of stressing the importance of what lay in wait for the future as history always has a tendency to repeat itself — if let unregulated. To that end, the Montreal annexationists failed miserably in getting any support from the people in their desire of wanting to have Canada become part of the United States. In fact, some Canadians regarded the members of the annexation movement as being nothing more than traitors willing to sell their own heritage in exchange for further economic prosperity. Although they failed to have Canada annexed to the United States, they were actually able to convince the British Government into negotiations on behalf of the Canadian colonies for a Free-Trade Agreement with our American cousins, or as they called it at that time, a Reciprocity Agreement — that agreement ran from 1854 to 1866. After it had been in effect for several years, the American Consul in Montreal stated with much satisfaction that in commercial terms, the treaty itself made Canada part of the American Union whether Canadians wanted it /or not. Then, in 1866, the United States Federal Government repealed the agreement because

It was strongly believed by the Americans that if the treaty had been canceled, they would be able to force the Canadian colonies (which at the time only consisted of few Provinces) into asking permission to join the American Masonic Family fold. The annexation of Canada under an American Freemasonry banner reached such a high feverish pace that on July 22ND, 1866 the fraternal Brethrenship introduced a piece of legislation into the U.S. Congress that was strictly designed for the admission of the States of Nova Scotia, New Brunswick, Canada East and Canada West into the American Union. The Bill, also incorporated the organization of the Territories of Selkirk, Saskatchewan and Columbia, as both new States and Territories of the United States of the America's. Two weeks prior to this, the Massachusetts Legislature passed a resolution for annexation of Canada as well.

Interestingly enough, when the Free-Trade Treaty was ended and the Americans were not successful in making Canada join their Freemasonry Family fold, the annexation forces in the United States turned once again to direct annexation as their method of operation. The theater of action once more turned to western Canada just as the first insurrection of the Metis population was still in its infancy. One of the agents representing the American Government was sent to the Manitoba region simply because of his ability to tow the fraternity line of "Manifest Destiny "by way of divine intervention. Saskatchewan Taylor thusly attempted to make Manitoba part of the American Union by designing a plan of action for its virtual acquisition through economic servitude whereas the United States of the America's would reign supreme.

The former Governor of Minnesota, William Marshall, arrived pledging military backing if Louis Riel and his Metis peoples agreed to the concept of joining the United States. In addition to supplying both men an guns, a total of $ 4 million in U.S. currency was also pledged to help annex western Canada into the American Union. Before long, an American businessman by the name of Robinson arrived on the scene and began publishing a newspaper which he coincidently called "The New Nation". The front page headlines of his worthy American rag interestingly enough read; "Consolidation: One Flag, One Empire "and "Natural Lines Must Prevail. "At that precise moment in time, the entire future of all North America west of the Great Lakes clear up to the Arctic Circle hung in the balance. From Ottawa, fraternity Brother Sir John A. MacDonald wrote: "It is quite evident to me that the U.S. Government is resolved to do all

285

IT CAN, SHORT OF WAR, TO GET POSSESSION OF THE WESTERN TERRITORY, AND WE MUST MAKE IMMEDIATE AND VIGOROUS STEPS TO COUNTERACT THEM."

NEEDLESS TO SAY, FREEMASONRY BROTHER MACDONALD DIDN'T HAVE ENOUGH TIME AT HIS IMMEDIATE DISPOSAL TO IMPLEMENT THE NECESSARY STEPS NEEDED IN ORDER TO PREVENT AN AMERICAN TAKE-OVER IN THE WESTERN TERRITORY AS THE CANADIAN FEDERAL GOVERNMENT HAD FEWER THAN 100 MEN IN MANITOBA. BECAUSE OF THIS, CANADA WAS THEREFORE DESTINED TO FALL UNLESS SOMEONE OUT WEST HAD THE GONADS TO STEP UP TO THE PLATE AND TAKE CHARGE OF THE SITUATION.

WHILE ALL OF THIS FREEMASONRY TURMOIL WAS TAKING PLACE, LOUIS RIEL WAS ONLY TWENTY-FIVE-YEARS-OLD, AND HE STOOD HIS GROUND IN DEFIANCE TO THE AMERICAN MASONIC RHETORIC OF THE "BROTHERHOOD OF MAN". RIEL THEREFORE ORDERED THE AMERICAN FLAG LOWERED OVER FORT GARRY AND SHUT DOWN THEIR NEWSPAPER. AND WHEN THE ADVANCED INVADING MILITARY FORCES CROSSED THE BORDER SOUTH OF WINNIPEG, THEY WERE MET BY RIEL'S GENERAL AMBROSE LEPINE, WITH 200 WELL-ARMED METIS HORSEMEN, WHO ARRESTED, DISARMED, AND ESCORTED THE AMERICANS BACK ACROSS THE BORDER. FOR HIS ROLE IN SAVING TWO-THIRDS OF THE ENTIRE LAND MASS OF PRESENT DAY CANADA FROM ANNEXATION BY THE UNITED STATES FREEMASONRY GOVERNMENT, LOUIS RIEL LATER MET HIS MASONIC REWARD ON A SCAFFOLD IN A MISERABLE REGINA JAIL.

FAILING IN THEIR BID TO TAKE CANADA PHYSICALLY, THE AMERICANS TURNED ONCE AGAIN TO COMMERCIAL TRADE — DURING THE LATE 1880'S, OUR COUNTRY WENT INTO A DEPRESSION — THERE WAS CERTAIN DESPERATION, AS THERE IS TODAY DURING THESE TRYING TIMES OF THE 21ST CENTURY. COMMERCIAL UNION WAS SAID TO BE THE ONLY ANSWER TO CANADA'S ECONOMIC WOES, THAT IS ACCORDING TO THOSE WHO WERE PUSHING FOR THE ANNEXATION OF CANADA WITH THE UNITED STATES. THE LIBERAL PARTY OF CANADA THUSLY ADOPTED A POLICY OF FULL AND UNRESTRICTED RECIPROCITY, WHICH IN ITSELF LITERALLY MEANT FULL FREE-TRADE. IN THE MEANTIME, THE UNITED STATES PASSED A COMMERCIAL BILL IN THE SENATE. IRONICALLY ITS SPONSOR, SENATOR JOHN SHERMAN OF OHIO, POINTED OUT THAT THE AMERICAN PEOPLE HAD LARGE SUMS OF MONEY INVESTED IN CANADA. HE FURTHER STATED: "ANYTHING THAT WOULD LEND TO PROMOTE FREE COMMERCIAL INTERCOURSE BETWEEN THE COUNTRIES, YES, ANYTHING THAT WOULD PRODUCE A UNION OF CANADA WITH THE UNITED STATES OF AMERICA, WILL MEET WITH MY HEARTY SUPPORT ... I WANT CANADA TO BE PART OF THE UNITED STATES ... CANADA SHOULD HAVE FOLLOWED THE FORTUNES OF THE COLONIES IN THE AMERICAN REVOLUTION. THE WAY TO UNION WITH CANADA IS NOT BY HOSTILE LEGISLATION BUT BY FRIENDLY OVERTURES. THIS UNION IS ONE OF THE EVENTS THAT MUST INEVITABLY COME IN THE FUTURE.

THE TRUE POLICY OF THIS GOVERNMENT THEN IS TO TENDER FREEDOM IN TRADE AND INTERCOURSE AND MAKE THIS OFFER IN SUCH A FRIENDLY WAY THAT IT SHALL BE AN OVERTURE TO THE PEOPLE OF CANADA TO BECOME PART OF THIS NATION. "AMERICAN MONEY SOON POURED INTO THE LIBERAL PARTY OF CANADA FUND. THE TORONTO GLOBE, (GLOBE AND MAIL FOUNDED IN 1844), WHICH WAS THE VOICE OF THE LIBERAL PARTY AT THE TIME, RECEIVED AN ESTIMATED $ 50,000.00 FROM ONE U.S. CORPORATION ALONE, THE J.J. RICHIE CORPORATION OF CLEVELAND, OHIO.

IN THE UNITED STATES, (1889), THE SECRETARY OF STATE, JAMES BLAINE, BETTER KNOWN AS "JINGO JIM "FOR HIS ATTITUDE TOWARDS RACIAL MINORITIES IN THE UNITED STATES, SUPPORTED BY HIS PRESIDENT, BENJAMIN HARRISON FIRMLY BELIEVED THAT A POLICY OF REFUSING TO DEAL WITH CANADA WOULD ULTIMATELY SUCCEED IN FORCING OUR COUNTRY INTO CONTINENTAL UNION WITHIN THE FREEMASONRY FAMILY FOLD. IRONICALLY, BLAINE HAD INADVERTENTLY STATED THAT CANADA WAS LIKE AN APPLE TREE THAT WAS JUST SLIGHTLY OUT OF REACH, BUT IN DUE TIME WOULD FALL INTO THEIR HANDS ONCE THE FRUIT WAS READY TO BE HARVESTED AND ALL THAT THEY (THE AMERICANS) HAD TO DO WAS WAIT FOR IT TO HAPPEN AS IT WAS PROCLAIMED BY **GOD** THAT THE UNITED STATES OF AMERICA WAS TO REIGN SUPREME ON THE NORTH AMERICAN CONTINENT.

IT SHOULD ALSO BE NOTED THAT FREEMASONRY LEADER, PRIME MINISTER JOHN A. MACDONALD REALIZED THE STRENGTH OF THE COMMERCIAL UNION MOVEMENT AND DECIDED TO DISSOLVE THE HOUSE OF COMMONS AND CALL A FEDERAL ELECTION. THE 1891 ELECTION COINCIDENTLY BECAME KNOWN AS CANADA'S VERY FIRST FULL BLOWN FREE-TRADE ELECTION. TORY LEADER MACDONALD THUSLY CAMPAIGNED VIGOROUSLY STATING THAT THE LIBERALS HAD BEEN PURCHASED WITH YANKEE GOLD AND THAT IF THEY (THE LIBERALS) WERE TO BE ELECTED INTO POWER, IT VIRTUALLY MEANT THE END OF CANADA AS AN INDEPENDENT NATION. EDWARD FARRER, WHO WAS AN EDITOR OF THE GLOBE, APPARENTLY HAD WRITTEN AN ARTICLE FOR THE U.S. SENATE OUTLINING WAYS THE UNITED STATES COULD UNDERMINE CANADA'S POLICY AND PUSH OUR COUNTRY INTO ANNEXATION. SIR JOHN A. RECEIVED A COPY OF THOSE PROOFS AND MADE THEM PUBLIC. AS FAR AS FRATERNITY BROTHER MACDONALD WAS CONCERNED, FARRER WAS NOTHING BUT A TRAITOR WHO WAS MORE THAN WILLING TO DELIVER CANADA TO THE AMERICANS ON A SILVER PLATTER. AGAINST THE ADVICE OF HIS DOCTORS, MACDONALD THREW HIMSELF INTO THE CAMPAIGN HOPING TO SAVE THE COUNTRY FROM AMERICAN FREEMASONS SOUTH OF THE 49TH PARALLEL. BORN A BRITISH MASONIC SUBJECT, HE WAS BOUND TO DIE THE SAME.

ON MARCH 5TH, 1891 CANADIANS WENT TO THEIR POLLING STATIONS TO VOTE ON THE ISSUE OF ANNEXATION WITH THE AMERICANS. WHEN ALL OF

THE VOTES WERE COUNTED, FREEMASONRY BROTHER MACDONALD CAME OUT THE VICTOR – FREE-TRADE HAD BEEN DEFEATED, AND SHORTLY THEREAFTER, THE UNITED STATES WENT INTO A DEPRESSION AND THE VOICES OF ANNEXATIONISTS DROPPED ABRUPTLY SILENT. THE LIBERAL PARTY OF CANADA QUICKLY DROPPED FREE-TRADE FROM THEIR POLITICAL AGENDA. IRONIC AS IT MAY SEEM, CANADIAN CITIZENS OF OUR MODERN DAY SOCIETY OF THE 21ST CENTURY WILL NEVER FULLY REALIZE AS TO HOW CLOSE THEY ACTUALLY CAME TO FLYING THE AMERICAN FLAG EVEN BACK THEN. IN EFFECT, THE 1891 FREE-TRADE CAMPAIGN WAS TO BE MASONIC BROTHER MACDONALD'S LAST – THREE MONTHS LATER, HE WAS DEAD.

BY 1902, THE AMERICAN FREEMASONS WERE AT IT AGAIN. THIS TIME, IT WAS THE DISPUTE OVER THE ALASKA BOUNDARY. CANADA LAID CLAIM TO THE CORRIDOR ACROSS THE ALASKAN PANHANDLE THAT GAVE ACCESS TO THE OCEAN FROM THE GOLD FIELDS OF THE KLONDIKE IN THE YUKON TERRITORY – U.S. PRESIDENT TEDDY ROOSEVELT (LIKE GEORGE WASHINGTON, BENJAMIN FRANKLIN AND THOMAS JEFFERSON, ROOSEVELT WAS ALSO OF THE SAME FREEMASONRY STOCK) AND NOT AT ALL AMUSED WITH CANADA'S CLAIM. HE THREATENED TO USE BRUTE FORCE TO MAINTAIN HIS AMERICAN SOVEREIGNTY IN THE DISPUTED REGION. FRATERNITY BROTHER TEDDY ROOSEVELT THEN SENT U.S. TROOPS UP TO THE ALASKA-B.C. BORDER TO RUN THE BOUNDARY LINES AS TO WHERE HE SAW FIT, WITH NO CONCERNS WHATSOEVER AS TO WHAT CANADA'S POLITICAL POSITION WAS ON THE SUBJECT. ROOSEVELT WANTED CANADA TO CEASE AND DESIST FROM ITS RIDICULOUS LAND CLAIM, THE AMERICAN MASONIC PRESIDENT WAS NOT INTERESTED IN NEGOTIATING WITH THE CANADIAN FEDERAL GOVERNMENT NOR WITH BRITAIN ON THE MATTER. THE U.S. FREEMASONRY LEADER'S MOTTO AT THE TIME TOWARDS ACHIEVING THE AMERICAN DREAM OF "**MANIFEST DESTINY** "WAS "**SPEAK SOFTLY AND CARRY A BIG STICK**."

THE END RESULT OF COURSE, IS WHAT WE NOW SEE TODAY – THE ENTIRE NORTHERN HALF OF BRITISH COLUMBIA'S COASTAL LINE FROM JUST NORTH OF PRINCE RUPERT ALL THE WAY UP TO ALASKA ITSELF IS AMERICAN TERRITORY. THE YUKON LOST ALL ACCESS TO THE PACIFIC OCEAN INCLUDING THE ENTIRE LYNN CANAL.

ALTHOUGH THEODORE ROOSEVELT WAS WELL-BORN, WELL-EDUCATED AND VERY WELL OFF FINANCIALLY, HE REPORTEDLY ENTERED THE POLITICAL ARENA AT THE BOTTOM OF THE FRATERNITY LADDER IN 1881 AS HE BECAME A REPRESENTATIVE IN THE NEW YORK STATE LEGISLATURE. AT THE TIME NEW YORK CITY AS WELL AS THE STATE OF NEW YORK WERE MASONIC STRONGHOLDS, FREEMASONS HELD HIGH POSITIONS IN BOTH GOVERNMENT AND BUSINESS. GOVERNMENTAL OFFICIALS LEVIED TAXES AND LITERALLY HANDED OVER CLUSTERS OF CONTRACTS FOR PAVING STREETS, BUILDING

SCHOOLS, AND OTHER PUBLIC WORKS TO THEIR FRATERNITY BRETHREN. THESE OFFICIALS ODDLY ENOUGH ALSO HAD THE POWER TO GRANT LUCRATIVE UTILITY FRANCHISES TO PRIVATE ENTERPRISES FOR STREET RAILWAYS, THE SUPPLY OF GAS, ELECTRIC POWER, AND WATER. HISTORICALLY, NEW YORK CITY VIRTUALLY FURNISHED THE UNITED STATES WITH OUTSTANDING EXAMPLES OF GOVERNMENTAL CORRUPTION AND OVER THE YEARS, MANY FINGERS HAD BEEN POINTED AT VARIOUS ASPECTS OF ORGANIZED CRIME BUT LITTLE /OR NOTHING HAS EVER BEEN MENTIONED AS TO THE IMPORTANT ROLE FREEMASONRY ACTUALLY PLAYED IN ITS INITIAL DEVELOPMENT.

IN 1881, TEDDY ROOSEVELT WON HIS WAY INTO THE FRATERNITY ORGANISM AS APPRENTICE POLITICIAN AND ALMOST IMMEDIATELY ACCEPTED THE PORTFOLIO IN THE HOUSE OF REPRESENTATIVES FOR THE NEW YORK STATE ASSEMBLY. ALL THIS BY THE TIME OF THE AGE 23 AS HE EAGERLY BEGAN MAKING HIS WAY UP THE FREEMASONRY LADDER AND HIS POLITICAL CAREER SOON TOOK OFF AT AN EXTREMELY FAST RATE OF SPEED. INTERESTINGLY, DURING HIS THREE YEARS IN THE LEGISLATURE, FRATERNITY BROTHER ROOSEVELT SUPPOSEDLY WORKED TOWARDS ESTABLISHING AN HONEST AND OPEN GOVERNMENT. HE FIRST MADE NEWSPAPER HEADLINES WHEN HE BEGAN PROMOTING AN INVESTIGATION INTO THE DISHONEST DEEDS OF NEW YORK STATE OFFICIALS. ONE YEAR LATER, (1882), HE WAS CHOSEN LEADER OF THE REPUBLICAN PARTY IN THE NEW YORK STATE ASSEMBLY. HAVING FURTHER MASONIC AMBITIONS IN 1884, ROOSEVELT SOUGH THE NOMINATION AS NATIONAL LEADER OF THE REPUBLICANS BUT HE WAS IRONICALLY DEFEATED BY "JINGO JIM "WHO RECEIVED IT INSTEAD. BOTH ROOSEVELT AND JAMES BLAINE THUSLY WORKED TOGETHER IN ATTEMPTING TO MAKE NORTH AMERICA ONE NATION UNDER **GOD** – TEDDY ROOSEVELT ESSENTIALLY BECAME A VERY IMPORTANT BACK ROOM PLAYER IN THE AMERICAN DREAM OF "**MANIFEST DESTINY**". TWO YEARS AFTER LOSING HIS BID TO OBTAIN THE POLITICAL POSTING ON A NATIONAL SCALE, THE REPUBLICANS CALLED UPON ROOSEVELT TO RUN AS A CANDIDATE FOR MAYOR OF NEW YORK CITY, BUT WAS UNSUCCESSFUL IN THAT BID AS WELL – THE ANTI-FREEMASONRY OPPOSITION FORCES WERE AGAINST HIM AS HE SEEMED DESTINED FOR OBSCURITY.

NOT BEING THE SORT OF PERSON TO CALL IT QUITS SO EASILY, BY 1889 FRATERNITY BROTHER ROOSEVELT RETURNED TO PUBLIC LIFE ONCE AGAIN WHEN U.S. PRESIDENT BENJAMIN HARRISON APPOINTED HIM AS A MEMBER OF THE CIVIL SERVICE COMMISSION. AS FATE WOULD HAVE IT, THE COMMISSION'S DUTY WAS TO GIVE EXAMINATION FOR GOVERNMENT JOBS SO THEY WOULD BE FILLED SUPPOSEDLY BY NON-FRATERNITY MEMBERS WHO HAD THE ABILITY TO DO THE WORK REQUIRED. GOVERNMENT OFFICIALS WHO WERE ALSO ACTIVE MEMBERS OF THE MASONIC CRAFT HAD A NASTY REPUTATION OF ALWAYS ALIGNING THEMSELVES WITH FELLOW BRETHREN WITHIN GOVERNMENTAL POSTINGS,

MANY OF THE ANTI-FREEMASONRY POLITICIANS ELECTED BY THE PEOPLE WERE AGAINST THE LAWS SET IN STONE BY THE HARRISON ADMINISTRATION AND HIS FELLOW SECRET FRATERNITY BRETHREN. FREEMASONS WANTED TO CONTINUE WITH THE USE OF THE "SPOILS SYSTEM "OF FILLING GOVERNMENT OFFICES AS A REWARD FOR SERVICES RENDERED, AND THE AMERICAN PRESIDENT WANTED TO CREATE THE ILLUSION THAT THE OPPOSITE WAS HAPPENING AND THEREFORE BROTHER ROOSEVELT WAS BROUGHT INTO THE PICTURE. ROOSEVELT REPORTEDLY WORKED AS HEAD OF THE COMMISSION FOR SIX LONG YEARS AND DESPITE THE FACT THAT HE HIMSELF WAS AN ACTIVE MEMBER OF THE MASONIC ORDER, AMERICAN HISTORIANS MAINTAINED THE ILLUSION THAT ROOSEVELT CONTINUALLY FOUGHT FOR AN HONEST AND OPEN GOVERNMENT. IN 1897, PRESIDENT WILLIAM MCKINLEY NAMED ROOSEVELT ASSISTANT SECRETARY OF THE AMERICAN NAVY. COINCIDENTLY, FRATERNITY BROTHER ROOSEVELT WANTED TO BUILD UP ITS ARMY AND NAVY FORCES IN ORDER TO EXPAND BY TAKING OVER LANDS THAT THE FREEMASONS NEEDED TO FULFILL ITS DREAM OF ACHIEVING THEIR **GOD** GIVEN RIGHT TO REIGN SUPREME. IT WAS UNDER THIS DECEPTION THAT TEDDY ROOSEVELT ORGANIZED A REGIMENT OF VOLUNTEER RENEGADES, THE INFAMOUS **"ROUGH RIDERS"**, A GROUP OF U.S. GOVERNMENTAL MILITARY TYPE ASSASSINS.

IN 1901, MASONIC BROTHER ROOSEVELT WAS APPOINTED TO THE PORTFOLIO OF VICE-PRESIDENT OF THE UNITED STATES UNDER THE MCKINLEY ADMINISTRATION. APPARENTLY, ONLY SIX MONTHS INTO HIS SECOND INAUGURATION, U.S. PRESIDENT WILLIAM MCKINLEY MADE A SPEECH AT BUFFALO, NEW YORK, IN WHICH HE EMPHASIZED THE END OF AMERICAN COMMERCIAL ISOLATION AND THE IMPORTANCE OF RECIPROCITY AS A MEANS OF PROMOTING FOREIGN TRADE. THE VERY NEXT DAY, SEPTEMBER 6TH, 1901 (DURING A RECEPTION), PRESIDENT MCKINLEY WAS ASSASSINATED SUPPOSEDLY BY AN ANARCHIST. AFTER HIS DEATH, VICE-PRESIDENT ROOSEVELT HUMBLY ACCEPTED THE OFFICE OF THE PRESIDENCY, SEPTEMBER 14TH, 1901. BE THAT AS IT MAY, FRATERNITY BROTHER ROOSEVELT DIDN'T APPOINT A REPLACEMENT UNTIL FOUR YEARS LATER, (CHAS. W. FAIRBANKS 1905). DURING HIS TERM IN THE WHITE HOUSE, SOME AMERICAN CITIZENS CALLED ROOSEVELT A RADICAL FOR THE WAY IN WHICH HE HAD THINGS DONE — POLITICALLY AND/OR OTHERWISE. WHILE IN OFFICE AS PRESIDENT, THE UNITED STATES ALSO GAINED CONTROL OF THE LANDS REQUIRED TO FULFILL ITS DREAM OF EXPANSION; A CANAL ACROSS THE ISTHMUS OF PANAMA. THIS DEED WAS ACCOMPLISHED IN 1903, DURING WHICH THE U.S. ADMINISTRATION PLACED A MILITARY COUP TO OVERTHROW THE PANAMANIAN GOVERNMENT. ROOSEVELT WAS LATER REPORTED TO HAVE BOASTED TO HIS MASONIC BRETHREN AND OTHERS THAT HE HAD TAKEN POSSESSION OF THE "CANAL ZONE".

At one time Teddy was seen as a friend of labor, but that misconception was quickly cleared up during the 1902 coal strike. Miners formed a nation wide union; the United Mine Workers of America, which asked for a nine-hour work day as well as an increase of wages. Needless to say, the mine owners were not at all impressed with the idea and 150,000 miners immediately went on strike. The strike continued all summer long, with coal piles dwindling and cold weather fast approaching, Roosevelt brought the strike to a rapid conclusion when he threatened to bring in the army to force miners back to work. The final outcome was a settlement of the strike itself, miners received a much longer work day for the exact same low pay structure. Miners were not overly impressed with the actions of their American President, a person could actually say that Freemasonry leader Roosevelt was giving the working class people the royal fraternal shaft in more ways than one. When Roosevelt first took office, many ordinary American citizens firmly believed that he was the President protecting them against the growing powers of big business and the threat of a foreign take-over. Roosevelt on the other hand, felt that he had the right to take any lawful action needed to benefit the nation and its people as a whole. According to the historians, Theodore Roosevelt thought of himself as a strong President like Andrew Jackson and Abraham Lincoln. Like Roosevelt, Andrew Jackson and Abe Lincoln were also members of the Masonic Order. Andrew Jackson in fact was a Grand Master of the Grand Lodge of Masons for the State of Tennessee once the Americans gained their independence from Britain during the Revolutionary War.

As the 1908 Presidential election approached, Roosevelt's popularity had dropped dramatically. The United States was suffering from a serious economic depression, and Roosevelt did very little to combat its affects on the American people. In fact, many American citizens strongly believed that he was the direct cause of it; no compromising, only confrontation. Roosevelt did not want to run again as the U.S. President, but maintained an overall desire of choosing his successor to the throne. His good friend and comrade at arms William Howard Taft was thusly anointed as the next President of the United States of America.

In 1890, President Benjamin Harrison appointed Taft Solicitor-General of the America's. He prepared cases for the Attorney-General and argued many of the U.S. Government's cases before the Supreme Court. During his many loyal years of service, Taft

MET MANY OF THE COUNTRY'S IMPORTANT AND MOST POWERFUL MEMBERS OF AMERICAN FREEMASONRY AND DID HIS DAMNEST TO PLEASE THEM. BY 1892, TAFT BECAME A JUDGE OF THE UNITED STATES CIRCUIT COURT OF APPEALS, HE SERVED EIGHT YEARS. IN 1900, PRESIDENT MCKINLEY APPOINTED HIM PRESIDENT OF THE PHILIPPINE COMMISSION – THE UNITED STATES HAD GAINED POSSESSION OF THE PHILIPPINE ISLANDS AS A RESULT OF THE SPANISH-AMERICAN WAR AND ONE YEAR LATER, TAFT BECAME THE FIRST GOVERNOR OF THE PHILIPPINES. BY 1904, TAFT RETURNED FROM THE PHILIPPINES AND BECAME ROOSEVELT'S SECRETARY OF WAR. TWO YEARS THEREAFTER, WAR SECRETARY TAFT SENT TROOPS INTO CUBA TO CONTROL A REVOLT, AND ACTED AS ITS GOVERNOR UNTIL ORDER WAS RESTORED. THE FOLLOWING YEAR, (1907), DICTATOR TAFT REORGANIZED THE POLITICAL STRUCTURE OF PANAMA, CUBA AND PUERTO RICO. DUE TO THE FACT THAT WILLIAM HOWARD TAFT WAS AN EXPERT CONSTITUTIONAL LAWYER, HE CONTINUED WITH ROOSEVELT'S NATIONAL POLICY OF "**MANIFEST DESTINY** "BY CARRYING AN EVEN BIGGER FREEMASONRY STICK TO HELP SWAY HIS OPPONENTS INTO SUBMISSION. LIKE TEDDY ROOSEVELT, MASONIC BROTHER TAFT ALSO FAVORED BIG BUSINESS.

NOT LONG AFTER HE SETTLED INTO THE WHITE HOUSE AS ROOSEVELT'S APPOINTED SUCCESSOR, EARLY IN 1910, THE AMERICANS APPROACHED CANADA BY MEANS OF A TELEGRAM CONVEYING UNITED STATES PRESIDENT TAFT'S URGENT DESIRE TO BEGIN EARLY NEGOTIATIONS FOR ANNEXATION INTO THE AMERICAN UNION. UPON HEARING THE NEWS, THE LIBERAL PARTY OF CANADA CHEERED AS WORD OF THE TALKS ENTERED INTO THE HOUSE OF COMMONS. THE CANADIAN FREEMASON CONSERVATIVE LEADER ROBERT BORDEN ONCE WROTE, "THERE WAS THE DEEPEST DEJECTION IN OUR PARTY AND MANY OF OUR MEMBERS WERE CONFIDENT THAT THE GOVERNMENT'S PROPOSALS WOULD APPEAL TO THE COUNTRY AND GIVE IT ANOTHER TERM IN OFFICE."

ALL WAS NOT WELL IN PARADISE AS DIRECT OPPOSITION TO FREE-TRADE SOON APPEARED WITHIN THE LIBERAL PARTY AS WELL. EIGHTEEN LIBERALS BROKE RANK WITH THEIR LEADER OVER THE QUESTION, INCLUDING CLIFFORD STIFTON, SIR WILFRID LAURIER'S FORMER MINISTER OF THE INTERIOR, WHO SAID HE DID NOT WANT TO SEE THE GREAT WEST COUNTRY WHICH HE LOVED "BECOME A BACKYARD TO THE CITY OF CHICAGO, "AS THE AMERICANS ONCE AGAIN REKINDLED ITS DREAMS OF "**MANIFEST DESTINY**". NEGOTIATIONS BEGAN INTRODUCING A NEW FREE-TRADE AGREEMENT WITH CANADA DURING A DEBATE IN A SPECIAL SUMMER SESSION OF THE U.S. CONGRESS IN JULY OF 1911 – IN WHICH THE SPEAKER OF THE U.S. HOUSE OF REPRESENTATIVES, JAY BEAUCHAMP CLARK STATED THAT HE WAS TOTALLY IN FAVOR OF IT BECAUSE HE HAD HOPES OF SEEING "THE DAY WHEN THE AMERICAN FLAG WILL FLOAT

OVER EVERY SQUARE FOOT OF BRITISH NORTH AMERICA CLEAR TO THE NORTH POLE."

STRANGE AS IT WAY SEEM, CANADIANS APPARENTLY BANDED TOGETHER IN PROTEST AGAINST THE PROPOSED FREE-TRADE AMERICANIZATION PLAN OF 1911 – CITIZEN GROUPS MET THE LEADER OF THE CONSERVATIVE PARTY LITERALLY TELLING HIM THAT HE WAS BEING FAR "TOO GENTLEMANLY AND POLITE IN THE BATTLE. "THEY URGED HIM TO STIFFEN UP HIS SPINE, AND MASONIC BROTHER BORDEN THUSLY ENDED UP PLEDGING TO FIGHT THE BATTLE TO THE BITTER END. THE TORIES KNEW THAT IF THEY DIDN'T FULFILL THE WISHES OF THE PEOPLE, THE CANADIAN CITIZENRY WOULD HAVE VOICED THEIR OPPOSITION AT THE VOTING BOOTHS WHICH WOULD HAVE VIRTUALLY WHIPPED THEM OFF THE POLITICAL MAP AND PLACED THEM INTO OBSCURITY. THE YEAR 1911 THUS BECAME AN ELECTION YEAR FOCUSING ON THE ISSUE OF FREE-TRADE WITH THE AMERICANS – CANADIAN SOVEREIGNTY WAS NOW HANGING IN THE BALANCE.

NEWSPAPERS THROUGHOUT THE COUNTRY IMMEDIATELY BEGAN QUESTIONING SIR WILFRID LAURIER AND HIS FEDERAL LIBERAL GOVERNMENT'S DESIRE TO DIVIDE CANADIAN UNIFICATION – BOTH THE MONTREAL STAR AND THE TORONTO STAR FOUGHT VALIANTLY AGAINST THE 1911 FREE-TRADE AGREEMENT WITH THE UNITED STATES. IN THE MONTREAL STAR'S LAST ISSUE BEFORE THE SEPTEMBER ELECTION, AN EDITORIAL COVERING THE ENTIRE FRONT PAGE HEADLINED; "UNDER WHICH FLAG?", AND BEGAN WITH THE FOLLOWING WORDS:

"THIS IS NOT A PARTY ELECTION. IT IS A NATIONAL CRISIS. WE ARE, IN TRUTH, AT THE HIGHWAY TOWARD NATIONAL GREATNESS WITH THE FLAG OF CANADA FLOATING IN OUR CLEAR NORTHERN AIR OVER OUR HEADS, OR WE WILL TURN ASIDE TOWARDS ABSORPTION IN THE GREAT AND GLORIOUS REPUBLIC TO THE SOUTH OF US– SURRENDERING TO A CALCULATING SMILE, WHAT WE HAVE LONG DEFENDED FROM HOSTILITY IN EVERY FORM – ARMED INVASION, TARIFF PERSECUTIONS, BULLYING OVER BOUNDARIES AND INSOLENT DISREGARD OF TREATY OBLIGATIONS."

IN HIS LAST CAMPAIGN SPEECH TO THE PEOPLE OF CANADA, FREEMASONRY BROTHER ROBERT BORDEN STATED:

"AS THIS CAMPAIGN CLOSES, THE SOLEMN DUTY CONFORMS US OF DECIDING, VERY PROBABLY FOR ALL TIME, THE MOST MOMENTOUS QUESTION EVER SUBMITTED TO THE CANADIAN ELECTORATE. THROUGHOUT THIS DOMINION, THE ELECTORATE NOW UNDERSTANDING THAT THEY ARE CALLED UPON TO DETERMINE, NOT A MERE QUESTION OF MARKETS, BUT THE FUTURE DESTINY OF

Canada — Even upon the economic side, reciprocity is but a step in a greater process. On each side of the boundary line its advocates realize perfectly that in its final outcome, this treaty undoubtedly means the commercial and fiscal union of Canada with the United States. Above all, do not forget that the momentous choice which you must make is for all time. If the tariffs of the two countries are interlocked, be assured that the stronger party will always carry the key. I believe that we are, in truth, standing at the parting of the ways. This compact, made in secret and without mandate, points indeed to a new path. We must decide whether a spirit of Canadianism or Continentalism shall prevail on the northern half of this continent."

On September 20TH, 1911, the day before the election, the Pro-Free-Trade Toronto Globe read with the following headlines: "Nothing To Prevent A Liberal Sweep — Reports Received From All Sections Are Most Encouraging — Sir Wilfrid Feels Confident. "While two days later, the front page of the Montreal Gazette told a totally different story than what was actually expected: "Laurier Defeated — Reciprocity Pact Rejected by the People — Majority Of 44 Which Will Probably Be Increased to Fifty — 8 Ministers Slain — Covenant of Treason Torn Into Tatters by the Electors — Bad Regime Is Ended — The Globe Says Ontario Evidently Does Not Like The Americans."

When the election votes were counted, the Laurier Government was swept from office — eight Cabinet Ministers were also thrown out of office by their constituency voters. Fraternity Brother Borden entered into "Ottawa in triumph, like a conqueror. A hundred men drew his carriage for miles through the streets which were packed with crowds and brave with fluttering flags. "At the time, (1911), only 23 percent of Canada's goods were traded with the United States, by the mid-1980's, that figure quickly rose to 80 percent.

The issue of annexation with the United States by way of Free-Trade reared its ugly head once again during the 1980's decade when the American people foolishly anointed a failed Hollywood actor, fraternity Brother Ronald Reagan, as their 40TH President in November of 1980. Little did the Canadian population realize that Reagan's secret Freemasonry mandate was to ultimately bring Canada into the U.S. Masonic Family fold. When he first took office in the White House, Reagan suggested that all trade barriers be lifted and Free-Trade with the entire North American Continent from

THE ARCTIC TO CENTRAL AMERICAN COUNTRIES BE IMPLEMENTED, A MEXICO AND BEYOND MENTALITY. THE GOVERNING BODIES OF ALL COUNTRIES WERE THUSLY MORE THAN WILLING TO ASSIST REAGAN IN HIS 1980 PRESIDENTIAL CAMPAIGN WHICH CALLED FOR A NORTH AMERICAN COMMON MARKET. CANADA'S INVOLVEMENT BEGAN SOON THEREAFTER, IN OTTAWA DURING 1982 AND 1983. THE UNITED STATES WAS NEGOTIATING A FREE-TRADE AGREEMENT WITH ISRAEL AND THEY WANTED TO HAVE ONE WITH CANADA NEXT. THE FREEMASONRY ADMINISTRATION OF FRATERNITY BROTHER RONALD REAGAN REALIZED THAT IF THE CANADIAN POPULATION HAD FOUND OUT THAT THEY (THE AMERICANS) HAD REVISED THEIR MASONIC GRANDMASTER PLAN OF HAVING THE **GOD** GIVEN RIGHT TO REIGN SUPREME BY ATTEMPTING TO OCCUPY THE ENTIRE NORTH AMERICAN CONTINENT, THERE WOULD HAVE BEEN A COMPLETE BACKLASH, AND CANADIANS WOULD HAVE FOUGHT BACK. SO, LIKE THE SECRET RITUALS OF THE MASONIC FRATERNITY, CANADA'S FREE-TRADE DEAL WITH THE UNITED STATES WAS THUSLY CONDUCTED UNDER A SHROUD OF ABSOLUTE SECRECY. BUT IN ORDER TO DO SO, CANADA HAD TO FIRST FULFILL CERTAIN CONTRACTUAL OBLIGATIONS TO HELP EASY THE PAIN OF SODOMIZATION. THE FIRST TASK WAS TO ESTABLISH A WRITTEN CONSTITUTION, ONE THAT COULD BE CHALLENGED IN A COURT OF LAW IF ITS POPULATION BECAME WISE TO THE GREAT AMERICAN DREAM GIVING ITS NEIGHBORS TO THE NORTH THE FRATERNAL SHAFT — THE COURTS IN TURN, WOULD KEEP THE DISGRUNTLED CANADIAN POPULATION AT BAY AND TOTALLY CONFUSED FOR MANY YEARS TO COME. ONCE OUR CANADIAN PRIME MINISTER PIERRE ELLIOTT TRUDEAU COMPLETED HIS TASK OF ENLIGHTENMENT, HE RECEIVED HIGH PRAISE FOR A JOB WELL DONE AND STEPPED ASIDE FOR THE NEXT PHASE OF AIDING AND ABETTING IN THE APPLICATION OF THE AMERICAN DREAM OF DIVINE INTERVENTION.

INTERESTING ENOUGH, PRESIDENT RONALD REAGAN REPORTEDLY STATED AT ONE TIME: "THE U.S.-CANADA FREE-TRADE AGREEMENT IS A NEW ECONOMIC CONSTITUTION FOR NORTH AMERICA. IT WILL I BELIEVE INAUGURATE A SIMILAR CONTINENT-WIDE ECONOMIC EXPANSION. "ALL TRADE BARRIERS IN EUROPE WERE LIFTED IN 1992 AS A WORLDWIDE FREE-TRADE COMMON MARKET HAD BEEN IMPLEMENTED AS PART AND PARCEL OF THE MASONIC **NEW WORLD ORDER** UNDER THE AUSPICES OF "THE BROTHERHOOD OF MAN — UNDER THE FATHERHOOD OF GOD."

IN THE MEANTIME BACK IN CANADA, THE OTTAWA BACK ROOM BOYS — WITH THE ASSISTANCE OF THE AMERICANS — PLACED YET ANOTHER ONE OF THEIR FRATERNAL PUPPETS INTO THE PRIME MINISTER'S OFFICE. ONLY MONTHS INTO HIS CANADIAN POLITICAL PORTFOLIO, THEN-CONSERVATIVE LEADER BRIAN MULRONEY PASSED INTO LAW PIERRE TRUDEAU'S HIGHLY CONTROVERSIAL CANADIAN SECRET POLICE BILL (C-9). IT WASN'T EXACTLY

THE SAME VERSION AS ORIGINALLY CONCEIVED, IT WAS SOMEWHAT MODIFIED, BUT STILL A FASCIST PIECE OF GOVERNMENTAL LEGISLATION NONETHELESS. TRUDEAU'S SECRET POLICE BILL WAS VETOED WHILE HE WAS STILL IN POWER BECAUSE OF PUBLIC OUTCRY. WHILE ACTING AS THE NEWLY ANOINTED CANADIAN PRIME MINISTER, MULRONEY MANAGED TO SECRETLY PASS THE BILL WITH THE HELP OF HIS POLITICAL COLLEAGUES AND MEDIA CONNECTIONS. THE REVAMPED LEGISLATION OF BILL C-9 THUSLY FORMED THE CANADIAN SECURITY INTELLIGENCE SERVICE – A.K.A. CSIS. NOT LONG AFTER IT WAS INITIALLY IMPLEMENTED BY THE CONSERVATIVE GOVERNMENT, CANADA'S SECRET POLICE FORCE BEGAN INVESTIGATING ALL ORGANIZED GROUPS THAT OPPOSED FEDERAL GOVERNMENT LEGISLATION, IT ENCOMPASSED ORGANIZED CITIZEN GROUPS THAT LEANED TO EITHER THE LEFT AND/OR TO THE RIGHT OF THE POLITICAL SPECTRUM. NO ONE WAS IMMUNE TO THE SURVEILLANCE TACTICS OF CANADA'S NEW AND IMPROVED SPY AGENCY. IT SHOULD ALSO BE NOTED THAT THE MAJORITY OF CSIS AGENTS WERE EX-RCMP OFFICERS, MOST OF WHOM RECEIVED THEIR TRAINING FROM VARIOUS U.S. SECRET SERVICE AGENCIES, (CIA, FBI). IT SHOULD FURTHER BE STATED THAT SOME MEMBERS OF THE NEWLY FORMED CANADIAN SECRET POLICE LATER QUIT THE FORCE CITING THAT IT WAS FAR TOO STRESSFUL OF A JOB. ANOTHER INTERESTING FACTOR IRONICALLY ENOUGH WAS THAT IN 1990, PRIME MINISTER BRIAN MULRONEY'S CSIS BUDGET WAS REPORTED AS BEING $189.9 MILLION, TO WHICH NOTHING WAS DISCLOSED AS TO WHERE AND HOW THE MILLIONS OF TAX DOLLARS WERE GOING TO BE SPENT.

IN SEPTEMBER OF 1984, A SECRET COMMUNICATIONS STRATEGY DOCUMENT ACCIDENTLY LEAKED OUT TO THE MEDIA. THE DOCUMENT APPARENTLY OUTLINED THE CANADIAN FEDERAL GOVERNMENT'S POSITION ON ESTABLISHING FREE-TRADE WITH THE AMERICANS. IT STATED IN PART: "THE HIGHER THE PROFILE THE ISSUE ATTAINS, THE LOWER THE DEGREE OF PUBLIC APPROVAL WILL BE ... OUR STRATEGY SHOULD RELY LESS ON EDUCATING THE GENERAL PUBLIC, THAN IN GETTING ACROSS THE MESSAGE THAT THE TRADE INITIATIVE IS A GOOD IDEA. IN OTHER WORDS: A SELLING JOB ... BENIGN NEGLECT FROM THE MAJORITY OF CANADIANS MAY BE THE REALISTIC OUTCOME OF THE WELL-EDUCATED COMMUNICATIONS PROGRAM."

THE TORONTO STAR PUBLISHED THE LEAKED DOCUMENT IN ITS ENTIRETY FURTHER STATING THAT "THE PROGRAM CALLS FOR BRIAN MULRONEY TO FOCUS EXCLUSIVELY ON THE POSSIBLE BENEFITS OF FREE-TRADE, TO AVOID MENTIONING JOB LOSSES, TO DISCREDIT OPPOSITION M.P.'S WHO RAISE CONCERNS ABOUT FREE-TRADE NEGOTIATIONS, AND TO ISOLATE GROUPS OPPOSED TO THE PENDING TALKS. IN MANY CASES, THE DOCUMENTS PURPOSE, THE BEST TACTIC WILL BE TO DIVIDE AND NEUTRALIZE GROUPS THAT OPPOSE THE FREE-TRADE OPTION."

Thus, in this land of social democracy – the year 1985 marked the beginning of the end of Canada as an independent nation, our country in effect was gradually becoming part of the United States. In March (St. Patrick's Day) protestors congregated around iron barricades and wrestled with police officers encircling Quebec City's majestic Chateau Frontenac while our very own Canadian Prime Minister began courting U.S. President Ronald Reagan – serenading the American Freemasonry leader with his rendition of the highly sentimental song **When Irish Eyes Are Smiling**. This political meeting, better known historically as the "Shamrock Summit "for the way in which Brian Mulroney so proudly executed his Irish comradery whereby the unification of Canada and our American cousins south of the 49TH parallel were to eventually merge as one under a free-trade deal. At the time of this impromptu duet of harmonious caterwauling by the western free-world leaders, no one fully realized the capability of the long-term political pain normally associated with sodomy that was about to be unleashed onto an unsuspecting Canadian population – the single most defining moment in the entire political history of our country whereas, we, as a nation collectively spread the cheeks of our ass wide open asking for more!!!

By November 1985 an External Affairs secret document was published in the Maclean's news magazine, it outlined the Conservative Government's sweeping program **"to reassure Canadians that Canadian sovereignty is not at risk. "**The Federal Government document recommended that billions of tax dollars be spend on the Department of Defense, including submarines (job creation programs) and hype up patriotism for British Columbia's EXPO 86 event as well as other national propaganda type programs to help Canadians forget about Free-Trade issues and ultimately wrap themselves up in the Canadian flag while rallying around all sorts of governmental false pretexts. Canadians were overjoyed with the prospects of making big bucks as three-quarters of the country's population was in the midst of an economic recession. At the time, most of the good paying jobs were in the Province of Ontario while in all of the other Provinces, the majority of the workforce was being paid minimum wage /or just slightly above it.

On October 3RD, 1987 the Canada-U.S. Free-Trade Agreement (FTA) was signed. Canadians literally had no say in this so-called **ACT OF DEMOCRACY** as it was signed, sealed and delivered strictly **BEHIND CLOSED DOORS**. Those who protested against the trade

AGREEMENT WERE EITHER ARRESTED BY THE POLICE ON THE SPOT, HARASSED /OR DETAINED WITHOUT JUST CAUSE. MANY **ANTI-FREE-TRADERS** WERE INSTANTLY LABELED AS BEING "**NAZIS** "/OR "**WIMPS** "AFRAID TO COMPETE WITH THE AMERICANS. IT GOES WITHOUT SAYING THAT MULRONEY'S TACTICS WORKED AS THE VAST MAJORITY OF THE CANADIAN POPULATION HAD ABSOLUTELY NO IDEA AS TO WHAT THE REAL ISSUE WAS, THEY WERE IN FACT, IN A TOTAL STATE OF CONFUSION. BATTLE LINES WERE THUSLY DRAWN, THE AMERICANS WERE THE CANADIAN ALLIES AND THE PROTESTORS, WERE THE ENEMY.

BY MAY 24TH, 1988 NEWFOUNDLAND'S CONSERVATIVE M.P. JOHN CROSBIE INTRODUCED BILL C-130 INTO THE HOUSE OF COMMONS, TO IMPLEMENT THE FREE-TRADE AGREEMENT. THE ACT STATED IN PART: "**NO PERSON SHALL, IN THE PURPORTED PERFORMANCE OF DUTIES OR FUNCTIONS UNDER ANY LAW OF CANADA, DO ANY ACT, EXERCISE ANY POWER OR CARRY ON ANY PRACTICE THAT IS INCONSISTENT WITH OR CONTRAVENES THIS ACT OR ANY REGULATION MADE UNDER THIS ACT, OR THE (FREE TRADE) AGREEMENT. "THE** ACT ITSELF WENT ON TO SAY THAT THE FREE-TRADE AGREEMENT OVERRIDES ANY CANADIAN LAW OR ANY OTHER ACT OF PARLIAMENT. IRONICALLY, IN 1949, WHEN NEWFOUNDLAND FINALLY JOINED CANADA IN CONFEDERATION, CROSBIE'S FAMILY WANTED THEIR BELOVED PROVINCE TO JOIN THE UNITED STATES INSTEAD.

THERE WERE MANY PROTESTS ORGANIZED ACROSS THE COUNTRY AGAINST ANNEXATION WITH THE AMERICANS, MOST OF WHICH WERE EXECUTED BY A 37-YEAR-OLD METIS PRAIRIE FARMER NAMED DAVID ORCHARD AND HIS GROUP OF CONCERNED CITIZENS FROM SASKATOON, SASKATCHEWAN. THE GROUP SIMPLY CALLED THEMSELVES "CITIZENS CONCERN ABOUT FREE-TRADE "AND HOUNDED MULRONEY EVERYWHERE HE WENT. IN FACT, ON MAY 7TH, 1987, DURING THE PRIME MINISTER'S TOUR OF WESTERN CANADA, MR. ORCHARD WAS DETAINED FOR 25 MINUTES BY MULRONEY'S SECRET POLICE. AS THE CANADIAN FEDERAL GOVERNMENT LEADER SHOOK HANDS AND KISSED OFF HECKLERS ON HIS WAY TO THE CENTENNIAL AUDITORIUM IN SASKATOON FOR THE VESNA FESTIVAL, ORCHARD APPARENTLY SHOUTED OUT "**MR. MULRONEY, YOU HAVE NO MANDATE TO NEGOTIATE FREE TRADE WITH THE UNITED STATES.**" THE CANADIAN PRIME MINISTER AND SASKATCHEWAN PREMIER GRANT DEVINE INSTANTLY LOOKED AT ONE ANOTHER AND SMIRKED. ALMOST IMMEDIATELY, DAVID ORCHARD WAS GRABBED BY A TALL GOOSE STEPPING GESTAPO AGENT OF THE CANADIAN SECRET POLICE. THE AGENT TOOK HOLD OF ORCHARD'S ARM AND BEGAN WALKING HIM TOWARDS A PARKING LOT AWAY FROM MULRONEY'S ENTOURAGE. WHILE GOOSE STEPPING, THE GOVERNMENT APPOINTED NATIONAL SECURITY AGENT BEGAN TO SAY SOMETHING ABOUT ORCHARD BEING TOTALLY "IMPOLITE". THAT'S WHEN THE DETAINED DISSIDENT MR. ORCHARD BEGAN TO REALIZE THAT HE WAS NOT GOING TO BE ALLOWED

TO EXPRESS HIS OWN PERSONAL OPINION TO THE CANADIAN PRIME MINISTER. SO, ORCHARD ONCE AGAIN SHOUTED OUT "YOU'VE GOT NO MANDATE TO NEGOTIATE A FREE TRADE AGREEMENT WITH THE UNITED STATES."

THE PRAIRIE FARMER WAS THUS FORCED NORTHWARD ACROSS THE PARKING LOT WHERE HE WAS HANDED OVER TO YET ANOTHER AGENT. WALKING FURTHER NORTH INTO THE PARKING LOT, THEY STOPPED BEHIND SOME PARKED CARS. ORCHARD THEN ASKED, "AM I UNDER ARREST? "THE DARK-SUITED THICKER-SET NATIONAL SECURITY AGENT THEN REPLIED, "RIGHT NOW YOU ARE. "THE DETAINED PROTESTOR RESPONDED BY SAYING THAT HE WANTED TO CONTACT HIS LAWYER. ONCE ORCHARD ASKED TO SPEAK WITH AN ATTORNEY, THERE WAS NO RESPONSE FROM THE GESTAPO AGENT AS HE CONTINUED TO HOLD ONTO THE IMPOLITE PROTESTOR. MOMENTS LATER, A CAR PULLED ALONG SIDE THE ROADWAY, STILL HOLDING ONTO ORCHARD'S ARM, THE AGENT THEN WALKED HIM TOWARDS THE CAR, OPENED THE BACK DOOR AND PLACED HIM INSIDE. ONCE MR. ORCHARD SLIDE OVER IN THE BACK SEAT, THE AGENT SAT BESIDE HIM. THE GOOSE STEPPING AGENT THEN ORDERED THE DRIVER TO LOCK THE DOORS, THERE WAS A CLICK SOUND AND ALL THE DOORS WERE INSTANTLY LOCKED. THE DRIVER WAS FURTHER INSTRUCTED TO DRIVE AROUND THE BLOCK. THE CSIS AGENT, THEN TURNED HIS HEAD SIDEWAY TOWARDS DAVID ORCHARD AND SAID; "WE KNOW YOU. YOU ARE THE INSTIGATOR OF THIS OPPOSITION. YOU WERE IN FRONT OF THE BESSBOROUGH LAST JULY WHEN THE PRIME MINISTER WAS HERE. YOU WERE WEARING THE SAME CHECKERED SHIRT AS YOU'VE GOT ON RIGHT NOW. YOU GAVE US TROUBLE. "ORCHARD QUICKLY ASKED; "WHAT KIND OF TROUBLE? "THE CSIS AGENT'S REPLY WAS; "YOU DIDN'T GET OFF THE SIDEWALK."

DISSIDENT DAVID ORCHARD WAS HELD FOR 25 MINUTES BY THE RCMP AND THEN RELEASED. HE WAS TOLD THERE WERE NO CHARGES AGAINST HIM, BUT THAT HE HAD "INVADED THE PRIVACY OF THE PRIME MINISTER. "THE SASKATCHEWAN PRAIRIE FARMER WAS FURTHER INFORMED BY THE POLICE THAT "WE ARE GOING TO LET YOU GO AND IF YOU GO WITHIN 100 YARDS OF THE AUDITORIUM, WE'RE GOING TO THROW YOU IN JAIL. "THIS BY NO MEANS WAS THE FIRST TIME DAVID ORCHARD HAD A RUN-IN WITH THE LAW. IN 1984, HE WAS ARRESTED FOR AN OUTSTANDING PARKING TICKET; WHICH AS IT TURNED OUT, HAD IN FACT BEEN PAID. ORCHARD WAS TAKEN TO THE POLICE STATION WHERE, HE WAS TREATED WITH UNNECESSARY FORCE. ONCE RELEASED, HE PRESSED FOR A $ 200,000.00 LAWSUIT AGAINST THE CITY OF SASKATOON AND THE POLICE, CLAIMING FALSE IMPRISONMENT, ASSAULT AND DENIAL OF HIS RIGHT TO LEGAL COUNSEL. ALMOST TWO YEARS LATER, HE SETTLED OUT OF COURT FOR $ 2,450.00 AS THE NEWS OF HIS INCARCERATION EXPERIENCE CROSSED THE COUNTRY THROUGH THE MOCCASIN TELEGRAPH SYSTEM. ORCHARD HAD INADVERTENTLY TAPPED INTO A CANADIAN NETWORK SYSTEM

FROM THE EAST COAST TO THE WESTERN SHORELINE OF THE PACIFIC OCEAN AND THE STAGE WAS THEREFORE BEING SET AS TO WHAT HAD TO BE DONE NEXT. DAVID ORCHARD AND HIS NEWFOUND GROUP OF DISSIDENT TAXPAYERS BANDED TOGETHER ORGANIZING DEBATES, SEMINARS, PROTEST RALLIES AND ISSUED NEWSLETTERS CONDEMNING THE MULRONEY ADMINISTRATION ON FREE-TRADE WITH THE AMERICANS.

IT EVEN GOT TO THE POINT WHERE ORCHARD AND HIS CITIZENS CONCERN ABOUT FREE TRADE PUBLISHED A BOOK EXPOSING THE TRUE LOGISTICS ABOUT FREE-TRADE, (MOST OF WHICH THIS CHAPTER IS USING ORCHARD'S MATERIAL TO HELP GET ITS POINT ACROSS REGARDING THE FREEMASONRY CONNECTION). DAVID ORCHARD'S BOOK, **"FREE TRADE: THE FULL STORY "**SOON WAS ABLE TO TRANSFORM ITSELF INTO VIDEO FORM — ALL IN PREPARATION FOR THE 1988 FEDERAL ELECTION AS IT WAS AN ELECTION BASED ON A SOMEWHAT LOW KEY FREE-TRADE ISSUE ON THE CANADIAN PRIME MINISTER'S PART. WHEN IT CAME DOWN TO THE ISSUES ASSOCIATED WITH FREE-TRADE WITH THE UNITED STATES, NOT VERY MANY CANADIANS WERE EDUCATED IN WHAT THE FTA ACTUALLY MEANT TO THE COUNTRY AS A WHOLE, THE CANADIAN POPULATION WAS PURPOSELY LEFT IN THE DARK CONCERNING THIS ISSUE. ORCHARD AND HIS GROUP THUSLY SET OUT TO EDUCATE THE UNINFORMED CITIZENRY.

AS THE ELECTION DREW NEAR, **ANTI-FREE-TRADE** CAMPAIGNERS STATED THEIR OPINIONS, MANY OF THE POSTERS WERE TORN DOWN IMMEDIATELY BY ORDER OF **GOVERNMENTAL OFFICIALS**. IN SIX MAJOR CITIES ACROSS THE COUNTRY — SAINT JOHN'S, MONTREAL, TORONTO, WINNIPEG, EDMONTON AND VANCOUVER — **ANTI-FREE-TRADE** CAMPAIGNERS WERE ARRESTED FOR "PUBLIC-MISCHIEF", A CRIMINAL OFFENCE, WHILE ERECTING POSTERS — AT LEAST TWO DOZEN PEOPLE WERE CHARGED UNDER THE CRIMINAL CODE OF CANADA.

IN THE NOVEMBER 1988 FEDERAL ELECTION, PRIME MINISTER BRIAN MULRONEY RECEIVED A THUMBS DOWN ON HIS DELIVERY OF CANADA TO THE UNITED STATES. ONLY 43 PERCENT OF THE CANADIAN POPULATION SUPPORTED HIM; 57 PERCENT REJECTED MULRONEY AND HIS ECONOMIC UNION WITH THE AMERICANS — 67 PERCENT IN THE YUKON AND NWT, 62 PERCENT IN SASKATCHEWAN AND 65 PERCENT IN BRITISH COLUMBIA, ALL VOTED AGAINST ANNEXATION. BUT YET, MULRONEY PROUDLY STATED THAT THE CANADIAN PEOPLE GAVE HIM AND HIS GOVERNMENT A MANDATE TO IMPLEMENT FREE-TRADE WITH THE UNITED STATES. ONLY SIX MONTHS AFTER THE FEDERAL ELECTION, POLLS INDICATED THAT 75 TO 85 PERCENT OF ALL CANADIANS FELT THAT THEY DID NOT KNOW ENOUGH INFORMATION ON WHAT THE FREE-TRADE DEAL WAS ALL ABOUT, BUT YET THEY VOTED ANYWAYS — ISN'T THAT TYPICAL OF OUR MODERN DAY CANADIAN SOCIETY. MUCH OF THE TURMOIL THAT CANADA HAS ENSURED SINCE THEN IS LARGELY DUE TO THE LACK OF KNOWLEDGE ON THE POPULATION OF COUNTRY'S PART. TO THAT END, MUCH OF THE MEDIA IS

TO BLAME AS WELL. FOR EXAMPLE, WHEN 700 ANGRY PEOPLE DEMONSTRATED AGAINST MULRONEY ON THE FREE-TRADE AGREEMENT IN VANCOUVER ON JUNE 8TH, 1989, CALLING HIM A TRAITOR TO HIS OWN COUNTRY, THERE WAS NO NEWS COVERAGE ON IT WHATSOEVER. IN ITS PLACE WAS INSTEAD LONG NEWS COVERAGE OF CHINESE EVENTS – THE BEIJING MASSACRE AT TIANANMEN SQUARE – AND OTHER VARIOUS NEWS STORIES SUCH AS MULRONEY'S AMICABLE MEETING WITH CHINESE BUSINESS LEADERS IN VANCOUVER, DURING WHICH TIME PERIOD HE MIMICKED NUMEROUS PLATITUDES ABOUT "LIBERTY "AND "DEMOCRACY".

THE FACT THAT CANADA ITSELF AT THAT PRECISE MOMENT IN TIME HAD A VERY FRAGILE DEMOCRACY THAT WAS TRYING ITS DAMNEST TO SURVIVE BUT WASN'T HAVING MUCH SUCCESS DUE TO WIDESPREAD MORAL CORRUPTION IN THE HOUSE OF COMMONS – IT WASN'T REALLY NEWS WORTHY MATERIAL AS BOTH OUR CANADIAN IDENTITY AND DEMOCRATIC PRINCIPLES WERE BEING VICIOUSLY VIOLATED BY THE CANADIAN POWERS THAT BE – AND IT WAS FURTHER PERCEIVED AS BEING NO REAL IMPORTANCE WHATSOEVER. A YEAR AFTER THE CHINESE UP-RISING AT TIANANMEN SQUARE, OUR COUNTRY'S NATIONAL MEDIA OUTLETS CONTINUED TO FOCUS ON THE MASSACRE BY DETAILING AN OVERALL ACCOUNT OF "CHINA AFTER TIANANMEN SQUARE "SO DEEMED AS THE "ASIA PACIFIC REPORT."

IN YET ANOTHER EXAMPLE OF MISGUIDED CANADIAN JOURNALISM WAS THE CASE OF AN UP-SIDE-DOWN CANADIAN FLAG THAT RECEIVED NATIONAL NEWS COVERAGE TEN WEEKS AFTER THE PROTESTORS CALLED PRIME MINISTER MULRONEY A TRAITOR TO HIS OWN COUNTRY. THE INCIDENT TOOK PLACE JUST A SHORT DISTANCE FROM VANCOUVER ITSELF, AS A LONE RESIDENT FROM GIBSONS, BRITISH COLUMBIA MADE THE HEADLINES: "TOWN IN UPROAR OVER FLAG FLIP "AS BENOIT J. LEPAGE FLEW HIS "MAPLE LEAF STEM-UP AND AT HALF-MAST, "MORNING THE DEATH OF CANADA. THE LONGTIME GIBSONS RESIDENT CALLED HIS "INVERTED FLAG A SYMBOLIC GESTURE AGAINST FREE-TRADE, "CITING THAT "THE YANKS WANT TO CONTROL THE ENTIRE NORTH AMERICAN CONTINENT AND THEY WILL. "BESIDE HIS UP-SIDE-DOWN MAPLE LEAF, LEPAGE ALSO FLEW THE STARS AND STRIPES – "RIGHT SIDE UP AND AT FULL MAST. "ADVOCATING HIMSELF AS A YOUTH ACTIVIST, HE WAS SENDING OUT A DISTRESS SIGNAL TO ALL CANADIANS; "OUR ONCE FREE NATION HAS BECOME THE 51ST STATE IN THE AMERICAN UNION. "LEPAGE'S PLAN WAS ORIGINALLY TO SEE HOW LONG IT WOULD TAKE COMMUNITY RESIDENTS TO FIGURE OUT WHAT THE FLAGS ACTUALLY STOOD FOR. BUT MUCH TO HIS SURPRISE, ONLY A VERY SMALL HANDFUL OF PEOPLE WERE WISE TO ITS TRUE MEANING. SHAKING HIS HEAD IN DISBELIEF, HE DECIDED TO TAKE IT ONE STEP FURTHER BY ISSUING INFORMATION LETTERS TO THE VARIOUS MEDIA OUTLETS IN THE VANCOUVER

AREA AND WAITED FOR THEIR REACTION TO HIS ANTICS OF **ANTI-FREE-TRADE** RHETORIC.

WHILE WAITING FOR SOME SORT OF A RESPONSE TO THE SITUATION AT HAND, THE GIBSONS SHIT DISTURBER RECEIVED A VISIT FROM THE RCMP. HE WAS THEN INFORMED THAT HE HAD TO TAKE DOWN THE MAPLE LEAF AND FLY IT UPRIGHT. WELL AWARE OF HIS LEGAL RIGHTS, BENOIT INJECTED BY ASKING "WHY, IT'S NOT ILLEGAL TO FLY A FLAG UPSIDE DOWN? "THE POLICE OFFICER THEN INSISTED THAT IT WAS INDEED ILLEGAL TO DO SO AND THAT UNDER CANADIAN LAW, HE COULD BE "CHARGED ACCORDINGLY. "SHAKING HIS HEAD TO-AND-FRO, LEPAGE SMILED AT THE RCMP CONSTABLE SAYING; "NO, IT'S NOT! "THE TWO PARTIES IN QUESTION THEN AGREED THAT IF SOME SORT OF CONFIRMATION COULD BE OBTAINED FROM OTTAWA, "HE COULD CONTINUE FLYING HIS INVERTED FLAG. "IT WAS A GENTLEMAN'S AGREEMENT AS THEY SHOOK HANDS ON IT — BOTH PARTIES THEN PROCEEDED TO TAKE DOWN THE INVERTED CANADIAN FLAG AND HOISTED IT RIGHT SIDE UP AT FULL MAST.

LEPAGE IMMEDIATELY MADE PHONE CALLS TO HAVE THE ISSUE RESOLVED. AFTER TALKING TO THE CANADIAN COAST GUARD AND THE SECRETARY OF STATE CANADA, THE MAPLE LEAF WAS ONCE AGAIN FLYING UP-SIDE-DOWN AND AT HALF STAFF. BY THIS TIME PERIOD, LEPAGE HAD RECEIVED MANY NASTY COMMENTS FROM LOCAL RESIDENTS FOR "DISHONOURING THE NATIONAL FLAG OF OUR COUNTRY. "HE WAS CURSED BY MANY AND LOOKED DOWN UPON BY OTHERS. AS FAR AS BENOIT LEPAGE WAS CONCERNED, THEY (THE LOCALS WHO CONDEMNED HIM FOR HIS ACTIONS) WERE NOTHING MORE THAN "OUTRAGED AMERICAN-CANADIANS. "EVEN MEMBERS OF THE GIBSONS ROYAL CANADIAN LEGION (BRANCH 109) CALLED IT AN "INSULT "STATING THAT "A FEW OF THE OLD SOLDIERS ARE KIND OF UPSET. "ONE LEGION OFFICER EVEN WENT ON PUBLIC RECORD STATING THAT HE, MEANING LEPAGE, "SHOULD HAVE SOME RESPECT FOR THEM THAT THINK IT'S MORE THAN JUST A GOLDARN RAG." HOW IRONIC COULD A SITUATION POSSIBLY BE, THERE HE STOOD, TRYING TO EDUCATE THE PEOPLE OF GIBSONS INTO REALIZING WHAT WAS ACTUALLY GOING ON BEHIND THE SCENE, AND ALL THEY COULD DO WAS CRITICIZE, JUDGE AND CONDEMN HIM BY SAYING THAT HE WAS BEING "DISRESPECTFUL."

IN SPEAKING OF IRONY, LEPAGE'S INVERTED FLAG DIDN'T REALLY BOTHER THAT MANY PEOPLE — THAT IS TO SAY UNTIL THE VANCOUVER BASED NEWSPAPER (THE PROVINCE) BEGAN PHONING AROUND GETTING A FEEDBACK FOR ITS PENDING NEWS STORY. WHEN THE NEWSPAPER CONTACTED CONNIE HARPER, SPOKESPERSON FOR THE FEDERAL SECRETARY OF STATE IN VANCOUVER, SHE STATED THAT LEPAGE WAS WELL WITHIN HIS RIGHTS TO FLY THE CANADIAN MAPLE LEAF UPSIDE-DOWN. FURTHERMORE, ACCORDING TO THE GIBSONS RCMP, ONCE THE VANCOUVER BASED NEWSPAPER HAD CONTACTED THEM — THE PROVINCE NEWSPAPER WAS IMMEDIATELY INFORMED THAT ONLY A SMALL

HANDFUL OF PEOPLE WERE DEEPLY UPSET BY THE INVERTED FLAG AND WERE FURTHER INFORMED BY THAT COMMUNITY'S RCMP "BUT THERE'S NOTHING LEGALLY WE CAN DO ABOUT IT. "COINCIDENTLY, ONLY HOURS AFTER THE NEWSPAPER CONTACTED THE GIBSONS ROYAL CANADIAN LEGION FOR THEIR REACTION; "THE FEUD HEADED UP, "AS "LEPAGE'S FLAG WAS TAKEN DOWN AND LEFT FOLDED ON HIS PORCH. "AFTER RETURNING HOME FROM WORK, BENOIT "IMMEDIATELY SENT IT BACK UP THE MAST" ACCORDING TO THE NEWSPAPER ARTICLE DATED; SUNDAY, AUGUST 13TH, 1989 "A CALLER TO THE PROVINCE" CLAIMED RESPONSIBILITY AND VOWED TO DO IT AGAIN. THE NEWS ARTICLE CONTINUED BY SAYING THAT AS FAR AS THE CALLER WAS CONCERN, "I THINK IT'S A DISGRACE." IN A FURTHER TWIST OF IRONY, THE INDIVIDUAL WHO INITIALLY TOOK DOWN THE INVERTED MAPLE LEAF WAS THE PERSONAL FRIEND OF AN AMERICAN CITIZEN WHO WAS LIVING IN THE TOWN OF GIBSONS – THIS AMERICAN CITIZEN LIVED JUST ACROSS THE ROAD FROM WHERE LEPAGE HAD FLOWN BOTH FLAGS ON HIS FRONT PORCH.

AFTER PROVING HIS POINT AS TO HOW UNINFORMED GIBSONS RESIDENTS ACTUALLY WERE ON THE SUBJECT OF FREE-TRADE WITH THE UNITED STATES, BENOIT J. LEPAGE CALLED IT QUITS AND TOOK DOWN BOTH HIS FLAGS, AND BEGAN WORKING ON THE NEXT VARIOUS PHASES OF HIS SCHEDULED LONG TERM RESEARCH PROJECT. BENOIT ANTICIPATED THAT IT WOULD BE TAKING HIM MANY YEARS TO UNRAVEL AS IT WAS A VERY COMPLEX WEB OF DECEIT AND MORAL CORRUPTION — FIRST BY RESEARCHING HIS FAMILY TREE AND THEN CONNECTIONS ALL OF THE FREEMASONRY DOTS TO ONE ANOTHER. AFTER TAKING DOWN HIS FLAGS, LEPAGE PHONED THE GIBSONS ROYAL CANADIAN LEGION SAYING TO THEM "I THINK I'VE PROVEN MY POINT! "HE KNEW THAT IT WOULD CREATE A BIT OF A RUCKUS, BUT "I NEVER THOUGHT THE REACTION WOULD BE SO NASTY. "THE NEWS CAPTION IN THE FOLLOWING DAY'S VANCOUVER BASED NEWSPAPER READ AS FOLLOWS: "FLAG FUROR ENDS; BENOIT LEPAGE HAS SURRENDERED AND PEACE HAS BEEN RESTORED IN GIBSONS. THE 34-YEAR OLD PAINTER CREATED A STORM OF PROTEST IN THE GATEWAY TO THE SUNSHINE COAST WHEN HE FLEW THE CANADIAN FLAG UPSIDE DOWN AND AT HALF-MAST TO PROTEST THE FREE TRADE AGREEMENT WITH THE U.S. "BUT IN REALITY, IT WAS NOTHING MORE THAN A 48-HOUR GUST OF NEWS HYPED WIND COMPLEMENTS OF THE NATIONAL MEDIA AS THEY VIEWED LEPAGE AS A VIRTUAL THREAT WHILE VERY POLITELY IMPLYING THAT HE WAS ESSENTIALLY PART OF THE LUNATIC FRINGE AND THEREFORE HAD NO OTHER ALTERNATIVE THAN TO SQUASH HIM LIKE A BUG BEFORE HE HAD AWAKEN THE "SLEEPERS "BY THE SHEER USAGE OF HIS **ANTI-FREE-TRADE** POLITICAL RHETORIC.

IT SHOULD ALSO BE MENTIONED THAT ONLY FIVE MONTHS PRIOR TO THE SIGNING OF THE FREE-TRADE AGREEMENT ON APRIL 30TH, 1987, THE CONSERVATIVE ADMINISTRATION OF THE CANADIAN FEDERAL GOVERNMENT

PROCEEDED WITH THE FINAL PHASE OF ITS PROPOSED ANNEXATION WITH THE UNITED STATES – KEEPING THE CANADIAN POPULATION IN A TOTAL STATE OF CONFUSION. THE MEECH LAKE CONSTITUTIONAL ACCORD, AS IT BECAME KNOWN AS, PROPOSED VARIOUS AMENDING FORMULA'S IN ORDER TO ACCEPT THE PROVINCE OF QUEBEC INTO TRUDEAU'S CONSTITUTIONAL ACT OF 1982. LIKE THE DENE NATION MANIFESTO OF THE NORTHWEST TERRITORIES, QUEBEC WANTED TO BE RECOGNIZED AS A "DISTINCT SOCIETY". AND JUST LIKE THE NWT, QUEBEC WANTED TO ESTABLISH SAFEGUARDS TO PROTECT ITS PEOPLE AND ITS CULTURE, BUT MOST IMPORTANTLY, ITS LANGUAGE. AS FAR AS THE FRANCOPHONE POPULATION OF QUEBEC WAS CONCERNED, THEY'VE BEEN A DISTINCT SOCIETY FOR WELL OVER 300 YEARS AND THEREFORE IT WAS PERCEIVED AS BEING NO REAL BIG DEAL IN HAVING THAT SAID STATED STIGMATISM IMPLEMENTED WITHIN THE CANADIAN CONSTITUTION ACT ITSELF. AND EXACTLY LIKE THE FREE-TRADE AGREEMENT, THE MEECH LAKE ACCORD ALSO BEGAN UNDER A COMPLETE SHROUD OF SECRECY WITH MUCH CLANDESTINE BACK ROOM MANEUVERING BEING INVOLVED.

ON JUNE 1ST, 1987, MICHAEL CHARETTE ENTERED THE CHAMBER OF THE HOUSE OF COMMONS, PICKED UP THE MACE, THE SYMBOL OF CANADIAN PARLIAMENTARY AUTHORITY, AND SAID: "MR. SPEAKER, I PROTEST THIS TREASON! I USE THAT WORD STRONGLY AND ADVISEDLY. CANADA IS UNDER ATTACK FROM WITHIN. "IT GOES WITHOUT SAYING THAT MONSIEUR CHARETTE WAS PROMPTLY ARRESTED, JAILED AND ORDERED TO UNDERGO A PSYCHIATRIC ASSESSMENT. IN A FURTHER STATE OF POLITICAL HYPOCRISY, THREE DAYS BEFORE THIS INCIDENT UNFOLDED ITSELF IN OTTAWA, THE FORMER PRIME MINISTER OF CANADA, P.E. TRUDEAU, ISSUED A PRESS RELEASE STATEMENT TO THE NATIONAL MEDIA CRITICIZING THE PROPOSED MEECH LAKE ACCORD. IN HIS PREPARED STATEMENT TO THE PRESS GALLERY, TRUDEAU STATED IN PART: "WHAT A DARK DAY FOR CANADA WAS THIS APRIL 30TH, 1987 ... THOSE CANADIANS WHO FOUGHT FOR A SINGLE CANADA, BILINGUAL AND MULTICULTURAL, CAN SAY GOOD-BYE TO THIS DREAM ... FOR THOSE CANADIANS WHO DREAMED OF THE CHARTER AS A NEW BEGINNING FOR CANADA ... THERE IS NOTHING LEFT BUT TEARS ... WHAT A MAGICIAN THIS MR. MULRONEY IS AND WHAT A SLY FOX ... HE HAS PUT CANADA ON THE FAST TRACK TO SOVEREIGNTY ASSOCIATION ... THE RT. HON. BRIAN MULRONEY, P.C., M.P., WITH THE COMPLICITY OF 10 PROVINCIAL PREMIERS, HAS ALREADY ENTERED INTO HISTORY AS THE AUTHOR OF A CONSTITUTIONAL DOCUMENT, WHICH – IF IT IS ACCEPTED BY THE PEOPLE AND THEIR LEGISLATORS – WILL RENDER THE CANADIAN STATE TOTALLY IMPOTENT."

ALTHOUGH EVERY PROVINCIAL PREMIER AND MOST POLITICIANS, ALONG WITH LITERALLY DOZENS OF MEDIA COMMENTATORS QUICKLY LEAPED AT THE OPPORTUNITY TO DISMISS TRUDEAU AS "THE VOICE OF THE PAST "WHO WAS

"SHRILL", "CONFRONTATIONAL", "EMBITTERED", A "RADICAL CENTRALIST", "IRRELEVANT "AND BASICALLY "PATHETIC", NO ONE DARED MENTION THAT HE TOO SHOULD HAVE UNDERGONE A PSYCHIATRIC ASSESSMENT FOR PUBLICALLY VOICING HIS DISCONTENT WITH WHAT BOTH THE MEECH LAKE CONSTITUTIONAL ACCORD AND THE FREE-TRADE AGREEMENT HAD IN SORE FOR CANADA AS A WHOLE.

BY JUNE 3RD, 1987 THE MEECH LAKE ACCORD WAS SIGNED BY THE PROVINCIAL PREMIERS AND THE PRIME MINISTER OF CANADA. WITHIN THE ACCORD, IT GAVE EACH PREMIER MORE POWER THAN STATE GOVERNORS IN THE U.S. OF A. – THUS SHIFTING POWER FROM FEDERAL TO PROVINCIAL GOVERNMENTS. UNDER THE MEECH LAKE ACCORD, THE SWEEPING NEW POWERS – TOTALLY UNHEARD OF IN ANY OTHER COUNTRY IN THE WORLD – WERE TO GIVE ALL CANADIAN PROVINCES THE POWER TO SELECT THE JUDGES FOR THE HIGHEST JUDICIAL POWER IN THE NATION, THE SUPREME COURT OF CANADA, AS WELL AS THE POWER TO SELECT THE MEMBERS OF THE UPPER HOUSE OF PARLIAMENT, THE SENATE. BUT THE MOST CRUCIAL ITEM OF ALL WAS THE SHIFTING OF POWER GIVING EACH AND EVERY PROVINCIAL PREMIER VETOING POWER OVER ANY FUTURE CONSTITUTIONAL AMENDMENTS. AS IF ALL THIS WASN'T BAD ENOUGH, UNDER THE ACCORD, THE YUKON AND THE NORTHWEST TERRITORIES – HAVING 40 PERCENT OF THE ENTIRE LAND MASS KNOWN AS CANADA – WERE BEING DENIED PROVINCIAL STATUS, AS THEY WERE ULTIMATELY EXCLUDED FROM THE ACCORD ITSELF. BY THE PROVISION THAT GAVE EACH AND EVERY PREMIER THE RIGHT TO BLOCK ANY NEW CONSTITUTIONAL AMENDMENTS, THE CANADIAN ARCTIC REGIONS DIDN'T HAVE A HOPE IN HELL OF SURVIVING POLITICALLY AS WELL AS ECONOMICALLY. AFTER THE YUKON WAS DENIED PROVINCIAL STATUS UNDER THE ACCORD, VOICES FROM THE NORTHLAND QUICKLY BEGAN TALKING WITH THEIR NEIGHBORING COUNTRY, THE STATE OF ALASKA. THE POSSIBILITY OF THE YUKON AND THE NWT JOINING THE NORTHERN AMERICAN STATE WAS DEFINITELY GREAT. BOTH OF THESE NORTHERN FRONTIER TERRITORIES IN THE PAST HAD BEEN DRASTICALLY MISTREATED BY THE CANADIAN FEDERAL GOVERNMENT, BY THE TORIES AS WELL AS BY THE LIBERALS. IRONICALLY, BOTH THE YUKON AND NORTHWEST TERRITORIES SOON BEGAN REDEFINING THE TERM KNOWN AS THE MEECH LAKE CONSTITUTIONAL ACCORD TO ONE OF SIMPLICITY "BEING MEECHED" BY THE CANADIAN FEDERAL GOVERNMENT. TO ANYONE WHO HAD SPENT TIME LIVING UP IN THE OUTER REACHES OF THE FROZEN FRONTIER NORTH OF THE 60TH PARALLEL, THE TERM SIMPLY MEANT THAT THE PEOPLE IN THE NORTHLAND WERE GETTING SEVERELY SCREWED OVER BY OTTAWA.

IN PROTEST OF THE CONSTITUTIONAL ACCORD, LATE 1989, THE GOVERNMENT LEADER OF THE YUKON TERRITORY (NDP's TONY PENIKETT) WAS GIVEN TITLE BY THE TERRITORIAL LEGISLATIVE ASSEMBLY IN WHITEHORSE

AS "PREMIER OF THE YUKON. "NEEDLESS TO SAY, PRIME MINISTER BRIAN MULRONEY WAS NOT AMUSED. TO FURTHER PRESS THE ISSUE OF THE YUKON ACTUALLY WANTING PROVINCIAL STATUS, PREMIER TONY PENIKETT ATTENDED THE FIRST MINISTER'S CONFERENCE (THURSDAY, NOVEMBER 9TH, 1989) IN OTTAWA. ALTHOUGH THE NEW DESIGNATED PREMIER WAS AT THE CONFERENCE PHYSICALLY, HE WASN'T ALLOWED TO FULLY EXPRESS HIS VIEWS – YUKON PREMIER PENIKETT WAS ALLOWED TO ATTEND STRICTLY AS AN OBSERVER AND NOTHING MORE. UNDER GOVERNMENTAL DEFINITION TERMS, THE GOVERNMENT LEADER, MUCH LIKE A PROVINCIAL PREMIER , IS THE LEADER OF THE POLITICAL PARTY SUPPORTED BY A MAJORITY OF THE ASSEMBLY'S ELECTED REPRESENTATIVES. AS FATE WOULD HAVE IT, IN SEPTEMBER OF 1988, THE FEDERAL GOVERNMENT AND THE NORTHWEST TERRITORIES SIGNED AN AGREEMENT-IN-PRINCIPLE OPENING THE WAY FOR NEGOTIATIONS THAT WOULD GIVE THE NWT PROVINCE-LIKE POWERS. IN ACTUAL FACT, TWO SEPARATE STATES; ONE DENE AND THE OTHER INUIT. ONCE THE FINAL AGREEMENT WAS COMPLETED, IT PROVIDED THE TERRITORY OF THE NWT GREATER CONTROL OVER ITS OIL AND GAS RESOURCES AS WELL AS CONTROL OF ITS OWN REVENUES FROM RESOURCE DEVELOPMENT. IN OTHER WORDS, THE CONSERVATIVE GOVERNMENT OF BRIAN MULRONEY ACCEPTED THE DENE NATION'S ORIGINAL CONCEPT OF BEING A DISTINCT SOCIETY AND THUS FORMED A "**DEUX NATIONS**" CONCEPT FOR THE NORTHWEST TERRITORIES INSTEAD OF TRUDEAU'S 1977 PROPOSAL OF DIVIDING IT UP INTO THREE SEPARATE ENTITIES.

AS FAR AS DAVID ORCHARD AND HIS GROUP OF **ANTI-FREE-TRADERS** WERE CONCERNED, THE COMBINED IMPACT OF THE CANADA-U.S. FREE-TRADE AGREEMENT AND THE MEECH LAKE ACCORD WAS STRIPPING CANADA OF ITS SELF-GOVERNING POWERS: **"BETWEEN THE BALKANIZATION OF THE MEECH LAKE ACCORD AND THE (FREE-TRADE AGREEMENT), CANADA WILL CEASE TO EXIST AS A SELF-GOVERNING COUNTRY.** "IT'S OBVIOUS TO SAY THAT MR. ORCHARD KNEW WHAT HE WAS TALKING ABOUT. IRONICALLY, WHEN THE FREE-TRADE-AGREEMENT WAS ORIGINALLY SIGNED, THEN-LIBERAL LEADER JOHN TURNER THREATENED TO TEAR IT UP IF HE HAD HIS WAY, WHILE NDP LEADER ED BROADBENT PLEDGED TO VETO ITS POWERS. BUT WHEN THE MEECH LAKE ACCORD WAS SIGNED, SEALED AND DELIVERED; THE OPPOSITION LEADERS ROSE FROM THEIR SEATS IN THE HOUSE OF COMMONS, CROSSED THE FLOOR AND SHOOK PRIME MINISTER MULRONEY'S HAND IN CONGRATULATIONS. AND IF THAT WASN'T BAD ENOUGH, BOTH MR. TURNER AND MR. BROADBENT WENT ON NATION WIDE TELEVISION SAYING THAT THEY SUPPORTED THE MEECH LAKE CONSTITUTIONAL ACCORD AND THAT THEIR RESPECTIVE POLITICAL PARTIES WOULD VOTE FOR IT IN THE HOUSE OF COMMONS WHETHER /OR NOT THE TORY ADMINISTRATION OF BRIAN MULRONEY MADE ANY AMENDMENTS. AS THE MONTHS QUICKLY PASSED, BOTH BROADBENT AND TURNER SOON BEGAN

TO REALIZE THAT THEIR VERY WORDS WOULD BE COMING BACK TO HAUNT THEM — VIRTUALLY BITING THEM IN THE ASS. SO, ON MARCH 4TH, 1989, ED BROADBENT ANNOUNCED THAT HE WAS RESIGNING FROM THE POLITICAL ARENA ALTOGETHER AFTER SPENDING 14 YEARS AS THE SOCIAL-DEMOCRAT'S NATIONAL LEADER — USING THE TERM SOCIAL-DEMOCRAT VERY LOOSELY NO DOUBT. AND ONLY WEEKS LATER, MAY 3RD, JOHN TURNER ALSO ANNOUNCED THAT HE TOO WAS STEPPING DOWN AS LEADER OF THE FEDERAL LIBERALS.

BY THE TIME THE 21ST CENTURY WAS STILL IN ITS INFANCY YEARS, DAVID ORCHARD LAUNCHED HIS CAMPAIGN TO SUCCEED JOE CLARK WHO HAD BEEN ANOINTED AS MULRONEY'S REPLACEMENT FOR THE CONSERVATIVE PARTY OF CANADA. FEELING A LITTLE BIT WISER TO THE WAY OF POLITICS, ORCHARD SET OUT TO RESTORE CANADA'S TRADE AND MILITARY INDEPENDENCE FROM OUR NEIGHBORS TO THE SOUTH ON A PLATFORM OF POLITICAL HONESTY AND TRUST. THE MAIN COMPONENT NATURALLY BEING CANADIAN SOVEREIGNTY AS HE FIRMLY BELIEVED THAT IT WAS BEING THREATENED BY U.S. CORPORATIONS BUYING UP CANADIAN COMPANIES IN AN ATTEMPT TOWARDS ELIMINATING THE CANADA-U.S. BORDER TO FURTHER ENHANCE AMERICAN OPPORTUNITIES INCORPORATED WITHIN THE FREE-TRADE AGREEMENT. ONLY FIVE YEARS PREVIOUS TO THE LAUNCHING OF HIS 21ST CENTURY CAMPAIGN, ORCHARD ATTEMPTED TO SEEK THE TORY LEADERSHIP IN 1998 AND PARTICIPATED IN THE FEDERAL ELECTION OF THE YEAR 2000 TRYING TO GAIN A SEAT IN THE HOUSE OF COMMONS FOR HIS RIDING OF PRINCE ALBERT, SASKATCHEWAN. BOTH OF WHICH PROVED UNSUCCESSFUL EVENTS IN HIS LIFE. CANADIANS OBVIOUSLY WEREN'T QUITE READY TO ACCEPT ORCHARD'S STERN WARNING OF WHAT THE POLITICAL ARENA HAD IN STORE FOR ITS UNEDUCATED JOE SIX PACK POPULATION.

PUTTING ALL OF THIS ASIDE FOR THE TIME BEING, THE MOST IMPORTANT POLITICAL RESIGNATION FOR THE YEAR 1989 ITSELF CAME FROM BRIAN PECKFORD, THE PREMIER OF NEWFOUNDLAND. ON JANUARY 21ST OF THAT YEAR, PECKFORD ANNOUNCED THAT HE WAS RESIGNING AS NFLD'S PREMIER, EFFECTIVELY BY MONTH'S END. AFTER TEN YEARS OF BEING THE PROVINCE'S CONSERVATIVE LEADER, (MARCH 27TH, 1979), HE ESSENTIALLY CALLED IT QUITS. INTERESTING AS OLD HELL WERE THE WORDS HE USED IN DESCRIBING THE POLITICIAN OF THE FUTURE; THE POLITICIAN OF THE FUTURE ACCORDING TO MR. PECKFORD HAD TO BE A RUTHLESS SON-OF-A-BITCH. OBVIOUSLY, ALL THREE OF THESE POLITICIANS (TURNER, BROADBENT AND PECKFORD) KNEW THAT THE FRATERNAL JIG WAS UP AND OPTED TO ABORT THE GRANDMASTER SCHEME OF DECEPTION FOR THEIR OWN PERSONAL SALVATION.

WITH THE DAWNING OF A NEW DECADE, SPRING OF 1990, THE MEECH LAKE CONSTITUTIONAL ACCORD BEGAN TO SPLIT THE COUNTRY RIGHT DOWN THE CENTER — EXACTLY AS TO WHAT THE MASONIC GOVERNING BODIES WANTED

– English Canada against French Canada. It was the exact same tactic that Prime Minister P.E. Trudeau used in our country's frozen frontier during the 1970's to help split its northern population, whites against all of the Arctic's native population. Like Trudeau, Brian Mulroney graduated from the same school of politics, the divide and conquer school of democracy. With the weakening of Canada as a nation by the Meech Lake Accord, the abject failure of the opposition parties to oppose Meech Lake, plus the weakness of their fight against Free-Trade, the defense of Canada was left in the hands of those organizations and/or individuals with the courage and fortitude to oppose the full force of both levels of Government – Provincially and Federally. The Meech Lake Accord in fact was part of the weakening of Canada that was necessary to get our country ready for economic union with the United States. By the early 1990's, it had led to countless squabbles all across the country – the West verbally attacking Quebec and Ontario, the Maritimes condemning Central Canada, Quebec and Ontario grappling at each others throats, and above all else, northerners in the frozen frontier of the Arctic regions disassociating themselves from the rest of Canada altogether.

Much like the Free-Trade Agreement, the Constitutional Accord was suppose to pass without incident. But the prospects of Americanizing Canadians had a reverse affect as various newly elected Premiers (Liberal Clyde Wells, NFLD; Liberal Frank McKenna, N.B.; and Progressive Conservative Gary Filmon, Manitoba), soon began to realize that if the Accord was to be passed into law, the end of Canada as a nation wasn't too far off the beaten path. For his part in attempting to save Canada from further annexation with the United States, in mid-May 1990, Newfoundland's Premier Clyde Wells had received two death threats promoted by his opposition to the Meech Lake Accord. Obviously, this is what Peckford meant by stating that the politician of the future had to be "ruthless" in his endeavors.

Little did the Canadian population realize that Prime Minister Mulroney's plan was to first get the Province of Quebec back into the Masonic Brotherhood as a fully recognized entity by enabling it to receive its Constitutional Right to co-exist as a "distinct society" under Canadian law. And once that was to be accomplished, Canada would have no other alternative but to turn to the Americans for guidance as Quebec was seriously considering the passing of legislation that would be closing its borders to all

Canadian citizens. Like the Northwest Territories, Quebec wanted to adopt the same policies of racial segregation. Quebec's various pieces of fascist legislation that were passed by the Provincial Legislature – Bills 101 and 178 – on language laws prohibiting the speaking of English within its jurisdiction are prime examples of the Francophone attitude of a "**distinct society**". And again just like the Northwest Territories, white English-speaking Canadians packed up their belongings and fled the Province for safety.

According to both Robert Bourassa (Quebec's now deceased French dictator) and Jean Chretien (the once Federally anointed Liberal leader of Canada), the "**distinct society**" clause contained within the Meech Lake Constitutional Accord did not violate the Canadian Charter of Rights and Freedoms under Trudeau's Canadian Constitution Act of 1982. But most Canadians saw it quite differently, and as per usual, citizens of Canada had no say in the matter whatsoever. Instead, Monsieur Chretien told the outraged population of Canada to calm down and that the country was not in a crisis mode. According to him, under a distinct society, no one's human rights were going to be violated and that the Charter of Rights was not going to be affected by the Accord. Like his former comrade and puppet master, Jean Chretien dazzled the public with his political bullshit as he showed more and more of his fraternity colors of the Institution of Prevost's Francophonism.

As the discussions on the Accord heated up with each passing day, Chretien took it one step further by publically stating that what Canada really lacked was real leadership and that the country actually needed someone in the Prime Minister's Office that could relate to the nation's population, "someone who will say the same thing to Canadians in two languages. "Less than a week after Newfoundland's Premier Wells received his death threats, newspaper headlines across the country stated that the Prime Minister of Canada (Brian Mulroney) actually did seek Chretien's assistance in the matter. And a week after that, further headlines stated that Jean Chretien also received death threats and that security was pumped up because of the threats as a Liberal leadership race was now looming. But in total honest, the supposed death threats on Monsieur Chretien actually sounded much like the news media hyped wind storm that Benoit LePage went through in Gibsons during the summer of 1989. According to LePage, he got the distinct impression that the national media outlets were trying to create the illusion that Jean Chretien was going to be the savior

OF OUR COUNTRY THUSLY PUTTING AN ABRUPT END TO ALL THE TURMOIL OF THE NATION AND THEREFORE HE DESERVED TO CONTINUE BEING THE FEDERAL LIBERAL LEADER. THE MEDIA THEN BEGAN PUBLICIZING THE BEEFED UP SECURITY AT THE LIBERAL LEADERSHIP FORUM IN MONTREAL.

AT THE SAME TIME ALL OF THIS POLITICAL MEANDERING WAS GOING ON, ONTARIO'S LIBERAL PREMIER DAVID PETERSON WAS EMBARRASSED AS OLD HELL AS A LEAKED DOCUMENT MADE ITS WAY TO OTHER MEDIA SOURCES. THE DOCUMENT DETAILED WAYS IN WHICH THE CREDIBILITY OF THE THREE DISSIDENT PREMIERS (MANITOBA, N.B. AND NFLD) COULD BE EXECUTED. IN THE LEAKED DOCUMENT, GARY FILMON WAS TO BE PORTRAYED AS "POLITICALLY ERRATIC", "INCONSISTENT "AND "UNPREDICTABLE." THE DOCUMENT RECOMMENDED THAT CLYDE WELLS' CONCERNS ABOUT THE ACCORD BE BEST DESCRIBED AS "OUT OF PROPORTION "AND BASICALLY RISING FROM HIS "OVERWEENING LACK OF TRUST. "NEW BRUNSWICK'S FRANK MCKENNA WAS TO BE PORTRAYED AS "PART OF THE PROBLEM "IF HE DID NOT MOVE SWIFT ENOUGH TO HAVE THE CONSTITUTIONAL ACCORD RATIFIED BY HIS PROVINCE'S LEGISLATURE. THE LEAKED DOCUMENT FURTHER STATED THAT IT WOULD BE RATHER EASY TO MANIPULATE THE MEDIA BECAUSE "THE NATIONAL MEDIA, ESPECIALLY THE C.B.C., WILL HAVE A BIAS TOWARDS MAKING A DEAL TO SAVE THE COUNTRY. "THE LEAKED DOCUMENT SOUNDED ALL TO FAMILIAR AS TO THE HYPOCRISY AND MANIPULATION OF THE TRUDEAU REGIME IN THE ARCTIC – TRUDEAU'S POLICY PAPER OF THE MID-1970'S TO DIVIDE THE NORTHWEST TERRITORIES INTO THREE SEPARATE REGIONS. NEEDLESS TO SAY, PREMIER PETERSON QUICKLY DENIED EVER SEEING THE DOCUMENT IN QUESTION, AND ALMOST IMMEDIATELY BLAMED BUREAUCRATS WITHIN THE ONTARIO GOVERNMENT'S OWN POLITICAL FRAMEWORK FOR THE PROPOSAL'S ACTUAL EXISTENCE. THE IMPORTANCE OF THE DOCUMENT ITSELF WAS THUSLY DOWN PLAYED BY ALL OF THOSE INVOLVED!!!

BUT 24-HOURS LATER, MAY 31ST, 1990, DENIS PRONOVOST (THE ASSISTANT DEPUTY SPEAKER OF THE HOUSE OF COMMONS), WAS FORCED TO RESIGN HIS PORTFOLIO FOR REMARKS MADE DURING AN OPEN-LINE RADIO TALK SHOW THE DAY THAT THE ONTARIO DOCUMENT LEAKED OUT. ON MAY 30TH, IN TROIS-RIVIERES, QUEBEC, CONSERVATIVE MP PRONOVOST, (ST. MAURICE, QUEBEC RIDING) CALLED NEWFOUNDLAND'S PREMIER CLYDE WELLS A "MENTAL CASE "FOR DRAGGING HIS FEET IN HAVING THE ACCORD RATIFIED IN THAT PROVINCE'S LEGISLATURE. THE TORY DEPUTY SPEAKER EVEN WENT SO FAR AS TO SAY THAT ALL OF THE PROVINCE OF NEWFOUNDLAND'S POPULATION WERE BASICALLY "ILLITERATE "AND THEREFORE SYMBOLIZED THE PEOPLE LIVING IN A "THIRD WORLD COUNTRY. "IN A TAPED CONVERSATION (CHLN), THE PROGRESSIVE CONSERVATIVE MP WENT ON RECORD FURTHER STATING THAT NEWFOUNDLAND AS A PROVINCE WAS NO GIFT TO CANADA,

AND"... THIS CRAZY MENTAL CASE, CLYDE WELLS. HE'S NOT WORTH MUCH. I'VE MET HIM. HE'S A DANGEROUS MAN. "IT WAS OBVIOUS TO EVEN A BLIND PERSON THAT CHRETIEN'S FEDERAL LIBERALS WERE SLEEPING WITH MULRONEY'S BACK ROOM BOYS AND DIDN'T REALLY GIVE A DAMN ONE WAY /OR THE OTHER ABOUT CANADA ACTUALLY REMAINING AS AN INDEPENDENT NATION — IT WAS ALL SMOKE AND MIRRORS. DENIS PRONOVOST HUMBLY APOLOGIZED TO WELLS AND THE PEOPLE OF NEWFOUNDLAND — WELLS ACCEPTED THE APOLOGY AND POLITICALLY, ALL WAS FORGOTTEN.

WHILE ALL OF THIS POLITICAL BULLSHIT WAS GOING ON, THE NEW DEMOCRATIC PARTY OF CANADA REMAINED SOMEWHAT SILENT ON THE MEECH LAKE CONSTITUTIONAL ACCORD. ONE MIGHT SAY THAT THEY HAD A SMALL GLIMMER OF SYMPATHY FOR THE CONSERVATIVES AS THE EMBARRASSMENT BECAME TOO MUCH FOR THEM TO BARE AS WELL. THE FEDERAL NEW DEMOCRATS' NEW LEADER AUDREY MCLAUGHLIN AND OTHER SOCIAL-DEMOCRATS INSTEAD LED AN ALL OUT ATTACK ON THE FEDERAL GOVERNMENT'S **GOODS AND SERVICES TAX**, AND EVERY ONCE IN A WHILE, WOULD MENTION MEECH LAKE IN PASSING. NOW, TALK ABOUT A POLITICAL PARTY WITH THEIR HEADS UP THE FRATERNAL BUTT!!!

THERE CANADA LAY, ON THE VERGE OF POLITICAL RUINATION AND THE SOCIAL-DEMOCRATS (A SO-CALLED POLITICAL PARTY OF THE COMMON WORKER), IGNORING THE MAIN ISSUE OF THE DAY; COMPLETE AND UTTER ANNEXATION BY THE AMERICAN MASONIC POLITICAL POWERS SOUTH OF THE 49TH PARALLEL. WITHIN THE MASONIC ORDER'S OWN FRATERNITY LITERATURE, IT OPENLY ADMITS TO THE FACT OF HAVING FULL FRATERNAL CONTROL OVER SOME OF OUR COUNTRY'S PRIME MINISTERS AS A LARGE PORTION OF THEM HAVE BEEN ACTIVE MEMBERS SINCE CONFEDERATION AND HAD PROVEN THEMSELVES WORTHY OF THE NOBLE AND ANCIENT CRAFT OF FREEMASONRY;

SIR JOHN ALEXANDER MACDONALD
RAISED 1844
PRIME MINISTER ....1867 - 1873
SECOND TERM.................1878 - 1891

SIR JOHN JOSEPH CALDWELL ABBOTT
RAISED 1847
PRIME MINISTER .... 1891 - 1892

SIR MACKENZIE BOWELL
RAISED 1864
PRIME MINISTER .... 1894 - 1896

SIR ROBERT LAIRD BORDEN

RAISED 1881
PRIME MINISTER .... 1911 - 1920

VISCOUNT RICHARD BEDFORD BENNETT
RAISED 1896
PRIME MINISTER .... 1930 - 1935

JOHN GEORGE DIEFENBAKER
RAISED 1922
PRIME MINISTER .... 1957 - 1963

WHILE CANADIAN FREEMASONRY PROUDLY BOASTED OF ALL SIX OF THESE PRIME MINISTERS BEING FINE OUTSTANDING MEMBERS OF THE ANCIENT CRAFT, THE PAPER TRAIL ON OTHER MASONIC PRIME MINISTERS DURING THE 1980'S AND 1990'S IS LESS FORGIVING AS OUR COUNTRY'S VERY OWN CITIZENRY BECAME TOTALLY DISILLUSIONED ALTOGETHER AT THE SO-CALLED CONCEPT KNOWN AS DEMOCRACY BY THE YEAR 2000. DURING THE FEDERAL ELECTION OF NOVEMBER 27TH, 2000 ONLY AN ESTIMATED 60.5 PERCENT OF CANADA'S ELIGIBLE VOTERS TURNED OUT AT THE POLLS EXERCISING THEIR DEMOCRATIC RIGHT OF CASTING THEIR BALLOTS. IN FACT, VOTER TURNOUT WAS SO LOW THAT BOTH OTTAWA BUREAUCRATS AND POLITICIANS ALIKE CONTEMPLATED THE IMMEDIATE INTRODUCTION OF LEGISLATION FORCING PEOPLE TO VOTE IN ORDER TO SUPPOSEDLY SAVE DEMOCRACY. THAT'S HOW CLANDESTINE CANADIAN POLITICS HAS ACTUALLY BECOME IN THE 21ST CENTURY, IS IT ANY WONDER AS TO WHY THE GENERAL POPULATION OF CANADA HAS BECOME TOTALLY DISGUSTED WITH THE POLITICAL AFFAIRS OF OUR NATION AND BASICALLY WANTED NO PART OF IT TO BEGIN WITH? CANADA HAD BEEN ESSENTIALLY BACKED INTO A CORNER BY ITS OWN POLITICAL STUPIDITY THANKS TO ANCIENT CRAFT OF FREEMASONRY AND ITS FRATERNAL **"BROTHERHOOD OF MAN – UNDER THE FATHERHOOD OF GOD."**

AS PART OF THIS GREAT ILLUSION KNOWN AS THE DEMOCRATIC PROCESS, MANDATORY VOTING IN FEDERAL ELECTIONS SOON BECAME THE TOPIC OF THE DAY AS CANADIAN POLITICIANS SERIOUSLY CONTEMPLATED DOING THE UNTHINKABLE BY FORCING AN INCREASED VOTER TURNOUT IN ORDER TO SUPPOSEDLY PRESERVE DEMOCRACY AND TO REAFFIRM THE FRATERNITY CAUSE OF DIVINE INTERVENTION BY **GOD** – AGAIN NOTHING BUT SMOKE AND MIRRORS ALL THE WAY AROUND!!!

COINCIDENTLY, THE MEECH LAKE CONSTITUTIONAL ACCORD WAS EVENTUALLY LAID TO REST AS ONE SINGLE INDIAN (ELIJAH HARPER) STOOD UP IN DEFIANCE TO THE POWERS THAT BE, REFUSING TO ALLOW HIS ELECTED COLLEAGUES TO RATIFY THE DOCUMENT IN THE PROVINCE OF MANITOBA'S LEGISLATURE. AS MANY TIMES BEFORE, CANADA WAS ONCE AGAIN SAVED BY

AN ABORIGINAL AS NO OTHER ELECTED OFFICIAL IN THE COUNTRY'S POLITICAL ARENA HAD THE GONADS TO DO IT AS FREEMASONRY'S LONG REACHING POWERFUL ARMS EXTENDED INTERNATIONALLY. THE ORGANISM ITSELF HAVING MILLIONS UPON MILLIONS OF MEMBERS ON ITS SECRET FRATERNITY ROSTER, MOST OF WHOM CONTROLLED THE GOVERNMENTAL INSTITUTIONS OF THE WORLD. SOME CALLING FREEMASONRY THE ANTI-CHRIST, WHILE OTHERS CALL IT AND ITS ORIGINS BACK TO THE DAYS OF THE PHARAOHS; A RELIGION. IT IS BELIEVED BY MANY, THAT THE ILLUMINATI (THE UPPER ECHELONS OF THE MASONIC ORDER) CONTROLS ALL FORMS OF HUMAN EXISTENCE; FROM BANKING TO PUBLISHING BOOKS AND PRINTING NEWSPAPERS AND MAGAZINES. FURTHER TO THIS, THE BLUE BLOOD MASTER MASONS WITHIN THE ILLUMINATI ARE ALSO BELIEVED TO BE THE CONTROLLING FACTORS BEHIND THE POLITICAL SCENES OF BOTH CANADA AND THE UNITED STATES. IT GOES WITHOUT SAYING THAT LIKE THE U.S. OF A., CANADIAN POLITICS IS DEFINITELY SHAPED ACCORDING TO THE ANCIENT CRAFT AND ITS MASONIC LEADERS.

TO FURTHER ADD CONFUSION TO THE ISSUE, CANADA'S FORMER PRIME MINISTER P.E. TRUDEAU ONCE URGED THE REWRITING OF THE MEECH LAKE CONSTITUTIONAL ACCORD MONTHS PRIOR TO ELIJAH HARPER'S REFUSAL TO ALLOW THE MANITOBA LEGISLATURE TO RATIFY IT. TRUDEAU ACCUSED THE FEDERAL POLITICIANS OF STONEWALLING, CITING THAT THEY (OTTAWA POLITICIANS SITTING IN THE HOUSE OF COMMONS) WERE AFRAID OF THE PROVINCE OF QUEBEC. THIS STATEMENT WAS MADE DURING A RECEPTION IN OCTOBER OF 1989 – PIERRE TRUDEAU WAS LAUNCHING A PUBLICITY CAMPAIGN FOR HIS NEW BOOK, TITLED OF ALL THINGS; **"TOWARD THE JUST SOCIETY: THE TRUDEAU YEARS."**

ACCORDING TO CO-EDITOR AND CONTRIBUTING WRITER TOM AXWORTHY, THE LIBERALS WANTED TO SET THE RECORD STRAIGHT. THAT IS TO SAY, ACCORDING TO WHAT THE LIBERALS SAW AS BEING THE TRUTH NO DOUBT. IN DOING SO, THEY BEGAN ATTACKING THE MULRONEY GOVERNMENT ON A VARIATION OF ISSUES THAT TRUDEAU HIMSELF VIEWED AS THE ULTIMATE TRUTH. IN HIS WRITINGS, TRUDEAU ACCUSED MULRONEY OF TRADING CANADA'S SOUL FOR AN ELECTORAL VICTORY AND FURTHER ACCUSED HIM OF DISMANTLING OUR COUNTRY FOR THE BENEFIT OF THE PROVINCES WITH HIS POLICY OF NATIONAL RECONCILIATION AND MEECH LAKE.

ACCORDING TO TRUDEAU: "THE MORE THEY HAVE LEARNED ABOUT WHAT MEECH LAKE REALLY MEANS, THE MORE INDIGNANT THESE PEOPLE HAVE BECOME THAT THEIR GOVERNMENTS HAVE SIGNED AN ACCORD THAT COULD BREAK UP THEIR COUNTRY, WEAKEN THE CHARTER OF 1982 AND UNDERMINE ESTABLISHED SHARED-COST PROGRAMS. "IT WAS OBVIOUS TO SAY, THAT TRUDEAU AND HIS FAITHFUL FOLLOWERS HAD SOMETHING ELSE UP THEIR

Maltese sleeves for the Canadian citizenry that didn't quite fit into the fraternal scheme of new things to come.

In one area of his writings, P.E. Trudeau talked of when Mr. Mulroney and Quebec's Premier Robert Bourassa conceived the Constitutional Accord: "It all happened in secret one dark night, beside a pretty little Quebec lake — Meech Lake. Canada was never before divided as it has been since that night."

A person must admit, it sure was an interesting statement of hypocrisy compared as to what Trudeau's own political track record was in both the Yukon and Northwest Territories when he was Prime Minister of Canada during the 1970's decade, (July 1977 policy paper on the Arctic). In attacking Free-Trade, Trudeau called the Canada-U.S. agreement "a monstrous swindle "that gave up "a large slice "of Canadian sovereignty. Trudeau's book was released by the end of March 1990 and by the first week of June of that same year, it hit The Globe and Mail's National Bestseller List. By this time period, the majority of Canada's population became totally confused as to who, politically, they should actually believe; the then-acting Prime Minister of the country, Brian Mulroney /or the Prime Minister of days-gone-by. Answer: neither really because only part of the actual fraternal truth was being told to the country's citizenry as everything else operated strictly under a shroud of total secrecy all in the name of a benevolent Brotherhood that had a very well documented hidden agenda. All a person has to really do is to patiently spend countless years putting all of the pieces of the puzzle together, one minuscule piece at a time!!!

For example; other than the friendship that Freemasonry Brother Ronald Reagan had with various Masonic P-2 members, Reagan also had a close personal/religious relationship with the Roman Catholic Church in Italy during his tenure years in the Oval Office as the 40TH President of the United States. Apparently the pontiff, Pope John Paul II collaborated with the U.S. Federal Government foreign policy makers to help wipe-out Communism on a global scale. The head of fraternity Brother Reagan's CIA, (Director William Casey), reportedly made numerous secret trips to the Vatican throughout the early 1980's as they, the Pope and Casey fine tuned a gentlemen's agreement that was to rid the world of the evil Communist menace once and for all. The Pope's main concern and first priority being of course the stranglehold that of which the Soviet Union had on his beloved homeland, Poland. The CIA, therefore financially supported Lech Walesa's Solidarity Trade

Union Movement in Poland using it as a catalyst for a fully fledged American made just cause. From there, the Communist regime fell like dominoes one-by-one.

Interestingly, while Communism was slowly being dismantled by the united allied American Freemasonry and Roman Catholic coalition forces, a couple of curious religious Italian onlookers began the tedious task of collecting documentation that was to verify the fact that Satan's Freemasonry forces had entered the Roman Catholic Church by way of the front door. Allegations of widespread corruption and abuse of religious/political powers soon turned into a full blown rhetoric battle of the many ism's; careerism, sexism and a host of others normally associated with the Ancient Craft of the Masonic Order. And when the book "Gone With The Wind in the Vatican "was finally published in the late 1990's, the Vatican tried its damnest to have the publication halted. Roman Catholic Church officials even went so far as to hold a McCarthy type hearing on the matter insisting that the book's authors violated the Vatican's judicial rights under Canon Law to be forewarned of the allegations being made against the Church itself. Although the book was first published in Italy during the month of February 1999 and only sold 100,000 copies in just four /or five short months, once it became public knowledge that the Sacred Roman Rota, the Holy See's highest appeals court had ordered the authors to attend its scheduled hearing in July 1999, the book was in more demand than ever before as it quickly obtained worldwide recognition!!!

Chapter 9 - THE ILLUMINATI: IN GOD WE TRUST

With the dawning of the 1990's, came a decade of unparalleled uncertainty and total confusion on a global scale. Many countries throughout the world became engulfed with widespread poverty and unemployment, with both high inflation rates and national debt loads. Most world economic specialists attributed the global crisis to a me-first attitude of the world's population and their outright desire to obtain instant gratification regardless of the consequences that it may have had on others, a.k.a. material greed in order to be recognized as a success in life. In accordance to the religious institutions, (the moral majority), the moral fibre of society had hit rock bottom and we, as a society in general, were virtually hell bound. But in reality, the IMF (International Monetary Fund) loan policies were the main contributing factors for many of the world's woes and were thusly cited as being the spring board since during mid-1989 when the Masonic Illuminati began taking drastic measures in curtailing its new loan agreements for Third World countries. The immediate world reaction to the IMF/Illuminati changes was violence in the streets in such countries as Jordan and Argentina. Non-violent protests of anger quickly turned into riots, (food riots as it were) that of which were brought on by the ever increasing prices when the two countries, under IMF urging, cut subsidies that had long kept down the price of bread, gasoline and electricity. At the time, it had been reported that the Third World debtors owed the Masonic world banking system $ 1.3 trillion in U.S. currency – one trillion dollars has twelve zeros attached to it. Each year, more and more money was leaving the Third World countries in order to pay down their debt. For example; countries in Africa, Asia and South America reportedly had a short fall of

$ 30 BILLION DURING THEIR FISCAL YEAR 1989/1990 BECAUSE OF THE IMF CURTAILMENT – MORE MONEY GOING OUT THAN WHAT WAS ACTUALLY COMING IN.

DURING THE SUMMER OF 1990, COUNTRIES SUCH AS THE DOMINICAN REPUBLIC AND PERU WERE FORCED TO INTRODUCE A NEW AUSTERITY PACKAGE IN ACCORDANCE TO THE IMF GUIDELINES. FOOD PRICES SOON SKYROCKETED OUT OF CONTROL AS BREAD INCREASED BY 300 PERCENT WHILE MILK PRICES TRIPLED AND NEWSPAPERS QUADRUPLED. THE FREEMASONRY CONTROLLED PERUVIAN GOVERNMENT THUSLY DEVALUED ITS COUNTRY'S PESO AND IMMEDIATELY RAISED THE MINIMUM SALARY FOR GOVERNMENT EMPLOYEES BY 30 PERCENT IN ORDER TO OFFSET THE TROUBLES THAT THEY REALIZED WERE COMING JUST AROUND THE FRATERNAL CORNER. INTERESTINGLY, MOST ECONOMISTS PRAISED THE GOVERNMENT PLAN AS A WAY AND MEANS OF RESCUING THE COUNTRY FROM SHEER BANKRUPTCY.

BUT NOT ALL OF THE WORLD'S GOVERNMENT LEADERS BEND OVER BACKWARDS TO SATISFY THE IMF AND THEIR CONCEPT OF WORLD DOMINATION VIA ECONOMIC SANCTIONS. AT THE TIME, SPECULATION EXISTED THAT PAKISTAN'S LATER TO BE OUSTED PRIME MINISTER BENAZIR BHUTTO WAS ABOUT TO COMPLY WITH THE IMF ORDER OF INTRODUCING A NEW ECONOMIC POLICY FOR THE PAKISTANI PEOPLE WHEN HER GOVERNMENT WAS DISSOLVED ON AUGUST 6TH, 1990. IN LIEU OF THAT SAID GOVERNMENT'S POSSIBLE ACTIONS, BHUTTO AND HER ADMINISTRATION WAS LITERALLY THROWN OUT OF OFFICE AND A STATE OF EMERGENCY WAS THUSLY DECLARED. THE COUNTRY'S NEWLY SELECTED CARETAKER PRIME MINISTER GHULAM MUSTAFA, ALONG WITH HIS SUPERIORS, CITED THE OUSTING BY ACCUSING BHUTTO AND HER GOVERNMENTAL OFFICIALS OF CORRUPTION AND NEPOTISM. FURTHER ALLEGATIONS EXISTED THAT BHUTTO'S POLITICAL PARTY, PAKISTAN PEOPLE'S PARTY WAS TOTALLY PREPARED TO SUPPORT THE AMERICAN FEDERAL GOVERNMENT AND THEIR CONCEPT OF "MANIFEST DESTINY "BY MAKING PAKISTAN A COLONY OF THE UNITED STATES.

BENAZIR BHUTTO WAS PAKISTAN'S FIRST WOMAN PRIME MINISTER TO LEAD A SO-CALLED MUSLIM NATION. SHE BECAME ITS LEADER IN NOVEMBER OF 1988 AND IN THOSE TWENTY MONTHS OF BEING IN POWER, HER GOVERNMENT BECAME PLAGUED WITH CHARGES OF MISMANAGEMENT AND ABUSE OF GOVERNMENTAL POWERS. BHUTTO HERSELF FACED CRIMINAL CHARGES AND APPEARED BEFORE THE JUDICIARY SYSTEM. PAKISTAN'S MUSLIM LEAGUE, A RELIGIOUS FACTION CONSISTING OF A NINE-POLITICAL PARTY SYSTEM FORMED AN ALLIANCE OF THE ISLAMIC DEMOCRATIC PARTY THUSLY USED ITS RELIGIOUS AND ANTI-U.S. FREEMASONRY CONNECTIONS TO FORCE BHUTTO OUT OF THE POLITICAL ARENA. ON WEDNESDAY, OCTOBER 24TH, 1990 BHUTTO AND HER POLITICAL PARTY WERE DEFEATED IN THE PAKISTAN ELECTORAL FINALS. ALTHOUGH

ALLEGATIONS EMERGED THAT A RIGGED ELECTION HAD TAKEN PLACE, THE ISLAMIC ALLIANCE WAS DECLARED THE VICTOR. THE FATE OF BENAZIR BHUTTO AND HER FOLLOWERS WERE THEREFORE PLACED IN THE HANDS OF THE ENEMY, MUSTAFA AND HIS ANTI-AMERICAN FAITHFUL FOLLOWERS.

ONCE THE NEWLY ANOINTED ISLAMIC GOVERNMENT OF PAKISTAN WAS IN PLACE, THEY THREATENED TO STOP PAYING INTEREST ON THEIR U.S. LOANS IF THE FREEMASONRY GOVERNMENT OF THE UNITED STATES REFUSED TO RESTORE ITS ECONOMIC AND AID PACKAGE WORTH AN ESTIMATED $ 564 MILLION TO THE PEOPLE OF PAKISTAN. AMERICAN FRATERNITY BROTHER GEORGE BUSH SENIOR HAD INTRODUCED SANCTIONS IN AN ATTEMPT TO HAVE THE PUPPET REGIME OF BENAZIR BHUTTO REINSTATED AS THE COUNTRY'S PRIME MINISTER. THE ECONOMIC AND AID PACKAGE SANCTIONS WERE INTRODUCED ON OCTOBER 1ST AS A WAY AND MEANS OF FORCING THE PEOPLE OF PAKISTAN TO VOTE THE WAY IN WHICH THE UNITED STATES HAD PERCEIVED AS BEING THE BEST POSSIBLE OUT COME FOR DEMOCRACY IN THE OCTOBER 24TH NATIONAL ELECTION. DUE TO THE U.S. GOVERNMENT BLACKMAIL TACTIC ALL IN THE NAME OF THE ILLUSIONARY DEMOCRATIC PROCESS, THE PAKISTANI PEOPLE HAD ONLY TWO CHOICES OF SURVIVAL; EITHER STAVE TO DEATH /OR STOP PAYING INTEREST ON THEIR LOANS ALTOGETHER. SINCE THEY WEREN'T WILLING TO COMPLY WITH THE AMERICAN FREEMASONRY ORDER FOR THE 1990'S, THE LATTER WAS CHOSEN.

EVIDENCE ALSO EXIST THAT EVEN IRAQI LEADER SADDAM HUSSEIN TOLD THE IMF WHERE TO STICK ITS NEW ECONOMIC LOAN POLICES FOR THE 1990'S DECADE. UNLIKE ALL THE OTHERS, THE IRAQI PRESIDENT WAS WILLING TO TAKE IT ONE STEP FURTHER IF NEED BE, AND THAT HE DID!!!

ONLY HOURS BEFORE HE INVADED THE MASONIC GOVERNMENT CONTROLLED OIL RICH NATION OF KUWAIT, SADDAM HUSSEIN REPORTEDLY DEMANDED THE IMMEDIATE WRITE-OFF OF AN ESTIMATED $ 14 TO $ 15 BILLION (U.S.) IN LOANS THAT THE IMF CONTROLLED GOVERNMENTS HAD PROVIDED HIS POLITICAL REGIME WITH DURING ITS EIGHT YEAR WAR WITH IRAN. THE IRAQI LEADER APPARENTLY THREATENED TO INVADE KUWAIT IF THE LOANS WERE NOT WRITTEN OFF. HUSSEIN WAS INSTANTLY CONDEMNED FOR HIS ACTIONS OF INVADING THE OIL FIELDS OF KUWAIT AS THE WORLD MEDIA OUTLETS COMPARED HIM TO ADOLF HITLER AND THE NAZI REIGN OF TERROR. WITHIN ONLY HOURS OF HUSSEIN'S INVASION, NEWSPAPERS IN THE WESTERN FREE-WORLD DENOUNCED IRAQ'S POLITICAL LEADER DESCRIBING HIM AS THE HATED AND MUCH FEARED BUTCHER OF BAGHDAD, AND FURTHER INSISTED THAT HE WAS A WORSHIPER OF HITLERISM.

ODDLY ENOUGH, AN AMERICAN NEWSPAPER (THE LOS ANGELES TIMES) GAVE FURTHER CHASE ON THE SUBJECT BY STATING THAT SADDAM HUSSEIN WAS BY NO MEANS PART OF THE LUNATIC FRINGE AND EVENT WENT SO FAR AS

TO GIVE A COUPLE OF CLUES PERTAINING TO HIS INVOLVEMENT WITH ISLAMIC FREEMASONRY BY FIRST CALLING THE IRAQI PRESIDENT A COLD-HEARTED RUTHLESS POLITICIAN HELL BENT ON SHEDDING THE BLOOD OF INNOCENT HUMAN BEINGS, THEN, STATING THAT HE ACTUALLY KNEW WHAT HE WAS DOING. THE NEWSPAPER ARTICLE WENT ON TO SAY THAT HUSSEIN WANTED TO LEAD A SUPERPOWER AND THAT SUCH A FEAT WAS BY NO MEANS A FOOLISH MANEUVER ON HIS PART AS HE HAD BY THAT TIME PERIOD MANAGED TO GAIN CONTROL OF A NOTEWORTHY FACTION OF THE WORLD'S OIL BEFORE ENTERING KUWAIT ANYWAYS. BUT THE REAL CLINCHER IN THE CALIFORNIA BASED NEWSPAPER WAS WENT IT STATED THAT SADDAM HUSSEIN WAS BASICALLY A BY-PRODUCT OF A BRUTAL DARWINIAN PROCESS THAT HAD ALLOWED HIM TO SURVIVE BY BEING MUCH SMARTER, TOUGHER, AND MORE RUTHLESS THAN HIS RIVALS.

TO ANYONE HAVING KNOWLEDGE OF FREEMASONRY, THE SINGLE WORD "DARWINISM "/OR ANYTHING FREELY ASSOCIATED WITH IT, SENDS UP A RED FLAG THAT REQUIRES SOME LOOKING INTO AS DARWINISM ITSELF IS CONSIDERED BY MOST AS BEING AN OCCULT SCIENCE NORMALLY ATTRIBUTED TO THE FUNDAMENTAL TEACHINGS OF THE MASONIC ORDER. WHAT OTHER REASON WOULD THERE HAVE BEEN FOR THE L.A. TIMES TO MAKE SUCH A RATHER BRAZEN STATEMENT CONCERNING SADDAM HUSSEIN IN THE FIRST PLACE???

THE NAME OCCULT, IS GIVEN TO THE SCIENCE OF ALCHEMY, MAGIC, AND ASTROLOGY, WHICH EXISTED IN THE MIDDLE AGES. TO THAT END, MANY OF THE SPECULATIONS OF THESE SCIENCES DURING THE EIGHTEENTH CENTURY WERE INCORPORATED WITHIN THE CONSTRUCTION OF FREEMASONRY OF THE HIGHEST DEGREES. MEMBERS OF THE MASONIC ORDER INTRODUCED THE "HERMETIC RITE "WHICH WAS BASED UPON THE DOGMAS OF ALCHEMY, WHILE "OCCULT MASONRY" CONSISTED OF THREE VARIATION DEGREES WHICH WERE THE SAME AS THOSE OF ANCIENT CRAFT MASONRY, ONLY THAT ALL THE SYMBOLS ARE INTERPRETED AFTER ALCHEMICAL PRINCIPLES. IT IS, IN FACT, THE APPLICATION OF MASONIC SYMBOLISM TO HERMETIC SYMBOLISM. COINCIDENTLY, THE SYMBOL FOR SADDAM HUSSEIN'S ISLAMIC SECRET POLICE FORCE WAS THE MASONIC ALL-SEEING-EYE OVER TOP THE MAP OF IRAQ.

THE HERMETIC RITE ITSELF ORIGINATED IN FRANCE, IT WAS FIRST INSTITUTED BY FRATERNITY BROTHER ANTOINE JOSEPH PERNETTI AT AVIGNON IN 1770, AND IS MORE COMMONLY KNOWN IN FREEMASONRY CIRCLES AS THE ILLUMINATI OF AVIGNON — HOLDING DEISTIC AND REPUBLICAN PRINCIPLES PROFESSING TO POSSESS SPECIAL ENLIGHTENMENT POWERS. BY 1778, AN INTERESTING TRANSFER TOWARDS THE FUNDAMENTALS OF PROTESTANT CHRISTIANITY OCCURRED AND THUSLY ESTABLISHED THE ACADEMY OF ILLUMINATI. THIS CAME ABOUT LARGELY DUE TO THE FACT THAT PERNETTI BECAME TOTALLY ENGULFED WITH THE MYSTICAL THEORIES OF EMMANUEL

Swedenborg, and published a translation of his works of the spiritual world known as **Wonders of Heaven and Hell**. The Academy of the Illuminati was based upon three primitive grades of Freemasonry, to which Pernetti added a mystical one known as the "True Masons." As time passed, the Academy of the Illuminati simply became known as the Academy of True Masons. Besides his laying of the footing foundation of the Illuminati, Pernetti's Masonic influences also saw the introduction of many additional degrees within the fellowship, the degree of the Knight of the Sun is a prime example. Pernetti was in fact a very learned individual, his authorship talents were endless as he published numerous writings on mythology, the fine arts, theology, geography, philosophy, and the mathematical sciences. At a very early age in his life's history, he was apparently affiliated with twenty-eight Masonic fraternities.

By the time Charles Darwin came onto the scene, Occult Masonry had already flourished on a global scale. With financial backing from the Masonic Brotherhood, Darwin developed his theory of man's evolution. He believed that all plants and animals alike were species of natural selection. Darwin further advanced his theory that men and apes were descended from a common anthropoid ancestor. Needless to say, his theories of evolution were not warmly taken by many people at the time. Like Freemasonry itself, most of Darwin's findings conflicted with the interpretations of the Holy Scriptures. In 1871, his theory of man's evolution **"THE DESCENT OF MAN"** was published, this enraged the hierarchy to such a degree that Darwin was instantly classified as a misguided crank who had gone completely mad. As the intellectual acceptance of Darwinian theories of enlightenment spread worldwide, new concepts of social justice were soon born. With this great awakening of ideas came the concept of socialism and its humanistic attributes. Although Charles Darwin was portrayed as a crackpot, nothing is mentioned whatsoever in the history books that he was in fact very active in the occult sciences of Freemasonry.

In accordance to Masonic philosophy, astrology is basically designed as a black art and is thus in a reflective sense, an occult science; a system of divination foretelling results by the relative positions of the planets and other heavenly bodies toward the earth. During ancient Masonic times, the days of the pyramids and pharaohs, this science was known as the divine art of magic. Despite the fact that some Masonic fraternities deny the existence of any connection between Freemasonry and magic itself, Magical

Masonry and Occult Masonry are one in the same as the fraternal forces of the "black art "of Freemasonry is essentially known as Masonic Magic. For instance; the Tarot Cards supposedly first used in Italy during the Fourteenth Century are better known to be the symbolic "Jewels of the Wise "of the Masonic Order. Each card has a significant meaning in accordance to the Masonic Tree of Life, the Tarot itself apparently represents the Path of Initiation and also depicts the workings of mind and soul on the way to enlightenment. The Tarot Cards on the other hand are a book of pictures, each depicting a different version of the universal truths, in symbolism common to all the sacred teaching of the Masonic fraternity since the beginning of time. Accordingly, these symbols were designed with very great care by the spiritual masters of wisdom.

Although many of the history books essentially state that the origins of the Tarot Cards are forever hidden in the archives of days-gone-by and that no one really knows as to where to place the actual beginning of this ancient book of pictures, the Tarot Cards in fact can easily be traced to the days long before the Crusades and the fraternal Order of the Knights Templar. These were the times in which spiritual knowledge was highly discouraged, and any form of written literature that did not agree with the Church and/or its political ruling class was being confiscated, then, burned to ashes. In a desperate attempt to preserve its ultimate mysteries of the universe, the sacred "Wisdom "was thus put in plain sight for all to see. By this time period, Freemasonry worldwide had been well driven underground in order to survive as a secret fraternity. This transposed imagery having its fraternal roots in the days and times of the pharaohs. In reviewing the Egyptian Book of the Dead about 3000 B.C. with an open mind, it becomes abundantly clear that many Egyptian legends indicate that their ancestors carried with them to the great beyond, most of the precious secrets of life's mysteries.

Like the great mysteries of life, the summer of 1990 will no doubt go down in the history books as one of the greatest mysteries of all as the IMF began flexing its fraternal muscles in preparation for world domination. At that time period, summer of 1990, the IMF owned and financially controlled 152 of the world's Governments, including Canada, as the international group of leaders dished out tens of billions of dollars each year to countries that temporarily couldn't pay their international debts. In recent years, more than 50 countries had borrowed extensively from the Illuminati fraternity – from Brazil to Malawi, Pakistan and Uganda. One of the main

CLAUSES IN BORROWING FREEMASONRY MONEY IS KNOWN AS THE KEY CLAUSE. BORROWING GOVERNMENTS HAD NO CHOICE BUT TO COMPLY WITH ALL OF THE IMF ECONOMIC POLICIES, WHICH USUALLY MEANT DEVALUING THEIR CURRENCIES, SLASHING SUBSIDIES, LAYING OFF GOVERNMENT WORKERS AND GETTING RID OF MONEY-LOSING GOVERNMENT COMPANIES. ALTHOUGH THE IMF PUBLICALLY STATES TIME AND TIME AGAIN THAT IT'S MAIN FUNCTION IS TO HELP TURN AROUND FAILED ECONOMIES WITH A GOOD DOSE OF FREE-MARKET CAPITALISM, IT ALSO HAD A WELL HIDDEN AGENDA. IT'S OBVIOUS TO SAY THAT THE IMF HAS MERELY REARRANGED THE FURNITURE INSIDE THE DEBTOR'S PRISON AND POSTPONED THE EXECUTION OF THE DEBTOR TO ANOTHER DATE AND TIME.

DURING THE SUMMER OF 1990, THE UNITED NATIONS SECRETARY-GENERAL, JAVIER PEREZ DE CUELLAR DID THE UNEXPECTED BY PUBLICALLY CRITICIZING THE IMF'S NEW ECONOMIC POLICIES AS HE STATED THAT THEY WERE IN AFFECT UNDERMINING THE MIDDLE CLASS AND IMPOVERISHING ALL OF THE WAGE EARNERS WHICH IN TURN WAS CLOSING THE DOORS TO THEIR BASIC NECESSITIES OF LIFE; EDUCATION, FOOD, HOUSING AND MEDICAL CARE. IN SHORT, THE NEW POLICIES WERE HAVING A DISASTROUS AFFECT ON ALL LEVELS OF THE UNEMPLOYMENT FRONT. THE MASONIC ILLUMINATI, (THE IMF), DID NOT APPRECIATE THE CRITICISM THAT THEY WERE GETTING FROM ONE OF THEIR OWN AND THEREFORE THE UNITED NATIONS' SPOKESMAN STATEMENTS TO THE WORLD MEDIA WERE ALMOST IMMEDIATELY PROCLAIMED AS BEING TOTALLY UNFOUNDED AND ABSOLUTELY LUDICROUS.

BIZARRELY ENOUGH, WHEN THE UNITED NATIONS WAS ORIGINALLY CONCEIVED IN THE EARLY 1940'S UNDER THE WATCHFUL EYE OF MASONIC PRESIDENT FRANKLIN D. ROOSEVELT, TWENTY-SIX RESPECTIVE STRONGHOLD GOVERNMENTS CONTROLLED BY THE FUNDAMENTAL PRINCIPLES OF FREEMASONRY'S ILLUMINATI FORCES PLEDGED THEIR COOPERATION IN THE STRUGGLE FOR VICTORY OVER HITLERISM.

A BRAZEN STATEMENT SUCH AS THIS CANNOT STAND ON ITS OWN MERIT AND THEREFORE A FURTHER ELABORATION MUST BE GIVEN IN ORDER TO SUBSTANTIATE IT'S BOLDNESS. CASE IN POINT; IN 1809, MASONIC BROTHER FILIPPO BUONARROTI FOUNDED THE ORDER OF THE SUBLIMES MAITRES PARFAITS (SMP FOR SHORT), IN GENEVA, IT WAS ONE OF THE WORLD'S VERY FIRST KNOWN INTERNATIONAL POLITICAL ENTITIES MARRYING ITSELF TO THE FUNDAMENTAL PRACTICES AND PRINCIPLES OF FREEMASONRY. SOME THREE YEARS AFTER ITS CONCEPTION, TALK SOON EMERGED OF AN INTERNATIONAL CONSPIRACY OF WORLD DOMINATION AND THE ANTI-MASONIC FORCES QUICKLY BEGAN BLOCKING THE ILLUMINATI CONCEPT BY MAKING ALL SECRET SOCIETIES ILLEGAL AND IMMORAL. APPARENTLY, ONLY 23 YEARS EARLIER BUONARROTI JOINED AN ITALIAN ILLUMINATI LODGE AND HIS ENTIRE LIBRARY

OF FREEMASONRY LITERATURE WAS CONFISCATED BY THE STATE AUTHORITIES. BY 1795, HE WAS CAPTURED AND JAILED ON CRIMINAL CHARGES IN PARIS, FRANCE. TWO YEARS LATER, HE BEGAN HIS CONSPIRATORIAL ORGANIZING WHILE SERVING HIS INCARCERATION TERM. IN 1806, HE WAS RELEASED AND FLED TO SWITZERLAND TO EXECUTE HIS DREAMS OF "MANIFEST DESTINY" BY WAY OF DIVINE INTERVENTION. BY 1830, BUONARROTI'S CONCEPT HAD SPREAD LIKE WILDFIRE THROUGHOUT EUROPE AND THE ENTIRE WORLD. THE ILLUMINATI REVOLUTIONARY PROGRAM OF GLOBAL DOMINATION GAINED SUCH A STRONG FOOTHOLD THAT WORLD LEADERS THEN BEGAN TALKING OF A DOOMED RACE, (THE HUMAN RACE), UNDER THE RULE OF FREEMASONRY. IN 1833, BUONARROTTI ONCE AGAIN WAS ARRESTED, BUT RELEASED SHORTLY THEREAFTER. FOUR YEARS LATER, ON SEPTEMBER 15TH, WHILE IN PARIS, FILIPPO MICHELE BUONARROTTI DIED.

ACCORDING TO WHAT THE HISTORY BOOKS WISH US TO BELIEVE IS TRUE, BUONARROTTI SUPPOSEDLY SPENT MOST OF HIS LIFE IN TOTAL POVERTY AND COMPLETE OBSCURITY. BUT IN REALITY, HE WAS A DESCENDANT OF MICHELANGELO'S BROTHER AS WELL AS A VERY STRONG ACQUAINTANCE OF NAPOLEON BONAPARTE. BUONARROTTI ALSO SHARED HIS VIEWS WITH MANY OF HIS MUTUAL FRIENDS, OF WHOM WERE KNOWN TO BE ACTIVE MEMBERS OF THE SUPERIOR FREEMASONRY FORCES – THE ILLUMINOIDS. AMONG ITS MEMBERS WERE; VICTOR HUGO, CHARLES NODIER, JEAN GIGOUX, JEHAN DUSEIGNEUR, LOUIS BLANC AND CELESTIN NANTEUIL. INTERESTINGLY, AT ONE TIME HUGO AND NODIER WERE GRAND MASTERS OF THE MASONIC UNDERGROUND ILLUMINATI FACTION, THE PRIEURE DE SION. NAPOLEON WAS REPORTEDLY ABLE TO RAISE TO POWER THROUGH HIS FRATERNITY FELLOWSHIP, THEREFORE, IT IS HIGHLY UNLIKELY THAT BUONARRITTI DIED A POOR MISUNDERSTOOD MAN AS TO WHAT THE HISTORIANS HAVE BEEN STATING OVER THE MANY YEARS SINCE HIS UNTIMELY DEATH. FURTHER GRAND MASTERS OF THE PRIEURE DE SION INCLUDED; LEONARD DE VINCI, SIR ISAAC NEWTON, CHARLES DE LORRAINE, AND MAXIMILIEN DE LORRAINE.

A PERSON MAYBE EXCUSED FOR ASKING THE MOST OBVIOUS QUESTION; WHAT IS THIS MASONIC ORDER DE SION???

IN ORDER TO FULLY ANSWER THAT QUESTION, A FRATERNAL PROBE INTO THE FIRST CRUSADE YEARS (1096-99) WOULD HAVE TO BE FIRST EXAMINED IN SOME DETAIL. AND SINCE THE ORDER DE SION ACTUALLY PLAYED A VERY IMPORTANT ROLE IN CONFINING CHRISTENDOM TO ITS PRESENT-DAY STRUGGLE FOR CONTROL OF THE HOLY LAND (ISRAEL), THE FOLLOWING MUST ALSO BE STATED. THE FIRST CRUSADE WAS INAUGURATED BY POPE URBAN II, UNDER HIS DIRECTION, URBAN ATTEMPTED TO BRING A UNION OF GREEK AND LATIN CHURCHES UNDER ONE WING, ROMAN EMPEROR RULE. THE FIRST CRUSADE WAS THUS MADE UP OF TWO BASIC GROUPS OF PEOPLE; I) UNORGANIZED BANDS

OF PEASANTS, MANY OF WHOM WERE KILLED ON THE OVERLAND JOURNEY TO CONSTANTINOPLE, AND 2) ORGANIZED COMPANIES UNDER FRENCH NOBLEMEN, THUS FORMING A SECRET SECT, THE PRIEURE DE SION.

AS THE STORY GOES ACCORDING TO FREEMASONRY LITERATURE, THE ORDER DE SION WAS FOUNDED ON THE ROCK OF SION BY GODFROI DE BOUILLON IN 1090, A FULL NINE YEARS BEFORE THE ACTUAL CONQUEST OF JERUSALEM. WHILE SOME HISTORIANS ON THE OTHER HAND STATE THAT ITS ORIGIN DIDN'T COME INTO EXISTENCE UNTIL 1099 ON MOUNT SION IN JERUSALEM, (THE FAMOUS HIGH HILL JUST SOUTH OF THE CITY). LIKE ALL OTHER RELIGIOUS ZEALOTS, DE BOUILLON CONSIDERED HIMSELF TO BE A DIRECT DESCENDANT OF CHRIST AND HE WAS WILLING TO EXPRESS IT TO THE FULLEST EXTENT OF THE LAW, **GOD'S LAW**. HENCE WITH THE GUIDANCE FROM THE ALMIGHTY GOD HIMSELF, GODFROI DE BOUILLON AND HIS DISCIPLES LAID THE MASONIC FOUNDATION FOR CONQUERING THE HOLY LAND. THIS IS WHY IT IS WRITTEN IN THE PRIEURE DOCUMENTS THAT BAUDOUIN I, GODFROI'S YOUNGER BROTHER, ESSENTIALLY OWNED HIS THRONE TO THE ORDER. WITH A ROLL OF TOILET PAPER IN HAND, GODFROI DE BOUILLO (THE DUKE OF LORRAINE) PASSED THE PORCELAIN THRONE DOWN TO HIS YOUNGER BROTHER BAUDOUIN THE FIRST. IT IS THEREFORE BELIEVED BY MANY THAT UPON THE DEATH BED OF GODFROI, HIS BROTHER GRACIOUSLY ACCEPTED THE CROWN THAT WAS OFFERED TO HIM AS BEING THE FIRST OFFICIAL KING OF JERUSALEM. IT IS ALSO INTERESTING TO NOTE THAT OVER THE MANY CENTURIES THAT HAVE FOLLOWED SINCE THEN, MOST, IF NOT ALL OF THE TRUTHFUL ASPECTS HAVE BEEN PURPOSELY REWRITTEN BY HISTORIANS IN ORDER TO CONCEAL WHAT ACTUALLY OCCURRED, ESPECIALLY CONSIDERING THE FACT THAT SINCE ITS ORIGINAL CONCEPTION EONS AGO THE ROMAN CATHOLIC CHURCH HAS BEEN AT ODDS WITH THE MASONIC ORDER. THE FACT OF THE MATTER WAS AND FOREVER WILL BE THAT THE ODER DE SION WAS ATTEMPTING TO INFILTRATE THE CHURCH, WHILE THE CHURCH WANTED TO HAVE NOTHING TO DO WITH THE ORDER AND WHAT IT STOOD FOR AS IT IN ITSELF WAS CONSIDERED TO BE THE ANTI-CHRIST.

BE THAT AS IT MAY, POPE URBAN II WAS THE 160TH SUPREME PONTIFF OF THE CATHOLIC CHURCH AND WAS REPORTEDLY KNOWN TO BE THE MOST ZEALOUS OF ALL THE POPES AS HE ENFORCED THE LAW OF PRIESTLY CELIBACY AND FORBADE THE CLERGY TO ACCEPT ECCLESIASTICAL OFFICES FROM LAYMEN. ON JULY 29TH, 1099 POPE URBAN DIED UNDER SOMEWHAT QUESTIONABLE CIRCUMSTANCES, HIS SUCCESSOR WAS PASCHAL II. ODDLY ENOUGH, POPE PASCHAL'S ADMINISTRATION WAS PLAGUED BY CONFLICTS OVER THE QUESTION OF THE INVESTITURE CONTROVERSY WITH ROMAN EMPERORS HENRY IV AND HENRY V. IN THE YEAR 1110, POPE PASCHAL II WAS IMPRISONED FOR TWO MONTHS AND DURING THAT TIME PERIOD MUCH PRESSURE WAS ADDED BY THE

EMPEROR (HENRY V) TO HAVE THE RIGHT OF INVESTITURE. PASCHAL WAS THUS FORCED TO RECOGNIZE LAY INVESTITURE, BUT ONCE HE WAS RELEASED FROM PRISON, HE WITHDREW IT BY WAY OF A ROYAL PAPAL PROCLAMATION. EIGHT YEARS LATER, HE TOO WAS DEAD. POPE PASCHAL'S REPLACEMENT WAS GELASIUS II. GELASIUS WAS CARDINAL AND CHANCELLOR UNDER BOTH URBAN AND PASCHAL, AND ON THE DEATH OF THE LATTER, HE WAS PURPOSELY SELECTED TO BE POPE BY THE PARTY HOSTILE TO THE EMPEROR HENRY V. INTERESTINGLY, THE RULERS OF THE HOLY ROMAN EMPIRE WERE OF SAXON-DYNASTY OF GERMAN KINGS. IN 1106, HENRY V WAS ALSO CROWNED THE GERMAN KING. HE WAS THE SON OF HENRY IV, WHOM WAS CROWNED GERMAN KING IN 1056 AND BECAME THE EMPEROR OF THE HOLY ROMAN EMPIRE TWENTY-EIGHT YEARS LATER. HENRY V, CONTINUED WITH HIS FATHER'S STRUGGLE WITH THE PAPACY UNTIL 1122 WHEN A SETTLEMENT WAS FINALLY REACHED BY "THE CONCORDAT OF WORMS "WHICH WAS CONCLUDED IN 1801 BETWEEN PIUS VII AND NAPOLEON.

ACCORDING TO THE ROMAN CATHOLIC CHURCH LEGEND, HENRY V WAS EXCOMMUNICATED FOR HIS ANTI-POPE ACTIVITIES AS GELASIUS II WAS FORCED TO FLEE FOR HIS LIFE. AFTER ONLY TWELVE MONTHS OF SITTING ON THE PAPAL PORCELAIN THRONE, GELASIUS DIED IN THE MONASTERY OF CLUNY, FRANCE, WHERE HE HAD BEEN HIDING OUT.

IN THE YEAR A.D. 31, ST. PETER WAS THE FIRST CATHOLIC POPE – FOR 2,000 YEARS THE CHURCH AND ITS TYRANTS CONTROLLED THE MASSES OF THE WORLD'S POPULATION. AND TWO-THOUSAND YEARS BEFORE THAT, THE PAGANS AND/OR HEATHENS WERE PERSECUTED, JUDGED AND CONDEMNED FOR WORSHIPING WOODEN IDOLS, STONE SCULPTURES, AND OTHER FALSE GODS WHILE THE RULING CLASS GOT RICHER AND THE POORER CLASSES GOT POORER; EXACTLY AS TO WHAT STILL EXIST TO THIS VERY DAY DURING THESE TRYING TIMES OF THE 21ST CENTURY.

UPON THE ARRIVAL OF THE ANOINTED KING OF THE JEWS, JESUS CHRIST CAME ONTO THE SCENE TO DAZZLE THE MASSES AND GUIDE THEM, LIKE A HEARD OF BLIND SHEEP – FOR THEIR OWN SALVATION TO THE PROMISED LAND. COINCIDENTLY, CHRIST WAS CONSIDERED TO POSSESS SUPERNATURAL POWERS AS HE WAS PROCLAIMED TO SIT AT THE RIGHT HAND OF GOD AND WAS ABLE TO DESTROY AND RECREATE AT WILL AS HE WENT ABOUT HIS DAILY DUTIES OF RIDDING THE EARTH OF ITS EVIL SATANIC FORCES. BUT IN ALL FAIRNESS, IT SOUNDS AS THOUGH THE BIBLE WAS ACTUALLY WRITTEN BY INDIVIDUALS WHO SUFFERED FROM THE MAIN CHARACTERISTICS OF SCHIZOPHRENIA; GOOD VERSUS EVIL.

AT TIMES, THE ROMAN CATHOLIC CHURCH CAN BE THE MOST ARROGANT RELIGIOUS INSTITUTION ON THE FACE OF THE EARTH – THE LIFE AND TIMES OF THE FAMOUS MASONIC COMPOSER MOZART IS A CASE IN POINT. WHAT

MOST PEOPLE CAN'T GRASP IS THE CORRELATION BETWEEN CHURCH AND STATE, JAHANNES CHRYSOSTOMOS WOLFGANGUS THEOPHILUS (THE REAL NAME OF WOLFGANG AMADEUS MOZART) IS THE PRIME EXAMPLE OF SUCH A CORRELATION. WHEN MOZART WAS BORN IN 1756, HIS FATHER WAS THE SUB-DIRECTOR OF MUSIC AT THE CATHEDRAL OF PRINCE SIGISMUND. AND WHILE STILL LIVING, MOZART WAS CLASSIFIED AS THE MASTER OF FREEMASONRY MUSIC ALTHOUGH HE WAS A SINCERE ORTHODOX ROMAN CATHOLIC. WHILE IN HIS LATE TWENTIES, HE WAS INITIATED INTO THE MASONIC ORDER ON DECEMBER 14TH, 1784 AS MOZART JOINED THE LODGE BENEVOLENCE OF CHARITY, ONE OF THE EIGHT LODGES THAT EXISTED IN VIENNA AT THE TIME.

TO MOST ROMAN CATHOLICS DURING THAT TIME PERIOD, THEY WERE UTTERLY SURPRISED IN HEARING THE NEWS THAT MOZART HAD BEEN ALLOWED TO JOIN A MASONIC LODGE IN A TOTALLY CATHOLIC COUNTRY CONSIDERING THE PAPAL BULLS OF 1738 AND 1751 THAT ESSENTIALLY FORBID IT. BUT THE FACT OF THE MATTER IS, FREEMASONRY THRIVED IN VIENNA DURING THE EIGHTEENTH CENTURY UNDER JOSEPH II AS ITS FUNDAMENTAL PRINCIPLES WERE ADMIRABLY SUITED TO WOLFGANG'S SENSITIVE DISPOSITION. IN A COMPLETE TWIST OF IRONY, MOZART DIED JUST BEFORE THE END OF THE CENTURY WHEN THE ACCESSION OF A NEW EMPEROR USHERED IN A PERIOD OF PERSECUTION OF FREEMASONRY WHICH WAS TO LAST FOR A GRAND TOTAL OF FIFTY YEARS.

DURING THE TIME PERIOD OF MOZART'S LIFE HISTORY — AUSTRIANS, RATHER HYPOCRITICALLY, USED A LEGAL NICETY TO OVERCOME THE PAPAL BULLS. TO BEGIN WITH, THEIR EMPEROR JOSEPH II, A MAN OF LIBERAL IDEAS, WAS KINDLY DISPOSED TO THE FUNDAMENTAL PRACTICES AND TEACHINGS OF FREEMASONRY. IN AUSTRIA THE PUBLICATION OF A PAPAL BULL DEPENDED UPON CIVIL AUTHORITY. IT ONLY BECAME OBLIGATORY AFTER IT HAD BEEN GAZETTED. AND WITH THINGS NOT BEING AS TO WHAT THEY SEEM AT THE BEST OF TIMES, THE PAPAL BULLS WERE NEVER PUBLICALLY GAZETTED AND WITH THIS BEING THE CASE, AUSTRIAN ROMAN CATHOLICS DID NOT CONSIDER THEMSELVES BOUND TO OBEY THE VATICAN AS LONG AS THIS LEGAL ELEMENT WAS LACKING. JOSEPH II, THE PEOPLE'S EMPEROR, REPORTEDLY WAS NOT AN ACTIVE MEMBER OF THE ANCIENT CRAFT OF FREEMASONRY. HIS MOTHER, MARIA THERESA, WAS OPENLY ANTAGONISTIC TO FREEMASONRY, WHILE HIS FATHER ON THE OTHER HAND, FRANCIS OF LORRAINE HAD BEEN INITIATED IN THE HAGUE IN 1731 BY A DELEGATION FROM THE GRAND LODGE OF ENGLAND.

ACCORDING TO MASONIC LITERATURE, MOZART BECAME AN INSTANT MEMBER OF GOOD STANDING AS HE PLAYED A VERY IMPORTANT ROLE PERFORMING A SERIES OF MUSICAL COMPOSITIONS, THAT MOZART HIMSELF ATTRIBUTED TO THE ANCIENT CRAFT AS IT TOOK A FIRM HOLD OF HIS ARTISTIC

IMAGINATION. APPARENTLY, MOZART DEVOTED MUCH OF HIS TIME TO THE FRATERNITY AS HE ATTENDED HIS LODGE REGULARLY AND VISITED OTHER LODGES FREQUENTLY. HE WAS A REGULAR GUEST AT THE TRUE HARMONY LODGE, AT THE TIME THE MOST INFLUENTIAL IN ALL OF VIENNA. IN FACT, IT WAS THE SPIRITUAL HOME OF AUSTRIAN FREEMASONRY WHERE WOLFGANG AMADEUS MOZART INSPIRED HIS FATHER LEOPOLD TO JOIN THE ANCIENT FRATERNITY AND UPON PASSING ONTO THE 2ND DEGREE AT TRUE HARMONY LODGE ON JANUARY 16TH, 1785, BOTH FATHER AND SON WERE PRESENT AT THE INITIATION. WOLFGANG AMADEUS MOZART WAS ALSO PRESENT AT FRANZ HAYDN'S INITIATION OF FEBRUARY 11TH OF THAT SAME YEAR. OTHER CLASSICAL COMPOSERS SUCH AS HANDEL, BACH AND BEETHOVEN WERE ALSO INITIATED INTO THE FRATERNAL "**BROTHERHOOD OF MAN**. "AS THE MASONIC ORDER BECAME A VERY POWERFUL FORCE TO BE RECKONED WITH, JOSEPH II BECAME WORRISOME. BY YEAR'S END, 1785, THE EMPEROR ISSUED A COURT DECREE REDUCING THE EIGHT VIENNESE LODGES TO THREE WITH AN OBLIGATION TO SUBMIT MEMBERSHIP LISTS TO THE AUTHORITIES. IN ACTUAL FACT, TWO NEW LODGES WERE FORMED FROM THE EIGHT; LODGE TRUTH AND LODGE NEW CROWNED HOPE. THE COMPOSER MOZART BECAME A MEMBER OF THE LATTER AND A REGULAR VISITOR TO THE OTHER.

ON FEBRUARY 20TH, 1790 THE PEOPLE'S EMPEROR JOSEPH II DIED, AND HIS SUCCESSOR QUICKLY SHATTERED THE MASONIC LOOKING GLASS AS FREEMASONRY IN AUSTRIA SOON WANED. ONLY THEN DID ROMAN CATHOLIC LEADERS BECOME OPENLY ANTAGONISTIC TO THE MASONIC FRATERNITY WHILE MOST AUSTRIAN LEADERS REGARDED IT ADVERSELY. BY 1795, FREEMASONRY WAS TOTALLY PROHIBITED BY LAW IN AUSTRIA ITSELF.

THE ULTIMATE IRONY IS THAT WOLFGANG AMADEUS MOZART AND HIS FATHER DIDN'T ALWAYS SEE EYE TO EYE WITH THE CATHOLIC CHURCH WHILE THEY, THE CHURCH, EXPLOITED THE MOZART FAMILY TALENT TO THE FULLEST EXTENT OF ROMAN CATHOLIC CANON LAW. IN 1772, CHURCH DIGNITARIES DEMANDED THAT MOZART AND HIS FATHER APPEAR BEFORE RELIGIOUS OFFICIALS AT THE VIENNA CATHEDRAL TO EXPLAIN THEMSELVES. AS IT TURNS OUT, BOTH WOLFGANG AND HIS FATHER WANTED TO GO ON A MUSICAL TOUR AND MADE A REQUEST WITH THE CATHOLIC CHURCH FOR A LEAVE OF ABSENCE TO UNDERTAKE THE TOUR, BUT IT WAS FLATLY REFUSED. NOTHING TAKING THE NEGATIVE RESPONSE TO THEIR REQUEST LAYING DOWN, BOTH FATHER AND SON RESUBMITTED THE REQUEST WHICH ULTIMATELY LED TO MOZART AND HIS FAMILY BEING INSTANTLY DISMISSED FROM THE CATHOLIC CHURCH ALTOGETHER AS THEY WERE CHALLENGING CHURCH AUTHORITY OVER THEM. WHEN TEMPERS FINALLY COOLED DOWN, LEOPOLD WAS REINSTATED BUT WOLFGANG AMADEUS MOZART WAS NOT OVERLY IMPRESSED WITH THEIR ACTIONS AND DEFIED THE SUPREME AUTHORITY THAT THE CHURCH HAD OVER

ITS PARISHIONERS BY TAKING HIS MOTHER ON TOUR TO ACCOMPANY HIM — THE VATICAN WAS NOT AMUSED WITH THE WHOLE UGLY/NASTY ORDEAL.

BY 1777, MOZART WAS FORCED TO RETURN TO THE CATHEDRAL AS ORGANIST UNDER HIS FATHER WHO HAD IN THE MEANTIME BEEN APPOINTED ITS FULLY FLEDGED MUSICAL DIRECTOR. FOR TWO LONG AGONIZING YEARS MOZART AND HIS FAMILY GRADUALLY BEGAN TO DESPISE THE CATHOLIC CHURCH EVEN MORE AND REFUSED TO ACCEPT THE VATICAN DISCIPLINE THAT WAS BEING DISPENSED ONTO THEM. THE INCREASING ANIMOSITY EVENTUALLY HEIGHTENED INTO AN EXTREMELY HEATED ARGUMENT IN 1781 WHICH LEAD TO WOLFGANG'S FULL EXPULSION FROM THE CHURCH — HE WAS LITERALLY KICKED IN THE SEAT OF THE PANTS DOWN THE CHURCH STAIRS. THIS RATHER UNDIGNIFIED EXIT, HOWEVER, SPELT COMPLETE MUSICAL FREEDOM AND TOTAL INDEPENDENCE FOR MOZART WHO REPORTEDLY "REJOICED" WITH THEIR UNGODLY MANEUVER OF DEALING WITH HIM.

FOR THE WAY IN WHICH THE ROMAN CATHOLIC CHURCH HAD UNJUSTLY TREATED HIM, MOZART IMMEDIATELY BEGAN TURNING TO THE FUNDAMENTAL PRACTICES AND TEACHING OF THE ANCIENT CRAFT OF FREEMASONRY FOR SPIRITUAL ENLIGHTENMENT AND SOON THEREAFTER HIS MUSICAL CAREER SHOT OUT LIKE A LOUD RELIGIOUS CANNON OVER THE HORIZON.

ON DECEMBER 5TH, 1791 AT VIENNA, JOHANNES CHRYSOSTOMOS WOLFGANGUS THEOPHILUS — A.K.A. WOLFGANG AMADEUS MOZART DIED — HE WAS BURIED WITH FULL MASONIC HONORS AND IN FULL ATTIRE. MOZART REPORTEDLY FIRST SAW THE MASONIC LIGHT IN 1770, AND INSTANTLY BECAME A NON-PRACTICING MEMBER OF THE LODGE "ZUR GEKRONTEN HOFFNUNG." MANY OF HIS MUSICAL COMPOSITIONS ARE IN FACT DEDICATIONS TO THE ANCIENT CRAFT ITSELF.

ONE OF MOZART'S LAST TRIBUTES TO FREEMASONRY WAS IN THE FORM OF AN OPERA, "THE MAGIC FLUTE "IN WHICH HE INCORPORATED THE BASIC PRINCIPLES OF A VARIATION OF MASONIC DEGREES WHEREBY LOVE AND HONOR WERE TO BE TESTED UNDER SOME RATHER BIZARRE CIRCUMSTANCES. THIS FAIRY-TALE TYPE OPERATIC ALLEGORY, WHICH FIRST OPENED IN VIENNA ON SEPTEMBER 30TH, 1791 WAS SAID TO BE A MIX OF SUBLIME MUSIC AND SLAPSTICK COMEDY THAT WAS INITIALLY DESIGNED FOR THE COMMON FOLK — A FAIRY-TALE OF GOOD VERSUS EVIL. INTERESTINGLY, THE STORY INVOLVED WILD BEASTS, A SERPENT, MUSIC CHIMES, FIRE AND WATER MACHINERY, AND OTHER INTERESTING ASPECTS WHICH MOZART INTENDED TO CAPTIVATE HIS AUDIENCE WITH.

ACCORDINGLY, THE QUEEN OF THE NIGHT APPEARS TO BE GOOD BUT IS IN FACT VERY EVIL IN ALL ASPECTS OF HUMAN NATURE. SHE SENDS PRINCE TAMINO, WHO COINCIDENTLY STUMBLED INTO HER REALM WITH HIS COMIC BIRD-CATCHER SIDEKICK PAPAGENO, ON AN ERRAND TO RESCUE HER DAUGHTER

PAMINA FROM THE SORCERER SARASTRO, WHO AS IT TURNS OUT APPEARS TO BE EVIL BUT IN FACT IS NOT THE VILLAIN AS HE SEEMS TO BE. MOZART EVEN WENT SO FAR AS TO INCORPORATE THINGS THAT WERE STILL IN ITS INFANCY STAGES OF DEVELOPMENT, SUCH AS THE THREE STRANGE BOYS /OR SPIRITS (THE QUEEN OF THE NIGHT'S EMISSARIES), WHO BOPPED TO-AND-FRO IN A FLOATING CONTRAPTION RESEMBLING THE JUST-INVENTED HOT-AIR BALLOON.

WITH REGARDS TO THE MASONIC REFERENCES, OF WHICH MANY HAD BEEN MADE, ONE NEED ONLY TO KEEP A STERN EAR OPEN FOR AS THE REFERENCES TO THE FRATERNAL RITUALS WERE SAID TO BE EVERYWHERE AND ULTIMATELY CAME IN THREESOMES THAT OF WHICH WAS A REFLECTION OF THE MASTER MASONS' THREE KNOCKS. THE KNOCKS IN MOZART'S THE MAGIC FLUTE BEING OF COURSE; THE THREE MYSTERIOUS LADIES, THE THREE BOYS /OR SPIRITS, THE THREE PRIESTS OF THE TEMPLE OF ISIS AND OSIRIS (MASONIC ORIGINS BEING TRACEABLE BACK TO ANCIENT EGYPT), THE THREE TRIALS THAT TAMINA AND PAMINA FACED, THE E-FLAT KEY SIGNATURE (WHICH CONTAINED THREE FLATS). THREE TIMES SIX IS 18 (THERE WERE 18 PLACES FOR THE PRIESTS' MEETINGS) AND THEIR MARCH TUNE COMPOSITION WAS 18 BARS LONG.

THE MAGIC FLUTE THEREFORE BECAME MOZART'S VEHICLE OF CHOICE FOR PLEDGING HIS DEEP DEVOTED AFFECTION TOWARDS — A PHILOSOPHICAL BROTHERHOOD THAT HAD BECOME AN IN SPIRITUAL INFLUENCE FOR HIM AS THE EVER INCREASING POLITICAL AND RELIGIOUS POWERS IN VIENNA AT THE TIME WERE DISPENSING MORE AND MORE OF THEIR DICTATORIAL POLICIES. ALL OF VIENNA'S INHABITANTS SOON COME UNDER AN EVER INCREASING STORM OF CRITICISM BY BOTH THE CATHOLIC CHURCH AND THE REIGNING HAPSBURG EMPIRE. PERHAPS THIS IS WHY MOZART WROTE THE OPERA THE WAY THAT HE DID, AS A WAY AND MEANS OF DEFYING BOTH CHURCH AND STATE ALL AT THE EXACT SAME TIME. NEEDLESS TO SAY, THE HOLY ROMAN EMPEROR OF AUSTRIA, LEOPOLD II PROHIBITED THE PRACTICE OF FREEMASONRY AND MOZART JUST DIDN'T SEEM TO GIVE A DAMN AS HE FORGED ONWARDS DESPITE THE ROYAL DECREE. HIS FRATERNITY OPERA TRIBUTE OPENED ON SCHEDULE, AND IN ACCORDANCE AS TO WHAT THE MASONIC LITERATURE HAD TO SAY ON THE SUBJECT, MOZART FELT THAT HIS OPERA DIDN'T HAVE THE SUCCESS THAT IT DESERVED AS BY THIS TIME PERIOD HIS HEALTH WAS FAILING MISERABLY AND HE WAS HOPELESSLY IN DEBT. JUST TEN WEEKS AFTER THE PREMIERE OF "THE MAGIC FLUTE", MOZART DIED A COMPLETELY SHATTERED AND PENNYLESS MAN.

IT IS ALSO INTERESTING TO OBSERVE THAT THE FIRST 100 YEARS OF ORGANIZED FREEMASONRY (1717-1817) COINCIDED WITH THE GREAT MASONIC CLASSICAL COMPOSERS AND OF ALL THESE, MOZART WITHOUT A DOUBT GAVE THE ANCIENT CRAFT OF FREEMASONRY ITS GRANDEST, GREATEST AND MOST BEAUTIFUL MUSIC!!!

Freemasonry in fact had much influence on both the political and social fibers of pretty well the entire world. Evidence of such is concealed within a list of prominent Freemasons of the Twentieth Century. Authors like Kurt Tucholsky and Carl von Osietzty, the hotel king Charles Hilton, and painter Lovith Corinth, the composer Jan Sibelius, the discoverer of penicillin Alexander Fleming, the classical comedian W.C. Fields, and Doctor Charles Mayo, the co-founder of the Mayo Clinic – are all prime examples of Freemasonry influences on the world. Additional names include such individuals as John Wayne, Mel Blanc, Gene Autry, General Douglas MacArthur, as well as German Chancellor, Gustav Streseman, the American FBI director John Edgar Hoover and U.S. Secretary of State Christian Herter.

According to Masonic legend, Freemasonry President Lyndon Johnson allowed FBI director Brother Hoover to stay on past the mandatory retirement age stating that he preferred having Hoover inside the tent and pissing outside, rather than having it the other way around. In 1935, the FBI under the fraternity administration of J. Edgar Hoover, began investigating Nazi spies within the United States. Contrary to public opinion, Freemasonry Brother Hoover and his agency lost their credibility long before the days of John Dillinger, Pretty Boy Floyd, and Bonnie and Clyde. Under Masonic President Warren Harding, the Special Investigations Unit of the FBI had consisted mainly of ex-convicts and con men on the take. And when it comes to corruption in the American administration of both the Central Intelligence Agency and the Federal Bureau of Investigation, they are one in the same – a Masonic Institution of money, power and greed. By the 1950's, Joseph Raymond McCarthy used his Freemasonry influences to orchestrate one of the greatest farces that the Twentieth Century had ever witnessed at its time – a ruthless campaign to promote his own political fortunes by raising the scary specter of Communist infiltration of the United States Government.

Hiding under fraternity Brother Hoover's cloak of the National Security Council established in 1947, Joseph McCarthy began his reign of terror while giving a speech in West Virginia in February of 1950. Then a Senator from Wisconsin, McCarthy announced that he had a list of known members of the Communist Party, who were gainfully employed with the State Department. McCarthy did not dare mention the existence of yet another known list containing the names of literally hundreds of thousands of active Freemasons

WHO HAD ALSO GAINED EMPLOYMENT WITHIN THE ADMINISTRATION OF THE AMERICAN GOVERNMENT – THAT LIST HE HELD CLOSE TO HIS CHEST. JOSEPH MCCARTHY AND HIS FAITHFUL FOLLOWERS OF BLIND SHEEP THUSLY ESTABLISHED THEIR WITCH HUNT ON COMMUNISM WHILE THE MASONIC BROTHERHOOD CONTINUED PLAYING OUT THEIR VISION OF GLOBAL DOMINATION **"MANIFEST DESTINY "**VIA **"THE BROTHERHOOD OF MAN – UNDER THE FATHERHOOD OF GOD."**

SINCE HISTORY HAS A NASTY HABIT OF ALWAYS REPEATING ITSELF, THE SAME RULE WAS APPLIED IN EUROPE DURING THE EARLY 1980'S AS THE ROMAN CATHOLIC CHURCH AND THE MASONIC FRATERNITY WERE ONCE AGAIN AT ODDS WITH ONE ANOTHER AS THE CHURCH ISSUED A DECLARATION OF WAR THAT WAS TO ROCK THE VERY FOUNDATIONS OF THE CATHOLIC CHURCH ITSELF – FROM THE VATICAN IN ROME TO EAST AND WEST GERMANY. THE DECLARATION OF WAR ESSENTIALLY STATED THAT WHOEVER WAS A MEMBER OF THE ANCIENT CRAFT OF FREEMASONRY HAD NO DAMN BUSINESS BELONGING TO THE CATHOLIC CHURCH AND WAS ISSUED IN GERMANY AS RUMORS FROM WITHIN THE RELIGIOUS SECTOR HAD BEEN CIRCULATING THAT VARIOUS STEPS WERE BEING TAKEN TO HAVE THE WALL THAT DIVIDED EAST AND WEST GERMANY (THE BERLIN WALL) TORN DOWN IN PREPARATION FOR THE MASONIC DEADLINE OF THE YEAR 2000. THE ROMAN CATHOLIC CHURCH SUPPOSEDLY WANTED ABSOLUTELY NOTHING TO DO WITH THE FREEMASONRY CONCEPT OF GLOBAL DOMINATION. TO THIS ILLUSIVE DECLARATION OF WAR, GERMAN MASONIC LEADERS, DESPITE BEING ROMAN CATHOLIC, WROTE A LETTER TO THE POPE SAYING IN PART: **"MAY HIS HOLINESS MAKE IT POSSIBLE, CONTRARY TO THE GERMAN BISHOP'S DECLARATION OF 1980, THAT FREEMASONS MAY OFFICIALLY BE ALSO MEMBERS OF THE CATHOLIC CHURCH?"**

INTERESTINGLY ENOUGH, THE PAPAL REPLY DIDN'T ARRIVE UNTIL THE BEGINNING OF MARCH 1981, OF WHICH IT WAS IN THE FORM OF A BRIEF DECLARATION OF THE CONGREGATION FOR THE INSTRUCTION IN FAITH: **"THE CORRESPONDING LAWFUL CHURCH REGULATION ... REMAINS FULLY IN EFFECT. MASONS ARE STILL EXCOMMUNICATED. ANY OTHER INTERPRETATION OF THE EXISTING NORM WERE ERRONEOUS AND TENDENCIOUS. "**AS FATE WOULD HAVE IT, THIS VATICAN VETO WAS NEVER MADE PUBLIC EVEN WHEN A WAVE OF RESIGNATIONS SWEPT THROUGH THE HIGH RANKS OF APPROXIMATELY 13,000 GERMAN FREEMASONS. MANY LEADING RELIGIOUS MASONS FELT THAT THEY WERE BEING TOTALLY MISUNDERSTOOD AND COMPLETELY EXPLOITED BY THE CATHOLIC CHURCH AS IT WAS FORCING THEM INTO CHOOSING BETWEEN CHURCH AND STATE, WHEN IN REALITY CHURCH AND STATE WERE ONE IN THE SAME. SOME GERMAN FREEMASONS FAVORED THEIR RELIGIOUS CONVICTIONS BUT THE VAST MAJORITY OF THEM CHOSE TO REMAIN ACTIVE MEMBERS OF THE

ANCIENT CRAFT OF FREEMASONRY DESPITE THE ROMAN CATHOLIC CHURCH DECREE.

OVER THE COURSE OF TIME TOWARDS MAN'S SUPPOSED PROGRESSION OF BEING A CIVILIZED RACE OF PEOPLE, THE ROMAN CATHOLIC CHURCH LOCKED HORNS WITH MEMBERS OF FREEMASONRY MANY, MANY TIMES. SINCE THE FIRST ESTABLISHING OF ORGANIZED FRATERNITY LODGERY (1717), THERE HAS BEEN WELL OVER 400 CHURCHLY BANS AGAINST MASONIC LODGES, FOURTEEN OF THESE BANS HAVE BEEN IN THE FORM OF PAPAL BULLS AND ENCYCLIA. FREEMASONRY, TO POPE PIUS XI (1846-78) FOR EXAMPLE WAS THE PERCEIVED AS BEING THE "**SYNAGOGUE OF SATAN** "AND TO POPE LEO XIII (1878-1903), MEMBERS OF THE ANCIENT CRAFT WERE CONSIDERED TO BE BOTH "**PESTILENCE AND SYPHILIS** "ALIKE, INCLUDING SUCH BRETHREN AS LESSING, GOETHE, MOZART /OR EVEN PRUSSIA'S KING, FREDERICK THE GREAT.

WITH THE TRADITIONAL ROMAN CATHOLIC ATTITUDE OF BEING HOLIER THAN THOU, CANON 2335 CAME INTO BEING (EFFECTIVE SINCE 1918) AND PLACED ON THE CATHOLIC LAWBOOK, CODEX LURIS CANONICI, MEMBERS OF FREEMASONRY WERE AUTOMATICALLY EXCOMMUNICATED, AND WERE TOTALLY PROHIBITED FROM RECEIVING THE HOLY SACRAMENTS – PURSUANT TO CANON 1240 THEY WERE NOT EVEN ALLOWED TO BE BURIED WITH CHURCH RITES. AT BEST FREEMASONS APPEAR TO BE VERY USEFUL TO THE CATHOLIC CHURCH AS MAINLY SCAPEGOATS BECAUSE POPE PIUS XII (1939-58) BLAMED THE MASONIC ORDER FOR ALL OF THE TROUBLES OF THE WORLD – FROM SCIENTIFIC MATERIALISM, RATIONALISM AND LOCOISM, AS WELL AS FOR THE MODERN DETERIORATION OF THE RELIGIOUS FAITH. TO THE TRADITIONALISTIC DEPOSED GERMAN ARCHBISHOP, MARCEL LEFEBVRE, THEY (THE MASONS) WERE RESPONSIBLE FOR THE RUIN OF THE CHRISTIAN CULTURE THROUGHOUT ITS HISTORY.

INTERESTINGLY, AT FIRST GLANCE THE GERMAN ARCHBISHOP APPEARED TO BE AN EXCEPTION TO THE RULE AS THE SECOND VATICAN COUNCIL (1962-65) SET OUT TO PUT AN END TO THE DAMNATION CRAZE: "THAT NOBODY IS FORCED IN MATTERS OF RELIGION, TO ACT CONTRARY TO HIS CONSCIENCE, AND THAT CATHOLICS MAY NOW SEARCH FOR THE TRUTH THROUGH FREE RESEARCH", (THE COUNCIL'S DECLARATION OF FREEDOM OF RELIGION) QUICKLY FELL ON THE POSITIVE SIDE OF THE LEDGER, AS FAR AS GERMAN FREEMASONS WERE CONCERNED.

BY 1968, THE VATICAN OFFERED GERMAN MASONIC LODGES OPEN DISCUSSIONS THROUGH THE APOSTOLIC PROTONARY, JOHANNES B. DE TOTH. FURTHERMORE, THE VATICAN APPOINTED THEOLOGIANS, AMONG THEM, THE MUENSTER PROFESSOR FOR DOGMA, HERBERT VORGRIMLER, TOGETHER WITH A GROUP OF GERMAN FREEMASONS, THEY APPEARED TO FINALLY MANAGED TO SET ASIDE OLD PREJUDICES IN ORDER TO ARRIVE AT SOME SORT OF CONSENSUS.

Two years later, the mixed group issued the "Lichmauer Declaration" literally stating that the Papal Bulls that were issued, concerned themselves mainly with the historical significance of Freemasonry and nothing more. This 1970 declaration thusly created a lot of resistance among Church leaders, the Vatican itself suffered the brunt of the consequences. In a letter dated July 18TH, 1974 Cardinal Franjo Seper, (Perfect of the Congregation of the Roman Faith) wrote the chairman of the German Bishop's Conference: "The Excommunication Canon 2335 affects only Catholics who join societies which really work against the church. Where the Bishop's Conference determines that lodges are not anti-churchly inclined, membership for Catholics is permitted."

Needless to say, the sudden about face with the Roman Catholic Church in Germany (East and West) had dire consequences at its main headquarters in the Vatican. The Bishop's Conferences of Great Britain, the Netherlands, Scandinavia, and the United States of the America's, including Canada, no longer saw any obstacles for Catholics wishing to join Masonic Lodgery. Even in Munich a lot of rumbling was going on as Archbishop Julius Cardinal Doepfner, the chairman of the German Bishop's Conference took first positive active steps by making it possible for Freemason Ludwig-Peter von Poelnitz, (Lord of the Manor of Aschbach, Franconia, Master of the Masonic Lodge of Research Quatuor Coronati of Bayreuth) who had left the Catholic Church, and suddenly fancied Catholicism once again, to officially rejoin the Church.

In 1977, the Archbishop Johannes Joachim Degenhardt found a more advanced correlation between Freemasonry and the Catholic Church than what was commonly assumed. And by January of 1980, the Italian priest and Roman Catholic historian, Don Rosario Esposito, sketched the connections between Catholicism and Masonic Lodgery in the official Radio Vaticano in which it was depicted that an absolute and total reconciliation had taken place between both the parties involved thus verifying the fact that the Catholic Church was actually being hypocritical as to what it had been stating publically and such that good will on the Church's part was just the tool needed for the German Freemasons. Upon hearing the news of this complete correlation between the Roman Catholic Church and Freemasonry, Baron von Poelnitz cited it as being insane insisting that if the two parties in question had in fact reconciled while preaching their own separate versions of goodness

And love, and tearing themselves into pieces for centuries, then that it was all for not.

With hypocrisy being the norm for Vatican officials, the year of reconciliation between the Roman Catholic Church and Masonic Lodgery ended for the German Freemasons with two bans. In May of 1980, the Brethren were shocked by a declaration of the German Bishop's Conference regarding the question of membership of Roman Catholics in Freemasonry. Page one of the twenty page paper put the six years of bitter dialogue between German Bishops, theologians and Freemasons into one complete sentence, **"The simultaneous membership in the Catholic Church and Freemasonry is incompatible."**

German Freemasons were even more upset by the Catholic foul play maneuver than by the ban itself. What initially began in 1974 as an open dialogue between members of the Ancient Craft of Freemasonry and the Roman Catholic Church suddenly announced itself in the Bishops' paper of 1980 as being that of an inquisition. Contrary to an agreement previously arrived at, the Bishops went being the backs of colleagues and published their own viewpoints without first consulting the German Freemasons. In their judgement, the Bishops often referred to text materials which were never the subject of the discussions. In fact, the dialogue attributed to the Masonic Order was hardly ever mentioned in this devastating one sided fiasco. While the Bishop of Augsburg, as chairman of the discussion group, praised the profound accuracy and foundation of the theologian inquisitors, the Masonic participant Baron von Poelnitz, found that the theologians hardly understood anything about Freemasonry itself. As far as the Baron was concerned, they didn't really want to understand. Far fetched as it may seem, one of the Bishops, Bishop Stimpfe had called the three most conservative German Professors of Theology into the group, to which the Munich church-law expert, Audomar Scheuerman almost instantly arrived with the prejudice statement **"The excommunication of the Freemasons must be preserved in any case, I will take care of that."**

According to most German Freemasons at the time, Scheuerman had an outrageous reputation of having all kinds of absurdities collected in his head — ridiculous conspiracy theories involving Freemasonry global domination. Outlandish firm beliefs such as the FDP (Free Democratic Party of Germany) actually being nothing else than the extended arm of the Ancient Craft, which according to Professor Scheuerman himself appeared to be very evident as the advertising for all the FDP propaganda material

ALWAYS CONTAINED THREE POINTS OF PUBLIC INTEREST AND THESE SAME THREE POINTS ALSO PLAYED A VERY IMPORTANT ROLE IN THE SYMBOLISM OF FREEMASONRY. THE MOST IMPORTANT POLITICAL PARTIES IN THE FEDERAL REPUBLIC OF GERMANY WERE THE CHRISTIAN DEMOCRATIC UNION (CDU), WITH ITS BAVARIAN SISTER-PARTY THE CHRISTIAN SOCIAL UNION (CSU), THE SOCIAL DEMOCRATIC PARTY (SDP), AND OF COURSE THE FDP. AS CONFUSING AS MOST THINGS MAY SOMETIMES APPEAR, IT ACTUALLY CONFORMED WITH THE MENTALITY BY WHICH THE INVESTITURE OF POPE JOHANNES PAULS II HAD BEEN ACCUSTOMED TOO, A CHURCHLY ORCHESTRATED MISCONCEPTION. THE PROFESSOR FOR CHURCH DOGMA IN MUENSTER, PROFESSOR HERBERT VORGRIMLER, ONCE HIMSELF DELEGATED AS CONSULTANT OF THE VATICAN SECRETARIAT FOR NON-BELIEVERS TO HELP OVERSEE DISCUSSIONS WITH GERMAN FREEMASONS, LOOKED UPON THE VATICAN DECLARATION AS BEING ADDED INTO THE COLLECTION OF ABSURD BANS BY THE ROMAN CATHOLIC CHURCH OVER THE PAST CENTURIES. VORGRIMLER'S COMMENTS OBVIOUSLY FELL ON DEAF EARS: **"THE CHURCH SHOULD NOT BE WONDERING IF SHE, IN VIEW OF SUCH DECLARATIONS, WILL NO LONGER BE CONSIDERED SERIOUSLY AS A PARTNER FOR DISCUSSIONS."**

LONG BEFORE GERMAN UNIFICATION IN LATE 1990, GERMANY HAD ALREADY ESTABLISHED THREE INDEPENDENT GRAND LODGES BASED ON PHILOSOPHICAL RATHER THAN GEOGRAPHICAL DIFFERENCES – IT WAS NO ACCIDENT OF FATE THAT THE BERLIN WALL CAME CRASHING DOWN, AND IT WAS BY NO MEANS A VOTE OF DEMOCRACY THAT THE EAST AND WEST WERE JOINING FORCES AS ONE SEPARATE ENTITY. THESE THREE INDEPENDENT GRAND LODGES OF FREEMASONRY, ALONG WITH THE BRITISH GRAND LODGE AS WELL AS AN AMERICAN-CANADIAN GRAND LODGE WERE REPRESENTED IN FOREIGN RELATIONS BY A FEDERATION KNOWN AS THE UNITED GRAND LODGE OF GERMANY.

COINCIDENTLY, MASONIC LODGERY IN GERMANY DATES BACK TO 1740 WHEN THE GRAND MOTHER LODGE OF THE THREE GLOBES WAS FIRST ESTABLISHED – IT WAS AND STILL IS TO THIS VERY DAY A CHRISTIAN ORGANISM BASED UPON THE GERMAN FREEMASON ORDER. THE ECLECTIC GRAND LODGE OF FRANKFURT WAS INSTITUTED TWO YEARS LATER, ITS ONLY REQUIREMENT IS THAT MEMBERS BELIEVE IN THE EXISTENCE OF GOD, /OR AS THE MASONS THEMSELVES SO KINDLY CALL HIM, **GAOTU**; THE GREAT ARCHITECT OF THE UNIVERSE.

THE DEEP PHILOSOPHICAL SIDE IN GERMAN FREEMASONRY IS EMPHASIZED IN THE WAY IT APPEARS DESIGNED FOR GERMANY'S "ELITIST. "IT IS NOT UNUSUAL FOR A GERMAN MASONIC BROTHER TO TAKE A YEAR /OR MORE TO ADVANCE IN DEGREE, NOT SURPRISING IF ONE CONSIDERS THAT THE DELIVERY OF A LEARNED TREATISE ON SOME PHILOSOPHIC SUBJECT MUST BE MADE

BEFORE ADVANCEMENT. THE GERMAN POPULATION ULTIMATELY PERCEIVES THE MASONIC CRAFT AS BEING A GROUP OF RICH PHILOSOPHERS AND/OR PROFESSIONAL PEOPLE, AN ELITE GROUP. ADOLF HITLER'S BLACK-CLAD SCHUTZSTAFFEL, (GOOSE STEPPING SS TROOPS) FOR EXAMPLE ORIGINATED FROM THE MILITARY-RELIGIOUS-CHIVALRIC ORDERS LIKE THE KNIGHTS TEMPLAR AND THE TEUTONIC KNIGHTS OF FREEMASONRY. CANDIDATES FOR THE MASONIC SUPERIOR WHITE RACE OF HITLERISM HAD TO PROVE AT LEAST 250 YEARS OF PURE ARYAN BLOODLINES — IN THE CASE OF PROSPECTIVE OFFICERS, A COMPLETE FAMILY TREE PROVIDING THREE FULL CENTURIES HAD TO BE SUBMITTED FOR APPROVAL.

CONTRARY TO THE MYTH OF HITLERISM ACTUALLY HAVING A SPUR OF THE MOMENT IDEOLOGY FOR ITS FAITHFUL FOLLOWERS, EACH AND EVERY SS CANDIDATE WAS INTERESTINGLY ENOUGH SUBJECTED TO A RELIGIOUS TYPE INITIATION CEREMONY SIMILAR IN NATURE TO THAT OF FREEMASONRY BEFORE HE WAS TO BE ACCEPTED INTO THE GERMAN VERSION OF A NEW WORLD ORDER.

THE TWIN S'S OF HITLER'S ELITE GOOSE STEPPING FORCES, IN THE FORM OF TWO JAGGED LIGHTING-FLASHES, IN ACTUAL FACT WAS USED BY THE ANCIENT GERMANIC TRIBES SIGNIFYING THE GREAT POWERS OF THE GODS; FRATERNAL LIGHTING BOLTS OF THE STORM GOD **THOR**. THOR'S GREAT WEAPON OF DESTRUCTION /OR FORCE WAS THE MIOLNER, THE HAMMER WHICH ACCORDING TO LEGEND HAD THE MARVELOUS PROPERTY OF INVARIABLY RETURNING TO ITS OWNER AFTER HAVING BEEN LAUNCHED UPON ITS MISSION AND HAVING PERFORMED ITS WORK OF DESTRUCTION. IN YET ANOTHER TWIST OF FATE, DURING THE MANY YEARS PRIOR TO THE BERLIN WALL FIRST BEING CONSTRUCTED ON AUGUST 13TH, 1961 BY EAST GERMANY, THE GERMAN DEMOCRATIC REPUBLIC OF EAST GERMANY ENDED UP FLYING A MASONIC ORIENTED FLAG CONSISTING OF A COMPASS AND THE FRATERNAL HAMMER OF THOR'S FORCE.

WHILE HITLER'S GOOSE STEPPING BLACK-CLAD SCHUTZSTAFFEL SS TROOPS WORE THE TWIN LIGHTENING BOLTS OF THE STORM GOD **THOR**, HIS WAFFEN SS TROOPS PARADED AROUND WITH A SKULL AND CROSS-BONES INSIGNIA ON THE COLLAR OF THEIR UNIFORMS. ACCORDING TO THE MASONIC ORDER'S OWN LITERATURE, THIS PROUDLY DISPLAYED INSIGNIA NOT ONLY SYMBOLIZED MORTALITY AND DEATH BUT WAS OFTEN USED BY FRATERNITY MEMBERS TO PUBLICIZE THE LONG LIFE ACHIEVEMENTS OF THE DEARLY DEPARTED — THEREFORE ASSISTING THEM INTO THE LIFE OF THE HEREAFTER. FURTHER TO THIS RATHER INTERESTING REVELATION AS A WAY AND MEANS OF EXPRESSION TO HELP EXTENUATE THE MINDS OF THE LIVING, THE SKULL AND CROSS-BONES INSIGNIA WAS ALSO INCORPORATED WITHIN THE FRENCH AND SCOTTISH RITES OF FREEMASONRY AND ALL THOSE OTHER DEGREES ASSOCIATED WITH THE

PRELIMINARY CEREMONIES OF INITIATION INTO THE ANCIENT CRAFT AS THE SKULL ITSELF WAS REPORTEDLY A SYMBOL IN THE MASONIC TEMPLARS ALSO DATING BACK THOUSANDS OF YEARS. MODERN DAY ENTITIES OF THE KNIGHTS TEMPLAR PUBLICALLY DENOUNCE THIS AS BEING A TRUE FACT OF THEIR RITUALISTIC CEREMONIES AND QUICKLY PROFESS THAT THEIR PREDECESSORS WERE DEEPLY INVOLVED WITH THE CRIME OF IDOLATRY AND INSTANTLY STATE THAT THE SKULL IS MERELY A SYMBOLIC DESIGN AND NOTHING MORE.

STRANGE AS IT MAY SEEM, ANOTHER INTERESTING QUIRK OF HISTORY THAT MOST HISTORIANS WERE NOT WILLING TO TALK ABOUT WAS THE FACT THAT ALL OF HITLER'S SS PERSONNEL WERE ENCOURAGED TO CONCEIVE THEIR OFFSPRING ON THE TOMBSTONES OF NOBLE "ARYANS. "THIS WAS LARGELY DUE TO THE BELIEF THAT IF CHILDREN WERE CONCEIVED IN GRAVEYARDS, THERE WOULD BE CLOSE CONTACT WITH THE SPIRITS OF THE DEAD. IN THE WORLD OF ANCIENT CRAFT FREEMASONRY, THE EGYPTIAN BOOK OF THE DEAD IS BETTER KNOWN AS THE BOOK OF THE MASTERS — CONTAINING THE ANCIENT EGYPTIAN PHILOSOPHY AS TO THE DEATH AND THE RESURRECTION THEREOF. APPARENTLY, A GOOD PORTION OF THESE SACRED WRITINGS WERE INVARIABLY BURIED WITH THE DEAD IN ORDER TO ASSIST THEM IN THE NEXT LIFE AND WITHIN THE CONTENTS OF THE EGYPTIAN BOOK OF THE DEAD, THERE EXIST AN UNQUESTIONABLE TIE WHICH BINDS FREEMASONRY TO THE NOBLEST OF THE CULTS AND MYSTERIES OF ANTIQUITY.

COINCIDENTLY, THE WORD FASCISM COMES FROM THE ITALIAN WORD "FASCIO "– REFERRING TO AN ANCIENT ROMAN SYMBOL OF AUTHORITY WHICH WAS AN APT SYMBOL OF THE UNITY OF THE PEOPLE UNDER THE SUPREME AUTHORITY OF THE STATE AND IN FREEMASONRY, THE SUPREME AUTHORITY IS THAT OF DOGMATIC POWER FROM WHOSE DECISIONS THERE IS ABSOLUTELY NO APPEAL. AT THE CLOSE OF THE SECOND WORLD WAR IN 1945, THE ALLIED FORCES ASSUMED GOVERNMENTAL POWER IN GERMANY "SUPREME AUTHORITY." FOUR YEARS LATER, THE FEDERAL REPUBLIC OF GERMANY WAS CREATED. THE TERRITORY WHICH BECAME THE SOVIET-OCCUPIED ZONE OF EAST GERMANY IN 1945 WAS GIVEN THE NAME OF THE GERMAN DEMOCRATIC REPUBLIC AND WAS GIVEN SOVEREIGN POWER OVER ITS FEDERAL AREA. AND IN 1959, THE FEDERAL REPUBLIC OF WEST GERMANY WAS THUSLY INCORPORATED AS YET ANOTHER MASONIC GOVERNMENT CONTROLLED STRONGHOLD. WITH THIS FREEMASONRY COLLABORATION, AN EVER INCREASING FORM OF ANIMOSITY SOON EMERGED AS BOTH EAST AND WEST NEEDED TO IRON OUT THEIR FRATERNAL DIFFERENCES OF OPINION AS THE YEAR 2000 WAS DRAWING CLOSER WITH EACH BRICK THAT WAS BEING PLACED ON THE BERLIN WALL IN ORDER TO DRIVE A WEDGE BETWEEN THEM EVEN FURTHER. IT WOULD TAKE NEARLY 30 YEARS FOR THE MASONIC BROTHERHOODS OF EAST GERMANY AND WEST GERMANY TO EVENTUALLY HAVE THE WALL REMOVED AFTER RECONCILING

THEIR FRATERNAL DIFFERENCES. ON OCTOBER 3RD, 1990 HELMUT KOHL BECAME THE FIRST CHANCELLOR OF BOTH GERMANIES SINCE HITLER'S RISE TO POWER IN 1933.

AT THE END OF THE NAZI REGIME'S REIGN OF TERROR, THE NUREMBERG TRIALS WERE HELD WHERE IN WHICH VARIOUS MEMBERS OF HITLER'S MILITARY MEN WERE TO RECEIVE THEIR JUDGEMENT PAPERS. SOME WERE ACQUITTED, WHILE OTHERS WERE ORDERED TO BE EXECUTED BY WAY OF HANGING /OR SENTENCED TO SERVE TIME IN PRISON; FROM LIFE SENTENCES TO 10 /OR 20 YEARS OF INCARCERATION. THE CHIEF PROSECUTOR AT THE NUREMBERG TRIALS WAS NONE OTHER THAN FREEMASONRY BROTHER ROBERT H. JACKSON, WHO AT THE TIME OF THE TRIBUNAL WAS AN ACTIVE MEMBER OF MOUNT MORIAH LODGE NO. 145 IN JAMESTOWN, NEW YORK. AS PRESIDENT OF THE UNITED STATES, FRATERNITY BROTHER HARRY S. TRUMAN REPORTEDLY APPROVED THE APPOINTMENT OF OTHER KNOWN MEMBERS OF THE ANCIENT CRAFT OF FREEMASONRY TO SIT ON THE TRIBUNAL BOARD THAT WAS GOING TO BE PASSING JUDGEMENT ON THE NAZI WAR CRIMINALS.

RIGHT AFTER THE SECOND WORLD WAR, WESTERN CIVILIZATION FACED YET ANOTHER CRISIS — THE SO-CALLED MENACE OF SOVIET COMMUNISM. IN DESCRIBING THE SCHISM BETWEEN COMMUNISM AND THE ANCIENT CRAFT OF FREEMASONRY, MASONIC ORDER LITERATURE DATED THE LATE 1940'S SAID IT BEST:

"IT IS A CHALLENGE THAT CANNOT BE DENIED OR IGNORED, AND ONE THAT CONFRONTS US IN EVERY PHASE AND ASPECT OF LIFE AND ACTIVITY. IT IS THE AGE-OLD STRUGGLE BETWEEN TYRANNY AND FREEDOM. OUR WORLD IS A BATTLEFIELD WHERE TWO IRRECONCILABLE SETS OF IDEAS, TWO PHILOSOPHIES OF LIFE AND GOVERNMENT, CONTEND FOR INTELLECTUAL SUPREMACY. OUR FUNDAMENTAL VALUES AND BELIEFS, THE CORNERSTONES ON WHICH WE HAVE ERECTED THE EDIFICE OF OUR CIVILIZATION, ARE UNDER ATTACK. THE FIGHT IS CAPTURE THE MINDS OF MEN; AND EACH PHILOSOPHY IS STRIVING MIGHTILY TO WIN OUR MENTAL ACCEPTANCE AND ALLEGIANCE."

AT THE TIME, NON-MASONS MAY HAVE BEEN EXCUSED FOR QUESTIONING THE MASONIC ORDER'S DEMOCRATIC PHILOSOPHY OF BOTH LIFE AND GOVERNMENT AS IT WAS DEEPLY ROOTED IN THE BASIC AFFIRMATIONS OF THE CHRISTIAN FAITH; THE SOVEREIGNTY OF GOD, THE ESSENTIAL DIGNITY AND WORTH OF THE INDIVIDUAL, AND THE SUPREMACY OF THE OBJECTIVE MORAL LAW. COMMUNISM AND THE THREAT OF IT, APPARENTLY MEANT A VIRTUAL SET BACK FOR AMERICAN FREEMASONRY AND THEIR DREAMS OF WORLD DOMINATION AS THE SOVIET FREEMASONS BROKE AWAY FROM THE PACT AND DECIDED TO GO OUT ON THEIR OWN.

According to Roman Catholic Church historians, at the outbreak of the Cold War, (as the threat of the so-called Communist menace was called back then), the majority of the Soviet Union's political power structure consisted principally of Jewish leaders who were acting in allegiance with the Masonic secret societies and had been totally financed with Jewish money. And while working in absolute secrecy from within the Bolsheviki Revolution of 1905 and onwards, the Jewish leaders along with their other Masonic Brethren were able to maintain political control of the masses; the basic fundamental building blocks of an International Jewish Masonic Conspiracy in accordance as to how the Vatican perceived it as being!!!

One of the Catholic Church's most recognized historians, Rev. E. Cahill, in fact stated in his published 1932 book **THE FRAMEWORK OF A CHRISTIAN STATE** that the Masonic Order along with its Jewish international financiers controlled both the media and the cinema of the United States, England, Germany and France. The Rev. Cahill went on referring to "the Press and Cinema as instruments of Masonic propaganda "as well as being part of "the anti- Catholic movement "that the Bolshevik influence (Socialism and/or Communism) had over the masses. Which in itself raises the question as to whether /or not Joseph McCarthy initially got the idea of going on his Communist hunting expedition from Cahill's published literary works. Afterall, McCarthy was said to have been a devoted Christian as well as having an outlandish Freemasonry tolerance when it came down to government held positions and according to Roman Catholic Church historian Cahill, any form of Communism was anti-Catholic while being Masonic in nature.

During Joseph McCarthy's witch hunt on known members of the Communist Party, February of 1950 until his death in 1957, Freemasonry was the central enemy of the Catholic Church and/ or everything Catholic in design – from Catholic governments to Catholic institutions throughout the world. The Church itself feared the ultimate establishing of a worldwide Masonic State that was in direct conflict with the instituting of a Roman Catholic State. According to the Catholic Church, the Communist regime of the Soviet Union was controlled entirely by people of the Jewish faith, since at that time period, Communist Russia contained a large of the world's Jewish population and further to this, the Church also believed that the Jewish people were at the center of all the subversive movements of past centuries. The Roman Catholic

Church even blamed subversive Jews for the establishing of many secret societies and fraternities worldwide. Perhaps this is why the Catholic Church sat back in silence while Adolf Hitler exterminated an estimated 6 million Jews during the Second World War, (1939-45). Afterall, Hitler was doing the work of the Catholic Church by reportedly ridding the world of the Jewish menace that Vatican officials supposedly feared the most. As far as the Roman Catholic Church was concerned, when Hitler first invaded Poland in 1939 which provoked the Second World War – the chief governmental officials of the Soviet Union were of the Jewish persuasion thus still possessing a deep seeded threat to Catholicism. Ever since then, the Vatican has been drastically watering down the true events of the Second World War and continually deny their rhetoric of anti-Semitism. That is to say until the Vatican anointed the first ever Polish Jew to the prestigious portfolio of being the Pontiff in 1978, (Karol Josep Woltyla of Wadowice, Poland). Pope John Paul II was also the first non-Italian pope to attain the Pontiff in over 450 years. In the true Roman Catholic fashion, all is well with the world once a parishioner's past sins are forgiven!!!

As the Roman Catholic Church continued sitting on its hands while Adolf Hitler prepared himself to exterminate millions of Jews during his many years of terror, Church officials condemned Freemasonry as being a growing cancer on society that was not to be tolerated and further urged all of its congregation members to stand up in defiance to the Masonic fraternity. Ironically, while all of this religious nonsense was going on, the Catholic Church was also busy making further allegations that the Ancient fraternal Order of Freemasonry had been corrupting and severely perverting the minds of the uninformed with shameful hypocrisies and lies of its origin. The Catholic Church even went so far as to stipulate that the Masonic league of instruction was to de-Christianize the Catholic State with its propaganda thus giving them (the Church) no other alternative but to once again remind all Catholics that they were prohibited from entering the Masonic Order /or giving it any assistance and/or support under the severe pain of being excommunicated.

Although the Roman Catholic Church has always seen itself as being the supreme power on a global scale, in the United States it took a back seat as the U.S. Supreme Court was the brain child of various members of the Ancient Craft of Freemasonry. This high end judiciary system was first conceived on May 29TH, 1787 when

Edmund Randolph (at the time, he was the Grand Master of Masons in Virginia and subsequently the nation's very first Attorney-General) rose to his feet at the Convention in Philadelphia to introduce the so-called Virginia Plan. This proposal interestingly called for a National Government composed of three co-equal branches; a legislature, an executive office and a judiciary system. It wasn't however, until several months later that an agreement was actually formulated. Under the Virginia Plan, the judiciary (as well as the executive) was to be chosen by the legislature. This naturally provoked a counterproposal that the selection be made by the executive officers of the White House. After a rather lengthy argument, octogenarian Benjamin Franklin, the saga of the Convention, offered an alternative solution to help ease Freemasonry tensions. Franklin recommended that his fellow delegation members (most of whom were lawyers) consider the traditional practice used in Scotland, where judges were ultimately nominated by members of the legal profession.

In the end, the U.S. Federal judiciary system was to be nominated by the executive and confirmed by the upper house of the legislature and was therefore written into the American Constitution as such. The Virginia Plan was also to provide the judiciary, as well as the executive, "with the revisionary power to review and invalidate acts of the legislature. "This of course was survived only in the form of "the Presidential veto. "Thus, the principle of judicial review was not expressly incorporated in the Constitution — it essentially remained in the hands of the Supreme Court itself to assume whether /or not this right was going to be executed in accordance to the law of the land.

Other Masonic friendly authors of the U.S. Constitution were Nicholas Gilman, Rufus King, David Brearly, William Paterson, Jona Dayton, Gunning Bedford Jr., John Dickinson, Jaco Broom, James McHenry, Daniel Carroll, John Blair, and of course George Washington, Thomas Jefferson and Ben Franklin. Furthermore, during the American Revolution for Independence from England, thirty-three General Officers held Freemasonry memberships. Of these, 16 were Brigadier Generals, 12 were Major Generals and five were Brigadiers who were breveted Major Generals before the war's end. The Brigadier Generals were Dayton, Gist, Greaton, Glover, Hand, Hogan, Maxwell, Mercer, Montgomery, Parsons, Rufas Putnam, Summer, Thompson, Varnum, Williams and Woodford. And those who were Brigadiers and then breveted to Major Generals were Muhlenberg, Nixon, Paterson, Stark and Weedon. The Major Generals were Arnold (before he turned traitor to the Masonic cause), Frye, Knox, Lafayette, Lincoln (who received the surrender at Yorktown), Herkimer, Parsons, Israel Putnam, St. Clair, von Steuben and Wooster.

On June 14TH, 1777 the Masonic controlled U.S. Congress declared the colors of their flag, the national anthem followed many years later. Ironically, the second verse of the Star Spangled Banner exposes the Freemasonry concept of global conquest for all to see as it contains the words "Then conquer we must, when our cause it is just; and this is our motto: **IN GOD IS OUR TRUST**. "In evaluating the Masonic influences on the U.S. White House, it is also interesting to note that during the early American formative years, which coincidently included the last decade of the Eighteenth Century and nearly all of the following century, Presidents who were Master Masons occupied the Oval Office 34 percent of the time. And during the entire Twentieth Century, the White House was occupied by practicing Freemasons 80 percent of the time. It should further be stated that during this same time period, (the Twentieth Century), the fraternity enjoyed its greatest growth and influence in the nation as well as around the world.

In properly analyzing the Masonic Order's own fraternity literature dated during the mid-1970's: "Fourteen Presidents and eighteen Vice-Presidents of the United States were Masons, including a majority of the Justices of the United Supreme Court, of the Governors of States, of the members of the Senate, and a large percentage of the Congressmen. Five Chief Justices of the United States were Masons and two were Grand Masters. The five were Oliver Ellsworth, John Marshal (also Grand Master of Masons in Virginia), William Howard Taft, Frederick M. Vinson and Earl Warren (also Grand Master of Masons in California)."

Other world famous members of the Ancient Craft of Freemasonry included Will Rogers, Simon Bolivar, James Boswell, Robbie Burns, King Edward VII, King George VI, Rudyard Kipling, Lord Kitchener, Giuseppe Mazzini, Jose Rizal, Cecil J. Rhodes, Sir Walter Scott, Jean Sibelius, Voltaire, John Molson (the Provincial Grand Master of Masons in the Province of Quebec), Sir George Prevost, Sir John Johnson (the Provincial Grand Master of Masons in Canada a.k.a. Ontario), the Masonic list of Freemasonry influence goes on and on. Among some of its members were well known astronauts of the Twentieth Century; Edwin E. Aldrin Jr., Donn F. Eisele, Leroy

Gordon Cooper, Virgil I. Grissom, Edgar D. Mitchell, Walter M. Schirra Jr., Thomas P. Stafford, Paul J. Weitz and James B. Irwin.

Further to this, according to the 1987 Freemasonry statistics: "It is estimated there are six million Masons worldwide, of which about three million reside in the United States. While there are no accurate figures available, it is believed there may have been as many as 100 million men over the past 300 years that have taken the vows of Masonry."

The many ancient mysteries of the Masonic Order are oddly enough incorporated within its most sacred book depicting the Three Great Lights of their antiquity; the Volume of Sacred Law, the Square and the Compasses, and of course the sacred writings that are understood to be revered by the individual Mason themselves. Contrary as to what many religious institutions may state as being a true fact of history (Protestants and Catholics alike), the Holy Bible is the most sacred book in both American and Canadian Freemasonry. In North America and most parts of Europe, it's the King James version of the Bible. The Holy Scriptures therefore contain the Three Great Lights of the secret ancient Order dating back thousands of years before Christ. In accordance to the Masonic doctrine, knowledge is power and each individual is encouraged to embrace it as they go on with their daily lives and become better human beings because of it. Although Freemasonry is said to be Satanic in nature by all forms of religion, each of its candidates are required to believe in God and the supreme power thereof. If the individual who wants to become a Mason does not believe in the existence of the Supreme Being, then, he /or she cannot be accepted into the ancient mystical Craft. In other words, atheists need not apply!!!

Notwithstanding, in accordance to many religious institutions within western civilization, the letter "G "that is incorporated within the compass and square of the Masonic Order's very own symbol (the Great Architect Of The Universe) is supposedly that of Satan when in fact it actually stands for **GOD** and its great strength, wisdom and beauty. Any other interpretation by the religious moral majority in the western hemisphere is pure religious rubbish as they (the religious moral majority members) are merely playing their part in adding more confusion to the issue in a desperate attempt to help conceal what is actually playing out behind the political scenes. Added confusion therefore enables numerous pieces of this gigantic puzzle to be spread out all over hell's creation as a way and means of desensitizing the North American citizenry.

In an attempt to fully understand the politics involved, one must first realize that politics is money, and with money comes power. For example; on the American one dollar bill, Masonic Brother George Washington is on the front, turn the bill over and the entire Freemasonry concept is at your immediate disposal. On the right, the shielded eagle holds the Illuninatus banner in its beak: **"E PLURIBUS UNUM"**, Latin meaning: **"ONE OUT OF MANY."** The eagle is also clutching 13 arrows in one claw and an olive branch containing 13 leaves in the other, supposedly symbolizing the Congressional powers of its administration. Above the head of the great American bird is a cloud with which a constellation of 13 stars. To the left of the Yankee bill is a 13 stepped pyramid with its top separated and an eye encased within it. This pyramid is supposedly a representation of the strength of the American Union and it is protected by the eye of God. The eye in fact represents the Masonic All-Seeing Eye which symbolizes God as he reportedly see's all and everything that is around him.

As Adolf Hitler and his fascist regime was slowly being elevated to power in Germany during the early 1930's, the American Masonic institution of Franklin D. Roosevelt (himself being a 32ND degree Master Mason at the time) authorized the usage of the Ancient Craft's All-Seeing Eye on the Yankee one dollar bill. It was ultimately a time period in U.S. history where in which a large number of American Freemasons on the North American Continent felt totally threatened by the schism activities that their German Brethren were performing on a grand scale and therefore because of it, became active members of the Illuminati as a way and means of keeping fraternity members in check throughout the western free-world.

In accordance to the Ancient Craft of Freemasonry and its membership of Illuminoids, the Masonic All-Seeing Eye actually pervades the inmost recesses of the human heart, and rewards its members according to their own merit. At the pyramid's base on the American one dollar bill in Roman numerals is the date 1776, the year that the U.S. Declaration of Independence was first instituted. At the top of the pyramid are the words: **"ANNUIT COEPTIS"**, once again Latin, meaning **"IT FAVORS OUR UNDERTAKING"**, while the bottom contains the Freemasonry motto: **"NOVUS ORDO SECLORUM** "identical to both times previously, Latin for the words enterprising the **"NEW ORDER OF THE AGES."**

The United States national emblem, the "American Eagle" contains 13 letters in its formation, the Mace in the House of Representatives is made of 13 rods of ebony fastened together by silver. The motto: **Annuit Coeptis** has 13 letters, as does the Freemasonry banner: **E Pluribus Unum**. America's shielded Illuminati eagle, a symbol of antiquity and power, has 13 feathers on its tail. According to Freemasonry theology, the eagle is also a symbol of Christ in His Divine character. For this reason, the American eagle has a direct link with **GOD**. The basic design of the Yankee one dollar bill for all intended purposes was reportedly approved by the Masonically controlled U.S. Congress on June 20TH, 1782.

Further to all of this, the Great Seal of America is characterized by the number 13 for a specific reason. When the U.S. of A. was originally conceived by members of the Ancient Craft of Freemasonry, thirteen U.S. States had already been initiated into the Masonic Family fold. Namely; Massachusetts, New Hampshire, Rhode Island, Connecticut, New York, New Jersey, Pennsylvania, Delaware, Maryland, Virginia, North Carolina, South Carolina, and Georgia. The American Declaration of Independence was signed by all thirteen of these Freemasonry stronghold States. The U.S. First Naval Fleet reportedly consisted of 13 ships, America's first independent national flag had 13 stars and 13 strips, and when first hoisted in dedication to their actual independent existence from England, a 13 gun saluted was said to have had taken place to help commemorate the festive occasion — one sounding gun echo for each U.S. State.

Ironically, while still seeking their independence from England, the American flag of Stars and Stripes was named the Grand Union and strange as it may seem, had the British Union Jack in its upper left corner, as did many colonial countries at the time. In accordance to British Freemasonry, the Union Jack and its blue color also represented the blue of Israel's national color. The nation of Israel was commanded to wear a ribbon of blue throughout its existence as a token of remembrance of God's eternal being, blue standing for faithfulness to the Almighty and His Supreme Powers. Red symbolizing the blood that was to be shed to protect the British Motherland, white naturally symbolizing the country's purity. Hence, the nation of Great Britain and a company of nations; Dominion of Canada, Commonwealth of Australia, Union of South Africa, Dominion of New Zealand, and yes, including the United

States of America were all colonial nations of the British Empire at one time /or another.

In reality, the thirteen steps up the pyramid, the thirteen stars, the thirteen leaves, the thirteen feathers and the thirteen arrows are in fact a representation of the Masonic Council of Thirteen, otherwise known as the Supreme Council Mother Jurisdiction Of The World /or simply put, Mother Council Of The World. These leaders of the Illuminati reportedly met once a year to discuss world affairs and their advancement within it.

Under Freemasonry terms, the severed top of the pyramid on the Yankee one dollar bill "the chief corner-stone "is actually a symbolic gesture referring to God's masterplan of establishing a "**New World Order** "through the Second Coming of Christ. Jesus Christ of course being the great antitype of the pyramid's top-stone, God's Divine Plan for all humanity. In the Holy Bible, Christ supposedly refers to Himself as "the stone which the builders rejected. "(Mark 12, 10). Ironically, in the same verse of these Scriptures, the Lord thy God reportedly describes the stone's position as "the head of the corner." Hence, the top-stone of the pyramid became the head honcho "chief corner-stone "of the American made new age movement. This can easily be verified by reading Apostle Paul's declaration in Ephesians 2, 20-21 where in which it is ironically stated"... Jesus Christ Himself being the chief corner-stone in whom all the building fitly framed together groweth unto an holy temple in the Lord."

In reviewing much of the Freemasonry literature, "the corner-stone does not appear to have been adopted by any of the heathen nations. "The symbolism of the corner-stone when duly laid with Masonic rites is essentially a corner-stone of immortality, "an emanation from that Divine Spirit which pervades all nature, and which, therefore, must survive the tomb, and rise, triumphant and eternal, above the decaying dust of death and the grave. "According to ancient Egyptian philosophy, "Book of the Dead", the pyramid is an "emblem of rule."

When the American Freemasons broke away from the Grand Lodge of England, they initially wanted to have absolutely nothing to do with British Freemasonry as they, (the Americans), also had visions of controlling the world. To that end, the United States national emblem, the American Masonic eagle having thirteen feathers on its tail thusly symbolizes the ultimate antiquity and power of the American breed Illuminati. And since the eagle is also a symbol

OF CHRIST AND HIS DIVINE POWERS, THE MASONIC EAGLE IS THEREFORE CONSTITUTED AS HAVING A DIRECT LINK TO THE ALMIGHTY GOD HIMSELF.

ACCORDING TO ANCIENT EGYPTIAN PYRAMID WRITINGS, (SOUTH WALL OF THE SUBTERRANEAN CAVITY) IT IS STATED THAT SATAN WAS TO BE ILLUMINATED FROM THE EARTH BETWEEN THE YEARS 1953 TO 1994 : "SATANIC POWER AND EVIL INFLUENCES WILL BE COMPLETELY RESTRAINED IS MARKED BY THE EXTREME END OF THE DEAD END PASSAGE. "THE DATE JANUARY 28TH, 1994 WAS THUS GIVEN AS TO WHEN ALL OF SATAN'S POWERS WERE TO BE ENTIRELY REMOVED FROM THE WORLD. IN A SURPRISING TWIST OF FATE, THE INSCRIBED ETCHING ALSO HAD A FURTHER SYMBOLIC MEANING FOR MEMBERS OF THE ANCIENT CRAFT OF FREEMASONRY – THE YEAR 1994 WAS EXACTLY 6,000 YEARS AFTER 4007 B.C. WHICH WAS SUPPOSEDLY THE DATE THAT ADAM AND EVE WERE IN THE GARDEN OF EDEN.

ALTHOUGH BOTH AMERICAN AND BRITISH FREEMASONS FIRMLY BELIEVED THAT THEY WERE IN FACT THE DIRECT DESCENDANTS OF CHRIST, ISRAEL IS RECOGNIZED AS BEING GOD'S NATION; BY BIBLICAL PROPHECY, GOD'S ISRAEL. KING GEORGE VI FOR EXAMPLE, ALLEGEDLY WAS ABLE TO TRACE HIS FAMILY TREE TO THE BIBLICAL KING DAVID OF ISRAEL. HER MAJESTY, QUEEN ELIZABETH (PARTS I AND II), LIKEWISE SO ILLUSTRIOUSLY ENDORSED THIS LINKAGE WITH KING DAVID OF THE BIBLE. THUS THE ROYAL CRY, GOD SAVE THE KING AND/OR QUEEN HAS A MUCH STRONGER MEANING TO THOSE OF LOYAL UNDERSTANDING TO THE BRITISH MONARCHY. IN THE EYES OF THE BRITISH-ISRAELITES, THE MONARCHY AND ITS ROYAL HOUSE IS ESSENTIALLY THE HOUSE OF KING DAVID. HENCE, MAKING THE ROYAL THRONE THE ACTUAL THRONE OF DAVID. AS FAR AS THE ROYAL MONARCHY WAS CONCERNED, JESUS CHRIST THROUGH HIS MOTHER IS A DIRECT DESCENDANT OF KING DAVID. JOSEPH, THE HUSBAND OF MARY, THE MOTHER OF JESUS, WAS LIKEWISE THE SAME, OF THE HOUSE AND LINEAGE OF DAVID, (LUKE 2, 4). FURTHERMORE, IN ACCORDANCE TO THE HOLY SCRIPTURES, THERE ARE TWO LINES OF DESCENT THAT CAN BE EASILY TRACED DOWN TO JESUS CHRIST FROM HIS ANCESTOR, KING DAVID, (ONE IN MATTHEW 1, 1-17, AND THE OTHER IN LUKE 3, 23-38).

IT IS FOR THIS REASON THAT THE BRITISH UNION JACK HAS SPECIAL MEANING FOR THOSE WHO UNDERSTAND BIBLICAL TEXT, "JACK "IN ENGLISH, "JACQUES "IN FRENCH, "JACOB "IN HEBREW; HENCE THE "UNION JACK "BEING EQUIVALENT TO A "UNITED JACOB "OF ISRAEL – JACOB BEING OF COURSE A DIRECT DESCENDANT OF BOTH CHRIST AND GREAT BRITAIN. IN USING BIBLICAL PROPHECY OF THE HOLY SCRIPTURES, IT IS SAID TO BE WRITTEN THAT; THE LORD GOD SHALL GIVE ONTO HIM (MEANING CHRIST) THE THRONE OF HIS FATHER DAVID; AND HE SHALL REIGN OVER THE HOUSE OF JACOB FOREVER MORE AND THAT IN HIS KINGDOM THERE SHALL BE NO END, (LUKE 1, 31-32).

Further to this, the King James version of the Bible is also quoted as saying: "At that time they shall call Jerusalem the throne of the **LORD**; and all nations shall be gathered unto it. "(Jeremiah 3, 17).

Only the misinformed ask as to why the Bible occupies itself as having a prominent place in national ceremonies worldwide. For instance, even before the political proceedings can begin in the British House of Commons as well as in the House of Lords, the 67th Psalm is always read thus elevating all of the British-Israelites even closer to their **GOD** given right of occupying the Throne of David.

Biblically, the number thirteen dates back to the "Twelve Tribes of Israel. "There were actually thirteen tribes, the Tribe of Joseph was originally split into two separate tribes; the Tribes of Ephraim and Manasseh. "The birthright was Joseph's "(1 Chronicles 5, 2) but with the division of the Tribe of Joseph, it was passed onto the Ephraim sect in particular for God supposedly had stated, "Ephraim is my first born." (Jeremiah 31, 9).

The evidence on hand notwithstanding the fact that Ephraim was also said to be the last born of all the thirteen tribal heads. In reality, the Holy Scriptures have many flaws within it since the tribes of Ephraim and Manasseh were actually adopted as two distinct entities after the rest were born, and since God supposedly set Ephraim up as a tribe before Manasseh; Manasseh is thusly constituted as being the thirteenth tribe of Israel. Plus in accordance to Masonic philosophy, it's a well known fact that the number 13 is stamped upon American history for that precise reason as they too see themselves as having Biblical rights to the Throne of David. And just like British Freemasonry, the American Master Masons also firmly believed by Biblical prophecy of the Holy Scriptures that they were the chosen people to sit at the right hand of God and therefore having the Lord thy God's ultimate blessings for the acquisition of the Throne of David. It is for this reason, and this reason alone that the American Freemasonry symbols have designated the number 13 of having divine powers as it by their own interpretation has a significant Biblical meaning.

Being a deeply devoted atheist, the whole thing is fickle no matter which way Biblical text is being interpreted for the self-serving interest of others!!!

Much like the United States, British Freemasons also wanted to laid claim to the Throne of David at any cost to human life. In fact, a large percentage of North America's closest fraternal political

ALLIES IN ENGLAND WERE OF THE UPPER ECHELONS PERSUASION OF THE MOST UNHOLY MASONIC ALLIANCES THAT WAS EVER FORMED AT THE DAWNING OF THE 21ST CENTURY AND CONTINUED TO THRIVE FOR MANY YEARS THEREAFTER. THIS FRATERNITY ALLIANCE OF THE 1990'S DECADE INCLUDED SUCH VERY HIGH PROFILE PROMINENT POLITICAL FIGURES AS THE RIGHT HONORABLE LORD CORNWALLIS (PRO GRAND MASTER FOR ENGLAND), THE RT. HON. LORD SWANSEA (PROVINCIAL GRAND MASTER FOR SOUTH WALES), THE RT. HON. LORD BURNHAN (PROVINCIAL GRAND MASTER FOR BUCKINGHAMSHIRE), THE RT. HON. THE EARL OF ELINTON AND WINTON (PRESIDENT OF THE MASONIC TRUST FOR GIRLS AND BOYS), THE RT. HON. LORD FARNHAM (ASSISTANT GRAND MASTER FOR ENGLAND), SIR LEONARD BARFORD (PROVINCIAL GRAND MASTER FOR SUSSEX), SIR KENNETH NEWTON (THE PRESIDENT OF THE MASONIC BOARD OF GENERAL PURPOSES), SIR JOHN WELCH (PRESIDENT OF GRAND CHARITY), HIS ROYAL HIGHNESS PRINCE MICHAEL, THE DUKE OF KENT (RE-ELECTED GRAND MASTER FOR ENGLAND) AND MANY, MANY MORE OF ENGLAND'S NOBILITY FACTIONS. PAST GRAND OFFICERS THAT OF WHOM DIED BETWEEN THE YEARS 1987 AND 1989 SWEARING ALLEGIANCE TO THE UNHOLY MASONIC ALLIANCE INCLUDED; SIR JOHN C. STEBBINGS, SIR ALAN ADAIR, THE REVEREND DOCTOR R.L. MACQUEEN, THE REVD. JOSEPH W. MARTINDALE, THE REVD. CANON JOHN R. LEWIS, THE REVD. ERIC H. MOSELEY, DOCTOR S. GUYER, DOCTOR A.H. BRIGGS, AND MANY OTHER HIGH RANKING INDIVIDUALS OF THE BRITISH INTELLIGENTSIA CITIZENRY.

ACCORDING TO BRITISH FREEMASONRY STATISTICS, MASONIC LODGERY HAD MANAGED TO STABILIZE ITSELF DURING THE LAST DECADE OF THE TWENTIETH CENTURY. FOR EXAMPLE, IN 1979, THERE WERE A REPORTED 1,679 LODGES IN THE LONDON AREA, AND TEN YEARS LATER, THAT NUMBER HAD BEEN DECREASED BY ONLY FIVE. IN THAT SAME YEAR, (1979), THE PROVINCIAL JURISDICTION TALLIED 5,568 MASONIC LODGES BUT THAT FIGURE HAD MANAGED TO INCREASE ITSELF TO 5,906 IN 1989 – IN 1979, AN ADDITIONAL 778 LODGES WERE OUTSIDE THE PROVINCIAL JURISDICTIONAL BOUNDARIES OF ENGLAND. THEREFORE, IN TOTAL 8,025 BRITISH FREEMASONRY LODGES EXISTED DURING THE YEAR 1979 AND TEN YEARS THEREAFTER, IT HAD BEEN INCREASED TO 8,358. AND ACCORDING TO THE 1989 STATISTICS, THERE WERE AN ESTIMATED 600,000 MEMBERS LISTED AS BEING ON THE MEMBERSHIP ROSTER OF ENGLAND WHILE NEW SOUTH WALES WAS SAID TO HAVE HAD A REPORTED 654 LODGES WITH 53,325 REGISTERED MEMBERS. FURTHERMORE, IN 1979, THERE WERE 17,336 GRAND LODGE CERTIFICATES ISSUED BY THE GRAND LODGE OF ENGLAND. BY 1989, THE WORLDWIDE BRITISH DISTRIBUTION FACTOR DECREASED ITSELF TO 13,520 GRAND LODGES UNDER ENGLISH COLONIAL RULE.

In accordance to the 1989 Masonic data, Scotland had over 481 overseas Lodges while England itself had more than 807. Under the Jurisdiction of the Grand Lodge of England, there were well over 344 Masonic Lodges in South Africa alone. At the time, South African President de Klerk's Freemasonry Lodge "De Broederbond No. 17 "was located in Pretoria. Other established fraternity Lodgery that was under the direct control of the Grand Lodge of England included; India with 331 well established Lodges, New Zealand with 425, and Brazil with over 1,406. Additional overseas Lodgery included; Hong Kong, Malaysia, Jamaica, Sierra Leone, Pakistan, Malawi, Uganda, Sri Lanka, Kuwait, Singapore, Trinidad, Berlin, and yes, even Montreal, Quebec in the disenfranchised country of Canada, (St. Paul's Lodge No. 874 and St. George's Lodge No. 440).

In reviewing additional Freemasonry material concerning the list of overseas Lodgery for both England and Scotland, Canada's most easterly Province of Newfoundland appears time and time again on the well documented literature. Under English Freemasonry control, twenty-seven NFLD Lodges are listed, (six of which are in St. John's alone). An additional 16 Masonic Lodges are registered within the Scottish jurisdiction, (four in St. John's). Further to this, under the **ROYAL** control of the British monarchy, three Lodges are listed as being in operation in Gander, Newfoundland (Gander Lodge No. 6860, Airways Lodge No. 8777 and Unity Lodge of Installed Masters No. 9145). Gander, Newfoundland being of course a long well established military post for both the British and Canadian Armed Forces. The Masonic overseas Lodgery of Scotland thus blessed the English Lodges with an increase of their everlasting presence, India's Lodgery increased with twenty-seven, New Zealand's increased with eleven and South Africa's increased with 118. Under the Scottish Rite, there were many other Lodgery increases; Ghana, Singapore, Trinidad, Nigeria, Malawi, Zimbabwe, Natal, Sierra Leone, Hong Kong, Jamaica, Malaysia, Lebanon and Pakistan. It is unknown as to what the British and Scottish overseas Freemasonry membership roster actually amounted too, speculation tallied the numbers somewhere in the millions.

Meanwhile, back in merry ole England things were slowly beginning to unravel for members of the Ancient Craft as two well documented book publications sent British Freemasons heading for cover as Great Britain's common folk wanted to learn as much as they possibly could about the secret world of Freemasonry. The growing

CONTROVERSY OF A POSSIBLE CONSPIRACY FOR WORLD DOMINATION HAD CAPTURED THE BRIT'S CURIOSITY WHOLEHEARTEDLY THAT IT CAUSED A FUROR FOR KNOWLEDGE TO BE QUENCHED. NOT LONG AFTER THE PUBLICATION OF AUTHORS STEPHEN KNIGHT (THE BROTHERHOOD: THE SECRET WORLD OF THE FREEMASONS PUBLISHED IN 1984) AND MARTIN SHORT'S SEQUEL (INSIDE THE BROTHERHOOD PUBLISHED FIVE YEARS LATER), A MASONIC CONSPIRACY OF CRIMINAL ACTIVITY SOON BEGAN TO UNFOLD IN ENGLAND.

IT WAS SAID TO HAVE BEEN ACCIDENTLY DISCOVERED THAT A LARGE MAJORITY OF BRITISH FREEMASONRY CONTROLLED MEMBERS OF THE JUDICIARY WERE PRESIDING OVER COURT CASES THAT SAW MOST OF THE CRIMINALS GETTING OFF EITHER SCOT-FREE /OR WITH VERY LENIENT SENTENCING BEING BESTOWED UPON THEM. FURTHER TO THIS RATHER INTERESTING REVELATION, THE VAST PERCENTAGE OF THE COURT CASES INVOLVED MEMBERS OF THE ANCIENT CRAFT WHO HAD BEEN CHARGED WITH KNOWN CRIMINAL OFFENCES AND WERE THEREFORE ISSUED WITH A SUBPOENA TO STAND BEFORE THE JUDICIAL SYSTEM. IT IN FACT BECAME SUCH A MEDIA CIRCUS FIASCO THAT IT EVEN CAUSED A FEW MEMBERS OF THE MASONIC ORDER ITSELF TO SAKE THEIR HEADS IN DISBELIEF AS ELECTED MEMBERS OF THE BRITISH PARLIAMENT IN FEBRUARY OF 1998 PASSED LEGISLATION FORCING ALL JUDGES, MAGISTRATES, POLICE OFFICERS, CROWN PROSECUTORS, PROBATION OFFICERS, AND EVEN PRISON STAFF TO DECLARE WHETHER /OR NOT THEY WERE ACTIVE MEMBERS OF FREEMASONRY.

THE WHOLE UGLY SCENARIO UNFOLDED LARGELY DUE TO THE FACT THAT A REVOLT HAD STARTED TO ERUPT IN THE BRITISH HOUSE OF COMMONS PITTING THE ELECTED MEMBERS OF PARLIAMENT AGAINST ONE ANOTHER AS IT WAS SLOWLY COMING TO LIGHT THAT A GROUP OF RENEGADE BRITISH FREEMASONS HAD LITERALLY ADOPTED A TERRORIST TACTIC OF SHOOT-TO-KILL WHEN DEALING WITH SERIOUS CRIMINAL OFFENDERS; A 21ST CENTURY STYLE **STAR CHAMBER** ACTING AS JUDGE, JURY AND EXECUTIONER. MASONIC INFILTRATION OF SELF-PROCLAIMED JUSTICE INCLUDED A VARIATION OF DOMESTIC TERRORIST CELLS THAT REPORTEDLY COVERED THREE SPECIFIC REGIONS OF ENGLAND — THE CASE OF THE BIRMINGHAM SIX; MEMBERS OF THE NOTORIOUSLY CORRUPT, AND LATER DISBANDED, WEST MIDLANDS SERIOUS CRIMES SQUAD, AND SEVEN INDIVIDUALS INVOLVED IN THE STALKER INQUIRY INTO AN ALLEGED SHOOT FIRST AND ASK QUESTIONS LATER POLICY THAT WAS STARTING TO REAL ITS UGLY HEAD IN ULSTER. FROM THERE, THINGS JUST SEEMED TO HAVE SPIRALED OUT OF CONTROL AS AN INVESTIGATION WAS CONDUCTED — LOOKING INTO THE EXISTENCE OF A POSSIBLE **MASONIC STAR CHAMBER** WHICH ESSENTIALLY BROUGHT ABOUT THE LIST OF MORE THAN 170 NAMES OF SOME OF ENGLAND'S MOST POWERFUL POLITICAL AND NOT SO POLITICAL PILLARS OF THE JUDICIAL

SYSTEM; FROM FELLOW MEMBERS OF THE BRITISH HOUSE OF COMMONS TO POLICE OFFICERS, JUDGES AND JOURNALISTS.

AFTER AN INTENSE INVESTIGATION – LASTING FOR SEVERAL MONTHS – THE MASONIC ADMINISTRATION OF THE UNITED GRAND LODGE OF FREEMASONS WERE HAULED IN ON THE CARPET AND IMMEDIATELY ASKED TO VERIFY AND/OR DENY THE NAMES LISTED AS BEING PARTY TO THE SHOOT-TO-KILL MENTALITY BY SOME OF ITS OWN MEMBERS OF THE ANCIENT CRAFT. AS THE INVESTIGATION CONTINUED TO INTENSIFY OTHER MEMBERS OF THE BRITISH FREEMASONRY WERE BROUGHT IN FOR QUESTIONING. DESPITE THE FACT THAT THEY FACED POSSIBLE INCARCERATION, NOT ONE MEMBER OF THE NATION'S MORE THAN HALF A MILLION MASTER MASONS DARED CONFIRM THE NAMES OF FELLOW BRETHREN TAKING PART IN THE MASONIC CONSPIRACY OF CRIMINAL TERRORIST ACTIVITY. BY THIS TIME PERIOD OF COURSE, FREEMASONRY WITHIN THE BRITISH COMMONWEALTH WAS VIRTUALLY UNDER ATTACK FROM ALL POSSIBLE ANGLES; IN THE NEWSPAPERS, ON TELEVISION AND RADIO, AND EVEN IN THE STREETS.

WHILE ALL CHAOS AND CONFUSION WAS BEING EXPOUNDED BY MEDIA OUTLETS, IN THE BRITISH HOUSE OF COMMONS STEPS WERE BEING TAKEN TO FORCE LEADERS OF THE BRETHERNSHIP TO COMPLY WITH THE COMMONS HOME AFFAIRS COMMITTEE'S REQUEST OF HAVING THE LIST OF TERRORIST NAMES COMPARED AGAINST MASONIC RECORDS. IN RESPONSE TO BEING FORCED TO DIVULGE THE NAMES LISTED AS ACTIVE MEMBERS OF THE ANCIENT CRAFT, THE LODGE'S GRAND SECRETARY, COMMANDER MICHAEL HIGHAM STEADFASTLY REFUSED TO COOPERATE WITH BRITISH AUTHORITIES DENOUNCING THE ENTIRE INVESTIGATION, LITERALLY CALLING IT NOTHING BUT A "FISHING EXPEDITION "TO HUNT AND TRACK DOWN MEMBERS OF THE CRAFT FOR THEIR OWN HIDDEN AGENDA PURPOSES. IN NOVEMBER OF 1997, THE 62-YEAR-OLD RETIRED NAVAL OFFICER SUPPOSEDLY HAD A CHANGE OF HEART WHEN HE WAS WARNED OF POSSIBLE CONTEMPT OF PARLIAMENT AND WAS ALL OF A SUDDEN, LOOKING AT SOME SERIOUS JAIL TIME IF HE PERSISTED WITH HIS LACK OF COOPERATION. AS FAR AS COMMANDER HIGHAM WAS CONCERNED, IT WAS NONE OF THE BRITISH PARLIAMENT'S DAMN BLOODY BUSINESS WHAT HIS FELLOW FRATERNITY MEMBERS WERE ACTUALLY UP TOO AS EVEN THEY (THE DISSIDENTS) ALSO HAD A RIGHT TO PRIVACY JUST LIKE EVERYONE ELSE – THE FACT THAT THEY HAD TURNED INTO A GROUP OF COLD-BLOODED KILLERS WAS OF LITTLE /OR NO INTEREST WHATSOEVER.

IN DEFENDING THE ACTIONS OF FELLOW FREEMASONS, HIGHAM ARGUED THAT DESPITE THE FACT THAT OF THE 96 NAMES THAT WERE SAID TO HAVE BEEN MEMBERS OF THE WEST MIDLANDS CRIME SQUAD, ONLY TEN OF THEM WERE POTENTIAL MATCHES FROM THE MASONIC RECORDS. THE MASONIC HIERARCHY OF THE JUDICIAL SYSTEM THEREFORE REMAINED IN COMPLETE TACT

AS COMMANDER HIGHAM HELD THAT LIST CLOSELY EMBEDDED TO HIS VEST. ALL-IN-ALL, THE COMMANDER-IN-CHIEF INSISTED THAT HIS FREEMASONRY MEMBERSHIP ROSTER CONSISTED LARGELY OF "DECENT CHAPS "WHO HAD A RIGHT TO PRIVACY DESPITE THE FACT THAT SOME OF ITS DISSIDENT MEMBERS HAD SUBSEQUENTLY FORMED AN EGOCENTRIC **MASONIC STAR CHAMBER**. IT WAS DURING THIS INTENSE HIGH DRAMA INTERROGATION PROCEDURE IN THE COMMONS COMMITTEE'S ROOM # 6 THAT THE GRAND SECRETARY OF THE UNITED GRAND LODGE OF ENGLAND INADVERTENTLY LET IT SLIP OUT THAT ONLY TEN NAMES ACTUALLY MATCHED THE FREEMASONRY MEMBERSHIP LIST. THE POWERS THAT BE INSTANTLY TOOK IT UPON THEMSELVES AS BEING A SIGN FROM THE HEAVENS ABOVE THAT THE MASONIC ORDER'S BRITISH ADMINISTRATOR WAS GOING TO BE SPILLING HIS GUTS OUT BEFORE THE COMMITTEE ITSELF ONCE THE THREAT OF SERIOUS JAIL TIME WAS USED AS FURTHER LEVERAGE TO EXTRACT MORE INFORMATION OUT OF HIM.

AND JUST WHEN EVERYONE THOUGHT THAT THE FRATERNITY DUST HAD FINALLY SETTLED ON ENGLAND'S MASONIC CONSPIRACY OF AN INSTITUTED **STAR CHAMBER**, OTHER INVESTIGATIONS INTO FREEMASONRY ACTIVITIES WERE SOON UNDERWAY AS FURTHER ALLEGATIONS EMERGED OUT OF THE WOODWORK – FROM PROBES INTO THE FAILING HEALTH CARE SERVICES OF 1998 TO THEN-BRITISH PRIME MINISTER TONY BLAIR'S SUPPOSED CRACKDOWN OF MASONIC INVOLVEMENT IN THE BRITISH ARMED FORCES IN THE YEAR 2000 AND BEYOND. MEMBERS OF GREAT BRITAIN'S BRITISH FREEMASONRY FORCES WERE ONCE AGAIN BEING RAKED OVER THE COALS FOR THEIR INVOLVEMENT IN A VARIATION OF UNSANCTIONED CONSPIRATOR DEEDS.

IN THE CASE OF THE DISMAL FAILURE OF HEALTH CARE, ALLEGATIONS EXISTED THAT A SELECT GROUP OF BRITISH FRATERNITY BRETHREN WERE PARTLY TO BLAME FOR ITS ILL-HEALTH DURING THE LAST REMAINING YEARS OF THE TWENTIETH CENTURY. ONCE THE PUBLIC INQUIRY WAS LAUNCHED, IT MARKED THE BIRTH OF ONE OF ENGLAND'S LARGEST PROBES EVER UNDER TAKEN INTO THE POSSIBLE EXISTENCE OF FREEMASONRY INVOLVEMENT ON A NATIONAL SCALE. ILL EQUIPPED AND UNDER FUNDED, HOSPITAL STAFF WERE BEING ORDERED TO PERFORM SURGERY DESPITE THE APPALLING HIGH RISK FACTOR CONDITIONS TO THEIR PATIENTS. THE DOCTOR WHO ENDED UP BLOWING THE WHISTLE ON THE WHOLE UGLY MESS WAS FORCED TO PACK UP HIS SURGICAL BAGS AND MIGRATE TO AUSTRALIA TO START A NEW LIFE AFTER BEING OSTRACIZED BY HIS FORMER COLLEAGUES – THE ORDEAL HAD BEEN DUBBED THE BRISTOL SCANDAL BY MEDIA OUTLETS. CONSULTANT ANAESTHETIST DR. STEPHEN BOLSIN LET IT BE KNOWN RIGHT FROM THE VERY BEGINNING THAT MASONIC ALLIANCES WERE AT THE ROOT OF THE PROBLEM AS FREEMASONRY FRIENDSHIPS WERE SAID TO HAVE BEEN SETTING OFF A "CULTURE OF COMPLACENCY "WITHIN THE MEDICAL PROFESSION. HIS ALLEGATIONS EVEN

WENT SO FAR AS TO BLAME THE POLITICS OF FREEMASONRY FOR THE DEATHS OF SEVERAL CHILDREN WHO WERE PATIENTS AT THE BRISTOL HOSPITAL. AND ONCE AGAIN, THE COMMONS HOME AFFAIRS COMMITTEE WAS DEMANDING THE NAMES OF KNOWN MEDICAL PERSONNEL WHO WERE ACTIVE MEMBERS OF THE FELLOWSHIP.

WITH THE PROBE INTO MASONIC HOSPITAL LINKS BEING EXPOSED VIA PUBLIC HEARINGS SIMILAR TO THAT OF WISCONSIN SENATOR JOSEPH MCCARTHY'S WITCH HUNT ON COMMUNISM, BRITISH PRIME MINISTER TONY BLAIR REPORTEDLY HAD HIS GOVERNMENT'S MINISTER OF DEFENSE ISSUE AN OFFICIAL ORDER BANNING ALL MEMBERS OF FREEMASONRY FROM STAGING MEETINGS ON ANY AND ALL PREMISES OCCUPIED BY MILITARY PERSONNEL, (DAILY MAIL, MARCH 5TH, 2000). ANGRY ENGLISH FREEMASONS ALMOST IMMEDIATELY BEGAN ACCUSING THE BRITISH PRIME MINISTER OF DISCRIMINATING AGAINST THEM AFTER INITIATING A CRACKDOWN ON ALL FORMS OF SECRET SOCIETIES WITHIN ENGLAND'S ARMED FORCES ONLY MONTHS PREVIOUSLY.

THE ANIMOSITY BETWEEN THE BRITISH PRIME MINISTER AND ENGLAND'S FREEMASONRY POPULATION GREW EVEN STRONGER AS MASONIC MEMBERS INSTANTLY ACCUSED TONY BLAIR OF HAVING A SECRET AGENDA OF WANTING TO REMOVE ALL ASPECTS OF THE ANCIENT AND NOBLE CRAFT FROM EVERY PART OF PUBLIC LIFE, INCLUDING THE CIVIL SERVICE, POLICE, GOVERNMENT, THE LAW AND MEDICINE. AS FAR AS THE BRITISH FREEMASONS WERE CONCERNED, THEY WERE AT WAR WITH THEIR COUNTRY'S OWN GOVERNMENT AS THE ULTIMATE ACT OF BETRAYAL HAD BEEN INITIATED AGAINST THEM BY ONE OF THEIR OWN KIND.

EVER SINCE THE DAWNING OF TIME, ENGLAND'S MINISTRY OF DEFENSE HAD ALWAYS EMPLOYED THE SERVICES OF LITERALLY THOUSANDS OF BRITISH FREEMASONS ON A YEARLY BASIS – GIVING THEM UNLIMITED ACCESS TO ALL MILITARY INSTALLATIONS NOT ONLY IN THE MOTHERLAND BUT WORLDWIDE AS WELL. IN FACT, THE DEFENSE MINISTRY OF THE TWENTIETH CENTURY HAD AN OPEN DOOR POLICY PERMITTING COUNTLESS MASONIC LODGES TO MET QUITE REGULARLY ON MOST OF ITS MILITARY BASES THROUGHOUT THE WORLD. FOR EXAMPLE, AT THE DUKE OF YORK'S BARRACKS IN CHELSEA, WEST LONDON, THE MINISTRY OF DEFENSE PERMITTED MORE THAN 40 MASONIC LODGES TO CONGREGATE FOUR TIMES A YEAR HOLDING MASSIVE MEETINGS AND BANQUETS. FURTHER TO THIS, BRITISH FREEMASONS WERE ALSO ALLOWED TO HOLD REGULAR TRAINING AND INSTRUCTION MEETINGS PERTAINING TO THE CIVILIAN NATIONAL GUARDS AND/OR CIVILIAN MILITIA. THEN ALL OF A SUDDEN AND WITHOUT WARNING, THEY ARE NOT PERMITTED TO EVEN SET FOOT ONTO THE PROPERTY. ADDING FURTHER INSULT TO INJURY WAS THE FACT THAT THE LAND ON WHICH THIS WORLD FAMOUS CHELSEA BARRACKS SAT UPON WAS

ACTUALLY LEGALLY OWNED BY THE EARL OF CADOGAN, A WELL KNOWN AND HIGHLY RESPECTED MASTER MASON HIMSELF. WHICH IRONICALLY, MADE THE MINISTRY OF DEFENSE DECREE NULL AND VOID ON THAT ONE PARTICULAR PIECE OF REAL-ESTATE.

FEELING SOMEWHAT ANNOYED AT THE EDICT, A LETTER WRITING CAMPAIGN WAS IMPLEMENTED TO TRY AN SWAY THE BRITISH GOVERNMENT'S STANCE ON CORRUPT DOMESTIC FRATERNITY TERRORIST POLITICS FROM BEING EXECUTED AGAINST THEM. WRITING ON BEHALF OF THE DUKE OF KENT, AT THE TIME PRO GRAND MASTER OF THE UNITED GRAND LODGE OF ENGLAND, LORD FARNHAM STATED IN HIS CORRESPONDENCE THAT THE DEFENSE MINISTRY WAS VIRTUALLY IMPLYING THAT NO MEMBER OF FREEMASONRY COULD EVER BE TRUSTED WHEN IT CAME TO MATTERS OF NATIONAL SECURITY. BUT THEIR EFFORTS WERE NOT ONLY FUTILE BUT ALSO REPORTEDLY WENT UNNOTICED AS TONY BLAIR'S MINISTRY OF DEFENSE PROCLAMATION WAS MADE CRYSTAL CLEAR IN JANUARY OF 2000 AS IT WAS SAID TO HAVE FURTHER BANNED FREEMASONRY RECRUITS FROM BEING INDOCTRINATED INTO THE BRITISH ARMED FORCES.

THE VIRTUAL RESULT OF ALL THE COMMONS HOME AFFAIRS COMMITTEE'S INVESTIGATIONS INTO THE ILLEGAL ACTIVITIES OF BRITISH FREEMASONS IN ENGLAND LED TO A FULL BLOWN GOVERNMENTAL REGISTRY FOR ALL MEMBERS OF THE ANCIENT CRAFT. AS PART OF THE PASSED LEGISLATION PACKAGE IN BRITISH PARLIAMENT, THE NEW REGISTER HAD TOTAL JURISDICTIONAL POWERS OF ENFORCEMENT AS WELL AS THE LEGAL RIGHT TO PENALIZE THOSE INDIVIDUALS WHO REFUSED TO COMPLY WITH THE LAW IF THEY WERE UNWILLING TO IDENTIFY THEMSELVES AS FREEMASONS. THIS LAW COVERED ALL GROUPS OF CIVIL SERVANTS AND/OR STATE EMPLOYEES, INCLUDING ALL ASPECTS OF THE JUDICIARY, THE POLICE, GOVERNMENT LAWYERS, PRISON AND PROBATION STAFF, BRITISH PARLIAMENT AS WELL AS THE MINISTRY OF DEFENSE — IT WAS ALL SMOKE AND MIRRORS AS FAR AS BRITISH FREEMASONS WERE CONCERNED!!!

FEARING SOME SORT OF RETALIATION IF IT HAD BEEN LEARNED THAT THEY WERE ACTIVE MEMBERS OF THE MASONIC ORDER ALWAYS PLAYING BOTH ENDS AGAINST THE MIDDLE, NUMEROUS MEMBERS OF THE CRAFT FELLOWSHIP ALMOST IMMEDIATELY DENOUNCED THE FUNDAMENTAL PRINCIPLES OF FREEMASONRY AND DULY SUBMITTED THEIR RESIGNATIONS FROM THE FRATERNAL **"BROTHERHOOD OF MAN"** CITING RECONCILABLE DIFFERENCES AS THEIR CAREERS WOULD HAVE SUFFERED DIRE CONSEQUENCES IF THEY WERE TO HAVE BEEN IDENTIFIED AS PARTICIPATING MASTER MASONS. POLICE OFFICERS, GOVERNMENTAL OFFICIALS AND OTHER WALKS OF LIFE THUSLY TURNED THEIR BACKS ON THE ANCIENT CRAFT JUST TO SAVE THEIR OWN SORRY ASSES. BEING PURELY OPPORTUNISTIC INDIVIDUALS AT HEART — SOME IN FACT EVEN WENT SO FAR AS TO CLAIM THAT IT WAS SOLELY FOR PERSONAL REASONS; ILL-HEALTH AND/

OR PSYCHOLOGICAL TRAUMA AND SUCH, THAT THEY HAD TAKEN THEMSELVES OFF THE MASONIC MEMBERSHIP ROSTER. HOW IRONIC, MEMBERS OF BRITISH FREEMASONRY DIDN'T MIND BEING ACKNOWLEDGED AS ACTIVE PARTICIPANTS OF THE CRAFT PROVIDING THE FACT OF COURSE THAT IT WOULDN'T INTERFERE WITH PROSPECTS OF REAPING THE REWARDS THAT WERE BEING BESTOWED ONTO THEM. BUT ONCE THE LID OF PANDORA'S BOX WAS BEING PRIED WIDE OPEN AS TO HOW CORRUPT AND DECEITFUL THEY HAD ACTUALLY BECOME OVER THE PASSAGE OF TIME, ALL OF A SUDDEN, IT WASN'T KOSHER TO BE RECOGNIZED AS BEING A WILLING PARTICIPANT IN GOD'S MASTERPLAN OF DIVINE INTERVENTION.

ALTHOUGH BOTH BRITISH AND AMERICAN FREEMASONS CONJOINTLY ATTEMPTED TO DISTANCE THEMSELVES FROM THE KNOWN FACT OF BOTH WANTING TO LAY CLAIM TO THE THRONE OF DAVID, BY ALL BIBLICAL AND MASONIC DEFINITION, UPON THE DEATH OF KING SOLOMON IN 922 B.C. WHEREAS HIS PEOPLE MOURNED HIM, THE DIVINE PROPHESY WAS FULFILLED AS THE HOUSE OF DAVID HAD BEEN ESTABLISHED AS THE RULERS OF ISRAEL (1 SAMUEL 7:16) – SOLOMON'S FATHER – TO WHOM THE LORD HAD SUPPOSEDLY SAID "OUT OF THY LOINS SHALL COME THE KINGS OF ISRAEL, TO RULE FOREVER". THIS, IF UNDERSTOOD PROPERLY MEANT THAT THE SONS, AND THEIR SONS AFTER THEM WOULD RULE ISRAEL TO THE END OF MAN'S EXISTENCE HERE ON THE PLANET EARTH. THE CHAIN OF COMMAND /OR THE LINE OF SUCCESSION WAS VIRTUALLY UNBROKEN FOR NINETEEN GENERATIONS, UNTIL THE FALL OF JERUSALEM IN 587 B.C. TO THE BABYLONIANS, THOUGH IN A DIVIDED FORM. OLD RELIGIOUS QUARRELS SOON FLARED UP ONCE AGAIN AND THEN, THE JEWISH PEOPLE REPORTEDLY TOOK THE ROAD OF INIQUITY WHEREUPON THE LORD WAS SAID TO HAVE ABANDONED THEM, LEAVING THEM TO THEIR ENEMIES. HOSTILE ARMIES THEN INVADED THE JEWISH PEOPLE FROM ALL SIDES, DRIVEN BY A THIRST FOR VENGEANCE AND THE MEMORY OF THE KING WHO HAD DOMINATED THEM, THE BABYLONIANS ALSO CAME WITH A THIRST FOR THE FABLED RICHES, WHOSE VALUE INCREASED IN THE TELLING OF THEIR EXISTENCE.

UNDER THE REIGN OF EZECHIAS IN JUDEAH, A MAJOR ATTACK WAS LAUNCHED BY KING SENNACHERIB OF ASSYRIA AGAINST THE CITADELS OF ISRAEL, AND THEY SOON CAPITULATED. THE GOLD AND OTHER RICHES WERE STRIPPED FROM THE TEMPLE. THE CITY WAS SPARED FOR A SHORT TIME PERIOD, WHEN THE CITY WAS ATTACKED BY NEBUCHADNEZZAR, THE KING OF BABYLON, WHO COMPLETED THE RAZING OF THE CITY AND THE TEMPLE. THE CITY OF JERUSALEM WAS SPARED NO MERCY AND THE KING, ZEDEKIAH THE LAST GENERATION KING, WAS BLINDED AND LED IN CHAINS TO BABYLON. AND THUS IN 587 B.C., FINALIZED NINETEEN GENERATIONS WHICH SAW THE END

OF THE HOUSE OF DAVID, IN THE DIVIDED KINGDOM CREATED BY SOLOMON'S SONS.

ACCORDING TO SOME BIBLICAL HISTORIANS, NEBUCHADNEZZAR HAD UNLEASHED HIS FORCES ON JERUSALEM IN A PAROXYSM OF RAGE AND JEALOUSLY. NOTHING WAS TO HAVE BEEN REPORTEDLY SPARED, NEITHER YOUNG WOMEN, CHILDREN NOR THE YOUNG MEN. ALL ABLE BODIED MEN WERE SOLD AS SLAVES AND THE CITY ITSELF WAS SYSTEMATICALLY DESTROYED. SOLOMON'S WALLS WERE RAZED TO THE GROUND AND EVERY HOUSE SET ABLAZE. THE CONQUERING HEROS RIFLED THE TEMPLE THAT WAS SAID TO HAVE SYMBOLIZED LOFTY POLITICAL IDEALISM AND FIVE FINGER DISCOUNTED ALL OF ITS PRECIOUS OBJECTS, INCLUDING THE BRONZE MURALS. AND KING SOLOMON'S TEMPLE WAS NO MORE THUSLY SETTING THE FRATERNAL STAGE FOR MORE BIBLICAL SECRETS AND LIES BY THE POWERS THAT BE.

IT IS ALSO INTERESTING TO NOTE THAT ACCORDING TO GENEALOGICAL RESEARCH STUDIES, EVEN SOME WELL KNOWN AMERICAN ICONS WERE SAID TO HAVE TRACED THEIR HERITAGE TO THE BRITISH MONARCHY AND ITS PROCLAIMED LINEAGE TO THE THRONE OF DAVID. SUCH AS IN THE CASE OF FORMER U.S. PRESIDENT GEORGE BUSH SR. AND HIS INEPT AMERICAN PRESIDENTIAL SON OF THE 21ST CENTURY. AS IT TURNS OUT, THE BUSH FAMILY NAME OF THE CONTINENTAL UNITED STATES WAS TRACED TO THE FIFTEENTH CENTURY – NORTHAMPTON SQUIRE HENRY SPENCER. WHICH IRONICALLY MADE THE AMERICAN PRESIDENT GEORGE BUSH JR. A DISTANT RELATIVE OF THE BRITISH MONARCHY THROUGH PRINCES WILLIAM AND HARRY ON THEIR LATE MOTHER'S SIDE, DIANA, THE PRINCESS OF WALES. FURTHER TO THIS, THE AMERICAN PRESIDENT'S FAMILY TREE WAS SAID TO HAVE ALSO BEEN LINKED TO SIR WINSTON CHURCHILL. THE BRITISH ICON CHURCHILL BEING OF COURSE ONE OF FREEMASONRY'S MOST WORLD FAMOUS MEMBERS OF THE ANCIENT CRAFT FOR THE TWENTIETH CENTURY. FRATERNITY BROTHER CHURCHILL WAS REPORTEDLY INITIATED IN 1903 AT MASONIC LODGE NO. 3000 IN MERRY OLE ENGLAND. WHICH IN ITSELF EXPLAINS AS WHY GEORGE BUSH JR.'S ADMIRATION FOR CHURCHILL ESCALATED EVEN FURTHER DURING THE AFTERMATH OF SEPTEMBER 11TH, 2001 AS THE ACTING AMERICAN PRESIDENT SOON BEGAN WOOING THE WORLD'S CITIZENRY BY UTILIZING BROTHER CHURCHILL'S RHETORIC OF THE SECOND WORLD WAR WHILE ADDRESSING THE U.S. CONGRESS CONCERNING THE ATTACKS IN THEIR OWN HOMELAND, THE UNITED STATES.

IN A SURPRISING TWIST OF FATE, IN APRIL OF 2001 THE SECRET MASONIC RITUALS OF THE BUSH FAMILY'S INFAMOUS ALL-MALE SKULL AND BONES ALMAMATER WAS REVEALED TO THE ENTIRE WESTERN HEMISPHERE AS A GROUP OF CURIOUS ONLOOKERS USED A NIGHT-VISION CAMERA TO CAPTURE THE INITIATION OF FRATERNITY CANDIDATES AT YALE UNIVERSITY. MUCH

LIKE HITLER'S WAFFEN SS SKULL AND CROSS-BONES INSIGNIA, THE SKULL AND BONES FRATERNITY HAS ITS ROOTS IN ANCIENT EGYPTIAN TIMES, AND EVENTUALLY MADE ITS WAY INTO YALE UNIVERSITY IN 1856. BESIDES THE BUSH FAMILY MEMBERS, THE SKULL AND BONES FRATERNITY HAS AMONG ITS MEMBERS SOME OF THE MOST POWERFUL FAMILIES RUNNING THE U.S. GOVERNMENTAL STRUCTURE BEHIND THE SCENES; INCLUDING WALL STREET BUSINESSMEN, AMBASSADORS, POLITICIANS AND JUDGES.

ONE OF THE VERY FIRST THINGS THAT THE NEWLY ANOINTED PRESIDENT GEORGE BUSH JR. DID AFTER SEIZING THE REIGNS OF POWER FROM VICE-PRESIDENT AL GORE AT THE BEGINNING OF THE 21ST CENTURY WAS TO HOLD A PRIVATE DINNER FOR HIS FELLOW FRATERNITY BRETHREN, "THE BONESMEN." BUT WHILE THE AMERICAN PRESIDENT BUSH WAS TRYING TO SEDUCE THE ENTIRE POPULATION OF THE WORLD, ALL WAS NOT WELL IN PARADISE LOST — MEANING THE GOOD OLD U.S. OF A. AS FAR AS THE RELIGIOUS ZEALOTS OF THE NORTH AMERICAN CONTINENT WERE CONCERNED, FREEMASONRY AND ITS TEACHINGS AND/OR PHILOSOPHIES WAS THE CURSE OF LUCIFER SPREADING ITS EVIL SATANIC WAYS ONTO THE WESTERN FREE-WORLD. CONTRARY AS TO WHAT THESE FANATICS MAY WISH TO BE TRUE, WITH ITS PAGAN AND OCCULT LIKE CEREMONIES, FREEMASONRY HAD IN FACT INDOCTRINATED SEVERAL MILLION OF THE CONTINENT'S INHABITANTS (PENTECOSTAL, EVANGELICAL, FUNDAMENTALIST PROTESTANTS AND ROMAN CATHOLICS ALIKE) INTO THE SPIRITUALLY ENLIGHTENED FAMILY FOLD OF SO-CALLED SATANISM AND ITS OCCULTIST DREAM OF A **ONE WORLD GOVERNMENT**, INCLUDING THE OFFICE OF THE U.S. PRESIDENCY.

THE RELIGIOUS FANATICS OPPOSING SUCH AN IMMORAL AND DEGRADATION LITERALLY CONDEMNED THE PONTIFF LEADERS OF LUCIFERIN FREEMASONRY TO THE DEPTHS OF HELL'S INFERNO AS THEY VERBALIZED THEIR DISSATISFACTION WITH THE RITUALISTIC CEREMONIES OF THE ANCIENT CRAFT WHICH THEY (THE HIGHLY RELIGIOUS ONES) PUT INTO MANY BOOK FORMS CALLING IT WITCHCRAFT AND/OR THE INNER WORKINGS OF THE DEVIL HIMSELF. IN THEIR FEEBLE ATTEMPT TO PERSUADE ITS READERSHIP INTO ACCEPTING THE CHRISTIAN WAY OF SEEING ALL ASPECTS OF FREEMASONRY ACTIVITY FROM THEIR POINT OF VIEW AND/OR UNDERSTANDING, **FOR AS SUCH IS THE KINGDOM OF GOD**, THE RELIGIOUS ZEALOTS OF THE WESTERN FREE-WORLD FAILED TO MENTION A FEW VERY IMPORTANT FACTORS. THE MOST CRUCIAL BEING THAT IN ACCORDANCE TO VARIOUS WRITINGS AND/OR SYMBOLS ON THE PYRAMIDS IN EGYPT, THE ANCIENT MYSTICAL CRAFT OF FREEMASONRY HAS VIRTUALLY BEEN IN EXISTENCE LONG BEFORE THE DAYS OF JESUS CHRIST AND THAT FOR MORE THAN 2,000 YEARS BOTH OF THESE FACTIONS, (THE MORAL MAJORITY AND THE ANCIENT CRAFT OF FREEMASONRY) HAVE BEEN FIGHTING AMONGST

Themselves on the world stage for ultimate supremacy over the political and religious affairs on a global scale.

Coincidently, during the 1950's in the United States, (1953-54 to be precise), a special Congressional Committee was formed to investigate the interlocking web of tax-exempt foundations just to see as to where they were spending their tax free money. Some Federal U.S. governmental watchdog members were said to have not been at all pleased with the fact that these large fraternal institutions never paid taxes. The Committee supposedly accidentally stumbled onto something that they themselves considered to be a sinister plot to rewrite American history and incorporate it into the new school textbooks. While conducting his research, Norman Dodd, the Committee's Research Director reportedly discovered a rather startling piece of documentation neatly tucked away in the achieves of the Carnegie Endowment for International Peace which was said to have been the Endowment's actual mission statement of purpose. In his final analysis of what had been unearthed in a mountain of archives, Dodd was said to have automatically concluded that a gigantic Freemasonry conspiracy existed to drastically alter the true facts of the past and was not at all impressed at what he had initially found:

> "The only way to maintain control of the population was to obtain control of education in the U.S. They realized this was a prodigious task so they approached the Rockefeller Foundation with the suggestion that they go in tandem and that portion of education which could be considered as domestically oriented be taken over by the Rockefeller Foundation and that portion which was oriented to International matters be taken over by the Carnegie Endowment."

According to his findings, the Rockefeller Foundation agreed to the terms set out by the Carnegie Endowment's mission statement of purpose and almost immediately began rewriting American history. Dodd also concluded from his study that the sole purpose of both the foundations in question was to destroy the United States of America by virtue of moral degradation as these educational changes were being gradually implemented right across the country by Federal and State authorities as they began aiding and abiding the Illuminoids in achieving their ultimate goal. Ironically, Dodd's findings were achieved mainly due to the Congressional Committee

TASK FORCE OF WISCONSIN SENATOR JOSEPH MCCARTHY'S NOTORIOUS WITCH HUNT HEARINGS THAT LAID THE ENTIRE BLAME OF AMERICAN PROBLEMS SOLELY ON THE SHOULDERS OF COMMUNISM INSTEAD OF A POSSIBLE MASONIC CONSPIRACY OF SORTS AS BY THIS TIME PERIOD OF THE WORLD'S HISTORY, THE COMMUNIST WERE PLOTTING TO TAKE-OVER THE WORLD AND NOT THE AMERICAN FREEMASONS AND THEIR SUPPOSED GOODWILL EFFORTS OF MAINTAINING DEMOCRACY UNDER THE AUSPICES OF **"THE BROTHERHOOD OF MAN – UNDER THE FATHERHOOD OF GOD."**

DODD'S RESEARCH INITIALLY FIRST BEGAN IN JULY OF 1953 AS A DIRECT OFF-SHOOT OF THE MCCARTHY HEARINGS WHEN IT BECAME APPARENT TO THE WISCONSIN SENATOR AND HIS TEAM OF INQUISITORS THAT SOME OF THE WEALTHIEST MEN IN THE UNITED STATES SET UP WELL-ENDOWED FOUNDATIONS TO STUDY THE VARIOUS ATTRIBUTES OF HOW THEY WERE GOING TO BE UNLEASHING THEIR FREEMASONRY GOALS OF GLOBAL DOMINATION ONTO AN UNSUSPECTING WORLD POPULATION. AS THE MCCARTHY HEARINGS DRAGGED ON, NOT ONCE DID IT EVER EXPRESS THE FACT THAT IT WAS THE AMERICAN FREEMASONS BEHIND THE PLOY TO CONTROL THE ENTIRE MOVIE INDUSTRY OF THE CONTINENTAL UNITED STATES AS A WAY AND MEANS OF DESENSITIZING THE WESTERN FREE-WORLD'S POPULATION. INSTEAD, JOSEPH MCCARTHY AND HIS COHORTS BLAMED THE COMMUNISTS LIVING ON THE NORTH AMERICAN CONTINENT FOR ATTEMPTING TO FORCE THE SO-CALLED MORAL DEGRADATION OF ONE OF THE WORLD'S MOST POWERFUL NATIONS.

AS THE DIRECTOR OF THE COMMITTEE'S RESEARCH DIVISION, DODD WAS VIRTUALLY ALLOWED TO EXAMINE ANY DOCUMENTS THAT HE SO DESIRED. THIS INCLUDED THE MINUTES OF THE BOARD OF TRUSTEES OF ALL THE FOUNDATIONS AND/OR ENDOWMENTS IN EXISTENCE WITHIN THE UNITED STATES ITSELF. ONE OF THE OLDEST OF THESE BEING OF COURSE THE CARNEGIE ENDOWMENT FOR INTERNATIONAL PEACE WHICH WAS FIRST INSTITUTED DURING THE YEAR 1908. WHILE SCRUTINIZING THE MINUTES OF THE CARNEGIE BOARD OF TRUSTEES, DODD WAS SAID TO HAVE NOTICED A RATHER ODD NOTE SENT TO U.S. PRESIDENT WOODROW WILSON REQUESTING THAT HE "SEE TO IT THAT THE WAR NOT END TOO QUICKLY. "THIS NOTE OF COURSE WAS REFERRING TO THE FIRST WORLD WAR WHICH REPORTEDLY ENABLED PRESIDENT WILSON'S FINANCIAL CAMPAIGN BACKER BERNARD BARUCH TO BE ANOINTED HEAD OF THE AMERICAN WAR INDUSTRIES BOARD WHERE HE AND THE ROCKEFELLER DYNASTY WERE SAID TO HAVE REAPED AN ESTIMATED $ 200 MILLION IN SHEER PROFIT FROM THE WAR EFFORT ITSELF. KNOWING FULL WELL THAT IN MOST FRATERNITY CIRCLES THE BANNER OF THE ILLUMINATUS ALWAYS PLAYED A VERY IMPORTANT ROLE IN EXECUTING WARFARE ONTO AN UNDESERVING PEOPLE, DODD WAS SAID TO BE NOT OVERLY IMPRESSED WITH WHAT HE HAD ACCIDENTLY STUMBLED INTO.

According to the moral majority themselves, the leaders of Luciferian Freemasonry and their dreams of a **ONE WORLD GOVERNMENT** were in actual fact the instruments behind all of the World Wars (Parts I and II) as they (the Illuminoids) began implementing a masterplan of destruction by way of a three-part resolution tactic — a grand design as it were, of ridding the entire world of Christianity and supposedly bringing it under the Illuminati dictatorship of Luciferian ideology. In this grand design of all things being virtually evil, the first of these World War's that was executed by the united Freemasons of the world, they were supposedly hoping to topple the Czarist Government of Russia and replace it with an Illuminati dictatorship enabling them to secure the vast natural resources of the Red Soviet Empire and lining their Freemasonry pockets with the untold fortunes of the Communist regime. The second of these World War's was to enable the conquering heros of the First World War to capture all of Europe which in turn was to give them full economic and political control as they executed European Union as well as one common currency.

And the Third World War, which was initially destined to take place in the Middle East between two of the world's most powerful religions (Islamic Freemasonry and those forces opposing it, Jewish Freemasonry) thus bringing about the Biblical Armageddon. As far as the fundamental ministerial and their religious institutions of the North American Continent were concerned, uniting the entire world under the deceptive banner of the **Luciferian New World Order** including Islamic and Jewish Freemasonry was something that required much negative publicity. They soon began publishing into book form their manuscripts of the Ancient Craft of Freemasonry's anti-Christian tactics of degradation and immoral conduct whereby putting them on the much unregulated Internet. Once on the Internet, a person and/or a group of individuals could literally say anything that they wanted without first verifying the contents of what they were writing about. Various conspiracy theories almost immediately began to formulate, flying fast and furious without proper verification, the moral majority instantly started exercising their democratic right to lay claim to a conspiracy existing against the Christian faith by the Freemasons of the North American Continent to de-Christianize the world and replace it with a Satanic cult hell bent on global domination.

While all of this was unfolding on the 21st Century world stage, the illusive U.S. made campaign – **The War On Terrorism** – American Freemasons were blaming other countries and their outlandish religious interpretations of the Holy Scriptures for the moral decay of not only the United States but also the entire world; the Islamic religion in particular and its declaration of war against the world's only superpower, the good old U.S. of A. With one group literally blaming the other, more and more anti-American Freemasonry literature was soon published which virtually added more confusion to the mix as by this time period, rhetoric of "us "versus "them "was being whispered from the lips of the American people. The good Christian folk of the United States obviously claiming that all forms of Freemasonry were the ultimate inner workings of the Devil himself as they firmly believed that the unholy trinity of the Masonic Deity was that of a three-headed pagan god that was so remote from the Christian faith and reportedly so blasphemous that all those who worshiped it were condemned to the pits of hell's everlasting inferno.

In fact, Luciferian Freemasonry and all of its pagan like traditions and/or ceremonies were said to have instituted such festive occasions as Easter, Christmas and Halloween. American fundamentalists of the moral majority even went so far as to insist that these occult practices were in direct opposition to the religious teaching of the Holy Scriptures thus intervening in God's word. The Satanic evil doers were further blamed for instituting other anti-Christian activities from the basic design of hot cross buns to hard-boiled eggs being brightly colored as Easter ornaments. Hell, they even laid blame onto Lucifer's fraternal army of evil doers for all of the ritualistic style killings being committed right across the Continental United States during most of the Twentieth Century. Serial killings performed by such mentally ill sufferers as Jeffrey Dahmer and his reported homosexual murders as well as the ceremonial style serial killer Richard Ramirez who forced his victims to bear witness to the ever powerful presence of Satan – forcing them to swear allegiance to the dark forces of the underworld, before butchering them. Psychotic schizophrenic serial killer Ramirez was better known as "The Night Stalker "so dubbed by media outlets throughout Canada and the United States for sensational type reasons as he often inscribed a Satanic pentagram on the mutilated bodies of his intended victims.

To further illustrate as to how the **Luciferian New World Order** was gaining momentum onto the citizenry of the Western free-world, the moral majority used examples as to how the American movie industry was not only desensitizing the people but brainwashing them as well. In using the movies such as Halloween, (Parts I, II and III), as prime examples; where blood and guts were the main components as a theme in all three of these movies with emphasis placed on the date October 31st as being the eve of all things evil. Capitalizing on this rhetoric even further, the religious ones used the serial killer Edward Gein as yet another example of Hollywood virtually going to hell in a handbasket. Gein reportedly committed such heinous crimes as grave robbing, necrophilia, mutilation, murder as well as cannibalism in the small Wisconsin town of Plainfield in the 1950's and was said to have been the main character source for Norman Bates in the movies Psycho, (Parts I, II and III), as well as for the character Leatherface in the movie creation Texas Chainsaw Massacre.

According to the moral majority movement in the United States of America, the evil world of Freemasonry and its occult like followers supposedly enabled Anton LaVey's version of Biblical text "**The Satanic Bible** "to become one of the nation's best selling items of the last century. Reportedly out selling the Holy Scriptures itself as a large portion of the American population was said to have been involved with the Black Mass ceremonies of worshiping the evil forces of darkness living in the Satanic underworld.

While painting a clandestine picture of the de-Christianizing of the entire world by virtue of these pagan like ceremonies of worship, the North American Continent's religious ones went about their daily business trying to regain control of the millions of people that Lucifer's fraternity forces were said to have had managed to seduce by casting a witch's spell upon them. Before long, a Biblical account of paganism was put forward which unbeknownst to the moral majority would be used to confirm the fact that Freemasonry did in fact exist during the days of old. In their self-righteous attempt to reiterate the myth that Satan's evil forces had actually gained a firm stranglehold onto the vast majority of the people living in the United States, the religious ones inadvertently admitted to the fact that the Ancient Craft of Freemasonry was literally tied to King Solomon. This despite the well known fact that the Lord thy God was said to have appeared before him not once but twice. And on both occasions of this supposed visitation of

THE SUPREME ENTITY, SOLOMON WAS SAID TO HAVE DISREGARDED WHAT THE LORD THY GOD HAD INSTRUCTED HIM TO DO AND REPORTEDLY WENT ON HIS OWN CHOSEN PATH OF SELF-DISCOVERY. WITH THEIR HOLY SCRIPTURES IN HAND, THESE RELIGIOUS ZEALOTS WRITE THAT DURING THE REIGNS OF KINGS DAVID AND SOLOMON, SATANIC INFILTRATION SLOWLY FILLED THE LAND AS THE PEOPLE OF THIS KINGDOM WERE VIRTUALLY POWERLESS TO PREVENT IT FROM HAPPENING. KING DAVID THEREFORE MAINTAINED TIGHT CONTROL OF HIS KINGDOM BY KEEPING A FAR DISTANCE FROM THE RELIGIOUS INFLUENCES OF SATANISM BUT ONCE HIS SON, SOLOMON TOOK CONTROL OF THE REIGNS OF POWER, ISRAEL WAS SAID TO HAVE LAID IN RUINS AS THE PAGANISM PRACTICES OF KING SOLOMON BEGAN DIVIDING THE ROYAL HOUSE OF DAVID. FROM THERE, THE RELIGIOUS FANATICS CONTINUE VERIFYING THE FACT THAT SOLOMON'S SUCCESSOR TO THE THRONE OF DAVID, HIRAM, ALSO WAS A PAGAN TYPE RELIGIOUS WORSHIPER WHOSE MANDATE IT WAS TO DIVIDE THE HOUSE OF DAVID EVEN FURTHER AS HIRAM HIMSELF WENT ON TO BECOME ONE OF FREEMASONRY'S MOST RENOWN TEACHERS OF PHILOSOPHY OF THE UNKNOWN MYSTICAL WORLD ASSOCIATED WITH THE ANCIENT CRAFT.

SUPPOSEDLY WITH THE **SATANIC BIBLE** IN HAND, AND AFTER HAVING EXECUTED TWO OF THE WARS OF MASSIVE DESTRUCTION PERTAINING TO ITS THREE-PART PLAN OF THE **ILLUMINATI: IN GOD WE TRUST**, THE CHRISTIAN COMMUNITY OF THE WESTERN FREE-WORLD REPORTEDLY WAITED WITH BAITED BREATH FOR THE IMPLEMENTATION AND/OR LIKELIHOOD OF WORLD WAR III ERUPTING IN THE MIDDLE EAST DURING THE BEGINNING STAGES OF THE 21ST CENTURY. THE ENTIRE WORLD SOON BEGAN WALKING ON A TIGHTROPE AS EXTREME FUNDAMENTALISTS OF ISLAM SENT A CLEAR MESSAGE TO THE AMERICAN FREEMASONRY INSTITUTIONS OF THE UNITED STATES BY LAUNCHING AN ALL OUT ATTACK ON SEPTEMBER 11TH, 2001 IN WHICH ONE OF THE MOST HIGHLY PROCLAIMED MASONIC SYMBOLS THAT WASHINGTON, D.C. HAD TO OFFER LAY UNDER SIEGE; THE PENTAGON. ACCORDING TO THE CHRISTIAN LITERATURE, THE STREETS OF THE CITY OF THE NATION'S CAPITAL WERE LAID OUT IN SUCH A WAY THAT THE FORMATION OF KEY MASONIC SYMBOLS (THE COMPASS, THE SQUARE AND THE PENTAGRAM) COULD BE FOUND. ON THE PROPERTY WHERE IN WHICH THE WHITE HOUSE IS LOCATED FOR EXAMPLE, IT IS SAID THAT AN INVERTED FIVE-POINT STAR /OR PENTAGRAM CAN BE VISIBLY SEEN FROM ABOVE – IT'S REPORTEDLY SITUATED "WITHIN THE INTERSECTIONS OF CONNECTICUT AND VERMONT AVENUES NORTH TO DUPONT AND LOGAN CIRCLES, WITH RHODE ISLAND AND MASSACHUSETTS GOING TO WASHINGTON CIRCLE TO THE WEST AND MT. VERNON SQUARE ON THE EAST."

AND SINCE THE PENTAGON ITSELF WAS SEEN AS BEING A SYMBOL OF WAR TO THE VAST MAJORITY OF THE WORLD'S POPULATION, IT ONLY MADE SENSE TO THE ISLAMIC FUNDAMENTALISTS THAT BECAUSE OF THIS SAID STATED

SYMBOLISM USED BY THE AMERICAN ILLUMINATI, THEN, THEY HAD NO OTHER CHOICE BUT TO TARGET THE PENTAGON AS WELL – AFTERALL, IT WAS PERCEIVED AS ACTUALLY BEING THE PENTAGRAM OF SATANISM.

AS THE NEIGHBORING COUNTRIES OF AFGHANISTAN AND IRAQ IN THE MIDDLE EAST BECAME THE SOURCES OF IRRITATION FOR THE AMERICAN FREEMASONRY DREAM OF "**MANIFEST DESTINY** "UNDER THE AUSPICES OF THEIR FRATERNAL ENTITY "**THE BROTHERHOOD OF MAN** – UNDER THE **FATHERHOOD OF GOD** "TENSIONS QUICKLY MOUNTED. THE WORLD PREPARED ITSELF FOR ARMAGEDDON AS THE FRATERNITY FORCES FIRST BOMBED THE LIVING JESUS OUT OF AFGHANISTAN, THEN, SET THEIR MASONIC SIGHTS ONTO IRAQ. AND BY SEPTEMBER OF 2002, (SATURDAY, SEPTEMBER 14TH), THE SITUATION ESCALATED EVEN FURTHER OUT OF CONTROL WHEN THE PRESIDENT OF THE UNITED STATES OF AMERICA, GEORGE W. BUSH DEMANDED THAT OTHER COUNTRIES WITHIN THE UNITED NATIONS LEAGUE SHOW SOME BACKBONE IN JOINING HIM AND HIS FRATERNAL CAUSE OF MAINTAINING FREEDOM AND DEMOCRACY BY BOMBING THE HELL OUT OF IRAQ AS HIS FATHER DID TEN YEARS PREVIOUSLY IN AN ATTEMPT TO TOPPLE THE ISLAMIC FREEMASONRY LEADER SADDAM HUSSEIN. ALMOST IMMEDIATELY, GEORGE BUSH JR. WAS CONSIDERED AS BEING THE ONE TERM WONDER OF THE OVAL OFFICE JUST LIKE HIS FATHER BECAUSE THE WARLORD AMERICAN PRESIDENT HAD LET IT BE KNOWN THAT IF NEED BE, THE U.S. OF A. WAS TOTALLY WILLING TO GO IT ALONE WITH THE IRAQI PEOPLE AS OUR AMERICAN COUSINS TO THE SOUTH OF THE 49TH PARALLEL FIRMLY BELIEVED THAT THE CIVILIZED FREE-WORLD HAD TO DEFEND ITS HONOR AGAINST ALL TYRANT LEADERS OF THE MIDDLE EAST.

THE AMERICAN ILLUMINATI FEELING THAT IT WAS THEIR GOD GIVEN RIGHT TO RULE SUPREME ON A GLOBAL SCALE WERE TOTALLY PREPARED TO EXERCISE THIS MASTERPLAN OF GLOBAL DOMINATION AT ANY COST TO HUMAN LIFE. THOSE WHO TRIED TO PREVENT GOD'S PLAN FROM BEING EXERCISED WITH DILIGENCE WERE THUSLY HELD DOWN WITH A FIRM FIST, LITERALLY SQUASHED LIKE A FRATERNAL BUG AS IT HAD BEEN SUPPOSEDLY WRITTEN IN THE HOLY SCRIPTURES THAT THE UNITED STATES OF THE AMERICA'S AND NO ONE ELSE WERE SAID TO BE GOD'S CHOSEN PEOPLE TO RULE THE WORLD.

WITHIN ONLY A MATTER OF A FEW DAYS AFTER MAKING HIS SEPTEMBER 14TH PITCH TO THE MASONIC ORDER'S FRATERNITY CONTROLLED UNITED NATIONS, THE AMERICAN PRESIDENT OF THE 21ST CENTURY WAS BEING COMPARED TO HITLER FOR HIS STANCE OF WARMONGERING AGAINST IRAQ'S ISLAMIC LEADER. WANTING TO SNIFF THE LIFE FORCE OUT OF FELLOW HUMAN BEINGS ESSENTIALLY PUT THE PRESIDENT OF THE WORLD'S ONLY SUPERPOWER ON THE EXACT SAME PLAYING FIELD AS THE ISLAMIC BUTCHER OF BAGHDAD. U.S. PRESIDENT GEORGE BUSH JR. HIMSELF, HAD VIRTUALLY TURNED INTO AN OUT OF CONTROL TIN-GOD WANTING TO RULE THE MIDDLE EAST AND

THE REST OF THE WORLD. AS THE INHABITANTS OF THE WORLD WATCHED, MOST FEARED FOR THE WORST, COMPLETE AND ABSOLUTE FULFILLMENT OF THE BIBLICAL PROPHECY – ARMAGEDDON.

Chapter 10 - EGYPT: THE CRADLE OF ANCIENT FREEMASONRY

Sometimes, being a devoted atheist is a godsend - no pun intended - which allows the individual to fully realize the magnitude of the true meaning of religious convictions, past as well as the present. Just like sometimes knowing that some sort of Supreme intelligence is out there but your not quite certain as to who /or what it actually is, also is a good thing. This Supreme Being that all forms of religion talk about could either be extraterrestrial /or a mere figment of man's imagination. No one knows exactly for certain who /or what this deity like creature actually is thus far. With the passage of time, the Holy Scriptures just seems to be something that has been conjured up in the form of a book of fairy tales written by a bunch of schizophrenic individuals who merely wanted to place themselves onto a pedestal in order to be glorified by all living beings. The word Free Mason for example does not belong to either Latin, Greek /or even English as far as that goes. Its origins in fact can be easily traced thousands of years before any of these languages. The name itself is said to have come from the Egypto-Coptic languages, the languages used by the Ancient Egyptians during the Golden Age of Egypt. Some historians in fact insist that the Copts are the lineal descendants of the people who emigrated from India to the Valley of the Nile River scrounging its banks with Cyclopean architecture and expressing themselves in three distinctive forms of the written language. These written languages were in;

1) Hieroglyphics
2) Hieratic
3) Demotic

THE PRIESTS AND LEARNED MEN OF EGYPT PRESERVED THEIR SACRED WRITINGS, SECRETS AND ANCIENT CEREMONIES IN THE FORM OF HIEROGLYPHICS AND HIERATIC. THE THIRD FORM OF THE WRITTEN LANGUAGE, DEMOTIC WAS USED BY THE COMMON PEOPLE PRINCIPALLY FOR COMMERCIAL PURPOSES. THIS DEMOTIC LANGUAGE WAS SAID TO HAVE BEEN VERY DIFFICULT TO TRANSLATE AS THERE WERE NO PROPERLY KEPT RECORDS OF THE LANGUAGE ITSELF BY THESE ANCIENT PEOPLE.

IN ACCORDANCE TO THE EGYPTO-COPTIC LANGUAGE **"PHREE"** MEANT CHILDREN /OR SONS OF LIGHT, WISDOM AND/OR INTELLIGENCE, WHILE **"MAiSSEN "**WAS THE PLURAL OF **"MES "**SIGNIFYING CHILDREN. FROM THESE WORDS, IT IS SAID THAT ANCIENT FREEMASONRY CAN BE TRACED AS THE ANCIENT CRAFT MEMBERS WERE ORIGINALLY KNOWN AS THE CHILDREN OF, /OR THE SONS OF LIGHT, WISDOM AND INTELLIGENCE, (**PHREE MAiSSEN**). THE LIGHT SIGNIFYING THE KNOWLEDGE OF FREEMASONRY TO THE CANDIDATE /OR INITIATE AND HIS QUEST FOR MORE OF THAT KNOWLEDGE. WHEN IT COMES TO DEALING WITH THE ORIGIN OF FREEMASONRY, THERE ARE INDISPUTABLE RECORDS FROM HIEROGLYPHICS THAT THE CRAFT EXISTED 2,000 YEARS BEFORE THE BUILDING OF KING SOLOMON'S TEMPLE. COINCIDENTLY, SOLOMON'S REIGN LASTED FROM 1033 B.C. TO 975 B.C. IT IS THEREFORE A FACT OF HISTORY THAT THE MASONIC ORDER ITSELF SURVIVED THE RAVISHES OF TIME CONTRARY AS TO WHAT SOME HISTORIANS WISH US TO BELIEVE IS TRUE. DESPITE WHAT WE ARE TOLD, THIS ANCIENT FRATERNITY HAS ENDURED THE FOLLOWING AGES;

BABYLONIAN	4,000 B.C.
EGYPTIAN	3,000 B.C.
GREEK	2,000 B.C.
ROMAN	1,000 B.C.

ANCIENT HISTORIANS IN FACT ASSURE MASONIC LINAGE DATING AS FAR BACK AS HUMANLY POSSIBLE WHEREAS THE HIGH PRIESTS OF THEBES WERE IN DIRECT LINE FOR 345 GENERATIONS. MANY INSTANCES ARE DULY RECORDED WHERE THE OCCUPATION OF ANCIENT CRAFT HAD BEEN PASSED FROM FATHER TO SON FOR COUNTLESS GENERATIONS. APPARENTLY IN THOSE EARLY DAYS, AT EVERY INITIATION, CERTAIN RITES AND CEREMONIES WERE PERFORMED AND EVERY FRATERNITY BROTHER HAD PROOF POSITIVE THAT THESE RIGHTS AND CEREMONIES ORIGINATED IN THE LAND OF VEDAS IN THE HIMALAYA MOUNTAINS. THUS WHILE FREEMASONRY IS SAID TO HAVE ORIGINATED IN ASIA, IT WAS CRADLED IN EGYPT. THESE SIGNS AND SYMBOLS, WE ARE TOLD BY HISTORIANS ARE IDENTICAL WITH THOSE USED BY THE ANCIENT BRETHREN

LONG CENTURIES BEFORE CHRIST. MANY OF WHICH ARE TO BE FOUND IN THE TOMBS AND TEMPLES OF EGYPT, ASSYRIA AND INDIA.

IN ANALYZING THE TRUE FACTS AS THEY ARE PRESENTED, IT IS OBVIOUSLY CONCLUDED THAT THE NILE RIVER PLAYED A VERY IMPORTANT ROLE IN ALLOWING THE ANCIENT CRAFT OF FREEMASONRY TO ENDURE THOUSANDS OF YEARS OF MAN'S INHUMANITY TO HIS FELLOW MAN. THE NILE, THE MOST IMPRESSIVE RIVER IN THE WORLD SECOND TO THE AMAZON, RISES IN CENTRAL AFRICA AND EVEN TO THIS VERY DATE IS IN THE EXACT SAME LOCATION OF ITS ORIGIN CHANGING JUST EVER SO SLIGHTLY DUE TO EROSION CAUSED BY THE RAVISHES OF TIME. AT THIS POINT IT SHOULD BE STATED THAT THROUGHOUT THE AGES, THE ESSENCE OF HUMAN EXISTENCE HAS ALWAYS BEEN CLOSELY CONNECTED TO THE GEOGRAPHY AND HISTORY OF A COUNTRY'S WATER SYSTEM. THE ORIGIN AND COURSE OF ITS RIVERS ENABLED THE DEVELOPMENT OF THE HUMAN RACE IN DIFFERENT REGIONS OF THE WORLD. AS EXAMPLES;

CHINA	YANG TSE
ASSYRIA	EUPHRATES
INDIA	GANGES
AFRICA	NILE AND CONGO
SOUTH AMERICA	AMAZON
LOUISIANA	MISSISSIPPI
QUEBEC	ST. LAWRENCE
BRITISH COLUMBIA	FRASER

BUT THE NILE WITHOUT A DOUBT HAS FIRST PLACE AS THE WONDER RIVER OF THE WORLD MAINLY BECAUSE OF ITS REGULAR ANNUAL INUNDATION OF THE VALLEY THROUGH WHICH IT PASSES, ENRICHING THE SOIL WHICH PRODUCES IN ABUNDANCE AND WITHOUT WHICH THE LAND OF EGYPT WOULD BE AS BARREN AS THE SAHARA. THE NILE RISES 6,500 FEET ABOVE SEA LEVEL AND ITS LENGTH IS WELL OVER 3,000 MILES — THE CURRENT IN EGYPT IS ESTIMATED IN BEING THREE MILES PER HOUR BUT INCREASES TO FOUR AND A HALF AT THE HEIGHT OF ITS INUNDATION. AT THE MOUTH OF THIS WONDERFUL AND NOBLE RIVER IS SITUATED THE ANCIENT CITY OF ALEXANDRIA, FOUNDED BY ALEXANDER THE GREAT IN 332 B.C. IT BECAME PART OF THE ROMAN EMPIRE IN 80 B.C. BUT IT WASN'T UNTIL FIFTY YEARS LATER THAT IT BECAME AN IMPERIAL CITY WITH A ROMAN GOVERNOR. HISTORY INFORMS US THAT IT WAS SECOND ONLY TO ROME WITH AN IMMENSE POPULATION, VERY HIGHLY CIVILIZED AND POSSESSED MOST, IF NOT ALL OF THE MYSTERIOUS KNOWLEDGE IN THE MECHANICAL ARTS AND SCIENCES. IN 640 A.D., IT WAS CAPTURED BY THE ARAB CALIPH UNDER AMRU, A SARACEN, WHO REPORTED TO HIS HIGH COMMANDER THAT HE HAD CAPTURED A CITY THAT HAD AN IMPRESSIVE INVENTORY OF;

4,000 PALACES

4,000 BATHS

12,000 GARDENS

400 THEATERS

12,000 DEALERS IN FRESH OIL

40,000 JEWS

AT THE TIME OF ITS CAPTURE BY THE ARABS, IT REPORTEDLY HAD TWO HUGE LIBRARIES (THE SOTER AND THE SERAPEUM) WHICH HAD BEEN FOUNDED AND LATER ENLARGED BY THE PTOLEMIES, ONE OF EGYPT'S MOST FAMOUS LINE OF KINGS. ACCORDING TO BIBLICAL TEXT, IT WAS IN THIS CITY THAT MARK SUFFERED MARTYRDOM AND PETER PREACHED CHRISTIANITY.

THE MODERN CITY NOWADAYS STANDS PARTY ON WHAT WAS IN THE OLDEN DAYS THE ISLAND OF PHAROS, THAT OF WHICH IS NOW A PENINSULA. THE OLD CITY ITSELF WAS BUILT ON THE MAINLAND AND THE RUINED WALLS OF THIS ANCIENT CITY ARE PLAINLY TRACED AND SOME OF THE OLD RESERVOIRS ARE STILL IN GOOD STATE OF PRESERVATION THOUGH BUILT 2,000 YEARS AGO. PTOLEMY SOTER (A.K.A. PTOLEMY THE FIRST), OBVIOUSLY SET OUT TO MAKE ALEXANDRIA THE CENTER OF LEARNING IN THE WORLD AS THIS POLICY WAS CAREFULLY CARRIED OUT BY HIS SUCCESSORS WHO NOT ONLY ENLARGED THE FIRST LIBRARY BUT ALSO BUILT A SECOND. IT IS CLEARLY ESTABLISHED THAT THE SPECIAL PURPOSE OF THESE LIBRARIES WAS THE CONCENTRATING OF THE MOST EMINENT SCHOLARS AND LEARNED MEN OF THE WORLD FOR THE IMPROVEMENT OF THE ARTS, SCIENCES AND PHILOSOPHIES. THE LEARNED MEN OF EGYPT WERE SENT TO ASIA AND GREECE TO COLLECT ALL THE VALUABLE MANUSCRIPTS THAT WERE PROCURABLE. MANY OF THESE BOOKS WERE COLLECTED WITHOUT COST AND UNDOUBTEDLY SOME WERE TAKEN UNDER DRESS BUT WHEN THIS PROCESS WAS LIKELY TO CAUSE TOO MUCH DISTURBANCE, A COPY WAS MADE OUT AND GIVEN TO THE OWNER. WITH THE PASSING OF TIME, AN ENORMOUS NUMBER OF BOOKS WERE THUSLY COLLECTED AND A CATALOGUE WAS LATER COMPLIED WHICH SHOWED THAT IN THE SOTER LIBRARY THERE WERE 700,000 VOLUMES, WITH ANOTHER 400,000 STOCKING THE SHELVES AT SERAPEUM. ALEXANDRIAN SCHOLARS WERE SAID TO HAVE TRANSLATED MANY OF THESE BOOKS INTO GREEK AND OTHER LANGUAGES AND DISTRIBUTED THEM TO MANY COUNTRIES THUS DISSEMINATING THE KNOWLEDGE CONTAINED IN THEM THROUGHOUT THE THEN KNOWN WORLD. BUT ACCORDING TO MOST HISTORIANS, IT IS BELIEVED THAT THE BULK OF THESE PRICELESS VOLUMES WERE DESTROYED BY THE SARACEN CALIPH AFTER HE HAD CONQUERED THE CITY AND PROMPTLY REPORTED TO HIS HIGH COMMANDER OF THE ATTAINED TROPHY.

HISTORY ALSO INFORMS US THAT ONE LONE INDIVIDUAL, JOHN THE GRAMMARIAN REQUESTED THAT CALIPH OMAR SURRENDER TO HIM ALL OF

THE BOOKS CONTAINED IN THESE LIBRARIES AND THAT THE SARACEN CALIPH REFUSED TO DO SO CITING FOR HIS REASONS FOR REFUSAL THAT IF THE BOOKS CONTAINED THE SAME RELIGIOUS DOCTRINE AS THE KORAN, THEN THE BOOKS THEMSELVES HAD NO GREAT VALUE AS THE KORAN WAS SAID TO HAVE CONTAINED ALL OF THE NECESSARY TRUTHS KNOWN TO MANKIND. CALIPH OMAR THEREFORE CONCLUDED THAT THE BOOKS HELD IN BOTH THE LIBRARIES CONTAINED WRITINGS THAT WERE CONTRARY TO THE TEACHING OF THE KORAN AND ALL THE BOOKS WERE ACCORDINGLY DESTROYED. ONE VERSION OF THE STORY OF THEIR DESTRUCTION IS ALONG THE LINES OF AN ORDER BEING GIVEN THAT THE MANUSCRIPTS BE USED FOR FUEL TO HEAT WATER FOR THE PUBLIC BATHS OF THE CITY. THIS PROCEDURE WAS REPORTEDLY CARRIED OUT AS BEING A FACT OF HISTORY AND IT IS FURTHER STATED THAT THE BOOKS PROVIDED FUEL FOR THESE BATHS FOR A PERIOD OF SIX MONTHS. AS FAR AS THAT GOES, HISTORIANS CAN'T SEEM TO EVEN AGREE ON THAT BEING A TRUE FACT OF HISTORY, THE SMALLER LIBRARY "THE SERAPEUM "WAS DESTROYED BY THE CHRISTIAN, THEODOSIUS WHO IS SAID TO HAVE RAM SACKED THE BUILDING, DESTROYING ALL OF THE BOOKS AND PILLAGED THE STATUARY. NEVERTHELESS, THE DESTRUCTION OF THESE LIBRARIES RESULTED IN THE SUPPRESSION OF THE GREEK SCHOOL OF PHILOSOPHY AND PLUNGED THE EUROPEAN WORLD INTO WHAT IS NOW SPOKEN OF AS THE DARK AGES BY CHRISTIANS WHICH LASTED 1,200 YEARS.

DURING ALL THIS TIME PERIOD, FROM THE FOURTH TO THE SEVENTEENTH CENTURIES IT SEEMS TO HAVE BEEN THE AMBITION OF THE GOVERNING AUTHORITIES TO COMPEL EVERY PERSON TO HAVE BUT ONE RELIGION AND ONE DOCTRINE AND THAT THE DOCTRINE AS AUTHORIZED BY THE GOVERNING BODY. ANYONE DEEMED GUILTY OF HAVING ANY RELIGION EXCEPT THE AUTHORIZED ONE WAS SEVERELY DEALT WITH. ALL LITERATURE HAD TO BE SANCTIONED BY THE RULING POWERS AND SUCH WAS THE SEVERITY WITH WHICH UNAUTHORIZED LITERATURE WAS DEALT WITH THAT SOME MEN WHO FEARED FOR THEIR LIVES TORCHED THEIR OWN LIBRARIES IN ORDER TO SAVE THEMSELVES AND THEIR FAMILIES FROM HAVING THE LIFE SNUFFED OUT OF THEM AT THE HANDS OF THE POWERS THAT BE. THESE WERE THE DAYS THAT WITCHES AND HERETICS WERE BURNED AT THE STAKE. DURING THE FOURTEENTH CENTURY FOR EXAMPLE, IT IS ESTIMATED THAT 100,000 OF GERMANY'S MOST INTELLIGENT MEN AND WOMEN WERE BURNED ALIVE FOR WITCHCRAFT ALONE. FURTHER TO THIS, BIBLICAL HISTORIAN JOHN WESLEY INFORMS US THAT DURING A FORTY YEAR TIME PERIOD OF THESE PERSECUTIONS AN ESTIMATED 40 MILLION PEOPLE WERE SLAUGHTERED ALL IN THE NAME OF RELIGION. ISN'T IT ANY WONDER AS TO WHY CHRISTIANS WORLDWIDE REFERRED TO IT AS BEING THE DARK AGES OF CHRISTIANITY.

Man's inhumanity to his fellow man really escalated out of control one day in November of 1095 as a group of Roman Catholics gathered in an open field outside a small French town in France, (Clermont). All forms of human life (nobles, knights as well as the country's peasantry) stood there listening to the words of their religious leader Pope Urban the Second. Apparently, the Pontiff was urging the crowd to take up arms and drive the much hated Muslims out of the country. At one time the Christians had ruled all of the Holy Land (Palestine) but the Muslims soon put an end to that by taking it away from them and by 1095, the Muslims virtually occupied every corner of the Roman Catholic domain both in Europe as well as in the East. For countless generations Europeans had an interest in what the Holy Land represented as they soon began visiting the places where Christ was said to have walked the earth. Although the Muslims permitted the Christian people to come and go freely, this was not good enough for the Roman Catholic Church as by this time period, vast fortunes were said to be had in the East.

The Catholic Church, wanting a piece of the action instigated a series of wars designed specifically to reclaim the Holy Land as their own;

First Crusade	(1096-99)
Second Crusade	(1147-49)
Third Crusade	(1189-92)
Fourth Crusade	(1202-04)
Fifth Crusade	(1218-21)
Sixth Crusade	(1228-29)
Seventh Crusade	(1248-54)
Eighth Crusade	(1270)

It is interesting to note that not only the Roman Catholic Pope Urban II despised the Muslims and everything that they stood for, but so did Pope Innocent III as well as Popes Eugenius III and Gregory VIII. Urban, being accredited for sparking the First Crusade and as the Muslims sought to reclaim their trophy, Pope Eugenius III sanctioned the military undertaking of keeping it under the Roman Catholic domain by appointing his own personal envoy to that specific cause; Bernard of Clairvaux, who just as it so happens went on to become known as a patron Saint of the Catholic faith. The Third Crusade came about largely due to the preaching tactics of Pope Gregory VIII who is said to have prophesied that it was God's

WILL THAT CHRISTIANS REIGN SUPREME IN THE HOLY LAND. WHILE THE FOURTH CRUSADE WAS INITIATED BY POPE INNOCENT III WHO'S SOLE PURPOSE IN LIFE WAS SUPPOSEDLY TO DRIVE THE MUSLIMS OUT OF THE HOLY LAND FOR ALL ETERNITY ENABLING CHRISTENDOM TO RULE THE ROOST. FOR 175 YEARS THE BATTLE FOR CONTROL OF THE HOLY LAND WENT ON LIKE A CHILDISH GAME OF TUG-OF-WAR.

NOT AT ALL SATISFIED WITH JUST CALLING THE RELIGIOUS SHOTS IN THE HOLY LAND, THE PAPACY SOON SOUGHT TO CONQUER EGYPT AS WELL, WHICH IN ESSENCE BECAME KNOWN AS THE FIFTH CRUSADE. THE SIXTH CRUSADE ON THE OTHER HAND ERUPTED WHEN FREDERICK THE SECOND (THE HOLY ROMAN EMPEROR) BEGAN CLAIMING WHAT HE PERCEIVED AS BEING HIS RIGHTFUL PLACE AT THE THRONE OF JERUSALEM. EVEN THE FRENCH MONARCHY GOT IN ON THE RELIGIOUS FESTIVITIES BY CLAIMING TO BE THE RIGHTFUL HEIR OF JERUSALEM AND EGYPT, THE SEVENTH CRUSADE WAS THE BRAIN CHILD OF KING LOUIS IX OF FRANCE. BUT KING LOUIS' DREAMS OF REIGNING SUPREME WERE SOON DASHED SOME YEARS LATER WHEN THE KING OF ENGLAND (EDWARD THE FIRST) PROCLAIMED ITS RIGHT TO SIT AT THE RIGHT HAND OF **GOD**. THIS, THE EIGHTH CRUSADE IS SAID TO HAVE BEEN THE LAST AS BY THIS TIME FRAME OF HISTORY, THE ROMAN CATHOLIC CHURCH HAD DEVELOPED A MORE SINISTER METHOD OF MAINTAINING ITS RIGHT TO SUPREMACY. THE INQUISITION, A SYSTEM OF TRIBUNALS WHEREBY A MANDATE WAS IMPLEMENTED TO EXTERMINATE THOSE WHO DID NOT HAVE THE EXACT SAME VIEWS AS THE CATHOLIC CHURCH ITSELF.

IRONICALLY, THE PAPAL INQUISITION WAS FIRST ESTABLISHED AT THE CLOSE OF THE SIXTH CRUSADE WHEN POPE GREGORY IX AND EMPEROR FREDERICK II HAD A MINOR DISAGREEMENT AS TO WHO WAS ACTUALLY IN CHARGE OF CHURCH MATTERS. AS THE STORY GOES, THE EMPEROR WANTED TO DICTATE HOW THOSE PRACTICING HERETIC BELIEFS WOULD BE PUNISHED WHILE LIVING IN HIS KINGDOM. IN RETALIATION, POPE GREGORY IX DECLARED THAT IT WAS NONE OF THE EMPEROR'S DAMN BUSINESS AND DECIDED TO DEAL WITH IT IN HIS OWN WAY. THIS IN EFFECT STARTED ONE OF HISTORY'S MOST NOTORIOUS BLOOD BATHS THAT WAS TO LAST SOME 600 YEARS.

THE FIRST WAVE OF INQUISITIONS KNOWN AS THE ROMAN INQUISITION WHICH EVENTUALLY LEAD TO THE SUPPRESSION OF THE MASONIC KNIGHTS TEMPLAR IN 1308 IS SAID TO HAVE LASTED WELL INTO THE SEVENTEENTH CENTURY. WHILE THE SECOND WAVE, SPANISH INQUISITION, WHICH WAS ORGANIZED IN 1480 WASN'T ABOLISHED UNTIL 1834. AND TO MAKE MATTERS EVEN WORST, THE ROMAN CATHOLIC CHURCH ESTABLISHED A THIRD WAVE IN 1542 UNDER THE WATCHFUL EYE OF POPE PAUL THE THIRD. THIS OFFSHOOT OCCURRED PRINCIPALLY BECAUSE OF THE FACT THAT IMPROVEMENTS TO THE PRINTING PRESS HAD BEEN MAKING IT POSSIBLE FOR NEW IDEAS TO

BE PUBLISHED AND READ WORLDWIDE AND THE CHURCH WAS NOT AT ALL IMPRESSED WITH THE CREATIVE WRITING STYLES OF THE BOOKS AUTHORS. IN A DESPERATE BID TO CONTROL THE THOUGHTS AND IDEAS OF OTHERS, BOTH THE PAPAL INQUISITION AND THE SPANISH INQUISITION WERE THUSLY AMALGAMATED INTO A NEW DECREE; THE HOLY ROMAN AND UNIVERSAL INQUISITION. POPE PAUL'S VERSION OF AN INQUISITION WAS IN THE FORM OF A COMMITTEE IN ROME WHOSE ONE SIMPLE TASK WAS TO GIVE FAIR WARNING TO PEOPLE WHO NOT ONLY PREACHED AGAINST THE CATHOLIC DOCTRINE BUT ALSO WROTE ABOUT IT AS WELL. IF THE PERSON AND/OR PERSONS DID NOT COMPLY WITH THE WISHES OF THE CHURCH, THEN THEY WERE ACCUSED OF SPREADING HERETICAL DOCTRINE THAT WAS IN DIRECT OPPOSITION TO THE ROMAN CATHOLIC CHURCH. AND IF THEY REFUSED TO CHANGE, THEY WERE EITHER THROWN INTO PRISON /OR DEALT WITH APPROPRIATELY BY OTHER MEANS.

INTERESTINGLY, DURING THE CRUSADES MANY A FREEMASON FOUGHT SIDE-BY-SIDE DEFENDING WHAT THEY HAD BELIEVED WAS THEIR GOD GIVEN RIGHT TO REIGN SUPREME; THE KNIGHTS TEMPLAR ALONG WITH THE TEUTONIC KNIGHTS AS WELL AS THE KNIGHTS OF MALTA. BUT WITH THE INSANITY OF THE INQUISITION, THE PAPACY BEGAN ITS LONG STRENUOUS INVESTIGATION INTO FREEMASONRY ACTIVITIES WHICH FORCED MANY A FREEMASON TO OPERATE UNDERGROUND IN TOTAL AND OUTRIGHT SECRECY. ACCORDINGLY, THE ROMAN CATHOLIC CHURCH ACCUSED THE MASONIC ORDER OF ENCOURAGING HUMAN BEINGS TO ACT IN MANY EVIL WAYS THAT WERE VERY DESTRUCTIVE TO THE HARMONIOUS AND PEACEFUL NATURE OF THE CATHOLIC FAITH.

MEANWHILE BACK IN EGYPT, ARTIFACTS WERE BEING DISCOVERED THAT LITERALLY BROUGHT INTO QUESTION THE VERY EXISTENCE OF BIBLICAL TEXT WHICH THROUGH THE AGES HAS CAUSED MAN TO REVISE AND/OR REWRITE WHAT HAD BEEN ORIGINALLY PERCEIVED AS BEING THE TRUE WORD OF GOD. MASONICALLY SPEAKING, POMPEY'S PILLAR AND CLEOPATRA'S NEEDLES ARE SAID TO BE PRIME EXAMPLES OF SUCH. POMPEY'S PILLAR IS LOCATED A SHORT DISTANCE FROM ALEXANDRIA AND BEARS A GREEK INSCRIPTION WHICH PROVED BEYOND A SHADOW OF A DOUBT THAT IT WAS ERECTED IN HONOR OF THE EMPEROR DIOCLETIAN. ITS BASE IS ABOUT 15 FEET SQUARE. THE SHAFT IS A SINGLE PIECE OF GRANITE, 73 FEET LONG AND 29 FEET 8 INCHES IN CIRCUMFERENCE. IT IS CROWNED WITH A CORINTHIAN CAPITAL 9 FEET HIGH. ITS TOTAL HEIGHT IS THUS 100 FEET. IT IS SAID THAT SOME ENGLISH SAILORS FOUGHT PAINSTAKINGLY TO CLIMB TO THE TOP AND ONCE THERE, FOUND A CAVITY WHICH SOME HISTORIANS DECLARED HELD YET ANOTHER STATUE AT ONE TIME /OR ANOTHER. THE CAUSE OF ITS ERECTION SEEMS TO HAVE BEEN

A thanksgiving to the Emperor in return for a gift of grain sent to the Alexandrians apparently in a time of famine.

Like Pompey's Pillar, Cleopatra's Needles also contained a historical significance pertaining to Biblical text. The Needles were originally erected at Heliopolis about 1500 B.C. but later moved by the Romans to Alexandria to decorate the "Caesareum" during the reign of Tiberius in about 14 B.C. Coincidently, one of these obelisks was given to the British Government by Mahommed Ali (no, not the American boxer Cassius Clay) and transported to England where it was eventually erected on the banks of the Thames River at London in 1878. Its dimensions are 68 feet long and 7 feet 7 inches across the base. The second of these obelisks was also given to another governing body as a symbolic gesture of good faith and in 1880 was erected in Central Park in New York City. It was slightly bigger than the other, standing 69 feet high with a base of 7 feet 9 inches and having a weight of 200 tons.

The granite used in both Pompey's Pillar and the Needles had been quarried from the same place undoubtedly in Syene, that of which is a great distance up the Nile River from Alexandria as the Hieroglyphics themselves are quite distinguishable in their form and meanings. To contemplate the craftsmanship of these ancients on the granite as well as the undertaking of removing such a huge piece of work for such a vast distance must surely make mouths drop in absolute and total awe. Since they were first quarried, nearly thirty-five centuries have passed thus heightening not only our opinion of the ability and ingenuity of those ancient peoples who made them but also peaking our curiosity of the historic value behind them. When the one which went to New York was being prepared for shipping, it was soon discovered that beneath the stone there existed a number of Masonic Emblems - an apron, a trowel, a trestles board and two ashlars - thus proof positive of Freemasonry's actual existence thousands upon thousands of years prior to the birth of Jesus Christ contrary as to what theologians wish us to believe is true.

Another interesting aspect of the Ancient Craft of Freemasonry is the fact that it is supposedly adverse to Christianity but yet it is said to be the purest of all other forms of religion devoting itself to not only to the teaching of the ultimate truth but the preaching of it as well. And part of that truth is its decalogue, which is a law passed down through the ages enabling Free Masons to stay on the path of righteousness. Incorporated within its own doctrine,

THE TEN COMMANDMENTS OF FREEMASONRY HELPS THE INITIATES ONTO THE HIGHER PLANE OF SPIRITUAL FULFILLMENT AND THE DESIRE TO OBTAIN MORE KNOWLEDGE OF HIS /OR HER'S HIGHER SELF; THUS BECOMING ONE WITH GOD, THE CREATOR OF THE UNIVERSE. IT'S A WELL KNOWN FACT OF HISTORY THAT IN ANCIENT TIMES, RELIGION AND SCIENCE CLASHED WITH ONE ANOTHER FOR HUNDREDS UPON HUNDREDS OF CENTURIES AS SPIRITUAL ADVISORS FELT THREATENED BY THIS UNQUENCHABLE THIRST FOR SCIENTIFIC KNOWLEDGE. WITH THE EROSION OF TIME, BOTH SCIENCE AND RELIGION SET ASIDE THEIR DIFFERENCES OF OPINION AND SOON WALKED THE SAME PATH IN THE FORM OF ONE SEPARATE ENTITY. IT WAS AS THOUGH A COLLABORATION OF SORTS HAD TRANSPIRED ALLOWING THE HUMAN RACE THAT SLIGHTEST CHANCE OF NOT WHIPPING ITSELF OFF THE FACE OF THE EARTH ALL IN THE NAME OF RELIGION.

ACCORDING TO ALL MASONIC LITERATURE, ATHEISTS AND AGNOSTICS ARE PERCEIVED AS BEING IN DIRECT OPPOSITION TO FREEMASONRY. OBVIOUSLY THIS IS CONTRARY TO POPULAR BELIEF AS IT IS NOT THE SAME RHETORIC THAT THEOLOGIANS HAVE BEEN PREACHING ON A GLOBAL SCALE SINCE TIME BEGAN. THUS FAR, ONE CANNOT BECOME A MEMBER OF THE ANCIENT CRAFT IF THEY DO NOT BELIEVE IN THE EXISTENCE OF A SUPREME BEING. THIS PHENOMENON OF DIVINE INTERVENTION TO SOME MAY SEEM LIKE A NOBLE IDEA, BUT TO AN ATHEIST IT'S ALL PART OF THE ILLUSION OF A FAIRY TALE AND ITS SCHIZOPHRENIC ACTIVITIES CONJURED UP BY THE POWERS THAT BE AS A WAY AND MEANS OF CONTROLLING A PERSON'S THOUGHTS, AMBITIONS AND IDEAS. WITH THIS PRECONCEIVED NOTION, THE ATHEIST AND/OR AGNOSTIC IS IN OPEN REVOLT AGAINST THE ATTRIBUTES OF ALL FORMS OF RELIGION, (ROMAN CATHOLIC AS WELL AS PROTESTANT). TO THEM, NO FORM OF RELIGION IS SACRED.

ALTHOUGH AN ATHEIST SEE'S RELIGION AS BEING UTTER POPPYCOCK, THE WORLD'S FREEMASONRY PAST IS VERY INTRIGUING TO RESEARCH. PERHAPS THIS IS MAINLY BECAUSE OF THE FACT THAT EVEN MASONIC HISTORIANS CAN'T SEEM TO DECIDE IF THE MASONIC ORDER IS A FORM OF RELIGION /OR NOT. INTERESTINGLY, THIS DENIAL OF BEING AN ACTUAL RELIGION IS SAID TO HAVE OCCURRED DURING THE DARK AGES OF CHRISTIANITY AS ALL MASONIC ACTIVITIES WAS FORCED TO OPERATE UNDERGROUND AS A WAY AND MEANS OF SURVIVAL. TO THIS VERY DAY, FREEMASONS WORLDWIDE DENY BEING A RELIGION AS THEY PRACTICE THE RITUALS AND CEREMONIES OF ANCIENT EGYPT.

THE ANCIENT ONES CAN NOT ONLY BE EASILY TRACED THOUSANDS OF YEARS BEFORE ANY WELL KNOWN LANGUAGES BUT ALSO 2,000 YEARS BEFORE THE ACTUAL BUILDING OF KING SOLOMON'S TEMPLE AS WELL AS LONG BEFORE THE BIRTH OF CHRIST. AFTER CAREFULLY EXAMINING THE TEMPLES AND THE RUINS OF THIS PREHISTORIC CIVILIZATION IN THE WONDROUS VALLEY OF THE NILE

River, Masonic scientists, historians, archaeologists, geographers and language experts throughout the world quickly concluded that their fraternity endured the ravishes of time as they soon began documenting their findings for all to see and examined as being a newfound truth of human existence. Before long, Biblical scholars began denouncing what science was attempting to make public knowledge and as time passed, only the selected few knew the actual truth of man's existence on this planet known as Earth. Since its earliest conception in Ancient Egypt, the philosophy of Freemasonry has been the teaching and preaching of the knowledge of the true God and its ultimate truths. With the unlocking of the secrets of the universe, the human race was supposedly going to be able to rise to its own glory thus distinguishing it from all other life forms. But the human animal being exactly as to what it is, waged war onto those who had opposing views and/or religious convictions. Thus proving that old adage that man's inhumanity to his fellow human being had not yet evolved from his animal instincts.

It goes without saying that every single one of the ancient philosophic craftsman lifted the veil of secrecy pertaining to the great mysteries of life as they received those sublime teachings, (which were the wonders of the ancient world) and began understanding there significance in the realm of spiritual fulfillment towards life's higher plane of existence. The first inhabitants of Egypt were said to have understood the vast meanings of the truths of all religions and philosophies, old as well as the new, and soon began writing them down onto anything that was available at the time, mostly skins of lambs and papyrus. The occasional temple /or pyramid would later provide them with the perfect canvas for their Hieroglyphic and Hieratic writing styles.

Masonically speaking, the Light and Wisdom of Phree Maissen is the very fiber of human existence as it is a normal human instinct to have thirst to obtain guidance through discovery and to be able to search and think for one's own self. With this unquenchable thirst comes developing the power of thought, which in most cases could not have otherwise been accomplished if man's thoughts, ideas and/or ambitions had been stifled. This oddly enough is where the term **"KNOWLEDGE IS POWER "** is said to have originated as the powers that be by this time period of history had snuffed out most, if not all of man's innovations as they did not coincide with Church doctrine. Nowadays, many people misinterpret the meaning of the phrase

FOR THE WRONG THING. TO THEM, IT SYMBOLIZES A SUPERFICIAL MEANING ENABLING A PERSON TO USE BRUTE FORCE ONTO OTHERS. WHEN IN REALITY, IT IS SIMPLY MEANT THAT THE INDIVIDUAL WHO WISHES TO POSSESS CERTAIN FACTS AND TRUTHS IS ON THE PATH OF ACQUIRING PERFECT KNOWLEDGE THAT IS TRUE IN EVERY SENSE OF THE WORD AND CANNOT BE DISPUTED BY ANYONE, NO MATTER WHO MAKES THE CLAIM OF DISCREDITING ITS AUTHENTICITY.

TO THAT END, THE CONSCIOUSNESS OF THE HUMAN MIND IS CONSIDERED TO BE THE *SIXTH SENSE*. THIS ASPECT OF DISCOVERY INVOLVES OPENING THE HUMAN MIND TO AN ENTOURAGE OF POSSIBILITIES RANGING FROM THE PERFORMANCE OF A PERSON THROWING THEIR VOICE TO HAVING SPOONS AND FORKS BENDING AT WILL. TO MANY DURING THE DARK AGES OF CHRISTIANITY, THIS *SIXTH SENSE* ENABLED THEM TO TAP INTO THEIR PSYCHE AND EXPLORE ASPECTS OF CLAIRVOYANCE. THE ROMAN CATHOLIC CHURCH BEING THE POWER OF AUTHORITY AT THE TIME LABELED THIS ABILITY AS BEING WITCHCRAFT AND BURNED ITS PERFORMERS AT THE STAKE. AS FAR AS THE CHURCH WAS CONCERNED, EACH AND EVERY AVENUE BEING EXPLORED BY THOSE ATTEMPTING TO EXERCISE THIS *SIXTH SENSE* ABILITY WERE UNBALANCING THE HARMONY OF NATURE'S LAWS WHICH WERE SAID TO HAVE BEEN ORDAINED BY THE ALMIGHTY GOD HIMSELF. MANIFESTING ITSELF LIKE A GROWING CANCER ON THE PLANET, MORE AND MORE OF MAN'S CONSCIOUSNESS ABILITY BEGAN TO SPREAD AS ITS POSSESSORS WANTED TO KNOW EXACTLY AS TO HOW THE HUMAN MIND WAS ABLE TO DO SUCH WONDROUS THINGS AT SO MUCH EASE AND REVERENCE. THE MORE MAN WANTED TO LEARN, THE HARDER IT BECAME JUST TO STAY ALIVE AS THE CHURCH WANTED TO RID THE PLANET OF ITS CANCEROUS TUMOR. IT THEREFORE CANNOT BE ARGUED BY ANYONE THAT THE HUMAN MIND DOES NOT LITERALLY HOLD THE KEY TO MOST OF THE MYSTERIES OF MAN'S EXISTENCE ON THIS GIGANTIC SWIRL OF MARBLE TYPE GLASS THAT'S JUST SUSPENDED IN THE UNIVERSE AS ONE WOULD HAVE ASSUMED THAT ALL MANKIND WOULD HAVE OBLITERATED ITSELF OFF THE FACE OF THE EARTH BY NOW.

OH, WHAT A THING IT WOULD BE IF ALL MANKIND USED THIS *SIXTH SENSE* TO END ALL OF ITS HOSTILITIES ON A GLOBAL SCALE WITHOUT THE RITUALS AND SACRIFICES THAT HAS BEEN NORMALLY ATTRIBUTED AND/OR DEMONSTRATED FOR THOUSANDS UPON THOUSANDS OF YEARS UNDER THE DECEPTION OF THE NON-RELIGIOUS TITLE OF THE **FATHERHOOD OF GOD** AND THE **BROTHERHOOD OF MAN** IN ITS ATTEMPTS OF FINALIZING A MASTERPLAN OF A ONE WORLD GOVERNMENT THROUGH THE AUSPICES OF A **NEW WORLD ORDER**. ONE OF THESE DAYS, ALL OF THE RELIGIOUS RHETORIC IS SIMPLY GOING TO JUMP UP AND BITE EVERYONE IN THE ASS AS THE HOSTAGES WAKE FROM THEIR DEEP SLEEP AND BEGIN TO REALIZE THAT ALL FORMS OF RELIGION ARE PURE BALDERDASH. GRANTED, THE HISTORY OF ANCIENT FREEMASONRY MAKES INTERESTING READING AND EVEN MAKES A DEVOTED ATHEIST SHAKE HIS /OR HER HEAD IN

WONDERMENT, THE FACT REMAINS PURE AND SIMPLE; GLOBAL DOMINATION IS THE INTENTION OF ALL THE PARTIES IN QUESTION.

SINCE THE DAWNING OF TIME, THE HUMAN RACE HAS ALWAYS USED BIBLICAL TEXT AS A WAY AND MEANS OF NOT ONLY CONTROLLING A PERSON'S THOUGHTS AND/OR IDEAS BUT ALSO AS AN INSTRUMENT OF JUSTIFYING ITS INHUMAN ACTS OF AGGRESSION ONTO HIS FELLOW MAN. FOR EXAMPLE, TOWARDS THE CLOSING OF THE TWENTIETH CENTURY SCHISM AMONGST THOSE WHO SOUGHT GLOBAL DOMINATION REARED ITS UGLY HEAD ONCE MORE AS ISLAMIC FRATERNITY LEADER SADDAM HUSSEIN MOVED HIS TROOPS INTO THE NEIGHBORING COUNTRY OF KUWAIT. WHICH IN ESSENCE SPARKED THE PERSIAN GULF WAR, AN ATTACK LEAD BY THE UNITED MASONIC ALLIED FORCES IN RETALIATION TO SADDAM'S OCCUPATION. WITH THE ANCIENT FREEMASONRY STAGE ALREADY SET, MEDIA OUTLETS THROUGHOUT THE WORLD SOON BEGAN INSISTING THAT IT WAS A WAR FOR DEMOCRACY AND THAT THE DEMOCRATIC PROCESS HAD DECREED THAT THE OIL RICK COUNTRY OF KUWAIT HAD TO BE PROTECTED AT ANY COST TO HUMAN LIFE AS THE BASIC PRINCIPLE OF DEMOCRACY WAS NOW SAID TO BE AT RISK. BEING OBLIVIOUS TO THE WHOLE ISSUE, THE VAST MAJORITY OF THE POPULATION LIVING IN THE WESTERN FREE-WORLD ACCEPTED THE RHETORIC AS BEING GOSPEL. AFTERALL, ONE OF THE WORLD'S MOST POWERFUL NATIONS (THE U.S. OF A.) WOULDN'T DARE LIE TO ITS PEOPLE!!! BUT BEFORE LONG, PROTESTS AND DEMONSTRATIONS WERE BEING ORCHESTRATED THROUGHOUT THE ENTIRE NORTH AMERICAN CONTINENT DEMANDING THAT NO BLOOD BE SHED FOR OIL AND THAT THE PERSIAN GULF WAR PART ONE BE STOPPED IMMEDIATELY. SURPRISINGLY, THE ONLY ONE TELLING THE ACTUAL TRUTH ON THE WHOLE MATTER WAS SADDAM HUSSEIN HIMSELF. HE WAS ODDLY ENOUGH CALLING IT A **HOLY WAR, ... A JIHAD.**

EVEN ONE OF AMERICA'S OWN MILITARY LEADERS BEGAN QUESTIONING THE WAY IN WHICH BRUTE FORCE WAS BEING EXPOUNDED ONTO THE IRAQI PEOPLE AS U.S. MILITARY PLANES BEGAN BOMBING THE HELL OUT OF BAGHDAD AS A MEANS OF ATTEMPTING TO CAPTURE SOMEONE WHO THE FRATERNITY DEEMED TO BE A TERRORIST OF SORTS FOR HIS HORRIFIC ACT OF MARCHING TO THE BEAT OF A DIFFERENT DRUMMER BY INVADING KUWAIT. ON MONDAY, SEPTEMBER 17TH, 1990 THE AMERICAN MASONICALLY CONTROLLED MILITARY INSTITUTION LOCATED IN WASHINGTON, D.C., KNOWN TO ALL AS THE PENTAGON, FIRED GENERAL MIKE DUGAN AS ITS U.S. AIR FORCE CHIEF OF STAFF AFTER DUGAN REPORTEDLY CRITICIZED THE PLANNING AND ATTACKING PROCEDURES SCHEDULED TO BE EXECUTED ON IRAQ AND THE TERMINATION OF ITS LEADER, SADDAM HUSSEIN. WITHIN ONLY MINUTES OF THE FIRING, U.S. DEFENSE SECRETARY (RICHARD CHENEY) STOOD BEFORE A PRESS GALLERY EXPLAINING HIS DECISION TO EXTINGUISH DUGAN'S CHAIN OF COMMAND BECAUSE OF COMMENTS MADE BY HIM IN PUBLIC. CHENEY

THEN EMPHASIZED THE IMPORTANCE OF SECRECY DURING SUCH MATTERS OF NATIONAL SECURITY AND THAT DUGAN WILLINGLY BREACHED BOTH SECURITY AND PROTOCOL WHEN HE BEGAN TO PUBLICALLY CONDEMN THE ACTIONS OF THE AMERICAN PRESIDENCY UNDER THE STEWARDSHIP OF MASONIC LEADER GEORGE BUSH SENIOR, (CHENEY WOULD LATER ON BE ANOINTED AS A WAR ADVISOR TO GEORGE BUSH JUNIOR DURING THE 21ST CENTURY HOSTILITIES IN THE MIDDLE EAST). UNSCATHED BY GENERAL MIKE DUGAN'S ATTEMPTS OF TELLING THE CITIZENRY OF THE WESTERN HEMISPHERE THAT A SECRET HIDDEN AGENDA HAD TRANSPIRED BEHIND THE SCENES DURING THE FIRST PERSIAN GULF WAR, LIFE WENT ON AS IT DID BEFORE AS THE VAST MAJORITY OF ITS POPULATION CONTINUED STICKING THEIR HEADS IN THE SAND HOPING THAT THINGS WOULD IRON ITSELF OUT IN THE END. EVEN THOSE WHO THOUGHT THAT THEY HAD THE WHOLE ISSUE FIGURED OUT WERE BLIND SIDED BY THEIR OWN IGNORANCE AS MORE PROTESTS AND DEMONSTRATIONS WERE BEING EXECUTED WITH PLACARDS STATING THE USUAL RHETORIC, **NO BLOOD FOR OIL** SOON BOMBARDED THE TELEVISION AIRWAVES NATION WIDE FOR DAYS AND WEEKS AT A TIME. WITHIN A MATTER OF DAYS, EACH AND EVERY LIVING SOUL SOON FORGOT THE WORDS OF FIRED GENERAL DUGAN AS THE CITIZENRY OF NORTH AMERICA BECAME DESENSITIZED AND BRAINWASHED BY THE AMERICAN POWERS THAT BE AND CONTINUED TO BE SO WELL INTO THE VARIOUS STAGES OF THE SECOND PERSIAN GULF WAR.

DESPITE THIS LITTLE SETBACK OF HUSSEIN'S INSURRECTION OF INVADING KUWAIT IN THE 1990'S, THE INTERCOURSE AND SUBSEQUENT MARRIAGE OF GLOBAL DOMINATION PROCEEDED AS PLANNED. COUNTLESS MEETINGS TOOK PLACE IN FINALIZING VARIOUS STAGES OF EUROPEAN UNIFICATION WITHIN ONLY MONTHS OF THE BERLIN WALL'S BEING DISMANTLED AND BY MIDNIGHT DECEMBER 31ST, 2001 EUROPE'S NEW EURO CURRENCY HAD MADE HISTORY AS IT BECAME A COMMON CURRENCY TO BE USED BY ALL EUROPEAN NATIONS. TO SOME, THIS MARKED THE DEMISE OF HUMAN CIVILIZATION AS THEY KNEW IT BECAUSE MOST OF THE CURRENCY BEING PHASED OUT BY THE MARRIAGE OF THE VARIOUS EUROPEAN NATIONS CONSISTED OF SOME OF THE OLDEST CURRENCY BEING USED IN THE WORLD. SOME OF THE COINS, HAVING A HISTORY GOING AS FAR BACK AS 2,650 YEARS EXISTING DURING THE TIME PERIOD OF ANCIENT FREEMASONRY. AND JUST LIKE WHAT THE WRITINGS ON THE WALLS OF THE GREAT PYRAMID IN EGYPT HAD PROPHESIED EVIL WAS SLOWLY BEING LIFTED FROM THE SHOULDERS OF THE WORLD.

IRONICALLY, NOT EVERYONE WAS ACCEPTING THIS ILLUMINATI CONCEPT OF GLOBALIZED DOMINATION. ON TUESDAY, SEPTEMBER 11TH, 2001 A CLEAR MESSAGE OF THEIR DISPLEASURE WAS DISPATCHED TO WHAT WAS PERCEIVED AS BEING THE ULTIMATE FORCE BEHIND THIS PLAN OF DEGRADATION. AIRLINE PASSENGER PLANES WERE FIRST HIJACKED FROM WITHIN THE UNITED STATES

OF AMERICA'S OWN HOMELAND, THEN FORCED TO CRASH LAND INTO SPECIFIC TARGETS. THE WORLD TRADE CENTER SYMBOLIZING AMERICA'S NEED TO OBTAIN MORE AND MORE MONEY IN ORDER TO ACHIEVE ITS GOAL AND THE PENTAGON, SYMBOLIZING THE MILITARY MIGHT BEHIND THE MASTERPLAN ITSELF. IT IS BELIEVED BY SOME THAT THIS ACT OF SO-CALLED TERRORISM ONTO THE UNITED STATES WAS EXECUTED LARGELY DUE TO THE FACT THAT IT WAS THE AMERICAN GOVERNMENT'S LONG TERM PLAN TO ERASE THE BORDER THAT SEPARATED CANADA FROM THE U.S. MAKING ALL CANADIAN SOIL NORTH OF THE 49TH PARALLEL THE 51ST STATE IN THE AMERICAN UNION. FURTHER TO THIS, IT IS ALSO BELIEVED THAT ONCE THE BORDER IS WHIPPED OUT TOTALLY CANADA WOULD HAVE NO OTHER ALTERNATIVE BUT TO ACCEPT THE AMERICAN CURRENCY AS ITS OWN ALL IN THE NAME OF THE FREE-TRADE AGREEMENT THAT WAS DULY SIGNED NOT SO LONG AGO ENABLING THE UNIFICATION OF THE ENTIRE NORTH AMERICAN CONTINENT. THE SAME PROCEDURE WAS BELIEVED TO ALSO APPLY TO MEXICO AS WELL. THIS PLAN OF **"MANIFEST DESTINY"** IS ALSO SAID TO HAVE BEEN INCORPORATED IN BOTH FREE-TRADE AGREEMENTS OF THESE COUNTRIES, THE UNITED STATES OF COURSE BEING THE VICTOR AS IT NOT ONLY HAD AN AGREEMENT WITH CANADA BUT ALSO WITH MEXICO. THUS FAR, MAKING EUROPEAN UNIFICATION A TEST CASE TOWARDS GLOBALIZATION. WITH THE HIJACKING OF PLANES FROM WITHIN ITS OWN BORDERS, THE MESSAGE OF DISSATISFACTION WAS CLEARLY UNDERSTOOD AS THE AMERICAN PRESIDENCY VOWED IMMEDIATE REVENGE ONTO THOSE WHO DARED INVADE THE MOST POWERFUL NATION IN THE WORLD ON ITS OWN TURF. IRONIC AS IT MAY SEEM, IT WAS O.K. FOR THE AMERICANS TO BOMB THE HELL OUT OF SOMEONE ELSE'S COUNTRY BUT IT WAS TABOO FOR OTHER COUNTRIES TO ATTACK THE UNITED STATES.

THE DOUBLE STANDARD INTERESTINGLY ENOUGH SEEMS TO HAVE COME ABOUT LARGELY DUE TO THE FACT THAT IN THE 1940'S WHILE TALKS WERE STILL IN THE PROCESS STAGES OF DEVELOPMENT BETWEEN THE AMERICAN AND JAPANESE FREEMASONS TRYING TO RECONCILE THEIR FRATERNAL DIFFERENCES OF OPINION CONCERNING GLOBAL DOMINATION, THE IMPERIAL GOVERNMENT OF JAPAN ATTACKED PEARL HARBOR DURING THE EARLY MORNING HOURS OF DECEMBER 7TH, 1941. AT THE TIME, PEARL HARBOR WAS THE SITE OF ONE OF THE UNITED STATES GOVERNMENT'S PRINCIPAL NAVAL BASES. IN 1887, THE U.S. GOVERNMENT RECEIVED AUTHORIZATION FROM THE HAWAIIAN GOVERNMENT TO ESTABLISH AND MAINTAIN FACILITIES FOR SHIPS DESTINED TO PARTS UNKNOWN IN THE SOUTH PACIFIC OCEAN. THE MILITARY INSTALLATION OF PEARL HARBOR WAS LOCATED IN A SECLUDED INLET ON THE SOUTH SHORE OF THE ISLAND OF OAHU, SIX MILES WEST OF HONOLULU. AS PART OF THEIR BELIEF OF HAVING **GOD'S** GIVEN RIGHT TO REIGN SUPREME, THE HAWAIIAN ISLANDS BECAME AMERICAN TERRITORY IN 1898.

Hawaii's Freemasonry history to say the least is that of a somewhat rather strange one as it was France who was said to have first established a Masonic Lodge in April of 1841. A French whaler by the name of Captain Georges LeTellier formed the French-speaking Lodge "le Progres de l'Oceanie 371 "in Honolulu. His barque, the Ajax, reportedly had broken down and had been towed into Honolulu Harbor for repairs. Although the date of the Lodge's initial Charter was originally believed to have been that of April 8TH, 1843, more recent documentation seems to indicate that the Lodge was first chartered one year previously, (April 8TH, 1842). But due to the fact that fraternity Brother LeTellier was always out on the high seas chasing whales and not maintaining his Masonic obligations that were normally associated with established Lodgery, France's Freemasonry leaders therefore canceled his Charter altogether and it was soon replaced with an American Freemasonry system. At this time period of history, France had amalgamated its fraternity causes towards global domination with American Freemasons. And nearly 150 years later, July of 1989, the State of Hawaii's Freemasonry membership were seeking political independence from the Grand Lodge of California as Honolulu's resident William K. McKee, Jr., (Waikiki Lodge No. 774) was installed as the Most Worshipful Grand Master while Brother Nelson A. Haina was duly elected Grand Secretary with their fraternal headquarters at the Honolulu Masonic Temple, 1227 Makiki Street. California's Most Worshipful Grand Master, Brother Stanley Channon was the installing officer of the festive ceremonies.

Within months after his Masonic appointment as Hawaii's new governing body, a much heated debate erupted during the first meeting of the Grand Lodge of the Hawaiian Islands. At its first recorded meeting, it was suggested that all Hawaiian Lodges be numbered according to the dates of their admission into the Grand Lodge of California rather than by the date of formation. Grand Master McKee intervened by declaring that all numbers should be abolished altogether: "The Lodges in the Grand Lodge of Hawaii are, therefore, not numbered." While under California's jurisdictional control for well over a century, all Hawaiian Lodgery maintained its numbering system but as the transformation was taking place in the early parts of 1990, so were its Freemasonry powers. The twelve California State controlled Hawaiian Lodges were; Kilauea Lodge No. 330, (Hilo, Hawaii); Kona Lodge No. 836, (Captain Cook, Hawaii); Kauai Lodge No. 589, (Lihue, Kauai); Koolau Lodge No. 801, (Kailua,

Hawaii); Lodge Maui No. 472, (Kahului, Hawaii); Schofield Lodge No. 443, (Wahiawa, Oahu). Honolulu, the Capital City of the Hawaiian Islands ironically had a total of six Lodges; Hawaiian Lodge No. 21, Honolulu Lodge No. 409, King Kalakaua Lodge No. 838, Pearl Harbor Lodge No. 598, and naturally Waikiki Lodge No. 774 and le Progres de l'Oceanie Lodge No. 371. The Hawaiian Grand Lodge's heated argument took place at its first Annual Communication meeting held in Honolulu on September 14TH through to the 16TH, 1990. In attendance, were many Masonic Grand Jurisdictional representatives from all parts of the world, not surprisingly, Canada included.

This grand Freemasonry year of 1990 thusly marked the birth of a totally recognized Masonic State of Hawaii, controlled by its Brethrenship in preparation for the **New World Order** deadline of the year 2000. In accordance to Freemasonry literature on this subject, "After several years of discussions and attempts to start, the Grand Lodge of Hawaii officially began on July 1ST, 1989 with the installation of officers. "This statement was obviously not displayed in the Masonic Bulletins for public consumption and/or scrutinizing. Due the fact that it was a Frenchman who originally set the fraternity wheels in motion during the mid-1800's to bring Hawaii into the American family fold, Canadian Freemasons were said to have not recognized the United States maneuver for full Masonic State of Hawaiian jurisdictional powers until the spring of 1990; nine full months after its conception for political independence. Hawaii therefore didn't actually become a fully recognized self-governing Masonic body until thirty years after it was originally declared a State within the American Union on August 21ST, 1959. With its official title of Masonic governing powers being recognized, the American State of Hawaii's implemented the Grand Lodge of the Hawaiian Islands which enabled them to became the 51ST Grand Lodge in the United States, one for each State in the Union and one for the nations capital in the District of Columbia. In accordance to Masonic doctrine, a State and/or country is not recognized as being a member of the Inter-American Masonic Federation, (sometimes known as the Masonic Family), if they do not have an established Grand Lodge to help guide the destiny of its people. Because of the fact that American Freemasons in the State of California were basically calling the fraternity shots, Hawaiian Freemasons somewhat resented this lack of political autonomy

AND THEREFORE WANTED TO CONTROL THEIR OWN LIVES AND NOT BE HELD ACCOUNTABLE BY THOSE LIVING ABROAD.

ONLY ONE YEAR PRIOR TO THE JAPANESE ATTACK ON PEARL HARBOR, THE VAST MAJORITY OF THE POPULATION OF THE CONTINENTAL UNITED STATES, (HAWAII INCLUDED), WERE DEAD SET AGAINST ENTERING THE WAR EFFORT OF THE SECOND WORLD WAR; EIGHTY-THREE PERCENT. AND FOLLOWING THE INITIAL JAPANESE ATTACK, THE FRATERNITY LEADER FOR THE UNITED STATES (MASONIC BROTHER F.D. ROOSEVELT) ALMOST IMMEDIATELY APPOINTED A COMMISSION OF INQUIRY TO DETERMINE WHAT EXACTLY WENT WRONG FOR SUCH A DIRTY DEED OF TERRORISM TO BE ABLE TO HAVE BEEN EXECUTED ON AMERICAN SOIL. ONLY WEEKS LATER, THE COMMISSION'S FINDINGS WERE MADE PUBLIC KNOWLEDGE, JANUARY 24TH, 1942. IT WAS THEREFORE CONCLUDED THAT THE COMMANDING OFFICERS OF THE HAWAIIAN MILITARY INSTALLATION (NAVAL AS WELL AS ARMY) WERE IN DIRECT DERELICTION OF THEIR DUTIES, A SLEEP AT THE SWITCH AS IT WERE. THOSE INDIVIDUALS RESPONSIBLE, TWO OF THE UNITED STATES OF AMERICA'S MOST DECORATED MILITARY OFFICERS, REAR ADMIRAL HUSBAND EDWARD KIMMEL AND MAJOR GENERAL WALTER CAMPBELL SCOTT WERE SUBSEQUENTLY FORCED TO RETIRE FROM SERVICE. IN THE MEANTIME, THE UNITED STATES WAS ALREADY IN THE MIDST OF RETALIATION PRACTICES SEEKING REVENGE FOR THE DESTRUCTION AND/OR DAMAGE OF EIGHT BATTLESHIPS AND TEN OTHER NAVAL VESSELS PLUS, AN ESTIMATED 200 AIRCRAFTS. AMONGST THE BILLOWS OF SMOKE AND DEBRIS WERE THE CAUSALITIES, APPROXIMATELY 3,000 NAVAL AND MILITARY PERSONNEL WERE EITHER KILLED /OR WOUNDED. THE UNITED STATES OF AMERICA THUSLY DECLARED WAR ON JAPAN ON THE FOLLOWING DAY OF ITS INITIAL ATTACK. INTERESTINGLY, AT THE CLOSE OF THE WORLD WAR II, THE EMPEROR OF JAPAN (HIROHITO) WAS SAID TO BE CONTEMPLATING THE TERMS OF A POSSIBLE SURRENDER, BUT THE POWERS THAT BE IN THE UNITED STATES WERE NOT ABOUT READY TO ACCEPT RHETORIC OF A PENDING SURRENDER AT THAT SPECIFIC MOMENT OF HISTORY AS THEY HAD PLANS OF EXECUTING EXPERIMENTAL TESTING OF A NEW ATOMIC BOMB THAT SCIENTISTS HAD JUST DEVELOPED. ON MONDAY, AUGUST 6TH, 1945 THE AMERICAN MASONIC ALLIED FORCES DROPPED MAN'S FIRST NUCLEAR BOMB ON HIROSHIMA AND THREE DAYS LATER (AUGUST 9TH) THEY DROPPED YET ANOTHER FOR FURTHER EXPERIMENTAL RESULTS, NAGASSAKI. AS A DIRECT RESULT OF BOTH THESE ATOMIC BOMBS BEING USED ONTO THE UNEXPECTED JAPANESE PEOPLES, HUNDREDS OF THOUSANDS OF INNOCENT MEN, WOMEN AND CHILDREN WERE BRUTALLY MURDERED, MAIMED /OR INJURED. THIS COWARDLY ACT OF REVENGE FOR THE INITIAL BOMBING OF PEARL HARBOR WAS REPORTEDLY SAID TO HAVE BEEN TOTALLY JUSTIFIABLE IN ITS ACTIONS AS JAPAN AND THE UNITED STATES

HAD ALREADY BEEN AT WAR WITH ONE ANOTHER WHEN BOTH ATOMIC BOMBS WERE DROPPED; THE ENDS THUSLY JUSTIFYING THE MEANS.

VOWING NOT TO FORGET PEARL HARBOR, THE U.S. PRESIDENT, FRATERNITY BROTHER HARRY S. TRUMAN UNLEASHED ONE OF THE WORLD'S BEST KEPT SECRETS ONTO THE PEOPLE OF HIROSHIMA AS AN AMERICAN B-29 BOMBER AIRCRAFT (ENOLA GAY) AND ITS PERSONNEL CIRCLED THE CITY OF 350,000 RESIDENTS TWO OR THREE TIMES AT AN ALTITUDE OF SLIGHTLY MORE THAN 10,000 FEET. AS THE PLANE CIRCLED THE SKY ABOVE, HIROSHIMA'S POPULATION BEGAN RUSHING TO AIR RAID SHELTERS AND FIFTEEN MINUTES LATER (8:15 A.M. JAPANESE TIME) MAN'S FIRST ATOMIC BOMB WAS DROPPED BY PARACHUTE TO ITS DESIGNATED TARGET BELOW. WHEN THE BLAST WAS FINALLY IGNITED, "IT SEEMED AS IF THE WORLD HAD SUDDENLY COME TO AN END. A TREMENDOUS FLASH, LIKE A BALL OF FIRE, ILLUMINATED EVERYTHING FOR SCORES OF MILES; IT WAS VISIBLE FROM THE AIR 170 MILES AWAY. THEN A FUNNEL OF SMOKE, DUST, FIRE, AND COLOR MOUNTED LIKE A WATERSPOUT UP, UP EVER HIGHER UNTIL THE PILLAR OF BOILING DUST HAD REACHED THE STRATOSPHERE. "IT FIRST CREATED A FIREBALL THAT WAS SAID TO HAVE REACHED THOUSANDS OF DEGREES FAHRENHEIT, THEN, THE MUSHROOM CLOUD WAS REPORTEDLY SAID TO FIRST GO TO 20,000 FEET, THEN WITHIN ONLY MINUTES A HEAD WAS FORMED REACHING THE ALTITUDE OF 40,000 FEET. "IT TOOK HOURS FOR THE AIR TO CLEAR SUFFICIENTLY TO SEE WHAT HAD HAPPENED." AND ONCE THE AIR DID CLEAR, THE AMERICAN MASONIC SUPREME ALLIED COMMAND TOOK PHOTOGRAPHS OF THE DESTRUCTION AT AN ALTITUDE OF 25,000 FEET AS ITS DESTRUCTIVE FORCES COULD BE SEEN FOR 4.1 MILES. "IN ONE SPLIT SECOND 60 PERCENT OF HIROSHIMA HAD BEEN WIPED OFF THE MAP ...IT OBLITERATED BUILDINGS, TREES, AND EVERYTHING ELSE WITHIN A WIDE RANGE. "THE SUPREME ALLIED COMMAND AT THE TIME REPORTED THAT NO LESS THAN ONE-TENTH OF HIROSHIMA'S POPULATION HAD BEEN KILLED AND APPROXIMATELY 176,987 PERSONS WERE LEFT HOMELESS AS THE BLAST LITERALLY REDUCED THE CITY TO MERE RUBBLE IN JUST ONE FOUL SWOOP. THE BLAST WAS REPORTEDLY SO POWERFUL THAT AN ESTIMATED 30,000 PEOPLE JUST DISINTEGRATED INTO THIN AIR AS THEY WERE SAID TO BE AT GROUND ZERO OF THE BLAST ITSELF. BUT WHEN THE FINAL TALLY OF THE CASUALTIES WAS EVENTUALLY TAKEN, IT WAS SOON DISCOVERED THAT THE ATOMIC BLAST HAD LITERALLY SNUFFED THE LIFE OUT OF WELL IN EXCESS OF 130,000 OF HIROSHIMA'S RESIDENT POPULATION. THE BLAST WAS IN FACT SO POWERFUL THAT IT LEFT THE IMPRINT OF HUMAN SKELETAL REMAINS EMBEDDED IN SLABS OF CONCRETE AS IT VIRTUALLY MELTED ALL SKIN AND MUSCLE TISSUE OFF OF ITS INTENDED VICTIMS WHO FELT AS THOUGH THEIR BODIES WERE ON FIRE. WHILE THE BLAST MADE SOME OF THE PEOPLE PERMANENT CONCRETE FIXTURES, THOSE WHO REMAINED ALIVE WENT SCREAMING IN AGONIZING PAIN

TO WHEREVER WATER WAS STILL ACCESSIBLE SO THAT THEY COULD EASY THEIR SUFFERING BY COOLING OFF THEIR RADIOACTIVE BODIES IN THE WATER.

THREE DAYS AFTER THE ATOMIC BOMB WAS INITIALLY DROPPED ON HIROSHIMA, THE MASONIC SUPREME ALLIED COMMAND DROPPED YET ANOTHER ONTO THE PEOPLE OF JAPAN. THIS TIME, IT WAS A SLIGHTLY IMPROVED VERSION OF THE FIRST THAT NEEDED TO BE FURTHER TESTED. ALTHOUGH THE MASSIVE DESTRUCTION OF THIS BLAST WASN'T QUITE AS GREAT AS THAT OF HIROSHIMA, ITS DEVASTATION WAS MORE COMPLETE AND FINAL AS SCIENTISTS HAD TWEAKED IT JUST A TAD. IN THE CENTER OF THE BLAST WHERE AN APPARENT VACUUM HAD BEEN CREATED, THERE WAS REPORTEDLY NO BUILDING TO BE SEEN ANYWHERE. ACCORDINGLY, EVERYTHING WAS SAID TO HAVE COMPLETELY VANISHED. "OF NAGASAKI'S 50,000 BUILDINGS 18,000 WERE DESTROYED AND FEW OF THE OTHERS ESCAPED DAMAGE. NEARLY 30,000 PERSONS WERE KILLED. "IN BOTH OF THESE BLAST TEST CASES, HUNDREDS OF THOUSANDS OF PEOPLE WERE SCARED FOR LIFE AS THEY SUSTAINED HORRIBLE INJURIES CAUSED BY RADIOACTIVE ELEMENTS. INJURIES THAT OF WHICH WERE TO FURTHER ASSIST AMERICAN RESEARCH STUDIES INTO THE EFFECT OF NUCLEAR SCIENCE. IN TOTAL, BOTH OF THESE EXPERIMENTAL ATOMIC BOMB BLASTS SAW 210,000 JAPANESE PEOPLE MASSACRED IN JUST ONE SPLIT SECOND. IRONICALLY, ALTHOUGH THE DECEMBER 7TH, 1941 ATTACK ON PEARL HARBOR ONLY KILLED 2,403 MILITARY PERSONNEL, THE DROPPING OF BOTH ATOMIC BOMBS TOTALLY DEVASTATED THE CO-PILOT OF THE B-29 BOMBER OF THE HIROSHIMA BLAST. THE DESTRUCTION OF BOTH BLASTS WERE SAID TO HAVE LEFT AN EVERLASTING IMPRESSION ON THE CO-PILOT HIMSELF AS HE (CAPTAIN ROBERT LEWIS) WAS NOT ONLY HAVING A HARD TIME SLEEPING AT NIGHT BUT WAS ALSO SAID TO BE HAVING RE-OCCURRING NIGHTMARES. IT REPORTEDLY EFFECTED HIM SO MUCH THAT SOME SAY HE LATER TOOK HIS OWN LIFE YEARS LATER AS THE PAIN HE WAS SUFFERING WAS BELIEVED TO HAVE BEEN A FAR GREATER BURDEN TO CARRY AROUND THAN ORIGINALLY ANTICIPATED. BE THAT AS IT MAY, WHILE ACTING AS CO-PILOT ABOARD THE BOMBER AIRCRAFT THAT DROPPED ITS PAYLOAD CODE-NAMED "LITTLE BOY "BY THE SUPREME MASONIC ALLIED COMMAND, LEWIS KEPT FINE DETAILS OF THE HIROSHIMA BLAST IN HIS LOGBOOK AS IT WAS UNFOLDING BEFORE HIS VERY EYES. ONCE THE PAYLOAD WAS DROPPED ONTO THE UNEXPECTED JAPANESE POPULATION BELOW, HE WROTE: "FOR THE NEXT MINUTE NO ONE KNEW WHAT TO EXPECT ... THE FLASH WAS TERRIFIC. FIFTEEN SECONDS AFTER THE FLASH THERE WERE TWO VERY DISTINCT SLAPS – AIR TURBULENCE – THAT WAS ALL THE PHYSICAL EFFECTS WE FELT ... WE THEN TURNED THE SHIP SO WE COULD OBSERVE RESULTS AND THERE WAS WITHOUT DOUBT THE GREATEST EXPLOSION MAN HAS EVER WITNESSED. I AM CERTAIN THE ENTIRE CREW FELT THIS EXPERIENCE WAS MORE THAN ANY ONE HUMAN HAD EVER THOUGHT POSSIBLE. IT JUST

SEEMS IMPOSSIBLE TO COMPREHEND. JUST HOW MANY DID WE KILL? ... I HONESTLY HAVE THE FEELING OF GROPING FOR WORDS TO EXPLAIN THIS OR MIGHT SAY ' MY GOD, WHAT HAVE WE DONE? ' IF I LIVE A HUNDRED YEARS I'LL NEVER GET THOSE MINUTES OUT OF MY MIND. EVERYONE ON THE SHIP IS ACTUALLY DUMBSTRUCK, EVEN THOUGH WE HAD EXPERIENCED SOMETHING FIERCE. "ONE OF THE FINAL ENTRIES IN LEWIS' LOGBOOK STATED THAT THE MUSHROOM CLOUD REMAINED VISIBLE "EVEN AFTER AN HOUR-AN-A-HALF, 400 MILES FROM THE TARGET."

FURTHER TO THIS, IN FREEMASONRY BROTHER TRUMAN'S RUSH TO TEST THE SECOND NUCLEAR BOMB ON NAGASAKI, THE AMERICANS ACCIDENTLY SNUFFED THE LIFE OUT OF SOME PRISONERS OF WAR WHO THE JAPANESE INTERNED IN A MITSUBISHI ARMORY PLANT. AMONGST THE P.O.W.'S THAT WERE BRUTALLY MURDERED BY THE ATOMIC BLAST WERE EIGHT ALLIED PRISONERS. AND WHEN IT WAS LEARNED THAT A GRAVE ERROR HAD BEEN MADE, FINGERS WERE INSTANTLY POINTED AT JAPAN'S BREAKING THE RULES AND REGULATIONS OF THE TREATMENT OF PRISONERS OF WAR. ACCORDING TO THE INTERNATIONAL RULES OF WAR, THE PRISONERS WERE NOT SUPPOSE TO BE AT THE MITSUBISHI PLANT. THE FACT THAT THEY (THE UNITED STATES) NEEDED TO TEST ITS WEAPON OF MASSIVE DESTRUCTION TO FIND OUT ITS FULL IMPACT OF DESTRUCTION ONTO THE HUMAN RACE WAS OF NO SIGNIFICANCE WHATSOEVER. WITHIN ONLY DAYS OF THIS INHUMANE ACT OF TERRORISM BEING EXECUTED UPON THE PEOPLE OF JAPAN (AUGUST 14TH, 1945), HIROHITO PUBLICALLY ANNOUNCED THE UNCONDITIONAL SURRENDER OF JAPAN TO THE MASONIC SUPREME ALLIED COMMAND. FRATERNITY BROTHER GENERAL DOUGLAS MACARTHUR THEN TOOK OVER ALL ASPECTS OF LIFE IN JAPAN AND IMPOSED U.S. INTERPRETATIONS OF DEMOCRATIC PROCEDURE ONTO ITS PEOPLE. COINCIDENTLY, THE CONTROVERSY CONCERNING THE TWO MILITARY OFFICERS THAT FRATERNITY BROTHER ROOSEVELT'S COMMITTEE HAD BLAMED FOR BEING A SLEEP AT THE SWITCH HAD BEEN BREWING THROUGHOUT THE ENTIRE TIME PERIOD OF THE SECOND WORLD WAR. IT IN FACT WAS SO CONTROVERSIAL THAT AN INDEPENDENT INVESTIGATION HAD TO BE CONDUCTED AS ALL MILITARY REPORTS WERE MADE PUBLIC KNOWLEDGE AFTER THE END OF THE WAR. ON NOVEMBER 15TH, 1945 THE INVESTIGATION BEGAN WITH VARIOUS TESTIMONIES FROM AN ASSORTMENT OF MILITARY PERSONNEL. ODDLY ENOUGH, THE INVESTIGATION SOON REVEALED THAT U.S. MILITARY INTELLIGENCE HAD AMPUL WARNING OF JAPANESE PLANS TO ATTACK PEARL HARBOR BUT CHOOSE TO DO ABSOLUTELY NOTHING TO PREVENT IT FROM HAPPENING. APPARENTLY, MILITARY INTELLIGENCE HAD SUCCEEDED IN BREAKING THE JAPANESE SECRET CODE PRIOR TO THE DECEMBER 7TH, 1941 ATTACK AND NO EFFORT WHATSOEVER WAS MADE TO AVERT WAR. ONCE THE AMERICANS HAD DECIPHERED THE JAPANESE CODED MESSAGE **"EAST WIND,**

RAIN "AS BEING A POSSIBLE WARNING CODE PERTAINING TO AN ALL OUT ATTACK ON PEARL HARBOR, REAR ADMIRAL RICHARD KELLY TURNER REFUSED TO ALLOW A REQUEST MADE BY ONE CAPTAIN ALAN KIRK TO SEND A DISPATCH TO HIS COMMANDING OFFICER, REAR ADMIRAL KIMMEL INFORMING HIM OF THE PENDING TERRORIST ATTACK. AT THE TIME, CAPTAIN KIRK WAS THE HEAD OF THE U.S. NAVY INTELLIGENCE SERVICE AND NOT LONG AFTER THE JAPANESE ATTACK ON AMERICAN SOIL, KIRK WAS RELIEVED OF HIS INTELLIGENCE SERVICE DUTIES SUPPOSEDLY FOR DERELICTION THEREOF.

FURTHER TO THIS, IT WAS ALSO LEARNED THAT EVEN AT THAT TIME PERIOD OF HISTORY, SOME AMERICAN MILITARY OFFICERS HAD A FIRM BELIEF THAT NO ONE IN THEIR RIGHT MINDS WOULD DARE ATTACK SUCH A POWERFUL NATION AS THE UNITED STATES AS THEY (THE AMERICANS) HAD PERCEIVED THEMSELVES AS BEING TOTALLY UNTOUCHABLE. DUE TO THEIR OUTRIGHT ARROGANCE AND SELF-RIGHTEOUSNESS, NOT ONE MEMBER OF THEIR SUPERIOR POWER'S MILITARY INTELLIGENCE OFFICERS TOOK HEED TO WHAT THE DECODED JAPANESE DISPATCHES WERE ACTUALLY TELLING THEM. ON JULY 26TH, 1946 THE INVESTIGATING COMMITTEE HEADED BY DEMOCRATIC SENATOR ALBEN WILLIAM BARKLEY RELEASED ITS FINDINGS. THREE YEARS LATER, BARKLEY WENT ON TO BECOME VICE-PRESIDENT OF THE UNITED STATES UNDER THE WATCHFUL EYE OF HARRY S. TRUMAN. INTERESTINGLY, WHILE TRUMAN WAS SERVING HIS TIME AS VICE-PRESIDENT OF THE UNITED STATES, (BEFORE BECOMING ITS PRESIDENT), HARRY S. TRUMAN WAS ALSO ACTING AS GRAND MASTER OF MISSOURI FROM OCTOBER 1940 TO OCTOBER OF 1941. AT ONE TIME PERIOD OF HIS LIFE, BROTHER TRUMAN ALSO SERVED AS THE DISTRICT GRAND MASTER AND WORSHIPFUL MASTER OF THE STATE OF MISSOURI. LIVING IN **INFAMY**, THE UNITED STATES OF THE AMERICA'S USED THE BOMBING OF PEARL HARBOR AS AN EXCUSE TO REFINE ITS TACTICS CONCERNING FOREIGN POLICY AND THUSLY IMPLEMENTED MASONIC BROTHER TEDDY ROOSEVELT'S POLICY OF CARRYING A BIG STICK AS A WAY AND MEANS OF BEATING SOME SENSE INTO THOSE WHO DARED QUESTION THE AMERICAN RIGHT OF DIVINE INTERVENTION.

IT SHOULD ALSO BE STATED THAT IT WAS FURTHER DISCOVERED THAT THE FREEMASONRY VICE-PRESIDENT HARRY S. TRUMAN DENIED EVER BEING TOLD OF THE PENDING TERRORIST ATTACK ON PEARL HARBOR DESPITE THE FACT THAT THE DECODED MESSAGE WAS EVENTUALLY DISPATCHED TO HIM THROUGH HIS LONGTIME FRIEND KIMMEL. STANDING BEFORE THE INVESTIGATING COMMITTEE AND SWEARING ON THE A STACK OF FREEMASONRY BIBLES, THE MASONIC GOVERNMENTAL LEADER TRUMAN LED THE COMMITTEE ASTRAY BY MAKING A FALSE STATEMENT BY IMPLYING THAT PRIOR TO THE JAPANESE ATTACK, HE AND REAR ADMIRAL KIMMEL WERE NOT ON SPEAKING TERMS WITH ONE ANOTHER AND THAT NO SUCH INFORMATION HAD NEVER BEEN RELAID TO HIM BY ANY

MEMBER OF KIMMEL'S U.S. NAVY INTELLIGENCE SERVICE PERSONNEL /OR EVEN BY KIMMEL HIMSELF. KIMMEL WAS SAID TO HAVE BEEN TOTALLY STUNNED AT WHAT HIS COMRADE HARRY S. TRUMAN WAS SAYING THAT HE WROTE A RATHER DISTRAUGHT LETTER TO TRUMAN ASKING THAT HE NOT ONLY EXPLAIN HIMSELF BUT ALSO MAKE A CORRECTION OF THE MISLEADING STATEMENTS THAT WERE BEING MADE. IN THE END, KIMMEL'S EFFORTS WENT UNANSWERED BY THE FRATERNITY LEADER. FURTHERMORE, IT WAS ALSO LEARNED THAT YET ANOTHER MEMBER OF THE MASONIC ORDER (LIEUTENANT COLONEL HENRY CHRISTIAN CLAUSEN) WAS USING BRUTE FORCE IN GETTING WITNESSES TO TESTIFY AT THE HEARINGS BY BROW-BEATING THEM INTO SUBMISSION. CLAUSEN, WHO WAS AN ASSISTANT RECORDER FOR THE ARMY BOARD'S TRIBUNAL WAS AN ATTORNEY FOR THE NORTHERN DISTRICT OF CALIFORNIA BEFORE THE OUTBREAK OF THE UNITED STATES' INVOLVEMENT IN WORLD WAR II. AS THE WAR WAS BEING UNLEASHED ONTO THE WORLD, CLAUSEN RECEIVED NUMEROUS LETTERS OF RECOMMENDATION FROM FELLOW FREEMASONS FOR A POSTING THAT OF WHICH HE SO DESPERATELY WANTED WITHIN THE U.S. GOVERNMENT'S WAR DEPARTMENT AS AN ACTIVE PARTICIPATING MEMBER ON THE STAFF OF JAG; **JUDGE ADVOCATE GENERAL.** IN FACT, ONE OF THOSE HIGHLY PHRASED LETTERS OF RECOMMENDATIONS FOR THE PRESTIGIOUS PORTFOLIO WAS DULY SUBMITTED TO MASONIC BROTHER CLAUSEN WAS FROM NONE OTHER THAN THE SENATOR FROM MISSOURI HARRY S. TRUMAN HIMSELF. AS A STRONG ADVOCATE OF COVERING ALL THEIR FREEMASONRY TRACKS, MASONIC BROTHER TRUMAN'S LETTER OF RECOMMENDATION ALMOST SINGLE HANDEDLY LEAD TO CLAUSEN BEING ASSIGNED TO THE ARMY'S PEARL HARBOR BOARD ONCE THE INVESTIGATION WAS UNDER WAY. IN A FRANTIC BID TO DRASTICALLY WATER DOWN THE TRUE FACTS SURROUNDING THE ACTUAL DETAILS OF WHAT WENT WRONG ON DECEMBER 7TH, 1941 A FREEMASONRY CONSPIRACY OF SORTS SOON BEGAN TO PLAY ITS DIRTY LITTLE HAND AS THE FRATERNAL POWERS THAT BE TRIED THEIR DAMNEST TO COVER-UP THE TRUE FACTS OF THE DILEMMA WHICH FORCED THE AMERICAN PEOPLE INTO TAKING PART IN THE WAR EFFORTS OF WORLD WAR II.

ONCE THE FRATERNITY DUST HAD FINALLY SETTLED MANY YEARS LATER, MASONIC BROTHER CLAUSEN WENT ON TO BECOME THE SOVEREIGN GRAND COMMANDER OF AMERICAN FREEMASONS FOR THE CONTINENTAL UNITED STATES. WHILE IN YET ANOTHER EXTREME TWIST OF IRONIC FATE, AT THE CLOSE OF THE SECOND WORLD WAR ANOTHER MEMBER OF THE ANCIENT FREEMASONRY CRAFT'S NAME EMERGED AS HE WAS PUT IN CHARGE OF THE ATOMIC WEAPONS RESEARCH PROGRAM FOR THE UNITED STATES GOVERNMENT. HE WAS MAJOR GENERAL JOHN E. HULL, COMMANDER OF THE U.S. ARMY JOINT TASK FORCE 7, WHICH IN THE YEARS 1947 AND 1948 CONDUCTED THE FIRST ATOMIC WEAPONS TEST AT ENIWEKOK, (A HIGHLY CLASSIFIED MILITARY

Installation located somewhere on the barren landscape of a desert). Brother Hull at the time was said to have been an active member of Oxford Lodge No. 67 in Oxford, Ohio.

Despite all their attempts to portray themselves as unwilling victims of circumstance, the facts cannot be denied by any member of the Ancient Craft as they (the Masonic powers who were representing the people of the United States of America), had ample knowledge of the Japanese attack on Pearl Harbor but yet, they issued no warning to the armed forces stationed at the military base. There is no doubt whatsoever that those occupying the White House and their military Chief-of-Staff were well aware of the fact that a huge Japanese convoy was making its way to Hawaii in order to launch an assault onto American soil. Not only did the U.S. President allow the destruction to occur, but extra measures were even initiated to guarantee its everlasting effectiveness as the downsizing of the Hawaiian Islands military might was being executed with most of its air defenses virtually being yanked from service shortly before the raid. With only one-third of its actual surveillance planes remaining on the base, Pearl Harbor lay in wait for the slaughter.

U.S. Freemasonry President Franklin D. Roosevelt was the fourth cousin of fraternity Brother Theodor Roosevelt. FDR married his sixth cousin, Anna Eleanor Roosevelt, a niece of cousin Teddy's. Franklin first took the oath of office as the 32ND President on March 4TH, 1933 and as part of his campaigning for the Oval Office, he pledged a new deal for the American people as their entire economy had been flushed down the toilet. Business and industry was at a standstill, a worldwide depression had existed. As far as FDR was concerned, the population of the Continental United States had a rendezvous date with destiny and it was his elected mandate to make it happen. In the meantime, Adolf Hitler was maneuvered into the post of Chancellor of Germany, (January 30TH, 1933) by the Masonically controlled Presidential Palace of Paul von Hindenburg. Once in power, Hitler had his political foes slain /or thrown into concentration camps and started a ruthless campaign to wipe out the Jewish population. Hitler's concept was to establish a "master race "and make away with all Jews. As far as the newly anointed German Chancellor was concerned, it was supposedly because of the Jewish people that Freemasonry was allowed to exist and he reportedly saw this race of people as a threat to society. Perhaps this was what he was said to have stated: "Must I do the

WORK OF THE LORD, AND MAKE AWAY WITH THIS JEWISH MENACE. "ALTHOUGH HISTORIANS TRY TELLING US THAT HE WAS A DEVOTED ROMAN CATHOLIC AND SUPPOSEDLY ANTI-MASONIC, THAT STILL DIDN'T GIVE HIM THE RIGHT TO PLAY **GOD** WITH OTHER PEOPLES LIVES. THE FACT ALSO REMAINS PURE AND SIMPLE THAT HITLER'S REGIME WAS FINANCIALLY SUPPORTED BY VARIOUS BUSINESS PEOPLE IN BOTH THE UNITED STATES AS WELL AS IN GERMANY, (INDUSTRIALISTS AND BANKERS). THESE BUSINESS ENTITIES OF MASONIC ORIGINS LITERALLY DISHED OUT MILLIONS OF DOLLARS TO THE EXTERMINATION FUND OF THE FASCIST DICTATOR; ILLUMINATI FINANCIERS.

AT THE START OF THE FIRST WORLD WAR, HITLER JOINED GERMANY'S ARMY. BY ITS DEFEAT IN 1918, HE NOT ONLY WAS SAID TO HAVE HATED THE JEWISH PEOPLE BUT WAS ALSO REPORTED TO HAVE BEEN SO ENRAGED AT ITS LOSS THAT HE FORMED THE NATIONAL SOCIALIST GERMAN WORKERS' PARTY, (A.K.A. THE NAZI PARTY). MUCH LIKE THE UNITED STATES, GERMANY'S FREEMASONS CONTROLLED EVERY ASPECT OF LIFE OF ITS CITIZENRY – HITLER, WHO WAS SAID TO HAVE BEEN AN ANTI-FREEMASON RIGHT TO THE CORE AND NOT OVERLY IMPRESSED WITH THE POLITICAL SITUATION OCCURRING IN HIS COUNTRY. DURING THE YEAR 1923, HE STAGED THE MUNICH "BEER-HALL" REVOLT WHICH IN AFFECT SEIZED FRATERNITY POWER FROM THE FREEMASONRY CONTROLLED GOVERNMENT OF GERMANY. HITLER WAS THEREFORE ARRESTED AND SUBSEQUENTLY SENT TO LANDSBERG PRISON. WHILE BEING INCARCERATED, HE WROTE HIS AUTOBIOGRAPHY, **MEIN KAMPF**; MY STRUGGLE. AFTER HIS RELEASE, HE WAS REPORTEDLY INSPIRED TO INSTITUTE AN ANTI-MASONIC MOVEMENT AND BY THE SUMMER OF 1932, HIS ASPIRATIONS WERE SLOWLY BECOMING A REALITY AS HE WAS BEING GROOMED TO BE THE GRAND-POOH-BAH IN ALL OF GERMANY. AT THE TIME, MANY GERMANS WERE GRUMBLING BECAUSE OF BAD ECONOMIC TIMES AND WIDESPREAD UNEMPLOYMENT. JUST LIKE ROOSEVELT, GERMANY'S NEW NATIONAL SOCIALIST LEADER PROMISED GREAT PROSPERITY FOR HIS MOTHERLAND AND ALL OF ITS PEOPLE. AND JUST AS THIS SUPPOSEDLY ANTI-MASONIC FORCE WAS REACHING ITS PEAK, A GROUP OF GERMAN AND AMERICAN INDUSTRIALISTS, WERE SAID TO HAVE CAPITALIZED ON HITLER'S POPULARITY AS IN JULY OF 1932, THE NAZI PARTY RECEIVED THIRTY-SEVEN PERCENT OF THE POPULAR VOTE. BUT BY NOVEMBER OF THAT SAME YEAR, HITLER'S POPULARITY STARTED TO DIMINISH AS OPPOSING RHETORIC TO HIS VISIONS OF FORMING A MASTER RACE WERE GAINING THE UPPER HAND. THIS WAS REPORTEDLY STATED AS HAVING A SOMEWHAT WORRISOME AFFECT ON HIS FINANCIAL BACKERS AND WITH THE AID OF THEIR POLITICAL FRATERNITY ALLIES, PERSUADED VON HINDENBURG TO APPOINT HITLER AS CHANCELLOR.

DESPITE THE FACT THAT HISTORIANS LIKE TELLING US THAT THE FASCIST DICTATOR HATED AND FEARED ALL FORMS OF MASONRY, THAT'S ONLY PARTLY TRUE AS IT WAS ONLY JEWISH FREEMASONRY THAT HE WAS ACTUALLY SAID TO

HAVE FEARED THE MOST, (PART OF HIS INTERNATIONAL JUDAEO-MASONIC CONSPIRACY THEORY). INTERESTINGLY ENOUGH IN ONE PARTICULAR INSTANCE, SOME MASONIC HISTORIANS HAVE QUOTED HITLER AS SAYING THAT FREEMASONRY HAD ALWAYS BEEN VIRTUALLY HARMLESS IN GERMANY AND THAT IT"... ACHIEVES THE FRUITION OF FANTASY THROUGH THE USE OF SYMBOLS, RITES AND MAGIC INFLUENCE OF EMBLEMS OF WORSHIP. HEREIN LIES THE GREAT DANGER WHICH I HAVE TAKEN IN HAND. DON'T YOU SEE THAT OUR PARTY MUST BE SOMETHING VERY SIMILAR, AN ORDER, AN HIERARCHIC ORGANIZATION OF SECULAR PRIESTHOOD? THIS NATURALLY MEANS THAT SOMETHING SIMILAR OPPOSING US MAY NOT EXIST. IT IS EITHER US, THE FREEMASONS OR THE CHURCH BUT NEVER TWO SIDE BY SIDE. THE CATHOLIC CHURCH HAS MADE ITS POSITION CLEAR, AT LEAST IN REGARD TO THE FREEMASONS. NOW WE ARE THE STRONGEST AND, THEREFORE, WE SHALL ELIMINATE BOTH THE CHURCH AND THE FREEMASONS."

BE THAT AS IT MAY, THE TRUE MASONIC HORROR OF ADOLF HITLER'S NAZISM WILL NEVER BE FULLY KNOWN. ACCORDING TO FREEMASONRY LITERATURE ON THE MANY HEINOUS ACTS OF MAN'S INHUMANITY TO MAN, A LARGE NUMBER OF GERMAN JEWISH FREEMASONS WERE NOT ONLY SENT TO THE CONCENTRATION CAMPS AND THE GAS CHAMBERS, BUT THEY WERE ALSO TORTURED AND MURDERED IN THEIR OWN HOMES AS WELL. FURTHER TO SUFFERING FROM THE MANY ADVERSE CONDITIONS BESTOWED ONTO THEM BY A FINANCIALLY FUNDED MASONIC MAD MAN, A REPORTED 80,000 MEMBERS OF THE GERMAN ANCIENT CRAFT OF FREEMASONRY WERE LISTED AS BEING BUTCHERED BY THE NAZI REGIME DURING THEIR REIGN OF TERROR. THEN OF COURSE THERE'S THE OTHER SIDE OF THE MASONIC COIN WHICH STATED THAT CONTRARY AS TO WHAT HAD BEEN ORIGINALLY PERCEIVED AS BEING A TRUE FACT OF HISTORY, ONLY TWO-THIRDS OF THE REGISTERED 85,000 MASONS IN GERMANY WERE INJURED IN SOME MANNER /OR ANOTHER, WHICH IN ESSENCE LITERALLY LEFT ONE-THIRD OF THAT COUNTRY'S FREEMASONRY POPULATION UNTOUCHED. ACCORDING TO AMERICAN MASONIC HISTORIANS, A FRENCHMAN NAMED BERNARD FAY WAS SAID TO HAVE BEEN THE PERSON WHO HANDED OVER A LIST OF KNOWN MEMBERS OF FREEMASONRY TO THE NAZIS. AS THE STORY GOES, ONE OF THEIR OWN KIND, FRATERNITY BROTHER FAY HAD SUPPOSEDLY OBTAINED THESE NAMES FROM AMERICAN MASONIC SOURCES NOT ONLY UNDER FALSE PRETENSES BUT BY MISREPRESENTATION AS WELL. BROTHER FAY WAS SAID TO HAVE BEEN WRITING A BOOK LEGITIMIZING THE TRUE HISTORICAL ACCOUNTS OF THE MASONIC ORDER AND HAD MANAGED TO CONVINCE SOME OF THE UNITED STATES OF AMERICA'S MOST HIGHLY PROFILED FREEMASONRY LEADERS INTO FURNISHING HIM WITH THIS LIST OF NAMES. BY THE EXACT SAME TOKEN, THESE SAME MASONIC HISTORIANS ALSO STATED THAT WHILE THE SECOND WORLD WAR WAS UNFOLDING BEFORE A WORLDWIDE STAGE, ALL

FREEMASONRY ACTIVITY WAS SUSPENDED IN THE PARTICIPATING COUNTRIES OCCUPIED BY THE NAZIS.

BUT IF ONE WERE TO BELIEVE EVERYTHING THAT HISTORIANS TRY TELLING US, WHAT A SAD WORLD IT WOULD BE AS IT HAS ALWAYS BEEN PART OF HUMAN NATURE TO ASK QUESTIONS BEFORE LAYING TO REST THE SO-CALLED FACTS OF MAN'S ACTUAL EXISTENCE. THEREFORE, IF ALL FREEMASONRY ACTIVITY HAD INDEED CEASED TO OPERATE DURING THE YEARS OF HITLERISM, THEN, WHY IS IT THAT IN ACCORDANCE TO THE MASONIC ORDER'S VERY OWN PAPER TRAIL MUCH OF THEIR FRATERNAL ACTIVITY WAS MERELY FORCED TO FIND OTHER MEANS OF SURVIVAL. FOR INSTANCE, IN THE INFAMOUS BUCHENWALD CONCENTRATION CAMP THE MASONIC POPULACE WAS SAID TO HAVE REACHED CLOSE TO ONE-HUNDRED BRETHREN IN OCTOBER OF 1944. MEETING DAILY, THEY OCCUPIED MOST OF THEIR TIME WITH MATTERS OF RITUALISTIC CEREMONIES AND THE TEACHING PHILOSOPHIES OF THE CRAFT. BY KEEPING THEIR MINDS OCCUPIED, THEY WERE ABLE TO EASE THE STRENUOUS TENSIONS OF JUST TRYING TO STAY ALIVE ON A DAILY BASIS. MASONIC SUBJECTS WERE CHOSEN AND BY VIRTUAL WORD OF MOUTH TRANSMITTED FROM ONE BUILDING TO ANOTHER, THUS ALLOWING QUICK DISCUSSIONS TO OCCUR. THEN, THE END RESULTS OF THE DISCUSSIONS WERE RELAID BACK TO ONE ANOTHER.

SOON AFTER HITLER'S RISE TO POWER, IT BECAME APPARENT THAT A GREAT POSSIBILITY EXISTED THAT JEWISH FREEMASONRY IN GERMANY WAS IN MUCH DANGER OF BEING EXTERMINATED ONCE AND FOR ALL AS IN THE SAME YEAR OF HIS INAUGURATION, THE GROSSLOGE ZUR SONNE (GERMAN GRAND LODGE OF THE SUN) IN BAYREUTH, ONE OF THE PRE-WAR GERMAN GRAND LODGES, REALIZED THE IMMINENT PROBLEMS FACING THEM AND DECIDED TO WEAR A LITTLE BLUE FLOWER, THE FORGET-ME-NOT IN LIEU OF THE TRADITIONAL SQUARE AND COMPASSES, AS A MARK OF IDENTITY FOR FREEMASONS. AND WHEN HITLER'S GERMAN MILITARY /OR GESTAPO INQUIRED, "WAS IST DAS?", THE SIMPLE REPLY WAS "EINE BLUME", A FLOWER. MANY A FREEMASON FELT THAT THE NEW SYMBOL WOULD NOT ATTRACT ATTENTION FROM THE NAZIS, WHO WERE IN THE PROCESS OF CONFISCATING AND APPROPRIATING ANYTHING AND EVERYTHING THAT THE JEWISH MASONIC LODGES HAD AS WELL AS ALL PROPERTY REAL AND/OR OTHERWISE HELD BY THE JEWISH PEOPLE. DUE TO HITLER'S HATRED FOR THE JEWISH PEOPLE, FREEMASONRY WAS ONCE AGAIN DRIVEN UNDERGROUND AND IT WAS NECESSARY THAT THE BRETHRENSHIP HAVE SOME SORT OF MEANS OF IDENTIFYING THEMSELVES TO ONE ANOTHER. THROUGHOUT THE ENTIRE NAZI ERA, A LITTLE BLUE FLOWER IN A LAPEL MARKED A FELLOW MEMBER OF THE ANCIENT CRAFT. IN THE CONCENTRATION CAMPS AND IN THE CITIES, A LITTLE BLUE FORGET-ME-NOT DISTINGUISHED THE LAPELS OF THOSE WHO REFUSED TO ALLOW THE LIGHT OF FREEMASONRY

TO BE EXTINGUISHED BY HITLER'S TERMINATION ORDER OF ITS JEWISH POPULATION.

UPON THE CLOSING DAYS OF WORLD WAR II, THE GERMAN GRAND LODGE OF THE SUN BEGAN TAKING THE NECESSARY STEPS OF HAVING ITS DOORS RE-OPENED IN BAYREUTH. IN 1947, A LITTLE BLUE PIN IN THE SHAPE OF A FORGET-ME-NOT WAS PROPOSED AS BEING THE OFFICIAL EMBLEM OF THE FIRST ANNUAL CONVENTION OF THOSE WHO HAD MANAGED TO SURVIVED THE BITTER YEARS OF DARKNESS, BRINGING THE LIGHT OF FREEMASONRY ONCE AGAIN INTO THE MASONIC TEMPLES. THE PROPOSAL WAS UNANIMOUSLY APPROVED AND ONE YEAR LATER, AT THE FIRST ANNUAL CONVENTION OF THE UNITED GRAND LODGES OF GERMANY, (EAST AND WEST GERMANY), THE PIN WAS ADOPTED AS AN OFFICIAL MASONIC EMBLEM HONORING THOSE FALLEN BRETHREN WHO HAD CARRIED ON WITH THEIR FREEMASONRY DUTIES UNDER HEINOUS/ADVERSE CONDITIONS. THE USAGE OF THIS ONE SIMPLE FLOWER THUSLY BLOSSOMED INTO AN INCREDIBLE AND MEANINGFUL EMBLEM OF THE FRATERNITY AS IT SOON BECAME THE MOST WIDELY WORN PIN AMONG FREEMASONS IN GERMANY AND IS STILL WORN BY SOME TO THIS VERY DAY. IN FACT, DURING THE YEAR 1972 A GROUP OF FREEMASONS FORMED THE MASONIC BROTHERHOOD OF THE BLUE FORGET-ME-NOT. THIS GROUP COMPRISED MOSTLY OF MASONIC WRITERS, HISTORIANS AND EDUCATORS. THEIR EMBLEM, ODDLY ENOUGH WAS THE LITTLE BLUE FLOWER, THE FORGET-ME-NOT.

EVEN MASONIC HISTORIANS COULDN'T SEEM TO AGREE ON WHERE THE ORIGINS OF THIS LITTLE BLUE FLOWER ACTUALLY CAME FROM. ONE HISTORIAN, CYRIL BATHAM OF GREAT BRITAIN CLAIMED THAT IT WAS ORIGINALLY ADOPTED IN THE 1920'S AS A FRATERNAL BADGE OF FRIENDSHIP THUS MAKING THE GERMAN/JEWISH CLAIM TO FAME OF EVADING THE GESTAPO PURE NONSENSE CITING THAT IT WAS SIMPLY AN EMBLEM SELECTED BECAUSE THE MASONIC SQUARE AND COMPASSES WERE NOT WORN BY GERMANY'S FREEMASONRY POPULATION.

SINCE ITS CONCEPTION THOUSANDS OF YEARS AGO, FREEMASONRY ACTIVITY IN BOTH GERMANY AND JAPAN WAS AS COMMON PLACE AS THE SCHISM THAT OCCURRED FROM WITHIN ITS OWN FRATERNITY MEMBERSHIP. PRIOR TO THE ATTACK ON PEARL HARBOR DURING THOSE EARLY MORNING HOURS OF DECEMBER 7TH, 1941, JAPANESE FREEMASONRY WAS SAID TO HAVE BEEN FLOURISHING AT A FAST FEVERISH PACE. BUT UNFORTUNATELY JUST LIKE JEWISH FREEMASONRY, MOST, IF NOT ALL THAT DOCUMENTATION ASSOCIATED WITH MASONIC ACTIVITIES IN JAPAN IS VIRTUALLY NON-EXISTENT. REPORTEDLY, WHEN THE SECOND WORLD WAR HAD COME TO A CLOSE AFTER THE MASONIC ALLIED FORCES DROPPED THE ATOMIC BOMBS ON HIROSHIMA AND NAGASAKI, JAPANESE FREEMASONRY WAS PERMITTED TO ONCE AGAIN GROW IN ACCORDANCE AS TO WHAT THE AMERICAN AND BRITISH MASONIC POWERS

THAT BE SAW AS A VIABLE COMPRISE. NOT LONG AFTERWARDS, BROTHERHOOD LITERATURE PERTAINING TO FREEMASONRY IN JAPAN SOON BEGAN TO EMERGE. FOR EXAMPLE, IN 1950 THE FRATERNAL POWERS THAT BE ALLOWED THE RE-SHUFFLING OF THE JAPANESE MASONIC LODGERY TO OCCUR. THE BRITISH STYLE BLUE LODGE HALL IN TOKYO, WHICH ILLUSTRATED THE REMARKABLE JAPANESE CAPABILITY OF UNDERSTANDING AND INTEGRATION, WAS THE FIRST OF THIS SHUFFLING OF THE FRATERNITY DECK AS A PIECE OF REAL-ESTATE WAS PURCHASED AND THE CONSTRUCTION OF THE TOKYO MASONIC BUILDING WAS SOON UNDERWAY. WHILE THE PROPOSED NEW BUILDING WAS BEING DECREED THE CENTER FOR ALL MASONIC ACTIVITY IN THE TOKYO AREA, THE TOKYO SCOTTISH RITE GOVERNING BODIES AMALGAMATED WITH THE ENGLISH BLUE LODGE AND TOGETHER THEY DEVELOPED THE PROPERTY MAKING IT THE FRATERNITY SITE FOR ALL THOSE WHO HAD SUFFERED VARIOUS FORMS OF PERSUASION AT THE HAND OF THE BROTHERHOOD ITSELF. WITHIN ONLY A FEW SHORT YEARS, IT HAD BEEN DETERMINED THAT THE PRINCIPLES AND TEACHINGS OF THE ANCIENT CRAFT WOULD BE BEST SERVED IF THE DEVELOPMENT PROPERTY WERE TO OPERATE STRICTLY AS A CHARITABLE ORGANIZATION. THE ZAIDAN HOJIN TOKYO MASONIC ASSOCIATION WAS THEREFORE FORMED AS A NON-PROFIT CHARITABLE FOUNDATION IN 1955. THE MISSION STATEMENT OF THE TOKYO MASONIC ASSOCIATION WAS THUSLY STATED AS BEING THE MAIN DRIVING FORCE TO PROMOTE CHARITY, LEARNING AND THE LOVE OF **GOD**. ACCORDING TO THE MASONIC LITERATURE, THE ACTUAL LOCATION OF THE TOKYO MASONIC BUILDING IS STATED AS BEING FUSSA-SHI-NISHITAMA-GUN, TOKYO, JAPAN. ITS INTERIOR WAS ADORNED WITH STAINED GLASS WINDOWS ILLUSTRATING BLUE LODGE SYMBOLISM AND OTHER APPENDANT FREEMASONRY SYMBOLS AND HAD A HUGE SEATING CAPACITY TO HELP HOUSE ITS RATHER EXTENSIVE MASONIC MEMBERSHIP. BY THE TIME THE 1990'S DECADE ROLLED AROUND, JAPANESE FREEMASONRY WAS SAID TO HAVE BEEN SUFFERING FROM A DECLINE IN MEMBERSHIP AS THE OLD GUARD MEMBERS OF THE WORLD WAR II ERA WERE BEING BURIED WITH FULL MASONIC HONORS AS THEY HAD REACHED THE FINAL STAGE OF LIFE'S VERY EXISTENCE; OLD AGE.

AT THE TIME OF THE JAPANESE ATTACK OF PEARL HARBOR, IT IS HIGHLY CONCEIVABLE THAT THE MAIN REASON BEHIND SUCH AN ASSAULT WAS LARGELY DUE TO THE FACT THAT JAPANESE FREEMASONS WANTED TO CONTROL THERE OWN DESTINY AND THIS THEREFORE LEAD TO DISSECTION WITHIN THE FRATERNITY ITSELF. AFTERALL, ACCORDING TO THEIR OWN PAPER TRAIL TERRITORIAL DISPUTES AND/OR DISAGREEMENTS WERE NORMAL OCCURRENCES FOR THE "BROTHERHOOD OF MAN – UNDER THE FATHERHOOD OF GOD". IN USING THE MASONIC ORDER'S VERY OWN DOCUMENTATION ONE CAN CLEARLY STATE WITH TOTAL AND ABSOLUTE CERTAINTY THAT THE SUBJECT OF GRAND LODGE RECOGNITIONS IS ONE OF THE MOST COMPLEX ISSUES SURROUNDING

THE ANCIENT CRAFT ITSELF. RECOGNITION OF MASONIC GOVERNING BODIES LITERALLY AFFECTS NOT ONLY THE GRAND LODGES THEMSELVES, BUT INDIVIDUAL LODGES AND BRETHREN THROUGHOUT THE WORLD. FOR IF A LODGE AND/OR GRAND LODGE WAS CONSIDERED TO BE "REGULAR", THEN IT WAS A TOTALLY RECOGNIZED INSTITUTION. BUT, IF THAT EXACT SAME LODGES WERE LISTED ON THE MASONIC BOOKS AS BEING "IRREGULAR", THERE WAS VIRTUALLY NO HOPE IN HELL OF EVER BECOMING A FULLY RECOGNIZED ORGANISM. THIS SORT OF FRATERNAL DISAGREEMENT WAS INDEED THE CASE WHEN IT CAME TO JAPANESE FREEMASONRY. WHILE THE GRAND LODGE OF SCOTLAND RECOGNIZED THE GRAND LODGE OF JAPAN, THE AMERICAN MASONIC GOVERNING BODY OF THE UNITED GRAND LODGE OF ENGLAND DID NOT. THIS, DESPITE THE FRATERNITY FACT OF COURSE THAT ENGLAND, SCOTLAND AND THE UNITED STATES LODGERY RECOGNIZED EACH OTHERS FREEMASONRY RIGHTS TO CO-EXIST. COINCIDENTLY, AT THE TIME THERE WERE NUMEROUS LODGES AND GRAND LODGES OPERATING IN A LARGE NUMBER OF COUNTRIES UNDER BOTH ENGLISH AND SCOTTISH RECOGNITION. IF A MEMBER OF JAPANESE FREEMASONRY WANTED TO VISIT SUCH LODGERY, HE WAS ONLY PERMITTED TO ATTEND THE SCOTTISH LODGES AND NOT THOSE UNDER THE ENGLISH DOMAIN. IN MOST INSTANCES, THE JAPANESE MASON WOULD FIND A MEMBER OF THE ENGLISH BRETHRENSHIP VISITING AT THE SCOTTISH LODGE WERE HE WAS ATTENDING. HE WOULD THEREFORE HAVE A RATHER DIFFICULT SITUATION ON HIS HANDS. IN ACCORDANCE TO THE MASONIC RULES OF ENGAGEMENT AS IT WERE, EITHER THE ENGLISH BRETHREN PRESENT /OR THE JAPANESE FREEMASON HAD TO IMMEDIATELY WITHDRAW THEMSELVES FROM ATTENDANCE AS THEY WERE NOT TO BE MASONICALLY ASSOCIATED WITH EACH OTHER. IN CASES SUCH AS THESE, THERE HAS BEEN SO MUCH ANIMOSITY CREATED WORLDWIDE WHICH EVENTUALLY CASED WARS TO BREAK OUT AND THE FRATERNAL RELATIONS BETWEEN THE UNITED STATES AND JAPAN WERE NO DIFFERENT.

WITHIN WEEKS AFTER THE ENDING OF WORLD WAR II, JOHN H. COWLES, THE GRAND COMMANDER OF THE SCOTTISH RITE FOR THE SOUTHERN JURISDICTION OF THE UNITED STATES OF AMERICA WROTE THE FOLLOWING:

"IT IS DIFFICULT SOMETIMES WHEN JOURNEYING THROUGH OUR LANDS, TO DISCOVER WHAT IS A REGULAR AND WHICH IS AN IRREGULAR MASONIC BODY. THERE ARE GRAND MASONIC POWERS IN EUROPE WHICH RECOGNIZE MASONIC BODIES IN OTHER COUNTRIES THAT GRAND LODGES IN THE UNITED STATES DO NOT RECOGNIZE AS REGULAR. SIMILARLY, IN THE UNITED STATES, THERE ARE GRAND POWERS WHICH RECOGNIZE AS REGULAR GRAND MASONIC BODIES IN FOREIGN LANDS WHICH REGULAR GRAND BODIES IN THOSE LANDS DO

NOT RECOGNIZE. LIKEWISE, SOME OF THE GRAND LODGES IN THE UNITED STATES RECOGNIZE AS REGULAR GRAND MASONIC POWERS IN OTHER COUNTRIES THAT SOME OF THE GRAND LODGES IN THE UNITED STATES DO NOT RECOGNIZE."

TO THE AVERAGE BRAINWASHED CITIZENRY OF THE NORTH AMERICAN CONTINENT, THIS KIND OF RHETORIC IS SOMEWHAT CONFUSING. ESPECIALLY CONSIDERING THE FACT THAT OVER RECENT YEARS, MOST OF THE POPULATION IN THE WESTERN FREE-WORLD HAVE BECOME NOTHING BUT COUCH-POTATOES ALLOWING THEIR BRAIN CELLS TO BE DAZZLED BY THE TELEVISION AIRWAVES. SIMPLY PUT, THESE TERRITORIAL DIFFERENCES OF OPINION ARE IN EFFECT SEVERING ALL DIPLOMATIC RELATIONS BETWEEN VARIOUS COUNTRIES AND THUSLY MAKING THEM ENEMIES OF THE DESIGNATED STATE.

BY MASONIC DEFINITION, A MASTER MASON IS CLASSIFIED AS AN UNWORTHY MEMBER WHEN HE WONDERS ASTRAY FROM THE TEACHINGS OF BROTHERLY KINDNESS AND ACCEPTS THE INSTRUCTION OF EVIL FORCES:

"MASONRY PRESCRIBES NO PRINCIPLES THAT ARE OPPOSED TO THE SACRED TEACHINGS OF THE DIVINE LAWGIVER, AND SANCTIONS NO ACTS THAT ARE NOT CONSISTENT WITH THE STERNEST MORALITY AND THE MOST FAITHFUL OBEDIENCE TO GOVERNMENT AND THE LAWS; AND WHILE THIS CONTINUES TO BE ITS CHARACTER,

IT CANNOT, WITHOUT THE MOST ATROCIOUS INJUSTICE, BE MADE RESPONSIBLE FOR THE ACTS OF ITS UNWORTHY MEMBERS. OF ALL HUMAN SOCIETIES, FREEMASONRY IS UNDOUBTEDLY, UNDER ALL CIRCUMSTANCES, THE FITTEST TO FORM THE TRULY GOOD MAN. BUT HOWEVER WELL CONCEIVED MAY BE ITS LAWS, THEY CANNOT COMPLETELY CHANGE THE NATURAL DISPOSITION OF THOSE WHO OUGHT TO OBSERVE THEM. IN TRUTH, THEY SERVE AS LIGHTS AND GUIDES; BUT AS THEY CAN ONLY DIRECT MEN BY RESTRAINING THE IMPETUOSITY OF THEIR PASSIONS, THESE LAST TOO OFTEN BECOME DOMINANT, AND THE INSTITUTION IS FORGOTTEN."

AS FAR AS THE ANCIENT CRAFT OF FREEMASONRY'S **BROTHERHOOD OF MAN** IS CONCERNED:

"A FREEMASON IS OBLIGATED, BY HIS TENURE, TO OBEY THE MORAL LAW; AND IF HE RIGHTLY UNDERSTANDS THE ART, HE WILL NEVER BE AN ATHEIST NOR AN IRRELIGIOUS LIBERTINE. HE, OF ALL MEN, SHOULD BEST UNDERSTAND THAT GOD SEETH NOT AS MAN SEETH; FOR MAN LOOKETH AT THE OUTWARD APPEARANCE, BUT GOD LOOKETH TO THE HEART. A FREEMASON IS, THEREFORE, PARTICULARLY BOUND NEVER TO ACT AGAINST THE DICTATES OF HIS CONSCIENCE.

Let a man's religion or mode of worship be what it may, he is not excluded from the Order, provided he believe in the glorious Architect of heaven and earth, and practice the sacred duties of morality. Freemasons unite with the virtuous of every persuasion in the firm and pleasing bond of fraternal love; they are taught to view the errors of mankind with compassion and to strive, by the purity of their own conduct, to demonstrate the superior excellence of the faith they may profess."

Outstanding members of the Ancient Craft, are "to be good men and true, or men of honor and honesty, by whatever denominations or persuasions they may be distinguished whereby Freemasonry becomes the center of union, and the means for conciliating true friendship among persons that must have remained at a perpetual distance."

It was no accident of fate that certain members of the Masonic Family waited for many years on the sidelines before they became high profile political leaders of a country, State and/or Province:

"A Freemason is a peaceable subject of Civil Powers, wherever he resides or works, and is never concerned in plots and conspiracies against the peace and welfare of the nation, nor to behave himself undutifully to interior Magistrates; for as Freemasonry hath always been injured by war, bloodshed and confusion, so ancient Kings and Princes have been men disposed to encourage the Craftsmen, because of their peaceableness and loyalty, whereby they practically answered the cavils of their adversaries and promoted the honor of the Fraternity, who ever flourished in times of peace. So that if a Brother should be a rebel against the State, he is not to be countenanced in his rebellion, however, he may be pitied as an unhappy man; and, if convicted of no other crime, though the loyal Brotherhood must and ought to disown his rebellion and give no umbrage or ground of political jealously to the Government for the time being; they cannot expel him from the Lodge, and his relation to it remains indefeasible."

Apparently, this was reported as being the case in most of the schism that was unfolding in the Middle East during the early stages of the 21ST Century. Dissident Islamic and Jewish Freemasonry leaders in such countries as Iraq, Afghanistan and Israel were said

TO HAVE BEEN CAUSING NOTHING BUT TROUBLE FOR MASONIC LEADERS IN OTHER COUNTRIES AS THE TWO POLITICAL FORCES, (REGULAR AND IRREGULAR GRAND MASONIC POWERS) FOUGHT IT OUT AMONGST THEMSELVES FOR A MUCH BIGGER SLICE OF THE FRATERNITY PIE LOOKING TO BE RECOGNIZED AS THE GOVERNING BODY FOR FULL POLITICAL AUTONOMY. AT THE TIME, ISLAMIC FREEMASONRY WAS CONSIDERED TO BE THAT OF AN "IRREGULAR "FRATERNITY INSTITUTION BY THE AMERICAN MASONIC GOVERNING BODY OF THE UNITED GRAND LODGE OF ENGLAND.

IN ORDER TO ACHIEVE THIS POLITICAL AUTONOMY ON A GLOBAL STAGE, A FREEMASON'S DESTINY WHICH IS NORMALLY BASED UPON HIS CHARACTERISTICS IS THUSLY CONCEIVED. THE MASONIC ORDER THEREFORE DESIGNS A CHART /OR TRACING BOARD DEPICTING THE DIRECTION OF HIS LIFE'S AMBITIONS ACCORDING TO WHAT THE BROTHERHOOD WISHES. THIS CHART IS SOMETIMES REFERRED TO AS THE MASTER'S CARPET. IN ANCIENT FREEMASONRY TIMES, "CARPETS" WERE ORIGINALLY DRAWN ON THE FLOOR WITH CHALK /OR CHARCOAL, AND AT THE DAWNING OF THE CRUSADES, MANY A FREEMASON WERE OBLITERATED ONCE IT HAD BEEN LEARNED AS TO WHAT PATH HIS LIFE WAS GOING TO BE TAKING AS PART OF HIS FUTURE'S DESTINY. IN ORDER TO AVOID THIS KIND OF FURTHER TROUBLE, THE CHARTS WERE SUBSEQUENTLY PAINTED ON CLOTH, WHICH WERE THEN LAID ON THE FLOOR. HENCE THEY WERE SIMPLY DUBBED CARPETS. IN FREEMASONRY, THERE ARE THREE GREAT STEPS /OR STAGES SYMBOLIZING HUMAN LIFE; YOUTH, MANHOOD AND OF COURSE OLD AGE. THESE SYMBOLS PLAY A VERY IMPORTANT ROLE IN THE WAY OF WHICH A MASONIC HOPEFUL WILL ACHIEVE HIS DESTINY. THEY ARE IN FACT THE SIMPLEST FORMS OF THE MYSTICAL LADDER, WHICH PERVADES ALL THE SYSTEMS OF INITIATION OF BOTH ANCIENT AND MODERN TIMES. NOWADAYS, THE CARPETS AND/OR CHARTS ARE GENERALLY SUSPENDED FROM THE WALL /OR FROM A FRAMEWORK WITHIN THE FREEMASONRY LODGE ITSELF.

CONTRARY TO PUBLIC OPINION, SADDAM HUSSEIN AND OSAMA BIN LADEN WERE NEVER REALLY ENEMIES OF THE STATE AS THERE ARE COUNTLESS MASONIC LODGERY SCATTERED THROUGHOUT THE MIDDLE EAST; INCLUDING IRAN, IRAQ, KUWAIT, JORDAN, AFGHANISTAN, ISRAEL AND SAUDI ARABIA. IRONICALLY, THERE ARE SIX ENGLISH-SPEAKING LODGES REGISTERED IN THE MIDDLE EAST UNDER THE MASONIC BANNER OF PEACE AND BROTHERLY LOVE; ARABIAN LODGE NO. 882, NEJAM LODGE NO. 897, RED SEA LODGE NO. 919, MILO LODGE NO. 938, PYRAMID LODGE OF PAST MASTERS NO. 962, AND JORDAN LODGE NO. 1339. ODDLY ENOUGH, ARABIAN LODGE NO. 882 IS LOCATED IN DHAHREN, SAUDI ARABIA, AND JORDAN LODGE NO. 1339 IS IN AMMAN, JORDAN. FIVE ARE REGISTERED UNDER THE UNITED GRAND LODGE OF GERMANY, WHILE THE OTHER (JORDAN) IS UNDER THE GRAND LODGE OF SCOTLAND. MANY OTHER FRATERNITY LODGES EXIST IN THE MIDDLE EAST,

BUT UNFORTUNATELY, NO REAL RELIABLE PAPER TRAIL CAN BE FOUND DUE TO THE FACT THAT MOST, IF NOT ALL OF THE FREEMASONRY'S POLITICAL ACTIVITIES ASSOCIATED WITH THE "BROTHERHOOD OF MAN "ARE UNWRITTEN LITERATURE. ONE SIMPLY HAS TO PUT ALL THE PIECES OF THIS GIGANTIC PUZZLE TOGETHER, ONE PIECE AT A TIME. BUILDING BLOCKS OF SELF-RELIANCE AND PRESERVATION SO TO SPEAK!!! FOR EXAMPLE, IN THE EARLY 1960'S MOST OF THE GRAND LODGES IN THE MIDDLE EAST WERE COMPLAINING OF PROBLEMS RELATING TO NON-ATTENDANCE OF MEMBERS AT LODGE MEETINGS AND SUGGESTED THAT EVERY LODGE APPOINT A COMMITTEE TO CONTACT THE BRETHRENSHIP WHO HAD CEASED TO ATTEND THE MEETINGS AND ASCERTAIN THE REASON FOR THEIR ABSENCE. AND BY THE LATER 1970'S AND EARLY 1980'S, STEPS WERE FINALLY BEING TAKEN TO FURTHER RESOLVE THE ISSUE. THE JEWISH STATE OF ISRAEL WAS THE FIRST TO SOLVE THE PROBLEM AS WIDESPREAD VIOLENCE HAD ERUPTED PITTING JEWS, CHRISTIANS AND ARABS AGAINST ONE ANOTHER CAUSING MUCH OF THEIR BLOOD TO BE SPILLED INTO THE STREETS. ACCORDING TO FREEMASONRY LITERATURE, "THE GRAND LODGE OF ISRAEL, WHICH COMPRISES SIXTY LODGES, OFFERS A FINE EXAMPLE OF TOLERANCE AND UNDERSTANDING. IN A COUNTRY OF VAST CONTRASTS AND DIVERSITY, FREEMASONRY IS THE ONLY MEDIUM WHERE JEWS, CHRISTIANS AND ARABS MIX IN HARMONY. INDEED IN 1981 A CHRISTIAN ARAB WAS ELECTED GRAND MASTER. THIS GREAT HARMONY IS EXEMPLIFIED BY THE COAT OF ARMS OF THE GRAND LODGE; WITH THE STAR OF DAVID, THE CHRISTIAN CROSS AND THE MOSLEM CRESCENT SUPER-IMPOSED IN THE SQUARE AND COMPASSES." THUSLY BECOMING A TRUE REPRESENTATION OF THE THREE MOST POWERFUL RELIGIONS WITHIN THE FRATERNITY BROTHERHOOD.

ON JUNE 23RD, 1981 A VERY UNIQUE EVENT WAS DULY NOTED TO HAVE TAKEN PLACE IN THE MASONIC HISTORY BOOKS IN TEL-AVIV; A CHRISTIAN ARAB, FRATERNITY BROTHER JAMIL SHALHOUB WAS ANOINTED AS THE NEW GRAND MASTER OF FREEMASONS OF ISRAEL. SHALHOUB WAS BORN IN HAIFA, AND WAS AN ACTIVE MEMBER OF THE GREEK ORTHODOX CHURCH. HE WAS "INSTALLED AS GRAND MASTER OF THE GRAND LODGE OF ANCIENT FREE AND ACCEPTED MASONS OF THE STATE OF ISRAEL, IN THE PRESENCE OF SOME 300 BRETHREN OF MANY RACES AND FAITHS, INCLUDING VISITORS FROM OVERSEAS." NEEDLESS TO SAY, THE NEW CHRISTIAN GRAND MASTER'S MASONIC CAREER WAS THAT OF A VERY IMPRESSIVE DOSSIER AS IT HAD SPANNED OVER MANY YEARS AS HE WAS SAID TO HAVE BEEN GROOMED FOR HIGH POLITICAL AND/OR RELIGIOUS PORTFOLIO'S WITHIN THE FRATERNAL "BROTHERHOOD OF MAN "UNDER THE AUSPICES OF THE "FATHERHOOD OF GOD". FREEMASONRY BROTHER SHALHOUB WAS A GRADUATE OF THE HEBREW UNIVERSITY OF JERUSALEM AS WELL AS OF LONDON UNIVERSITY. HE INTERESTINGLY OPERATED A RATHER BUSY LAW PRACTICE IN HAIFA DURING HIS MASONIC TENURE OVER THE JEWISH STATE OF

Israel reportedly specializing in the "Personal Status "of its people. According to the Israelite Freemasonry literature from Tel-Aviv: "He has the unusual authorization to plead before the Christian, Jewish and Muslim esslesiastical courts in the Holy Land, where for many centuries matters pertaining to marriage, divorce and 'personal status' have been judged and not as in other countries before civil courts. "Fraternity Brother Shalhoub's long-standing family connections ironically enough was in the world of money lending as well as insurance for "his father having been a Lloyds Underwriter; he is a Director of the Arab-Israel Bank, and has a fine record of public service, particularly in activities connected with inter-faith and inter-race understanding and co-operation."

Masonic Brother Jamil Shalhoub was first Initiated into Freemasonry in the "Eliyahu Hanavi" (Elijah the Prophet) Lodge No. 16 in Haifa, in 1959. By 1966, he had advanced to the posting of Master of the Prophet Lodge, so named because the Prophet was born in Haifa, and its Lodge workings were therefore in Arabic and Hebrew. Once fraternity Brother Shalhoub had stepped forefront of the Israelite Masonic Order's Light of Wisdom, he also brought with him into the Ancient Craft the Greek Orthodox Bishop of Haifa. Brother Jamil Shalhoub was appointed as the Grand Worshipful Overseer of its Lodge in 1968, and "has since served almost continuously in different offices in Grand Lodge, culminating with his unanimous election in May 1981 as Grand Master. "His popularity was witnessed by the attendance at his Installation ceremony as the Grand Master of all Israelite Freemasonry at the Masonic Temple in Tel-Aviv. The temple itself was said to have been literally packed to capacity, standing room only as he was Installed Grand Master of the State of Israel by the Most Worshipful Brother Shlomo Gross, I.P.G.M. with the assistance of M.W. Brother Shalmo Kassan, P.G.M. As per usual, all three Sacred Law reading took place, "the Old Testament, the New Testament and the Koran. "It is also interesting to note that the new Grand Master chose to take his secret Masonic oaths of office in the Old Testament, from which he took the theme **"Brotherhood Universal "**for his reportedly highly emotional charged inaugural address, given in Arabic, English and Hebrew. It was also at this gathering that "Brethren of many different faiths were appointed to offices in the Grand Lodge, including, as a Senior Grand Chaplin, V.W. Bro. Labib Abu-Rukun. "The newly appointed Chaplin ironically enough was "a highly respected leader of the Druse sect, dressed in his robes and distinguished head-dress."

Once the ancient mystical ceremonies were completed, a festive dinner was held that very evening, "when the Brethren were joined by the Ladies and many non-Masonic personalities, including the Speaker of the Knesset (Parliament), and the Mayor of Haifa, the home city of the new Grand Master."

From what Tel-Aviv's Masonic Temple data had stated, fraternity Brother Shalhoub was a highly decorated Master Mason who was climbing up the Freemasonry ladder at an alarming rate of speed. He was a "Past Principle of Jaffa Royal Arch Chapter, which works the Mark, Excellent Mater and Royal Arch Degrees under the Supreme Grand Royal Arch Chapter of the State of Israel, under which it also worked the degree of Royal Ark Mariner, the Cryptic Series and the Babylonish Pass. "Brother Jamil Shalhoub was also a holder of the 33RD Degree in the Ancient and Accepted Scottish Rite of Freemasonry for the Jewish State of Israel; Sublime Master Mason of the 33RD Degree. One of the very first things that the duly anointed Grand Master of the Israelites did was spread his message of **Universal Brotherhood** in the Holy Land not only to the 3,000 brethren listed on the Grand Lodge's membership roster but to all of the sixty-seven Lodges scattered throughout the Holy Land whose **ANCIENT** workings were in Arabic, English, French, German, Hebrew, Rumanian and/or Spanish in accordance to their recognized Masonic Constitutions throughout the world. Further to this, the new Grand Master also preached universality to the whole entire world as he stood on his pulpit proclaiming brotherly love for all mankind. "There can be no doubt that there will be many Brethren in the four quarters of the globe who will wish to join in congratulating M.W. Shalhoub on his Installation, and in the prayer that he may be granted good health, happiness and peace to enable him to carry out the duties of his office "is how the June 24TH, 1981 Freemasonry Bulletin from Tel-Aviv concluded its dedication to its Masonic Christian Arab Grand Master. By 1989-90, another Israelite was chosen as the Grand overseer of the Jewish Masonic State of Israel, Mordechai Falkovitch of Tel-Aviv. It should also be stated that the Grand Lodge of Israel allows plural memberships within the Jewish State as well as dual memberships outside of the State. In addition to this, the Grand Lodge of Israel maintained Foreign Relations with her fraternity Lodgery in Nicaragua throughout its transformation years under the American Masonic administration of fraternity Brothers Ronald Reagan and George Bush Senior. And once the Islamic fundamentalist Ayatollah Khomenini ceased power

FROM THE UNITED STATES GOVERNMENTAL PUPPET REGIME OF THE SHAH OF IRAN AND PASSED A DECREE BANNING ALL AMERICAN FREEMASONRY ACTIVITIES TO EXIST WITHIN HIS PROSPECTIVE COUNTRY'S JUDICIAL BOUNDARIES, THE GRAND LODGE OF ISRAEL SEVERED ALL OF ITS FRATERNITY TIES WITH IRAN – ALL THE WORLD'S A STAGE!!!

FURTHER TO ALL OF THIS RELIGIOUS/POLITICAL BULLSHIT TAKING PLACE THROUGHOUT THE 1980'S AND 1990'S DECADES, IN JUNE OF 1990 A GROUP OF SIXTY-THREE BRITISH FREEMASONS HOPPED ABOARD AN AIRCRAFT IN LONDON, ENGLAND TO PARTICIPATE IN VARIOUS GRAND MASONIC EVENTS THAT WERE TAKING PLACE IN ISRAEL. DURING THEIR INITIAL VISIT TO THE HOLY LAND OF ALL FREEMASONRY WORLDWIDE, THEY MET WITH MANY OF THE BRETHRENSHIP FROM OTHER PARTS OF THE GLOBE. ON THE LAST DAY, THEY ATTENDED A MEETING OF THE THREE LOCAL LODGES IN FREEMASONS' HALL IN TEL-AVIV. THE HEBREW-SPEAKING OFFICERS OF THE AVIV LODGE THUSLY OPENED THE PROCEEDING AND THEN, SURRENDERED THE GAVEL OVER TO SHARON LODGE, WHICH INTERESTINGLY ENOUGH IS LISTED AS BEING THE OLDEST ENGLISH-SPEAKING LODGE WITHIN THE JEWISH STATE OF ISRAEL'S JURISDICTIONAL BOUNDARIES. THIS LODGE WAS SAID TO HAVE BEEN MADE UP OF MANY ETHNIC ORIGINS AND FAITHS, INCLUDING A ROMAN CATHOLIC MEMBER OF THE UNITED STATES GOVERNMENT'S DIPLOMATIC SERVICES WHO WAS REPORTEDLY TAKING PART IN THE CEREMONY IN ENGLISH. AS THE ENGLISH CEREMONIAL ACTIVITY CAME TO A CLOSE, THE CHAIRMAN AND HIS DELEGATION OF FAITHFUL OFFICERS THEN HANDED THE TRAVELING GAVEL OVER TO THE MASTERS OF THE AKKO LODGE, IN WHICH THE BRETHRENSHIP WAS COMPRISED OF MUSLIM /OR CHRISTIAN ISRAELI ARABS, WHO IN TURN CONDUCTED THE CLOSING CEREMONIES IN ARABIC. DESPITE THE FACT THAT ACCORDING TO THE MORAL MAJORITY MEMBERS LIVING ON THE NORTH AMERICAN CONTINENT FIRMLY BELIEVED THAT ALL FORMS OF FREEMASONRY WERE THE INNER WORKINGS OF **SATAN**, THE USUAL THREE SACRED BOOKS OF THE MASONIC **BROTHERHOOD OF MAN** WERE USED AT THIS GATHERING; THE TENACH (OLD TESTAMENT) IN HEBREW, THE NEW TESTAMENT IN ENGLISH AND THE KORAN IN ARABIC.

IRONICALLY, WHILE THE BUSH FAMILY'S ANCESTOR WINSTON CHURCHILL WAS PRIME MINISTER OF ENGLAND HE REPORTEDLY STATED THAT THE JEWISH STATE WAS "ESPECIALLY IN HARMONY WITH THE TRUEST INTEREST OF THE BRITISH EMPIRE. "IN THE MEANTIME, BOTH THE AMERICAN AND THE CANADIAN FREEMASONS VIEWED ISRAEL AS AN "UNSINKABLE AIRCRAFT CARRIER "DESIGNED TO WIN THE FRATERNAL BATTLE OF THE VERY FIBER OF ITS EXISTENCE. IT SHOULD ALSO BE STATED THAT AFTER MANY YEARS OF NOT RECEIVING ANY COMMUNICATIONS FROM THE MIDDLE EAST, THERE WAS MUCH ACTIVITY IN FOREIGN RELATIONS BETWEEN THE UNITED STATES, CANADA

AND ITS ISRAELITE LODGERY IN THE HOLY LAND BY THE MID-1980's. IN FACT, DURING THE YEAR 1986, THE FIRST COMMUNIQUE IN MORE THAN TEN YEARS WAS RECEIVED FROM THE BARKAI LODGE LOCATED IN THE WORLD'S LARGEST ALL-JEWISH CITY IN THE STATE OF ISRAEL.

BY MASONIC INTERPRETATION, ISRAEL'S STAR OF DAVID, KNOWN BY THE JEWISH PEOPLE AS THE SHIELD OF DAVID, IS MORE COMMONLY KNOWN BY ITS BIBLICAL SYMBOL, THE SEAL OF SOLOMON WHICH WAS CONSIDERED BY THE ANCIENT JEWS AS A TALISMAN OF GREAT EFFICACY:

"THE SEAL OF SOLOMON OR SHIELD OF DAVID, FOR UNDER BOTH NAMES THE SAME THING WAS DENOTED, IS A HEXAGONAL FIGURE CONSISTING OF TWO INTERLACED TRIANGLES, THUS FORMING THE OUTLINES OF A SIX- POINTED STAR. UPON IT WAS INSCRIBED ONE OF THE SACRED NAMES OF GOD, FROM WHICH INSCRIPTION IT WAS SUPPOSED PRINCIPALLY TO DERIVE ITS TALISMANIC POWERS. THESE POWERS WERE VERY EXTENSIVE, FOR IT WAS BELIEVED THAT IT WOULD EXTINGUISH FIRE, PREVENT WOUNDS IN A CONFLICT, AND PERFORM MANY OTHER WONDERS. THE JEWS CALLED THE SHIELD OF DAVID IN REFERENCE TO THE PROTECTION WHICH IT GAVE ITS POSSESSORS. BUT TO THE OTHER ORIENTALISTS IT WAS MORE FAMILIARLY KNOWN AS THE SEAL OF SOLOMON. AMONG THESE IMAGINATIVE PEOPLE, THERE WAS A VERY PREVALENT BELIEF IN THE MAGICAL CHARACTER OF THE KING OF ISRAEL. HE WAS ESTEEMED RATHER AS A GREAT MAGICIAN THAN AS A GREAT MONARCH, AND BY THE SIGNET WHICH HE WORE, ON WHICH THIS TALISMANTIC SEAL WAS ENGRAVED, HE IS SUPPOSED TO HAVE ACCOMPLISHED THE MOST EXTRAORDINARY ACTIONS, AND BY IT TO HAVE ENLISTED IN HIS SERVICES THE LABORS OF THE GENII FOR THE CONSTRUCTION OF HIS CELEBRATED TEMPLE."

OF ALL TALISMANS, THERE IS NONE SO POWERFUL, EXCEPT PERHAPS, THE CHRISTIAN CROSS, WHICH WAS SO GENERALLY PREVALENT AMONG THE ANCIENTS AS THE GREAT SEAL OF SOLOMON AND/OR THE SHIELD OF DAVID. ALL OF WHICH TO SAY THE LEAST, ARE PURELY BASED UPON THE LEGENDS AND/OR FABRICATED NONSENSE CONTAINED IN THAT GREAT BOOK OF FAIRY TALES KNOWN AS THE HOLY SCRIPTURES. LIKE ALL ASPECTS OF OUR SO-CALLED DEMOCRATIC PROCEDURE, ALL FORMS OF RELIGION ARE BASED UPON THE HYPOCRITICAL TEACHINGS OF DECEPTION. CANADA'S VERY OWN MASONIC BIBLE, THE AUTHORIZED KING JAMES VERSION BY HIS MAJESTY'S SPECIAL COMMAND, (COPYRIGHT 1951), IS THE PRIME EXAMPLE OF SUCH TRIPE.

WHEN IT COMES TO MASONIC CONCEPTS OF DECEPTION, THE AMERICAN FREEMASONS ARE DEFINITELY THE MASTERS OF THEIR FELLOW-CRAFT. FOR INSTANCE, IN ACCORDANCE TO THE **"BROTHERHOOD OF MAN "**UNDER

THE AUSPICES OF THE **"FATHERHOOD OF GOD** "THE U.S. GOVERNMENTAL ADMINISTRATION OF GEORGE BUSH SENIOR DURING THE DAYS LEADING UP TO THE PERSIAN GULF CRISIS OF THE 1990'S WAS THE GREATEST OF ALL THESE DECEPTIONS PERTAINING TO THE LAST CENTURY. THIS 41ST PRESIDENT OF THE UNITED STATES WAS CONSIDERED TO HAVE BEEN THAT COUNTRY'S MOST HIGHLY RESPECTED PROTECTOR OF AMERICAN FREEMASONRY NOT ONLY GRADUATED FROM YALE UNIVERSITY BUT ALSO BECAME A MEMBER AND DIRECTOR OF THE FOREIGN RELATIONS COMMITTEE, BETTER KNOWN BY ALL AS THE COUNCIL ON FOREIGN RELATIONS. THROUGHOUT HIS MASONIC CAREER, BROTHER BUSH HELD MANY IMPORTANT FRATERNITY PORTFOLIO'S; SUCH AS THE U.S. REPRESENTATIVE TO "COMMUNIST CHINA "IN 1974-75; HEAD DIRECTOR OF THE CIA IN 1976; AND LATER, AMBASSADOR TO THE UNITED NATIONS. SOME FORTY-FOUR YEARS BEFORE FREEMASONRY BROTHER GEORGE HERBERT WALKER BUSH BECAME KNOWN AS THE EL PRESIDENTE OF THE CONFEDERACAO MASONICA INTER-AMERICANNA, HE SERVED WITH THE MASONIC ALLIED FORCES DURING THE SECOND WORLD WAR AS A NAVY FIGHTER PILOT. A YOUNG GEORGE BUSH WAS DECORATED AS A NATIONAL HERO WHEN HIS TORPEDO BOMBER TURNED INTO A DIVE WITH SMOKE POURING INTO THE COCKPIT AND FLAMES RIPPLING ACROSS THE WINGS. RISKING HIS OWN LIFE, THE YOUNG NAVY FIGHTER REPORTEDLY SPOTTED HIS JAPANESE TARGET AND RELEASED HIS PAYLOAD OF FOUR 225-KILOGRAM BOMBS ONTO THE UNSUSPECTING TARGET BELOW. HE THEN, BAILED OUT OF HIS BURNING BOMBER SOMEWHERE OVER THE PACIFIC OCEAN. IN AN ATTEMPT TO FULFILL HIS LIFE'S AMBITIONS, ONCE RESCUED FROM THE COLD WATERS OF THE PACIFIC AND REGAINING HIS COMPOSURE, BROTHER BUSH MOUNTED ANOTHER AIRCRAFT AND CONTINUED WITH THE PROCEEDINGS OF THE MASTER'S CARPET.

DURING HIS TENURE AS THE PROTECTOR OF AMERICAN FREEMASONRY, THE 41ST PRESIDENT OF THE GOOD OLD U.S. OF A. GAVE CLUES TO HIS MASONIC INVOLVEMENT IN THE **UNIVERSAL BROTHERHOOD** OF GLOBAL DOMINATION IN JANUARY OF 1991 WHEN HE ANNOUNCED TO THE ENTIRE WORLD THAT HIS ATTEMPTS OF CURTAILING THE ISLAMIC FREEMASONRY LEADER OF IRAQ WERE THAT OF A JUST CAUSE FIGHTING FOR FREEDOM AND DEMOCRACY. IT GOES WITHOUT SAYINGS THAT VERY FEW PEOPLE LIVING IN THE WESTERN FREE-WORLD TOOK HEED TO THESE CLUES AS BY THIS TIME PERIOD, SADDAM HUSSEIN WAS CONSIDERED TO BE THE EVIL CHARACTER IN THIS FRATERNAL PLAY OF PLAYS.

ON WEDNESDAY, JANUARY 16TH, AT 3:40 P.M. (PACIFIC STANDARD TIME), 2:40 A.M. OVER BAGHDAD, MASONIC PRESIDENT GEORGE BUSH SR. GAVE THE ORDER FOR OPERATION DESERT SHIELD TO EXECUTE OPERATION DESERT STORM. WITHIN TWO HOURS AFTER DROPPING ITS FRATERNITY BOMBS ON IRAQ AND ITS POPULATION OF 17.6 MILLION, THE AMERICAN

Freemasonry dictator addressed the nation giving his reasons for the obliteration of human life and their anti-democratic rhetoric on the peace loving nations incorporated within the International Masonic Family of Man. The following is in part what the protector of American Freemasonry stated in his dictatorial speech to the nation:

"...This is a historic moment, we in this past year made great progress in ending the long era of conflict and Cold War. We have before us the opportunity to forge for ourselves and for future generations a **New World Order**. A world of rule of law, not the law of the jungle, governs the conduct of nations. When we are successful, and we will be, we have a real chance at this **New World Order**. An Order in which a credible United Nations can use its peacekeeping role to fulfill the promise and vision of the U.N.'s founders ..."

According to the American news media, the U.S. President was said to have worked on honing his speech for two /or three weeks prior to the actual bombing of Baghdad. In his twelve minute propaganda address to the entire world, the United States protector of American Freemasonry waved the U.S. flag around by glorifying the brave efforts of the fighting forces involved with Operation Desert Storm. To those with the knowledge of what was really transpiring behind the scenes, the speech itself was the most hypocritical rhetoric ever witnessed on a worldwide scale as less than an hour after the American pitch for the formation of a **New World Order** was publicized by George Bush Sr., other Masonically controlled countries quickly stood before the news cameras pledging their allegiance to the fraternity cause. Canada's Prime Minister Brian Mulroney was one of the first to step up to the Freemasonry plate demanding that Saddam Hussein vacate the premises of Kuwait immediately /or else suffer the consequences of the Brotherhood's wrath.

As Ted Turner's global-spanning Cable News Network (CNN) broadcasted the Persian Gulf War, (the First Gulf War), efforts in over 100 different countries, more than 53 million American households were literally glued to their television sets. Only seven days previous to the spilling of Iraqi blood, the U.S. Pentagon issued strict guidelines for all news reporters covering the war to follow, and as the entire scenario began to unfold before everyone's very eyes over CNN's airwaves, the American military directors and

PRODUCERS CONTINUALLY EDITED AND RE-WROTE THE FRATERNITY SCRIPT IN AN ATTEMPT TO DISTORT THE TRUTH BEHIND HUSSEIN'S DISSIDENT ACTIONS.

WHILE THE CRISIS WAS BEING PLAYED OUT ON WORLDWIDE TELEVISION, PROTEST DEMONSTRATIONS PLAGUED THE ENTIRE WORLD; **"NO BLOOD FOR OIL "**CHANTED THE DEEPLY CONFUSED PROTESTERS. ANTI-WAR RALLIES WERE SOON EXECUTED IN ENGLAND, FRANCE GERMANY, ITALY, AUSTRALIA, SWITZERLAND, THE PHILIPPINES, CANADA, THE UNITED STATES AND EVEN IN THE MIDDLE EAST. HERE IN CANADA, ALL THE MAJOR CITIES ACROSS THE COUNTRY TOOK PART IN THE ANTI-WAR FESTIVITIES. PROTESTERS MARCHED ON PARLIAMENT HILL IN DEFIANCE OF CANADA'S INVOLVEMENT IN THE PERSIAN GULF. IN WASHINGTON, D.C. DEMONSTRATORS GATHERED OUTSIDE THE CAPITAL BUILDINGS TO DENOUNCE AMERICA'S PUSH FOR THE OBLITERATION OF LIVES IN THE MIDDLE EAST. AS THEY GATHERED IN FRONT OF AT THE ALL POWERFUL WHITE HOUSE, THEY CHANTED; **"HELL NO, WE WON'T GO. WE WON'T DIE FOR TEXACO. "**DEMONSTRATORS IN BATON ROUGE, LOUISIANA MARCHED IN BODY BAGS WHILE MUSICAL PERFORMERS WILLIE NELSON AND KRIS KRISTOFFERSON STRUTTED THEIR STUFF AT THE PEACE RALLY IN AUSTIN, TEXAS. IN BERLIN, PROTESTERS ROLLED OIL BARRELS DOWN THE CITY STREETS TO SHOW THEIR OUTRAGE OVER THE PERSIAN GULF CONFLICT. MEANWHILE IN ISTANBUL AND BAGHDAD, PROTESTERS DEMONSTRATED THE RUTHLESS IDEOLOGY OF THE AMERICAN AGGRESSOR AND ITS ALLIED COALITION. AS THE UNITED NATIONS JANUARY 15TH 1991 DEADLINE FOR SADDAM HUSSEIN TO GET THE HELL OUT OF KUWAIT DREW CLOSER WITH EACH PASSING DAY, TENSIONS QUICKLY MOUNTED ON A WORLDWIDE SCALE. PROTESTERS THEN STEPPED UP THEIR ANTI-WAR RHETORIC IN AN ATTEMPT TO DERAIL THE AGGRESSION IN THE MIDDLE EAST.

ON THE LAST DAY OF HUSSEIN'S OPPORTUNITY TO VACATE THE KUWAIT PREMISES, HIGH SCHOOL STUDENTS ACROSS CANADA SKIPPED CLASSES AND MARCHED FOR WORLD PEACE. IN BRITISH COLUMBIA'S METROPOLIS OF VANCOUVER, THOUSANDS OF STUDENTS BLOCKED STREETS, SINGING **"GIVE PEACE A CHANCE "**AND CHANTING **"NO BLOOD FOR OIL! "**LIKE A DEEP PENETRATING REPETITIOUS INTERCOURSE OF THE VIETNAM CONFLICT, THE SLOGANS **"HELL NO, WE WON'T GO "**AND **"ONE, TWO, THREE, FOUR WE DON'T WANT YOUR FUCHIN WAR "**BROUGHT REMINDING SHIVERS OF BLOOD AND CARNAGE TO THE ADULT POPULATION. IN VICTORIA, OVER ONE-THOUSAND STUDENTS MARCHED ONTO THE LAWN OF THE LEGISLATURE DEMANDING CANADA'S IMMEDIATE WITHDRAWAL FROM THE PERSIAN GULF. BEFORE LONG, DEMONSTRATIONS BROKE OUT IN SURREY, MAPLE RIDGE, PRINCE GEORGE AND JUST ABOUT EVERY LITTLE HOLE IN THE WALL WITHIN THE PROVINCIAL JURISDICTION. THE CITIZENRY WAS VIRTUALLY BROUGHT TO ITS KNEES AS MANY ADULTS WIPED TEARS FROM THEIR EYES AND

CONTEMPLATED THE PAST WARS OF THE TWENTIETH CENTURY THAT CLAIMED MORE THAN 80 MILLION LIVES. IN GIBSONS, B.C. WELL OVER 100 STUDENTS LEFT CLASSES AND BLOCKED TWO LANES OF THE MAIN HIGHWAY IN FRONT OF THEIR HIGH SCHOOL, (ELPHINSTONE SECONDARY). AS IN ALL PROVINCIAL WIDE DEMONSTRATIONS, THE QUEEN'S SEMI-MILITARY POLICE FORCE MEMBERS WERE CALLED IN TO MAINTAIN THE ROYAL BRITISH MOTTO OF PUBLIC ORDERLY CONDUCT. WHILE CHANTING THE USUAL SLOGANS NORMALLY ATTRIBUTED A TOTALLY CONFUSED AND UNINFORMED POPULATION, THE STUDENTS WERE CLEARED OFF THE HIGHWAY AND ORDERED ONTO THE SIDEWALKS. THE PROTESTING STUDENTS THEN COLLECTED PAGES OF SIGNATURES SAYING **NO** TO THE WAR IN THE MIDDLE EAST. THE PETITION WAS ADDRESSED TO THE MASONICALLY CONTROLLED GOVERNING BODY OF THE UNITED NATIONS SECURITY COUNCIL, IT SIMPLY STATED; "TO THE UNITED NATIONS ASSEMBLY: WE, THE YOUTH OF THE WORLD SAY TO YOU - **NO WAR**, GIVE PEACE A CHANCE." THE ENTIRE YOUTH POPULATION OF THE SUNSHINE COAST STOOD UP TO BE COUNTED THAT DAY AS YET ANOTHER PETITION HAD BEEN CIRCULATED THE PREVIOUS DAY AND FAXED TO THE OFFICE OF THE CANADIAN PRIME MINISTER. ADDRESSED TO BRIAN MULRONEY, THIS PETITION INFORMED THE CANADIAN FREEMASONRY ESTABLISHMENT THAT THE FUTURE LEADERS OF TOMORROW WERE NOT AT ALL PREPARED TO PUT UP WITH THE BROTHERHOOD'S STYLE OF DEMOCRACY: "WE ARE SETTING THE TONE FOR THE 21ST CENTURY. YOU HAVE THE POWER TO STOP THE PROGRESSION TOWARDS WAR IN THE PERSIAN GULF. PLEASE USE THIS POWER. "FOR GIBSONS AND THE SURROUNDING COASTAL REGION, THIS SORT OF OUTBURST WAS TOTALLY OUT OF CHARACTER FOR THEM. AS MANY TIMES IN THE PAST, COMPLACENCY HAD BEEN THE NORMAL TREND FOR MOST, IF NOT ALL OF THE SUNSHINE COAST RESIDENTS. ALTHOUGH THEIR EFFORTS WERE GALLANT, IN THE END EVERYTHING WAS NONE THE LESS FUTILE AS THE TRUE DEMOCRATIC-DICTATORIAL COALITION NATIONS DROPPED THEIR FRATERNITY BOMBS ON BAGHDAD.

EVER SINCE THE BOMBING OF PEARL HARBOR IN 1941, AMERICAN FOREIGN POLICY IS WITHOUT A DOUBT DRAPED IN BLOOD; BOTH THE KOREAN AND VIETNAM WARS ARE PRIME EXAMPLES OF SUCH. WITH OTHER OFFSHOOT EXAMPLES OF THIS POLICY BEING IMPLEMENTED IN SUCH COUNTRIES AS SOUTH AND CENTRAL AMERICA AS WELL AS IN THE MIDDLE EAST. THE MOST MEMORABLE BEING OF COURSE THE IRAN-CONTRA AFFAIR OF THE 1980'S UNDER THE COMMAND OF MASONIC LEADERS RONALD REAGAN AND GEORGE BUSH SENIOR; REAGAN BEING PRESIDENT OF THE UNITED STATES AND BUSH THE UNDERLING VICE-PRESIDENT. THE SCANDAL ITSELF ERUPTED AFTER AN ILLEGAL TRANSACTION HAD TAKEN PLACE IN 1987 IN WHICH THE UNITED STATES OF AMERICA AGREED TO SELL ARMS TO IRAN IN RETURN FOR THE RELEASE OF U.S. HOSTAGES. THE UNITED STATES, THEN USED THE PROFITS

FROM THE SALE OF WEAPONRY TO SECRETLY SUPPORT NICARAGUA'S CONTRA REBELS IN THEIR ATTEMPT TO OVERTHROW THAT COUNTRY'S GOVERNMENT. FURTHER TO THIS LITTLE CAPER, THE UNITED STATES HAD SUPPLIED GUNS AND AMMUNITION TO SADDAM HUSSEIN ONLY YEARS PREVIOUSLY AS IRAQ AND IRAN BEGAN SQUABBLING AMONGST THEMSELVES OVER A BORDER DISPUTE, SEPTEMBER 1980. AND WHEN HUSSEIN INVADED KUWAIT, HE USED THOSE EXACT SAME WEAPONS TO WARD OFF AMERICA SOLDIERS IN THE PERSIAN GULF WAR – IRONY IN ITS ABSOLUTE BEST FORM!!!

BY THE TIME THE EVENTS OF SEPTEMBER 11TH, 2001 BEGAN TO UNFOLD BEFORE OUR VERY EYES, THE U.S. ECONOMY HAD ALREADY BEEN IN AN ECONOMIC SLUMP FOR ABOUT ELEVEN /OR TWELVE MONTHS AFTER REAPING THE WEALTH OF A FULL TEN YEARS OF ECONOMIC BLISS. COMPANIES WERE EITHER DOWN SIZING /OR CONTEMPLATING BANKRUPTCY PROCEDURES ALTOGETHER. AFTER THE ATTACK, NEWS OUTLETS IN BOTH CANADA AND THE UNITED STATES ATTEMPTED TO LAY BLAME TO THE ECONOMIC WOES OF NORTH AMERICAS AS BEING A DIRECT CAUSE OF THE INVASION ON AMERICAN SOIL AS MORE AND MORE COMPANIES BEGAN LAYING OFF PEOPLE /OR SHUTTING DOWN THEIR OPERATIONS TOTALLY AND CLAIMING BANKRUPTCY PROTECTION. WITH UNEMPLOYMENT SLOWLY REACHING AN ALL TIME HIGH IN BOTH COUNTRIES PRIOR TO SEPTEMBER 11TH, WHAT ELSE WAS TO BE EXPECTED FROM THE POWERS THAT BE. AFTERALL, IT WAS THROUGH NO FAULT OF THEIR OWN THAT THE WORLD ECONOMY WAS HEADING FOR THE CRAPPER SIMPLY BECAUSE OF THE FACT THAT NO ONE WANTED TO DARE ADMIT TO A RECESSION ACTUALLY EXISTING IN HIS /OR HER OWN PROSPECTIVE COUNTRY. SEPTEMBER 11TH JUST SEEMED TO BE AN IDEAL SITUATION, THE ENDS OBVIOUSLY JUSTIFYING THE MEANS AS AFTER THE INITIAL ATTACK EVERYONE FEARED THE WORST WHEN THE U.S. PRESIDENT (GEORGE BUSH JUNIOR) VOWED TO SEEK REVENGE. A WORLD'S ECONOMY ALWAYS SEEMS TO IMPROVE WHEN A GROUP OF STUPID DEGENERATE BONEHEADS DECIDE TO WAGE WAR ONTO A COUNTRY AND/OR A PEOPLE JUST TO PROVE A POINT OF SUPERIORITY. CASE IN POINT; THE U.S. ECONOMY FLOURISHED AFTER DECEMBER 8TH, 1941 AS DID CANADA'S DURING THAT SAME TIME PERIOD OF HISTORY.

IRONICALLY ENOUGH, AN ESTIMATED TWO MONTHS PRIOR TO THE SEPTEMBER 11TH ATTACK BEING EXECUTED ONTO THE WORLD TRADE CENTER AND THE PENTAGON, ITALY'S SECRET SERVICE AGENCY (SISDE, EQUIVALENT TO BRITAIN'S MI5 AND THE UNITED STATES OF AMERICA'S CIA) APPARENTLY WARNED U.S. INTELLIGENCE OFFICERS AS WELL AS THE AMERICAN PRESIDENT GEORGE W. BUSH THAT THEY SHOULD BE EXPECTING AN AIRBORNE ASSAULT ON THEIR HOME TURF AND THAT THERE EXISTED A PLOT TO KILL THE U.S. PRESIDENT IN HIS OWN COUNTRY. AS BEFORE, NO INITIAL MEASURES WERE TAKEN TO PREVENT SUCH AN AIRBORNE ATTACK TO TRANSPIRE. THE REPORT

ITSELF WAS SAID TO BE SENT TO SISDE's WESTERN COUNTERPARTS ON JULY 6TH, 2001, NINE FULL WEEKS BEFORE THE SEPTEMBER 11TH TRAGEDY. ODD AS IT MAY SOUND, THE REPORT EVEN SPECIFIED WHO THE INSTIGATORS OF THE ATTACKS WERE GOING TO BE THUSLY ENABLING U.S. INTELLIGENCE OFFICERS AMPLE TIME TO CONDUCT THEIR OWN STRATEGY AS A WAY AND MEANS OF PREVENTING SUCH A MANOEUVRE TO OCCUR. BUT JUST LIKE PEARL HARBOR, THE AMERICANS QUICKLY ASSUMED THAT SUCH A DEED WAS AN IMPOSSIBILITY AS THEY WERE AFTERALL UNTOUCHABLE. WITH THEIR BANNERS OF ARROGANCE AND SELF-RIGHTEOUSNESS RAPPED AROUND THE FLAG OF STARS AND STRIPES, ITALY'S SECRET SERVICE REPORT FELL ON DEAF EARS AND ON SEPTEMBER 11TH ITS CONTENTS BECAME A FULL BLOWN REALITY CHECK FOR THE UNITED STATES. AND JUST LIKE PEARL HARBOR, THE REACTION OF OUR AMERICAN COUSINS SOUTH OF THE 49TH PARALLEL WAS IDENTICAL TO THAT OF SIXTY YEARS PREVIOUSLY; REVENGE!!!

IT SHOULD ALSO BE STATED THAT AT THIS EXACT SAME TIME FRAME OF HISTORY, ISLAMIC FREEMASONRY WAS STILL IN TOTAL CHAOS AS SADDEM HUSSEIN HAD MANAGED TO TURN THE TABLES ON ITS MEMBERSHIP YEARS PREVIOUSLY AND THEIR DIFFERENCES OF OPINION WITH AMERICAN FREEMASONS HADN'T BEEN WORKED OUT AS OF YET. WITH THE DETERIORATION OF THE INTERCOURSE AND MARRIAGE OF ISLAMIC AND AMERICAN FREEMASONRY, CAME THE EXPLOSION OF A FEEDING FRENZY FOR DOMINATION, ONE GROUP WANTING MORE POWER THAN THE OTHER. AND SINCE THE OVAL OFFICE WAS NOW OCCUPIED BY THE SON OF A MASTER MASON, THE SEPTEMBER 11TH ATTACK ON AMERICAN SOIL WAS INSTANTLY LABELED AS AN ACT OF TERRORISM AND RETALIATION WAS VOWED ONTO THOSE WHO INSTIGATED IT. ON SUNDAY, OCTOBER 7TH (ONLY 27 DAYS AFTER THE SO-CALLED TERRORIST ATTACK ON THE AMERICAN PEOPLE) FRATERNITY LEADER GEORGE W. BUSH AUTHORIZED THE BOMBING OF AFGHANISTAN AS A MEANS OF FLUSHING OUT THE MAIN PERSON WHO THE ITALIAN SECRET SERVICE REPORT DEEMED TO BE BEHIND THE AIRBORNE ASSAULTS, OSAMA BIN LADEN. FOR DAYS AND WEEKS AT A TIME, AIRCRAFTS DROPPED THEIR PAYLOAD ONTO THE AFGHANISTANI POPULATION KILLING INNOCENT MEN, WOMEN AND CHILDREN AND THEN DROPPING HUMANITARIAN AID PACKAGES OF FOOD AND MEDICAL SUPPLIES AFTER THE END OF EACH EVENINGS ATTACK THUS CREATING THE ILLUSION THAT THE AIR STRIKES WERE NOT DIRECTED AT INNOCENT CIVILIANS. THIS ACT OF KINDNESS WAS PERFORMED LARGELY DUE TO THE FACT THAT THE ENTIRE WORLD WAS WATCHING EVERY MOVE THAT WAS BEING MADE ON THEIR TELEVISION SETS VIA SATELLITE AS THE AMERICANS RE-DEFINED THE GUIDELINES OF WAR TACTICS FOR THE 21ST CENTURY. AND JUST AS BEFORE, THEIR ACTIONS WERE DEEMED TO BE JUSTIFIED AS THE UNITED STATES OF AMERICA HAD DECLARED WAR ON TERRORISM. WHILE HIDING BEHIND THEIR SHIELD OF NATIONAL

SECURITY, THE U.S. GOVERNMENT VOWED NOT TO REST UNTIL BIN LADEN AND HIS FOLLOWERS WERE BROUGHT TO JUSTICE IN ACCORDANCE TO WHAT THE AMERICAN MASONIC **BROTHERHOOD OF MAN** FELT WAS JUSTIFIABLE. BY THE END OF SEPTEMBER 2001, A BOUNTY WAS THUS PLACED ON OSAMA BIN LADEN'S HEAD SAYING THAT THE BOUNTY ITSELF ($ 30 MILLION U.S.) WOULD BE PAID OUT TO ANYONE WHO HELPED CAPTURE BIN LADEN DEAD /OR ALIVE. ANY PROSPECTIVE TAKERS ON GEORGE W. BUSH'S OFFER WERE THUSLY ENCOURAGED TO CONTACT EITHER BRANCHES OF THE UNITED STATES SECURITY AGENCIES, CIA /OR FBI. BOUNTY HUNTERS FROM AROUND THE WORLD THEN BEGAN SCOUTING THE COUNTRYSIDE OF AFGHANISTAN TRYING TO BE THE FIRST ONES TO CLAIM THE 30 MILLION DOLLAR DOOR PRIZE. THREE WEEKS LATER, OCTOBER 21ST, 2001 THE AMERICAN PRESIDENT AUTHORIZED CIA OPERATIVES TO ASSASSINATE BIN LADEN AND TO HAVE HIS NETWORK OF FOLLOWERS DISMANTLED. THE U.S. GOVERNMENT IN ESSENCE BECAME NO BETTER THAN THOSE INDIVIDUALS WHO THEY WERE TRYING TO EXTERMINATE AS $ 1 BILLION IN U.S. CURRENCY WAS SET ASIDE SPECIFICALLY FOR THAT JUST CAUSE.

MEANWHILE NORTH OF THE 49TH PARALLEL, SYMPATHY FOR THE UNITED STATES WAS REACHING AN ALL TIME HIGH AS CANADIANS CONSOLED WITH THEIR AMERICAN COUSINS TO THE SOUTH. AS FAR AS THE VAST MAJORITY OF THE CANADIAN POPULATION WAS CONCERNED, THE AMERICANS WERE TOTALLY JUSTIFIED IN TAKING THE RETALIATORY ACTIONS AGAINST THE ISLAMIC TERRORISTS ASSUMED TO BE HIDING OUT SOMEWHERE IN THE CAVES OF THE MOUNTAINS OF AFGHANISTAN. IT WAS IN THESE MOUNTAINS THAT THE UNITED STATES STARTED BOMBING THE HELL OUT OF TRYING TO FLUSH OUT BIN LADEN. THREE MONTHS AFTER THE BOMBING OF AFGHANISTAN HAD INITIALLY STARTED, IT WAS STILL BEING EXECUTED AS THE NEW YEAR CELEBRATIONS BEGAN TO UNFOLD IN THE WESTERN FREE-WORLD. THE BOMBING ITSELF WAS SO FAR OUT OF CONTROL THAT THE U.S. PRESIDENT EVEN BEGAN CONTEMPLATING DROPPING AIRCRAFT PAYLOADS ONTO IRAQ AS AN EXTRA MEASURE OF GETTING THE MESSAGE ACROSS THAT AMERICAN FREEMASONRY WAS NOT ABOUT READY TO TOLERATE ANY ACTS OF DEFIANCE AGAINST ITS JUST CAUSE OF **"MANIFEST DESTINY"**. RIGHT FROM THE OUTSET OF SEPTEMBER 11TH, CANADIANS BECAME SO DESENSITIZED TO WHAT WAS REALLY GOING ON THAT THEY TOTALLY DENIED KNOWING ANYTHING OF BOTH U.S. FOREIGN POLICY AS WELL AS AMERICAN HISTORY CONCERNING GLOBAL CONQUEST. THIS BRAIN DEAD CANADIAN ATTITUDE REARED ITS UGLY HEAD EVEN FURTHER WHEN AN ASSISTANT PROFESSOR OF WOMEN'S STUDIES AT THE UNIVERSITY OF BRITISH COLUMBIA, SUNERA THOBANI, BEGAN SPEAKING IN OTTAWA AT A WOMEN'S CONFERENCE ON MONDAY, OCTOBER 1ST, 2001. THOBANI PUBLICALLY ATTACKED U.S. FOREIGN POLICY BY SAYING THAT THE

AMERICANS WERE NOT ONLY "BLOODTHIRSTY "VENGEFUL PEOPLE BY NATURAL DESIGN BUT THAT THEIR ACTS OF AGGRESSION IN OTHER COUNTRIES HAD HISTORICALLY BEEN "SOAKED IN BLOOD. "FURTHER STATING: "TODAY IN THE WORLD THE UNITED STATES IS THE MOST DANGEROUS AND THE MOST POWERFUL GLOBAL FORCE UNLEASHING HORRIFIC LEVELS OF VIOLENCE ALL OVER THE WORLD. "IN HER SPEECH, THE UNIVERSITY PROFESSOR ACCUSED U.S. PRESIDENT GEORGE W. BUSH OF IMPOSING HIS OWN HIDDEN AGENDA ONTO OTHER COUNTRIES WHERE NON-WHITE WOMEN ALL OVER THE WORLD WOULD END UP CARRYING THE BRUNT OF THE PUNISHMENT IN A TRADITIONALLY MALE DOMINANT SOCIETY.

SOMEWHAT HORRIFIED AT WHAT THOBANI WAS SAYING IN FRONT OF THE TELEVISION AND NEWSPAPER CAMERAS, SOME OF THE CONFERENCE ORGANIZERS BEGAN TO FEEL A LITTLE UNEASY AS THE CANADIAN FEDERAL GOVERNMENT WAS FOOTING THE BILL FOR THE CONFERENCE ITSELF ($ 80,000.00 CANADIAN) AND AT THE TIME, TWO VERY HIGH PROFILE FEDERAL LIBERALS WERE IN ATTENDANCE; VANCOUVER-CENTER M.P. HEDY FRY AND LIBERAL SENATOR LANDON PEARSON. APPARENTLY, BOTH FRY AND PEARSON WERE DEEPLY OFFENDED AT WHAT WAS BEING STATED AT THE CONFERENCE. FEARING THAT THE FUNDING WOULD BE CANCELED ALTOGETHER, SOME ORGANIZERS OF THE CONFERENCE BEGAN SENDING THOBANI NOTES TO TRY AND GET HER TO CEASE AND DESIST IN USING SUCH DEFAMATORY RHETORIC AGAINST THE UNITED STATES. DISREGARDING THE HEATED POLITICAL TENSION, THE UBC PROFESSOR FORGED ONWARDS WITH HER SPEECH CITING THAT WHILE THE AMERICANS WERE PORTRAYING THE TERRORISTS AS "EVIL DOERS" HELL BENT ON DESTROYING CIVILIZATION AND DEMOCRACY, THEY (THE UNITED STATES) WERE ONLY OUT TO TRY AND GAIN CONTROL OF THE VAST OIL AND GAS RESOURCES OF THE MIDDLE EAST "FOR WHICH AFGHANISTAN IS A KEY, STRATEGIC POINT!"

BY DAY'S END, THE MEDIA HEADLINES RIGHT ACROSS THE COUNTRY CALLED THOBANI'S COMMENTS THE RANTING OF A NUTTY PROFESSOR WHO HAD A SOMEWHAT DISTORTED VIEW OF WORLD POLITICS AND WAS DETERMINED TO FORCE HER RACIST IDEOLOGIES DOWN THE THROATS OF OTHERS. HER SPEECH, WHICH WAS SAID TO HAVE CONTAINED A FULL 40 MINUTES OF ANTI-AMERICAN RHETORIC WAS EVEN CONDEMNED BY OUR VERY OWN THEN-CANADIAN PRIME MINISTER, JEAN CHRETIEN AS WELL AS OTHER HIGH PROFILE POLITICAL FIGURES FROM THE EASTERN MARITIME PROVINCES TO BRITISH COLUMBIA'S CAPITAL CITY ON THE PACIFIC. CANADIAN MEDIA COVERAGE OF THOBANI'S SPEECH WAS TO SAY THE LEAST DEPLORABLE AS THEY TRIED THEIR DAMNEST TO PORTRAY HER AS BEING PART OF THE LUNATIC FRINGE THAT SIMPLY HATED THE UNITED STATES. AS THE MEDIA BEGAN PUTTING THEIR OWN SPIN ON WHAT WAS ACTUALLY BEING STATED AT THE CONFERENCE, A FEW OF THE CONFERENCE

ORGANIZERS ARGUED BITTERLY WITH THE MEDIA ACCUSING THEM OF TRYING TO SUPPRESS THOBANI'S ATTEMPTS TO PROVIDE ALTERNATIVE SOLUTIONS TO WAGING WAR ONTO A COUNTRY AND/OR A PEOPLE.

IN YET ANOTHER TWIST OF IRONY, NEWS OUTLETS IN BOTH CANADA AND THE UNITED STATES COMPARED THE AFTERMATH OF THE SEPTEMBER 11TH ATTACK OF AMERICA EXACTLY TO THAT OF PEARL HARBOR SAYING THAT THE DESTRUCTION WAS IN THE SAME CATEGORY AS WELL AS ITS MAGNITUDE OF CAUSALITIES. THE ONE LITTLE ITEM THAT ALL OF THEM WERE NEGLECTING TO STRESS WAS THE FACT THAT LIKE THE ATTACK ON PEARL HARBOR, U.S. GOVERNMENTAL OFFICIALS HAD AMPLE TIME TO AVERT ITS DESTRUCTIVE FORCE. BUT SINCE THINGS AREN'T EXACTLY AS TO WHAT THEY SEEM TO BE MOST OF THE TIME, BUSH'S AMERICAN ADMINISTRATION WAS BEING VINDICATED FROM ANY WRONGDOINGS PERTAINING TO THEIR PLAYING AN IMPORTANT ROLE IN THE SO-CALLED TERRORIST ATTACK IN ITS OWN HOMELAND. OBLIVIOUS TO THE PAST, THE CITIZENRY OF THE NORTH AMERICAN CONTINENT RALLIED AROUND THE RHETORIC BEING USED BY THE UNITED STATES AND FROM THAT POINT ONWARDS HISTORY WAS ALL OF A SUDDEN RE-WRITTEN AS THE U.S. OF A. WAS NOW THE GOOD GUY WHILE BIN LADEN AND HIS FOLLOWERS WERE THE ENEMY. THE BLIND SHEEP CHARACTERISTICS THAT PEOPLE OF THE WESTERN HEMISPHERE HAD ADOPTED, DISALLOWED ANYONE TO SPEAK ILL OF THE AMERICANS AND WHAT HAD JUST HAPPENED TO THEM. ANY RHETORIC THAT DARED EMPHASIZE THE UNITED STATES BLOOD SOAKED PAST AS BEING A MATTER OF PUBLIC RECORD WAS AUTOMATICALLY LOOKED DOWN UPON AND QUICKLY LABELED AS BEING ANTI-AMERICAN. AND FOR THOSE INDIVIDUALS WHO FURTHER QUESTIONED THE EXISTENCE OF U.S. FOREIGN POLICY BEING EXACTLY AS TO WHAT IT WAS, THEY WERE SIMPLY CALLED BIGOTED PERSONS MAKING RACIST COMMENTS. THE PHYSIOLOGICAL WARFARE USED ONTO THE PEOPLE GOT TO THE POINT WHERE HARDLY ANYONE IN THE WESTERN FREE-WORLD WAS EVEN ABLE TO THINK FOR THEMSELVES AS THEY BECAME TOTALLY MESMERIZED BY THE AMERICAN PROPAGANDA MACHINES, GOVERNMENTAL SPIN DOCTORS AS IT WERE.

WHEN IT COMES TO PUTTING A SPIN ON THINGS, THE AMERICAN ARE THE MASTERS OF THIS NOBLE ANCIENT CRAFT BECAUSE AFTER THE GENERAL POPULATION HAD ENOUGH TIME TO DIGEST ALL OF THE RHETORIC BEING USED, THE ORIGINAL THOUGHT THAT THEY (THE CITIZENRY) MAY HAVE HAD IN THE BACK OF THEIR COLLECTIVE MINDS WAS TOTALLY DISSOLVED BY THE PROPAGANDA MACHINES. FOR EXAMPLE, WHILE THE BOMBING OF AFGHANISTAN WAS REACHING ITS THIRD FULL MONTH OF OCCURRENCE (JANUARY 5TH, 2002) A 15-YEAR-OLD STUDENT PIOLET, CHARLES BISHOP, COMMANDEERED A SMALL PLANE THAT HE WAS LEARNING TO FLY FROM HIS INSTRUCTOR IN TAMPA, FLORIDA AND CRASHED IT INTO A 42-STOREY HIGH-RISE KNOWN AS THE

Bank of America Tower. Apparently, the youth left a suicide note expressing sympathy for Osama bin Laden and the events of September 11TH. As a symbolic gesture for the youth's undying admiration for bin Laden and his faithful followers, the 15-year-old hijacked a Cessna 172 and flew it right into the Bank of America Tower. Just like the World Trade Center, the Bank of America Tower symbolized America's need to obtain more and more money to achieve its goal of global domination. Unlike Canada, the United States thrives on all attributes of symbolism.

As a way and means of destroying all aspects of the youth's actions as being an act of domestic terrorism, governmental officials in Washington, D.C. almost instantly proclaimed it as being no such thing. Within only a few hours, media outlets in the United States had decreed the boy's actions as being those of a very troubled teenager, someone who had few friends and was said to have been strictly a loner. As an extra measure to further discredit any second thoughts that someone may have had in the back of their minds, the powers that be attributed the youth's strange behavior to a prescription drug that he was taking for severe acne, Accutane. Determined not to allow the citizenry of North America the privilege of the though process, the drug was thusly used as being the main contributing factor that lead to the youth's strange bouts of depression concerning the September 11TH tragedy which in essence was said to be not allowing him to live in the real world. By this time period of course, we, the people of the western free-world took it all in as being the whole truth and nothing but the honest truth. Any thoughts of domestic terrorism that we may have originally had, quickly evaporated within 48 hours of the small plane's crashing into the Bank of America Tower.

Chapter 11 - ISRAEL: THE HOLY LAND OF ALL FREEMASONRY

In the Middle East during ancient times, it was said to be the custom when a contract was about to be made that a shoe /or sandal be taken from the right foot as an offering, and was handed either to a neighbor as a witness /or to the other party involved, as a guarantee that the contract /or agreement would be honored. This ancient ritual is still enacted as part of the Masonic ceremonies in Israel and other parts of the world. It is conducted by all new candidates before they are allowed to enter the fraternal Lodgery and/or Temple of the designated deity. When the candidate arrives at the Temple, he is allowed to enter the Ante-Room only. Of his own free will and accord, he enters a preparation room where he does exactly as he is told, not knowing /or even understanding why. He has to honestly and to the best of his ability answer certain questions. He then obediently for some obscure reason takes off his right shoe, hears a short preamble and is told to put it back on. By Biblical definition, the prophet was told to take off his shoes for he was now standing on Holy Ground. As the Masonic candidate enters into the realm of the unknown, he is then told to remove his shoes and all of his clothing as they are said to be a representation of the unclean unregenerate of the world. He then puts on some sort of unusual looking garments. Then he is blind-folded and is allowed to enter the Temple under the complete trust of his sponsor, walking into the unknown with his sponsor as guide. Psalm 24 of the Holy Scriptures is then read and upon its completion, the question is asked as to *WHO SHALL ASCEND INTO THE HILL OF THE LORD?* Whereupon the candidate is to reply that it is he who enters with clean hands

AND A CLEAN HEART. IN OTHER WORDS, HE IS NOT ONLY WORTHY AND FULLY QUALIFIED TO ENTER THE KINGDOM OF THE LORD BUT IS ALSO DULY AND TRULY PREPARED TO DO SO, SACRIFICING HIS OWN LIFE IF NEED BE. JUST PRIOR TO HIS ENTERING THE TEMPLE OF THE DESIGNATED GOD, HE HANDED OVER HIS RIGHT SHOE (THE RIGHT SIDE OF COURSE BEING THE STRONG SIDE OF MAN), ESSENTIALLY SAYING THAT HIS SHOE, BOUND HIM TO THE RIGGERS OF THE FRATERNITY AND THAT HE WAS WILLING TO WALK BLINDLY INTO THE DARKNESS IN ORDER TO SEARCH FOR THE LIGHT OF TRUTH. THE CANDIDATE IS THEN ALLOWED TO TAKE HIS RIGHTFUL PLACE AT THE RIGHT HAND OF GOD AND BEGINS HIS LONG JOURNEY INTO THE LIGHT OF KNOWLEDGE THAT OF WHICH HE SEEKS.

THE ULTIMATE GOAL OF EVERY FREEMASON WORLDWIDE IS SUPPOSEDLY TO STUDY, UNDERSTAND AND TO APPLY THE TENETS AND PRINCIPLES OF THE ANCIENT CRAFT. A CLEAR KNOWLEDGE AND UNDERSTANDING OF FREEMASONRY AND WHAT IT INITIALLY STANDS FOR IS THEREFORE NECESSARY BEFORE IT CAN ACHIEVE ITS SAID STATED ULTIMATE GOAL. ACCORDING TO SOME MASONIC SCHOLARS, FREEMASONRY IS NEITHER A RELIGION NOR A CULT BUT RATHER A WAY OF LIFE. HISTORICALLY, FREEMASONRY IS SCATTERED OVER THE HABITABLE WORLD AND HAS AN OUTRAGEOUS TRACK RECORD CONCERNING THE CONQUEST OF OTHERS. BUT YET MEMBERS OF THIS ANCIENT FRATERNITY PROFUSELY STATE THAT THE MASONIC ORDER IS NOT A FORCE DESTINED TO TAKE-OVER THE GOVERNMENTS OF THE WORLD NOR IS IT A REPRESENTATION OF THE ENLIGHTENED INTELLIGENTSIA OF THE WORLD. TO THE MASONIC MEMBERSHIP, FREEMASONRY IS MERELY A MESSENGER TO HELP HUMBLE THOSE WHO HAVE BROKEN AWAY FROM THE TRADITIONAL WAYS IN SEARCH FOR A MORE ENLIGHTENED WAY OF LIFE. THE BASIC TENETS AND PRINCIPLES OF FREEMASONRY ARE SAID TO BE AS RELEVANT TO THOSE WHO DWELL IN THE CAVES OF THE MOUNTAINS OF AFGHANISTAN TO THOSE SUPER POWERS WHO PLACE BOUNTIES ON THE HEADS OF ITS ENEMIES. THE GOAL OF A FREEMASON IS SAID TO IMPROVE THE RELATIONSHIP OF MAN TO MAN IN ALL WALKS OF LIFE. AND THAT NOT ALL MEN NEED TO BE FREEMASONS IN ORDER TO ACHIEVE SUCH A GOAL BUT THAT THEY MUST BE ABLE TO ACCEPT THE FAVORABLE INFLUENCES THAT THE PRINCIPLES OF FREEMASONRY POSSESSES. IT'S NOT EXACTLY CERTAIN AS TO WHETHER /OR NOT OSAMA BIN LADEN WAS AN ACTIVE MEMBER OF THE MASONIC **BROTHERHOOD OF MAN**. IF HE WAS AT ONE TIME /OR ANOTHER, HE SURELY ISN'T ANY LONGER!!!

IN ACCORDANCE TO THEIR OWN PHILOSOPHIES, FREEMASONRY IS SAID TO CULTIVATE AND IMPROVE THE MINDS OF ALL ITS GENUINE POSSESSORS. IN DOING SO, IT IS BELIEVED THAT IT CREATES A FAVORABLE IMPRESSION ON EVERYONE WITH WHOM THEY COME IN CONTACT. HERE IN NORTH AMERICA FOR EXAMPLE, MEMBERS OF THE CRAFT STRONGLY FEEL THAT THEY HAVE LEFT A

FAVORABLE IMPRESSION ON ALL WALKS OF LIFE AROUND THE WORLD. INSISTING THAT THEY HAVE INFLUENCED OTHERS TO PRACTICE THE FOUR CARDINAL VIRTUES OF TEMPERANCE, PRUDENCE, FORTITUDE AND JUSTICE COMBINED WITH FAITH, HOPE AND CHARITY TO ALL. DURING THE SEPTEMBER 11TH TRAGEDY, FREEMASONS WERE ENCOURAGED TO CONSIDER EVERY DECISION IN THEIR DAILY LIFE AS THOUGH THEY WERE LIVING IN A FISH BOWL. EVERY ACT, DEED AND YES, EVEN THOUGHT WAS VIEWED AS BEING SCRUTINIZED BY THE GREAT ARCHITECT OF THE UNIVERSE. WITH THE ENCOURAGEMENT OF DIVINE INTERVENTION, MEMBERS OF THE MASONIC ORDER IN BOTH CANADA AND THE UNITED STATES CONSOLED ONE ANOTHER AS EVERY ASPECT OF THEIR DAILY LIVE WAS ABOUT TO CHANGE FOR ALL ETERNITY AS THE NORTH AMERICAN CONTINENT'S POWERS THAT BE SOON IMPOSED STRICT SECURITY MEASURES ONTO ALL OF ITS INHABITANTS. THE FREEDOMS ONCE EXPERIENCED BY ALL WALKS OF LIFE WAS NOW GONE AS THE POWERS THAT BE IN BOTH COUNTRIES HEIGHTENED SECURITY PROCEDURES BY INTRODUCING ANTI-TERRORIST LEGISLATION AND IMPOSING STRICT RESTRICTIONS OF TRAVEL ONTO THE GENERAL POPULATION. THE INFLUENTIAL EVILS OF THOSE WHO WANTED TO DESTROY WESTERN CIVILIZATION AND ITS SUPPOSEDLY TRUE DEMOCRATIC PROCESS WERE SAID TO BE BEHIND THIS EVER INCREASING ESCALATING VIOLATION OF OUR ESSENTIAL FREEDOMS. AND THE ONLY WAY IN WHICH THE INFLUENCES OF THE EVIL DOERS COULD BE COMBATED WAS IN THE FORM OF PUTTING ALL CITIZENS OF NORTH AMERICA ON HIGH ANTI-TERRORIST ALERT.

WITH THE VARIOUS RESTRICTIONS BEING IMPOSED ONTO A ONCE FREE PEOPLE, THE INHABITANTS OF THE NORTH AMERICAN CONTINENT BEGAN TO SLOWLY FEEL THE IMPACT OF MAN'S INHUMANITY TO HIS FELLOW MAN. SOME IN FACT BEGAN TO QUESTION WHETHER /OR NOT SUCH ACTIONS WERE JUSTIFIABLE GIVEN THE CIRCUMSTANCES AND THE TRUE DETAILS LEADING UP TO THE SEPTEMBER 11TH TRAGEDY ITSELF. IT THEREFORE BECAME QUITE APPARENT THAT IN ORDER FOR THE POWERS THAT BE TO PROPERLY EXECUTE ITS FAVORABLE INFLUENCES AROUND THE WORLD, IT MUST FIRST CULTIVATE AND IMPROVE THE MINDS OF OTHERS CREATING THE ILLUSION THAT THE PRACTICE OF LIFE, LIBERTY AND THE PURSUIT OF HAPPINESS WAS BEING EXERCISED WHILE IN THE ACT OF SEEKING VENGEANCE IN THE NAME OF DEMOCRACY. IT IS SAID AMONGST THOSE OF FREEMASONRY THAT THERE EXIST A NEW MASONIC WORLD THAT IS AS LAWFUL AS A WORLD COULD POSSIBLY BE. A WORLD WITH WHICH IT HAS A NATURE ALL OF ITS OWN, BEING COMMITTED TO WELL-DEFINED AIMS. ITS MEMBERS APPARENTLY CANNOT MAKE IT OVER TO SUIT THEIR OWN PARTICULAR WHIMS AS THEY MUST ALWAYS CONFORM TO ITS REQUIREMENTS. THIS **NEW WORLD ORDER** OF FREEMASONRY IS ALSO SAID TO BE A COMPLETE WORLD; IT SATISFIES THE NEEDS OF THE WHOLE MAN; PHYSICAL, MORAL, INTELLECTUAL, SOCIAL AND SPIRITUAL. ANYONE ENTERING

THE THRESHOLD OF THIS DOMAIN MUST POSSESS CERTAIN QUALIFICATIONS; MAINLY OBEDIENCE, HUMILITY AND INDUSTRIOUSNESS, FOR HE WHO ENTERS IS SWORN TO SECRECY.

HISTORICALLY, FREEMASONRY IS THE OLDEST FRATERNAL RELIGION IN EXISTENCE TODAY. WHICH IS PERHAPS WHY A LARGE PERCENTAGE OF THEIR ANCIENT SECRET CEREMONIES CAN BE FOUND WITHIN BIBLICAL SCRIPTURES SUCH AS IN RUTH, CHAPTER 4, VERSES 7 AND 8. IN USING THAT WORLD-FAMOUS HYPOCRITICAL RELIGIOUS LINE, "__IT IS WRITTEN__" IN THE BOOK OF RUTH IN THE OLD TESTAMENT THAT NO CASH AND/OR LEGAL TENDER WAS TO BE INVOLVED. BEFORE READING THE PASSAGE AT HAND, ONE MUST FIRST CONSIDER THE BACKGROUND INVOLVED SO AS TO BETTER UNDERSTAND WHAT WAS HAPPENING. BOAZ, THE MAIN BIBLICAL ACTOR IN THIS PLAY OF PLAYS, WANTED TO BUY A VALUABLE PIECE OF PROPERTY. HOWEVER, HE COULD NOT DO SO AS SOMEONE ELSE HAD PRIOR CLAIM. IN A DISCUSSION THAT FOLLOWED BETWEEN THE TWO WOULD-BE PURCHASERS, IT WAS DISCOVERED THAT BESIDES THE USUAL MATTERS THAT ARE LOOKED INTO WHEN BUYING LAND, THERE WAS A RATHER INTERESTING STRING ATTACHED. IT SEEMS THAT THE PREVIOUS OWNER OF THE PROPERTY, HAD DIED, LEAVING A WIDOW, WHO IN TURN HAD A DAUGHTER NAMED RUTH. IN THE AGREEMENT OF SALE THERE WAS A STIPULATION THAT THE NEW OWNER HAD TO TAKE THE HAND OF RUTH IN MARRIAGE. AS IT TURNED OUT, THE MAN WHO HAD FIRST CLAIM ON THE PROPERTY IN QUESTION, ALREADY HAD A PROBLEM AT HOME, AND HE CERTAINLY WASN'T ABOUT READY TO ADD TO THEM BY BRINGING ANOTHER WOMAN INTO HIS HOUSEHOLD, HE WAS ALREADY IN THE DOGHOUSE WITH HIS FIRST WIFE. SO HE THEN TURNED TO BOAZ AND IN EFFECT SAID THAT HE WASN'T WILLING TO COMPLY WITH THE TERMS OF THE AGREEMENT OF SALE. HE THEN TOOK OFF HIS RIGHT SANDAL AND GAVE IT TO A NEIGHBOR AS A WITNESS THAT HE WOULD HONOR THE CHANGE IN OWNERSHIP OF THE PROPERTY.

BOAZ THUSLY ACQUIRED THE LAND AS HE TOOK RUTH AS HIS WIFE.

ACCORDING TO YET ANOTHER MASONIC LEGEND, SOME EIGHTY-THOUSAND WORKERS HEWED THE STONES FOR THE ERECTION OF KING SOLOMON'S TEMPLE AND THE TEMPLE OF JERUSALEM FROM THE CAVES OF ZEDEKIAH. FOR HUNDREDS OF YEARS THE CAVES WERE BLOCKED. IT IS BELIEVED THAT THEY WERE BLOCKED DURING THE TIME OF THE CRUSADERS OUT OF FEAR THAT DEFENSE POSITIONS WOULD BE TAKEN UP THERE. THE CAVES WERE REDISCOVERED SOME CENTURIES AFTER THE CRUSADES BY ACCIDENT WHEN AN AMERICAN MASTER MASON, AN ARCHEOLOGIST, WHILE OUT WALKING HIS DOG. THE DOG REPORTEDLY BEGAN DIGGING INTO THE HILLSIDE AND AN OPENING WAS THUSLY REVEALED. THE AMERICAN ARCHEOLOGIST WENT INTO THE OPENING WITH LIGHTED CANDLES AND OBSERVED A SPACIOUS CAVE WITH HUGE CURVED CEILINGS SUPPORTED BY NUMEROUS PILLARS. HEBREW AND ARABIC WRITINGS, DIFFICULT TO DECIPHER

WERE DISCOVERED ON THE WALLS OF THE CAVE. AFTER HEARING MANY RUMORS CONCERNING THE CAVE, AMONG OTHERS, THAT PEOPLE ENTERED THE CAVE AND NEVER CAME OUT AGAIN. THE GOVERNMENT OF PALESTINE CLOSED THE ENTRANCE IN ABOUT 1879, THUS BARRING ANY FURTHER ADMITTANCE. WITH LEGENDS AND BELIEFS ABOUND TO THE EFFECT THAT SOMEWHERE DEEP DOWN IN THE CAVE TREASURES OF THE HOLY UTENSILS AND INSTRUMENTS OF THE TEMPLE WERE TO BE FOUND, THESE HAVING BEEN HIDDEN THERE AT THE TIME BY THE PRIESTS, WHEN THE ROMAN LEGIONS, LED BY TITUS, PLACED JERUSALEM UNDER SIEGE. LESS THAN 100 YEARS AFTER THE ENTRANCE WAS FIRST SEALED OFF TO THE PUBLIC, THE ISRAELI GOVERNMENT REOPENED THE CAVE FOR PUBLIC VIEWING (MID-1970'S). LIGHTING WAS INSTALLED, AS WELL AS STONE STEPS. IN ONE OF THE RECESSES IN THE FAR CORNER OF THE SECOND HALL OF THE CAVE, WATER DRIPPED FROM THE HIGH ROCK CEILING, FORMING A SMALL POOL BELOW. ACCORDING TO THE LEGEND, THESE DROPS OF WATER ARE SAID TO BE THE **TEARS OF KING ZEDEKIAH** WHICH HE SUPPOSEDLY SHED WHILE ESCAPING FROM CASDITES.

BY MASONIC DEFINITION, THE CAVES OF ZEDEKIAH WERE SAID TO HAVE AWAKEN THE HIDDEN THOUGHTS IN THE HEARTS OF FREEMASONS. MASONIC RITUALS IN VARIOUS DEGREES WERE CARRIED OUT THERE. BOTH KING SOLOMON'S TEMPLE AND THE TEMPLE OF JERUSALEM ARE HOLY SYMBOLS TO ALL FREEMASONS THROUGHOUT THE WORLD, IRRESPECTIVE OF CREED, COLOR /OR RACE. ZEDEKIAH'S CAVE IS VEILED IN LEGENDS AND SECRECY AND NO DOUBT FREEMASONS BOTH FROM ISRAEL AND ABROAD WOULD GATHER THERE TO CARRY OUT THEIR MASONIC WORK AND RITUALS IN A VERY SPECIAL ATMOSPHERE AND SUPPOSEDLY BRING PEACE AND FRATERNITY TO ALL OF HUMANITY. ACCORDING TO A BRITISH JOURNALIST, ROY BRONTON OF THE LONDON "OBSERVER", DURING THE BRITISH OCCUPATIONAL MANDATE YEARS OF ISRAEL, UP TO THE YEAR 1949, LARGE CHUNKS OF STONE WERE QUARRIED FROM THE ROCK IN THE CAVE AND DISPATCHED BY SEA TO VARIOUS COUNTRIES THROUGHOUT THE WORLD TO BE USED AS FOUNDATION STONES FOR NEWLY ERECTED MASONIC LODGES.

SINCE THEY WERE FIRST DRIVEN UNDERGROUND DURING THE CRUSADES, FREEMASONRY HAS DONE VERY LITTLE TO IMPROVE ITS PUBLIC IMAGE, WITH THE EXCEPTION OF THE SHRINERS OF COURSE. BY ALL ACCOUNT, THIS ANCIENT MYSTICAL BROTHERHOOD IS OBSESSIVELY SECRETIVE AND STUBBORNLY DEFENSIVE THAT IT ONLY REINFORCES THE IMPRESSION THAT FREEMASONS HAVE SOMETHING TO HIDE. THE ONLY WAY FOR A PERSON TO PROTECT THEMSELVES FROM HARMS WAY IS BY USING ITS OWN PROPAGANDA TO SEEK THE TRUE MEANING OF LIFE'S MYSTERIES. SECRETIVENESS, EVASIVENESS AND THE UNWILLINGNESS TO ANSWER REASONABLE QUESTIONS ARE BY NO MEANS THE WAY TO CONDUCT THE AFFAIRS OF ONE'S DAILY LIFE. SOMETIMES, A PERSON'S

GENUINE CURIOSITY IS PEAKED BY THE LACK OF CO-OPERATION ONE GETS BY ASKING ALL OF THE RIGHT QUESTIONS BUT NO ONE SEEMS TO WILLINGLY ANSWER THEM FOR FEAR OF RETRIBUTION.

IN ACCORDANCE TO FREEMASONRY, ISRAEL IS THE KEY TO ITS SURVIVAL, THE HOLY LAND WITH ITS MYSTICAL CHARM HAS BEEN CLOSELY CONNECTED TO THE HISTORY OF FREEMASONS WORLDWIDE. THERE STOOD, AT ONE TIME, THE TEMPLE OF SOLOMON, TO WHICH SOME HISTORIANS HAVE TRACED THE ORIGIN OF THE MASONIC ORDER AND FURTHER TO THIS THERE WERE THE CRUSADERS, THAT OF WHICH CAUSED OTHER HISTORIANS TO IMMEDIATELY SEARCH THE ARCHIVES TO FIND THE CRADLE OF THE FRATERNITY AS A WAY AND MEANS OF FINALLY DETERMINING THE FATE OF THE ORDER OF THE KNIGHTS TEMPLAR WHOSE SUBSEQUENT HISTORY HAD ALSO BEEN CLOSELY MINGLED WITH THE HOLY LAND. BY MASONIC DEFINITION, FREEMASONRY IS MENTIONED IN THE SCRIPTURES. AT THE TIME THAT THE ISRAELITES ENTERED THE PROMISED LAND, THE CITY OF JERUSALEM WAS IN THE POSSESSION OF THE JEBUSITES, FROM WHOM, AFTER THE DEATH OF JOSHUA, IT WAS CONQUERED, AND AFTERWARD INHABITED BY THE TRIBES OF JUDAH AND BENJAMIN. THE JEBUSITES WERE NOT, HOWEVER DRIVEN OUT. ACCORDING TO BIBLICAL BELIEF, MOUNT MORIAH WAS PURCHASED BY KING DAVID AS A SITE FOR THE TEMPLE OF JERUSALEM. COINCIDENTLY, SOME HISTORIANS INSIST THAT IT IS ONLY IN REFERENCE TO THIS TEMPLE THAT JERUSALEM IS CONNECTED WITH THE LEGENDS OF ANCIENT CRAFT FREEMASONRY THEREFORE DISREGARDING ALL OF THE FACTUAL DOCUMENTATION CONTAINED IN THE ARCHIVES.

LIKE ALL OTHER NATIONS CONTROLLED BY THE MASONIC **BROTHERHOOD OF MAN**, CANADA ALSO PLAYED AN IMPORTANT ROLE IN THE DEVELOPMENT OF FREEMASONRY IN ISRAEL. "MODERN SPECULATIVE MASONRY WAS INTRODUCED INTO JERUSALEM BY THE ESTABLISHMENT OF A LODGE IN 1872, THE WARRANT FOR WHICH, ON THE APPLICATION OF ROBERT MORRIS AND OTHERS, WAS GRANTED BY THE GRAND LODGE OF CANADA. "SPECULATIVE FREEMASONRY IS A SYSTEM OF ETHICS WHICH IS DIVIDED INTO THREE DISTINCT CLASSES / OR DOCTRINES; THE MORAL, THE RELIGIOUS AND THE PHILOSOPHICAL. THE MORAL DOCTRINES, ARE BASED UPON THE GOOD SOCIAL CHARACTER OF MAN'S KINDNESS TO HIS NEIGHBOR, TO HIMSELF AND TO HIS **GOD**. WHILE THE RELIGIOUS DOCTRINES STAND FOR HIS INTELLIGENCE AND THE IMMORTALITY OF HIS SOUL. INTERESTINGLY ENOUGH, THE PHILOSOPHICAL DOCTRINES OF MASONRY ARE THE TEACHINGS OF MUTUAL LOVE, UNDERSTANDING AND AIDING IN MAN'S SOCIAL INSTITUTION OF A UNIVERSAL BROTHERHOOD. "THERE IS A SOCIALISM IN FREEMASONRY FROM WHICH SPRING ALL MASONIC VIRTUES — NOT THAT MODERN SOCIALISM EXHIBITED IN A COMMUNITY OF GOODS, WHICH, ALTHOUGH IT MAY HAVE BEEN PRACTICED BY THE PRIMITIVE CHRISTIANS, IS FOUND TO BE UNCONGENIAL WITH THE INDEPENDENT SPIRIT

OF THE PRESENT AGE — BUT A COMMUNITY OF SENTIMENT, OF PRINCIPLE, OF DESIGN, WHICH GIVES TO MASONRY ALL ITS SOCIAL AND HENCE ITS MORAL, CHARACTER. "THE OBJECT OF THESE MASONIC SOCIALIST TEACHINGS ARE THUSLY DESIGNED TO MAKE THEM ZEALOUS MASONS FOR HE WHO KNOWS NOTHING OF THE PHILOSOPHY OF FREEMASONRY WILL UNDOUBTEDLY BECOME IN TIME LUKEWARM AND INDIFFERENT WHILE HE WHO DEVOTES HIMSELF TO ITS CONTEMPLATION WILL FEEL AN EVER-INCREASING ARDOR IN THE STUDY OF ITS DOCTRINES.

ACCORDING TO THE PHILOSOPHY OF FREEMASONRY, IT BRINGS THE INDIVIDUAL INTO CLOSE RELATIONSHIP WITH "THE PROFOUND THOUGHTS OF THE ANCIENT WORLD, AND MAKES US FAMILIAR WITH EVERY SUBJECT OF MENTAL SCIENCE THAT LIES WITHIN THE GRASP OF HUMAN INTELLECT. SO THAT, IN CONCLUSION, WE FIND THAT THE MORAL, RELIGIOUS AND PHILOSOPHICAL DOCTRINES OF FREEMASONRY RESPECTIVELY RELATE TO THE SOCIAL, THE ETERNAL, AND THE INTELLECTUAL PROCESS OF MAN."

THE JEWISH HOMELAND OF ISRAEL AT ONE TIME WAS SIMPLY KNOWN AS PALESTINE — IT STRETCHED FROM LEBANON SOUTH TO THE BORDERS OF EGYPT, AND FROM THE THIRTY-FOURTH TO THE THIRTY-NINTH DEGREES OF LONGITUDE. IT WAS CONQUERED FROM THE CANAANITES BY THE HEBREWS UNDER JOSHUA 1450 B.C. THEY DIVIDED IT INTO TWELVE CONFEDERATE STATES ACCORDING TO THE TRIBES. BY 1040 B.C., PALESTINE BEGAN ENLARGING ITS TERRITORY BUT MANY OF THE TRIBES BEGAN FIGHTING AMONGST THEMSELVES FOR POLITICAL CONTROL AND IN THE YEAR 975 B.C. IT WAS DIVIDED INTO THE TWO KINGDOMS OF ISRAEL AND JUDAH, THE LATTER CONSISTING OF THE TRIBES OF JUDAH AND BENJAMIN, AND THE FORMER OF THE REMAINING TRIBES. ABOUT 740 B.C., BOTH KINGDOMS WERE SUBDUED BY THE PERSIANS AND BABYLONIANS, AND AFTER THE CAPTIVITY ONLY THE TWO TRIBES OF JUDAH AND BENJAMIN RETURNED TO REBUILD THE TEMPLE. THE HISTORY OF THE PROMISED LAND IS THAT OF BLOODSHED, ALL IN THE NAME OF RELIGION. LIKE THE PERSIANS, PHILISTINES AND BABYLONIANS, THE BRITISH ISRAELITES WANTED TO CONTROL THE HOLY LAND. ENGLAND'S DESIRE TO OBTAIN AN ACCURATE KNOWLEDGE OF THEIR PROMISED LAND THUS GAVE RISE TO THE FORMATION OF AN ASSOCIATION IN 1866, WHICH WAS PERMANENTLY ORGANIZED IN LONDON, AS THE "PALESTINE EXPLORATION FUND "WITH QUEEN VICTORIA "AS THE CHIEF PATRON, AND A LONG LIST OF THE NOBILITY AND THE MOST DISTINGUISHED GENTLEMEN IN THE KINGDOM, ADDED TO WHICH FOLLOWED THE GRAND LODGE OF ENGLAND AND FORTY-TWO SUBORDINATE AND PROVINCIAL GRAND LODGES AND CHAPTERS." THE ROYAL BRITISH ISRAELITES WERE DETERMINED TO FULFILL GOD'S PROMISE OF WORLD DOMINATION. EARLY IN THE FOLLOWING YEAR, (1867), A COMMITTEE BEGAN EXAMINATION OF THE ARCHEOLOGICAL SURROUNDINGS OF THE

ANCIENT CITY WHICH HAD BEEN COVERED UP BY VARIOUS FORMS OF DEBRIS OVER THE AGES.

IN JANUARY OF 1867, ENGLAND'S FREEMASONRY MEMBERSHIP SENT FRATERNAL BROTHER LIEUTENANT CHARLES WARREN TO ACT AS THE OVERSEER OF THE PROJECT. HE ARRIVED IN JERUSALEM ON FEBRUARY 17TH OF THAT SAME YEAR AND BEGAN EXCAVATING IN MANY PARTS OF THE CITY WITH A FEW INTERRUPTIONS UNTIL 1871 WHEN HE RETURNED BACK TO ENGLAND. DURING HIS OPERATIONS, BROTHER WARREN KEPT THE FRATERNITY IN LONDON CONSTANTLY INFORMED OF THE PROGRESS OF HIS DIGS, IN WHICH HE AND HIS ASSOCIATES WERE SO ZEALOUSLY ENGAGED. UPON COMPLETION OF THE DESIGNATED TASK IN THE HOLY LAND, WARREN WAS ADVANCED TO THE FRATERNAL PORTFOLIO OF LIEUTENANT-GENERAL AND THEREUPON KNIGHTED FOR HIS SERVICES RENDERED IN THE PROMISED LAND. HIS OFFICIAL NEW FREEMASONRY TITLE WAS "LIEUTENANT-GENERAL SIR CHARLES WARREN, G.C.M.G., K.C.B., F.R.S. "THE RESULT OF HIS LABORS THUS PROPHESIED ENGLAND'S INALIENABLE RIGHT TO GOVERN THE PROMISED LAND OF PALESTINE AND THE ENTIRE WORLD. "THE RESULT OF THESE LABORS HAS BEEN A VAST ACCUMULATION OF FACTS IN RELATION TO THE TOPOGRAPHY OF THE HOLY CITY WHICH THROW MUCH LIGHT ON ITS ARCHEOLOGY. "NOT LONG AFTER FRATERNITY BROTHER CHARLES WARREN RETURNED BACK TO ENGLAND TO DISCLOSE HIS FINDINGS BY WAY OF A BOOK TITLED; "THE RECOVERY OF JERUSALEM", BRITISH FREEMASONS INSTANTLY ESTABLISHED A BRANCH OF THE PALESTINE EXPLORATION FUND SOCIETY IN THE UNITED STATES OF AMERICA. ENGLISH AND AMERICAN FREEMASONS JOINED FORCES AND LAID CLAIM TO THE HOLY LAND. BY 1881, INVISIBLE BOUNDARIES IN THE SAND WERE BEING DRAWN UP BY THE MASONIC ALLIED FORCES, EVERYONE WANTED A PIECE OF THE ACTION; FRANCE, GERMANY AND ITALY INCLUDED. IT TOOK THE MASONIC ALLIED FORCES LESS THAN 50 YEARS TO GAIN FULL CONTROL OF THE HOLY LAND, (FROM 1881 TO 1918). ON NOVEMBER 2ND, 1917 THE FAMOUS BALFOUR DECLARATION WAS SIGNED WHICH ESTABLISHED PALESTINE AS THE SITE OF A NATIONAL HOME FOR THE JEWISH PEOPLES, AND AROUSED BITTER ARAB OPPOSITION. WHILE THE TWO RACES (JEWS AND ARABS) FOUGHT AMONGST THEMSELVES, THE BRITISH AND AMERICANS BEGAN CARVING UP THE MIDDLE EAST AS THEIR VERY OWN MASONIC POSSESSION. THIRTY-NINE DAYS AFTER FRATERNITY BROTHER ARTHUR JAMES BALFOUR (THE FIRST EARL OF BALFOUR) SIGNED THE HISTORICAL DOCUMENT, BRITISH TROOPS ENTERED PALESTINE ON DECEMBER 11TH, 1917.

SINCE THE DAWNING OF TIME, HUMAN BEINGS HAVE HAD A NEED FOR SPIRITUAL DIMENSION IN EVERY ASPECT OF THEIR DAILY LIVES. RIGHT FROM THE VERY BEGINNING OF RECORDED TIME, MAN HAS SOUGHT AND CONTINUES TO THIS VERY DAY TO SEEK ASSURANCE FROM HIS BELIEF IN SOME POWER

BEYOND HIMSELF. THE WORLDWIDE PROLIFERATION OF RELIGION ATTESTS TO THE FACT THAT AS MAN SPREAD OUT ACROSS THE FACE OF THE EARTH, HE TOOK WITH HIM WHAT HE COULD OF HIS OLD FAITH AND ADAPTED HIS BELIEFS TO FIT HIS NEW ENVIRONMENT. THIS PROCESS OBVIOUSLY TOOK MANY CENTURIES TO ACCOMPLISH AS ISOLATION AND THE LACK OF OUTSIDE COMMUNICATION ALLOWED THESE BELIEFS TO BECOME PART AND PARCEL OF MANY A NATIONS RELIGIOUS HERITAGE. REPETITION AND A DESIRE OF THE PRIESTHOOD TO MAINTAIN THE STATUS QUO LED TO AN INDELIBLE PERMANENCY OF THESE SPECIAL BELIEFS AND SUCH BELIEFS THUSLY BECAME TO BE THE TRUE FACTS IN THE EYES OF PEOPLE HOLDING STEADFAST TO ONE /OR THE OTHER RELIGIOUS CONVICTIONS.

ACCORDINGLY, FREEMASONRY IS SAID TO HAVE ACTED AS A STEPPING STONE TO HELP BRIDGE THE GAP THAT LONG EXISTED BETWEEN ALL FORMS OF RELIGION. WITH A VESTED INTEREST IN THE PROCEEDINGS, MASONRY WON EARLY ACCEPTANCE BY FOREIGN NATIONS ALL OVER THE WORLD WHERE IT WAS FIRST INTRODUCED. THE LINK BETWEEN FREEMASONRY AND ANCIENT RELIGION SUCH AS THE DRUIDS ARE SAID TO BE PRIME EXAMPLES, BOTH OF COURSE HAVING A SPECIAL VENERATION FOR LIGHT; SYMBOLIZED BY THE SUN AND COMMENSURATE WITH THE CREATION OF THE UNIVERSE IN THE DOCTRINE THAT LIGHT CAME BEFORE MAN AND PREPARED HIM A SUITABLE HABITATION AND THAT LIGHT ITSELF IS SUPPOSEDLY THE SCOPE AND SYMBOL OF FREEMASONRY. THE DRUIDS WORSHIPED THE SUN AND LIT FIRES IN THE RENFREWSHIRE HILLS OF SCOTLAND TO ENTICE AND WELCOME IT BACK TO ITS SUMMER HAUNTS. THIS RITUAL OF COURSE DATING AS FAR BACK AS THE FIRST CENTURY B.C. AND JUST LIKE THE RITUALISTIC CEREMONIES OF ANCIENT EGYPT, THE FOLLOWERS OF DRUIDISM FIRMLY BELIEVED THAT THEY WERE THE DIRECT DESCENDANTS OF THE SUPREME BEING. FREEMASONS WITHOUT A DOUBT ACKNOWLEDGE THEIR LINKS WITH THE PREHISTORIC RELIGIONS, PERHAPS THIS IS WHY MASONIC LITERATURE DESCRIBES ITSELF AS BEING THE ONLY REMAINING SURVIVOR OF THE ANCIENT MYSTERIES AND GUARDIAN OF ITS HISTORY. DRUIDISM FIRST SHOWED SIGNS OF BEING EXTINGUISHED WHEN THE ROMANS SUBSEQUENTLY BEGAN CONVERTING THEM TO CHRISTIANITY DURING THE SECOND CENTURY A.D. AND TWO /OR THREE CENTURIES LATER WAS TOTALLY ALIENATED IN PARTS OF BRITAIN WHERE THEY EVENTUALLY SUCCUMB TO CHRISTIANITY. IN CERTAIN DEGREES, THE DRUIDS AND FREEMASONS FACED THE EXACT SAME COMPLICATIONS OF PERSECUTION BY THE ACTING POWER OF AUTHORITY. BUT DESPITE ALL ATTEMPTS BY THE ROMAN CATHOLIC CHURCH TO SNUFF OUT THE VERY EXISTENCE OF THE MASONIC ORDER, ENGLISH FREEMASONRY SOON BEGAN TO FLOURISH DURING THE PERIOD OF DEVELOPMENT OF THE BRITISH EMPIRE AS ENGLISHMEN, WHO WERE TRAINED AT HOME IN THE ANCIENT CRAFT BEGAN CARRYING THEIR MASONRY PRINCIPLES TO EVERY CORNER

OF THE GLOBE. CONTRARY TO THE MYTH THAT THE PROTESTANT MASONIC CRAFT WAS DEBUNKED INTO OBSCURITY BY THE CATHOLIC CHURCH FOR ITS SATANICAL RITUALS AND/OR CEREMONIES, THE CRAFT SPREAD LIKE WILDFIRE FROM BEING A SINGLE CELL IN ENGLAND TO THAT OF A VERY POWERFUL FORCE TO BE RECKONED WITH ON A GLOBAL SCALE MANY CENTURIES LATER. THE PROBLEM NOWADAYS IS OF COURSE MAN'S BASIC INSTINCTS OF GREED AND DISHONESTY, BOTH IN GOVERNMENTS AND IN THEIR OWN PERSONAL LIVES. THAT OF WHICH EVEN FREEMASONRY IS NOT IMMUNE DESPITE EFFORTS BY THOSE WHO MAKE THE CLAIM STATING OTHERWISE.

IN ORDER TO HAVE A MUCH BETTER UNDERSTANDING AS TO HOW EVEN MEMBERS OF THE MASONIC FRATERNITY CAN WONDER ASTRAY FROM THEIR OWN IDEOLOGIES, FURTHER EXPLORING MUST BE CONDUCTED. FOR INSTANCE, THROUGHOUT ITS ENTIRE FREEMASONRY PAST BRITISH COLUMBIA HAS PRODUCED MANY MASONIC POLITICIANS, JUDGES, LABOR LEADERS, POLICE OFFICERS, DOCTORS, LAWYERS, FILM MAKERS, JOURNALISTS, BUSINESSMEN, SO ON AND SO FORTH. AND WITH THIS BEING THE CASE, IT MAKES IT MUCH EASIER TO PUT THOSE MEMBERS OF THE FRATERNAL ORDER UNDER A MICROSCOPE. BRITISH COLUMBIA OF COURSE BEING THE MOST CORRUPT PROVINCE WEST OF THE ROCKY MOUNTAINS, TEN FULL YEARS OF SOCIALIST DOMINATION – OCTOBER 1991 TO MAY 2001 – UNDER THE NDP BANNER HAS THUS PROVEN THIS BEYOND A SHADOW OF A DOUBT. SOME OF ITS MOST POWERFUL POLITICAL PLAYERS AND LAW ENFORCEMENT PERSONNEL WERE MASTER MASONS, SUCH PEOPLE AS BOTH THE NDP AND LIBERAL PARTY OF B.C. – IN PARTICULAR FROM CONFLICT-OF-INTEREST COMMISSIONER H.A.D. OLIVER FOR THE 21ST CENTURY AND ON DOWNWARDS TO THE MASONIC ADMINISTRATION OF W.A.C. BENNETT OF THE 1950'S. WHILE THOSE WHO ENFORCED THE LAWS OF THE LAND ON THE OTHER HAND WERE AN OBSCURITY OF RCMP OFFICERS (RCMP MASONIC DEGREE TEAM), PROSECUTORS AND MAGISTRATES FROM THE DAWNING OF B.C.'S BECOMING PART OF THE DOMINION OF CANADA IN 1871. FOR EXAMPLE; A.M. MANSON WAS BRITISH COLUMBIA'S GRAND MASTER OF ALL MASONS IN 1926. HE WAS ALSO A FORMER ATTORNEY-GENERAL WHO LATER WENT ON TO BECOME A JUSTICE OF THE BRITISH COLUMBIA SUPREME COURT.

THERE WERE MANY OTHER JUDGES SITTING ON THE BENCH WHO HAD JOINED THE ANCIENT CRAFT. ONE OF THE MOST HIGH PROFILE NORTHWEST TERRITORIAL SUPREME COURT JUDGES DURING THE 1970'S WAS THEN MR. JUSTICE ORVAL JOHN THOMAS TROY. FRATERNITY BROTHER JUDGE TROY WAS FIRST INITIATED INTO FREEMASONRY IN 1958 AT THE ROBERT BURNS LODGE NO. 10 IN HALIFAX, NOVA SCOTIA. WHILE SERVING AS JUDGE IN CANADA'S UNEXPLORED FROZEN FRONTIER, JUDGE TROY BECAME A MEMBER OF YELLOWKNIFE LODGE NO. 162 WHERE HE REMAINED BEING A MEMBER

UNTIL 1990. IN ACCORDANCE TO MASONIC LITERATURE, (JUNE 1992 MASONIC BULLETIN), WHILE SITTING ON THE BENCH IN THE ARCTIC, JUDGE TROY WAS SAID TO HAVE HAD MUCH RESPECT AND COMPASSION FOR THE NATIVE PEOPLES AND THEIR CUSTOMS WHEN DEALING WITH ABORIGINAL ISSUES THAT WERE OFTEN BEFORE THE COURTS. TO THAT END, THE NATIVE PEOPLE OF THE NORTHWEST TERRITORIES BESTOWED MANY GIFTS IN HONORING HIM UPON HIS RETIREMENT FROM THE JUDICIAL BENCH MANY YEARS LATER. FRATERNITY BROTHER ORVAL JOHN THOMAS TROY DIED IN PENTICTON, BRITISH COLUMBIA ON MARCH 19TH, 1992 AND WAS BURIED WITH FULL MASONIC HONORS.

ONLY NINE MONTHS PREVIOUS TO FORMER JUDGE TROY'S PASSING, YET ANOTHER FORMER JUDGE, FRATERNITY BROTHER LAWRENCE (LARRY) ECKARDT ALSO MET HIS DEMISE. BROTHER LARRY ECKARDT PASSED AWAY ON JUNE 14TH, 1991, HE WAS A PAST MASTER OF AVIATION LODGE NO. 175 AND AN ACTIVE MEMBER OF ANCIENT LIGHT LODGE NO. 88. HE PRACTICED LAW IN THE CITY OF VANCOUVER, BRITISH COLUMBIA FOR MANY YEARS AND SERVED AS A PROVINCIAL COURT JUDGE, (OCTOBER 1991 MASONIC BULLETIN).

THE ANCIENT MYSTICAL PRACTICES OF FREEMASONRY REACHED ALL ASPECTS OF LIFE IN BRITISH COLUMBIA, ESPECIALLY THOSE OF POLITICAL ORIENTATION. FOR EXAMPLE; FRATERNITY BROTHER EDWARD DUNK, WHO ONCE SERVED IN THE CANADIAN ARMY DURING THE TIME OF CONFLICT, IMMEDIATELY JOINED THE B.C. PROVINCIAL POLICE UPON BEING DISCHARGED FROM THE ARMY, (THE B.C. PROVINCIAL POLICE SUBSEQUENTLY MERGED WITH THE RCMP IN 1950), MADE IT ALL THE WAY UP THE RCMP RANKS TO STAFF-SERGEANT WHEN HE OFFICIALLY RETIRED IN 1971. MASONIC BROTHER DUNK IS ALSO SAID TO HAVE EVEN ACTED AS CHAUFFEUR FOR THEN-PREMIER W.A.C. BENNETT FOR A SHORT TIME PERIOD. DURING FRATERNITY BROTHER BENNETT'S POLITICAL REIGN IN THE PROVINCE OF BRITISH COLUMBIA, HE ALIGNED HIMSELF WITH MANY FRATERNAL BRETHREN BY VIEWING ITS MEMBERSHIP ROSTER WITH AN IRON HELD FIST NORMALLY ATTRIBUTED TO A FASCIST REGIME SUCH AS ADOLF HITLER/OR BENITO MUSSOLINI. BROTHER BENNETT AND HIS SOCIAL CREDIT GOVERNMENT CONVERTS FIRST TOOK OFFICE ON AUGUST 1ST, 1952 AND WERE RE-ELECTED MANY TIMES THEREAFTER. IN ACCORDANCE TO MASONIC LITERATURE, THE MAJORITY OF BENNETT'S GOVERNMENT CONSISTED LARGELY OF FREEMASONS WHO WERE LOYAL TO THE ANCIENT CRAFT. THE 1970 SOCIAL CREDIT PROVINCIAL CABINET FOR INSTANCE CONSISTED OF THE MOST WELL SEASONED MEMBERS THAT THE MASONIC ORDER HAD TO OFFER DURING ALL THE YEARS IT WAS IN POWER;

WESTLEY DREWETT BLACK   VICTORIA-COLUMBIA LODGE NO. 1 (VICTORIA)

MINISTER OF HIGHWAYS; APRIL 25TH, 1968

MINISTER OF HEALTH SERVICES AND HOSPITAL INSURANCE,
DECEMBER 12TH, 1966 TO APRIL 24TH, 1968
MINISTER OF SOCIAL SERVICES,
MARCH 20TH, 1959 TO DECEMBER 11TH, 1966
MINISTER OF MUNICIPAL AFFAIRS,
AUGUST 1ST, 1952 TO MARCH 19TH, 1964

ROBERT WILLIAM BOWSER   GOLDSTREAM LODGE NO. 161 (LANG-
FORD)
    ATTORNEY-GENERAL; AUGUST 1ST, 1952 TO MAY 26TH, 1968
    MINISTER OF COMMERCIAL TRANSPORT,
    MARCH 20TH, 1964 TO MARCH 26TH, 1968
    MINISTER OF INDUSTRIAL DEVELOPMENT, TRADE AND COM-
    MERCE,
    MARCH 28TH, 1957 TO MARCH 19TH, 1964
    MINISTER OF EDUCATION,
    OCTOBER 19TH, 1953 TO APRIL 13TH, 1954

DONALD LESLIE BROTHERS   EMULATION LODGE NO. 125 (TRAIL)
    MINISTER OF EDUCATION; MARCH 7TH, 1968
    MINISTER OF MINES AND PETROLEUM,
    MARCH 20TH, 1964 TO MARCH 26TH, 1968

EINAR MAYNARD GUNDERSON   EVERGREEN LODGE NO. 148 (VANCOUVER)
    MINISTER OF FINANCE,
    AUGUST 1ST, 1952 TO FEBRUARY 14TH, 1954

ERIC FITZGERALD CHARLES MARTIN   VICTORIA-COLUMBIA LODGE NO.
1 (VICTORIA)
    MINISTER OF HEALTH SERVICES AND HOSPITAL INSURANCE,
    MARCH 20TH, 1959 TO DECEMBER 11TH, 1966
    MINISTER OF HEALTH AND EDUCATION,
    AUGUST 1ST, 1952 TO MARCH 19TH, 1959

LESLIE RAYMOND PETERSON   MAPLE LEAF LODGE NO. 74 (VANCOUVER)
    MINISTER OF LABOUR; NOVEMBER 28TH, 1968
    ATTORNEY-GENERAL; MAY 27TH, 1968
    MINISTER OF EDUCATION
    SEPTEMBER 27TH, 1956 TO MAY 26TH, 1968

WALDO MCTAVISH SKILLINGS   VICTORIA-COLUMBIA LODGE NO. 1 (VIC-
TORIA)

Minister of Industrial Development, Trade and Commerce,
April 25TH, 1968

Newton Phillip Steacy   Nanaimo Lodge No. 110 (Nanaimo)
Minister of Agriculture,
September 13TH, 1957 to November 27TH, 1960

Earl Cathers Westwood   Doric Lodge No. 18 (Nanaimo)
Minister of Commercial Transport,
November 28TH, 1960 to December 3RD, 1963
Minister of Recreation and Conservation,
March 28TH, 1957 to December 3RD, 1963
Minister of Trade and Industry,
September 27TH, 1956 to March 28TH, 1957

Lyle Wicks   St. Andrew's Lodge No. 49 (Victoria)
Minister of Railways,
September 27TH, 1956 to March 19TH, 1959
Minister of Labour,
August 1ST, 1952 to November 27TH, 1960

Ray Gillis Williston   Victoria-Columbia Lodge No. 1 (Victoria)
Minister of Lands, Forests and Water Resources; March 30TH, 1962
Minister of Lands and Forests,
February 28TH, 1956 to March 29TH, 1962
Minister of Education,
April 14TH, 1954 to September 26TH, 1956

Other members of the Ancient Craft who were elected to British Columbia's 29TH Legislative Assembly on August 27TH, 1969 were:

Dennis Geoffrey Cocke   New Democratic Party MLA
Prince Arthur Lodge No. 82 (Vancouver)

William Harvey Murray   Social Credit MLA
Tsimpsean Lodge No. 58 (Prince Rupert)
Speaker of the Legislative Assembly; January 23RD, 1964

George Mussalllem   Social Credit MLA
Prince David Lodge No. 101 (Haney)

Dean Edward Smith   Social Credit MLA

FORT ST. JOHN LODGE NO. 131 (FORT ST. JOHN)

ROBERT MARTIN STRACHAN   NEW DEMOCRATIC PARTY MLA
        ST. JOHN'S LODGE NO. 21 (LADYSMITH)
        LEADER OF HER MAJESTY'S LOYAL OPPOSITION,
        APRIL 1956 TO APRIL 1969

HUNTER BERTRAM VOGEL   SOCIAL CREDIT MLA
        EUREKA LODGE NO. 103 (LANGLEY)

CONTRARY AS TO WHAT THE PROVINCE'S OWN HISTORIANS AND/OR JOURNALISTS WRITE AS BEING A POLITICAL FACT OF DAYS-GONE-BY, THE ACTUAL TRUTH OF THE MATTER IS AND ALWAYS WILL BE THAT DURING THE FIRST 100 YEARS OF BRITISH COLUMBIA'S JOINING THE DOMINION OF CANADA (1871/1970) MOST OF ITS PREMIERS AND LIEUTENANT-GOVERNORS WERE MEMBERS OF THE MASONIC ORDER. OF ALL ITS PREMIERS DURING THIS FULL 100 YEARS OF HISTORY, FOURTEEN OF THEM WERE SAID TO HAVE BEEN MASTER MASONS AND OF ALL ITS LIEUTENANT-GOVERNORS, ONLY EIGHT WERE STATED AS BEING PARTICIPATING MEMBERS OF THE ANCIENT FRATERNAL CRAFT.

JOHN FOSTER MCCREIGHT 1ST PREMIER - NOVEMBER 13TH, 1871 TO DECEMBER 20TH, 1872
        VICTORIA LODGE NO. 783 (VICTORIA)
        FIRST INITIATED IN 1866 AND LATER BECAME

        DEPUTY GRAND MASTER OF B.C. FREEMASONS

AMOR DE COSMOS 2ND PREMIER - DECEMBER 23RD, 1872 TO FEBRUARY 9TH, 1874
        VICTORIA LODGE NO. 1085 (VICTORIA)
        A CHARTER MEMBER IN 1860 BY AFFILIATION FROM
        OROVILLE, CALIFORNIA, HE BECAME THE FIRST MASONIC
        SECRETARY IN BRITISH COLUMBIA

GEORGE ANTONY WALKEM 3RD PREMIER - FEBRUARY 11TH, 1874 TO JANUARY 27TH, 1876
        KAMLOOPS LODGE NO. 10 (KAMLOOPS)
        A CHARTER MEMBER IN 1886 BY AFFILIATION FROM
        KING SOLOMON'S LODGE NO. 22 AT TORONTO, ONTARIO

GEORGE ANTONY WALKEM 5TH PREMIER (1878-82)

ROBERT BEAVEN 6TH PREMIER - JUNE 13TH, 1882 TO JANUARY 27TH, 1883

Quadra Lodge No. 8 (Victoria)
Alexander Edmund

Batson Davie   8th Premier - May 15th, 1887 to August 1st, 1889

A devoted Roman Catholic, his name first appeared
as an affiliated member of Cariboo Lodge No. 4 in
Quesnel on November 30th, 1874

John Herbert Turner 11th Premier - March 4th, 1895 to August 8th, 1898

First Agent-General for the Province of British
Columbia in London, England in 1901
A charter member in 1868 by affiliation from
Victoria Lodge No. 2 at Charlottetown, PEI

Edward Gawlor Prior 15th Premier - November 21st, 1902 to June 1st, 1903

(also was Lieutenant-Governor)
Victoria Lodge No. 1 (Victoria)
First initiated in 1891

Sir Richard McBride 16th Premier - June 1st, 1903 to December 15th, 1915

Later Agent-General for the Province of British
Columbia in London, England
Union Lodge No. 9 (New Westminister)

William John Bowser 17th Premier - December 15th, 1915 to November 23rd, 1916

Mount Hermon Lodge No. 7 (Vancouver)
First initiated in 1895

Harlan Cary Brewster 18th Premier - November 23rd, 1916 to March 1st, 1918

Vancouver and Quadra Lodge No. 2 (Victoria)
First initiated in 1909

John Duncan MacLean   20th Premier - August 20th, 1927 to August 20th, 1928

Later chairman of the Canadian Farm Loan Board
in Ottawa, Ontario
Pacific Lodge No. 16 (Mission City)

FIRST INITIATED IN 1896

SIMON FRASER TOLMIE   21ST PREMIER - AUGUST 21ST, 1928 TO
NOVEMBER 15TH, 1933
            VICTORIA-COLUMBIA LODGE NO. 1 (VICTORIA)

BYRON INGEMAR JOHNSON   24TH PREMIER - DECEMBER 29TH, 1947
TO AUGUST 1ST, 1952
            SAINT ANDREW'S LODGE NO 49 (VICTORIA)
            FIRST INITIATED IN 1929

WILLIAM ANDREW CECIL BENNETT 25TH PREMIER - AUGUST 1ST, 1952
            SAINT GEORGE'S LODGE NO. 41 (KELOWNA)
            FIRST INITIATED IN 1932

SOME OF THE MASONIC LIEUTENANT-GOVERNORS INCLUDED:

THOMAS ROBERT MCINNES, M.D.   6TH LIEUT.-GOVERNOR NOVEM-
BER 15TH, 1897 TO JUNE 21ST, 1900
            UNION LODGE NO. 9 (NEW WESTMINISTER)

SIR FRANK STILLMAN BARNARD   10TH LIEUT.-GOVERNOR DECEM-
BER 5TH, 1914 TO DECEMBER 9TH, 1919
            VICTORIA-COLUMBIA LODGE NO. 1 (VICTORIA)
            FIRST INITIATED IN 1882
            THE SON OF FRANCIS JONES BARNARD
            WHO IN 1865 OPERATED THE BARNARD EXPRESS
            FROM YALE ON THE LOWER FRASER RIVER
            TO RICHFIELD, BARKERVILLE AND CAMERONTON
            IN THE CARIBOO, WHO HAD BEEN INITIATED INTO
            THE ANCIENT CRAFT ON DECEMBER 4TH, 1872

COL. EDWARD GOWLOR PRIOR   11TH LIEUT.-GOVERNOR DECEM-
BER 9TH, 1919 TO DECEMBER 12TH, 1920
            VICTORIA-COLUMBIA LODGE NO. 1 (VICTORIA)
            FIRST INITIATED IN 1891

WALTER CAMERON NICHOL   12TH LIEUT.-GOVERNOR DECEMBER 24TH,
1920 TO FEBRUARY 24TH, 1926
            CASCADE LODGE NO. 12 (VANCOUVER)
            FIRST INITIATED IN 1899

ROBERT RANDOLF BRUCE 13TH LIEUT.-GOVERNOR FEBRUARY 24TH, 1926 TO
AUGUST 1ST, 1931 COLUMBIA LODGE NO. 38 (INVERMERE)

Col. William Cultham Woodward 16TH Lieut.-Governor   August 29TH, 1941 to October 1ST, 1946
    Acacia Lodge No. 22 (Vancouver)
    first initiated in 1901

Col. Clarence Wallace   18TH Lieut.-Governor October 1ST, 1950 to October 3RD, 1955
    Saint Andrew's Lodge No. 49 (Victoria)
    first initiated in 1951 and raised while
    still holding the office of Lieut.-Governor
    on May 23RD, 1952

Col. John Robert Nicholson 21ST Lieut.-Governor July 2ND, 1968
    Adoniram Lodge No. 118 (Vancouver)

According to further fraternity documentation contained within its own monthly bulletins, there were also other Masonic Premiers of British Columbia along with various elected members of the Provincial Legislative Assembly who were actively practicing the Ancient fraternal Craft, such as Cariboo North's MLA Alex Fraser (now deceased). Fraser was an active member of the Cariboo Lodge No. 69 in Quesnel for most of his life and was a dedicated card carrying member of the Social Credit Party of British Columbia. Further to these interesting political revelations, in the January 1992 issue of the Masonic Bulletin the fraternity congratulated one of its own members of the New Democratic Party who had been elected into the Legislature of British Columbia: "We congratulate Brother Fred Randall of Park Lodge No. 63 on being elected to the Provincial Legislature for the Burnaby-Edmonds riding. "While yet another Masonic Bulletin from the previous month (December 1991) congratulated the newly elected NDP Premier of the Province and his family for being elevated as British Columbia's new fraternity lord of the manor. NDP Premier Mike Harcourt was the son of Masonic Brother Frank Harcourt of Commonwealth Lodge No. 156. Even the social-democrat Dave Barrett who replaced the W.A.C. Bennett regime during the 1972 Provincial election came from Masonic stock, as did Barrett's replacement as Premier in December of 1975, Bill Bennett, the son of W.A.C.

Throughout British Columbia's Freemasonry past, there has been many secrets and lies passed down by countless generations. For instance, during the decade of the 1990's while researching

THE MASONIC ARCHIVES FOR THE FRATERNITY DOCUMENTATION ASSOCIATED WITH HIS FAMILY TREE, IT SOON BECAME APPARENT TO THE GIBSONS SHIT DISTURBER THAT THE MANY UNTOLD STORIES HAD TO BE DIRECTLY CONNECTED TO THE FREEMASONRY WRITERS OF DAYS-GONE-BY. DUE TO THE FACT THAT HIS FRENCH ANCESTRAL HERITAGE DID NOT HAVE A LONG HISTORY IN BRITISH COLUMBIA, BENOIT LEPAGE BEGAN RESEARCHING NAMES OF THE JEWISH/GERMAN PERSUASION AS HE HAD KNOWN A COUPLE FREEMASONS LIVING IN HIS COMMUNITY WHO WERE SAID TO HAVE JEWISH BLOODLINES (ROMANIAN/JEWISH AND GERMAN/JEWISH). THIS COMBINED WITH THE FACT THAT HIS VERY OWN ANCESTORS IN LOUISIANA HAD LONG AGO FEARED THE JEWISH POPULATION AS A RACE OF PEOPLE. WANTING TO KNOW MUCH MORE ABOUT JEWISH FREEMASONRY, HE SOON BEGAN DIGGING JUST A LITTLE BIT DEEPER INTO THE BRITISH COLUMBIA'S MASONIC PAST. IT DIDN'T TAKE VERY LONG BEFORE A RATHER LONG LIST OF THE PROVINCE'S WELL KNOWN JEWISH FREEMASONRY POPULATION APPEARED AS MEMBERS OF UPPER SOCIETY AT THE TURN OF THE TWENTIETH CENTURY.

THE GREAT EXODUS OF GERMANY'S POPULATION IN 1848 (THE YEAR OF REVOLUTION IN EUROPE) FOR EXAMPLE SAW A LARGE NUMBER OF JEWISH PEOPLE FLEE BECAUSE OF THE POLITICAL TURMOIL THAT WAS BEING CREATED. IN THAT EXACT SAME YEAR, FOUR YOUNG MEMBERS OF A JEWISH FAMILY REPORTEDLY LEFT GERMANY FOR NORTH AMERICA WITH JUST THE SHIRTS ON THEIR BACKS. THEY WERE GODFREY, CHARLES, DAVID AND ISAAC OPPENHEIMER. FIRST MAKING THEIR WAY TO NEW ORLEANS, WHERE DAVID WAS SAID TO HAVE STUDIED BOOKKEEPING AS HE WAS BELIEVED TO BE WORKING AT A GENERAL STORE AT THE TIME. BUT THE LURE OF MAKING VAST FORTUNES IN THE GOLD FIELDS OF CALIFORNIA SOON FOUND BROTHERS CHARLES AND DAVID MAKING THEIR WAY TO THE PACIFIC OCEAN. AND ON FEBRUARY 27TH, 1851 THEY ARRIVED IN SAN FRANCISCO BY WAY OF PANAMA. BROTHER ISAAC JOINED THEM A LITTLE LATER ON. BY 1852, DAVID HAD SETTLED IN PLACER COUNTY, CALIFORNIA, (THEN THE HEART OF THE GOLD FIELDS) WORKING AS A TRADER WITH BROTHERS CHARLES AND ISAAC. FIVE YEARS LATER, THE OPPENHEIMER BROTHERS WERE BECOMING MEMBERS OF UPPER SOCIETY AS THEIR BUSINESS VENTURES IN THE CALIFORNIA GOLD FIELDS ENABLED THEM TO EXPAND INTO THE LUCRATIVE PROFESSION OF REAL-ESTATE DEVELOPMENT PROPERTIES AS WELL AS EATERIES, (RESTAURANT BUSINESS VENTURES). BY THIS TIME PERIOD OF COURSE, RUMORS OF A GOLD FIND IN BRITISH COLUMBIA HAD CAUGHT THE ATTENTION OF ALL THREE BROTHERS AS THINGS IN CALIFORNIA WERE NOW BEGINNING TO TEETER OUT AS THE GOLD RESOURCES WERE SLOWLY BEING DEPLETED AND NO ONE WAS MAKING ANY MORE MONEY AT IT. ONLY TWO YEARS AFTER THE IMPERIAL EDICT OF 1858 HAD DECREED THAT BRITISH COLUMBIA WAS NOW PART OF THE BRITISH EMPIRE, THE OPPENHEIMER BROTHERS SEVERED ALL

TIES WITH THE CALIFORNIA BRETHRENSHIP AND MIGRATED NORTHWARD AS IN 1858-59 CHARLES HAD ESTABLISHED A SMALL SUPPLY BUSINESS IN VICTORIA ON THE PACIFIC JUST IN CASE THINGS DIDN'T WORK OUT DOWN SOUTH. WHILE OTHER FREEMASONRY BUSINESSMEN CHOSE TO ESTABLISH THEMSELVES IN VICTORIA AND NEW WESTMINISTER, BROTHERS CHARLES, DAVID AND ISAAC DID AS BEFORE, MIGRATED RIGHT INTO THE HEARTLAND OF THE GOLD FIND. BROTHER CHARLES SUPPLIED THE GOLD SEEKERS WITH THEIR GRUB STAKES FROM HIS YALE COMPANY STORE WHERE BUSINESS QUICKLY FLOURISHED. AS THE GOLD SEEKERS SLOWLY MADE THEIR WAY UP THE FRASER CANYON AND DEEP INTO THE PROVINCE'S INTERIOR, THE OPPENHEIMER BROTHERS SAW AN OPPORTUNITY TO FOLLOW THEM. BEFORE LONG, THE BUSINESS VENTURE EXPANDED, ESTABLISHING NEW STORES AND WAREHOUSES IN HOPE, LYTTON, BARKERVILLE AND FISHERVILLE.

IN 1862, BROTHER CHARLES REPORTEDLY LEFT THE BUSINESS VENTURE TO EXPLORE NEW FRATERNITY ADVENTURES WITH MASONIC BROTHER WALTER MOBERLY, AN ENGINEER WHO WAS CONTRACTED TO BUILD A SECTION OF THE CARIBOO ROAD TO THE GOLD FIELDS OF BRITISH COLUMBIA. FREEMASONRY BROTHER CHARLES OPPENHEIMER HAD MANAGED TO SECURE A CONTRACT TO BUILD PART OF THE CARIBOO ROAD. HE REPORTEDLY NEGLECTED TO COMPLETE HIS CONTRACTUAL OBLIGATIONS WHICH IN TURN COST THE BRITISH GOVERNMENT EVEN MORE MONEY TO HAVE COMPLETED IN THE END. (OPPENHEIMER'S CONTRACT WAS TO CONSTRUCT THE SECTION OF THE CARIBOO ROAD BETWEEN LYTTON AND SPENCES BRIDGE). COINCIDENTLY, BROTHER MOBERLY WAS LATER IMMORTALIZED AS THE MOBERLY SCHOOL IN VANCOUVER WAS NAMED IN HIS HONOR. WHILE BROTHER CHARLES WAS OUT MINGLING WITH THE UPPER ECHELONS OF B.C.'S FREEMASONRY ELITE, BROTHERS DAVID AND ISAAC WERE EXTREMELY BUSY BUYING UP PROPERTY THAT WAS ONCE OCCUPIED BY THE INDIANS. BY THE SUMMER OF 1866, THE OPPENHEIMER BROTHERS HAD ACQUIRED MANY ACRES OF LAND IN LYTTON AS WELL AS OTHER PROPERTIES SCATTERED ALONG THE NEWLY CONSTRUCTED CARIBOO ROAD THAT MADE ITS WAY UP TO BARKERVILLE. BUYING PARCELS OF LAND FOR NEXT TO NOTHING, THEN, DEVELOPING THEM AND LATER SELLING AT A HIGH PRICE. THIS MANEUVER WAS ALSO APPLIED TO THE SELLING OF LOTS IN THE HEART OF BARKERVILLE'S DOWNTOWN CORE AS IT WAS MAKING BROTHERS DAVID AND ISAAC VERY WEALTHY MEN. IT IN FACT BECAME SUCH A LUCRATIVE BUSINESS THAT ISAAC WAS FORCED TO MOVE FROM YALE TO THE NEW TOWN OF BARKERVILLE AS PROSPECTORS WERE BEING EXPLOITED BY JUST ABOUT EVERYONE, INCLUDING THE OPPENHEIMER BROTHERS. BUT MOST OF THEIR DREAMS WERE SOON SHATTERED AS FIRE RAVAGED THROUGH BARKERVILLE IN 1868, LEAVING THE OPPENHEIMER'S WITH VIRTUALLY NOTHING AS IT HAD

BEEN REPORTED THAT THEIR LOSSES WERE AN ESTIMATED $ 100,000.00 (NO FIRE INSURANCE).

BY THIS TIME PERIOD, THE OPPENHEIMER BROTHERS WERE DEEPLY IN DEBT DESPITE THE FACT THAT THEY WERE SAID TO HAVE BEEN WEALTHY MEN. APPARENTLY, THEY WERE LAND RICH BUT CASH POOR AS THEY WERE CONSTANTLY ROBBING PETER TO PAY PAUL AS THEIR BUSINESS VENTURES CONTINUALLY EXPANDED WITH EACH PASSING YEAR. IN OCTOBER OF 1866, CHARLES OPPENHEIMER'S COMPANY WAS FORCED INTO TRUSTEESHIP AS CREDITORS FEARED THAT THEY WOULD NOT BE PAID. AT THE TIME, BRITISH COLUMBIA'S NORTHERN ECONOMY WAS SOLELY DEPENDED UPON THE MEN AND WOMEN WORKING THE GOLD FIELDS. AND BY SEPTEMBER OF THE FOLLOWING YEAR, BROTHERS DAVID AND ISAAC WERE PROHIBITED FROM PLAYING ANY ROLE IN THE COMPANY'S AFFAIRS AS IT WAS SLOWLY BEGINNING TO CRUMBLE BECAUSE OF MISMANAGEMENT AND NEGLECT. THE BUSINESS VENTURE WAS SUBSEQUENTLY SOLD TO A COMPETITOR WHICH IN ESSENCE FORCED BROTHERS DAVID AND ISAAC TO RETHINK THEIR BUSINESS TACTICS AND BROTHER ISAAC THEREFORE UP ROOTED HIMSELF, MOVING TO BARKERVILLE. BY MARCH OF 1868, THE OPPENHEIMER BROTHERS HAD MANAGED TO REGENERATE SOME OF THEIR LOSES DUE TO A COMPETITOR (CARL STROUSS) TAKING OVER THE YALE OPERATION AND NOT LONG AFTER THAT BROTHERS DAVID AND ISAAC BEGAN TO REBUILT THE BUSINESS IN BARKERVILLE. SIX MONTHS LATER, SEPTEMBER 16TH, 1868 A RAVING FIRE SPREAD THROUGH THE WOODEN STRUCTURE TOWN REDUCING EVERYTHING IN ITS PATH TO ASHES, WITH THE EXCEPTION OF ONE BUILDING (SCOTT'S SALON) AND MOST OF CHINATOWN WHICH WAS VIRTUALLY UNTOUCHED. MORE THAN A HALF MILLION DOLLARS WORTH OF BUSINESSES LAY IN RUINS AFTER THE SMOKE HAD FINALLY CLEARED ONCE THE TWO HOUR BLAZE HAD COMPLETED ITS DEVASTATION. A FEW BUSINESS PEOPLE PACKED UP WHAT THEY COULD SALVAGE FROM THE RUINS WHILE OTHERS ALMOST IMMEDIATELY BEGAN TO REBUILD. THE BARKERVILLE FIRE WAS REPORTEDLY SAID TO HAVE HAD A PSYCHOLOGICAL AFFECT ON THE OPPENHEIMER BROTHERS THAT WHILE ISAAC WAS BUSY ORGANIZING THE WILLIAMS CREEK FIRE BRIGADE, DAVID MADE ONE OF HIS FIRST CIVIC CONTRIBUTIONS TO THE COMMUNITY, A FIRE-WAGON COMPLETE WITH HOSES MADE OF BUFFALO HIDE, PUMPS, LADDERS AND HOOKS FOR PULLING DOWN FLAMING WALLS. IN 1871, CHARLES OPPENHEIMER WAS ONCE AGAIN PART OF THE BUSINESS VENTURES AS HE WAS SAID TO HAVE BEEN ABLE TO ACQUIRE CONTROL OF CARL STROUSS' BUSINESS ENTERPRISES AND INSTANTLY INSTALLED BROTHERS DAVID AND ISAAC AS ITS PARTNERS IN THE NEWLY FORMED FAMILY FIRM SIMPLY DUBBED THE OPPENHEIMER BROTHERS. STROUSS' GENERAL STORE IN BARKERVILLE WHICH WAS REBUILD AFTER THE FIRE WAS SOLD TO CHARLES IN 1871 AND A

YEAR LATER (SEPTEMBER 1872) RESOLD TO F. NEUFELDER AND IN 1880, WAS BOUGHT OUT BY THE HUDSON'S BAY COMPANY.

DURING THE EARLY DAYS OF BRITISH COLUMBIA'S ENTRANCE INTO THE FEDERALLY CONTROLLED MASONIC FAMILY OF MAN (A.K.A. CONFEDERATION), THE GOLD RUSH OF THE CARIBOO'S INTERIOR REGIONS WERE BEGINNING TO DECLINE AND BARKERVILLE WAS SOON PLAYING A LESS IMPORTANT ROLE IN THE PROVINCE'S HISTORY. ALTHOUGH THE LATTER PARTS OF THE DECADE OF THE 1870'S SAW THE OPPENHEIMER BROTHERS USING YALE AS THEIR COMPANY'S BASE OF OPERATION, THAT TOO WAS SLOWING ERODING AWAY AS OTHER MEANS OF BUSINESS SURVIVAL HAD TO BE IMPLEMENTED. USING THEIR FREEMASONRY CONNECTIONS FOR AN ADVANTAGE, DAVID OPPENHEIMER JOINED A FRATERNITY SYNDICATE IN JANUARY OF 1880 TO HELP RAISE MONEY FOR THE CONSTRUCTION OF THREE DIFFERENT SECTIONS OF MASONIC BROTHER JOHN A.'S DREAM OF A TRANSCONTINENTAL RAILWAY NEAR YALE. THE SYNDICATE WAS NATURALLY SPEARHEADED BY FRATERNITY BROTHER ANDREW ONDERDONK (KING SOLOMON'S PRIMITIVE LODGE NO. 91). IN NOVEMBER OF THAT YEAR, (1880), AS OPPOSITION FORCES RALLIED TO PROTECT GOVERNMENTAL PLANS OF DIVERTING RAILWAY FUNDS FROM THE PROVINCE'S INTERIOR TO VANCOUVER ISLAND, DAVID OPPENHEIMER LET IT BE KNOWN THAT HE WAS NOT AT ALL PLEASED WITH FREEMASONRY LEADERS IN BOTH VICTORIA AND OTTAWA'S SUDDEN ABOUT FACE WITH THE FUNDING THAT OTHER MEMBERS OF THE ANCIENT CRAFT HAD INVESTED HEAVILY IN TO HELP SEE THE LINES ACTUAL COMPLETION. WITH THE DIVERSION OF RAILWAY FUNDS, THE OPPENHEIMER BROTHERS BUSINESS VENTURE HAD LOTS TO LOOSE AS IT HAD BEEN GUARANTEED WITH ALMOST CERTAINTY BY THE SYNDICATE LEADERS INVOLVED THAT THE ALLOCATED OF THE FINANCIAL FUNDS WERE TO REMAIN IN PLACE AS THESE MONIES WERE NEEDED FOR THREE VERY DIFFICULT SECTIONS OF THE LINE THAT OF WHICH REQUIRED THE EXPERTISE OF AN EXTREMELY SKILLED WORK FORCE; A CHINESE LABOR FORCE AS MUCH BLASTING OF ROCKS HAD TO BE DONE FROM THE MOUNTAIN SIDES SO THAT THE TRACKS COULD BE LAID.

ONCE THE FRATERNITY SCHISM WAS FINALLY RESOLVED, THE OPPENHEIMER BROTHERS HAD MORE THAN A MILLION DOLLARS WORTH OF BUSINESS FROM THE CANADIAN PACIFIC RAILWAY BEING FUNNELED THROUGH THEIR VARIOUS BUSINESS VENTURES AS THEY SUPPLIED RAILWAY CONTRACTORS WITH THE GOODS THAT THEY NEEDED TO CONSTRUCT THE LINE. AND AS BEFORE, CREDITORS THREATENED TO FORCE THE OPPENHEIMER BROTHERS WITH LEGAL ACTION IF PAYMENT FOR THE GOODS SUPPLIED TO THEM FOR RESALE WAS NOT PAID OFF IN FULL. IN APRIL OF 1881, THE COMPANY HAD DEBTS WORTH MORE THAN $ 80,000.00 AGAINST ASSETS OF $187,000.00, WHICH FORCED THE IMPLEMENTATION OF A CASH ON DELIVERY POLICY. THIS **C.O.D.** POLICY NOT ONLY APPLIED TO THE OPPENHEIMER BROTHERS AND THEIR

COMPANY BUT TO ALL OF ITS CUSTOMERS AS WELL. BY MID-AUGUST 1881, THE RESTRUCTURING OF THE COMPANY HAD TAKEN PLACE WHICH SAW CONTROL BEING TURNED OVER TO BOTH DAVID AND ISAAC. TWO WEEKS LATER, FIRE DESTROYED ALL OF YALE'S BUSINESS SECTION OF TOWN AND ONCE AGAIN, THE OPPENHEIMER BROTHERS LOST BIG TIME. THEIR STOREY-AND-A-HALF STORE AND ALL OF ITS INVENTORY WAS THUSLY LIQUIFIED BY THE FLAMES, TOGETHER WORTH APPROXIMATELY $170,000.00 BUT ONLY INSURED FOR LESS THAN ONE-QUARTER ITS DECLARED VALUE, ($ 49,000.00). APPARENTLY, THE ONLY THING THAT THEY WERE ABLE TO SALVAGE WAS MOST OF THE CONTENTS OF THEIR HOME AS THE HOUSE ITSELF WAS SAID TO HAVE BEEN TOTALLY GUTTED.

ACCORDINGLY, THE GOLD RUSH OF THE FRASER CANYON BY THIS TIME PERIOD OF HISTORY HAD LONG LOST ITS NOVELTY AND THE OPPENHEIMER BROTHERS WERE OBVIOUSLY GETTING SOMEWHAT ANNOYED AT THE STRIKE OF MISFORTUNE THAT SEEMED TO FOLLOW THEM AROUND NO MATTER WHERE THEY WENT. JUST LIKE THE GOLD FIELDS OF CALIFORNIA AND BARKERVILLE, BROTHERS DAVID AND ISAAC LATER TOOK FULL ADVANTAGE OF THEIR YALE SITUATION AND BEGAN CONTEMPLATING THE TASK OF MIGRATING IN THE SAME DIRECTION THAT THE RAILWAY BUILDERS WERE HEADED; DOWN INTO THE LOWER SECTIONS OF THE FRASER VALLEY. IN JANUARY OF 1882, THE OPPENHEIMER BROTHERS AND THEIR COMPANY OPENED A LARGE IMPORT-WHOLESALE BUSINESS ON WHARF STREET IN VICTORIA ON THE PACIFIC AND FOR THE NEXT FEW YEARS PROSPERED AS THE CAPITAL CITY BECAME THE MAIN SUPPLY CENTER FOR THE ENTIRE PROVINCE. WITH THE EMERGING OF CPR'S MOVE TO VANCOUVER, IT SOON BECAME APPARENT TO BROTHERS DAVID AND ISAAC THAT THEIR EXISTED A MUCH GREATER OPPORTUNITY TO MAKE VAST QUANTITIES OF MONEY AT THE TERMINUS OF THE FRATERNITY'S CPR INVESTMENT. SO IN THE FALL OF 1885, FREEMASONRY MEMBERS DAVID AND ISAAC MOVED TO VANCOUVER WHERE BROTHER DAVID HAD BEGUN TO ACQUIRE PRIME DEVELOPMENT PROPERTIES AS EARLY AS 1878 WHEN HE HAD MANAGED TO CONVINCE OTHER MEMBERS OF THE CRAFT TO PURCHASE 300 ACRES OF LAND ON THE BURRARD INLET. FURTHER TO THIS, DURING THE SUMMER OF 1884 HE AND OTHER VICTORIA FREEMASONS BOUGHT MORE LAND AT COAL HARBOUR AND ENGLISH BAY, THEN, LOBBIED THE MASONICALLY CONTROLLED GOVERNMENT'S OF BRITISH COLUMBIA AND OTTAWA TO ASSIST THE CPR IN EXTENDING ITS LINE WESTWARD FROM PORT MOODY. THE FREEMASONRY PACT ALSO ENCOURAGED OTHER LANDOWNERS (NON-MASONS AS WELL) TO JOIN THEM IN THE DONATING ABOUT 175 ACRES OF THEIR LANDS TO THE RAILWAY LINE. RIGHT UP TO THE VERY LAST DAYS OF THE CPR'S OFFICIAL ANNOUNCEMENT OF ITS EXTENSION OF THE GRANVILLE LINE, THE OPPENHEIMER BROTHERS CONTINUED TO BUY MORE AND MORE LAND AT GOVERNMENT AUCTIONS. ONLY SIXTEEN YEARS INTO B.C.'S ENTRANCE INTO

Confederation with the Masonic controlled Government of Sir. John A. MacDonald, (1887), the declared value of the Oppenheimer land holdings through their Vancouver Improvement Company was listed as being $ 125,000.00, reportedly the third largest holding company after the CPR ($ 1,000,000.00) and the Hastings Saw Mill ($ 250,000.00).

With their wealth accumulating with each passing day, the Oppenheimer Brothers opened the first wholesale grocery warehouse in Vancouver in July of 1887. While Brother Isaac was managing the store, Brother David reportedly concentrated all of his efforts on promoting the full development of the City. As their aspirations for wealth increased, so did their political involvement in public affairs. Brother Isaac, a member and past master of Mount Hermon Lodge No. 7 as well as a member of the Cariboo Lodge No. 4 became an elected public official in December of 1886. Brother David, a member of Cascade Lodge No. 12 was also anointed Alderman of the City at the exact same time as Brother Isaac. While Brother Isaac maintained his Masonic political portfolio as Alderman until some years later, Brother David went on to become Vancouver's Mayor.

Despite the fact that a large majority of the City's population (business as well as residents) publically opposed Brother David's politics, he was still maneuvered into office as the crowning Mayor. During this time period of British Columbia's democratic history, any and all candidates running for public office had to have at least $ 2,000.00 worth of property in the community that of which they were running in, (that was equivalent to nearly an entire City block of houses). The policy itself was initially implemented solely for the purpose of making sure that unqualified political candidates were unable to run for public office, (Chinese, Japanese, East Indian and such). This was especially true when it came down to mayoralty candidates as British Columbia was strictly a whiteman's playing ground for capitalist ventures where the rich got richer off the sweat of others. And since B.C. was originally the most racist region in the land, even more so than in French Canada, it only made sense that some sort of protectionism be implemented in the political arena on the municipal level. Both politicians (David and Isaac) represented the sparsely settled area on the east side of Vancouver where most of their land development properties were located. Critics of Masonic Brother David accused him of being in a direct conflict-of-interest as he continually promoted development on the east side. The situation in fact had gotten so far out of control

THAT IN 1888 NO ONE DARED CHALLENGE HIM FOR THE MAYOR'S THRONE AS HE RAN FOR A SECOND TERM IN OFFICE. WINNING BY ACCLAMATION, AN ANTI-MASONIC MOVEMENT WAS SOON BORN AND LED BY WILLIAM TEMPLETON, A GROCER WHO PUBLICALLY DENOUNCED THE MAYOR OF VANCOUVER BY THE FOLLOWING YEAR CITING THAT FRATERNITY BROTHER DAVID WAS SPENDING FAR TOO MUCH TIME AND MONEY BUILDING HIS CASTLES IN THE SKY AND NOT ENOUGH ON CIVIC ADMINISTRATION AND LAW ENFORCEMENT. UNDER THE WATCHFUL FREEMASONRY EYE OF BROTHER DAVID OPPENHEIMER, THE CITY OF VANCOUVER WAS SAID TO HAVE BEEN BACKSLIDING AS UNBRIDLED CORRUPTION ASSOCIATED WITH PAY-OFFS AND BACKROOM DEALS BECAME THE NORMAL PRACTICE FOR BUSINESS TRANSACTIONS TO TRANSPIRE. BY THE TIME THE BALLOTS WERE COUNTED, TEMPLETON LITERALLY WENT DOWN IN DEFEAT AS MAYOR OPPENHEIMER'S CHALLENGER. SURPRISINGLY, THOSE WHO CRITICIZED THE ANTICS OF THE MAYOR THE MOST, SIMPLY DIDN'T BOTHER CASTING A VOTE FOR THE MAYORALTY CANDIDATES BUT DID CAST A VOTE FOR THE ALDERMANIC CANDIDATES. THIS IRONICALLY TOOK PLACE MERELY BECAUSE OF THE FACT THAT THE VAST MAJORITY OF THE ALDERMANIC HOPEFULS OPPOSED OPPENHEIMER FOR HIS STANCE ON LEADING THE CITY'S EAST SIDE INTERESTS.

DESPITE THE FACT THAT THE FRATERNITY ICON WAS PROMOTING HIS OWN SELF-SERVINGS INTERESTS, THE CITY OF VANCOUVER'S ECONOMY WAS STILL GROWING STRONG UNDER THE STEWARDSHIP OF ITS LIVING IDOL. BUT IN DECEMBER OF 1891, FRATERNITY BROTHER DAVID OPPENHEIMER DECLINED A REQUEST MADE BY SOME 400 RESIDENTS, INCLUDING MANY PROMINENT FREEMASONRY BUSINESSMEN FOR HIM TO SEEK A FIFTH TERM IN OFFICE. CITING ILL-HEALTH AND BUSINESS CONCERNS, BROTHER DAVID WITHDREW FROM ACTIVE POLITICAL LIFE AND CONCENTRATED ON MANAGING HIS OWN INVESTMENTS. HE THEN TURNED ALL OF HIS ENERGY TOWARDS THOSE BUSINESS VENTURES THAT OF WHICH WERE SAID TO HAVE BEEN IN SOME FINANCIAL DIFFICULTY, SUCH AS THE VANCOUVER ELECTRIC RAILWAY AND LIGHT COMPANY WHICH HE FORMED IN 1890 AND THE VANCOUVER TRAMWAY, A 13-MILE ELECTRIC RAILWAY WHICH WAS FORMED IN 1888 LINKING VANCOUVER TO NEW WESTMINISTER AND PASSED RIGHT THROUGH THE AREA OF EAST VANCOUVER WHERE THE OPPENHEIMER FAMILY HAD EXTENSIVE LAND HOLDINGS SUITABLE FOR RESIDENTIAL DEVELOPMENT. IN JUNE OF 1893, TRUSTEES FOR THE DEBENTURE HOLDERS TOOK OVER THE RAILWAY AND IN AUGUST OF THE FOLLOWING YEAR, THE TRAMWAY WENT INTO RECEIVERSHIP.

AFTER LICKING HIS FREEMASONRY WOUNDS, MORE AND MORE OF BROTHER DAVID'S BUSINESS VENTURES BEGAN TO FALL PREY TO HIS FRATERNITY CREDITORS. AT THE TIME OF HIS DEATH ON JANUARY 1ST, 1897, DAVID OPPENHEIMER'S VAST FORTUNE HAD DEPLETED SO MUCH THAT ACCORDING TO THE PROVINCIAL GOVERNMENT'S RECORDS, THE PROVINCIAL

FINANCE MINISTER (MASONIC BROTHER JOHN HERBERT TURNER) ESTIMATED THAT A FAIR MARKET VALUE FOR HIS ENTIRE ESTATE WAS SOMEWHERE IN THE NEIGHBORHOOD OF $20,000.00 AND NO MORE. THROUGHOUT HIS FREEMASONRY CAREER, AS WELL AS WHILE ACTING AS MAYOR OF VANCOUVER, FRATERNITY BROTHER DAVID OPPENHEIMER REPORTEDLY MADE A LOT OF ENEMIES. DESPITE THIS LITTLE KNOWN FACT OF HISTORY, HIS OBITUARY STATED THAT HE WAS BASICALLY A WELL LIKED MAN AND WAS GENERALLY LOVED BY ALL. AT THE AGE OF 64, BROTHER DAVID RECEIVED A MASONIC FUNERAL WHERE HE LAY IN STATE AT THE MASONIC TEMPLE IN VANCOUVER WHEREBY HE RECEIVED FULL FRATERNITY HONORS AS THE CEREMONY WAS CONDUCTED BY THE WORSHIPFUL MASTER AND BRETHREN OF HIS LODGE, CASCADE LODGE NO. 12. AFTER THE SERVICE, HIS REMAINS WERE TRANSPORTED TO THE STATE OF NEW YORK WHERE THEY WERE INTERRED IN THE HEBREW CEMETERY IN BROOKLYN, NEW YORK. BROTHER ISAAC REPORTEDLY LEFT VANCOUVER IN 1901 TO TRAVEL EXTENSIVELY THROUGHOUT EUROPE AND THE UNITED STATES BEFORE TAKING UP RESIDENCE IN SPOKANE, WASHINGTON, WHERE HE DIED AT THE AGE OF 88 YEARS. CHARLES AND GODFREY HAD MET THAT GREAT ARCHITECT OF THE UNIVERSE LONG BEFORE BROTHERS DAVID AND ISAAC.

LIKE JEWISH FREEMASONRY, THE SACRED INSTITUTION OF CHINESE FREEMASONRY ALSO PLAYED A VERY IMPORTANT ROLE IN THE PROVINCE'S ACTUAL DEVELOPMENT OVER THE MANY YEARS. IN FACT, THE SUBJECT OF CHINESE FREEMASONRY IS THAT OF A HISTORY OF COMPLETE WONDERMENT AND ABSOLUTE AWE. BY MASONIC DEFINITION, THERE IS AN IMMENSE BIBLIOGRAPHY COVERING THE MANY ASPECTS OF BOTH ITS PRESENT AND PAST HISTORY. OF MOST IMPORTANCE IS THE TERM FREEMASONRY ITSELF FOR THERE IS NO SUCH ORGANIZATION WITHIN THE CHINESE CULTURE WHICH IS CLOSELY COMPARED TO THE MASONIC CONCEPTS OF THE BROTHERHOOD MEANING OF UNIVERSALITY AS "IT IS TRUE THAT, ON THE HIGHEST MORAL AND PHILOSOPHICAL PLAIN THERE ARE MANY SIMILARITIES, QUOTATIONS, AND PHRASES WHICH HAVE BEEN TRANSLATED, PERHAPS WISHFULLY, TO CORRESPOND WITH OUR MASONIC RITUALS AND LITERATURE. "DESPITE THIS, MANY FREEMASONRY AUTHORITIES AGREE THAT A STRONG ALLEGIANCE EXIST BETWEEN THE MOTHER COUNTRY OF CHINA AND ITS BROTHERHOOD REPRESENTATIVES OF THE MASONIC GOVERNING POWERS THAT BE.

HISTORIAN AUTHORITIES ON THE EARLY PEOPLE OF CHINA AGREE THAT TRACES OF NEOLITHIC PEOPLES ARE FOUND IN THE VALLEY OF THE YELLOW RIVER. ACCORDING TO THE INSTITUTION OF FREEMASONRY, "THESE ARE THE PEOPLE WHO DEVELOPED A CULTURE WHICH GIVES THE FIRST RECORDED HISTORY OF THIS GREAT LAND. THESE PEOPLE OF THE MIDDLE KINGDOM GIVE US THE NAME ' CHINA '; AND IT IS PROBABLE THAT THE CHHIN DYNASTY OF 221 TO 207 B.C. BROUGHT ABOUT THE FIRST UNIFICATION OF CHINA.

There were rulers of a limited central area long before that, but history gradually recedes into mystical kings and emperors starting with the Three Emperors, probably somewhere around 3000 B.C. "By Masonic interpretation, the **"NEW AGE "**movement that some years ago ran a series of articles entitled "Ancient Chinese Masonry "by Bishop W.C. White makes very interesting reading. In accordance to his research into the earliest sources of Freemasonry, "on an operative level, "aroused many Masonic attitudes of the last two decades of the Twentieth Century:

"Among ancient writings on rites and ceremonies they give such in great detail; these practices date back to before the time of Solomon, and some of them are carried on to the present, though their origin is lost in the mists of antiquity. In the spoken and written language the common term for proper conduct, orderliness, and exactitude is, literally ' compass-square'. In an ancient stone frieze in Shantung, dated 2000 years ago, is a carved depiction of the first mystical man and woman, — one holding a carpenters square, and the other an ancient type of compass."

The Masonic **Brotherhood of Man** felt very proud of their new found ties to Chinese Freemasonry: "From western archaeologists we learn that stone tools are found in the valley of the Yellow River, and believed to have been used for ritualistic purposes. Jade was often used, though jade was exhausted in China in the second century B.C. Jade to the Chinese was the stone of immortality, and was particularly used in burials. The jade artifacts were purely symbolic." It is also interesting to note that according to Freemasonry, "Ra, the Sun God of Egypt, "is depicted by the hieroglyphic circle, sometimes with a point in the center, and that the earliest Chinese ideograph for the sun is exactly the same. "During these formative centuries, agriculture superceded hunting and fishing, rice and millet were grown, (it wasn't for centuries later that wheat was cultivated); pigs and poultry were domesticated, as were cattle, sheep and dogs. It was during this period that silk was developed into a major industry. Expansion proceeded from the Middle Kingdom. The pictograph for ' China ' — ..... is a square, representing the earth; and a vertical line through it representing ' the center' — because, as all people of the Celestial Kingdom knew, China was the center of the world."

Over the centuries, there has been many articles written about the earliest recorded societies of China. Most of which, must be taken

WITH A VERY LARGE GRAIN OF SALT!!! THE WRITINGS WHICH HAVE DESCENDED TO US FOR SEVERAL MILLENNIA ARE AMBIGUOUS TO A DEGREE. ORIENTAL WRITING IS CHARACTERIZED BY ITS FLOWERY LANGUAGE AND IMPRECISE TERMINOLOGY. ANYONE STUDYING LAO TZU AND HIS "TAO TE CHING "IS CONFRONTED WITH MANY VERSIONS AND TRANSLATIONS. MOST ARE UNIQUE TO THE EXTENT THAT A PERSON WOULD NEVER RECOGNIZE THE FACT THAT THEY ACTUALLY CAME FROM THE EXACT SAME SOURCE. THE TRADITIONAL VIEW IS THAT LAO TZU WAS AN OLD CONTEMPORARY OF CONFUCIUS, WHICH DATES HIS WORK TO THE FOURTH CENTURY B.C. THE DATES GENERALLY GIVEN ARE 551 TO 479 B.C. FOR THE LIFE OF THE GREAT MASONIC MASTER OF CHINESE PHILOSOPHY. IN REALITY, THERE IS NO CLAIM THAT CONFUCIUS HAD ANY INFLUENCE OF WHAT THE MASONIC ORDER "MAY LOOSELY DEFINE AS MASONIC PHILOSOPHY. "BUT BY THEIR OWN DEFINITION, CONFUCIUS WAS A VERY PRAGMATIC MAN; "HE HAD A REPUTATION FOR HONESTY, SO CONSEQUENTLY WAS NEVER EMPLOYED BY ANY OF THE RULING PRINCES. HE HAD A DEVOTED FOLLOWING AND HIS STATEMENTS, APPARENTLY VERBATIM, HAVE BEEN HANDED DOWN TO US OVER THE CENTURIES. "IRONIC AS IT MAY SEEM, MANY MASONIC BRETHREN COMPARE CONFUCIUS TO SAMUEL JOHNSON, A FRATERNITY BROTHER AND A "GREAT ENGLISH LEXICOGRAPHER "WHO BY THE BROTHERHOOD'S OWN ADMITTANCE WAS ALSO "A LAW UNTO HIMSELF ."

HISTORICALLY SPEAKING, CONFUCIUS AND MANY OF HIS DISCIPLES CONTRIBUTED A GREAT DEAL TO THE WAYS IN WHICH CHINESE PHILOSOPHERS THOUGHT. THE LIFE AND DOCTRINE OF THE GREAT CHINESE PHILOSOPHER MENCUIS FOR EXAMPLE IS OF A GREAT INTEREST TO FREEMASONRY. MENG K'O (MENCUIS) WAS A NATIVE OF TSOU, IN SHANGTUNG, AND STUDIED WITH A FAMOUS CHINESE PUPIL OF K'UNG CHI (CONFUSIUS' GRANDSON). AFTER LEARNING HIS TEACHER'S PROCEDURES MENCUIS WENT OFF TO SERVE KING HSUAN OF CH'I, WHO FOUND NO POSTING FOR HIM. HE THEN WENT TO KING HUI OF LIANG, BUT THE KING WAS NOT AFFECTED BY HIS RHETORIC BECAUSE HE APPARENTLY FELT THAT EVERYTHING MENCUIS SAID WAS WAY TOO FAR-FETCHED AND IMPRACTICAL. AT THAT SAME TIME PERIOD, AFTER ADOPTING THE POLICIES OF LORD SHANG, THE STATE OF CH'IN WAS ENRICHING ITSELF AND STRENGTHENING ITS ARMY. ADVISED BY THE STRATEGIST WU CH'I, THE CHINESE STATES OF CH'U AND WEI WERE THUS ATTACKED AND DEFEATED AS WERE MANY OTHER WEAKER STATES. KINGS WEI AND HSUAN OF CH'I, WERE ABETTED BY SUCH STRATEGISTS AS SUN WU AND T'IE CHI, WITH THE RESULTS THAT THE FEUDATORS PAID THEIR COURT TO CH'I, AND THE WHOLE WORLD BECAME DEVOTED TO THE FORMING OF THE NORTH-SOUTH AND EAST-WEST ALLIANCES, AND ATTACK THUS CAME TO BE LOOKED UPON AS AN ACT OF THE HIGHEST CALIBER. IT WAS UNDER SUCH CIRCUMSTANCES THAT MENCIUS TAUGHT ABOUT THE EXCELLENCE OF YAO, SHUN AND THE THREE DYNASTIES.

So, finding himself at odds wherever he went, Meng K'o withdrew home and with such pupils as Wan Chang, summarizing the poems and the writings of old as well as the teachings of Confucius' ideas, composed the book Mencius in seven volumes.

According to pious legends, Meng K'o lost his father at a very young age. The home being near graves, he was said to have played among them. His mother disliked this area for her son and moved closer to the market district. Here, the young boy reportedly played marketeering, which his mother was also said to have disapproved of. Then, they moved near a school where the young future scholar played at arranging sacrificial vessels and performing the bowing, advancing, and with drawings of a polite well balanced society. Here they stayed and Meng K'o attended school. His mother was once said to have inquired as to how far the class had advanced on this one particular day and the lad pretended not to hear her. There upon she slashed the threat of her loom and stated: "If you fail to study you will be like by ruined cloth. "And this reportedly frightened the soon to be philosopher so much that thereafter, he kept hard at his studies from morning til night, and thusly became known as a world famous Confucianist called Mencuis.

In accordance to Chinese philosophers, the most important development of the Confucius School was in the teaching of Mencius (372-289 B.C.). After the death of the great Confucius, the teachings were divided into two schools; one of Hsuntse and one of Mencius. The former believing in the wickedness of human nature and the necessity of restraint and the latter believing in the sheer expansiveness of the good heart of man. Mencius once said: "The great man is one who has not lost the heart of a child." Interestingly, he started out from the assumption that man has the innate capacity for good and loves what is good, that it is through corruption that man deteriorates, and that therefore, the essence of self-cultivation, of preserving ones moral character, consists merely in "finding the lost heart of the child. "This, according to most historians became the orthodox school. Ironically, Mencius has been given a place next to Confucius, and it is common to speak of Confucian doctrines as the "teachings of Kung-Meng, "naturally meaning Confucius (Kung) and Mencius (Meng). As far as the Chinese philosophers were concerned, it was the faith in the innate goodness of human nature which the later Confucian scholars so loved and which had been incorporated into the body politic of Confucian humanism. Furthermore, according to many historians,

WHEN THE SUNG NEO-CONFUCIANISTS CAME, THEY SAW THE TREMENDOUS IMPORT OF MENCIUS, AND CONSEQUENTLY INCLUDED HIS WORKINGS INTO THE CONFUCIAN FOUR BOOKS TO BE LEARNED BY ALL CHINESE SCHOOL CHILDREN. MENCUIS, "DEVELOPED THE THEORY OF MAN'S HIGHER SELF AND HIS LOWER SELF. "AT ONE POINT, MENCIUS ASKED: "WE ARE ALL HUMAN BEINGS. WHY IS IT THAT SOME ARE GREAT MEN AND SOME ARE SMALL MEN? "TO THIS HE SIMPLY REPLIED: "THOSE WHO ATTEND TO THEIR GREATER SELVES BECOME GREAT MEN, AND THOSE WHO ATTEND TO THEIR SMALLER SELVES BECOME SMALL MEN. "HOW IRONIC ARE HIS WORDS OF WISDOM AND HIS TEACHINGS OF THE SELF, MENCIUS SPOKE OF THE "GREAT MAN", RATHER THAN THE CHUNTSE /OR THE "GENTLEMAN."

INTERESTINGLY, MANCIUS WAS THE FAVORED DISCIPLE OF CONFUCIANISM. HE REPORTEDLY WROTE: "MAN SHOULD APPLY THE SQUARE AND THE COMPASSES MORALLY TO THEIR LIVES, AND THE LEVEL AND MARKING LINE BESIDES IF THEY WOULD WALK IN THE STRAIGHT AND EVEN PATH OF WISDOM, AND KEEP THEMSELVES WITHIN THE BOUNDS OF HONOR AND VIRTUE. "AND THEN THERE'S THAT WELL-KNOWN QUOTATION FROM THE WORKINGS OF MENCIUS, THE GREAT MASTER OF CHINESE FREEMASONRY: "A MASTER MASON, IN TEACHING HIS APPRENTICES, MAKES USE OF THE COMPASSES AND THE SQUARE. YE WHO ARE ENGAGED IN THE PURSUIT OF WISDOM MUST ALSO MAKE USE OF THE COMPASSES AND THE SQUARE. "BY MASONIC DEFINITION, THESE TWO WORDS, "COMPASSES "AND "SQUARE "IN THE CHINESE LANGUAGE VIRTUALLY REPRESENTS "ORDER, REGULARITY, AND PROSPERITY. "THE OLDEST OF THESE ANCIENT CHINESE CUSTOMS AND/OR LITERATURE CLASSICS, "WHICH EMBRACES A PERIOD FROM THE TWENTY-FOURTH TO THE SEVENTY CENTURY BEFORE CHRIST, "INTERESTINGLY ENOUGH ARE DISTINCT SYMBOLS OF FREEMASONRY. ALTHOUGH THE MASONIC ORDER TAKES CREDIT FOR MOST CHINESE ATTRIBUTES OF WISDOM, IT IS AGREED BY MOST AUTHORITIES THAT THE CHINESE USE OF THE TERM "SQUARE AND COMPASSES "SYMBOLIZE PRECISELY THE MEANING OF MORAL CONDUCT AS IN AN OPEN AND HONEST SOCIETY BASED UPON HUMANIST PRINCIPLES. "SINCE 620 B.C. THE CHINESE HAVE HAD FREEMASONRY WITH RITES AND RITUALS ALMOST IDENTICAL WITH FREEMASONRY TODAY," WROTE THE WELL RESPECTED CHINESE HISTORIAN DR. HSIEH IN HIS MASONIC ACCOUNTS OF CHINA. WITHIN THE GREAT WALL OF CHINA, THERE EXISTED MANY SECRET SOCIETIES OF THE YEARS GONE BY; "THE HUNG, THE LOTUS, THE TRIAD LEAGUE, AND SAM HO HUI. "AS FAR AS THAT GOES, CHINA AS IN ALL OTHER COUNTRIES, SECRET SOCIETIES HAVE EXISTED FROM THE VERY BEGINNING OF TIME. ACCORDING TO THE MASONIC ORDER'S OWN LITERATURE FOR EXAMPLE, THERE ARE EVEN "SECRET SOCIETIES AMONGST THE INDIANS OF NORTH AMERICA." BUT IN THE EXACT SAME BREATH ANY RESEMBLANCES, OTHER THAN PURELY SUPERFICIAL, IS QUICKLY DENOUNCED BY

THE ORDER. IT SEEMS THAT THE ONLY TIME PERIOD THAT THE FREEMASONRY CONCEPT OF THE **BROTHERHOOD OF MAN** IS WILLING TO ACKNOWLEDGE THEIR ACTUAL EXISTENCE, IS WHEN IT WILL BENEFIT THE MOVEMENT AND ITS JUST CAUSE TOWARDS GLOBAL DOMINATION AS THEY ARE BASICALLY CONSIDERED TO BE "IRREGULAR"OFFSHOOTS OF THE ANCIENT CRAFT.

A NUMBER OF WELL-KNOWN MASONIC WRITERS HAVE STUDIES CHINESE SECRET SOCIETIES EXTENSIVELY. SOME CALL THEM AS SUCH, WHILE OTHERS LUMP ALL SUCH SOCIETIES INTO ONE CLASSIFICATION, "FREEMASONRY." TODAY'S CHINESE FREEMASONS ARE DIRECT DESCENDANTS OF THESE ANCIENT SECRET MASONIC SOCIETIES, "THE PRESENT USE OF THE TERM ' FREEMASONRY ' BY ORIENTALS IS MERELY A CONVENIENCE. "AT LEAST THAT'S WHAT FREEMASONRY HISTORIANS ARE STATING FOR THE TIME BEING. WITH FURTHER EMPHASIS BEING STATED: "AND CHINESE THEMSELVES DO NOT CLAIM ANY OVERT CONNECTION WITH OUR OWN FREEMASONRY. "THIS BY ALL MEANS DOES NOT PROHIBIT ANY CHINESE PERSON FROM BECOMING A MEMBER OF A REGULARLY INSTITUTED LODGE OF FREEMASONRY THAT OF WHICH IS RECOGNIZED BY ALL MAJOR MASONIC JURISDICTIONS. IN J.S.M. WARD'S PUBLICATION OF "FREEMASONRY AND THE ANCIENT GODS "HE WROTE: "IN CHINA MANY SECRET SOCIETIES ABOUND, OR AT LEAST, DID UNTIL RECENT YEARS. THEY APPEAR TO BE OFTEN TIMES OF POLITICAL CHARACTER: THEY DID HAVE SIGNS OF RECOGNITION, OATHS, AND RITUALS. SEVERAL EMPERORS PERSECUTED THESE SOCIETIES MERCILESSLY AND RECORDS ARE EXTANT OF ENTIRE LODGES BEING PUT TO DEATH. MUCH OF OUR KNOWLEDGE COMES TO US FROM UNFRIENDLY ACCOUNTS OF THE POLITICAL OPPONENTS OF THESE ORDERS. "UNFORTUNATELY, MR. WARD DID NOT MENTION THE VARIOUS ORGANIZATIONS AND THEIR SIMILARITIES TO THE MODERN-DAY MASONIC FRATERNITY. ALTHOUGH NOT MENTIONED, "ONE SUCH GROUP IS REPUTED TO REFER TO BROTHERLY LOVE, RELIEF AND TRUTH AS THE PRINCIPLES OF THE ORDER. "LIKE ALL OTHER MASONIC LODGERY, ITS MEMBERS MUST HELP EACH OTHER WHEN IN DISTRESS, AND OBEY THE WISDOM AND COMMANDS OF ITS ELDERS.

INTERESTINGLY, IN 1945 THE MASONIC LODGE OF RESEARCH (NO. 218) LISTED FOUR MAJOR SOCIETIES IN CHINA WITH FRATERNAL RELATIONS TO FREEMASONRY. "CHINESE MASONIC SOCIETIES HAVE THEIR ORIGIN IN THE EAST; WESTERN INFLUENCE, MASONIC OR OTHERWISE, HAS NEVER INFLUENCED IT. CHINESE RECORDED HISTORY MAY BE TRACED BACK TO 2205 B.C. "ACCORDING TO THE RESEARCH LODGE MATERIAL, THE FOUR CHINESE SOCIETIES THAT COMPRISED OF A MASONIC CHARACTERISTIC WERE;

THE HUNG   : THE SOCIETY OF HEAVEN AND EARTH
THE LOTUS   : THE WHITE LILY SOCIETY
THE TRIAD LEAGUE : TIEN HAN HUI TONG

Masonic research scientist J.G. Naismith thus concluded his findings by stating the following: "From my study of this great and intriguing subject I believe the society was formed to the glory of **GOD** and the welfare of **MAN**, and that its' members see in its development an approach to the time when mankind will brothers be, and the Eternal Father reign **SUPREME**."

By Masonic understanding, one of the major problems relating to the topic of Chinese Freemasonry is the language itself; "there are today approximately one billion Chinese people, presumably all of them speak one or more of the seven or eight dialects or languages. Of the 4,000 or so languages in the world, Chinese is by far the most widely spoken. Somewhat surprisingly the dialects of Chinese are so different that they are mutually unintelligible. The written language is more or less common to all of the sub-languages. The languages are tonal in that syllables have a pitch relative to each other. A word of similar sound to our ears, may have quite a different meaning if the pitch is changed. There is no relationship between Chinese and Japanese or Korean."

Furthermore, according to the Masonic Order, British Columbia's leading Chinese Freemasonry expert Dr. So Won Leung summed it up best while reviewing all the evidence on hand: "To me there is something mystical in the striking similarity between rites and ceremonies of these old Chinese Secret Societies and Freemasonry as we know it. This is more remarkable when one recalls the antiquity of both and the lack of opportunity for either to have been patterned after the other. "Coincidently, fraternity Brother Leung received full Masonic honors when he died on August 3RD, 1992 at the age of 77 after suffering from a long illness. He was born in China in 1915 and came to Canada while still a child in 1922. He graduated from the University of B.C. and the University of Toronto where he received his medical credentials. He not only served in the Second World War but also became a Master Mason where he slowly began climbing the fraternal ladder of success. Serving as past master of Fellowship Lodge No. 137 as well as District Deputy Grand Master of District No. 26 fifteen years prior to his death.

Undoubtedly, the first established Masonic Lodgery in China was in 1759 at Canton by officers of a Swedish ship, the "Prince Carl", after which the Lodge was named. Interestingly enough, the

SHIP REPORTEDLY CARRIED A SORT OF A FRATERNITY "TRAVELLING WARRANT" THAT OF WHICH WAS ISSUED AT GOTHENBURG, "ALLOWING THE SHIP'S COMPANY TO MET AS A LODGE WHENEVER IT CAME ASHORE. "IT THUS LEFT BEHIND IN MANY PORTS OF CALL, A MASONIC CLUB WHICH WAS EXPECTED TO INSTITUTE A WARRANT FROM ENGLAND, THAT IS TO SAY OF COURSE IF ANY MEMBERS OF THE FREEMASONRY FRATERNITY WISHED TO STAY ASHORE. BE THAT AS IT MAY, THE UNITED GRAND LODGE OF ENGLAND EIGHT YEARS LATER, ALSO ESTABLISHED A LODGE AT CANTON. IT IS INTERESTING TO NOTE THAT THERE WEREN'T ENOUGH EUROPEANS TO CONTINUE THE MEETINGS AND BY THE EARLY 1800'S, BOTH OF THE FRATERNITY LODGES CEASED TO EXIST. BY 1844, THE GRAND LODGE OF ENGLAND RE-ESTABLISHED ITS MASONIC STRONGHOLD IN CHINA, (IN SHANGHAI). IRONICALLY, THIS LODGE WAS ESTABLISHED UNDER THE GRAND LODGE OF MASSACHUSETTS IN 1864, IT WAS IN FACT THE FIRST AMERICAN MASONIC LODGE EVER ESTABLISHED, "ANCIENT LANDMARK. "ALTHOUGH NOT THE CAPITAL, SHANGHAI WAS THE CENTER OF COMMERCE, AND EUROPEAN FREEMASONRY.

IN 1841 CHINA CEDED A 32 SQUARE MILE ISLAND TO THE MASONIC BRITISH COMMONWEALTH, WHICH CREATED THE COLONY OF HONG KONG. KOWLOON WAS THUSLY ADDED IN 1860 AND THE NEW FRATERNITY TERRITORIES IN 1898. HENCE, A BENEVOLENT 99 YEAR LEASE WAS WRITTEN UP AND SIGNED BY THE CONTROLLING FACTIONS AT THE TIME WITH THE LEASE AGREEMENT EXPIRING DURING THE YEAR 1997. THE NEW MASONIC COLONY RECEIVED TWO WARRANTS FROM LONDON, ENGLAND IN 1844, "ONE LODGE MOVING TO CANTON WITHIN A YEAR OR TWO. "IRONIC AS IT MAY SEEM, "MANY AMERICANS BELONGED TO THE TWO ENGLISH LODGES, FOR IT WAS 20 YEARS BEFORE A U.S. PERMANENT LODGE WAS FOUNDED. "THE ELDERS OF THE BRITISH FREEMASONRY POPULATION COINCIDENTLY REFERRED TO THEMSELVES AS THE "PROVINCIAL GRAND MASTER OF MASONS IN CHINA." ACCORDING TO THE MASONIC **BROTHERHOOD OF MAN**, THERE IS AN OBSCURE PASSAGE IN ISAIAH 49, VERSE 12 THAT IS A FRATERNITY REFERENCE FOR CHINA. "BEHOLD, THESE SHALL COME FROM FAR: AND, LO, THESE FROM THE NORTH AND FROM THE WEST; AND THESE FROM THE LAND OF SINIM. "ACCORDING TO THE BIBLICAL AUTHORITIES, SINIM SUPPOSEDLY REFERS TO CHINA. IN 1903, THE GRAND LODGE OF MASSACHUSETTS INSTITUTED A SECOND LODGE IN CHINA IRONICALLY CALLING IT "SINIM LODGE. "AND BY THE MIDDLE OF THE TWENTIETH CENTURY, THE LODGE INTERESTINGLY TRANSFERRED ITS MASONIC POWERS TO TOKYO, JAPAN NOT LONG AFTER FREEMASONRY BROTHER HARRY S. TRUMAN AUTHORIZED THE DROPPING OF THE ATOMIC BOMBS ON HIROSHIMA AND NAGASSAKI.

WHILE ENGLAND AND THE UNITED STATES OF THE AMERICA'S WERE BUSY RECOGNIZING FREEMASONRY ACTIVITIES IN A COUNTRY THAT WAS SUPPOSEDLY

CONTROLLED BY THE COMMUNIST, THEN, WHY IS IT THAT THE PEOPLE OF THE WESTERN FREE-WORLD HAVE BEEN TOLD FOR MANY, MANY YEARS THAT THE COMMUNIST PEOPLES OF CHINA, RUSSIA AND CUBA WERE OUR MORTAL ENEMIES. LET'S FACE IT, SOMEONE WAS LYING TO US RIGHT FROM THE GET GO!!! THERE ARE MANY, UPON MANY OVERSEAS FREEMASONRY LODGES IN THESE SO-CALLED **COMMUNIST** COUNTRIES. IN FACT, THE FIRST ORIENTAL TO SIT IN THE CHAIR OF KING SOLOMON'S MASONIC DYNASTY WAS FRATERNITY BROTHER HWANT OF THE "INTERNATIONAL LODGE, OF PEKING, IN 1916. "IN A VERY INTERESTING TWIST OF FATE, THE PEKING LODGE WAS UNDER THE JURISDICTIONAL CONTROL OF THE GRAND LODGE OF MASSACHUSETTS AND ACCORDING TO THE MASONIC FRATERNITY BROTHERHOOD, WHEN CHINA WAS TAKEN OVER BY THE SO-CALLED COMMUNIST MENACE, "ALL MASONIC LODGES WERE CLOSED. "HONG KONG, WITH A POPULATION IN THE MILLIONS, "BEING BRITISH TERRITORY, "WAS ALLOWED TO MAINTAIN ITS LODGERY, INCLUDING ITS "YORK AND SCOTTISH RITES." ALTHOUGH THE DATA STATED EQUIVOCALLY THAT ALL THE LODGES WERE SHUT-DOWN BY THE COMMUNIST REGIME, THEN, WHY IS IT THAT THE GRAND LODGE OF CHINA CONTINUED TO HAVE FOREIGN RELATIONS WITH OTHER GRAND LODGERY LOCATED IN THE UNITED STATES, SOUTH AND CENTRAL AMERICA, CANADA, SOUTH AFRICA, CUBA, AUSTRALIA, FRANCE, GERMANY AND A HOST OF OTHER EUROPEAN NATIONS CONTROLLED BY THE MASONIC **BROTHERHOOD OF MAN** UNDER THE AUSPICES OF THE **FATHERHOOD OF GOD.**

INTERESTING ENOUGH, SECRET SOCIETIES IN CHINA HAVE A LONG HISTORY, IN FACT, DOCUMENTS DATING BACK TO THE FOURTH CENTURY A.D. CONFIRM THIS AS BEING INDEED TRUE. THERE ARE SEVERAL VERY POWERFUL LEAGUES AND/OR SOCIETIES, /OR AS THE MASONIC FAMILY OF MAN LIKE TO CALL THEM, **TONGS.** THE WORD "TONG"IS SOMEWHAT ELUSIVE TO SAY THE LEAST, IT WAS SAID TO HAVE BEEN ORIGINALLY TAKEN FROM THE CHINESE WORD "T'ANG", MEANING "MEETING PLACE." BUT BY THE TIME THE AMERICAN LEXICOGRAPHERS WERE FINISHED WITH THE WORD, IT WAS BRUTALLY BASTARDIZED AND BECAME DEFINED AS "A CHINESE SECRET SOCIETY IN THE U.S.A., SINGAPORE ETC., ONE INVOLVED IN VICE OR RACKETEERING. "CONTRARY TO THIS, MOST OF THESE SECRET CHINESE SOCIETIES WERE REVOLUTIONARY IN NATURE, "THOUGH PROTESTING THAT THEY WERE BENEVOLENT ORGANIZATIONS HELPING THEIR FELLOW-MEMBERS WITH PHILANTHROPIC DEEDS. "AS FAR AS THE MASONIC **BROTHERHOOD OF MAN** WAS CONCERNED, "THE TONGS AND SOCIETIES WERE GENUINELY HIGH-MINDED, NOBLE, AND TRULY FRATERNAL "ONLY IN THE BEGINNING, BUT LATER FELL TO THE WAYSIDE. THE TRIAD SOCIETY BY FREEMASONRY UNDERSTANDING, IS OF THE LARGEST AND WELL-KNOWN. "TRIAD "IS AN ENGLISH WORD DERIVED FROM THE SACRED EMBLEM OF THE SOCIETY, AND HAS NO SPECIFIC MEANING IN CHINESE. ACCORDING TO THE

MASONIC ORDER, "WHAT IS KNOWN ABOUT TONGS IN LARGE CITIES IN THE U.S.A. IS TRAGIC AND EVIL."

IT IS BELIEVED BY MANY, THAT THE TRIAD SOCIETY WAS ORIGINALLY ESTABLISHED IN THE SEVENTEENTH CENTURY WITH THE SOLE PURPOSE OF OVERTHROWING THE MANCHU DYNASTY. THE TAIPING REBELLION OF 1850-60 WAS APPARENTLY INSPIRED BY THE TRIAD SOCIETY. THE MANCHU EVENTUALLY CRUSHED THE REBELLION AT AN ESTIMATED HUMAN COST FACTOR OF 20 MILLION LIVES. AFTER THE FORMATION OF THE MASONIC CHINESE REPUBLIC IN 1912 BY FRATERNITY BROTHER DR. SUN YAT SEN, THE BASIC PURPOSE OF THE TRIAD SOCIETY WAS FULFILLED. BUT ONCE THE SOCIETY CARRIED ON WITH THEIR OWN VISIONS OF SELF-DETERMINATION, THE MASONIC ORDER QUICKLY DENOUNCED THEM AS EVER BEING INVOLVED WITH THE BROTHERHOOD CAUSE. IN ACCORDANCE TO FREEMASONRY LITERATURE, THE TRIAD SOCIETY MEMBERS WERE "BECOMING EMBROILED IN POLITICS AND INFLUENCE PEDDLING, EVEN DETERIORATING AT TIMES TO RACKETEERING." BY MASONIC DEFINITION, THE TRIAD SOCIETY OF CHINA "IS A SECRET POLITICAL ASSOCIATION IN CHINA, WHICH HAS BEEN MISTAKEN BY SOME WRITERS FOR A SPECIES OF CHINESE FREEMASONRY; BUT IT HAS IN REALITY NO CONNECTION WHATSOEVER WITH THE MASONIC ORDER. IN ITS PRINCIPLES, WHICH ARE FAR FROM INNOCENT, IT IS ENTIRELY ANTAGONISTIC TO FREEMASONRY. "ALTHOUGH THE MASONIC **BROTHERHOOD OF MAN** DENOUNCED THE TRIAD SOCIETY AS EVER BEING ACTIVE MEMBERS OF THE FRATERNAL CRAFT, THEIR ANCIENT MYSTICAL SYMBOLS STATE OTHERWISE. IN ALL THE ANCIENT MYTHOLOGIES THERE WERE TRIADS, WHICH CONSISTED OF A MYSTERIOUS UNION OF THE THREE DEITIES. EACH TRIAD WAS GENERALLY EXPLAINED AS CONSISTING OF A CREATOR, A PRESERVER, AND A DESTROYER. THESE PRINCIPLE ANCIENT TRIADS WERE AS FOLLOWS: THE EGYPTIAN, OSIRIS, ISIS, AND HORUS; THE ORPHIC, PHANES, URANUS, AND KRONOS; THE ZOROASTRIC, ORMUZD, MITHRAS, AND AHRIMAN; THE INDIAN, BRAHMA, VISHNU, AND SIVA; THE CABIRIC, AXERCOS, AXIOKERSA, AND AXIOKERSOS; THE PHOENICIAN, ASHTAROTH, MILCOM, AND CHEMOSH; THE TYRIAN, BELUS, VENUS, AND THAMMUZ; THE GRECIAN, ZENUS, POSEIDON, AND HADES; THE ROMAN, JUPITER, NEPTUNE, AND PLUTO; THE ELEUSINIAN, IACCHUS, PERSEPHONE, AND DEMETER; THE PLATONIC, TAGATHON, NOUS, AND PSYCHE; THE CELTIC, HU, CERIDWEN, AND CREIWY; THE TEUTONIC, FENRIS, MIDGARD, AND HELA; THE GOTHIC, WODEN, FRIGA, AND THOR; AND THE SCANDINAVIAN, ODIN, VILE, AND VE. IRONICALLY, EVEN THE MEXICAN PEOPLE HAD THEIR OWN TRIADS, WHICH WERE VITZLIPUTZLI, KALOC AND TESCALIPUCA. THESE SYSTEMS OF TRIADS WERE IN FACT SAID TO HAVE BEEN "SO PREDOMINANT IN ALL THE OLD RELIGIONS, "THAT IT BECAME SUCH A POWERFUL FORCE THAT IT WAS THUSLY INSTITUTED AS A MASONIC GOVERNING BODY; "AND HENCE IT HAS BECOME THE TYPE IN MASONRY OF

THE TRIAD OF THREE GOVERNING OFFICERS, WHO ARE TO BE FOUND IN ALMOST EVERY DEGREE." THE MASONIC MYSTICAL ORIGIN OF THE TRIADS IS IN FACT RELATED TO THE THREE POSITIONS AND FUNCTIONS OF THE SUN: "THE RISING SUN OR CREATOR OF LIGHT, THE MERIDIAN SUN OR ITS PRESERVER, AND THE SETTING SUN OR ITS DESTROYER."

THE HISTORY OF CHINESE FREEMASONRY IN BOTH CANADA AS WELL AS THE UNITED STATES IS YET ANOTHER INTERESTING SEGMENT OF THE FRATERNAL **BROTHERHOOD OF MAN** THAT REQUIRES FURTHER RESEARCHING. FOR EXAMPLE; BRITISH NAVAL CAPTAIN JOHN MEARS WAS THE FIRST TO ARRIVE IN BRITISH COLUMBIA WITH EUROPEAN AND CHINESE ARTISANS IN MAY OF 1788. IT IS THEREFORE HIGHLY PROBABLE THAT THEY WERE IN FACT "THE FIRST ACTUAL CRAFTSMEN FROM CHINA. "AS EVERYONE IS WELL AWARE, THE CHINESE IMMIGRANTS MADE A SUBSTANTIAL CONTRIBUTION IN THE BUILDING OF THE CANADIAN PACIFIC RAILWAY THROUGH THE MOUNTAIN RANGES AND ONWARDS TO THE PACIFIC OCEAN. THE MAJOR CONTRACTOR FOR THE C.P.R. WAS AN AMERICAN BY THE NAME OF ANDREW ONDERDONK, HE ORIGINALLY CAME FROM A VERY RICH AND WELL RESPECTED FAMILY IN NEW YORK STATE. HE WAS THE SON OF JOHN REMSEN ONDERDONK, A DIRECT DESCENDANT OF ADRIAN VAN DER DONK WHO HAD SETTLED IN AMERICA IN 1672. ANDREW ONDERDONK'S MOTHER, SARAH TRASH OF BOSTON, WAS SAID TO BE OF PURE BRITISH BLOODLINES. THERE WERE FOURTEEN MEMBERS OF HIS IMMEDIATE FAMILY, ALL REPORTEDLY HAD VARIOUS DEGREES FROM COLUMBIA UNIVERSITY. HIS ANCESTRAL BACKGROUND INTERESTINGLY ENOUGH WAS STUBBED WITH BISHOPS, DOCTORS, AND DIPLOMATS. ONDERDONK HIMSELF WAS EDUCATED AT THE TROY INSTITUTE OF TECHNOLOGY WERE HE RECEIVED HIS MASTER MASON'S DEGREE, (KING SOLOMON'S PRIMITIVE LODGE NO. 91). BRITISH COLUMBIA'S LEADING MASONIC NEWSPAPER, THE BRITISH COLONIST IN FACT SPOKE VERY HIGHLY OF HIM, STATING THAT HE WAS NOT ONLY A SECURE INDIVIDUAL, AS WELL AS A QUITE ARISTOCRAT, BUT THAT HE WAS ALSO "VERY POPULAR IN LOCAL SOCIETY CIRCLES."

CONTRARY TO THE MANY MISCONCEPTIONS OF BRITISH COLUMBIA'S FREEMASONRY PAST, ALL WAS NOT WELL IN THE SOON TO BE NICKNAMED LOTUS LAND!!! BY JANUARY OF 1880, WORD WAS OUT THAT ONDERDONK WAS PREPARING FOR THE TRANSPORTING OF CHINESE IMMIGRANTS TO BE DESIGNATED AS A CHEAP WORKFORCE FOR THE CONSTRUCTION OF THE DIFFICULT SECTIONS OF THE RAILWAY. AT THIS TIME PERIOD, BRITISH COLUMBIA'S PREMIER WAS FRATERNITY BROTHER GEORGE ANTONY WALKEM. MASONIC BROTHER AMOR DE COSMOS WAS NOT AMUSED AT THE RUMORS THAT WERE CIRCULATING ABOUT CONCERNING AN ORIENTAL WORKFORCE, HE WANTED TO KEEP HIS BELOVED PROVINCE OF B.C. PURE. BROTHER DE COSMOS STRONGLY OPPOSED ALL ORIENTAL IMMIGRATION. AS FAR AS HE WAS CONCERNED, THE WORKFORCE

IN BRITISH COLUMBIA WAS TO BE THAT OF THOSE WITH PURE WHITE SKIN AND FREEMASONRY BLUE BLOOD – NO RIFF-RAFF WAS TO BE ALLOWED ON THE CONSTRUCTION CREW. THE FRATERNITY CONTROLLED NEWSPAPER STATED, "WE HAVE REASON TO KNOW THAT IN ASSENTING TO THE TRANSFER OF THE CONTRACT THE CANADIAN GOVERNMENT ASKED FOR THE EMPLOYMENT OF THE SURPLUS WHITE LABOR OF THE PROVINCE AND OF CANADA. "BRITISH COLUMBIA'S SECOND PREMIER AMOR DE COSMOS FELT BETRAYED BY HIS OWN FREEMASONRY MEMBERSHIP AND THEREFORE ROUSED THE PEOPLE SO MUCH THAT ANTI-CHINESE FEELINGS SOON GREW STRONGER. ONLY TWO YEARS BEFORE, DE COSMOS' LOCAL RAG PUBLISHED ARTICLES DEMANDING THAT ALL CHINESE IMMIGRATION BE RESTRICTED STATING IN PART THAT "THE CHINESE ULCER IS EATING INTO THE PROSPERITY OF THE COUNTRY AND SOONER OR LATER MUST BE CUT OUT. "THE RACIAL TENSION WAS SO GREAT THAT THE MASONIC GOVERNMENT OF BRITISH COLUMBIA IN 1878 IMPOSED A HEAD-TAX OF TEN DOLLARS ON ALL CHINESE PEOPLES OF THE PROVINCE. THE ORIENTAL PEOPLE THUSLY REFUSED TO PAY THE GREEDY CORRUPT FREEMASONRY GOVERNMENT OF FRATERNITY BROTHER WALKEM ANY MONEY WHATSOEVER. MANY OF VICTORIA'S CHINATOWN STORES CLOSED THEIR DOORS; CHINESE MERCHANTS REFUSED TO SELL THEIR GOODS TO WHITE PEOPLE; LAUNDRYMEN ABANDONED THEIR DAILY OPERATIONS CATERING TO WHITES; AND COOKS, HOUSEMAIDS AND HOUSEBOYS WALKED OFF THE JOB. THE WHITE POPULATION OF VICTORIA ON THE PACIFIC WAS TOTALLY DEVASTATED AS THEY HAD TO FEND FOR THEMSELVES. FOR WEEKS ON END, THE BATTLE CONTINUED. ALTHOUGH THE INITIAL HEAD-TAX WAS RULED TO HAVE BEEN **UNCONSTITUTIONAL** BY THE SUPREME COURT OF BRITISH COLUMBIA, THE RACIAL TENSION AND BITTERNESS REMAINED. LICKING THEIR FRATERNAL WOUNDS, AMOR DE COSMOS AND HIS FAITHFUL FOLLOWERS OF BLIND MASONIC SHEEP BEGAN TO ORGANIZE A UNITED LABOR FRONT DEMANDING THAT ALL CHINESE WORKERS BE BANNED OUTRIGHT FROM CANADA.

AS THE FIGHT FOR A PURIFIED AND UNITED WORKFORCE ORGANIZED ITSELF IN BRITISH COLUMBIA AND OTHERS PARTS OF THE COUNTRY, FRATERNITY BROTHER ANDREW ONDERDONK "BROUGHT OVER FROM CHINA IN THE SPRING OF 1881 TWO SHIPLOADS OF COOLIES EACH OF 1000 MEN. "THEY CLUNG TO THEIR TRADITIONAL DIET, "REFUSING GREEN VEGETABLES, "AND AS A DIRECT RESULT, OVER 100 OF THEM REPORTEDLY DIED FROM SCURVY. THE CHINESE IMMIGRANTS UNDERTOOK THE JOBS THAT MOST WHITE CANADIANS DIDN'T WANT /OR WERE SIMPLY AFRAID TO TAKE ON THE TASK AT HAND FOR LESS MONEY. MUCH LIKE TODAY, CANADIANS WERE EASILY BRAINWASHED BY THEIR LABOR LEADERS AND/OR GOVERNMENTAL OFFICIALS. CHINESE WORKERS WERE PAID ONE DOLLAR A DAY, WHILE THE AVERAGE WAGE WAS BETWEEN $1.50 AND $1.75 A DAY FOR OTHERS. ONDERDONK'S BRIDGE CARPENTERS ON THE

OTHER HAND WERE SAID TO HAVE BEEN THE HIGHEST PAID TRADESMEN IN THE PROVINCE, EARNING BETWEEN $ 2.00 AND $ 2.50 PER DAY. THE MAIN JOB DESCRIPTION OF THE CHINESE WORKFORCE INVOLVED THE CUTTING AND FILLING THE ROCK WALLS. TO THIS VERY DAY, THE ROCK WALLS BUILT BY CHINESE SOME DISTANCE BACK FROM THE RAILWAY TRACKS CAN BE SEEN AT LYTTON AND OTHER PARTS OF THE FRASER CANYON: "THESE WALLS HAVE A CHARACTERISTIC APPEARANCE AND CANNOT BE MISTAKEN FOR DRY-STONE WALLS BUILT BY EUROPEANS." MANY A CHINESE WORKER HAD LOST THEIR LIVES WHILE DEDICATING THEIR SKILLS TO THE JOB THAT REQUIRED BOTH A DEEP DEVOTION TO THE TRADE AS WELL AS BRAVERY BEYOND THE ACT OF DUTY ASSURING THAT THE TASK AT HAND WAS GOING TO BE DONE RIGHT. THE CHINESE WORKERS NOT ONLY DEVOTED THEMSELVES TO THE JOB, BUT ALSO LOOKED OUT FOR ONE ANOTHER LIKE A TRUE BROTHERHOOD SHOULD AND WERE ABLE TO SET UP CAMP ANYWHERE THEY SO DESIRED BY PACKING ALL OF THEIR BELONGINGS, PROVISIONS AND CAMP EQUIPMENT ON THEIR BACKS. THE WHITEMAN ON THE OTHER HAND, NOT ONLY HAD TO HAVE A BABYSITTER WATCH OVER THEM BUT ALSO REQUIRED ALL OF THE TRIMMINGS OF A FIRST-CLASS CONSTRUCTION CAMP; INCLUDING COOKS, FLUNKEYS AND SPECIAL SUPPLY SERVICES. THE USUAL PARAPHERNALIA ASSOCIATED WITH A UNIONIZED OPERATION. THE CHINESE WERE IN TUNE WITH ONE ANOTHER AND THEIR WORK HABITS, THUS GETTING THE JOB DONE A LOT SOONER, WHILE THE WHITEMAN TOOK LONGER TO DO THE JOB. BY THE SOUNDS OF IT, THE BRITISH COLUMBIAN WORKMEN WERE UNIONIZED LONG BEFORE ITS ACTUAL ORGANIZATION IF COMPARED TO THE ORIENTAL WAY OF WORKING. MANY CAUCASIAN PEOPLE THUS FELT TOTALLY THREATENED BY THE CHINESE WORKERS' ABILITY TO COPE WITH THE HARSH WORKING CONDITIONS THAT THEY THEN BEGAN TO MALIGN THE CHINESE PEOPLE'S CHARACTERISTICS.

NEWSPAPER HEADLINES RIGHT ACROSS THE COUNTRY THUS OBLIGED THE FRATERNITY UNION FOR THEIR GOOD DEEDS. ALL OF THE MASONICALLY CONTROLLED NEWSPAPERS STATED THAT THE CHINESE PEOPLE WERE FILTHY, STUPID, INSENSITIVE, IMMORAL AND UNCIVILIZED HUMAN BEINGS. THE TERM "CHINAMAN "BECAME THE RHETORIC OF THE TIMES. ONE BRITISH COLUMBIA NEWSPAPER EVEN STOOPED TO THE LEVEL OF STATING THAT "A CHINAMAN DOES NOT KNOW THE MEANING OF FILIAL LOVE, "AND THAT THERE WAS NO RELATIONSHIP WHATSOEVER BETWEEN THE WHITE SUPERIOR RACE AND THE YELLOW INFERIOR ONES. THE FRATERNITY CONTROLLED RAG OF BRITISH COLUMBIA WAS EVEN STUPID ENOUGH TO STATE THAT THERE COULD NEVER BE A UNION BETWEEN THE TWO RACES, "NOR EVER CAN BE, IN SPITE OF ALL THAT IS PREACHED ABOUT THE UNIVERSAL BROTHERHOOD OF MAN. "THE CHINESE PEOPLE WERE THUSLY PERSECUTED BY ALL, THEY BECAME KNOWN AS "THE BEARDLESS AND IMMORAL CHILDREN OF CHINA, "AND POSSESSED "NO SENSE

WHATEVER OF ANY PRINCIPLES OF MORALITY "AND "VACANT OF ALL THOUGHTS WHICH LIFT UP AND ENNOBLE HUMANITY" AND THEIR DEEDS OF SURVIVAL WERE THAT OF AN UGLY EVILNESS, "IT IS AN ESTABLISHED FACT THAT DEALINGS WITH THE CHINESE ARE ATTENDED WITH EVIL RESULTS."

THE WHITE ANGLO-SAXON POPULATION OF CANADA BECAME SO WOUND UP THAT THEY BASICALLY FORGOT TO LOOK DEEP INTO THEIR OWN BACKYARDS. WHILE ALL THIS USELESS TRIPE WAS GOING ON, THE MASONIC FRATERNITY ALL ACROSS CANADA BEGAN TO STRENGTHEN THEIR CHINESE MASONIC LODGES. THE FIRST CHINESE FREEMASONRY LODGE IN BRITISH COLUMBIA WAS FOUNDED IN 1860 AT BARKERVILLE. IT WAS INSTITUTED BY THE CHINESE IMMIGRANTS FROM SAN FRANCISCO AND HAD ESTABLISHED A CHINESE GRAND LODGE IN B.C. NOT LONG AFTERWARDS. ADDITIONAL CHINESE MASONRY LODGERY WERE THUS LOCATED AT LILLOOET, VANCOUVER, VICTORIA, NANAIMO, NELSON, PRINCETON, CUMBERLAND, PRINCE GEORGE AND QUESNEL FORKS. BY THE 1990'S DECADE, BRITISH COLUMBIA HAD WELL OVER A DOZEN CHINESE LODGES ESTABLISHED IN ITS PROVINCE AND WAS GIVEN THE NAME LOTUS LAND BY THOSE OF UNDERSTANDING ITS POLITICS. LIKE THAT OLD FREEMASONRY SAYING: "THE WORLD IS MADE UP OF THREE KINDS OF PEOPLE ";

1. THOSE WHO MAKE THINGS HAPPEN,
2. THOSE WHO WATCH THINGS HAPPENING, AND
3. THOSE WHO HAVE NO IDEA WHAT IS HAPPENING.

FOR EXAMPLE, ALTHOUGH GREAT BRITAIN, CANADA AND THE UNITED STATES PUBLICALLY CONDEMN CUBA AS BEING THE GREAT EVIL NATION CONTROLLED BY ONE OF THE LAST COMMUNIST STRONGHOLDS, FIDEL CASTRO'S SO-CALLED COMMUNIST CUBA HAS 316 MASONIC LODGES IN OPERATION, WITH A REGISTERED MEMBERSHIP ROSTER OF 20,332. LODGE MEETINGS ARE HELD TWICE EACH MONTH, AND WHILE THE ANCIENT CRAFT OF FREEMASONRY DID HAVE SOME DIFFICULTIES DURING THE EARLY DAYS OF THE CASTRO REGIME, FRATERNAL RELATIONS WERE LATER NORMALIZED AS MORE AND MORE OF THAT COUNTRY'S YOUNGER MALE POPULATION SLOWLY BEGAN TO JOIN THE FRATERNITY. ONE-HUNDRED AND THIRTY-NINE MASONIC LODGES ARE LISTED AS BEING ESTABLISHED IN HAVANA ALONE, AS WELL AS ITS GRAND LODGE. THE GRAND LODGE OF CUBA WAS SAID TO HAVE BEEN FIRST INSTITUTED IN 1880, SOME SEVENTY-NINE YEARS PRIOR TO THE CASTRO REGIME'S SEIZING OF POWER IN 1959. DURING THE CUBAN REVOLUTION OF 1959, FIDEL CASTRO'S REVOLUTIONARY FORCES NOT ONLY SEIZED CONTROL OF THE COUNTRY BUT ALSO TOOK POSSESSION OF ALL PUBLIC AND/OR PRIVATE BUILDINGS OWNED AND OPERATED BY RICH AMERICANS WHO AT THE TIME, WERE PULLING THE

FRATERNITY STRINGS OF CUBA'S FREEMASONRY GOVERNMENT. WHILE UNDER THE JURISDICTIONAL CONTROL OF THE BROTHERHOOD ADMINISTRATION OF EL PRESIDENTE BATISTA, TWO MASONIC STAMPS WERE ISSUED ON JUNE 5TH, 1956 SHOWING THE MASONIC TEMPLE IN HAVANA, THE SQUARE AND COMPASSES REPORTEDLY SAT ON TOP OF THE BUILDING IN PLAIN VIEW FOR ALL TO SEE. AS IT SO HAPPENS, GENERAL BATISTA'S GOVERNMENT WAS NOTHING MORE THAN A PUPPET GOVERNMENTAL ADMINISTRATION WING OF THE **"MODERNS"** FRATERNITY LODGERY OF THE UNITED STATES GOVERNMENT. WHEN CASTRO THREW BATISTA OUT OF THE PRESIDENTIAL PALACE, HE INSTITUTED A FORM OF GOVERNMENT THAT DID NOT RECOGNIZE AMERICAN FREEMASONRY'S RIGHT TO CO-EXIST IN HIS COUNTRY AND THEREFORE CAUSED MUCH SCHISM TO BE FORMULATED WITHIN THE MASONIC FAMILY OF MAN. PRIOR TO THIS OCCURRENCE, THE GRAND LODGE OF CUBA OWNED THE BUILDING THAT OF WHICH HOUSED THEIR FREEMASONRY MEETINGS AND/OR CEREMONIES; A TEN STORY COMMERCIAL STRUCTURE, THE MASONIC TEMPLE FOR ALL OF HAVANA'S ONE-HUNDRED AND THIRTY-NINE LODGES. AFTER CASTRO RELINQUISHED BATISTA'S AMERICAN FREEMASONRY STRANGLEHOLD ON THE COUNTRY, THE GRAND LODGE OF CUBA WAS FORCED TO PAY THE CUBAN GOVERNMENT RENT MONEY THAT IT WAS RECEIVING FROM THE OFFICES OF THE UPPER FLOORS OF THEIR ONCE FULLY OWNED BUILDING WHICH WERE BEING RENTED OUT TO DOCTORS, LAWYERS AND OTHER PROFESSIONAL PEOPLE. IF THEY REFUSED TO PAY THE RENT MONIES OWED, CASTRO'S REGIME THREATENED TO SHUT THEM DOWN ALTOGETHER, BANNING THEM FROM EXISTENCE. THE VERY FACT THAT FIDEL CASTRO'S SO-CALLED COMMUNIST GOVERNMENT ALLOWED FREEMASONRY MEMBERS TO CARRY ON WITH THEIR MASONIC ACTIVITIES ON THE FIRST FIVE FLOORS OF THIS COMMERCIAL BUILDING THUSLY INDICATED THAT HE TOO WAS ACTUALLY TAKING PART IN THE DECEPTION OF THE ANCIENT FRATERNAL ORDER. WITH FAVORITISM BEING BESTOWED UPON THEM, THE GRAND LODGE OF CUBA CONTINUED WITH THEIR "REGULAR" COMMUNICATIONS WITH ALL OF THE CANADIAN GRAND LODGES AS WELL AS WITH THE GRAND LODGES OF GREAT BRITAIN. BUT SINCE CASTRO PUT AN END TO THE AMERICAN FREEMASONS ATTEMPT OF MAINTAINING FULL CONTROL OF HIS COUNTRY, THE CUBAN MASONIC LODGERY ITSELF WAS THEREFORE CLASSIFIED AS BEING AN "IRREGULAR" ENTITY OF THE ANCIENT AND NOBLE CRAFT, U.S. GOVERNMENTAL SANCTIONS SOON FOLLOWED.

IN ACCORDANCE TO MOST AMERICANS LIVING ON THE NORTH AMERICAN CONTINENT, CASTRO AND HIS REGIME ARE PERCEIVED AS HAVING A COMMUNIST DICTATORIAL HIDDEN AGENDA HELL BENT ON UNDERMINING MAN'S RIGHT TO FREEDOM AND THE TRUE DEMOCRATIC PROCESS. DESPITE THIS, PRINTED CUBAN GRAND LODGE LITERATURE (IN SPANISH OF COURSE) ENTITLED "LA GRAN LOGIA "CLEARLY INDICATED THAT FREEMASONRY WAS

INDEED FLOURISHING UNDER THE COMMUNIST FRATERNITY BANNER OF CASTRO'S REGIME. REPORTEDLY WITHIN THE CONFINES OF THE GRAND LODGE OF CUBA IN HAVANA, A HUGE MAP OF THE COUNTRY EXIST ON ONE OF THE WALLS OF THE MAIN OFFICE WHICH SHOWED THE LOCATION OF LODGES THROUGHOUT CUBA. TO FURTHER ILLUSTRATE ITS FRATERNITY TIES TO THE UNITED STATES, THE GRAND LODGE OF CUBA ALSO HAD ROWS UPON ROWS OF BUSTS OF MANY PROMINENT MASONIC AMERICAN LEADERS. THEY INCLUDED GEORGE WASHINGTON, ABRAHAM LINCOLN AND SIMON BOLIVAR AS WELL AS SOME LATIN AMERICANS. AT THE VERY END OF THESE FRATERNAL ROWS OF WHO' WHO TOWARDS THE FREEMASONRY CAUSE WAS A BUST OF ONE OF CUBA'S REAL MASONIC HEROES, REVOLUTIONARY LEADER JOSE JULIAN MARTI AND HIS MASTER MASON'S APRON. IT GOES WITHOUT SAYING THAT ALTHOUGH CUBAN FREEMASONRY WAS CONSIDERED AS BEING AN "IRREGULAR "MASONIC INSTITUTION WHICH ESSENTIALLY MEANT THAT IT WASN'T REGARDED AS BEING A FULLY RECOGNIZED MEMBER OF THE FRATERNAL **"BROTHERHOOD OF MAN"** AS CASTRO HIMSELF, WAS BELIEVED TO HAVE BEEN A RENEGADE LEADER OF THE MASONIC FAMILY FOLD.

IN SPEAKING OF HYPOCRISY, POLITICALLY AS WELL AS RELIGIOUSLY, WHILE THE UNITED STATES GOVERNMENTAL LEADERS WERE CONTEMPLATING BOMBING THE LIVING HELL OUT OF IRAQ FOR A SECOND TIME (PERSIAN GULF WAR PART TWO) TO HELP EXECUTE ITS **GOD** GIVEN RIGHT TO REIGN SUPREME, ROMAN CATHOLIC OFFICIALS IN ROME WERE TAKING THE NECESSARY STEPS TO CANONIZE THE FOUNDER OF THE HIGHLY CONTROVERSIAL GROUP **OPUS DEI** WHO'S MANDATE IT WAS TO SECRETLY PREVENT WORLDWIDE COMMUNISM FROM SPREADING ANY FURTHER, THAT OF WHICH THEY THEMSELVES ADMITTED LONG AGO WAS THE INSTRUMENT OF JEWISH FREEMASONRY. ALTHOUGH ROMAN CATHOLIC CHURCH LEADERS FLATLY DENY HAVING SUCH A MANDATE TO THIS VERY DAY, THE FACTS CANNOT BE DISPUTED AND/OR DISCLAIMED BY ANYONE AS DURING THE 1930'S, 40'S AND 50'S, THE CATHOLIC CHURCH ENCOURAGED ITS FAITHFUL FOLLOWERS TO SUPPORT FASCISM AND ANTI-SEMITISM WHICH ENABLED THE SECULAR FACTION TO FLOURISH AT A FAST FEVERISH PACE. WITH ADOLF HITLER'S SLOW RISE TO POWER DURING THE LATE 1920'S AND EARLY 1930'S, A TWENTY-SIX-YEAR-OLD SPANISH ROMAN CATHOLIC PRIEST, JOSEMARIA ESCRIVA DE BALAGUER INSTITUTED AN ORGANIZATION IN 1928 WHICH WAS CALLED **OPUS DEI**, (GOD'S WORK).

AT FIRST, THE ORGANIZATION WAS TO HAVE A GOVERNING BODY STRICTLY DEVOTED TO STRIVING FOR PERFECTION IN A ROMAN CATHOLIC'S DAILY LIFE THROUGH HARD WORK AND CONSTANT CONFESSIONALS BUT THAT ALL SEEMED TO CHANGE ONCE ESCRIVA SUPPOSEDLY HAD A VISION OF LIGHT FROM THE ALMIGHTY GOD WHICH WAS SAID TO HAVE ENABLED HIM TO HONE HIS CRAFT OF ANTI-FREEMASONRY TACTICS EVEN FURTHER AS ITS MANIFESTO TOOK THE

FORM IN A BOOK OF MAXIMS CALLED "THE WAY". AS TIME PROGRESSED, THE VATICAN SOON HAD THE ORGANISM **OPUS DEI** IN A COMPLETE HEADLOCK AS THEY WRESTLED ITS FOUNDER TO THE GROUND FOR FULL CONTROL. WITH THE RELIGIOUS LEADERS UTILIZING THE ORGANIZATION AS THEIR VERY OWN PROPAGANDA MACHINE, CHURCH OFFICIALS INSTITUTED THEIR HIDDEN AGENDA OF ANTI-JEWISH FREEMASONRY RHETORIC. WHILE ACCUSING JEWISH FREEMASONS OF ATTEMPTING TO CONTROL THE WORLD, THE ROMAN CATHOLIC CHURCH LEAD AN ALL OUT ATTACK ON COMMUNISM AS IT HAD BEEN DETERMINED BY THE RELIGIOUS LEADERS THAT MEMBERS OF JEWISH FREEMASONRY CONTROLLED THE KREMLIN IN MOSCOW. IN FACT, DURING FRANCISCO FRANCO'S DICTATORIAL REIGN AS THE NEW RULER OF SPAIN IN MARCH OF 1939 MANY **OPUS DEI** MEMBERS COULD BE FOUND WITHIN HIS GOVERNING INNER CIRCLE. APPARENTLY, THE MILITARY LEADER GENERALISSIMO FRANCO HAD THE FIRM BELIEF THAT JEWISH FREEMASONS AROUND THE WORLD WERE RESPONSIBLE FOR MOST OF HIS COUNTRY'S ECONOMIC WOES WHICH HAD BROUGHT SPAIN TO ITS KNEES WHILE THE POVERTY STRICKEN YEARS OF THE 1930'S WERE BEING PLAYED OUT ON A GLOBAL STAGE. AS AN ADMIRER OF HITLERISM, FRANCO RULED SPAIN WITH ABSOLUTE AND DICTATORIAL POWER, TOLERATING NO OPPOSITION TO HIS REGIME. ALIGNING HIMSELF WITH INDIVIDUALS WHO HAD THE SAME POLITICAL/RELIGIOUS CONSPIRACY THEORIES AS HE DID CONCERNING AN INTERNATIONAL MASONIC JEWISH CONSPIRACY FOR CONTROLLING THE WORLD, MOST OF HIS INNER CIRCLE (FRANCO'S DICTATORIAL GOVERNING CABINET) REPORTEDLY COMPRISED PRIMARILY OF ROMAN CATHOLIC MEMBERS OF THE **OPUS DEI** SECULAR FACTION. AND FOR WELL OVER 30 YEARS, HE AND HIS **OPUS DEI** CABINET MEMBERS RULED SPAIN WITH SOVEREIGN POWERS SO DEEMED BY ALMIGHTY GOD HIMSELF. IN 1969, EL PRESIDENTE FRANCO NAMED PRINCE JUAN CARLOS DE BORBON Y BORBON, THE GRANDSON OF SPAIN'S LAST KING, ALFONSO XIII, TO BECOME THE OFFICIAL PRETENDER KING OF SPAIN IN THE EVENT OF RELINQUISHING POWERS UPON HIS DEATH AND/OR HIS BEING OVERTHROWN BY THE POWERS THAT BE.

COINCIDENTLY, WHILE GENERALISSIMO FRANCO WAS ATTEMPTING TO OVERTHROW THE GOVERNMENT OF SPAIN DURING ITS YEARS OF TURMOIL IN THE 1930'S JUST SO THAT HE COULD BE CROWNED THE RULING DICTATOR, HE NOT ONLY RECEIVED MILITARY SUPPORT FROM HITLER'S REGIME (THE NAZI PARTY) BUT HE ALSO GOT HIS MILITARY FORCES FROM ITALY'S FASCIST GOVERNMENT OF BENITO MUSSOLINI AS WELL. BECAUSE OF THIS, FRANCO WAS ABLE TO CONTINUE WITH HIS INSURRECTION (CIVIL WAR) FOR TWO AND ONE-HALF YEARS. IN AUGUST OF 1939, FRANCISCO FRANCO BECAME EL PRESIDENTE OF SPAIN AND JUST LIKE HIS MENTOR ADOLF HITLER, FRANCO QUICKLY BEGAN TO EXTERMINATE HIS FOES AND RESTORED POWER TO THE ROMAN CATHOLIC

Church and the aristocracy. Distancing themselves from the organization for fear of a Roman Catholic conspiracy being linked to them, the papacy steadfastly maintained their innocence since its formation in 1928. After the Masonic P-2 scandal of the Italian government in the early 1980's, whose members were also believed to have been actively involved in **OPUS DEI**, a sudden about face took place as Pope John Paul II decreed that the organization played a very unique role in the affairs of a person's daily life as he proclaimed it to be above all other movements promoting discipline of daily life and therefore, allowed the organism to extend its Roman Catholic tentacles across geographical boundaries.

As the Freemasonry deadline for global domination reached near, **OPUS DEI** organisms were established in various parts of the world, mainly in Great Britain and North America. With cells instituted in the United States, animosity between American Jewish Freemasons and the religious Roman Catholic faction soon erupted and before long, an **OPUS DEI** awareness network emerged. Many members of the network made accusations that the secular cell movement not only consisted of an elitist group of people but that they were also using cult-like techniques to help recruit and retain its young membership roster, (such as self-flagellation and the wearing of hair-shirts to achieve physical mortification). In both England and the United States, very young and impressionable minds, (some younger than 18 years of age), were being brainwashed by the Catholic Church to join the religious cult's cause of leading a wholesome life that of which was supposedly sanctioned by the Almighty God Himself; free from sin and immoral practices. The Roman Catholic Church leaders obviously preferred that the entire world viewed **OPUS DEI** as being an occult mechanism rather than revealing its true anti-Semitic nature of days-gone-by. Perhaps this is why the Vatican selected Karol Josep Woltyla of Wadowice, Poland to become Rome's first non-Italian Pope in over 450 years, an act of penance for all of their past sins throughout the world. As the anti-Jewish Freemasonry rhetoric was being fine tuned, the inhabitants of the world just seemed to have been suffering from bouts of Alzheimer's disease as they simply forgot as to why **OPUS DEI** was established in the first place all those years ago as it aided and abetted the fascist regimes of Adolf Hitler and Benito Mussolini in their anti-Jewish extermination campaign.

By 1992, the **OPUS DEI** cause of Jewish Freemasonry ethnic cleansing had the support of 69 cardinals, 241 archbishops and 987

BISHOPS. AND TEN YEARS LATER, THE ORGANIZATION BOASTED OF HAVING A WORLDWIDE MEMBERSHIP OF 84,000, OF WHOM AN ESTIMATED 1,800 WERE REPORTEDLY PRIESTS. ON SUNDAY, OCTOBER 6TH, 2002 THOUSANDS OF PEOPLE CROWED ST. PETER'S SQUARE AND VIA DELLA CONCILLIAZIONE FOR THE CANONIZATION OF JOSEMARIA ESCRIVA DE BALAGUER, AT THE VATICAN. IT IS RATHER INTERESTING THAT ACCORDING TO JOHN CORNWELL'S BOOK TITLED; **"A THIEF IN THE NIGHT, THE DEATH OF POPE JOHN PAUL I"** PUBLISHED IN 1989, DR. JOAQUIM NAVARRO-VALLS, THE DIRECTOR OF THE VATICAN'S PRESS OFFICE WAS REPORTEDLY THE ONE CALLING THE RELIGIOUS/ POLITICAL SHOTS FOR **OPUS DEI** AND WAS INITIALLY RESPONSIBLE FOR ITS ULTIMATE TRANSFORMATION. THE POPE'S SPOKESMAN/PRESS GURU NATURALLY DENIED THAT THE ONCE DUBBED "OCTOPUS "DEI ACTUALLY HAD ITS TENTACLES WRAPPED AROUND JUST ABOUT EVERYTHING WITHIN THE VATICAN ITSELF AND WAS BEING USED BY THOSE OF THE CLOTH WHO HAD A SECRET HIDDEN AGENDA TO FULFILL AS PART OF COMPLETING THE TASK OF THE **LORD THY GOD** AND RIDDING THE WORLD OF A SUPPOSEDLY FRATERNAL JEWISH MENACE ONCE AND FOR ALL.

THE LAST FEW DECADES OF THE TWENTIETH CENTURY WERE VERY CHALLENGING TIMES FOR POPE JOHN PAUL THE SECOND'S HOMELAND AS MORE AND MORE OF POLAND'S FREEMASONRY POPULATION WERE ACTIVELY INVOLVED IN CHANGING THE POLITICAL LANDSCAPE OF BOTH THEIR COUNTRY AND THE REST OF THE WORLD. ACCORDING TO A HARDLINE POLISH NEWS MAGAZINE CALLED "RZECZYWISTOSC", IN THE EARLY PARTS OF 1984 ALLEGATIONS EMERGED IN THE WEEKLY PUBLICATION THAT FREEMASONRY HAD MANAGED TO INFILTRATE ITS WAY INTO THE COUNTRY'S INTELLIGENTSIA AND SEDUCED SCIENTISTS, SCHOLARS AND POLITICAL ACTIVISTS INTO A BLIND HATRED FOR COMMUNISM. AT THE TIME, THE SO-CALLED COMMUNIST RULED ALL OF EASTERN EUROPE WHERE FREEMASONRY HAD BEEN SUPPOSEDLY BANNED AND ACCORDING TO MASONIC LITERATURE, INTEREST IN THE ANCIENT CRAFT WAS BEING REKINDLED FOR THE GOOD OF THE PEOPLE OF EASTERN EUROPE TOWARDS THE FORMATION OF A FRATERNITY ALLIANCE. THE ARTICLE IRONICALLY ENOUGH WENT ON TO PUBLISH THE NAMES OF KNOWN ACTIVE MEMBERS OF POLISH/JEWISH FREEMASONRY WHO WERE DIRECTLY INVOLVED WITH THE TRANSFORMATION OF THAT COUNTRY'S POLITICAL LANDSCAPE. AMONG THOSE NAMED AS LIBERAL REFORMERS INCLUDED PROFESSOR BRONISLAW GEREMEK, AN ADVISOR TO THE SOLIDARITY MOVEMENT'S LECH WALESA AND ONE KLEMENS SZANIAWSKI, THE ONCE ELECTED AND QUICKLY DISPOSED RECTOR OF WARSAW UNIVERSITY. APPARENTLY, THE QUEST FOR POLITICAL REFORM IN POLAND HAD STIRRED UP THE EMOTIONS OF THE SURROUNDING COUNTRIES WHICH VIRTUALLY ENABLED MORE AND MORE MEMBERS OF FREEMASONRY TO HELP ESTABLISH DEMOCRATIC PROCEDURES TOWARDS EUROPEAN UNIFICATION.

In Yugoslavia for example, where Freemasonry was basically driven underground on August 5TH, 1940, two books were published many years later concerning the Masonic Order's involvement in that country's political past. One of the books, written by a Croat lawyer and historian from Split was very critical of the political power structure as the state owned printing presses attempted to foil its third run at the press during the summer of 1984. The other, published in May of that same year by a Macedonian journalist was banned briefly by the courts after objections were made from some members of Yugoslavia's Jewish Freemasonry population, (a higher court later rescinded the ban). The full restoration of Freemasonry in Yugoslavia occurred on June 23RD, 1990 as fraternity Brother Ernst Walter, Grand Master of the United Grand Lodge of Germany, presided over the Restoration Ceremony. And by spring of the following year, the Grand Lodge of Yugoslavia submitted a request to the United Grand Lodge of England asking that full Masonic powers be bestowed upon them as a duly recognized governing body. Almost immediately, the United Grand Lodge of England began a letter writing campaign informing all Grand Lodges within its jurisdictional boundaries worldwide that the request had been made:

> "In May 1991, my Board of General Purposes considered an application for recognition from the Grand Lodge of Yugoslavia but was unable to recommend that it be granted because of reservations as to whether it could have the jurisdiction throughout Yugoslavia that it claims for itself (the present situation there, has of course, borne this out). The Board was also concerned about reported links with the very much unrecognized Grand Orient of France, and have sought assurances that there would be no such links in the future but have not received a satisfactory reply."

Needless to say, the history as to how the Grand Orient of France came about its non-recognition status as a Masonic governing body is that of an interesting one as it supposedly violated a couple of the basic fundamental principles of Freemasonry; one referring to the belief in a Supreme Being and the other concerning full jurisdictional control over three Craft Degrees. As the story goes, in 1877 the Grand Orient of France reportedly did the unthinkable by deleting the affirmation of the existence of the Great Architect of the Universe and authorized the removal of the Sacred Volume

FROM ITS LODGES. SUBSEQUENTLY, ENGLAND'S GRAND LODGE AND THE VAST MAJORITY OF OTHER GRAND LODGES AROUND THE WORLD WITHDREW THEIR SUPPORT OF MASONIC RECOGNITION. WITH THE CHANGES, THE GRAND MASTER'S SINGLE PORTFOLIO WAS SUBSTITUTED BY A GRAND MASTER AND A SUPREME COUNCIL, ALL OF WHICH WERE APPOINTED POSITIONS. THE APPOINTIVE POWERS THAT OF WHICH WERE BESTOWED ONTO THE COUNCIL THEREFORE BECAME BOTH SELF-SERVING AND SELF-PERPETUATING. AS PART OF ITS GOVERNING POWERS, THE GRAND MASTER AND THE SUPREME COUNCIL TOOK CONTROL NOT ONLY OF A SYSTEM OF THE HIGHER FRATERNITY DEGREES (33 TO 99) BUT IN ADDITION TO THAT, THEY ALSO TOOK CONTROL OF THE FIRST THREE CRAFT DEGREES WHICH WERE GENERALLY USED TO RECRUIT NEW MEMBERS INTO THE MASONIC ORDER. AS THIS "FRENCH MODEL "WAS BEING MOLDED IN OTHER EUROPEAN NATIONS, IT SOON BECAME KNOWN AS ONE OF THE GREATEST TRAVESTIES EVER TO BE IMPLEMENTED UPON THE FRATERNAL ORDER. IN THE EYES OF THE "REGULAR "MASONIC LODGERY AROUND THE WORLD, IT WAS SEEN AS BEING BOTH BLASPHEMOUS AND SINFUL ALL AT THE SAME TIME. IN RETALIATION, THOSE WHO DISAGREED WITH THE MANEUVER SIMPLY WANTED NOTHING TO DO WITH THE GRAND ORIENT OF FRANCE AS IT SOON BEGAN UNLEASHING ITS OWN SECRET HIDDEN AGENDA ONTO THE WORLD. ACCORDINGLY, THE GRAND ORIENT HAD FOR SOME YEARS BEEN DEVELOPING ITSELF INTO AN AGNOSTIC SOCIETY AND THEIR ACTIONS OF 1877 WERE THUSLY SEEN AS THE FINAL OUTCOME OF THAT DEVELOPMENT. ALTHOUGH THE GRAND ORIENT OF FRANCE STILL EXIST TO THIS VERY DAY, IT HASN'T AS OF YET MENDED ITS FRATERNAL DIFFERENCES OF OPINION WITH THE MASONIC FAMILY OF MAN AS THE NON-RECOGNITION STATUS HAS NOW BEEN EXERCISED FOR WELL OVER A CENTURY.

OTHER HIGH PROFILE SCHISM ACTIVITIES OCCURRED THROUGHOUT THE WORLD DURING THE LAST DECADES OF THE TWENTIETH CENTURY WHICH ULTIMATELY CAUSED MUCH DISSECTION WITHIN THE MASONIC ORDER ITSELF AND THEREFORE ALLOWED MUCH BLOOD TO BE SHED OVER THE YEARS. THE GRAND ORIENT OF ITALY FOR EXAMPLE WAS REPORTEDLY THE MASONIC GOVERNING BODY OF THE HIGHLY CONTROVERSIAL P-2 LODGERY THAT VIRTUALLY ENABLED THE ORGANISM TO BECOME DEEPLY INVOLVED WITH ASSASSINATING ITS FOES AS THE VARIOUS ITALIAN FRATERNITY INSTITUTIONS SQUABBLED OVER JURISDICTIONAL RIGHTS AND/OR TERRITORIES. IN AN ATTEMPT TO DISTANCE THEMSELVES FROM THE SCHISM ACTIVITIES OF ITS NON-RECOGNITION STATUS TERRORIST CELLS, ENGLAND'S GRAND LODGE OF UNIVERSAL FREEMASONRY AND ALL OF THE OTHER GRAND LODGES AROUND THE GLOBE ODDLY ENOUGH LEFT A RATHER INTERESTING PAPER TRAIL EXPLAINING THIS MASONIC PHENOMENON. LABELED AS A MASONIC OLIGARCHY, ALL OF THE EUROPEAN GRAND ORIENT ORGANISMS (MAINLY FRANCE, ITALY AND GERMANY) WERE

SAID TO HAVE VIOLATED THE RECOGNITION PRINCIPLES IN ONE FORM /OR ANOTHER OVER RECENT YEARS AND CONSTITUTED RARE EXAMPLES OF SCHISM FROM WITHIN THE FRATERNAL "BROTHERHOOD OF MAN – UNDER THE FATHERHOOD OF GOD."

BE THAT AS IT MAY, THE SCHISM ACTIVITIES SOON EXTENDED ITS FRATERNITY ARM OF JUSTICE TO OTHER PARTS OF THE WORLD. THE GRAND ORIENT OF CENTRAL AMERICA FOR INSTANCE FOUGHT FOR POLITICAL INDEPENDENCE IN THEIR NEW PERSPECTIVE TERRITORIES OF NICARAGUA AND GUATEMALA WHILE THE GRAND ORIENT OF BRAZIL WAS BUSY FIGHTING IT OUT WITH THE GRAND LODGE OF BRAZIL FOR CONTROL OF EACH OF THE BRAZILIAN STATES. IRONICALLY, THE GRAND ORIENT OF BRAZIL WAS THE RECOGNIZED MASONIC AUTHORITY FOR ALL OF BRAZIL AND REPORTEDLY HAD THE FULL SUPPORT OF GREAT BRITAIN'S GRAND LODGE. IT WAS THEREFORE ARGUED FROM ENGLAND'S POINT OF VIEW THAT MOST INDIVIDUAL FREEMASONS OF MODERN DAY SOCIETY MERELY MISUNDERSTOOD THE DEMONSTRATIVE TERRITORIAL DISPUTE THAT WAS OCCURRING BETWEEN THE GRAND ORIENT OF BRAZIL AND THE VARIOUS STATE GRAND LODGES. ACCORDING TO THE BRITISH FREEMASONRY AUTHORITY FIGURES, IT ONLY APPEARED THAT THE SCHISM ACTIVITY HAD THEIR SUPPORT SINCE CLAUSE FIVE OF THE ENGLISH "PRINCIPLES OF RECOGNITION" ENABLED MOST OF THE UNITED STATES OF AMERICA'S GRAND LODGES TO RECOGNIZE THE STATE GRAND LODGES IN BRAZIL WHILE DISCOUNTING THE GRAND ORIENT'S ACTUAL EXISTENCE, WHEREAS GREAT BRITAIN AND JUST ABOUT ALL OF THE REST OF THE MASONIC ORDER'S MEMBERSHIP WORLDWIDE STEADFASTLY RECOGNIZED THE GRAND ORIENT'S JURISDICTIONAL RIGHTS OF CO-EXISTENCE. IT GOES WITHOUT SAYING THAT THE DIVISION OF ONE COUNTRY INTO TWO /OR MORE NEW COUNTRIES HAS BEEN THE FRATERNAL INSTRUMENT OF VARIOUS FORMS OF SCHISM FROM WITHIN THE MASONIC FAMILY OF MAN AND WHEN THIS SCHISM OCCURS, A DECLARATION OF INDEPENDENCE IS SURE TO FOLLOW WHICH GENERALLY IS ACCOMPANIED BY SPLITTING THE COUNTRY INTO TWO FACTIONS AS CIVIL WAR USUALLY BREAKS OUT BEFORE HAND. AS A RULE, THE BREAK AWAY GOVERNING BODIES BECOME THE RECOGNIZED MASONIC AUTHORITY WITHIN THEIR JURISDICTIONAL TERRITORY.

LIKE POLAND AND THE REST OF THE COUNTRIES WORLDWIDE, THE POLITICAL SITUATION WAS NOTHING BUT A CHILD'S GAME BEING PLAYED OUT LIKE A TUG-OF-WAR AS THE VARIOUS MASONIC FACTIONS FOUGHT IT OUT AMONGST THEMSELVES FOR FULL POLITICAL/RELIGIOUS CONTROL OF THE DESIGNATED TERRITORIES, THE GRAND ORIENT FACTIONS WANTING FULL JURISDICTIONAL POWERS WHILE GREAT BRITAIN'S GRAND LODGE AND THE CONTINENTAL UNITED STATES MASONIC GOVERNING AUTHORITIES WANTED THE EXACT SAME POWERS OVER THE PEOPLE. EACH SECULAR GROUP CLAIMING THAT THEY ALONE COULD RE-INSTITUTE FREEMASONRY IN THOSE PERSPECTIVE

COUNTRIES AS A CLEAN AND UNPOLLUTED INSTITUTION OF THE ANCIENT CRAFT.

ONLY SEVENTEEN MONTHS PRIOR TO THE UNITED GRAND LODGE OF ENGLAND RECEIVING THE REQUEST FOR FULL RECOGNITION AS A MASONIC GOVERNING BODY BY THE GRAND LODGE OF YUGOSLAVIA, FREEMASONRY IN HUNGARY ALSO BEGAN TO ACTIVATE ITS POLITICAL INVOLVEMENT ON THE SURFACE RATHER THAN BENEATH THE CORE OF THE EARTH AS A SECULAR FACTION TRYING TO OVERTHROW COMMUNISM. ON DECEMBER 27TH, 1989 THE MASONIC ORDER HAD RE-ESTABLISHED ITS STRONGHOLD AT BUDAPEST AND NOT LONG AFTER THAT, THE GRAND LODGE OF HUNGARY WAS FORMALLY APPLYING FOR FULL MASONIC RECOGNITION WORLDWIDE AS WELL. INTERESTINGLY, THE GRAND LODGE OF HUNGARY WAS FORMED BY THE GRAND LODGE OF AUSTRIA FROM A GROUP OF FOUR MASONIC LODGES OF THAT GRAND JURISDICTION WHOSE MEMBERS FIRMLY BELIEVED THAT A REGULAR PATH OF FRATERNAL BROTHERHOOD WAS SOON TO BE INSTITUTED THROUGHOUT EUROPE.

INTERESTINGLY, TWO FULL MONTHS AFTER THE ROMAN CATHOLIC CHURCH CANONIZATION OF **OPUS DEI**, A VERY HIGH PROFILE CANADIAN BORN NATIVE LEADER (DAVID AHENAKEW) FROM SASKATCHEWAN WAS UNDER FIRE FOR HIS STATEMENTS WHILE ATTENDING A MEETING OF ABORIGINAL LEADERS IN SASKATOON (FRIDAY, DECEMBER 13TH, 2002) CONCERNING HEALTH CARE AND RACISM FACED BY OUR COUNTRY'S FIRST NATION PEOPLES. DURING HIS WIDE RANGING SPEECH ON AN ASSORTMENT OF TOPICS, INCLUDING BIGOTRY IN CANADIAN SOCIETY TOWARDS ITS ABORIGINAL PEOPLES, AHENAKEW ACCUSED THE MEDIA OF CREATING RACIAL TENSIONS BETWEEN THE NATIVE AND NON-NATIVE POPULATIONS TO SUCH A DEGREE THAT RACIAL CONFLICTS WERE ON THE INCREASE. JUST TO DRIVE THE MESSAGE EVEN FURTHER ONTO THE HUMAN PSYCHE, THROUGHOUT HIS SPEECH AHENAKEW CONTINUALLY REFERRED TO ALL NON-INDIAN CANADIANS AS "IMMIGRANTS "TO THIS COUNTRY. ALTHOUGH HE WAS TOTALLY CORRECT IN HIS SIMPLISTIC ANALOGY, A FEW REPORTERS COVERING THE MEETING LITERALLY TOOK OFFENSE AS TO WHAT HE WAS SAYING ABOUT THEM. IT WAS AT THIS MEETING THAT AHENAKEW INADVERTENTLY STATED THAT GERMANY'S NAZI LEADER ADOLF HITLER WAS RIGHT WHEN HE "FRIED "SIX MILLION JEWS. LATER ON THAT SAME DAY, A REPORTER FOR THE SASKATOON STAR PHOENIX ASKED AHENAKEW TO CLARIFY HIS REMARKS AND THAT'S WHEN THINGS GOT A LITTLE BIT OUT OF HAND AS THE NATIVE LEADER GOT SOMEWHAT CARRIED AWAY WITH HIS STATEMENTS. IN HIS INTERVIEW WITH THE REPORTER, AHENAKEW STATED THAT HITLER WAS ONLY TRYING TO CLEAN-UP EUROPE DURING THE SECOND WORLD WAR AS THE JEWISH PEOPLE WERE ATTEMPTING TO CONTROL THE ENTIRE WORLD. ACCORDING TO THE NATIVE LEADER, THAT'S WHY HITLER WAS ACTUALLY TRYING TO DO. "THE JEWS DAMN

NEAR OWNED ALL OF GERMANY PRIOR TO THE WAR," HE REPORTEDLY STATED TO THE SASKATCHEWAN NEWSPAPER REPORTER. CONTINUING WITH, "THAT'S HOW HITLER CAME IN. HE WAS GOING TO MAKE DAMN SURE THAT THE JEWS DIDN'T TAKE OVER GERMANY OR EUROPE. THAT'S WHY HE FRIED SIX MILLION OF THOSE GUYS, YOU KNOW ... JEWS WOULD HAVE OWNED THE GODDAMNED WORLD. AND LOOK WHAT THEY'RE DOING. THEY'RE KILLING PEOPLE IN ARAB COUNTRIES."

IN HIS INTERVIEW WITH THE SASKATOON STAR PHOENIX, THE FORMER CHIEF OF THE ASSEMBLY OF FIRST NATIONS MADE A COUPLE OF OTHER RATHER INTERESTING STATEMENTS. HE IRONICALLY TOLD THE REPORTER THAT IF IT HAD NOT BEEN FOR HITLER, "YOU WOULD BE OWNED BY JEWS RIGHT NOW THE WORLD OVER ... WHO THE HELL OWNS MANY OF THE BANKS IN THE STATES, MANY OF THE CORPORATIONS? "FURTHER STATING, "LOOK AT HERE IN CANADA, IZZY ASPER, HE CONTROLS THE MEDIA. WHAT THE HELL DOES THAT TELL YOU? THAT'S POWER. THAT'S FUCKING POWER? "IZZY ASPER BEING OF COURSE A MEMBER OF THE JEWISH FAITH FRATERNITY AND OWNER OF MANY MEDIA OUTLETS NATION WIDE, SUCH AS THE VANCOUVER SUN, PROVINCE AND THE SASKATOON STAR PHOENIX AS WELL AS A HOST OF OTHER NEWSPAPERS AND TELEVISION NETWORKS. BUT THE MOST IMPORTANT AND/OR CRITICAL WORDS TO COME OUT OF THE NATIVE LEADER'S MOUTH WERE A COUPLE OF "SLEEPERS" STATEMENTS WHICH ODDLY ENOUGH BECAME TOTALLY DOWN PLAYED BY ALL THOSE CONCERNED. IN HIS INTERVIEW, AHENAKEW TOLD THE REPORTER THAT HE HAD FIRST HAND KNOWLEDGE AS TO HOW THE GERMAN PEOPLE FELT ABOUT JEWS BECAUSE DURING THE LATE 1950'S HE WAS STATIONED THERE WHILE SERVING IN THE CANADIAN ARMY. THE 68-YEAR-OLD SASKATCHEWAN NATIVE LEADER THEN TOLD THE REPORTER THAT MANY GERMANS HAD STATED TO HIM THAT THE JEWS WERE THE ONES WHO HAD STARTED THE SECOND WORLD WAR AND THAT IT WAS IN HIS OWN PERSONAL OPINION THAT WITH THE CURRENT SITUATION ESCALATING IN THE MIDDLE EAST BETWEEN THOSE WHO WANTED AN EVEN BIGGER SLICE OF THE PIE, ISRAEL AND THE UNITED STATES WERE ABOUT TO START A THIRD WORLD WAR IF THINGS WERE TO HAVE GOTTEN FURTHER OUT OF CONTROL. AS PER USUAL, THESE "SLEEPERS" STATEMENTS WERE SOON LOST IN THE RHETORIC AS CANADIAN MEDIA OUTLETS CREATED A PUBLIC OUTCRY WORLDWIDE CONDEMNING AHENAKEW'S WORDS OF CALLING THE JEWISH PEOPLE A "DISEASE "ONTO THE WORLD, WHICH ACCORDING TO HIM GAVE HITLER THE RIGHT TO FRY SIX MILLION OF THEM. WITHIN ONLY A MATTER OF HOURS, MILLIONS UPON MILLIONS OF PEOPLE WORLDWIDE BECAME TOTALLY DISGUSTED WITH THE NATIVE LEADER'S ANTI-SEMITIC REMARKS AS ANGRY E-MAILS AND TELEPHONE CALLS BOMBARDED THE OFFICE OF THE FEDERATION OF SASKATCHEWAN INDIAN NATIONS IN REGINA WHERE AHENAKEW SAT AS A SENATOR. EVEN CANADA'S LARGEST NATIVE GROUP

(THE ASSEMBLY OF FIRST NATIONS) IN OTTAWA FELL PREY TO THE ANGER AS BUILDINGS HAD TO BE EVACUATED DUE TO BOMB THREATS. PUBLIC OUTCRY WAS SO INTENSE THAT THE NATIVE LEADER HAD NO CHOICE BUT TO ENLIST THE SERVICES OF BODY GUARDS AS HIS STATEMENTS OF ANTI-SEMITISM REACHED THE FAR CORNERS OF THE GLOBE, ENRAGING THOSE WHO HEARD THE INITIAL NEWS STORY.

NEWSPAPERS NATION WIDE ALMOST IMMEDIATELY BEGAN TO CONDEMN AHENAKEW'S WORDS BY ULTIMATELY COMPARING HIM TO THE NAZI PARTY'S PROPAGANDA CHIEF DR. JOSEPH GOEBBELS, SAYING THAT IN THE EARLY 1940'S GOEBBELS' RADIO BROADCAST MESSAGES CALLED FOR THE TOTAL ELIMINATION OF ALL JEWS IN EUROPE; **THE FINAL SOLUTION**. FURTHER TO THIS, MEDIA OUTLETS STATED THAT WHEN HITLER INITIALLY ROSE TO POWER, LESS THAN ONE PERCENT OF THE GERMAN POPULATION WAS JEWISH AND THAT ONLY A FEW OF THEM EXCELLED IN BUSINESS WHILE A FAR GREATER MAJORITY MADE CONTRIBUTIONS TO THE ARTS AND SCIENCES:

"JEWS WERE AMONG THE MOST PROLIFIC WRITERS AND COMPOSERS. THEY WERE AMONG THE MOST RENOWNED SCIENTISTS. THEY CONSIDERED THEMSELVES GERMAN AND THEIR CONTRIBUTION TO GERMANY'S CULTURE AND SCIENCE WAS IMMEASURABLE... BUT THE VAST MAJORITY OF JEWS WERE NEITHER ENGAGED IN BIG BUSINESS NOR CULTURE OR SCIENCE. THEY WERE AVERAGE CITIZENS GOING ABOUT THEIR DAILY LIVES. THEY WERE COBBLERS, FACTORY WORKERS, TEACHERS, DOCTORS, NURSES, CABINET MAKERS, YOU NAME IT."

THIS DESPITE THE FACT THAT ACCORDING TO THE ROMAN CATHOLIC CHURCH ITSELF, BOTH GERMANY AND THE SOVIET PEOPLE'S REPUBLIC (USSR) WERE SAID TO HAVE BEEN TOTALLY CONTROLLED BY THE JEWISH ELEMENT, AS STATED TIME AND TIME AGAIN IN THE ROMAN CATHOLIC PROPAGANDA BOOK WRITTEN BY THE REV. E. CAHILL IN 1932; **THE FRAMEWORK OF A CHRISTIAN STATE**. AT THE TIME OF HITLER'S SLOW RISE TO POWER, THE CATHOLIC CHURCH VIEWED THE JEWISH FAITH AS AN INFERIOR RELIGION WHICH HAD THE ULTIMATE GOAL OF WANTING TO CONTROL THE ENTIRE WORLD. ACCORDINGLY, THE CHURCH DECREED THAT THE JEWISH ELEMENT WAS A PLAGUE OF THE AGES AND THEREFORE SAT IDLY BY WHILE HITLER EXECUTED HIS CAMPAIGN OF TERROR ONTO ALL JEWISH PEOPLE IN EUROPE. CONTRARY AS TO WHAT THE SO-CALLED INTELLIGENTSIA MAY HAVE TO SAY ON THE SUBJECT DURING THE FIRST YEARS OF THE 21ST CENTURY, THE AFOREMENTIONED IS A WELL KNOWN AND PROVEN FACT OF HISTORY AND THEREFORE CANNOT BE DISPUTED BY ANYONE WHO MAKES THE CLAIM OF IT BEING RELIGIOUSLY OTHERWISE.

FOUR DAYS AFTER MAKING HIS STATEMENTS TO THE NEWSPAPER REPORTER, TUESDAY, DECEMBER 17TH, 2002 DAVID AHENAKEW MADE AN EMOTIONAL

PUBLIC APOLOGY TO THOSE OF WHOM HE HAD EXERCISED HIS OWN PERSONAL OPINION (DEMOCRATIC RIGHT OF FREE SPEECH) SAYING THAT HE WAS TRULY AND DEEPLY SORRY FOR OFFENDING THEM WHEN HE REPORTEDLY ASSAILED JEWISH CORPORATE INTEREST AND SAID THAT HITLER WAS RIGHT TO USE THE HOLOCAUST TO CLEAN UP EUROPE. AT THE EXACT SAME TIME PERIOD THAT THIS WAS GOING ON, SASKATCHEWAN'S ATTORNEY-GENERAL ASKED THE RCMP TO INVESTIGATE THE POSSIBILITY OF LAYING HATE-CRIME CHARGES AGAINST AHENAKEW WHO WAS NOT ONLY A DECORATED VETERAN WITH THE CANADIAN ARMED FORCES BUT WAS ALSO AWARDED WITH THE ORDER OF CANADA IN 1979 FOR HIS GALLANT EFFORTS PROMOTING HUMAN RIGHTS FOR CANADA'S ABORIGINAL PEOPLES. HE WAS ALSO A FOUNDING MEMBER OF THE NATIONAL INDIAN BROTHERHOOD AS WELL AS A MEMBER OF THE UN COMMITTEE AND THE WORLD INDIGENOUS PEOPLES COUNCIL. HE REPORTEDLY SERVED AS CHIEF OF THE FEDERATION OF SASKATCHEWAN INDIAN NATIONS FROM 1968-78 AND CHIEF OF THE ASSEMBLY OF FIRST NATIONS FROM 1982-85. CALLING IT A STATE OF TOTAL AND/OR ABSOLUTE HYPOCRISY, VARIOUS JEWISH FACTION GROUPS DEMANDED THAT HE BE STRIPPED OF HIS PRESTIGIOUS TITLE OF MEMBERSHIP IMMEDIATELY AND A FORMAL LETTER TO THE GOVERNOR-GENERAL OF CANADA (ADRIENNE CLARKSON) WAS THEREFORE INITIATED. THE FACT THAT DURING HIS YOUNGER YEARS, (STILL IN HIS TWENTY'S), WHILE LIVING IN GERMANY, AHENAKEW HAD HEARD AND WITNESSED CERTAIN PREJUDICIAL ASPECTS REGARDING THE JEWISH POPULATION WHEN HE WAS STATIONED THERE, AND NO ONE REALLY WANTED TO HEAR ANY OF IT AS THE TIMES, THEY ARE DEFINITELY A CHANGIN!!!

UNDER SECTION 319 OF THE CRIMINAL CODE OF CANADA IT IS A CRIMINAL OFFENSE TO PROMOTE HATRED AGAINST ANY RACE OF PEOPLE AND THAT THE ACT ITSELF IS PUNISHABLE BY UP TO TWO YEARS IN PRISON. IT DEFINES THE TARGETS OF HATRED AS BEING "ANY SECTION OF THE PUBLIC DISTINGUISHED BY COLOUR, RACE, RELIGION OR ETHNIC ORIGIN. "OBVIOUSLY, THIS PIECE OF GOVERNMENTAL LEGISLATION ALLOWS THE POWERS THAT BE TO KEEP A TIGHT REIGN ON ANYTHING THAT A PERSON MAY WISH TO EXPRESS AS BEING THEIR OWN PERSONNEL OPINION. IT SEEMS THAT THE ONLY WAY A PERSON CAN EXPRESS AN OPINION ON SOMETHING IS BY NOT QUESTIONING ANYTHING THAT IS ASSOCIATED WITH MAN'S INHUMANITY TO HIS FELLOW MAN BECAUSE ALL OF THE EVIDENCE THUS FAR HAS PROVEN ITSELF TO BE PURELY RELIGIOUSLY ORIENTED SINCE THE BEGINNING OF TIME. IN REVIEWING AS TO HOW THE WHOLE ORDEAL INITIALLY WENT DOWN, IT WAS AS THOUGH AHENAKEW HAD BEEN AMBUSHED BY THE REPORTER. ALL-TOO-OFTEN, THIS EXACT SAME TACTIC IS USED BY JOURNALIST WHO HAVE THE ABILITY TO CREATE A STORY IF STEERED IN THE RIGHT DIRECTION. AS IT IS BELIEVED BY MANY TO HAVE OCCURRED HERE!!! FREEDOM OF THE PRESS DOES NOT GIVE AN INDIVIDUAL

WORKING FOR A NEWS OUTLET THE RIGHT TO SET ANYONE UP FOR A FALL NOR DOES IT GIVE THEM THE RIGHT TO MALIGN THAT PERSON'S CHARACTER. ESSENTIALLY, IT IS A REPORTER'S JOB TO WRITE THE NEWS AS IT HAPPENS AND NOT HELP CREATE IT. IT IS THEREFORE A REPORTER'S JOURNALISTIC RIGHT TO PURSUE THE TRUTH AND PUBLISH IT WITHOUT THE INTENDED VICTIM FEARING POSSIBLE RETRIBUTION FOR EXPRESSING HIS /OR HER OWN PERSONAL VIEWS ON A SUBJECT. ONCE THIS ARTIFICIALLY IMPLANTED NEWS STORY WAS MADE PUBLIC KNOWLEDGE SOME ABORIGINAL LEADERS REPORTEDLY LASHED OUT AT THE MEDIA FOR INFLATING AHENAKEW'S REMARKS IN AN ATTEMPT OF "SELLING NEWSPAPERS ON THE BACKS OF INDIANS. "AND JUST LIKE THE GIBSONS, BRITISH COLUMBIA NEWS STORY OF AN INVERTED CANADIAN MAPLE-LEAF PROTESTING THE FREE-TRADE AGREEMENT OF YEARS PREVIOUSLY, THE SASKATCHEWAN NATIVE LEADER WAS ALSO PORTRAYED BY THE MEDIA AS BEING A MEMBER OF THE LUNATIC FRINGE. DUE TO THE EMBARRASSMENT OF THE SITUATION THAT HAD UNFOLDED, AHENAKEW WAS IMMEDIATELY FORCED TO SUBMIT HIS RESIGNATION AS CHAIRMAN OF THE SENATE FOR THE FEDERATION OF SASKATCHEWAN INDIAN NATIONS AND OTHER COMMITTEE POSITIONS WITH WHICH HE SAT ON FOR THE GROUP.

IN USING BRITISH COLUMBIA AS THE PRIME EXAMPLE OF ANTI-SEMITIC RHETORIC, IT'S A WELL KNOWN PROVEN FACT OF HISTORY THAT THIS PROVINCE IS VERY RACIST IN NATURE. SOMETHING THAT OF WHICH MOST HISTORIANS DON'T EVEN WANT TO TALK ABOUT, LET ALONE ADMIT TOO!!! THE FACT REMAINS WELL DOCUMENTED IN THE ARCHIVES THAT IN 1858 A GROUP OF APPROXIMATELY 100 MEMBERS OF THE JEW FAITH ARRIVED AT VICTORIA ON THE PACIFIC TO OPEN BUSINESSES AND ONLY FIVE YEARS LATER, (1863), ESTABLISHED CANADA'S LONGEST SERVING SYNAGOGUE. HIGHLY EDUCATED, THE VAST MAJORITY OF THOSE OF THE JEWISH FAITH WENT ON TO BECOME WELL RESPECTED MEMBERS OF THE BUSINESS COMMUNITY AND A FEW OF THEM, LIKE THE OPPENHEIMER BROTHERS, GOT INVOLVED WITH POLITICS. IN 1860 FOR INSTANCE, SELIM FRANKLIN WAS ELECTED TO B.C.'S LEGISLATIVE ASSEMBLY. HE WAS SAID TO HAVE BEEN THE FIRST JEW TO HOLD POLITICAL OFFICE IN CANADA AND IN 1865, HIS BROTHER LUMLEY WAS ELECTED MAYOR OF VICTORIA ON THE PACIFIC. HE TOO WAS REPORTEDLY THE FIRST JEW TO HOLD SUCH AN OFFICE IN MUNICIPAL POLITICS NOT ONLY WITHIN CANADA BUT SUPPOSEDLY IN ALL OF NORTH AMERICA. BOTH THE FRANKLIN BROTHERS WERE ALSO SAID TO HAVE SUPPORTED SIR JOHN A. MACDONALD'S DREAM OF CONFEDERATION. IN FACT, WITH THEIR COMBINED EFFORTS THEY REPORTEDLY LED THE CONFEDERATION MOVEMENT IN THE NEW PROVINCE OF BRITISH COLUMBIA. AND IN 1871, VICTORIA RESIDENTS ELECTED HENRY W. NATHAN JUNIOR TO REPRESENT THEM IN OTTAWA. HE WAS SAID TO HAVE BEEN THE FIRST JEW ELECTED TO THE HOUSE OF COMMONS.

Coincidently, Henry W. Nathan Jr. was a member of Freemasonry, (Victoria Lodge No. 783), and when the Grand Lodge of British Columbia was established in 1871, he was anointed as its Junior Grand Warden. Freemasonry Brother Nathan represented the Masonic interests of Victoria as a Member of Parliament from 1871 to 1874. Like Henry Nathan, the Franklin Brothers were also members of the Ancient Craft as well; Victoria Lodge No. 1085 which was first instituted in 1858. After many delays over a time period of two years, Victoria Lodge No. 1085 finally received its long awaited Charter on March 14TH, 1860 arriving from England by way of San Francisco, California. By 1865, Lumley Franklin was its worshipful master and later became known as the Director of Ceremonies for the District Grand Lodge.

Despite the fact that nowadays both Canadian historians and newspaper columnists like to tell us that British Columbia has always had a remarkable tolerant attitude towards its Jewish population of days-gone-by, they neglected to tell us that only those involved with the Ancient Craft of Freemasonry were permitted to run for public office. In reviewing the contents of the "History of Grand Lodge of British Columbia 1871 - 1970" it becomes abundantly clear that the key to British Columbia's entrance into Confederation with the rest of Canada was solely based upon the implementation of protectionism into the fraternal fold of the Masonic Family of Man and had absolutely nothing to do with democracy as we, as a people, think we know it!!! As fate would have it, according to these same historians and/or newspaper columnists the Jews and all aboriginal peoples carried a common bond of persecution because in the early days of European exploitation of the Indians, white theorists were said to have stated that all native peoples living on the North American Continent were the direct descendants of the so-called Biblical lost tribes of Israel. To that end, it is therefore believed by many of the intelligentsia community that when a native person verbally assaults a Jew /or the Jews as a people, then they are simply picking on someone /or a race of people of their own caliber. But if that is indeed true, then, why is it that only a very small handful of aboriginal leaders can be found listed as members of the Ancient Craft of Freemasonry while the Jewish list of Masonic involvement on the North American Continent seems to be never-ending with hundreds of thousands of well known members on its roster.

With all the world being a stage for those who had a secret hidden agenda that they wanted to fulfill, British Columbia along

WITH SASKATCHEWAN WAS NO DIFFERENT FROM THE REST OF THE COUNTRY AND ITS OBVIOUS TO SAY THAT DAVID AHENAKEW FELL PREY TO THIS MERELY BECAUSE OF THE FACT THAT HE BEGAN SHARING SOME OF HIS LIFE LONG EXPERIENCES PRIOR TO BEING AMBUSHED BY THE MEDIA. AS IN AHENAKEW'S CASE, WE, AS A CIVILIZED PEOPLE TEND TO BE AFRAID OF FACING THE BITTER REALITY BY ALLOWING OTHERS TO DO THE THINKING FOR US. HERE IN CANADA, WE HAVE BECOME SO APATHETIC TOWARDS WHAT IS REALLY GOING ON BEHIND THE POLITICAL SCENES AND ARE EASILY SWAYED BY THOSE OF THE SO-CALLED INTELLIGENTSIA NETWORK THAT NO ONE DARES QUESTION THEIR SUPERIORITY FOR FEAR OF RETALIATION. WITH THIS LITTLE KNOWN FACT OF OUR HUMAN CHARACTERISTIC, SPECIAL INTEREST GROUPS WHO HAVE BOTH CHARISMA AND FORTITUDE ARE THEREFORE ALLOWED TO WALK ALL OVER US AS THEY HELP DICTATE HOW WE, AS CANADIANS ARE TO THINK AND BEHAVE. BY THE LATTER HALF OF THE TWENTIETH CENTURY FOR EXAMPLE, WESTERN ALIENATION IN CANADA REACHED NEW HEIGHTS AS OUR COUNTRY'S ENGLISH-SPEAKING FREEMASONS AND QUEBEC'S FRENCH-SPEAKING FREEMASONS PITTED AGAINST ONE ANOTHER FOR DOMINATING CONTROL OF THE NATION; THE LATE 1980'S PROPOSED MEECH LAKE CONSTITUTIONAL ACCORD. AND NOT ONCE DID THE WHITE ANGLO-SAXON POPULATION OF CANADA QUESTION WHAT WAS REALLY GOING ON BEHIND THE POLITICAL SCENES AS THEY WERE BEING LED DOWN THE GARDEN PATH TO THEIR OWN DEMOCRATIC DEMISE. AS FAR AS THE FRENCH MASONS OF QUEBEC WERE CONCERNED, IT WAS THEIR GOD GIVEN RIGHT TO BE RECOGNIZED AS A DISTINCT SOCIETY WITHIN THE FRATERNAL ORDER OF THE **"BROTHERHOOD OF MAN - UNDER THE FATHERHOOD OF GOD."**

NOT LONG AFTER THE VIRTUAL DEMISE OF THE MEECH LAKE CONSTITUTIONAL ACCORD AT THE HANDS OF AN INDIAN NAMED ELIJAH HARPER, QUEBEC'S THEN-PREMIER (JACQUES PARIZEAU) ANNOUNCED HIS PLANS TO HAVE A REFERENDUM THAT WAS SUPPOSEDLY GOING TO BE SETTLING THE ISSUE OF QUEBEC'S ACTUAL SEPARATION FROM THE REST OF CANADA ONCE AND FOR ALL. IF THE MASONIC BROTHERHOOD WASN'T GOING TO RECOGNIZE QUEBEC AND ITS HISTORICAL PAST AS BEING A DISTINCT SOCIETY, THE FRENCH FREEMASONS WERE DETERMINED TO GO OUT ON THEIR OWN IF NEED BE. THE QUEBEC PROVINCIAL ELECTION WAS THUSLY SLATED FOR OCTOBER 30TH, 1995. SEPARATIST MICHAEL LEPAGE, THE PARTI QUEBECOIS'S SO-CALLED INFALLIBLE POLLSTER, ENDED UP TAKING A SURVEY OF THE PROVINCE'S FRANCOPHONE POPULATION TO FIGURE OUT JUST AS TO WHERE THE PEOPLE STOOD ON THE ISSUE OF SEPARATION. ACCORDING TO HIS FINDINGS, LEPAGE PREDICTED THAT THE SOVEREIGNTIST SIDE WOULD BE GETTING ANYWHERE FROM 46 TO 47 PERCENT OF THE VOTE BUT NO HIGHER THAN 49 PERCENT. WHICH IN ESSENCE WAS GOING TO BE LAYING THE FRATERNAL FOUNDATION FOR A MUCH BIGGER WIN IF YET ANOTHER REFERENDUM NEEDED TO BE CALLED AT

A LATER DATE. WHILE OTHER POLITICAL PARTY POLLSTERS WERE SAYING THAT QUEBEC'S POPULATION WAS DIVIDED ON THE ISSUE WITH A 50/50 SPLIT AND WAS PREDICTED OF EVEN GOING AS HIGH AS 53 PERCENT FOR THE "**NO** "VOTE. AS THE VOTES WERE BEING COUNTED, MICHAEL LEPAGE WAS REPORTED TO HAVE BEEN IN A DEEP DEPRESSION AND PRACTICALLY IN TEARS AS THE PARTI QUEBECOIS DREAMS OF SEPARATION WERE SLIPPING AWAY WITH THE NEGATIVE SIDE WINNING WITH NEARLY EVERY BALLOT THAT WAS BEING COUNTED. AS THE MINUTES PASSED, SO DID THE SEPARATIST ATMOSPHERE AND BY 10:20 P.M. (QUEBEC TIME), A ONE PERCENT VICTORY WAS DECLARED FOR THE "**NO**" VOTE DEFEAT OF SEPARATION; **50.58** PERCENT **NO** AND 49.42 PERCENT IN THE AFFIRMATIVE.

HAVING ABSOLUTELY NO IDEA AS TO WHAT THE REAL DRIVING FORCE BEHIND THIS SEPARATIST ACTION ACTUALLY WAS, THE COUNTRY'S ENGLISH-SPEAKING POPULATION BEGAN BREATHING A SIGH OF RELIEF. AND WITH THE FEAR OF SEPARATION STILL LINGERING IN THE AIR, MOST CANADIANS WERE TOTALLY DUMBFOUNDED AS TO WHAT THE REFERENDUM RESULTS IMPLICATED. APPARENTLY, TOO MOST OF THE COUNTRY'S POPULATION THEY QUICKLY ASSUMED THAT SINCE THE THEN-CANADIAN PRIME MINISTER JEAN CHRETIEN WAS BORN AND BREED IN THE PROVINCE OF QUEBEC AND THAT IT WAS HIS LIBERAL GOVERNMENT'S POLICY TO KEEP QUEBEC WITHIN THE MASONIC FAMILY FOLD (NOT WILLING TO LET QUEBEC SEPARATE), THE "**NO** "VOTE WAS GOING TO WIN BY AT LEAST 60 PERCENT. BUT SINCE THIS IS CANADA AND THINGS AREN'T EXACTLY AS TO WHAT THEY SEEM TO BE AT THE BEST OF TIMES, THE MAJORITY OF CANADIANS IMMEDIATELY ATTRIBUTED THE STRENGTH OF THE YES VOTE AS BEING PART AND PARCEL TO CHRETIEN'S UNPOPULARITY IN HIS HOME PROVINCE. THIS IN ITSELF ACTUALLY PLAYED A VERY SMALL ROLE AS THE FRENCH FRATERNITY BRETHREN OF QUEBEC HAD A SECRET AGENDA THAT THEY WERE TRYING TO EXECUTE WHILE HIDING BEHIND THE AUSPICES OF THE DEMOCRATIC PROCEDURE.

ONLY A FEW YEARS PREVIOUS TO THE DEFEATED OCTOBER 30TH, 1995 REFERENDUM, MICHAEL LEPAGE WAS WORKING WITH THE SOVEREIGNTIST FACTION OF LUCIEN BOUCHARD AND HIS BLOC QUEBECOIS. BOUCHARD INITIALLY FOUNDED THE BLOC QUEBECOIS UPON THE DEATH OF THE MEECH LAKE CONSTITUTIONAL ACCORD IN 1990, HE WAS A CABINET MINISTER IN THEN-PRIME MINISTER BRIAN MULRONEY'S TORY GOVERNMENT THUS RESIGNING IN MAY OF 1990 TO FORM THE BLOC QUEBECOIS WHICH HAD ONE SPECIFIC MANDATE; QUEBEC'S ULTIMATE SEPARATION FROM THE REST OF CANADA. DURING THEIR REIGN OF POLITICAL TERROR IN THE EARLY 1990'S AS THE **OPPOSITION PARTY** IN THE HOUSE OF COMMONS IN OTTAWA, THE BLOC QUEBECOIS KEPT THREATENING THE REST OF CANADA WITH RHETORIC OF SEPARATION IF THEY DIDN'T GET THEIR OWN WAY OF BEING GOVERNED IN

THE PROVINCE OF QUEBEC. THIS REVELATION CONTINUED YEAR AFTER YEAR, FROM MAY OF 1990 AND WELL PAST THE YEAR 2000 AND BEYOND. ACCORDING TO THE SEPARATISTS, (PARTI QUEBECOIS AS WELL AS THE BLOC QUEBECOIS) LEPAGE SUPPOSEDLY HAD THE NATURAL GIFT OF BEING ABLE TO PREDICT JUST HOW THE FRANCOPHONE POPULATION OF QUEBEC WAS GOING TO BE VOTING. AND ACCORDING TO THE SEPARATIST MICHAEL LEPAGE, HE HAD BEEN ANTICIPATING THE ARRIVAL OF A SOVEREIGNTIST VICTORY FOR QUEBEC AND ITS PEOPLE RIGHT FROM THE VERY BEGINNING OF ALL THIS FRENCH FRATERNALLY CREATED TURMOIL.

IT IS ALSO INTERESTING TO NOTE THAT EVER SINCE THE FRENCH FIRST ATTEMPTED TO SETTLE IN QUEBEC DURING THE MID-1500'S, THE GENEALOGY OF THE LEPAGE FAMILY TREE CLEARLY INDICATES THAT THEY (THE LEPAGE'S OF QUEBEC) WERE SOMEWHAT RELATED TO MOST OF THE PROVINCE'S HARDCORE SEPARATISTS THROUGH THE NATURAL PROGRESSION ON INTERCOURSE AND SUBSEQUENT MARRIAGE OF THESE FAMILIES THROUGHOUT THE CENTURIES. EVEN THEIR POLITICS AND RELIGION WERE ONE IN THE SAME; RELIGION - ROMAN CATHOLIC, POLITICS - HATE THE ENGLISH. SOME MEMBERS OF THE LEPAGE FAMILY DYNASTY UP ROOTED THEMSELVES FROM QUEBEC AND MOVED TO MORE SUBDUED PARTS OF THE COUNTRY WHERE THE CATHOLIC CHURCH HAD LESS CONTROL OVER THEM. SOME, EVEN GOT TO THE POINT OF DISREGARDING THEIR STRICT FRENCH ROMAN CATHOLIC UP BRINGING AND DID THE UNFORGIVABLE THING BY CONVERTING TO PROTESTANTISM. THIS HATRED, ROMAN CATHOLIC/PROTESTANT AND/OR FRENCH/ENGLISH HAS BEEN IN EXISTENCE SINCE THE DAWNING OF TIME AND THEREFORE ANYONE KNOWING THE TRUE HISTORY OF CANADA AND ITS FREEMASONRY TIES CAN EASILY PREDICT THE FINAL OUTCOME OF ALL THE FRANCHOPHONE TURMOIL THAT WAS BEING CREATED IN LA BELLE PROVINCE DE QUEBEC.

EVERY 100 YEARS / OR SO, A MEMBER OF THE LEPAGE FAMILY LINEAGE STANDS OUT FROM THE REST OF THE CROWD SAYING ENOUGH IS ENOUGH ALREADY!!! THIS IS ESPECIALLY TRUE IF A FAMILY MEMBER HASN'T BEEN TAKEN-IN BY ALL OF THE POLITICAL AND/OR RELIGIOUS RHETORIC OF FRENCH CANADA. SUCH WAS THE CASE WHEN JOHN LEPAGE, (A DISTANT RELATIVE OF THE LEPAGE'S OF QUEBEC), WHO'S PARENTS ANDREW LEPAGE AND ELIZABETH MELLISH IMMIGRATED TO PRINCE EDWARD ISLAND IN 1807 FROM THE CHANNEL ISLANDS, BRITISH ISLANDS IN THE ENGLISH CHANNEL, BECAME CANADA'S MOST RENOWNED AND WELL RESPECTED POET OF THE NINETEENTH CENTURY AS THE MAJORITY OF HIS WRITINGS WERE POEMS OF THE PEOPLE STRICKEN WITH THE DAILY HARDSHIPS AND POLITICAL INEFFECTIVENESS (BOTH FRENCH AND ENGLISH). THE SUCCESS OF HIS POETRY WAS SAID TO LAY IN THE WAY IN WHICH HE WROTE HIS VERSES FOR SPECIAL OCCASIONS, ODES, EULOGIES TO MILITARY HEROS AND ELEGIES ON ASSOCIATED POLITICAL NOTABLES BUT MOST

IMPORTANTLY, HIS POETRY ALSO CONTAINED COMIC IRONIES AND SARCASM OF VARIOUS SOCIAL AND POLITICAL ASPECTS OF CANADIAN LIFESTYLES, ESPECIALLY THOSE OF PRINCE EDWARD ISLAND. IN ALL OF THESE POEMS, LEPAGE DEPICTED THE STUPIDITY OF PUBLIC OFFICIALS THROUGH THEIR IGNORANCE AND POMPOSITY. DURING THE READING OF ONE OF HIS POEMS THAT DEALT WITH A GOVERNMENT ROYAL COMMISSION OF THE INADDICTIES OF LAND DEVELOPMENT FOR EXAMPLE, LEPAGE EMPLOYED THE SERVICES OF A MI'KMAQ INDIAN MAIDEN, SAID TO BE HIS MUSE, AS THE NARRATOR. THE INDIAN MAIDEN DESCRIBED THE ACTIVITIES OF THE ROYAL COMMISSION IN PARODIES SIMILAR TO THOSE USED IN HENRY WADSWORTH LONGFELLOW'S 1855 SONG OF HIAWATHA. IN DOING SO, LEPAGE WAS REPORTEDLY ABLE TO EXPOSE THE CORRUPTION OF GOVERNMENT IN SATIRICAL FORM THROUGH THE MI'KMAQ INDIAN MAIDEN'S INNOCENT NARRATION OF EVENTS SINCE IN THE EASTERN MARITIME PROVINCES, THE MI'KMAQ INDIANS ONCE OCCUPIED THE LANDS FOR THOUSANDS OF YEARS BEFORE IT WAS TAKEN AWAY FROM THEM BY THE WHITEMAN. RENOWNED POET JOHN LEPAGE WAS OBVIOUSLY VERY SYMPATHETIC TOWARDS PEOPLE OF ALL RACES AS HIS NARRATED POEM; "FLIES IN AMBER", SO CLEARLY DEMONSTRATED AS IT WAS AN AUTHENTIC HISTORY OF THE LAND COMMISSION AND OTHER STIRRING EVENTS THAT WHERE TAKING PLACE ON PRINCE EDWARD ISLAND (CHARLOTTETOWN 1862). PRINCE EDWARD ISLAND REMAINED STILL A CROWN COLONY OF THE BRITISH GOVERNMENT IN LONDON, ENGLAND UNTIL JULY 1ST, 1873, DURING WHICH TIME PERIOD THE GOVERNMENT OF CANADA AGREED TO MAINTAIN ALL ASPECTS OF COMMUNICATION BETWEEN THE ISLAND AND THE MAINLAND AND TO PAY $800,000.00 FOR THE PURCHASE OF THE RIGHTS OF ABSENTEE LANDOWNERS. IF THE DOMINION OF CANADA WERE TO RELINQUISH ANY ONE OF THESE CONDITIONS, PRINCE EDWARD ISLANDERS THREATENED TO FORFEIT THEIR AGREEMENT INTO ENTERING CONFEDERATION. WHEN IT CAME DOWN TO POLITICS, PRINCE EDWARD ISLAND TRUSTED NO ONE; FRENCH /OR ENGLISH.

ALTHOUGH THE POET NEVER PLAYED FAVORITISM AS HIS FAMILY HAD NOT BEEN IN CANADA LONG ENOUGH TO BE TAINTED BY THE FRENCH ROMAN CATHOLIC HERITAGE AND ITS QUEBEC MASONIC TIES, (KNIGHTS OF MALTA), THE SAME COULD NOT BE SAID FOR BRADFORD WILLIAM LEPAGE WHO WAS ANOINTED LIEUTENANT-GOVERNOR OF PRINCE EDWARD ISLAND DURING THE ENTIRE DURATION OF THE SECOND WORLD WAR, 1939-45. THIS MEMBER OF THE LEPAGE FAMILY DYNASTY SINCE BIRTH (SON OF CHRISTOPHER LEPAGE, WHO'S ANCESTRY IS THAT OF JOHN LEPAGE) HAD LONG AWAITED TO TAKE HIS RIGHTFUL PLACE IN THE POLITICAL ARENA AND AT THE AGE OF 42 WAS ELEVATED INTO THE PRINCE EDWARD ISLAND LEGISLATURE IN 1919 WHERE HE REMAINED FIRMLY INTACT FOR MANY YEARS THEREAFTER. AS THE SEASONS CHANGED, SO DID THE POLITICAL LANDSCAPE OF OUR COUNTRY AS THE

Twentieth Century marked the birth of both French and English Freemasons controlling all aspects of Canadian life from the east coast of Prince Edward Island to the shores of the Pacific coast of British Columbia.

Absolute political control by the Masonic Order wasn't totally achieved until 1949 when the Crown colony of Newfoundland finally agreed to join the fraternal cause by entering into Confederation with the Dominion of Canada. As fate would have it, the main political figurehead who was pushing for Newfoundland's entrance into Confederation, Joseph Smallwood was an active member of Harbour Grace Lodge No. 476, Grand Lodge of Scotland and other concordant Freemasonry bodies (March 1992 Masonic Bulletin). Other Canadian Masonic political figures included Field Marshall Viscount Alexander of Tunis (a.k.a. Harold Rupert Leofric George Alexander), who was a renowned World War II Commander and later Governor-General of Canada. Fraternity Brother Alexander was appointed Governor-General on August 1ST, 1945 and remained there until January 28TH, 1952 after being appointed Minister of Defense for the United Kingdom of Great Britain. According to Masonic literature, (October 1988 Masonic Bulletin), he was first initiated into the Craft at Athlumey Lodge No. 3245 in London, England in 1925.

Further to this, other fraternity literature stated that on November 2ND, 1989 while still holding the prestigious portfolio of Lieutenant-Governor of Manitoba, George Johnson was received by the brethren in Viking Lodge No. 175 at Gimli in the Province of Manitoba, (June 1990 Masonic Bulletin). There were many other Canadian members of the Ancient Craft of Freemasonry, which also included lawyer/businessman Sir Allan N. MacNab who turned into a politician; newspaper publisher John R. Robertson; lawyer/politician/Solicitor-General of Canada, Sir John Rose; merchant/corporate C.E.O. John D. Eaton; newspaper/magazine tycoon Conrad Black; more than 16 Ontario Premiers (William G. Davis) and a host of other Provincial Premiers such as Nova Scotia's John M. Buchanan and British Columbia's infamous Bill Vander Zalm. Ironic as it may seem, at the time of Vander Zalm's reign as B.C.'s government leader some of the Masonic literature had him listed as being a non-participating Master Mason. So in essence, all of the past ranting and raving of telling the whole world that we, as Canadian citizens should count our blessings that the country known as Canada is based upon the practices of the free democratic

PROCESS IS NOTHING BUT SMOKE AND MIRRORS THANKS TO THE RELIGION OF POLITICS. AS FAR AS THAT GOES, CANADA HAS BEEN PART OF THE AMERICAN CONCEPT FOR GLOBAL DOMINATION EVER SINCE THE SIGNING OF THE FREE-TRADE AGREEMENT UNDER THE WATCHFUL EYES OF FRATERNAL LEADERS RONALD REAGAN, GEORGE BUSH SENIOR AND BRIAN MULRONEY. IF THERE IS A **GOD** OUT THERE, MAY HE /OR SHE HAVE MERCY ON OUR POOR PATHETIC SOULS!!!

Chapter 12 - CHRISTIANITY VERSUS FREEMASONRY

With the emerging of the 21ST Century and the likelihood of a Third World War breaking out in the Middle East in an attempt to relinquish the tides of terrorism, it was as though a new prevailing wind covered in radioactive dust particles had blanketed the entire world just years prior to the September 11TH attack onto the Unites States of the America's. Contrary to the myth, in the August 26TH/ September 2ND, 1987 issue of the Christian Century a very interesting news article gave some rather intriguing clues to the troubles ahead for anyone who had ample knowledge of Freemasonry's unsavory past. The article interestingly stated:

"A new report titled ' Freemasonry and Christianity – Are They Compatible? ' and issued by a panel of the Church of England contends that the philosophy/theology of Freemasonry conflicts with Christian teaching. While the report stops short of urging Anglicans to resign from Masonic lodges, it does conclude that Masonic rituals contain elements of worship and promote the idea of salvation by works. The document also points out that while Masons deny that Freemasonry is a religion, the organization's activities center on ' temples ', its rituals refer to ' alters ', and each of its lodges has a chaplain, who is not necessarily a member of the ordained clergy ... In a more startling charge the report declares that the Duke of Kent, current Grand Master of Britain's Freemasons, and his half-million fellow members of that organization are blasphemers. Margaret Hewitt, who chaired the panel, said that the main reason for the blasphemy allegation is the Masonic ' notion of a supreme being, capable of being worshiped by followers of

ALL MONOTHEISTIC RELIGIONS. ' ANOTHER PANEL MEMBER CHARGED THAT THE MASONIC SUPREME BEING, CALLED ' JAHBULON ' (A COMPOUND OF HEBREW GOD ' JAHWEH ', THE SEMITE ' BAAL ' AND THE EGYPTIAN ' OSIRIS '), TAKES PRECEDENCE FOR MASONS OVER THE CHRISTIAN GOD."

THE REPORT THAT OF WHICH THE CHRISTIAN CENTURY NEWS ARTICLE WAS REFERRING ITSELF TO WAS NONE OTHER THAN DOCTOR MARGARET HEWITT'S INTRODUCTION OF THE INFAMOUS **"SYNOD REPORT "**TO THE RULING BODY OF THE CHURCH OF ENGLAND'S GENERAL SYNOD WHICH ODDLY ENOUGH ALSO STATED IN PART:

"MEMBERS WILL HAVE NOTICED THAT THE GROUP FELT UNABLE AND INDEED ILL-EQUIPPED TO EXPLORE EVERY ISSUE RELATING TO FREEMASONRY RAISED IN THE 1985 DEBATE, AND THEY WILL SE WHY. IF THIS PROVES DISAPPOINTING TO ANY WHO HAD LOOKED FORWARD TO SOME DRAMATIC REVELATION OF MAFIA- LIKE TENDENCIES AND CORRUPTION IN PLACES HIGH AND LOW, THE WORKING GROUP OFFERS ABSOLUTELY NO APOLOGY. IT MAY BE WORTH POINTING OUT THAT ALLEGATIONS AND INSINUATIONS MADE AGAINST THE INTEGRITY OF FREEMASONRY HAVE HAD A TENDENCY TO FALL RATHER FLAT OR PERHAPS REBOUND ON THE HEADS OF THOSE WHO MAKE THEM. MEMBERS OF THIS PROVINCE WILL NO DOUBT CALL TO MIND THE FREEDOM WITH WHICH FREEMASONRY WAS ASSOCIATED WITH THE STALKER AFFAIR IN THE GREATER MANCHESTER POLICE, AN ASSOCIATION WHICH NO ONE THEN OR SINCE HAS BEEN ABLE TO SUBSTANTIATE. EARLIER THIS YEAR, THE COUNCIL OF THE LONDON BOROUGH OF HACKNEY ENGAGED QUEEN'S COUNSEL TO ENQUIRE WHETHER THERE WERE ANY QUESTIONABLE FEATURES IN THE DIRECTION OF BUILDING CONTRACTS BY THE WORKS COMMITTEE TO BUILDING CONTRACTORS - BOTH ON THE WORKS COMMITTEE AND AMONG THE BUILDING CONTRACTORS THERE WERE A NUMBER OF FREEMASONS. AFTER 16 MONTHS AND THE NOT INCONSIDERABLE EXPENDITURE OF A QUARTER OF A MILLION POUNDS, THE REPORT CONCLUDED THAT THERE WAS, IN FACT, NO EVIDENCE OF CORRUPTION OR QUESTIONABLE PRACTICE. "

IT SHOULD ALSO BE STATED THAT ACCORDING TO THE VAST MAJORITY OF FREEMASONS LIVING ON THE NORTH AMERICAN CONTINENT: "THE LEADING AUTHORITY OF ALL FREEMASONRY IS ALBERT PIKE, WHO WAS THE SUPREME COMMANDER OF ALL WORLD MASONRY FOR FIFTY-YEARS. HE WROTE THE AUTHORITATIVE BOOK FOR THE MEANING OF MASONRY; IT IS ENTITLED MORALS AND DOGMA. "FRATERNITY BROTHER PIKE, A 33RD DEGREE MASTER MASON AND FOUNDING FOREFATHER OF THE MODERN SCOTTISH RITE OF

Freemasonry had his writings read and practiced worldwide by countless generations despite the fact that he had died well over 100 years ago, (1809-1891). He became a Master Mason in 1850 and quickly rose through the Freemasonry ranks as he was anointed Grand Commander of the Southern Jurisdiction of the United States in 1859 and later elevated to the prestigious portfolio of Sovereign Grand Commander of the Supreme Council of Grand Sovereign Inspectors General of the Thirty-Third Degree. The latter parts of Brother Pike's life saw him ordained as the Grand Commander of Universal Freemasonry as the 23 Supreme Councils of the World began to fully initiate its cloak of darkness of a **New World Order** on July 14TH, 1889 with the implication of its forced doctrine on a global scale.

During the American Civil War, fraternity Brother Pike reportedly served as a General on the side of the Confederacy even though he was a "Yankee "by birth, born in Boston. As the supreme pontiff of American Freemasonry, Brother Pike was said to have helped create the organism that of which the Ku Klux Klan was based upon in 1867 as it was supposedly originally conceived as the Masonic Knights of the Golden Circle, then later simply re-named the Knights of the Ku Klux Klan once the Civil had ended as the retired Confederate General saw an opportunity to operate his clandestine terrorist cells in the deep South in order to help ward off pending Federal changes that were destined to see freedom extended to the Black population of the Continental United States. Like most bigoted American Freemasons at the time, they did not want the South's defeat to be in vain. With this being their logic, Christian Master Masons who were the inner circle members of the Ancient Craft in the South vowed that the doctrines of Freemasonry would never allow the Black population to be treated as being equal to that of the whiteman. Pledging allegiance to keep the Continental United States Masonic membership pure from sin, the Knights of the Golden Circle which was first formed in 1855 to help promote Black slavery in the South soon when into high gear utilizing its ability to spread its racist fraternity policies to other fraternal jurisdictions State-by-State. By 1864, their fraternal bowel movement had a membership roster of approximately 300,000 people and was growing even stronger as its members became actively involved in treasonous behavior such as spying and planning armed insurrections against the governing Masonic powers of fraternity Brother Abraham Lincoln. At the end of the Civil War, the organism

CEASED TO EXIST BUT LATER RE-EMERGED AS SIX FORMER CONFEDERATE OFFICERS HELD SECRET MEETING IN 1866 VOWING TO RE-ESTABLISH WHITE SUPREMACY IN THE STATES THAT WERE PART OF FRATERNITY BROTHER ANDREW JOHNSON'S RECONSTRUCTION POLICIES AFTER LINCOLN'S ASSASSINATION BY BOOTH. REPORTEDLY, ALL OF THE TOP OFFICIALS THAT WERE RESPONSIBLE FOR INITIATING THE KLAN WERE SAID TO HAVE BEEN DISSIDENT FREEMASONS OF THE SCOTTISH RITE WHO WERE NOT ONLY ANTI-NEGRO BUT WERE ALSO ANTI-CATHOLIC AS WELL.

ALTHOUGH MASONIC LEADER ALBERT PIKE WAS A MYSTIC, A SYNCRETIST AS WELL AS A DEEPLY DEVOTED BIGOT, HIS 800-PLUS PAGE WORKS (**MORALS AND DOGMA**) WAS PREREQUISITE READING MATERIAL FOR MILLIONS OF NEW MEMBERS OF FREEMASONRY TO FOLLOW WHOLEHEARTEDLY FOR THE BETTER PART OF A CENTURY AND ONLY QUITE RECENTLY HAS BEEN DISCONTINUED AS IT HAD TO CHANGE WITH THE TIMES BECAUSE SOME MEMBERS OF THE ANCIENT CRAFT SAW IT AS ANTI-MASONIC AMMUNITION FOR THE 21ST CENTURY – POLITICAL CORRECTNESS BEING THE ULTIMATE KEY TO FREEMASONRY'S SUCCESS FOR THE YEAR 2000 AND BEYOND. BROTHER PIKE WAS THE ONLY MASONIC AUTHOR TO BE MENTIONED IN THE OUTLANDISH SYNOD COMMITTEE'S RESEARCH DEBATE FOR THE CHURCH OF ENGLAND AND IT WAS IN DR. HEWITT'S OPINION THAT THE FREEMASONRY AUTHOR ALBERT PIKE WAS NUTTIER THAN A FRUITCAKE. OR, AS SHE SO ELEGANTLY CALLED HIM, A "NUTTER. "

IT GOES WITHOUT SAYING THAT THE ARTICLE THAT APPEARED IN THE CHRISTIAN CENTURY PUBLICATION WAS OF SOME INTEREST TO FREEMASONS WORLDWIDE AS IT WAS GIVING A FEW CLUES AS TO THE CORRUPT RELATIONSHIP BETWEEN THE VARIOUS FACTIONS OF CHRISTIANITY AND FREEMASONRY. THE ANGLICAN CHURCH REPORT THUS EXPOSED THE DEEP RELIGIOUS WOUNDS THAT EXISTED BETWEEN FREEMASONRY AND ITS MOTHER CHURCH OF ENGLAND. IN THE UNITED KINGDOM FOR EXAMPLE, BOTH THE CHURCH OF ENGLAND AND THE METHODIST CHURCH HAVE QUESTIONED THE ABILITY OF A PERSON TO BE A FREEMASON AND A CHRISTIAN. FURTHER TO THIS, THE CHURCH OF SCOTLAND IN THE 1980'S ALSO BEGAN EXAMINING THE SAME QUESTION. AND HERE IN CANADA (1986), A SERIES OF LETTERS IN THE PRESBYTERIAN RECORDS RAISED THE ISSUE IN A HIGHLY PARTISAN MANNER. UNFORTUNATELY FOR US LIVING IN THE 21ST CENTURY, THROUGHOUT THE 1980'S AND 1990'S DECADES AND WELL BEYOND THE YEAR 2000, TENSION BETWEEN THE CHRISTIAN CHURCH AND THE CHRISTIAN FREEMASONS GREW TO AN EXTREME LEVEL OF DISTRUST. EACH APPARENTLY HAD THEIR OWN VISION AS TO HOW A **NEW WORLD ORDER** WAS TO BE ESTABLISHED BASED UPON CHRISTIAN PRINCIPLES.

AS FATE WOULD HAVE IT, THE CHURCH OF SCOTLAND, JUST LIKE THE CHURCH OF ENGLAND, PRODUCED A RATHER SCATHING ANTI-MASONIC REPORT,

WHICH ESSENTIALLY FORCED THE FRATERNITY LEADERS OF THE GRAND LODGE OF SCOTLAND TO OPENLY CRITICIZE CHURCH OFFICIALS AS IT APPARENTLY CAUSED MUCH MORE ANIMOSITY TO FLOURISH DUE SOME MEMBERS OF FREEMASONRY RE-ASSESSING THEIR RELIGIOUS CONVICTIONS. TORN BETWEEN THEIR LOVE OF GOD AND THEIR DEEP DEVOTION TO THE ANCIENT CRAFT OF FREEMASONRY, MANY A SCOTTISH FREEMASON CONTEMPLATED WITHDRAWING FROM THE CHURCH WHILE OTHERS SERIOUSLY THOUGH OF SUBMITTING THEIR RESIGNATIONS AS MEMBERS OF THE CRAFT ALTOGETHER. IN THE GRAND LODGE OF SCOTLAND'S COMMENTS CONCERNING THIS ISSUE, IT REITERATED TO ITS MEMBERS THAT THEIR DUTY WAS NOT ONLY TO GOD, BUT TO THEIR COUNTRY, THEIR NEIGHBORS, THEIR FAMILIES AND TO THE CHURCH ITSELF:

"SO WHERE DO WE GO FROM HERE? WHAT SHOULD BE OUR RESPONSE? FIRST AND FOREMOST I SERIOUSLY ENJOIN YOU, BRETHREN, NOT TO RESIGN FROM YOUR CHURCH. TO DENY YOUR CHURCH CAN ALL TOO EASILY BECOME THE FIRST STEP DOWN THE SLIPPERY SLOPE TOWARDS DENYING GOD. FURTHERMORE, TO DO SO IS TO PLAY INTO THE HANDS OF OUR DETRACTORS WHO WILL IMMEDIATELY SAY THAT YOUR RESIGNATION IS A TACIT ADMISSION THAT FREEMASONRY AND MEMBERSHIP OF THE CHURCH ARE INCOMPATIBLE.

WE MUST ADOPT A HIGHER PROFILE; WE ARE NOT ON THE RUN; WE HAVE NOTHING TO BE ASHAMED OF, INDEED WE HAVE A VERY GREAT DEAL TO BE PROUD OF. THEREFORE, LET US LET THE WORLD KNOW WHAT WE ARE AND WHAT WE STAND FOR; LET THE WORLD KNOW THE HIGH MORAL STANDARDS WE DEMAND OF OUR MEMBERS, AND OUR DISCIPLINE; THAT WE WILL NOT EMBRACE ANY SERIOUS WRONG-DOERS. SADLY WE HAVE ALREADY SEEN THIS AFTERNOON THE ACTION WHICH IS SOMETIMES NECESSARY TO MAINTAIN OUR STANDARDS: STANDARDS WHICH VERY FEW, IF ANY, OTHER ORGANIZATIONS ENFORCE SO RIGIDLY. LET THE WORLD KNOW OF OUR THREE GREAT LIGHTS OF BROTHERLY LOVE, RELIEF AND TRUTH. LET THE WORLD KNOW OF OUR CHARITABLE WORK AND WHAT WE DO WITHIN THE CRAFT AND WITHIN THE COMMUNITY. LET THE WORLD KNOW, PERHAPS MOST IMPORTANTLY OF ALL, THAT WE ARE AN ORGANIZATION WHERE ANY MAN REGARDLESS OF RACE, CREED, RELIGION, COLOUR, RICH OR POOR, OLD OR YOUNG, CAN MEET HIS FELLOW- MEN ON THE FLOOR OF THE LODGE AS AN EQUAL, BECAUSE THERE IS NO OTHER ORGANIZATION IN THE WORLD WHERE THAT HAPPENS.

IN THE PAST, FREEMASONRY HAS DONE LITTLE TO IMPROVE ITS PUBLIC IMAGE. INDEED, BY ITS OBSESSIVE SECRECY AND STUBBORN

DEFENSIVENESS IT HAS ONLY REINFORCED THE IMPRESSION THAT IT HAS SOMETHING TO HIDE. BRETHREN, WE LIVE IN AN OPEN SOCIETY. PEOPLE ARE INTERESTED; THEY DO WANT TO KNOW WHAT FREEMASONRY IS ABOUT AND, IN MY VIEW, THEY HAVE A RIGHT TO KNOW. SECRETIVENESS, EVASIVENESS AND UNWILLINGNESS TO ANSWER REASONABLE QUESTIONS CAN AT BEST ONLY CREATE A BAD IMPRESSION AND AT WORST DO IRREPARABLE HARM, AND WHEN ONE COMES DOWN TO IT, THERE IS REALLY VERY LITTLE ABOUT FREEMASONRY WHICH IS GENUINELY SECRET AND, OF COURSE, THAT WHICH IS SECRET, WE MUST GUARD JEALOUSLY AND NEVER REVEAL. ON THE OTHER HAND, HOW DO WE EXPECT TO GET INTELLIGENT CANDIDATES TO COME FORWARD BECAUSE ' OF A GOOD OPINION PRECONCEIVED' IF NO QUESTIONS CAN BE ANSWERED AND SECRECY PREVAILS. NOW SOME OF YOU HAVE HEARD ME SAY THIS BEFORE AND I AM NOT ASHAMED TO REPEAT IT, THE 9TH CHARGE WHICH IS READ AT EVERY INSTALLATION STATES ' YOU AGREE TO PROMOTE THE GENERAL GOOD OF SOCIETY, TO CULTIVATE THE SOCIAL VIRTUES AND TO PROPAGATE THE KNOWLEDGE OF THE ART OF FREEMASONRY SO FAR AS YOUR INFLUENCE AND ABILITY CAN EXTEND,' AND I ASK YOU, BRETHREN, HOW MANY OF US ARE DOING THAT AT THE PRESENT TIME?"

HISTORICALLY, THERE SEEMS TO HAVE ALWAYS BEEN SOME SORT OF LEVEL OF DISTRUST BETWEEN ONE BRANCH /OR ANOTHER OF THE CHRISTIAN CHURCH AND FREEMASONRY, SUCH AS THE CRUSADES AND THE THREE WAVES PERTAINING TO THE INQUISITION. IN HIS BOOK "ROMAN CATHOLICISM AND FREEMASONRY "WRITTEN IN 1922, DUDLEY WRIGHT WROTE:

"AT FREQUENT INTERVALS NOW FOR NEARLY TWO HUNDRED YEARS, THE HEADS OF THE ROMAN CATHOLIC CHURCH HAVE BEEN LAUNCHING THEIR PAPAL THUNDERS AGAINST FREEMASONRY, ALLEGING THAT IT IS NOT ONLY ANTI-CHRISTIAN, BUT ATHEISTIC IN ITS CONSTITUTION; THAT AT ITS DOORS LIE THE MANY WARS WHICH HAVE TAKEN PLACE DURING THAT PERIOD; AND THAT IT HAS BEEN RESPONSIBLE FOR THE INNUMERABLE REVOLUTIONS THAT HAVE DISTURBED NATIONS, AND THE MYRIADS OF SEDITIOUS PLOTS WHICH HAVE BEEN HATCHED, PARTICULARLY SINCE 1717, WHEN THE MOTHER GRAND LODGE OF THE WORLD WAS FIRST ORGANIZED."

SINCE THE DAWNING OF TIME, FREEMASONRY HAS BEEN SEEN AS THE GREAT EVIL BY THE ROMAN CATHOLIC CHURCH. ITS SECRETS AND ITS CLOSE IDENTIFICATION WITH PROTESTANTISM, MADE IT A VAST MOVEMENT TO BE FEARED. BUT THE GREATEST THREAT OF ALL WAS THE FACT THAT ITS MEMBERSHIP TRADITIONALLY CAME FROM FREE-THINKERS WHO ENJOYED THE

SPECULATIVE NATURE OF THE CRAFT ITSELF. THIS IN ESSENCE WORRIED THE CATHOLIC CHURCH OFFICIALS BECAUSE IT WAS AGAINST THEIR RELIGIOUS DOCTRINE TO HAVE PEOPLE BASICALLY THINKING FOR THEMSELVES. AS A RESULT, THE CATHOLIC CHURCH OFTEN SAW THE EXISTENCE OF A CONSPIRACY IN EVERYTHING THAT THEY FEARED AS IT PERTAINED TO THE PRACTICE OF FREEMASONRY. A CONSPIRACY THAT OF WHICH WAS DESIGNED TO DESTROY ALL THAT FREEMASONS WORLDWIDE HELD DEAR TO THEIR HEARTS AND IDENTIFIED WITH BY CALLING THEMSELVES TRUE CHRISTIANS. AFTERALL, THE ROMAN CATHOLIC FAITH WAS SAID TO BE THE ONLY TRUE RELIGION BY PAPAL DECREE IN ROME. FOR EXAMPLE, A ROMAN CATHOLIC THEOLOGIAN (MONSIGNOR DILLON) WAS SAID TO HAVE STATED:

"EVERY SECRET SOCIETY IS FRAMED AND CREATED TO MAKE MEN THE ENEMIES OF GOD AND HIS CHURCH, AND TO SUBVERT FAITH; AND THERE IS NOT ONE, NO MATTER ON WHAT PRETEXT IT MAY BE FOUNDED, WHICH DOES NOT FALL UNDER THE MANAGEMENT OF A SUPREME DIRECTORATE GOVERNING ALL SECRET SOCIETIES ON EARTH. THE ONE AIM OF THIS DIRECTORATE IS TO UPROOT CHRISTIANITY AND THE CHRISTIAN SOCIAL ORDER, AS WELL AS THE CHURCH, FROM THE WORLD — IN FACT, TO ERADICATE THE NAME OF CHRIST AND THE VERY CHRISTIAN IDEA FROM THE MINDS AND HEARTS OF MEN."

ACCORDING TO FURTHER FREEMASONRY LITERATURE, THERE WERE ONLY TWO MAIN REASONS FOR THE CATHOLIC CHURCH TO SPEAK SO DISRESPECTFULLY OF THEM. ONE BEING OF COURSE THAT AS FAR AS THE CHURCH WAS CONCERNED, FREEMASONS WERE WORSHIPERS OF THE DEVIL AS THEY WERE PERCEIVED AS BEING NOTHING MORE THAN A BUNCH OF HEATHENS PERFORMING PAGAN LIKE RITUALS OF WORSHIP AND THE SECOND BEING THAT THE MAJORITY OF FREEMASONRY PRINCIPLES WERE MOSTLY KEPT SECRET. BUT IN REALITY THERE WAS A THIRD AS WELL AS A FOURTH REASON!!! THE THIRD NATURALLY WAS THE FACT THAT ALL OF THE MASONIC PHILOSOPHIES AND THEIR TEACHINGS WEREN'T EXACTLY AS TO WHAT THE CATHOLIC CHURCH HAD BEEN SAYING ALL ALONG — FREEMASONRY WENT AGAINST THE FUNDAMENTAL PREACHING OF THE ROMAN CATHOLIC DOCTRINE BY INSISTING THAT EACH ONE OF ITS MEMBERS BE ABLE TO THINK FOR THEMSELVES. AND THE FOURTH ULTIMATE REASON WAS THAT FREEMASONS WORLDWIDE WERE CLAIMING THAT THEIR FRATERNITY EXISTED LONG BEFORE CHRIST. THIS ESSENTIALLY PISSED THE CATHOLIC CHURCH RIGHT OFF AS THEY (THE ROMAN CATHOLIC FAITH) FOR 2,000 YEARS HAD BEEN DEPICTING THEMSELVES AS BEING THE ONLY TRUE RELIGION HAVING DIRECT GENEALOGICAL TIES TO JESUS CHRIST. FREEMASONRY WAS THEREFORE UNDER ATTACK LARGELY DUE TO THE FACT THAT IT WAS INSTANTLY PERCEIVED AS BEING A THREAT TO THE CATHOLIC FAITH. AS THE

POLITICAL LANDSCAPE BEGAN TO CHANGE GLOBALLY AND WAS THROWN INTO CHAOS BY THE TWO WORLD WARS, WILD IDEAS OF CONSPIRACIES BEGAN TO EMERGE AS THEY HELPED TO EXPLAIN SO MANY THINGS THAT WERE HAPPENING AT THE TIME AS THE CATHOLIC CHURCH LOOKED ONWARDS AT SURVEYING ITS DOMAIN. IT IS INTERESTING TO NOTE THAT EVEN TODAY, MOST MOVEMENTS THAT SEEK TO DENY CHANGE AND/OR TO RETURN TO A FAMILIAR PAST USUALLY SEE SOME SORT OF WORLD CONSPIRACY AND OFTEN TIE FREEMASONRY INTO THE EQUATION. IT IS ONE THING TO DREAM UP A CONSPIRACY THEORY TO HELP EXPLAIN SOMETHING BUT IT'S A TOTALLY DIFFERENT BALL GAME WHEN A PERSON UTILIZES AN ORGANIZATIONS OWN PAPER TRAIL TO HELP EXPLAIN TO THE ENTIRE WORLD WHAT THE TRUTH OF THE MATTER ACTUALLY IS IN ACCORDANCE TO THE DOCUMENTATION SUBMITTED. IT IS NOT THE INTENTION OF THIS BOOK TO BELABOR /OR EVEN CONVINCE THE READERSHIP INTO ACCEPTING ANY /OR ALL OF THESE WORDS AS BEING THE GOSPEL ACCORDING TO THE AUTHOR. THE HUMAN MIND IS A BEAUTIFUL AND WONDERFUL THING, THE MAIN FUNCTION OF THIS BOOK IS THEREFORE DESIGNED TO ASSIST THE READER INTO THINKING FOR THEMSELVES AS ALL THE FACTS PERTAINING TO THIS GIGANTIC PUZZLE ARE ALL LAID OUT BEFORE THEIR VERY EYES. GRANTED, THE AUTHOR HAS EXPRESSED HIS OWN PERSONAL OPINION FROM TIME TO TIME, BUT THE FACTS CAN EITHER BE ACCEPTED AND/OR REJECTED BY THE READER. THINKING FOR ONE'S OWN SELF IS SOMETHING THAT OF WHICH NOT TOO MANY PEOPLE ARE DOING NOWADAYS AS THEY WATCH TELEVISION /OR SIT IN FRONT OF THEIR HOME COMPUTERS FOR HOURS ON END WASTING THEIR LIVES AWAY. LIKE THE RECYCLE BIN ICON ON THE COMPUTER SCREEN, GARBAGE IN/GARBAGE OUT!!!

THE FACT REMAINS PURE AND SIMPLE, TO FULLY UNDERSTAND THE RELATIONSHIP OF CHRISTIANITY AND FREEMASONRY TODAY A FEW OTHER DETAILS MUST BE THROWN INTO THE EQUATION AS IT WERE. WHICH IN ONE SENSE MAY RAISE THE EYEBROWS OF MANY CHRISTIANS AND MASONRY LEADERS AS THE ARGUMENTS PUT FORWARD ARE TOTALLY DIFFERENT THAN THOSE USED IN THE PAST IN A NUMBER OF WAYS;

1) THE CHURCHES THAT ARE DIRECTLY INVOLVED ARE DIFFERENT. IT WAS HISTORICALLY THE ROMAN CATHOLIC CHURCH THAT SAW FREEMASONRY AS A THREAT. TODAY IT IS WHAT USED TO BE THE FERTILE GROUND FOR PERSPECTIVE MASONS, THE MAINLINE PROTESTANT CHURCHES.

2) THE THEORIES OF CONSPIRACY HAVE GENERALLY DISAPPEARED.

3) THE BASIC COMPLAINT HAS CHANGED FROM FREEMASONRY BEING ATHEISTIC TO BEING A FORM OF RELIGION IN ITS OWN RIGHT. HOWEVER, THERE ARE A NUMBER OF IMPORTANT SIMILARITIES.

THE FIRST BEING OF COURSE THAT THE ESTABLISHED CHURCH AGAIN SEE'S ITSELF AS BEING UNDER ATTACK. THIS TIME, THE ENEMY IS NOT A NEW RATIONALISM BUT RATHER NEW RELIGIONS. WITH THE GROWTH OF SECTS AND CULTS, AND THE APPEARANCE OF THE EASTERN RELIGIONS IN WESTERN SOCIETY THROUGH TERRORIST CELL GROUPS, THE CHURCH AGAIN SEE'S A NEED TO DEFINE ITSELF MORE RIGOROUSLY SO AS TO KEEP OUT THE UNWANTED. AND SECONDLY, THE MOST IMPORTANT ISSUE OF ALL, THE SECRECY OF FREEMASONRY CONTINUES TO CAUSE IT TO BE SEEN AS A LIKELY TARGET, SINCE NO ONE IS QUITE SURE WHAT REALLY IS GOING ON WITHIN ITS OWN RANKS. AN ARTICLE IN THE OCTOBER 1987 MASONIC BULLETIN FROM M.B.S. HIGHAM GAVE A MORE CONVINCING VIEW OF THE ISSUES THAT WERE STAINING THE RELATIONSHIP BETWEEN CHRISTIAN CHURCHES AND FREEMASONRY. IN PARAGRAPH 5, HE WAS REPORTEDLY TO HAVE STATED:

"THE REPORT (OF THE PANEL OF THE CHURCH OF ENGLAND CONCERNING THE COMPATIBILITY OF FREEMASONRY AND CHRISTIANITY) CONCLUDES THAT PART OF THE ROYAL ARCH RITUAL MUST BE CONSIDERED BLASPHEMOUS. IT CRITICIZES FREEMASONRY IN GENERAL AS SYNCRETISTIC (I.E. ATTEMPTING TO UNIFY OR RECONCILE DIFFERENT RELIGIONS); GNOSTIC (HAVING ITS OWN SPIRITUAL KNOWLEDGE); PELAGIAN (PROVIDING SALVATION THROUGH WORKS); DEIST (PROMOTING NATURAL RELIGION, OR A RELIGION WITHOUT DIVINE AUTHORITY) AND INDIFFERENT TO THE CLAIMS OF CHRISTIANITY. IT INSISTS THAT MASONIC CEREMONIES INVOLVE WORSHIP, AND COMPLAINS THAT CHRISTIAN REFERENCES HAVE BEEN REMOVED FROM FAMILIAR PRAYERS."

THE INTERCOURSE AND MARRIAGE BETWEEN CHRISTIANITY AND FREEMASONRY WAS SO INTENSE THAT MANY A FREEMASON ONCE AGAIN BEGAN DENYING THE FACT THAT THEIR FRATERNAL INSTITUTION WAS A RELIGION CONTRARY TO THE RELIGIOUS WORDS AND SYMBOLS USED BY MASONS STATING OTHERWISE. HIDING BEHIND A THIN VALE OF SECRECY, MASONIC HISTORIANS ONCE AGAIN BEGAN INSISTING TO THE CHRISTIAN OUTSIDER THAT THEIR FRATERNITY WAS BY NO MEANS A RELIGION. INSISTING THAT THE TERMS USED DID NOT NECESSARILY IMPLICATE RELIGIOUS WORSHIP THAT WAS SEEN AS BEING PARTICULARLY CHRISTIAN. THIS DESPITE THE FACT THAT THE USE OF THE TERMS SUCH AS "ALTER "AND/OR "TEMPLE "WOULD SEEM TO INDICATE A PLACE OF RELIGIOUS WORSHIP. FOR EXAMPLE, THE HOLY BIBLE IS THE "VOLUME OF THE SACRED LAW "TO THE MASONIC ORDER AND **GOD** IS

REFERRED TO UNDER VARIOUS ALIASES. ACCORDINGLY, MASONIC HISTORIANS CONTINUED INSISTING THAT THE COMBINATION OF SEEMING TO BE RELIGIOUS AND SEEMING NOT TO BE CHRISTIAN WAS INITIALLY THE COMBINING CATALYSIS THAT MADE FREEMASONRY APPEAR TO BE THE THREAT TO THE CHRISTIAN FAITH. THIS COMBINING CATALYSIS WAS THUSLY PROCLAIMED AS BEING TOTALLY UNDERSTANDABLE AS IT SEEMED TO BE A NATURAL PROGRESSION SINCE THE EARLY AUTHORS OF THEIR RITUALS WERE MOSTLY RELIGIOUS MEN TO BEGIN WITH. FOR INSTANCE, THE AUTHOR OF AN ELABORATE VERSION OF THE OLD MASONIC CHARGES (DISCIPLINARY AND ADVANCEMENT OF CANDIDATES AND MEMBERS) FOUND IN THE BOOK OF CONSTITUTIONS WAS NONE OTHER THAN DR. JAMES ANDERSON (1684-1739) WHO INTERESTINGLY ENOUGH WAS A MINISTER OF THE CHURCH OF SCOTLAND. FRATERNITY BROTHER ANDERSON WAS SAID TO HAVE TRIED TO TRACE HIS FAMILY TREE TO THE DAYS OF ADAM AND EVE. NEEDLESS TO SAY, HE WAS UNSUCCESSFUL IN HIS ENDEAVORS!!! IT SHOULD ALSO BE POINTED OUT THAT IN NORMAN MACKENZIE'S BOOK "SECRET SOCIETIES "PUBLISHED IN 1968 HE STATED:

"AFTER THE RELIGIOUS PASSIONS OF THE PRECEDING CENTURY, THE MOOD FAVORED A REJECTION OF DOGMA AND A TOLERANCE OF ANY PERSONAL BELIEF THAT DID NOT EXCLUDE THE IDEA OF A SUPREME BEING. DEISM — A SYCRETIC BELIEF IN GOD DISTINCT FROM THEOLOGICAL DOCTRINE — WAS WIDESPREAD AMONG THE EDUCATED PEOPLE AND THE WEALTHIER CLASSES FROM WHICH FREEMASONRY DREW ITS MEMBERS, UNTIL A MORE ORTHODOX CHRISTIAN FAITH BECAME SOCIALLY NECESSARY IN THE 19TH CENTURY. THIS RELIGIOUS TOLERANCE WAS REFLECTED IN THE FIRST MASONIC ' BOOK OF CONSTITUTIONS '(1722-23), WHICH LAID DOWN THAT MASONS MIGHT BELONG TO ANY RELIGIOUS SECT, BUT THAT THEY COULD NOT BE ATHEISTS."

IT HAS BEEN SAID THAT THE PROMINENT THEOLOGICAL POSITION OF THOSE ATTRIBUTED TO FREEMASONRY, THEN AS NOW WAS SOME SORT OF DIVINE INTERVENTION; **DEISM** AS IT WERE. RATIONAL THOUGH WAS THE RAGE OF THE DAY, AND TOLERANCE OF OTHER BELIEFS WAS TO BE EXPECTED. ACCORDING TO SOME FREEMASONRY HISTORIANS, THE USE OF RELIGIOUS SYMBOLS WAS NOT INTENDED TO CREATE A NEW RELIGION BUT RATHER TO BROADEN THE AVAILABLE LIMITS TO INCLUDE OTHERS WHO BELIEVED IN A DIFFERENT WAY. OVER THE MANY YEARS, THE DEIST THEOLOGY MAY HAVE DISAPPEARED, BUT THE LEVEL OF RELIGIOUS TOLERANCE HAS REMAINED EXACTLY THE SAME. THESE SAME MASONIC HISTORIANS BELIEVE THAT IT IS THIS INCLUSIVE QUALITY TO THE RITUAL OF THE MASONS THAT IS THE MAIN DRIVING FORCE BEHIND THE PRESENT RELIGIOUS TENSIONS IN THE RELATIONSHIP BETWEEN

Christianity and Freemasonry. When the ecumenical currents were flowing strongly in the Church, the tolerance of Freemasonry was a positive thing but as the Church felt the sectarian influences that caused it to embrace less and less. With the ideas of ecumenicity and a move to a more strict understanding of what a Christian actually was, the Church became more exclusive (that is, it excluded people), and allowed less and less variation of beliefs. This bowel movement is evident in many ways as denominations over the years had been actively seeking spiritual union (if not organic union) with sister denominations but since then have retreated more and more into their own denominational understanding. To any given system of faith that is becoming more aware of how it is different from others, it isn't long before a system that promotes an inclusive view of faith that is introduced becomes a threat.

Unfortunately for the human race, this distrust of an inclusive attitude is not reserved for only Freemasonry. In the same report presented to the Church of England, the authors attached what they saw as other possible back-sliders – the Roman Catholic Pope, and the Archbishop of Canterbury:

> "Only last year, the Bishop of Rome was himself in Assisi praying for peace alongside Buddhists, Sikhs, Jews and medicine men of North American Indian tribes. When he listened attentively to their prayers, was he joining in them or unobtrusively dissociating himself from what was going on? Was the whole affair, in which the Archbishop of Canterbury was himself prominent, just an exhibition of spiritual sleight-of-hand, or esslesiastical hypocrisy."

With the stench of religious words flying every which way in the report submitted to the Church of England, the Archbishop of York let his feelings be known in a speech to the General Synod of the grand-pooh-bah of England:

> "I think that it is worthy of a church document. We badly need good contexts in which people with different religious convictions can work together, without abandoning those convictions or without ignoring them."

Be that as it may, the constant religious bickering amongst themselves extended well into the 21ST Century. To a certain degree it created more problems which in essence lead to higher tensions between Christianity and Freemasonry that in reality, it became

MORE OF A PROBLEM FOR THE CHURCH THAN IT WAS FOR THE MASONS THEMSELVES. ALTHOUGH THE MAJORITY OF FREEMASONS WORLDWIDE WERE SAID TO HAVE NOT SEEN IT AS BEING TOO MUCH OF A PROBLEM, THEY STILL DECIDED TO WALK EVER SO SOFTLY AS THEY DIDN'T WANT TO ADD ANY FUEL TO THE FIRE THAT WOULD HAVE IGNITED MORE TENSIONS. PROCEEDING, BUT WITH EXTREME CAUTION THEY WITHHELD FROM USING PARTICULAR TERMS AND/OR ACTIONS THAT MIGHT HAVE BEEN SEEN AS BLASPHEMOUS TO THE DEVOUT CHRISTIAN. AS FAR AS THE FREEMASONS WERE CONCERNED, IT WAS SOMETHING THAT HAD TO BE DONE IN ORDER TO REBUILD THE RELATIONSHIP BETWEEN FREEMASONRY AND CHRISTIANITY. WANTING TO BE EXTRA SENSITIVE TO THE FEELINGS AND EMOTIONS OF THOSE AROUND THEM NATURALLY BEING THE KEY TO THE REBUILDING PROCESS. THIS SENSITIVITY LATER EVOLVED INTO POLITICAL CORRECTNESS FOR ALL INHABITANTS OF THE WESTERN FREE-WORLD.

AFTER NEARLY 15 YEARS OF REBUILDING THE RELATIONSHIP BETWEEN CHRISTIANITY AND FREEMASONRY, TENSIONS ONCE AGAIN ESCALATED OUT OF CONTROL AS A FORMER PRACTICING ROMAN CATHOLIC WAS THE FRONT RUNNER FOR BECOMING ENGLAND'S NEXT ARCHBISHOP OF CANTERBURY; THE BISHOP OF ROCHESTER, THE RT. REV. MICHAEL NAZIR-ALI. AS SOON AS IT HAD BECOME APPARENT THAT THE BISHOP OF ROCHESTER WAS THE MORE FAVORED WINNER, THE CHURCH OF ENGLAND BEGAN CONDUCTING A CONFIDENTIAL INVESTIGATION INTO HIS BACKGROUND; INCLUDING ALLEGATIONS THAT BEFORE HE BECAME A DEVOTED PROTESTANT HE WAS A PRACTICING ROMAN CATHOLIC. RUMORS EVEN HAD IT THAT HE WAS ALSO A MEMBER OF THE FRATERNAL ORDER. ALMOST IMMEDIATELY TENSIONS ROSE TO NEW HEIGHTS AS PRINCE CHARLES WAS REPORTED TO HAVE STATED THAT WHEN HE WOULD EVENTUALLY BECOME THE KING OF GREAT BRITAIN AND THE **SUPREME** GOVERNING POWER OF THE CHURCH OF ENGLAND HE WANTED THE BISHOP OF LONDON, THE RT. REV. RICHARD CHARTRES TO BE THE NEXT ARCHBISHOP OF CANTERBURY. BUT SINCE MOMMY DEAREST WAS STILL THE PROTECTRESS OF ENGLISH FREEMASONRY WHILE SHE SAT ON THE PORCELAIN THRONE, NAZIR-ALI WAS STILL THE FAVORED CONTENDER. NEWSPAPERS IN ENGLAND AND NORTH AMERICA HIGHLY PUBLICIZED THE PLIGHT OF THE RT. REV. MICHAEL NAZIR-ALI'S ORDEAL AS RACIST OVERTONES WERE SAID TO BE ATTRIBUTING TO THE CHURCH OF ENGLAND'S INITIAL INVESTIGATION AS THE BISHOP OF ROCHESTER WAS A BLACKMAN. LIKE ALL OTHER FORMS OF RELIGION, HYPOCRISY WAS THE OVER-RIDING FACTOR WHICH GOVERNED THEM BECAUSE IN THE END, A COMPROMISE OF SORTS WAS IMPLEMENTED IN DECEMBER OF 2002 WHEN PRINCE CHARLES AND THEN-BRITISH PRIME MINISTER TONY BLAIR CONJOINTLY APPOINTED ROWAN WILLIAMS THE FORMER ARCHBISHOP OF WALES AS THE 104TH ARCHBISHOP OF CANTERBURY.

Williams, a self-proclaimed leftist member of the fraternal cause was in direct opposition to the American Freemasonry led actions being taken against the people of Iraq in the proposed Persian Gulf War Part Two. It was obviously a public relations appointment as Tony Blair himself was backing the American Freemasonry ploy of ousting Saddam Hussein as the Iraqi leader and just as the British and American troops were building up their military might forces in the Middle East, the Archbishop of Canterbury Rowan Williams was officially installed into his prestigious portfolio as head of the Church of England on Thursday, February 27TH, 2003 in a pompous ceremony which took place at Canterbury Cathedral in London, England.

It can therefore be safely stated that the relationship between Christianity and Freemasonry has always been a somewhat stormy adventure with one part of the Church /or the other, and it is often as much tied to how the Church see's itself as open to new /or different ways of worshiping **GOD**. And when it see's good arising from the different faiths coming together in respect to sharing in common tasks, then the open and vague religious language of Freemasonry seems less threatening, and more acceptable. Since time began, the Church (Protestant and/or Roman Catholic) has always felt the need to more clearly define the edges of its faith and when it see's other faiths as greater /or lesser a threat to its existence blasphemous /or racist overtones are quite often used to ward off the unwanted. All-too-often numerous forms of religion hide behind a shroud of secrecy as they feel threatened by the rituals and symbols of Freemasonry and proclaims heresy as being present in the actions of the Lodgery, as many of the previous Chapters have indicated in this book. A full examination of this relationship between Church and state raises many questions in the minds of others concerning man's inhumanity to his fellow human beings. It in fact raises more questions then there are actual answers as well. Only one thing is for certain, the ritualistic faith of Freemasonry has lead the way for many of the world's conflicts over thousands of years to unfold. Which in itself makes a person wonder as to where he /or she is to turn for their own personal salvation???

To further inscribe the events of September 11TH, 2001 into the human psyche, the powers that be bombarded the entire population of the Western free-world with additional desensitizing propaganda programming on such weekly television series such as Touched By An Angle with Della Reese and Roma Downey; The District with Creg

T. Nelson; The Education of Max Bickford with Richard Dreyfuss; Law & Order with Sam Waterson, Jerry Orbach and Jesse L. Martin; JAG with David James Elliott, and a host of other weekly program series. Knowing full well that the television airwave transmission was essentially the best medium to utilize aspects of brainwashing tactics, the powers that be went into full gear depriving the inhabitants of Western civilization of the thought process. Far too many people were busy worshiping the boob tube and whatever this false god had to say, people literally took it as being the gospel since the television airwaves wouldn't dare lie to its faithful followers of misguided blind sheep as they were being led down the wrong path of discovery.

By the time the bombing of Afghanistan had been executed by the American Masonic Supreme Allied Command, brainwashing tactics had virtually become a work of art as the science of it all had been formulated during the initial bombing of Baghdad during the First Persian Gulf War only a few years previously. Less than 48 hours after the United States and its Masonic Allied forces launched its military assault on Iraq during the 1990's decade, a linguist professor of the Massachusetts Institute of Technology made an impressive presentation in London, England at the annual conference of the Catholic Institute for International Relations. The Massachusetts professor, Norman Chomsky denounced the Persian Gulf War by saying that it had absolutely nothing to do with maintaining a **"New World Order "**as to what U.S. President George Bush Senior and his western allied forces were claiming. Professor Chomsky emphasized that the War in the Middle East was basically being waged to save the Old World Order in which the United States of America historically savagely repressed former colonial empires to protect its own economic interest. Oddly enough, as the professor was making his allegations of Western Imperialism, he was warmly applauded by the Roman Catholic upper echelons of the Church. Chomsky, reiterated the U.S. Federal Government's willingness to spill blood while being one of the western hemisphere's most influential intellectuals in the cause of peace and further argued that the American governmental structure and its Masonic "business elite "saw oil as a Natural Resource belonging to them. As far as professor Chomsky was concerned, the fact that the oil was located in a foreign country was merely a geographical accident.

In a paper accompanying his speech, Chomsky wrote: "The cynicism is transparent. Until August 1ST, Saddam Hussein was an

ALLY AND FAVORED TRADING PARTNERS. HIS CRIMINAL ATROCITIES WERE EASILY OVERLOOKED; OTHERS WHOSE RECORDS ARE AS UNSAVORY AS HIS CONTINUE TO BE AMIABLE FRIENDS ... IN REALITY, SADDAM HUSSEIN BECAME THE NEW INCARNATION OF HITLER AND GENGHIS KHAN WHEN HE REVEALED HIMSELF TO BE A ' RADICAL NATIONALIST ' WHO REJECTS THE DOCTRINE THAT THE ENERGY RESERVES OF THE GULF ARE TO BE CONTROLLED BY THE U.S. AND RELIABLE CLIENT STATES. AT THAT POINT, HIS MONSTROUS RECORD CAN BE INVOKED AS A PROPAGANDA DEVICE." CHOMSKY CONCLUDED HIS INFAMOUS JANUARY 18TH, 1991 SPEECH BY SUMMARIZING SIMILAR EXAMPLES OF WESTERN IMPERIALIST TACTICS OF A "QUICK TRANSITION FROM AMITY TO ENEMY. "INTERESTINGLY, ONE OF THE EXAMPLES INCLUDED GENERAL MANUEL NORIEGA OF PANAMA, "WHO HAD BEEN AIDED AND SUPPORTED BY THE U.S. UNTIL HE CEASED TO SERVE ITS INTERESTS. "OTHER COMPARISONS INCLUDED INDONESIA AND NICARAGUA – AND ACCORDING TO CHOMSKY, IF THE TRUE DETAILS OF ITS WESTERN AGGRESSION WERE KNOWN, THAT SUPPRESSION WOULD "MAKE SADDAM HUSSEIN LOOK LIKE A BOY SCOUT."

PROFESSOR CHOMSKY WASN'T THE ONLY ONE SPEAKING OUT DURING THE PERSIAN GULF WAR AND ITS AMERICAN MASONIC ORIENTATION. DON MCGILLIVRAY, AT THE TIME A NATIONAL POLITICAL COLUMNIST WITH THE SOUTHAM NEWS, HAD LOTS TO SAY IN HIS JANUARY 21ST COLUMN IN THE VANCOUVER SUN. REPORTING FROM OTTAWA, MCGILLIVRAY'S ARTICLE WAS INTERESTINGLY TITLED; "LIKE BUSH, HITLER ALSO OFFERED A NEW WORLD ORDER OF PEACE. "THE WELL KNOWN AND HIGHLY RESPECTED CANADIAN POLITICAL EXPERT STATED IN PART: "THE GULF WAR IS BEING FOUGHT FOR A BRIGHT AND SHINING UTOPIA. PEOPLE WHO BACK IT AS A NECESSARY WAR BELIEVE VICTORY FOR THE U.S. OVER IRAQ WOULD USHER IN A GOLDEN AGE CALLED THE NEW WORLD ORDER. "IN COMPARING BUSH TO HITLER, COLUMNIST MCGILLIVRAY TOOK HIS READERS BACK TO JANUARY 30TH, 1941 IN WHICH HITLER GAVE A LONG RANTING SPEECH IN BERLIN. FRATERNITY GERMAN LEADER ADOLF HITLER REPORTEDLY STATED THE FOLLOWING: "I AM CONVINCED THAT 1941 WILL BE THE CRUCIAL YEAR OF A GREAT NEW ORDER IN EUROPE ... THE WORLD SHALL OPEN UP FOR EVERYONE. PRIVILEGES FOR INDIVIDUALS, THE TYRANNY OF CERTAIN NATIONS AND THEIR FINANCIAL RULERS SHALL FALL. AND LAST OF ALL, THIS YEAR WILL HELP TO PROVIDE THE FOUNDATIONS OF A REAL UNDERSTANDING AMONG PEOPLES, AND WITH IT THE CERTAINTY OF CONCILIATION AMONG NATIONS. "ACCORDING TO MCGILLIVRAY, "HITLER'S NEW ORDER WAS A CONTINUING THEME. "IN 1941, A COLLECTION OF ADOLF HITLER'S SPEECHES WERE PUBLISHED "AS A SEQUEL TO MEIN KAMPF" AND WAS DULY TITLED; **"MY NEW ORDER.** "MCGILLIVRAY STATED THAT HITLER'S **NEW WORLD ORDER** WAS NOTHING MORE THAN "A MAD TYRANT'S CRUEL HOAX ON A WORLD GROANING UNDER HIS WAR MACHINE. "THE HIGHLY

ACCLAIMED NEWSPAPER COLUMNIST WENT ON TO FURTHER EMPHASIZE THAT "HITLER'S DESCRIPTION OF THE PROMISED UTOPIA IS NOT MUCH DIFFERENT FROM TODAY'S PROMISES. "FURTHER NOTING THAT HITLER "CLAIMED NATIONS WOULD SETTLE THEIR DISPUTES PEACEFULLY BY CONCILIATION. "McGILLIVRAY FURTHER OBSERVED THAT "THAT'S ONE OF THE KEY CLAIMS FOR THE NEW WORLD ORDER."

THE SOUTHAM NEWS POLITICAL EXPERT WAS A FIRM BELIEVER THAT ONCE SADDAM HUSSEIN HAD BEEN PROPERLY DISPOSED OF, "OTHERS OF HIS SORT WILL KNOW THAT THEY MUST SETTLE DISPUTES PEACEFULLY OR THE UNITED NATIONS "WOULD USE THE UNITED STATES "AS ITS POLICEMAN "AND SETTLE THE ISSUE WITH A BIG FRATERNAL STICK. OR, AS McGILLIVRAY SO DIPLOMATICALLY PUT IT; "THIS IS THE WAR-TO-END-WARS ILLUSION. "ONE ADDITIONAL PIECE OF IMPORTANT INFORMATION WAS ALSO STATED IN HIS JANUARY 21ST, 1991 COLUMN, THAT BEING, WHILE THE PRESIDENT OF THE UNITED STATES ADDRESSED A JOINT SESSION OF CONGRESS ON SEPTEMBER 11TH, 1990 HE STATED THAT THE PERSIAN GULF CRISIS OFFERED THE PEOPLE OF AMERICA "A RARE OPPORTUNITY TO MOVE TOWARD AN HISTORIC PERIOD OF COOPERATION ... A NEW WORLD ORDER CAN EMERGE, FREER FROM THE THREAT OF TERROR, STRONGER IN THE PURSUIT OF JUSTICE AND MORE SECURE IN THE QUEST FOR PEACE. "THIS WAS OBVIOUSLY PART OF THE AMERICAN MASONIC ORDER'S HIDDEN AGENDA AS THEY SO WISELY INITIATED AS A "CALL TO ACTION "PROGRAM. AS FAR AS DON McGILLIVRAY WAS CONCERNED, U.S. PRESIDENT GEORGE BUSH SENIOR "PICKED UP THE NEW WORLD ORDER IDEA FROM MIKHAIL GORBACHEV. AND PRIME MINISTER BRIAN MULRONEY PICKED IT UP FROM BUSH. "CLOSE, BUT STILL NO CIGAR!!!

WHILE ALL OF THESE EXTRAORDINARY EVENTS WERE BEING PLAYED OUT BEFORE OUR VERY EYES, SOMETHING ELSE WAS HAPPENING BEHIND THE SCENES WHICH WENT VIRTUALLY UN-NOTICED BY MOST OF THE INHABITANTS OF THE WESTERN FREE-WORLD. AS NORTH AMERICA'S WHITE ANGLO-SAXON AND FRENCH FREEMASONS WERE BUSY FLEXING THEIR FRATERNAL MUSCLES AND PORTRAYING THEMSELVES AS BEING THE CREAM OF THE FRATERNITY CROP, ALL HELL WAS BREAKING LOOSE AS MEMBERS OF PRINCE HALL FREEMASONRY SOUGHT TO BE RECOGNIZED AS A LEGITIMATE GOVERNING ENTITY, (PRINCE HALL FREEMASONRY BEING OF COURSE BLACK FREEMASONRY). IN THE UNITED STATES FOR EXAMPLE WHERE BLACK FREEMASONRY WAS BEING HELD DOWN IN A COMPLETE STRANGLEHOLD, TENSIONS SOON MOUNTED DURING THE EARLY PARTS OF THE 1990'S DECADE AS FRATERNITY LEADERS ON BOTH SIDES OF THE CANADA/U.S. BORDER BEGAN STUDYING THE POSSIBILITY OF FINALLY RECOGNIZING BLACK MASONRY AS AN ACTUAL LIVING ORGANISM WITH FULL JURISDICTIONAL POWERS UNDER THE VERY WATCHFUL MASONIC EYE OF THE 41ST AMERICAN PRESIDENT, GEORGE BUSH SENIOR.

Historically, American Black Freemasonry initially began some years prior to the Revolutionary War for political independence from the Grand Lodge of England. In most fraternity circles, Black Freemasonry was believed to have been conceived by a Blackman named Prince Hall and fourteen other men of African bloodlines as they reportedly established a Masonic Lodge in Boston, Massachusetts which they called African Lodge No. 459. This Lodge was said not to have been recognized by the Grand Lodge of Massachusetts as the Black African Lodge refused to acknowledge any allegiance whatsoever to the Grand Lodge of Massachusetts which was first instituted in the year 1733. Then on March 2ND, 1784 white American Freemasons had no choice but to acknowledge the fact that Prince Hall and his small band of faithful followers had received a Charter from England authorizing the establishment of Masonic Lodges for African/American men. This came about mostly due to the fact that during the Revolutionary War, Prince Hall and his fourteen faithful followers had been initiated into the many mysteries of Freemasonry in a Military Lodge that had been warranted by the Grand Lodge of England. After feeling somewhat betrayed by the white American Freemasonry members, (it was alright for Black Freemasons to fight and die for the fraternal cause for political independence from England but when it came to being treated as their social equals; nada, zip, zero, nothing), a petition was submitted for full Masonic recognition within the **Brotherhood of Man**.

Be that as it may, on September 29TH, 1784, His Royal Highness the Duke of Cumberland, (the Grand Master of the Grand Lodge of England at the time), granted permission for the establishing of Black Freemasonry Lodgery not only within the State of Massachusetts but beyond as well. The Duke of Cumberland, then appointed a Negro resident of Boston (Prince Hall) as the caretaker of Black Freemasonry in the State of Massachusetts. It should also be stated that throughout the Revolutionary War years, Black Freemasonry continued to operate in some form /or another until the death of Prince Hall and his colleges some years later. By 1827, Black Freemasonry was slowly being rekindled amongst the Black population as more and more men of African descent decided to govern themselves accordingly by not acknowledging the whiteman's Masonic authority over them. Having the will of self-determination, it was therefore decreed that the knowledge they possessed of the Ancient Craft literally gave them the right to be free and independent members of all the existing white Masonic

LODGERY AS IT HAD BEEN INCORPORATED INTO FREEMASONRY LAW THAT NO PERSON OF THE BLACK RACE WAS EVER TO BE CONSIDERED AND/OR ADMITTED AS A VISITOR OF ANY LODGE OF MASONRY UNDER THE VAST MAJORITY OF THE FREEMASONRY JURISDICTIONS WITHIN THE CONTINENTAL UNITED STATES. ALL FORMS OF AFRICAN/AMERICAN BLACK LODGERY ON THE ENTIRE NORTH AMERICAN CONTINENT WAS CONSIDERED TO BE WITHOUT LEGAL AUTHORITY. THIS NEGRO MASONIC SYSTEM ODDLY ENOUGH BECAME KNOWN AS A COUNTERFEIT VERSION OF THE WHITEMAN'S NORTH AMERICAN FREEMASONRY CONCEPT, SUPPOSEDLY AN ILLEGITIMATE IMITATION OF THE REAL THING DESPITE THE FACT THAT ALL FORMS OF FREEMASONRY WERE SAID TO HAVE BEEN BASED UPON THE FUNDAMENTAL PRINCIPLES OF BROTHERLY LOVE FOR ALL MANKIND. IN TRIBUTE TO ITS ORIGINAL FOUNDER, PRINCE HALL LODGERY WAS ESTABLISHED WHICH WAS IN NO WAY, SHAPE /OR FORM ASSOCIATED WITH THE WHITEMAN'S AMERICAN MASONIC RACIST CONCEPTS OF DISCRIMINATION. IT ESSENTIALLY BECAME A TOTALLY SEPARATE ENTITY ALL OF ITS OWN. THESE LODGES WERE REPORTEDLY CREATED TO HELP APPEASE PRESSURE FROM WITHIN THE VARIOUS BLACK COMMUNITIES THAT OF WHICH WANTED TO MAINTAIN SOME SORT OF MASONIC INFLUENCE IN THEIR PERSPECTIVE COMMUNITY. AS TIME PROGRESSED, THE TERMINOLOGY PRINCE HALL FREEMASONRY REPLACED ALL WORDINGS OF BLACK AND/OR AFRICAN/AMERICAN FREEMASONRY.

AS THE WHITE AMERICAN FREEMASONRY LEADERS EXERCISED THEIR GOD GIVEN RIGHT OF **"MANIFEST DESTINY "**FROM THE EAST COAST TO THE WESTERN SHORES OF THE PACIFIC OCEAN, PRINCE HALL FREEMASONRY CONTINUALLY GREW WITH EACH PASSING GENERATION. THE MORE POWERFUL THE BLACK FREEMASONRY MOVEMENT BECAME, THE LESS INTERESTED THE WHITE POWER STRUCTURE WAS IN RECOGNIZING THEM AS THEIR SOCIAL EQUALS. AFTER WELL OVER 200 YEARS OF THEIR LACK OF AND UNWILLINGNESS TO ALLOW FULL RECOGNITION TO BE EXPOUNDED UPON THE BLACK MEMBERS OF THE ANCIENT CRAFT OF FREEMASONRY, THE ENTIRE SCENARIO FINALLY BLEW TO A HEAD AT THE ANNUAL MEETING OF THE GRAND MASTERS OF NORTH AMERICA HELD IN WASHINGTON, D.C. DURING THE MONTH OF FEBRUARY 1989. THE SUBJECT OF RECOGNITION WAS RAISED AT THE CONVENTION AND BROUGHT TO THE FLOOR FOR DISCUSSION AND, THEN A VOTE. IN THEIR DISCUSSION, WHITE FREEMASONS WEIGHED THE PROS AND CONS OF THE TOPIC AS THEY SEARCHED FOR LEGAL REASONS PERTAINING TO WHETHER / OR NOT IT WAS ACTUALLY A GOOD THING TO DO FOR FURTHER EXPANSION OF THE YEAR 2000 DEADLINE. AS THE GRAND LODGE OF WISCONSIN HAD ALREADY INSTITUTED STEPS TOWARDS A RESOLUTION OF RECOGNITION FOR PRINCE HALL FREEMASONRY IN THEIR PERSPECTIVE STATE, RESOLUTION NO. 16 WAS THEREFORE TABLED AT THE NATION'S CAPITAL CONVENTION. THE CONSENSUS OF THIS PENDING RESOLUTION WAS TO SAY THE LEAST AN

INSTRUMENT OF MUCH HEATED DEBATE. ONCE THE RESOLUTION CAME TO THE FLOOR FOR DISCUSSIONS, A LEGAL ARGUMENT ENSUED PERTAINING AS TO WHICH GROUP OF FREEMASONS HAD THE LEGAL AND MORAL RIGHT TO MAKE SUCH A PROPOSAL. FOR LEGAL REASONS, NORTH AMERICA'S WHITE GRAND MASTER MASONS STATED THAT THEY REQUIRED A LETTER FROM THE GRAND LODGE OF PRINCE HALL REQUESTING THE SAID RECOGNITION. FURTHER TO THIS, IT WAS ALSO RECOMMENDED THAT THE WHOLE ISSUE ITSELF BE HANDED OVER TO THE MASONIC FOREIGN RELATIONS COMMITTEE FOR AN IN-DEPTH STUDY. AND DUE TO THE FACT THAT NEITHER HAD TRANSPIRED, RESOLUTION NO. 16 WAS THEREFORE WITHDRAWN SOME MONTHS LATER.

THROUGHOUT THE CONTINENTAL UNITED STATES, PRINCE HALL FREEMASONRY WAS THE SUBJECT OF MUCH DISCUSSION DURING THE LATE 1980's AND EARLY 1990's. WHILE THERE WERE THOSE WHO WANTED BLACK FREEMASONRY TO BE RECOGNIZED AS A VERY VALUABLE PIECE OF MASONIC HISTORY, THOSE OPPOSING IT WERE TENFOLD. INDIVIDUAL FREEMASONS WHO WERE FIGHTING FOR BLACKS TO BE ACCEPTED AS THEIR FRATERNITY EQUALS ARGUED THAT IT WAS THE MASONIC ORDER'S SACRED CONSTITUTIONAL DUTY UNDER THE LAWS OF THE LAND TO INCORPORATE PRINCE HALL FREEMASONRY AS A FULLY RECOGNIZED FRATERNAL INSTITUTION. IF THAT ARGUMENT FAILED TO GET A POSITIVE RESPONSE OUT OF THE BRETHRENSHIP, RHETORIC OF THE ORDER'S BENEVOLENT **"BROTHERHOOD OF MAN "**POLICY OF ELIMINATING DISCRIMINATION FROM THE AMERICAN SOCIAL FABRIC WAS THROWN INTO THE MIX. AND ONCE ALL THIS HAD FAILED, WORDS OF POSSIBLE GOVERNMENTAL TAX REFORMS WERE UTILIZED AS MANY OF THE MASONIC LODGES NATION WIDE STOOD TO LOOSE THEIR TAX EXEMPT STATUS UNDER GEORGE BUSH SENIOR'S PENDING RESTRUCTURING POLICIES AS THE U.S. GOVERNMENT WAS SCRAMBLING TO FIND ADDITIONAL TAX REVENUES TO HELP FINANCIALLY FUND ITS JUST CAUSE OF PROMOTING DEMOCRACY AND FREEDOM AROUND THE WORLD UNDER THE FRATERNAL AUSPICES OF THE **"FATHERHOOD OF GOD."**

ON NOVEMBER 30TH, 1989 MASONIC HISTORY WAS REPORTEDLY MADE IN THE STATE OF NEW YORK AS WHITE AMERICAN ANGLO-SAXON FREEMASONS AND THEIR WIVES FROM WITHIN THAT GRAND JURISDICTION MET WITH PRINCE HALL FREEMASONS AND THEIR WIVES AT A "FELLOWSHIP DINNER "BEING HELD AT THE CAVALIER RESTAURANT IN AMHERST, N.Y. THE FESTIVE OCCASION WAS SPONSORED BY A JOINT COMMITTEE OF PERSEVERANCE LODGE NO. 948 OF THE FIRST ERIE DISTRICT AND PARAMOUNT LODGE NO. 73 OF PRINCE HALL LODGERY. THE NEW YORK STATE'S GRAND MASTER, BROTHER BOSWELL T. SWITS AND THE WHITE BRETHRENSHIP OF THE ERIE DISTRICTS BROKE BREAD WITH FRATERNITY BROTHER SOLOMON WALLACE (THE GRAND MASTER OF THE MOST WORSHIPFUL PRINCE HALL GRAND LODGE OF THE NEW YORK STATE JURISDICTION) AND THE BRETHREN OF THE PRINCE HALL MASONIC

Lodges of Erie County. All parties involved were said to have had a great time as they enjoyed the good food and shared each others enlightening stories of mutual respect for one another. Although this festive occasion reportedly went off without a hitch, all was not well in paradise lost as dissection amongst the American Anglo-Saxon Freemasonry population began to grow even stronger as more and more white members of the Ancient Craft demanded that Black Freemasonry be fully recognized as a living, breathing organism of the Masonic Family of Man.

Bitterly divided on the subject of recognizing Black Freemasonry, it was as though the hands of time had been turned back to the days of Abraham Lincoln's posting in the Oval Office. Despite the fact that the Masonic deadline for full global domination was merely ten years away, not all members of the Ancient Craft of Freemasonry felt obligated to eliminate the racial barriers at the close of the Twentieth Century. Just the very though of recognizing American Black Masonry as their social equal was like waving a blood soaked U.S. Confederate flag in the deep South while those in the northern States continued pointing fingers at the South for not wanting to remove the shackles of the Black populations never-ending fraternity bondage.

As more and more Masonic Lodges in the northern U.S. States adopted a resolution giving recognizable powers to the Prince Hall Grand Lodge of their designated jurisdictions, opposing Freemasonry forces issued edicts prohibiting its members from visiting and/or attending those Lodges adopting the resolution. With the edicts flying fast and furious, numerous Grand Lodges severed all Masonic relations and/or communications with other American Grand Lodges. The Grand Lodge of Louisiana for example broke off all contact with the Grand Lodge of Connecticut on the basis that the Grand Lodge of Connecticut and the Prince Hall Grand Lodge of Connecticut had recognized each others Constitutional Right to co-exist. While everlasting Freemasonry tensions mounted with each passing day, the Grand Lodge of Rhode Island issued its own form of edict questioning the jurisdictional rights of all those involved in the dilemma. An argument was thusly put forward in written form stating that although the Grand Lodge of Rhode Island had no formal agreement with the Grand Lodge of Connecticut nor with that State's Prince Hall Grand Lodge, it was business as usual as the State of Rhode Island's Freemasonry population recognized each Lodge's right to freely visit all Masonic

Lodgery anywhere within the Continental United States. As far as the Grand Lodge of Rhode Island was concerned, if its members wanted to visit any of the Black Masonic Lodges they were totally allowed to do so on their own free will and accord despite the fact that some of the Masonic governing powers that be preferred otherwise. Perhaps it was for this reason that both the Grand Lodge of Rhode Island and the Prince Hall Grand Lodge of Rhode Island established a committee to initiate meaningful dialogue with prospects of legitimatizing Black Freemasonry.

Just as the Islamic Freemasonry leader of Iraq had acquired control of Kuwait during the summer of 1990, a long list of Grand Lodges within the Continental United States appointed special committees to study the feasibility of recognizing Prince Hall Freemasonry. According to these members of the country's white Masonic Brotherhood, it only made sense that Black Masonry be recognized as it was afterall, historically older than the country itself. Just to name a few of the other Grand Lodges that were willing to go that extra mile for the Black members of the Craft were as follows; Grand Lodge of the State of Iowa, Grand Lodge of the State of Washington, Grand Lodge of the State of Nebraska, Grand Lodge of the State of Idaho, and Grand Lodge of the State of Oregon. In Nebraska for example, both the Prince Hall Grand Lodge as well as that State's white Freemasonry Grand Lodge officially recognized each other as legal Masonic Grand Lodges on February 3rd, 1990 as simultaneous resolutions were passed acknowledging this as being a fact of life. These actions therefore officially ended the many years of misunderstanding and bloodshed that had come between the two fraternity bodies concerning the Masonic legitimacy of each organizations Constitutional Right of existence. As Grand Master Norman C. Hall of the Prince Hall Grand Lodge and Grand Master Thomas W. Tye of the Nebraska Grand Lodge celebrated the passing of the resolutions, it was duly noted as a historical milestone for the Ancient Craft, as this mutual respect and fraternal understanding literally meant unrestricted Masonic recognition for all of the State of Nebraska's Black Freemasonry population. In that same year, the Grand Lodge of Washington State also extended recognition rights to the Prince Hall Grand Lodge of Washington "with rights of visitation only. "In return, the Prince Hall Grand Lodge passed a resolution in identical terms to be bestowed onto that State's white American Anglo-Saxon Freemasonry population. With communications being opened at an extremely slow pace, the Grand

LODGE OF WISCONSIN IN JUNE OF 1990 AGREED TO RECOGNIZE THE PRINCE HALL GRAND LODGE OF WISCONSIN "FOR VISITATION PURPOSES ONLY." THE PRINCE HALL GRAND LODGE THEN IN RETURN AGREED TO RECOGNIZE THE GRAND LODGE OF WISCONSIN "FOR VISITATION PURPOSES ONLY. "AS THIS FRATERNITY GAME OF CHESS WAS BEING PLAYED OUT STATE-BY-STATE, MORE AND MORE MASONICALLY CONTROLLED GOVERNMENTAL JURISDICTIONS WITHIN THE CONTINENTAL UNITED STATES BEGAN TO FINALLY OPEN THEIR HEARTS TO THE BLACK FREEMASONRY POPULATION OF THE GOOD OLD U.S. OF A.

UPON HEARING THE NEWS OF SOME AMERICAN FREEMASONS WANTING FULL RECOGNITION TO BE IMPLEMENTED FOR BLACK MEMBERS OF THE ANCIENT CRAFT OF FREEMASONRY, THE UNITED GRAND LODGE OF ENGLAND WAS NOT AL ALL AMUSED AS THE RIFF THAT WAS BEING FELT IN NORTH AMERICA WAS SLOWLY MAKING ITS WAY ACROSS THE WATERS TO GREAT BRITAIN. BEFORE LONG, ENGLAND'S FREEMASONRY LEADERS WERE GIVING THEIR BRETHRENSHIP STERN WARNINGS TOWARDS THE POSSIBILITY OF EXPULSION BEING EXERCISED ONTO THEM IF THEY DARED PAY A VISIT TO THE HIGHLY UNRECOGNIZED BLACK LODGES WHILE TRAVELING ABROAD. LIKE MOST OF THE AMERICAN FREEMASONRY LODGES OF NORTH AMERICA, THEIR GOVERNING MASONIC BODY IN GREAT BRITAIN ALSO DID NOT RECOGNIZE BLACK FREEMASONRY'S U.S. CONSTITUTIONAL RIGHT OF CO-EXISTENCE WITHIN THE BROTHERHOOD ITSELF.

BY SPRING OF 1991, IT SEEMED AS THOUGH THE VAST MAJORITY OF AMERICAN FREEMASONS WERE ABOUT TO CHANGE THEIR MINDS CONCERNING THE HARD NOSED STANCE THAT WAS BEING TAKEN TOWARDS NOT RECOGNIZING BLACK FREEMASONRY AS AN ASSET TO THE CRAFT. BUT LIKE EVERYTHING ELSE IN THE WORLD OF MASONIC POLITICAL ACTIVITIES, THIS WAS NOT TO BE AS FURTHER EDICTS WERE BEING ISSUED FORBIDDING MEMBERS OF THE NOBLE AND ANCIENT CRAFT TO BE PRESENT IN LODGES UNDER THE JURISDICTIONS OF THE GRAND LODGES OF CONNECTICUT, WISCONSIN, NEBRASKA, WASHINGTON AND ALL THOSE OTHER GRAND LODGES WHO WERE ATTEMPTING TO MAKE BLACK FREEMASONS EQUAL UNDER THE CONSTITUTIONAL LAWS OF THE UNITED STATES OF THE AMERICA'S. THE GRAND LODGE OF WEST VIRGINIA FOR EXAMPLE WAS ONE OF THE VERY FIRST GRAND LODGES TO ISSUE SUCH AS EDICT IN RETALIATION. AS THE FREE-FOR-ALL BEGAN TO ESCALATE TO EPIDEMIC PROPORTIONS, THE AMERICAN FREEMASONRY BROTHERHOOD MEMBERS WERE SOON AT EACH OTHERS THROATS FIGHTING AMONGST THEMSELVES EVEN FURTHER AS ATTEMPTS WERE MADE TO DOUSE THE FLAMES OF FRATERNITY RACISM.

MEANWHILE NORTH OF THE 49TH PARALLEL, CANADIAN FREEMASONS ALMOST IMMEDIATELY BEGAN TAKING THE NECESSARY MEASURES OF ACCEPTING

ALL BLACK MEMBERS OF FREEMASONRY AS THEIR SOCIAL EQUAL WHILE OPEN DISCUSSIONS ON PRINCE HALL MASONRY WERE THE MAIN TOPICS OF MOST GRAND LODGES RIGHT ACROSS THE NATION. THIS ACT WAS EVIDENT AT THEIR 1992 WINNIPEG, MANITOBA CONFERENCE HELD DURING THE MONTH OF MARCH, (MARCH 20TH AND 21ST), WHERE IT WAS DECREED THAT PRINCE HALL MASONRY WITHIN THE JURISDICTIONAL BOUNDARIES OF THE CANADIAN MASONIC FAMILY OF MAN HAD A LEGITIMATE CLAIM FOR FULL RECOGNITION BY THE BROTHERHOOD. A RESOLUTION WAS THEREFORE ADOPTED ENCOURAGING ALL CANADIAN GRAND LODGES TO ACKNOWLEDGE THIS LEGITIMACY IN THEIR PERSPECTIVE PROVINCIAL AND TERRITORIAL JURISDICTIONS. MEMBERS OF FREEMASONRY IN BRITISH COLUMBIA FOR INSTANCE WERE PERMITTED TO ATTEND WHITE LODGE MEETINGS WITHIN SUCH STATES AS WASHINGTON AND OTHER JURISDICTIONS IF THEY SO DESIRED BUT WERE STILL DENIED THE PRIVILEGE OF ATTENDING ANY PRINCE HALL LODGERY MEETINGS WITHIN THE CONTINENTAL UNITED STATES. LESS THAN A MONTH PRIOR TO THE WINNIPEG CONFERENCE TAKING PLACE, OVER 100 BRITISH COLUMBIA FREEMASONS FROM 15 MASONIC LODGES ON THE SOUTHERN PORTION OF VANCOUVER ISLAND, (VICTORIA DISTRICTS NO. 1 AND 21 IN CONJUNCTION WITH THE VICTORIA LODGE OF EDUCATION AND RESEARCH), WERE THROWING A SHIN-DIG OF SORTS HELD AT ONE OF THEIR LODGES. ALSO IN ATTENDANCE AT THE FEBRUARY 29TH, 1992 FESTIVE CELEBRATION WAS FRATERNITY BROTHER BILL RHEUBOTTOM, THE GRAND SENIOR WARDEN OF THE PRINCE HALL MASONS OF THE STATE OF WASHINGTON. BROTHER RHEUBOTTOM REPORTEDLY GAVE A BRIEF HISTORY AND THE NEVER-ENDING CONFLICTS WHICH HAD TRANSPIRED BETWEEN BLACK FREEMASONS AND MANY CAUCASIAN GRAND LODGES. NEEDLESS TO SAY, THE BRETHRENSHIP HAD LOTS OF QUESTIONS FOR THE GUEST SPEAKER. ACCORDING TO THE CONTENTS OF THEIR OWN PAPER TRAIL, MASONIC BROTHER RHEUBOTTOM WAS SIMPLY REFERRED TO AS MR. RHEUBOTTOM WHICH WITHOUT A DOUBT STRESSED THE IMPORTANCE OF FACT THAT EVEN THE GRAND LODGE OF BRITISH COLUMBIA DID NOT RECOGNIZE BLACK FREEMASONRY'S CONSTITUTIONAL RIGHT TO CO-EXIST.

AS THE EVER INCREASING TENSIONS MOUNTED ON THE NORTH AMERICAN CONTINENT, THE PRINCE HALL GRAND LODGE OF WASHINGTON MADE A FORMAL REQUEST FOR FULL FRATERNAL RECOGNITION FROM THE UNITED GRAND LODGE OF ENGLAND. WITH THIS ULTIMATE REQUEST FOR RECOGNITION BEING MADE, IT VIRTUALLY SET THE WHEELS IN MOTION FOR THE UNITED GRAND LODGE OF ENGLAND'S ABILITY TO RELINQUISH THE TIDES OF RACISM BY ACKNOWLEDGING FULL MASONIC POWERS TO ALL OF THE AMERICAN PRINCE HALL LODGES WITHIN THE UNITED STATES. ON OCTOBER 11TH, 1991 BROTHER OSCAR F. BOEHRINGER (CHAIRMAN OF THE EXTERNAL RELATIONS COMMITTEE OF THE BOARD OF GENERAL PURPOSES OF THE UNITED

GRAND LODGE OF ENGLAND), CONTACTED FRATERNITY BROTHER JAMES O. WOOD (PAST GRAND MASTER OF THE GRAND LODGE OF WASHINGTON), REQUESTING THAT HE ACT AS A EMISSARY TO THE PRINCE HALL GRAND LODGE OF WASHINGTON STATE. AS FAR AS THE UNITED GRAND LODGE OF ENGLAND WAS CONCERNED, BROTHER WOOD WAS TOTALLY QUALIFIED TO FULFILL THE SHOES OF THE POSTING LARGELY DUE TO THE FACT THAT HE HAD SERVED AS THE CHAIRMAN OF THE GRAND LODGE OF WASHINGTON'S COMMITTEE WHICH WAS SPONSORING THE MOVE FOR A RESOLUTION TO RECOGNIZE THE PRINCE HALL GRAND LODGE OF WASHINGTON AND WAS ALSO PRESENT DURING THE INITIAL TALKS THAT WERE CONDUCTED IN APRIL OF 1991 IN BOSTON BETWEEN ENGLAND'S GRAND SECRETARY M.B.S. HIGHAM, OSCAR BOEHRINGER AND REPRESENTATIVES OF THE SEVERAL AMERICAN GRAND LODGES THAT HAD RECOGNIZED BLACK FREEMASONRY'S U.S. CONSTITUTIONAL RIGHT OF EXISTENCE. WITH THE PRINCE HALL GRAND LODGE OF WASHINGTON TAKING THE FIRST STEP TO SECURE THE VALUABLE INFORMATION THAT WAS NEEDED FOR FULL MASONIC RECOGNITION, THE UNITED GRAND LODGE OF ENGLAND WAS THEREFORE OBLIGATED BY ITS SACRED DUTY TO CONDUCT AN INVESTIGATION INTO PROSPECTS OF ACKNOWLEDGING BLACK FREEMASONRY'S RIGHT TO HAVE ALL FRATERNAL POWERS BESTOWED ONTO THEM. WHILE ACTING AS AN OFFICIAL EMISSARY TO THE PRINCE HALL GRAND LODGE OF WASHINGTON STATE, BROTHER WOOD ANTICIPATED THAT ENGLAND'S GOVERNING MASONIC BODY WOULD ESSENTIALLY "SOFTEN" ITS DICTATORIAL BAN ON LODGE VISITATIONS IN STATES WERE BLACK FREEMASONRY HAD BEEN RECOGNIZED BY THE WHITE BRETHRENSHIP AS APPARENTLY MOST OF THE HIGH RANKING BRITISH MASTER MASONS HAD MANAGED TO CIRCLE THE WAGONS, FORMING A "CHARMED CIRCLE" FOR WHOM THE BAN DID NOT APPLY.

AS IT TURNS OUT, BLACK FREEMASONRY IN THE STATE OF WASHINGTON WAS IN FACT ONCE A FULLY RECOGNIZED MASONIC INSTITUTION AS THE ACTIONS OF ONE OF THE GRAND LODGE'S PAST GRAND MASTER'S, FRATERNITY BROTHER WILLIAM H. UPTON LITERALLY FORCED THE MASONIC POWERS THAT BE IN ENGLAND TO ACKNOWLEDGE PRINCE HALL MASONRY'S CONSTITUTIONAL RIGHT FOR CO-EXISTENCE IN THAT STATE. THIS CAME LARGELY DUE TO THE FACT THAT TWO BLACK SEATTLE RESIDENTS SUBMITTED A PETITION TO THE GRAND LODGE OF WASHINGTON STATE IN 1898 ASKING TO BE RECOGNIZED AS A FRATERNAL ORGANISM WITHIN THE FAMILY FOLD. AFTER ANALYZING THE SITUATION BEFORE HIM, THE GRAND MASTER OF THE GRAND LODGE OF THE STATE OF WASHINGTON ESTABLISHED A COMMITTEE TO REVIEW THE REQUEST MADE BY THE BLACK FREEMASONS. IN THE COMMITTEE'S REPORT, THE QUESTION OF BLACK FREEMASONRY WAS DETAILED IN LONG LENGTH AND FOUR POSSIBLE RESOLUTIONS WERE THUSLY PUT FORWARD FOR CONSIDERATION;

1) FREEMASONRY BEING UNIVERSAL, AND HOLDING NO RESTRICTIONS TOWARDS RACE AND/OR COLOR WERE BOUND BY ITS OWN FUNDAMENTAL PHILOSOPHIES AND TEACHINGS.

2) BLACK FREEMASONRY WAS HISTORICALLY LEGITIMATE.

3) FREEMASONRY WAS THAT OF A SOCIAL INSTITUTION AND THAT PERHAPS IT WOULD BE BETTER SERVED IF CITIZENS OF AFRICAN DECENT BE PERMITTED TO MINGLE AMONGST OTHER MEMBERS OF THEIR OWN KIND.

4) DO ABSOLUTELY NOTHING.

ALTHOUGH FRATERNITY BROTHER UPTON WAS GIVEN THE OPPORTUNITY TO PASS THE BUCK BY FORWARDING THE APPLICATION FOR FULL MASONIC RECOGNITION BACK TO THE PETITIONERS, HE CHOOSE TO RECOGNIZE BLACK FREEMASONRY'S RIGHT TO CO-EXIST. REPORTEDLY MANY OF THE GRAND LODGES WITHIN THE CONTINENTAL UNITED STATES WERE MORTALLY OFFENDED BY THE ACTIONS TAKEN BY THE GRAND LODGE OF WASHINGTON STATE, DISSENSION QUICKLY ROSE TO NEW EVERLASTING HEIGHTS AS MASONIC LODGES IN THE DEEP SOUTH BROKE OFF ALL CONTACT WITH MEMBERS OF THE ANCIENT CRAFT IN THE WEST. IN AN INSTANT REVOLT, MANY OF THE SURROUNDING MASONICALLY CONTROLLED AMERICAN STATES WITHDREW THEIR FRATERNITY TIES WITH THE RENEGADE STATE OF WASHINGTON FOR INITIATING SUCH AN OUTRAGEOUS MANEUVER. AS THE WAR OF WORDS SOON ESCALATED OUT OF CONTROL, THE RESOLUTIONS SUBMITTED BY THE COMMITTEE WERE SOMEWHAT MODIFIED BY THE GRAND LODGE OF WASHINGTON IN AN ATTEMPT TO REKINDLE FRATERNAL RELATIONS WITH THE DISGRUNTLED MEMBERS OF THE **"BROTHERHOOD OF MAN. "** BY THIS TIME PERIOD OF COURSE, BROTHER UPTON WAS FORCED TO VACATE HIS OFFICE AS GRAND MASTER AND SHORTLY THEREAFTER, (1899), THE GRAND LODGE OF WASHINGTON RESCINDED ITS ORIGINAL CLAIM OF BLACK FREEMASONS HAVING THE EXACT SAME CONSTITUTIONAL RIGHTS AS WHITE AMERICAN FREEMASONS.

IN THE SAME YEAR THAT WASHINGTON STATE PASSED INTO LAW REVOKING BLACK FREEMASONRY'S RIGHT TO CO-EXIST, THE GRAND LODGE OF BRITISH COLUMBIA REFERRED TO THIS GROWING CONTROVERSY AS THOUGH THEY WERE WALKING ON EGG SHELLS. APPARENTLY, SOME MEMBERS OF BRITISH COLUMBIA'S FREEMASONRY POPULATION FELT SOMEWHAT SYMPATHETIC TOWARDS THE ACTIONS OF THE GRAND LODGE OF WASHINGTON STATE AS THE GRAND LODGE OF BRITISH COLUMBIA HAD NEVER RECOGNIZED BLACK FREEMASONRY'S CONSTITUTIONAL RIGHT TO CO-EXIST. WASHINGTON STATE'S FORMER GRAND MASTER UPTON WASN'T EXONERATED BY THE AMERICAN BRETHRENSHIP FOR HIS ACT OF BETRAYAL AGAINST THE MASONIC BROTHERHOOD FOR TAKING BOLD NEW STEPS OF TREATING BLACK MASTER MASONS AS BEING EQUAL TO WHITE MASTER MASONS UNTIL 1990. FRATERNITY BROTHER UPTON THEREFORE

RECEIVED FULL FREEMASONRY HONORS AS A MEMORIAL STONE WAS THUSLY PLACED AT HIS GRAVE SITE AT MOUNTAIN VIEW CEMETERY IN WALLA WALLA, WASHINGTON.

IT GOES WITHOUT SAYING, THAT THE VAST MAJORITY OF ENGLAND'S HIGH RANKING FRATERNITY LEADERS DIDN'T WANT A REPEAT PERFORMANCE OF BROTHER UPTON'S WASHINGTON STATE SCHISM ACTIVITIES TO OCCUR SO DAMN BLOODY CLOSE TO THE NEW MILLENNIUM DEADLINE. BY MARCH 13TH, 1991 THE UNITED GRAND LODGE OF ENGLAND WAS REVIEWING REPORTS THAT THE GRAND LODGES OF CONNECTICUT, WISCONSIN, NEBRASKA AND THE STATE OF WASHINGTON WERE EXCEEDING THEIR JURISDICTIONAL POWERS BY FULLY RECOGNIZING BLACK FREEMASONRY'S U.S. CONSTITUTIONAL RIGHT TO CO-EXIST AMONGST THOSE OF WHITE AMERICAN ANGLO-SAXON FREEMASONRY BLOODLINES. IT WAS THEREFORE REPORTED THAT IF FOUND GUILTY OF BREACHING THEIR FRATERNAL GOVERNING POWERS, THE UNITED GRAND LODGE OF ENGLAND HAD THE LEGAL RIGHT NOT TO RECOGNIZE THESE FOUR GRAND LODGES OF THE UNITED STATES OF THE AMERICA'S AS BEING MASONIC ENTITIES. UNTIL A RULING WAS DECREED BY LAW, THE FREEMASONRY BRETHREN OF ENGLAND AND THE ENTIRE NORTH AMERICAN CONTINENT, (CANADA INCLUDED), WERE PROHIBITED FROM VISITING ALL FOUR OF THE GRAND LODGES DESIGNATED JURISDICTIONS. ALTHOUGH FREEMASONS OF NORTH AMERICA WERE FORBIDDEN TO VISIT THOSE DISSIDENT MEMBERS OF THE FOUR U.S. STATES, BRETHREN FROM ALL OF THE RECOGNIZED MASONIC JURISDICTIONS IN THE WESTERN FREE-WORLD (INCLUDING THOSE JURISDICTIONS OF THE FOUR DISSIDENT GRAND LODGES) WERE ABLE TO CONTINUE VISITING THE UNITED GRAND LODGE OF ENGLAND'S JURISDICTION IF THEY SO DESIRED. IN TOTAL, THE UNITED GRAND LODGE OF ENGLAND RECOGNIZED AN ESTIMATED 117 GRAND LODGES FROM ALL OVER THE WORLD WHILE COUNTLESS OTHERS REMAINED TOTALLY UNRECOGNIZED AS THEY WERE LEGALLY NON-EXISTENT ENTITIES OF THE ANCIENT CRAFT.

AT THE EXACT SAME TIME PERIOD THAT THE UNITED GRAND LODGE OF ENGLAND BEGAN CONTEMPLATING AS TO WHAT WAS THE EASIEST AND BEST WAY OF DEALING WITH THE CRISIS THAT HAD MANAGED TO UNFOLD ITSELF ACROSS THE WATERS IN NORTH AMERICA, AN ALL CANADA CONFERENCE IN WINNIPEG WAS BEING ATTENDED BY THE GRAND MASTERS, DEPUTY GRAND MASTERS AND GRAND SECRETARIES OF ALL JURISDICTIONS FROM THE EASTERN SHORES OF NEWFOUNDLAND TO VICTORIA ON THE PACIFIC AS WELL AS CANADA'S NORTHERN FRONTIER, (MARCH 15TH AND 16TH, 1991). TOPPING THE AGENDA NATURALLY WERE DISCUSSIONS ON BLACK FREEMASONRY AS BOTH THE PROVINCES OF ONTARIO AND QUEBEC HAD PRINCE HALL GRAND LODGES OPERATING WITHIN THEIR JURISDICTIONAL BOUNDARIES. AT THE TIME, BLACK FREEMASONRY POSED NO INITIAL THREAT TO THE CANADIAN MASONIC FAMILY

OF MAN AS THEY WERE NOT SEEKING FULL FRATERNITY RECOGNITION AS OF YET. TABLED AT THE 1991 WINNIPEG CONFERENCE WAS A DISCUSSION PAPER ENTITLED; "PRINCE HALL FREEMASONRY – A CANADIAN APPROACH. "THIS DISCUSSION PAPER ESSENTIALLY GAVE WAY TO THE TABLING OF A RESOLUTION TO ACKNOWLEDGE THE LEGITIMACY OF BLACK FREEMASONRY IN CANADA AT THE 1992 WINNIPEG CONFERENCE WHICH TOOK PLACE ON MARCH 20TH AND 21ST OF THAT YEAR.

BY THE TIME THE NEW MILLENNIUM AND ITS PREDESTINED DEADLINE POKED ITS HEAD AROUND THE FRATERNITY CORNER – ALL OF THE ANIMOSITY THAT WAS BEING GENERATED BETWEEN PRINCE HALL FREEMASONRY AND THEIR WHITE COUNTERPARTS ON BOTH SIDES OF THE 49TH PARALLEL, IT SEEMED AS THOUGH EVERYONE WAS WAITING WITH BAITED BREATH FOR SOME SORT OF CHARISMATIC PERSONALITY. SOMEONE ABLE TO SPEAK SOFTLY BUT YET STILL CAPABLE OF SWINGING TEDDY ROOSEVELT'S BIG FREEMASONRY ENLIGHTENMENT STICK TO BECOME NORTH AMERICA'S VERY FIRST HIGH PROFILE BLACK AMERICAN PRESIDENT OF THE UNITED STATES TO HELP CALM THE TURBULENT WATERS BY UNIFYING ALL MEMBERS OF THE MASONIC ORDER INTO ONE BENEVOLENT BROTHERHOOD ONCE AGAIN.

HISTORY HAS PROVEN THUS FAR THAT WHILE FREEMASONRY IS SUPPOSEDLY THAT OF A BENEVOLENT BROTHERHOOD STANDING FOR **FREEDOM** AND **DEMOCRACY** FOR ALL OF THE WORLD'S INHABITANTS, IT IS ACTUALLY A FRATERNITY OF POWER SEEKING DICTATORS HELL BENT NOT ONLY ON RULING THE ENTIRE WORLD BUT ALSO FORCING THEIR OPINIONATED VIEWS ONTO OTHERS. THIS DESPITE THE FACT THAT IN ACCORDANCE TO THEIR OWN LITERATURE, THEY ARE SUPPOSEDLY NOT INVOLVED WITH THE POLITICAL AFFAIRS OF A WELL ORCHESTRATED HIDDEN AGENDA. ACCORDING TO THE DATA AVAILABLE, THE FOLLOWING IS A LIST OF WHITE U.S. LODGERY AND ITS MEMBERSHIP NUMBERS CONTAINED WITHIN THE 1989 LIST OF MASONIC LODGES SUBMITTED TO THE GRAND LODGE OF BRITISH COLUMBIA;

STATE	REGULAR LODGES	MEMBERS	YEAR GRAND LODGE INSTITUTED
ALABAMA	391	58,462	1821
ALASKA	16	2,006	1981
(EXCLUDING 6 ALASKA LODGES UNDER THE GRAND LODGE OF WASHINGTON)			
ARIZONA	70	15,417	1882
(WITH 3 RESEARCH LODGES)			
ARKANSAS	347	40,320	1838

California	561	159,567	1850
		(Including Hawaiian Lodges)	
Colorado	165	28,749	1867
Connecticut	131	28,542	1789
Delaware	31	7,967	1806
District of Columbia	31	8,120	1811
Florida	329	78,450	1830
Georgia	456	81,646	1735
Idaho	78	9,122	1867
Illinois	688	127,690	1840
Indiana	536	134,252	1818
Iowa	421	49,882	1844
Kansas	345	59,156	1856
Kentucky	458	83,862	1800
Louisiana	284	38,518	1812
Maine	200	34,642	1820
Maryland	129	34,348	1787
Massachusetts	317	78,850	1733
Michigan	462	92,707	1826
Minnesota	222	37,958	1853
Mississippi	296	40,838	1818
Missouri	503	78,546	1821
Montana	125	13,149	1866
Nebraska	213	27,723	1857
Nevada	43	7,317	1865
		(Interestingly, there are 5 Lodges in Las Vegas and 6 in Reno)	
New Hampshire	78	21,318	1789
New Jersey	193	58,343	1786
New Mexico	68	10,268	1877
New York	795	124,737	1781
		(Plus 10 overseas Lodges)	

NORTH CAROLINA	394	70,224	1787
NORTH DAKOTA	87	6,922	1889
OHIO	658	196,362	1808
OKLAHOMA	296	50,750	1892
OREGON	166	24,167	1851
PENNSYLVANIA	537	187,361	1730
RHODE ISLAND	44	9,574	1791
SOUTH CAROLINA	331	69,060	1737
SOUTH DAKOTA	126	10,940	1875
TENNESSEE	378	88,659	1813
TEXAS	951	186,088	1837
UTAH	31	3,883	1872
VERMONT	95	11,135	1794
VIRGINIA	357	62,000	1778
WASHINGTON STATE	253	37,132	1858

(INCLUDING 6 LODGES IN THE STATE OF ALASKA)

WEST VIRGINIA	152	36,603	1865
WISCONSIN	255	31,721	1843
WYOMING	52	8,872	1874

FOR A TOTAL OF 50 STATES WITH 13,228 RECOGNIZED MASONIC LODGES WITH A REGISTERED MEMBERSHIP ROSTER OF 2,762,115 PROMINENT COMMUNITY FIGURES OF THE GOOD OLD U.S. OF A. ALSO CONTAINED WITHIN THE 1989 LIST OF MASONIC LODGES SUBMITTED TO THE GRAND LODGE OF BRITISH COLUMBIA WAS FURTHER DOCUMENTATION PERTAINING TO SOME OF THE MOST POWERFULLY RECOGNIZED GRAND LODGES OF THE WORLD AS THEY BECAME POLITICAL ACTIVATED ORGANISM WITH A MANDATE TO HELP TO ORCHESTRATE A BENEVOLENT BROTHERHOOD OF THE FRATERNITY'S **NEW WORLD ORDER** CONCEPT;

GRAND LODGE	**REGULAR LODGES**	**MEMBERS**	**YEAR INSTITUTED**
ARGENTINA	73	2,500	1857

NEW SOUTH WALES	654	53,325	1888
QUEENSLAND	461	26,400	1921
SOUTH AUSTRALIA	194	12,000	1884
TASMANIA	77	5,928	1890
VICTORIA, AUSTRALIA	700	50,000	1889

(THE HON. JUSTICE WILLIAMS OF THE AUSTRALIAN SUPREME COURT WAS THE GRAND MASTER 1989-90)

AUSTRIA	48	1,900	1784
BELGIUM	23	NO DATA	1979
BOLIVIA	30	1,880	1929
CHILE	162	NO DATA	1862
DENMARK	77	NO DATA	1745
DOMINICAN REPUBLIC	32	NO DATA	1858
ECUADOR	8	NO DATA	1921
FINLAND	102	4,400	1924
FRANCE	566	NO DATA	1743
GARBON	8	NO DATA	1983
GERMANY	396	21,000	1737
GREECE	68	NO DATA	1811
GUATEMALA	31	825	1903
HONDURAS	13	325	1922
ICELAND	13	2,429	1951
ITALY	568	NO DATA	1805
NETHERLANDS	148	7,010	1756
NORWAY	37	15,812	NO DATA
PANAMA	10	NO DATA	1916
PARAGUAY	11	850	1869
PERU	154	6,240	1882
PUERTO RICO	71	4,000	1885
EL SALVADOR	15	NO DATA	1912

SPAIN	38	NO DATA	1982
SWEDEN	67	NO DATA	1765
	(DURING 1989-90, HIS ROYAL HIGHNESS PRINCE		
	BERTIL OF SWEDEN WAS THE GRAND MASTER)		
SWITZERLAND	62	3,703	1844
TURKEY	81	6,700	1909
VENEZUELA	91	NO DATA	1824

UNFORTUNATELY, MUCH OF THE DATE CONTAINED WITHIN THE LIST OF MASONIC LODGES ON A GLOBAL SCALE REGARDING THE MEMBERSHIP OF MOST OF THE CONTROLLED FRATERNITY COUNTRIES ARE ACTUALLY INCOMPLETE PIECES OF THE PUZZLE. DESPITE THIS LITTLE KNOWN QUIRK, ONE CAN STILL ARRIVE AT THE CONCLUSION THAT THE MASONIC INFLUENCE IS STILL A VERY POWERFUL FORCE WORLDWIDE. TO FURTHER ADD CONFUSION TO THE ISSUE, ISRAEL REPORTEDLY HAD 63 MASONIC LODGES LISTED WITH A MEMBERSHIP ROSTER OF ABOUT 3,000 PEOPLE, (EIGHT IN HAIFA, NINE IN JERUSALEM AND 18 IN TEL-AVIV). FURTHER TO THIS, ACCORDING TO THE SAME DOCUMENTATION, WHILE JAPAN'S MASONIC LODGERY REPORTEDLY CONSISTED OF 21 IN TOTAL WITH OVER 3,052 MEMBERS LISTED, COMMUNIST CHINA HAD 9 LODGES WITH UNDER 1,000 MEMBERS. ISRAEL'S GRAND LODGE WAS THEREFORE LISTED AS BEING FIRST INSTITUTED IN 1932, JAPAN'S 1957 AND CHINA'S 1949.

ACCORDING TO THE FURTHER DOCUMENTATION, THE GRAND LODGE OF IRAN WAS SAID TO HAVE BEEN FORMED ON MARCH 1ST, 1969 UNDER THE JOINT SPONSORSHIP OF THE GRAND LODGE OF SCOTLAND, THE NATIONAL GRAND LODGE OF FRANCE AND THE UNITED GRAND LODGE OF GERMANY, WITH AN OFFICIAL REPRESENTATIVE OF THE GRAND LODGE OF ENGLAND PRESENT. INTERESTINGLY, ONCE THE UNITED STATES PUPPET THE SHAH OF IRAN (SHAH MOHAMMED REZA PAHLAVI) SEIZED POWER IN 1953 WITH HIS AMERICAN CIA BACKED COUP, THE IRANIAN PRIME MINISTER MOHAMMED MOSSADEZ WAS FORCED TO FLEE FOR HIS LIFE AS THE CONJOINT TERRORIST PLOY (CIA AND BRITISH MI6) TO HAVE HIM TOPPLED AS THE RULING GOVERNING BODY NOW WANTED HIS HEAD ON A SLIVER PLATTER. WITH THE SHAH OF IRAN IN PLACE AS THE MAIN FIGUREHEAD IN THE MIDDLE EAST, THE MASONIC **BROTHERHOOD OF MAN** WAS ONCE AGAIN ABLE TO FLOURISH AT A MUCH IMPROVED RATE OF SPEED. AS THE VARIOUS MASONIC LODGES IN IRAN BEGAN TO INCREASE THROUGHOUT THE 1950'S AND 1960'S, POLITICAL AUTONOMY WAS ESSENTIALLY GUIDED BY THE DESIGNATED GRAND LODGE OF IRAN IN 1969 WITH BOTH THE UNITED STATES AND GREAT BRITAIN PULLING THE PUPPETRY STRINGS. BEFORE LONG, FULL MASONIC RECOGNITION WAS BEING BESTOWED UPON THE

COUNTRY OF IRAN ON A GLOBAL SCALE BY SUCH COUNTRIES AS SCOTLAND, FRANCE, GERMANY, ARGENTINA, SOUTH AFRICA, INDIA, ISRAEL, VENEZUELA, COLUMBIA, AS WELL AS SEVERAL GRAND LODGES IN CANADA AND MOST OF THE GRAND LODGES WITHIN THE CONTINENTAL UNITED STATES. AND BY THE TIME THE IRANIAN LEADER AYATOLLAH RUHOLLAH KHOMEINI ROSE TO POWER IN A 1979 RELIGIOUS COUNTER-REVOLUTION, THE U. S. GOVERNMENT DECIDED TO USE ISLAMIC FREEMASONRY LEADER SADDAM HUSSEIN AS A POND IN AN ATTEMPT TO RE-GAIN THE STRANGLEHOLD THAT THE AMERICAN AND BRITISH MASONIC LEADERS HAD LOST WHILE THE AYATOLLAH RULED THE COUNTRY.

WHEN AN INDIVIDUAL STUDIES FREEMASONRY JUST FOR THE SAKE OF HAVING A MUCH BETTER UNDERSTANDING OF ITS FUNDAMENTAL PRINCIPLES, IT DOESN'T TAKE THE STUDENT VERY LONG BEFORE HE /OR SHE FINDS THEMSELVES DABBLING INTO THE SUBJECT OF COMPARATIVE RELIGIONS. IN RESEARCHING RELIGION, A VERY LONG LIST OF REFERENCE BOOKS ARE NEEDED. THE PROBLEM BEING OF COURSE THAT NO TWO BOOKS ARE ALIKE AS ONE BOOK MAY STATE SOMETHING AS BEING A TRUE FACT, WHILE THE OTHER STATES THAT IT ISN'T. WHEN IT COMES TO RELIGION, THE DATA CAN GET SOMEWHAT CONFUSING AS VARIOUS WRITERS (RELIGIOUS AND/OR OTHERWISE) CREATE A MAZE OF POLITICAL/RELIGIOUS DOUBLE-TALK. TO HELP ILLUSTRATE HOW WRITTEN OPINIONS CAN SOMETIMES DIFFER, A BOOK PUBLISHED IN 1888, COMPILED BY A FREEMASON, BROTHER W.J. WHYMPER TITLED; "THE RELIGION OF FREEMASONRY "WHICH REPORTEDLY EXPOSED THE MASONIC ORDER AS BEING A CHRISTIAN INSTITUTION, HAS A FOREWORD BY W.J. HUGHAN, A MASTER MASON IN THE 32ND DEGREE, WHO DISAGREED WITH THE AUTHOR. IT IS ALSO INTERESTING TO NOTE THAT THIS SAME BOOK WAS EDITED BY YET ANOTHER MASON, BROTHER G.W. SPETH WHO DISAGREED WITH BOTH THE AUTHOR AS WELL AS WITH BROTHER HUGHAN. THE END RESULT, NATURALLY WAS A DRASTICALLY WATERED DOWN VERSION OF WHAT THE ORIGINAL MANUSCRIPT CONTAINED IN THE FIRST PLACE. IN ACCORDANCE TO WHAT WAS EVENTUALLY PUBLISHED AFTER IT WAS BUTCHERED ALL TO FRATERNAL HELL, WHYMPER INSISTED THAT FREEMASONRY BECAME CHRISTIAN IN FAITH AND EFFECTIVELY EXCLUDED ALL OTHER FAITHS. NEEDLESS TO SAY, HIS BOOK NEVER MADE THE AMERICAN BEST SELLER'S LIST.

WHEN IT COMES TO EXPOSING THE TRUE ELEMENTS OF FREEMASONRY AND ITS CHRISTIAN FAITH OF ESTABLISHING A **NEW WORLD ORDER**, THE INDIVIDUAL IS PLACING HIS /OR HER LIFE ON THE LINE. AT LEAST SUCH WAS THE CASE OF WILLIAM MORGAN IN 1826, WHEN HE PUBLISHED HIS EXPOSE OF FREEMASONRY IN THE UNITED STATES. MORGAN WAS A VIRGINIA BORN FREEMASON, WHO CLIMBED TO SUCCESS DUE TO HIS MASONIC CONNECTIONS. HE WAS A U.S. CAPTAIN DURING THE WAR OF 1812 AS WELL AS AN ACTIVE MEMBER OF THE

ANCIENT CRAFT'S FRATERNAL ORDER OF THE ILLUMINATI WHICH AT THE TIME WAS DEEPLY INVOLVED WITH NORTH AMERICAN FREEMASONRY, INCLUDING PLANS OF THE EXECUTION AND/OR IMPLEMENTATION OF A **NEW WORLD ORDER** WITHIN THE POLITICAL FRAMEWORK OF THE CONTINENTAL UNITED STATES. IN 1821, MORGAN MOVED TO CANADA, (TORONTO), WHERE HE SOON BECAME A BREWER. NOT LONG AFTER, HE MOVED BACK TO THE UNITED STATES AND BEGAN COMPILING SOME NOTES. IT HAD BEEN REPORTED THAT AFTER CONVERTING TO THE CHRISTIAN FAITH, (AS OPPOSED TO THE SO-CALLED THREE HEADED-GOD OF FREEMASONRY), FRATERNITY BROTHER WILLIAM MORGAN WAS SAID TO HAVE RENOUNCED HIS INVOLVEMENT IN FREEMASONRY AND BEGAN COLLECTING THE NECESSARY DOCUMENTATION TO EXPOSE ITS PLANS OF TAKING OVER THE GOVERNMENTAL STRUCTURE OF NORTH AMERICA. IN AUGUST OF 1826, BROTHER MORGAN WAS EXTREMELY BUSY AS RUMORS HAD SURFACED THAT HE HAD BEEN BURNING THE MIDNIGHT OIL IN ATTEMPTS OF GETTING HIS MANUSCRIPT COMPLETED AND READY FOR THE PRINTING PRESS WHICH WAS TO SAID TO HAVE REVEALED THE SECRET NATURE OF THE MASONIC ORDER, INCLUDING ALL OF THE OATHS AND SECRET PASSWORDS. MORGAN'S BOOK WAS INDEED PUBLISHED, IT WAS IRONICALLY TITLED; "ILLUSTRATIONS OF FREEMASONRY, BY ONE OF THE FRATERNITY WHO HAS DEVOTED THIRTY YEARS TO THE SUBJECT." SUBSEQUENTLY, HE WAS JAILED FOR HIS DIRTY DEED, THEN RELEASED AND FINALLY ABDUCTED, THEN, SILENCED FOREVER. ON WEDNESDAY, SEPTEMBER 20TH, 1826 WILLIAM MORGAN WAS REPORTEDLY MURDERED BY THREE MEMBERS OF THE ANCIENT CRAFT OF FREEMASONRY. WHILE FRUITLESS SEARCHES WERE SAID TO BE MADE THROUGHOUT THE AREA FROM WHICH HE WAS LAST SEEN, FREEMASONS REPORTEDLY MAINTAINED THEIR ENIGMATIC SILENCE. BOTH VERBALLY AS WELL AS IN NEWSPAPERS, MEMBERS OF THE ANCIENT CRAFT WERE DENOUNCED BY ALL AS THEY WERE CALLED MURDERERS AND TRAITORS. A CORPSE WAS EVENTUALLY FOUND AT THE MOUTH OF THE NIAGARA RIVER, IT WAS THUSLY CLAIMED BY MORGAN'S FAMILY. DUE TO PUBLIC OUTCRY, HIS ABDUCTORS WERE THEN BROUGHT BEFORE THE COURTS. ACCORDING TO THEM, THEY SUPPOSEDLY LEFT MORGAN IN A MILL, BELIEVING THAT HE WOULD EVENTUALLY HEAD BACK TO CANADA FROM THERE. CITING LACK OF EVIDENCE AND THE FACT THAT AT THAT TIME PERIOD OF HISTORY, KIDNAPING WAS CONSIDERED TO BE ONLY A MISDEMEANOR, THE CHARGES WERE FORMALLY DISMISSED.

UPON HEARING THE NEWS OF MORGAN'S DEATH, RUMORS QUICKLY BEGAN TO CIRCULATE THAT VARIOUS MEMBERS OF THE ANCIENT CRAFT OF FREEMASONRY HAD BEEN SOMEHOW CONNECTED. OUTRAGED CITIZENS WERE THEREFORE FORCED TO TAKE MATTERS INTO THEIR OWN HANDS AS THEY HAD AUTOMATICALLY CAME TO THE INSTANT CONCLUSION THAT THE PROPER AUTHORITIES WERE ALSO DEEPLY INVOLVED IN A CONSPIRACY TO SUPPRESS

EVIDENCE AS NO ONE WITHIN THE JUSTICE SYSTEM REALLY WANTED TO INVESTIGATE THE CRIME. TO THESE CITIZENS, THE PROPER AUTHORITIES WERE MEMBERS OF FREEMASONRY OBEYING THE GRAND LODGE OF NEW YORK'S DECREE TO CONCEAL ALL OF THE EVIDENCE AS IT PERTAINED TO MORGAN'S DEATH. BECAUSE OF THIS PRECONCEIVED NOTION THAT A CONSPIRACY HAD ACTUALLY TRANSPIRED, SEVEN CITIZEN COMMITTEES WERE THUSLY FORMED IN AS MANY COUNTIES TO INVESTIGATE THE CRIMES COMMITTED. THE VIGILANTE CITIZEN COMMITTEES CONDUCTED THEIR INVESTIGATION ACTIVITIES FOR NEARLY A YEAR, TAKING TIME OFF FROM WORK AND PAYING THEIR OWN EXPENSES IN PURSUIT OF JUSTICE. WHEN THEY COMPLETED THEIR RESEARCH STUDIES INTO THE MASONIC ORDER'S INVOLVEMENT OF WILLIAM MORGAN'S ABDUCTION, MURDER AND SUBSEQUENT COVER-UP, THE CITIZEN GROUPS PRESENTED THEIR EVIDENCE AND DEMANDED QUICK ACTION. IN TOTAL, THE CITIZEN COMMITTEES HAD LEARNED THAT AT LEAST 136 MEMBERS OF AMERICAN FREEMASONRY WERE DIRECTLY INVOLVED WITH THE ORDEAL. THESE CONSPIRATORS WERE REPORTEDLY NOT ALL FROM THE SAME LOCALITY, BUT WERE LITERALLY SCATTERED ALONG A COUPLE HUNDRED SQUARE MILES OF COUNTRYSIDE. THE CONSPIRACY ORGANISM WAS SAID TO HAVE WORKED IN PERFECT HARMONY INSURING THAT THOSE INVOLVED WOULD NEVER HAVE TO FEAR THE RISK OF FULL CONVICTION AND/OR PUNISHMENT FOR THE CRIMES OF ABDUCTION, MURDER AND COVER-UP. MANY OF THOSE INVOLVED WERE WELL RESPECTED FREEMASONS WHO HAD TAKEN THE OATHS OF THE KNIGHTS TEMPLAR DEGREES WHICH FORBID ITS MEMBERS OF DIVULGING ALL CRIMINAL ACTS OF THEIR FELLOW BRETHRENSHIP, INCLUDING MURDER AS WELL AS TREASON.

ACCORDING TO VARIOUS PUBLICATIONS, THE END RESULT OF THE CITIZEN GROUPS INVESTIGATION ACTIVITIES ENABLED THE JUDICIAL SYSTEM TO BRING FORMAL CHARGES AGAINST INDIVIDUAL FREEMASONS AND THE MASONIC INSTITUTION AS A WHOLE. FURTHER TO THIS, IT WAS ALSO STATED THAT THE OCTOPUS LIKE TENTACLES OF FREEMASONRY VIRTUALLY MADE IT AN IMPOSSIBILITY TO GET A CONVICTION AS JUST ABOUT EVERYONE INVOLVED HAD SOME SORT OF A MASONIC CONNECTION ATTACHED TO THEM. THE SHERIFFS IN ALL OF THE COUNTIES IN WHICH THE DEEDS OF VIOLENCE HAD BEEN COMMITTED AGAINST MORGAN FOR EXAMPLE, WHOSE OFFICIAL DUTY IT WAS UNDER THE CRIMINAL CODE OF NEW YORK STATE TO SELECT AND SUMMON THE GRAND JURIES, WERE NOTABLY ALL MEMBERS OF THE ANCIENT CRAFT. SOME IN FACT WERE SAID TO HAVE BEEN PARTY TO THE CRIME ITSELF. IT WAS EVEN EMPHASIZED THAT MOST OF THE JURORS SELECTED BY THE SHERIFFS WERE FELLOW FREEMASONS AS WELL. REPORTEDLY, SOME OF THEM WERE WILLING PARTICIPANTS OF THE CRIMES AS THE SUBSEQUENT COVER-UP THEN BECAME PART OF THEIR CIVIL DUTY BY MASONIC DEFINITION. THE LEGAL WEAVING OF

THIS TWISTED WEB OF DECEPTION WENT ON FOR NEARLY FIVE FULL YEARS AS BY THIS TIME PERIOD, IT HAD MANAGED TO CONSUME MOST PEOPLE'S DAILY LIVES IN THE PURSUIT OF JUSTICE. DESPITE THE FACT THAT SOME OF THE SUSPECTS DID INDEED STAND TRIAL, NOT MUCH ACTUALLY BECAME OF IT AS THE BULK OF THE BRETHRENSHIP MAINTAINED THEIR CODE OF SILENCE IN THE JURY BOX. CONSEQUENTLY, THEIR ACTS OF LOYALTY TO THE MASONIC FAMILY OF MAN ENABLED ALL OF THEM TO EXERCISE A UNITED FRONT IN THE MOMENT OF THEIR UTMOST NEED OF FRATERNAL RESCUE.

AS THE COURT PROCEEDINGS SLOWLY BEGAN TO UNFOLD LIKE A BADLY WRITTEN MOVIE SCRIPT, WITNESSES TO THE CRIME REPORTEDLY VANISHED FROM THE SCENE WHILE OTHERS WERE BEING CARRIED OFF AT THE MOMENT THEIR EVIDENCE WAS DEEMED INDISPENSABLE AND PLACED BEYOND THE JURISDICTIONAL BOUNDARIES OF THE STATE AUTHORITIES. THOSE INDIVIDUALS WHO WERE IN FACT CALLED TO TESTIFY, WERE QUICKLY ADVISED BY LEGAL COUNSEL TO PROTECT THEMSELVES FROM INCRIMINATION. IN THE MEANWHILE, MASONIC LODGES FROM VARIOUS REGIONS OF THE UNITED STATES RESPONDED FAVORABLY TO THE BATTLE CRY OF SENDING FINANCIAL AID TO HELP PAY THE COST OF DEFENDING ITS ENDANGERED BRETHREN FROM FURTHER PROSECUTION. OF THE 136 MEMBERS OF THE ANCIENT CRAFT WHO WERE SAID TO HAVE BEEN INVOLVED, SIXTY-NINE OF THEM WERE REPORTED AS BEING ACTUAL PARTICIPANTS IN THE ABDUCTION AND MURDER OF MORGAN. THEIR DEEDS WERE SO WELL HIDDEN THAT THE VAST MAJORITY OF PEOPLE LIVING AT THE TIME FIRMLY BELIEVED THAT ALL OF THE INDIVIDUALS WHO HAD AMPLE KNOWLEDGE OF THE EVENTS LITERALLY UP ROOTED THEMSELVES, (MIGRATING OUTSIDE OF THE UNITED STATES), IN ORDER TO EITHER TAKE THEIR FAMILIES OUT OF HARMS WAY /OR TO SIMPLY EVADE THE DANGER OF LEGAL PUNISHMENT. IN YET ANOTHER MISCONCEPTION IS THE FACT THAT ACCORDING TO SOME AMERICAN HISTORIANS, THE CITIZEN GROUPS EVIDENCE AGAINST FREEMASONRY WAS SO COMPELLING THAT IT LITERALLY CAUSED A MASS EXODUS FROM THE BROTHERHOOD ITSELF AS 45,000 FREEMASONS WITHIN THE CONTINENTAL UNITED STATES SUBMITTED THEIR RESIGNATIONS AND FORCED THE CLOSURE OF MORE THAN 3,000 MASONIC LODGES. FURTHER TO THIS, HISTORIANS ALSO TELL US THAT THE LEGISLATURES OF THE STATE OF NEW YORK, MASSACHUSETTS AND PENNSYLVANIA LATER INITIATED INVESTIGATIONS INTO FREEMASONRY ACTIVITY WITHIN THEIR PERSPECTIVE STATES. THEIR FINDINGS REPORTEDLY REVEALED THAT THE MASONIC FRATERNITY WAS A STATE WITHIN A STATE AND WAS BOUND BY ITS GRUESOME OATHS OF SECRECY. IN THE INITIAL REPORT OF THE NEW YORK STATE SENATE COMMITTEE, IT WAS NOTED THAT AT THE TIME THERE WERE APPROXIMATELY 30,000 FREEMASONS IN THE STATE OF NEW YORK WHICH ACCOUNTED FOR ONE-FOURTH OF THE ELIGIBLE VOTING POPULATION AND THAT THOSE SAME MEMBERS OF THE ANCIENT CRAFT HELD

75 PERCENT OF ALL THE PUBLIC OFFICES IN THE STATE AND HAD DONE SO FOR 40 YEARS. COMMENTING ON THE WAY IN WHICH THE NEWSPAPERS WERE BEING USED AS A SELF-SERVING SPRING BOARD OF FREEMASONRY INTEREST, THE REPORT STATED IN PART:

> "THE PUBLIC PRESS, THAT MIGHTY ENGINE FOR GOOD OR FOR EVIL, HAS BEEN, WITH A FEW HONORABLE EXCEPTIONS, SILENT AS THE GRAVE. THIS SELF-PROCLAIMED SENTINEL OF FREEDOM, HAS FELT THE FORCE OF MASONIC INFLUENCE, OR HAS BEEN SMITTEN WITH THE ROD OF ITS POWER."

AS FAR AS THE AMERICAN MASONIC ORDER WAS CONCERNED, MORGAN'S BOOK "ATTRACTED MORE ATTENTION THAN IT DESERVED. "ACCORDING TO FREEMASONRY DATA, WILLIAM MORGAN WAS CLASSIFIED AS "A MAN OF QUESTIONABLE CHARACTER AND DISSOLUTE HABITS, "AND THE MASONS OF LEROY, NEW YORK STATE – OLIVE BRANCH LODGE NO. 9 – REFUSED TO ADMIT HIM INTO THEIR LODGE AND CHAPTER. THE OLIVE BRANCH LODGERY AT THAT TIME HAD A DIRECT LINK TO THE OFFICE OF THE PRESIDENT OF THE UNITED STATES AND HIS FRATERNAL ADVISORS. CONTRARY TO POPULAR BELIEF, THERE ARE COUNTLESS THEORIES AND/OR MYTHS CONCERNING BOTH WILLIAM MORGAN DISAPPEARANCE AND SUBSEQUENT DEATH. IN A VARIETY OF THE FRATERNITY PUBLICATIONS ON THIS ONE PARTICULAR TOPIC, IT HAD BEEN DECREED THAT DESPITE ALL OF THE OVERWHELMING EVIDENCE AGAINST THE GUILTY PARTIES IN QUESTION NO ONE WAS LEGALLY AT FAULT. AS THE GENERAL POPULATION CONTINUALLY POINTED FINGERS AT MEMBERS OF CRAFT FOR BEING INVOLVED IN A CONSPIRACY OF COVERING UP THE WHOLE DILEMMA, LEGAL AMERICAN HISTORY WAS BEING MADE BEHIND CLOSED DOORS; "BUT IT IS CERTAIN THAT THERE IS NO EVIDENT OF HIS DEATH THAT WOULD BE ADMITTED IN A COURT OF PROBATE "STATED LITERATURE OF THE MASONIC ORDER OF THE UNITED STATES OF THE AMERICA'S.

THE TRUE DETAILS OF WILLIAM MORGAN'S DEATH WERE NOT ACTUALLY KNOWN UNTIL MANY YEARS LATER, (1848), WHEN ONE OF THE THREE MEMBERS OF THE ANCIENT CRAFT INVOLVED IN THE CRIME SUPPOSEDLY CONFESSED TO THE CRIME ON HIS DEATH BED IN HOPES OF RECEIVING RELIGIOUS ABSOLUTION. WANTING TO CLEAR HIS GUILTY CONSCIENCE BEFORE MEETING THE GREAT ARCHITECT OF THE UNIVERSE, FRATERNITY BROTHER HENRY L. VALANCE CONFESSED TO THE CRIME AS HIS DOCTOR LISTENED IN HORROR WHILE THE DIRTY DEED WAS BEING EXPLAINED TO HIM IN MINUTE DETAIL. THE STORY WAS THEN SAID TO HAVE BEEN PUBLISHED IN NEWSPAPER FORM EXPOSING ALL OF THE GRUESOME DETAILS OF BOTH THE ABDUCTION AND THE SUBSEQUENT KILLING OF MORGAN AT THE HANDS OF HIS FELLOW MASONIC BRETHREN. APPARENTLY, AFTER KIDNAPING MORGAN AND THEN TRYING TO GET HIM TO

FESS UP AS TO WHY HE VIOLATED THE SACRED BLOOD OATH OF THE CRAFT, WEIGHTS WERE WRAPPED AROUND HIM, THEN, PUSHED OFF A BOAT AND INTO THE DEPTHS OF THE NIAGARA RIVER HE WENT.

THE MASONIC **BROTHERHOOD OF MAN** THUSLY RE-WROTE THE DEATH OF WILLIAM MORGAN A FEW YEARS LATER, ROBERT MORRIS 1852, "THE HISTORY OF THE MORGAN AFFAIR. "IN 1883, MORRIS WAS ALSO RESPONSIBLE FOR THE WRITING OF "POLITICAL ANTI-MASONRY, IT'S RISE, GROWTH AND DECADENCE." THE AUTHOR OF THESE TWO FINE WORKS WAS A DEDICATED FREEMASON AND A WRITER OF MASONIC LITERATURE. ROBERT MORRIS WAS INITIATED INTO THE FRATERNAL ORDER ON MARCH 5TH, 1846 AT OXFORD LODGE IN THE STATE OF MISSISSIPPI. "THE LIFE OF BRO. MORRIS WAS SO ACTIVE AND UNTIRING FOR THE BENEFIT OF THE INSTITUTION OF MASONRY, THAT HE HAD THE OPPORTUNITY OF FILLING VERY MANY POSITIONS IN ALL THE DEPARTMENTS OF MASONRY, AND WAS GRAND MASTER OF MASONS OF THE GRAND LODGE OF KENTUCKY IN 1858-59. "HIS CREATIVE WRITING SKILLS ENABLED HIM TO COVER ALL AREAS OF THE MASONIC JURISPRUDENCE, RITUALS AND HANDBOOKS, MASONIC BELLES-LETTRES, HISTORY AND BIOGRAPHY. MORRIS TRAVELED EXTENSIVELY THROUGHOUT THE UNITED STATES CONTRIBUTING TO MANY OF HIS WRITING STYLE OF LITERARY WORKS TOWARDS THE JUST CAUSE OF THE FRATERNITY CONTROLLED NEWSPAPERS. JUST BEFORE HIS DEATH IN 1888, MORRIS COMPOSED THE HIGHLY PROCLAIMED **"WE MEET UPON THE LEVEL** "WHICH ACCORDING TO AMERICAN FREEMASONS RENDERED HIS NAME IMMORTAL. IF ONE WERE TO COMPILE ALL THE WRITINGS OF ROBERT MORRIS, "A COMPLETE BIOGRAPHY WOULD FILL VOLUMES. "IT GOES WITHOUT SAYING THAT ROBERT MORRIS WAS A RICH AND HIGHLY RESPECTED CITIZEN OF THE UNITED STATES. COINCIDENTLY, MASONIC BROTHER MORRIS WAS 70 YEARS OLD WHEN HE FINALLY GOT TO MET THAT **GREAT ARCHITECT OF THE UNIVERSE.**

IN THE UNITED STATES, WHERE THERE ARE NEITHER POPES TO ISSUE BULLS NOR KINGS TO PROMULGATE EDICTS, THE OPPOSITION TO FREEMASONRY HAD TO TAKE THE FORM OF A POLITICAL PARTY. SUCH WAS THE CASE OF THE ANTI-MASONIC PARTY THAT WAS ORGANIZED SOON AFTER THE DISAPPEARANCE AND SUBSEQUENT DEATH OF ONE WILLIAM MORGAN. BY MASONIC DEFINITION, "THE OBJECT OF THIS PARTY WAS PROFESSEDLY TO PUT DOWN THE MASONIC INSTITUTION AS SUBVERSIVE OF GOOD GOVERNMENT, BUT REALLY FOR THE POLITICAL AGGRANDIZEMENT OF ITS LEADERS, WHO USED THE OPPOSITION TO FREEMASONRY MERELY AS A STEPPING-STONE TO THEIR OWN ADVANCEMENT TO OFFICE. BUT PUBLIC VIRTUE OF THE MASSES OF THE AMERICAN PEOPLE REPUDIATED A PARTY WHICH WAS BASED ON SUCH CORRUPT AND MERCENARY VIEWS, AND ITS EPHEMERAL EXISTENCE WAS FOLLOWED BY A TOTAL ANNIHILATION. "BUT IN REALITY, THE ANTI-MASONIC PARTY WAS

FORMED MAINLY AS A CAMPAIGN TO AVENGE THE DEATH OF WILLIAM MORGAN AND TO IMPRISON THE CONSPIRATORS OF A GOVERNMENT BASED UPON THE CORRUPT IMMORAL TEACHING OF FREEMASONRY. MORGAN'S MURDERERS WERE EVENTUALLY PUT ON TRIAL BETWEEN THE YEARS 1827 AND 1830, A FEW OF THEM WERE THUSLY CONVICTED AND RECEIVED SOMEWHAT RATHER EXTREMELY LENIENT SENTENCING, MOST OF WHOM PLEADED GUILTY IN ORDER TO SAVE THEMSELVES FROM REVEALING THE SECRET HIDDEN AGENDA OF THE MASONIC BROTHERHOOD. DUE TO THE FACT THAT THE ENTIRE JUSTICE SYSTEM WAS LITERALLY CONTROLLED BY THE AMERICAN FREEMASONS, A GOOD PORTION OF MORGAN'S MURDERERS WERE NOT HELD RESPONSIBLE FOR HIS DEATH. THE SUPREME COURT RULING WAS THAT NO ONE INVOLVED WITH THE BRUTAL MUTILATION OF WILLIAM MORGAN COULD NOT BE HELD ACCOUNTABLE FOR THE CRIMES OF THE FRATERNITY. DUE TO WIDESPREAD HOSTILITY AND PUBLIC OUTCRY UPON THE FINAL JUDICIARY DECISION OF THE KILLERS OF MORGAN, THE ANTI-MASONIC PARTY WAS BORN. HATRED FOR THE MASONIC ORDER VIRTUALLY SPREAD LIKE WILDFIRE THROUGHOUT THE NORTHEASTERN UNITED STATES. THE ANTAGONISM WAS REPORTEDLY SO STRONG THAT ACCORDING TO MOST HISTORIANS, MORE THAN 3,000 LODGES ACROSS THE U.S. SUPPOSEDLY SURRENDERED THEIR CHARTERED WARRANTS AND ULTIMATELY FORCED THE AMERICAN MASONIC ORDER OUT OF EXISTENCE ALTOGETHER. ACCORDING TO THESE SAME HISTORIANS, THE ANTI-MASONIC PARTY THUSLY ACHIEVED SOMETHING THAT OF WHICH NEITHER THE CRUSADES NOR THE THREE WAVES OF THE INQUISITION COULD ACCOMPLISH, FORCE THE ANCIENT CRAFT OF FREEMASONRY TO BE DISMANTLED ONCE AND FOR ALL AS IT WAS SAID TO HAVE BECAME A TOTALLY DEFUNCT ORGANISM NOT LONG AFTER THE TRIAL OF MORGAN'S KILLERS. BUT CONTRARY AS TO WHAT THESE SO-CALLED INSTANT HISTORICAL EXPERTS WISH US TO BELIEVE IS A TRUE FACT OF HISTORY, THE MASONIC ORDER WAS MERELY FORCED TO OPERATE EVEN DEEPER UNDERGROUND AS A SECRET SOCIETY WITHIN THE CONTINENTAL UNITED STATES.

IN THE SAME YEAR THAT THE MASONIC JUSTICE SYSTEM PASSED JUDGEMENT OF MORGAN'S MURDERERS, THE ANTI-MASONIC FORCES WERE BUSY ORGANIZING A CONVENTION TO ESTABLISH A NATIONAL PARTY. IN THE NATIONAL ELECTION OF 1830 FOR EXAMPLE, THE ANTI-MASONIC POLITICAL PARTY ONLY MANAGED TO MUSTER 130,000 VOTES. SO, IT WAS THEREFORE FORCED TO ENLIST THE SERVICES OF MANY PROMINENT STATESMEN WITHIN ITS RANKS, AND IN SEPTEMBER OF 1831 NOMINATED WILLIAM WIRT OF MARYLAND AND AMOS ELLMAKER OF PENNSYLVANIA AS ITS CANDIDATES FOR THE OFFICES OF THE PRESIDENCY AND VICE-PRESIDENCY OF THE UNITED STATES OF THE AMERICA'S. IN ACCORDANCE AS TO HOW THE MASONIC ORDER DESCRIBED THE END RESULTS OF THE ELECTION IN AN ATTEMPT OF OCCUPY THE OVAL OFFICE,

IT STATED: "EACH OF THESE GENTLEMEN RECEIVED BUT SEVEN VOTES, BEING THE WHOLE ELECTORAL VOTE OF VERMONT, WHICH WAS THE ONLY STATE THAT VOTED FOR THEM. SO SIGNAL A DEFEAT WAS THE DEATH BLOW OF THE PARTY, THAT IN THE YEAR 1833 IT QUIETLY WITHDREW FROM PUBLIC NOTICE, AND NOW IS HAPPILY NO LONGER IN EXISTENCE. "MUCH LIKE THE AMERICAN MASONIC ORDER OF TODAY, THE BROTHERHOOD FRATERNITY IN THE 1830'S WAS SO POWERFUL AND INFLUENTIAL THAT IT LITERALLY BROKE THE SPIRIT OF THE ANTI-MASONIC PARTY AS IT WAS FORCED TO JOIN THE RANKS OF THE NEWLY FORMED WHIG PARTY. IN ESSENCE, THE WHIG PARTY WAS NOTHING MORE THAN ANOTHER CONTROLLED TROPHY OF THE AMERICAN FREEMASONRY GOVERNMENTAL STRUCTURE OF THE MASONIC FAMILY OF MAN.

THIS IS HOW THE HIGHLY RESPECTED HISTORIAN WILLIAM LEETE STONE SUMMARIZED HIS OPINION OF THE CHARACTER OF THE ANTI-MASONIC PARTY, "THE FACT IS NOT TO BE DISGUISED – CONTRADICTED IT CANNOT BE –THAT ANTI-MASONRY HAD BECOME THROUGHLY POLITICAL, AND ITS SPIRIT WAS VINDICTIVE TOWARDS THE FREEMASONS WITHOUT DISTINCTION AS TO GUILT OR INNOCENCE. "THE MASONIC HISTORIAN WRITER WILLIAM STONE WAS RESPONSIBLE FOR MANY HISTORICAL WORKS OF CREATIVITY. HE PUBLISHED "THE LIFE AND TIMES OF SIR WILLIAM JOHNSON "AND "THE LIFE OF GOVERNOR GEORGE CLINTON." BOTH OF WHOM WERE NATURALLY MEMBERS OF THE ANCIENT CRAFT OF FREEMASONRY. SOME OF STONE'S OTHER REMARKABLE WORKS INCLUDED; "REVOLUTIONARY LETTERS "AND "THE HISTORY OF NEW YORK CITY. "WILLIAM STONE WAS A UNIVERSITY GRADUATE, HE WAS RAISED INTO THE MASONIC FRATERNITY IN 1859 AND PRESENTED A MOVING SPEECH AT INDEPENDENCE HALL IN NEW YORK CITY IN 1876 CELEBRATING AMERICA'S 100TH BIRTHDAY. MANY HISTORIANS OF THE TIME, WHOLEHEARTEDLY AGREED WITH STONE: "THE OBJECT OF ANTI-MASONRY, IS NOMINATING AND ELECTING CANDIDATES FOR THE PRESIDENCY AND VICE-PRESIDENCY, IS TO DEPRIVE MASONRY OF THE SUPPORT WHICH IT DERIVES FROM THE POWER AND PATRONAGE OF THE EXECUTIVE BRANCH OF THE UNITED STATES GOVERNMENT. TO EFFECT THIS OBJECT, WILL REQUIRE THAT CANDIDATES BESIDES POSSESSING THE TALENTS AND VIRTUES REQUISITE FOR SUCH EXALTED STATIONS, BE KNOWN AS MEN DECIDEDLY OPPOSED TO SECRET SOCIETIES. "THE MASONIC ORDER THUSLY DEFENDED ITS DOCTRINE BY FURTHER STATING THAT THE ISSUE HAD BEEN BOLDLY "ACCEPTED BY THE PEOPLE; AND AS PRINCIPLES LIKE THESE WERE FUNDAMENTALLY OPPOSED TO ALL THE IDEAS OF LIBERTY, PERSONAL AND POLITICAL, INTO WHICH CITIZENS OF THE COUNTRY HAD BEEN INDOCTRINATED, THE BATTLE WAS MADE, AND THE ANTI-MASONIC PARTY WAS NOT ONLY DEFEATED FOR THE TIME, BUT FOREVER ANNIHILATED."

During the disappearance and subsequent murder of William Morgan, the President of the United States was none other than John Quincy Adams. According to historians, Mr. Adams' characteristics consisted of the spirit of anti-Masonry. The 6TH President of the U.S. of A. by Masonic definition was "a man of strong points and week ones, of vast reading and wonderful memory, of great credulity and strong prejudices." Speculation existed that President John Quincy Adams was indeed a member of the fraternity, but later turned against them once the Morgan Affair began to unfold. According to the fraternal Masonic Brotherhood: "He hated Freemasonry, as he did many other things, not from any harm that he had received from it or personally knew respected it, but because his credulity had been wrought upon and his prejudices excited against it by dishonest and selfish politicians, who were anxious, at any sacrifice to him, to avail themselves of the influence of his commanding talents and position in public life to sustain them in the disreputable work in which they were enlisted. In his weakness, he lent himself to them. He united his energies to theirs in an impracticable and unworthy cause. "A year before his death in 1848, a collection of Masonic letters were published titled; "Letters On The Masonic Institution, by John Quincy Adams. "Its contents were reportedly said to have been 284 pages long and was published in Boston, in the year 1847.

This was by no means the first of his anti-Masonic published writings. Between the years 1831 and 1833, John Quincy Adams leaked many letters on Freemasonry's activities in the United States as well as anti-Masonry letters addressed to him personally. American Freemasons quickly denounced their fraternity Brother: "Deceived and excited by the misrepresentations of the anti-Masons, he united himself with the party, and threw all his vast energies and abilities into the political contests then waging. The result was this series of letters, abusive of the Masonic Institution, which he directed to leading politicians of the country, and which were published in public journals from 1831 to 1833. These letters which are utterly unworthy of the genius, learning, and eloquence of the author, display a most egregious ignorance of the whole design and character of the Masonic Institution. "Further to this, according to the Freemasons of America, the "oath "and the "murder of Morgan" of which Adams became continual harpist "from the first to the last page "of his writings, was literally viewed as being nothing more than a continually floatation of excitement for the author.

Most of John Quincy Adams' anti-Masonic literature was filtered through to Henry Gassett of Boston, "a most virulent anti-Mason, "and distributer of anti-Masonic books, which he published at his own expense during the Morgan excitement. According to the Masonic Order, all the books that were ever published by Gassett are still sitting in many of the principal libraries of the United States, "on whose shelves they are probably now lying covered with dust; and, that the memory of his good deed might not altogether be lost, he published a catalogue of these donations in 1852, to which he was prefixed an attack on Masonry. "It should also be noted that according to further Masonic literature, the highly respected historian Mr. Stone had "been compelled, by the force of truth, to make many admissions which are favorable to the Order. "According to Stone, "Masonry should be suppressed because a few of its members are supposed to have violated the laws in a village of the State of New York. "The end result of Mr. Stone's observations, history was thusly rewritten for the benefit of the Masonic **Brotherhood of Man** and its **God** given right of establishing a **New World Order**, otherwise fulfilling the American Freemasonry dream of **"Manifest Destiny."**

During the Twentieth Century, there has been many books written condemning the ritualistic practices of Freemasonry. For instance, in 1995 a group of Danish members of the Ancient Craft were outraged when a Norwegian book was published that went into great detail describing their secret rituals and ceremonies; "Freemasonry – Mysteries, Community and Personality Development". The Norwegian author, Sverre Dag Mogstad was totally dumbfounded when some 10,000 Danish Freemasons asked a bailiffs court to ban the book on the bases that it violated the group's privacy rights. Apparently, the book was receiving so much interest in Norway and Sweden that it had virtually backed the Danish Freemasons into a corner and the only course of action left to them was to try and have the book banned not only from being sold but further publication as well. Accordingly, the Danish Freemasons insisted that secrecy was the whole point of Freemasonry and that Mogstad nor anyone like him had the right to peek inside their Ancient fraternal Craft and expose it to the entire world without proper authorization from the powers that be.

Only six years previous to this, further secrets of Freemasonry had been published in Great Britain; "Inside The Brotherhood "by Martin Short. The English author's book was an explosive sequel to

Stephen Knight's book that was titled "The Brotherhood "of which was first published in 1984. Just eighteen months after Knight's book was published some say that he died under somewhat questionable circumstances in July of 1985 at the tender age of thirty-three. Some said supposedly at the hand of the English Freemasons as they were some how able to have poisoned him, while others claimed that the Masonic Order members had put a curse on him because of the significance numbers of his age. Thirty-three obviously referring to the thirty-third degree of the fraternal Rose Croix Order. With all of the wild conspiracy theories flying around, the fact remained pure and simple; Stephen Knight died of natural causes relating to a brain tumor and not at the hands of the Freemasons. But as time went on, more and more conspiracy theories soon began to emerge. Theories so far fetched that none of them made any sense whatsoever and not worthy of even putting down on paper. Like Mogstad's published works, Stephen Knight's book became an instant hit with most people around the world. It stirred up such an interest that even after his death, Knight was still being a thorn in Freemasonry's side as his book went into reprint in 1985 (twice) and again in 1986, also twice.

According to Masonic literature, Martin Short's book; Inside The Brotherhood wasn't treated with much Freemasonry fanfare. In fact, the Grand Secretary of the United Grand Lodge of England issued a rather interesting statement following its publication in 1989:

"From all the ' trailers ' it is clear that the book is short on facts and long on innuendo.

The author has been described as an investigative journalist, but he reports improbable generalistions, and anonymous ' evidence'. His flawed belief that Freemasonry can be held responsible for everything a Freemason does is akin to blaming the Church of England for the views of the Bishop of Durham.

Understanding research would have allowed him to appreciate that whilst Freemasonry supports religion it is not a religion.

His comments on Freemasonry in relation to the police, the administration of justice, and national and local

GOVERNMENT DO NOT STAND UP TO SCRUTINY, ESPECIALLY IN THE LIGHT OF THE FACT THAT THERE IS NOTHING IN A FREEMASON'S OBLIGATIONS TO CAUSE CONFLICT WITH PUBLIC DUTY. DESPITE ALL HIS CLAIMS TO THOROUGHNESS, MR. SHORT HAS PRODUCED NO EVIDENCE — NAMES AND FACTS, AS OPPOSED TO ANONYMOUS ALLEGATIONS AND HEARSAY — TO SHOW THAT FREEMASONRY OR FREEMASONS HAVE EVER PROTECTED ANY LAW BREAKERS."

ENGLISH FREEMASONS HAD JUST CAUSE TO WORRY AS ACCORDING TO MARTIN SHORT'S PUBLISHED WORKS, HE NOT ONLY RAISED ISSUES CONCERNING THE FACTS BEHIND ALLEGATIONS REGARDING FREEMASONRY'S ROLE IN THE DEATH OF STEPHEN KNIGHT BUT ALSO EXPOSED THE MASONIC ORDER'S INVOLVEMENT IN THE ROMAN CATHOLIC/PROTESTANT UPRISINGS OF NORTHERN IRELAND, RACKETEERING IN LOCAL GOVERNMENTS AS WELL AS "INSIDER TRADING "ON A GRAND SCALE, PERVERSIONS OF JUSTICE AND EVEN MARTIAL BREAK-UPS. IT GOES WITHOUT SAYING THAT FREEMASONS BASICALLY COULDN'T HANDLE THE CRITICISM NOR WERE THEY WILLING AND ABLE TO TOLERATE THE FACT THAT THEIR DIRTY LITTLE SECRETS BEING DIVULGED TO NON-PRACTICING MEMBERS OF THE ANCIENT CRAFT. JUST LIKE ONE OF THE MOTTO'S OF THE TELEVISION SERIES THE X-FILES; **THE TRUTH IS OUT THERE**, IT ONLY MADE SENSE TO INCORPORATE THE HISTORY OF FREEMASONRY INTO THE SECOND PART OF THIS BOOK SINCE THE LEPAGE'S OF QUEBEC AND LOUISIANA WERE ESSENTIALLY MASONIC WRITERS OF HISTORICAL FACTS, RITUALS AND CEREMONIES. AND THIS BEING PART OF THE LEPAGE FAMILIES ANCESTRAL HERITAGE, IT CANNOT BE DISPUTED BY ANYONE AS THE PERSPECTIVE DOCUMENTATION DEEMS IT SO. WHILE RESEARCHING THE FAMILY TREE, BENOIT J. LEPAGE WAS QUITE STUNNED IN FINDING WHAT HE HAD SOON BEGAN TO REALIZE WAS ACTUALLY A TRUE FACT OF HIS FAMILY'S PAST AND SINCE HE HAD ACQUIRED ACCESS TO AN ASSORTMENT OF MASONIC LITERATURE, EVERYTHING JUST SEEMED TO FIT INTO PLACE. IT WAS SORT OF LIKE WHAT ROMAN CATHOLIC OFFICIALS FELT IN THE EIGHTEENTH CENTURY WHEN THEY HAD LEARNED THAT A VAST MAJORITY OF ITS OWN HIGH-RANKING RELIGIOUS FIGURES HAD SECRETLY JOINED THE MASONIC ORDER. THIS WAS SAID TO HAVE SPARKED A FOUR YEAR LONG INVESTIGATION INTO FREEMASONRY DURING THE 1740'S; SPANISH INQUISITION. AFTER COMPLETING ITS RESEARCH STUDIES IN 1748, ALL FREEMASONS BELONGING TO THE CATHOLIC CHURCH WERE AUTOMATICALLY EXCOMMUNICATED. THIS INCLUDED MANY NOBLES, SOME PRIESTS AND A FEW MEMBERS OF FRANCE'S FRENCH MONARCHY. EVEN THE PAPACY WAS SAID TO HAVE BEEN OCCUPIED BY AN ACTIVE MEMBERSHIP OF THE ANCIENT MASONIC CRAFT FROM THE END OF THE EIGHTEENTH CENTURY WELL INTO THE NINETEENTH CENTURY. AMONG THE LIST OF

HIGH-RANKING CATHOLIC FREEMASONS (NUMEROUS ABBOTS AND BISHOPS, IMPERIAL CHAPLAINS, CARDINALS AND AT LEAST FIVE ARCHBISHOPS) WAS NONE OTHER THAN POPE PIUS IX. AS IT SO HAPPENS, EVEN NAPOLEON BONAPARTE'S FOREIGN AFFAIRS MINISTER CHARLES MAURICE DE TALLEYRAND-PERIGORD WAS EXCOMMUNICATED FROM THE ROMAN CATHOLIC CHURCH FOR BEING A FREEMASON. TALLEYRAND WAS ORIGINALLY ORDAINED A PRIEST IN 1779, THEN BECAME ABBOT OF SAINT-DENIS AND IN 1780 WAS APPOINTED AGENT-GENERAL OF THE FRENCH CLERGY. BY 1789, HE WAS NAMED BISHOP OF AUTUN AND FORCED TO RESIGN ONLY TWO YEARS LATER WHEN POPE PIUS VI FINALLY LEARNED OF HIS MASONIC CONNECTIONS. THE LITTLE TIN-GOD EMPEROR NAPOLEON TOOK TALLEYRAND UNDER HIS FRATERNAL WING SOMETIME LATER AS BONAPARTE WAS WELL AWARE OF THE FACT THAT THE EXCOMMUNICATED ROMAN CATHOLIC HAD A LOT OF FRIENDS IN HIGH PLACES IN BOTH THE UNITED STATES AND GREAT BRITAIN. SOME OF TALLEYRAND'S CLOSEST ALLIES WERE SUCH FRATERNITY MEMBERS AS VOLTAIRE, BENJAMIN FRANKLIN, THE MARQUIS DE LAFAYETTE, CLAUDE-LOUIS BERTHOLLET, JOHANN WOLFGANG VON GOETHE AND A LONG LIST OF OTHER WELL KNOWN AND HIGHLY RESPECTED AMERICAN REVOLUTIONARY WAR SUPPORTERS LIVING IN VARIOUS PARTS OF THE WORLD, (MAINLY ENGLAND, FRANCE AND THE U.S. OF A.).

COINCIDENTLY, NOT ALL MEMBERS OF THE MASONIC ORDER ACTUALLY CARED FOR FRATERNITY BROTHER TALLEYRAND. FOR EXAMPLE, NOT LONG AFTER HE WAS ANOINTED BISHOP OF AUTUN A POMPOUS CEREMONY WAS TAKING PLACE AT A GALA AFFAIR COMMEMORATING THE ACHIEVEMENTS OF THE RICH AND FAMOUS OF FRANCE, MAY 5TH, 1789. AS ABOUT 285 NOBLES GATHERED TOGETHER TO PAT EACH OTHER ON THE BACKS FOR A JOB WELL DONE IN MAKING THE DIVIDED NATION (THE THIRD ESTATE) BECOME ONE AGAIN, 308 MEMBERS OF THE ROMAN CATHOLIC CHURCH'S FINEST CLERGY MINGLED WITH THE NOBLES AS 621 COMMONERS LOOKED ON. THIS ALL TRANSPIRED APPROXIMATELY FOUR-HUNDRED YARDS FROM THE ROYAL PALACE OF THE KING AND QUEEN OF THE THIRD ESTATE. AMONG THE CLERGY AT THE GALA AFFAIR WAS NONE OTHER THAN CHARLES MAURICE DE TALLEYRAND-PERIGORD, THE BISHOP OF AUTUN. APPARENTLY, BONAPARTE WAS ALSO IN ATTENDANCE AND HE WAS SAID TO HAVE BEEN NOT AT ALL IMPRESSED WITH THE FESTIVITIES AND MADE SOME RATHER NASTY COMMENTS ABOUT IT INSISTING THAT THE GATHERING ITSELF WAS NOTHING MORE THAN "MUD IN SILK STOCKING". WHICH IN ESSENCE WAS SAID TO HAVE SPARKED YET ANOTHER INTERESTING COMMENT REGARDING NAPOLEON'S FUTURE FOREIGN AFFAIRS MINISTER. FRATERNITY BROTHER VICTOR RIQUETI, THE MARQUIS DE MIRABEAU THUSLY LET IT BE KNOWN THAT AS FAR AS HE WAS CONCERNED, THE BISHOP OF AUTUN WAS "A VILE, GREEDY, BASE, INTRIGUING FELLOW, WHOSE ONE DESIRE IS MUD AND MONEY; FOR MONEY HE WOULD SELL HIS

SOUL; AND HE WOULD BE RIGHT, FOR HE WOULD BE EXCHANGING A DUNGHILL FOR GOLD. "AMONG THE NOBLES WHO REPORTEDLY WITNESSED MIRABEAU'S COMMENTS OF CHARACTER ASSASSINATION WERE THE MARQUIS DE LAFAYETTE; ANTOINE-NICOLAS CARITAT, THE MARQUIS DE CONDORCET; THE COMTE THOMAS-ARTHUR DE LALLY, THE BARON DE TOLLENDAL; THE VICOMTE LOUIS-MARIE NOAILLES; ARMAND DE VIGNEROT, THE DUC D'AIGUILLON; THE DUC FRANCOIS-ALEXANDRE DE LA ROCHEFOUCAULD-LIANCOURT; AND BOTH THE DUCS D'ORLEANS, LOUIS-PHILIPPE-JOSEPH AND HIS SON LOUIS-PHILIPPE WHO INTERESTINGLY ENOUGH WENT ON TO BECOME KING OF FRANCE IN 1830. THIS GROUP OF FRENCH FREEMASONS FORMED THE INNER CIRCLE OF "LES TRENTS", A SECRET ORGANISM COMPRISING OF THIRTY TO FORTY-SEVEN NOBLE MASTER MASONS WANTING TO MAKE EVERLASTING CHANGES WITHIN THE FRENCH MONARCHY. CHANGES THAT OF WHICH FRENCH FREEMASONS KNEW FULL WELL WOULD NOT BE AGREEABLE TO THE GOVERNMENT UNDER ANY CIRCUMSTANCES. OTHER MEMBERS OF THIS INNER CIRCLE INCLUDED MIRABEAU HIMSELF, EMMANUEL-JOSEPH SIEYES, JEAN-JOSEPH MOUNIER, ANTOINE-PIERRE-JOSEPH BARNAVE, JEAN-SYLVAIN BAILY (THE ASTRONOMER) AND OF COURSE MAXIMILIEN DE ROBESPIERRE. THE GROUPS LEADER; LOUIS-PHILIPPE-JOSEPH, THE DUC D'ORLEANS MET THAT GREAT ARCHITECT OF THE UNIVERSE IN 1793 WHEN HE WAS GUILLOTINED FOR TRYING TO OVERTHROW THE FRENCH FRATERNAL MONARCHY.

OBVIOUSLY MASONIC BROTHER MIRABEAU KNEW TALLEYRAND VERY WELL BECAUSE EIGHT YEARS AFTER THE 1789 GALA EVENT, FRATERNITY BROTHER TALLEYRAND WAS TRYING TO SOLICIT BRIBES FROM U.S. NEGOTIATORS AS TENSIONS MOUNTED EVEN HIGHER BETWEEN THE UNITED STATES AND FRANCE. THE APPARENT SOLICITATION OF FUNDS HAD OCCURRED WHEN FRENCH FREEMASONS BEGAN INTERFERING WITH U.S. COMMERCE AS A WAY AND MEANS OF FORCING AMERICAN CONGRESS TO CHANGE ITS FOREIGN POLICY CONCERNING CONFLICTS ABROAD. AT THE TIME, FRATERNITY BROTHER JOHN ADAMS WAS THE ELECTED PRESIDENT OF THE UNITED STATES (1797-1801) AND HE HAD APPOINTED THREE MEN TO ACT AS MEDIATORS TRYING TO RESOLVE THE SCHISM THAT HAD LONG EXISTED BETWEEN AMERICAN FREEMASONS, BRITISH FREEMASONS AND FRENCH FREEMASONS, THE UNITED STATES WAS SUPPOSEDLY PREPARED TO SEVER ALL FRATERNAL TIES WITH FRANCE, EVEN AT THE COST OF WAR IF NEED BE. FRANCE WAS TRYING TO CONVINCE THE AMERICAN FREEMASONS TO JOIN IN THE FIGHT AGAINST GREAT BRITAIN'S MASONIC INSTITUTIONS, BUT THE UNITED STATES DIDN'T WANT TO GET INVOLVED WITH ANYTHING THAT THE FRENCH KNIGHTS OF MALTA WERE TRYING TO STIR UP AS BY THIS TIME PERIOD, THEY (THE AMERICANS) HAD PLANS OF THEIR OWN THAT WERE NOW IN THE WORKS. ONCE THE TRIO OF NEGOTIATORS ARRIVED IN PARIS IN 1797, TALLEYRAND INFORMED THEM (C.C. PINCKNEY, JOHN MARSHALL AND

Thomas Gerry) that he had three secret agents waiting in the wings ready to negotiate some sort of a compromise but nothing was going to be happening until the U.S. agreed to give the French Government the equivalent of ten-million dollars in American currency and to further give an estimated $ 250,000.00 (U.S.) payable directly to him personally as a gift for being so kind and generous to his American Masonic Brethren. This little bit of American history became known as the **XYZ AFFAIR** simply because of the fact that Freemasons in France, England and the United States didn't want to disclose who Talleyrand's co-conspirators actually were. When the attempted extortion tactic was finally made public in the United States of the America's (April of 1798), the letters **X**, **Y**, and **Z** were substituted for the names of Talleyrand's emissaries. The French Government in turn denied knowing anything of the affair and denounced the so-called **X**, **Y**, and **Z** agents by instantly calling them charlatans not looking out for the best-interest of the French population. This despite the fact that Talleyrand was the French Government's specially appointed Foreign Affairs Minister. Almost immediately, tensions mounted even further as France's governmental officials kept denying knowing anything about it. Late in 1799, American Masonic Government leader Adams sent yet another entourage to stem the tides as by this time period war seemed to be the only way to resolve the issue once and for all.

When fraternity President Thomas Jefferson sent Livingston and Marshall to negotiate the terms of the Louisiana Purchase in 1803, he couldn't trust anyone else for the job as the vast majority of the American Masonic administration were corrupt son-of-bitches just like Talleyrand. In order to avoid another fraternal scandal like the well publicized **XYZ AFFAIR**, the Masonic President of the U.S. of A. sent two fellow Freemasons; Brother Robert R. Livingston and Brother John Marshall. So in reality, it was no real big surprise with the fraternity brethrenship of the Ancient Craft when Freemasonry Brother Talleyrand was left with instructions to up the ante by French Masonic leader Napoleon Bonaparte contrary as to what historians have been saying after all of these years.

Some two-hundred years later, American Freemasons continued hiding behind their shroud of secrecy in order to fulfill dreams of "Manifest Destiny "by verbalizing that their cause was that of a just cause as it was said to have been the sacred duty of the United States of America to fight for democratic freedom of peoples throughout the world. Ironically, some members of North American Freemasonry

FELT THAT THEY WERE SUFFERING FROM WHAT THEY THEMSELVES CALLED OF ALL THINGS "THE MUSSOLINI SYNDROME. "BENITO MUSSOLINI'S GREATEST ACHIEVEMENT WAS REPORTEDLY MAKING THE TRAINS RUN ON TIME IN ITALY DURING HIS INITIAL REIGN OF TERROR (1922-45). DUE TO THE FACT THAT THE ITALIAN DICTATOR WAS NOTHING MORE THAN A PUPPET GOVERNMENT SET UP BY GERMANY'S NAZI PARTY, WHEN THE FASCIST GOVERNMENT OF ADOLF HITLER COLLAPSED IN APRIL OF 1945 WHICH ENDED GERMANY'S INVOLVEMENT IN THE SECOND WORLD WAR, MUSSOLINI WAS SUBSEQUENTLY CAPTURED, TRIED IN A SUMMARY COURT-MARTIAL AND THEN EXECUTED ON APRIL 28TH, 1945. ALTHOUGH THE ENTIRE COUNTRY ITSELF MAY HAVE BEEN IN TOTAL CHAOS, AT LEAST THE TRAINS LEFT THE STATION ON TIME - EACH AND EVERY TIME WHILE MUSSOLINI WAS IN CHARGE OF STATE AFFAIRS. THIS IS EXACTLY THE WAY THAT FREEMASONRY HAD BEEN OPERATING IN BOTH CANADA AND THE UNITED STATES AS EACH COUNTRY'S POLITICAL AND ECONOMIC CIRCUMSTANCES SLOWLY BEGAN HEADING DOWN THE CRAPPER WHILE MOST FRATERNITY BRETHREN SAT ON THEIR HANDS DOING ABSOLUTELY NOTHING ABOUT IT. FOR EXAMPLE; DURING THE 1990'S, THE GOVERNOR OF WISCONSIN, MASONIC BROTHER TOMMY THOMPSON RECEIVED THE THREE DEGREES OF THE FRATERNAL ORDER AT A SPECIAL CEREMONY (JULY 9TH, 1990) IN MADISON, WISCONSIN AND FRATERNITY BROTHER JESSE A. HELMS JR. (SENATOR JESSE HELMS THAT IS) GAVE THE GRAND ORATOR'S ADDRESS AT THE 1991 COMMUNICATION OF THE GRAND LODGE OF NORTH CAROLINA. THEN IN 1993, AMERICAN FREEMASONS RE-ENACTED THE POMPOUS CEREMONY THAT TOOK PLACE ON SEPTEMBER 18TH, 1793 WHEN FREEMASONRY LEADER GEORGE WASHINGTON LAID THE CORNERSTONE OF THEIR SEATED POWER STRUCTURE, THE WHITE HOUSE, WHILE ACTING AS THE NATION'S FIRST PRESIDENT. TWO-HUNDRED YEARS AFTER IT WAS FIRST PLACED, THE GRAND LODGE OF AMERICAN MASONRY F.A.A.M., OF THE DISTRICT OF COLUMBIA COMMEMORATED THE BICENTENNIAL OF THE WHITE HOUSE. BROTHER WASHINGTON'S OLD FRATERNITY ALMAMATER, THE GRAND LODGES OF MARYLAND AND VIRGINIA PARTICIPATED IN THE CORNERSTONE RITUAL THAT TOOK PLACE AT PRESIDENT'S PARK NEXT TO THE WHITE HOUSE. THIS RE-ENACTMENT WAS THUSLY GLORIFIED AS BEING THE TURNING POINT OF FREEMASONRY AS IT CELEBRATED OVER 200 YEARS OF DEDICATED SERVICE IN AMERICA. IN THE MEANTIME, CHAOS AND VARIOUS FORMS OF UPHEAVALS HAD PLAGUED THE CONTINENTAL UNITED STATES FROM ONE END OF THE COUNTRY RIGHT TO THE OTHER, BUT AT LEAST THE AMERICAN FREEMASONS WERE ABLE TO CONTINUE REACHING THEIR MEETING DEADLINES AND PERFORMING THEIR POMPOUS CEREMONIES AND/OR RITUALS.

THE MAJORITY OF THE CHAOS THAT WAS OCCURRING IN THE UNITED STATES OF AMERICA AS IT TURNED OUT WAS THE CREATION OF AMERICAN FREEMASONRY'S OWN DOING. FOR INSTANCE, DURING THE LAST DECADE OF THE

TWENTIETH CENTURY, FREEMASONS OF THE WESTERN FREE-WORLD WANTED TO EXPOSE THE POPULATION OF THE NORTH AMERICAN CONTINENT TO THE POSITIVE ASPECTS OF THEIR ANCIENT CRAFT. FREEMASONS IN BOTH CANADA AND THE UNITED STATES WERE THUSLY ADVISED TO TAKE BOLD NEW STEPS BY GETTING THE MASONIC ORDER IN THE LIME LIGHT OF TELEVISION AND NEWSPAPERS AS THE DEADLINE OF THE YEAR 2000 WAS FAST APPROACHING. ALTHOUGH IT WAS FREEMASONRY LEADERS WHO POSSESSED A NEW VISION FOR THEIR FRATERNITY FOR THE YEAR 2000 AND PART OF THAT VISION INCLUDED PUTTING FREEMASONRY ON THE MAP WHERE IT SUPPOSEDLY BELONGED, NO ONE, NOT EVEN THE FREEMASONS THEMSELVES COULD HAVE ANTICIPATED THE FLOOD OF NEWS COVERAGE THAT IT WAS ABOUT TO BE RECEIVING DUE TO THEIR OWN STUPIDITY. OR, COULD THEY???

ON SEPTEMBER 4TH, 1991 A VERY INTERESTING STORY RAN ON THE FRONT PAGE OF A FLORIDA NEWSPAPER (THE ST. PETERSBURG TIMES) REPORTING OF AN $ 8 MILLION SETTLEMENT THAT WAS AWARDED TO A FORMER FREEMASON WHO WAS PARALYZED FROM THE NECK DOWN DURING A MASONIC LODGE INITIATION RITUAL. THE FORMER MASON WAS GUARANTEED $ 8,500.00 (U.S.) PER MONTH FOR THE REST OF HIS NATURAL LIFE. ACCORDING TO THE NEWSPAPER ARTICLE, THIRTY-FOUR-YEAR-OLD VERN JOHNSON "WAS BLINDFOLDED, PUSHED ONTO A CANVAS BLANKET AND TOSSED INTO THE AIR. "HE CLAIMED TO HAVE BEEN BOUNCED OVER AND OVER AGAIN, SOMETIMES AS HIGH AS FOUR FEET IN THE AIR. AT ONE POINT, JOHNSON REPORTEDLY LANDED IN THE BLANKET ON THE BACK OF HIS NECK INJURING HIS SPINAL CORD. HE WAS SAID TO NEVER BE ABLE TO WALK AGAIN DUE TO THE INJURIES SUSTAINED. JOHNSON'S LAWYER, JON KRUPNICK OF FORT LAUDERDALE FILED LAWSUITS AGAINST ALL THE GUILTY PARTIES INCLUDING THE ATTENDING PARAMEDICS, THE AMBULANCE COMPANY AND SEVERAL DOCTORS FOR POOR CARE AS THE INJURIES PERMANENTLY CRIPPLED HIS CLIENT. BY THE TIME THE CASE EVEN GOT TO SEE THE INSIDE OF A COURT ROOM, ATTORNIES FOR THE DEFENDANTS CLAIMED THAT JOHNSON HIMSELF WAS PARTLY TO BLAME FOR THE INJURIES BECAUSE HE ORIGINALLY REFUSED TO TELL MEDICAL PERSONNEL WHAT HAD ACTUALLY HAPPENED AT THE INITIATION CEREMONY. WHILE IN EXCRUCIATING PAIN, JOHNSON SIMPLY TOLD THE MEDICAL PERSONNEL THAT "HE WAS SWORN TO SECRECY BY THE MASONS. "AFTER MANY YEARS OF LITIGATIONS, THE LAST OF SEVERAL SETTLEMENTS WAS MADE IN SEPTEMBER OF 1991 WITH ONE OF THE DOCTORS WHO INITIALLY TREATED JOHNSON WHICH IN ESSENCE CLOSED THE BOOKS ON THE ENTIRE ORDEAL ONCE AND FOR ALL.

ALTHOUGH THE INJURIES SUSTAINED BY JOHNSON WOULDN'T HAVE OCCURRED IN THE FIRST PLACE IF THE AMERICAN FREEMASONS HADN'T BEEN SO IRRESPONSIBLE, THEY STILL MAINTAINED THEIR INNOCENCE RIGHT UP TO THE BITTER END. THIS, DESPITE THE FACT THAT JOHNSON'S ATTORNEY

REPORTED THE EVENTS OF THE NIGHT OF OCTOBER 20TH, 1983 TO THE PROPER AUTHORITIES IN PREPARATION FOR HIS PENDING COURT PROCEEDINGS.

IF THE NEGATIVE PUBLICITY FROM THE SEPTEMBER 4TH NEWS ARTICLE WASN'T BAD ENOUGH, IT WAS NOTHING IN COMPARISON AS TO WHAT WAS DISCLOSED IN THE WALL STREET JOURNAL TWO MONTHS LATER. IN BIG BOLD LETTERS, THE FRONT PAGE HEADLINES READ; **"IN THE HOT SEAT: JOINING THE SHRINERS CAN BE ELECTRIFYING"** AND **"MICHAEL VAUGHN WAS JOLTED BY A SHOCKING INITIATION; SECRET RITES LAID BARE."** THE STORY REPORTED IN THE NOVEMBER 4TH, 1991 ISSUE OF THE JOURNAL STATED THAT A FORTY-FOUR-YEAR-OLD KENTUCKY BRICK LAYER (MICHAEL VAUGHN) SUED THE OLEIKA SHRINE TEMPLE FOR INJURIES THAT HE HAD RECEIVED DURING HIS INITIATION IN JUNE OF 1989. IN DESCRIBING THE INITIATION CEREMONY, VAUGHN STATED THAT IT INCLUDED "THE USE OF ELECTRICAL SHOCKS APPLIED TO THE BARED BOTTOMS OF INITIATES FOR THE AMUSEMENT OF THE MEMBERSHIP. "AN ASSOCIATED PRESS ARTICLE COVERING THE HIGHLY DESPICABLE COURT PROCEEDINGS REPORTED THAT "A COURT-ORDERED VIDEO TAPE OF THE TEMPLE'S INITIATION DEVICES CONFIRMED MUCH OF VAUGHN'S STORY, INCLUDING THE EXISTENCE OF AN ELECTRIFIED BENCH AND MAT. "ODDLY ENOUGH, A CINCINNATI LAWYER, ROBERT E. MANLY WHO SPECIALIZED IN FRATERNITY LAW WAS INTERVIEWED IN THE NEWS ARTICLE AND WAS REPORTED TO HAVE STATED THAT "THE EVENT SOUNDS LIKE HAZING, AND THAT IS GENERALLY LOOKED UPON AS UNLAWFUL."

IN YET ANOTHER TWIST OF FRATERNAL IRONY WAS THAT ONCE THE PRESIDING JUDGE (JUDGE GEORGE BARKER) GOT AROUND TO HEARING ALL OF THE EVIDENCE ASSOCIATED WITH THE CASE, HE WAS QUOTED AS SAYING: "SOME PEOPLE WOULD LAUGH THE PLAINTIFF OUT OF COURT. OTHERS WOULD SOCK IT TO THE SHRINERS FOR BEING A BUNCH OF IDIOTS. "THE OVERALL END RESULT OF THE COURT PROCEEDING WAS THE WELL PUBLICIZED FACT THAT ON DECEMBER 13TH, 1991 A LEXINGTON JURY REJECTED A DAMAGE CLAIM OF $ 236,000.00 AGAINST THE MASONIC ORDER'S OLEIKA SHRINE TEMPLE. VAUGHN'S ATTORNEY, JOHN HAMILTON, HAD ASKED JURORS TO GIVE HIS CLIENT $ 20.00 A DAY FOR THE NEXT THIRTY YEARS FOLLOWING THE JUNE 1989 INITIATION INCIDENT. ONCE THE VERDICT WAS FINALLY HANDED DOWN, VAUGHN STATED THAT HE HARBORED NO ILL WILL TOWARDS THE SHRINERS AND ACCEPTED THE VERDICT OF THE JURY DESPITE THE FACT THAT THEY DID NOT SEE IT HIS WAY.

ACCORDING TO OTHER NEGATIVE PUBLICITY OF THE MASONIC ORDER'S FRATERNAL SHRINERS (ANCIENT ARABIC ORDER OF NOBLES OF THE MYSTIC SHRINE) WHOSE GROUP OF FREEMASONS ARE PRIMARILY KNOWN FOR THEIR HUMANITARIAN ACTIVITIES ASSOCIATED WITH CHILDREN'S HOSPITALS, A RATHER BIZARRE ALLEGATION WAS PUBLISHED IN THE SOUTHAVEN, MICHIGAN,

Daily Tribune on April 24TH, 1987. The news article alleged that although the Shriners organization was the richest charity of the entire North American Continent, it reportedly gave less than one-third of all the monies collected from the general population of the United States in 1984 to its twenty-two hospitals for children that were scattered across the nation. The remaining portions of the money collected were said to have been used on travel, entertainment, fraternity ceremonies, fund-raising, food, accommodation, etc., etc. Of the $ 21.7 million raised in the United States, the Shriners allegedly kept 71 percent of the proceeds for their own administrative purposes. Only ten months previous to this, (June 29TH, 1986), shocking allegations were being publically exposed in the Orlando Sentinel as it ran a special four-part series of its six-month long investigation into Shrine charity expenditures using U.S. Internal Revenue Services records (IRS income tax returns) to help confirm as to what members of the Ancient Craft of Freemasonry's Shriners were spending money on and exactly as to how much they were raising on a yearly basis. The Shrine Circus in the United States for example generated $ 23 million in 1985 but less than two percent of all the proceeds were said to have gone to the medical care of children. Also in 1984, the twenty-two Shrine hospitals reportedly received only one percent of the estimated $17.5 million collected from the Shrine circuses.

Like all other Freemasonry organisms, the basic objectives of the Ancient Arabic Order of Nobles of the Mystic Shriners was to promote truth, justice and good fellowship. The Shriner spirit was therefore based on the spreading of smiles, laughter and sunshine in a world which spoke far too much of war, bombs, guided missiles and pushbutton warfare. As far as some members of the Masonic Order were concerned, there was a drastic need to bring some sunshine and laughter into the world as most people within North America at the time, (1930's, 40's, 50's and 60's) had a doomsday outlook on life as religious zealots were continually prophesying the occurrence of the Biblical Armageddon with the arrival of the four horsemen of the Apocalypse and that charge was supposedly being led by the Satanic underlings of Freemasonry. Because of this, Freemasonry Shrinedom was able to re-define itself as it became a separate living Masonic organism as people were slowly beginning to escape the clutches of the doomsday sayers. Contrary to public belief, (religious and/or otherwise), Shrinedom within the Continental United States had existed long before the Twentieth Century. In

Fact, these type of Lodges were operating in the American Colonies prior to the Revolutionary War for political independence from the Grand Lodge of England. These forms of Masonic Lodges were ironically enough called **"PRESCRIPTIVE RIGHT "**Lodgery. As the story goes, a number of Christian Freemasons wanted to open a Lodge promoting Shrinedom but according to the new regulations concerning the establishment of Masonic Lodgery, (English regulations adopted in 1717), the group apparently did not have the right amount of members within its fraternal flock. Disregarding Great Britain's authority over them, the Christian renegade Freemasonry population went ahead anyways and began instituting Shrinedom within the British Colonies of North America. As the numbers slowly increased, England's reluctance to recognize the prescriptive right Lodges as actual living organisms of the Ancient Craft began to diminish. It wasn't until 1730 that North American Shrinedom received full Masonic recognizable powers from the Grand Lodge of England and had the legal authority to expand its tentacles westward to the Pacific Ocean.

By the 1870's, these prescriptive right Lodges began to shed its snake like skin as two theatrical type New York Freemasons decided to hone the Lodgery with Arabic and Muslim folklore. Before long, they developed ritualistic ceremonies in which the Masonic Deity of a Supreme Being (the Great Architect of the Universe) was simply referred to as "Allah", "Father "and/or the "Grand Geometrician." Further to this being implemented, when in prayer, the fraternity members were to face towards Mecca (the most Holy City in Islam) and initiate the many ceremonies normally attributed to the holy devotions of God's sacred laws.

Nearly three centuries after its first North American conception, the total membership of American Freemasonry's population participating in the Shrinedom experience of laughter and good cheer reached 500,000 strong for the year 2000. Some world famous members of the Shriners included entertainers, heads of government as well as governmental officials and statesmen. Canada's very own Prime Minister, Masonic Brother John Diefenbaker for instance was also a Shriner, as were U.S. Presidents Harry S. Truman, Franklin D. Roosevelt, Gerald Ford and Warren G. Harding. Some American political icons who were both members of the Ancient Craft of Freemasonry and Shrinedom included some very high profile individuals such as the F.B.I.'s director J. Egar Hoover and the United States military leader General Douglas

MacArthur. Other members included Hubert Humphrey, Sam Nunn, Jack Kemp and of course Robert Dole. The list of North American Shriners further included a host of actors; Harold Lloyd, John Wayne, Glenn Ford, Red Skelton, Clark Gable, Danny Thomas, Bud Abbott, Roy Rogers and Ernest Borgnine just to name a few. Even sports legends, astronauts, musical conductors and race car drivers were known members of Shrinedom. This group included baseball players Ty Cobb and Earl Combes, football players Bart Starr and Ray Nitschke and auto racer Marvin "Doc "Dee and David Pearson. Boxing legend Jack Dempsey, musical conductor John Phillip Sousa, cartoon voice character Mel Blanc and astronaut Buzz Aldrin were all known Shrine members promoting laughter and good cheer.

With the ever increasing demand to have their own place of worship, Shrine Temples were build in various regions of the Continental United States. For example, in 1965 there were approximately 832,000 members attending all the Shrinedom Temples in the U.S. of A. and according to those same numbers, it literally meant that for every one Shriner there were at least five Master Masons of Freemasonry as the American Masonic population was now being counted in the millions. By the early 1970's, the Shriners membership numbers reached slightly less than a million and began to continually decline throughout the 1980's and 1990's as the Baby Boombers refused to grow up while circling around in mini-motorcycles adorned with the pseudo-Middle Eastern gobbledygook regalia of Shrinedom. Besides their Twentieth Century interest of creating laughter and good cheer, the modern-day Shrine spirit supported many aspects of health as they generated billions upon billions of dollars for the building of their Shriner Hospitals for Crippled Children and provided equipment for treating the deformed children who entered them. Hiring fully qualified orthopedic surgeons in their hospitals who were the leading experts in the field of medical research studies, the number of the Shriners Hospitals continually increased as the need to do so often exposed itself while the years passed.

As the Shriners membership numbers began to increase during the 1960's to the height of its very ambitious endeavors of the 1970's, conspiracy theories began to emerge amongst the religious zealots of the moral majority. They accused the Shriners of being worshipers of the underworld who had initiated the Satanic ceremonies of Lucifer himself within their fraternity and thus violated the sacred fundamental principles and teachings of God's

GIVEN LAWS. BY THE 1980'S, SHRINERS WERE ACCUSED OF BEING THE SECRET RULERS OF THE WORLD WHO HAD VIRTUALLY CREATED ALL OF THE BLOODY WARS ON THE PLANET WHILE SERVING AS SATAN'S EVIL NEGATIVE FORCES OF EARTH. THIS DESPITE THE FACT THAT IT WAS STILL A MANDATORY REQUIREMENT FOR ALL MEMBERS OF SHRINEDOM TO ADHERE TO THE ACCEPTANCE OF THE SUPREME BEING OF GOD IN THE SHRINE TEMPLES – SO ESSENTIALLY, ONLY THE NAME WAS CHANGED TO MAKE IT MORE MYSTICAL!!! IF A PERSON DIDN'T KNOW ANY BETTER, ALL OF THIS ANIMOSITY CAN BE EASILY INTERRUPTED AS BEING THE FACT THAT THE MORAL MAJORITY MEMBERS WERE MERELY JEALOUS OF THE SHRINERS SIMPLY BECAUSE THEY WERE MAKING MORE PROGRESS IN THEIR BENEVOLENT EFFORTS WHILE NOT BEING TO JUDGMENTAL OF ALL THE OTHER RELIGIOUS FAITHS THAT HAD EXISTED AROUND THE WORLD. AFTERALL, IT WAS SAID TO BE PART OF THE MASONIC CODE OF CONDUCT NEVER TO GIVE OFFENCE TO THE OTHER RELIGIONS OF MANKIND. SIMPLY PUT, NO REFERENCE TO CHRISTIANITY /OR OTHER SECTS /OR RELIGIONS WERE TO BE MADE BY ANY MEMBER OF SHRINEDOM AT ANY TIME OF THE DAY /OR NIGHT. SHRINEDOM MEMBERS WERE AUTOMATICALLY EXPECTED TO RESPECT THE HOLY BIBLE FOR THE CHRISTIAN, THE TORAH FOR THE JEWS, THE KORAN FOR THE MUSLIMS, THE BHAGVADA GITA FOR THE HINDUS, THE GRANTH SAHIB FOR THE SIKHS, ETC., ETC., ETC.

THE MOST SYMBOLIC ATTIRE ASSOCIATED WITH SHRINEDOM ODDLY ENOUGH IS THE RED FEZ, THE OFFICIAL HEADGEAR OF A SHRINER. THIS RED BRIMLESS, CYLINDRICAL FELT HEAD GARMENT REPORTEDLY RECEIVED ITS NAME FROM FEZ, A CITY IN MOROCCO AND TO THIS VERY DAY IS STILL REGARDED AS A SACRED STRONGHOLD COMMUNITY OF ISLAM AND ITS RELIGIOUS FAITH. THE RED FEZ OF SHRINEDOM THUSLY SYMBOLIZES THE FREEMASONRY CONNECTION TO THE MUSLIMS AS IT HAD BEEN WORN BY MANY OF THEM FOR COUNTLESS GENERATIONS. FOR LITERALLY HUNDREDS OF YEARS, THE CITY OF FEZ HAD A MONOPOLY ON THE MANUFACTURING OF THE CAPS. APPARENTLY, IT WAS SUPPOSEDLY THAT THE DYE WHICH GAVE THE HEAD DRESS ITS DULL CRIMSON HUE COULD NOT BE OBTAINED ANYWHERE ELSE IN THE WORLD. BUT AS THE TIMES BEGAN TO CHANGE, SO DID THIS MONOPOLY AS IT COULD NOW BE MANUFACTURED AT A MUCH MORE CHEAPER PRICE ELSEWHERE. MASONICALLY SPEAKING, THE CITY OF FEZ HAD LONG BEEN REGARDED AS A SEAT OF ARABIC LEARNING IN AFRICA DATING AS FAR BACK TO THE DAYS OF ITS FIRST BEING FOUNDED IN 808 A.D. BY THE MOROCCAN RULER IDRIS II, WHO WAS SAID TO HAVE BUILT THE SCARED MOSQUE OF MULAI IDRIS.. SINCE SHRINEDOM WAS AN AMERICAN FREEMASONRY CONCEPT, THERE WERE NO SHRINE TEMPLES OUTSIDE OF THE NORTH AMERICAN CONTINENT. THAT IS TO SAY OF COURSE UNTIL THE LATTER PARTS OF THE TWENTIETH CENTURY. PROHIBITED BY MASONIC DEFINITION OF ARABIC AND MUSLIM FOLKLORE,

NO SHRINE TEMPLE WITHIN THE CONTINENTAL UNITED STATES WERE TO CONTAIN A Q /OR AN X IN THEIR TEMPLE NAMES. IN 1965 FOR EXAMPLE, THE ONLY NON-ARABIC /OR MUSLIM TEMPLE NAMES WERE THOSE OF THE ALOHA TEMPLE LOCATED IN HONOLULU, HAWAII AND THE SHARON TEMPLE LOCATED IN TYLER, TEXAS. WITH THEIR U.S. MEMBERSHIP ROSTER PEAKING AT NEARLY ONE-MILLION DURING THE EARLY 1970'S, A DECREE WAS LATER IMPLEMENTED FOR WORLDWIDE RECOGNITION AS THE ANCIENT ARABIC ORDER OF NOBLES OF THE MYSTIC SHRINERS EXTENDED ITS OCTOPUS LIKE TENTACLES TO THE FAR CORNERS OF THE GLOBE INITIATING LAUGHTER WHEREVER THEY PLANTED THEIR FRATERNITY ROOTS.

ACCORDING TO THE RELIGIOUS ZEALOTS OF THE MORAL MAJORITY OF THE LAST TWO DECADES OF THE TWENTIETH CENTURY, THE SHRINERS RED FELT HEADGEAR SUPPOSEDLY HAD A DOUBLE MEANING BEHIND MOST OF THE MASONIC ORDER'S FACADE OF ACTIVITIES WITHIN THE CONTINENTAL UNITED STATES WHICH ENABLED SATAN HIMSELF TO START KNOCKING ON THE DOORS OF AMERICA TRYING TO PERSUADE GOOD CHRISTIAN FOLK INTO ACCEPTING ITS FALSE BIBLICAL TEACHINGS AND/OR PHILOSOPHIES. THE RED HEAD DRESS THUSLY REKINDLED IMAGES OF RELIGIOUS TEACHINGS OF THE MUSLIMS TAKING REVENGER FOR THE BUTCHERY OF 50,000 MEN, WOMEN AND CHILDREN DURING THE CRUSADE YEARS AT THE CITY OF FEZ ITSELF. IN A SATANIC TYPE RITUALISTIC CEREMONY, UNBORN BABIES WERE SAID TO HAVE BEEN REMOVED FROM THE WOMBS OF THEIR MOTHERS AND IMMEDIATELY HAD THEIR HEADS, ARMS AND LEGS HACKED OFF WITH THE SCIMITAR, A LARGE SWORD WITH A CURVED BLADE. AS THE STREETS OF FEZ WERE REPORTEDLY FILLED WITH BLOOD OF THE SLAUGHTERED CHRISTIANS, THE MUSLIM EXECUTIONERS SUPPOSEDLY DIPPED THEIR WHITE HATS INTO THE CHRISTIANS' BLOOD AND SO PROUDLY PLACED THE NOW RED BLOOD SOAKED HATS ON THEIR HEADS AS A SYMBOLIC GESTURE OF THEIR VENGEFUL TRIUMPH. ACCORDING TO THE RELIGIOUS ZEALOTS OF THE MORAL MAJORITY'S NORTH AMERICAN POPULATION, THAT'S EXACTLY HOW THE SHRINERS RED HEAD GARMENT CAME INTO BEING. FURTHER LINKING THE SHRINERS RED FEZ TO THE REVENGEFUL TACTICS OF AN EYE FOR AN EYE OF ISLAMIC FREEMASONRY, RELIGIOUS PUBLICATIONS EMPHASIZED THEIR BELIEF THAT THE SHRINE CEREMONIAL RITUALS WERE DEEPLY IMBEDDED IN THE DEMONIC ISLAMIC RELIGION AND THE SHRINERS THEMSELVES SWORE ALLEGIANCE TO THE ISLAMIC GOD NAMED ALLAH. CONSIDERING THE FACT THAT IN ACCORDANCE TO THE MORAL MAJORITY'S OTHER BELIEF, (THE MASONIC DEITY BEING THAT OF A THREE-HEADED PAGAN GOD), THIS WASN'T AT ALL SURPRISING AS IT HAD LONG BEEN THE MORAL MAJORITY'S RELIGIOUS POSITION THAT NEITHER THE ISLAMIC ALLAH NOR THE FREEMASONRY GREAT ARCHITECT OF THE UNIVERSE WERE SEEN AS THE TRUE REPRESENTATIONS

OF THE GOD CONTAINED WITHIN THE HOLY SCRIPTURES. TO THAT END, THE MORAL MAJORITY'S GOD WAS THEREFORE THE ONLY TRUE GOD OF THE BIBLE.

MEANWHILE HERE IN CANADA, MEDIA OUTLETS NATION WIDE PORTRAYED THE SHRINERS AS AN HONORABLE ORGANISM PROMOTING LAUGHTER AND GOOD CHEER AS THEY PARADED AROUND LIKE WOO WOO THE CRYING CLOWN, (FRATERNITY BROTHER ASHER SMITH OF THE SMITHRITE GARBAGE DISPOSAL FAME WHO AS A BOY RAN AWAY FROM HOME AT THE AGE OF 13 TO JOIN THE RINGLING BROTHERS CIRCUS). MASONIC FRATERNITY BROTHER SMITH IRONICALLY ENOUGH LATER ON IN LIFE BECAME AN ACTIVE MEMBER OF THE CRAFT AND BECAME LISTED AS A PARTICIPANT OF VIMY LODGE NO. 97. AS FAR AS THE VAST MAJORITY OF CANADA'S NEWS MEDIA MEMBERS WERE CONCERNED, ANY AND ALL FORMS OF SHRINEDOM ACTIVITY WAS GREAT FOR THE COUNTRY'S ECONOMY AS THE VARIOUS SHRINER ASSOCIATIONS HAD A WELL KNOWN REPUTATION OF SPENDING LARGE AMOUNTS OF MONEY WHEREVER THEY WENT ALL IN THE NAME OF GOOD CLEAN FUN. DURING THE SUMMER OF 2002 FOR EXAMPLE, THE INTERNATIONAL SHRINERS' CONVENTION WHICH WAS HELD IN THE CITY OF VANCOUVER HAD MANAGED TO PUMP AN ESTIMATED $ 28 MILLION INTO THAT PART OF THE PROVINCE'S ECONOMY AS 15,100 SHRINERS DESCENDED ONTO THE LOWER MAINLAND. AN ESTIMATED $ 4.8 MILLION WAS REPORTEDLY SPENT ON ACCOMMODATIONS; NEARLY $ 3 MILLION ON FOOD AND BEVERAGES AT RESTAURANTS AND STORES; $ 2.2 MILLION ON INDIVIDUAL SHOPPING SPREES; $ 1.4 MILLION ON RECREATION AND ENTERTAINMENT AND $1.8 MILLION ON TRANSPORTATION. THE ENTIRE DOWNTOWN CORE OF VANCOUVER WAS LITERALLY PACKED TO THE BRIM AS THE ESTIMATED 10,000 HOTEL ROOMS WERE MOSTLY OCCUPIED BY SHRINERS. ONCE THE WEEK LONG REGALIA EVENTS HAD ENDED, (JUNE 23RD TO THE 29TH), AN ESTIMATED 1,200 SHRINERS CONTINUED ON THEIR MERRY WAY AS THEY BOARDED A U.S. BASED CRUISE SHIP "THE INFINITY "THAT WAS HEADING UP TO ALASKA WHILE APPROXIMATELY 3,000 OTHERS TOOK PART IN THE VARIOUS TOUR GROUPS DESTINED FOR WHISTLER, VICTORIA ON THE PACIFIC AND BANFF, ALBERTA.

HERE IN BRITISH COLUMBIA, POSITIVE NEWS COVERAGE OF FREEMASONRY ACTIVITIES HAS ALWAYS BEEN A FAVORABLE APPROACH TO JUST ABOUT EVERYTHING; VIRTUALLY RANGING FROM A VARIATION OF NEWS WORTHY ARTICLES. THIS MIGHT TAKE THE FORM OF STORIES BEING TOLD OF THE INDIVIDUAL HEROIC DEEDS OF MEMBERS OF THE ANCIENT CRAFT TO COMMUNITY INVOLVEMENTS SUCH AS FUND RAISING ACTIVITY TO GRACE HOSPITAL FOR RESEARCH ON IMPROVING THE RATES OF SUCCESSFUL BIRTHS FOR SUBSTANCE DEPENDENT MOTHERS TO INITIATING TRAINING SEMINARS FOR THE RECIPIENTS OF SEEING-EYE DOGS FROM THE CANADIAN NATIONAL INSTITUTE OF THE BLIND. OTHER STORIES MAY HAVE INVOLVED GIVING PUBLIC RECOGNITION TO THE B.C. AND YUKON DIVISION OF THE CANADIAN

CANCER SOCIETY IN APPRECIATION OF THE CANCER CAR PROJECT AND THE DIRECTION IT WAS TAKING UNDER THE WATCHFUL EYE OF BRITISH COLUMBIA'S FREEMASONRY POPULATION, (VANCOUVER SUN, JANUARY 31ST, 1992). THIS ARTICLE, WHICH WAS FIVE-COLUMNS LONG SHOWED THE PICTURE OF MASONIC BROTHER JIM MILLET OF AVIATION LODGE NO. 175 BEHIND THE WHEEL OF ONE OF THE MASONIC ORDER'S VEHICLES USED TO TRANSPORT CANCER PATIENTS TO AND FROM CANCER CLINICS. AS PART OF THEIR CANCER CAR PROJECT, THE VANS, SUPPLIED BY THE MASONIC FRATERNITY WERE BEING DRIVEN BY ITS VOLUNTEER DRIVERS. THESE DRIVERS, DONATED THEIR TIME ENSURING THE SUCCESS OF THE PROJECT WHILE THE ANCIENT CRAFT OF FREEMASONRY CONTINUALLY SOUGHT FINANCIAL ASSISTANCE FROM BOTH ITS BRETHRENSHIP AND THE COMMUNITY AT LARGE TO HELP KEEP THE VEHICLES IN OPERATION, PAYING FOR THE COST OF FUEL, MAINTENANCE AND INSURANCE OF ALL THE CANCER CARE VEHICLES THAT WERE UP AND RUNNING THROUGHOUT THE PROVINCE.

COINCIDENTLY, ONLY A WEEK PRIOR TO THE VANCOUVER SUN'S WRITING OF THE FIVE-COLUMN ARTICLE, A NEWS STORY WAS PUBLISHED IN THE PROVINCE NEWSPAPER (JANUARY 23RD, 1992) REGARDING FRATERNITY BROTHER STUART ROSS OF EMPIRE LODGE NO. 85. THE STORY GAVE A RATHER INTERESTING ACCOUNT OF SOME OF HIS LONG LIST OF COMMUNITY INVOLVEMENTS DURING HIS 75 YEARS OF LIFE WHICH OF ALL THINGS ALSO INCLUDED BEING THE BANDMASTER OF THE B.C. SHRINER'S CONCERT BAND. AND SIX DAYS AFTER THAT, YET ANOTHER NEWS STORY WAS PUBLISHED IN A MUCH SMALLER NEWSPAPER (VANCOUVER COURIER, JANUARY 29TH, 1992) WHICH FEATURED A FRONT-PAGE ARTICLE OF FRATERNITY BROTHER ASHER SMITH'S LIFE LONG ACHIEVEMENTS WHICH JUST AS IT SO HAPPENS ALSO INCLUDED BEING A MEMBER OF THE ORDER OF CANADA. THE PHOTOS IN THE NEWS WORTHY ARTICLE CONCERNING SMITH WERE TAKEN BY MASONIC HISTORIAN BROTHER JIM HARRISON OF MOUNT MORIAH LODGE NO. 82. BROTHER HARRISON, WHO WAS NOT ONLY A MEMBER OF THE ANCIENT CRAFT BUT OF SHRINEDOM AS WELL WAS ODDLY ENOUGH EXTREMELY BUSY DOCUMENTING THE ACHIEVEMENTS OF THE MASONIC ORDER AS HE HAD BEEN COMPLYING A BOOK ON MEMBERS OF BRITISH COLUMBIA'S FREEMASONRY POPULATION AND THEIR POSITIVE CONTRIBUTIONS TO SOCIETY AS A WHOLE. AS FATE WOULD HAVE IT, THE GIBSONS SHIT DISTURBER KNEW ABSOLUTELY NOTHING WHATSOEVER OF MASONIC BROTHER ASHER SMITH UNTIL HIS NAME WAS BROUGHT UP AS A POTENTIAL INVESTOR IN THE COMMERCIAL DEVELOPMENT OF A PIECE OF PROPERTY THAT LEPAGE HAD OWNED FOR A FEW OF YEARS. APPARENTLY, ONE OF THE OTHER INVESTORS IN THE DEVELOPMENT PROJECT (JIM ROLLERSON, THE FORMER OWNER OF HENRY'S BAKERY IN GIBSONS DURING THE 1980'S AND EARLY 1990'S) WAS TRYING TO FORCE LEPAGE

AND HIS THREE PARTNERS (RALPH SCHULTZ, DAVE PEERS AND DONALD M. HAUKA) INTO ACCEPTING ASHER SMITH AS A POTENTIAL INVESTOR IN THE PROJECT AND ONLY WEEKS PREVIOUS TO THIS MANEUVER BEING EXECUTED THE PROJECT SEEMED DOOMED TO FAILURE AS ROLLERSON HAD ALSO BEEN TRYING TO FORCE THE GROUP TO INCORPORATE A "STRATA TITLE "APPROACH TO THEIR COMMERCIAL DEVELOPMENT CONCEPT WHICH LITERALLY JEOPARDIZED ALL OF ITS ALLOCATED FUNDING. AS CHAIRMAN OF THE GROUP'S DEVELOPMENT COMMITTEE, FRATERNITY BROTHER DON HAUKA KNEW SOMETHING ABOUT SMITH'S BUSINESS PRACTICES THAT HE WAS NOT ABOUT READY TO SHARE WITH HIS INVESTMENT PARTNERS. IT WAS THEREFORE UNANIMOUSLY DECIDED THAT THEY WOULD NOT ONLY DECLINE ON THE OFFER RAISED BY THE BAKER, BUT THAT THE DEVELOPMENT PROJECT ITSELF WAS FOR THE TIME BEING GOING TO BE SHELVED AS THE GROUP'S KEY DRIVING FORCE (DONALD MITCHELL HAUKA) WAS NOW SUFFERING FROM SERIOUS HEALTH ISSUES AS HE HAD BEEN DIAGNOSED WITH CANCER YEARS PREVIOUSLY. ONCE THE REMISSION HAD SUBSIDED, THE DOCTORS NOW GAVE HIM ONLY A FEW SHORT MONTHS TO LIVE. AS HIS BODY BEGAN TO RAPIDLY DETERIORATE, BROTHER HAUKA WAS FORCED TO FACE THE FACT THAT HIS DAYS WERE NOW BEING NUMBERED. LEAVING THE CONFINES OF THE HOSPITAL, NOT WANTING TO DIE IN THE MIDST OF TOTAL STRANGERS PLUS A LOUSY VIEW OF THE HUSTLE AND BUSTLE OF THE CITY OF VANCOUVER, HAUKA WANTED TO SPEND THE LAST REMAINING DAYS OF LIVE AT HOME IN HIS OWN BEDROOM WHICH HAD THE MILLION DOLLAR VIEW OF HIS BELOVED HOWE SOUND AND THE MOUNTAINS. AFTER SPENDING 43 YEARS OF HIS LIFE LIVING IN GIBSONS, FRATERNITY BROTHER DONALD M. HAUKA SHOOK HANDS WITH THE GREAT ARCHITECT OF THE UNIVERSE AS HE ENTERED THE REALM OF THE GREAT UNKNOWN ON JANUARY 9TH, 1993 AT THE AGE OF 70 ON HIS OWN TERMS AMONGST FAMILY AND FRIENDS.

WHILE HE LIVED, THERE WAS ALWAYS A PATIENT EAR TO LISTEN AND HELP GUIDE THE INDIVIDUAL THROUGH TROUBLED AND VERY CONFUSING TIMES. IF A PERSON WAS TOLD BY OTHERS THAT SOMETHING WASN'T WORKABLE AND/OR TOTALLY IMPOSSIBLE TO ACCOMPLISH, DON HAUKA WAS ALWAYS RIGHT THERE TO HELP PROVE OTHERWISE BECAUSE TIME WASN'T OVERLY IMPORTANT TO HIM. HE WASN'T ONE TO WATCH THE CLOCK /OR EVEN THE CALENDAR TOO CLOSELY. PART OF HIS NEVER-ENDING CHARM WAS UNDOUBTEDLY HIS UNCONVENTIONAL APPROACH TO MOST THINGS IN LIFE THAT TO SOME WERE EXTREMELY COMPLICATED AND/OR COMPLEX. TO DON HAUKA, THESE ISSUES WERE MEANINGLESS AS HE ALWAYS HAD A POSITIVE AND EASYGOING OUTLOOK ON LIFE THAT WOULD BRING A SMILE TO ANYONE'S FACE AND INSTANTLY MAKE ANY PROBLEM SEEM SURMOUNTABLE. HAVING A DEEP SENSE OF LOVE AND DEVOTION FOR THE SUNSHINE COAST AND ALL OF ITS PEOPLE, FRATERNITY BROTHER HAUKA RARELY LOCKED THE DOORS OF HIS HOME AS HE WAS ALWAYS

FRIENDLY AND HELPFUL TO THOSE WHO OFTEN REQUIRED HIS SERVICES FOR ONE THING /OR ANOTHER. AS A HIGHLY RESPECTED MEMBER OF THE MASONIC ORDER AND AS THE LODGE SECRETARY FOR MOUNT ELPHINSTONE LODGE NO. 130, FRATERNITY BROTHER DONALD M. HAUKA TRIED WITHOUT ANY SUCCESS WHATSOEVER TO SWAY THE POLITICAL ANTICS OF HIS UNDERLING. ALTHOUGH BROTHER HAUKA WAS TRYING TO EDUCATE LEPAGE IN THE MANY POSITIVE ASPECTS OF THE ANCIENT CRAFT, IT WAS BASICALLY TO HARD FOR THE THIRTY-SOMETHING-YEAR-OLD PROTÉGÉE TO SWALLOW AS OVER THE MANY YEARS OF HIS LIFE, LEPAGE HAD WONDERED ASTRAY FROM HIS STRICT FRENCH ROMAN CATHOLIC UPBRINGING AND DENOUNCED ALL FORMS OF RELIGION AS HE NOW NO LONGER BELIEVED IN THE EXISTENCE OF A SUBLIME **SUPREME BEING**.

IN FACT, WHEN BENOIT J. LEPAGE FLEW HIS INVERTED CANADIAN FLAG DURING THE MONTH OF AUGUST 1989 TO PROTEST CANADA'S SIGNING OF THE NORTH AMERICAN FREE-TRADE AGREEMENT WITH THE UNITED STATES, HE WAS ASSISTED BY A VERY UNLIKELY SOURCE, HIS NEXT DOOR NEIGHBOR FRATERNITY BROTHER HAUKA. DON HAUKA, WHO AS A YOUNG LAD IN HIS EARLY 20'S SERVED IN THE ROYAL CANADIAN NAVY ABOARD THE "STRATHROY "DURING WORLD WAR II AS A PETTY OFFICER AND SOME YEARS LATER BECAME KNOWN AS ONE OF OUR COUNTY'S PIONEERS IN SUB-SEA TECHNOLOGY. THROUGHOUT THE 1950'S, 60'S AND 70'S, BROTHER HAUKA WAS CONSTANTLY EXPERIMENTING ON SUBMERSIBLES TO PHOTOGRAPH THE TREASURES THAT LAY BENEATH THE WATERS OF HOWE SOUND. ON THE EXACT SAME DAY THAT LEPAGE HOISTED UP HIS INVERTED CANADIAN MAPLE LEAF, HAUKA WAS SAID TO HAVE GIVEN THE GIBSONS SHIT DISTURBER A CRASH COURSE IN INTERNATIONAL MARINE LAW. AS A MEMBER OF THE GIBSONS ROYAL CANADIAN LEGION (BRANCH # 109), FRATERNITY BROTHER HAUKA KNEW EXACTLY AS TO HOW THE LEGION MEMBERS WERE GOING TO BE REACTING TO THE POLITICAL STATEMENT AND NOT BEING A PERSON TO JUDGE OTHERS FOR THEIR MISGUIDED ANTICS, A HEART-TO-HEART TALK WAS IMPLEMENTED AS LEPAGE WAS SUMMONED TO HIS NEXT DOOR NEIGHBOR'S HOME WHERE HE FIRST REPORTEDLY BECAME A PROTÉGÉE OF INSTRUCTION AND THEN AN INSTRUMENT OF NEGATIVE MEDIA COVERAGE BY THE PROVINCE NEWSPAPER. LIKE HIS APPRENTICE, FRATERNITY BROTHER HAUKA HAD AN ABIDING DISTRUST OF ANY AUTHORITY, BE IT POLITICIANS, MILITARY OFFICERS /OR EVEN THE GRIM REAPER AS FAR AS THAT GOES. DON'S STRAIGHTFORWARD AND HONEST APPROACH NEEDLESS TO SAY MADE HIM ONE OF THOSE RARE MEN WHO ALWAYS CALLED THINGS AS HE SAW THEM. PERHAPS THIS WAS WHY HE AND LEPAGE BECAME SUCH GOOD FRIENDS OVER THE YEARS SINCE BOTH OF THESE INDIVIDUALS IRONIC AS IT MAY SEEM, ALWAYS QUESTIONED THE WAY IN WHICH THE POWERS THAT BE GOVERNED THEM.

AS A YOUNG PROTÉGÉE, MANY INTERESTING STORIES WERE PASSED DOWN FROM HIS TEACHER. STORIES THAT OF WHICH CONFIRMED THE FACT THAT

THE VARIOUS MEDIA OUTLETS IN THE PROVINCE OF BRITISH COLUMBIA HAS ALWAYS HAD A VERY WELL KNOWN REPUTATION FOR POSITIVE NEWS COVERAGE OF MOST OF THE PROVINCIAL MEMBERS OF THE ANCIENT CRAFT AND HAS BASICALLY BEEN RESPONSIBLE FOR MUCH OF ITS FRATERNAL SUCCESS OVER THE YEARS. FOR EXAMPLE, ON REMEMBRANCE SUNDAY OF NOVEMBER OF 1991, THE VANCOUVER COURIER RAN THE STORY OF AN 18-YEAR-OLD MEMBER OF THE SEAFORTH HIGHLANDERS WHO WAS AWARDED WITH THE VICTORIA CROSS FOR CONSPICUOUS GALLANTRY IN THE FIRST WORLD WAR. HE WAS NONE OTHER THAN FREEMASONRY BROTHER ROBERT GORDON MACBEATH. IN 1921, FRATERNITY BROTHER MACBEATH BECAME A MEMBER OF THE VANCOUVER CITY POLICE FORCE. AS THE STORY GOES, ALTHOUGH HE HAD MANAGED TO ESCAPE THE WAR TOTALLY UNSCATHED, MACBEATH WAS KILLED BY A CRIMINAL'S BULLET ON OCTOBER 10TH, 1922. HIS FUNERAL PROCESSION WAS REPORTED TO HAVE HAD STRETCHED LITERALLY FOR BLOCKS. IT INCLUDED THE MAYOR AND THE ENTIRE CITY COUNCIL, POLICE PIPE BAND, UNITS OF THE SEAFORTH HIGHLANDERS AND IRISH FUSILIERS, AND FELLOW MEMBERS OF HIS MASONIC FRATERNITY, MOUNT HERMON LODGE NO. 7, WHICH AS IT SO HAPPENS ALSO CONDUCTED THE FUNERAL CEREMONY. FRATERNITY BROTHER MACBEATH'S VICTORIA CROSS WAS REPORTED AS NOW BEING PROUDLY DISPLAYED IN THE CITY OF VANCOUVER'S POLICE MUSEUM.

FURTHER TO THIS HAVING OCCURRED, WHILE GOING THROUGH THE MASONIC ARCHIVES FOR RESEARCH STUDIES OF HIS SOON TO BE RELEASED MANUSCRIPT CONCERNING THE POSITIVE CONTRIBUTIONS MADE BY THE VARIOUS MEMBERS OF BRITISH COLUMBIA'S FREEMASONRY POPULATION, MASONIC HISTORIAN JIM HARRISON DISCOVERED THAT ON THE FRONT COVER OF THE 1991 B.C. TELEPHONE DIRECTORY THERE WAS A PHOTO OF A PERSON THAT HAD BEEN ASSUMED BY THE TELEPHONE COMPANY (TELUS, FORMERLY B.C. TEL) TO HAVE BEEN THAT OF ALEXANDER GRAHAM BELL. BUT MUCH TO THE ASTONISHMENT OF BROTHER HARRISON, THE PHOTO ITSELF WAS ACTUALLY THAT OF ROBERT BURNS MCMICKING, THE 16TH GRAND MASTER OF THE GRAND LODGE OF BRITISH COLUMBIA (1894-95) WHO REPORTEDLY FOUNDED THE FIRST CHARTERED TELEPHONE COMPANY IN THE PROVINCE; THE ESQUIMALT AND VICTORIA TELEPHONE COMPANY WHICH BEGAN ITS BUSINESS OPERATIONS ON MAY 8TH, 1880.

WHILE MEMBERS OF CANADIAN FREEMASONRY WERE RECEIVING A MOSTLY FAVORABLE REVIEW NATION WIDE, THE ANCIENT CRAFT WAS BEING PUBLICALLY HUMILIATED ON THE DAILY TELEVISION AIRWAVES AND IN NEWS PRINT WITHIN THE CONTINENTAL UNITED STATES DURING THE LAST TWO DECADES OF THE TWENTIETH CENTURY. AS THIS HIGHLY CHARGED NEGATIVE PUBLICITY WAS BEING BOMBARDED ON ALMOST ALL THE FORMS OF MEDIA COVERAGE, AMERICAN FREEMASONS WENT ON WITH THEIR DAILY LIVES AS

THOUGH NOTHING WAS HAPPENING OUT OF THE ORDINARY. IT WASN'T UNTIL A HIGHLY ENERGIZED SOUTHERN BAPTIST MOVEMENT BEGAN INVESTIGATING MASONIC ACTIVITIES IN THE UNITED STATES THAT CAUSED MOST AMERICAN FREEMASONS TO FINALLY START WORRYING JUST A LITTLE BIT. THE MOVEMENT INITIALLY BEGAN IN THE SPRING OF 1992 WHEN JAMES "LARRY "HOLLY, A PHYSICIAN OF BEAUMONT, TEXAS MAILED OUT INFORMATION PACKAGES TO MORE THAN FIVE-THOUSAND SOUTHERN BAPTIST LEADERS WHO WERE SCHEDULED TO HAVE THEIR ANNUAL CONVENTION IN INDIANAPOLIS, (JUNE 9-11). CONTAINED WITHIN THESE INFORMATION PACKAGES WERE VARIOUS PIECES OF DOCUMENTATION CONDEMNING FREEMASONRY ACTIVITIES WITHIN THE UNITED STATES. THE 5,000 SOUTHERN BAPTIST LEADERS, THEN IN TURN PASSED THE INFORMATION ON TO ANOTHER FIVE-THOUSAND DELEGATES SCHEDULED TO BE ATTENDING THE CONVENTION. HAVING THE EXACT SAME AFFECT AS A CHAIN LETTER, THE MOVEMENT SOON GAINED MOMENTUM AS MORE AND MORE PEOPLE JUMPED ONTO THE RELIGIOUS BANDWAGON CONDEMNING FREEMASONRY FROM THE EAST COAST TO THE WEST COAST AND BACK AGAIN. THE ENTIRE COUNTRY WOULD LATER BE UP IN ARMS ABOUT WHAT THE AMERICAN FREEMASONS WERE DOING TO THEIR BELOVED NATION RELIGIOUSLY, POLITICALLY AND MORALLY AS A COMPLETE WOMANIZER WAS SOON ELEVATED INTO THE WHITE HOUSE. THE U.S. PRESIDENTIAL PALACE WAS SAID TO HAVE BEEN OCCUPIED BY YET ANOTHER FREEMASON AS GEORGE BUSH SENIOR HAD VACATED THE PREMISES AND MADE WAY FOR THE NEW ACTING LEADER OF THE NATION. BEFORE LONG, MORAL MAJORITY MEMBERS WERE BUSY AS OLD HELL CONNECTING THE FRATERNITY DOTS TO U.S. PRESIDENT BILL CLINTON'S ANCESTRAL PAST LINKING IT TO LUCIFERICAN FREEMASONRY. FOR EXAMPLE, ON JULY 16TH, 1782, THE YEAR AFTER THE BRITISH SURRENDERED TO THE AMERICAN FREEMASONS, REPRESENTATIVES OF THE WORLD'S SECRET SOCIETIES REPORTEDLY CONVENED THE CONGRESS OF WILHELMSBAD IN EUROPE AND FORMALLY JOINED MASONRY AND THE ILLUMINATI. DURING THE NEXT FOUR YEARS, THE MASONIC ORDER'S ILLUMINATI MEMBERS WERE ABLE TO SECRETLY ESTABLISH SEVERAL LODGES WITHIN THE CONTINENTAL UNITED STATES AND IN 1785, THE COLUMBIAN LODGE OF THE ORDER OF THE ILLUMINATI WAS ESTABLISHED IN NEW YORK CITY. AMONG ITS MEMBERS INCLUDED GOVERNOR DEWITT CLINTON, HORACE GREELY AND CLINTON ROOSEVELT. WITH THE 1990'S COMING TO A FAST CLOSE AND THE DAWNING OF THE 21ST CENTURY JUST AROUND THE FRATERNAL CORNER, THE OFFICE OF THE UNITED STATES PRESIDENCY WAS VIRTUALLY STRIPPED OF ALL ITS MORAL FIBER AS THE AMERICAN PEOPLE WERE BEING TOLD THAT WHATEVER THE SEXUAL PREFERENCE OF THE U.S. PRESIDENT MAY HAVE BEEN, IT WAS LITERALLY NONE OF THEIR DAMN BLOODY BUSINESS. ALTHOUGH THE PRESIDENT OF THE MOST POWERFUL NATION IN THE ENTIRE WORLD HAD SCREWED THE POOCH so to speak, it had been decreed that if he wanted to fondle and/or sexually exploit young female interns working at the White House, than it was the American President's right to do so as his sex life was that of his own personal business and not that of the nation. As far as the Ancient Craft of Freemasonry was concerned, the country may have been going to hell in a handbasket, but at least the trains were running on time!!! This undoubtedly frustrated the moral majority to no end as those members of the Craft governing the affairs of the nation virtually refused to change their evil Satanic ways of womanizing and/or other immoral acts of common indecency all in the name of an American Freemasonry Deity.

At this point it should also be stated that just like U.S. President Jimmy Carter of the 1970's, the American Freemasonry leaders of the Bilderberg's elite Illuminati group also hand picked Arkansas Governor Bill Clinton to become the President of the most powerful nation in the world for the last decade of the Twentieth Century. Masonic Brother Bill Clinton reportedly attended his first Bilderberg meeting in 1991 which in essence saw him elevated into the prestigious portfolio of the Oval Office not long afterwards. It is without a doubt that both of these U.S. Presidents were by-products of the Rockefeller empire because like Brother Carter, American President Bill Clinton was also an active member of the Trilateral Commission. At the time, he was also a potential candidate for the Freemasonry Council on Foreign Relations as he had been enlisted by two of the most influential Masonic families within the Continental United States; the Rockefeller's and the Rothschild's. In September of 1998 while speaking to the faithful followers of the cause towards the ends justifying the means, U.S. President Bill Clinton gave a few clues to the Western free-world as to his involvement in a Freemasonry style conspiracy for global domination;

> "...by the time you become the leader of a country, someone else makes all the decisions. You may find you can get away with virtual Presidents, virtual Prime Ministers, virtual everything."

At the Southern Baptist Convention of 1992, a motion was passed enabling them to study the compatibility of Freemasonry with Christian and Southern Baptist doctrine. The research studies which included various forms of Masonry activities, philosophies and teachings of the Masonic Lodges and their rituals and/

OR CEREMONIES. FURTHER TO THIS, IT WAS ALSO DECREED THAT THE END RESULTS OF THE STUDY SHOULD BE SUBMITTED TO THE FOLLOWING YEAR'S CONVENTION SLATED TO TAKE PLACE IN HOUSTON, TEXAS IN JUNE OF 1993. ALMOST IMMEDIATELY, AMERICAN FREEMASONS WENT ON THE DEFENSIVE TRYING TO DISCREDIT THE TEXAS PHYSICIAN FOR HIS PART IN STIRRING UP THE SOUTHERN BAPTIST CONGREGATION MEMBERS AND THE REST OF THE COUNTRY. ONE OF THE VERY FIRST THINGS THAT THE AMERICAN MASONIC ORDER DID WAS OPENLY CRITICIZE HOLLY'S PUBLISHED FINDINGS, A 58 PAGE BOOK PACKET TITLED; "THE SOUTHERN BAPTIST CONVENTION AND FREEMASONRY." ACCORDING TO THE MASONIC ORDER'S OWN LITERATURE ON THIS TOPIC, THE BOOK "PRODUCED BY MR. HOLLY, IS A LENGTHY DISSERTATION OF THE EVILS OF FREEMASONRY, CALLING IT A SATANIC RELIGION AND A CULT. HE SPENDS MANY PAGES AND MUCH RHETORIC ON THIS SUBJECT, DEFINING THE OCCULT. SATAN WORSHIP, ANCIENT SOCIETIES AND THEIR EVIL TEACHINGS AND PRACTICES. HE THEN ASSOCIATES FREEMASONRY WITH THESE AS HE TAKES PART OF MASONIC RITUAL AND TRADITION, AND WRITING OF THOSE WHOM HE DEEMS AS MASONIC AUTHORITIES, AND USES THEM FOR HIS PURPOSE. THIS BOOK IS ESPECIALLY CRITICAL OF THE DEGREES OF THE SCOTTISH RITE, PARTICULARLY THE 30TH DEGREE. HE ALSO CITES IN LENGTHY DETAIL THE WRITINGS OF ALBERT PIKE AND ALBERT G. MACKEY'S ENCYCLOPEDIA OF FREEMASONRY. "THE MASONIC LITERATURE WENT ON CRITICIZING THE DEEDS OF THE SOUTHERN BAPTIST MOVEMENT EVEN FURTHER BY ATTRIBUTING THEIR FEARS OF THE UNKNOWN TO THE FACT THAT MUCH CHAOS AND CONFUSION HAD PLAGUED THE UNITED STATES AND WERE SAID TO HAVE BEEN THE MAIN COMPONENTS BEHIND THE MOVEMENT ITSELF. BUT WITH MANY THANKS TO THAT GREAT ARCHITECT OF THE UNIVERSE AT LEAST THE TRAINS WERE STILL RUNNING ON TIME!!!

THE COMPATIBILITY OF FREEMASONRY AND CHRISTIANITY AT THE SOUTHERN BAPTIST CONVENTION OF 1993 WAS TO SAY THE LEAST A VERY INTERESTING SHOW OF FORCE, BUT ALL RELIGIOUS HELL BROKE LOOSE WEEKS LATER ONCE IT HAD BEEN DISCOVERED THAT THE PERSON IN CHARGE OF COMPILING THE REPORT, DR. GARY LEAZER, HAD BEEN GETTING SOME OF HIS INSTRUCTIONAL GUIDANCE FROM VARIOUS AMERICAN FREEMASONRY ALLIES. DURING THE COMPATIBILITY STUDY, A LETTER WRITTEN BY THE GOOD DOCTOR TO ONE OF HIS MASONIC BUDDIES, WHO JUST SO HAPPENED TO BE ONE OF THE UNITED STATES' FOREMOST FREEMASONRY LEADERS, INADVERTENTLY APPEARED OUT OF NO-WHERE WHICH LITERALLY GAVE THANKS FOR ALL OF THE ASSISTANCE IN RESEARCHING THE MANY FACETS OF THE ANCIENT CRAFT. APPARENTLY, THIS MASONIC COMRADE HAD ALSO FURNISHED LEAZER WITH SEVERAL REMARKS CONCERNING THOSE INDIVIDUALS WHO WERE HARSHLY CRITICIZING FREEMASONRY. DESPITE THE FACT THAT IN ANY TRUE ANALYSIS OF AN ISSUE BOTH SIDES ARE TO BE WEIGHTED OUT EQUALLY, THE SOUTHERN

Baptist leaders were not at all impressed with Dr. Leazer's approach to the matter at hand. In the end, the letter written by the good doctor forced the Southern Baptist leaders to take a second look at the person in charge of the compatibility study group as it had been reported that Leazer was getting way too friendly with his Masonic allies. Although the Southern Baptist movement didn't like the idea that some Freemasonry officials had been furnishing information for a proper diagnosis of the study itself, they were said to have allowed Leazer's contents of the report to stand unchanged. The compatibility report was then submitted to the floor for a vote as prepared by both Dr. Leazer and his Freemasonry tutors. Which as it turned out condemned Freemasonry to the depths of hell for its Satanic like upbringing of paganism and Christianity. In a twist of ironic fate, Leazer became so impressed with the Ancient Craft that he later on became an active member of Freemasonry once he was ultimately forced to resign as the investigating officer for the Southern Baptist movement. Contained within the religious writings of a U.S. propaganda news service, a newspaper (The Columbus Dispatch) printed an explanation to Leazer's removal in their November 6TH, 1993 edition. It stated in part:

"Larry Lewis, president of the Home Missions Board, said he requested Leazer's resignation for 'Gross insubordination' following publication in October of a speech Leazer gave to a Masonic group.

Lewis said Leazer's Aug. 8 speech violated an order to 'refrain from any and all involvement in the Freemasonry issue.' Lewis told Baptist Press, the denomination's official news agency, he had accepted Leazer's resignation Oct. 22.

' He has clearly violated that direction and in doing so has demonstrated his unwillingness to submit to the authority of his superiors, ' Lewis said. Whether Baptists can also be members of a Masonic Lodge has been a volatile issue."

Only a few short months prior to this interesting article being published in the Ohio newspaper, the Religious News Service of the Continental United States gave a few clues to the animosity that was brewing as it stated the following in their August 9TH, 1993 issue of The Banner concerning the religious/political atmosphere both before and after the convention. The headline caption, which

READ IN BIG BLACK BOLD LETTERS, **"A MATTER OF CONSCIENCE"**, WENT AS FOLLOWS:

"YOU CAN BE A MASON IF YOU'RE SOUTHERN BAPTIST EVEN THOUGH MANY OF FREEMASONRY'S TEACHINGS ARE NOT COMPATIBLE WITH CHRISTIANITY.

THAT'S WHAT DELEGATES TO THE SOUTHERN BAPTIST CONVENTION'S ANNUAL MEETING IN HOUSTON, TEXAS, DECIDED IN JUNE. THEY RULED THAT LODGE MEMBERSHIP IS A MATTER OF PERSONAL CONSCIENCE.

PRIOR TO THE CONVENTION THE MASONS, WHO HAVE AN ESTIMATED MEMBERSHIP OF 2.5 MILLION IN THE UNITED STATES, TOOK OUT FULL-PAGE ADS IN BOTH OF HOUSTON'S NEWSPAPERS, URGING BAPTISTS NOT TO TAMPER WITH SECTIONS OF A CONTROVERSIAL CHURCH REPORT ON FREEMASONRY THAT ADVISED DELEGATES TO LEAVE MEMBERSHIP UP TO INDIVIDUALS.

DELEGATES APPROVED THE REPORT WITHOUT AMENDMENTS BY ABOUT A 5-1 MARGIN, TURNING BACK AN ATTEMPT TO TOUGHEN IT BY LABELING FREEMASONRY A ' MIXTURE OF PAGANISM AND CHRISTIANITY ' THAT IS ' CONDEMNED BY GOD. '

CRITICS OF FREEMASONRY WERE SATISFIED WITH THE REPORT'S CONCLUSION THAT SOME MASONIC PRACTICES, SUCH AS THE USE OF BLOODY OATHS, ARE INCOMPATIBLE WITH CHRISTIANITY. BUT THE REPORT ALSO SAID THAT OTHER MASONIC PRACTICES, SUCH AS BELIEF IN GOD, ARE SUPPORTIVE OF CHRISTIANITY.

THE SOUTHERN BAPTIST CONVENTION IS THE LARGEST PROTESTANT DENOMINATION IN THE UNITED STATES. THIS YEAR'S CONVENTION IN HOUSTON ATTRACTED 17,000 MESSENGERS, OR VOTING DELEGATES."

AS FAR AS BIBLICAL TEXT GOES, MUCH OF THE RANTING AND RAVING THAT WAS BEING CONDUCTED BY THE VARIOUS RELIGIOUS INSTITUTIONS WAS HYPOCRITICAL TO SAY THE LEAST. FOR INSTANCE, ALTHOUGH THE PRESBYTERIAN CHURCH OF CANADA WAS ALSO OPENLY CRITICIZING THE ANCIENT CRAFT OF FREEMASONRY FOR REFERRING TO **GOD** AS THE GREAT ARCHITECT OF THE UNIVERSE (1986 PRESBYTERIAN RECORD, A PUBLICATION OF THE PRESBYTERIAN CHURCH IN CANADA), CONTAINED WITHIN THE ORIGINAL TEXT OF CALVINISM, THE PROTESTANT FAITH REPEATEDLY CALLED THEIR GOD "THE ARCHITECT OF THE UNIVERSE" AND REFERRED TO HIS WORKS IN NATURE

AS BEING THE "ARCHITECTURE OF THE UNIVERSE." THIS REFERENCE TO GOD'S WORKS OF ARCHITECTURE WITHIN THE UNIVERSE WAS REPEATED TEN TIMES IN THAT CHRISTIAN RELIGION ALONE. BECAUSE OF THIS CONSTANTLY REPEATED REFERENCE, THE REVD. DR. JAMES ANDERSON, A GRADUATE OF THE ABERDEEN UNIVERSITY AND MINISTER OF THE SCOTCH PRESBYTERIAN CHURCH ON SWALLOW STREET, PICCADILLY, LONDON, ENGLAND FROM 1710 TO 1734 WAS REPORTEDLY COMPELLED TO INCORPORATE THOSE PHRASES INTO FREEMASONRY AS HE WROTE THE FIRST MASONIC BOOK OF CONSTITUTIONS IN 1723. CONTRARY TO THE RELIGIOUS MYTH THAT FRATERNITY BROTHER ANDERSON TOOK IT UPON HIMSELF TO CALL THE MASONIC DEITY THE GREAT ARCHITECT OF THE UNIVERSE, HE MERELY TOOK IT OVER FROM WHERE JOHN CALVIN HAD LEFT OFF IN HIS COMMENTARY OF PSALM 19 WHEREAS IT WAS STATED THAT THE HEAVENS "WERE WONDERFULLY FOUNDED BY THE GREAT ARCHITECT". THE FOUNDING FOREFATHER OF THE PROTESTANT FAITH FURTHER STATED IN THAT EXACT SAME PARAGRAPH, "WHEN ONCE WE RECOGNIZE GOD AS THE ARCHITECT OF THE UNIVERSE, WE ARE BOUND TO MARVEL AT HIS WISDOM, STRENGTH AND GOODNESS. "SO MUCH FOR RELIGIOUS HONESTY BEING PASSED DOWN THROUGHOUT THE AGES!!!

IN SPEAKING OF HONESTY, (RELIGIOUSLY AND/OR OTHERWISE), WHILE THE SOUTHERN BAPTIST MOVEMENT WAS SLOWLY GAINING MOMENTUM WITHIN THE CONTINENTAL UNITED STATES, IT WAS BUSINESS AS USUAL NORTH OF THE 49TH PARALLEL FOR THE CANADIAN FREEMASONRY FAMILY OF MAN. FOR INSTANCE, DUE TO THE FACT THAT BRITISH COLUMBIA'S RULING POLITICAL PARTY (THE NDP) WAS THAT OF A SACRED MASONIC INSTITUTION, FREEMASONS LIVING IN THE PROVINCE WERE QUICKLY REMINDED THAT THEIR LOYALTY WAS FIRST TO THE ANCIENT CRAFT, THEN, TO THE PROVINCE, AND LASTLY, TO THEIR COUNTRY; IN THAT SPECIFIC ORDER. AT THE 121ST ANNUAL COMMUNICATION MEETING OF THE GRAND LODGE OF BRITISH COLUMBIA, WHICH WAS HELD AT THE RECREATION CENTRE IN VERNON ON JUNE 18TH AND 19TH, 1992 A REPORT OF THE MASONIC CONSTITUTION COMMITTEE WAS TABLED BY FRATERNITY BROTHER H.A.D. OLIVER, THE NEWLY ELECTED NDP GOVERNMENT OF BRITISH COLUMBIA'S VERY OWN FUTURE POLITICAL CONFLICT-OF-INTEREST GURU. THIS SPECIAL COMMITTEE'S REPORT CONTAINED SOME RATER STARTLING REVELATIONS THAT WOULD HAVE MADE ANY PERSON'S HAIR STAND UP IN ATTENTION FROM FRIGHT. CONTAINED WITHIN ITS WRITINGS WERE REMINDERS OF THE FACT THAT IT WAS THE DUTY OF ALL MEMBERS OF THE PROVINCE OF BRITISH COLUMBIA'S FREEMASONRY POPULATION NOT ONLY TO REMAIN LOYAL TO THE CRAFT BUT TO ALSO REFRAIN FROM EXPRESSING THEIR OWN PERSONAL POLITICAL OPINIONS BECAUSE APPARENTLY, NOT EVERYONE WITHIN THE MASONIC BROTHERHOOD WAS PLEASED WITH THE ELECTION RESULTS OF OCTOBER 1991 WHICH SAW THE FRATERNAL REIGNS OF POWER

BEING HANDED OVER TO A "LEWIS "MEMBER OF MASONRY. IT WAS THEREFORE RECOMMENDED THAT THE GRAND LODGE OF BRITISH COLUMBIA FURTHER RESERVE THE RIGHTS OF INDIVIDUAL FREEMASONS AS GUARANTEED RIGHTS OF FREE-SPEECH UNDER THE CANADIAN CHARTER OF RIGHTS AND FREEDOMS, BE RELINQUISHED AS IT PERTAINED TO THAT INDIVIDUAL'S RIGHTS TO EXPRESS HIS OWN OPINION WITH REGARDS TO PUBLIC AFFAIRS. ALTHOUGH THEY WERE PERMITTED TO EXPRESS THEIR VIEWS ON THEOLOGY, THE POLITICAL THOUGHT PROCESS WAS LITERALLY PROHIBITED BY MASONIC DECREE. FURTHER TO THIS DICTATORIAL RECOMMENDATION BEING TABLED WITHIN THE CONFINES OF THE SPECIAL REPORT, BRITISH COLUMBIA FREEMASONS WERE THEN REMINDED OF THEIR SACRED DUTIES OF LOYALTY AND CITIZENSHIP TO THE ANCIENT NOBLE CRAFT.

THE OTHER INTERESTING THING REGARDING BRITISH COLUMBIA'S MEETING OF THE MIMES WAS THE FACT THAT NOT ALL OF THE INVITED DELEGATES WERE IN ATTENDANCE. OF THE 170 INVITED MASONIC LODGERY FROM WITHIN THE JURISDICTIONAL BOUNDARIES OF THE PACIFIC NORTHWEST, 166 OF THEM WERE REPRESENTED AT THE GALA EVENT. DISTINGUISHED GUESS FROM MANY MASONIC JURISDICTIONS WERE IN ATTENDANCE, INCLUDING 73 REGISTERED VISITORS FROM ALBERTA, ALASKA, WASHINGTON, IDAHO, MONTANA, UTAH AND NEVADA. FOR THE FIRST TIME IN ITS RECORDED HISTORY, DELEGATES FROM THE STATES OF CALIFORNIA AND OREGON WERE NOT PRESENT. SOME MEMBERS OF THE ANCIENT CRAFT ATTRIBUTED THIS LACK OF REPRESENTATION STEMMING FROM THE FACT THAT BOTH THE GRAND LODGES OF CALIFORNIA AND OREGON WERE AT ODDS WITH THE GRAND LODGE OF IDAHO FOR THEIR DIRTY DEED OF RECOGNIZING PRINCE HALL FREEMASONRY AS A VALUABLE ASSET TO THE HISTORY OF AMERICAN FREEMASONRY. AS THE 759 DELEGATES VOTED ON THE ISSUES TABLED, 198 DELEGATES WHO REPORTEDLY BOYCOTTED THE EVENT VOTED BY PROXY. APPARENTLY, OTHER RIFFS WITHIN THE FREEMASONRY FOLD WERE EXPOSED AS SOME OF THE UNRECOGNIZED MASONIC GOVERNING BODIES HAD BEEN PASSING THEMSELVES OFF AS LEGITIMATE REPRESENTATIVES OF THE ANCIENT CRAFT WHEN IN FACT THEY HAD NO FRATERNAL AUTHORIZATION TO DO SO; PRINCE HALL FREEMASONRY AND OTHER NON-RECOGNIZED MASONIC LODGERY WHO HAD BEEN OSTRACIZED BY THE FRATERNAL **"BROTHERHOOD OF MAN – UNDER THE FATHERHOOD OF GOD. "**THE GRAND LODGE OF BRITISH COLUMBIA THEREFORE LET IT BE KNOWN AT THIS GATHERING THAT IT HAD NO INTENTION WHATSOEVER, AT LEAST AT THAT TIME, TO ADHERE TO SUCH ACTIONS AND ABSOLUTELY REFUSED TO HAVE ANY FURTHER DISCUSSIONS ON THE MATTER. FURTHER TO THIS, IT WAS DECREED THAT THE GRAND LODGE OF BRITISH COLUMBIA OUTRIGHT REFUSE TO PARTICIPATE IN ANY CONFERENCES WITH THE SO-CALLED INTERNATIONAL ASSOCIATIONS CLAIMING TO REPRESENT FREEMASONRY AS A WHOLE, WHICH AS IT JUST SO HAPPENED WERE ALSO

ADMITTING MEMBERSHIP TO DOMESTIC LODGES OF THE ANCIENT CRAFT WHO HAD FAILED TO CONFORM WITH THE FUNDAMENTAL PRINCIPLES OF THE BROTHERHOOD'S DOCTRINE OF RECOGNIZABLE POWERS. THE DELEGATES IN ATTENDANCE WERE THUSLY FORCED TO ACCEPT AND PRACTICE THE DECREE INITIATED BY THE GRAND LODGE OF BRITISH COLUMBIA IF THEY WISHED TO REMAIN RECOGNIZED MEMBERS OF THE MASONIC FAMILY OF MAN. LIKE THE GRAND LODGES OF ENGLAND, IRELAND AND SCOTLAND, THE GRAND LODGE OF BRITISH COLUMBIA WAS TOTALLY CONVINCED THAT IF THE AIMS AND RELATIONSHIPS OF THE CRAFT WERE AT ALL COMPROMISED BY THE CONSTANT CHANGING OF THE WORLD AROUND THEM, FREEMASONRY WAS DOOMED TO FAIL IN ITS MAIN OBJECTIVE TOWARDS GLOBAL DOMINATION. WITH THAT BEING INGRAINED WITHIN THE HUMAN PSYCHE, THE GRAND LODGE OF BRITISH COLUMBIA REGISTERED ITS STRONG OPPOSITION TO ANY AND ALL OF THE MANY FRATERNAL CHANGES THAT WERE GOING TO BE OCCURRING DURING THE FIRST FEW DECADES OF THE 21ST CENTURY.

CONTAINED WITHIN THE TEXT OF THE HISTORY OF THE GRAND LODGE OF BRITISH COLUMBIA IS BY THEIR VERY OWN ADMISSION AS MEMBERS OF THE CRAFT BEING OPENLY PROUD OF THE FACT THAT THE UNITED NATIONS IN NEW YORK IS THAT OF A MASONIC INSTITUTION DESIGNED TO PROMOTE WORLD PEACE, HUMAN RIGHTS AND DEMOCRACY ON A GLOBAL SCALE WHILE OPERATING UNDER THE AUSPICES OF THE **BROTHERHOOD OF MAN AND THE FATHERHOOD OF GOD**. AND THAT BRITISH COLUMBIA FREEMASONS, LIKE THEIR BRETHREN RIGHT ACROSS THE NORTH AMERICAN CONTINENT CONTRIBUTED A GREAT DEAL TO THAT CAUSE EVER SINCE ITS FORMATION. REPORTEDLY, BRITISH COLUMBIA'S MAIN CONTRIBUTING FACTOR WAS SAID TO HAVE BEEN WHEN FRATERNITY BROTHER JOHN THORNTON MARSHALL (PAST WORSHIPFUL MASTER OF VICTORIA-COLUMBIA LODGE NO. 1 IN VICTORIA ON THE PACIFIC) WAS SENT INTO EXILE BY HIS APPOINTMENT IN OTTAWA TO BECOME PRIME MINISTER WILLIAM LYON MACKENZIE KING'S NEW GURU FOR THE DOMINION OF CANADA'S BUREAU OF STATISTICS IN AUGUST OF 1941. KING AND MARSHALL NATURALLY BEING ADVOCATES OF THE AMERICAN **NEW WORLD ORDER** CONCEPT!!! APPARENTLY, BROTHER MARSHALL HAD BEEN THE DIRECTOR OF VITAL STATISTICS FOR THE GOVERNMENT OF BRITISH COLUMBIA FOR SOME TIME WHEN THE PREMIER (THOMAS DUFFERIN PATTULO) MADE PRIVATE ARRANGEMENTS WITH THE GOVERNMENT OF CANADA TO HAVE MARSHALL TRANSFERRED OUT OF THE PROVINCE. THE APPOINTMENT WAS MADE BY SPECIAL ORDER-IN-COUNCIL AS ALL FEDERAL CIVIL SERVICE POSITIONS HAD BEEN FROZEN DUE TO THE OUTBREAK OF THE SECOND WORLD WAR AND AT THAT PRECISE MOMENT OF OUR COUNTRY'S HISTORY, AN AMERICAN BORN POLITICIAN (C.D. HOWE) WAS IN CHARGE OF RUNNING CANADA'S WAR-PRODUCTION PROGRAM. HOWE HAD BEEN DUBBED

THE MINISTER OF EVERYTHING BY HIS FRATERNITY COLLEAGUES AS HE BECAME A VERY POWERFUL POLITICAL PLAYER NOT ONLY WITHIN MACKENZIE KING'S RULING LIBERAL CABINET BUT ALSO WITHIN THE LIBERAL PARTY OF CANADA ITSELF THROUGHOUT MOST OF MARSHALL'S TENURE YEARS WITH THE UNITED NATIONS.

COINCIDENTLY, BROTHER MARSHALL WAS FIRST ANOINTED INTO THE GOVERNMENT OF BRITISH COLUMBIA ON FEBRUARY 14TH, 1916 FOLLOWING THE DEATH OF HIS FATHER, WHO ACCORDING TO THE MASONIC LITERATURE WAS SAID TO HAVE DIED "IN ACTION "DURING THE FIRST WORLD WAR IN BELGIUM ON OCTOBER 6TH, 1915. BROTHER MARSHALL'S FATHER WAS THE PAST MASTER OF GRANVILLE LODGE NO. 1787 IN BUCKINGHAM, ENGLAND. FRATERNITY BROTHER WILLIAM JOHN BOWSER WAS PREMIER OF THE PROVINCE WHEN MARSHALL'S APPOINTMENT TO THE GOVERNMENT WAS MADE IN 1916. THROUGHOUT THE 1940's, 50's AND EARLY 1960's, FREEMASONRY BROTHER MARSHALL MADE GOOD ON HIS SECRET OATH TO THE ANCIENT CRAFT AS HE SAT ON VARIOUS UNITED NATIONS COMMITTEES AND QUICKLY ROSE UP THROUGH THE FRATERNITY RANKS OF MANY INTERNATIONAL SUB-COMMITTEES. BETWEEN THE YEARS 1947-49, MASONIC BROTHER MARSHALL REPRESENTED CANADA AT THE U.N. AND CONTINUED TO DO SO FOR MANY YEARS THEREAFTER; 1954-60. IN 1955, HE WAS ELECTED CHAIRMAN OF THE POPULATION COMMISSION FOR THE UNITED NATIONS AND AGAIN IN 1957. BOTH OF THESE PRESTIGIOUS PORTFOLIO'S EACH COMPRISED OF TWO YEAR TERMS RESPECTIVELY. AS A HIGHLY RESPECTED MEMBER OF THE UNITED NATIONS, BROTHER MARSHALL GAINED WORLDWIDE RECOGNITION FROM HIS FELLOW BRETHREN WHO ALSO SAT ON NUMEROUS INTERNATIONAL COMMITTEES AND/OR SUB-COMMITTEES. IN JUNE OF 1953, HE WAS AWARDED THE MASONIC CORONATION METAL AND BECAME AN HONORARY MEMBER OF THE UNITED STATES BUREAU OF THE CENSUS STAFF IN WASHINGTON, D.C.

MEANWHILE BACK IN LOTUS LAND, IN JUNE OF 1963 BROTHER MARSHALL WAS ELEVATED TO THE TASK OF GRAND HISTORIAN FOR THE PENDING WORKS OF THE HISTORY OF THE GRAND LODGE OF BRITISH COLUMBIA. HIS ELEVATION APPOINTMENT TERM WAS SUPPOSEDLY TO LAST FOR ONE YEAR, ENDING ON JUNE 4TH, 1964 AND HAD BEEN SCHEDULED TO MAKE HIS FIRST PRESENTATION AS GRAND HISTORIAN TO THE GRAND LODGE MEMBERS ONLY DAYS LATER. BUT JUNE 18TH, 1964 CAME AND WENT AS NO REPORT HAD BEEN SUBMITTED BY THE GRAND HISTORIAN. A VERY HIGHLY KNOWLEDGEABLE GRAND HISTORIAN WAS THEN ANOINTED (BROTHER WILLIAM GEORGE GAMBLE) TO ASSIST MARSHALL IN HIS TASK OF DATA COLLECTING. AND ON JUNE 17TH, 1965 MARSHALL SUBMITTED HIS FIRST REPORT AS GATE KEEPER OF MASONIC EVENTS FOR THE PROVINCE OF BRITISH COLUMBIA. BY THIS TIME PERIOD OF COURSE, THE ENTIRE PROVINCIAL GOVERNMENT WAS TOTALLY CONTROLLED BY MEMBERS

OF THE MASONIC ORDER, WAC BENNETT WAS PREMIER. IN HIS REPORT, BROTHER MARSHALL LET IT BE KNOWN THAT MUCH OF THE INFORMATION THAT WAS REQUIRED FOR A FULLY DOCUMENTED DIAGNOSIS OF BRITISH COLUMBIA'S FREEMASONRY PAST WAS EITHER MISPLACED /OR POSSIBLY LOST ALTOGETHER. REQUIRING FURTHER ASSISTANCE TO LOCATE THE LOST FILES, BROTHERS GAMBLE AND MARSHALL USED WHATEVER INFLUENCES THEY COULD POSSIBLY MUSTER AS SOME OF THE DOCUMENTATION PERTAINING TO THE MASONIC ORDER'S ACTIVITIES IN BRITISH COLUMBIA HAD TO BE RETRIEVED FROM ARCHIVAL CLUTCHES IN OTTAWA. THE FILES, REPORTEDLY AMOUNTING TO SEVERAL LARGE CARDBOARD BOXES OF LOOSE-LEAF PAGES LITERALLY TOOK MONTHS TO SORT OUT. NOT LONG AFTERWARDS, COMPILING THE BOOK WAS SOON UNDERWAY AS NUMEROUS GOVERNMENTAL AGENCIES (FEDERAL, PROVINCIAL AS WELL AS MUNICIPAL) BEGAN SECURING INFORMATION THAT WAS NEEDED TO HELP THE RESEARCHERS WITH THE TASK OF HAVING THE BOOK BOTH WRITTEN AND PUBLISHED. EVEN CLASSIFIED REPORTS THAT WERE DEEMED TO BE OF GREAT HISTORICAL SIGNIFICANCE MANAGED TO MAKE THEIR WAY INTO THE HANDS OF THOSE SEEKING THEM. ALL DOCUMENTATION PERTAINING TO ANY MASONIC INVOLVEMENT, (FEDERALLY AND/OR PROVINCIALLY), WERE EASILY OBTAINED FROM THE NATIONAL AND PROVINCIAL ARCHIVES. BY JUNE 22ND, 1967 A FULL CARD CATALOGUE INDEX OF ALL MASONIC SOURCES OF INFORMATION OF HISTORICAL VALUE HAD BEEN FORMULATED. THE GRAND LODGE OF BRITISH COLUMBIA THEN ESTABLISHED A SPECIAL CENTENNIAL COMMITTEE TO OVERSEE THE TASK OF THE WORKS PROJECT, WHICH IN TURN INSTITUTED THE HISTORY SUB-COMMITTEE WHEREUPON VARIOUS HIGH PROFILE MEMBERS OF THE ANCIENT CRAFT SAT ASSURING THAT ONLY THE PROPER DOCUMENTATION MADE ITS WAY INTO THE HISTORY BOOK. ONE OF THESE MEMBERS INTERESTINGLY ENOUGH WAS A SUPREME COURT JUDGE, FRATERNITY BROTHER VICTOR L. DRYER, A.K.A. THE HONORABLE MR. JUSTICE DRYER OF MOUNT LEBANON LODGE NO. 72 IN VANCOUVER, B.C. TWENTY-THREE YEARS AFTER ITS ORIGINAL CONCEPTION, (FIRST PROPOSED BY BROTHER GAMBLE ON JUNE 19TH, 1947 AND SLOWLY EXECUTED BY HIM OVER THE YEARS), A PRESENTATION WAS MADE TO THE GRAND LODGE OF BRITISH COLUMBIA ON JUNE 18TH, 1970 LETTING THEM KNOW THAT THE WORKS PROJECT WAS REACHING ITS FINAL WRITING STAGES AND ALL THAT WAS NOW LEFT TO DO WAS FORMULATE THE TABLE OF CONTENTS. A DRAFT COPY OF THE TABLE OF CONTENTS WAS THEN SUBMITTED TO THE GRAND LODGE FOR ITS SCRUTINIZING JUDGEMENT CALL. ALSO SUBMITTED WAS A REPORT OUTLINING THE GRATITUDE THAT MEMBERS OF THE MASONIC ORDER WISHED TO EXPRESS TO VARIOUS MEMBERS OF THE PROVINCIAL GOVERNMENT'S ARCHIVAL RESEARCHERS FOR THE COUNTLESS HOURS THEY DONATED TO THE CAUSE OF COLLECTING THE NECESSARY MATERIALS AS IT PERTAINED TO FREEMASONRY

IN BRITISH COLUMBIA AND SO GRACIOUSLY EXPRESSED THEIR MANY THANKS WITHIN THE TEXT OF THE NEW HISTORY BOOK. AFTER READING THROUGH ITS TOTAL CONTENTS AND GIVING THE FRATERNAL SEAL OF APPROVAL ON IT, THE AUTHORIZED VERSION OF THE HISTORY OF THE GRAND LODGE OF BRITISH COLUMBIA 1871-1970 WAS PUBLISHED BY THE COLONIST PRINTERS LIMITED OF VICTORIA ON THE PACIFIC UNDER CANADIAN COPYRIGHT LAWS IN 1971.

IRONICALLY, A PERSON DOESN'T GET THE FULL POLITICAL AND/OR ECONOMICAL LOGISTICS OF THE ANCIENT CRAFT OF FREEMASONRY ON A PROVINCIAL SCALE UNTIL HE/OR SHE READS THE CONTENTS OF THE HISTORY OF THE GRAND LODGE OF THE PROVINCE OF BRITISH COLUMBIA. FOR INSTANCE, THERE HAS BEEN MANY WELL KNOWN MEMBERS OF BRITISH COLUMBIA'S MASONIC PAST WHO HAVE BEEN IMMORTALIZED. SOME OF THEM INCLUDED;

MEMBER'S NAME	AFFILIATED LODGE	IMMORTALIZED COMMUNITY
DR. ISRAEL WOOD POWELL	ELGIN LODGE NO. 348 MONTREAL, QUEBEC	POWELL RIVER, B.C.
CAPT. DANIEL PENDER	NANAIMO LODGE NO. 1090 NANAIMO, B.C.	PENDER HARBOUR, B.C. & THE PENDER ISLANDS
ROBERT BURNABY	FREDERIC LODGE OF UNITY NO. 661 CROYDON, SOUTH LONDON, ENGLAND	BURNABY, B.C.
SEWELL PRESCOTT MOODY	UNION LODGE NO. 899 NEW WESTMINISTER, B.C.	MOODYVILLE, B.C.
THOMAS LADNER	UNION LODGE NO. 9 NEW WESTMINISTER, B.C.	LADNER, B.C.
THE PRINCE OF WALES, LATER CROWNED KING EDWARD VII	PRINCE OF WALES LODGE NO. 250 LONDON, ENGLAND	PRINCETON, B.C.
GUISEPPE GARIBALDI	ELECTED GRAND MASTER OF THE GRAND LODGE OF ITALY IN 1865	GARIBALDI, B.C. MOUNT GARIBALDI & GARIBALDI PROVINCIAL PARK
ISAAC LEHMAN	UNION LODGE NO. 9 NEW WESTMINISTER, B.C.	MOUNT LEHMAN, B.C.

Many other British Columbia communities also immortalized the Freemasonry membership roster of days-gone-by — communities such as; Prince George, Prince Rupert, McBride, Oliver, Nelson, Stewart, Vernon, Dunsmuir, Hudson's Hope, Comox, Cumberland, Greenwood, Lytton, Fort Steele, Taylor, Pemberton and a never-ending host of other villages, towns and/or cities scattered throughout the Province. Although the list of immortalization is that of a long one, not all of the Province's communities had a happy Masonic relationship. In using the history of Gibsons, British Columbia as a prime example, (The West Howe Sound Story 1886-1976, The Gibson's Landing Story, and The History of the Grand Lodge of British Columbia 1871-1970), it becomes abundantly clear that despite the fact that this community may have had a humble beginning as a fishing and logging settlement throughout the latter parts of the Nineteenth Century and most of the next century as well, fully recognized Freemasonry actually didn't set up housekeeping until the late 1940's, (June 19TH, 1948), when Mount Elphinstone Lodge No. 130 received its official Charter from the Grand Lodge of British Columbia. Prior to that date, bitter battle lines had been drawn between members of the Orange Order and other members of the Ancient Craft of Freemasonry as some of the community's founding forefathers were active members of Orangism. In 1912, the Orange Lodgery having fully established themselves in the lower section of the community down in the bay area not very far from where the new LePage's Glue Factory had been constructed a dozen years previously, felt that they had full Masonic jurisdictional powers in the community as they were said to have been promoters of equal rights for all individuals with no special rights /or privileges for anyone, especially for the aboriginal peoples living on the Sechelt Indian Reserve Lands. Only eleven years after the Imperial Edict of August 20TH, 1858 which authorized the legalized theft of Indian lands, a company of Royal Engineers were sent to lay out the survey pegs for the Sechelt Indian Reserve in 1869.

With their bigoted opinions and self-righteous views, the Masonic Order's Orangism members began spreading their hatred up and down the coastline even more as a group of high profile Freemasonry dignitaries from Vancouver had arrived in Gibsons to establish a base of operation. Among these dignitaries was none other than fraternity Brother William H. Dunmore, (the Past Grand Master of Vancouver's Orange Lodgery itself), who as it turned out spent many years of his life spreading a lot of anti-native

RHETORIC THROUGHOUT THE SUNSHINE COAST. BY THE LATE 1920'S AND EARLY 1930'S, THE ORANGISM MEMBERSHIP BEGAN REACHING AN ALL TIME LOW AS THE DEPRESSION YEARS OF THE "DIRTY THIRTIES "HAD BESIEGED THE ENTIRE NORTH AMERICAN CONTINENT TO WHICH MOST INHABITANTS LATER LABELED AS BEING THE "HUNGRY THIRTIES." BROTHER NELSON WINEGARDEN, A MEMBER OF THE LOCAL ORANGE ORDER'S LODGERY IN GIBSONS HAD APPLIED FOR A JOB WITH THE MASONICALLY CONTROLLED PROVINCIAL POLICE FORCE IN MID-FEBRUARY OF 1930. FEELING SOMEWHAT ANXIOUS TO SEE THEIR FELLOW MEMBER OF THE ANCIENT CRAFT SUCCEED IN HIS ENDEAVORS AS HE HAD JUST TAKEN ON THE RESPONSIBILITY OF RAISING HIS OWN FAMILY, (MARRIED ONE OF THE LOCAL GALS ON FEBRUARY 23RD, 1930), GIBSONS MASONIC LODGE MEMBERS SUBMITTED A LETTER OF RECOMMENDATION TO THE FREEMASONRY PROVINCIAL GOVERNMENT OF FRATERNITY BROTHER SIMON FRASER TOLMIE, (THE 21ST PREMIER OF THE PROVINCE), VOUCHING FOR BROTHER WINEGARDEN'S GOOD CHARACTER AND COMMITMENTS TO THE FRATERNAL CAUSE. HIS APPLICATION FOR EMPLOYMENT WAS THEREFORE FAST TRACKED FOR APPROVAL ON MARCH 27TH, 1930 AND BY THE TIME THE POLICE FORCE EVENTUALLY CAME UNDER RCMP JURISDICTIONAL POWERS IN 1950, ORANGEMAN NELSON WINEGARDEN ALREADY HAD A FULL TWENTY YEARS UNDER HIS FRATERNAL BELT. AND IT WAS MORE THAN LIKELY A GOOD THING BECAUSE BY THE TIME WORLD WAR II HAD BROKEN OUT IN 1939, THE ORANGE ORDER IN GIBSONS AND THE SURROUNDING AREA WAS VIRTUALLY BECOMING NON-EXISTENT AS PEOPLE BY THIS TIME PERIOD NOW HAD MORE IMPORTANT ISSUES ON THEIR MINDS TO CONTEND WITH.

ACCORDING TO THE MASONIC ORDER'S OWN LITERATURE, THE ORANGE LODGERY HAS ALWAYS HAD A SOMEWHAT RATHER EXTREMELY ROCKY RELATIONSHIP WITH MANY OF THE FREEMASONRY MEMBERS LIVING WITHIN THE PROVINCE OF BRITISH COLUMBIA ITSELF. PERHAPS THIS ANIMOSITY WAS LARGELY DUE TO THE FACT THAT MOST OF THE ORANGISM MEMBERS HAD ADOPTED THE AMERICAN RITUALISTIC ATTITUDE AS PART OF ITS MASONIC CEREMONIES WHEREBY IT WAS EITHER THEIR WAY /OR THE HIGHWAY WHEN DEALING WITH CERTAIN CONTROVERSIAL ISSUES REGARDING POLITICAL AFFAIRS AND/OR THE FIRST NATION PEOPLES OF OUR COUNTRY.

BE THAT AS IT MAY, AFTER THE SECOND WORLD WAR A NEW STOCK OF FREEMASONRY VISIONARIES WANTED TO ESTABLISH THEMSELVES IN GIBSONS BUT THINGS REPORTEDLY GOT A LITTLE UGLY AS THE REMAINING ORANGE ORDER MEMBERS BEGAN CLAIMING SQUATTERS RIGHTS TO THE JURISDICTIONAL BOUNDARIES OF THE SUNSHINE COAST. THE SITUATION WAS SO INTENSE THAT THE GRAND MASTER OF THE GRAND LODGE OF BRITISH COLUMBIA (BROTHER KILBURN KING REID), HAD TO ISSUE HIS **DISPENSATION NOTICE** FOR THE GIBSON'S LANDING MASONIC LODGE IN PERSON ON JANUARY 11TH,

1947. After trying to resolve the differences of opinion amongst its own membership with no success whatsoever, the dispensation otherwise known as a legal written document authorizing Lodge members to conduct their affairs in a lawful Masonic manner in accordance to the Freemasonry doctrine without prejudice was ordered to be extended for a full twelve months on June 19TH, of that same year. By June 19TH, 1948 peace was finally restored as a compromise of sorts was reached when the Grand Lodge of British Columbia granted a new Charter to the Sunshine Coast Freemasons as they instituted Mount Elphinstone Lodge No. 130 in Roberts Creek. The Lodge was constituted by fraternity Brother George Roy Long, the Grand Master of all Freemasons for British Columbia which in turn enabled members of the Masonic Order to mold the political landscape of the entire coastal region into what they had envisioned for the 21ST Century with Master Masons becoming elected political figures; mayors, councilmen, regional board directors, municipal administrators and planners, as well as Provincially elected Members of the Legislative Assembly.

Like anything else in the Freemasonry world, everything is enshrined with both mysticism and symbolism. To that end, the establishing of the Roberts Creek Masonic Lodge was no different. Taking its name from a mountain close by that dominated the western entrance to the Howe Sound, which had been dubiously dubbed Mount Elphinstone supposedly to immortalize a fellow fraternity member, Captain J. Elphinstone whom was reportedly the First Lord of the British Admiralty Fleet during the time of Captain George Vancouver's exploration trips of the Pacific Coastal regions between the years 1792 and 1794. Folklore has it that Captain Elphinstone was the commanding officer of the English monarchy's ship the **HMS GLORY** when his name quickly rose up through the ranks of the British naval forces as a very powerful military leader destined for much greatness in an adaptation of Earl Howe's famous naval victory in 1794 known as "The Glorious First of June. "Howe being of course the First Lord of the Admiralty between the years 1783-1788 to which Captain George Vancouver named the Howe Sound after.

Historically, Captain Elphinstone was better known by his fraternity colleagues as the Eleventh Lord Elphinstone since his Freemasonry ancestry was said to have possibly gone as far back as the Biblical times of Jesus Christ himself. Further to this, William Elphinstone, the first member of the Elphinstone Klan to be raised to

THE PRESTIGIOUS TITLE OF NOBILITY BECAME KNOWN AS BISHOP ELPHINSTONE, (BISHOP OF ROSS), IN 1481 AND THEN DEEMED LORD HIGH CHANCELLOR OF SCOTLAND SEVEN YEARS LATER, (1488). THE FIRST LORD ELPHINSTONE REPORTEDLY FOUNDED THE UNIVERSITY OF ABERDEEN, SCOTLAND IN 1494. AS FATE WOULD HAVE IT, THE FIRST LORD ELPHINSTONE WHO WAS ALSO KNOWN AS BISHOP ELPHINSTONE OF THE ROMAN CATHOLIC CHURCH IN ABERDEEN WAS SAID TO HAVE FIRST SUGGESTED THAT THE UNIVERSITY BE ESTABLISHED IN THE PRESENCE OF POPE ALEXANDER VI, (1492-1503), WHO IN TURN REPORTEDLY ISSUED A BULL DEEMING IT SO. THE FIRST LORD ELPHINSTONE, THEN SPENT THE REST OF HIS NATURAL LIFE DEDICATING TIME TO ITS BEING INSTITUTED AS A LEARNING CENTER. BY ALL ACCOUNT, BISHOP ELPHINSTONE WAS IMMEDIATELY IMMORTALIZED IN NORTHEASTERN SCOTLAND AS MONUMENTS TO HIS GREATNESS WERE PLACED ON THE FLOORS OF THE UNIVERSITY'S CHAPEL WHICH WAS CONSTRUCTED IN THE EARLY PARTS OF THE 1500'S. REPORTEDLY, THE BUILDING OF THE UNIVERSITY BEGAN IN 1506 AND TOOK MANY YEARS TO COMPLETE. ACCORDING TO VARIOUS SCOTTISH HISTORIANS, THE NEW SEAT OF LEARNING WAS USED AS A STEPPING STONE FOR THE ESTABLISHING OF THE PROTESTANT CHURCH OF SCOTLAND DURING WHICH TIME PERIOD BOTH THE ROMAN CATHOLICS AND THE PROTESTANTS BEGAN INSISTING THAT THEIR SPECIFIC FORM OF RELIGION WAS MORE SUPERIOR THAN THE OTHER. AND SINCE ALL OF THIS HAD INITIALLY TRANSPIRED, IT ONLY MADE SENSE THAT THE GOOD FAMILY SURNAME OF **ELPHINSTONE** BE INDOCTRINATED WITHIN THE VERY WALLS OF THE SUNSHINE COAST INSTITUTIONS OF LEARNING. ON JUNE 12TH, 1890 THE HOWE SOUND SCHOOL DISTRICT WAS FORMED FOR THE IMMEDIATE AREAS SURROUNDING GIBSON'S LANDING AND IN 1910, A TWO-ROOM SCHOOL WAS BUILD IN GIBSONS TO ACCOMMODATE STUDENTS. ONE YEAR LATER, (1911), THE ELPHINSTONE BAY ELEMENTARY SCHOOL WAS ESTABLISHED IN ROBERTS CREEK AND FORTY-ONE YEARS AFTER THAT, (1952), THE ELPHINSTONE JUNIOR-SENIOR HIGH SCHOOL WAS ERECTED IN GIBSONS ENABLING THE COMMUNITY LEADERS TO CARRY ON WITH ITS OLD FAMILY TRADITIONS OF TEACHING HALF TRUTHS TO THE YOUNG IMPRESSIONABLE MINDS OF THE SURROUNDING AREAS.

JUST LIKE SAMUEL DE CHAMPLAIN'S CLAIMING OF HIS TERRITORY IN FRENCH CANADA FOR THE CONSTRUCTION OF QUEBEC CITY IN 1608, CANINE URINATION WAS ALSO TAKING PLACE IN ENGLISH CANADA AS WELL WITH ALMOST EVERYTHING IN SIGHT BEING SPRAYED UPON IN THE NAME OF THE SCOTTISH LORDS OF ELPHINSTONE;

MOUNT ELPHINSTONE CHAPTER OF THE ORDER OF THE EASTERN STAR
MOUNT ELPHINSTONE CHAPTER OF THE ORDER OF DEMOLAY
MOUNT ELPHINSTONE CHAPTER OF THE INTERNATIONAL ORDER OF JOB'S DAUGHTER

Elphinstone Chapter of the International Order of the Daughters of the Empire

Elphinstone Chapter of the Victorian Order of Nurses

Mount Elphinstone Community Cemetery

Elphinstone Pioneer Museum

Elphinstone Hospital Committee

Elphinstone Co-Operative Store

Elphinstone Bay Farmer's Institute

Elphinstone Ski Club

Elphinstone Cannery

Elphinstone Bay Road

Elphinstone Road

YMCA's Camp Elphinstone

and so on and so forth.

It seemed as though everyone living in and around Gibsons itself had lost the ability to use their own imaginations when trying to pick a name to which their endeavors were to be incorporated in daily life — lack of originality simply because of the fact that they wanted to fit into the community and be totally accepted by all. No matter where a person went on the Sunshine Coast, (Gibsons, Roberts Creek, Sechelt), there it was hitting them smack in the face; Elphinstone this and Elphinstone that. This lack of originality therefore blossomed during the early years of the community's development as the blind were virtually leading the blind down the path to their own egocentric ignorance towards other human beings living amongst them. Unfortunately for most people, this form of mentality spilled itself over well into the 21ST Century!!!

Not long after the book titled "The Gibson's Landing Story" was first published in 1962, a resident of the Gibsons community had paid a visit to Drunkilbo, Scotland (the home of the Sixteenth holder of the distinguished title Lord Elphinstone and cousin to Queen Elizabeth II) asking permission to use his Lordship's family crest as the Junior-High School's educational facility Coat of Arms. Fraternal authorization to do so was then granted and as a gesture of appreciation, a suitably inscribed copy of Lester R. Peterson's book was thusly sent to the Sixteenth Lord Elphinstone. Only 83 years previous to this glorious occasion taking place, the Fifteenth Earl of Elphinstone had sanctioned the usage of his good family name in promoting a settlement situated south of Riding Mountain National Park and northwest of Neepawa in the Province of Manitoba. The community was thusly named Elphinstone by the chief factor of

THE HUDSON'S BAY COMPANY AT THE TIME (JOHN A. LAUDER) AFTER LORD ELPHINSTONE, WHO OWNED THIRTEEN SECTIONS OF PRAIRIE LAND THAT WAS NOW IN THE PROCESS OF BEING DEVELOPED INTO A COMMUNITY. THE AREA HAD BEEN SURVEYED IN 1876 AND FOUR YEARS LATER, LORD ELPHINSTONE WAS VISITING HIS FRATERNITY FRIENDS ON THE LITTLE SASKATCHEWAN RIVER WHERE THE HUDSON'S BAY COMPANY CHIEF FACTOR ALREADY HAD DREAMS OF ESTABLISHING A SMALL POST OFFICE AND HAVING SETTLERS FROM ONTARIO TENDING TO THE FIELDS OF THEIR NEWLY ACQUIRED PROPERTIES. IN THE MEANTIME, THE HUDSON'S BAY COMPANY ITSELF HAD A POST FIVE MILES DUE NORTH OF THE PROPOSED SETTLEMENT WITH PLANS OF EXPANSION. BETWEEN THE YEARS 1879-80, THE HUDSON'S BAY COMPANY BUILT A GRIST MILL, A SAWMILL AND A STORE IN THE SETTLEMENT TO WHICH LORD ELPHINSTONE WAS MORE THAN WILLING TO ACCOMMODATE HIS GOOD FRIENDS AND PLACING HIS NAME ONTO IT. THE POST OFFICE AT ELPHINSTONE, MANITOBA BECAME A REALITY DURING THE YEAR 1887 WHICH ENABLED THE NEW SETTLEMENT TO FLOURISH THROUGHOUT THE TWENTIETH CENTURY AS WELL AS INTO THE NEXT.

MOST OF THE TIME, A COMMUNITY'S HUMBLE BEGINNING ARE DRASTICALLY ALTERED DUE TO VARIOUS HISTORICAL INFRACTIONS. IN COMPARING THE HISTORY OF HOW THE TOWN OF GIBSONS CAME INTO BEING WITH THAT OF ANOTHER COMMUNITY IN B.C.'S KOOTENAY COUNTRY, (ROSSLAND), SOME VERY INTERESTING DETAILS SUDDENLY BEGIN TO EMERGED. FOR INSTANCE, THE FOUNDING FOREFATHER OF GIBSON'S LANDING WAS NONE OTHER THAN AN AFFILIATED ORANGISM MEMBER NAMED GEORGE WILLIAM GIBSON FROM THE PROVINCE OF ONTARIO WHO WAS ORIGINALLY BORN IN LINCOLN, ENGLAND ON JANUARY 31ST, 1829, THEN SERVED FOR A TIME IN THE BRITISH NAVY AND EVENTUALLY RETIRING AS A LIEUTENANT. WHILE HE WAS STILL IN HIS MID-FIFTY'S, GEORGE GIBSON AND HIS FAMILY MIGRATED TO BRITISH COLUMBIA IN 1885 VIA SAN FRANCISCO WHICH WAS STILL A HOTBED OF FREEMASONRY ACTIVITY. SEEKING FRATERNAL SECURITY FOR HIS NEWFOUND FAMILY AND BRINGING THEM OUT WEST, THE GIBSON FAMILY FIRST SETTLED ON VANCOUVER ISLAND AMONGST THE FREEMASONRY POPULATION. AFTER SPENDING SOME TIME IN THE MASONIC STRONGHOLD COMMUNITIES OF VICTORIA AND NANAIMO, GIBSON AND HIS TWO SONS SET SAIL IN A FLAT BOTTOM BOAT SEARCHING FOR LAND THAT THEY COULD CALL THEIR OWN. THEN ON MAY 24TH, 1886 A COUPLE OF STAKES WERE DRIVEN INTO THE GROUND AND THE SETTLEMENT OF GIBSON'S LANDING WAS BORN. INTERESTINGLY ENOUGH, THE LAND THAT OF WHICH THE GIBSON FAMILY WERE NOW CLAIMING AS THEIR VERY OWN WAS ONCE OCCUPIED BY THE SQUAMISH INDIAN TRIBES AS PART OF THE FIRST NATION PEOPLES TRADITIONAL HUNTING GROUNDS ALTHOUGH

THE AUGUST 20TH, 1858 IMPERIAL EDICT STATED OTHERWISE. (THE SECHELT INDIANS OCCUPIED THE OTHER END OF THE SUNSHINE COAST).

WHEN THE GIBSON FAMILY DROVE THE STAKES INTO THE GROUND CLAIMING VARIOUS DISTRICT LOTS AS THEIR NEWFOUND TROPHIES, (DISTRICT LOTS 685, 686 AND 697), A MEMBER OF THE ANCIENT CRAFT OF FREEMASONRY AND HIS COHORTS WERE STILL THE RULING GOVERNMENTAL BODY FOR THE ENTIRE PROVINCE. PREMIER WILLIAM SMITHE (1883-87) WHO IN TURN ENABLED OTHER WELL KNOWN MEMBERS OF THE ANCIENT CRAFT OF FREEMASONRY TO MAKE THEIR WAY OUT WEST FROM ONTARIO AND MANITOBA TO HELP ESTABLISH THE NEW SETTLEMENT OF GIBSON'S LANDING. FAMILIES SUCH AS THE WINEGARDEN'S AND THE GRANTHAM'S AS WELL AS MANY OTHER PROMINENT FAMILY NAMES ENSHRINED IN THE CLOAK OF SECRECY AND DECEPTION SUPPOSEDLY ALL IN THE NAME OF DEMOCRACY AND/OR MAN'S ABILITY OF PROGRESSING TOWARDS BEING A MORE CIVILIZED RACE OF PEOPLE.

WHILE ALL THIS BLATANT THEFT OF INDIAN LAND WAS OCCURRING ON THE SUNSHINE COAST, ANOTHER PIONEER OF SORTS NAMED ROSS THOMPSON SLOWLY BEGAN PICKING AWAY AT HIS GOLD CLAIM IN THE KOOTENAY DISTRICT OF THE TRAIL REGION. BY JULY OF 1890, MINING CLAIMS WERE BEING STAKED ON RED MOUNTAIN, NEAR WHERE A STREAM KNOWN AS TRAIL CREEK CROSSED THE OLD DEWDNEY TRAIL, ON ITS WAY TO JOIN THE MIGHTY COLUMBIA RIVER AND SOME TEN MILES FROM THE PRESENT CITY OF TRAIL. THE FIRST MINE WAS REPORTEDLY LOCATED IN THE ROSSLAND CAMP, OTHERS LATER FOLLOWED; THE CENTRE STAR, WAR EAGLE, IDAHO AND VIRGINIA, AND SHORTLY THEREAFTER CAME THE GREAT LE ROI MINE WHICH BECAME KNOWN AS A FAMOUS GOLD AND COPPER PRODUCER. BY THIS TIME PERIOD OF COURSE, THE USUAL RUSH TOOK PLACE IN THE GOLD FIELDS OF THE KOOTENAY COUNTRY AS MANY THOUSANDS TREKKED THEIR WAY INTO THE SURROUNDING AREA AFTER ROSS THOMPSON'S PREEMPTION CLAIM TO WHICH THE COMMUNITY WAS NAMED AFTER. AND ACCORDING TO MASONIC LITERATURE, MANY OF THOSE INDIVIDUALS WHO FLOCKED INTO ROSSLAND BELONGED TO THE ANCIENT CRAFT OF FREEMASONRY. JUST LIKE THE NEWLY SETTLED COMMUNITY OF GIBSON'S LANDING, VARIOUS MEMBERS OF THE CRAFT ALSO WANTED TO CONTROL THE DESTINY OF ITS POPULATION. ON JUNE 19TH, 1896 THE GRAND LODGE OF BRITISH COLUMBIA ISSUED A CHARTER FOR THE ESTABLISHING OF CORINTHIAN LODGE NO. 27 FOR THE MASTER MASONS OF ROSSLAND AND THE LODGE WAS THEREFORE CONSTITUTED FIVE MONTHS LATER ON NOVEMBER 18TH OF THAT SAME YEAR.

IRONICALLY, WHILE GLANCING THROUGH THE PAGES DEPICTING THE SO-CALLED TRUE HISTORY OF THE COMMUNITY OF GIBSON'S LANDING, A FORMER HIGH SCHOOL STUDENT OF LESTER PETERSON'S (BENOIT J. LEPAGE) RECOGNIZED A LOT OF FAMILIAR NAMES THAT WERE ONCE LOCALLY ASSOCIATED

WITH THE ANCIENT CRAFT OF FREEMASONRY. NAMES THAT OF WHICH HELPED MOLD THE COMMUNITY INTO WHAT IT HAS BECOME IN THE 21ST CENTURY;

THE REVEREND JAMES SHAVER WOODSWORTH – MINISTER OF THE GIBSON'S LANDING METHODIST CHURCH IN 1917, LATER BECAME A MEMBER OF PARLIAMENT IN OTTAWA AND THE FIRST NATIONAL LEADER OF THE CO-OPERATIVE COMMONWEALTH FEDERATION (CCF BIRTH CHILD OF THE NDP).

GEORGE H. HOPKINS – LAND SPECULATOR AND FOUNDER OF HOPKINS LANDING IN THE EARLY 1900's. BORN IN IRELAND ON DECEMBER 31ST, 1853, BROTHER HOPKINS WAS AN ADVOCATE OF ORANGISM, HE DIED IN MAY OF 1931 AND WAS BURIED WITH FULL MASONIC HONORS. HE REPORTEDLY BECAME A JUSTICE OF THE PEACE IN 1915.

JAMES SINCLAIR – ENGINEER TURNED POLITICIAN IN THE EARLY 1940's, HE REPRESENTED THE PEOPLE OF THE SUNSHINE COAST AS THEIR DULY ELECTED LIBERAL MEMBER OF PARLIAMENT IN OTTAWA FROM 1949 UNTIL THE CONSERVATIVE LANDSLIDE VICTORY OF FRATERNITY BROTHER DIEFENBAKER IN MARCH OF 1958 AS CANADA'S NEWLY CROWNED MASONIC PRIME MINISTER. IN 1971, P.E. TRUDEAU WOULD EVENTUALLY MARRY INTO THE FRATERNAL SINCLAIR'S FAMILY FOLD.

ERNEST PARR-PEARSON – FOUNDER OF THE WEEKLY PUBLISHED "COAST NEWS "IN 1945. HE BECAME A MASTER MASON IN THE LATE 1940's AS HIS NAME IS NOTED IN THE ROBERTS CREEK MASONIC LODGE RECORDS AS BEING AN ENTERED APPRENTICE IN 1948.

RICHARD (DICK) FITCHETT – THE FOUNDER OF THE FIRST KNOWN BUILDING MATERIAL SUPPLY OUTLET DUBBED "GIBSONS BUILDING SUPPLIES" IN 1947. HONOURARY MEMBER OF MOUNT ELPHINSTONE LODGE NO. 130 AS HE BECAME ACTIVELY INVOLVED WITH MUNICIPAL POLITICS.

EDWARD J. SHAW – BUSINESSMAN AND OWNER OF SHAW'S TRUCKING AND TRANSPORT COMPANY. BROTHER SHAW WAS ALSO A FOUNDING CHARTERED MEMBER OF MOUNT ELPHINSTONE LODGE NO. 130 IN ROBERTS CREEK.

JAMES H. DRUMMUND – ENTREPRENEUR AND PILLAR OF THE COMMUNITY AS HE IS OF THE DRUMMUND REALITY AND INSURANCE AGENCY FAME. BROTHER DRUMMUND WAS ALSO A FOUNDING CHARTERED MEMBER OF MOUNT ELPHINSTONE LODGE NO 130.

WALTER J. PETERSON – COMMERCIAL LAND DEVELOPER DURING THE 1940's AND 50's. HONOURARY MEMBER OF MOUNT ELPHINSTONE LODGE NO. 130 IN ROBERTS CREEK.

CECIL P. BALLINTINE – COMMERCIAL LAND DEVELOPER DURING THE 1940's AND 50's. BROTHER BALLINTINE WAS ALSO A FOUNDING CHARTERED MEMBER OF MOUNT ELPHINSTONE LODGE NO. 130.

Benjamin J. Lang – businessman and owner of Lang Drug Stores, one in Gibsons and another in Sechelt during the 1940's, 50's and 60's. He became a Master Mason in the 1940's just prior to his establishing the Gibsons branch of the drug stores. His name is duly noted in the Roberts Creek Masonic Lodge records as being an Entered Apprentice in 1948.

Robert L. Jackson – part of the infamous Jackson Brothers logging fame. He became a Master Mason in the late 1940's as his name is noted in the Roberts Creek Masonic Lodge records as being an Entered Apprentice in 1948.

Allan S. Truman – longtime resident and principle of the Elphinstone Junior-Senior High School during the 1950's. Honourary member of Mount Elphinstone Lodge No. 130 in Roberts Creek.

A.K. (Keith) Wright – commercial developer from the 1950's and well into the next decades. Honourary member of Mount Elphinstone Lodge No. 130 in Roberts Creek.

Jack Marshall – businessman and owner of Peninsula Plumbing and Supplies as well as being a plumbing contractor in the 1960's,70's and 80's. Honourary member of Mount Elphinstone Lodge No. 130 as he became actively involved with municipal politics.

Norman Hough – a new comer to the community of Gibsons in 1950, he purchased a 100 acre parcel of land and almost immediately became the largest supplier of local farm products for the surrounding area. Brother Hough was a member of Mount Elphinstone Lodge No. 130 through his affiliation with Freemasonry in the Province of Saskatchewan where he had just moved from.

According to LePage, there were countless other members of the Ancient Craft of Freemasonry mentioned in the book written by his former teacher. Chuckling at the whole distorted affair of days-gone-by, who would have ever imagined that a former student of Lester Peterson's actually had the ability to put all of the pieces of this gigantic puzzle together many years after dropping out of high school simply because of the fact that even back then, he felt as though he didn't fit into the community because of his strict no nonsense French Roman Catholic upbringing.

Perhaps his ability to do so stemmed mainly from the fact that he had lived up in the Northwest Territories during the early to mid-1980's and felt somewhat sympathetic towards the native peoples. Or maybe it even had something to do with an accidental discovery while researching his family tree in the 1990's where he had learned

THAT A MEMBER OF THE LePAGE FAMILY DYNASTY HAD MOVED UP TO THE YUKON TERRITORY IN THE 1940'S ERA AND BECAME AN ACTIVE MEMBER IN WHITEHORSE LODGE NO. 48, (MASTER MASON AIME R. LePAGE). UPON HIS ARRIVAL INTO THE FROZEN FRONTIER, FRATERNITY BROTHER AIME LePAGE ALMOST IMMEDIATELY BECAME ACTIVELY INVOLVED WITH THE TERRITORIAL GOVERNMENT'S POLICY OF IMPLEMENTING AN APARTHEID SYSTEM OF GOVERNMENT NORTH OF THE 60TH PARALLEL. ONCE THIS BECAME APPARENT TO BENOIT LePAGE, EVERYTHING CAME INTO FULL FOCUS MERELY BECAUSE OF THE FACT THAT ACCORDING TO THE HISTORY OF BRITISH COLUMBIA'S FREEMASONRY PAST THEY WERE TRYING TO CONTROL THE DESTINY OF THE YUKON IN THE EARLY DAYS, GRAND LODGE OF BRITISH COLUMBIA'S ISSUING OF A **DISPENSATION NOTICE** IN 1898 FOR MEMBERS OF VICTORIA-COLUMBIA LODGE NO. 1 WHO WERE NOW RESIDING IN THE YUKON TERRITORY WHILE MASTER MASONS FROM THE JURISDICTION OF THE GRAND LODGE OF MANITOBA WERE ALSO STAKING CLAIMS TO THE YUKON ITSELF.

IN JUNE OF 1898 A LETTER WRITTEN TO THE GRAND LODGE OF MANITOBA, THE GRAND LODGE OF BRITISH COLUMBIA CAME RIGHT OUT AND ASKED THE MANITOBA FREEMASONS AS TO WHAT THEY SPECIFICALLY WANTED TO CONTROL THE MASONIC REIGNS OF POWER WITHIN THE JURISDICTIONAL BOUNDARIES OF THE YUKON TERRITORY. INTERESTINGLY, THE REPLY FROM THE GRAND LODGE OF MANITOBA STATED THAT THEY CLAIMED NO EXCLUSIVE JURISDICTIONAL RIGHTS TO THE YUKON BUT THAT THEY WERE ALSO OPEN TO ANY SUGGESTIONS THAT THE GRAND LODGE OF BRITISH COLUMBIA MAY HAVE HAD PROVIDED OF COURSE THAT MANITOBA FREEMASONS WOULD BE PERMITTED TO CONTINUE OPERATING THEIR MASONIC LODGES THAT CAME UNDER THE AUSPICES OF MANITOBA FREEMASONRY CONTROL. THE GRAND MASTER OF THE GRAND LODGE OF BRITISH COLUMBIA THEREFORE AGREED WITH THE TERMS SUBMITTED BY THE GRAND LODGE OF MANITOBA ALLOWING THEM TO CONTINUE HAVING MASONIC GOVERNING POWERS WITHIN THE IMMEDIATE JURISDICTION OF ITS DESIGNATED LODGERY AND THE PROVINCE OF BRITISH COLUMBIA FREEMASONRY POPULATION EVENTUALLY GAINED FULL MASONIC AUTHORITY OF THE TERRITORY DUE TO ITS GEOGRAPHICAL POSITION WITHIN THE FAMILY FOLD NOT LONG AFTER THE TURN OF THE TWENTIETH CENTURY.

PREVIOUS TO THE GRAND LODGE OF BRITISH COLUMBIA'S GAINING FULL MASONIC CONTROL OF THE YUKON TERRITORY, NUMEROUS ATTEMPTS WERE MADE BY BRITISH COLUMBIA FREEMASONS TO ESTABLISH LODGES NORTH OF THE 60TH PARALLEL BUT ALL VISIBLE ATTEMPTS FAILED MISERABLY SIMPLY BECAUSE OF THE FACT THAT MEMBERS OF B.C.'S FREEMASONRY POPULATION WERE BUSY FIGHTING IT OUT WITH MANITOBA'S FREEMASONRY POPULATION FOR SUPREMACY IN THE NORTHLAND. FOR EXAMPLE, MEMBERS OF THE

Grand Lodge of Manitoba already had everything in the works towards establishing Masonic Lodges in both of the key populated communities, Dawson City and Whitehorse when British Columbia Master Masons tried to set up housekeeping in Dawson City under the auspices of the Grand Lodge of British Columbia. Needless to say, the Manitoba Master Masons were not at all impressed and the B.C. proposed Lodge in Dawson City failed to materialize due to the schism activity that it had created. It was largely due to this schism activity that led the Grand Lodge of British Columbia to compile the letter to the Grand Lodge of Manitoba asking for a clear concise definition of the terms as both of these Grand Lodges viewed the Yukon as open territory although neither one of them had real tangible proof to verify their claim on the land. And since this was indeed the case, the two existing Masonic Lodges at the time that were operating under the Manitoba Freemasons eventually handed the reigns of power over to British Columbia Freemasons in 1907 when the Grand Lodge of Manitoba surrendered its remaining claim to the Yukon Territory to the Grand Lodge of British Columbia.

With British Columbia Freemasons having full jurisdictional control of the Yukon, native self-determination North of the 60TH parallel thusly became virtually non-existent as by this time period of Canada: A People's History; the whiteman literally controlled everything in the northern frontier and before long, all aboriginal peoples North of 60 became an enslaved race in their own homeland. Controlling the political destiny of the Yukon Territory, British Columbia Freemasons began implementing their own kind of justice in the Arctic as more and more members of the Ancient Craft became duly elected public officials representing all walks of life on various levels of government, (municipal, territorial as well as federal).

Neither the schism activity North of the 60TH parallel nor the January 1947 dispensation on the Sunshine Coast were isolated cases for the Province's Freemasonry population where a notice to cease and desist had to be issued by the Grand Lodge of British Columbia. For instance, during the First World War some members of the City of Vancouver's elite Master Masons went behind the backs of others and began organizing a **"Masonic Senate "** to promote their own hidden agenda onto the Province's Freemasonry and non-Masonic population. Feeling that the Government of the day was neglecting to execute the Freemasonry vision of the political landscape for the Province of B.C., a group of radical Freemasons

VIOLATED THE FUNDAMENTAL PRINCIPLES OF THE CRAFT AND DECIDED TO TAKE MATTERS INTO THEIR OWN HANDS BY ESTABLISHING A SENATE THAT WAS TO HAVE OVER-RIDING FRATERNAL POWERS FOR THE ALREADY INSTITUTED MASONIC GOVERNING BODIES. THEY WERE LITERALLY TRYING TO OVERTHROW THE GRAND LODGE OF BRITISH COLUMBIA'S JURISDICTIONAL POWERS OVER THEM. ON JUNE 17TH, 1915 FRATERNITY BROTHER JAMES STARK (THE GRAND MASTER OF THE GRAND LODGE OF BRITISH COLUMBIA FROM JUNE 18TH, 1914 TO JUNE 18TH, 1915), VOICED HIS OPPOSITION TO THE UNTIMELY ORGANIZING OF THE MASONIC SENATE VOWING TO HAVE IT IMMEDIATELY DISMANTLED FOR THE GOOD OF THE PROVINCE AND ITS PEOPLE. A COMMITTEE WAS THEN FORMED BY THE NEW GRAND MASTER BROTHER WILLIAM CAREY DITMARS (JUNE 18TH, 1915 TO JUNE 23RD, 1916) TO LOOK INTO THE DISSENSION AND TO IMMEDIATELY IMPLEMENT SOME SORT OF RECOMMENDATION TO HAVE THE ISSUE RESOLVED QUICKLY AND WITHOUT FURTHER INCIDENT. BY THE TIME THE COMMITTEE HAD COMPLETED ITS INTERNAL INVESTIGATION, THE INDIVIDUALS WHO HAD ORIGINALLY INSTIGATED THE INSURRECTION IN THE FIRST PLACE WERE SIMPLY DEEMED TO HAVE BEEN OVERLY ENTHUSIASTIC FREEMASONS WHO WERE MERELY ANXIOUS TO PROMOTE THE CRAFT. WITH THE VIRTUAL DOWN PLAYING OF THE ISSUE AT HAND, EVERYTHING WAS IMMEDIATELY SWEPT UNDER THE FRATERNAL CARPET AND NEVER SPOKEN OF EVER AGAIN AS THE LODGE IN QUESTION AND ITS DISGRUNTLED MEMBERS WERE WRITTEN OFF THE MASONIC RECORD BOOKS WITH AN EXTREMELY LARGE ERASER.

LESS THAN FIFTY YEARS PREVIOUS TO THIS UNTIMELY INSURRECTION HAVING REARED ITS UGLY HEAD, TROUBLE HAD MANAGED TO SPILL ITSELF OVER TO THE BOILING POINT WHEN IT WAS DISCOVERED AT A MASONIC MEETING BEING HELD AT YALE, B.C. ON SEPTEMBER 14TH, 1868 THAT VARIOUS MEMBERS OF THE ANCIENT CRAFT WERE ABOUT TO DO THE UNTHINKABLE BY DIPLOMATICALLY TRYING TO OVERTHROW THE GOVERNMENT OF THE DAY WITH THE BRUTE FORCE OF ARM TWISTING. BACKROOM DEALS WERE BEING MADE BY THOSE WHO WANTED THE PROVINCE TO ENTER INTO THE CANADIAN MASONIC UNION OF CONFEDERATION WHILE OTHER MEMBERS OF THE CRAFT HELD A WAIT-AND-SEE PHILOSOPHY TO THE MATTER AT HAND. THOSE MEMBERS WANTING TO TAKE A SLOW APPROACH APPARENTLY ALSO WANTED THE BEST DEAL HUMANELY POSSIBLE FOR THE PROVINCE AND ITS PEOPLE BUT ALSO WANTED TO ESTABLISH POLITICAL AUTONOMY FROM BOTH OTTAWA AND ENGLAND. KNOWN HISTORICALLY IN FREEMASONRY CIRCLES AS THE "YALE CONSPIRACY "SIMPLY BECAUSE OF THE FACT THAT THIS SEPTEMBER MEETING WAS A POLITICAL CONVENTION OF ALL BRITISH COLUMBIA FREEMASONS THAT WERE SCATTERED THROUGHOUT THE PROVINCE AS TWENTY-SIX DELEGATES GATHERED TOGETHER TO DISCUSS THE PROSPECTS OF CONFEDERATION.

All forms of Masonic interests were conducted and/or performed at this gathering of British Columbia Freemasons. Representatives from Victoria, Metchosin, Salt Spring Island, Esquimalt, New Westminister, Burrard Inlet, Harrison River, Yale, Lytton, Lac La Hache, Williams Lake, Quesnel and the entire interior of the Province were all present and accounted for. It was at this meeting of the fraternal mimes that a committee was formed to negotiate terms of making a Province within MacDonald's Freemasonry fold. Some very high profile members of the Ancient Craft were also appointed to the committee; the Honorable Amor de Cosmos of Victoria, the Honorable John Robson of New Westminister and the Honorable Hugh Nelson of Burrard Inlet. Convention members condemned the actions of their fellow Freemasonry Brethren opposing the Masonic union and further stressed the fact that as far as they were concerned, political independence from Great Britain was a no brainer situation because of how the Imperial Government in England viewed their newfound territory of British Columbia as merely the means to an end in the grand scheme of things. It was therefore concluded at this convention that Governor Seymour and his entire Executive Council were in reality pulling the puppetry strings of the Legislature of British Columbia and that new bold measures had to be taken in order to insure Freemasonry's success west of the Rocky Mountains. With that logic being the driving force, the committee to negotiate the Terms of Union was then implemented.

Just like the 43RD President of the United States' outright hatred for Saddam Hussein, over the course of time the **"Yale Conspiracy "**erupted into a battle of words as one group condemned the other for not divulging the true details which had transpired during the Yale Convention of 1868. Those opposing Confederation insisted that deceit and deception had taken place while the ruling Masonic governing body was trying to force others into accepting the concept that it was all God's will and not the ultimate creation of man himself. Before long, dissension amongst British Columbia Freemasons reached new heights as unwavering Master Masons from all walks of life exercised their discontentment for one another with fist fights breaking out into the streets while utter lawlessness quickly began to serge. Those possessing a more subdued /or passive approach to the crisis chose other means of expressing their opinions on the matter. For example, the Brethrenship in the Masonic Lodge located at Barkerville decided to hoist the Freemasonry Protestant

Canadian flag up the flag-pole that was situated on the roof top of their Lodge. This fraternity Canadian flag at that time period consisted of "a Union Jack in the fly and a beaver surrounded by a wreath of Maple Leafs, on a white background."

Although members of Freemasonry continually profess that their Ancient Craft is not a form of religion, the history of British Columbia's Masonic past seems to state otherwise. For example, the first recorded instance of laying a fraternal cornerstone took place in 1863 during the construction of our country's oldest Jewish synagogue in the City of Victoria on the Pacific. The placement of this cornerstone was duly noted in the Masonic record books as a glorious occasion for members of the Craft who were of the Hebrew race and that many of the new synagogue congregation in Victoria not only helped establish the Jewish faith but also had a hand in instituting various Masonic Lodges Province wide as well. Apparently, it was at the request of these members of Jewish Freemasonry that a Masonic ceremony be performed in connection with the laying of the synagogue cornerstone. At the time, there were only two Masonic Lodges in the City of Victoria; the Victoria Lodge which had received its Charter from the Grand Lodge of England and the Vancouver Lodge with a Charter from the Grand Lodge of Scotland. Accordingly, both of these Lodges were more than willing to perform the ceremony. The ceremony itself was then set for June 1ST, 1863 but later postponed to the following day due to an extremely heavy down pour of rain.

On June 2ND, 1863 the ceremony was underway as the day reportedly was warm and sunny. Three platforms had been built; one for Victoria's Freemasons, one for members of the Jewish congregation and the third for the ladies as gender segregation had been in full bloom during this time period of history. At precisely 2:00 P.M. things got underway as musicians played and prayers were being read out loud as part of the festive occasion. Sometime after 3 o'clock that afternoon, fraternity Brother Robert Burnaby of the Victoria Lodge laid the cornerstone into place and a few more pompous words were read thus immortalizing the synagogue into the Masonic history books. A couple of very high profile Freemasonry names were also duly noted as being in attendance; Israel Wood Powell – Provincial Grand Master of the Provincial Grand Lodge of Scotland, the Honorable Judge David Cameron – Masonic Bible Bearer for the ceremony and of course the Chaplin who conducted

THE ORATION – THE REVEREND RICHARD L. LOWE OF THE ANGLICAN CHURCH'S OUR LORD'S CHURCH IN VICTORIA ON THE PACIFIC.

ON THE FOLLOWING DAY, (JUNE 3RD, 1863), ARMOR DE COSMOS AND HIS MASONICALLY CONTROLLED NEWSPAPER, (THE BRITISH COLONIST), DEVOTED THE VAST MAJORITY OF ITS NEWS COVERAGE TO THE EVENT PROCEEDINGS OF LAYING THE CORNERSTONE AT THE SYNAGOGUE SAYING IN PART:

"THE ISRAELITES IN VICTORIA ARE A LARGE AND HIGHLY RESPECTED BODY. MANY OF THEM HAVE RESIDED IN THE CITY FROM THE DATE OF ITS EARLIEST EXISTENCE AND THEIR CONDUCT AND BEARING HAS INVARIABLY BEEN SUCH AS TO EARN THEM THE GOOD WISHES AND ESTEEM OF THEIR FELLOW CITIZENS OF OTHER PERSUASIONS."

FOR THE NEXT FORTY YEARS /OR SO, MEMBERS OF BRITISH COLUMBIA'S FREEMASONRY POPULATION LAID COUNTLESS CORNERSTONES ON VARIOUS RELIGIOUS INSTITUTIONS THROUGHOUT THE PROVINCE, INCLUDING THEIR OWN MASONIC TEMPLES AS WELL AS ON BENEVOLENT JUST CAUSES;

ST. ANDREW'S PRESBYTERIAN CHURCH IN VICTORIA – AUGUST 20TH, 1869

MORTUARY CHAPEL OF THE MASONIC CEMETERY AT SAPPERTON NEAR NEW WESTMINISTER – JULY 30TH, 1872

NANAIMO MASONIC TEMPLE – OCTOBER 15TH, 1873

PROTESTANT ORPHAN'S HOME IN THE CITY OF VICTORIA – JULY 28TH, 1883

EPISCOPAL CHURCH IN SURREY – AUGUST 4TH, 1884

NEW MASONIC TEMPLE IN THE CITY OF NEW WESTMINISTER – AUGUST 27TH, 1887

SAINT PAUL'S EPISCOPAL CHURCH IN KAMLOOPS – MAY 22ND, 1888

MASONIC TEMPLE IN KAMLOOPS – JULY 2ND, 1888

ST. LEONARD'S MASONIC HALL IN NEW WESTMINISTER – MARCH 18TH, 1890

YOUNG MEN'S CHRISTIAN ASSOCIATION BUILDING IN THE CITY OF VANCOUVER – JULY 24TH, 1890

ALEXANDRA HOSPITAL FOR WOMEN AND CHILDREN IN THE CITY OF VANCOUVER – APRIL 30TH, 1891

ST. ALBAN'S EPISCOPAL CHURCH IN NANAIMO – JUNE 22ND, 1891

St. Peter's Episcopal Church in Comox – July 23RD, 1891

First Presbyterian Church in the City of Vancouver – November 26TH, 1892

Protestant Orphan's Home in the City of Victoria – June 24TH, 1893

Saint Andrew's Presbyterian Church in the City of Nanaimo – July 18TH, 1893

Christ Church Episcopal in the City of Vancouver – July 28TH, 1894

Methodist Church in the Town of Wellington – December 14TH, 1895

St. Saviour's Episcopal Church in the Town of Nelson – August 12TH, 1898

Masonic Hall in the City of New Westminister – March 31ST, 1899

Despite the fact that it had long been a Masonic policy not to place cornerstones within the foundation works of schools and/or other public buildings, this policy seemed to have changed at the turn of the Twentieth Century when a request was made by Victoria's Freemasons to have Lodge members lay a cornerstone at the newly constructed Victoria High School on October 3RD, 1901. Less than six months later, (March 29TH, 1902), a Masonic cornerstone was laid to rest on the new Vancouver Public Library better known historically by present day Vancouverites as the Andrew Carnegie Building on the corner of Main and Hastings. Further to this having occurred, British Columbia Freemasons were invited to participate in the laying of a cornerstone at the new Masonic Temple that was being constructed in Tacoma, Washington on May 22ND, 1903 – Fraternity Brother Theodore Roosevelt (the President of the United States at the time) was reportedly the master of ceremonies.

Throughout British Columbia's Freemasonry past there has been numerous members of the clergy, (Protestant as well as Roman Catholic), who were reportedly active participants of the Masonic Order;

The Reverend Thomas Somerville – St. Andrew's Presbyterian Church in the City of Victoria, a devoted Freemason, he was said to have been the first Provincial Grand Chaplin for Victoria's Master

Masons. He was also the first Pastor of the newly constructed Church.

The Reverend F. B. Gribble – St. John's Anglican Church in Victoria, historically known as "The Iron Church "which stood on Douglas Street. Brother Gribble was the Chaplin for British Columbia Lodge No. 1187 in Victoria during the 1860's.

The Reverend Canon W. H. Cooper – the assistant Anglican Priest at Kamloops. Brother Cooper was a chartered member of Kamloops Lodge No. 10 as well as Mountain Lodge No. 11 which was located in a tiny railway "Tent Town "at the junction of Kicking Horse River and the Columbia River during the summer of 1884.

The Right Reverend Acton Windeyer Sillitoe – a.k.a. the Bishop of New Westminister. He assisted with the cornerstone placement at Christ Church in Surrey on August 24TH, 1884 as well as the placement of the Masonic cornerstone at Saint Paul's Episcopal Church in Kamloops on May 22ND, 1888. Brother Sillitoe was an active member of Union Lodge No. 9 in New Westminister.

The Reverend John A. Logan – Worshipful Master of Ionic Lodge No. 19 at Chilliwack in 1893.

The Reverend L. Norman Tucker – Rector of the Christ Church Episcopal in the City of Vancouver. His name is proudly displayed on a plaque commemorating the cornerstone placement of July 28TH, 1894.

The Reverend Cato Ensor Sharp – a Priest of the Holy Order in the Anglican Church. Brother Sharp also served as the Grand Master of the Grand Lodge of British Columbia June 19TH, 1903 to June 24TH, 1904.

The Reverend John A. Cleland – reportedly the first permanent minister at Saint Saviour's Anglican Church in Penticton. In 1908, he played a very important role in obtaining a Masonic Charter for Orion Lodge No. 51 in that community.

The Right Reverend W. W. Perrin – a.k.a. the Lord Bishop of the Diocese of Columbia. Brother Perrin presided over the Masonic service on May 20TH, 1910 mourning the death of King Edward VII which was held in the Masonic Temple at Victoria on the Pacific.

The Reverend Charles Collins Hoyle – Vicar at the All Saints Church at Ladner 1911 to 1914. Professor at St. Mary's Hall of the Anglican College 1912 to 1913. Brother Hoyle was the Chaplin at Union Lodge No. 9 in New Westminister and appointed Grand Historian for the Grand Lodge of British Columbia from 1912 to 1915.

The Reverend A. D. de Pencier – a.k.a. his Lordship the Bishop of New Westminister during the roaring 1920's.

The Reverend F. A. D. Chadwick – Rector of the Saint John's Church in Victoria during the infamous 1920's. In March of 1915 while acting as Grand Chaplin at the time, Brother Chadwick conducted the Masonic funeral services for fraternity Brother Israel Wood Powell who had been summoned by the Great Architect of the Universe on February 25TH of that year.

The Reverend James Sutherland Henderson – a Doctor of Divinity with the United Church of Canada cum Presbyterian persuasion. Grand Master of the Grand Lodge of British Columbia from June 18TH, 1937 to June 24TH, 1938. An active member of Union Lodge No. 9 in New Westminister and Acacia Lodge No. 22 in the City of Vancouver. Brother Henderson received the Good Citizen's Award (a bronze medallion) which was presented to him in 1939 by the Freemasonry population of Vancouver as part of the Fraternal Order of the Native Sons of British Columbia which had been established after the First World War.

The Reverend James George Brown – a Doctor of Divinity with the United Church of Canada and subsequent founder of Union College in the City of Vancouver. Brother Brown was the Grand Master of the Grand Lodge of British Columbia from June 18TH, 1943 to June 23RD, 1944.

The Right Reverend D. Swanson – on October 9TH, 1949 the unveiling of a plaque took place to commemorate the 50TH year anniversary of laying the cornerstone at Christ Church Cathedral in the City of Vancouver under the supervision and guidance of fraternity Brother Swanson and two Masonic Lodges, Western Gate Lodge No. 48 and Mount Lebanon Lodge No. 72. At the time, Brother Swanson was the Grand Chaplin for the Grand Lodge of British Columbia. He also held the portfolio of being a Doctor of Divinity for the **Masonic Brotherhood of Man** within the Provincial jurisdiction.

The Reverend Federic Pike – an active member of Victoria-Columbia Lodge No. 1 during the 1950's. Brother Pike conducted the services held at Christ Church Cathedral in Vancouver, (late 1950's), where in which his Lodge members were celebrating the first 100 years of full active service within the Province of British Columbia.

The Right Reverend Fred P. Clark – a.k.a. the Anglican Bishop of B.C.'s Kootenay country who as it so happened conducted the

Masonic oration in the placement of a cornerstone for the new Freemason's Hall that had transpired at Salmo in 1954. At the time, Brother Clark was also the Grand Chaplin for the Grand Lodge of British Columbia.

The Reverend Alex Calder – spent 62 years with the United Church of Canada, serving in various locations throughout the country received his 50-year pin from the Masonic Order in 1989 and further received full Masonic honors when he died on October 5TH, 1991. He was affiliated with Russell Lodge No. 62 in the Province of Manitoba and had his membership transferred to British Columbia's Haida Lodge No. 166 in Victoria on January 15TH, 1969.

The Reverend Donald John Gilles – Minister at the Vancouver Heights Presbyterian Church. He was also a member of Mount Shepherd Lodge No. 159, having affiliated from Zenith Lodge No. 104 in 1967. Brother Gilles was originally initiated into the Ancient Craft of Freemasonry at St. Mark's Lodge No. 35 within the jurisdiction of the Grand Lodge of Manitoba. On December 31ST, 1989, the Grand Lodge of British Columbia presented him with a 60-year pin of dedicated service to the Craft.

The Reverend H.R. Whitmore – Grand Chaplin of the Grand Lodge of British Columbia and an active member of Summerland Lodge No. 56 in Summerland, B.C. during the 1970's.

The Reverend W. E. Greenhalgh – Rector of the St. Matthias Church in the City of Victoria during the 1970's. On Sunday, May 16TH, 1971 Brother Greenhalgh conducted a special religious service for the Victoria brethrenship at St. Michael's and All Angels Church. The service was reportedly enjoyed by all.

The Right Reverend John S.P. Snowden – a.k.a. Bishop Snowden of the Anglican Church as well as the Freemasonry representative of Cariboo Lodge No. 4 and Kamloops Lodge No. 10 during the 1980's and 1990's.

The Reverend William B. Mundy – Grand Chaplin for the Grand Lodge of British Columbia in the late 1980's and early 1990's. Brother Mundy was also the Worshipful Master of Cayoosh Lodge No. 173 in the very early 1990's.

The Reverend Lloyd Northcott – minister of St. Peter's Anglican Church in Revelstoke. Brother Northcott was the worshipful Master of Kootenay Lodge No. 15 in 1991 as well as the Grand Chaplin for the Grand Lodge of British Columbia.

The Reverend Warren V. Marsh – Rector of the Anglican Church's St. John the Divine in the City of Quesnel reportedly

CONDUCTED THE RELIGIOUS SERVICES CELEBRATING THE 125TH ANNIVERSARY OF MASONIC MEETINGS BEING HELD IN THE WILLIAMS CREEK AREA OF THE CARIBOO DURING AUGUST 10-11, 1991 FESTIVITIES SPONSORED BY CARIBOO LODGE NO. 4 (BARKERVILLE, B.C.). THE RELIGIOUS SERVICES WERE HELD AT ST. SAVIOUR'S ANGLICAN CHURCH LOCATED IN THIS HISTORICAL WESTERN TOWN ON THE VERY LAST DAY OF THE FESTIVE OCCASION, (SUNDAY, AUGUST 11TH, 1991). A TOTAL OF MORE THAN 60 MASTER MASONS AND THEIR IMMEDIATE FAMILY MEMBERS PACKED THE SMALL CHURCH. REPRESENTATIVES FROM AT LEAST 38 BRITISH COLUMBIA MASONIC LODGES WERE PRESENT, INCLUDING SOME SISTER LODGES FROM WASHINGTON STATE WHO WERE REPRESENTED BY 14 WASHINGTON STATE LODGE MEMBERS FROM VARIOUS JURISDICTIONS.

CONTRARY TO THE MYTH THAT IS BEING PROJECTED BY THE VARIOUS RELIGIOUS FAITHS, THERE ARE LITERALLY THOUSANDS UPON THOUSANDS OF MEMBERS OF THEIR CLERGY WHO ARE ACTIVE MEMBERS OF THE ANCIENT CRAFT OF FREEMASONRY LIVING AMONGST US TO THIS VERY DAY WITHIN THE NORTH AMERICAN CONTINENT ITSELF. THE LIST IN FACT IS SO BLOODY LONG THAT IT WOULD EVEN MAKE AN ATHEIST SHED A TEAR FOR ALL MANKIND!!! DESPITE THIS GRAND ILLUSION, MASONIC HARMONY AT THE TURN OF THE TWENTIETH CENTURY WAS NO DIFFERENT THAN PAST LEVELS OF EXTREME UNHAPPINESS. IN 1907 FOR EXAMPLE, DISSENSION AMONGST BRITISH COLUMBIA FREEMASONS BEGAN TO INCREASE AS REPRESENTATIVES OF UNION LODGE NO. 9 IN NEW WESTMINISTER BEGAN ABUSING THEIR MASONIC POWERS BY DELIBERATELY ATTEMPTING TO ADMIT A PERSON INTO THE MEMBERSHIP THAT OTHERS FELT WAS AN APPLICATION THAT SHOULD HAVE NEVER BEEN PROCESSED IN THE FIRST PLACE. IT WAS BELIEVED BY MANY MASTER MASONS THAT A CONSPIRACY HAD EXISTED TO UNDERMINE THE AUTHORITY OF THE GRAND LODGE OF BRITISH COLUMBIA AS IT HAD BEEN FRATERNITY POLICY NOT TO RECOGNIZE BLACK FREEMASONRY'S RIGHT TO CO-EXIST AS AN OFFSHOOT ORGANISM OF THE WHITE ANGLO-SAXON BROTHERHOOD. AFTERALL, ONLY NINE YEARS PREVIOUS TO THIS MASONIC INSURRECTION THE GRAND LODGE OF WASHINGTON STATE HAD IMPLEMENTED A POLICY TO RECOGNIZE THAT STATE'S BLACK MEMBERS AS BEING THEIR SOCIAL EQUALS. AN INTERNAL INVESTIGATION WAS THUSLY ORDERED BY THE MASONIC GOVERNING BODY OF THE GRAND LODGE OF BRITISH COLUMBIA AND AT ITS COMPLETION, DECLARED THAT NO INITIAL CONSPIRACY HAD ACTUALLY TRANSPIRED BUT DID FIND THAT SOME MEMBERS OF THE PROVINCE'S OLDEST LODGE WITHIN THAT JURISDICTION HAD IN FACT STEPPED OVER THE LINE AND HAD TO BE PUNISHED FOR THEIR DEEDS OF UN-MASONIC CONDUCT. THE SPECIAL COMMITTEE APPOINTED TO INVESTIGATE THE ALLEGATIONS OF A CONSPIRACY RECOMMENDED THAT THE WORSHIPFUL MASTER OF UNION LODGE NO. 9 BE STRIPPED OF HIS FREEMASONRY DUTIES FOR A PERIOD OF SIX MONTHS AND HIS TWO CO-CONSPIRATORS BE SUSPENDED FOR

THREE MONTHS AS WELL. AFTER READING THE EVIDENCE THAT WAS PRESENTED TO THE GRAND LODGE OF BRITISH COLUMBIA OFFICIALS, THE CHAIRMAN OF THE INVESTIGATING COMMITTEE READ OUT HIS RECOMMENDATIONS, WHICH IN TURN WERE APPROVED BY THE GRAND LODGE MEMBERS. THE GRAND LODGE OF BRITISH COLUMBIA THEREFORE SEIZED THE JURISDICTIONAL POWERS OF UNION LODGE NO. 9 AND SUSPENDED ALL OF ITS MASONIC ACTIVITIES FOR THE RECOMMENDED SIX MONTH PERIOD.

TEN YEARS LATER, MORE DISSENSION ERUPTED AMONGST BRITISH COLUMBIA'S FREEMASONRY POPULATION. IT IN FACT HAD REACHED THE POINT WHERE A MASONIC LODGE LITERALLY HAD TO BE WRITTEN OFF THE RECORD BOOKS AND OUT OF EXISTENCE FOREVER MORE. APPARENTLY, ARROWSMITH LODGE NO. 62 AT ALBERNI HAD BEEN SQUABBLING WITH FELLOW MEMBERS OF THE ANCIENT CRAFT OF FREEMASONRY DURING THE ENTIRE TIME PERIOD OF THE FIRST WORLD WAR TO WHICH YET ANOTHER INTERNAL INVESTIGATION HAD TO BE CONDUCTED. ON FEBRUARY 25TH, 1918 IT WAS RECOMMENDED THAT THE GRAND MASTER OF THE GRAND LODGE OF BRITISH COLUMBIA (BROTHER DOUGLAS CORSAN, M.D. JUNE 22ND, 1917 TO JUNE 21ST, 1918), REVOKE THE LODGE'S CHARTER IF THE SCHISM ACTIVITY WAS UNABLE TO RESOLVE ITSELF. THE CHARTER WAS THEREFORE SUSPENDED PENDING FURTHER TALKS IN ATTEMPTS OF RESTORING PEACE AND TRANQUILITY TO THE **MASONIC BROTHERHOOD OF MAN**. AFTER TRYING TO ARRIVE AT A PEACEFUL COMPROMISE TO THE SITUATION FOR MONTHS ON END, A DECREE WAS ISSUED BY FRATERNITY BROTHER JOHN SHAW (GRAND MASTER OF ALL FREEMASONS JUNE 21ST, 1918 TO JUNE 20TH, 1919) ON JUNE 19TH, 1919 ORDERING THE BRETHREN OF THE ARROWSMITH LODGE TO CEASE ITS MASONIC ACTIVITIES FORTHWITH. THE LODGE NAME WAS THEN DELETED FROM THE ROSTER OF THE GRAND LODGE OF BRITISH COLUMBIA ON THE FOLLOWING DAY AND ITS MEMBERS WERE DULY NOTED AS BEING NON-RECOGNIZABLE MEMBERS OF THE CRAFT. IT WAS REPORTEDLY THE SECOND TIME IN THE RECORDED HISTORY OF BRITISH COLUMBIA'S FREEMASONRY PAST WHERE THE PROVINCE'S GRAND LODGE HAD BEEN FORCED TO ACT WITH EXTREME PREJUDICE IN ORDER TO SAVE FACE AND ERASE ALL TRACES OF A LODGE'S ACTUAL EXISTENCE.

COINCIDENTLY, DURING THE OUTBREAK OF THE FIRST WORLD WAR THE UNITED GRAND LODGE OF ENGLAND ISSUED A DECREE TO ALL OF ITS MASONIC LODGERY WORLDWIDE INFORMING THEM THAT ANY FREEMASON OF ENEMY ALIEN BIRTH WAS PROHIBITED FROM ATTENDING MEETINGS WITHIN ITS JURISDICTIONAL BOUNDARIES WHILE THE WAR WAS GOING ON. ONCE THIS BARRING BEGAN TAKING PLACE, HARSH CRITICISM WAS SOON BESTOWED ONTO THE FREEMASONRY LEADERS IN GREAT BRITAIN AS FURTHER FRIENDLY RELATIONS ALSO BEGAN TO BREAK-OFF IN THE NON-ENEMY COUNTRIES WITH A WAR OF CLANDESTINE WORDS AS AMERICAN FREEMASONS GOT IN ON THE ACT.

Reportedly, one Freemason of German birth living in the United States accused his fellow Master Masons of having absolutely no idea as to what World War I was actually all about and stated categorically that "some of us are not so sure but what the War in Europe is after all a struggle for commercial supremacy. "Even non-German Master Masons expressed their displeasure to the shocking revelation to the actions instituted by the United Grand Lodge of England. In 1916, allegations of un-Masonic conduct began to emerge on the North American Continent as Ohio Freemasons accused various Masonic leaders in both the United States and Great Britain of violating all of the fundamental principles of Masonic duty and **Masonic Brotherhood.**

Before long, Master Masons in Kentucky and Missouri also began expressing their utter discontentment saying that it was the first time in Freemasonry history that the right of **Masonic Brotherhood** had been disregarded by a Masonic governing body insisting that the decree itself was going to ultimately be repudiated by the United Grand Lodge of the United States as the vast majority of America's Freemasonry population were said to have viewed it as being a violation of their Anglo-Saxon Constitutional Rights. Dissension amongst white American Freemasons soon escalated out of control as further Master Masons in New Hampshire, North Carolina and Utah exercised the democratic right of expressing their opposition to the United Grand Lodge of England's decree while those living in Connecticut and California for example voiced their opinions in approval of the actions being implemented by Great Britain.

The growing controversy apparently even made its way North of the 49TH parallel into Canada during the early days of the First World War's breaking out. Contained within the text of the history of the Grand Lodge of British Columbia 1871-1970, it is interestingly stated that the Grand Lodge of Quebec virtually had no choice but to take swift affirmative action on the issue because of what had transpired against a member of the Craft who was a skilled mechanic of German birth holding down a position in a factory manufacturing munitions for the British Government. As the story goes, the Grand Lodge of Quebec was said to have had originally disagreed with the decree introduced by the Grand Lodge of England and thusly permitted the German Craftsman to attend the local meetings of his Masonic Lodge. A few weeks later, he was reportedly arrested in one of Canada's Maritime Provinces as the British authorities had suspected him of espionage activities.

After his capture and subsequent arrest, he was said to have had papers in his possession that were deemed to have been valuable pieces of information critical to the war effort. Unfortunately, the Masonic authors of the history book pertaining to British Columbia's Freemasonry past not only neglected to mention as to who this German born Freemason actually was but they also failed to include any further documentation stipulating as to what he was said to have had in his possession when he was arrested in 1914. The only other thing that they did mention on this subject was that immediately following the outbreak of the First World War, the Grand Lodge of Freemasons in Germany had issued edicts severing fraternal relations with all Grand Lodges in their enemy countries. Thus enabling the Ancient Craft of Freemasonry to hide behind its shroud of secrecy even further.

It should also be stated that the entire controversy itself, (dissension amongst North American Freemasons because of the decree by the United Grand Lodge of England), was forever silenced once the United States of the America's 28TH President Woodrow Wilson declared war on the German Government on April 6TH, 1917. Because of the U.S. involvement of World War I, American Freemasons quickly began applying their own kind of logic to the global crisis that was at hand by continually insisting that it was each and every Master Masons duty to protect the fundamental practices of democracy from those aggressors wishing to force their own self-righteous views onto others. In an address to the Grand Lodge of Alabama membership, the American Masonic leaders stressed the importance of taking part in the war effort in the most prolific way that it seemed as though the words had been repeated in fraternity Brother George Bush Junior's deeds of retaliation during the 21ST Century:

> "Our reasons for entering are the most logical and convincing that could be conceived. Our existence as a nation has been imperilled, our honor and our rights upon sea and land have been violated; and notwithstanding the voice of the pacifist, the socialist, and the pro-German, we have cast our lot with those whom we conceive are fighting for the upholding of the right. To those of our countrymen who are opposed to war on principle, or whose views give them the opinion that war could have been avoided, let me state that the time has passed for such arguments as they advance; the only aim now

CONSIDERED IS A SUCCESSFUL AND VICTORIOUS ENDING AT THE EARLIEST POSSIBLE MOMENT THAT OUR MEN, OUR GUNS, OUR EXPLOSIVES, AND ALL OTHER MEANS AT OUR COMMAND CAN ACCOMPLISH, AND THE MAN WHO OPPOSES THIS AIM, HAS NO RIGHT TO THE PROTECTION OF OUR FLAG OR OF OUR ORGANIZATION."

DESPITE THE FACT THAT THE AMERICAN FREEMASONRY POPULATION WAS STILL BITTERLY DIVIDED ON THEIR INVOLVEMENT DURING THE ENTIRE TIME PERIOD THAT THE FIRST WORLD WAR WAS TAKING PLACE, A FACADE OF BOTH FALSENESS AND A SENSE OF SECURITY WAS IMMEDIATELY IMPLANTED AS FRATERNAL RELATIONS WITH ENGLAND AND THE UNITED STATES HAD CONTINUED TO EXIST THROUGHOUT THE WAR YEARS. FREEMASONRY BRETHREN ON ACTIVE SERVICE WERE SAID TO HAVE HAD AN EXTREMELY DIFFICULT TIME UNDERSTANDING AS TO WHY THEY COULD NOT HAVE THE EXACT SAME RIGHTS AND PRIVILEGES IN FRANCE /OR OTHER COUNTRIES AS THEY ORIGINALLY HAD IN ENGLAND /OR THE UNITED STATES. AT THE TIME, SOME LODGES IN GREAT BRITAIN, CANADA AND THE UNITED STATES HAD SEVERED ALL MASONIC TIES WITH VARIOUS FREEMASONRY LODGES ABROAD AND HAD PROHIBITED ITS MEMBERS FROM VISITING ANY OF THE EXISTING LODGERY. UPON HEARING THE DISCONTENTMENT OF FREEMASONRY SERVICEMEN WHO WERE ON ACTIVE DUTY ABROAD, FELLOW MASTER MASONS WITHIN THE CONTINENTAL UNITED STATES CONTINUALLY EXPRESSED THEIR DISPLEASURE TO THE MASONIC LEADERS OF THE HOMELAND SECURITY DIVISION OF THE **BROTHERHOOD OF MAN**. BUT TO THE DISMAY OF THOSE VOICING THEIR GRIEVANCES, THE COMPLAINTS FELL ON DEAF EARS AS IT WAS BUSINESS AS USUAL UNTIL SOMETIME IN THE 1920'S WHEN FENCE MENDING SLOWLY BEGAN BETWEEN THE BRITISH AND AMERICAN FREEMASONS.

BY THE TIME THE SECOND WORLD WAR HAD COME INTO BEING AND THE JAPANESE BOMBED PEARL HARBOR, BOTH THE GRAND LODGE OF THE UNITED STATES AND THE UNITED GRAND LODGE OF ENGLAND HAD A NEW ENEMY AND COVERTLY BEGAN ISSUING A DECREE TO ALL OF ITS MASONIC LODGERY WORLDWIDE INFORMING THE FRATERNAL MEMBERSHIP THAT ANY FREEMASONS OF ENEMY ALIEN BIRTH WERE PROHIBITED FROM ATTENDING MEETINGS WITHIN ITS PERSPECTIVE JURISDICTIONAL BOUNDARIES. WITH THIS DECREE, JAPANESE INTERNMENT CAMPS WERE THAN SET-UP IN SPECIFIC LOCATIONS AS PEOPLE OF ALL JAPANESE ORIGIN INSTANTLY BECAME THIRD RATE CITIZENS EVEN IF THEY WERE BORN IN THIS DEMOCRATIC SOCIETY THAT WE, AS A SO-CALLED CIVILIZED PEOPLE CALL THE WESTERN FREE-WORLD.

BY THEIR VERY OWN ADMISSION, THE HISTORY OF THE GRAND LODGE OF BRITISH COLUMBIA'S FREEMASONRY PAST IS DESCRIBED AS BEING THE BRIDE WHO FAILED TO PERFORM HER WOMANLY DUTIES ON THE CEREMONIAL

WEDDING NIGHT, INTERESTINGLY DUBBED "THE BRIDE THAT FAILED". DESPITE THE FACT THAT THIS WAS USED MERELY AS AN ANALOGY, THE ENTIRE POPULATION OF THE PROVINCE OF BRITISH COLUMBIA WAS BEING SEVERELY SCREWED OVER BY MEMBERS OF THE MASONIC ORDER. THIS WAS ESPECIALLY TRUE WHEN IT CAME TO THE ROMAN CATHOLICS SINCE THEY THEMSELVES HAD NEGLECTED TO BOLT THE FRONT DOOR OF THE CHURCH WHICH HAD ENABLED THE PROTESTANT FREEMASONRY DEITY TO ENTER IN GLORIOUS TRIUMPH.

HISTORICALLY, FREEMASONRY AND THE ROMAN CATHOLIC CHURCH IN THE PROVINCE OF BRITISH COLUMBIA HAVE ALWAYS BEEN AT ODDS WITH ONE ANOTHER COMPETING FOR THE SOULS OF OTHERS. DURING THE LATE 1800's, A MEMBER OF MIRIAN LODGE NO. 20 IN THE OKANAGAN VALLEY, (VERNON, B.C.), WAS REFUSED THE LAST RITES OF HIS ROMAN CATHOLIC CHURCH SIMPLY BECAUSE OF THE FACT THAT HE WOULD NOT DENOUNCE FREEMASONRY. ON HIS DEATH BED, (JANUARY 22ND, 1895), FRATERNITY BROTHER LUCIEN GIROUARD WAS ASKED TO RELIEVE THE SATANIC FORCES OF THE ANCIENT CRAFT FROM HIS SOUL BUT VERY POLITELY TOLD THE ROMAN CATHOLIC PRIEST TO GO TO HELL. AS IT TURNS OUT, BROTHER GIROUARD BELONGED TO A VERY WELL KNOWN AND RESPECTED FRENCH ROMAN CATHOLIC FAMILY WHO'S MASONIC TIES WERE THAT OF THE KNIGHTS OF MALTA IN THE PROVINCE OF QUEBEC.

BRITISH COLUMBIA FREEMASONRY HAS ALWAYS HAD A STORMY RELATIONSHIP WITH THE ROMAN CATHOLIC CHURCH. GRANTED, THERE ARE A FEW REPORTED CASES WHERE THE CHURCH, AFTER ADDING MUCH RELIGIOUS PRESSURE, ROSE VICTORIOUS IN THE FIGHT FOR SUPREMACY. FOR INSTANCE, WHEN THE EIGHTH PREMIER OF THE PROVINCE TOOK OFFICE ON MAY 15TH, 1887, FRATERNITY BROTHER ALEXANDER EDMUND BATON DAVIE, BOTH HE AND HIS WIFE WERE REPORTEDLY MEMBERS OF THE ROMAN CATHOLIC CHURCH. ACCORDINGLY, THE MASONIC RECORDS INDICATE THAT ONLY FIVE YEARS PREVIOUS TO HIS TENURE AS PREMIER, BROTHER DAVIE'S NAME WAS OMITTED AS BEING A MEMBER OF THE ANCIENT CRAFT, (1882), THUS ENABLING HIM TO ACT AS A NON-PARTICIPATING MASTER MASON WHILE BEING A MEMBER OF THE CATHOLIC FAITH. THEN THERE'S THE CASE WHEN THE FIRST DEPUTY GRAND MASTER OF THE GRAND LODGE OF BRITISH COLUMBIA (BROTHER MR. JUSTICE JOHN FOSTER MCCREIGHT OF THE SUPREME COURT OF B.C.) WAS WITHIN EASY REACH OF THE GRAND MASTER'S THRONE IN 1873. HE WAS SAID TO HAVE DECLINED THE OFFER AS IT WOULD HAVE MEANT POLITICAL SUICIDE AND THE ULTIMATE DEMISE OF HIS PROFESSIONAL CAREER AS HE HAD ALSO BEEN A MEMBER OF THE ROMAN CATHOLIC FAITH. BECAUSE OF THE TREMENDOUS PRESSURE THAT WAS BEING DIVESTED UPON HIM, (BEING FORCED TO CHOSE ONE RELIGION OVER THE OTHER), THE MASONIC JUDGE IN WAITING IMMEDIATELY SEVERED ALL TIES WITH THE FRATERNITY AND BECAME A NON-PARTICIPATING MASTER MASON. TO THAT END, HISTORIANS (MASONIC

AND/OR OTHERWISE), ATTRIBUTED MCCREIGHT'S SUCCESS TO BEING APPOINTED TO THE JUDICIAL BENCH AND THE PREMIERSHIP OF THE PROVINCE AS HAVING ABSOLUTELY NOTHING TO DO WITH BACK ROOM WHEELING AND DEALING. THE WILL OF THE PEOPLE LIVING IN A FREE DEMOCRATIC SOCIETY IS THUSLY STATED AS BEING THE END RESULT OF HIS SUCCESS IN BOTH INSTANCES. FACT OF HISTORY FOLKS; FREEMASONRY BROTHER MCCREIGHT BECAME THE FIRST PREMIER OF THE PROVINCE OF BRITISH COLUMBIA ON NOVEMBER 13TH, 1871 AND ON DECEMBER 26TH OF THAT EXACT SAME YEAR, HE WAS ALSO INSTALLED AS THE FIRST DEPUTY GRAND MASTER OF THE NEW GRAND LODGE OF BRITISH COLUMBIA. BY 1880, HE WAS ANOINTED AS JUDGE FOR THE SUPREME COURT OF B.C.

AND WHEN BROTHER MCCREIGHT'S TERM AS BRITISH COLUMBIA'S FIRST PREMIER HAD EXPIRED ON DECEMBER 20TH, 1872, THE VERY COLORFUL FRATERNITY BROTHER AMOR DE COSMOS (FOUNDING EDITOR OF THE BRITISH COLONIST NEWSPAPER AND SECRETARY OF THE PROVINCE'S FIRST MASONIC LODGE) WAS ELEVATED TO THE PREMIERSHIP ON DECEMBER 23RD, 1872 HOLDING OFFICE UNTIL FEBRUARY 9TH, 1974. ONCE DE COSMOS' OFFICE HAD BEEN VACATED, YET ANOTHER MEMBER OF THE **MASONIC BROTHERHOOD OF MAN** CEASED THE REIGNS OF POWER ON FEBRUARY 11TH, 1874. BRITISH COLUMBIA'S THIRD PREMIER FREEMASONRY BROTHER GEORGE ANTONY WALKEM WAS NOT ONLY A STRONG SUPPORTER OF POLITICAL AUTONOMY FOR THE PROVINCE BUT ALSO AN ADVOCATE FOR ESTABLISHING THE GRAND LODGE OF BRITISH COLUMBIA WHICH IN ESSENCE MEANT HOME-RULE FOR MEMBERS OF THE MASONIC ORDER LIVING WITHIN ITS JURISDICTIONAL BOUNDARIES. IN ORDER TO ASSURE ECONOMICAL SUCCESS IN HIS CHOSEN FIELD OF EXPERTISE, (HE WAS A LAWYER BY PROFESSION), FRATERNITY BROTHER WALKEM JOINED KAMLOOPS LODGE NO. 10 ONCE IT RECEIVED A CHARTER FROM THE GRAND LODGE OF BRITISH COLUMBIA IN 1886. AMONG THE FIRST OFFICERS OF THIS LODGE WAS NONE OTHER THAN FRATERNITY BROTHER HARRY JOHN CAMBIE, FOR WHOM CAMBIE STREET IN THE CITY OF VANCOUVER IS NAMED. PRIOR TO HIS CHARTERED MEMBERSHIP WITH THE KAMLOOPS LODGE, BROTHER WALKEM'S ASSOCIATION TO THE PROVINCE'S FREEMASONRY POPULATION WAS SAID TO HAVE BEEN STRICTLY THROUGH HIS AFFILIATION WITH KING SOLOMON'S LODGE NO. 22 IN TORONTO, ONTARIO. WHILE STILL MAINTAINING THE THRONE OF THE PREMIERSHIP, BROTHER WALKEM REPORTEDLY SECURED A SEAT ON THE JUDICIAL BENCH FOR THE PORTFOLIO OF A SUPREME COURT JUDGE FOR THE PROVINCE OF BRITISH COLUMBIA AND THUSLY SUBMITTED HIS RESIGNATION AS PREMIER IN 1882 MAKING WAY FOR EVEN MORE MEMBERS OF THE ANCIENT CRAFT OF FREEMASONRY TO SEIZE THE REIGNS OF POWER. BROTHER WILLIAM SMITHE FOR EXAMPLE WAS THE SEVENTH PREMIER OF THE PROVINCE FROM JANUARY 29TH, 1883 TO MARCH 28TH, 1887 WHO BECAME

A NON-AFFILIATED FREEMASON OF BRITISH COLUMBIA LONG BEFORE HE SET FOOT INTO CANADA AS HE WAS ORIGINALLY FROM ENGLAND, (MATFEN, NORTHCUMBERLAND), AND HAD MIGRATED TO THE COWICHAN DISTRICT ON VANCOUVER ISLAND IN 1862. BY ALL ACCOUNT, BROTHER SMITHE WAS SAID TO HAVE BEEN A NON-PARTICIPATING MASTER MASON OUT OF SHEER NECESSITY IF NOTHING ELSE AS HIS FATHER AND HIS FATHER BEFORE HIM WERE ALSO MEMBERS OF THE ANCIENT CRAFT.

FURTHER TO THIS INTERESTING REVELATION, THE PROVINCE'S NINTH PREMIER FRATERNITY BROTHER JOHN ROBSON SEIZED THE REIGNS OF POWER AFTER THE UNTIMELY DEATH OF HIS FREEMASONRY COLLEAGUE BROTHER DAVIE WHO IRONICALLY DIED DUE TO ILLNESS ON AUGUST 1ST, 1889 WHILE STILL ACTING AS B.C.'S EIGHTH PREMIER. FRATERNITY BROTHER ROBSON WAS THE REPRESENTATIVE OF THE MASONIC ORDER'S NEW WESTMINISTER BRETHRENSHIP DURING THE YALE CONVENTION THAT WAS HELD ON SEPTEMBER 14TH, 1868. AND WHEN FRATERNITY BROTHER ROBSON SUDDENLY DIED AS A RESULT OF AN ACCIDENT, (CRUSHING THE TIP OF HIS LITTLE FINGER IN THE DOOR OF A HANSOM CAB ON JUNE 20TH, 1892 WHILE VISITING IN LONDON, ENGLAND AND DYING NINE DAYS LATER DUE TO BLOOD POISONING SETTING IN) WAS IMMEDIATELY REPLACED AS HIS THRONE IN VICTORIA WAS NOW SITTING EMPTY. HIS FIGUREHEAD REPLACEMENT WAS NONE OTHER THAN ONE OF FREEMASONRY BROTHER DAVIE'S VERY OWN RELATIVES, HIS YOUNGER BROTHER THEODORE DAVIE WHO INTERESTINGLY ENOUGH SERVED AS THE PROVINCE'S ATTORNEY-GENERAL IN FRATERNITY BROTHER ROBSON'S PROVINCIAL CABINET ONLY MONTHS PRIOR TO HIS ACCIDENTAL DEATH IN THE YEAR 1892. UPON HEARING THE NEWS OF ROBSON'S ILL HEALTH AND SUBSEQUENT DEATH, A NEW CHOSEN LEADER WAS ANOINTED AS THE CROWNING MASONIC AUTHORITY FOR THE PROVINCE OF BRITISH COLUMBIA. BOTH OF THE FRATERNITY DAVIE BROTHERS WERE DEVOTED ROMAN CATHOLICS ATTENDING ST. ANDREW'S CATHEDRAL IN THE CITY OF VICTORIA. AND JUST LIKE FREEMASONRY BROTHER WALKEM, THE TENTH PREMIER OF THE PROVINCE SECURED A SEAT ON THE JUDICIAL BENCH FOR THE PORTFOLIO OF A SUPREME COURT JUDGE FOR THE PROVINCE OF B.C. AND THEN SUBMITTED HIS RESIGNATION ON MARCH 2ND, 1895 TO FILL THE SHOES OF YET ANOTHER MEMBER OF THE MASONIC ORDER WHO HAD VACATED DUE TO MEETING THAT GREAT ARCHITECT OF THE UNIVERSE. EVEN BEFORE THE BODY HAD A CHANCE TO GET COLD, THE VULTURES WERE CIRCLING OVERHEAD TRYING TO REPLACE HIM. CHIEF JUSTICE MATTHEW BAILLIE BEGBIE DIED ON JUNE 11TH, 1894 IN VICTORIA AND WITHIN MERE HOURS, DAVIE WAS REPORTEDLY WOOING THE BRETHRENSHIP FOR A FAVOR. ON MARCH 11TH, 1895, AFTER DEFEATING HIS MAIN OPPONENT FRATERNITY BROTHER HENRY PERING PELLOW CREASE FOR THE PRESTIGIOUS APPOINTMENT, THE JUDICIAL CAREER OF MR. JUSTICE THEODORE DAVIE WAS LAUNCHED INTO FRATERNAL

ACTION AS HE SWORE ALLEGIANCE ON A MASONIC BIBLE. ONLY A WEEK PRIOR TO HIS TAKING THE OATH OF JUDICIAL OFFICE, (MARCH 4TH, 1895) AND ONLY TWO DAYS AFTER SUBMITTING HIS RESIGNATION AS PREMIER, DAVIE'S REPLACEMENT FRATERNITY BROTHER JOHN HERBERT TURNER BECAME THE ELEVENTH PREMIER OF THE PROVINCE. THIS FORM OF DEMOCRACY FOLLOWED THE EXACT SAME PATTERN FOR THE BULK OF BRITISH COLUMBIA'S POLITICAL LIFETIME SPANNING WELL INTO THE 21ST CENTURY WITH BACKROOM DEALS BEING MADE WITHIN THE VERY WALLS OF THE PROVINCIAL LEGISLATURE AS MEMBERS OF THE MASONIC ORDER RECEIVED PATRONAGE APPOINTMENTS TO VARIOUS GOVERNMENTAL PORTFOLIOS SUCH AS LIEUTENANT-GOVERNORS, CHIEF JUSTICES, PROSECUTORS, MAGISTRATES, COMMISSIONERS, ETC., ETC., ETC.

IN THE EARLY DAYS OF BRITISH COLUMBIA'S FREEMASONRY PAST, MEMBERS OF THE MASONIC ORDER CONTROLLED MOST, IF NOT ALL OF THE GOVERNMENTAL AFFAIRS AFTER THE PROVINCE ENTERED INTO SIR JOHN A. MACDONALD'S FAMILY FOLD. FOR INSTANCE, ONE OF THE FIRST CHARTERED MEMBERS OF KING SOLOMON LODGE NO. 17 LOCATED AT NEW WESTMINISTER (RECEIVING ITS FULL CHARTER OF RECOGNITION ON JUNE 23RD, 1892), WAS FRATERNITY BROTHER FREDERICK W. HOWAY WHO IN 1907 WENT ON TO BECOME A JUDGE FOR THE COUNTY OF NEW WESTMINISTER. IF WHAT HISTORIANS TELL US IS TRUE, FREEMASONRY BROTHER HOWAY ALSO WENT ON TO BECOME ONE OF THE PROVINCE'S MOST LEADING EXPERTS AND/OR AUTHORITY ON B.C. HISTORY, ESPECIALLY ON THE SUBJECT OF THE FUR TRADE INDUSTRY. ACCORDINGLY, BROTHER HOWAY WAS THE AUTHOR OF NUMEROUS LARGE NEWSWORTHY ARTICLES AS WELL AS SEVERAL PUBLISHED BOOKS. IN 1914, BROTHER HOWAY'S PUBLISHED VERSION OF HISTORY WAS RELEASED TO THE GENERAL PUBLIC IN A TWO VOLUME SET AS IT PERTAINED TO BRITISH COLUMBIA IN THE EARLY TIMES OF ITS DEVELOPMENT TO THE PRESENT, MEANING 1914 OF COURSE. IN HIS CREATIVE WRITING STYLE, HOWAY THE MASTER MASON NEGLECTED TO MENTION THE FACT THAT HE AND HIS COHORTS OF THE ANCIENT CRAFT OF FREEMASONRY WERE THE DRIVING FORCE BEHIND RULING THE ROOST WEST OF THE ROCKY MOUNTAINS. HIS PUBLISHED WORKS WERE THEN USED AS TOOLS OF LEARNING WITHIN THE EDUCATIONAL FACILITIES OF JUNIOR-SENIOR HIGH SCHOOLS AS WELL AS IN UNIVERSITIES AND COLLEGES. FURTHER TO THIS HAVING OCCURRED, BROTHER HOWAY REPORTEDLY MARRIED SARAH LOUISE LADNER, THE DAUGHTER OF WILLIAM H. LADNER FOR WHICH THE COMMUNITY OF LADNER WAS NAMED; BOTH WILLIAM AND HIS BROTHER THOMAS TO BE PRECISE.

GETTING BACK TO THE ESTABLISHING OF KING SOLOMON LODGE NO. 17 FOR A MOMENT / OR TWO, WHEN FRATERNITY BROTHER HOWAY AND HIS FELLOW MASTER MASONS PETITIONED THE GRAND LODGE OF BRITISH COLUMBIA FOR

A Charter on the symbolic day of July 1ST, 1891 a very interesting event later unfolded, (something that of which wouldn't be found anywhere in Brother Howay's version of B.C. history). After receiving the petition for a Charter, Freemasonry Brother A.W. Sillitoe of Union Lodge No. 4 was sent out to conduct personal interviews on the Brethrenship who had submitted the proposal for the establishing of a new Masonic Lodge. Brother Bishop Sillitoe in turn submitted a favorable report and the Charter was approved by the Grand Lodge of British Columbia on June 23RD, 1892 and on August 9TH of that same year, King Solomon Lodge No. 9 came into being.

Like Brother Howay, other high profile members of the Masonic Order quickly rose up through the fraternity ranks after they took part in establishing new Freemasonry Lodges within the Province. For example, Alta Lodge Lodge No. 29 was constituted during the late 1890's at Sandon in the Slocan Valley. Upon receiving its Charter on June 24TH, 1899 fraternity Brother William-Henry Lilley was listed as being the Lodge's Secretary. Brother Lilley was thusly anointed a magistrate of the courts. And when members of North Star Lodge No. 30 asked for the establishing of the Masonic Lodge in 1899 at Fort Steele located on the Kootenay River in the East Kootenay at its junction with a tributary known as Wild Horse Creek, (a small stream flowing through a narrow gulch), fraternity Brother Israel Powell, the first Grand Master of the Grand Lodge of British Columbia, was the Superintendent of Indian Affairs for the Province. Brother Powell, wanting to subdue an Indian uprising only years earlier notified the Northwest Mounted Police that they were going to be establishing a barracks for its semi-military officers and men, who were to be under the direct command of Freemasonry Brother Colonel S.B. Steele. Upon receiving its Charter on June 24TH, 1899 some rather interesting names are listed as being chartered members; a couple of future Cabinet Ministers in the Federal and Provincial Governments as well as Civil Servants, a Judge and even a famous poet.

Among the membership roster of North Star Lodge No. 30 in its infancy years, the name of a young lawyer appears, Brother William Roderick Ross who later on became the Minister of Lands and Forests in the Provincial Masonic Governments of McBride and Bowser. Freemasonry records indicate that Brother Ross practiced his skills as a lawyer not only with other members of the Ancient Craft who were stationed at Fort Steele but also with those who

WERE SCATTERED THROUGHOUT THE TOWNS AND SETTLEMENTS OF THE SURROUNDING DISTRICT AS WELL. WHILE BROTHER ROSS WAS EXERCISING HIS CRAFTSMANSHIP WITH THE FELLOW BRETHREN, BROTHER CHARLES MAIR, THE POET WENT ON TO BECOME ONE OF THE FOUNDING FOREFATHERS OF THE COMMUNITY OF KELOWNA IN THE CENTRAL OKANAGAN VALLEY. INTERESTINGLY, BROTHER MAIR'S MOST IMPORTANT CONTRIBUTION TO BRITISH COLUMBIA'S FREEMASONRY PAST CAME IN THE FORM OF HIS WRITING ABILITY SURROUNDING THE RED RIVER SETTLEMENT OF 1869-70 DURING THE FIRST INSURRECTION OF LOUIS RIEL AND THE METIS OF THE WESTERN PLAINS. AT THE TIME OF THE INSURRECTION, BROTHER MAIR WAS WRITING FOR TWO OF THE COUNTRY'S MAJOR NEWSPAPER OUTLETS — THE TORONTO GLOBE AND MAIL, AND THE MONTREAL GAZETTE WHICH IN TURN ENABLED HIM TO SPREAD HIS ANTI-NATIVE RHETORIC THROUGHOUT BOTH ENGLISH AND FRENCH CANADA. ORIGINALLY AFFILIATED WITH THE GRAND LODGE OF CANADA (IN ONTARIO), FRATERNITY BROTHER MAIR PLAYED AN IMPORTANT ROLE IN THE FORMATION OF A POLITICAL NATIONALIST GROUP CALLED **"CANADA FIRST "**AS THEY PROMOTED SIR JOHN A.'S CONCEPT OF A UNITED CONFEDERATION IN 1867. BY THE TIME LOUIS RIEL AND HIS RENEGADE HALF-BREED INDIANS BEGAN QUESTIONING THE SUPREMACY OF THE MASONIC ORDER TWO YEARS LATER, BROTHER MAIR ALONG WITH BROTHERS JOHN CHRISTIAN SCHULTZ AND THOMAS SCOTT WERE CAPTURED AND SUBSEQUENTLY IMPRISONED BY REBELS. THE ORANGEMEN, BROTHERS MAIR AND SCHULTZ EVENTUALLY ESCAPED AND RETURNED BACK TO ONTARIO AND THE REST IS AS THEY SAY, HISTORY AS THE EMOTIONS OF EVERY MAN, WOMAN AND CHILD RIGHT ACROSS THE NATION BECAME SO ENRAGED THAT THE QUEST FOR THE TRUTH GOT HIDDEN IN THE PAGES OF TIME.

AND WHEN THE METIS OF THE WEST ROSE UP AGAINST THE MASONIC ORDER FOR A SECOND TIME, (THE NORTHWEST REBELLION OF 1885), FRATERNITY BROTHER MAIR SERVED AS AN OFFICER IN THE GOVERNOR GENERAL OF CANADA'S BODY GUARDS, FREEMASONRY BROTHER LORD LANSDOWNE WHO WAS ALSO KNOWN AS THE MARQUESS OF LANSDOWNE BEFORE BECOMING THE GOVERNOR GENERAL OF CANADA IN 1883. DURING THE TIME OF HIS ACTIVE SERVICE IN THE FREEMASONRY BODY GUARDS REGIMENT, BROTHER MAIR TOOK HIS MARCHING ORDERS FROM YET ANOTHER MEMBER OF THE ANCIENT CRAFT, FRATERNITY BROTHER LORD MELGUND A.K.A. GILBERT JOHN MURRAY KYNYNMOND ELLIOT, THE FOURTH EARL OF MINTO WHO LATER ON BECAME KNOWN AS CANADA'S GOVERNOR-GENERAL IN NOVEMBER OF 1898. FOR HIS DEED OF DISCREDITING THE METIS PEOPLES' CLAIM OF HAVING LAND RIGHTS WITHIN THE DOMINION OF CANADA DURING THE FIRST INSURRECTION AS WELL AS HIS TAKING UP OF ARMS AGAINST THEM IN 1885, FREEMASONRY BROTHER CHARLES MAIR BECAME A CIVIL SERVANT FOR THE

Masonically controlled Government of British Columbia. In 1868, Brother Mair reportedly married Elizabeth Louise Mackenney, the niece of fraternity Brother Schultz and twenty-two years after that, (1889), became an honorary member of the F.R.S.C., (Fellow of the Royal Society of Canada). The Canadian history books therefore glorify Charles Mair as being a renowned poet and/or journalist but failed to mention anything of his being an active member of the very bigoted Freemasonry Orangism klan.

While fraternity Brother Mair was busy re-writing the pages of history with Freemasonry Brother Howay, the Grand Lodge of British Columbia issued a special decree in 1895 permitting Brother Robert F. Green to be anointed as the second Worshipful Master of Kaslo Lodge No. 25 located at Kaslo, in the Province of British Columbia. Brother Green later on became the Minister of Mines in the Provincial Masonic Government of McBride at the turn of the Twentieth Century and then elevated to the portfolio of the Canadian Senate in Ottawa. It should also be stated that between the years 1902-1910, members of the Masonic Order literally controlled the entire Provincial Legislature holding most, if not all of the important political portfolios. For example, during his tenure years as British Columbia's sixteenth Premier, Masonic Brother Richard McBride totally surrounded himself with fellow Brethren of the Craft as his Cabinet Members were reportedly all Freemasons;

Attorney-General – Brother Charles Wilson of Cascade Lodge No. 12 (Vancouver)

Minister of Mines – Brother Robert F. Green of Kaslo Lodge No. 25 (Kaslo)

Provincial Secretary – Brother Arthur S. Goodeve of Corinthian Lodge No. 27 (Rossland)

Minister of Education – Brother Henry Esson Young of Atlinto Lodge No. 42 (Atlin)

Attorney-General – Brother William J. Bowser of Mount Hermon Lodge No. 7 (Vancouver) Bowser also served as Grand Master of the Grand Lodge of British Columbia from June 24TH, 1904 to June 23RD, 1905

Minister of Lands – Brother William Roderick Ross of North Star Lodge No. 30 (Fort Steele)

Minister of Public Works – Brother Thomas Taylor of Kaslo Lodge No. 25 (Kaslo)

Some of the other members of the Ancient Craft of Freemasonry who were duly elected public officials (MLA's) were as follows;

Brother Henry Federick William Behnsen of Vancouver-Quadra Lodge No. 2 (Victoria)

Brother Charles Edward Tisdall of Cascade Lodge No. 12 (Vancouver) Tisdall would later become Mayor of the City of Vancouver in the 1920's and also the Grand Master of the Grand Lodge of British Columbia from June 22ND, 1923 to June 20TH, 1924

Brother Lytton Wilmot Shatford of Hedley Lodge No. 34 (Hedley)

Brother William Henry Hayward of Temple Lodge No. 33 (Duncan)

Brother James Hargrave Schofield, founder of Fidelity Lodge No. 32 (Trail) Schofield also served as Grand Master of the Grand Lodge of British Columbia from June 22ND, 1906 to June 21ST, 1907

Brother James Pearson Shaw of Kamloops Lodge No. 10 (Kamloops)

Brother Harry Holgate Watson of Cascade Lodge No. 12 (Vancouver) Watson also served as Grand Master of the Grand Lodge of British Columbia from June of 1900 to June of 1901.

The fraternal list of Provincially elected Masonic Brethren goes on and on and on for the next one-hundred years /or so, spanning well into the 21ST Century. Not at all to shabby for an International Institution that is continually insisting that they and their group of Ancient Craft Freemasonry Brethrenship have no interest whatsoever in the political affairs of a Province, State and/or Country. Can you say **"YALE CONSPIRACY "**with an extremely straight face without bursting into sheer laughter as nothing has really changed since then — it's still the same old, same old — political back room wheeling and dealing all in the name of the illusional process known as democracy.

Although the published authorized version of the history of the Grand Lodge of British Columbia down played the possibility of an everlasting conspiracy throughout the entire duration of the Twentieth Century, the facts speak for themselves. Especially considering that according to their own published paraphernalia, Masonic Bulletins and other pieces of documentation that verify the fact that other B.C. Premiers such as James Dunsmuir (the fourteenth Premier), John Oliver (the nineteenth Premier) and Thomas Dufferin Pattullo (the twenty-second Premier) were said to have all been non-participating Master Masons prior to the inauguration of WAC Bennett as the twenty-fifth Freemasonry Premier of the Province of British Columbia on August 1ST, 1952. And

WHEN WAC RETIRED FROM ACTIVE PROVINCIAL POLITICS IN 1974 AS LEADER OF THE SOCIAL CREDIT PARTY OF B.C., AFTER ENABLING THE FRATERNITY BANNER TO BE HOISTED UP THE OLD FLAG-POLE UNDER THE SOCIAL-DEMOCRATS OF THE DAVE BARRETT REGIME OF COURSE, THE FREEMASONRY BENNETT LEGACY LIVED ON AS A LEWIS MASTER MASON SEIZED THE REIGNS OF POWER, (MEANING BILL BENNETT), WHO IN TURN PASSED THE LEGACY TORCH ONTO A NON-PARTICIPATING MASTER MASON BILL VAN DER ZALM. PREMIER VAN DER ZALM AND THE SOCIAL CREDIT PARTY OF BRITISH COLUMBIA THEN HANDED THE REIGNS OF POWER OVER TO THE SON OF FRATERNITY BROTHER FRANK HARCOURT OF COMMONWEALTH LODGE NO. 156, WHO IN TURN PASSED IT ONTO ... YOU GET THE PICTURE!!!

LIKE AN EXTREMELY BAD CHAIN LETTER BEING HANDED DOWN THROUGH VARIOUS GENERATIONS, THE DEMOCRATIC PROCEDURE WAS DOOMED TO FAILURE AS IT LITERALLY BECAME A STACKED DECK IN FAVOR OF THE MASONIC ORDER'S MANDATED DEADLINE FOR THE YEAR 2000. FRATERNITY BROTHER H.A.D. OLIVER, THE THEN-NDP'S CONFLICT-OF-INTEREST COMMISSIONER AIDED AND ABIDED IN PAVING THE WAY FOR THE POLITICALLY ELECTED BRETHRENSHIP AS MORE AND MORE OF THEM BECAME ACTIVELY INVOLVED WITH CRIMINAL ACTIVITIES (INFLUENCE PEDDLING, BREACH OF TRUST, RECEIVING A BENEFIT, ETC., ETC., ETC.), WHICH IN TURN HAD THREATENED TO BRING DOWN THE HOUSE THAT KING SOLOMON HAD BUILT OVER THE THOUSANDS OF YEARS SINCE ITS FIRST CONCEPTION. FEARING THAT THEIR HOUSE OF CARDS WAS GOING TO BE CRUMBLING BEFORE THEIR VERY EYES, THE MASONICALLY CONTROLLED GOVERNMENT OF BRITISH COLUMBIA HAD NO CHOICE BUT TO IMPLEMENT SOME FORM OF PROTECTIONISM IN ORDER TO KEEP ITS DULY ELECTED PUBLIC OFFICIALS WHO HAD MANAGED TO TURN INTO CORRUPT DESPERADOES FROM SEEING THE INSIDE OF A PRISON CELL.

ONLY THREE YEARS PRIOR TO WAC'S RETIRING FROM THE POLITICAL SCENE, A CELEBRATION TO NEARLY A FULL CENTURY OF MASONIC CONTROL OF THE POLITICAL AFFAIRS WITHIN THE PROVINCE OF BRITISH COLUMBIA TOOK PLACE AS A BRONZE MEDAL COMMEMORATING THIS GLORIOUS OCCASION WAS FORGED IN 1971 AND DULY ISSUED TO OUTSTANDING MEMBERS OF THE CRAFT. THE CENTENNIAL MEDALLION WHICH DEPICTED IN RELIEF THE BUSTS OF TWO PROMINENT MEMBERS OF THE ANCIENT CRAFT OF FREEMASONRY – THE FIRST PREMIER OF THE PROVINCE FRATERNITY BROTHER MCCREIGHT AND THE RULING MASONIC GOVERNING BODY OF THE DAY, FRATERNITY BROTHER WAC BENNETT. REPORTEDLY, BOTH OF THESE MEMBERS OF THE MASONIC ORDER PLAYED VERY IMPORTANT KEY POLITICAL ROLES FOR THE GRAND LODGE OF BRITISH COLUMBIA. LIKE BROTHER MCCREIGHT, FREEMASONRY LEADER BENNETT ROSE UP THROUGH THE FRATERNITY RANKS SERVING AS THE

Worshipful Master of his perspective Lodge (St. George's Lodge No. 41 in Kelowna) near the close of the Second World War 1944-45.

The medallion itself was supposedly conceived by the Vancouver Numismatic Society to help commemorate the centennial of the entry of the United Colony of British Columbia into the Canadian Confederation which had taken place on July 20TH, 1871. Wanting to partake in the celebration a 100 years later, the Numismatic Society decided that it was fitting to produce a commemorative medal depicting on its obverse side the two Premiers of the Province. The **Centennial Medal** which was two inches in diameter and forged in silver and in bronze from designs done in relief, prepared by the Society was said to have been entirely minted in the Province. One of the medallions, was struck in gold and presented to the then-Premier in 1971. It is interesting to note that the Vancouver Numismatic Society was no stranger to Province's Freemasonry past and therefore used the centennial celebration of British Columbia's entrance into the Masonic family fold as an excuse to boost its own agenda by promoting the medallion. By 1974, WAC retired from active British Columbia politics in order to make way for other members of the Masonic Order to control the Freemasonry destiny of the Province.

According to further Freemasonry documentation, the Grand Lodge of British Columbia's own fraternity paper trail (Masonic Bulletins) contained some rather unique pieces of information that would have made even Senator Joe McCarthy and his witch hunt on Communism do a complete about face on its blacklisting writers, actors, producers and directors of the motion picture industry. During the month of April 1990 for example, British Columbia Freemasons living in and around the Greater Vancouver Regional District, (including Vancouver Island and Victoria on the Pacific), attended a fraternal dinner meeting held at Vancouver Lodge of Instruction, Education and Research which had a highly respected Masonic writer as its main guest speaker; Allen Earl Roberts. Fraternity Brother Allen Roberts as it so happened was famous for his long list of accomplishments, which included a host of book publications on the Ancient Craft of Freemasonry (over 20 of them) as well as more than 15 motion pictures on Masonic subjects. Some of the books included;

TITLE OF BOOK	**YEAR PUBLISHED**

TITLE OF BOOK	YEAR PUBLISHED
HOUSE UNDIVIDED: THE STORY OF FREEMASONRY AND THE CIVIL WAR	1961
FREEMASONRY IN HIGHLAND, VIRGINIA	1962
A DAUGHTER OF THE GRAND LODGE OF VIRGINIA	1963
SWORD AND TROWEL: THE STORY OF MILITARY LODGES	1964
MASONRY UNDER TWO FLAGS	1968
KEY TO FREEMASONRY'S GROWTH	1969
FIFTY GOLDEN YEARS: THE HISTORY OF WARWICK LODGE	1972
THE CRAFT AND ITS SYMBOLS	1974
GEORGE WASHINGTON: MASTER MASON	1976
BROTHERHOOD IN ACTION! THE STORY OF THE VIRGINIA CRAFTSMEN	1977
A CHRONICLE OF VIRGINIA RESEARCH LODGE	1978
FRONTIER CORNERSTONE: THE HISTORY OF THE GRAND LODGE OF OHIO	1980
WHO IS WHO IN FREEMASONRY 1984	1984
FREEMASONRY IN AMERICAN HISTORY	1985
BROTHER TRUMAN: THE MASONIC LIFE AND PHILOSOPHY OF HARRY S. TRUMAN	1985
WHO IS WHO IN FREEMASONRY 1986	1986
THE DIAMOND YEARS: SEVENTY-FIVE YEAR HISTORY OF BABCOCK LODGE	1987
THE SEARCH FOR LEADERSHIP	1987
SEEKERS OF TRUTH: THE STORY OF THE PHILALETHES SOCIETY 1928 - 1988	1988
THE MYSTIC TIE	1991
MASONIC LIFELINE: LEADERSHIP	1992
MASONIC TRIVIA AND FACTS	1994
WHO IS WHO IN FREEMASONRY 1996	1996

COINCIDENTLY, IN THE FORWARD WRITTEN FOR HIS BOOK "FREEMASONRY IN AMERICAN HISTORY", IT DESCRIBES THE AUTHOR AS BEING THE MOST

KNOWLEDGEABLE MASONIC EDUCATOR LIVING IN THE WESTERN FREE-WORLD. THE BOOK ITSELF IS A COMPLETE HISTORY OF THE UNITED STATES AND THE ROLE VARIOUS MEMBERS OF THE ANCIENT CRAFT PLAYED IN ITS DEVELOPMENT OVER THE SPAN OF ITS EXISTENCE.

IN 1969, FREEMASONRY BROTHER ROBERTS FOUNDED A COMPANY, (IMAGINATION UNLIMITED), TO HELP SERVE AS A VEHICLE TO PROMOTE MASONIC TEACHINGS AND PHILOSOPHIES ON THE SILVER SCREEN FOR THE SOLE PURPOSE OF EDUCATING THE UNINFORMED POPULATION. THE FIRST OF THESE PROPAGANDA FILMS, (WRITTEN, PRODUCED AND DIRECTED BY BROTHER ROBERTS HIMSELF), COMPRISED OF MOTION PICTURES IN WHICH HE DUBBED; THE MASONIC LEADERSHIP SERIES: GROWING THE LEADER (1970), BREAKING BARRIERS TO COMMUNICATION (1971), PLANNING UNLOCKS THE DOOR (1972), AND PEOPLE MAKE THE DIFFERENCE (1973). THE PRODUCTION OF THESE NAZI LIKE PROPAGANDA FILMS WERE ALL BASED UPON HIS BOOK, "KEY TO FREEMASONRY'S GROWTH "AND WERE ALL MADE AVAILABLE FOR PUBLIC VIEWING ON A SINGLE VIDEO TAPE IN 1989. LIKE HITLER'S NAZI PARTY PROPAGANDA MINISTER JOSEPH GOEBBELS, (1928-45), ROBERTS MADE CYNICAL USE OF PSYCHOLOGICAL METHODS TO SWAY THE MASSES. AS FRATERNITY BROTHER ALLEN ROBERTS' NOTORIETY BECAME A HOUSEHOLD WORD WITHIN THE MASONIC ORDER ITSELF, HE REPORTEDLY PRODUCED SEVERAL FILMS FOR VARIOUS GRAND LODGES THROUGHOUT THE CONTINENTAL UNITED STATES. JUST TO NAME A FEW OF THEM; CHALLENGE! (1977) FOR THE GRAND LODGE OF VIRGINIA, PRECIOUS HERITAGE (1977) FOR THE GRAND LODGE OF OHIO, LIVING STONES (1984) FOR THE GRAND LODGE OF GEORGIA. WITH THE PROPAGANDA MACHINES CONTINUALLY WORKING OVERTIME, A HOST OF OTHER MOTION PICTURES WERE MADE TO HELP PROMOTE JUSTIFICATION OF THEIR JUST CAUSE TOWARDS THE AMERICAN BELIEF OF HAVING GOD'S DIVINE POWERS OF ESTABLISHING A **"NEW WORLD ORDER "**ON A GLOBAL SCALE. SOME OF THESE WORKS OF DIVINE INTERVENTION INCLUDED; THE SAGA OF THE HOLY ROYAL ARCH OF FREEMASONRY (1973), THE BROTHERHOOD OF MAN (1975), LONELY WORLD (1979), FRATERNALLY YOURS (1979), AND OF COURSE VIRTUE WILL TRIUMPH (1982).

DURING THE RONALD REAGAN YEARS AS PRESIDENT OF THE UNITED STATES, FRATERNITY BROTHER ROBERTS AND OTHERS FORMED ANCHOR COMMUNICATIONS IN ORDER TO ASSIST MEMBERS OF THE MASONIC ORDER TO HAVE THEIR BOOKS PUBLISHED ON FREEMASONRY. ANCHOR COMMUNICATIONS WAS IN FACT SO SUCCESSFUL THAT BEFORE LONG IT BECAME A SUBSIDIARY OF IMAGINATION UNLIMITED AND CONTINUED WITH ITS PROPAGANDA PROGRAM TO EDUCATED THE UNINFORMED IN ALL FORMS OF THE SPECTRUM.

FREEMASONRY BROTHER ROBERTS IS ALSO KNOWN FOR A COUPLE OF OTHER RATHER INTERESTING JUST CAUSES. ON JANUARY 1ST, 1972 HE WAS THE

DRIVING FORCE BEHIND THE FORMATION OF THE MASONIC BROTHERHOOD OF THE BLUE FORGET-ME-NOT. AND IN FEBRUARY OF 1989, HE WAS SAID TO HAVE GIVEN A SPEECH AT THE CONFERENCE OF GRAND MASTERS THAT WAS BEING HELD IN ALEXANDRIA, VIRGINIA WHICH HE ARGUED BITTERLY THE LEGITIMACY OF PRINCE HALL FREEMASONRY TO HIS FELLOW BRETHREN. AS A SOMEWHAT DIRECT RESULT OF HIS RHETORIC USED, THE GRAND LODGE OF CONNECTICUT REPORTEDLY BEGAN TO INVESTIGATE THE POSSIBILITY OF RECOGNIZING BLACK FREEMASONRY MEMBERS OF THE PRINCE HALL GRAND LODGE OF CONNECTICUT AS THEIR CO-EQUALS ON OCTOBER 14TH, 1989. BUT BROTHER ROBERTS WOULD NEVER SEE HIS VISION OF SOCIAL EQUALITY BEING IMPLEMENTED ON A NATIONAL SCALE FOR BLACK MEMBERS OF THE ANCIENT CRAFT. AFTER SUFFERING FROM A BRIEF ILLNESS, HE DIED IN THE HOSPITAL AT RICHMOND, VIRGINIA ON MARCH 13TH, 1997, (HE WAS 80-YEARS-OLD). A DEVOTED MEMBER OF FREEMASONRY SINCE THE END OF THE SECOND WORLD WAR, HE CONTINUALLY ROSE UP THROUGH THE FRATERNITY RANKS LITERALLY WRITING HUNDREDS OF NEWS WORTHY ARTICLES PROMOTING THE MASONIC ROLE IN AMERICAN SOCIETY. ON APRIL 1ST, 1948 ROBERTS BECAME A FULLY FLEDGED MASTER MASON AT BABCOCK LODGE NO. 322 IN HIGHLAND SPRINGS, VIRGINIA, AND SERVING AS ITS WORSHIPFUL MASTER IN 1955. AS TIME PROGRESSED, BROTHER ROBERTS JOINED AN ASSORTMENT OF MASONIC GOVERNING BODIES. HE WAS WORSHIPFUL MASTER OF THE VIRGINIA RESEARCH LODGE NO. 1777 BETWEEN THE YEARS 1965-67 AND LATER SERVED AS ITS SECRETARY FROM 1973 TO 1996. ROBERTS WAS REPORTEDLY ALSO THE SOVEREIGN GRAND MASTER OF THE ALLIED MASONIC DEGREE TEAMS IN 1990 WHEN HE ATTENDED THE GRAND FESTIVE ACTIVITIES IN BRITISH COLUMBIA. BEING AN AVID HISTORY BUFF, HE WAS FURTHER INSTRUMENTAL IN FORMING THE VIRGINIA CRAFTSMEN IN 1962, A FRATERNITY DEGREE TEAM THAT WORE CONFEDERATE UNIFORMS SYMBOLIZING THOSE MEMBERS OF THE ANCIENT CRAFT WHO AT THE TIME OF THE CIVIL WAR WERE NOT AT ALL IMPRESSED WITH THE ANTICS OF THEIR AMERICAN PROTECTOR OF FREEMASONRY; U.S. PRESIDENT ABE LINCOLN.

FOR A PERIOD OF 32 YEARS, ROBERTS TRAVELED EXTENSIVELY THROUGHOUT THE CONTINENTAL UNITED STATES, CANADA AND GREAT BRITAIN PROMOTING THE FUNDAMENTAL TEACHINGS AND PRACTICES OF FREEMASONRY. THIS ENSUED LARGELY DUE TO THE FACT THAT HE WAS IN CONSTANT DEMAND AS A GUEST SPEAKER AT VARIOUS MASONIC GATHERING HERE IN NORTH AMERICA AS WELL AS ABROAD. HIS ENDEAVORS ON THE LECTURE CIRCUIT WERE SO SUCCESSFUL THAT SOME MEMBERS OF THE ANCIENT CRAFT INSTANTLY LABELED HIM AS BEING THE MOST PROLIFIC AUTHOR AND HISTORIAN OF MASONIC EVENTS KNOWN TO ALL MANKIND. IN 1988, ROBERTS WAS AWARDED WITH THE GEORGE WASHINGTON DISTINGUISHED SERVICE METAL OF THE GRAND LODGE OF

Virginia and on July 9TH, 1994, the Grand Lodge of Virginia renamed its fraternal library and museum in his honor. It goes without saying that a few of his propaganda films were regarded as being highly acclaimed productions as the writer/producer/director received worldwide recognition for his efforts and was the reception of many prestigious awards at International Film and T.V. Festivals held in New York and Houston, Texas over the course of his life's long list of accomplishments. Only two years prior to his death, (1995), fraternity Brother Roberts was bestowed with the highest Masonic recognition of merit award in the Continental United States, a Master Mason of the 33RD degree. It should also be stated that in 1969, Roberts urged the establishing of a central based "clearing house "for Masonic information, insisting that the Order had no choice but to chance with the times. By spring of 1993, the Masonic Information Center in Washington, D.C. was formed and designed to serve as "a clearing house, processing information of interest to the Masonic community "not only within North America but also beyond its jurisdictional boundaries.

Like the investigation into the bombing of Pearl Harbor and the Nuremberg Tribunal which saw countless Nazi War Criminals either executed, imprisoned and/or acquitted all together, various members of the Ancient Craft of Freemasonry were also personally hand picked to look into the events which enabled the terrorist attacks to occur on September 11TH, 2001. In late November of 2002, fraternity Brother George Bush Jr. appointed the former Secretary of State Henry Kissinger to probe the reasons as to why the Masonic controlled Government of the 43RD President of the United States failed to foil the attacks. It was just like the appointing of Freemasonry Brother Chief Justice Earl Warren to conduct the hearings on John F. Kennedy's assassination in order to cover-up the true details of a possible American governmental conspiracy. Kissinger interestingly was secretary of state and national security advisor for Masonic Presidents Richard Nixon and Gerald Ford.

Just to give a further example as to how hypocritical all of these types of investigations actually are in its proper light, not long after fraternity Brother Ronald Reagan appointed a panel to investigate the Iran-Contra Affair, he too testified before the committee reportedly insisting that he had no recollection of what had transpired. And Gerald Ford swore on a Masonic Bible as he testified before a House of Representatives' sub-committee which was investigating the possibility of granting Tricky Dick Nixon a

FULL PRESIDENTIAL PARDON FOR HIS INVOLVEMENT IN VARIOUS VIOLATIONS AGAINST HUMANITY.

IT SHOULD ALSO BE STATED THAT LESS THAN ONE YEAR PREVIOUS TO KISSINGER'S FRATERNAL APPOINTMENT, HE ATTENDED THE CARNATION OF CANADA'S NEWSPAPER BARON, (CONRAD BLACK), AS LORD BLACK OF CROSSHARBOUR IN LONDON, ENGLAND. ALSO IN ATTENDANCE WERE OTHER WELL KNOWN MEMBERS OF THE ANCIENT CRAFT OF FREEMASONRY; EX-BRITISH PRIME MINISTER BARONESS MAGGIE THATCHER AND LORD CARRINGTON JUST TO NAME A COUPLE OF THEM. LORD BLACK IN TURN SOLD THE VAST MAJORITY OF HIS CANADIAN OUTLETS TO MEDIA MAGNATE IZZY ASPER, WHO THEN WENT ON TO HELP MOLD THE WAY IN WHICH CANADIAN PUBLIC OPINION WAS TO PRESENT ITSELF. WITH U.S. PRESIDENT GEORGE BUSH JR. RATTLING HIS FRATERNAL SWORD, AMERICAN ANTI-ISLAMIC RHETORIC THREATENED TO ANNIHILATE THE ENTIRE HUMAN RACE AS A THIRD WORLD WAR LOOKED EMINENT. COINCIDENTLY, IN JANUARY OF 1980 ARGUMENTS WERE PUT FORWARD BY THE GRAND LODGE OF SCOTLAND THAT LITERALLY THROUGH FREEMASONRY INTO A COMPLETE TAILSPIN WORLDWIDE AS IT DECREED THAT FREEMASONRY WAS IN FACT A RELIGION BUT NOT IN ACCORDANCE TO THE NORMAL SENSE OF THE WORD — IT WAS SAID TO BE A RELIGION OF FAITH WITHOUT THE USUAL WORSHIP ATTACHED TO ANY ONE SPECIFIC ALTER. THEN SEVERAL MONTHS LATER, NOVEMBER 1981, THE MASONIC RESEARCH LODGE OF TEXAS PUBLISHED A REBUTTAL STATING THAT FREEMASONRY WAS BY NO MEANS A RELIGION DESPITE AS TO WHAT THE GRAND LODGE OF SCOTLAND HAD PREVIOUSLY STATED. AS FAR AS THE AMERICAN FREEMASONS WERE CONCERNED, THEIR FRATERNAL ORDER WAS NEITHER RELIGIOUS NOR ANTI-RELIGIOUS BUT RATHER A COMPLETELY TOLERANT ORGANIZATION THAT REPRESENTED THE TRUE VALUES THAT WERE SUPREME IN THE LIFE OF THE CHURCH. IN ITS STATEMENT OF DISCLAIM, THE TEXAS LODGE OF RESEARCH CONTAINED STATEMENTS BY TWO DOCTORS OF DIVINITY IN REBUTTAL TO THE EXACT SAME ISSUE RAISED AT THE MASONIC CONVENTION HELD IN BALTIMORE IN 1843 WHEREAS IT WAS STATED THAT "CHRISTIANITY IS CONSIDERED THE ESTABLISHED RELIGION OF AMERICAN FREEMASONRY."

APPARENTLY, THE QUESTION OF WHETHER/OR NOT FREEMASONRY WAS A RELIGION HAD PLAGUED ITS MEMBERSHIP FOR MANY, MANY YEARS. AMERICAN FREEMASONS IN FACT HAVE BEEN TRYING TO RESOLVE THE ISSUE EVER SINCE THE BALTIMORE CONVENTION. FOR INSTANCE, IN 1952 THE MASONIC REV. BROTHER THOMAS D. ROY STATED: "FREEMASONRY IS NOT EVEN IN THE REMOTEST SENSE A RELIGION "AND IN 1970, YET ANOTHER MASONIC MEMBER, REV. BROTHER FORREST D. HAGGARD STATED: "THERE IS NO LINKAGE OR AFFILIATION BETWEEN THE SYMBOLIC LODGE AND THE CHRISTIAN FAITH."

One maybe excused for asking the most obvious question as to why such a misinterpretation of beliefs and/or understandings has been taking place ever since the building of King Solomon's Temple thousands of years ago.

Well as it turns out in England during the mid-1950's (1956 to be precise), the Grand Lodge of England sought a concession in taxes on the Freemasons' Hall in London and made application with the British Courts citing that a statute affording relief to non-profit organizations whose main objects were concerned to be the advancement of religion. The court ruling found that as long as a man had some sort of religion /or mode of worship believing in a Supreme Creator and lead a good moral life, Freemasonry was sort of like a religion but in all likelihood did not advance religion per se. This debate has thus far lingered on throughout the entire world and continues to haunt Freemasons to this very day and will more than likely continue to do so for the rest of all eternity. Especially since the United States of the America's had showed a total willingness of risking the chance of starting a Third World War in the Middle East all in the name of religion by attempting to wipe out Islamic Freemasonry and ridding the world of people such as Saddam Hussein and their renegade Ancient Craft policies that were interfering with U.S. visions of having a **NEW WORLD ORDER** in place as the deadline itself had already come and gone with the celebrated new millennium festivities. Once Iraq and its people were liberated, (Shock-and-Awe attack on Iraq during the spring of 2003 and forcing its inhabitants into submission), American Freemasonry leaders on the North American Continent then began setting their fraternal sights on neighboring countries in the Middle East as a way and means of implementing their own interpreted version of the **"Brotherhood of Man – under the Fatherhood of God."**

According to Freemasonry's military code of conduct, it is written that during the time of conflict a member of the Ancient Craft is strictly prohibited from killing another known member of the Brotherhood no matter as to which side of the religious/ political spectrum they maybe on. For example, at the height of the Revolutionary War for political independence from the Grand Lodge of England, the Mohawk Indian Chief Joseph Brant was in command of a group of aboriginal warriors who were fighting off the Americans while they served on the British side of the schism activity when a member of the United States Army (Captain McKinsty) was captured by the Indians. Brant reportedly ordered

HIS MOHAWK WARRIORS TO TIE THE PRISONER TO A TREE AND THEN TOLD THEM TO TORTURE HIM IN AN ATTEMPT TO EXTRACT INFORMATION. BUT JUST AS THE INDIANS WERE ABOUT TO FOLLOW THROUGH ON THE ORDERS ISSUED BY THE BRITISH CHAIN OF COMMAND, MCKINSTY MADE THE MYSTIC APPEAL OF A FREEMASON IN THE MOMENT OF IMMINENT DANGER. RECOGNIZING THE BATTLE CRY OF A FELLOW MEMBER OF THE ANCIENT CRAFT, MASONIC BROTHER JOSEPH BRANT THEN LEAPED TO BROTHER MCKINSTY'S RESCUE BY INTERVENING IN THE TORTURE PROCEEDINGS AND QUICKLY WHISKED HIM OFF TO FRENCH CANADA, (QUEBEC), WHERE THE BRITISH NOW RULED SUPREME AND PLACED HIM IN THE CARE OF ENGLISH MASTER MASONS WHO IN TURN BROUGHT THE SOMEWHAT BEWILDERED CAPTAIN BACK TO THE U.S. MILITARY FORCES STATIONED AT ONE OF THE NEARBY AMERICAN OUTPOSTS TOTALLY UNSCATHED AND/OR UNINJURED BY THE OCCURRING EVENTS.

PERHAPS THIS EXACT SAME COURTESY WAS BESTOWED ONTO SADDAM HUSSEIN WHEN U.S. PRESIDENT GEORGE W. BUSH WENT ON WORLDWIDE TELEVISION MARCH 17TH, 2003 GIVING THE ISLAMIC FREEMASONRY LEADER 48 HOURS TO GET THE HELL OUT OF IRAQ /OR ELSE HE AND HIS RENEGADE REGIME WOULD BE FACING THE FIVE POINTS OF MASONIC FELLOWSHIP IN THE FORM OF BOMBS AND BULLETS. LIKE ALL ELSE IN THE FREEMASONRY WORLD, NOTHING IS EVER LEFT TO CHANCE ITSELF AS EVERYTHING IS ALWAYS A STACKED DECK PURELY IN FAVOR OF THE AGGRESSOR.

<u>ONE FINAL POSTSCRIPT TO THIS CHAPTER.</u>

IN ACCORDANCE AS TO WHAT HAS BEEN STATED THUS FAR REGARDING THE CATHOLIC CHURCH AND THE MASONIC INSTITUTION, THE MOST POWERFUL ENTITY OF FREEMASONRY KNOWN TO ALL MANKIND WITHIN THE WESTERN FREE-WORLD, (**THE ILUMINATI: IN GOD WE TRUST**), ODDLY ENOUGH JUSTIFIED THEIR ACTIONS TOWARDS GLOBAL DOMINATION BY STATING THAT THE ROMAN CATHOLIC JESUIT ORDER ALSO IMPLEMENTED VARIOUS DEGREES OF THE ANCIENT CRAFT INTO CATHOLICISM AS THEY TOO POSSESSED THE FUNDAMENTAL DESIRE TO BECOME MASTERS OF THE UNIVERSE HERE ON EARTH. THIS PRIESTLY VISION WAS IN FACT REPORTEDLY SANCTIONED BY A PAPACY DECREE BUT LATER QUICKLY LABELED "LA FABLE DE LA FRANC-MACONNERIE JESUITIQUE "BY THOSE WHO CHOSE NOT TO ACCEPT SUCH A MANEUVER BY ROMAN CATHOLIC CHURCH OFFICIALS IN THE VATICAN. LIKE THE MIXTURE OF OIL AND WATER, PROTESTANT FREEMASONRY AND THE ROMAN CATHOLIC FAITH WERE SAID TO BE TOTALLY INCOMPATIBLE SINCE MAN FIRST TAUGHT HIMSELF HOW TO COOK HIS FOOD WITH FIRE. BUT AS THE TWO MAIN RELIGIOUS INSTITUTIONS CONSTANTLY CLASHED WITH ONE ANOTHER FOR ULTIMATE SUPREMACY, THE ROMAN CATHOLIC CHURCH INADVERTENTLY LEFT

A RATHER INTERESTING TRAIL OF HORSE DROPPINGS BEHIND THEM AS THEY SOUGHT TO CIVILIZE THE SAVAGES OF CANADA'S WILDERNESS AND TO IMPROVE THE POLITICAL INTEGRITY OF THE COUNTRY WHILE STILL MAINTAINING THEIR RELIGIOUSLY STYLED BIGOTRY. TO THAT END, THE JESUITS WERE SAID TO HAVE INVENTED VARIOUS DEGREES INTO THEIR FRATERNAL **ORDER OF CHRIST** WHICH WAS TOTALLY OVERHAULED WITH THE INTENT OF ASSISTING THE EXILED HOUSE OF STUART IN ITS EFFORTS TO RE-GAIN THE ENGLISH THRONE BECAUSE AT THAT TIME PERIOD OF HISTORY, (MID-1600'S THROUGHOUT THE 1700'S), THERE EXISTED A LACK OF WILLINGNESS TO RESTORE THE ROMAN CATHOLIC FAITH'S RELIGIOUS STRANGLEHOLD ON GREAT BRITAIN AND THE REST OF THE WORLD. KNOWN HISTORICALLY AS STUART FREEMASONRY, WHICH WAS SUPPOSEDLY IMPLEMENTED BY THE EXILED DYNASTY THEMSELVES AS A WAY AND MEANS OF RE-GAINING POSSESSION OF THEIR BRITISH TITLE OF NOBILITY AFTER BEING OVERTHROWN BY OPPOSING FORCES SUCH AS THOSE OF THE PROTESTANT HERO WILLIAM OF ORANGE, WHO AS IT TURNS OUT WAS SECRETLY RECEIVING FINANCIAL FUNDING FROM THE ROMAN CATHOLIC CHURCH ITSELF TO HELP TOPPLE THE HOUSE OF STUART.

IN RETALIATION, THE STUART FAMILY DYNASTY CONCEIVED A PLAN THAT WAS DESIGNED TO FULLY RESTORE THEIR RIGHTFUL PLACE ON THE THRONE. IT WAS THE INTENTION OF THE HOUSE OF STUART TO FIRST HAVE JAMES II RE-INSTATED AS THE GOVERNING POWERS THAT BE IN ENGLAND, IRELAND AND SCOTLAND, AND AFTERWARDS HIS SON AND GRANDSON, JAMES FRANCIS EDWARD AND CHARLES EDWARD, RESPECTIVELY KNOWN IN HISTORY AS THE CHEVALIER ST. GEORGE AND THE YOUNG PRETENDER. BUT THE MAIN STUMBLING BLOCK WAS SAID TO HAVE BEEN THE LACK OF A PROPER FREEMASONRY PAPER TRAIL THAT WAS TO ENABLE THE STUART LEGACY TO ONCE AGAIN RULE SUPREME. WHAT WAS REPORTEDLY NEEDED WAS SOME SORT OF MASONIC INFLUENCE ON BEHALF OF THE FAMILY, WHICH WAS TO BE ATTRIBUTED TO JAMES THE SECOND AS HIS ABDICATION TO THE THRONE IN 1688 WAS NOT DESTINED TO GO DOWN IN THE HISTORY BOOKS WITHOUT A FIGHT. TURNING TO THE FRENCH MONARCHY FOR ASSISTANCE IN THE MATTER, THE JESUITS WERE AUTHORIZED TO INCORPORATE CERTAIN FREEMASONRY DEGREES WITH THE ULTERIOR MOTIVE OF CARRYING OUT THE ROMAN CATHOLIC CHURCH'S OWN PERSONAL HIDDEN POLITICAL AGENDA IN GREAT BRITAIN AS BY THIS TIME PERIOD, PROTESTANTISM WAS RULING THE ROOST ACROSS THE ENGLISH CHANNEL.

UPON THE DEATH OF JAMES II, WHICH TOOK PLACE AT THE PALACE OF SAINT-GERMAIN-EN-LAYE (FRANCE) IN 1701, HE WAS SUCCEEDED IN HIS CLAIMS TO THE BRITISH THRONE BY HIS SON, WHO BY THIS TIME PERIOD OF HISTORY WAS DULY RECOGNIZED BY THE KING OF FRANCE LOUIS XIV AS BEING A MEMBER OF THE ANCIENT CRAFT OF FREEMASONRY UNDER THE HONOURARY TITLE OF JAMES III FOR MASONIC REASONS OF ENLIGHTENMENT. IN AN ATTEMPT TO

WHITEWASH THE ROMAN CATHOLIC CHURCH'S INVOLVEMENT OF HAVING THE HOUSE OF STUART RE-INSTATED TO THE BRITISH THRONE, THE PAPACY KEPT RE-WRITING THE PAGES OF HISTORY AT EVERY OPPORTUNE MOMENT DENYING THE FACT THAT THE JESUITS PLAYED A CRUCIAL ROLE IN THIS SLEIGHT-OF-HAND TRANSACTION. APPARENTLY, A LARGE COLLECTION OF LIBRARY BOOKS ON THIS SPECIFIC TOPIC EXIST IN SUCH COUNTRIES AS GERMANY AND FRANCE BUT ONLY MADE AVAILABLE TO THE SELECTED FEW.

AS THE STORY GOES, THE JESUITS HAD INTRODUCED THESE DEGREES INTO THEIR ORDER WHICH DEPICTED THE ENTIRE HISTORY OF THE KNIGHTS TEMPLAR, (FROM ITS FIRST CONCEPTION TO ITS SO-CALLED DEMISE), AND EVEN THREW IN A COUPLE OF DEGREES ASSOCIATED WITH THE DOCTRINE OF VENGEANCE FOR THE POLITICAL AND RELIGIOUS CRIME OF THEIR DESTRUCTION FOR EXTRA MEASURE. ALL OF THESE DEGREES WERE SUPERIMPOSED OVER THE ALREADY EXISTING FOUR VOWS OF CONDUCT THAT THEIR CONGREGATION MEMBERS HAD TO SWEAR ALLEGIANCE AND BE FAITHFUL FOLLOWERS OF. IN THE PUBLISHED WORKS OF FRENCH FREEMASON NICOLAS DE BONNEVILLE, (BORN AT EVREUX, IN FRANCE, MARCH 12TH, 1760), HE MADE THIS DOCUMENTATION PUBLIC KNOWLEDGE FOR THE VERY FIRST TIME IN 1788 AND WAS LATER LOCKED IN SHACKLES AND THROWN INTO PRISON FOR BEING A GIRONDIST (1793). ONLY ONE YEAR PREVIOUS TO HIS BEING INCARCERATED BY ORDER OF THE KING OF FRANCE LOUIS XVI FOR PARTAKING IN THE FRENCH REVOLUTION, DE BONNEVILLE WROTE AND PUBLISHED THE ACCLAIMED "HISTORY OF MODERN EUROPE." THE THREE VOLUME PUBLISHED WORKS REPORTEDLY EXPOSED MANY HIDDEN UNTOLD SECRETS OF THE ANCIENT CRAFT AND HOW MEMBERS OF FRENCH FREEMASONRY VIEWED THE WORLD UNDER THEIR NEW AND IMPROVED STEWARDSHIP.

IN THE MEANTIME, THE LEPAGE'S FROM FRANCE WHO WERE NOW HIDING OUT IN NORTH AMERICA TRYING TO AVOID THE GUILLOTINE AS SOME OF THEM WERE NOT ONLY ACTIVELY INVOLVED WITH THE GIRONDIST MOVEMENT BUT ALSO HAD BEEN SECRETLY COLLABORATING WITH THE FRENCH MONARCHY IN AN ATTEMPT OF HAVING THE HOUSE OF STUART RE-INSTATED IN ENGLAND. AS THEY PLAYED BOTH ENDS AGAINST THE MIDDLE AND HOPED THAT NO ONE WAS GOING TO CATCH ONTO THIS, THEY ALSO DIDN'T LIKE THE IDEA OF BEING BEHEADED ONE DAMN BIT. FEARING THAT IT WOULD EVENTUALLY COME BACK AND BITE THEM IN THE ASS, THE LEPAGE'S TOOK HOLD OF A GIGANTIC ROMAN CATHOLIC ERASE AND ALMOST IMMEDIATELY BEGAN WHIPPING OUT ALL TRACES OF THEIR DIRTY LITTLE DEEDS. AND WHILE THEY KICKED UP THEIR HEELS IN GLORIOUS TRIUMPH IN PARTS OF THE FRENCH NORTH AMERICAN CONTINENT, LOUIS XVI WAS FOUND GUILTY OF TREASONOUS BEHAVIOR BY THE GIRONDINS AND ORDERED TO BE EXECUTED ONCE THEY AND THEIR DISGRUNTLED COHORTS FINALLY SEIZED THE REIGNS OF POWER. ON JULY 8TH,

1793 an order was thusly given for the immediate arrest of the King of France and soon thereafter, he was guillotined. Those members of the Masonic LePage family name who evaded uncertain death by way of fleeing the scene of the crime, then, went on to become highly respected members of Freemasonry once again. Continuing to make their presence well known with contributions to the never-ending Ancient Craft of Freemasonry, the LePage's achieved greatness in the form of a collection of initiation degrees in Roman Catholic's fraternity Order of Christ and Catholic Church's Portugese entity of the Knights Templar. Once this was accomplished, all was forgiven once more!!! These degrees known in French as "Souverain des Souverain Grands Commandeur du Temple" were said to have been valuable contributions to the Ancient Craft on a worldwide scale for its ultimate goal of globalized conquest. That of which the LePage's undoubtedly agreed and eventually had all of their highly praised Freemasonry degrees published in manuscript form known in Brotherhood circles as a cahier, a number of sheets of parchment /or paper fastened together at the tail end of a Masonic Institution being implemented for its initiated members.

During this time period of the LePage family name being raised to Freemasonry splendor and wonderment, the word "cahier "was often used by French Freemasons to designate a small book printed in manuscript form containing the ritual of a degree of the said Institution. The word itself was reportedly borrowed from French history where it denoted the reports and/or proceedings of certain assemblies such as the clergy /or the States-General. In the year 1815, another French Masonic writer named Claude Antoine Thory had his Freemasonry works published; "Acta Latomorum". Contained within these writings, Thory interestingly alluded to the LePage's and their uncanny ability to constantly being a valuable asset to the Ancient Craft despite the fact that they were not very well liked by most of the English-speaking North American Freemasonry population. Knowing as to how the Protestant Freemasons viewed both the French Roman Catholic faith and the LePage's of Quebec and Louisiana, it was only fitting that this portion be incorporated within the very last pages of this Chapter since everything seems to go hand-in-hand with all of the other schism activity that has been unfolding before our own eyes during the first few years of the 21ST Century in the name of religion and its globalized conquest.

Chapter 13 - Man's Only Salvation

INTRODUCTION

The Gibson's Landing Story; Lester R. Peterson, Gibsons, British Columbia, 1962

The West Howe Sound Story 1886 - 1976; Francis J. Van Den Wyngaert, Gibsons, B.C., 1980

The Province; B 11, Monday, November 30th, 1998 (But Quebeckers aren't amused – Quebec director Robert LePage is in the middle of a growing controversy while promoting his movie creation " No " which is set in 1970 during the FLQ crisis).

Maclean's Newsmagazine; Page 60, January 29th, 2001 (**Puzzles and predators**. Some of the brilliant sleight-of-hand artistic antics conducted by Robert LePage).

The Vancouver Sun; D 1, Thursday, September 12th, 2002 (**LePage's magic spell:** Robert LePage, perhaps the world's greatest contemporary theatre maker, brings his acclaimed one-man show The Far Side of the Moon to Vancouver).

The Vancouver Sun; D 14, Thursday, September 12th, 2002 (From here to infinity – The Far Side of the Moon stretches to the heavens in a multmedia exploration of space, time and Robert LePage himself).

I Know That Name!; Pages 153 - 155, Mark Kearney and Randy Ray, Toronto, Ontario, 2002

Coast Reporter, Gibsons, British Columbia; A 8, Sunday, December 1st, 2002 (Movie – Vocal beachcombers crowd screens TV pilot).

Coast Reporter, Gibsons, British Columbia; A 4, Sunday, January 5th, 2003 (Movies – Lights, camera, action! Local film commission aims to lure movie magic to the coast).

Chapter 1 - DIEU ET MON DROIT

The Expanding World; Hamlyn Publishing Group Limited, London, England, 1979

CANADA: A Modern History; J. Bartlet Brebner, University of Michigan 1960

The Founding of Canada: Beginnings to 1815; Stanley B. Ryerson, 1963

History of Canada For High Schools; Duncan McArthur, M.A., F.R.S.C., Douglas Professor ofColonial and Canadian History, Queen's University, Kingston, 1930

Our Canada; Arthur G. Dorland, M.A., Ph.D., University of Western Ontario, 1949

A Nation Developing; J.A. Lower, 1970 (Brief History of Canada for Secondary Schools for the Province of British Columbia)

General History For Colleges and High Schools; Philip Van Ness Myers, Historian College Hill, Ohio, 1906

Feudal Canada: The Story Of The Seigniories Of New France; Thomas Guerin, Montreal, 1926

Essai Sur L'Industrie au Canada, sous le regime Francais; Joseph-Noel Fauteux, Professor of Social Sciences and Political Sciences, University of Montreal, 1927

The Seigniorial System in Canada: A Study In French Colonial Policy; William Bennett Munro, Ph.D., Assistant Professor of Government at Harvard University, 1907

PERSPECTIVES IN CANADIAN HISTORY: No. 3, THE SEIGNIORIAL REGIME IN CANADA; DOROTHY A. HENEKER, FIRST EDITION 1927, REPRINTED 1980

THE WHITE AND THE GOLD: THE FRENCH REGIME IN CANADA; HISTORIAN THOMAS B. COSTAIN, 1954

A HISTORY OF FRENCH LOUISIANA: VOLUME ONE, THE REIGN OF LOUIS XIV 1698-1715; MARCEL GIRAUD, TRANSLATED FROM FRENCH TO ENGLISH BY JOSEPH C. LAMBERT, 1974

A HISTORY OF FRENCH LOUISIANA: VOLUME FIVE, THE COMPANY OF THE INDIES 1723-1731; MARCEL GIRAUD, TRANSLATED FROM FRENCH TO ENGLISH BY BRIAN PEARCE, 1987

THE ATLANTIC CANADIANS: 1600-1900, VOLUMES 1, 2, AND 3; THE GENEALOGICAL RESEARCH LIBRARY, TORONTO, ONTARIO, 1994

THE FRENCH CANADIANS: 1600-1900, VOLUMES 1, 2, AND 3; THE GENEALOGICAL RESEARCH LIBRARY, TORONTO, ONTARIO, 1992

THE WESTERN CANADIANS: 1600-1900, VOLUMES 1, 2 AND 3; THE GENEALOGICAL RESEARCH LIBRARY TORONTO, ONTARIO, 1992

LE GRAND ARRANGEMENT DE ACADIENS AU QUEBEC 1625-1925; VOLUMES 1 THROUGH TO 10, 1981

UNION LIST OF MANUSCRIPTS 1600-1900: VOLUMES 1 AND 2; PLUS VARIOUS SUPPLEMENTS 1975

PASSENGER AND IMMIGRATION LISTS INDEX 1600-1900; PLUS SUPPLEMENTS 1983/84/85/91

FINDING YOUR FRENCH-CANADIAN ANCESTORS; LOUISE ST. DENIS, DATE UNKNOWN

DICTIONNAIRE GENEALOGIQUE DES FAMILLES DU QUEBEC; LES PRESSES DE L'UNIVERSITE DE MONTREAL, 1983

BIOGRAPHY AND GENEALOGY MASTER INDEX LIST 1ST AND 2ND EDITION; PLUS VARIOUS SUPPLEMENTS, 1980

Dictionnaire Genealogique des Familles Canadiannes; Volume 1, Cyprien Tanguay, date unknown

Archives Canadiennes: Genealogie des familles de L'Ile D'Orleans; author and date unknown

Genealogie de la famille LePage (Branche du Rimouski); National Archives of Canada, Ottawa, Ontario – Catalogue Reference Number MG 25668

Pedigree Chart of LePage Lineage; Ted and Denise Lanning, December 18th, 1997

Genealogie de la famille LePage; Jacqueline St. Laurent, Montreal, Quebec, 1964

The Page Family History in the United States, (a Branch of the LePage Family from Canada); Ivan S. Page, Pasadena, California, 1965

Coat of Arms: Historiography of the LePage Family Crest; date unknown

The Ancient History of the Distinguished Surname LePage; date unknown

Les LePage, au coeur de notre histoire; **ASSOCIATION DES FAMILLES LePAGE D'AMERIQUE INC., RIMOUSKI, QUEBEC, 1996**

CELEBRATION EUCHARISTIQUE –
DESCENDANTS DE LA FAMILLE AMABLE ET JOSEPH LePAGE;
Saint-Benoit de Balmoral, Nouveau Brunswick
LE 12 OCTOBRE 1996

La Famille LePage au Canada; Leo LePage, **1996**

Chapter 2 - MOI BEAU PAYS DE QUEBEC

Masonic Bible: Authorized King James Version; William Collins Sons and Company Ltd., 1951

Holman's Edition: The Holy Bible; A.J. Holman & Company, 1877

Ancient Secrets Of The Bible; SUN-PKO Productions Inc., 1992

Picturesque Scotland; Francis Watt, M.A. and the Rev. Andrew Carter, M.A., Frederick Warne and Company, London, England date unknown (at least the mid to late 1800's)

The English Parliament; Kenneth R. Mackenzie, 1950

A Monarchy Transformed: Britain 1603 - 1714; Mark Kishlanshy, 1996

The Master Christian; Marie Corelli, 1900

The Divine Plan; author unknown as well as its date (at least the very early 1900's)

The World Problem and The Divine Solution; Charles S. Eby, 1914

In The Steps Of The Master; H.V. Morton, 1934

Europe and A Wider World: 1415-1715; Edited by Sir Maurice Powicke, M.A., D. Litt., F.B.A., late Regius Professor of Modern History at the University of Oxford, 1965

The Framework Of A Christian State; Rev. E. Cahill, Dublin, Ireland, 1932

Feudal Canada: The Story Of The Seigniories Of New France; Thomas Guerin, Montreal, 1926

Essai Sur L'Industrie au Canada, sous le regime Francais; Joseph-Noel Fauteux, Professor ofSocial Sciences and Political Sciences, University of Montreal, 1927

The Seigniorial System In Canada: A study In French Colonial Policy; William Bennett Munro, Ph.D., Assistant Professor of Government at Harvard University, 1907

Perspectives In Canadian History: No. 3, The Seigniorial Regime in Canada; Dorothy A. Heneker, first edition 1927, reprinted 1980

The White And The Gold: The French Regime In Canada; Historian Thomas B. Costain, 1954

A History of Political Theory; George H. Sabine, Professor of Philosophy, Cornell University, 1950

The Inquisition; Michael Baigent and Richard Leigh, 1999

Born Again; Charles W. Colson, 1976

The Vancouver Sun; A 10, Tuesday, September 11TH, 2001 (**Vatican to allow changes in Bible.** Dead Sea Scrolls revelations are the basis for new material).

The Province; A 11, Tuesday, September 11TH, 2001 (**Vatican unrolls Dead Sea Scrolls for Bible changes**).

The Province; A 34, Sunday, September 23RD, 2001 (King Billy on papal payroll).

CHAPTER 3 - JE ME SOUVIENS

CANADA: A Modern History; J. Bartlet Brebner, University of Michigan, 1960

The Founding Of Canada: Beginnings to 1815; Stanley B. Ryerson, 1963

History Of Canada For High Schools; Duncan McArthur, M.A., F.R.S.C., Douglas Professor ofColonial and Canadian History, Queen's University, Kingston, 1930

Our Canada; Arthur G. Dorland, M.A., Ph.D., University of Western Ontario, 1949

A Nation Developing; J.A. Lower, 1970 (Brief History of Canada for Secondary Schools for the   Province of British Columbia).

General History For Colleges And High Schools; Philip Van Ness Myers, Historian College Hill,   Ohio, 1906

Feudal Canada: The Story Of The Seigniories Of New France; Thomas Guerin, Montreal, 1926

Essai Sur L'Industrie au Canada, sous le regime Francais; Joseph-Noel Fauteux, Professor ofSocial Sciences and Political Sciences, University of Montreal, 1927

The Seigniorial System In Canada: A Study In French Colonial Policy; William Bennett Munro, Ph.D., Assistant Professor of Government at Harvard University, 1907

Perspectives In Canadian History: No. 3, The Seigniorial Regime in Canada; Dorothy A. Heneker, first edition 1927, reprinted 1980

The White And The Gold: The French Regime In Canada; Historian Thomas B. Costain, 1954

Canadian History In Documents: 1763-1966; Edited by J.M. Bliss, 1966

A History Of American Democracy; John D. Hicks, George E. Mowry and Robert Burke, 1966

The Story Of Civilization: Part X – Rousseau And Revolution; Will and Ariel Durant, 1967

Our Land: Building The West; Gage Educational Publishing Company for High Schools in   Canada, 1987

Canada: A People's History (Episode 1: When The World Began); CBC, MM

Canada: A People's History (Episode 2: Adventurers And Mystics); CBC, MM

Canada: A People's History (Episode 3: Claiming The Wilderness); CBC, MM

Canada: A People's History (Episode 4: Battle For A Continent); CBC, MM

Canada: A People's History (Episode 5: A Question Of Loyalties); CBC, MM

Canada: A People's History (Episode 6: The Pathfinders); CBC, MMI

Canada: A People's History (Episode 7: Rebellion And Reform); CBC, MMI

Canada: A People's History (Episode 8: The Great Enterprise); CBC, MMI

Canada: A People's History (Episode 9: From Sea To Sea); CBC, MMI

Canada: A People's History (Episode 10: Taking The West); CBC, MMI

Canada: A People's History (Episode 11: The Great Transformation);
    CBC, MMI

Canada: A People's History (Episode 12: Ordeal By Fire); CBC, MMI

Canada: A People's History (Episode 13: Hard Times); CBC, MMI

Canada: A People's History (Episode 14: The Crucible); CBC, MMI

Canada: A People's History (Episode 15: Comfort And Fear); CBC,
    MMI

Canada: A People's History (Episode 16: Years Of Hope And Anger);
    CBC, MMI

Canada: A People's History (Episode 17: In An Uncertain World);
    CBC, MMI

Origins: A History Of Canada (The Origins of Canada's
    Indigenous Peoples); TV Ontario, The Ontario Educational
    Communications Authority, MCMLXXXVI

Origins: A History Of Canada (Displaced Persons); TV Ontario,
    The Ontario Educational Communications Authority,
    MCMLXXXVI

IKWE; National Film Board Of Canada, 1986

1867: How The Fathers Made A Deal; Christopher Moore, 1997

British North America Acts And Selected Statutes 1867-1962;
    Maurice Ollivier, Q.C., LL.D, F.R.S.C., Parliament Counsel,
    House Of Commons, Government Of Canada, Ottawa, 1962

CHAPTER 4 - LE PAYS DE DROIT FRANCAIS

FEUDAL CANADA: THE STORY OF THE SEIGNIORIES OF NEW FRANCE;
THOMAS GUERIN, MONTREAL, 1926

ESSAI SUR L'INDUSTRIE AU CANADA, SOUS LE REGIME FRANCAIS; JOSEPH-
NOEL FAUTEUX, PROFESSOR OF SOCIAL SCIENCES AND POLITICAL
SCIENCES, UNIVERSITY OF MONTREAL, 1927

THE SEIGNIORIAL SYSTEM IN CANADA: A STUDY IN FRENCH COLONIAL
POLICY; WILLIAM BENNETT MUNRO, PH.D., ASSISTANT PROFESSOR
OF GOVERNMENT AT HARVARD UNIVERSITY, 1907

PERSPECTIVES IN CANADIAN HISTORY: NO. 3, THE SEIGNIORIAL REGIME IN
CANADA; DOROTHY A. HENEKER, FIRST EDITION 1927, REPRINTED
1980

THE WHITE AND THE GOLD: THE FRENCH REGIME IN CANADA; HISTORIAN
THOMAS B. COSTAIN, 1954

THE FOUNDING OF CANADA: BEGINNINGS TO 1815; STANLEY B. RYERSON,
1963

CANADA: A MODERN HISTORY; J. BARTLET BREBNER, UNIVERSITY OF
MICHIGAN, 1960

A HISTORY OF FRENCH LOUISIANA: VOLUME ONE, THE REIGN OF LOUIS
XIV 1698-1715; MARCEL GIRAUD, 1953, TRANSLATED FROM FRENCH
TO ENGLISH BY JOSEPH C. LAMBERT, 1974

A HISTORY OF FRENCH LOUISIANA: VOLUME FIVE, THE COMPANY OF THE
INDIES 1723-1731; MARCEL GIRAUD, TRANSLATED FROM FRENCH TO
ENGLISH BY BRIAN PEARCE, 1987

DICTIONARY OF AMERICAN BIOGRAPHY; VOLUME III, PAGE 534, DATE
UNKNOWN

Louisiana History; Volume III, Number 1, Pages 21 and 22, Free Persons Of Color in Colonial   Louisiana by Donald E. Everett, Professor of History, Trinity University, San Antonio, Texas, date unknown

Letter from The Natchitoches Genealogical and Historical Association in Louisiana to Benoit J. LePage, dated June 2ND, 1999

An American Dilemma: The Negro Problem And Modern Democracy; Gunnar Myrdal with the assistance of Richard Sterner and Arnold Rose, 1944

The Great Events by Famous Historians; Volume 15, National Alumni of the United States, 1905

A History of American Democracy; John D. Hicks, George E. Mowry and Robert Burke, 1966

LORD DURHAM'S REPORT; edited and with an Introduction by Gerald M. Craig, 1963

Canada: A People's History (Episode 1: When The World Began); CBC, MM

Canada: A People's History (Episode 2: Adventurers And Mystics); CBC, MM

Canada: A People's History (Episode 3: Claiming The Wilderness); CBC, MM

Canada: A People's History (Episode 4: Battle For A Continent); CBC, MM

Canada: A People's History (Episode 5: A Question Of Loyalties); CBC, MM

Canada: A People's History (Episode 6: The Pathfinders); CBC, MMI

Canada: a People's History (Episode 7: Rebellion And Reform); CBC, MMI

Canada: A People's History (Episode 8: The Great Enterprise); CBC, MMI

Canada: A People's History (Episode 9: From Sea To Sea); CBC, MMI

Canada: A People's History (Episode 10: Taking The West); CBC, MMI

Canada: A People's History (Episode 11: The Great Transformation); CBC, MMI

Canada: A People's History (Episode 12: Ordeal By Fire); CBC, MMI

Canada: A People's History (Episode 13: Hard Times); CBC, MMI

Canada: A People's History (Episode 14: The Crucible); CBC, MMI

Canada: A People's History (Episode 15: Comfort And Fear); CBC, MMI

Canada: A People's History (Episode 16: Years Of Hope And Anger); CBC, MMI

Canada: A People's History (Episode 17: In An Uncertain World); CBC, MMI

Origins: A History Of Canada (The Origins of Canada's Indigenous Peoples); TV Ontario, The Ontario Educational Communications Authority, MCMLXXXVI

Origins: A History Of Canada (Displaced Persons); TV Ontario, The Ontario Educational Communications Authority, MCMLXXXVI

IKWE; National Film Board of Canada, 1986

Chapter 5 - LA FAMILLE LePAGE APRES LA CONFEDERATION CANADIENNE

Our Canada; Arthur G. Dorland, M.A., Ph.D., University of
Western Ontario, 1949

A Nation Developing; J.A. Lower, 1970 (Brief History of Canada for
Secondary Schools for the Province of British Columbia).

History Of Canada For High Schools; Duncan McArthur, M.A.,
F.R.S.C., Douglas Professor of Colonial and Canadian
History, Queen's University, Kingston, 1930

General History For Colleges And High Schools; Philip Van Ness
Myers, Historian College Hill, Ohio, 1906

To A Non-Mason: You Must Seek Masonic Membership; Henry
C. Claussen, 33RD degree, Sovereign Grand Commander,
The Supreme Council, 33RD degree, Ancient And Accepted
Scottish Rite Of Freemasonry, Mother Jurisdiction Of The
World, 1976

A History Of American Democracy; John D. Hicks, George E.
Mowry and Robert Burke, 1966

The Armed Forces Of Canada 1867-1967; Directorate of History,
Canadian Forces Headquarters, Ottawa, 1967

The Great Events by Famous Historians; Volume 15, National
Alumni of the United States, 1905

The New Mexico Freemason; Volume 53, Number 4, July-August,
1988

United Masters Lodge No. 167, Lodge of Masonic Research;
Volume 24, Number 10, April 1982

The Northern Light: A Window For Freemasonry; Volume 21, Number 1, February 1990

Free Trade: The Full Story; David Orchard, 1988

Lincoln: The Unknown; Dale Carnegie and Associates Inc., Garden City, New York, 1959

Abraham Lincoln: A New Birth Of Freedom; made for television series, date and propaganda production unknown during the last century

American Historical Documents; Barnes & Noble Inc., College Outline Series, 1970

History Of The Grand Lodge Of British Columbia 1871-1970; Grand Lodge Of British Columbia A.F. & A.M., 1971

The Old West: Cowboys; Time-Life Books, Alexandria, Virginia, 1973

Encyclopedia of Freemasonry Volumes 1 & 2; The Masonic History Company (U.S.A.), 1924

The Quebec Masonic Journal, Grand Lodge Of Quebec A.F. & A.M.; Summer 1989

Canada: A People's History (Episode 1: When The World Began); CBC, MM

Canada: A People's History (Episode 2: Adventurers And Mystics); CBC, MM

Canada: A People's History (Episode 3: Claiming The Wilderness); CBC, MM

Canada: A People's History (Episode 4: Battle For A Continent); CBC, MM

Canada: A people's History (Episode 5: A Question Of Loyalties); CBC, MM

Canada: A People's History (Episode 6: The Pathfinders); CBC, MMI

Canada: A People's History (Episode 7: Rebellion And Reform); CBC, MMI

Canada: A People's History (Episode 8: The Great Enterprise); CBC, MMI

Canada: A People's History (Episode 9: From Sea To Sea); CBC, MMI

Canada: A People's History (Episode 10: Taking The West); CBC, MMI

Canada: A People's History (Episode 11: The Great Transformation); CBC, MMI

Canada: A People's History (Episode 12: Ordeal By Fire); CBC, MMI

Canada: A People's History (Episode 13: Hard Times); CBC, MMI

Canada: A People's History (Episode 14: The Crucible); CBC, MMI

Canada: A People's History (Episode 15: Comfort And Fear); CBC, MMI

Canada: A People's History (Episode 16: Years Of Hope And Anger); CBC, MMI

Canada: A People's History (Episode 17: In An Uncertain World); CBC, MMI

Origins: A History Of Canada (The Origins of Canada's Indigenous Peoples); TV Ontario. The Ontario Educational Communications Authority, MCMLXXXVI

Origins: A History Of Canada (Displaced Persons); TV Ontario, The Ontario Educational Communications Authority, MCMLXXXVI

Maclean's Newsmagazine; Pages 58 & 59, July 1ST, 2001 (**DISTINCT SOCIETY – In Quebec, WHERE NOTHING IS SIMPLE, PEOPLE ENJOY TWO NATIONAL HOLIDAYS**).

Encyclopedia Canadiana; Volume 6, Pages 17 and 18, Canadiana Company Limited, a subsidiary company of the Grolier Society of Canada Limited, Ottawa, 1960

The Brotherhood: The Explosive Expose of the Secret World of The Freemasons; Stephen Knight, 1986

Inside The Brotherhood: The Explosive Sequel to Stephen Knight's The Brotherhood; Martin Short, 1989

The Hiram Key: Pharaohs, Freemasons and The Discovery of The Secret Scrolls of Jesus; Christopher Knight and Robert Lomas, 1997

The Inquisition; Michael Baigent and Richard Leigh, 1999

The Expanding World; Hamlyn Publishing Group Limited, London, England, 1979

The Old West: The Canadians; Time-Life Books, Alexandria, Virginia, 1977

The White And The Gold: The French Regime in Canada; Historian Thomas B. Costain, 1954

The Story Of Civilization: Part X – Rousseau And Revolution; Will and Ariel Durant, 1967

The Holy Blood And The Holy Grail; Michael Baigent, Richard Leigh and Henry Lincoln, 1982

The Mitrokhin Archive, The KGB in Europe and the West; Christopher Andrew and Vasili Mitrokhin, 1999

The Vancouver Sun; B 5, Monday, February, 28TH, 2000 (Soviets feared Quebec ' fascists '. War documents show that

DIPLOMATS WERE WORRIED THAT NEWSPAPERS IN QUEBEC COULD CUT SUPPORT FOR THE SOVIET COMBAT EFFORT).

THE NORTHWEST WASHINGTON MASONIC NEWS, DEVOTED TO THE INTERESTS OF FREEMASONRY WHEREVER DISPERSED; VOLUME XXVIII, NUMBER 4, BELLINGHAM, WASHINGTON, DECEMBER 1989

THE MONTANA MASONIC NEWS; VOLUME 42, NUMBER 404, OCTOBER 1989

THE KANSAS MASON; VOLUME 28, ISSUE 3, JUNE 1989

GENEALOGIE DE LA FAMILLE LePAGE (BRANCHE DU DISTRICT DE RIMOUSKI) ARCHIVES PUBLIQUES DU CANADA, OTTAWA, ONTARIO FILE NUMBER MG 25668

THE METIS IN THE CANADIAN WEST, VOLUMES 1 & 2; MARCEL GIRAUD, TRANSLATED FROM FRENCH TO ENGLISH BY GEORGE WOODCOCK, 1986

ENCYCLOPEDIA CANADIANA; VOLUME 10, PAGES 5 AND 6, CANADIANA COMPANY LIMITED, A SUBSIDIARY COMPANY OF THE GROLIER SOCIETY OF CANADA LIMITED, 1960

CANADA: A POLITICAL & SOCIAL HISTORY; EDGAR MCINNIS, FORMERLY A PROFESSOR OF HISTORY, YORK UNIVERSITY, 1982

CANADIAN HISTORY IN DOCUMENTS, 1763-1966; EDITED BY J.M. BLISS, 1966

PERSPECTIVES IN CANADIAN HISTORY: NO. 3, THE SEIGNIORIAL REGIME IN CANADA; DOROTHY A HENEKER, FIRST EDITION 1927, REPRINTED 1980

THE SEIGNIORIAL SYSTEM IN CANADA: A STUDY IN FRENCH COLONIAL POLICY; WILLIAM BENNETT MUNRO, PH.D., ASSISTANT PROFESSOR OF GOVERNMENT AT HARVARD UNIVERSITY, 1907

LE CAPITALISME MARCHAND ET LA PECHE A LA MORUE EN GASPESIE: LA CHARLES ROBIN ET COMPAGNIE DANS LA BAIE DES CHALEURS (1820 - 1870); ANDRE LePAGE, 1983

PEDIGREE CHART OF LEPAGE LINEAGE; TED AND DENISE LANNING,
    DECEMBER 18TH, 1997

GENEALOGIE DE LA FAMILLE LEPAGE; JACQUELINE ST. LAURENT, MONTREAL,
    QUEBEC, 1964

THE PAGE FAMILY HISTORY IN THE UNITED STATES, (A BRANCH OF
    THE LEPAGE FAMILY FROM CANADA); IVAN S. PAGE, PASADENA,
    CALIFORNIA, 1965

COAT OF ARMS: HISTORIOGRAPHY OF THE LEPAGE FAMILY CREST; DATE
    UNKNOWN

THE ANCIENT HISTORY OF THE DISTINGUISHED SURNAME LEPAGE; DATE
    UNKNOWN

LES LEPAGE, AU COEUR DE NOTRE HISTOIRE; **ASSOCIATION DES
    FAMILLES L**E**PAGE D'AMERIQUE INC. RIMOUSKI,
    QUEBEC, 1996**

**CELEBRATION EUCHARISTIQUE –
DESCENDANTS DE LA FAMILLE AMABLE ET JOSEPH L**E**PAGE**
SAINT-BENOIT DE BALMORAL, NOUVEAU BRUNSWICK
LE 12 OCTOBRE 1996

LA FAMILLE LEPAGE AU CANADA; LEO LEPAGE, **1996**

Chapter 6 - To Be An Indian, In A Whiteman's World

Statement of the Government of Canada on Indian Policy, 1969; presented to the First Session ofthe Twenty-eighth Parliament by the Honourable Jean Chretien, Minister of Indian Affairs and Northern Development

Canada: A People's History (Episode 1: When The World Began); CBC, MM

Canada: A People's History (Episode 2: Adventurers And Mystics); CBC, MM

Canada: A People's History (Episode 3: Claiming The Wilderness); CBC, MM

Canada: A People's History (Episode 4: Battle For A Continent); CBC, MM

Canada: A People's History (Episode 5: A Question Of Loyalties); CBC, MM

Canada: A People's History (Episode 6: The Pathfinders); CBC, MMI

Canada: A People's History (Episode 7: Rebellion And Reform); CBC, MMI

Canada: A People's History (Episode 8: The Great Enterprise); CBC, MMI

Canada: A People's History (Episode 9: From Sea To Sea); CBC, MMI

Canada: A People's History (Episode 10: Taking The West); CBC, MMI

Canada: A People's History (Episode 11: The Great Transformation); CBC, MMI

Canada: A People's History (Episode 12: Ordeal By Fire); CBC, MMI

Canada: A People's History (Episode 13: Hard Times); CBC, MMI

Canada: A People's History (Episode 14: The Crucible); CBC, MMI

Canada: A People's History (Episode 15: Comfort And Fear); CBC, MMI

Canada: A People's History (Episode 16: Years Of Hope And Anger); CBC, MMI

Canada: A People's History (Episode 17: In An Uncertain World); CBC, MMI

Origins: A History Of Canada (The Origins of Canada's Indigenous Peoples); TV Ontario, The Ontario Educational Authority, MCMLXXXVI

Origins: A History Of Canada (Displaced Persons); TV Ontario, The Ontario Educational Communications Authority, MCMLXXXVI

Summer Of The Loucheux: Portrait Of A Northern Indian Family; Tamahack Films, MCMXXXIII

Make Prayers to the Raven: The Bible and the Distant Time; KUAC-TV, University of Alaska- Fairbanks, 1987

IKWE; National Film Board of Canada, 1986

Kaneshsatake: 270 Years of Resistance; National Film Board of Canada, 1993

Incident At Oglala; Carolco International & Spanish Forks Motion Picture Company, 1991

Northland (Summer Edition); CBC North, 1992

British North America Acts and Selected Statutes 1867-1962; Maurice Ollivier, Q.C., LL.D, F.R.S.C., Parliament Counsel, House of Commons, Government of Canada, Ottawa 1962

The Canadian Encyclopedia, Pages 1052-1059, Volume 2, Second Edition; Hurtig Publishers Ltd., 1988

Consolidation of Indian Legislation Report: Volume I, United Kingdom and Canada; Gail Hinge under contract to the Department of Indian and Northern Affairs, Ottawa, date unknown

History of Grand Lodge of British Columbia 1871-1970; Grand Lodge of British Columbia, A.F. & A.M.,1971

Old Square-Toes and His Lady: The Life of James and Amelia Douglas; John Adams, 2001

Frontier Days in British Columbia; edited by Garnet Basque, Sunfire Publications Ltd., 1993

The Carrier: My People; Lizette Hall, Quesnel, British Columbia, 1992

Dakelh Keyoh: The Souther Carrier in Earlier Times; Elizabeth Furniss, Quesnel, B.C., 1993

Justice in Paradise; Bruce Clark, Montreal, Quebec, 1999

The Province; A 46, Sunday, April 4TH, 1999 (**Clark finally disbarred. Ontario ruling kills courtroom career of outspoken advocate of native land claims**).

The Old West: The Canadians; Time-Life Books, Alexandria, Virginia, 1977

The Metis In The Canadian West, Volumes 1 & 2; Marcel Giraud, translated from French to English by George Woodcock, 1986

THE METIS: CANADA'S FORGOTTEN PEOPLE; D. BRUCE SEALEY AND ANTOINE S. LUSSIER, 1975

CANADIAN DIMENSION; PAGES 2 - 6, VOLUME 19, NUMBER 5, DECEMBER 1985 (CANADA'S METIS PEOPLES OF THE WEST).

ENCYCLOPEDIA OF FREEMASONRY VOLUMES 1 & 2; THE MASONIC HISTORY COMPANY (U.S.A.), 1924

THE GLOBE & MAIL; D 4, SATURDAY, JULY 11TH, 1992 (**LOUIS RIEL**; WAS HE MARTYR, TRAITOR, MADMAN OR SAINT?).

THE VANCOUVER SUN; B 1, SEPTEMBER 12TH, 1998 (BATTLE OF BATOCHE WAS LOUIS RIEL'S WATERLOO).

MACLEAN'S NEWSMAGAZINE; PAGES 68 & 69, JULY 1ST, 2001 (**A REBEL AT HEART? A YOUNG WILFRID LAURIER PUSHED FOR QUEBEC SOVEREIGNTY**).

THE VANCOUVER SUN; A 1 AND A 8, SATURDAY, AUGUST 25TH, 2001 (LEGISLATURE IS ON OUR LAND: B.C. NATIVES, GOVERNMENTS ARE ' TRESPASSING, ' BANDS CLAIM IN LAWSUIT).

THE VANCOUVER SUN; A 15, (COMMENTARY PAGE), THURSDAY, AUGUST 29TH, 2001 (**A CAPITAL IDEA**. CLAIMS BY TWO INDIAN BANDS THAT THE B.C. LEGISLATURE IS AN UNWELCOMED SQUATTER ON THEIR LAND PROVIDED A WONDERFUL OPPORTUNITY TO MOVE THE SEAT OF GOVERNMENT BACK TO WHERE IT SHOULD BE).

THE ARMED FORCES OF CANADA 1867-1967; DIRECTORATE OF HISTORY, CANADIAN FORCES HEADQUARTERS, GOVERNMENT OF CANADA, OTTAWA 1967

MEN IN THE SHADOWS: THE SHOCKING TRUTH ABOUT THE RCMP SECURITY SERVICE; JOHN SAWATSKY, 1983

RCMP VS THE PEOPLE: INSIDE CANADA'S SECURITY SERVICE; EDWARD MANN, PROFESSOR OF SOCIOLOGY, YORK UNIVERSITY AND JOHN ALAN LEE, ASSOCIATE PROFESSOR OF SOCIOLOGY, UNIVERSITY OF TORONTO, 1979

Imperfect Union: Canadian Labour & the Left (Part 1: International Background – CanadianRoots); CBC, date unknown

Imperfect Union: Canadian Labour & the Left (Part 2: Born On Hard Times); CBC, date unknown

The Hammer, The Sickle and the Maple Leaf; Simon Fraser University, 1989

Canada's Sweetheart: The Saga of Hal C. Banks; CBC, date unknown

Angry Society; Colin Alexander, Yellowknife, Northwest Territories, 1976

Dene Nation, **the colony within**; edited by Mel Watkins for the University League for Social Reform, University of Toronto Press, 1977

Dene Nation Annual Report 1983; Dene National Assembly, Yellowknife, Northwest Territories

Maclean's Newsmagazine; Page 48, January 14TH, 2002 (**The founding scoundrel. A wee bit of a peek into Sir John A. MacDonald's good qualities as a human being**).

The English Parliament; Kenneth R. Mackenzie, 1950

A Monarchy Transformed: Britain 1603-1714; Mark Kishlansky, 1996

1867: How The Fathers Made A Deal; Christopher Moore, 1997

The Unjust Society: the tragedy of Canada's Indians; Harold Cardinal, 1969

The Vancouver Sun; A 12, Wednesday, April 26TH, 2000 (Native kids ' used for experiments '. Federal health tests in B.C. and Ontario residential schools in the 1940's and '50's).

Letter from RCMP Security Classification Office, Ottawa, May 17th, 1999 (Informing Benoit LePage that they received his application form for a photo-copy of the 1975 Report titled "RED POWER - CANADA").

Letter from RCMP Security Classification Office, Ottawa, June 3rd, 1999 (In response to Benoit LePage's request for a photo-copy of the 1975 Report titled "RED POWER - CANADA". RCMP Ottawa in turn gave LePage the necessary access file numbers to retrieve the files from the National Achieves of Canada).

Letter from National Archives of Canada, Ottawa, May 16th, 2000 (Informing Benoit LePage that they received his letter of request, asking for a photo-copy of the 1975 RCMP Report in accordance to the Freedom of Information Act. Also contained in this letter were details letting it be known to the person requesting the information that a search had been conducted using the reference and catalogue numbers submitted to them but the documentation was not to be found).

Priorities In Policing - Terrorism and V.I.P. Security; compiled by RCMP Ottawa, 1975

Protests & Demonstrations By North American Indians 1973 to 1977; National Archives of Canada, Record of the Canadian Intelligence Service, RG 146, Volume 26, File Number 93-A-00048 Part 1

The Ottawa Journal, Ottawa, Ontario: August 7th, 1975 (Red Power ' threat ' defused).

Globe & Mail, Toronto, Ontario; August 7th, 1975 (Red Power groups called threat to stability).

UNNAMED NEWSPAPER, Montreal, Quebec; August 7th, 1975 (Red Power poses no threat to security, says Mountie).

The Vancouver Sun; A 4, Monday, March 18th, 2002 (**RCMP** kept secret ' **Red Power** ' file on dissident natives. Fear of armed

CONFRONTATION WITH NATIVES REVEALED IN NEWLY RELEASED DOCUMENTS FROM '70'S).

LETTER FROM KEN RUBIN CONSULTING SERVICES, OTTAWA, MARCH 26TH, 2002 (PHOTO-COPIES OF THE DOCUMENTATION AS IT PERTAINED TO THE **RED POWER-CANADA PHOTOGRAPH ALBUM**).

THE GLOBE & MAIL; A 2, DECEMBER 3RD, 1997 (A MISSION TO EMBARRASS THE BIGWIGS. WHEN KEN RUBIN DIGS FOR INFORMATION THE NATION'S BUREAUCRATS START TO SWEAT).

MACLEAN'S NEWSMAGAZINE; PAGES 16 - 19, OCTOBER 9TH, 2000 (**FAREWELL TO A TITAN**, PIERRE ELLIOTT TRUDEAU PASSES AWAY — AND THE COUNTRY RESPONDS WITH AN OUTPOURING OF EMOTION).

MACLEAN'S NEWSMAGAZINE; T 1 - T 32, OCTOBER 9TH, 2000 (PIERRE ELLIOTT TRUDEAU 1919 - 2000, CANADA'S CHAMPION).

CANADIAN DIMENSION; PAGE 5, VOLUME 19, NUMBER 5, DECEMBER 1985 (NORTH AMERICAN INDIANPOPULATION STATISTICS).

CHAPTER 7 - RED POWER – CANADA

A History Of French Louisiana: Volume Five, The Company of The Indies 1723-1731; Marcel Giraud, translated from French to English by Brian Pearce, 1987

Men In The Shadows: The Shocking Truth About The RCMP Security Service; John Sawatsky, 1983

RCMP vs The People: Inside Canada's Security Service; Edward Mann, Professor of Sociology, York University and John Alan Lee, Associate Professor of Sociology, University of Toronto, 1979

Imperfect Union: Canadian Labour and the Left (Part 1: International Background – CanadianRoots); CBC, date unknown

Imperfect Union: Canadian Labour and the Left (Part 2: Born On Hard Times); CBC, date   unknown

The Hammer, The Sickle and the Maple Leaf; Simon Fraser Universtity, 1989

Canada's Sweetheart: The Saga of Hal C. Banks; CBC, date unknown

Justice in Paradise; Bruce Clark, Montreal, Quebec, 1999

The Province; A 46, Sunday, April 4TH, 1999 (**Clark finally disbarred. Ontario ruling kills courtroom career of outspoken advocate of native land claims**).

Angry Society; Colin Alexander, Yellowknife, Northwest Territories, 1976

Dene Nation, **the colony within**; edited by Mel Watkins for the University League for Social Reform, University of Toronto Press, 1977

MACLEAN'S NEWSMAGAZINE; PAGES 34 - 36, JULY 17TH, 2000 (NEW PIPE DREAMS. IN THE 1970'S, NATIVE PROTESTS HELPED STOP THE MACKENZIE VALLEY PIPELINE. NOW, NATIVE LEADERS WANT TO SEE IT BUILT).

TIME MAGAZINE; PAGES 22-24, JULY 20TH, 1998 (**MARCHING TO THE BRINK**. NORTHERN IRELAND'S MUCH-VAUNTED PEACE AGREEMENT IS BEING PUT TO A FIERY TEST, BUT THERE ARE ALSOENCOURAGING SIGNS THAT THIS LATEST CRISIS IS DIFFERENT... THOUSANDS OF PROTESTANT ORANGE ORDER MEMBERS MARCH FOR PEACE OR BACK TO WAR).

MACLEAN'S NEWSMAGAZINE; PAGE 32, JULY 17TH, 2000 (THE ORANGE ORDER THREATENS IRISH PEACE).

MACLEANS NEWSMAGAZINE; PAGES 28 - 30, JULY 30TH, 2001 (**POLICING HATRED**. A CANADIAN COP IS HELPING OVERSEE THE TOUGH JOB OF BRINGING NORTHERN IRELAND'S POLICE FORCE INTO THE 21ST CENTURY).

THE FRAMEWORK OF A CHRISTIAN STATE; REV. E. CAHILL, DUBLIN, IRELAND, 1932

MASONIC BULLETIN, GRAND LODGE OF BRITISH COLUMBIA; VOLUME LII, NUMBER 2, OCTOBER 1988

ENCYCLOPEDIA OF FREEMASONRY VOLUMES 1 & 2; THE MASONIC HISTORY COMPANY (U.S.A.), 1924

THE GLOBE & MAIL; D 4, SATURDAY, JULY 11TH, 1992 (**LOUIS RIEL**; WAS HE MARTYR, TRAITOR, MADMAN OR SAINT?).

THE PROVINCE; A 14, MONDAY, NOVEMBER 26TH, 2001 (HALF NATIVE, HALF FRENCH – HALF FORGOTTEN).

CANADIAN DIMENSION; PAGES 2 - 6, VOLUME 19, NUMBER 5, DECEMBER 1985 (CANADA'S METISPEOPLES OF THE WEST).

CANADIAN GEOGRAPHIC; PAGES 36 - 48, VOLUME 115, NO. 2, MARCH/APRIL 1995 (KEEPING THE METIS FAITH ALIVE, ST. LAURENT, MANITOBA IS A FOCUS OF METIS HISTORY AND PRIDE).

MACLEAN'S NEWSMAGAZINE; PAGES 18 & 19. JULY 31ST, 2000 (RETURN OF AN ICON. A HISTORIC CHURCH   BELL MAY BE RESTORED TO ITS METIS ROOTS).

THE VANCOUVER SUN; B 1, SEPTEMBER 12TH, 1998 (BATTLE OF BATOCHE WAS LOUIS RIEL'S WATERLOO).

MACLEAN'S NEWSMAGAZINE; PETER C. NEWMAN ARTICLE, APRIL 12TH, 1999 (**REWRITING HISTORY: LOUIS RIEL AS A HERO**).

NATIONAL POST; FRONT PAGE COVERAGE, THURSDAY, OCTOBER 24TH, 2002 (**CBC TELEVISION BROADCAST –THE RETRIAL OF LOUIS RIEL**).

NATIONAL POST; A 12, THURSDAY, OCTOBER 24TH, 2002 (**THE RETRIAL OF LOUIS RIEL**).

NATIONAL POST; A 21, (EDITORIAL PAGE), THURSDAY, OCTOBER 24TH, 2002 (RIEL REBELLION).

MACLEAN'S NEWSMAGAZINE; PAGES 49 & 50, SEPTEMBER 4TH, 2000 (REOPENING THE HISTORY BOOKS. CANADIANS ARE WOEFULLY IGNORANT OF THE PAST).

THE VANCOUVER SUN; A 3, MONDAY, OCTOBER 9TH, 2000 (**CBC GAMBLES $25 MILLION ON OUR HISTORY**).

MACLEAN'S NEWSMAGAZINE; PAGES 62 - 66, OCTOBER 23RD, 2000 (**CBC'S CANADA: A PEOPLE'S   HISTORY ARRIVES AMID RENEWED FIXATION ON THE COUNTRY'S PAST. NOT THE SAME OLDSTORY**).

THE OLD WEST: THE CANADIANS; TIME-LIFE BOOKS, ALEXANDRIA, VIRGINIA, 1977

THE METIS IN THE CANADIAN WEST, VOLUMES 1 & 2; MARCEL GIRAUD, TRANSLATED FROM FRENCH TO ENGLISH BY GEORGE WOODCOCK, 1986

THE METIS: CANADA'S FORGOTTEN PEOPLE; D. BRUCE SEALEY AND ANTOINE S. LUSSIER, 1975

A Portrayal Of Our Metis Heritage; Metis Association of the Northwest Territories, 1976

Canada: A People's History (Episode 1: When The World Began); CBC, MM

Canada: A People's History (Episode 2: Adventurers And Mystics); CBC, MM

Canada: A People's History (Episode 3: Claiming The Wilderness); CBC, MM

Canada: A People's History (Episode 4: Battle For A Continent); CBC, MM

Canada: A People's History (Episode 5: A Question Of Loyalties); CBC, MM

Canada: A People's History (Episode 6: The Pathfinders); CBC, MMI

Canada: A People's History (Episode 7: Rebellion And Reform); CBC, MMI

Canada: A People's History (Episode 8: The Great Enterprise); CBC, MMI

Canada: A People's History (Episode 9: From Sea To Sea); CBC, MMI

Canada: A People's History (Episode 10: Taking The West); CBC, MMI

Canada: A People's History (Episode 11: The Great Transformation); CBC, MMI

Canada: A People's History (Episode 12: Ordeal By Fire); CBC, MMI

Canada: A People's History (Episode 13: Hard Times); CBC, MMI

Canada: A People's History (Episode 14: The Crucible); CBC, MMI

Canada: A People's History (Episode 15: Comfort And Fear); CBC, MMI

Canada: A People's History (Episode 16: Years Of Hope And Anger); CBC, MMI

Canada: A People's History (Episode 17: In An Uncertain World); CBC, MMI

Origins: A History Of Canada (The Origins of Canada's Indigenous Peoples); TV Ontario, The Ontario Educational Communications Authority, MCMLXXXVI

Origins: A History Of Canada (Displaced Persons); TV Ontario, The Ontario Educational Communications Authority, MCMLXXXVI

Summer Of The Loucheux: Portrait Of A Northern Indian Family; Tamahack Films, MCMXXXIII

Make Prayers to the Raven: The Bible and the Distant Time; KUAC-TV, University of Alaska- Fairbanks, 1987

IKWE; National Film Board of Canada, 1986

Kanehsatake: 270 Years of Resistance; National Film Board of Canada, 1993

Incident At Oglala; Carolco International & Spanish Fork Motion Picture Company, 1991

Northland (Summer Edition); CBC North, 1992

Masonic Antient News; Brother Francis " Frank " Goodwillie, Editor and Publisher , Surrey, British Columbia, Fall 1987

History of Grand Lodge of British Columbia 1871 - 1970; Grand Lodge of British Columbia, A.F. & A.M., 1971

The Northern Light: A Window For Freemasonry; Volume 21, Number 1, February 1990

Masonic List of Lodges; Grand Lodge of British Columbia, 1989

Masonic Bulletin, Grand Lodge of British Columbia; Volume LIII, Number 3, November 1990

Grand Lodge Bulletin, Volume 89, Number 1;Grand Lodge of Iowa, A.F. & A.M., March 1988

The Vancouver Sun; A 7, Tuesday, December 12th, 2000 (**MOVEMENT TO FREE LEONARD PELTIER GROWS**. Canada's application for clemency handed to U.S.   ambassador).

The Vancouver Sun; A 11, Saturday, December 16th, 2000 (FBI agents oppose clemency for Peltier. Hundreds of agents march around White House to show their opposition to freeing U.S. Indian activist).

Maclean's Newsmagazine; Pages 26 & 27, April 23rd, 2001 (Death Of A Warrior, Anna Mae Pictou-Aquash).

Letter from Canadian Security Intelligence Service, Ottawa, March 8th, 2000 (Informing Benoit LePage that Canada's very own spy agency was unable to locate the requested document titled " Red Power-Canada " but instead sent him Priorities In Policing - Terrorism and V.I.P.Security).

Letter from the Office of the Information Commissioner of Canada, Ottawa, March 23rd, 2000 (Letting Benoit LePage know that they received his initial complaint regarding the lack of co operation by our nation's very own spy agency).

Letter from the Office of the Information Commissioner of Canada, Ottawa, June 29th, 2000 (In response to Benoit LePage's complaint regarding CSIS).

Letter from the Office of the Information Commissioner of Canada, Ottawa, July 7th, 2000 (End result of the investigation concerning Benoit LePage's complaint against CSIS as it pertained to his request for the 1975 RCMP Report **RED POWER-CANADA**).

Letter from the Security Intelligence Review Committee, Ottawa, August 4TH, 2000 (Acknowledging that they had received his complaint concerning CSIS).

Letter from the Solicitor General of Canada, Ottawa, August 24TH, 2000 (In response to Benoit LePage's concerns regarding the lack of co-operation from CSIS).

Priorities In Policing - Terrorism and V.I.P. Security; compiled by RCMP Ottawa, 1975

Protests And Demonstrations By North American Indians Surveillance Report 1973-77; National Archives of Canada, Record of the Canadian Intelligence Service, RG 146, Volume 2676 File Number 93-A-00048

Maclean's Newsmagazine; Page 53, August 18TH, 1997 (**How Indian self-rule can bring prosperity**. While other bands dream of becoming provinces, the Sechelt, B.C., chiefs go about creating jobs and a better life).

The Province; A 6, Wednesday, January 27TH, 1999 (' **Sechelt got it right** '. Clark describes deal with Sunshine Coast band as 'real model ').

The Vancouver Sun; A 5, Saturday, April 17TH, 1999 (**Sechelt band-governments sign treaty**. The 900-member band is granted $ 42 million and 933 hectares of land).

The Vancouver Sun; A 1 & A 2, Saturday, May 15TH, 1999 (Indians irked as Ottawa upsets 11 band elections. Two band elections set aside in B.C. as the Indian affairs department defends its position by saying the complaints were initiated by members of the bands).

The Vancouver Sun; Front Page Coverage, Wednesay, May 31ST, 2000 (**Sechelt band to reject treaty that was hailed as ' shining light'**. The agreement provided the 900 members with land and $ 42 million).

The Vancouver Sun; A 2, Wednesday, May 31ˢᵀ, 2000 (Sechelt Band wants to keep tax exemptions. The agreement will be rejected today as part of a day of ceremonies).

The Province, A 5, Wednesday, May 31ˢᵀ, 2000 (**Sechelt Indian Band will sue for land**).

The Province; A 6, Thursday, June 1ˢᵀ, 2002 (In Sechelt: BC native groups say treaty process is dying — or dead).

The Vancouver Sun; B 10, Tuesday, November 26ᵀᴴ, 2002 (Sechelt band wants voice on local school board. ' Consistent representation ' required, says Chief Garry Feschuk).

The Province; A 26, (Editorial Page), Wednesday, April 5ᵀᴴ, 2001 (**Whose Roads?** Cheam Indian band members threaten an Oka-style confrontation on blockade).

The Vancouver Sun; B 8, Thursday, April 6ᵀᴴ, 2000 (Valley Indian band drops threats of toll booths. The Cheam band will meet today with provincial authorities to discuss a dispute over land use in the Rosedale-Agassiz area around an intersection of Highway 9).

The Province; A 33, (Letters to the Editor), Thursday, April 6ᵀᴴ, 2000 (**Let's blockade them**).

The Province; Front Page Coverage, Sunday, April 16ᵀᴴ, 2000 (**Quiet now, but will it Spread ?**Worried Frazer Valley residents fear a native roadblock will escalate into another summer of confrontation).

The Province; A 3, Sunday, April 16ᵀᴴ, 2000 (A line in the asphalt. Cheam block road in rural Aggasiz, threaten bridge toll in protest over park).

The Province; A 2, Monday, April 17ᵀᴴ, 2000 (RCMP ' keep the peace ' at Cheam Indian band blockade).

The Vancouver Sun; A 5, Monday, April 17ᵀᴴ, 2000 (Both sides talking tough in Cheam land dispute).

The Province; A 37, (Letter to the Editor), Wednesday, April 19th, 2000 (Warrior wear hurts natives. Plus 2nd letter; What else can they do? Negotiation just a sham).

The Province; A 8, Friday, April 21st, 2000 (Natives disrupt media briefing because of the total lack of news coverage concerning aboriginal grievances).

The Province; A 32, Sunday, April 23rd, 2000 (Cheam ' pawns ' in premier's plans).

The Ottawa Journal, Ottawa, Ontario; August 7th, 1975 (Red Power ' threat ' defused).

Globe & Mail, Toronto, Ontario; August 7th, 1975 (Red Power groups called threat to stability).

UNNAMED NEWSPAPER, Montreal, Quebec; August 7th, 1975 (Red Power poses no threat to security, says Mountie).

Letter from United Nations, Vienna International Centre in Austria, September 20th, 2000 (Acknowledging the receiving of Benoit LePage's letter of August 14th asking for whateverassistance they might be able to offer him).

Fifth United Nations Congress On The Prevention Of Crime And The Treatment Of Offenders; Geneva, 1-12 September, 1975, United Nations, New York, 1976

Sixth United Nations Congress On The Prevention Of Crime And The Treatment Of Offenders; Caracas, Venezuela, 25 August - 5 September 1980, United Nations, New York, 1981

The Vancouver Sun; Front Page Coverage, Tuesday, October 16th, 2001 (**Police get new powers to fight terrorism. ' Peace and security ' of Canadians at stake, federal minister says**).

Maclean's Newsmagazine; Pages 16-21, June 26th, 2000 (**ABUSE OF TRUST**. What happened behind the walls of residential church schools is a tragedy that has left native victims traumatized).

Maclean's Newsmagazine; Pages 22 & 23, June 26ᵀᴴ, 2000 (**NO FORGIVING.** Canada's largestchurches are reeling under litigation costs arising from their days running native residential schools).

The Vancouver Sun; A 9, Thursday, January 18ᵀᴴ, 2001 (Compensation claims to skyrocket, says   Chief. Coon Come is confident up to 60,000 people aren't included in the legal action over residential schools).

A Thief In The Night: The Death of Pope John Paul I; John Cornwell, 1989

Monopoly Men: The Distant Murmuring Of A Secret Government, (Phenomenon: The Lost Archives); Liberty International Entertainment Inc., 1999

www.**THE MONEY MASTERS.COM**

United Masters Lodge No. 167, Lodge of Masonic Research, Volume 24, Number 10; Grand Lodge of New Zealand, April 1982

American Historical Documents; Barnes & Noble Inc., College Outline Series, 1970

The New Webster's Encyclopedic Dictionary Of The English Language; Lexicon Publications Incorporated, New York, 1988

A History Of American Democracy; John D. Hicks, George E. Mowry and Robert Burke, 1966

The Vancouver Sun; A 3, Monday, August 27ᵀᴴ, 2001 (Native leader vows to expose Canada's ' ongoing racism ', Chief fears government ' will not tell the truth ' at UN conference in South Africa).

The Province; A 2, Wednesday, August 29ᵀᴴ, 2001 (Canada leery of UN conference that would brand Israel ' racist ').

The Province; A 24, (Editorial Page), Wednesday, August 29th, 2001 (Racism conference will do anything but reconcile our differences).

The Vancouver Sun; A 4, Wednesday, August 29th, 2001 (Canada may avoid conference on racism. Foreign affairs minister cites concerns about draft text condemning Israel as racist).

The Vancouver Sun; A 18, (Editorial Page), Thursday, August 30th, 2001 (Coon Come marginalizes himself and his people).

The Province; A 24, Friday, August 31st, 2001 (Manley won't talk racism).

The Province; A 24, Friday, August 31st, 2001 (Political disputes rule Durban talks).

The Province; A 31, (Editorial Page), Friday, August 31st, 2001 (Canada should recall UN racism delegation).

The Vancouver Sun; A 10, Friday, August 31st, 2001 (Manley won't attend UN conference on racism, Canada's foreign minister said the level of criticism against Israel ' is extreme ').

The Vancouver Sun; A 10, Friday, August 31st, 2001 (' Zionism is racism ' claim threatens UN conference, Arab activists disrupt press conference by Jewish groups at gathering in South Africa).

The Vancouver Sun; A 10, Saturday, September 1st, 2001 (Protesters peaceful at anti-racism conference).

The Vancouver Sun; A 16, (Editorial Page), Saturday, September 1st, 2001 (UN conference against racism is anything but. We should ignore whatever comes out of this farce).

The Vancouver Sun; A 9, Monday September 3rd, 2001 (Durban, South Africa – Outrage voiced at slavery talks, American black politicians angered by lack of African support for reparation, apology).

THE PROVINCE; A 14, TUESDAY, SEPTEMBER 4ᵀᴴ, 2001 (DURBAN, SOUTH AFRICA – CANADA DECLARES; WE WON'T QUIT RACISM MEET).

THE VANCOUVER SUN; A 3, TUESDAY, SEPTEMBER 4ᵀᴴ, 2001 (CANADA STAYS AT RACISM CONFERENCE).

THE VANCOUVER SUN; A 5, (NATIONAL NEWS) TUESDAY, SEPTEMBER 4ᵀᴴ, 2001 (ABORIGINAL CASES SWAMP COURTS).

THE GLOBE AND MAIL; A 12, TUESDAY, SEPTEMBER 4ᵀᴴ, 2001 (UN CONFERENCE AGAINST RACISM – U.S AND ISRAEL WITHDRAW DELEGATES).

THE VANCOUVER SUN; A 9, WEDNESDAY, SEPTEMBER 5ᵀᴴ, 2001 (MANLEY HINTS CANADA WILL WITHDRAW FROM RACISM TALKS OVER ISSUE OF ISRAEL).

THE VANCOUVER SUN; A 14, (EDITORIAL PAGE), WEDNESDAY, SEPTEMBER 5ᵀᴴ, 2001 (NO REASON TO STAY IN DURBAN. PLUS 2ᴺᴰ EDITORIAL COMMENT; UN BLABFEST ON RACISM A WASTE OF MONEY).

THE PROVINCE; A 12, WEDNESDAY, SEPTEMBER 5ᵀᴴ, 2001 (CANADA STAYS AT RACISM TALKS).

THE PROVINCE; A 20, (EDITORIAL PAGE), WEDNESDAY, SEPTEMBER 5ᵀᴴ, 2001 (HEDY FRY MUST WITHDRAW FROM UN RACISM CONFERENCE).

THE PROVINCE; A 3, THURSDAY, SEPTEMBER 6ᵀᴴ, 2001 (FRY GAVE $ 2 MILLION TO GROUPS FOR RACISM MEETING).

THE PROVINCE; A 3, THURSDAY, SEPTEMBER 6ᵀᴴ, 2001 (UN DELEGATES HUNT FOR COMPROMISES).

THE VANCOUVER SUN; A 5, (NATIONAL NEWS), THURSDAY, SEPTEMBER 6TH, 2001 (OTTAWA FINANCED RACISM LOBBYING TO THE TUNE OF $ 2 MILLION).

THE VANCOUVER SUN; A 11, THURSDAY, SEPTEMBER 6ᵀᴴ, 2001 (CANADA STILL TRYING TO END IMPASSE AT RACISM TALKS. DELEGATION LEADER HEDY FRY SAYS PROCEEDINGS IN SOUTH AFRICA ARE AT A CRITICAL STAGE).

THE VANCOUVER SUN; A 17, (COMMENTARY PAGE), THURSDAY, SEPTEMBER 6TH, 2001 (TRUTH ABOUT SLAVERY NOT THAT SIMPLE).

THE VANCOUVER SUN; A 7, FRIDAY, SEPTEMBER 7TH, 2001 (RACISM CONFERENCE USELESS, CHRETIEN SAYS. THE PRIME MINISTER CRITICIZES THE MEETING'S ISRAEL-BASHING AND FIRST NATIONS' COMPLAINT ABOUT OTTAWA'S TREATMENT OF NATIVES).

THE VANCOUVER SUN; A 17, (COMMENTARY PAGE), FRIDAY, SEPTEMBER 7TH, 2001 (**A NATION IN DENIAL**. IN CONTRAST TO CANADIANS' AWARENESS ABOUT NATIVE RESIDENTIAL SCHOOLS, AMERICANS ARE IGNORANT ABOUT THEIR OWN SAD INDIAN LEGACY).

THE VANCOUVER SUN; A 12, SATURDAY, SEPTEMBER 8TH, 2001 (ANTI-RACISM CONFERENCE GOES INTO OVERTIME).

THE PROVINCE; A 33, SUNDAY, SEPTEMBER 9TH, 2001 (CANADA RAPS ATTACK ON ISRAEL).

THE VANCOUVER SUN: A 8, MONDAY, SEPTEMBER 10TH, 2001 (UGLY RACISM CONFERENCE ENDS).

MACLEAN'S NEWSMAGAZINE; PAGES 14 & 17, SEPTEMBER 10TH, 2001 (**FURORE AT RACISM CONFERENCE**, PAGE 14 WHILE ON PAGE 17; **DURBAN'S TIN-POT TYRANTS**).

THE PROVINCE; A 10, THURSDAY, JULY 19TH, 2001 (HALIFAX – WE CAN BRING CANADA TO A STANDSTILL: CHIEFS SAY).

THE PROVINCE; A 24, SUNDAY, JULY 29TH, 2001 (CHIEFS' HOSTILITY TO NEW RULES HURTS MEMBERS AS COAST-TO-COAST BLOCKADES ARE THREATENED).

MACLEAN'S NEWSMAGAZINE; PAGE 13, JULY 30TH, 2001 (HALIFAX – **NOTHING TO LOOSE**).

THE PROVINCE; A 25, WEDNESDAY, DECEMBER 5TH, 2001 (CHIEFS WORKING ON INDIAN ACT STANCE).

THE VANCOUVER SUN; A 8, (EDITORIAL PAGE), MONDAY, JUNE 17TH, 2002 (**CHANGES TO INDIAN ACT ARE ALL ABOUT POWER.** IF NATIVES HAVE A WORKABLE ALTERNATIVE ON ACCOUNTABILITY, LETS HEAR IT).

NATIONAL POST; B 3, THURSDAY, JULY 11TH, 2002 (OTTAWA AIMS TO RESTART STALLED TALKS ON TREATIES).

THE VANCOUVER SUN; A 7, SATURDAY, JULY 15TH, 2002 (INDIAN ACT CHANGES GET COLD RECEPTION FROM NATIVE CHIEFS).

THE REPORT NEWSMAGAZINE; PAGES 14 - 18, VOLUME 29, NUMBER 16, AUGUST 12TH, 2002 (FURTHER AND FURTHER APART: OTTAWA SEEMS DETERMINED TO BUILD A PERMANENT GULF BETWEEN CANADA'S INDIANS AND NON-NATIVES).

THE PROVINCE; A 20, MONDAY, AUGUST 27TH, 2002 (INDIAN ACT TALKS BACK ON AFTER HIATUS).

THE PROVINCE; A 2, TUESDAY, JULY 31ST, 2001 (O CANADA LYRICS CALLED SEXIST).

THE VANCOUVER SUN; A 1 & A 4, MONDAY, JANUARY 15TH, 2001 (**NO MORE MR. NICE GUY,** NATIVE ACTIVIST VOWS. BILL WILSON TAKES AGGRESSIVE PATH FOR REFORM IN B.C. TREATY PROCESS).

THE VANCOUVER SUN; A 7, THURSDAY, MAY 10TH, 2001 (WHEN DELGAMUUKW SPEAKS, THE PREMIER LISTENS. A NATIVE INDIAN LEADER AND DOSANJH AGREE THE LIBERAL'S PLEDGE OF A REFERENDUM ON TREATIES IS RECIPE FOR DISASTER).

THE PROVINCE; FRONT PAGE COVERAGE, FRIDAY, JULY 20TH, 2001 (NATIVES THREATEN B.C. BLOCKADES OVER REFERENDUM).

THE PROVINCE; A 3, FRIDAY, JULY 20TH, 2001 (**" WAR COUNCIL "** TO BATTLE LAND-CLAIM REFERENDUM).

THE PROVINCE; A 4, WEDNESDAY, JULY 25TH, 2001 (NATIVE REFERENDUM ' STUPID IDEA ', SAYS LEADER).

THE VANCOUVER SUN; A 3, THURSDAY, JULY 26TH, 2001 (FEDERAL MINISTER CALLS FOR CALM ON LAND CLAIMS. NAULT SAYS REFERENDUM NOT PREFERRED OPTION).

The Province; A 11, Friday, July 27th, 2001 (Nault stares down Campbell on treaties).

The Vancouver Sun; A 9, (Commentary Page), Monday, July 30th, 2001 (An olive branch is extended as First Nations' leader Bill Wilson complains that his moderate messages have been ignored by the media).

Maclean's Newsmagazine; Pages 23 & 24, September 3rd, 2001 (Time for amends. A land- claims referendum could derail key negotiations with B.C.'s natives).

The Vancouver Sun; A 10, Tuesday, June 8th, 1999 (' **Oldest Indian** ' sues federal government for **$ 1.5** million, for land. The Paul Cree band has been pressing its claim for decades).

The Vancouver Sun; A 1 & A 8, Saturday, August 25th, 2001 (Legislature is on our land: B.C. natives, Governments are 'trespassing, ' bands claim in lawsuit).

The Vancouver Sun; A 15, (Commentary Page), Thursday, August 29th, 2001 (**A capital idea**. Claims by two Indian bands that the B.C. legislature is an unwelcomed squatter on their land provided a wonderful opportunity to move the seat of government back to where it should be).

The Province; Front Page Coverage, Tuesday, October 31st, 2000 (Gitxsan lay claim to ' every in of land ').

The Province; A 3, Tuesday, October 31st, 2000 (Gitxsan seek absolute title. Natives return landmark case to Supreme Court for title over private land).

Financial Post; C 1, Tuesday, August 7th, 2001 (B.C. natives threaten to cap massive gasfield development, ' We have to protect our rights, our lands ').

Financial Post; C 6, Tuesday, August 7th, 2001 (Industry urges B.C. to resolve native issues).

The Province; Front Page Coverage, Wednesday, March 6th, 2002 (**Offshore oil is ours, say Haida**).

The Province; A 3, Wednesday, March 6th, 2002 (**Queen Charlottes and offshore oilfields are ours, Haida say**).

The Province; Front Page Coverage, Thursday, March 7th, 2002, ('**This is our land to keep, ' claim Haida**).

The Province; A 3, Thursday, March 7th, 2002 ('**We were here first'** claim the Haida First Nation Peoples and threaten to establish own sovereign state if things can't be worked out).

The Province; Front Page Coverage, Friday, March 8th, 2002 (**Now natives sue to evict our ferries!**).

The Province; A 3, Friday, March 8th, 2002 (**Natives try to shut down superport and ferry terminal**).

The Vancouver Sun; A 1 - A 4, Friday, November 22nd, 1996 (**The Royal Commission on Aboriginal Peoples.** Schools aimed to 'kill the Indian in the child.' A royal commission reveals the horrors that the church-run, state-regulated residential schools inflicted on aboriginals).

The Vancouver Sun; A 11, Tuesday, October 31st, 2001 (Natives offered deal on abuse claims. The federal government acting without the churches, offers settlement on Indians).

The Vancouver Sun; A 9, Friday, June 28th, 2002 (Churches may get charity credit to pay for residential school lawsuits. Ottawa reconsiders a plan first proposed by ecumenical group that would put federal government on the hook for a bigger proportion of damages for 11,000 lawsuits).

The Vancouver Sun; A 8, Wednesday, November 20th, 2002 (**Anglican Church, Ottawa reach abuse-compensation deal.** Church could pay up to $ 25 million to native Indians sexually abused at residential schools).

National Post; A 10, Thursday, November 21ST, 2002 (Compensation plan reached for residential school abuse).

The Vancouver Sun; A 4, Saturday, December 14TH, 2002 (**Church settles claims.** National Presbyterians second to agree with government on native students' compensation).

The Vancouver Sun; A 16, Saturday, December 21ST, 2002 (Ottawa speeds up abuse suits. Natives choosing to take advantage of a faster process would have to waive rights).

The Province; Front Page Coverage, Friday, June 22ND, 2001 (Majority backs B.C. referendum on native treaties in our poll taken).

The Province; A 7, Friday, June 22ND, 2001 (Majority of B.C. residents back referendum on native treaties).

The Province; A 25, Wednesday, December 5TH, 2001 (Sham treaty referendum leaves Ottawa cold).

The Province; A 12, Wednesday, March 27TH, 2002 (Referendum ballot mail out).

The Province; A 12, (Letters to the Editor), Wednesday, March 27TH, 2002 (No point to 'referendumb').

Coast Reporter, Gibsons, British Columbia; A 1 & A 7, Sunday, April 7TH, 2002 (Treaty Ballot – Mistrust deepens over vote).

Coast Reporter, Gibsons, B.C.; A 11, (Letters to the Editor), Sunday, April 14TH, 2002 (Referendum ballot boycott wrong answer).

The Province; Front Page Coverage, Friday, April 5TH, 2002 (Angry bishops bash native   referendum).

The Province; A 3, Friday, April 5TH, 2002 (Anglicans and natives challenge referendum).

THE PROVINCE; A 4, MONDAY, APRIL 8TH, 2002 (CONGREGATIONS TOLD TO SAY NO TO REFERENDUM. ANGLICANS PRAISE BISHOPS, EVEN IF THEY DON'T AGREE).

THE PROVINCE; A 14, (LETTERS TO THE EDITOR), MONDAY, APRIL 8TH, 2002 (ANGLICAN CHURCH CONDEMNING NATIVE TREATY REFERENDUM SUSPICIOUS).

THE VANCOUVER SUN; A 10, (EDITORIAL PAGE), TUESDAY, APRIL 9TH, 2002 (RELIGIOUS LEADERS ARE RIGHT TO SPEAK OUT ON REFERENDUM).

THE VANCOUVER SUN; A 11, (LETTERS TO THE EDITOR), TUESDAY, APRIL 9TH, 2002 (THE REFERENDUM SPIN. WHILE SOME READERS COMPLAIN THAT THE LIBERALS HAVE STACKED THE DECK, OTHERS ARE HAPPY TO BE ASKED THEIR OPINION. MEANWHILE, THE CLERGY IS REMINDED ABOUT THE SEPARATION OF CHURCH AND STATE).

THE VANCOUVER SUN; B 1, TUESDAY, APRIL 9TH, 2002 (LIBERALS LIKENED TO DICTATORSHIP ON TREATY VOTE. DISCOUNTING ' NO ' VOTES REMINDS CLERIC OF ONE-PARTY STATE TACTICS).

THE PROVINCE; A 8, TUESDAY, APRIL 9TH, 2002 (REFERENDUM BALLOTS POURING IN).

THE PROVINCE; A 19, (LETTERS TO THE EDITOR), WEDNESDAY, APRIL 10TH, 2002 (THE NATIVE TREATY REFERENDUM SHAM ALL THE WAY AROUND).

THE PROVINCE; A 18, (OPINION PAGE), THURSDAY, APRIL 11TH, 2002 (AND NOW, RAFE'S REASONS FORRETURNING BLANK REFERENDUM).

THE PROVINCE; A 18, (OPINION PAGE), FRIDAY, APRIL 12TH, 2002 (VOTE 'NO ' IF YOU WANT – BUT VOTE).

THE PROVINCE; A 19, (LETTERS TO THE EDITOR), FRIDAY, APRIL 12TH, 2002 (REFERENDUM JUST ' MORE GOV'T WASTE ').

THE PROVINCE; A 12, MONDAY, APRIL 15TH, 2002 (FIRST NATIONS FIND SUPPORT IN SMALL TOWNS).

THE PROVINCE; A 23, THURSDAY, MARCH 28TH, 2002 (COURT WON'T HALT TREATY REFERENDUM).

THE PROVINCE; A 10, THURSDAY, MAY 16TH, 2002 (NATIVES LOSE BID TO BLOCK BALLOT COUNT).

THE VANCOUVER SUN; B 4, THURSDAY, MAY 16TH, 2002 (**34 PER CENT OF BALLOTS RETURNED.** REFERENDUM ON TREATY TALKS SENT TO 2.1 MILLION PEOPLE).

NATIONAL POST; A 1, THURSDAY, JULY 4TH, 2002 (**TREATY PLAN WINS LARGE MAJORITY.** PROVINCE READY TO ' GET ON WITH THE TASK ' AFTER CONTROVERSIAL REFERENDUM, PREMIER SAYS).

NATIONAL POST; A 6, THURSDAY, JULY 4TH, 2002 (PROVINCE ' NOT ON SAME PLANET ' AS NATIVES).

CARIBOO OBSERVER, QUESNEL, BRITISH COLUMBIA; A 2, SUNDAY JULY 7TH, 2002 (TREATY REFERENDUM WINS MAJORITY, NORTH CARIBOO SUPPORTS HARD LINE).

CARIBOO OBSERVER, QUESNEL, BRITISH COLUMBIA; A 8, (OPINION PAGE), SUNDAY, JULY 7TH, 2002 (REFERENDUM UNDERWHELMING).

CARIBOO OBSERVER, QUESNEL, BRITISH COLUMBIA; PAGES A 1 & A 20, WEDNESDAY, JULY 10TH, 2002 (RED BLUFF INDIAN BAND CHIEF SLAMS REFERENDUM).

Chapter 8 - THROUGH A MASONIC LOOKING GLASS

CANADA SINCE 1945: POWER, POLITICS, AND PROVINCIALISM; ROBERT BOTHWELL, IAN DRUMMOND AND JOHN ENGLISH, 1981

ONE CANADA: MEMOIRS OF THE RIGHT HONOURABLE JOHN G. DIEFENBAKER; JOHN DIEFENBAKER, 1975

CANADA: A POLITICAL & SOCIAL HISTORY; EDGAR MCINNIS, FORMERLY A PROFESSOR OF HISTORY, YORK   UNIVERSITY, 1982

READINGS IN CANADIAN HISTORY: POST-CONFEDERATION; R. DOUGLAS FRANCIS AND DONALD B. SMITH, 1982

SEPARATISM: A POSITIVE RESPONSE FROM ENGLISH CANADA; BRIAN A. BROWN, WITH A FORWARD BYRENE LEVESQUE, 1976

THE NEW CONFEDERATION: FIVE SOVEREIGN PROVINCES; BRIAN A. BROWN, WITH A FORWARD BY W.A.C. BENNETT, 1977

CITY FOR SALE: INTERNATIONAL FINANCIERS TAKE A MAJOR NORTH AMERICAN CITY BY STORM; HENRY AUBIN, MONTREAL, QUEBEC, 1977

THE EGYPTIAN BOOK OF THE DEAD; E.A. WALLIS BUDGE, LATE KEEPER OF ASSYRIAN AND EGYPTIAN ANTIQUITIES IN THE BRITISH MUSEUM, ORIGINALLY PUBLISHED IN 1895BY THE TRUSTEES OF THE MUSEUM, REPRINTED 1967

THE FRAMEWORK OF A CHRISTIAN STATE; REV. E. CAHILL, DUBLIN, IRELAND, 1932

CULTS AND NEW FAITHS; JOHN BUTTERWORTH, 1981

IRAN 1979; CHANNEL 4 TELEVISION COMPANY LIMITED, 1989

Portraits of Power: Remaking The World (Islam); a Steven York Film, date unknown

The Iran-Contra Affair; Frontline, April 23rd, 1991 (Corporation For Public Broadcasting)

The Secret Government: The Constitution In Crisis, (an expose of the Iran-Contra Affair and other U.S. Governmental imposed wars against various nations worldwide); Public Affairs Television Inc., 1987

The Secret Files: Washington, Israel & The Gulf; The Washington Post Company Television Production, 1992

The Bank of Crooks and Criminals: The World's Sleaziest Bank; Frontline, April 21st, 1992

Washington Monument: The Unraveling of the Bank of Credit and Commerce; CBS News 60 Minutes, date unknown

The Man Who Made Saddam Hussein's Supergun: Canadian Scientist Gerald Bull; Frontline, February 12th, 1991

Gerald Bull's Supergun; BCTV Evening News, October 8th, 1991

The Heroes of Desert Storm; a 1991 made for T.V. movie which aired throughout North America on October 6th, 1991 glorifying the Persian Gulf war (Part One), with an introduction by U.S. President George Bush Senior

Iraq: The Cradle of Civilization, (Legacy); date and production unknown

The Diabolical Minds of Adolf Hitler and Saddam Hussein, (Unsolved Mysteries); date and production unknown

Saddam's Killing Fields; Frontline, March 31st, 1992 (Corporation For Public Broadcasting)

Saddam's Killing Fields; CBS News 60 Minutes, date unknown

United States Government Funnels Arms and Money to Iraq Through an Italian Banking System (BNL in Atlanta, Georgia); ABC News Nightline, May 2ND, 1991

U.S. President George Bush Under Investigation Regarding the BNL Scandal and Its Subsequent Cover-Up By His Administration; ABC News Nightline, July 7TH, 1992

The Arming of Saudi Arabia; Frontline, February 16TH, 1993

Saddam Hussein & King Hussein of Jordan; CBS News 60 Minutes, 1991

Hell Fighters of Kuwait; Nova, 1991

Jews, Movies, Hollywoodism and the American Dream; 1171086 Ontario Ltd., 1997

The Hollywood 10 Blacklist; date and production unknown

G-MEN: The Rise of J. Edgar Hoover, (The American Experience); date and production   unknown

Watergate: The Secret Story; CBS Inc. and Post/Newsweek Television Stations, MCMXCII

The Kennedy Assassinations: Coincidence Or Conspiracy; Entertainment Tonight, July 6TH, 1992

I Know What I Saw, (JFK's Assassination); ABC News 20/20, date unknown

CIA Assassinated JFK, (an interview with Mark Lane the author of " Plausible Denial " implicating the CIA's involvement); Northwest Afternoon, 1992

The Plot To Kill President Kennedy: From The De-Classified Files; date and production unknown

The Knights Templar; Sophistory & Westbrook Films, MM

Monopoly Men: The Distant Murmuring Of A Secret Government, (Phenomenon: The Lost Archives); Liberty International Entertainment Inc., 1999

www.THE MONEY MASTERS.COM

Secret Societies: Freemasonry and the Bonesmen, (The Unexplained); A & E Television Network, 1998

The Skulls, (a suspense made for T.V. movie of the Bonesmen); Universal Pictures, 2000

Inspector Morse: In The Masonic Mysteries, (a series of Three Freemasonry Stories of Murder and Betrayal); BBC Television, MCMXC

The Northern Light: A Window For Freemasonry; Volume 21, Number 1, February 1990

History Of Canada For High Schools; Duncan McArthue, M.A., F.R.S.C., Douglas Professor of Colonial and Canadian History, Queen's University, Kingston, 1930

Our Canada; Arthur G. Dorland, M.A., Ph.D., University of Western Ontario, 1949

A Nation Developing; J.A. Lower, 1970 (Brief History of Canada for Secondary Schools for the Province of British Columbia).

Our Land: Building The West; Gage Educational Publishing Company for High Schools in Canada, 1987

Canada: A People's History (Episode 1: When The World Began): CBC, MM

Canada: A People's History (Episode 2: Adventurers And Mystics); CBC, MM

Canada: A People's History (Episode 3: Claiming The Wilderness); CBC, MM

Canada: A People's History (Episode 4: Battle For A Continent); CBC, MM

Canada: A People's History (Episode 5: A Question Of Loyalties); CBC, MM

Canada: A People's History (Episode 6: The Pathfinders); CBC, MMI

Canada: A People's History (Episode 7: Rebellion And Reform); CBC, MMI

Canada: A People's History (Episode 8: The Great Enterprise); CBC, MMI

Canada: A People's History (Episode 9: From Sea To Sea); CBC, MMI

Canada: A People History (Episode 10: Taking The West); CBC, MMI

Canada: A People's History (Episode 11: The Great Transformation); CBC, MMI

Canada: A People's History (Episode 12: Ordeal By Fire); CBC, MMI

Canada: A People's History (Episode 13: Hard Times); CBC, MMI

Canada: A People's History (Episode 14: The Crucible); CBC, MMI

Canada: A People's History (Episode 15: Comfort And Fear); CBC, MMI

Canada: A People's History (Episode 16: Years Of Hope And Anger); CBC, MMI

Canada: A People's History (Episode 17: In An Uncertain World); CBC, MMI

Free Trade: The Full Story; David Orchard, 1988

The Star-Phoenix, Saskatoon, Saskatchewan; (Opinion/Commentary) Thursday, June 22ND, 1989 (Anti-free traders try to cash in on tragedy).

The Star-Phoenix, Saskatoon, Saskatchewan; A 5, (Forum), Wednesday, July 19TH, 1989 (Media coverage warps anti-free trade message).

The Vancouver Sun; A 8, Wednesday, January 22ND, 2003 (Undaunted Orchard aims to lead Tories. The Saskatchewan farmer is noted for his opposition to the free trade agreement).

The Vancouver Sun; A 22, (Editorial Page), January 25TH, 2002 (Maverick Orchard shakes up Tory race again).

A History of American Democracy; John D. Hicks, George E. Mowry and Robert Burke, 1966

Egypt: The Cradle Of Ancient Masonry; Volume 1, Norman Frederick de Clifford, Macoy Publishing and Masonic Supply Company, New York, 1907

Encyclopedia of Freemasonry Volumes 1 & 2: The Masonic History Company (U.S.A.), 1924

Masonic Ancient News; Brother Francis " Frank " Goodwillie, Editor and Publisher, Surrey, British Columbia, Fall 1987

Masonic Bulletin, Grand Lodge of British Columbia; Volume XL, Number 3, November 1976

Masonic Bulletin, Grand Lodge of British Columbia; Volume LIII, Number 9, May 1991

To A Non-Mason: You Must Seek Masonic Membership; Henry C. Claussen, 33RD degreeSovereign Grand Commander, The Supreme Council, 33RD degree, Ancient And Accepted

Scottish Rite Of Freemasonry, Mother Jurisdiction Of The World, 1976

The High Twelvian; Volume 63, Number 3, George Washington - Master Mason, Our FirstPresident, Winter 1989

How To Respond To The Lodge; L. James Rongstad, 1977

Should A Christian Be A Mason?; E.M. Storms, 1980

The Facts On The Masonic Lodge, Does Masonry Conflict With The Christian Faith?; John Ankerberg and John Weldon, 1989

Freemasonry: The Invisible Cult In Our Midst, A Biblical Expose of Freemasonry; written by a former Worshipful Master, Jack Harris, 1983

Men In The Shadows: The Shocking Truth About The RCMP Security Service; John Sawatsky. 1983

RCMP vs The People: Inside Canada's Security Service; Edward Mann, Professor of Sociology, York University and John Alan Lee, Associate Professor of Sociology, University of Toronto, 1979

Imperfect Union: Canadian Labour and the Left (Part 1: International Background – CanadianRoots); CBC, date unknown

Imperfect Union: Canadian Labour and the Left (Part 2: Born On Hard Times); CBC, date   unknown

The Hammer, The Sickle and the Maple Leaf; Simon Fraser University, 1989

Canada's Sweetheart: The Saga of Hal C. Banks; CBC, date unknown

Friends In High Places: Politics and Patronage in the Mulroney Government; Claire Hoy, 1987

CANADA AND THE REAGAN CHALLENGE: CRISIS AND ADJUSTMENT, 1981-85; STEPHEN CLARKSON, 1985

THE PROVINCE; PAGE 5, SUNDAY, AUGUST 13TH, 1989 (**TOWN IN UPROAR OVER FLAG FLIP**).

THE PROVINCE; PAGE 12, MONDAY, AUGUST 14TH, 1989 (**FLAG FUROR ENDS**).

THE VANCOUVER SUN; C 1, WEDNESDAY, SEPTEMBER 11TH, 2002 (**ADOPTING U.S.** GREENBACK ' KISS OF DEATH, ' FORMER PRIME MINISTER **MULRONEY** SAYS).

MACLEAN'S NEWSMAGAZINE; PAGES 18 & 19, JANUARY 8TH, 2001 (AN EXTENSIVE ESSAY WRITTEN BY CANADIAN HISTORIAN PETER C. NEWMAN INTERESTINGLY TITLED, **THE END OF CANADA?** MEASURES TO EXPAND FREE TRADE WILL INEVITABLY LEAD TO THE END OF FIRST OUR DOLLAR — AND THEN OUR SOVEREIGNTY).

PIERRE TRUDEAU SPEAKS OUT ON MEECH LAKE; PIERRE E. TRUDEAU, FIRST PUBLISHED IN 1988, REPRINTED 1990

LUCIEN BOUCHARD: ON THE RECORD; TRANSLATED BY DOMINIQUE CLIFT, FIRST PUBLISHED IN FRENCH 1992, REPRINTED INTO ENGLISH 1994

BEHIND THE EMBASSY DOOR: CANADA, CLINTON AND QUEBEC; JAMES J. BLANCHARD, 1998

TOWARD THE JUST SOCIETY: THE TRUDEAU YEARS; PIERRE ELLIOTT TRUDEAU, 1989

CONSPIRACY AND ROMANCE: STUDIES IN BROCKDEN BROWN, COOPER, HAWTHORNE, AND MELVILLE; ROBERT S. LEVINE, 1989

THE ILLUMINOIDS; NEAL WILGUS, 1979

MACLEAN'S NEWSMAGAZINE; PAGES 14 & 15, JUNE 19TH, 2000 (JUNE 23RD, 1990 — THE DAY THAT   CHANGED CANADA).

MACLEAN'S NEWSMAGAZINE; PAGES 16 - 20, JUNE 19TH, 2000 (A LIFE OF ITS OWN — MEECH LAKE MAY HAVE DIED, BUT CANADA IS STILL LIVING WITH THE CONSEQUENCES).

Maclean's Newsmagazine; Pages 26 - 28, June 19ᵀᴴ, 2000 (' I Did What I Had to do, ' Brian Mulroney says Canada would have been better off with Meech).

Maclean's Newsmagazine; Pages 18 - 21, December 4ᵀᴴ, 2000 (Jean Chretien gambled on an early election call — and then led his Liberals to a resounding victory: Majority Rules).

A Thief in the Night: The Death of Pope John Paul I; John Cornwell, 1989

The Hiram Key: Pharaohs, Freemasons and The Discovery of The Secret Scrolls of Jesus; Christopher Knight and Robert Lomas, 1997

The Vancouver Sun; A 3, Thursday, July 15ᵀᴴ, 1999 (Satan has entered Vatican, prelate claims).

Chapter 9 - THE ILLUMINATI: IN GOD WE TRUST

Women In Politics: Corazon Aquino; BBC Television Wales, MCMLXXXIX

Women In Politics: Benazir Bhutto; BBC Television Wales, MCMLXXXIX

Armageddon in the Middle East; Dana Adams Schmidt, 1974

The Unholy War: Oil Islam, and Armageddon; Marius Baar, 1980

Iran 1979; Channel 4 Television Company Limited, 1989

Portraits of Power: Remaking The World (Islam); a Steven York Film, date unknown

The Iran-Contra Affair; Frontline, April 23RD, 1991 (Corporation For Public Broadcasting)

The Secret Government: The Constitution In Crisis, (an expose of the Iran-Contra Affair and other U.S. Governmental imposed wars against various nations worldwide); Public Affairs Television Inc., 1987

The Secret Files: Washington, Israel & The Gulf; The Washington Post Company TelevisionProduction, 1992

The Bank of Crooks and Criminals: The World's Sleaziest Bank; Frontline, April 21ST, 1992

Washington Monument: The Unraveling of the Bank of Credit and Commerce; CBS News 60 Minutes, date unknown

The Man Who Made Saddam Hussein's Supergun: Canadian Scientist Gerald Bull; Frontline, February 12TH, 1991

Gerald Bull's Supergun; BCTV Evening News, October 8TH, 1991

THE HEROES OF DESERT STORM; A 1991 MADE FOR T.V. MOVIE WHICH AIRED THROUGHOUT NORTH AMERICA ON OCTOBER 6TH, 1991 GLORIFYING THE PERSIAN GULF WAR (PART ONE), WITH AN INTRODUCTION BY U.S. PRESIDENT GEORGE BUSH SENIOR

IRAQ: THE CRADLE OF CIVILIZATION, (LEGACY); DATE AND PRODUCTION UNKNOWN

THE DIABOLICAL MINDS OF ADOLF HITLER AND SADDAM HUSSEIN, (UNSOLVED MYSTERIES); DATE AND PRODUCTION UNKNOWN

SADDAM'S KILLING FIELDS; FRONTLINE, MARCH 31ST, 1992 (CORPORATION FOR PUBLIC BROADCASTING)

SADDAM'S KILLING FIELDS; CBS NEWS 60 MINUTES, DATE UNKNOWN

UNITED STATES GOVERNMENT FUNNELS ARMS AND MONEY TO IRAQ THROUGH AN ITALIAN BANKING SYSTEM (BNL IN ATLANTA, GEORGIA); ABC NEWS NIGHTLINE, MAY 2ND, 1991

U.S. PRESIDENT GEORGE BUSH UNDER INVESTIGATION REGARDING THE BNL SCANDAL AND ITS SUBSEQUENT COVER-UP BY HIS ADMINISTRATION; ABC NEWS NIGHTLINE, JULY 7TH, 1992

THE ARMING OF SAUDI ARABIA; FRONTLINE, FEBRUARY 16TH, 1993

SADDAM HUSSEIN & KING HUSSEIN OF JORDAN; CBS NEWS 60 MINUTES, 1991

HELL FIGHTERS OF KUWAIT; NOVA, 1991

JEWS, MOVIES, HOLLYWOODISM AND THE AMERICAN DREAM; 1171086 ONTARIO LTD., 1997

THE HOLLYWOOD 10 BLACKLIST; DATE AND PRODUCTION UNKNOWN

G-MEN: THE RISE OF J. EDGAR HOOVER, (THE AMERICAN EXPERIENCE); DATE AND PRODUCTION UNKNOWN

1999 VICTORY WITHOUT WAR; RICHARD MILHOUS NIXON, 1988

NIXON, (The American Experience); date and production unknown
George Washington: The Man Who Wouldn't Be King; date and
    production unknown

Watergate: The Secret Story; CBS Inc. and Post/Newsweek
    Television Stations, MCMXCII

The Kennedy Assassinations: Coincidence Or Conspiracy;
    Entertainment Tonight, July 6th, 1992

I Known What I Saw, (JFK's Assassination); ABC News 20/20, date
    unknown

CIA Assassinated JFK, (an interview with Mark Lane the author
    of " Plausible Denial "implicating the CIA's involvement);
    Northwest Afternoon, 1992

The Plot To Kill President Kennedy: From The De-Classified Files;
    date and production unknown

The Knights Templar; Sophistory & West brook Films, MM

Monopoly Men: The Distant Murmuring Of A Secret Government,
    (Phenomenon: The Lost Archives); Liberty International
    Entertainment Inc., 1999

www.THE MONEY MASTERS.COM

Secret Societies: Freemasonry and the Bonesmen, (The
    Unexplained); A & E Television Network, 1998

The Skulls, (a suspense made for T.V. Movie of the Bonesmen);
    Universal Pictures, 2000

Inspector Morse: In The Masonic Mysteries, (a series of Three
    Freemasonry Stories of Murder and Betrayal); BBC
    Television, MCMXC

The Logic of International Relations; Walter S. Jones, Professor of
    Political Science, Senior Vice-President for Academic Affairs
    and Provost, Wayne State University, 1985

Behind The Embassy Door: Canada, Clinton and Quebec; James J. Blanchard, 1998

Canada: A People's History (Episode 1: When The World Began); CBC, MM

Canada: A People's History (Episode 2: Adventurers And Mystics); CBC, MM

Canada: A People's History (Episode 3: Claiming The Wilderness); CBC, MM

Canada: A People's History (Episode 4: Battle For A Continent); CBC, MM

Canada: A People's History (Episode 5: A Question Of Loyalties); CBC, MM

Canada: A People's History (Episode 6: The Pathfinders); CBC, MMI

Canada: A People's History (Episode 7: Rebellion And Reform); CBC, MMI

Canada: A People's History (Episode 8: The Great Enterprise); CBC, MMI

Canada: A People's History (Episode 9: From Sea To Sea); CBC, MMI

Canada: A People's History (Episode 10: Taking The West); CBC, MMI

Canada: A People's History (Episode 11: The Great Transformation); CBC, MMI

Canada: A People's History (Episode 12: Ordeal By Fire); CBC, MMI

Canada: A People's History (Episode 13: Hard Times); CBC, MMI

Canada: A People's History (Episode 14: The Crucible); CBC, MMI

Canada: A People's History (Episode 15: Comfort And Fear); CBC, MMI

Canada: A People's History (Episode 16: Years Of Hope And Anger); CBC, MMI

Canada: A People's History (Episode 17: In An Uncertain World); CBC, MMI

Time Weekly News Magazine; Pages 10-16, January 30TH, 1989 (**A New Breeze Is Blowing.** The Bush Era Begins with George Bush Senior taking allegiance as the 41ST President).

Time Weekly News Magazine; Pages 20 & 21, January 30TH, 1989 (**The Gipper Says Goodbye.** As a new cast moves onstage, the Reagans leave to a standing ovation).

The Occult: A History; Colin Wilson, 1971

War Stories: The Schutzstaffel SS; Thames Television Ltd., 1981

War Stories: The Waffen SS; Thames Television Ltd., 1981

Encyclopedia of Freemasonry Volumes 1 & 2; The Masonic History Company (U.S.A.), 1924

The Egyptian Book of The Dead; E.A. Wallis Budge, Late keeper of Assyrian and Egyptian Antiquities in the British Museum, originally published in 1895 by the Trustees of the Museum, reprinted 1967

The Framework Of A Christian State; Rev. E. Cahill, Dublin, Ireland, 1932

Cults and New Faiths; John Butterworth, 1981

Conspiracy And Romance: Studies in Brockden Brown, Cooper, Hawthorne, and Melville; Robert S. Levine, 1989

Reveille in Washington: 1860-1865; Margaret Leech, 1941

The Illuminoids; Neal Wilgus, 1979

The Inquisition; Michael Baigent and Richard Leigh, 1999

The Holy Blood And The Holy Grail; Michael Baigent, Richard Leigh and Henry Lincoln, 1982

The Messianic Legacy; Michael Baigent, Richard Leigh and Henry Lincoln, 1986

A Thief In The Night: The Death of Pope John Paul I; John Cornwell, 1989

The Brotherhood: The Explosive Expose of the Secret World of the Freemasons; Stephen Knight, 1986

Inside The Brotherhood: The Explosive Sequel to Stephen Knight's The Brotherhood; Martin Short, 1989

The Hiram Key: Pharaohs, Freemasons and The Discovery of The Secret Scrolls of Jesus; Christopher Knight and Robert Lomas, 1997

The Story Of Civilization: Part X – Rousseau And Revolution; Will and Ariel Durant, 1967

Masonic Bulletin, Grand Lodge of British Columbia; Volume XLVII, Number 3, November 1983

To A Non-Mason: You Must Seek Masonic Membership; Henry C. Claussen, 33 rd degree, Sovereign Grand Commander, The Supreme Council, 33RD degree, Ancient And Accepted Scottish Rite of Freemasonry, Mother Jurisdiction Of The World, 1976

Masonic Bulletin, Grand Lodge of British Columbia; Volume XL, Number 3, November 1976

Grand Lodge Bulletin, Grand Lodge of Iowa, A.F. & A.M.; Volume 89, Number 1, March 1988

Gizeh Gazette, The Communication Lifeline Of Gizeh Temple;
Volume 36, Number 4, November 1991

The Northwest Washington Masonic News, Devoted To The
Interests Of Freemasonry Wherever Dispersed; Volume
XXVIII, Number 4, Bellingham, Washington, December 1989

The Northern Light: A Window For Freemasonry; Volume 21,
Number 1, February 1990

The High Twelvian; Volume 63, Number 3, George Washington –
Master Mason, Our First President, Winter 1989

Freemasonry: A Journey Through Ritual and Symbol; W. Kirk
MacNulty, 1991

Men In The Shadows: The Shocking Truth About The RCMP
Security Service; John Sawatsky, 1983

RCMP vs The People: Inside Canada's Security Service; Edward
Mann, Professor of Sociology, York University and John Alan
Lee, Associate Professor of Sociology, University of Toronto,
1979

Imperfect Union: Canadian Labour and the Left (Part 1:
International Background – CanadianRoots); CBC, date
unknown

Imperfect Union: Canadian Labour and the Left (Part 2: Born On
Hard Times); CBC, date   unknown

The Hammer, The Sickle and the Maple Leaf; Simon Fraser
University, 1989

Canada's Sweetheart: The Saga of Hal C. Banks; CBC, date unknown

Masonic Bulletin, Grand Lodge of British Columbia; Volume XLVI,
Number 9, May 1983

Proceedings Of The Most Worshipful Grand Lodge Of Ancient,
Free and Accepted Masons Of British Columbia; Seventy-

SEVENTH ANNUAL COMMUNICATION HELD AT VANCOUVER, B.C., 17TH AND 18TH DAYS OF JUNE 1948

ISRAEL-BRITAIN; ADAM RUTHERFORD, LONDON, ENGLAND, 1939

FREEMASONRY: THE INVISIBLE CULT IN OUR MIDST, A BIBLICAL EXPOSE OF FREEMASONRY; WRITTEN BY A FORMER WORSHIPFUL MASTER, JACK HARRIS, 1983

HOW TO RESPOND TO THE LODGE; L. JAMES RONGSTAD, 1977

THE FACTS ON THE MASONIC LODGE, DOES MASONRY CONFLICT WITH THE CHRISTIAN FAITH?; JOHN ANKERBERG AND JOHN WELDON, 1989

REACHING JUDGEMENT AT NUREMBERG: THE UNTOLD STORY OF HOW THE NAZI WAR CRIMINALS WERE JUDGED; BRADLEY F. SMITH, 1977

MASONIC BULLETIN, GRAND LODGE OF BRITISH COLUMBIA; VOLUME LIII, NUMBER 8, APRIL 1991

MASONIC BULLETIN, GRAND LODGE OF BRITISH COLUMBIA; VOLUME LVI, NUMBER 4, DECEMBER 1992

THE SOUTHERN BAPTIST CONVENTION AND FREEMASONRY, VOLUMES I & II; JAMES L. HOLLY, M.D., 1993

MASONIC BIBLE: AUTHORIZED KING JAMES VERSION; WILLIAM COLLINS SONS AND COMPANY LTD., 1951

THE ROCKEFELLERS: AN AMERICAN DYNASTY; PETER COLLIER AND DAVID HOROWITZ, 1976

THE ROTHSCHILDS: A FAMILY PORTRAIT; FREDERIC MORTON, 1962

THE CANADIAN ESTABLISHMENT; VOLUME 1, PETER C. NEWMAN, 1975

THE CANADIAN ESTABLISHMENT VOLUME II, THE ACQUISITORS; PETER C. NEWMAN, 1981

THE VANCOUVER SUN; A 11, THURSDAY, SEPTEMBER 19TH, 2002 (ANCESTRY LINKS BUSH TO HIS HERO WINSTON CHURCHILL, U.S. PRESIDENT

IS ALSO RELATIVE OF PRINCES WILLIAM AND HARRY, GENEALOGISTS DISCOVER).

THE VANCOUVER SUN; A 10, WEDNESDAY, APRIL 25TH, 2001 (**BIZARRE SECRET RITUALS OF BUSH FAMILY'S SKULL AND BONES FRATERNITY CLUB REVEALED**).

MACLEAN'S NEWSMAGAZINE; PAGES 108 - 112, DECEMBER 25TH, 2000/ JANUARY 1ST, 2001 (**VICTORY AT LAST**. GEORGE W. BUSH FINALLY CAPTURES THE U.S. PRESIDENCY AFTER TURBULENT AND DIVISIVE POST-ELECTION BATTLE THAT LASTED 36 DAYS).

MACLEAN'S NEWSMAGAZINE; PAGES 24 & 25, JANUARY 29TH, 2001 (**BUSH COUNTRY**. A NEWPRESIDENT IS INAUGURATED BUT HIS POLITICAL HONEYMOON IS LIKELY TO BE SHORT).

FREEMASONRY ON TRIAL; VARIOUS AUTHORS (20) IN TOTAL, CHOOSING TRUTH MINISTRIES, ABBOTSFORD,B.C., 1998

THE COURT SYSTEM AND FREEMASONRY; VARIOUS AUTHORS, CHOOSING TRUTH MINISTRIES, ABBOTSFORD, B.C., JUNE 2001

PAGAN TRADITIONS; DAVID INGRAHAM, HEARTHSTONE PUBLISHING, OKLAHOMA CITY, OKLAHOMA, 2000

TRICK OR TREAT: THE HISTORY OF HALLOWEEN; BILL USELTON, HEARTHSTONE PUBLISHING, OKLAHOMA CITY, OKLAHOMA, 1994

THE PROVINCE; A 8, SUNDAY, SEPTEMBER 15TH, 2002 (BUSH URGES UN TO SHOW BACKBONE ON IRAQ).

Chapter 10 - EGYPT: THE CRADLE OF ANCIENT FREEMASONRY

Egypt: The Cradle Of Ancient Masonry; Volume 1, Norman Frederick de Clifford, Macoy Publishing and Masonic Supply Company, New York, 1907

The Egyptian Book Of The Dead; E.A. Wallis Budge, Late keeper of Assyrian and Egyptian Antiquities in the British Museum, originally published in 1895 by the Trustees of the Museum, reprinted 1967

Encyclopedia of Freemasonry Volumes 1 & 2; The Masonic History Company (U.S.A.), 1924

The Holy Blood And The Holy Grail; Michael Baigent, Richard Leigh and Henry Lincoln, 1982

The Messianic Legacy; Michael Baigent, Richard Leigh and Henry Lincoln, 1986

The Inquisition; Michael Baigent and Richard Leigh, 1999

The Framework Of A Christian State; Rev. E. Cahill, Dublin, Ireland, 1932

Cults and New Faiths; John Butterworth, 1981

The Hiram Key: Pharaohs, Freemasons and the Discovery of The Secret Scrolls of Jesus; Christopher Knight and Robert Lomas, 1997

Masonic Bible: Authorized King James Version; William Collins Sons and Company Ltd., 1951

The Unholy War: Oil, Islam, and Armageddon; Marius Baar, 1980

Armageddon in the Middle East; Dana Adams Schmidt, 1974

Iran 1979; Channel 4 Television Company Limited, 1989

Portraits of Power: Remaking The World (Islam); a Steven York
Film, date unknown

The Iran-Contra Affair; Frontline, April 23ʳᵈ, 1991 (Corporation
For Public Broadcasting)

The Secret Government: The Constitution In Crisis, (an expose of
the Iran-Contra Affair and other U.S. Governmental imposed
wars against various nations worldwide); Public Affairs
Television Inc., 1987

The Secret Files: Washington, Israel & The Gulf; The Washington
Post Company Television Production, 1992

The Bank of Crooks and Criminals: The World's Sleaziest Bank;
Frontline, April 21ˢᵗ, 1992

Washington Monument: The Unraveling of the Bank of Credit and
Commerce; CBS News 60 Minutes, date unknown

The Man Who Made Saddam Hussein's Supergun: Canadian Scientist
Gerald Bull; Frontline,   February 12ᵀᴴ, 1991

Gerald Bull's Supergun; BCTV Evening News, October 8ᵀᴴ, 1991

The Heroes of Desert Storm; a 1991 made for T.V. movie which aired
throughout North America on October 6ᵀᴴ, 1991 glorifying
the Persian Gulf War (Part One), with an introduction by
U.S. President George Bush Senior

Iraq: The Cradle of Civilization, (Legacy); date and production
unknown

The Diabolical Minds of Adolf Hitler and Saddam Hussein,
(Unsolved Mysteries); date and production unknown

Saddam's Killing Fields; Frontline, March 31ˢᵗ, 1992 (Corporation
For Public Broadcasting)

SADDAM'S KILLING FIELDS; CBS NEWS 60 MINUTES, DATE UNKNOWN

UNITED STATES GOVERNMENT FUNNELS ARMS AND MONEY TO IRAQ
THROUGH AN ITALIAN BANKING SYSTEM (BNL IN ATLANTA,
GEORGIA); ABC NEWS NIGHTLINE, MAY 2ND, 1991

U.S. PRESIDENT GEORGE BUSH UNDER INVESTIGATION REGARDING
THE BNL SCANDAL AND ITS SUBSEQUENT COVER-UP BY HIS
ADMINISTRATION; ABC NEWS NIGHTLINE, JULY 7TH, 1992

THE ARMING OF SAUDI ARABIA; FRONTLINE, FEBRUARY 16TH, 1993

SADDAM HUSSEIN & KING HUSSEIN OF JORDAN; CBS NEWS 60 MINUTES,
1991

HELL FIGHTERS OF KUWAIT; NOVA, 1991

JEWS, MOVIES, HOLLYWOODISM AND THE AMERICAN DREAM; 1171086
ONTARIO LTD., 1997

THE HOLLYWOOD 10 BLACKLIST; DATE AND PRODUCTION UNKNOWN

G-MEN: THE RISE OF J. EDGAR HOOVER, (THE AMERICAN EXPERIENCE);
DATE AND PRODUCTION   UNKNOWN

1999 VICTORY WITHOUT WAR; RICHARD MILHOUS NIXON, 1988

NIXON, (THE AMERICAN EXPERIENCE); DATE AND PRODUCTION UNKNOWN

GEORGE WASHINGTON: THE MAN WHO WOULDN'T BE KING; DATE AND
PRODUCTION UNKNOWN

WATERGATE: THE SECRET STORY; CBS INC. AND POST/NEWSWEEK
TELEVISION STATIONS, MCMXCII

THE KENNEDY ASSASSINATIONS: COINCIDENCE OR CONSPIRACY;
ENTERTAINMENT TONIGHT, JULY 6TH, 1992

I KNOW WHAT I SAW, (JFK'S ASSASSINATION); ABC NEWS 20/20, DATE
UNKNOWN

CIA Assassinated JFK, (an interview with Mark Lane the author of " Plausible Denial " implicating the CIA's involvement); Northwest Afternoon, 1992

The Plot To Kill President Kennedy: From The De-Classified Files; date and production unknown

The Knights Templar; Sophistory & Westbrook Films, MM

Monopoly Men: The Distant Murmuring Of A Secret Government, (Phenomenon: The Lost Archives); Liberty International Entertainment Inc., 1999

www.THE MONEY MASTERS.COM

Secret Societies: Freemasonry and the Bonesmen, (The Unexplained); A & E Television Network, 1998

The Skulls, (a suspense made for T.V. movie of the Bonesmen); Universal Pictures, 2000

Inspector Morse: In The Masonic Mysteries, (a series of Three Freemasonry Stories of Murder and Betrayal); BBC Television, MCMXC

History Of World War II; War Department of the Supreme Allied Command of the United States, Canada and Great Britain, 1946

INFAMY: Pearl Harbor And Its Aftermath; John Toland, 1983

Hirohito: Behind The Myth; BBC Television, date unknown

The Vancouver Sun; A 20, Wednesday, March 27TH, 2002 (' **My God, what have we done? 'Logbook from Enola Gay recalls first dropping of an atomic bomb**).

The Province; A 2, Wednesday, March 27TH, 2002 (' **My God – what have we done? '**).

The Vancouver Sun; B 19, Saturday, June 15th, 2002 (**Hiroshima A-bomb parts can be sold, judge rules**).

The Vancouver Sun; A 6, Monday, December 31st, 2001 (Europe's euro revolution begins at midnight. While many fear upheaval as the common currency begins circulation, some officials say it will bring prosperity).

The Vancouver Sun; A 6, Monday, December 31st, 2001 (Conversion brings retirement for   Europe's oldest currency).

Maclean's Newsmagazine; Pages 36 & 37, January 8th, 2001 (European Blues. Plans to less- affluent East worry EU members).

The Vancouver Sun; A 6, Monday, March 18th, 2002 (Gibraltarians offered $ 72 million to surrender their Mediterranean colony to the U.K. for European Unification purposes).

National Post; A 12, Monday, July 15th, 2002 (Britain & Spain talk of accord as the majorityof the residents of Gibraltar refuse to join European Union).

Funk & Wagnalls New Encyclopedia; Volume 18, Pages 369 and 370, Funk & Wagnalls Inc., New York, 1973

Veil: The Secret Wars of The CIA 1981-1987; Bob Woodward, 1987

Masonic Bulletin, Grand Lodge of British Columbia; Volume LN, Number 1, September 1990

New Zealand Freemason; Volume 15, Number 2, Winter 1987

The Vancouver Sun; D 11, Wednesday, August 23rd, 2000 (**U.S. economy slows down after 10 years of economic blist**).

Maclean's Newsmagazine; Pages 20-23, January 15th, 2001 (**AVOIDING THE MELTDOWN.**How the Canadian economy can weather a U.S. slump by relying on its own strengths).

Maclean's Newsmagazine: Pages 24 & 25, January 15th, 2001
(**GREENSPAN TO THE RESCUE**, U.S. Federal Reserve
unexpectedly slashes interest rates amid fears of recession).

The Vancouver Sun; Front Page Coverage, Saturday, September 22nd,
2001 (**Stock market loss the worst since Great Depression. In
one week, Dow stocks lose $ 1.4 trillion US in value**).

The Vancouver Sun; A 14, Saturday, September 22nd, 2001 (The
Aftermath of 9/11; the U.S. economy is proclaimed " in
recession, " and not expected to recover until next year).

The Vancouver Sun; D 4, Thursday, October 25th, 2001 (Terrorist
attacks stall U.S. economy. No area of the United States has
been spared from the economic fallout, Federal Reserve says).

The Vancouver Sun; C 1, (Business Section), Saturday, October 6th,
2001 (**Don't blame September 11th, Wall Street tells firms**).

The London Times; Page 4, Saturday, September 29th, 2001 (**Thirty
attacks against West are still to come, says Italy. Secret Service
Report issued to the United States and Britain warning of
terrorist attacks**).

New York Post; Pages 1 & 2, Thursday, May 16th, 2002 (**9/11
BOMBSHELL: BUSH KNEW. Prez was warned of possible
hijackings before terror attacks**).

The Vancouver Sun; A 2, Thursday, May 16th, 2002 (**U.S. had warning
of bin-Laden hijacking plan**).

The Province; A 18, Friday, May 17th, 2002 (9/11 families demand
probe).

The Vancouver Sun; A 19, Thursday, November 28th, 2002 (Kissinger
to head 9/11 investigation. Bush ally appointed to probe of
U.S. aviation security, intelligence).

The Vancouver Sun; A 17, Saturday, May 18th, 2002 (' **Why didn't
lights go off in their heads? ' Warnings about terrorist plans
and bin Laden links not heeded**).

THE VANCOUVER SUN; A 17, SATURDAY, MAY 18TH, 2002 (**BUSH TRIES TO EVADE FALLOUT FROM TIP-OFF DISCLOSURES. PRESIDENT CLAIMS HE WAS NOT INFORMED ABOUT A SPECIFIC THREAT TO ATTACK U.S.**).

MACLEAN'S NEWSMAGAZINE; PAGES 14 - 22, OCTOBER 1ST, 2001 (**AMERICA'S READY:** SO IS BRITAIN. BUT IS THE REST OF THE WORLD PREPARED TO JOIN THE WAR ON TERROR?).

MACLEAN'S NEWSMAGAZINE; PAGES 32 - 36, OCTOBER 1ST, 2001 (GUNNING FOR OSAMA. THE U.S. HOPES TO TRAP AND KILL BIN LADEN IN A MASSIVE MILITARY ASSAULT).

MACLEAN'S NEWSMAGAZINE; PAGES 46 - 48, OCTOBER 1ST, 2001 (**A MIXED RECEPTION. A**MID THE SUPPORT FOR **B**USH**,** SOME THOUGHT THE U.S. GOT WHAT IT DESERVED).

MACLEAN'S NEWSMAGAZINE; PAGES 19- 41, OCTOBER 15TH, 2001 (**WAR – OCT. 7, 9 P.M., AFGHAN TIME: THE BOMBING BEGINS**).

MACLEAN'S NEWSMAGAZINE; PAGES 26 - 31, OCTOBER 22ND, 2001 (**CANADA GOES TO WAR**).

MACLEAN'S NEWSMAGAZINE; PAGES 36 & 37, OCTOBER 22ND, 2001 (WALKING A FINE LINE. MUSLIM COUNTRIES SUPPORTING THE U.S. - LED WAR ON TERRORISM FACE DOMESTIC MILITANTS OPENLY HOSTILE TO AMERICA — AND HAILING OSAMA BIN LADEN AS A HERO).

MACLEAN'S NEWSMAGAZINE; PAGES 58 & 59, OCTOBER 22ND, 2001 (**THOSE DAMN YANKEES.** THE HARDY PERENNIAL OF CANADIANS ANTI-AMERICANISM IS BACK — IN FULL FLOWER).

MACLEAN'S NEWSMAGAZINE; PAGES 26 - 28, DECEMBER 3RD, 2001 (**IS SADDAM NEXT?**).

THE PROVINCE; A 14, MONDAY, JUNE 17TH, 2002 (**BUSH ORDERS CIA TO** FORCE **I**RAQ'S **S**ADDAM FROM   OFFICE).

THE VANCOUVER SUN; A 8, TUESDAY, JULY 23RD, 2002 (POLITICAL MANOEUVRES PRESAGE U.S. WAR ON IRAQ: U.S. SABRE-RATTLING AND WARNINGS FROM BAGHDAD RAISE FEARS OF CONFLICT).

The Vancouver Sun; A 13, Friday, September 13TH, 2002 (' A grave and gathering danger ' VERBATIM: U.S. President George Bush tells the UN that Saddam Hussein has answered a decade of its demands with a decade of defiance).

The Vancouver Sun; A 5, Monday, October 1ST, 2001 (Bounty hunters stalk Osama bin Laden for $ 30 million in rewards. Mercenaries are allegedly infiltrating Afghanistan to find suspected terrorist).

The Vancouver Sun; A 5, Monday, October 22ND, 2001 (Bush orders bin Laden killed. Expanded powers for CIA are part of wider moves to restructure U.S. covert forces).

The Vancouver Sun; A 6, Saturday, December 15TH, 2001 (Bin Laden ' dead or alive ': Bush says it doesn't matter).

The Vancouver Sun; A 12, Monday, December 16TH, 2002 (Bush allows CIA to kill 25 terrorists if necessary).

National Post; A 10, Friday, July 12TH, 2002 (**BUSH RECEIVED BOARDROOM LOAN: RECORDS. DEMOCRATS CRY HYPOCRISY;** Low-interest deal would be banned under President's new crackdown).

The Vancouver Sun; Front Page Coverage, Tuesday, October 2ND, 2001 (Feminist's anti-U.S. speech causes uproar. Hedy Fry jeered by opposition for sitting silent).

The Vancouver Sun; A 2, Tuesday, October 2ND, 2001 (Fry says she didn't applaud speech).

National Post; Front Page Coverage, Tuesday, October 2ND, 2001 (B.C. feminist lays blame on U.S. and its ' foreign policy soaked in blood ' — 500 cheer Thobani's critique).

National Post; A 14, Tuesday, October 2ND, 2001 (Speaker cites 'victims of U.S. aggression ').

The Province; A 14, Tuesday, October 2ND, 2001 (MP's upset by view of leading feminist).

THE VANCOUVER SUN; FRONT PAGE COVERAGE, WEDNESDAY, OCTOBER 3RD, 2001 (THOBANI SPEECH DISGRACEFUL, PREMIER SAYS OF U.S. BASHING. ' THE COMMENTS SHE MADE WERE HATEFUL ').

THE VANCOUVER SUN; A 2, WEDNESDAY, OCTOBER 3RD, 2001 (' **THEY WERE SENDING MESSAGES, TRYING TO GET HER TO SHUT UP** ').

THE VANCOUVER SUN; A 6, WEDNESDAY, OCTOBER 3RD, 2001 (' IT'S BLOODTHIRSTY VENGEANCE '. TRANSCRIPT OF UBC PROFESSOR SUNERA THOBANI'S SPEECH AT THE WOMEN'S RESISTANCE CONFERENCE).

THE VANCOUVER SUN; A 7; WEDNESDAY, OCTOBER 3RD, 2001 (FREE SPEECH IN A PRISTINE VACUUM. UNIVERSITY DEFENDS ' NUTTY PROFESSOR ').

THE VANCOUVER SUN; A 7, WEDNESDAY, OCTOBER 3RD, 2001 (STUDENTS SUPPORT THOBANI'S COMMENTS).

THE VANCOUVER SUN; A 19, (LETTERS TO THE EDITOR), WEDNESDAY, OCTOBER 3RD, 2001 (FEMINIST'S SPEECH RIPS OPEN DEBATE ON AMERICA'S GLOBAL ROLE).

THE PROVINCE; A 4, WEDNESDAY, OCTOBER 3RD, 2001 (ANTI-U.S. SPEECH BLASTED. CAMPBELL, DAY AND MANLEY DENOUNCE UBC PROFESSOR'S ' SOAKED IN BLOOD ' TIRADE).

THE PROVINCE; A 28, (EDITORIAL PAGE), WEDNESDAY, OCTOBER 3RD, 2001 (A SPATE OF HATE).

THE PROVINCE; A 29, (LETTERS TO THE EDITOR), WEDNESDAY, OCTOBER 3RD, 2001 (SOME HAILED THOBANI'S WORDS, OTHERS RAILED THEM).

NATIONAL POST; A 1, WEDNESDAY, OCTOBER 3RD, 2001 (THOBANI ' RANT ' CALLED HATEFUL: B.C. PREMIER, LIBERAL SENATOR VOICE DISGUST).

NATIONAL POST; A 10, WEDNESDAY, OCTOBER 3RD, 2001 (ANTI-AMERICAN SPEECH WAS ' MANIPULATIVE RANT ': SENATOR).

NATIONAL POST; A 18, WEDNESDAY, OCTOBER 3RD, 2001 (A PRODUCT OF CHRETIEN'S CANADA).

The Vancouver Sun; A 14, Thursday, October 4th, 2001 (PM condemns ' terrible ' Thobani speech. But Chretien and Secretary of State Hedy Fry defend government's funding of conference).

The Province; A 37, (Letter to the Editor), Thursday, October 4th, 2001 (Speech ' completely irresponsible ').

The Vancouver Sun; Front Page Coverage, Saturday, October 6th, 2001 (Americans denounceThobani – and Canada. ' With friends like Canada, who needs Third World enemies? ').

The Vancouver Sun; A 6, Saturday, October 6th, 2001 (The New McCarthyism. Calls for the head of Hedy Fry in the Sunera Thobani affairs raise memories of the bad old days).

The Vancouver Sun; A 7, Saturday, October 6th, 2001 (' With friends like Canada, who needs enemies? ').

The Vancouver Sun; A 22, (Editorial Page),Saturday, October 6th, 2001 (' Blame the victim 'the price of democracy).

The Vancouver Sun; A 23, (Letters to the Editor), Saturday, October 6th, 2001 (Thobani's credibility attacked. Plus a 2nd letter; Courage to speak out).

The Vancouver Sun; A 8, Wednesday, October 10th, 2001 (UBC prof shocked by hate mail she has received).

The Province; A 15, Friday, October 12th, 2001 (RCMP urged to apologize for releasing Thobani's name).

The Vancouver Sun; A 3, Thursday, October 18th, 2001 (I was vilified for being an ungrateful immigrant: Thobani. UBC professor sees reaction to her fiery speech as a response to an' uppity woman of colour ').

The Vancouver Sun; A 4, Thursday, October 25th, 2001 (Hate-crime charges against Thobani ' unfounded '. UBC professor's lawyer says Ontario police have dropped the complaint).

THE PROVINCE; A 7, THURSDAY, OCTOBER 25TH, 2001 (PROF WON'T BE CHARGED OVER SPEECH).

THE PROVINCE; A 6, SUNDAY, JANUARY 6TH, 2002 (**PLANE CRASHES INTO BUILDING. STUDENT PILOT, 15, KILLED;** ' NO INDICATION ' OF TERRORISM).

THE VANCOUVER SUN; A 1 & A 2, MONDAY, JANUARY 7TH, 2002 (**TEEN PILOT'S SUICIDE NOTE SPOKE OF HIS** ' SYMPATHY ' FOR BIN LADEN).

THE PROVINCE; A 12, WEDNESDAY, JANUARY 9TH, 2002 (**STUDENT PILOT PRESCRIBED DRUG LINKED TO SUICIDES**).

THE GLOBE AND MAIL; A 7, THURSDAY, JANUARY 10TH, 2002 (PILOT SUICIDE DIDN'T SPUR DRUG STUDY, FIRM SAYS).

CHAPTER 11 - ISRAEL: THE HOLY LAND OF ALL FREEMASONRY

THE FRAMEWORK OF A CHRISTIAN STATE; REV. E. CAHILL, DUBLIN, IRELAND, 1932

CULTS AND NEW FAITHS; JOHN BUTTERWORTH, 1981

IRAN 1979; CHANNEL 4 TELEVISION COMPANY LIMITED, 1989

PORTRAITS OF POWER: REMAKING THE WORLD (ISLAM); A STEVEN YORK FILM, DATE UNKNOWN

THE IRAN-CONTRA AFFAIR; FRONTLINE, APRIL 23RD, 1991 (CORPORATION FOR PUBLIC BROADCASTING)

THE SECRET GOVERNMENT: THE CONSTITUTION IN CRISIS, (AN EXPOSE OF THE IRAN-CONTRA AFFAIR AND OTHER U.S. GOVERNMENTAL IMPOSED WARS AGAINST VARIOUS NATIONS WORLDWIDE); PUBLIC AFFAIRS TELEVISION INC., 1987

THE SECRET FILES: WASHINGTON, ISRAEL & THE GULF; THE WASHINGTON POST COMPANY TELEVISION PRODUCTION, 1992

THE BANK OF CROOKS AND CRIMINALS: THE WORLD'S SLEAZIEST BANK; FRONTLINE, APRIL 21ST, 1992

WASHINGTON MONUMENT: THE UNRAVELING OF THE BANK OF CREDIT AND COMMERCE; CBS NEWS 60MINUTES, DATE UNKNOWN

THE MAN WHO MADE SADDAM HUSSEIN'S SUPERGUN: CANADIAN SCIENTIST GERALD BULL; FRONTLINE, FEBRUARY, 12TH, 1991

GERALD BULL'S SUPERGUN; BCTV EVENING NEWS, OCTOBER 8TH, 1991

THE HEROES OF DESERT STORM; A 1991 MADE FOR T.V. MOVIE WHICH AIRED THROUGHOUT NORTH AMERICA ON OCTOBER 6TH, 1991 GLORIFYING THE PERSIAN GULF WAR (PART ONE), WITH AN INTRODUCTION BY U.S. PRESIDENT GEORGE BUSH SENIOR

Iraq: The Cradle of Civilization, (Legacy); date and production
unknown

The Diabolical Minds of Adolf Hitler and Saddam Hussein,
(Unsolved Mysteries); date and production unknown

Saddam's Killing Fields; Frontline, March 31ST, 1992 (Corporation
For Public Broadcasting)

Saddam's Killing Fields; CBS News 60 Minutes, date unknown

United States Government Funnels Arms and Money to Iraq
Through an Italian Banking System (BNL in Atlanta,
Georgia); ABC News Nightline, May 2ND, 1991

U.S. President George Bush Under investigation Regarding
the BNL Scandal and Its subsequent Cover-Up By His
Administration; ABC News Nightline, July 7TH, 1992

The Arming of Saudi Arabia; Frontline, February 16TH, 1993

Saddam Hussein & King Hussein of Jordan; CBS News 60 Minutes,
1991

Hell Fighters of Kuwait; Nova, 1991

Jews, Movies, Hollywoodism and the American dream; 1171086
Ontario Ltd., 1997

The Hollywood 10 Blacklist; date and production unknown

G-MEN: The Rise of J. Edgar Hoover, (The American Experience);
date and production   unknown

1999 Victory Without War; Richard Milhous Nixon, 1988

NIXON, (The American Experience); date and production unknown

George Washington: The Man Who Wouldn't Be King; date and
production unknown

Watergate: The Secret Story; CBS Inc. and Post/Newsweek
Television Stations, MCMXCII

The Kennedy Assassinations: Coincidence Or Conspiracy;
Entertainment Tonight, July 6th, 1992

I Know What I Saw, (JFK's Assassination); ABC News 20/20, date
unknown

CIA Assassinated JFK, (an interview with Mark Lane the author
of " Plausible Denial " implicating the CIA's involvement);
Northwest Afternoon, 1992

The Plot To Kill President Kennedy: From The De-Classified Files;
date and production unknown

The Knights Templar; Sophistory & Westbrook Films, MM

Monopoly Men: The Distant Murmuring Of A Secret Government,
(Phenomenon: The Lost   Archives); Liberty International
Entertainment Inc., 1999

www.THE MONEY MASTERS.COM

Secret Societies: Freemasonry and the Bonesmen, (The
Unexplained); A & E Television Network, 1998

The Skulls, (a suspense made for T.V. movie of the Bonesmen);
Universal Pictures, 2000

Inspector Morse: In The Masonic Mysteries, (a series of Three
Freemasonry Stories of Murder and Betrayal); BBC
Television, MCMXC

Encyclopedia of Freemasonry Volumes 1 & 2; The Masonic History
Company (U.S.A.), 1924

Egypt: The Cradle Of Ancient Masonry; Volume 1, Norman
Fredrick de Clifford, Macoy Publishing and Masonic Supply
Company, New York, 1907

The Hiram Key: Pharaohs, Freemasons and The Discovery of The
    Secret Scrolls of Jesus; Christopher Knight and Robert
    Lomas, 1997

WAC Bennett and the Rise of British Columbia; David J. Mitchell,
    Vancouver, B.C., 1983

Israel-Britain; Adam Rutherford, London, England, 1939

American Historical Documents; Barnes & Noble Inc., College
    Outline Series, 1970

Masonic Bulletin, Grand Lodge Of British Columbia; Volume XLVI,
    Number 9, May 1983

Masonic Bulletin, Grand Lodge Of British Columbia; Volume LV,
    Number 1, September 1991

Masonic Bulletin, Grand Lodge Of British Columbia; Volume LVI,
    Number 1, September 1992

Masonic Bulletin, Grand Lodge Of British Columbia; Volume LIII,
    Number 2, October 1989

Masonic Bulletin, Grand Lodge Of British Columbia; Volume LV,
    Number 10, June 1992

Masonic Bulletin, Grand Lodge Of British Columbia; Volume LV,
    Number 2, October 1991

Masonic Bulletin, Grand Lodge Of British Columbia; Volume LIII,
    Number 3, November 1990

History Of The Grand Lodge Of British Columbia 1871-1970;
    Grand Lodge Of British Columbia A.F. & A.M., 1971

Masonic Bulletin, Grand Lodge Of British Columbia; Volume LV,
    Number 4, December 1991

Masonic Bulletin, Grand Lodge Of British Columbia; Volume LV,
    Number 5, January 1992

Lucien Bouchard: On The Record; translated by Dominique Clift, first published in French 1992,reprinted into English 1994

Behind The Embassy Door: Canada, Clinton and Quebec; James J. Blanchard, 1998

Canada: A People's History (Episode 1: When The World Began); CBC, MM

Canada: A People's History (Episode 2: Adventurers And Mystics); CBC, MM

Canada, A People's History (Episode 3: Claiming The Wilderness); CBC, MM

Canada: A People's History (Episode 4: Battle For A Continent); CBC, MM

Canada: A People's History (Episode 5: A Question Of Loyalties); CBC, MM

Canada: A People's History (Episode 6: The Pathfinders); CBC, MMI

Canada: A People's History (Episode 7: Rebellion And Reform); CBC, MMI

Canada: A People's History (Episode 8: The Great Enterprise); CBC, MMI

Canada: A People's History (Episode 9: From Sea To Sea); CBC, MMI

Canada: A People's History (Episode 10: Taking The West); CBC, MMI

Canada: A People's History (Episode 11: The Great Transformation); CBC, MMI

Canada: A People's History (Episode 12: Ordeal By Fire); CBC, MMI

Canada: A People's History (Episode 13: Hard Times); CBC, MMI

Canada: A People's History (Episode 14: The Crucible); CBC, MMI

CANADA: A PEOPLE'S HISTORY (EPISODE 15: COMFORT AND FEAR); CBC, MMI

CANADA: A PEOPLE'S HISTORY (EPISODE 16: YEARS OF HOPE AND ANGER); CBC, MMI

CANADA: A PEOPLE'S HISTORY (EPISODE 17: IN AN UNCERTAIN WORLD); CBC, MMI

MASONIC BULLETIN, GRAND LODGE OF BRITISH COLUMBIA; VOLUME LV, NUMBER 7, MARCH 1992

MASONIC BULLETIN, GRAND LODGE OF BRITISH COLUMBIA; VOLUME LII, NUMBER 2, OCTOBER 1988

MASONIC BULLETIN, GRAND LODGE OF BRITISH COLUMBIA; VOLUME LIII, NUMBER 10, JUNE 1990

MASONIC BULLETIN, GRAND LODGE OF BRITISH COLUMBIA; VOLUME LVI, NUMBER 4, DECEMBER 1992

BARKERVILLE: A GOLD RUSH ADVENTURE; RICHARD THOMAS WRIGHT, 1984

MASONIC BULLETIN, GRAND LODGE OF BRITISH COLUMBIA; VOLUME XLIII, NUMBER 7, MARCH 1980

MASONIC BULLETIN, GRAND LODGE OF BRITISH COLUMBIA; VOLUME LVI, NUMBER 2, OCTOBER 1992

MASONIC BULLETIN, GRAND LODGE OF BRITISH COLUMBIA; VOLUME LIII, NUMBER 8, APRIL 1990

THE VANCOUVER SUN; A 18, SATURDAY, OCTOBER 5TH, 2002 (**POPE WILL CANONIZE FOUNDER OF CONTROVERSIAL OPUS DEI. ESCRIVA'S GROUP HAS INSPIRED SUSPICION AND ADMIRATION**).

THE VANCOUVER SUN; A 8, MONDAY, OCTOBER 7TH, 2002 (THOUSANDS ATTEND CANONIZATION CEREMONY FOR THE FOUNDER OF OPUS DEI).

UNITED MASTERS LODGE NO. 167, LODGE OF MASONIC RESEARCH, VOLUME 24, NUMBER 10; GRAND LODGE OF NEW ZEALAND, APRIL 1982

THE VANCOUVER SUN; A 4, MONDAY, DECEMBER 16TH, 2002 (NATIVE LEADER'S COMMENTS STIR TALK OF HATE CRIME).

THE VANCOUVER SUN; A 5, TUESDAY, DECEMBER 17TH, 2002 (RCMP WILL BE ASKED TO PROBE ANTI-SEMETIC REMARKS. REQUEST TO BE MADE BY SASKATCHEWAN'S ATTORNEY-GENERAL).

THE VANCOUVER SUN; A 14, (EDITORIAL PAGE), TUESDAY, DECEMBER 17TH, 2002 (JEWS LEFT WORRYING ABOUT TOLERANCE IN CANADA. PLUS A 2ND ARTICLE; AHENAKEW MUST LOSE HIS PLACE IN ORDER OF CANADA).

THE VANCOUVER SUN; A 11, WEDNESDAY, DECEMBER 18TH, 2002 (NATIVE LEADER APOLOGIZES. JEWISH GROUPS SAY HIS REMARKS ABOUT HOLOCAUST STILL CONSTITUTE A CRIME).

THE VANCOUVER SUN; A 21, WEDNESDAY, DECEMBER 18TH, 2002 (CHRISTIANS, JEWS, MUSLIMS, STRUGGLING TO FIND LIGHT IN THESE DARK TIMES).

THE VANCOUVER SUN; A 23, (LETTERS TO THE EDITOR), WEDNESDAY, DECEMBER 18TH, 2002 (NO ROOM FOR RACISM. READERS STAND UP AGAINST ANTI-SEMITISM IN CANADA).

CARIBOO OBSERVER, QUESNEL, BRITISH COLUMBIA; A 8, WEDNESDAY, DECEMBER 18TH, 2002 (THIS GUY GETS ORDER OF CANADA).

THE VANCOUVER SUN; A 22, (EDITORIAL PAGE), THURSDAY, DECEMBER 19TH, 2002 (ANTI-SEMITISM RUNS DEEPEST IN MAINSTREAM).

THE VANCOUVER SUN; A 14, (EDITORIAL PAGE), MONDAY, DECEMBER 23RD, 2002 (JEWS AND ABORIGINAL PEOPLE ARE NATURAL ALLIES).

THE VANCOUVER SUN; A 7, THURSDAY, JANUARY 9TH, 2003 (ALTERNATE JUSTICE PROPOSED FOR AHENAKEW. B'NAI BRITH LEADERS ENDORSE HEALING, SENTENCING CIRCLE).

MASONIC BULLETIN, GRAND LODGE OF BRITISH COLUMBIA; VOLUME LIII, NUMBER 6, FEBRUARY 1990

CHAPTER 12 - CHRISTIANITY VERSUS FREEMASONRY

THE CHRISTIAN CENTURY; VOLUME 104, NUMBER 24, PAGE 714, AUGUST 26/SEPTEMBER 2ND, 1987

MASONIC BULLETIN, GRAND LODGE OF BRITISH COLUMBIA; VOLUME LIII, NUMBER 10, JUNE 1991

ROMAN CATHOLICISM AND FREEMASONRY; DUDLEY WRIGHT, RIDER AND SON PUBLISHING LTD., 1922

MONSIGNOR DILLON, " WAR OF ANTICHRIST WITH THE CHURCH " AS QUOTED BY ALEX MELLOR IN HIS BOOK, OUR SEPARATED BRETHREN THE FREEMASONS; GEORGE G. HARRAP AND COMPANY, 1964

MASONIC BULLETIN FROM M.B.S. HIGHAM, VOLUME 51, NUMBER 2, PAGE 13, OCTOBER 1987

SECRET SOCIETIES; NORMAN MACKENZIE, CRESCENT BOOKS, 1968

MASONIC BULLETIN FROM M.B.S. HIGHAM, VOLUME 51, NUMBER 2, PAGE 16, OCTOBER 1987 (REPORT TO THE GENERAL SYNOD OF THE CHURCH OF ENGLAND, 1987, AS QUOTED BY DR. JOHN HABGOOD, ARCHBISHOP OF THE CHURCH OF ENGLAND IN A SPEECH TO THE GENERAL SYNOD ON JULY 13TH, 1987).

MASONIC BULLETIN FROM M.B.S. HIGHAM, VOLUME 51, NUMBER 2, PAGE 16, OCTOBER 1987 (REPORT OF SPEECH GIVEN BY THE ARCHBISHOP OF YORK, DR. JOHN HABGOOD, AT THE GENERAL SYNOD ON JULY 13TH, 1987).

THE HIRAM KEY: PHARAOHS, FREEMASONS AND THE DISCOVERY OF THE SECRET SCROLLS OF JESUS; CHRISTOPHER KNIGHT AND ROBERT LOMAS, 1997

THE INQUISITION; MICHAEL BAIGENT AND RICHARD LEIGHT, 1999

The Story Of Civilization: Part X – Rousseau And Revolution; Will and Ariel Durant, 1967

The Framework Of A Christian State; Rev. E, Cahill, Dublin, Ireland, 1932

Encyclopedia of Freemasonry Volumes 1 & 2; The Masonic History Company (U.S.A.), 1924

Cults and New Faiths; John Butterworth, 1981

Iran 1979; Channel 4 Television Company Limited, 1989

Portraits of Power: Remaking The World (Islam); a Steven York Film, date unknown

The Iran-Contra Affair; Frontline, April 23RD, 1991 (Corporation For Public Broadcasting)

The Secret Government: The Constitution In Crisis, (an expose of the Iran-Contra Affair and other U.S. Governmental imposed wars against various nations worldwide); Public Affairs Television Inc., 1987

The Secret Files: Washington, Israel & The Gulf; The Washington Post Company Television   Production, 1992

The Bank of Crooks and Criminals: The World's Sleaziest Bank; Frontline, April 21ST, 1992

Washington Monument: The Unraveling of the Bank of Credit and Commerce; CBS News 60Minutes, date unknown

The Man Who Made Saddam Hussein's Supergun: Canadian Scientist Gerald Bull; Frontline, February 12TH, 1991

Gerald Bull's Supergun; BCTV Evening News, October 8TH, 1991

The Heroes of Desert Storm; a 1991 made for T.V. movie which aired throughout North America on October 6TH, 1991 glorifying

the Persian Gulf War (Part One), with an introduction by
U.S. President George Bush Senior

Iraq: The Cradle of Civilization, (Legacy); date and production
UNKNOWN

The Diabolical Minds of Adolf Hitler and Saddam Hussein,
(Unsolved Mysteries); date and production unknown

Saddam's Killing Fields; Frontline, March 31ST, 1992 (Corporation
For Public Broadcasting)

Saddam's Killing Fields; CBS News 60 Minutes, date unknown

United States Government Funnels Arms and Money to Iraq
Through an Italian Banking System (BNL in Atlanta,
Georgia); ABC News Nightline, May 2ND, 1991

U.S. President George Bush Under Investigation Regarding
the BNL Scandal and Its subsequent Cover-Up By His
Administration; ABC News Nightline, July 7TH, 1992

The Arming of Saudi Arabia; Frontline, February 16TH, 1993

Saddam Hussein & King Hussein of Jordan; CBS News 60 Minutes,
1991

Hell Fighters of Kuwait; Nova, 1991

Jews, Movies, Hollywoodism and the American Dream; 1171086
Ontario Ltd., 1997
The Hollywood 10 Blacklist; date and production unknown

G-MEN: The Rise of J. Edgar Hoover, (The American Experience);
date and production   unknown

1999 Victory Without war; Richard Milhous Nixon, 1988

NIXON, (The American Experience); date and production unknown

George Washington: The Man Who Wouldn't Be King; date and
      production unknown

Watergate: The Secret Story; CBS Inc. and Post/Newsweek
      Television Stations, MCMXCII

The Kennedy Assassinations: Coincidence Or Conspiracy;
      Entertainment Tonight, July 6TH, 1992

I Know What I Saw, (JFK's Assassination); ABC News 20/20, date
      unknown

CIA Assassinated JFK, (an interview with Mark Lane the author
      of " Plausible Denial " implicating the CIA's involvement);
      Northwest Afternoon, 1992

The Plot To Kill President Kennedy: From The De-Classified Files;
      date and production unknown

The Knights Templar; Sophistory & Westbrook Films, MM

Monopoly Men: The Distant Murmuring Of A Secret Government,
      (Phenomenon: The Lost Archives); Liberty International
      Entertainment Inc., 1999

www.THE MONEY MASTERS.COM

Secret Societies: Freemasonry and the Bonesmen, (The
      Unexplained); A & E Television Network, 1998

The Skulls, (a suspense made for T.V. movie of the Bonesmen);
      Universal Pictures, 2000

Inspector Morse: In The Masonic Mysteries, (a series of Three
      Freemasonry Stories of Murder   and Betrayal); BBC
      Television, MCMXC

The Last Communist: Fidel Castro; Frontline, February 11TH, 1992

A History of American Democracy; John D. Hicks, George E.
      Mowry and Robert Burke, 1966

The Province; A 39, Sunday, January 13ᵀᴴ, 2002 (Racism row now over top Anglican post).

The Vancouver Sun; A 10, Friday, February 28ᵀᴴ, 2003 (Anglicans install ' lefty ' as head of Church. The provocative Rowan Williams becomes Archbishop of Canterbury).

The Vancouver Sun; A 2, Saturday, May 20ᵀᴴ, 2000 (Catholics, Anglicans discuss union. A historic meeting between the churches ends with the creation of a commission to investigate how to reunite after 466 years).

Who is David Duke? Americans Ask Themselves; Frontline, March 3ᴿᴰ, 1992

A Black Person in White America; ABC News 20/20, 1992

The New Plantations: Hilton Head Island, South Carolina; CBS News 60 Minutes, 1991

Canada: A People's History (Episode 1: When The World Began); CBC, MM

Canada: A People's History (Episode 2: Adventurers And Mystics); CBC, MM

Canada: A People's History (Episode 3: Claiming The Wilderness); CBC, MM

Canada: A People's History (Episode 4: Battle For A Continent); CBC, MM

Canada: A People's History (Episode 5: A Question Of Loyalties); CBC, MM

Canada: A People's History (Episode 6: The Pathfinders); CBC, MMI

Canada: A People's History (Episode 7: Rebellion And Reform); CBC, MMI

Canada: A People's History (Episode 8: The Great Enterprise): CBC, MMI

Canada: A People's History (Episode 9: From Sea To Sea); CBC, MMI

Canada: A People's History (Episode 10: Taking The West); CBC, MMI

Canada: A People's History (Episode 11: The Great Transformation); CBC, MMI

Canada: A People's History (Episode 12: Ordeal By Fire); CBC, MMI

Canada: A People's History (Episode 13: Hard Times); CBC, MMI

Canada: A People's History (Episode 14: The Crucible); CBC, MMI

Canada: A People's History (Episode 15: Comfort And Fear); CBC, MMI

Canada: A People's History (Episode 16: Years Of Hope And Anger); CBC, MMI

Canada: A People's History (Episode 17: In An Uncertain World); CBC, MMI

C.D. Howe: The Minister of Everything; CBC Television, date unknown

History Of The Grand Lodge Of British Columbia 1871-1970; Grand Lodge Of British Columbia A.F. & A.M., 1971

Proceedings Of The Most Worshipful Grand Lodge Of Ancient, Free And Accepted Masons Of British Columbia; Seventy-seventh Annual Communication held at Vancouver, B.C., 17th and 18th days of June 1948

Masonic Bulletin, Grand Lodge Of British Columbia; Volume LIII, Number 1, September 1989

Masonic Bulletin, Grand Lodge Of British Columbia; Volume LIII, Number 6, February 1990

Masonic Bulletin, Grand Lodge Of British Columbia; Volume LIII, Number 7, March 1990

Masonic Bulletin, Grand Lodge Of British Columbia; Volume LIII, Number 9, May 1990

Masonic Bulletin, Grand Lodge Of British Columbia; Volume LIII, Number 10, June 1990

Masonic Bulletin, Grand Lodge Of British Columbia; Volume LN, Number 1, September 1990

Masonic Bulletin, Grand Lodge Of British Columbia; Volume LN, Number 2, October 1990

Masonic Bulletin, Grand Lodge Of British Columbia; Volume LN, Number 3, November 1990

Masonic Bulletin, Grand Lodge Of British Columbia; Volume LN, Number 9, May 1991

Masonic Bulletin, Grand Lodge Of British Columbia; Volume LV, Number 3, November 1991

Masonic Bulletin, Grand Lodge Of British Columbia; Volume LV, Number 4, December 1991

Masonic Bulletin, Grand Lodge Of British Columbia; Volume LV, Number 9, May 1992

Masonic Bulletin, Grand Lodge Of British Columbia; Volume LV, Number 10, June 1992

Masonic List Of Lodges, Grand Lodge Of British Columbia, 1989

Masonic Bulletin, Grand Lodge Of British Columbia; Volume LV, Number 7, March 1992

Masonic Bulletin, Grand Lodge Of British Columbia; Volume LVI, Number 3, November 1992

Gizeh Gazette, The Communication Lifeline Of Gizeh Temple; Volume 36, Number 4, November 1991

The Freemason Of Portland; Grand Lodge Of Oregon, Volume 42, Number 11, April 1965

The Gibson's Landing Story; Lester R. Peterson, Gibsons, B.C., 1962

The West Howe Sound Story 1886-1976; Francis J. Van Den Wyngaert, Gibsons, B.C., 1980

Barkerville: A Gold Rush Adventure; Richard Thomas Wright, 1984

Masonic Bulletin, Grand Lodge Of British Columbia; Volume XXXIX, Number 10, June 1976

Masonic Bulletin, Grand Lodge Of British Columbia; Volume XL, Number 3, November 1976

Masonic Bulletin, Grand Lodge Of British Columbia; Volume XLIII, Number 10, June 1980

Masonic Bulletin, Grand Lodge Of British Columbia; Volume LIII, Number 5, January 1991

Masonic Bulletin, Grand Lodge Of British Columbia; Volume LIII, Number 9, May 1991

Masonic Bulletin, Grand Lodge Of British Columbia; Volume LV, Number 2, October 1991

Masonic Bulletin, Grand Lodge Of British Columbia; Volume LV, Number 5, January 1992

Masonic Bulletin, Grand Lodge Of British Columbia; Volume LV, Number 6, February 1992

Masonic Bulletin, Grand Lodge Of British Columbia; Volume LV, Number 8, April 1992

Masonic Bulletin, Grand Lodge Of British Columbia; Volume LVI, Number 4, December 1992

The Southern Baptist Convention and Freemasonry, Volumes I & II; James L. Holly, M.D., 1993

Freemasonry On Trial; various authors (20) in total, Choosing Truth Ministries, Abbotsford, British Columbia, 1998

The Court System And Freemasonry; various authors, Choosing Truth Ministries, Abbotsford, British Columbia, June 2001

How To Respond To The Lodge; L. James Rongstad, 1977

Should A Christian Be A Mason?; E.M. Storms, 1980

The Facts On The Masonic Lodge, Does Masonry Conflict With The Christian Faith?; John Ankerberg and John Weldon, 1989

Freemasonry: The Invisible Cult In Our Midst, A Biblical Expose of Freemasonry; written by a former Worshipful Master, Jack Harris, 1983

The Vancouver Sun; December 22nd, 1995 (Copenhagen – Freemasons want book stonewalled).

Masonic Bulletin, Grand Lodge Of British Columbia; Volume LV, Number 5, January 1992

Masonic Bulletin, Grand Lodge Of British Columbia; Volume LIII, Number 1, September 1989

The Brotherhood: The Explosive Expose of the Secret World of The Freemasons; Stephen Knight, 1986

Inside The Brotherhood: The Explosive Sequel to Stephen Knight's The Brotherhood; Martin Short, 1989

THE VANCOUVER SUN; A 12, FRIDAY, JANUARY 12TH, 2001 (CLINTON'S
PENSION TO TOP $ 7 MILLION. TAXPAYERS GROUP COMPLAINS
PRESIDENT WILL BE THE RICHEST PENSIONER IN U.S. HISTORY).

THE VANCOUVER SUN; A 5, FRIDAY, JULY 20TH, 2001 (' SIR KEN ' OF
WEST VAN TO LEAD 530,000 SHRINERS. HE'S ONLY THE SIXTH
CANADIAN NAMED AS ' IMPERIAL POTENTATE ' – WEST VANCOUVER
BUSINESSMAN KENNETH (KENNY) SMITH).

THE PROVINCE; A 42, THURSDAY, JANUARY 31ST, 2002 (SHRINERS' BASH
WORTH $ 30 MILLION TO THELOWER MAINLAND'S ECONOMY).

THE VANCOUVER SUN; B 6, MONDAY, APRIL 1ST, 2002 (FREEMASONS, ABOUT
GIVING BACK TO THE COMMUNITY).

THE VANCOUVER SUN; B 2, SATURDAY, JUNE 15TH, 2002 (SHRINERS'
CONVENTION ROLLS INTO VANCOUVER. CLUB WILL STAGE GIANT
PARADES ON PACIFIC BOULEVARD).

THE VANCOUVER SUN; B 1 & B 2, MONDAY, JUNE 24TH, 2002 (VANCOUVER
BECOMES A SHRINER'S PARADISE.7,500 CONVENTIONEERS AND THEIR
FAMILIES BRING COMPETITION, MIRTH AND FESSES TO TOWN).

THE VANCOUVER SUN; B 5, TUESDAY, JUNE 25TH, 2002 (WHY I BECAME A
SHRINER: THERE ARE 7,500 SHRINERS IN VANCOUVER FOR THE 128TH
IMPERIAL COUNCIL SESSION, AND 497,000 SHRINERS WORLDWIDE.
WE ASKED SOME OF THEM WHY THEY JOINED).

THE VANCOUVER SUN; B 5, TUESDAY, JUNE 25TH, 2002 (SHRINERS ASKED
WHY THEY WEAR A FEZ. FEW MEMBERS GATHERED IN VANCOUVER
COULD EXPLAIN THE MEANING OF THE HEADDRESS OR WHY THEY
INCLUDE A LONG BLACK TASSEL).

THE VANCOUVER SUN; B 5, TUESDAY, JUNE 25TH, 2002 (YOUR GUIDE TO THE
SHRINE SYMBOLS).

THE VANCOUVER SUN; A 17, (COMMENTARY PAGE), FRIDAY, JUNE 28TH, 2002
(**DESPITE THEIR RITUALS, SHRINERS SHY AWAY FROM SPIRITUAL NATURE**).

THE VANCOUVER SUN; B 3, FRIDAY, JUNE 28TH, 2002 (SHRINERS VACATION AFTER CONVENTION. ABOUT 4,000 OF THE SHRINERS VISITING VANCOUVER HAVE DECIDED TO STAY IN B.C. A WHILE LONGER).

THE VANCOUVER SUN; B 3, FRIDAY, JUNE 28TH, 2002 (I FEZZ UP: I DO NOT GET THE SHRINERS. THE GOBBLEDYGOOK, THE HIERACHY: DON'T THEY SUFFER ENOUGH KLOWNS AND POTENTATES AT WORK?).

THE VANCOUVER SUN; (EDITORIAL PAGE), A 22, NOVEMBER 27TH, 2002 (B.C. LIBERALS RAMROD A SECOND TERM FOR OLIVER).

MASONIC BULLETIN, GRAND LODGE OF BRITISH COLUMBIA; VOLUME LVI, NUMBER 1, SEPTEMBER 1992

MASONIC BULLETIN, GRAND LODGE OF BRITISH COLUMBIA; VOLUME LVI, NUMBER 2, OCTOBER 1992

THE NORTHERN LIGHT: A WINDOW FOR FREEMASONRY; VOLUME 21, NUMBER 1, FEBRUARY 1990

HTTP://WWW.FREEMASONRY.ORG/PSOC/ALLENROBERTS.HTM

HTTP://WWW.GEOCITIES.COM/CAPECANAVERAL/2903/BKARL.HTML

THE PROVINCE; A 44, WEDNESDAY, SEPTEMBER 12TH, 2001 (CONRAD BLACK'S A LORD — AT LAST. NEWSPAPER BARON GAVE UP CANADIAN CITIZENSHIP IN ROW OVER PEERAGE).

THE PROVINCE; A 66, WEDNESDAY, SEPTEMBER 12TH, 2001 (HOLLINGER MAY BECOME PRIVATE).

THE VANCOUVER SUN; A 13, THURSDAY, NOVEMBER 1ST, 2001 (CONRAD BLACK TAKES HIS SEAT IN BRITAIN'S HOUSE OF LORDS. EX-CANADIAN LORD BLACK OF CROSSHARBOUR TAKES NAME FROM A LONDON DISTRICT).

THE VANCOUVER SUN; A 19, THURSDAY, NOVEMBER 28TH, 2002 (KISSINGER TO HEAD 9/11 INVESTIGATION. BUSH ALLY APPOINTED TO PROBE OF U.S. AVIATION SECURITY, INTELLIGENCE).

THE VANCOUVER SUN; A 14, OCTOBER 17TH, 2002 (SADDAM, THE SOLE
CANDIDATE, SWEEPS **100%** OF IRAQ VOTE. ' THIS IS A UNIQUE
MANIFESTATION OF DEMOCRACY, ' SAYS ONE MEMBER OF THE
GOVERNMENT IN BAGHDAD).

TIME NEWSWEEK; (**SPECIAL REPORT**), PAGES 16-27, MARCH 10TH,
2003 (**LIFE AFTER SADDAM**: IF INVADING TROOPS TOPPLE IRAQ'S
DICTATOR, WASHINGTON WILL INHERIT RESPONSIBILITIES FOR A BITTER,
FACTIOUS COUNTRY. HERE'S **TIME'S** LOOK AT THE BLUEPRINT FOR
REMAKING THE NATION — AND THE MIDDLE EAST).

NATIONAL POST; (FRONT PAGE COVERAGE), MARCH 17TH, 2003 (BUSH TO
GIVE DIPLOMACY ONE FINAL TRY IN WHAT HE CALLS A ... ' **MOMENT
OF TRUTH FOR THE WORLD**).

THE VANCOUVER SUN; (FRONT PAGE COVERAGE), MARCH 17TH, 2003
(**BUSH's: ' MOMENT OF TRUTH** ' – U.S. IMPOSES DEADLINE ON
DIPLOMATIC NEGOTIATIONS — SADDAM THREATENS WORLD   WAR IF
ATTACKED).

THE VANCOUVER SUN; (FRONT PAGE COVERAGE), MARCH 18TH, 2003
(**BUSH TO SADDAM: '** LEAVE IRAQ WITHIN **48** HOURS ' – CITING
DANGER TO AMERICA, HE PREPARES NATION FOR WAR).

THE PROVINCE; (FRONT PAGE COVERAGE), MARCH 18TH, 2003 (**BUSH
TELLS SADDAM: GET OUT NOW OR FACE WAR**).

NATIONAL POST; (FRONT PAGE COVERAGE), MARCH 18TH, 2003 (' **48
HOURS** ').

NATIONAL POST; (FRONT PAGE COVERAGE), MARCH 20TH, 2003 (**THE WAR
HAS BEGUN**).

THE VANCOUVER SUN; (FRONT PAGE COVERAGE), MARCH 20TH, 2003 (**U.S.
ATTACKS**).

THE PROVINCE; (FRONT PAGE COVERAGE), MARCH 20TH, 2003 (**U.S.
MISSILES TARGET SADDAM**).

THE VANCOUVER SUN; (FRONT PAGE COVERAGE), MARCH 24TH, 2003 (
'SHAME ON YOU, MR. BUSH ' – FILM DIRECTOR MICHAEL

Moore was both booed and applauded Sunday night when he made anti-war remarks after accepting the Oscar for best documentary feature for the gun-culture film **Bowling for Columbine** at the Academy Awards in Los Angeles. Moore said later he wasn't worried about being blacklisted. " I don't work in Hollywood, I'm funded by Canadians. ").

The Province: B 6, March 30TH, 2003 (Moore to take on Bush and bin Laden in his next documentary **Fahrenheit 911**).

Chapter 13 - Man's Only Salvation

Masonic Bible: Authorized King James Version; William Collins Sons and Company Ltd., 1951

Masonic List Of Lodges; Grand Lodge OF British Columbia, 1989

Encyclopedia of Freemasonry Volumes 1 & 2; The Masonic History Company (U.S.A.), 1924

Egypt: The Cradle Of Ancient Masonry; Volume 1, Norman Frederick de Clifford, Macoy Publishing and Masonic Supply Company, New York, 1907

History Of The Grand Lodge Of British Columbia 1871-1970; Grand Lodge Of British Columbia A.F. & A.M., 1971

Proceedings Of The Most Worshipful Grand Lodge Of Ancient, Free and Accepted Masons Of British Columbia; Seventy-Seventh Annual Communication held at Vancouver, B.C. on the 17th and 18th days of June 1948

To A Non-Mason: You Must Seek Masonic Membership; Henry C. Claussen, 33rd degree, Sovereign Grand Commander, The Supreme Council, 33rd degree, Ancient And Accepted Scottish Rite Of Freemasonry, Mother Jurisdiction Of The World, 1976

The Quebec Masonic Journal, Grand Lodge Of Quebec A.F. & A.M.; Volume 2, Number 1, Summer 1989

Entered Apprentice Degree: Grand Lodge Of British Columbia through the Committee on Masonic Education and Research, 1957

The Freemasons Of Portland, Oregon; Volume 42, Number 11, April 1965

12 Questions On Freemasonry; Grand Lodge of Free and Accepted Masons of Washington State, Tacoma, Washington, date unknown

The Northern Light: A Window For Freemasonry; Volume 21, Number 1, February 1990

The Northwest Washington Masonic News, Devoted To The Interests Of Freemasonry Wherever Dispersed; Volume XXVIII, Number 4, Bellingham, Washington, December 1989

The New Mexico Freemason; Volume 53, Number 4, July-August, 1988

The Montana Masonic News; Volume 42, Number 404, October 1989

The Kansas Mason; Volume 28, Issue 3, June 1989

The New Zealand Freemason, Volume 15, Number 2, Winter 1987

United Masters Lodge No. 167, Lodge of Masonic Research; Volume 24, Number 9, March 1982

United Masters Lodge No. 167, Lodge of Masonic Research; Volume 24, Number 10, April 1982

Masonic Antient News; Brother Francis " Frank " Goodwillie, Editor and Publisher, Surrey, British Columbia, Fall 1987

Masonic Antient News; Brother Francis " Frank " Goodwillie, Editor and Publisher, Surrey, British Columbia, September 1988

Masonic Antient News; Brother Francis " Frank " Goodwillie, Editor and Publisher, Surrey,British Columbia, June 1989

The High Twelvian; Volume 63, Number 3, George Washington - Master Mason, Our First President, Winter 1989

Grand Lodge Bulletin, Grand Lodge Of Iowa, A.F. & A.M.; Volume 89, Number 1, March 1988

Grand Lodge Bulletin, Grand Lodge Of Alberta; Volume 56, Number 10, December 1991

Gizeh Gazette, The Communication Lifeline Of Gizeh Temple; Volume 36, Number 4, November 1991

1994 Masonic Calendar; Grand Lodge A.F. & A. M. of Canada, in the Province Of Ontario,Celebration of its 200 years of Masonic History in the Province of Ontario.

Will Of The Lodge: A Parliamentary Law Guide for Freemasons; Richard L. Ashby M.M., Registered Procedural Parliamentarian, 1990

Quarterly Communication, United Grand Lodge of Ancient, Free And Accepted Masons of England; held at Freemason's Hall, 60 Great Queen Street, London, England on Wednesday,the 8TH day of March 1989 (whereas His Royal Highness the Duke of Kent was slated to be re-elected as its Grand Master).

Quarterly Communication, United Grand Lodge of Ancient, Free And Accepted Masons of England; held at Freemason's Hall, 60 Great Queen Street, London, England on November 27TH, 1987 (whereas HRH The Duke of Kent, KG, GCMG, GCVO, ADC, was the Most Worshipful Grand Master).

The St. Clair News, The Monthly Journal of the Grand Lodge Of Scotland; Glasgow St. Clair Lodge No. 362, Volume 3, Number 1, September 1988 (whereas the Grand Master HRH reportedly had a rather long winded account of the Royal family's happy affiliation with Freemasonry).

Constitution Of The Most Excellent Grand Chapter Of Royal Arch Masons Of British Columbia; Clarke & Stuart Company Limited, Vancouver, B.C., August 1971

The Book Of Constitutions Of The Grand Lodge Of Ancient, Free And Accepted Masons Of British Columbia; Central Printers & Stationers, Published Under The Authorization Of The Grand Lodge Of British Columbia, 1982

THE DUTIES, RIGHTS AND PRIVILEGES OF A MASTER MASON; A SPEECH
GIVEN BY R. W. BROTHER HEAPS OF MOUNT ELPHINSTONE LODGE
No. 130, TO A DISTRICT No. 24 WORKSHOP HELD ON DECEMBER 6TH,
1975

SOME MASONIC SYMBOLISM IN DAILY LIFE; A SPEECH GIVEN BY W. BROTHER
RON CLOUGH OF CAPILANO LODGE No. 164, TO A DISTRICT No. 24
WORKSHOP HELD ON DECEMBER 6TH, 1975

LODGE ADMINISTRATION AND BUSINESS; A SPEECH GIVEN BY R.W. BROTHER
W. WOODWARD OF TRIUNE LODGE No. 81, TO A DISTRICT No. 24
WORKSHOP HELD ON DECEMBER 6TH, 1975

IMPROPER SOLICITATION; A SPEECH GIVEN BY R.W. BROTHER W.J.
MASON OF HOLLYBURN LODGE No. 135, TO THE NINTH ANNUAL
EDUCATIONAL SEMINAR OF DISTRICT No. 24 HELD ON NOVEMBER
24TH, 1983

INNOVATION – THROUGH A MASONIC LOOKING GLASS; A SPEECH GIVEN BY
V.W. BROTHER HARLEY G. SCALES OF MOUNT ELPHINSTONE LODGE
No. 130, TO THE TENTH ANNUAL DAY OF ENLIGHTENMENT DISTRICT
No. 24 HELD ON DECEMBER 1ST, 1984. (BROTHER SALES WAS ALSO
A PAST DISTRICT MASTER OF THE UNITED   GRAND LODGE OF
GERMANY).

CHARITY AND FREEMASONRY; A SPEECH GIVEN BY R.W. BROTHER RON
CLOUGH OF CAPILANO LODGE No. 164, TO THE TENTH ANNUAL DAY
OF ENLIGHTENMENT DISTRICT No. 24 HELD ON DECEMBER 1ST, 1894

A TESTIMONIAL FROM ISRAEL; A SPEECH GIVEN BY R.W. BROTHER ED
NICHOLSON OF MOUNT ELPHINSTONE LODGE No. 130, TO THE
BRETHRENSHIP ON NOVEMBER 8TH, 1986

MASONIC FUNERAL SERVICE; MOUNT ELPHINSTONE LODGE No. 130,
ROBERTS CREEK, B.C., THE RICHARDSON PRESS LTD., VANCOUVER,
BRITISH COLUMBIA, DATE UNKNOWN

SPEECHES OF DISTRICT No. 9; GRAND MASONIC DAY, VANCOUVER, B.C.,
OCTOBER 15TH, 1983

Speeches And Discussion Papers; Grand Lodge Of British Columbia for the Grand Masonic Day, October 20TH, 1984

Speeches of District No. 24; Mini Masonic Day, Roberts Creek, British Columbia, November 30TH, 1985

Agenda And Proceedings; Minutes of the 42ND Annual Inter-Provincial Conference of the Officers Of The Four Western Canadian Masonic Jurisdictions held at Banff, Alberta (September 2ND, 3RD and 4TH, 1982).

Agenda And Proceedings; Minutes of the 43RD Annual Inter-Provincial Conference of the Officers Of The Four Western Canadian Masonic Jurisdictions held at Banff, Alberta(September 1ST, 2ND and 3RD, 1983).

Agenda And Proceedings; Minutes of the 100TH Annual Communication of the Grand Lodge Of British Columbia held in the City of Victoria in June of 1971 in celebration of their 100 years of Masonic history in the Province of British Columbia.

Agenda And Proceedings; Minutes of the 112TH Annual Communication of the Grand Lodge Of British Columbia held at Penticton, British Columbia (June 23RD and 24TH, 1983).

Agenda And Proceedings; a brief break down of the 115TH annual Communication of the Grand Lodge Of British Columbia held at the Civil Centre, Prince George, B.C. on Thursday and   Friday, the 19TH and 20TH days of June 1986

Agenda And Proceeding; Minutes of the Seventy-Eighth Session of the Grand Chapter of the British Columbia and Yukon Order of the Eastern Star held in Vancouver, British Columbia (May 29TH, 30TH and 31ST, 1989).

Agenda And Proceedings; Minutes of the Seventy-Ninth Session of the Grand Chapter of the British Columbia and Yukon Order of the Eastern Star held at the Chilliwack Coliseum, Chilliwack, British Columbia (May 28TH, 29TH and 30TH, 1990).

Grand Master's Address; a speech given by fraternal Brother
    Douglas R. Grant, the Grand Master of the Grand Lodge Of
    British Columbia at the 120th Annual Communication June
    1991

Speeches of The Grand Lodge Of British Columbia A.F. & A.M.,
    Sixth Annual Grand Masonic Day, Saturday, October 17th,
    1987

Freemasonry Rituals – The B.C. Ancient Work Explained; The
    Educational Committee of Mount Elphinstone Lodge No.
    130, date unknown

Freemasonry Rituals – The Canadian Working Explained; The
    Educational Committee of Mount Elphinstone Lodge No.
    130, date unknown

Freemasonry Enlightenment – Look To The Light; The Educational
    Committee of Mount Elphinstone Lodge No. 130, 1984

Bylaws And Regulations of Mount Elphinstone Lodge No. 130,
    Roberts Creek, B.C. (1981)

Membership Roster of Mount Elphinstone Lodge No. 130, Roberts
    Creek, B.C. (1987)

Masonic Bulletin, Grand Lodge Of British Columbia; Volume
    XXXIV, Number 10, June 1971

Masonic Bulletin, Grand Lodge Of British Columbia; Volume
    XXXIX, Number 10, June 1976

Masonic Bulletin, Grand Lodge Of British Columbia; Volume XL,
    Number 3, November 1976

Masonic Bulletin, Grand Lodge Of British Columbia, Volume XL,
    Number 5, January 1977

Masonic Bulletin, Grand Lodge Of British Columbia; Volume XL,
    Number 8, April 1977

Masonic Bulletin, Grand Lodge Of British Columbia; Volume XLIII, Number 7, March 1980

Masonic Bulletin, Grand Lodge Of British Columbia; Volume XLIII, Number 10, June 1980

Masonic Bulletin, Grand Lodge Of British Columbia; XLVI, Number 9, May 1983

Masonic Bulletin, Grand Lodge Of British Columbia; Volume XLVII, Number 3, November 1983

Masonic Bulletin, Grand Lodge Of British Columbia; Volume XLVIII, Number 1, September 1984

Masonic Bulletin, Grand Lodge Of British Columbia; Volume XLIX, Number 9, May 1986

Masonic Bulletin, Grand Lodge Of British Columbia; Volume LI, Number 3, November 1987

Masonic Bulletin, Grand Lodge Of British Columbia; Volume LII, Number 2, October 1988

Masonic Bulletin, Grand Lodge Of British Columbia; Volume LII, Number 5, January 1989

Masonic Bulletin, Grand Lodge Of British Columbia; Volume LII, Number 6, February 1989

Masonic Bulletin, Grand Lodge Of British Columbia; Volume LII, Number 7, March 1989

Masonic Bulletin, Grand Lodge Of British Columbia; Volume LIII, Number 1, September 1989

Masonic Bulletin, Grand Lodge Of British Columbia; Volume LIII, Number 2, October 1989

Masonic Bulletin, Grand Lodge Of British Columbia; Volume LIII, Number 6, February 1990

Masonic Bulletin, Grand Lodge Of British Columbia; Volume LIII, Number 7, March 1990

Masonic Bulletin, Grand Lodge Of British Columbia; Volume LIII, Number 8, April 1990

Masonic Bulletin, Grand Lodge Of British Columbia; Volume LIII, Number 9, May 1990

Masonic Bulletin, Grand Lodge Of British Columbia; Volume LIII, Number 10, June 1990

Masonic Bulletin, Grand Lodge Of British Columbia; Volume LN, Number 1, September 1990

Masonic Bulletin, Grand Lodge Of British Columbia; Volume LN, Number 2, October 1990

Masonic Bulletin, Grand Lodge Of British Columbia; Volume LIII Number 3, November 1990

Masonic Bulletin, Grand Lodge Of British Columbia; Volume LIII, Number 5, January 1991

Masonic Bulletin, Grand Lodge Of British Columbia; Volume LIII, Number 6, February 1991

Masonic Bulletin, Grand Lodge Of British Columbia; Volume LIII, Number 8, April 1991

Masonic Bulletin, Grand Lodge Of British Columbia; Volume LIII, Number 9, May 1991

Masonic Bulletin, Grand Lodge Of British Columbia; Volume LIII, Number 10, June 1991

Masonic Bulletin, Grand Lodge Of British Columbia; Volume LV, Number 1, September 1991

Masonic Bulletin, Grand Lodge Of British Columbia; Volume LV, Number 2, October 1991

Masonic Bulletin, Grand Lodge Of British Columbia; Volume LV, Number 3, November 1991

Masonic Bulletin, Grand Lodge Of British Columbia; Volume LV, Number 4, December 1991

Masonic Bulletin, Grand Lodge Of British Columbia; Volume LV, Number 5, January 1992

Masonic Bulletin, Grand Lodge Of British Columbia; Volume LV, Number 6, February 1992

Masonic Bulletin, Grand Lodge Of British Columbia; Volume LV, Number 7, March 1992

Masonic Bulletin, Grand Lodge Of British Columbia; Volume LV, Number 8, April 1992

Masonic Bulletin, Grand Lodge Of British Columbia; Volume LV, Number 9, May 1992

Masonic Bulletin, Grand Lodge Of British Columbia; Volume LV, Number 10, June 1992

Masonic Bulletin, Grand Lodge Of British Columbia; Volume LVI, Number 1, September 1992

Masonic Bulletin, Grand Lodge Of British Columbia; Volume LVI, Number 2, October 1992

Masonic Bulletin, Grand Lodge Of British Columbia; Volume LVI, Number 3, November 1992

Masonic Bulletin, Grand Lodge Of British Columbia; Volume LVI, Number 4, December 1992

The Vancouver Sun; A 1 & A 2, Tuesday, December 26TH, 2000 (Holy Grail may be hidden on a Baltic island, new book says – Book links crusading Knights Templar with forgotten treasures).

THE VANCOUVER SUN; A 6, TUESDAY, JANUARY 14TH, 2003 (CONTROVERSIAL TABLET LINKED WITH BIBLICAL STORY OF SOLOMON'S TEMPLE).

HTTP://WWW.FREEMASONRY.ORG/PSOC/ALLENROBERTS.HTM

HTTP://WWW.GEOCITIES.COM/CAPECANAVERAL/2903/BKARL.HTML